Praise for
Texas Rich

"A steaming, sprawling saga . . . As always, Fern Michaels writes a full story with bigger-than-life characters we would look forward to meeting. . . . A rags-to-riches saga that would make a colorful movie."

—*Romantic Times*

"Talk about action! There is more in this epic than in five novels. And it's fascinating, interesting, and exciting. One of those rare books, the kind the reader doesn't want to end. A real winner!"

—*Green Bay Press Gazette*

"Fine fare for Fern Michaels's fans!"

—*The Philadelphia Inquirer*

By Fern Michaels
(published by The Random House Publishing Group)

ALL SHE CAN BE
CINDERS TO SATIN
DESPERATE MEASURES
FOR ALL THEIR LIVES
FREE SPIRIT
SEASONS OF HER LIFE
SERENDIPITY
TENDER WARRIOR
TO HAVE AND TO HOLD
TO TASTE THE WINE
VALENTINA
VIXEN IN VELVET

The Captive series
CAPTIVE PASSIONS
CAPTIVE EMBRACES
CAPTIVE SPLENDORS
CAPTIVE INNOCENCE
CAPTIVE SECRETS

The Texas series
TEXAS HEAT
TEXAS RICH
TEXAS FURY
TEXAS SUNRISE

The Sins series
SINS OF OMISSION
SINS OF THE FLESH

TEXAS RICH
&
TEXAS HEAT

TWO NOVELS

FERN MICHAELS

BALLANTINE BOOKS • NEW YORK

2006 Ballantine Books Mass Market Edition

Texas Rich copyright © 1985 by Fern Michaels
Texas Heat copyright © 1986 by Fern Michaels

Published in the United States by Ballantine Books, an imprint of The Random House Publishing Group, a division of Random House, Inc., New York.

BALLANTINE and colophon are registered trademarks of Random House, Inc.

ISBN 0-345-49563-2

Printed in the United States of America

www.ballantinebooks.com

OPM 9 8 7 6 5 4 3 2 1

TEXAS RICH

ACKNOWLEDGMENTS

Recently I had the opportunity to visit the tiny dot in the Pacific known as Guam. I found it to be a land of warm smiles, laughing eyes, blue skies, and what seemed like perpetual sunshine. To compare this beautiful, progressive paradise to Hawaii and Palm Beach would not be unjust. Like Riley and Otami my heart shattered when it was time to leave.

Because of the devastation created by Typhoon Karen on the island of Guam it was necessary to take certain liberties in my early descriptions of specific locales and buildings. All references are true and accurate to the rebuilt Guam.

I particularly want to thank Louise and the entire Crisostomo family along with Mary James, Astrid Hertslet, and Ben Blaz for being so generous with their time and making my visit so memorable. My sincere thanks to all of you.

Fern Michaels

The Coleman Family Tree

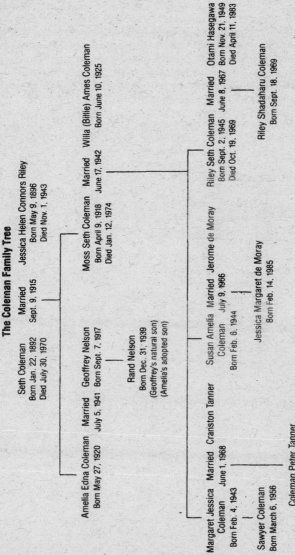

Seth Coleman
Born Jan. 22, 1892
Died July 30, 1970

Married
Sept. 9, 1915

Jessica Helen Connors Riley
Born May 9, 1896
Died Nov. 1, 1943

Moss Seth Coleman
Born April 9, 1918
Died Jan. 12, 1974

Married
June 17, 1942

Willa (Billie) Ames Coleman
Born June 10, 1925

Amelia Edna Coleman
Born May 27, 1920

Married
July 5, 1941

Geoffrey Nelson
Born Sept. 7, 1917

Rand Nelson
Born Dec. 31, 1939
(Geoffrey's natural son)
(Amelia's adopted son)

Susan Amelia Coleman
Born Feb. 6, 1944

Married
July 9, 1966

Jerome de Moray

Jessica Margaret de Moray
Born Feb. 14, 1985

Riley Seth Coleman
Born Sept. 2, 1945
Died Oct. 19, 1969

Married
June 8, 1967

Otami Hasegawa
Born Nov. 21, 1949
Died April 11, 1983

Riley Shadaharu Coleman
Born Sept. 18, 1969

Margaret Jessica Coleman
Born Feb. 4, 1943

Married
June 1, 1968

Cranston Tanner

Sawyer Coleman
Born March 6, 1956

Coleman Peter Tanner
Born April 2, 1969

PART I

{{{{{{{{{{ CHAPTER ONE }}}}}}}}}

The crisscross-patterned lace curtains, which should have been silk organdy but were rayon instead, billowed in the soft May breeze. The chitterings of birds and new green scents drifted into Billie Ames's room. She drew in her breath, savoring the tantalizing fragrances. Spring was her favorite time of year and this year it had seemed such a long time coming. In thirty-seven days she would graduate from high school. Adulthood. Grown-up. She bent to tie her saddle shoes, brushing impatiently at her ash-blond hair, which fell over her eyes, and frowned. Multistriped shoelaces and white anklets? Some grown-up! She should be wearing nylon stockings and heels, not these remnants of girlhood. But the war had been on in Europe for some time now and since the attack on Pearl Harbor last December, Billie had wondered if sheer stockings would go the way of the passenger pigeon: extinct. Not that it mattered, because they were beyond the limits of her clothing allowance anyway. Lots of women wore leg makeup and drew seams on the backs of their legs. But only pagans and Philistines did such things, declared Billie's mother. And Agnes Ames rarely, if ever, admitted she was wrong.

Billie's thoughts circled back to graduation. When she flipped the tassel of her mortarboard from one side to the other it would be the beginning of her last free summer and then off to Penn State. She'd already signed up for a major in English, because she had to pick something; but the truth was she hated the whole idea. What Billie wanted, really wanted, was to go to a good design and textile school. Agnes said that wouldn't be seemly. The best schools were in New York City and young girls just didn't live there alone. Not nice girls, at any rate. Later, after Billie had her degree, she could fool with such notions.

But Billie suspected the real reason was that the cost of design school was prohibitive. She wished she knew more about the family finances. Were they comfortable or merely keeping their heads above water? Agnes said that was hardly the concern of a young girl. Study, socialize with "acceptable youngsters," and dress well. That was Agnes's credo, and it always ended with: "Then you'll marry a young man from an old mainline family and your future will be secured. And always remember that no man wants used merchandise. Virginity is your most prized possession. Guard it well!" It was hard not to giggle when Agnes began preaching.

Sighing, Billie buttoned the straps of her jumper, which she'd made herself. It was such a beautiful shade of lavender and it had huge pearl buttons on the shoulder straps and two smaller ones on the patch pockets. Instead of hemming the skirt, she'd fringed it. She was the only girl in school with a fringed skirt, so far. By next week there would be at least twenty others; she was certain of it. Billie Ames enjoyed being something of a style setter.

Virginity. Agnes put great store in preserving it. Temptation was something to be fought and conquered until one's wedding night.

Billie sighed again, this time more deeply. Temptation wasn't a problem for her. She had no steady boyfriend, didn't want one, either. And the boys she knew were certainly not worth wasting her virginity on. They had pimply faces, sloppy clothes, and bicycles with chipped paint and chains that always slipped off when they rode double. There was nothing at all romantic about them! Besides, most of the boys had nothing except the war on their minds, hardly able to wait for graduation when they could enlist and prove what big men they were. Girls were only secondary to the German and Japanese armies.

Billie's world was simply too narrow, she thought. She wished she had more opportunities to travel, see things, do things. Even her trips downtown had been severely limited by Agnes ever since the arrival of military personnel. She thought of all the young men in their uniforms and grinned wickedly at her reflection in the mirror. The navy uniforms were the best, especially now in the warmer weather when they'd switched to whites. The men looked so dashing and debonair, like Tyrone Power or Errol Flynn. Imagine walking into her senior prom on the arm of a tall dark navy man! That was another thing. She didn't have a date for the prom. A dress . . . but no date. Agnes was beginning to worry, Billie could tell. But a senior prom was special, and you had to go with someone special. Several boys had asked her, but she'd declined. Even she, with all her romantic notions, didn't really expect the white knight to come charging down Elm Street to swoop her off to the dance. . . . Yet surely something or someone better would come along. At the last minute, she could always snag Tim Kelly. Ungainly Tim, who would make chopped liver of her feet on the dance floor. Still, he was a basketball captain and would make a respectable escort. Another sigh. Being one of the prettiest girls in the graduating class, and one of the most popular, didn't ensure romance.

A glance at the clock on her nightstand told Billie she'd have to hurry and she experienced a small skitter of excitement. She loved Saturday afternoons and the matinee at the Loews Theatre. It meant she could leave her sewing and piano lessons behind for a few hours. Saturday afternoon meant walking downtown with her two girlfriends and meeting the gang at the corner. No one paired off, exactly, but they did walk side by side down the tree-lined streets. They were friends, and after this summer they'd all go their different ways. Billie decided she wouldn't miss them, not the way some of the kids said they would. She'd be going off to a new school, where she could pick and choose her own friends, new friends. Ones that wouldn't have to pass Agnes's muster. Friends that might or might not be "acceptable."

Billie closed the lid of her tinkling music box, a Christmas gift from her father when she was four years old. She looked at it fondly for a moment. She would not take it with her when she left for college; nor would she take the photograph of her parents smiling on the last day of their honeymoon. For an instant she felt a twinge of disloyalty. Her father had died before she and Agnes moved into Grandmother's house on Elm Street. One day he was there and the next he wasn't. It wasn't as though she missed having a father, not exactly, but in some ways she did think of herself as deprived. It made her different from the other girls, whose fathers sat on Sunday afternoons reading the newspaper and took them out for a driving lesson in the family automobile. She wouldn't want Agnes to know she'd left the music box or photograph behind. If worse came to worse, she could pack them at the bottom of a trunk in the attic and leave them there. Billie felt better immediately. She was a good child. A dutiful daughter. And she was still a virgin, which was more than some of the girls at school could say. Already there were whispers that Cissy had given her all to an army corporal.

Billie ran a brush through her thick blond hair, pinned it back with two heart-shaped barrettes, then closed the door on her pink-and-white bedroom. "Mother, I'm leaving now," she called to Agnes from the foot of the stairs, then she waited.

Some people could walk into a room; others could make an entrance. Agnes Ames just appeared. One minute she wasn't there and the next she was. It always amazed Billie.

She managed to keep her voice just a notch above conversational—Agnes said shouting was unladylike—as she went through the weekly litany for Agnes's benefit. "We may stop for a cherry phosphate after the show. If we do, I'll be home by five. If we decide to go for hamburgers, I'll be home by five-thirty. The boys like to see the newsreel a second time. So it may be six at the very latest. I have my purse and enough change to pay for myself and enough for a phone call. I'm wearing my best underwear and I only put cologne on my wrists, not behind my ears. I polished my shoes and buffed the white part."

Billie smiled at her mother and stood still for her silent inspection. Agnes's dark brown gaze snapped and clicked as it monitored her daughter. From long experience Billie recognized the invisible signal that said she had passed standards. "What are you going to do this afternoon, Mother?"

"Today is Saturday. I have to clean the two front bedrooms. Our roomers are out, so this is the best time. Miss Carpenter is working overtime at the Navy Yard today. She certainly must make a princely wage." This might be the time to think about raising the room rent a little, Agnes thought, maybe a dollar or so a week. Or perhaps she could offer breakfast and charge three dollars more. . . . God, how she hated this penny-pinching! "Miss Addison is away for the weekend. Did she pay you for hemming her skirt, Billie?"

"Yes, Mother. And there's another for me to do this week."

"Good. We don't want to be taken advantage of, do we? I still haven't resigned myself to opening my home to total strangers. Of course, what else could I do? I'm as patriotic as the next person and, considering the housing shortage in Philadelphia and having the space, I couldn't very well not, could I?"

"They're both nice ladies," Billie said. "They're quiet and they don't mess up the bathroom." She hoped Agnes wasn't having second thoughts about taking in roomers, because now there always seemed to be a little extra money.

Agnes Ames was tall and thin, stylishly so. Her expertise with the needle proved that clothing need not be padded or flounced to make a garment appear custom tailored. Today she wore a beige-and-brown street dress with a wide chocolate sash. Adorning her long aristocratic neck were her grandmother's pearls. *Severe* was a word that came to mind when one thought of Agnes Ames. Just as the pearls were always around her neck, so there was the calculating expression in her eyes. She had good clear skin, thanks to Pond's Cold Cream and Dream Puff Powder. They were the only cosmetics she allowed to touch her face, aside from lipstick. Agnes never wore rouge: that was for wantons and streetwalkers. She preferred to pinch her cheeks. She did her own hair, out of necessity and frugality, and had become expert at using Nestle's thick green wave set and the metal clamps that guaranteed a tight crimp. Small, imitation pearl clip-on earrings completed the outward appearance of Agnes Ames.

She poked her long thin arms through the holes of a pinafore-style apron, which she wore to save her dress. "Yes, they are quiet and neat, aren't they? However, that was not happenstance, Billie—I was quite careful in choosing them and it always pays to have a clear-cut understanding from the beginning." Switching to Billie's plans for the afternoon, Agnes asked, "Are all of you going to the matinee?"

Billie took her cue. "Carl, Joey, Chester, and Tim. Bernice, Barbara, Dotty, and myself. That's all."

Agnes rolled the names over on her tongue. Hardly old Philadelphia mainline society, but they were acceptable. No old money there, but a lot of new money, most of it profits of war. New money could be offensive, almost threatening, because it had to be earned. Old money was comforting, a state of being.

"Enjoy the movie, Billie. I'll hold dinner. Something light. Perhaps some of that new lettuce from our Victory garden. There are still four eggs left on our rations." Agnes's lip curled when she mentioned the Victory garden and food rationing. Billie suspected that the careful tending of the garden out back was less an effort of patriotism than an outward sign of Agnes's driven desire to be like everyone else, only better.

"It sounds fine, Mother. Don't work too hard. Perhaps I should stay home and give you a hand."

"Nonsense. You go out with your friends. I'll be done in no time. If it weren't for this ridiculous war, decent people would still have cleaning help. It seems anyone who's able to give a full day's work has gone on to greener pastures at the Navy Yard or in factories. Help is so difficult to find."

After Billie had left, Agnes looked about the small living room. It was neat, tidy and gleaming. Agnes liked soap and water. With her daughter out of the house this might be a good time to move Billie's things downstairs to the study. There was no sense letting an extra room go to waste, and they certainly could use the money it would bring. By Tuesday the room could be rented. She should have done it long before this. It never occurred to her that Billie might object. Billie never objected. She was such a good child. The study had a window seat where Billie could sit and read for hours. No one could ever point a finger at Agnes and say she wasn't doing her duty for the war effort. It wasn't her fault she didn't have a son to give for her country. Renting out her spare rooms and having a Victory garden were her contributions.

Agnes wrapped a bandanna around her head to protect her wave and went about getting her cleaning products in order. Oxydol, Old Dutch Cleanser, and a supply of rags. A feather duster under one arm, the mop in the other, she climbed the stairs. It was such an awful way to spend a Saturday afternoon. She should be taking a leisurely tea at someone's house and talking about what was on everyone's minds, the war. She'd love to be a hostess at a formal tea and serve thin cucumber sandwiches. Instead, she was cleaning rented bedrooms and a community bathroom. She didn't want this kind of life for Billie; she didn't want it for herself, either.

Billie walked alongside Tim Kelly. There was something different about the sandy-haired Tim today. His tall thin body looked ready to explode. Whatever it was, the other boys were in on it, too.

"If you walk any faster, you'll meet yourself coming," Billie teased.

"You always say that, Billie." Tim laughed. "You just take short little steps. How come you aren't wearing your penny loafers?"

"Because I polished these and I wanted to show them off."

Tim laughed again. "I like girls who wear silk stockings and high heels," he teased.

"You can't get silk stockings anymore because they need

every bit of it to make parachutes," Billie countered. "The best you can get is nylon, but they cost a fortune."

"Cissy always seems to have enough money for them, and don't they look great on her!" Tim started smacking one fist into the palm of the other. He didn't seem to notice that at the mention of the notorious Cissy he had gained everyone's attention. "You aren't going to believe what I did yesterday. You just won't believe it!"

The girls stopped in their tracks while the boys laughed. "If it's something dirty, Tim Kelly, we don't want to hear it," one girl said excitedly.

"Yes we do." Another giggled.

"No we don't!" Billie said firmly.

"Well, you're gonna hear it anyway. I signed up. I went and did it. I didn't even tell my parents yet," Tim said proudly.

"Oh, no," Billie whispered. Suddenly she wished they could all be little kids again, roller-skating down Elm Street, setting up lemonade stands. Tim was the first of their bunch to enlist and it seemed an omen of things to come, judging by the awe on the other boys' faces.

"I leave a couple of weeks after graduation. I'll be eighteen by then," Tim said quietly. "I want to get into it. We all do, don't we, fellas? It's just a matter of time now. We'll write you girls, and you've got to promise to write back. We've decided we want to pay back the Japs for what they did to Pearl Harbor."

"What about college?" Billie asked inanely, still stunned by the news, yet feeling very grown-up now and already mourning carefree childhood.

"Is that all you have to say? Jesus H. Christ! I'm talking about war! About serving my country! I'm going off to fight for the American way of life and for girls like you, Billie! If those Japs can do what they did to Pearl, they could just march across this country and kill us in our beds. Everybody knows how sneaky they are!"

"I don't feel like going to the movies now," Dotty said, sitting down on the low stone wall that surrounded the Cummingses' front yard. The thought of yellow-faced men with bloody fangs marching across the U. S. of A. made her gulp.

"Hey, Dotty, what's the matter?" Carl challenged. "You scared of those Japs? What would you do if they said they'd kill me if you didn't sleep with them? What would you do then, huh?" Carl's eyes glimmered, waiting for his steady girl-friend's answer. Dotty recognized the old no-win predicament. It was a question that usually arose at Brummers Ice Cream Parlor while they were sipping rainbow cokes. If she said she would never sleep with a Jap, Carl would say she didn't care enough about him to spare his life. If she said she'd do *anything* to save him, he'd sneer and question her morals. Either way, a girl couldn't win. The recognition of the dilemma on her face softened Carl. "Don't worry, Dotty, I wouldn't let a 'monkey man' lay a finger on you. I'd kill myself first." Tenderly, he placed a hand on Dotty's shoulder.

"Let's go downtown to the Navy Yard instead," Tim suggested. "We can hang around outside and watch the ships in the harbor." The girls' eyes lit up. It was certainly better than trying to figure out what had gotten into the boys. Once they were there, the boys would meander around acting like big shots and talking about the ships, and the girls could watch the uniforms.

The boys led the way while the girls hung back, huddling as they walked. "Does anyone have any rouge or lipstick?"

"I have some Tangee. It's not very good, pink coral, or something. It was all I could sneak off my sister's dresser."

"It's good enough," Dotty encouraged. "We'll just use lots of it. Just think, we might meet some of those handsome sailors and maybe Carl won't think I'm such a kid if he sees some real men interested in me." She dabbed furiously at her cheeks and lips, watching her reflection in the window of a parked car.

One by one, the girls took turns, to the boys' whistling approval. Then they paired off and walked casually, the boys with their arms flung around their girls' shoulders. Billie felt strange walking beside Tim this way; part of her world was slipping away. The first step in becoming an adult and it had to be learning to say good-bye. Of their little group, the gang, four of her friends from as far back as she could remember were leaving to fight a war. Her mouth was dry and she licked her lips. The waxy lipstick felt thick and greasy. She'd never used so much rouge before. What would Mother say? The problem was where she was going to wash it off? If they'd gone to the movies as they'd intended, she could have washed it off in the ladies' room.

"Do you think the MPs will chase us away?" Billie questioned.

"Not when I tell them Tim already enlisted and the rest of us go down Monday morning," Carl said with more bravado than he felt.

The sight of the Philadelphia Navy Yard frightened Billie. This wasn't a Movietone newsreel; this was the real thing. Battleships, destroyers, cruisers, all with their camouflaged green-and-brown superstructures reaching for the sky. Even from this distance and seen through the chainlink fence, they seemed enormous and ominous. The boys pointed out the classification of each ship, but it all remained a mystery to Billie, who couldn't tell a battleship from a cruiser. Only the aircraft carrier, with its long flat deck, was easily distinguishable from the rest. How could a plane take off from that dock? Worse yet, how did it land? She'd seen the newsreels and marveled at the skill of the pilots. Once she'd heard that from the air the carrier's deck looked like a tombstone. The thought gave her chills.

"How do you like them?" a masculine voice drawled at Billie's elbow. She turned and stared up into incredible, summer-blue eyes.

"They're frightening, but beautiful," Billie said honestly. Handsome. Tall. Beautiful. Simply beautiful. The man, not the ship.

"I kind of like them myself. Especially the carrier. But my favorite is the *Enterprise*. I trained on her. Moss Coleman," he introduced himself. "Lieutenant, junior grade. And you're . . . ?"

"Billie. Billie Ames. Actually it's Willa, but no one calls me that, not even my mother." Now why had she said that? How gauche and immature she must seem to him with her round circles of rouge. She could just kick herself for putting it on. He must be at least twenty-five. Too old for her. Too old for what? All he was doing was talking to her. His brilliant eyes seemed amused and she realized how unsophisticated she must seem to him. His dark hair was almost black against the stark white of his naval officer's uniform. He was as handsome as sin, as Grandmother used to say. His deep tan so early in the year made Billie wonder where he'd been before coming to Philadelphia.

The same amusement was in his voice when he spoke again. "Billie it is. Willa sounds like an old maiden aunt. Do you live here in Philly?"

Billie nodded. "All my life. We live on . . . we live not far from here," she answered, suddenly shy.

Moss stood back for a better look at the girl. She was young, too young. Younger than the girls who hung out at the USO. Soft ash-blond hair framed her face and was held back from her temples by two barrettes. Bright, intelligent hazel eyes were fringed by smoky lashes and naturally arched brows. Her pretty face was smooth-skinned, color marking the high cheekbones. A delicately formed mouth, beneath the lipstick, was generous and yielding, vulnerable with youth. She was a sweet thing, keeping her eyes lowered, her voice soft and shy. His sense of chivalry rose to the surface. If some of his buddies spotted her, she wouldn't have a prayer. They were animals, pure and simple, and the fact that she'd be seen talking to Moss Coleman, Reaper of Virgins, would make her fair game. He'd be willing to bet her mother didn't know she was here or that she wore rouge and lipstick. He grinned. She was innocent. He could see it in her face. Nice bones, good figure. Old Seth would look at that first. Carry on the Coleman line, good breeding, all the shit that went with settling down and marrying the right girl. A closer look made him think she probably didn't know where babies came from, something he could change within two days, three at the most.

His friends constantly kidded Moss about his lady-killer charm and kept track of his score. The latest count since he'd hit Philly was eleven. But these were dangerous times and a man had to take what he could when he could. They offered, he accepted. It was that simple. This little girl standing beside him wouldn't offer. She was what the guys called a good girl. Though some claimed all good girls had wet bloomers.

"So, you live around here. Do you come here often to look around?"

"No. I've only been here once before, on a class trip. I came down with some of my friends. They're around here somewhere. One of the boys enlisted and the others are going down to enlist on Monday. We're supposed to be at the movies," she blurted, looking around for her friends with a worried expression, as though needing to be saved from this stranger in his immaculate uniform.

For the first time in his life Moss found himself uncertain. She was looking at him in a way that made him feel he was being inspected and falling short. His appearance flashed before him. He was perfect: shoes shined, belt buckle polished, all the brass in shining order. Every hair in place, Ipana smile.

{ 12 }

Suntan just the right shade. Creases so sharp they could slice bread. It must be his imagination, this dissatisfaction he felt from her.

Moss knew he should leave. There was nothing for him here. "Would you like to see the carrier up a little closer?" he heard himself asking. "I can get you through the gate."

Billie frowned. She remembered her mother's warning of strangers. "Yes, thank you, I would."

Moss cupped her elbow and took her around to the guard at the gate, who offered him a smart salute. He showed his identification and waited while Billie signed in. He watched while she registered her address, 479 Elm Street, and smiled. I have *one* of your secrets, little girl, he thought with satisfaction.

The yard was peopled with sailors and busy work crews, their young faces either wreathed with smiles or studies of concentration. Moss was quick to see the admiring glances that came Billie's way and his hand tightened on her elbow possessively. Battleships and destroyers bound for Europe huddled around the dock. Their decks, dotted with white T-shirts and blue denims, were being scraped and primed, painted and polished, before they took their cargos of men and machines out to sea.

"This is about as far as I can take you. These are great ships, but I'll always think of the flight deck of the USS *Enterprise* as home. There's nothing like the feeling of landing gear touching that deck or of being hoisted backward by the landing hook."

Billie's eyes grew round with admiration. "You're a flyer? You really fly one of those planes and land on that little deck?"

"It's really not that little, Billie." He found he liked saying her name. "I've been flying since I was fourteen on our ranch in Texas and there's more space on a carrier deck than on the old dirt road back home."

There was such naked admiration in Billie's eyes, Moss felt himself blush at his own braggadocio. "I've got to admit to overshooting the landing deck a couple of times, but I've never ditched. That means going over the side, plane and all. Some guys are really good. There's a fella in my barracks who has never made a mistake. Not one."

"That's amazing," Billie said in a hushed whisper. "How long have you been in Philly?"

"A month. I came in from San Diego. That's why the suntan."

There was something bitter about his expression. "That's where I should be now, getting ready to push off for the Pacific."

"Why aren't you?"

"I've been assigned to Admiral McCarter, as his aide. I suppose lots of guys would give their eyeteeth for this duty, but I'd rather be flying." She watched as he lifted his head and tracked a pigeon headed for the superstructure, as though he wished he, too, could just spread wings and fly. Billie was quiet for a long moment, aware of his sadness. It made her almost hurt for him. She reached out to lay her hand on the sleeve of his white tunic.

Moss dropped his gaze to her, seeing her smile and the compassion in her hazel eyes. "My father's an influential man," he told her, something he'd never confided to another soul. "I'm the only son and Pap doesn't cotton to the idea of me flying. He arranged this assignment with the Admiralty." It was there again, the bitterness.

"Couldn't you ask to be reassigned?"

"Yeah, I could, but I couldn't do it to Pap," Moss said quietly. "He hangs a lot on me, wanting me to carry on the family and the business. I could be madder'n hell, but I'm not. He loves me and he's afraid of losing me."

"Texas, you said?" That explained the slight drawl.

"Texas. Austin."

"Then you're a cowboy!"

Moss laughed, a nice easy sound, as though laughing were second nature to him. She liked the way his eyes crinkled at the corners and just the barest dimple showed in his firm, chiseled jaw. "Hardly. Texans don't ride horses to get anywhere. They fly. Seems like most of the people I know have their own planes. Or else they rent them. Just like folks here in Philly hire taxicabs."

Billie couldn't imagine flying anywhere, much less owning her own plane. "All Texans own a plane?" she asked naively.

"Well, not all, but the ones I know do. Say, you've never been up, have you? You've never flown?"

Billie shook her head, following his gaze once again to the birds perched on the carrier. "Never. And I don't suppose I ever will. What's it like?"

Moss took her hand, taking her over to a stack of crates and sitting beside her. "Billie, honey, you're going to be sorry you asked that question." For the next hour Lieutenant (j.g.) Moss Coleman described to Billie the exhilaration he felt when his wheels left the ground. He told her about flying a wrecked old crop duster around the ranch and the way his father had tanned his hide when he'd found out about it. Moss had Billie laughing, exclaiming, shuddering. He sparked her imagination and made her wish that just once she could fly.

"There's a little airport around here where they have planes for hire. I'd like to take you up, Billie, just so you'll know I'm not crazy and everything I've told you is true."

"I'd like that," she answered quickly, cheeks flushed with the anticipated excitement, eyes bright and eager. "Oh, but I don't think my mother would like that— Mother! What time is it?"

Moss glanced at his watch. "Five-thirty."

"Omigosh! I've got to get going." For the first time in hours Billie remembered her friends. They must think she'd gotten lost or gone home by herself. They wouldn't still be hanging around the yard. "It was nice of you to show me around, Lieutenant. I know you must be busy and I've got to start for home. My mother will worry if I'm not home by six." She felt so silly, telling this man that she had to be home by six o'clock. It was so babyish. She felt humiliated by the restrictions, especially since he'd spent the afternoon talking to her as though she were his own age and not an empty-headed schoolgirl.

"Do you see your friends anywhere? You don't suppose they left without you, do you?" he asked, concerned.

"It doesn't matter. I know my way home. Thank you again." Billie began to walk away. Moss was stunned. Girls never walked away from him, not at five-thirty in the afternoon. He was about to speak when Billie turned. "Lieutenant, since you're so far from Texas and your family, perhaps you'd like to come to dinner on Sunday." She almost gasped with astonishment at her invitation. What in the world had made her ask him to dinner? She could already hear Agnes's objections. Still, lots of families invited servicemen for a home-cooked meal. Meal. Food. Oh, God! Agnes was going to complain about the food ration coupons. Still, she'd made the offer and she had to follow up on it. "Four seventy-nine Elm Street. Gray-and-white house."

"Wait a second, Billie. Two miles is a long walk and you'll never make it home in time. Let me see if I can borrow a car and I'll drive you. By the way, thanks for the invitation. Tomorrow's Sunday, you know." He grinned as though he guessed her second thoughts.

Billie flushed under the dazzling smile. "It really isn't necessary. I've still got the money for the movies and I can take a cab if I have to, really."

"I won't hear of it. If I hadn't pulled your ear about flying, you wouldn't be stranded. Please, let me help." He was so sincere, Billie just nodded.

While Billie waited, she contemplated her predicament. She didn't want Agnes to know that she'd spent Saturday afternoon at the Navy Yard, much less that she'd been talking to a military man and had lost her friends. What if someone called or stopped by the house to ask about her? What if Moss came to dinner? He'd surely tell Agnes how he'd met Billie.

Moss returned dangling the keys to a 1938 Nash parked near the guardhouse. Billie felt so grown-up when Moss held the door open for her. Agnes was going to have a fit. Nice girls didn't get into cars with strange boys. Or men. Moss Coleman, Lieutenant (j.g.), was no boy. Agnes wouldn't miss that fact. In spite of herself, Billie was excited and flattered.

"How long will you be in Philly?" Billie asked when Moss had maneuvered through the traffic and swung out onto the main road.

"Probably through the summer. At least, that's the way it looks right now. Or until I can get myself assigned to where the action is. Being an errand boy for a hotshot admiral isn't my idea of doing my part for the war effort. I'm a pilot, Billie, and a damn good one. That's what I want to do."

Billie nodded. She knew all there was to know about a protective parent. Moss interpreted her expression correctly. "You too, huh?"

"It's because I'm an only child. My father died when I was little. I suppose it's natural for a parent to be protective. They want what's best for us." To Moss it sounded like a recital of what her mother must have said hundreds of times. Just the way Seth Coleman had preached to him.

"I've got a sister, but I'm the only son. Pap is up there in years and he's afraid for me. But I can't let his fear rub off on me. Flying is what I do and what I do best. I don't plan to run around for some two-star admiral whose only idea of action is signing papers and drinking scotch. Scotch that I have to procure for him."

"What will you do?"

"It's not what I'll do, Billie; it's when I'll do it! Pap can get me assigned to fat man's duty, but he can't keep me here. I can speak up for myself and there's not a damn thing he can do about it. But I hate to hurt him. He's a great guy and I know how much I mean to him. It's just that sometimes I really feel the weight of that responsibility pressing down on me. Being the apple of ole Pap's eye isn't what it's cracked up to be." Moss could hardly believe he was telling her these things. He was used to keeping his personal life and his problems to himself.

"Turn here. It's two blocks down and then take the next right. Gray-and-white house. I'll say a prayer you get what you want."

Moss almost braked the car. Any other girl would have said she would keep her fingers crossed. This one was going to pray for him. Impulsively, he reached across the seat and took her hand. It felt small and fragile in his. He released it a moment later to shift gears and pull to a stop in front of the house. He glanced at his watch. "Five minutes to six," he announced proudly, as though getting her home on time had been a monumental task.

Billie wondered where her friends were. Were they worrying about her? "Would you like to come in and meet my mother? Oh, but you've probably got other things to do, and I do appreciate your taking the time to bring me home. I'm sorry I've been such a nuisance."

"You, sweet Billie, are anything but a nuisance." He smiled, realizing he'd meant what he said. But Jesus, he didn't want to go in and meet her mother. He loved his mother but other people's made him nervous, especially girls' mothers. Hell, he was here . . . maybe she was afraid she was going to catch it and he could help matters. All in the line of duty. "I'd like to meet your mother," he lied.

Billie almost fainted. That wasn't what he was supposed to say. Didn't he know she was only trying to be polite? She didn't wait for him to come around to open the door for her. Instead, she leaped out, smoothing down the skirt of her jumper. Suddenly, the fringe along the hem seemed girlishly silly and trendy, and for the second time that day she wished she were wearing stockings and heels.

Agnes Ames's eyes narrowed when she heard the sound of a car door closing in front of the house. None of Billie's friends drove a car. She parted the lace curtains slightly and peered out. Billie and a navy man. An officer, considering the dress whites. What could have happened? She wouldn't panic. Billie was a responsible child. A serious, responsible child.

"Mother! I'm home. Come and meet someone."

Moss Coleman stood a good six inches taller than Agnes, yet he was immediately aware of her strength, as if she were his height or even taller. It was in the measuring, brown eyes and in the subtle squaring of the shoulders. . . . He'd seen the same signs of character in Seth. Pearls. Why did they always wear pearls? It seemed every girl's mother he'd ever met was adorned with them.

Billie broke the silence. "Mother, this is Moss Coleman. He was nice enough to bring me home so I wouldn't be late. Moss, this is my mother, Mrs. Ames." He waited to see if Mrs. Ames would offer her hand. She didn't.

Billie was beginning to feel desperate. Agnes was standing her ground, staring at Moss with suspicion. "I've invited Moss to dinner tomorrow. He's from Texas and it's been a long time since he's had a home-cooked meal. I knew you wouldn't object," Billie prompted hopefully.

"Dinner. Of course. We'd like to have you for dinner, Lieutenant," Agnes offered.

Moss wondered if Mrs. Ames meant she'd like to have him as a guest or for the main course! But hold on a minute, he'd never accepted the invitation. Somebody was being railroaded here and he thought he knew who. "I wouldn't want to impose, Mrs. Ames," he said in his best-bred Texan, just a shade short of humble. Before he could politely make excuses, Agnes forced something that passed for a smile.

"Fine. Shall we say around two? I want to thank you for bringing my daughter home. It was very considerate of you. She's very young and I worry when she's late." There it was, the gentle nudge, the reminder that he was suspected of being a troll who lived under a bridge and preyed on innocent young girls.

"It was my pleasure, ma'am," Moss drawled. "Billie, thank you for the invitation. I have to get the car back to the yard. Nice meeting you, ma'am."

He still hadn't said if he was coming to dinner and Billie felt wretched as she watched him walk out to the car, Agnes's words about her youth still smarting.

Outside in the car, Moss exhaled a long, gusty sigh. He didn't think he wanted to come to dinner. But Sundays were always so boring you could want to tear your hair out, and it had been nice talking with Billie. If he didn't have anything better to do, he'd show up around two o'clock. If something came up, he'd send a note.

Before Agnes could question her daughter, Billie rushed into a lengthy explanation. "I think it was very nice of him to bring me home, don't you, Mother?"

"Billie, you broke how many rules this afternoon?" Agnes said frigidly.

"Mother, please. Do we have to go into all of this? I'm home, safe and sound. Nothing happened. The lieutenant is charming. He didn't say he was coming to dinner and I'm certain he has other plans, so don't count on it. I'm sorry if I upset you."

Agnes sniffed. It was her usual reaction to Billie's apologies. Once, just once, Billie would have liked to hear that she was forgiven, or at least that her mother understood.

"I think I'll go up to my room and get ready for supper."

"I moved your room downstairs to the study. Mr. Campbell from next door and his nephew helped move down the furniture. I'm going to rent your room. We really have to do our bit, Billie. The housing situation is reaching crisis proportions."

Billie only knew that someone else was going to live in her room, the only place she'd been able to call her own since she was a little girl. "I wish you had told me, Mother. I don't mind the change, but I would have liked to pack my things myself. Did you go through everything? Even my pictures?" Billie felt violated.

"Everything. Go see for yourself. Now you'll have the window seat. You can sit there tomorrow and watch the road to see if your handsome lieutenant shows up for dinner." Agnes smiled.

Billie glanced at her mother. She'd just been bought. Agnes's seeming acceptance of having Moss for Sunday dinner was supposed to soothe the wound of having been moved lock, stock, and barrel out of her room. And she had to accept the terms of truce; otherwise, if Moss did come tomorrow, she could count on Agnes's sulky indifference, which could make Billie squirm as though she had fire ants in her bloomers.

It wasn't fair. It just wasn't fair. At least Agnes could have asked before renting out her bedroom from under her. Billie wandered into the study and looked at the window seat with its velvet cushion. It would be a delightful place to curl up with a book. She had a clear view of the drive and the street.

Perhaps it wasn't so bad after all.

Agnes remained in the hall at the bottom of the stairs, head cocked to one side as though she were listening to a distant noise. The sound she heard was her inner voice murmuring questions concerning Billie. Her perfectly nice and gifted daughter had returned to the house this evening and there was something different about her that had nothing to do with the lipstick or with the artificial blush applied to her cheeks.

{{{{{{{{ CHAPTER TWO }}}}}}}}

Agnes Ames bent down to baste the roasting chicken. As with almost everyone else in Philadelphia—and Agnes did aspire to being like everyone else, only better—after coming home from Sunday service the first order of the day was to dress the chicken and stick it in the oven. It was one thing to invite a guest to Sunday dinner and quite another to plan a meal that was acceptable yet not expensive.

The chicken was a delectable golden brown, the bread stuffing savory with herbs. Her practiced eye took in the bowl of garden salad and the fresh string beans, which, being out of season, had cost more than she cared to spend. Mashed potatoes and gravy would be more than enough when she'd added her homemade biscuits. The butter, dearer than dear since rationing, was first allowed to soften, then whipped with ice water to increase its volume, and chilled again. It was one of her little tricks and it worked quite well. Agnes Ames could not abide white, unpalatable oleo. She had prepared a deep-dish apple pie the night before and it would be mouth-watering. If there was one culinary talent she possessed, it was making pies. The secret was using rendered suet instead of shortening, which cost a fortune, for the crust. She did not like to think about the dent in her sugar supply for the sweet dessert.

The music coming from the living room had a mournful sound. That wasn't like Billie. Normally, she'd be playing light, popular tunes after her practicing was done. Once, Agnes had had dreams of her daughter becoming a concert pianist and she'd been told by experts that Billie had the talent. But after learning the prohibitive cost of schooling and lessons and recitals, Agnes had regretfully abandoned the idea and turned her ambitions for Billie along less flamboyant lines.

Agnes listened for a moment. Billie must have learned a new piece. Perhaps it wasn't mournful, just sad. Her thoughts immediately went to the young lieutenant. Moss Coleman frightened her. Or was it the way Billie looked at Moss Coleman? A Texan! No doubt he was a ranch hand—or did they call them cowpokes? And that atrocious drawl! Not for Billie. Definitely not for Billie. She'd been worrying all morning what she would do if the cowboy did show up for dinner and managed, despite her, to ask Billie for a date. Up to now, Billie had always listened to her, always behaved and followed her advice. Agnes's stomach fluttered.

If the lieutenant was still around through summer, what would that do to Billie's chances with Neal Fox? Neal Fox, whose father owned the bank. Neal Fox, who was more than acceptable with his studious habits, family money, and 4F classification. Martha Fox, a member of Agnes's garden club, had eagerly arranged a date for the two youngsters. Comparing the Fox boy with someone like Lieutenant Coleman . . . Agnes shuddered and almost cut her thumb as she peeled the potatoes. She hoped—no, prayed—that the lieutenant wouldn't come for dinner. He had thanked them for the invitation but never actually accepted. No manners. Ignorant cowhand. Agnes supposed this was the way cowboys did things. Neal was the kind of boy who would arrive exactly fifteen minutes early for dinner, carrying a bouquet of flowers for her and a box of candy for Billie. That was the way it should be done. The lieutenant would arrive, maybe, with his hat in his hand, eat three helpings of everything, hold the chicken in his fingers and lick them afterward. She'd been to the movies; she knew cowboys cooked over open fires and ate out of cans. But was the handsome young lieutenant actually one of those? There'd been something about him when he'd met her penetrating gaze. It was as though he'd been trying to figure *her* out. A Texan!

Today would be a good time to talk to Billie about Neal. After their guest left and they were doing the dishes. A nice mother-to-daughter talk. Billie seemed to like that Sunday bit of intimacy. Agnes personally found it especially boring. Her own life was uneventful and Billie's was so placid and predictable that it didn't leave much room for conversation. Usually they ended up discussing a book or the progress of the garden, or exchanging pieces of gossip.

Agnes glanced at the clock. It was one-forty-five. Fifteen minutes till their guest arrived. Billie stopped playing. She closed the piano. She was going into her room. Agnes knew her daughter was perched on the window seat, book in hand, staring out at the road. Waiting for a white uniform.

The telephone rang at three minutes of two. Billie almost broke her neck running out to the hall to pick up the receiver. "Hello," she breathed.

"Billie?"

"Yes." It was him. "Yes, yes, it's me. Moss?"

A low chuckle came over the wire. "I'm sorry, Billie, but I won't be able to come to dinner. The admiral wants to play golf this afternoon and can't find a partner. I'm the best he can come up with. Perhaps you'll invite me another time?"

Billie sucked in her breath. He wasn't coming. Somehow, she'd known he wouldn't. She wanted so badly to see him walk up to her front door. She couldn't remember ever wanting something so badly, unless it was the Christmas she'd wanted a two-wheeled bike. She hadn't gotten that, either. "Anytime," she said brightly, hiding her disappointment. "Our Sundays are open. You don't need an invitation." There. Short of begging, what else could she say?

"That's very kind of you. Please thank your mother. Listen, Billie, if you're ever at the Front Street USO on a Saturday night, I hope you'll save me a dance."

USO. Dance. Save him a dance. "I'll do that, Lieutenant. Thank you for calling," Billie said pleasantly. When she hung up the phone, she forced a smile to her lips. She knew Agnes was standing in the doorway and had probably heard every word. She had to turn and face her mother. Do it. Do it now before your face cracks with the strain.

"Oh, Mother—there you are. That was Lieutenant Coleman. He won't be able to make dinner. He has to play golf with the admiral. I told him he had an open invitation. Was that all right, Mother?"

Relief coursed through Agnes. Neal was still in the running. "Of course, dear. We must do our part, small as it may seem. I'm certain that one day, when he has nothing better to do, he'll drop by for a home-cooked meal."

Billie wanted to run to her room and cry. Cry when things got too bad. But it wouldn't be the same now. Now she was sleeping in the study because her room, a room that had been hers and hers alone, was to be rented! How she had loved it, the small windows under the eaves, the shelves holding all her books. Her music scores in neat stacks, the pictures she'd painted, and her bulging portfolio of designs that leaned against the wall. Now it was all a jumble in the study. A study wasn't a bedroom. She was sick with disappointment.

"Well, since there are just the two of us, we might as well eat now." Agnes turned and went back into the kitchen. "We'll eat in here; no sense going to all the trouble of messing up the dining room, is there?"

Billie followed after her mother, knowing how difficult it was going to be to swallow even one bite. She adjusted her features into a pleasant mask of indifference. It was going to be just another Sunday.

As Moss replaced the phone, his eyes went to the golf bag in the corner of Admiral McCarter's office. The admiral was entertaining a visiting three-star at the Officers Club. Moss's conscience pricked slightly as he made his way down the long battleship-gray hallway. He joined three of his friends who waited impatiently at the curb in the parking lot.

"New York City, here we come!" one of the j.g.'s shouted hoarsely. Moss grinned and climbed into the backseat of the Ford.

He didn't think about Billie Ames again until the next Sunday morning, when he awoke feeling achy and out of sorts. He brushed his teeth and swallowed three aspirin. When was he going to learn that Saturday-night hangovers hung on like leeches and were the ruination of a good Sunday? As long as he was going to be miserable, he might as well salve his conscience and go to dinner at Billie's house.

For a long moment he looked at the pay phone on the wall outside his quarters. Who was he kidding? Last night at the USO, he'd hung about the doorway watching for her. It was only after eleven o'clock, when nice girls like Billie would already be home, that he'd gone out to the local bar to tie one on. Now, he quickly dropped his nickel into the slot before he could talk sense to himself.

Billie picked up the phone on the first ring. She tilted her hat slightly to the side so she could comfortably place the receiver against her ear. She expected to hear her girlfriend's voice.

"Billie?"

When she heard his low, husky drawl, she felt her knees buckle. Her knuckles whitened on the prayer book in her hand. He'd called. Her eyes lifted upward, acknowledging the power of prayer.

Cool and calm. "Lieutenant, how are you? Did you have a nice golf game last Sunday with the admiral?" she asked for want of anything better and needing a moment to compose herself. Lordy, why couldn't she be more sophisticated?

"Golf? Oh, that golf game. Par." His conscience pricked again and he quickly squelched it. His head was killing him and he shouldn't be doing this; he didn't even know why he was doing it. She was a nice girl, a nice young girl, and there was nothing there for him. He remembered how he'd looked for her the night before. "How are you, Billie? Am I calling too early?" He massaged his temples, wondering what time it was.

The low, throaty laugh felt good in his ear. "No, of course not. I've been up for hours. As a matter of fact I was just on my way to church. Another five minutes and you'd have missed me." She waited expectantly.

"Church?" Where people go to pray. Did she pray for him as she'd promised? "Are you Catholic?"

"Yes, I am."

"I'm Catholic also. So's my mother. There aren't very many of us in Texas. Not a very good one, I'm afraid. I don't attend mass regularly." Hell, what was he, really? More agnostic than anything else, he supposed. The day his mother had told him he was old enough to attend services on his own he'd stopped going. Instead of attending the ten o'clock service as his sister Amelia did, he'd hung around the airfield. Seth never went to church.

Billie was unsure of what comment she could make to another of his confessions. Out of the corner of her eye she could see Agnes standing by the front door, waiting impatiently. Did Agnes know who was on the other end of the phone?

Moss saved her from making a reply. "I'd like to come to dinner today, if the invitation is still open."

Moss heard the slight gasp over the wire. "Of course. Dinner is at two. I'll look forward to seeing you again, Lieutenant."

"Do you think you could call me Moss, instead of lieutenant?"

"Of course . . . Moss. I'll see you this afternoon."

"Don't forget you promised to pray for me," he joked.

"I won't."

She dropped the receiver and turned to face Agnes. "Mother, do you know who that was? Lieutenant Coleman is coming to dinner. Isn't that nice?" She adjusted her hat in the front hall mirror, afraid to face her mother's scowl.

"We'll have to hurry dinner through if you're going to visit your girlfriend this afternoon." Agnes made a supreme effort to keep her tone light and conversational. Inside, she was having difficulty resigning herself to the threat of the handsome lieutenant. She'd thought that matter closed.

Billie turned. "There. How do I look?"

Agnes detected a change in her daughter. In the passing of an instant she seemed to have bloomed. She was so pretty, this daughter of hers. In a few years she'd be a raving beauty. Billie had her bones, her carriage. Good, clear skin with soft melting eyes that changed from green to brown to gray. Hazel eyes. Much too good for a Texas cowpoke. Another week or so and Neal Fox would be home from college.

As they walked the four blocks to St. Elias they were regaled with the chiming of the carillon. Agnes was worried. Perhaps a prayer would help. It seemed like such a long time since she'd believed in prayer. She only attended church because it was expected of her; it was the right thing to do and most of the right people were there. Agnes was a convert to Catholicism. That jackass she'd married to spite her parents had insisted she convert and raise the children in his religion. She'd done her duty, but as far as she was concerned religion was just a lot of hokus-pokus. She never held with going to confession and abstaining from meat on Fridays, but, good mother that she was, she'd seen to it that Billie had made her first communion and been confirmed when she was eleven. Once a month she sent her off to confession. How bored that priest must have been listening to Billie's little sins! Communion on every Sunday was a must. For Billie. Billie was a good girl and would stay a good girl. And it wasn't the power of prayer that would do it. That was Agnes's job!

Billie dreamed her way through mass and her mother had to nudge her gently when it was time to go to the altar rail for communion. Her prom was just weeks away. Was it possible to invite someone like Moss Coleman to be her escort? Would he think a senior dance silly and young? She was counting on too much, looking too far ahead. Coming to dinner was one thing; what she wanted and hoped for was another. She had to be patient. She would pray for that, for patience. Still, she'd be the envy of every girl there if she showed up with a tall handsome navy man. A lieutenant, a fly-boy. The girls would drop dead.

In just a few hours she'd see him again. Prickly fingers of excitement ran up and down her arms. She bowed her head and prayed Moss Coleman would get what he wanted, everything he wanted.

Billie sat on the window seat pretending to read, watching for Moss. She'd brushed her teeth twice and kept glancing in the mirror to be sure the breeze hadn't disturbed her hair. It was smooth and sleek, a shining cap of ash blond, curved under in a pageboy. She wished it would fall over one eye like Veronica Lake's, but its own natural tendency to curl forced her to tame it back with a barrette. When the car slid to a stop at the curb, Billie felt positively light-headed. She forced herself to take two or three deep breaths as she did before playing in a piano recital. She allowed the bell to ring before she opened the door and found herself held in the gaze of those smiling summer-blue eyes. She smiled the dazzling smile Moss remembered and his head felt better already.

Agnes walked into the front room and was stunned to see Moss extending a huge bouquet of flowers toward her. "For your table, Mrs. Ames. Billie, the chocolates are for you." This was all wrong. It was Neal Fox who was supposed to bring the candy and flowers. For a moment, Agnes was unnerved. But only for a moment. She smiled her smile that never reached her eyes.

He grinned. He knew she didn't want him here and it didn't make any difference to him. He turned to Billie. "If dinner isn't ready, why don't you show me your garden? I could see from the front that your property goes pretty far back."

"I'd like that. Mother, you don't need me in the kitchen, do you?"

Moss's eyes went to Agnes again. He waited, almost daring her.

"No, you two young people go along. I can manage. I'll serve in twenty minutes." Agnes hadn't failed to notice the time. Moss had arrived fifteen minutes early. Neal Fox was the one who was supposed to have such impeccable manners. She felt confused and irritable as she went back to the kitchen. Stooping to reach under the sink, she rummaged for a suitable vase. The flowers stopped just short of being ostentatious. They must have cost him a fortune. The candy, too. The most expensive there was. And it wasn't a measly little one-pound box. No, it was a full five pounds and tied with a big red bow. How much did junior lieutenants make a month? Not enough to pay for such costly gifts, she was certain. Agnes sniffed. She thought she smelled money. Was it possible that this drawling, brash young man with the perceptive eyes could be something other than a cowhand? She'd quiz him during dinner. Agnes was good at quizzing. Most of the time people weren't aware of just how much they were telling her. She'd somehow underestimated this handsome flyer and she wouldn't make that mistake again.

As she stirred the gravy she watched Billie and Moss through the kitchen window. They did make a handsome couple. What were they talking about? The weather? Hardly. Him? More than likely. Billie was a good listener.

She grimaced. The gravy was lumpy; now she was going to have to strain it.

Dinner was a puzzling affair to Billie. Conversation was rapid and nonstop between her mother and Moss. She'd been worried that Agnes would be frigidly aloof and make the strain of conversation unbearable. Instead, her mother appeared animated and interested. Moss answered Agnes's questions with an exaggerated drawl, all the while wearing a most disconcertingly amused expression. He never spoke that way, Billie thought, when he was talking to her.

"I understand Austin is quite large," Agnes was saying. "Billie and I have never been further south than Virginia. Have you lived there long?"

"All my life," Moss drawled. "So have my folks. This is sure mighty good chicken, ma'am."

So much for his hearty cowhand appetite, Agnes thought. He'd done little more than pick at his food. But she had noticed that he had no difficulty selecting the proper fork and, to her relief, he hadn't tucked his napkin under his chin. Agnes tried again. "I assume your parents still live there?"

"Yes, ma'am. My mother always served her green beans this way, with bits of bacon and onion." His gaze went to

Agnes's narrowing eyes. He smiled, enjoying his success at baiting her. He knew she was fishing for information and he was being polite but evasive.

"Billie, dear, don't you like the stuffing? You aren't eating. Is anything wrong, don't you feel well?"

"I'm fine, Mother." Quickly, before Agnes could dominate the conversation, Billie asked a question of her own. "Tell us about Admiral McCarter. What's it like to work for him?"

Moss laughed. "Boring. All admirals are boring. They sit and shuffle papers when they aren't out on the golf course or having dinner at the Officers' Club. They moan and groan and complain about how lonely it is at the top."

"What is it you'd rather be doing, Lieutenant?" Agnes interjected.

The drawl was more pronounced when he spoke to Agnes. "Well, ma'am, I joined up to fly. And that's what I intend to do, if there's such a thing as having prayers answered." His eyes flicked to Billie and she felt warmed by his smile and by the confidence between them.

"How do your parents feel about your flying? I'd think your mother in particular would be concerned. Of course, I've never had a son, but I'd think your father would be very proud of you. Is he a flyer, too?"

"No, ma'am. Pap's retired, I suppose you could say." He loved the look of frustration on Agnes's face. "My mother was concerned at the beginning, but she said whatever makes me happy makes her happy. She has my sister, Amelia, to fuss over."

He was being too respectful to be considered a smart aleck. Yet he was evading her questions. "I've heard Texans live on ranches. Do you?"

"Live on a ranch?" Moss repeated. "We have a spread. We call it a spread in Texas." He turned to Billie and asked her if she'd like to go to the movies after dinner.

"Yes, I would." Mother, you don't mind, do you?" Billie's tone and the look in her eyes told Agnes she didn't care if her mother minded or not. She was going. It was shocking. Things were going on here. Things she couldn't put a name to and wasn't sure she liked. She'd had such grand plans for Neal Fox and Billie, and she knew now that the girl would never look at the banker's son without comparing him with this exceedingly handsome, if somewhat dull, young lieutenant. She seethed inwardly.

"No, I don't mind." She'd had enough. "Why don't you two leave just after dessert. I'll do the dishes. You can do them next Sunday, Billie."

This Sunday dessert was cherry pie and it was delicious. Both Billie and Moss gulped it down. Agnes served Moss coffee and gave her daughter a glass of milk. Billie was well aware this was her mother's silent reminder that she was a child and Moss was a man; she left the milk untouched.

"The next feature is at four o'clock, Moss. We'd better hurry. I don't like to walk in during the picture, do you?" Not waiting for a reply, Billie walked ahead to the parlor for her purse.

"Mrs. Ames, it was a delicious dinner. It was nice to eat home-cooked for a change. Thank you for having me, and I'll be sure to tell my mother that you use the same string bean recipe."

There was nothing to do except be agreeable. She'd been had. This brash young man had outmaneuvered her. "Thank you for the flowers, Lieutenant. That was very kind of you. We'll have to wait for summer, I suppose, to have flowers from our own garden. Spring flowers are so fragile, wilting and dying almost immediately after they're picked." She was talking too much and he was letting her. When he joined Billie in the front hall, Agnes stared at them for a long moment. He reminded her of a hawk circling its prey and she almost objected when he reached for Billie's hand. She wanted to stop Billie before it was too late. Too late for what? Too late for Neal Fox, for God's sake!

Moss turned, his face half in shadow. "Good-bye, Mrs. Ames. I'll have Billie home before dark." Agnes didn't need to see his eyes; she knew what would be there. Satisfaction. A battle well won.

He escorted Billie down the aisle, careful not to spill the two containers of popcorn. He didn't like two people fishing out of the same box. What was his was his.

Billie sat beside Moss: their shoulders touched. He liked this sweet young girl. She reminded him of his sister in so many ways. Even Seth would approve of Billie. There was something gentle about her, almost old-world. He was beginning to suspect that she was deeper and more complex than she appeared on the surface. She was so young and innocent, without the pseudosophistication that he'd become accustomed to in girls. How had that buzzard back in the house on Elm Street come by a daughter like this? By God, Agnes Ames had to have been cut from the same bolt of cloth as Pap. Traits that he admired in his father were almost unpalatable in a woman. Still, Moss realized the deep vein of loyalty that ran through people like Seth Coleman and Agnes Ames. Loyalty and strength and intelligence. He wouldn't fault her for that.

They sat quietly together watching the newsreel and the cartoon before the main feature. Betty Grable was showing her legs and it wasn't even ten minutes into the movie. Moss reached out and took Billie's hand. For some reason, couples always held hands in the movies. Is that how he was thinking of himself and Billie? As a couple? Billie's hands were soft, just like the rest of her. He knew she was smiling in the darkness. He smiled, too. She was a nice kid. A very nice kid. He wondered when she would be eighteen. Pretty, too. Billie had the kind of beauty that came from within, arresting the beholder. He supposed she was what they called "the girl next door," and he'd heard some guys say that was what the war was about. Moss knew it wasn't. Power, that was the reason for the war. Something people like himself and Pap and Agnes Ames understood.

Another ten minutes into the movie and he leaned over to whisper, "Billie, this is a terrible movie and we both know how it's going to turn out. Why don't we leave and go some place we can talk. I'd like to get to know you better."

"All right," Billie agreed, frowning slightly. She'd told Agnes they'd be at the movies. It seemed whenever she was with Moss she broke another rule.

"Are you always so agreeable?" There was an edge to his voice, as though he were annoyed.

"Only when it's something I want to agree to."

"I've got a blanket in the car. What say we go to the park and sit by the lake?"

Billie's pulses sped. If Agnes ever got wind of this, she'd be very disapproving. Before she could reconsider, she stood up and waited for Moss to lead her up the aisle and out into the sunshine.

It was a beautiful day. If Billie had ordered it from Sears Roebuck, she couldn't have done better. Marshmallow clouds drifted across an incredibly blue sky. The grass never seemed greener, the sun never warmer. The park lake rippled and glistened. It was perfect.

The minutes and hours passed with hardly a notice. Together they sat or reclined on the blanket, talking and talking and talking. She found herself telling Moss things she'd never told anyone. Her desire to go to design and textile school instead of becoming an English or history teacher. How she felt being without a father and how she'd learned to cope with Agnes's protectiveness. When she told him of her aptitude as a pianist, it was a revelation and not a boast.

Moss sprawled out on the blanket, his dark shining head resting in Billie's lap. He reached up and touched a finger to her lips. "No lipstick today," he said, looking up at her. The fringe of dark lashes hemming his eyes cast shadows into the blue.

"Not on Sunday." Billie laughed. "Do you mind?"

"Not on Sunday." He grinned. "I should be taking you home now. I told your mother I'd have you home by dark. By the time we get there it'll be past dark."

"I don't want to go home," Billie told him.

"I don't either."

"Why haven't you kissed me?" she blurted.

Moss laughed. "Did you want me to? Would you like it if I kissed you, Billie Ames?" He tried to keep his voice light and teasing. He'd wanted to kiss her for hours. He could almost taste her, could almost feel her lips soft and yielding beneath his. There was something about this sweet innocent he wanted to leave untouched, undisturbed. He didn't realize he was holding his breath for Billie's answer until she replied.

"I wanted it to be your idea, Lieutenant. Now that I've embarrassed myself by asking, I don't want to kiss you. Come on, we'll be late." Wordlessly, she stood up and yanked the blanket out from under him, folding it meticulously before starting back to the car.

"Billie! Wait!" Suddenly, it was important to make her understand. What exactly she should understand he didn't know. "Look at me when I talk to you. I've wanted to kiss you all afternoon, especially when you had cherry pie right there on the corner of your mouth." He touched her lips with his finger. "I'll know when you're ready to be kissed, Billie. Trust me?"

Billie smiled, his gesture lighting her face. That meant he wanted to see her again. She decided she would invite him not to her prom but to her graduation dance. Perhaps she wouldn't even go to her prom. It held no allure for her now.

They rode home in silence, Moss holding her hand. He

liked the way it felt in his. He liked Billie Ames. He should have kissed her. "I want to see you again. Will you let me?"

"I told you I'd pray for you to get what you wanted."

"How about the USO on Saturday? Does your mother allow you to go there?"

"I've only been there once for a welcoming tea in the afternoon; my mother is a volunteer for the Red Cross. I'll ask her. I think she'll say yes." Even if Agnes said absolutely no, Billie would find a way to get there. She was going to see as much of Moss as she could.

"Okay, I'll see you there, then. Hold on, I'll walk you to the door. We don't want your mother thinking I'm the kind of guy who pulls up and blows the horn and dumps you out on the street."

"Mother would never think that," Billie said loyally, but she knew it was a lie and so did Moss. "I had a wonderful time. Thank you. And thank you for the chocolates."

"Hey, I enjoyed it, too." He realized it was true. He did enjoy Billie's company, was enchanted with it. She made him feel good. She listened and cared and didn't talk too much.

She knew Moss was going to kiss her. It wasn't a soul-searing experience, and rockets didn't shoot off into the night. Instead, the kiss was soft, gentle, with the promise of so much more. More than Moss was ready to give or ask of her. She didn't feel dizzy or weak-kneed. A slow-spreading warmth enveloped her and she wanted him to hold her, just for a moment, just until she could remember that the world consisted of more than Moss Coleman. Her eyes were shining in the porch light. Someday there would be more—she was sure of it—because she would make it happen.

"Good night, Billie. I'll see you on Saturday."

"G'night, Moss. Drive carefully."

His mother was the only one who told him to drive carefully, and then, as if to spite authority, he would drive like a bat out of hell. Tonight he drove carefully, all the way back to the Navy Yard.

Agnes stood in the darkened parlor watching through the lace curtains. Her back stiffened. She'd heard the low, throaty laughter that was Billie's. She'd never heard her daughter laugh that way; it was a woman's laugh. Quickly, she moved to the kitchen, waiting for the front door to open. "How was the movie?" she asked.

"It was awful. Just awful. Neither of us liked it." There,

that was the truth. She simply felt no need or desire to tell Agnes when, where, why, or what. "How was your afternoon, Mother?"

"Oh, I played canasta with the neighbors and I've only just come home. I was going to listen to *Amos 'n' Andy*. Join me?"

"No thanks, Mother, I have to read a couple of chapters for a history quiz tomorrow. I think I'll have a sandwich and get started."

There was no quiz; neither was she hungry. She just wanted to be alone and think about today. She wanted to remember every look, every word, everything about Moss. Saturday was only six days away.

{{{{{{{ CHAPTER THREE }}}}}}}}

Agnes appeared in the kitchen to gather her scouring cleansers and wash bucket. Billie stood at the sink clearing away the last of the breakfast dishes. The old wringer washer on the back service porch sloshed rhythmically. "You'll have to hurry along, Billie, if you're going to the movies this afternoon with your nice friends."

All of a sudden she had "nice friends," Billie noticed. "I'm not going to the movies today. I thought I'd stay home and give you a hand. And besides, I want to wash my hair."

At this deviation from her daughter's Saturday routine, Agnes's eyes widened as she waited for the explanation she knew would come. Billie always washed and waved her hair on Saturday night in time for Sunday mass. Billie was struggling with the words. Agnes could sense it.

"Moss invited me to the dance at the USO tonight," Billie said. "I'm going." It was a flat statement, not a challenge.

"You know how I feel about the USO," Agnes countered. "It's perfectly fine for all those boys so far from home and it may be perfectly respectable for all those other girls, but not for you, Billie. When Lieutenant Coleman comes to call, I'll suggest he take you somewhere else, somewhere not quite so controversial."

"He's not coming to call, Mother. I'm going to meet him there. And the only controversy concerning the USO is yours."

"Would it make any difference to you if I said I didn't want you to go?" Agnes pretended to fuss with the cleaning rags and cleansers. This stubborn determination was so unlike Billie that it frightened her.

"Of course it makes a difference. But I'm going anyway." Billie felt her knees quaking and her breath caught in her throat. Never had she deliberately disobeyed her mother, but being with Moss, seeing him again, was almost a tangible need.

Agnes did not speak to her for the rest of the day. The sounds of scrubbing and moving furniture upstairs said all there was to say. There was no supper that night. Billie stood in front of the refrigerator and picked. Agnes was in her upstairs front bedroom, listening and waiting for Billie. She never came. Agnes heard the front door close at 7:18.

The USO was near the Navy Yard, a good walk, and Billie wasn't used to being out at night alone. Thankfully, it wouldn't be dark for almost an hour and she'd be with Moss by that time.

Her heels clicked on the sidewalk, not saddle shoes this time, but the high heels she'd been saving for the prom. Nylon stockings—"Starlight" was the name of the light beige shade—made her feel very adult even though her new garter belt felt a little loose. She'd finished making her dress only yesterday. It was one of her own designs, a soft navy-blue georgette that had cost a fortune at the drygoods. She'd adapted the little Peter Pan collar the pattern called for into a portrait neckline and the intricate puffed sleeves ended in a band just above her elbows. The skirt was full and hung in soft gathers from the tiny waistline, and the taffeta underslip rustled pleasantly with each step she took. Tiny smoke-pearl buttons retrieved from an old dress she'd outgrown marched down the front closing. Agnes hadn't seen it. She would have decreed the style and color too severe for Billie's soft blond coloring, but Billie's sense of color and style told her Agnes would have been wrong. The dress was perfect for her.

Even a block away Billie could hear the strains of Glenn Miller's band coming through the open doors of the USO. Men in uniform hung around outside and the dark armbands of the military police were in evidence. She stopped in the shadows for a moment to run a comb through her hair. Tonight it was pulled up from her ears and puffed over the forehead in a pompadour, allowing the back to fall long and soft to her shoulders. Just a touch of lipstick and powder completed her toilette. Tonight Billie Ames was feeling very far from being a schoolgirl and much closer to the woman she wanted to be, for Moss.

He saw her immediately and ran across Front Street to meet her. He was aware of the change in her and his grin said he knew it was for him. "You're terrific," he told her, looking down into her eyes. He realized how glad he was that she'd come, how relieved. Her hand was warm in his and she smiled up at him, making him feel as though he were the only man in the world. Moss was used to female attention and flattery, but there was nothing of the coquette about Billie Ames. As a Southern buddy would say, she was "gen-*you*-ine"!

The lighting on the dance floor was subdued but not dim. The Victrola attached to speakers played Dick Haymes's "If You Were the Only Girl in the World." Moss held her close, his cheek resting against her brow, and hummed along with the music—the sound was exciting, masculine, in her ear. She never remembered being so happy, so lovely, so much a woman.

Girls and chaperones served punch and cookies at one of the long tables set off to the side of the converted storefront dance hall. Another table held coffee and doughnuts. Khaki-green and navy-blue uniforms lined the walls, swirling skirts and the aroma of toilette water filled the air. No smoking was allowed and Billie had gone to the powder room while Moss went outside for a cigarette. She'd noticed last Sunday that he smoked Old Gold. The aroma of the tobacco clung to him when he again took her into his arms.

As they danced, Moss felt a hand clap onto his shoulder and Billie looked up to see a tall attractive lieutenant smiling down at her. "Thought I'd cut in here, Coleman," the officer said mildly. "Won't you introduce me to the lady?" His accent was crisp, the vowels slightly flat, and Billie fixed him as a New Englander.

For a moment, Moss appeared annoyed. "Billie Ames, Lieutenant Thad Kingsley." Thad stepped forward, forcing Moss to relinquish her into his arms.

As Billie stepped into Thad's embrace she felt his soft gray eyes smiling down at her. He had nice eyes, ready to brighten with laughter and soften his chisled, craggy features. Taller and leaner than Moss, he modified his long steps to accommodate her as they danced.

"You look like the angel from the top of a Christmas tree."

"And you look like one of the posters outside the post office. *'Uncle Sam wants you!'*" she bantered, his compliment pleasing her.

"I'll try to think of that as flattery." He laughed easily, his eyes brightening the way she had known they would.

He seemed to spend a lot of time in the sun; his skin was shades darker than his hair, which was the mellow gold of a summer's day. Billie liked Thad and his quiet way. Sometimes Moss's intensity made her uncomfortable and stirred mysterious emotions within her. Thad was refreshing and had a knack for putting people at their ease.

"Are you from Philadelphia?" he was asking. "It's a nice city and the people have been especially kind to servicemen."

"The City of Brotherly Love," she reminded him. "You're from New England?"

"Shows that much, does it?" He laughed at himself. "Vermont. Top western corner of the state. My family has been there for generations and they actually claim to favor the climate. I prefer somewhere warmer myself. Guess I'll get enough of the tropics if I'm sent to the Pacific."

"Do you think you will?" she asked. An icy finger touched her heart at the thought of all these beautiful young men going off to war. Especially when she thought about Moss leaving Philadelphia.

"Loose lips sink ships," Thad teased, sensitive to her sudden melancholy. "Actually, none of us knows where we'll end up, but I know for a fact Moss is itching to get back to the *Enterprise*, where we trained together. For the moment, I'm assigned to the *Sarasota*, but she's in for repairs."

As Thad took Billie around the dance floor, he looked down at this fresh young thing who was softer than cotton in his arms. What the hell was Coleman doing with her? Little Billie was hardly Moss's type. She was young, too young, and sweet.

Several times during the evening other men cut in on Moss to dance with her. She felt his eyes follow her around the dance floor and it made her feel all shivery inside. "It's time I took you home, Billie. It's nearly ten and I couldn't borrow a car tonight."

"I'll have to meet you outside," she told him. "You know the USO doesn't allow girls to leave with the servicemen. If someone sees us, I won't be allowed back."

"You're not coming back," Moss growled. "I don't like sharing you with other men. You belong to me, Billie." He put his arm around her shoulder and led her outside, ignoring the stares of several girls and servicemen standing near the door.

Outside Billie's front door, Moss took her into his arms. She liked the way she fit against him, liked the feel of his strong thighs pressing through the thin fabric of her dress. He tilted up her chin with the tip of his finger and she saw his dark brows draw together as he looked down at her. It was almost as if he were thinking that he didn't quite know what to do with her. Then he kissed her, a slow, warm caress of his lips on hers. She gave herself up to him, parting her lips, aware of the hard bite of his teeth behind that kiss. There was a power about Moss Coleman, carefully hidden behind those careful manners and tender kisses, and Billie was drawn to it, taking some of it for herself. She heard his soft intake of breath. This was a very different kiss from the first. There was a possession in it and a yielding. His hands cupped the back of her head, prolonging the contact, bringing her mouth to his with a hungry yearning. When his hands slid down her back, resting just above the slender curve of her buttocks, he bent lower to bury his face in the hollow of her throat, nipping the softness of her skin, inhaling the fragrance of her. "Oh, Billie," she heard him say, "you shouldn't let me feel this way about you."

In response, Billie cradled his head against her, her fingertips grazing the crisp dark waves at the back of his neck. "I want you to feel this way, Moss," she whispered, "I want..."

The next contact of his mouth on hers was sudden, demanding, and quickly over. "Go inside, Billie, for God's sake, go inside."

He released her so suddenly that it left her trembling, confused, and a little frightened. But if she had never known another thing, Billie Ames knew she had wanted that kiss to go on forever. Before her hand touched the doorknob, Moss had disappeared down the front walk, already lost in the shadows of the overhanging trees.

From the upstairs bedroom window Agnes watched. Because of the porch roof she hadn't seen what transpired outside the front door, but she'd seen Billie and Moss come up to the house. Nine minutes later she watched him streak down the front path.

Agnes watched the relationship between Billie and Moss change from a casual friendship to something deep and warm. Moss came several nights a week after dinner and there were phone calls during which Billie would laugh that new woman's laugh. She knew her daughter was untouched, still innocent. She could read it in Moss's eyes, but the hunger she read in Billie's was disconcerting. Each night when he brought Billie home he would come in for a few minutes. Agnes dreaded those brief encounters when she was forced to look into the lieutenant's eyes for reassurance. Despite her misgivings, which were mostly due to Billie's behavior, Agnes trusted Moss. There was a certain nobility about him, which she suspected would prevent him from taking unfair advantage of Billie's innocence. At least she hoped such was the case. Agnes was not certain of anything any longer, and it was this that caused her the most distress.

Her fond hopes of an alliance between the Fox family and her own were hardly more than a memory. The most she could hope for at this point was that Moss Coleman would leave Philadelphia and leave soon. It was all he talked about during Sunday dinner, which was now a ritual. He hoped to be attached to a fighter squadron in the Pacific. The shadow of pain in Billie's eyes whenever he expressed such desires pierced Agnes's heart. If only it would happen before Billie left for college; then she would have time to recover before embarking on a new life.

This brought a fresh fear to Agnes. She was well aware of the impetuosity of youth and she prayed Moss didn't fill Billie's head with the sense of urgency that was the downfall of so many good girls these days. The uncertainties of wartime, living for today because there mightn't be a tomorrow . . . it had been more than one girl's undoing. Marriage would never come into the conversation. She couldn't help wondering how many casualties Moss Coleman had left behind. She only knew she didn't want Billie added to the list. Billie was all she had. Billie was Agnes's hope for the future. If only she knew more about Moss, it might ease her mind. He might even have a wife somewhere already!

Billie came home from school and straight into the kitchen. "Mother, I'm home. Did Moss call, by any chance?"

"No. Billie, you haven't given any serious practice at that

piano for weeks. You're not being fair to me. The lessons are expensive and you have to do your part."

"I don't want any more lessons. I'm never going to be a concert pianist and I don't have time for it anymore. Tell Mr. Trazzori I want to stop. Stop, Mother, as in finish. No more. What are we having for dinner?"

"Lamb chops. I managed to get four of them today. I had to stand in line over two hours. I wish this rationing would end." Agnes spoke matter-of-factly, but she was shaken about Billie's decision. Eleven years of study and practice gone to waste because of a cowboy. Even at college Billie would have continued her lessons, but it had been weeks since college was mentioned—the weeks since Moss Coleman had first come to the house. Suddenly Agnes blurted, "Billie, I have to talk to you. You still have two weeks of school left. I received a call this afternoon asking why you didn't attend today. I want an explanation and I want it now."

"Mother, all the marks are in. Really, it isn't important. I was with Moss. We took a ride up to the Jersey shore. There's nothing to be upset about. Why is it so awful to skip school for once? Other kids do it all the time."

"That's just it. You've never done anything like this. Billie, ever since you've met that fly-boy you've changed. You aren't the same anymore, and I don't like what I see. You're spending entirely too much time with him." She hated to ask, fearing the answer, but she had to do it. "Just how fond are you of this Moss Coleman?"

"Mother, I wish you wouldn't ask questions like that. I'm grown now, and it's really none of your business."

"Oh, isn't it my business! It's my business when I have to lie to the school and tell them you've got the sniffles. As soon as I heard you weren't in school, I knew whom you were with and I don't like it."

"I'm a big girl now, Mother, and I can take care of myself. If you're worried that I might . . . that I might . . ."

Agnes spoke before she'd really found the words. "It's not you who worries me. I know you're a good girl. But that young man isn't going to wait forever. Billie, do you understand what I'm saying?" There was an edge of desperation in Agnes's tone.

"Don't worry, Mother." Billie's voice had softened in sympathy. If theirs was a more demonstrative relationship, she'd have given Agnes a hug to reassure her. "Moss hasn't touched me. He kisses me good night, but so does Tim Kelly. I wish you'd trust me. You always have before. Why not now? What makes Moss so different in your eyes? Is it because he's older?"

I wish I knew, Agnes thought to herself. "Moss isn't a boy, like Tim Kelly. He's a man, and men have certain needs and desires."

"I really don't want to talk about this." Billie shifted her clear hazel eyes away from her mother. She didn't need to be told about men's desires; she'd already guessed at them, had experienced a taste of them in Moss's strong embrace, in the hardness of his body as it pressed against hers so urgently. Billie had found the echo of those same needs in herself, and Moss knew it. That was why he kept pushing her away, muttering to himself under his breath. He knew that his was the only control.

"I have to work on my graduation dress if I'm to finish it in time. Call me if you need help with dinner." Impetuously, she kissed Agnes on the cheek to take the sting out of her words, then went to her room.

Billie closed the door behind her, wishing it had a lock. Four more hours and she'd be with Moss again. The admiral had taken personal leave and that left Moss pretty much on his own, he'd told her. He'd still have the car tonight and they'd drive down to the park. After that first time they'd never gone to the USO again. He still didn't want to share her with anyone else. His possessiveness made her feel all warm and soft inside. Later, when he drove her home, he would wrap his arms around her and kiss her. Again and again. She shivered when she thought of the way he whispered a groan and grew hard against her. He laughingly called her a tease. If he could have seen her eyes in the darkness of the front porch, he would see her silent dare, the loving challenge to go beyond the limits he had set.

What would she do when he left? The unknown hung over her like a pall. She never told him that she didn't pray for him anymore. Not for his reassignment, anyway. Now she prayed for other things: for him to love her, for him never to forget her.

Moss had agreed to attend her graduation and the dance afterward. He'd wear his dress whites, and the girls were going to die when she walked in on his arm, simply die. Once it would have been important; now it seemed silly and girlish. Now she only wanted to have him to herself, to be alone with him. She knew she was in love. Moss's feelings were still a mystery. He liked her; that much she knew. He enjoyed kissing her and dancing with her and being with her. He'd told her. But when he wasn't with her, did he think of her the way she thought of him?

It was after nine when the phone rang. Agnes laid down her needlepoint canvas and took it on the third ring. "Father Donovan, how nice of you to call," she said quietly, then took a deep breath, almost afraid to hear what he would say.

"Mrs. Ames, I did as you asked. I called Chaplain Franklin at the Navy Yard. I think I told you I was acquainted with him. Chaplain Franklin assures me that Lieutenant Coleman is a very fine young man from a distinguished Texas family. It happens that the chaplain is quite friendly with the admiral's wife. That personal reference concurs with the lieutenant's records—he's not married."

Agnes listened while Father Donovan told her about the Colemans of Texas, her ears perking when he said that the father, Seth, had his fingers in many profitable pies. Oil, beef, aviation, and electronics.

"The lieutenant is well recommended, Mrs. Ames, and has an excellent record. All in all, I don't think you've a thing to worry about where Billie is concerned. I hope this puts your mind at ease. I wish more parents were as concerned about their children as you are. A few discreet questions could save them a lot of grief."

"Father, I appreciate all you've done. You must come to dinner one day soon."

"Anytime I can be of help, just call me. That's why I'm here. Good night, Mrs. Ames."

Agnes's eyes were sparkling like newly cut diamonds when she picked up her needlework again. Beef. Oil. Electronics. Money. Lots of it. Tomorrow she'd go to the main library and check out the city of Austin and what was, apparently, one of its leading families. She snorted in a very unladylike manner when she thought of Neal Fox and his father's bank.

As she stitched along with a bright vermilion length of Persian yarn, listening to the *Longines Wittnaur Music Hour*, Agnes thought that her clever little ploy of attempting to intimidate a cowboy certainly hadn't backfired. She was glad now she'd used her best china and crystal along with her mother's lace tablecloth. At least he could see the Ameses weren't peasants, but examples of good breeding and manners who could hold up their heads with the Colemans of Austin, Texas.

Had Father Donovan said she hadn't a thing to worry about? That was because he hadn't seen the look in Billie's eyes whenever the young lieutenant was near. That look told Agnes all she needed to know. If Moss crooked his finger, Billie would run. He could easily take advantage of her. And if he did, where would that leave Billie? Deflowered at seventeen. She could become pregnant and then what? Still, Agnes had a strong hunch that Moss would keep his head. He knew he was tormenting her; he also knew he held all the cards where her daughter was concerned. But there was something in his eyes that said he played fair.

It was five minutes to ten when Moss and Billie walked through the front door. Agnes was gathering up her needlepoint to retire for the evening. "Good night, Moss, Billie," she said quietly. Not for the world was she going to meet the young man's stare *this* evening. "I have a frightful headache, Billie. Be sure all the lights are out and the door locked when you go to bed." Without another look at either of the young people, Agnes climbed the stairs.

Moss was vaguely disappointed. Of late he'd actually enjoyed his little staring game with Agnes. Something was up. Tonight there was a nervousness and excitement about Agnes that made him wonder.

"It's a shame Mother has a headache," said Billie, "but that means we have the living room all to ourselves. We can listen to the radio or just sit here and talk. You don't have to rush back to the yard, do you?"

Moss's mind raced. He supposed he could stay awhile. The others would wait for him. He'd never told Billie that when he left her most evenings he didn't go back to the base. He didn't have to report in until seven in the morning, so usually he went with the others to an after-hours club. "I can stay for a while. But I'll have to get back soon, early duty in the morning."

Billie sat on the sofa and was disappointed when Moss sat at the other end. Did he think Agnes was going to spy on them? The news report came on the radio and they listened silently. She saw how alert Moss became at the mention of the USS *Enterprise* in the Pacific. H. V. Kaltenborn was speaking.

"Today is June eighth. Less than a week ago a triumph was declared in the Pacific by our naval and air forces off the shores of the tiny island of Midway. It was a day of reckoning for the Empire of Japan, which met with the strength of American aircraft carriers *Hornet*, *Yorktown*, and *Enterprise*. Four Japanese carriers were sent to the bottom. The *Soryu*, the *Hiryu*, *Kaga*, and *Akagi* will never sail into Tokyo Harbor again."

Moss listened with rapt attention. If there was one thing Billie had learned early on, it was Moss's interest in every bit of news. Especially about the war. He could lose track of time when he talked about it. She'd listen with interest until he got to the part where he said he couldn't wait to be reassigned. She always had to bite her tongue to keep from asking, "What about me?"

Moss glanced at his watch. Kaltenborn's news seemed to have shaken him. "I've got to get back, Billie. Tell your mother I hope her headache is better."

"Moss, isn't the *Enterprise* the ship you trained on last fall? Where is Midway? What does it all mean?"

Moss placed his hand on her shoulders, looking down at her. "It means that if I don't hurry and get myself over there, it's all going to be over." He ran a hand through his thick dark hair. "I don't know what to do, Billie. I don't want to go against Pap, but I know I've got to get in there and do my share." His sudden grin relieved the worry lines between his eyes. "Can't let all the other guys have the fun, can I?"

He wrapped his arms around her and kissed her lightly, shifting his brain into what he called neutral, allowing himself to relax. Billie was so soft, so feminine, her lips so tender and gentle, promising more if only he dared to take it. He didn't want to hurt her. Neither did he want to take advantage of her. He cared for her, was enchanted by her, but he didn't love her. At least, he didn't think he did. He couldn't let himself love anyone, not even a nice girl like Billie. Love made too many demands and got in the way of plans and dreams. Seth loved him, too much, and the responsibility of that love prevented him from pursuing something he wanted very badly. He didn't need or want another tie or obligation to anyone, not even Billie.

Besides, she was one of those nice girls who would never understand that a guy could mess around and not want anything lasting or permanent. He'd have to stop seeing so much of her. She was getting under his skin and it was becoming more and more difficult to put honor and respect first. He should see other women, women who weren't so nice and didn't have any false illusions. Women who wouldn't be hurt by an occasional roll in the hay and who wouldn't expect marriage in return for virginity.

When Moss released Billie, he saw the tears in her eyes. "Hey, don't ever cry for me, Billie." And then he was gone.

Billie sat on her bed for a long, long time, warm tears trickling down her cheeks. How could she not cry for Moss? He wanted to be in the Pacific, flying into battle, risking his life. Why couldn't he want her that much? If he did, he'd never want to leave her.

Billie came instantly awake and knew what day it was. Graduation. Her sleepy eyes went to the hook on the back of the closet door where her dress hung. It was beautiful, almost a bridal dress, virginal in its whiteness. The thought suddenly annoyed her. Perhaps she should have threaded some of the eyelet with a colored ribbon or made a colored sash. It wasn't too late; she still had all day. She decided a colored sash was the answer. She'd wear the completed white one for the graduation ceremonies and change to the pastel one for the dance. It would hardly take ten minutes to whip up on the machine. That's what she would do. She wanted to stand out from the other girls, to look just a little different, for Moss.

This was a night she wanted him to remember, herself a vision that he could take with him when he left. How long would she have him with her? Not very long, she realized. For weeks he'd been filled with the news of the *Enterprise* and its part in the battle of Midway. It made Moss "chomp at the bit," as he called it, to get into the fray before it was over. If only it *was* over, all of it; then he wouldn't have to leave her.

Billie felt she didn't really understand Moss Coleman any better than on the first day she'd met him more than a month ago. This was already June. June was a month for brides. Yesterday she'd heard that two of her classmates were marrying before their men shipped out. Simple, hurried ceremonies with only family present.

Billie ached.

By the middle of July Tim would be gone. The other boys would soon follow. Her girlfriends were going off to college and she herself was to leave for Penn State at the end of August. Everyone promised to write everyone, but Billie knew that soon each would find a life and interests of his own. Slowly but surely the letters would cease. Oh, they'd see one another over the holidays or during the summer, but this part of their lives was over. God alone knew when they'd see any of the boys again, if ever. It was sad and it made tonight seem even more special.

There was going to be an all-night party at a classmate's after the dance. Agnes had already given permission for her to stay out until after the champagne breakfast the parents planned to serve. Billie giggled to herself. The poor girl. Billie knew for a fact that most of the couples had other plans. Oh, they'd make an appearance at the party, but then they'd leave. That's exactly what she'd like to do, only she didn't know how to broach the subject with Moss. She knew he'd be bored. Maybe she could suggest driving up to Atlantic City. They could walk on the beach and watch the sunrise. That would be the perfect ending to a perfect night.

Just the thought of spending an entire night with Moss, of lying beside him on a blanket on the beach, was so romantic that she rolled over on her bed and pressed her face into the pillow. Strange things were happening inside her, dark longings and a yearning ache that quickened her pulses whenever she was with him, whenever he touched her. She'd looked in the mirror to see if this change showed on her face. It seemed to be Billie Ames's face but she didn't feel like Billie Ames inside. She ached, her breasts tingled, there was an emptiness in the center of her. She wanted Moss to touch her breasts and fill this emptiness. She wanted it so badly that there seemed to be a bubble of sadness at the back of her throat. Tears were always so near the surface that she found herself biting them back throughout the days until she was with him again. The romance magazines called this feeling passion. But they never said passion could hurt this way.

Moss buttoned the last button on his white jacket. He knew he was going to take a lot of ribbing when he made his way out to the officers' lounge. A high school graduation! That was for sailors.

"Wheweee," Thad Kingsley whistled. "You're gonna throw all those little ladies into a tailspin."

"Smell him!" heckled his buddy Jack. "Smells like he's been in a French whorehouse. All them mamas of all them little girls are gonna have heart palpitations."

"Knock it off," Moss said, grinning.

"Handsome devil, but," said another young officer, wagging

a finger, "it ain't no fun being just a plain old handsome devil unless he's planning on being a sinful handsome devil." The others laughed, enjoying Moss's discomfort.

"How old you say this little gal is? Seventeen, you say? For shame, man, you're robbing the cradle. Pure as the driven snow, right?" Jack cackled.

"Shut the hell up, Jack. Don't you have anything better to do than ride me?"

"Not unless we all dress up like you and stand outside. What say we do that, guys? Maybe some of them little girls will fall all over us and invite us for Sunday dinner. Why should Moss have all the fun? Does that little gal know you been laying every girl between here and New York City?"

"I told you to knock it off—I mean it," Moss snarled. The fun was getting out of hand. Truth always bothered Moss when it was delivered by someone else.

"What are you going to do, sic the admiral on us?" Thad teased. "Come on, guys, let's go find some fun of our own. Coleman has things to do and places to go." To show that it was all in fun, the guys clapped Moss on the back as they left the lounge.

Thad swung around for one last barb. "I want you in by sunup and I expect that uniform to be in the same condition it's in now," he said in what he hoped was a motherly tone. "You hear me?"

Moss laughed and waved as he went out the door.

They were good guys. And if Moss could, he'd pick Thad Kingsley for a brother. Thad was probably the best damn flyer he knew. He was one cool man under pressure and never made a mistake.

Agnes's eyes were unreadable when she opened the door to admit Moss. He looked as if he were born to navy whites. "Come in, Moss. Billie will be ready in a moment." She admired the creamy white camelias he was carrying. "What a lovely corsage!"

Moss stared straight into Agnes's eyes. When he spoke, his drawl was more pronounced. "I'm thinkin' I'll be outa here by September. Leastwise, that's the way it looks now." He watched for her reaction, expecting relief. He frowned. Hell, wasn't that what she wanted? For him to be gone so her little Billie would be safe? That wasn't panic he saw in her face, or was it?

* * *

The small band hired for the graduation dance was making a valiant effort to accomplish the big band sound of Glenn Miller. A young woman was making a fair stab at sounding like Helen O'Connell, to the delight of everyone in the hall. Billie danced with Moss, her head cradled against his chest. She felt so good, so right being in his arms. She'd noticed every female head in the gym turn when she'd walked in on his arm. Even the teachers had cast more than one admiring glance in his direction as he led her around the dance floor.

Agnes stood at the table serving punch from the huge bowl. She preened as she heard the principal beside her acclaim Billie as the prettiest girl at the dance. "And who's the young man with her, Mrs. Ames? It's obvious he's well bred."

"He's Lieutenant Moss Coleman, from Austin, Texas. Confidentially, he's from a very important family, if you know what I mean."

The principal, sensing Agnes's excitement, knew exactly what she meant. Moss Coleman must be a very wealthy man indeed.

"Billie, the band is going to take a break," Moss said against her cheek. "This is a good time for me to check in with Admiral McCarter. Why don't you go over and get some punch and I'll meet you at the refreshment table."

Agnes, standing guard over the punch bowl so none of the more rambunctious students would spike it, saw Billie coming toward her, saw the flush on her daughter's cheeks, the full smiling lips, the glow in her eyes. Billie had a look about her that would throw fright into any mother's heart. A look that said she was full grown and had found the man she would have.

"Mother, are you having a good time?" Even her voice was different, Agnes decided. Warm and vibrant, holding an assurance and confidence. A woman's confidence. Billie was a girl no longer. Agnes had felt that way once, experienced those same tensions and desires, and she knew where they led. Directly to the bedroom.

"It's a wonderful dance and a very special night for you, isn't it, Billie? Especially since Moss thinks he'll be shipping out before September." She pretended not to notice Billie's distress, waiting to hear if Moss had confided his plans or made promises for the future.

"Did he tell you that?" Billie asked, her hands trembling.

"Oh, I'm so sorry, dear. Did I let a cat out of the bag? Yes, he told me just this evening." Agnes stared at her daughter, thoughts ricocheting through her head. Her own hand shook slightly as she ladled out the punch. What a silly little girl Billie actually was. Perhaps she shouldn't have been so protective of her all these years; perhaps then Billie would know how to reach out and take what she wanted. She herself had been much smarter at seventeen than Billie, Agnes thought. She took a deep breath and came to an instant decision. "Take this, dear. You look as though you need it," she said, serving her daughter a cup of punch.

Billie reached for the punch cup and at that instant Agnes's hand flew upward, the bright red drink splattering all over the front of Billie's white dress.

Coming around the corner from the hallway just then, Moss saw Billie step backward, but not in time. Her dress was ruined. He stood still for a minute. There was no point in ruining his uniform. When Billie finished wiping at the deep red stains, he walked forward.

"Oh, Moss, I'm so glad you're here," Agnes said anxiously. "Will you please take Billie home so she can change her dress? Billie, I'm so sorry. I thought you had the cup in your hand. You don't mind, do you, Moss?"

"Of course not." His eyes searched Agnes's. He'd been wrong; it wasn't panic at all. It was fear. A tight smile escaped him as he took Billie past the small, knotted crowds.

Agnes watched them leave. Her glance went to the oversized clock on the wall, somewhat difficult to see with all the crepe-paper decorations hanging above. Ten minutes to drive home, another fifteen for Billie to change, ten for them to return. She would wait. This would be Billie's chance and it might be the only one she'd get. Agnes pushed down all maternal uncertainties. It was a terrible gamble, but she was doing it for Billie's sake. Her daughter was going to be one of the Colemans of Austin. Agnes smiled. And one way or another, she'd be one of them, too.

{{{{{{{{{ CHAPTER FOUR }}}}}}}}}

Moss took the latchkey from Billie's hand and opened the front door. He admired the way she was handling her disappointment and embarrassment. Other girls, he knew, would have fretted and complained about the ruined dress, making the situation miserable for everyone. Not Billie. During the ride home she'd laughed and joked and teased him about being the most popular man at the dance.

"I'll only be a minute. Maybe two." She laughed. "I'm afraid I'm soaked clear through to the skin. Why don't you turn on the radio to keep you company?"

"I'm sorry about your dress, Billie," he told her sincerely. "You were the prettiest girl at the dance. No, not just pretty, beautiful."

Billie felt his words warm her. Now it didn't matter if she had to wear sackcloth and ashes. Moss had said she was beautiful and she felt beautiful when he looked at her this way, with fires glowing behind his eyes.

He watched her disappear into the room off the parlor. After tuning in a radio station, he jammed his hands in his pockets and paced the darkened room. There was a line of light seeping from under Billie's door; he could see it flicker and waver as she moved about inside.

Billie stripped off her dress, knowing she'd find that the red punch had seeped through to her white taffeta slip. Even her skin was sticky and she needed a quick wash. How could Mother have been so careless? She'd need a complete change of clothes, everything.

Moss opened the door to Billie's bedroom; the soft, pink light from the bedstand shafted into the open closet door where he could hear her rummaging. He leaned against the doorjamb, hands stuffed into his trouser pockets, his cap tilted low over his eyes.

Unaware of his intrusion, Billie reached for her terry robe

{ 49 }

and stepped out of the closet, humming softly to the tune of "I'll Be Seeing You" playing on the radio in the parlor. Moss surveyed her from the shadow of his cap, seeing the long naked length of her back, her small round rump, and her tapering legs, firm and lightly muscled. Her bare shoulders were dusted with the dark gold of her hair. She turned slightly, affording him a view of her small uptilted breasts with nipples as pink as the inside of seashells. Her waist was tiny and he grinned at her little round tummy, a vestige of girlhood.

Billie shrugged into her robe, gathering it closed with the belt before turning to see him, her face registering surprise. Moss looked at her, his gaze never wavering from her face. It was there, the woman's heat. It had turned her hazel eyes to gold.

A flush of warmth crept down Billie's body, touching embers to her breasts, her belly, between her legs. Still staring into his eyes, she opened her robe, allowing it to slip off her shoulders and caress her arms as it slid to the floor. Just as she discarded the scruffy white robe, so did she cast off her girlhood. It was a woman's arms that lifted to welcome him.

Agnes kept watching the clock on the wall. All around her, skirts swirled and music played. She was oblivious to everything save the passing of time. Nearly an hour had gone by since Billie had left with Moss. Agnes walked to the cloakroom for her sweater. Her step was determined as she left the high school and went out to the street.

Her movements were controlled as she drove her seldom used Studebaker, both hands clutched on the wheel. Instead of coming in from the south end of her block, she drove an extra two blocks so she could swing around and come in from the north and park on the opposite side of the street. There she sat, staring across at the gray-and-white house on Elm Street. Moss's borrowed car was parked in the drive. The house was dark and uninviting.

The light from the outside streetlamp filtered through Agnes's rayon curtains into Billie's darkened bedroom, splashing onto her narrow, girlish bed and puddling a silvery sheen onto their nakedness. She lay close in Moss's embrace, sensually aware of his coarse chest hairs tickling her breasts. His lips nuzzled her neck, trailing familiarly now to the hollow between her breasts and beneath them. He cupped and caressed their swollen firmness and seemed to take such pleasure in them that she wished they were bigger, fuller, for him.

"I don't know what's sweeter, Billie, you or the fruit punch. You're still sticky with it and delicious," he murmured against her flesh, rekindling the throbbing of her pulses. She wanted to be sweet for him. She wanted to be everything for him.

Billie sighed, stretching languorously beside him. She was a woman now. Moss had made love to her and made her a woman. His woman. He'd been so tender with her, so careful, arousing her to such a fever pitch before penetrating her flesh with his that she'd hardly noticed the quick, sudden rending of her maidenhead. Then, as he'd moved slowly within her, she'd felt herself dissolve wetly, her flesh opening itself to him, taking him fully inside her. She'd imagined that she was his canvas and he the artist, painting her with the vivid colors of her awakened sexuality, designing her to his pleasure as he traced intricate patterns along her body with his lips and hands. His wonderful hands. There was not an inch of her unkissed or unloved, and Billie Ames felt she had metamorphosed from a dun-colored caterpillar into an exotic butterfly.

Leaning up on one elbow, Moss trailed a teasing finger from the hollow of her throat down her body to the mossy bank of her sex, still moist and warm from their loving. "It'll be better for you next time, Billie. I didn't want to hurt you."

"You didn't. It was wonderful. I've never felt this close to anyone before, Moss. I love it. I love you."

His only answer was to kiss her, softly, his lips lingering on hers in an intimate caress. She parted her lips, allowing him entrance just as easily as she'd allowed him to enter her body. She was sweet and warm with the aftermath of their loving, but he knew she hadn't come to a climax and this was something he wanted to share with her, wanted to give her. "Being close isn't enough," he breathed. "There's so much more, and I want to show you."

"More? Show me, Moss. Show me now," she insisted, feeling a growing pressure at the center of herself that she knew he alone could assuage. Was it possible to be closer to him than she felt this minute? Was it possible to take a part of him that she could keep for her own and never lose no matter what happened, no matter how far away he would go?

Moss was shaken by her invitation. He had expected to find pleasure in making love to her, but he'd never guessed at the depth of that pleasure or anticipated such uninhibited willingness. She'd been wonderful, accepting his caresses, the possession of her body, offering herself to him as though she were a gift created for him alone. Their eyes met in the dimness, clear and level, heated and eager without a trace of regret or embarrassment. Seeing her lips part in anticipation of his kiss, he lowered his mouth to hers, touching and seeking that special sweetness that was Billie's alone. He felt her fingers graze his back, lowering to his haunches, reawakening his desire for her. At that moment he believed he could never be sated in his hunger. Billie was special, unexpectedly so. She enchanted him with her responses, enthralled him with her eager, unpracticed touch. She was an untapped spring of sensuality and he determined to follow her courses to the deeply hidden source.

Her body turned in his arms, offering itself to his explorations. Her skin was soft, supple beneath his touch. He watched her face as he caressed her breasts, slowly, intriguingly, lowering to her belly, between her parted thighs. The upsweep of her lashes lowered sleepily as she gave herself over to him, trusting him to take her to that place he had promised.

His hand roamed the soft flesh of her thighs, rising upward. He watched her expression of wonder as she moved against his touch and she heard his response to her passion in the catch of his breath and the husky sound of his voice. "I love to touch you this way," he whispered. "I love to watch you surrender yourself to me. Touch me, Billie," he encouraged. "Touch me."

She sought him with her hands, eager to know him, to explore the mystery that promised such pleasure. Her own excitement grew as she realized his delight. The hardness of his sex was somehow vulnerable and tender, throbbing with desire. His body delighted her, tempting her fingers to find the breadth of his chest and the flatness of his belly and the strength of his thighs. The sound of her own heart thundered in her ears as she explored the fragility between his legs and the round firmness of his buttocks.

Moss found himself breathless from her touch, seeing in her eyes that she took as much pleasure in him as he did in her. Her lashes fluttered and the tip of her tongue moistened her lips as though she were about to taste a delicious morsel. He brought his mouth to hers once again, hungering for it, darting his tongue against the silky underside of her full lower lip. His hands never broke contact with her body, following the rhythmic rise and fall as she pressed herself against him, following his hand, seeking passion's reward.

Billie was ravaged by this hunger he created in her, confused by it, not knowing where it would end, afraid it would. There was an emptiness at her center that craved him, demanded release. There was an exquisiteness in this contact and it was as though she were being fragmented, separated from herself, and nothing existed in the world but her body and his hand.

Moving over her, he placed himself between her thighs, his eyes igniting embers wherever they touched her. The gold spill of her hair on the pillow, her white skin, her gentle curves that were young and appealing, all beckoned to him. His eyes locked with hers as he continued his caress; his passions were fired as she met his gaze with abandon, letting him see the desire that dwelt there and echoed in the trembling of her loins. "Billie, Billie." He murmured her name as if it were a love lyric. "You're lovely, so lovely."

He fed her passions, gentled her desires, and brought her slowly and inexorably to the point of no return, smiling tenderly when she gasped with the sweetness of her release. She climaxed beneath his touch, crying her surprise, rolling her head back and forth as she called his name. He eased the tension in her thighs, pressed his palm into the contractions of her belly, smiling down at her reassuringly and persuading her doubts away. When she calmed, she smiled with the wonder of this discovery he had unfolded for her, and Moss had never felt such a surge of tenderness as he did for Billie at that moment. He wanted to be her lover, to carry her over the threshold of her passions, to explore the mysteries of her sensuality.

"Tell me you want more, Billie. Tell me again how you want me to show you more." His voice was so deep, a rumble in her ears, but she understood and eagerly whispered the words he wanted to hear.

He leaned forward, entering her, gently, so gently, filling her with himself. Her flesh closed around him, capturing him in an exquisite embrace. She caressed the smooth expanse of his back, arched her breasts against his chest. Her mouth yielded to his, deeply, lovingly. She encouraged his embrace, heightened his passions, grasping his buttocks and holding him deep within her. She felt the heat rise again from the contact of their flesh. She felt herself matching the slow sensual rhythm he initiated. She was aware of the building of tension again at her center, driving herself and him once more to that sweet release.

He felt her tighten and become rigid with her climax, her pulsations beckoning him to his own release. He raised himself up, grasping her bottom in his hands, lifting her, thrusting himself into her with shorter, quicker strokes.

Her body was a delight, her responses instinctive, and the expression of complete surrender on her lovely face brought him to the edge of passion and he plummeted over to the other side to join her in the celebration of her womanhood.

Their bodies glistened with the sheen of their pleasure and satisfaction. They lay side by side on the narrow bed, legs entwined, her head resting upon his shoulder. He brought her back from the far side of passion with caresses to her breasts and throat. He kissed her brow and inhaled the fragrance of her hair. His voice was soft and husky as he exulted in the delight he had found in her, enumerating those qualities he found so beautiful.

"I love you," she breathed, nuzzling her lips into the furring on his chest.

"I know you do, Billie. I know." And his answer was a kiss, so gentle and tender that it brought a tear to her eye.

Agnes walked across the front yard, keeping to the grass so her heels wouldn't click on the flagstones, and let herself in through the kitchen door. Laying her purse on the kitchen table, she went into the darkened living room. Frank Sinatra was crooning on the radio. Billie's bedroom door was closed and Agnes drew in her breath when she heard Moss's soft, intimate-sounding laughter and Billie's urgent whispers.

Sitting down on the dark brown Morris chair that had been her mother's favorite, Agnes faced the door to Billie's room and contemplated the quiet sounds she heard from within. She was aware that Moss was in there with Billie and she knew what they were doing.

It seemed strange to Agnes to be sitting out here when any decent mother would be breaking down the door to save her daughter. But, in many ways, Agnes *was* saving Billie—and herself as well. In all likelihood, considering Billie's recent behavior and the glow in her eyes, Moss would have landed her in bed sooner or later. The trick was to turn every disadvantage—such as having a lovestruck daughter who no longer wanted to be a virgin—into an advantage. Deliberately spilling the punch down the front of Billie's dress and arranging for her to be alone with Moss had been a terrible gamble, but so far things seemed to be going just as she'd planned. Taking a deep breath, Agnes waited. The next move in this little game had to be well played and she had to keep her head about her.

Hands folded in her lap, her face expressionless, time had no meaning as Agnes waited. When the door finally opened and Moss, naked except for his white slacks, stepped out, the first thing he saw as the Andrews Sisters sang "Boogie Woogie Bugle Boy" was Agnes glaring at him with icy calm. Billie, her robe clutched tightly about her, bumped into him and saw immediately what had brought him up short.

"Mother!"

Agnes stared first at Billie and then at Moss. Yes, it was a terrible gamble to take. Moss grinned at her, his eyes saying he knew what she'd done. Agnes recoiled slightly, but she knew she'd won. She could feel it in her bones, in every breath she took. Billie was going to be Mrs. Moss Coleman. What was disturbing Agnes at this moment was the knowledge that she hadn't won this little game by outsmarting Moss. No, Lieutenant Coleman had *allowed* her this victory.

As he'd walked out into the living room, Moss's thoughts had been filled with Billie. What an exciting bed partner she was! Willing. So very willing to please. And she was beautiful, in her soft, sweet way. Even now, thinking about it, he could hardly believe her boldness. One minute she'd had the robe on and the next, after seeing him in the doorway, she was lifting those warm tender arms to him, inviting him to be her lover. A wry, satisfied grin was stretching across his face—and then he saw *her* sitting in the chair watching the door. Agnes. He hadn't needed a bolt of lightning to tell him she'd been sitting there for a very long time. And the look in her eyes reminded him of Pap's just after he'd closed a very profitable business deal. In that split second, Moss knew that if he had a chance to do it all over again, he'd do it. Agnes or no Agnes. Billie was worth it.

One of Pap's famous admonishments skittered through his brain. Mothers automatically think in terms of rape; they can never accept that their darling daughters are ready and willing. Their second thought is of bastard children and social embarrassment. Their last—and most comforting—thought is of marriage.

"Close your zipper, Lieutenant," Agnes said softly. "It's getting late. There's no point in going back to the dance. It would be a good idea if you got dressed and left."

Dismissed. Caught just like a kid with his fist in the cookie jar. Moss wanted to laugh. He'd just stolen her daughter's innocence and virginity and she was dismissing him. But Moss knew she wasn't finished with him, not yet, not till she'd gotten what she wanted. He saw her eyes flick to Billie and realized that Agnes would say what she had to say when Billie wasn't around to hear or object. The urge to laugh was so strong that his throat began to tickle. Pap, you old bastard, you didn't tell me there were mothers like this one.

Billie, standing just behind Moss, pulled the belt of her terry robe tighter. The sight of her mother calmly sitting there made her feel faint. Grasping Moss's arm, more to keep herself steady than in any gesture of protectiveness, she protested Agnes's sending him away like a naughty boy. "Mother, this wasn't Moss's fault. I made him do it. I wanted to and I'm not sorry!" she cried defiantly. "You have to believe me. I love him. You have to understand that."

Moss felt Billie's nails digging into his bare arm. Noble. Little Billie was making her declaration of love and defending him to Agnes. He should be saying all the things Billie was saying. She was stealing his thunder. This time there was no controlling the laughter that bubbled out of him. He put his arm around Billie's shoulder and drew her to him. That little movement, that little declaration of his own, was all Agnes needed. She bit back her smile, lowering her head to cloak her face in the semidarkness.

Billie sat on the edge of her bed watching Moss dress. She needed reassurance; she wanted to hear the words that would tell her he loved her, but she couldn't ask. What would happen once Moss left the house? Would he come back? If he asked her to leave with him now, this minute, she would. Please, God, let him come back. She was silent as she watched him button his white tunic with slow, unhurried hands.

Moss was avoiding Billie's eyes. Her naked love for him was almost more than he could handle. All his life he'd known that when someone loved you that way it demanded something in return. With Seth, the demand had been responsibility and obligation. He refused to imagine what Billie would demand in return. Closer to the truth, it was what Agnes would demand that made him cringe. He knew he had to look at Billie, knew he must take her in his arms. Poor little thing, she looked so frightened. What did she fear most—Agnes's anger or that he wouldn't return her love? Billie had nothing to fear from Agnes. Things had gone exactly the way she'd planned from the moment she'd doused Billie with punch. That left only himself. Love? Not yet.

He gathered Billie into his arms. She felt so good, all warm and soft. He felt himself stiffening. Billie smiled up at him and then laid her head against his chest. How right she felt, how good. She fit just right in the crook of his arm. Think. He had to think. But not here. He had to get out of here. He kissed Billie lightly on the lips, on the tip of her nose, on her closed eyes, and again on her lips. "I'll call you tomorrow, between eleven and noon. The admiral is playing golf then and I'll have the office all to myself. We'll talk. Good night, Billie."

"Good night, Moss," Billie said, choking back a sob. She looked so abandoned and lost and afraid.

"Don't worry, Billie. Things'll work out." He hated to see a woman cry. They got all red-eyed and sniffly and then they had to blow their nose. His sister was forever crying and blowing. Jesus, the things a guy had to tolerate. "Don't cry." The depths of his caring stunned him. Yes, he did care about Billie. "Stay here. I'll let myself out. Call you tomorrow."

Billie nearly collapsed on the bed once she'd heard the door close. She clenched her hands in her lap and waited for her mother. Billie's heart thumped madly all the while she waited. She wasn't sorry for what she'd done. She'd never be sorry. He'd faced Agnes. He'd said he'd call tomorrow. He *would* call tomorrow. Her eyes went to the rumpled bed and the wrinkled sheets. Emotionally drained, she fell back against the pillows and her eyes burned with tears when the scent of Moss's after-shave caressed her cheek.

. It had been wonderful, everything she thought it would be. She pleased him, she knew she did; he'd told her. She smiled when she remembered his gentleness, his wildness. She flushed when she thought of her own abandon. How could something so wonderful between two people be wrong? Moss didn't think it was wrong or he wouldn't have made love to her. How she hated now the phrase the kids used. "Doing it." It sounded like two dogs in heat. Moss and she hadn't "done it." They'd made love. Inexperienced as she was, she knew the difference.

Where was her mother? Why hadn't she come into the room to express her disappointment and disgust? To shout, to chastise and issue dire warnings and threats. When the little enamel clock with the painted fleur-de-lis read one o'clock, Billie turned off the lamp and lay back against the pillow Moss had lain on.

Moss drove slowly, savoring the warm summer breezes that blew in through the car window. It had been damn close to a perfect evening. Caught. Caught like two kids behind the barn. He laughed, a rich sound that began in his middle and bellowed out his throat. Damn near perfect. But his thoughts didn't take him beyond the following day. There would be no more nights like tonight. Agnes had allowed him to sample the merchandise and it was to be his one and only. From here on in, he either made arrangements to buy the goods—and this meant marriage—or else removed himself from the situation entirely.

Moss whipped out his ID and idled past the guard at the gatehouse. He had some deep thinking to do. He parked the car, went to his quarters, and changed. Dressed in fatigues, he made his way back to the admiral's office. Now was a good time to take apart the maritime compass on the admiral's desk and put it in working order, as he'd promised. The admiral liked to avail himself of Moss's expertise with anything mechanical, and there was always a radio or clock or something on the car awaiting his attention.

He worked slowly and methodically, and was surprised to find that the sun was rising as he finished. He replaced the antique compass on the admiral's desk and devilishly propped up a sign that read KILROY WAS HERE, complete with the caricature of the little bald guy with a bulbous nose peeping over the fence. The sign struck him as funny and he wondered briefly about the origin of the popular slogan, but instead of laughing he felt like crying. Sitting at an admiral's desk fixing little contraptions wasn't Moss's idea of fighting a war. There was an aching at his center to be airborne, skidding off the flat deck of a carrier and rushing off to face his destiny. There had to be some way of getting out of this stinking assignment. But he couldn't go against his father. Seth was an old man and Moss was the apple of his eye, the old man's chance for immortality, as Pap liked to put it. Seth loved him and in return for that love, Moss owed it to Pap to go along. Seth was set on creating a dynasty, a Coleman dynasty, and his fierce pride demanded that Moss produce future generations of Colemans to inherit the fabulous wealth he'd created out of nothing but shrewd business dealings and a lot of luck. But maybe, just maybe, there was a way to appease Pap and still get what he wanted. To fly. To test his mettle. To pit himself against an enemy and win. Moss wanted it so badly he could taste it, and he worried that it would all be over before he could get in.

Wearily, Moss stepped out into the dawn, heading back to the barracks he shared with other officers for a much needed shower. Reveille was just sounding as he stepped out from the steamy spray and tied a towel around his middle.

"Okay, you wing-tailed bastards, let's get the lead out and move," Thad Kingsley shouted to the men lying sprawled in their bunks. "Let's all look alive like Coleman here. We're looking at navy, men. Real navy. Move it!"

"Knock it off," Moss growled irritably. "I'm not in the mood this morning."

"Get him! Big night last night. High school graduation. Ah, youth! Did you get to keep her out all night? Tell us about it!"

Moss endured the heckling of his friends until Jack Taylor ripped away his towel, hooting and catcalling. "Looks like our man had himself a big night."

Moss was on him like a shot. The men flinched at the sound of his fist hitting Taylor's jaw.

"Jesus!" Taylor complained. "What's gotten into you, Coleman? Can't you take a little ribbing?" He rubbed his swelling jaw. "You can hand it out, so why can't you take it? So who cares if you struck out? You can't win 'em all."

"It's none of your business if I struck out or not," Moss said. "Just stay out of my life, okay? And you better get some ice on that jaw." He headed for the latrine.

Thad Kingsley shrugged. "So the guy's in love. Leave him alone, Taylor. He's got something eating him, and if and when he's ready to tell us, he will."

Thad thought about the little fresh-faced blonde Moss had met at the USO several weeks before and frowned. He hadn't been serious when he'd said Moss was in love, but now he wondered. Could it be that a pretty little thing as sweet and naive as Billie Ames could break through that tough Texan veneer when other, more sophisticated women had failed? Kingsley felt a surge of envy that Coleman always managed to find pie in the sky, and at the same time he almost pitied Billie.

Billie heard the sounds of Agnes preparing breakfast in the kitchen and smelled the inviting aroma of brewing coffee. Just before six o'clock that morning she'd heard their roomers leave for work. Now Agnes and Billie were alone in the house. Now she had to go out and face her mother.

Bravado at seven-thirty in the morning was not something Billie could muster and her hand shook as she poured the coffee. She steeled herself and waited for Agnes to open the conversation. When Agnes nibbled her toast and sipped her coffee, Billie could feel her stomach tighten. She could see Agnes's reasoning. Billie was the guilty one, the offender; therefore, she should be the first to speak. Billie took a deep breath. "Mother, about last night. I know you're disappointed in me. I understand why you would be. I'm not asking your forgiveness; I'm asking you to understand. I love Moss. And none of it was his fault. It was me, Mother. I instigated—"

"Somehow, Billie, that doesn't make me feel one whit better," Agnes said sternly. "It's difficult for me to believe you could be so wanton."

"Mother, I didn't feel wanton last night and I don't this morning," Billie said firmly. "When two people love each other they want to be together. They want to make love." And then they marry each other, Billie said to herself.

"I see," Agnes said coolly. "Have you given any thought to the fact that you may be pregnant? It's been known to happen, you know. What if you're pregnant and Moss is shipped out? He wants to go. He's not interested in spending the duration in the Philadelphia Navy Yard."

"I'll talk to him. Let's not blow this all out of proportion."

"Billie, my concern is you. Nice girls do not go to bed before they're married. I don't want you to be like Cissy. Oh, yes, I've heard the rumors," Agnes answered Billie's surprise. "How that girl's mother holds her head up is beyond me!"

Agnes occupied herself with her coffee cup, carefully hiding her smugness. Everything was going as planned. She had to remind herself to be careful, to say just the right thing at just the right time. She sipped the hot brew, not wanting to admit to herself that Billie's statement had rocked her severely. Strength was not a trait she associated with her lovely daughter. When Moss Coleman entered their lives she'd seen that strength grow and bloom. She mustn't let Billie think she was being manipulated. Agnes sighed, wishing for those easier days when Billie was a little girl and had been so amenable and willing to see her mother's way and adhere to her mother's ideals. Everyone knew that Billie Ames was a talented, lovely girl. Why else would Mrs. Fox have entertained the notion of a match between

Billie and Neal? It was because Agnes had been farsighted, grooming and training Billie for a better life than this one. Carefully now, Billie had to think she was following her own lead. "Billie, you're so young. Moss is older, more sophisticated. You are certainly no match for him. I imagine he's had many women and he's the type to have many, many more. I don't want to see you hurt. Worse, I don't want you used and left behind. That kind of thing can become a habit. Look at Cissy. It's not what I want for you, Billie. It would be best if you didn't see Moss anymore, forget last night, and go on from there."

"No! I love Moss and he loves me. He's going to ask me to marry him and I will. And if he doesn't ask me, I'll wait for him, forever if necessary. I love him!" Tears were bright in Billie's eyes and Agnes felt pity for her daughter. Still, she mustn't allow it to interfere. Billie tossed her napkin onto the table and fled from the room.

Agnes finished her coffee and set the cup in the sink. She marched through the living room to Billie's room and closed the door behind her. "I detest such behavior, Billie. If you want to be grown-up and do the things adults do, then behave like one. I want you to take my place at the Red Cross today. You have to be there by nine and expect to work through lunch. Take a shower and get there as soon as you can. I'll call ahead and tell them you're taking my place. I'm much too upset to go myself," she added, knowing Billie's sense of guilt wouldn't let her refuse. She was right. Again.

The minute Billie had left the house, Agnes called the Navy Yard and asked to be put through to Lieutenant Moss Coleman in Admiral McCarter's office. While she waited, she let her eyes wander to the desk calendar near the phone. She counted the days since she knew Billie'd had her last period. The Moss Colemans of this world didn't believe in things like protection. Agnes would bet next month's ration stamps on that. She swallowed hard, not liking to think of the gamble she was taking. That it was Billie who might be pregnant and therefore Billie who would be taking the risk didn't enter Agnes's mind.

"Admiral Noel McCarter's office. Lieutenant Coleman speaking."

"Lieutenant, this is Agnes Ames. I'd like to talk with you when you get off duty. What time shall I meet you outside the gates?"

Hers was a no-nonsense tone. She meant business. Moss

grinned. She was one hour and fifteen minutes late. He'd expected the call before eight. "Yes, ma'am. I'll be off duty at three this afternoon. Good-bye, Mrs. Ames."

Beef. Oil. Something called electronics. A spread. Acres and acres of land. Money. Respectable money. Power. Prestige. All the things Agnes ever hoped and dreamed for could be Billie's. Billie would share.

Agnes settled herself at the kitchen table and penned off two notes to her roomers. She apologized for such short notice, but she could no longer rent the rooms. She sealed the envelopes and slipped them under the bedroom doors. She felt absolutely wonderful.

The Philadelphia Navy Yard was not one of Agnes's favorite places. As she waited for Moss she watched the activity taking place around her. She was still a young woman by some standards and she had to admit that there was something about a uniform that enhanced a man. For a few brief moments she wished again for youth with its highs and lows. She hastily amended the thought to include "providing I knew what I know now."

The Studebaker was hot and airless and smelled of the brake fluid the idiot at the garage had spilled on the floor mat. She checked her lipstick in the rearview mirror. She wanted to be in command and to be in command one must look one's best.

Moss Coleman walked through the gates at three-forty. Forty minutes late. He didn't apologize or make excuses when he opened the car door and sat down. "Ma'am," he said, smiling a greeting.

"Good afternoon, Lieutenant," Agnes said coolly as she slid the car into gear and away from the gate.

Moss was amused at the situation. If Pap knew, he'd be wetting his pants. Squared off against a woman. At the same time he was finding himself annoyed that she wasn't jittery or just plain mad. She shouldn't be so controlled. He had stolen away her daughter's virginity! She was more controlled than Pap was at times. Agnes Ames was a bitch. Well, Pap was a bastard. He supposed he was a bastard, too, junior grade and working toward first class. Agnes knew he'd make it. He could feel it and almost smell her triumph. That was okay, but he wasn't going to make it easy for her.

"You look fit this afternoon, Lieutenant. This heat is oppressive, don't you think? I'm hoping it will rain so my Victory garden will grow."

"I feel fit, ma'am." He stopped just short of returning the compliment and adding that he thought she looked victorious.

"Did you speak with Billie today?" Agnes asked bluntly.

"She called me from the Red Cross. She said you weren't feeling well so she took your place. My mother always uses a vinegar rag when she has a headache."

"Spare me your little home-grown homilies, Lieutenant, and let's get down to business." She pulled into the A&P parking lot. "I'm not in the mood for coffee and neither are you, so we'll dispense with that idea."

She was reading his mind; shades of Pap. Her coming declaration neither surprised nor offended him. In fact, Pap couldn't have done it better. The lady had what Seth would call spunk.

"I don't think there's any doubt in either of our minds that you will do right by my daughter." Moss knew his shrug irritated Agnes.

"It's quite possible—more than likely, in fact—that Billie will be pregnant," Agnes said flatly. "In your impetuosity last night, I doubt either of you gave any thought to the possible consequences or took any precautions to prevent them. In any case, any doctor could tell you it was the wrong time of month."

Wrong for Billie. Right for Agnes. What was it for him? Less than twenty-four hours and already she had Billie pregnant. There was a lot to be said for seizing opportunity when it knocked. "What is it you want from me, Mrs. Ames? Spell it out so this okey-dokey cowpoke can understand." Moss enjoyed the pink flush that stained Agnes's cheeks. All semblance of his drawl was gone; so was his humor. This was business now. Billie was a commodity. He wished he could hate this old buzzard but if he did, he'd have to hate himself.

"It's not what *I* want from you, Moss; it's what Billie is going to need. In case you aren't aware of it, Billie loves you, is deeply in love with you. You will notice I am not questioning your feelings—at this point they are immaterial. I want and expect you to marry my daughter to protect her reputation and your own as well."

Protect *his* reputation? What was she getting at? Besides wanting him to marry Billie, that is. It surprised him that Agnes could speak so glibly and forwardly about sex and pregnancy instead of alluding to it through euphemisms. Something was

{ 63 }

wrong here. Agnes was looking like the cat who swallowed the canary and he had a feeling those were his tail feathers tickling her chin.

Moss was about to give Agnes his answer but decided to make her sweat for it. Agnes deserved to sweat. Earlier that morning while tinkering with the admiral's compass, Moss had already made his decision. Certainly he would marry Billie. Aside from the fact that she really was a lovely girl and a surprisingly inventive bed partner, Billie Ames would be the perfect solution to his problems with Seth. Pap was hot spit on carrying on the Coleman line. Billie and a baby would free him of responsibility and obligation and he could ask for reassignment to the Pacific. Billie and a baby would free him from spending the duration in the Philadelphia Navy Yard pushing papers and arranging golf dates.

"I'll ask Billie to marry me tonight," Moss drawled, unable to contain the wide grin that spread over his features.

For an instant, Agnes was taken aback. She hadn't contemplated it would be this easy; she'd expected more of a fight from this tall Texan. She had the uncomfortable feeling that instead of her using him, Moss was using her for his own purposes. However, Agnes was not about to look a gift horse in the mouth. Without another word, she pulled the choke and started the car. As she pulled out of the A&P parking lot, Moss reached forward and turned on the radio, tuning in the ongoing drama of Helen Trent and her trials and tribulations. He lounged back in the seat and stretched his long legs, cap pulled forward so the shiny visor shadowed his eyes. His attitude annoyed her, but then she supposed that's the way they did things in Texas. Texas.

The sky was already darkening when Agnes dropped Moss off at the gates to the navy base. She had driven less than a mile when the cloudburst struck. Cautiously, she steered her car to the side of the road. This was no time to chance an accident, not now, when the golden gates of Texas were ready to open for her in welcome. It took cleverness to lift the Agnes Ameses of this world out of self-sacrifice and privation into the lap of luxury. Coleman luxury. At last she was achieving everything that was meant to be hers since the day she'd entered the world already screaming her head off at the injustice of it all. And it had been unjust, she reflected, all of it, from being born to Maude and Matthew Neibauer, those God-fearing, self-righteous parents, to her sorry marriage to Thomas Ames, made in spite and endured in sour resignation. . . .

Even as a child Agnes wondered if perhaps things would have been different if the Neibauers had not lived on Elm Street in the house Maude had inherited from her mother. Maude had married Matthew, a simple laborer, against her mother's wishes and the whole town knew it. They sniffed through their proper, middle-class noses in disapproval that one of their own should marry beneath her station.

Maude, always high-strung and nervous, anguished daily over what she imagined were intentional slights. Tearfully, she hung her wash at the crack of dawn before the neighbors could see her and be reminded that she did not have a colored woman to do it. Underwear was hung between sheets so it wouldn't be seen and NoWorry bleach was added by the gallon to the wash water. A white wash was synonymous with virtue, according to Maude. Matthew's dirty plumber's overalls were hung in the basement. No need to remind the neighbors he didn't wear a suit and tie. Life, to Maude, was a series of obstacles never to be conquered.

It had been Agnes's job from the time she was very young to clean the house each Saturday morning, before ten o'clock, in case company should come. They never did. In the front parlor she dusted her grandmother's brown horsehair furniture, replaced the crocheted doilies on the arms with freshly starched ones, and polished the whatnot. No one ever sat in the parlor, not even Maude and Matthew. Agnes scrubbed the front porch on her hands and knees and waxed it. She scoured the white columns with Bab-O and waxed them until the gleam could be seen from the bottom of the hill.

Once, her father suffered a back injury and couldn't work for almost an entire summer. They lived off the garden and ate sliced bacon only occasionally. She never complained, even when she left the table hungry, but sometimes she still cringed remembering the threats her parents had made to keep her from telling her few friends that they had no meat.

Friends; how few there were while growing up, and the front porch was the only place she was allowed to entertain them. She could never invite them back to the kitchen for cookies. The kitchen linoleum was cracked, the glasses weren't right, the plates were old-fashioned, and Maude feared the children would report all this back to their parents.

Agnes used to wonder if she'd been adopted. She hoped she was—she hated to think that she shared the same blood with these fearful, passionless people. There was no way she could imagine Maude taking off her pajama bottoms for Matthew, and there was never a sound from their room. It was always as silent as a tomb.

Thomas Ames drew her with his flashing dark eyes and ready smile. It was with him that she found the affection, approval, and easygoing ways she'd needed for so long. Maude was horrified. Thomas simply wasn't good enough. He was lazy, shiftless, a reprobate. The only home he'd known were the tiny rooms over the Twelfth Street saloon. He could never offer Agnes Neibauer a future.

Agnes, however, was much more interested in the very real and very passionate present. Thomas's smile, his gentle nature, intoxicated her. She was determined to have him.

Once, she heard Maude and Matthew fighting. "Why I never listened to my mother I don't know," Maude screamed. "She was right about you! Just like I'm right about Agnes and that Ames boy."

Agnes married Thomas Ames at the age of seventeen in a civil ceremony in Elkton, Maryland. Predictably—it wasn't long after Billie's birth—she came to the conclusion that she'd traded one life for another just like it. Once passion's glow dimmed, she merely tolerated Thomas, forcing herself to share her body with him on Friday nights. When Maude and Matthew died of influenza, she and Thomas took Billie, her few toys, and the cheap living room suite, and moved back to the house on Elm Street. Nothing had changed. Agnes carried on as Maude had done, living the same life and hating every minute of it.

She'd always wanted more, but how did you get more? Prayer wasn't the answer, as any fool could see, and hard work brought no miracles. Power and brains, that's what it took, along with a healthy dose of imagination.

Thomas Ames, husband, father, mediocre provider, died of a lack of imagination. Oh, he'd had it once; that was what had drawn Agnes to him. But time and worry and bills had taken their toll. He had tried his best, that she grudgingly admitted, but he outdid himself the day he took one gasping breath, one last exhale, and died on the kitchen floor. It was over before she could open her mouth in surprise.

She spared no expense on the handsome Springfield metallic

casket. Their neighbors and the whole Parish touched the bronzed metal at Thomas's wake, and their eyebrows rose in respect. Agnes was satisfied. None of them knew how many meatless meals she and Billie had eaten until the casket was paid.

Two hours after the Springfield casket was lowered into the ground, Thomas Ames's scanty wardrobe was packed and delivered to the church poor box. The mattress was turned and fresh linens, the ones embroidered for her hope chest, were put on the bed. She'd then dropped to her knees and thanked God for taking Thomas so quickly. Having to nurse him would have been unjust in a life that was already too one-sided.

The cloudburst was over. Agnes rolled down the window and then wiped the windshield with her linen handkerchief. Everything looked so green. The trees, the shrubbery, even the dress she was wearing was green. Green, the color of money.

It was a glorious day.

{{{{{{{{{ CHAPTER FIVE }}}}}}}}}

Agnes Ames met with Father Donovan that very evening, even before Moss came to the house. She stretched the truth, just a bit, saying Moss was due to be shipped out any time now, so could the Father please dispense with the banns that should be read three Sundays in a row?

"Dispensation is not given freely, Mrs. Ames," Father Donovan said with a sigh, "but neither is it unusual during these times of war." Little Billie Ames was getting married. How could he refuse this child her precious request? He'd baptized her, confirmed her, and after all, Lieutenant Coleman was a Catholic—on his mother's side, at least. Most unusual for a Texan, the priest thought, but he was naturally pleased. "I'll make the arrangements, Mrs. Ames. It's usual in cases where the banns cannot be announced three Sundays in a row to have them announced in three different churches." He paused a moment. "There *will* be at least one week before the wedding, won't there?" he asked sternly. He was willing to go just so far.

"Oh, yes," Agnes hastily assured him. "Today is Thursday, so this Sunday makes one week. And since the wedding will be next Sunday, that gives us two weeks!" Her mind was clicking with the relentlessness of a metronome. Invitations. Only close friends, of course, and Father Donovan. Caterer. Champagne, something light and elegant. Accommodations . . . the Latham Hotel, downtown. Simple yet elegant. The word that kept coming to Agnes's mind was "small," but then she amended it to "hurried." She wanted this over and done with quickly, before any of the Colemans got the idea of coming up from Texas and talking "sense" to Moss.

The following days were spent on the telephone, readying the house and making arrangements. She explained to friends that "this war" made it impossible to do anything right, but Agnes knew Billie didn't care a whit if it was a formal wedding at a mass or simply repeating vows in the rectory. All she wanted was the ring on her finger that said she was Mrs. Moss Coleman.

Moss had voiced no objections and silently agreed to Agnes's little fabrication that he might be shipped out at any moment. Everyone appeared to be happy. Moss and Billie were to have the upstairs to themselves now, taking over Agnes's room with its big double bed. The roomers were gone, much to Agnes's relief. Everyone would share the kitchen and bath, but Agnes would move down to Billie's bedroom study. Moss would contribute to the household expenses, and of course there would be a nice little allotment for Billie once he went away.

Agnes was in the kitchen, her mind half on the unfinished letter before her and half on what to have for dinner. Her eye fell on the calendar hanging beside the refrigerator. Billie's period should have begun two days ago. Billie was pregnant. She had to be. She was going to bear the Coleman heir and secure her own and Agnes's future.

Billie wandered in and listlessly poured herself a glass of lemonade. She was thirsty yet almost afraid to drink it because her stomach had been so upset these past three or four days. Billie attributed the queasiness to the excitement of the wedding, but when she'd mentioned it to Agnes she'd been shocked to see satisfaction on her mother's face. Surely her own mother wouldn't wish this misery upon her.

"What are you doing, Mother?"

"Oh, I thought I'd write to the Colemans. I think it's about time, don't you? I discussed it with Moss last night and he gave me the address. It's such a long trip for them to make that I thought it would be nice to write about a few of the details so they won't feel left out."

"You didn't say anything to me about it, Mother. Neither did Moss. Why do you always confer with Moss and then I find out what you've decided after the fact? I'm beginning to feel left out."

Agnes stared across the table at her daughter. "You're getting cranky, Billie, and that isn't good for you or the baby."

Billie sighed. "You don't know I'm pregnant. I really wish you wouldn't talk like that."

"All right, let's say you're on edge—does that make you feel better?"

"No. Let's just drop it. I think I'll take a shower and lie down for a while. I feel a headache coming on."

"Is there anything you want me to say to the Colemans?"

"How can I say anything? I don't even know them. I've never even spoken to them, and neither have you. Since you're so bent on doing everything exactly right, Mother, don't you know that it's the *groom's* family who should make the first gesture?"

"Well, *I* know that, Billie, and *you* know that, but perhaps *they* don't know it," Agnes replied defensively. She was well aware of her breach of etiquette and admittedly somewhat unnerved by it. Certainly a family as affluent and influential as the Colemans was aware of its duties and obligations. In fact, this was the only fly in Agnes's ointment: the Colemans might disapprove of Moss's decision to marry; if so, then either they would convince him that he was acting hastily and should cancel the wedding, or they would ignore the situation entirely and never accept Billie or the baby as one of their own.

Billie rubbed her temples and relented, too queasy and achy to argue. "All right, Mother, you take care of it. You usually do. As long as Moss approves, it's all right." It wasn't all right. Why hadn't Moss said something to her? But if he had, it would have been one of those little "don't worry your pretty little head about things like that" speeches. She *was* being cranky, but it was only because she wouldn't be seeing Moss tonight. He had to attend a social function with Admiral McCarter, meeting and dancing with other women. She remembered how Moss had been the focus of female attention at the graduation dance, and even at the USO he'd attracted women like bees to honey. She tried to reason with herself that Moss loved her, that he'd asked her to marry him, but jealous fear bit into her like the teeth of a dragon.

She felt better after her shower, more relaxed. Curling herself onto the window seat, she rested her head on her knees and gazed out at the green lawn and summer flowers through the dark rusty screen, thinking about Moss. She always thought about him; even when she was doing other things, thinking other things, he was always there, like a friendly shadow, smiling down at her. How she loved him! It came from somewhere deep within her, welling, rising like a mountain river during spring thaw, rushing and turbulent until it found its own level. She knew Moss loved her; otherwise he'd never have asked her to marry him, but she guessed it wasn't with the overwhelming, consuming love she felt for him. To Billie, Moss was all that was exciting and beautiful. He was the focus of her passions and the man of her dreams. He was love. If he didn't love with the same devotion and depth, it was all right, she thought. Someday he would. He would grow to love her and she would become his world just as he was already hers. Somewhere in her heart, though, Billie was aware that Moss loved her as much as he could love anyone. It would have to be enough.

A delicious feeling of wickedness rushed through Billie. She dreamed of sleeping in the same bed all night with Moss. She wanted to reach out and touch him, warm with sleep, feel herself turning into his arms and resting her head on his chest. She wanted to awaken in the morning and see him before she saw anyone else, hear the sound of her name on his lips, have him crush her against him, have him make love to her. She hugged her knees to her chest. Life couldn't be more wonderful or perfect if God had stepped down from the heavens and personally handed Moss to her, to keep and to love. If she really was pregnant, it would be wonderful. Moss's baby. Their child. How she would love it. Moss would adore her because she'd given him a child.

A frown puckered Billie's brow. She wasn't certain how Agnes would react to a baby in the house. Babies meant work and confusion, Agnes always said. They demanded and needed attention. Yet whenever Agnes alluded to the possibility of pregnancy, there was something smug and satisfied about her.

Billie was so caught up in her daydreams she almost missed hearing the jangling phone in the front hall. When she realized it wasn't the church bells ringing in the noon Angelus, she scurried to the phone and lifted the receiver. She was breathless.

"Billie?"

"Yes, Moss." He'd called. He wanted to talk to her. How wonderful it was to hear him say her name.

"I can't talk for long. We've got a lot of visiting brass here today. I'm behind in my work and the admiral is edgy. He gets nervous when too many stars are around, especially when they've got more brass than he does."

"Maybe you'll be more sympathetic when you're an admiral," Billie teased.

"Billie, I don't want to be an admiral. All I want is to fly. I want to take my place up there with the rest of the guys."

Billie's heart flopped over. Every day, it seemed, the news was filled with stories of downed pilots. She childishly crossed her fingers to wish that Moss would spend the war with Admiral McCarter. She knew it was selfish of her, but she loved him and wanted to keep him safe. What was wrong with that? "I know. I didn't mean to upset you. I was only teasing."

"I know, honey, but I want you to understand that I could never be happy unless I'm flying. I've told you that all along."

It sounded like a warning to Billie. She'd ignore it. "Yes, you did, and I'm sure you'll get your wish when it's time."

"Hey, Billie, do you still pray for me?" he asked, his voice warm and intimate, sending shivers up her spine.

"You know I do," she whispered. She prayed. She prayed he'd always be safe and never taken from her.

"Good girl. What are you doing today?" he asked. "Will you think of me?"

"All day, every day," she told him, her pulses quickening. She imagined she could see his smile, his thick dark hair brushing his tanned brow, and those summer blue eyes that winked out from under thick black brows. Smiling eyes in an otherwise serious face. "I guess I'll weed the garden and then I'll move some of my things upstairs." She felt herself flush, remembering that just minutes before she had been daydreaming about sharing a room and a bed with him.

As though reading her thoughts, Moss whispered huskily, an intimate sound that made her blood sing, "Will you be moving them up to *our* room? I like having your little-girl things around me, Billie. And then what will you do? I want to know so I can think about you."

"Then I suppose I'll have to help Mother with the arrangements for the wedding." She laughed, gloriously happy. "If she'll let me, that is. She seems to be enjoying each little agonizing detail. Right now she's writing to your parents and seems to think I should do the same. What do you think, Moss?"

"Don't you worry your pretty little head about that. Just let your mother handle it. There'll be plenty of time for you to think about other things besides me." The old girl wasn't letting any grass grow under her feet, Moss thought. Pap, you're gonna whizz in your pants when you get that letter. He hoped Billie wouldn't think to ask him if he'd called his folks. Amusing. It was all so damned amusing.

"Did you know Mother was writing to your parents?" Billie asked hesitantly.

Injured feelings here, Moss concluded. How often he'd dealt with them where Amelia was concerned. Play the game. Lie if you must. "Not actually, but it's not such a bad idea, don't you agree?"

"I suppose so. But Moss, shouldn't you be the one writing to them? You've never said if you called them or what they said about our getting married. Aren't they even curious?"

"Billie, don't worry. Everything is fine. Trust me, won't you?"

"I do, Moss. I feel guilty, I guess, because I told Mother I didn't want to add a note. Lord, she even wants to send a picture of me."

Trust Agnes to come up with that idea. He smiled. Seth would study the photo with a magnifying glass. "A looker" is what he'd call Billie. "We'll call them the day we get married. That way they'll be talking to their new daughter. Tell me you love me, Billie."

"I love you, Moss. I'm miserable when I'm not with you. Tomorrow seems like forever away. I dream about us all the time and what it's going to be like when we're married."

"Good" was all he said. Hell, he had dreams, too. Of taking off from the deck of a carrier and soaring upward into blue Pacific skies. Wing pilot. Squadron commander. Pap, you ain't seen nothin' yet! I've got me a war to fight and you're gonna take care of my wife and baby. Moss knew there was a baby. Even Billie had confessed she was late. It was just a matter of time until a doctor verified the fact. Pap, you're getting a bonus and you don't even know it. Another Coleman. Carry the name, continue the line. It damn well better be a boy—Pap would never settle for less. Moss brought his attention back to Billie. "Tomorrow isn't so far away. Look, honey, I've gotta go now. The admiral is coming up the walk. I'll call you tomorrow and come by for dinner."

"Good-bye, Moss. Think about me?"

"I will, Billie. Now, don't you do anything too strenuous. If you're going outside, wear a hat. The heat is brutal."

The lilt in Billie's voice was like a birdsong. He'd made her happy and that was good. When she was happy she didn't think a lot and if she didn't think a lot, Agnes didn't look for problems.

"I'll do that, Moss. I love you."

Moss leaned back in his swivel chair. Admiral McCarter was nowhere in sight. He wondered how the admiral's golf game was going. If nothing else, he could write some letters. The kind Pap wrote when he wanted something from someone. In this case, Moss was applying for a transfer, listing his first preference as the USS *Enterprise*. He'd get what he wanted; he knew it. He'd graduated top of his class and was known as a good pilot.

Before he'd had a chance to begin, the phone rang four times in rapid succession. He doodled on the blotter in front of him, drawing a sleek plane. His pencil slid over the blotter, honing its lines.

Agnes licked the envelope flap and sealed it. There, it was done. She did not plan to send the letter air mail. The Colemans would receive it after the wedding. Even if they managed to work in a phone call, it would be too late.

Agnes shrugged. Moss was expendable. Once he'd pronounced his vows—she was counting on his sense of duty—and the marriage certificate was in Billie's hands, he could fly off directly to Tokyo as far as she was concerned. It was Billie who was important. Billie and the baby. Of course she was pregnant; she already had the symptoms. And if by some strange chance of fate she wasn't, Agnes would be sure to give them lots of time alone. There would be a baby within the month.

Would Billie make a good mother? She was very young. Agnes didn't know. Agnes didn't care. The Colemans could afford nursemaids and nannies.

Little bumps like those on a fresh-plucked chicken rose on Agnes's arms. She swore she could feel the weight of the Coleman money. First she'd smelled it. Now she could feel it. The heavier it felt, the better she liked it. Billie Ames Coleman. Billie Coleman's mother.

Billie and Moss were married and the day of their wedding was perfect. The sun shone. The garden bloomed. Billie was radiant. Moss was handsome and dashing in his navy whites. Agnes was victorious.

The entire party, including Father Donovan, numbered thirty-five, and the reception was held at the Latham Hotel in downtown Philadelphia. Every time a champagne cork popped Agnes cringed. It was so expensive, even the house brand they were serving. Moss had offered to pay for the wedding but she'd refused. There were *some* things she had to do. This was one of them.

Moss found a quiet corner and for company had taken half a bottle of bubbly and a glass. He watched his beautiful bride as she laughed with her friends and danced with his from the Navy Yard. Thad Kingsley seemed especially attentive to Billie, and Moss was enjoying it. Now that Billie was his, all his, he could afford to be generous. He snickered as he remembered his own jealousy that night at the USO. What he'd said was true. He didn't want to share her with anyone and he'd never taken her there again.

Married. Good God, he was married and had a wife. Moss guzzled the champagne and had to fight to keep from standing on the table and making a toast. Not to his bride, but to his old man. Pap, it was a hell of a wedding. We all got drunk, all but the bride and her mother. We nibbled on strawberries and scrambled eggs and something called crepes. I've got me a wife, you old bastard, and I got her by myself. No picking and choosing. No running her past the Coleman receiving line. His eyes went to his radiant bride. A new Coleman. He held his glass aloft and winked at Billie.

Agnes's party was over. This was *his* time now.

The Hotel Latham was one of the best. The dining rooms were opulent; the little bistro at ground level fashionable and intimate. The service was discreet; carpeted halls muffled footsteps. This was where Billie would spend her wedding night.

It could have been a soddy hut and she wouldn't have noticed, not if Moss was with her.

Outside their room, Moss swept Billie into his arms and carried her over the threshold, his mouth warm and exciting against her ear. "You're mine now, Billie Coleman, all mine!" His arms were strong and she felt small and vulnerable in them, clinging to his neck. He echoed her own thoughts: he belonged to her now, and nothing would ever take him from her.

Their overnight cases had been placed near the bed and roses filled the room. Billie gasped her delight, knowing they were from Moss. A bucket of champagne and two glasses had been placed on the bedstand. Suddenly Billie was shy. It was still daylight. Going to bed was expected. On graduation night the lights had been turned off; their lovemaking had just happened, her passions rising to the surface. Hectic color bloomed on her cheeks.

Moss removed his white tunic. His undershirt emphasized his burnished, tanned skin and snugly fit the contours of his broad chest and manly arms. Peeking above the V neck was a dark curling of chest hairs. His waist was slim, his hips flat, his thighs filled the legs of his trousers. He was beautiful, and Billie felt pale and dun-colored beside him. Why would this beautiful man have wanted to marry her? she wondered. Yet it seemed right that she should find him more physically striking than herself; in nature the male of the species was more colorful and beautiful than the female.

Moss pulled the shades, dimming the room, casting Billie into half shadow. When he turned to look at her he saw the radiance that had surrounded her downstairs in the ballroom had flickered and died. She sat on the edge of the bed, watching him, her chin lifted and her mouth was set as though to keep from crying. He understood and a wave of pity washed over him. She was probably overexcited by the wedding, exhausted by the preparations, and overwhelmed with her new role as his wife. "Let me help you with your dress, Billie," he offered quietly, waiting for her to accept before moving toward her. Ordinarily, Moss was an impatient lover, but with Billie he wanted to take his time; he wanted to arouse her and have her come to him in the wild abandon she had shown in her own little room.

Billie stood and turned her back, letting him work the tiny buttons of her gown. But first he removed her veil and Juliet cap, his fingers smoothing her sleek ash-blond hair, lifting it off her neck to place a kiss that reverberated through her. Tender fingers and loving hands helped her out of her gown, leaving her in her slip. Moss's hands ached with the need to caress her and his body ached with a stronger need as he gazed at her. She was lovely, his Billie, built on delicate, slender lines, her breasts round and perfect for her figure. Her waist was slim above the gentle slope of her hips and soft curve of her thighs. He felt her shiver beneath his touch.

Moss wrapped his arms around her waist, standing behind her, pressing his lips into the hollow between her shoulder and neck. "Don't be afraid of me, Billie. Don't ever be afraid." His voice was warm and loving, cracking the veneer of her shyness. She leaned back against his lean, hard body. "I'll pour us some champagne and you slip into something comfortable," he murmured.

When Billie stepped out of the bathroom into the cool, shade-darkened room, the radio was playing softly and Moss was waiting for her on the bed. She drew in her breath apprehensively, knowing she was being silly; but the sight of his naked chest both excited and intimidated her, until she saw that he was reclining on top of the covers, still wearing his white trousers.

"You're beautiful." He smiled up at her, his intense blue eyes skimming over her nightie. "Come and lie down here beside me. I want to hold you."

Billie crept into his embrace, resting her head against his shoulder. His arms brought her close, warming her skin, giving her solace, demanding nothing. From time to time his lips caressed her brow and he inhaled the fragrance of her hair. He was gentleness. He was understanding. And she loved him.

Street sounds wafted through the windows and seemed in harmony with the music on the radio. The bed seemed strange, longer than her own and wider, alien. The furnishings of the room were impersonal, used by hundreds of other people. Everything was strange, everything was unfamiliar, except the touch of Moss's hand stroking her hair and the clean masculine scent of him and the heat of his body beside hers. Billie turned to that familiarity, seeking reassurance from it, hoping to find the security she did not feel.

He took her hand in his and brought it to his lips, caressing her fingertips, nibbling, tickling her palm with the tip of his tongue. Shyly, she withdrew her hand.

"What's my Billie thinking?" he asked softly.

After a long moment: "I'm afraid. I'm silly, I know, but I'm afraid. You cause such feelings in me, Moss, and they scare me."

"Would it help you to know that you cause the same feelings in me? The very same, Billie."

"I do?" She turned her head, looking up into his face, and saw the truth of his words in his eyes.

"You do. I've never been a husband before, either. I want things to be exactly right. I don't want to disappoint you, Billie. We've been together before, but it was different then, wasn't it? I was Moss Coleman. You were Billie Ames. Now we're married, Mr. and Mrs., and there's a whole life ahead of us. But we're still the same people, Billie. And we can grow together, can't we?"

His words released her fears. He understood. Billie felt such a rush of love for him that she wound her arms around his neck and kissed him, pouring out her emotions in the sweet contact between them. His hand caressed her shoulder; his arm tightened about her waist. "Oh, yes, Billie," he murmured against her mouth, "I want everything to be perfect for you. You do things to me, Billie, in here." He pressed the flat of her hand against his heart.

Billie melted against him, giving herself up to him, rejoicing in the feel of his lips brushing against hers so gently, so very gently. He kissed the curve of her chin, traced the length of her throat and the cleft between her breasts. The ribbons at the bodice of her nightie gave way to his fingers, baring her for his kisses and the easy caress of his hand.

She shuddered with the first wave of passion, closing her eyes and welcoming the sensation. He left her for a moment and when he returned he was naked, the strength of his long legs and firm thighs pressing against hers. He helped her remove her nightie, seeing how she kept her eyes lowered and averted. Tenderly, he lifted her chin, willing her to look into his eyes, to see him, to find what she most wanted to see. He smiled, that slightly askew grin that could turn her heart over in her chest. "My Billie," he whispered, "my beautiful, adorable Billie."

He lay down beside her, drawing her into his arms, kissing her again and again with a passion that was answered by her own. He traced delicate patterns over her face and brow, nibbled at her ears and lowered to the hollow of her throat and across the fullness of her breasts, circling but not touching the taut rosy crests, before returning again to her mouth. He savored the young clean scent of her and sampled the sweet taste of her skin. His hands stroked the velvet of her thighs and belly but refrained from going further.

Moss sensed that he was breaking through the barrier of Billie's insecurity. It would be so easy to sweep her over the edge with him, but somehow he knew it wouldn't be enough. Passion was never enough. It was hollow and meaningless unless it was accompanied by some deeper emotion, a lasting commitment, a joining of hands before taking that leap together. He almost laughed at himself; with other women passion had always been its own reward, but not with Billie. He wanted, no, needed her to love him. "Do you want me, Billie? Do you love me?"

He waited for her answer, wanting to hear her commit herself to him. He hadn't wanted to rush her; he didn't want to reveal his own burning need for her that could leave him feeling vulnerable and uncertain. But a deeper need made him insist. "Tell me, Billie," he whispered against the beating pulse of her throat, sending little tremors vibrating through her.

"Yes, I want you. Yes, yes, I love you. I'll always love you," she told him, her gaze melting into his, willing him to know how much she loved him, how much she needed him. "I want you to make love to me," she said in a hungry, husky voice she hardly recognized as her own. "I want you to teach me to make love to you."

Moss was excited by her admission, all sensation heightened. He captured her mouth with his own, evoking a low, sensual groan. He placed her hand on his body, teaching her the rhythm, and he became helpless beneath her touch, awarding to her the power and the control over his desire. He invited her caresses, inspired them. He wanted to please her, to have her find him pleasing.

Billie's eyes shone victorious at this new conquest. His tremors and shudders echoed her own. She smoothed the flat of her palms over his body, delighting in the comparison between the silky thicket of hairs on his chest and the rougher coat surrounding his sex. Her mouth found the pulse at the base of his neck and the ruddy flesh of his nipples that responded just like her own, forming into hard little nubs that teased the tongue and invited her suckling. She tasted and licked, following her whims, excited by her explorations of the flatness of his belly and the firmness of his thighs. He gave himself over to her, reveling in the feel of her mouth on his body and rejoicing in the fire that burned in her eyes.

Billie exulted in the power of her sensuality, delighted in the dominion of her femininity. She sought him with fevered lips, possessed him with seeking hands, her own passions erupting and overflowing with the realization that she could give him this pleasure. The unfamiliarity of his sex intoxicated her, beckoning her caress, revealing its strength and yet evoking tenderness with its vulnerability. She wanted to find each hollow of his body, trace every line with her fingers and lips. She wanted to possess him, to make his body as familiar to her as her own.

Moss gritted his teeth to retain control of himself. It would be so easy to give in to this driving need for release. But he wanted to make love to her, to prompt her own driving ambitions for satisfaction. With a groan of regret, he seized her haunches and brought himself on top of her. He returned her caress, answered her hungry kisses. His hands never left her body, smoothing, tempering, yielding, following her sensations and silent demands.

He kissed her eyes, her nose, her mouth, before pulling himself from her embrace to position himself between her parted thighs. His eyes devoured her as she waited for him. Her tumble of soft golden hair shone against the pillow; her skin was bathed in a sleek sheen that silkened the contact between them. She trembled uncontrollably. Fire flickered through her as his mouth moved down her body, and then the fire raged from the most intimate of kisses. Billie felt herself flying upward, like a cinder in an autumn breeze, floating toward the sun. Suddenly the sun was within her, bright and glowing, consuming her reserve and making her part of the universe.

Her body opened to him, needing him, knowing that only he could fill this vast space within her that had once been the sun. His body became a part of her own, completing her.

He watched her face as he moved within her, seeing the passions that he had ignited and that were now consuming him. Sheath and shaft embraced as he drove himself deep within her, thrusting harder, faster, blindly seeking the far side of passion and holding her fast as he tumbled them over the edge.

Billie fell asleep in her husband's arms. The last vestiges of girlhood had been shattered and broken and she had been afraid she would never be whole again. But the fragments had fallen away to reveal the warm, loving woman who lived beneath. This, then, had been her first step into womanhood and Moss had led her to victory.

{{{{{{{{{ CHAPTER SIX }}}}}}}}

"I don't know, Moss." Billie pulled back on his hand, feet dragging as they crossed the tarmac to the little plane straining in the wind against the wires that anchored her to the ground.

"Come on, Billie. I want to take you up. It's important to me," he insisted, urging her forward. "Look at her sitting out there, just waiting for us. You'll love her. I promise you will."

"No, Moss, please," she pleaded. "Can't I just wait here?"

"No, Billie, you can't wait here. I want you up there with me. You're married to a flyer and I want you to know what it's like. Don't you trust me?"

There was such hurt in his eyes that Billie would have done anything to assuage it. She could never bring herself to cause him pain or disappointment, especially in herself. "Of course I trust you. It's that machine I don't trust. Mother says if God meant for us to fly, He would have given us wings."

"But He did, Billie. Only He didn't attach them to our backs. Those are the wings He gave us. Now, will you stop being a silly little girl and take to the air with your man?"

Billie followed behind Moss as though she were being led before a firing squad.

"She's a beauty, isn't she? She's a PT nineteen, a trainer, and safer than Ivory Soap."

The craft's fuselage was painted a dark meridian blue and her wings, carried low under the main body, were painted a garish yellow. Billie saw nothing of beauty here, only that the cockpit was open to the sky. She knew a terrible fear. "Moss! There's no roof! I'll fall out!"

"Not roof," he corrected, "canopy. And no, you won't fall out. You'll be safely strapped in. You'll love it, Billie. You will."

Moss was already involved in his ground check. His hands smoothed over the wafer-thin edge of the wings, testing the elevator flaps and trailing beneath to some unseen gadgetry. Billy watched him, eyes focused on those sensitive fingers as they ran over the skin of the aircraft. It was the way a man would caress a woman; delicately, worshipping, exploring.

The hot wind blew relentlessly across the tarmac, ballooning Moss's shirt and ruffling his dark, crisp hair. Her own slacks were flapping violently against her legs and the sun was already burning the tip of her nose. But Moss was oblivious to everything but the craft. He checked something near the tail, and as a final gesture he kicked one of the balloon tires.

"She's in great shape," he declared. "C'mon, Billie, up you go!"

Showing her where to step, Moss placed his hands firmly on her neat little bottom and shoved as she gracelessly climbed onto the plane and then down into the front seat.

"Now tuck your hair up onto your head and put this on." He handed her a leather helmet. "Without a canopy the wind'll blow you to kingdom come. Be sure to pull it down firmly over your ears and watch out for that wire—it goes to the headset and plugs into the instrument panel."

Her fingers frozen with terror, Billie fumbled with the wind-tangled strands of hair, pushing them beneath the leather helmet. Moss was spitting on the inside lenses of the goggles and wiping them with the sleeve of his shirt. "Can't have them fogging up, want you to see what it's all about," he said, handing them to her and instructing her to pull the band at the back of her head to secure them.

She didn't want to do this—she hated it already—but most of all, she hated Moss's condescending tolerance. The excitement lighting his eyes wasn't for her. It was for this garishly painted aircraft that could offer him something she couldn't.

Billie watched with dread as Moss released the guide wires holding the craft to the ground. The space inside the cockpit was small and narrow with barely enough shoulder room for herself, much less a man, but the space beneath the instrument panel was deep and long, built to accommodate long legs. Billie's feet fell far short of the interior bulkhead, where they could have found purchase and helped to brace her against the motion of the plane. She felt as though she were dangling on her seat, frail and vulnerable.

Moss slapped the fuselage twice at Billy's left elbow before climbing into the seat behind her. The few inches of bulkhead separating them seemed miles wide, robbing her of his much needed closeness. When the sudden spurt of engine power turned the prop, slowly at first and then with the alarming speed and thrust of a turbine, Billie's fingernails bit into the palm of her hands. The soft balloon tires bounced them down the runway as they gathered speed, jostling her in her seat, feet reaching for purchase to steady herself. She was unaware of a crackle in her ears until she heard Moss's voice coming over the headset. "Take it easy, Billie. We're almost up and then the going is smooth."

Billie squeezed her eyes shut against the sight of the tarmac speeding beneath the wings. A sudden burst of power, a last bounce, and they left the ground. "Atta girl," Moss was saying, "easy now, easy." Billie hung on to the sound of his voice, taking the reassurances deep inside her. It was the only contact between them and she clung to it. "Give the little lady a nice ride; it's her first time up. Easy, sweetheart, easy."

Billie's eyes popped open behind the protection of the goggles. Moss was sweet-talking the plane! That familiar loving note in his voice wasn't for her at all, but for this damn piece of machinery with her bumpy riveted skin and whorish paint!

"We're going up, Billie. Hold on!" And the nose of the little trainer plane shot upward vertically. Billie gulped, swallowing past the painful lump of fear. Her eyes squeezed shut again and she decided not to open them again until she was once more standing on God's own earth. She felt the wind against the exposed portions of her face, whistling past her ears. The engine vibrated, sending shivers through her body. She held a white-knuckled grip on the edges of her seat, praying that she would live past this moment into the next and the next until she was once again on the ground. A terrible heart-squeezing fear iced her veins and stole her air.

"That's my girl! You're a beauty! A real beauty!" Moss cried, exhilarated.

They were up for more than an hour, Billie clutching furiously to the sides of her seat, her stomach heaving. When Moss finally set the craft onto the runway and taxied to her reserved space on the tarmac, Billie had to pry her stiffened fingers loose, pressing them against her legs in order to work them out of their clawed posture.

She had hated it, every minute of it. Worse, she now understood fully that airplanes were her rivals for Moss's affection. An acid jealousy stirred in her at the realization, as though airplanes were flesh-and-blood women.

After reattaching the guide wires, Moss came to help her out of the cockpit. His face was beaming, wreathed with smiles. "God, I can't tell you how good that was. Every day I don't fly I only feel half-alive!" His hand reached out beyond Billie to once again appreciate the sweep of the wing tip. "You're a sweet little thing," he said. "And you're a sweet little copilot." He threw his arms around Billie's shoulder to hug her against him, leading her with long strides across the tarmac back to the hangar.

When she came abreast of it, she abruptly tore away from Moss and entered the door marked "Ladies." Staggering to her knees, she knelt before what she'd heard Moss call the "porcelain princess" and vomited.

Billie and Moss moved into the master bedroom on the second floor of 479 Elm Street. Privacy was theirs.

June gave way to July and the days were long and hot. Billie was plagued with morning sickness, which she tried to cover by not rising for the day until after Moss left for the Navy Yard. But Agnes had the eyes of a hawk and always seemed to be standing outside the bathroom door just as Billie made her wild dash each morning to retch in the bowl. And always there was the satisfied expression in Agnes's eyes, which Billie mistook for a gloating judgment. "Bad things happen to bad girls." How often she'd heard Agnes repeat that smug little saying as she was growing up. By now her mother should have forgiven her little indiscretion. After all, she was married now. Happily married to a wonderful man.

There was no doubt in Billie's mind that she was pregnant. Still, she never spoke the word aloud. Until a physician made it official, she was simply a young married woman with a delicate stomach. Every so often Billie was aware of how Moss's glance went to Agnes, and sometimes it seemed that they had more in common than she had first realized. Moss didn't exactly defer to Agnes, but he did seem to discuss things with her first. Where had this understanding between them come from? How had it happened? Hesitantly, she spoke of it to Moss, and he was quick to tell her it was her imagination. She believed him.

Dinner was over—breaded pork chops, to which Moss had added ketchup. He liked to add a variety of spicy condiments to his food, especially to Agnes's plain home-style meals. He liked to sink his teeth into thick rare beef or juicy fried chicken, not a pork chop that had been cooked to kingdom come or an indefinable meat loaf. The pork chops hadn't even been center cuts. Rationing was something that never concerned the Colemans of Texas.

"Whose turn is it to wash, yours or mine?" Billie asked, smiling across the table at her handsome husband.

"You two argue it out. I have a meeting," Agnes declared, rising from the table.

Moss volunteered to dry. He disliked soapy water up to his elbows and under any other circumstances would have refused any kitchen duty at all. At home, they had cooks and housekeepers who handled the mundane chores of living.

Billie liked being alone in the kitchen with Moss, doing all the little things that married couples did. Someday, they'd have a little house all their own and a swing in the backyard for their baby. "I heard the news this morning," she said, scraping the plates into the trash. "The USS *Enterprise* has been assigned a new commander. A Captain Davis. Did you know that, Moss?" Now why had she said that? Why must she persist in punishing herself by mentioning ships and carriers and airplanes and then watch for the eager expression in his eyes?

"Yes, I heard." Christ, he'd give his right arm to be on that ship. Davis. Should he tell Billie now or later? Later always made more sense. Why mention it when he didn't know if Captain Davis would remember him? Just because Davis had been in San Diego while Moss was in flight training didn't mean the captain would go out of his way to honor Moss's request for transfer to the Big E. He had never in his life wanted anything as badly as he wanted out of the Navy Yard and an assignment in the Pacific.

He looked at Billie, who was humming along with the radio as she rinsed the dinner plates. She was all most men would dream of, but Moss knew he needed more than a pretty wife. He needed adventure, challenge; he needed to fly. His gaze lowered to Billie's waistline. Once the pregnancy was confirmed, he'd make his move.

Billie's voice was so soft Moss had to strain to hear it. "They were talking about Midway," she said, her arms immersed in dishwater. "You were talking about it only last week. Remember?"

"How can I forget? The Big E proved herself and closed the argument against aircraft carriers." Always when he talked about carriers Moss's eyes lit from within and his slow, easy drawl quickened to a staccato. Billie felt the stirrings of panic. "Shore-based aviation had only a minor effect on Midway. High-level horizontal bombing is okay for land targets, but it's ineffective against ships at sea. That's why the Flying Fortresses failed where the fighter planes succeeded."

Moss was thinking of the Pacific map hanging in his quarters. He'd bet anything Guadalcanal was next on the Big E's agenda. When he noticed Billie's silence he looked up to see a great tear rolling down her cheek. "Hey, Billie, what's wrong?" He dropped the dishtowel and gathered her into his arms.

She cried softly into his chest. "I was just thinking of all those men and how they died. Moss, if anything ever happened to you, I'd die. I'd just die!"

"Billie, nothing's going to happen to me. Don't cry." He held her, soothing her, comforting her, thinking all the while what a bastard he was because soon, very soon, he'd leave her to join the ranks of the Pacific vanguard.

Routine in the Coleman/Ames household had taken on new life. Billie busied herself with small chores around the upstairs bedroom, trying to make it as inviting as possible. She spent hours standing in line at the butcher shop for something she knew Moss would especially like for dinner. On occasion, she squandered the precious coupons on steak—he'd taught Agnes and Billie just how he liked his steak done, charred on the outside, raw on the inside—and then pleaded an upset stomach at dinner, settling happily for a poached egg. Moss seemed unaware of the sacrifices Billie made, although they didn't go unnoticed by Agnes.

As activities in the Pacific intensified, Moss spent more time at the Navy Yard, sometimes coming home well after midnight and going immediately to bed. While operations for the Pacific were sent directly through the West Coast and not Philadelphia, information did leak through and he was hungry for every morsel. He was well apprised of the escalation of the war in Europe, as it was part of his job, but it was always to the western skies that his attention would drift.

When Moss arrived home late, Billie was satisfied to lie

beside him propped up on a pillow and stroke his dark head. And every night, she'd pray that he would stay at the Navy Yard and not be sent off into battle.

By the first weeks of August, Billie had resigned herself to morning sickness. She had missed her second period and was one week into her next cycle. It seemed to Billie that all of Moss's and Agnes's attention was focused on her belly. It was two days now since Billie had been to the doctor. Agnes had made the appointment. She had to know, and Moss needed to know. Billie told them she had a lifetime ahead of her to have babies.

It was three in the afternoon when the telephone rang. Agnes, who was hovering about in the living room picking lint off the sofa, reached for it on the first ring.

She found Billie in the kitchen drinking lemonade. Billie couldn't remember her mother smiling this way before.

"That was Dr. Backus. He says the rabbit died. That means you're pregnant, Billie. Moss will be delighted."

Pregnant. It was official now. She was going to have a baby, Moss's baby. She should be happy, ready to share in the joy; instead she was a tangle of confused emotions. She didn't think she was ready to become a mother. Not yet. She still wanted to have Moss all to herself. She needed this time with him, wanted it. She would become big and ungainly, uncomfortable and awkward. Would Moss still want her? Would he still be as passionate and demanding in bed? She couldn't comprehend how a couple could make love when the woman's belly was sticking out to here! "You're happy, aren't you, Mother?" Billie asked quietly.

"Certainly I'm happy, for *you*, Billie. And I'm sure that Moss will be just as delighted. You'll see. I think we should wait until after dinner to tell him, don't you? This isn't something you just announce over the telephone."

Agnes was jubiliant. She felt as though a load of bricks had been lifted from her shoulders. It was a fact. Billie carried the Coleman heir. Moss Coleman, Jr. It was done. Now Billie's and her future was secured, regardless of what happened or didn't happen to Moss. The baby's future, too. It was an afterthought.

"Mother, I'm going upstairs for a while. If Moss calls, call me, all right? Even if I'm sleeping."

"Of course, Billie. You do seem a little peaked today. It

must be the heat." It couldn't be anything else, Agnes thought. She wouldn't allow it to be anything else.

Billie lay back amid the mound of pillows with their lace edging. She was feeling an apprehension and dread that she couldn't explain. She should be happy, exuberant. Instead she just wanted to cry. This pregnancy was going to make a difference, she knew it would. No matter what her mother or Moss said. It was going to make a difference. She slept, her pillow wet with tears.

Billie was setting the table when the phone rang. Agnes answered, listened, mumbled something Billie couldn't hear, and then hung up. "Moss won't be home tonight. Take away his plate."

Take away his plate, as though he were already gone. "Mother, why didn't you let me speak to him? Didn't he ask for me?"

Agnes stared at her daughter. It was only natural that she was disappointed, although Agnes would never become used to Billie's romanticism. "Dear, he recognized my voice and he just said to give you the message. I think he was in a hurry. There seemed to be quite a bit of commotion in the background."

Billie sank down into a chair, worry and disappointment dimming her features. "You really are a lucky girl, Billie," Agnes said mildly, disguising her impatience. "You're married to a man in the military and you must accept the fact that he will have duties to perform. Think of all those other wives whose husbands are thousands of miles away."

"What time is it?" Billie asked anxiously. "Let's put on the radio and listen for the news. I just know something awful happened." And then she exploded. "I hate this damn war!"

Moss didn't come home that night. The following night he didn't appear or call. Billie felt a terrible, urgent need to talk to Moss. It had been two whole days. Didn't he miss her? Was what he was doing more important than her and the baby? He didn't even *know* about the baby.

Dabbing her eyes, she went to the phone, dialed the Navy Yard, and asked to be put through to Admiral McCarter's office. An unfamiliar voice answered the phone and explained that Lieutenant Coleman was not at his desk. Was there a message? Billie muttered something that passed for a negative and hung up. She hated the pitying expression in Agnes's eyes that seemed to be saying there were going to be many times like this and the quicker she got used to it, the better. She'd never get used to it. Never.

The next day, just when Billie was anticipating still another night without seeing her husband, Moss staggered up the walk. It was noon; she could hear the Angelus ringing. His eyes were red-rimmed and bloodshot from lack of sleep and too many hours in smoke-filled rooms. His uniform, usually impeccable, was wrinkled and mussed. Kissing Billie briefly on the lips, he shook off her clinging arm. "I need a shower and I could go for a cold beer. I've got three hours before I have to get back and I haven't had any sleep to speak of for two days, and no, Billie, I can't discuss it with you. I should've stayed on the base, but I wanted to see you. Now I'm so damned tired I'm hardly worth your trouble. Get me that beer, won't you?"

When Billie climbed the stairs with a tray holding the beer and a single rose in a bud vase, Moss was asleep. Three hours, he'd said. He looked so tired that it nearly broke her heart. Carefully, so as not to awaken him, Billie untied and removed his shoes and socks. There was a fresh uniform hanging in the closet; and she'd take it downstairs with her and give it a pressing. It would give her something to do. She bent over the bed to kiss him lightly on the cheek, hoping against hope that he'd awaken and take her in his arms. He didn't.

At the bottom of the stairs she met Agnes, who was carrying a small Big Ben alarm clock. "I'll just take this up and set it on the dresser. Your little clock will never wake Moss. He needs a cowbell."

Billie's glance flicked away from her mother to hide her resentment. Moss was *her* husband and *she* wanted to do for him, and she didn't need Agnes's interference. Agnes thought of everything. It was always her decision what they would have for dinner, what mass they would go to on Sundays, what day the sheets should be changed, whether or not the windows should be opened, when and how Moss should be told about the baby. Since her marriage, Billie had experienced a growing sense of powerlessness and inconsequence. Every choice or decision seemed to have been taken out of her hands by Agnes's greater wisdom and experience. It rankled. It was a small wonder that Agnes had not told Moss about the baby.

Billie had been fantasizing about the moment when she would announce her pregnancy to Moss. In the movies the wife always prepared an intimate little dinner and then afterward snuggled into the husband's lap and shyly made the announcement. None of Billie's daydreams were coming true. This was the first time Moss had been home in two days. When could she tell him? On the run, when he had a few minutes for her before rushing back to the base? It wasn't fair. If only she knew what was going on at the Navy Yard...

A feeling of dread stayed with her as she sharpened the creases in Moss's trousers and ironed his shirt. Moss had seemed exhausted but exhilarated. The thought made her queasy.

When Moss's freshly pressed uniform hung on the back of the closet door and his newly shined shoes stood in military line beneath, Billie took the morning paper into the living room. Her eyes raked the columns of the *Philadelphia Inquirer*. News of the war on both fronts leaped at her, but she could find nothing to explain Moss's absence. It was hateful. She wished it would all end so people could get on with their lives.

With nothing better to do, she sat on the front porch and worked the crossword puzzle, her concentration broken by thoughts of Moss lying upstairs on their bed.

When Moss loped down the steps a short while later, he found Billie dozing in the wicker chair. "Hey, is this how you spend your time, lazybones?" he teased lightly. He was already dressed in the freshly pressed uniform and his hair was still wet from his shower and shave. "I've gotta go now. If I get a chance, I'll call you later. Don't wait up for me."

"Moss, wait!" Billie pleaded, running down the walk behind him. "We really didn't get a chance to talk. I have so much to tell you. What's going on at the yard? Why aren't you coming home? Is something wrong?"

"Can't talk now, honey. The admiral'll have my hide if I'm not back on time. You be good and I'll call you later, if I can." He kissed her soundly and drove away. Billie watched after him, feeling foolish and ashamed and damned angry. He still didn't know about the baby.

Moss could see Billie standing on the sidewalk in the rearview mirror. For a brief moment his conscience pricked him, but then his thoughts leaped forward to the yard. Admiral McCarter and big brass from the Pentagon were debriefing West Coast command on the success of the air-sea strike and occupation of Guadalcanal. It was a foregone conclusion that the enemy would attempt to retake the island and reestablish strategic control of the South Pacific. When they did, the *Enterprise* would be there to meet them. Things were moving and Moss was determined to move with them.

Poor Billie, Moss thought. Maybe tomorrow he'd wrangle some free time and take her to the movies. It would be nice to make long, leisurely love to her afterward. Very nice indeed... But it was not bedroom action that he wanted now. Fighting, that was what he wanted. He refused to think of how he and Agnes had used Billie. She was a wonderful girl, soon to be the mother of his child, and she meant the world to him.

When Moss returned to the house on Elm Street, Agnes took one look at him and sat down on the hard kitchen chair. She told him Billie was out back weeding the pole beans. "When do you leave?" she asked quietly.

"Day after tomorrow. I got it, the Big E. She's coming into Pearl for repairs and that's where I'll meet her," Moss said, and realized that Agnes was neither surprised nor upset by his news. She'd been expecting it.

"Before you go out to Billie I want to remind you . . . she'll want to tell you about the baby herself."

"I won't forget. You know, don't you, that I didn't act on this transfer until I knew definitely that she was pregnant. Now I have to call my father and tell him," Moss said thoughtfully. Call Pap and give him the double whammie. The shock of knowing his son was about to be transferred to the Pacific front would be softened by the news of his first grandchild.

Billie felt herself being picked up off the ground and then turned around to face her husband. "Moss!" The happy surprise that had brightened her features faded into disappointment when she looked into his eyes. "Mother told you!" she accused. "I wanted to tell you."

Moss squeezed her tight, burying his face into her neck. "What difference who told me, little mama. C'mere and give me a kiss. I can't tell you how happy I am!"

Billie's disappointment ebbed with the force of his kiss and his warm arms holding her tight. What difference who told him, as long as he was happy, as long as he loved her this way.

As Moss held her, inhaling her sunshine fragrance, he reminded himself what a bastard he was. Not enough of a bastard to spoil this moment for her, though. His own news would wait until dinnertime when Agnes was there to soften the shock. Tender lovemaking would take the edge off later. He, Moss Coleman, was finally out from under; no one was going to jerk his strings anymore. Not Seth, not Agnes, not even Billie.

Together, arms around each other, they walked toward the house. "We're having roast beef, rare. Mother said it's the only rump roast she ever cooked that could still wink at her."

Moss laughed. They did try to please him, he knew, and he appreciated it. There would be the inevitable string beans made the way his mother prepared them. Small new potatoes with the skins on, fresh biscuits to dip in his gravy, and strawberry-rhubarb pie for dessert. He'd announce his news over the pie—after he finished it. He did love pie. "I can hardly wait until later," he said, leering at Billie. "I haven't been much of a husband for you lately." She grinned and made a grab for his leg, but he was too quick for her. "I'm going to jump into the shower. Help your mother in the kitchen. It's like a steam room in there. Why don't we eat on the back porch?"

"Would you like that?" Moss nodded. "All right, the back porch it is. Mother, we're eating on the back porch. I'll clean off the table and set it. Hurry up, Moss. The gravy cools quickly."

Agnes chattered nonstop through dinner. She felt anxious yet triumphant. It was as if she were conducting a symphony and it was being played chord by chord, note by note, building to the crescendo. She could sense it and so could Billie. It was in her eyes.

Moss laid aside his fork and leaned back in his chair. "You should give my mother the recipe for that pie." There was no easy way. Straight out. Say it. "Billie," he said softly, "I got my orders today. I leave day after tomorrow."

Billie's fork clattered on her plate. She knew it, just knew it. "Where? Where will you go?" she managed to croak.

"Pearl Harbor. The Big E is in for repairs and I'm assigned as a pilot. It's what I want, Billie. I have to do it. Can't you see that?"

Billie lowered her head, her soft blond hair hiding her bitterness. "Even knowing about the baby, you still want to go?"

"Yes. But I don't want to think of you here alone. I've given it thought and I want you and your mother to go to Austin. I can make all the travel arrangements. You'll live with my family until this is all over and I come home to you."

"Go to Texas!" Billie gasped, feeling as though the world were caving in under her feet. She didn't want to leave Philadelphia, leave everything that was familiar to her. She wanted to stay right here, have her baby here, be here when Moss came home.

Moss's eyes linked with Agnes's across the table. "I guess I shouldn't have included you along with Billie without asking you first."

Bitter tears stung Billie's yes. He hadn't asked *her*. The urge to scream was so strong that she choked and reached for her water. Moss was off his chair in an instant, clapping her on the back. Again he looked at Agnes. They were in agreement. It would be all right. Agnes would make it all right.

"You're going to love Texas, honey," he said. "You too, Agnes. You'll have the entire right wing of the house if you want it. I'm calling home tonight and I want both of you to talk to my parents. I don't want you to worry, Billie. Promise me. It's only right that our baby be born in Texas, in my home. You and your mother will have everything you need. It's a big house, Billie. You won't find my family getting under your feet, if that's what worries you. And you'll have the right kind of care for the baby. Neither of you will want for anything."

"I have everything I want right here and now," Billie murmured, lifting her gaze to meet Moss's eyes. "As long as I have you, that's everything to me."

"I know, honey, and the same goes for me. You know that. It's only that I'll feel better knowing you and Agnes have someone to take care of you. And I want my son to know his heritage. You understand, don't you?"

A son, he was saying, Billie thought. What if the baby was a girl? Heritage? What heritage? A ranch somewhere in Texas? Milking cows and planting corn? What was Moss talking about?

Moss realized her confusion and grinned. "Honey, I guess there's something you and your mother don't know about me." He looked at Agnes to include her. "Remember when I said my folks had a spread in Texas? Well, that's true, but I didn't tell you how far it spread. Sunbridge isn't just a little ole ranch, honey. It's an empire, built by my father. Naturally, someday it's going to be mine and our baby's. And it's not out in the sticks, either. Austin is a city, bigger than Philadelphia, with good schools and paved streets, honest," he teased, trying to lighten the situation. "You'll have your own car and anything else you want. But most important, Billie, I'll know someone is looking out for you."

Billie was listening so intently she failed to see the smug

confirmation on Agnes's face. "Tell me the truth, Moss. You put in for the transfer, didn't you? You asked for it. You pulled strings and did what you had to do to get to the Big E, didn't you? I thought all that stopped once we were married."

The truth. When caught with your pants down, always opt for the truth. "I told you from the beginning I'd do anything to get out of here. There's a war on and I want to be part of it. I didn't lie to you, Billie. I never lied to you."

"But that was before the baby. What about me and the baby?"

"Go to Sunbridge, Billie. For me and the baby. You're a Coleman now, and that's where you belong. You'll have everything you'll ever need or want. Give it a chance, honey."

"I don't want or need anything or anyone but you!"

Agnes took over. "Billie, we're going to Austin. It's settled. Moss is right. This is best for you and the baby. I'll be there so you won't feel alone among strangers. And I'm certain you will love the Colemans once you get to know them." Sunbridge. He'd said the name of the ranch was Sunbridge. "It's a good idea, Moss. Billie should be with family at a time like this. What do you think I should do with this house?"

"Put it in the hands of a good realtor and do your business through the mail. My father will handle it for you if you don't want to be bothered."

It was settled. Agnes was as excited as a child at Christmas. Sell the house. Nothing to come back to even once the baby was born. Sunbridge would be her home, too. It was more than she'd dared hope for, but it had all fallen into place. It was perfect and, given time, Billie, too, would see how perfect it was.

"I'll wash the dishes. Why don't you take Billie for a walk? Or ride down to the park; exercise is important for her now."

"That sounds good to me," Moss said with forced brightness. Why couldn't Billie understand? Why did women have to be so emotional? He hated what he was doing to her, but he refused to let himself brood about it. Moss linked Billie's arm through his and patted her hand reassuringly as they walked down the front steps. It would be all right. He'd see to it.

Billie fell into step beside her husband. She had to accept his decision. To fight him would be to alienate him, perhaps lose him, and that she would never do. If she felt betrayed, she would simply have to deal with it. For now, time was precious and she wasn't going to spoil it. Making things unpleasant wouldn't change a thing. Except, perhaps, how Moss would feel about her. Swallowing down her tears, she smiled up at him, a smile that came from her heart.

Moss put his arm around Billie, relieved by her smile. She was so warm and sweet. So endearing, so pregnant. He smiled in return. He'd love her for what she was to him, his wife, the mother of his child. Without Billie loving him the way she did there would be no baby, no way out of the Navy Yard. He'd always love her for that.

It was just before nine when Billie and Moss returned home. Time to call Texas. Agnes watched as Moss shifted from one foot to the other. He was nervous and she realized this was the first time she'd ever seen him so. Usually his brash confidence, just bordering on insolence, carried him through everything. Everything but with his father, evidently.

Moss covered the mouthpiece of the phone. "The operator is having some trouble getting through. There's the time difference, too." When Seth Coleman's voice came booming over the wire, Moss held the receiver away from his ear.

"Moss! Son! It's good to hear your voice. Got a letter not too long ago from a woman who says she's your mother-in-law. We decided to sit on it till we heard from you. What's this all about?"

"It's true, Pap." Moss glanced over at Billie, who was watching him intently. He hoped Pap wouldn't demand explanations he couldn't make. Hell, he'd postponed this phone call too long. He should have called from the yard, where he'd have had relative privacy.

"Why'd you do a fool thing like that? Wartime is no time to get married. A man isn't thinking straight. There's a lot of women willing to give tail without your marrying them!" There was a pause; an idea had just occurred to Seth. "Did you *have* to get married, son?"

"That's about the size of it, Pap," Moss said uneasily, glancing again at Billie, wondering how much of Seth's conversation she could hear.

"What's she like, this filly you married?"

"Aces, Pap. Remember that colt you gave me when I was ten and how I loved her?"

"I remember that you rode her to death," Seth growled harshly.

Moss's eyes clouded. Why did Seth have to be such a

bastard? He'd loved that horse. Zap him now. Get it out. "I'm sending Billie and her mother to Austin. I'm being reassigned to the USS *Enterprise*. I leave in thirty-six hours. I'm going, Pap. It's hands off this time around. The only thing I want from you is to take good care of my wife and her mother. You make sure that my son gets into this world the way he should." The silence on the other end of the phone didn't surprise Moss. Seth was going to chew on that little tidbit for a long time to come.

"That's the third dumbest thing you've done since you got shipped to Philadelphia. If you'd kept your pants zipped, you wouldn't be married. . . ."

"I don't want to hear it, Pap." He forced a smile for Billie's sake. "You're going to have a grandson, Pap."

"It's my *own* son I want right now!" Seth shouted. "Just stay put. I'll get on the phone and call in some favors. Twenty-four hours is all I need and you can forget shipping out."

"Pap, you lift one finger and I'll never forgive you. This is what I want. Leave it alone. I mean it." He waited for silence. He wanted to make sure Pap had heard and was listening. "You're going to love Billie. Think about it, Pap. You're going to be a grandfather." Bait. Throw the old man a little bait and see if he grabs it.

A thick rattly cough came over the wire. Moss could just picture the speculations, the choices, that were running through the old man's head. The baby was going to clinch it. Seth would never chance alienating his son and grandchild. "What's the mother like?" Pap asked.

Moss almost laughed. How could he tell Pap that Agnes was a ring-tailed bitch? "Just like you, Pap. You're going to love her, too."

"Your mother wants to speak with you," Seth said coldly. "Don't hang up when you're done talking to her. We aren't finished yet."

"Yes we are. You just haven't accepted it yet." Moss grinned down at Billie and drew her close. It was done. The old man wouldn't cross him now, not with the heir to the Coleman empire in the offing.

"Mam! It's good to hear your voice. You feeling all right?"

The voice was wavery and tearful. It saddened Moss. "We miss you, son. I'm so happy for you. I'm certain Billie is a wonderful girl and we're going to love her just the way we love you. When will we get to meet her?"

"Soon. Pap will explain it all. Billie and her mother are coming to Austin. Take care of them for me, Mam. Promise me."

"I promise, darlin'. What does this mean? Are you being reassigned? I thought your father took care of that. . . ."

"He did, Mam, but I undid it." Before she could ask any more questions, he handed the phone to Billie.

Startled, Billie swallowed hard. "Mrs. Coleman. This is Billie Ames. No, I mean Coleman." Moss grinned down at her flustering. "It's so nice to talk to you. I'm looking forward to meeting you and Mr. Coleman. I just hope our coming to Austin isn't going to be an imposition."

"Dear child, I wouldn't have it any other way. I'm delighted. In fact, I can hardly wait to get everything ready for you. Billie, I do want us to get on together, for Moss's sake."

"Thank you, Mrs. Coleman. I'll put Moss back on. He wants to talk to his father again."

Moss took the phone. This time there was something different in Pap's voice. Was it acceptance of his reassignment? Never. It was the baby. He'd probably enrolled it in Texas A&M by now. A trust fund and the kid's first pony were already on order. Seth would handle it all. "Send your family on, son. We'll take care of them for you. Take care of yourself, son. You're a damn fool. You know that, don't you?"

"I had a hell of a teacher. I love you, Pap."

"I know you do, son. Knock them on their ass for all of us."

The connection was broken.

In Austin, Texas, Seth Coleman rose abruptly from his oversized desk in the library and went to stand before the long windows that overlooked the back gardens of Sunbridge and the rolling hills of the cattle range beyond. He deliberately turned his back on his wife so she wouldn't see his defeat. The call from Moss had come as a crushing blow. The boy was going off to war and the sudden news of a grandchild was a trade-off.

Jessica Coleman watched her husband, wringing her hands in sympathy. Seth's love for Moss was obsessive and the thought of losing his son to the war was crippling. Jessica loved her son no less, and her fears were just as great; but her love was tender and maternal, without the driving power and possessiveness of Seth's. It was the way Seth loved—or hated—and she had come to accept it years ago, had learned to live with it. And what Seth neither loved nor hated did not exist for him. She, Jessica, did not exist.

"You've got yourself a daughter-in-law, Jess," Seth told her. He turned to face her and she saw he'd come to terms with Moss's decision. "But I've got myself a grandson!"

Billie lay beside Moss, watching him sleep. She needed to commit him to memory, so when she closed her eyes she could bring him back to her and conjure every line, every detail of him. She wanted to remember how his hands felt on her body as he loved her, slowly, completely. Her heart was breaking at the thought of his leaving, but it was a burden she wouldn't ask him to take to war.

She snuggled down against him, taking his warmth, resting her head against his shoulder. It was impossible not to touch him, not to smooth her hand over the breadth of his chest and the flatness of his belly. She loved him, and for this time at least, he was hers.

He stirred beneath her touch and turned his face to kiss her brow. His arms wrapped her in his embrace and he murmured her name. Billie's hand slipped lower, brazenly awakening him, sliding beneath him as he rolled toward her. At least she would have this to take to Texas with her.

{{{{{{{{{ CHAPTER SEVEN }}}}}}}}}

The week-long train trip to Austin, with its stopovers and delays and bone-rattling clackety-clack, was pure torture for Billie. Morning sickness, which continued for most of the day, had struck again within an hour of Moss's leaving. She was nauseated from waking till midafternoon, and then was so debilitated and exhausted that she spent the entire trip in her lower berth with a bucket provided by a kindly conductor. Agnes fussed and clucked for the first two days but gave it up after Billie cried to be left alone to die in misery.

Agnes absented herself somewhat gratefully and dined in style three times a day in the luxurious dining car, where she made it her business to tell anyone who'd listen that she belonged to the Coleman family of Austin. She never considered this a direct lie, leaving it to the listener to assume she was a blood Coleman or to wonder just who or what a Coleman was. Her entire attention was taken up by the adventure of it all; this trip was like an overture to the opening act. Not once did Moss Coleman enter her mind; from the moment he had stepped aboard the transport that would take him to San Diego and then on to Hawaii, he had been forgotten. Moss Coleman had served his purpose.

The Southern-Pacific superliner pulled into the Austin station the morning of August 25, 1942. Billie held her mother's arm and fought down the bile that was rising in her throat. Her eyes were rimmed with purple shadows. Her legs trembled from lying in her berth for almost seven straight days, jarring her spine and increasing her queasiness. She looked gaunt and sick.

"Mrs. Coleman?" A white-jacketed porter approached them, smile gleaming.

"Yes," Agnes answered for Billie, who sank down again on the edge of the lower berth.

"If you'll follow me, Mrs. Coleman, I'll take you to your party. They're waiting on the platform. If you give me your stubs, I'll get your bags and bring them out to the car."

Obviously, the Colemans tipped generously, Agnes thought; this explained the porter's toothy grin. She dug into her purse and extracted the baggage claim stubs. "Come along, Billie. We mustn't keep everyone waiting."

The porter led them to the back of the train and positioned a little stepstool to help them disembark. The capped head and uniformed shoulders of a chauffeur were visible behind a white-haired woman and a tall, bulky-shouldered man leaning on a cane. They stood apart from the station throng.

Billie's eyes met those of her father-in-law and she was sure of what she read in them: So this was the fragile, sickly female that Moss had the misfortune to marry! She turned to Moss's mother and saw compassion and understanding in the soft gray gaze. Billie found herself heading for the woman's outstretched arms.

"You're ill, child," Jessica Coleman said. "You come along

with me. Tita—that's our housekeeper—has a cure for everything, and that includes morning sickness. We'll have you right as sagebrush in a few days." She didn't even have to look at her husband to know he must be thinking that Moss had gotten himself an ox in a ditch when he'd chosen this ashen-faced child to produce the Coleman heir.

Jessica turned to Agnes. "I hope you'll enjoy Sunbridge as much as we do, Mrs. Ames," she said quietly, and Billie recognized the soft drawl that was Moss's.

Agnes's polite response was designed to make perfectly clear right from the beginning that her coming to Texas had been Moss's idea entirely—it had seemed to ease his mind before he went away, and so, of course, she'd been prompted to oblige. This Agnes said without gushing, without any display of emotion. Her manner was subdued, exactly correct. Seth observed the performance and remembered Moss's remark when asked what the mother was like: "Just like you, Pap." Well, here she was. Agnes Ames in her severely tailored suit and small black hat atop her chestnut curls. A woman of few words and with a no-nonsense look about her. Seth approved. He looked at Billie and thought how unfortunate it was that Moss's tastes didn't run along the same lines.

"Why don't you take the little gal to the car, Jess," Seth suggested. "Poor li'l thing looks about done in. Mrs. Ames and I will be along shortly. Carlo," he addressed the chauffeur, "take care of the baggage."

Seth took Agnes's arm as they walked behind Jessica and Billie. "I wonder if you'd mind if we let Jess and your daughter go ahead to Sunbridge. I'm going to the office and we can take a company car home from there." Seth had no intention of riding forty miles in a car with a retching mother-to-be and this was as good a time as any to get to know Agnes.

"I wouldn't mind at all. Billie is hardly fit company these days. The baby, you know."

Seth forced a smile and his blue eyes beneath the thick gray hair glittered in a way remarkably like Moss's. Agnes watched to see if he carried the cane for effect or out of need. He did walk with a slight limp, but not enough, she thought, to warrant the cane. There was nothing of the invalid about this tall, powerful man, whose eyes seemed to see everything and whose words said only half of what he meant. Agnes already felt completely comfortable with him but she knew instinctively that hers was the exceptional reaction: Seth Coleman would be intimidating to most women and especially someone as young and naive as Billie.

Agnes missed nothing, from the uniformed chauffeur to Seth's white custom Stetson to Jessica's expensive silk-blend suit and Stone Marten stole. When the baggage had been stowed in the trunk of the luxurious black Packard, Agnes climbed in the backseat, beside Jessica and Billie; Seth sat in front, with Carlo.

"Jess, Carlo will drop Mrs. Ames and me at the office. There's something I have to sign. We'll follow you in one of the company cars."

"Perhaps Mrs. Ames is tired and would prefer to go directly to Sunbridge," Jessica said, offering Agnes the opportunity to decline Seth's arrangement.

"Nonsense!" Seth declared.

"Actually, I had a very good night, Mrs. Coleman. I'd be delighted to accompany Mr. Coleman to the office and follow later."

Jessica smiled and nodded.

"She's Jessica and I'm Seth," her husband growled from the front seat.

"And I'm Agnes," she replied, mimicking his tone.

In spite of himself, Seth grinned. So the old girl could give as good as she got. Perhaps there was hope for the daughter after all. Perhaps in a few years she'd lose that soft edge and smarten up, be more like her mother. He was going to enjoy having Agnes about, Seth decided, as he decided most things, instantly. The women in his household were just too soft, too easily brought to tears. Agnes would be a refreshing change.

Agnes had been expecting Austin to be a frontier town, like in a western movie, but she couldn't have been more wrong. They drove down wide-paved streets, between sidewalks almost as wide. The downtown shopping area, while less developed and hectic than New York, certainly could rival Philadelphia's. The long black Packard came to a stop before a tall building with a pink Italian marble façade. Engraved in the lintel over the brass-and-glass revolving doors was the name *Coleman*. Agnes was impressed but kept her counsel, as though she were used to associating with people who owned their own skyscrapers. Remembering Billie, she said, "You will be all right, won't you, dear? I'm certain I'll be joining you before long."

Billie, her eyes closed against the bright sunlight and the motion of the car, simply nodded. She'd be glad when Agnes left the car, taking the overpowering scent of her Tabu perfume with her.

"Billie will be fine, Agnes," Jessica reassured her. "We're heading straight home and I'll put her right to bed. Seth, why don't you take Agnes out to lunch? It will be well past noon before you'll be able to get out to Sunbridge, anyway."

"I'll do that, Jess," Seth said politely. Why did Jess think people needed three squares a day to survive? He could remember a time when if he ate once a day, he could consider himself lucky.

Billie slept the forty-odd miles to Sunbridge and Jessica found herself patting Billie's arm. She wanted to gather the young girl close to her but was afraid to disturb her.

Billie Ames Coleman, Moss's wife, her son's wife, and within her she carried Moss's child. Her own honest-to-goodness grandchild. There was a time, so long ago, when she was as bright and hopeful and young as Billie. Time and Seth had changed that.

She was being bitter, something she usually reserved for the early hours of the morning when she awoke in her bed, alone. A body had a right to feel bitter at such times. Was it too much to ask to have affection and tenderness and perhaps just a tiny dose of companionship at her age? She wished fervently she could point to a time, a place, when things had changed between herself and Seth. If she had to choose, it would be the day of Moss's birth. She'd done what was expected, given him a son. His *first* son, he'd declared, the first of many! When Amelia had been born it was a disappointment that had turned bitter when it was discovered Jessica could bear no more children. Yes, that's when things went wrong, when Seth no longer came to her bed. . . .

Jessica had been wildly in love with the larger-than-life, rawboned Seth Coleman. She always laughed when he told her she was just what he needed, a refined gentle lady to upgrade the Coleman bloodline. "Jess, you have class," he would tell her, sweeping her into his arms. He knew what he wanted and he wanted her. He made no secret of his desires, telling anyone who would listen. She couldn't resist the handsome, aggressive young man, though he had worked with his hands in the oil fields and still had the dirt under his fingernails two years after they were married. He shared his dreams of owning the biggest, grandest spread in all of Texas, and she had known that he would claw it out of the bare earth. Once she had thought he had wanted it for her. Now she knew better. He had wanted it for himself, just as he wanted her refinement and respectability. She had given it gladly, thinking she would receive love and tenderness in return.

She could have done so much better, her family had told her. Carl Bowdrie from the Austin bank had wanted her almost as much as Seth. But there hadn't been the challenge in Carl's eyes that there was in Seth's.

Living with her parents hadn't prepared her for a life with Seth Coleman. Her father had been a gentleman with a classical education and a small family fortune. Her mother had been a lady. They hadn't been rich, merely comfortable. Life had been pleasant—filled with affection, genuine affection and love—and simple: church suppers, quiet dinner parties with well-bred people carrying on intelligent conversations, good wine, delicately prepared food, discreet service.

She'd never gotten used to the shindigs Seth threw. Raw whiskey, beer by the keg, and the "wheeling-dealing," as Seth called it; that was the underlying reason. Things had changed recently, though. Instead of raw whiskey there was champagne and the wheeler-dealers had somewhere come by parlor manners. But underneath it was all the same, attended by the same people for the same reasons: money.

Just once she had asked Seth for something that had been important to her. She'd wanted to keep the house she'd inherited from her parents. She would have been able to go there, to escape to her girlhood home with her children and show them that not all of life was focused on one man's personality and wealth. But this had been denied her. Seth had refused her request, had taken it all away from her. Just as he'd taken her children.

She had been a young debutante when she'd met Seth. Now she was an old lady living in a monstrous house she detested, with a man who didn't care if she took the next breath.

Jessica reached out and took Billie's hand in her own, wishing she could impart the strength she herself had never possessed. "You have to be strong, Billie," she whispered. "Not tough, strong. There's a difference."

Just before they turned into the drive Jessica shook her

lightly. "Wake up, Billie. I thought you'd like to get your first glimpse of Moss's home—Sunbridge."

Billie rubbed the sleep from her eyes and looked through the split windshield of the Colemans' Packard. They passed under a high wooden arch that was emblazoned with the name "Sunbridge." Miles of white rail fencing stretched into the distance. Tall oak trees lined the winding drive and on either side were expanses of bright green lawn with sprinklers pulsing rhythmically.

Billie felt as though they were journeying through a tunnel of dappled green. Far up the drive, bright daylight shone, and when they achieved the final turn the house came into view.

Sitting upon a gently sloping rise, the great house basked beneath the blue Texas sky and was caressed by the sun. Billie thought, as they came out from under the dark of the trees, that only here, in this place called Sunbridge, could the sun seem so warm and golden.

The house was a three-story brick of the palest pink, flanked by two wings, which were also three-storied but set back several feet from the main body. This expanse of prairie rose was accented by white columns that supported the roof of the verandah sweeping the entire frontage. A multipaned fan light crested the huge double front door and the design was repeated again over each window on the top floor. Ornamental topiary trees and crepe myrtle hugged the foundation, and surrounding the house was a magnificent rose garden complete with trellises and statuary. Billie gasped with awe. "Moss never told me about Sunbridge. He just called it a spread!"

Jessica laughed. "How like Moss. Sunbridge is a spread; it spreads over two hundred and fifty thousand acres. We raise thoroughbreds and thousands of head of cattle. They're kept on the back acres, and other, smaller ranches are commissioned by Seth for breeding. But this is only a small part of the Coleman holdings and business interests. Seth built all of this himself." Jessica sounded proud but Billie noticed a sadness in her eyes.

"The name Sunbridge fits it so well," Billie said.

"Yes. When Seth first saw the land he says he felt as though he could almost reach up and touch the sun. He came from very dark beginnings, Billie, and building this place was a major achievement for him. He hoped that a great house upon this rise would bridge his past with what he wanted for the future. Seth's not a romantic, not by any means, but the name of Sunbridge was entirely his own conception." The sadness had remained in Jessica's eyes, and as though to break herself from her solemn thoughts she forced a smile in Billie's direction. "We'll get you inside, Billie, where it's much cooler. Then I'll have the housekeeper fix something for you. I know you're not feeling well, so I'll spare you a formal introduction to the servants."

At the front portico Carlo opened the door for them and tipped his hat. Jessica gave him instructions concerning the baggage. The ethereal grace of the rose garden and the feminine sweep of the clematis vine surrounding the heavy oak doors did nothing to prepare Billie for the inside of the house. Shining oaken floors, massive beams studding the ceilings, thick dark Oriental carpets, and man-sized leather furniture. As Jessica took her on a tour of the downstairs rooms, it was easy for Billie to imagine them filled with smoke and noisy with deep masculine voices and thudding high-heeled cowboy boots. Panoramic paintings filled the walls, all of them depicting burly, tanned men at some masculine endeavor: branding steers, breaking horses, riding the range. It seemed that Jessica's feminine influence stopped in the gardens. The great house of Sunbridge was Seth Coleman's domain and every detail of the furnishings stated that fact.

"Come upstairs, Billie," Jessica said. "We've opened the second floor of the east wing for you and Agnes, and of course for Moss when he comes home. I hope you'll like what I've done with your room."

Here Jessica had exerted her influence. Pastel-colored walls, vases of fresh flowers, lighter, feminine furnishings. Billie's own bedroom was larger than the entire downstairs of the house on Elm Street. Soft mint-green silk moiré covered the walls, while pinks and golds were used for the draperies and bedspread. A luxurious carpet in a soft green-and-beige pattern quieted footsteps.

"It's such a large house," Billie said with wonder. "Our house back in Philadelphia could fit in this one at least six times. You don't try to keep it up yourself, do you?"

"My, no! The rose garden alone would put me under." Jessica laughed lightly. "There's Carlo, whom you've met. He chauffeurs and acts as a general handyman about the house. He's married to Tita, our cook, and he does the shopping for her, as well as other errands. Besides Tita, there are two or three other young Mexicans who come in for general cleaning and laundry. Then there are the stablehands and of course Julio, our gardener. Sunbridge supports quite a few people, Billie. Ever since Amelia—that's Moss's sister, you know—left for England, I'm quite grateful for female companionship. And now that you and your mother are here, I couldn't be more delighted. I want us to be friends, Billie. More than that, I'd like it if you learned to think of me as a second mother, if it's possible."

Billie was so heart-touched that she found herself rising above her initial shyness and stepping into Jessica's outstretched arms. "Moss loves you very much," she whispered, "and I know I'm going to love you, too."

Jessica's eyes were bright with tears. "It's going to be so good to have you here, child. And a baby on the way! Sunbridge has been lonely without young people and children. Now off to bed with you. I can imagine how nice it will be to be in a bed that isn't rocking back and forth."

During her first days at Sunbridge, Billie kept very much to her room. A stationary bed did not work its prescribed miracle. Billie still teetered on the edge of nausea for most of the day, and when she didn't, she was so exhausted from retching that she confined herself to the bedroom. Jessica fussed and fretted over her. Billie had never felt more loved than by this gentle white-haired mother-in-law, who spent hours with her to keep her from being lonely. Everything about Moss's mother was kind, gentle, considerate. Billie saw very little of Agnes during this time except for morning and evening visits, when she regaled Billie with her observations of Sunbridge. Agnes was very busy these days, familiarizing herself with every detail of the Colemans' house and family history.

One morning when Agnes came to sit with Billie over a cup of tea, Billie mentioned how helpful and concerned Jessica was. "Well, she should be," Agnes stated flatly, fussing with her ever-present rope of pearls. "After all, you are going to bring her first grandchild into the world."

Billie blinked and stared at Agnes. This was going to be her mother's first grandchild, also.

"Oh, I know what you're thinking, Billie, and you're wrong. I'm delighted about the baby and I do worry about you. It's just that... well, I'm much younger than Jessica, you must realize. I haven't really adjusted to the thought of becoming a grandmother. I feel as though a whole new world has opened up for us and I'm determined to explore it. You understand, don't you, dear." It wasn't a question but a statement. "Besides, I mustn't be selfish. I've had a lovely daughter and Jessica hasn't been quite so lucky with Amelia. You've never given me a day's trouble, but, from what I understand, Moss's sister has been quite a hellcat, rebellious since the day she was born. Certainly not the kind of daughter that brings a mother gratification."

"But Jessica loves Amelia dearly!" Billie exclaimed.

"Of course she does—Amelia *is* her daughter. But from what I gather, Amelia's running off to England was more to get out of a rather nasty scrape here than from any display of patriotism. Besides," Agnes added, lowering her voice, "we all know what kind of girls join the military, don't we?"

"Amelia didn't 'run off' to England, Mother; she was assigned there," said Billie. "She joined the Women's Army Corp right here in Texas and the WACs are important to the war effort. I just hope you never hurt Jessica by insinuating anything else."

Agnes interrupted with a change of subject. "Has Seth come to see you this morning?"

"Yes, he did, but I don't think he likes me, Mother."

"Don't be silly, and don't you antagonize Seth, Billie. He's simply a very autocratic man and autocratic men find it very difficult to show affection."

At this, Billie raised her eyebrows. "And did you learn this from the same person who told you about Amelia? I find it strange that you'd defend Seth and at the same time be critical of Jessica."

"I wasn't being critical, just observant." Agnes placed her cup and saucer back on Billie's breakfast tray and then stood up, smoothing her russet silk dress.

"Isn't that a new dress, Mother?"

"Yes, and don't you think it's the perfect color for me? It's been so long since I've had anything as nice as this and there are several more on order. The sale of the house should go through anytime now, so I'm not afraid to dip into my savings, just a bit."

Billie, who had an eye for fabric and fashion, realized that it had taken more than a bit of dipping to buy this dress. She looked at her mother objectively. There were subtle changes about Agnes. . . . She seemed more polished and put together, somehow. Was it that she was wearing more makeup these days? Or was it just being here at Sunbridge that put color in her cheeks and a glow in her eyes? Billie sighed. She supposed she'd been selfish. She hadn't noticed the strain her mother had been under for so many years to provide for both of them. Now mundane worries like taxes and grocery bills were no longer her concern.

"You look wonderful, Mother," Billie said.

"I wish I could say the same for you, Billie. Why, you're positively haggard—no wonder Seth doesn't like to come up to visit! When are you going to get out of that bed and come downstairs? The Texas sun is wonderful and at least it would help you get rid of that sickroom pallor. Pregnancy isn't a disease, you know, Billie!"

"I *do* get out of bed." Tears came unbidden to Billie's eyes. She cried so easily these days. And she was always so sleepy when she wasn't sick.

"Oh, for goodness' sake, don't cry. I didn't mean to upset you." Agnes was halfway to the bed to embrace Billie when she remembered her silk dress. Even one tear would stain it beyond repair. "It's only that I worry about you. Perhaps you can go down and sit on the verandah. That wouldn't hurt, would it?"

"No, I suppose not." Billie lay back against her pillows. The tea she sipped was roiling through her stomach and she recognized the signal. Agnes also recognized the green tinge to Billie's complexion.

"I'll be downstairs, Billie. Call if you need me," Agnes said over her shoulder as she made a hasty exit.

During the second week at Sunbridge, when Billie was feeling no better, she resentfully surrendered to Seth's authority. He arranged a series of tests at the hospital in Austin. Dr. Adam Ward became Billie's physician on call. What this meant, Seth explained, was that he was available for the slightest problem. If even a headache lasted more than an hour or two, Adam was to be summoned. It was an order. Billie nodded her compliance. Later Agnes told Billie that the entire third floor wing of the hospital had been donated by the Colemans and it was there that the baby would be born. The Coleman heir.

Dr. Ward prescribed vitamins for Billie and a daily regimen of diet and exercise. There were to be twice-weekly vitamin B injections as well, which the doctor administered himself at Sunbridge. That a busy physician would drive the forty-plus miles from Austin was her first realization of Seth Coleman's clout. In Philadelphia, a doctor made house calls only if his patient was completely unable to make the trip to his office.

Aside from a telegram informing them that he'd arrived safely in San Diego, there had been no word from Moss. Billie wrote him care of an APO number, San Francisco. V-mail was notoriously slow, she'd been told when she'd fretted about Moss's not answering her letters. She wrote every night, using the onionskin paper commonly known as V-mail stationery that Jessica had brought her from the post office.

After the very first vitamin B injection Billie began to feel more like herself. But the days were still long and lonely for her. It was Jessica who kept Billie company on those afternoons when she was feeling better. Billie welcomed Jessica's attentions and company. She liked to hear stories about Moss when he was a child, and looking through the family photo album was one of her favorite pastimes. One day, Jessica asked Billie if she would like to see Moss's room.

Jessica opened the door to a room on the second floor, west wing. "This was Moss's room when he was a boy," Jessica explained. "When he was seventeen he moved to the room next to yours. And then, of course, he went off to college." Billie stepped inside and immediately felt herself immersed in Moss's life. School banners almost covered the walls by the narrow low bed. Books, hockey sticks, baseball bats, and other assorted sports equipment littered the corners. Dresser tops and bookshelves were studded with sports trophies, and from the ceiling, on fine, almost invisible wires, hung model planes, put together by Moss himself with painstaking attention to detail.

"Why don't I just leave you here, Billie? That's the first smile I've seen on your face in almost a week," Jessica said. "If you need me, I'll be in the kitchen with Tita, going over next week's shopping list. When you're through here, I've something else to show you."

Jessica closed the door quietly, a sympathetic smile touching her lips. Poor Billie, she missed Moss so. Such a quick courtship, so little time to get to know each other. And now there was a baby on the way. As she walked to the kitchen, she thought of Seth's disapproval of Billie—"not the stuff Colemans are made of." But there was one thing Seth and that lovely girl had in common: their love for Moss. The thought occurred to Jessica that perhaps Seth was so disagreeable to

Billie for just that reason—he saw the girl as a rival for Moss's affections. Well, Jessica sighed, hadn't that always been the case? Since the day of Moss's birth nothing and no one else had existed for Seth, and that included herself and poor Amelia, who had tried her whole life to gain her father's love. And when she'd failed, Amelia had opted for her father's attention instead. That was the reason for most of her scrapes and rebellion. It seemed that all of them, Moss included, thought nothing was as important as being worthy of Seth's love. A love so grudgingly given.

Billie hardly heard the door close, so enthralled was she at being surrounded by Moss's things. It wasn't difficult to imagine his young dark head bent over the scarred and battered desk as he studied his schoolwork or meticulously painted one of his model planes—and so many of them! It was easy to see that his love of flying had begun at an early age. Her eyes wandered over a cabinet filled with athletic trophies, the floor-to-ceiling shelves littered also with books, some of them read over and over again, judging by the tattered corners and dog-eared pages. Photographs hung on the walls—Moss playing baseball, football, one with his arm around a pretty girl at what must have been his senior prom. She was a slender girl with dark hair and angular features. Several photographs were of Moss with this girl. One, bent and dog-eared, as though it had been carried for a long time inside a wallet, was of the girl, stylishly dressed in ski togs, smiling up at Moss, who had his arm around her possessively. Across the bottom, Moss had scrawled, "Alice 'n' me."

Billie knew a pang of jealousy. Who was Alice?

Several photographs were of himself with his sister, Amelia, whom Billie recognized from pictures Jessica had shown her. Two sleek dark heads close together, Amelia's arm around a pony's neck, Moss grinning into the camera while he authoritatively held the animal's bridle.

Sinking down onto the foot of the narrow bed, Billie smoothed her hand over the green wool sweater that lay beside her. There was so much about Moss she didn't know, couldn't even imagine. He was still a stranger, she realized sadly, a man who had come into her life and taken her heart. There had never seemed to be time for questions, for delving into the past. All that had mattered was the present, the all-too-short present. And now here she sat among his things, in this room that seemed to be maintained as a shrine to his youth. She felt as though she'd been sent here to Texas to be stored among his possessions and to wait for his return, something more that belonged to Moss. Unthinkingly, her hand went protectively to her middle, where the life their love had created nestled warm and safe within her. This was Moss's also. And the baby would wait, just as she would, to be reclaimed.

The feelings of an echoing past stayed with Billie when Jessica took her later to the little workroom behind the stable. Here an older Moss had littered the small space with radio innards, electric motors, screwdrivers. Here, too, was the sense that Moss had only just left for a little while, that any instant he would appear at the door to finish a project or begin another.

"This should have been cleared out long ago," Jessica complained good-naturedly, "but Seth wouldn't hear of it. That man's as stubborn as a sore-toed mule. It's not as though Moss will ever use this place to tinker again, not when he's got factories and laboratories with all the latest equipment."

Billie's brows lifted in question. "That's right, dear. Didn't Moss tell you? Or was he too busy sweeping you off your feet?" Jessica laughed indulgently. "Seth's business isn't just cattle and oil. Heavens, no. The Colemans are involved in aeronautics and electronics. Moss always was bright when it came to new ideas or new uses for old ones. That's a direct quote from Seth, but I was always proud of Moss, too. Considering the way his father dotes on him—and certainly he never wanted for anything money could buy—Moss was never spoiled or lazy, never what you'd call a playboy. He gets more pleasure from his little inventions than he would from a new sports car." Jessica's pride in her son was evident in her glowing smile. "Moss always had good judgment, I'm glad to say, and he's shown extraordinary taste when it comes to choosing a wife."

Jessica threw her arms around Billie and hugged her. "You've become very dear to me, child. I won't pretend it doesn't have something to do with the baby, but I'm so glad you've come to Sunbridge."

"Moss's good judgment extends to his choice of mothers," Billie teased, returning the hug. "And thank you for showing me his room and his workshop. There's so much about my husband I don't know."

"The Coleman men are a hard lot to understand, Billie. There's a lot of Seth in Moss, and even being married for almost thirty years I still can't say I know my husband. But this is Moss's world, Billie, and it must become yours if you're ever to be happy. Your child will belong to Sunbridge. And while you're discovering Moss's world and his work, I hope it will bring him closer to you, ease some of the loneliness."

Together, Billie and Jessica stepped out of the workshop and into the bright Texas sun. When Billie looked over the expanse of lawn and the pastures beyond, she tried to see through Moss's eyes. Sunbridge. Moss's home. Would it ever be home to her?

Seth was taking unusually long to select his dinner clothes. Normally he reached into the closet and whatever his hand touched was what he wore. Tonight there were guests. Guests, he snorted. Moss's sickly-looking wife and her mother, who could double as a barracuda. He withdrew a five-hundred-dollar, custom-made suede jacket that was the color of tumbleweed. He had a shirt to match and he'd even wear a tie. Dress up, spruce up, show off a little. Agnes Ames would catalog his entire outfit complete with prices. He hadn't managed to get this far in life without knowing something about people, and Seth had seen Agnes before, in himself. There was a burning fever in her eyes that had once been in his own.

The pier glass threw back his reflection. He looked fine. Fitter than a tick on a brown dog, and the image of success. Not long ago *Texan* magazine had done a spread on him, noting his humble beginnings. Humble my ass, Seth snorted. Born to an abjectly poor tenant farmer, he had worked by day beside his five brothers and his father to eke out a living from the barren land. By night, he'd huddled on a bare mattress with only unwashed brothers for warmth. He would never forget the stink. He would never forget any of it.... His ma was always carrying a big belly or spewing another life into the already too crowded shack. The naked defeat in her eyes and the stench of moonshine on his father's breath convinced him at an early age that life on someone else's land would never bring a man a good meal or a clean bed.

He was twelve years old, scared of the big world but scareder still of what staying in that tenant shack would make of him, when he cut and ran with the rags on his back and sixty cents stolen from the cracked milk jug. He poked around some for a year or two, begging and finding odd jobs. But most men took him for older than he was because of his size and the curiously solemn expression in his eyes, and he talked himself into a job in the oil fields. He worked like a slave and was treated like one, but at the end of the first month he had fourteen dollars and eighty-five cents and that was all that mattered. He saved, spending only what was necessary to survive: a warm coat, sturdy boots, and a stupid old mule to carry him about. And at the end of each year the sock in his bedroll bulged fatter and fatter.

He was twenty when he met Skid Donovan, an old catter with a lease on a pumped-out well but no money. There was still oil in that old hole; Seth could smell it. All around them the black stuff was making men rich. It was a chance, a gamble, and he took it. They became partners.

Seth worked like a mule and sharpened his business savvy. That other companies wanted to take over Skid's lease confirmed Seth's opinion that there was more oil down there. He had to fight and develop eyes in the back of his head. Luck decided to ride with him and the well proved. But while he did all the work, Skid drank away his half of the profits. After two years Seth had enough and sold the partnership out from under Skid without guilt. Hell, Skid would guzzle himself to death in another six months anyway, so what difference did it make that he'd gotten his signature while the old man was blind with rotgut whiskey? The world was made of survivors. . . .

The mirror was showing Seth something he didn't want to see. He was aging just like his father. The grooves and trenches in his face were the same ones he'd despised in the old man. Without a second thought, he raised his booted foot and smashed the pier glass into thousands of sparkling shards.

He supposed that somewhere down the line he should have sent some money to the old man and those shiftless, sorry creatures who were his brothers. But hell, if they wanted to wallow in poverty, who was he to stop them? Sending them money would have been like pissing in the ocean. They were all too stupid. He didn't owe them anything. He couldn't even remember if the old man had ever called him anything besides "boy." And when he'd left, he was sure, it had been a relief to his family that there was one less mouth to feed. They hadn't exactly sent out a search party for him.

Seth had never wanted Jessica to know the whole truth. Once he'd set his sights on her, he'd wanted nothing to stand in the way of making her his wife. She knew he came from modest beginnings, but he'd never told her how sorry it had all been—it never did for a woman to have something to hold over a man's head.

Yes, he'd wanted Jess. Good family, good bloodlines, a little short on money—but that was all right; he was going to have more than enough. Poor Jessica. Pretty as a picture and crazy in love with him. But weak, no grit, no starch, too emotional. He'd been expecting a passel of robust sons and what he'd gotten was a worthless daughter who had made it impossible for Jess to bear more children. Sometimes there was no justice. And of course, she'd given him Moss. For his one magnificent son, Seth did have to thank Jessica. He'd given her an easy life and she had no complaints.

Agnes Ames, now that was some woman. He admired her rigid posture and her capable hands. A strong woman, damned attractive, too. He wished he could say the same for the pitiful little gal Moss had married. Billie would have to toughen up if she was going to fit into the Coleman family. He hoped he was wrong, but he thought he saw many of Jessica's weaknesses in the girl. Too thin and narrow-hipped.

Yes sir, he'd come a long way by the shortest possible route. He made the rules. The legacy he would leave behind to his son and future grandsons had been worth it. His family, his legacy. No guilt, no remorse. When you won, you won all the way.

Seth Coleman presided over the cherrywood dining table in proper patriarchal form. His thick, freshly combed gray hair brought his healthy tanned features into relief beneath the glow of the Victorian globe chandelier. A russet-brown, western-cut jacket fit snugly about his broad shoulders and he wore a silk waistcoat that belonged to another age. Billie tried to see something of Moss in Seth's face but could recognize only the summer-blue eyes; they were older and wiser, of course, but they lacked the warmth and humor that were in her husband's. Those qualities, she decided, he'd inherited from Jessica.

"What's for supper?" Seth growled in his peculiarly graveled voice. "I don't mean to offend you ladies," he said with a smile toward Agnes, "but I hope to hell we've having something a man can sink his teeth into."

"Now, Seth, you know what the doctor said about your

diet." Jessica kept her words light but there was a loving chastisement in her tone. "As it happens, tonight we're having roast beef and potatoes. That should suit any man, Seth, even you."

"Damn the doctor. What I've been needing is a mess of ribs or maybe some chicken-fried steak. Now that's man food. Tita! Bring on that beast you've roasted and I hope to hell it's still bloody in the middle. If we've got any delicate appetites at this table, they can have the end slices."

Billie knew the "delicate appetite" Seth referred to was her own. She determined not to think about the blood-rare beef Seth preferred and hoped her stomach didn't begin to churn halfway through dinner. Her eyes went across the table to Agnes for encouragement, but her mother was already dipping her spoon into the thick corn soup, another of Seth's favorites. Billie glanced away from the lump of butter floating on its surface.

"I took Billie to Moss's old room today, Seth, and out to the workshop," Jessica said. She was optimistic; perhaps with more frequent exchanges between Seth and Billie their relationship would improve. Her technique had never helped reconcile Seth and Amelia, but with a father and daughter, emotions always ran too high.

Billie felt Seth's eyes on her. "What'd you think gal? Quite a little display, wasn't it?" Seth always brightened when the subject of Moss came up. "That boy's got a head on his shoulders. I can remember him taking a jolt or two from an electrical short in those little inventions of his, but that never stopped him from setting out to do what he intended."

"What was he trying to do?" Billie asked innocently. "I know he likes to tinker with things, but I didn't understand any of what I saw in the workshop."

Seth's expression was disdainful. "Of course you wouldn't. Before that boy was twelve years old he'd redesigned the pump station we use for irrigation," he said, pointing his fork at her for emphasis, "and it's still in use today. That boy can do anything he sets his mind to, and don't think otherwise. Through-and-through Coleman and the nut doesn't fall far from the tree. He's got a few things to learn and I'm here to teach him. If this war hadn't come along, my son never would've left Sunbridge—or Texas, either—to find himself a wife. The Colemans, and Jessica's family, too, for that matter, have been in Texas for damn near a century. Texas born and Texas bred. And that's the way it's going to be for Moss's sons, even if his wife is a Yankee from Pennsylvania." Seth's voice was thundering now, and his eyes pierced the distance between Billie and himself, leaving her dumbstruck.

Jessica's fingers frayed the edges of her linen napkin. Agnes sat silent and tall, her mouth pinched into a sour line as she stared across at Billie, willing her daughter to stand up to this cantankerous old man before he devoured her. When Billie's shoulders hunched forward in defeat, Agnes tossed her napkin onto the table like a fighter throwing his hat into the ring—Seth had not only insulted Billie's heritage but her own as well.

"The Colemans may have been in Texas for nearly a century, but long before any of them saw their first Indian *my* family fought in the Revolutionary War!" Agnes bristled. "I'm a member of the DAR, just like my mother before me and her mother before her! And since you've openly admitted that the bloodline has been stagnant for too long, it seems to me Moss showed good sense in looking elsewhere for a wife."

The room was still. Even chubby, dark-skinned Tita ceased rattling dishes in the adjoining kitchen. Jessica's gentle blue eyes went to her husband in a silent plea for domestic peace. Suddenly a great sound filled the room, booming from the rafters. Billie quickly lifted her eyes to see Seth with his head thrown back in laughter, shoulders shaking and belly bouncing. When he'd dried his eyes on the back of his hand, he smiled across at Agnes. "Good for you, Aggie! I guess I've been told, haven't I? Between you and me we're gonna have ourselves one hell of a grandson!"

Agnes accepted this as a compliment and retrieved her napkin. "Eat your soup, Seth, while you can still choke it down," she said, and went back to the business of eating. Jessica and Billie were bewildered, Jess because it was the closest she'd ever heard her husband come to complimenting a woman, Billie because it was the first time she'd known her mother to allow herself to be called Aggie.

When coffee was served, black and aromatic the way Seth liked it, he made his announcement. "Got an invite in the mail today" was his offhand remark to Jessica as he added a third lump of sugar to his cup. "We're flying over to Dallas sometime before Thanksgiving; the date's not set. The Barretts are having a shindig for Lyndon Johnson. A real down-home Texas barbecue. It's something we should have done, instead of letting the Barretts get the jump on us. Lyndon's decided he'll be more useful in the navy than in Washington. Leastwise, that's what he's saying. It's really only because he thinks it'll add to his political image."

"When did Lyndon decide this?" Jessica asked worriedly. "Poor Claudia, she must be beside herself!"

"Lady Bird will do all right," Seth said. "She always does all right. Luckiest day of Lyndon's life was when that woman agreed to marry him; otherwise he'd still be a no 'count teacher in the sticks somewhere. She told him he could do anything and he believed her. When she pointed him in the direction of politics he took to it natural as a newborn calf to its mother's teat."

"Now, Seth, that isn't saying much for Lyndon, and you know he's an able man. I've heard you say so yourself."

"Lots of men are able, Jess, and lots of men never get anywhere. That's because they've hooked up with the wrong woman. We leave Friday, just after lunch."

Jessica wrung her hands in her lap, clearly distressed. "Seth, couldn't I take the train and meet you? You know how I hate to fly."

"No, you cannot take the train. Who'd run the house from now till Friday? You'll fly with me."

Jessica paled. "What about Billie and Agnes?"

"What about them?" Seth dug his fork angrily into his lemon pie.

"It's just... it's just that I don't think it's a good idea for Billie to fly, do you? Considering the baby and the way she's been feeling? Billie and I could take the train together."

Seth swallowed another gulp of scalding coffee. "You ever been up in a plane, gal?" he said to Billie, who shrank back against her seat and nodded, remembering how she'd squeezed her eyes shut the entire time. Just the thought made her feel sick. "Well, Jess might be right. How about you, Aggie? You like to fly?"

"I love it," Agnes stated, ignoring Billie's amazement. "Or at least I know I'd love it. We usually drove to parties in Philadelphia, but I'm willing to try flying. According to Moss, it's an experience everyone should have."

"Believe him." Seth laughed. "Of course, I don't like that stunt-flying Moss is so crazy about. Just a nice safe, level trip. You'd better rest up, gal," he ordered Billie. "This family has got to be represented at this shindig and you're going, pukey or not. Lyndon Johnson has done a lot for this family with his connections in Washington, and we've got to show our appreciation."

"Billie will be just fine," Agnes assured him. "Billie, why don't you play a few piano pieces for us after dinner? You haven't been at the piano since before we left Philadelphia."

"I didn't know you played," Jessica interjected. "How nice it will be to hear that old piano again. Amelia had quite a bit of talent. Remember how Amelia used to play for our friends, Seth?"

When there was no answer, Jessica hastily went on to recall for Agnes and Billie some of the big parties that had been held at Sunbridge. But Agnes's attention was on Seth, who leaned back in his chair and lighted a thick brown cigar. She'd noticed that whenever Amelia's name was mentioned he withdrew from the conversation. Evidently, he didn't share Jessica's fondness for their daughter. Billie's child, she thought with satisfaction, would always hold a position of importance in the Coleman household, and without competition from Amelia or any of her future progeny.

Seth settled himself into a worn leather wing chair in the living room and frowned at his wife, who was busily uncovering the baby grand piano that stood in the bay of long-curtained windows. It wasn't until Agnes brought him a large snifter of cognac that his expression brightened.

"It's probably terribly out of tune," Jessica apologized. "I don't remember the last time it was played." Billie tried a few scales. The tone was acceptable but the instrument did need attention. Soon she broke into the beginning strains of Dvorak's "Humoresque," playing softly and haltingly at first until her fingers remembered their stretch and reach. Measure by measure her volume increased and the music filled the high-vaulted room with the lilting quality of her interpretation.

Jessica was impressed, smiling over at Agnes with pleased astonishment. "I never knew Billie was so accomplished," she whispered. She glanced over at Seth, who was clearly unmoved by his daughter-in-law's performance. Talent, unless it would enhance the power and property of Sunbridge, was unappreciated. When Billie broke into the waltz from Tchaikovsky's *Sleeping Beauty*, Seth was heard to growl, "Doesn't that gal know any saloon music? Some good old ricky-ticky tunes." Then, louder: "How about 'Red River Valley' or 'My Darlin' Clementine'? Why do women always like funeral marches?"

Jessica was embarrassed, Agnes annoyed. But Billie heard and immediately switched to a bouncing rendition of "Red River Valley," which brought a grudging smile of pleasure to Seth's face. He wanted saloon music, she'd give him saloon music—"Clementine," "The Cowboy's Lament," "Deep in the Heart of Texas." Soon Seth's feet were tapping with the rhythms and he was clapping his hands. Now Agnes's expression was bored, Jessica's hopeful. In time, she thought, and the Lord willing, Seth just might come to appreciate this new daughter of theirs.

It was then that the phone rang. After the third ring Tita picked up the receiver in the hall and quickly came to announce long distance, San Diego. "It's Señor Moss!"

Billie's hands froze in midair and she leaped to her feet. But she was no quicker than Seth, who struggled from his chair and then had to lean on his cane for balance. For one moment their eyes locked, and Billie was the first to look away. Seth would speak to his son before she could speak to her husband.

Agnes and Jessica followed Seth and Billie out to the hall, gathering close. "That you, son?" Seth barked into the receiver. "'Bout time we heard from you! Still in San Diego?"

"How you doing, Pap? Are you treating my girl right? Not pulling any of your tricks, are you, Pap?"

Seth's answer was a noncommittal growl. "When the hell are you coming home? Have you gotten those ideas about war and glory out of your thick head yet?"

"I'm calling to say I'm leaving for Hawaii at oh three hundred tomorrow, California time."

"Why the hell you want to go all the way over there? If you're fighting for this country, then that's where you should stay, right here in the States! You've got a wife here and a son on the way. This is where you should be. I can still fix it, you know. Why don't you let me?"

"Pap, this is what I want. I'm being assigned to the USS *Enterprise*. You take care of Billie and the baby for me. I'm counting on you. Where is Billie?"

"Right here. Listen, son, there's something I want to ask you. Remember that well we pulled in out over to Waco? They're telling me she's going dry and we should pull out before we lose money on her. My gut tells me there's still a lode down there and we just haven't tapped it. Christ, the whole area is pulling in oil and I can't see any reason why we shouldn't. What do you think about drilling another well along the same ridge? You were out there before you got that fool notion to enlist in the navy—what d'you think?"

Billie hovered near, with clenched fists, straining to hear the sound of Moss's voice. Frustration screamed through her. *Why* was Seth talking about oil wells and money. She thought she'd faint if she didn't speak to Moss this instant! She looked at Jessica, who signaled to her to be patient.

"That's not what those smart-assed geologists have been telling me," Seth complained. "They're saying those pumps south of ours are pulling and we're bottoming out. A slant rig, you say? Do you know where it's been tried?... Yeah, I've heard of him. He's a wildcatter out of Oklahoma, isn't he?" Another pause. "Hell, son, why don't you come on home? Turn in that leather jacket and come be where you'll do the most good. Those planes don't run on water, you know. This country needs all the fuel oil it can get."

Seth listened, the lines in his face deepening with discouragement. "Yes, your mother's right here and so's Aggie.... Yes, she's here, too." Without another word, Seth handed the phone to Jessica, who kept her loving remarks brief before turning the phone over to Billie.

"Moss? Darling, how are you?"

"Fine. How's my girl? Not letting the old man make you sorry you married into the Colemans, are you?"

"Never. Never ever. Are you still in San Diego? Have you written? I didn't receive any letters. Did you get mine?"

"Every single one of them, honey. I didn't write; they've been keeping me pretty busy. I'm being shipped to Hawaii along with my squadron. Thad Kingsley's here, too, and shipping out with me. You remember him, don't you? Tall guy from New England."

"How could I forget? I danced with him at our wedding. Will you write when you get to Hawaii? I miss you, Moss." Billie glanced over at Seth, who was standing beside Agnes and Jessica. There was so much she wanted to say to Moss, but how could she with everyone listening to her every word?

"I miss you, too, Billie. Take care of yourself and the baby. Do what your mother tells you and everything will be okay. Hear?"

She wanted to ask if he really missed her. She wanted him to say he loved her. "Moss, when do you think we'll be together again? Will you be home for Christmas?"

"Don't think so, honey. Hawaii's half a world away, don't

forget. Write to me, Billie. I love hearing from you. Write me all the news, okay?"

"Okay. And Moss?"

"Yeah, Billie?"

"Take care of yourself, won't you? I worry."

"Don't worry. I'm going to come home as good as I left. I've got to go now, honey. There's a hundred guys waiting to use the phone. Take care of yourself. I miss you."

Billie gulped, trying to ignore the three pairs of eyes that watched her. She wished for one instant of privacy. Turning her back, she whispered into the phone, "Moss, I love you."

"I know you do, Billie." Click.

Billie held the dead receiver in her hand, feeling it grow cold in her grip. "Well, what did he say?" Seth demanded.

"He . . . he said he missed me."

"No, I mean did he say anything important? When is he coming home? Will he be coming back to the States?"

Wordlessly, Billie turned and climbed the stairs to her room. She wanted to be alone with her thoughts of Moss, and more than anything she wanted to spare herself Seth's inquisition.

Moss pushed his cap back at a jaunty angle and crossed the hotel lobby to where Thad Kingsley waited. "Didn't I tell you," Thad said, "it'd be better coming into town to call Billie? At least you didn't have to compete with two hundred men for use of the phone. Besides, sometimes the lines from the base are so jammed it takes an hour for a call to go through."

Moss signaled the barman for another drink. "Pap's having trouble with a well in Waco. That old man thinks I've got the answer to every one of Sunbridge's problems. I told him to get hold of a wildcatter I know in Oklahoma. If anybody can find oil, that bastard can."

Thad's brow wrinkled as he balanced his long lean body on the high bar stool. "Wasn't Billie home? Didn't you get to talk to her?"

"Billie's fine, or so she says. She was having a little morning sickness last time I saw her, but I guess that's passed."

"Don't you know?"

"How should I know?" Moss asked honestly. "I'm here in San Diego and she's in Texas."

"Didn't you ask her?" Thad persisted.

"Hell, I just phoned to tell my wife I'm leaving for Hawaii

and I don't know when I'll see her again. Do you think I want to talk about vomit at a time like that?"

Thad considered himself properly chastened. Moss's relationship with Billie was really none of his concern. It was just that his impression of Billie was that she was fragile and too terribly vulnerable. And Moss Coleman could be such a bastard. "I suppose a phone call like that can get pretty heavy. It can't be easy to leave a girl like Billie, especially when she's carrying your first child."

"Pap'll take good care of her." Moss sipped his drink, oblivious to the frown creasing his friend's brow.

{{{{{{{{{ CHAPTER EIGHT }}}}}}}}

Billie was determined to make Moss's home her own. But so many things puzzled her; Texas was so different from Philadelphia. Seth entertained business friends and associates at Sunbridge, for instance, often completing financial transactions right on the front porch. Soft voices would discuss details over and over and then the deal would be formalized with a hearty handshake. Only later would contracts and agreements be put on paper; a man's hand on a promise held more weight than his legal signature.

And Billie's own life became internalized, as her focus turned more and more to the small life within her. The changes in her body came quickly and were always accompanied by a fresh bout of queasiness, if not sickness. Her breasts were swollen and painful, her balance seemed awkward, and she noticed in the mirror that her pelvis was tilting forward, which made the hem of her dresses hang unevenly. Agnes decided it was time for maternity smocks and skirts with tummy holes. Often, Billie yearned for the familiarity of Philadelphia. It would be nice to go shopping with a girlfriend or just walk into town and look in the windows. She had to remind herself that all her friends were at college and the only window-shopping available was nearly forty miles away in Austin.

When the subject of Billie's pregnancy came up at the supper table, Seth insisted on referring to his grandchild as a boy—and his tone said he'd accept nothing less. Jessica had told her kindly, "Billie, it doesn't do any good to argue with Seth. I've been married to him for nearly thirty years and you can believe me." She knew Jessica commiserated with her during these conversations and that was comforting. After all, once the baby was born, regardless of its sex, it couldn't be sent back. As long as it was healthy, what did it matter? Nevertheless, Billie wisely never mentioned the words *baby girl* or even hinted at a feminine name. But the pressure of Seth's possible disappointment was giving her headaches even Tita's potions or the doctor couldn't cure. She kept her miseries to herself and spent hours rereading Moss's sparse letters, which ran a half to a whole page, never more. At least she'd heard from him; for that she was grateful. If his letters were less than romantic, she would accept it. She spent long hours writing letters that she was certain he never read. It was something to do.

Billie found herself upset over Agnes's silent aversion to Jessica's company: her mother seemed to prefer accompanying Seth whenever she could on his rounds of the ranch, and she sat with him in his study listening to the radio news. While Billie and Jessica read Moss's letters, Agnes was reading prospectus reports on Seth's latest venture into the electronics industry. They got along well, these two, seeming to have a quiet understanding of one another. Cantankerous as Seth was, he had met his match in Agnes and he respected her for it.

Billie was seeing her mother as if for the first time. No longer did Agnes appear matronly and middle-aged. Now, with her new upswept hairdo, stylish dresses, and dainty shoes (instead of the durable, sensible ones she'd always bought in Philadelphia), Agnes was a very attractive woman. Even some of Seth's associates who came to the house seemed impressed with the Colemans' Yankee kin, and she'd been invited to dinner several times.

Agnes had set Seth straight almost from the beginning. She let him know that as Billie's mother she was in control of her daughter and of the child she carried. Sons left home. Daughters stayed and obeyed. Seth was to understand that if things didn't go well at Sunbridge, Agnes would pick up her daughter and return to Philadelphia. She should have been a man, Seth found himself thinking.

On the last day of September Billie and Jessica were sitting outdoors in the rose arbor drinking iced fruit punch when Tita wobbled out waving an airmail letter. Jessica's hand went to her throat in alarm; Billie rushed to her while snatching the letter from Tita's outstretched hand. "It's all right, Jessica. It's from England." She handed the letter to her mother-in-law and sat down opposite her, feeling the same relief that was evident on Jessica's face.

"It's from Amelia! I've been worried about her. I think the last I heard from her was just before you came to Sunbridge, Billie." Quickly, Jessica skimmed the contents, her face brightening and softening with maternal love. "Amelia has married! An RAF pilot, and she now has a small stepson. Isn't that wonderful?" There was a shadow lurking in Jessica's expression. "I would have liked to give her a wedding, but I suppose that's unreasonable, considering she's in England, and then there's the war, of course. But I'm very happy for her, nevertheless."

"A ready-made family," said Billie.

"Amelia deserves happiness," Jessica went on. "She has so much love to give. She'll be a wonderful mother. Both my children married, and we didn't get to attend either wedding."

Moss Coleman stood on the ramparts of Fort Kamehameha and looked down into Pearl Harbor at the lady he loved. She was 827 feet long, 114 feet wide, and displaced 20,000 tons empty and unarmed. His lady was both a warship and an airfield, the USS *Enterprise*. Four huge bronze propellers driven by steam turbines gave her more than thirty knots of speed, and behind the props a single rudder as big as the side of a barn swung at a touch from the bridge to provide an enviable maneuverability. In her breast she carried a new and secret device called "radar," which could find the enemy in the black of night or shrouding fog. Captain and mess cook, firemen and pilots, and more than two thousand men lived and fought on her. Her pilots, who romanced her from high above her decks, knew a special love for their lady. It was from her that they went to do battle, but it was always to her that they prayed to return. And no pilot's love was greater than Moss's own.

As Moss's eyes squinted lovingly over her, from the superstructure to the aft deck, he knew the reason for her existence was the flight deck that covered her from stem to stern. Her deck was broken only by the island amidships on the starboard side where the control centers of the ship were housed. On both bows were catapults to launch the planes, and forward, aft, and amidships heavy-duty elevators lifted the planes from the cavernous hangar deck below. Over eighty aircraft were stored below—stubby Grumman F4F Wildcats with squared-off wing tips.

Moss throbbed with anticipation. Today was October 16, 1942, and his lady had taken a new master, Captain Osborne B. Hardison. Preparations were being made to get under way. In the month since he'd arrived, he'd been engaged in practice flights and drills. He was ready, like the lady, to engage the enemy. The controls of his Wildcat—affectionately christened the Texas Ranger—felt right in his hand. His ear was tuned to the drone of the engine and the lift of her wings. In less than an hour he would report to duty, along with his team of eager pilots. In a few hours the lady's lines would be cast off and she would cruise out into the narrow channel toward the blue Pacific, past Hospital Point and Fort Kamehameha. And when Diamond Head was lost beyond the horizon, scuttlebutt had it that she would turn her bow toward the Solomon Islands. The Japanese troops on Guadalcanal were pressing hard against the marine lines that protected Henderson Field.

One week later, Moss and Thad Kingsley stood bareheaded on the *Enterprise*'s aft flight deck, their gazes turned to Rear Admiral Thomas Kinkaid as he inspected the decks of the floating airfield. That morning, at dawn, they'd met their supporting ships and the tanker *Sabine*. Hours ago the carrier class *Hornet* had joined the task force.

"Kinkaid's briefing was an eye-opener," Thad said, exhaling a cloud of smoke that was drawn away in a thin stream by the wind.

Moss agreed. "Let him handle the tactics and we'll do the rest. Some of the guys are worried he'll get so fancy with his moves that we'll never find the ship before we run out of fuel on our return scat. Not me, though. I'd find this beauty if she was six fathoms under."

Thad laughed guardedly. Moss's bravado sometimes worried him. It was too easy to be too cocky. "Just follow orders, Coleman, and the Big E will be waiting for us. Remember the objective."

Moss tossed his butt over the side. "We have to stop the

Japs from taking Henderson Field. It's an important link in the U.S.–Australian lifeline. And the Japs' strongest naval forces since Midway are at sea: four carriers, eight heavy cruisers, two light cruisers, and twenty-eight destroyers. That's a hell of a lot of targets and I'm going to get my shot at them!"

"We've got targets of our own to protect, don't forget. The *Saratoga*, the *Wasp*, now us and the *Hornet*. The battleship *Washington* will look mighty good to those zeros. Kinkaid's worried that we're undermanned and he may be right." Moss's seeming overconfidence was a trait Thad knew was keeping his friend from making full lieutenant. The command worried that he'd take unnecessary risks with men and machines.

An announcement came over the loudspeaker:

"All pilots to the wardroom. All pilots to the wardroom."

"That'll be for Crommelin's briefing," Moss said. There was admiration in his voice for their flight trainer. His combat record was impeccable and when training the *Enterprise* pilots under his command, he'd given them confidence in their F4Fs by showing them a slow roll at under a thousand feet: he required nothing of them he was not able to perform himself. Moss could still hear Crommelin's voice coming over the radio: ". . . over and over and over and over again."

Thad and Moss sat together among the other pilots. Everyone wore open-necked khaki. The green-covered tables held brimming coffee mugs, and cigarette smoke rose in blue clouds up to the cables overhead.

"You've all been thoroughly and carefully trained," Crommelin began. "You know how to drop a bomb and hit a target, and that's what I damn well expect you to do. Our marines have had a long, miserable struggle for Guadalcanal and now they're depending on us. There's no room for waste, no excuse for misses. If you can't do the job, it'd be better if you stayed back in the States and give men who could do it your bunks and your crack at the Japs." There was a long moment of silence. "Now I want you to get some rest, write a few letters, eat light, and lay off the coffee. Come morning, I expect you to knock those Jap sons of bitches right off the face of this earth!"

The sound of the men's uplifting cheer was still ringing in Moss's ears as he wrote to Billie.

Darling Billie,

Things are happening quickly around here and I wanted

to write. I know I have been remiss in the letter department, honey, but it hasn't been because I don't think about you and our child. I left for San Diego so suddenly that we hadn't even had a chance for those little games parents-to-be like to play. We never even discussed a name for our son. Mam's family name was Riley and I'd like it if that's what he is named. Expect to get some objection from Pap but stand firm, won't you?

I miss you, honey. More than you know. But I know I'm doing what I have to do and there is consolation in that. You are so young, Billie darling, and I was so selfish to send you off to Sunbridge, especially at this time when you would probably like to be in familiar surroundings with friends you have known all your life. Sunbridge is my life, Billie, and it's a good one and one I want for you and our child.

I guess it is at times like these that a man takes stock of who he is and what he has done. Little wife, if I have anything to be proud of, anything to fight for, it is you. From the first, your trust and belief in me have made me a better man. I'll come home to you, Billie. I will.

Moss

Before dawn on October 26, while first-shift breakfast was being served to sailors still grumpy with sleep, a message was received from the headquarters of the commander, South Pacific Force. It was in the familiar style of Admiral Bill Halsey. Three words:

ATTACK. REPEAT. ATTACK.

The flight deck of the *Enterprise* was a confusion of efficiency as aircraft were raised from the hangar bay and rolled to the catapult mechanisms on the runway. Yellow-jacketed men wearing radio headsets listened for the order to signal takeoff amid the roaring whine of the engines and the thrum of the props.

Moss stood among the pilots, helmet and goggles in hand, waiting for his squadron to be signaled. His leather jacket was opened to the early-morning wind. Thad Kingsley pushed through the others and grasped Moss's hand in a firm shake. If there was a time for farewell, this was it. He knew without doubt that Moss held him in great affection and friendship but that it wasn't his style to initiate the gesture. "Hey, buddy, don't get too eager for those meatballs," he said, referring to the Japanese flags that were affixed to a pilot's plane to indicate a kill. He clapped Moss on the shoulder affectionately. "I'll meet you back in the wardroom for debriefing when this is over, you Texas bastard."

"I'll be there, you Yankee cracker. Make certain you are." Moss flashed a white smile. "There's my plane." As he loosened his grip on Thad's hand and moved forward, he turned suddenly and grinned, shouting above the roar. "Hey, Thad, did I tell you what my son's name is? Riley! Riley Moss Coleman!" Turning again, he sprinted for the Texas Ranger, his mind shifting gears from the elusive reality of his unborn child to the business at hand.

In the cockpit, eyes forward, expression grim, he adjusted his headset and tested the elevator flaps. Efficiently he performed his checklist, switching on controls and inspecting gauges. His parachute pressed into his back but he disregarded it. Mentally, he became one with his machine; if she went down, so did he.

The battlefield had been chosen; a thousand square miles of South Pacific lying just north of the Santa Cruz Islands. The sea was calm except for the long ground swells that never ceased. Above, at approximately 1,500 feet, drifted white-and-gold clouds. As the Big E probed ever westward, the scouting fighter squadrons would return by appointment for refueling. Again and again they would land and depart in their relentless search, until the enemy was met.

Watching from amidships, Thad saw the Texas Ranger catapult into the air, her wheels leaving the deck before she reached the edge. He'd been astounded and pleased at the mention of the baby. It was rare that Moss was sentimental, but hell, when a guy was about to fly his first mission, what else could be on his mind but what he'd be leaving behind? He prayed Moss would be around to meet little Riley Coleman. Thad pushed his fingers through his sandy hair and grinned. Moss even had him believing the baby would be a boy.

Navy Fighter Squadron 4 took to the air, circling wide of the mother ship and setting a northward course, eight pairs of glinting wings in the early sun. Moss flew starboard wingman for his squadron leader, Lieutenant Commander Jimmy McVey, holding slightly aft in the V formation. They settled into a hunt-and-search pattern, eyes scanning above and below for the enemy.

When only ten minutes of flying time remained, a voice rasped over the headset: "Zeros, up-sun, twelve o'clock!" Moss looked up, squinting, and had his first sight of the enemy. The bright sunlight at 14,000 feet beat into the cockpit, but it couldn't warm the cold at the pit of his stomach. His experienced eye read the fuel gauge. Bursts of speed and fuel-consuming maneuvers could mean a sudden point of no return. He felt his teeth bite-down on his lower lip.

The attack came from the rear, arrow straight and just as deadly. Curses were mumbled into headsets; grim and determined faces peered through cockpit windshields. Explosive firepower flew all about the American fighters and they were helpless to return it without coming about and taking the zeros head-on. McVey radioed their position back to headquarters. The return message was to pursue and attack—where there were zeros there would be Japanese carriers. Two were known to be in the area. Moss once again glanced at the fuel gauge.

"Break formation," came McVey's voice. "Spiral down and jump from the rear." It was a maneuver that didn't generate the squadron's faith. It was already known that zeros could outclimb and outmaneuver American fighters.

One by one, the squadron spiraled portside and dropped to 11,000 feet. The maneuver wasn't working—the zeros were still on their tails. Mooney, second port wingman, broke radio silence. "Squad four, two zeros hanging back. Repeat, two enemy hanging back. Total nine enemy."

"Coleman, MacGuire, drop back and take them. Squadron ready and ahead," McVey commanded.

Two machines, one order. Moss and MacGuire held back on the throttles, losing air speed, allowing the rest of the squad to shoot ahead. Accomplishing a forty-degree turn to port, they climbed to seek their zeros. The Japanese craft flew toward them at a thirty-degree angle, coming from above. Moss saw MacGuire veer eastward. The zeros went after him, increasing air speed and losing altitude. MacGuire was a sitting duck. A long burst and MacGuire's Wildcat was a burning pyre. Moss watched for signs of a bailout, ready to cover his partner, praying to see a cloud of silk. There was no sign except for vapor trail.

Moss clamped his teeth shut against the roiling in his gut.

He gripped the control stick as though it were a lifeline, his finger tickling the trigger. He could sense the zeros hot on his trail, hungry for the kill. A part of his mind wondered how the rest of the squad was doing. Would McVey send a craft to double back? Instinctively he led his pursuers north, away from American territory. His eye judged the fuel gauge. It had to be now or never.

The enemy dove down on him, closing the distance, coming within firing range. Moss throttled back, hoping they'd overshoot. As they flashed past, he poured on the coal, got on their tails, and fired. He felt the burst from his guns send vibrations through the cockpit, jiggling the needles on his instrument panel. He hadn't known he'd squeezed his eyes shut until he looked to see both of them falling, bursting into flames, paper lanterns crashing toward the sea.

Taking a wide circle that would set him on a course for the *Enterprise*, Moss headed home to refuel. It was only the beginning of a very long day.

Later, much later, after long hours of battle between ships and aircraft, after the Japanese navy retreated, leaving Guadalcanal and marine bases intact, Moss would acknowledge two enemy zeros destroyed, but he would take credit for only one. Lieutenant MacGuire would be credited for the other.

On the third of November, at the barbecue at the Barretts' ranch outside Dallas, Representative Lyndon Baines Johnson told Seth in confidence that the *Enterprise* had engaged in battle. She was now known to be anchored in the hill-rimmed tropical harbor of Nouméa, New Caledonia. She'd been hit and was under emergency repair. No list had yet been released of wounded and fatalities.

Seth kept the news to himself. It wouldn't do to have Jessica become anxious or for that fragile little gal from Philadelphia to get hysterical and jeopardize the only chance for the Coleman bloodline. It was Agnes who took up the reins after Seth finally confided in her. She saw that the gaiety of the party was gnawing on his nerves and that he'd rather await any news at Sunbridge. She resourcefully claimed to have received an important phone message; Seth was needed back home immediately. Grateful, and happy for her company, Seth asked Agnes to go with him and together they boarded his private plane and departed for Austin.

Jessica and Billie returned to Sunbridge the following Thursday. They knew something was deeply troubling Seth. He claimed it was a business problem and for Billie's sake Jessica did not challenge him, but she knew, somehow, that it had to do with Moss. When they were alone, Seth put her fears to rest, or tried to, by telling her it was that damn oil well that had tapped out. Again, she didn't believe him, but nearly thirty years of marriage had taught Jessica not to contradict her husband or test his patience. She watched as Seth paced the floor or rode old Nessie until the mare nearly dropped in her tracks. Day after day she suffered, silently, praying for her son and worrying over her husband. Migraine headaches kept Jessica to her room, and she reluctantly handed over the household management to an eager Agnes. It was all becoming too much. Moss at war, Amelia marrying, Billie's pregnancy, and Agnes's increasing closeness to Seth. And Jessica knew her health wasn't what it should be, but she kept it to herself. Seth disliked what he called "ailing females."

Relief came nearly three weeks later when two letters arrived from Moss. One was addressed to Billie. In it he said he'd like the baby to be named Riley, Jessica's family name. The other was sent after Guadalcanal. He was fine. Only a small note was enclosed for Billie, half a page. The other nine pages of bold scrawl were directed to Seth. Moss told of his first kill, but the bulk of the letter was devoted to describing how Thad Kingsley and his wingman had caught an unprotected Japanese light carrier. The two of them alone had sent her to the bottom of the South Pacific.

"Who the hell is this Kingsley fella?" Seth growled. "Seems like he's gotten himself pretty close to Moss, if you ask me. If Moss had found that Jap ship, he wouldn't have needed any help in sending her to the bottom. And what the hell is a meatball?"

The next week a truly grateful Thanksgiving was spent at Sunbridge.

{{{{{{{{{ CHAPTER NINE }}}}}}}}}

In the study, Agnes sat back in her chair across the massive desk from Seth. She had just completed taking down a letter he'd dictated and later she would type it. When he was at home, Agnes acted as his secretary. Today, she was marveling at Seth's expertise in manipulation. There were lessons to be learned here and learn them she would. For the first time in years she felt her talents were being put to use. First the house, which Jessica was relinquishing to her care, and now working beside Seth. She knew that Sunbridge was a family-held business, all of it. Any fool could see that Jessica was in failing health and that Seth was a prime candidate for a stroke if he didn't ease up a bit. With Moss off to war, that would leave only empty-headed Billie to handle things for the Colemans. Learning as much as she could about the business was not only a pleasure; it was a necessity.

Agnes nodded her approval as she typed up the letters Seth wanted sent to his contacts in Washington. Moss was building an honorable reputation for himself as a fighter pilot. Within the last few weeks he'd been promoted to squadron commander; lieutenant commander was only a step away. Surely the boy was entitled to leave. To have Moss home for Christmas was not, Seth felt, a request out of bounds. And he was offering a prime dressed beef to grease the gears.

Within two weeks Seth was notified that Moss would be sent to San Diego to assemble a group of replacement pilots and would be given a seven-day leave to join his family in Texas.

Billie's joy knew no bounds when she received the news. She didn't know or care how it had all come about; all she knew was that her husband was coming home and she would be in his arms again.

The news of her son's homecoming roused Jessica sufficiently to join the holiday preparations. Agnes prepared the menus and scrupulously oversaw the holiday cleaning, but it was Jessica who knew how to bring Christmas to Sunbridge. The house was bedecked with holly and evergreens and awash with the fragrances of Christmas. Gifts arrived by the carload, wrapped and beribboned and making Billie's eyes widen with disbelief.

Jessica took Billie into Austin to shop for presents. It was an experience to sit in a comfortable store lounge and have items paraded before them for their approval. Billie missed the frantic hustle and bustle of Philadelphia and the taste of snow in the air. But she resigned herself to Jessica's pace, knowing she wasn't capable of much activity herself. A few weeks of relief from morning sickness had come to an end and she was once again suffering the full range of pregnancy symptoms.

Three days before Moss was due to come home, Billie awakened early, crawled out of bed, and headed straight for the commode. She retched miserably and then sat on the edge of the bathtub while she bathed her face in cold water. Nothing was helping. Not Tita's home remedies or Dr. Ward's prescriptions and vitamin injections. Billie felt a mess and looked a mess. Her ankles were so swollen that she'd been reduced to scuffling around in a pair of Agnes's large house slippers. She needed a haircut and a permanent wave, but the thought of the smelly chemicals she'd have to endure made her queasy. A new dress was a must. Lord, what was Moss going to think when he saw her? When he'd left she still had a waistline! Her breasts had become fuller, but now they showed faint stretch-marks as they lay heavily against her burgeoning middle. It would have been all right if Moss had been with her day after day, accepting the changes in her body; but now, after so long an absence, he couldn't help being shocked, possibly even revolted. Billie tipped her face into her hands and cried. She was still dabbing at her tears when she sat down at the breakfast table.

Seth's eyes went to Agnes, who answered his silent question with a shrug. He stole another look at Billie. The little gal looked terrible. Moss was in for a shock when he got home. Seth disliked pregnancies. A woman changed and became an awkward, ungainly, puffy individual, a caricature of herself. Billie's appearance annoyed him, just the way Jessica's had annoyed him when she'd carried his children. But he was tolerant—or rather, he was forcing himself to be tolerant. After all, this young lady *was* carrying his future grandson.

"Three more days and your son will be home," Agnes said brightly as she cut into a succulent sausage. Billie's head went up and her eyes narrowed. His son? Moss was *her* husband. Agnes took note of Billie's look. "We have to do something about your appearance," she said. "Why don't we go into town and get your hair done and perhaps pick up a new dress? One that isn't so . . . so . . ."

"So like a tent, Mother? I need the room, or haven't you noticed how much weight I've put on? I'm afraid there aren't too many styles that will fit me."

"You can try," Seth said coolly. There it was. Agnes's backup. She was to go into town. Seth excused himself, and when he returned he laid a check next to Billie's plate. She looked down at it and winced. A thousand dollars to get her hair done and a new dress. "Buy yourself some pretties," Seth said. His tone clearly stated that he thought she needed *something*. Regardless of how she felt, she knew she had to go to town. Seth tolerated no excuses. Agnes smiled benignly. Seth was so good to them.

The entire day was just one long trial of misery for Billie. At the hairdresser's she'd sat with her shoeless feet propped up while lotions and the heat-wave machine were applied to her hair. Between bouts of nausea she kept reminding the beautician that she wanted a *soft* curl, no frizz! Twice she'd had to retch into a wastepaper basket while the clamps and wires were still attached to her head, making it impossible for her to bend over. In the end, her hair looked as though she'd stuck her finger into a live light socket and she nearly sobbed when she was told it would relax within a few weeks. It was cut too short, it was permed too curly, and she thought she resembled a bowling pin when she hazarded a look in a full-length mirror. Thankfully, after the setting and an eternity under the dryer, the effect was not quite so bad.

When Agnes saw Billie's haircut and permanent wave she had to refrain from gasping her shock. "Did you choose that particular style from a magazine, Billie?" she asked off-handedly. Suddenly, Agnes felt very old, hardly a strong-spirited active woman of forty-three. A forty-three-year-old woman couldn't possibly have a woman of forty for her child. And that was exactly how Billie looked, old and worn. Even her pink-and-gold complexion had faded into something resembling jaundice. For the first time Agnes was truly alarmed for her daughter's health. "Billie, what did Dr. Ward say the last time you saw him? I've tried not to be an interfering mother, but . . ."

"Lately, Mother, you've hardly been interfering. Not interested is closer to the truth. Dr. Ward said I should have my teeth checked. Pregnancies are hard on women's teeth. Lord." She managed a grudging laugh. "My teeth are the only part of me that don't hurt! Can we go back to Sunbridge now?"

"Absolutely not. First we're going to have lunch. Seth took me to the Paladian once and their food is wholesome and simple. Next we're going shopping for some new dresses for you. Now that I've finally gotten you away from the house, we're going to accomplish what we've set out to do. Honestly, Billie, you're getting to be a drudge, just like Jessica."

Billie shot Agnes a warning glance but was feeling too ill to pursue a defense of her mother-in-law. "Whatever we're going to do, let's do it quickly. My feet are swollen and my shoes are pinching and I just want to go home."

Back at Sunbridge, Billie immediately went to her room. All she wanted was to take her shoes off and have a nice warm bath. She sat on the edge of her bed looking down at her swollen feet with clinical interest. And to think she'd been a double-A narrow only months ago. Would things ever be the same again?

After her bath, Billie went to see how Jessica was feeling, and spent the time before dinner reading the daily paper to her mother-in-law. Jessica's headaches had been too severe to allow her to use her eyes for either reading or working on the baby sweater she was knitting.

"You'd better run along and dress for dinner, Billie. You look so tired. I think the day in town was too much for you. Tell me what you bought. Was Seth generous with his check?"

"More than generous," Billie assured her, remembering for the first time that she hadn't spent anywhere near the entire sum. The remainder must still be tucked away in Agnes's purse. Would she return it to Seth? "I bought a few dresses and tops. One I especially like is a soft sage color with long sleeves and a bias-cut bodice that buttons off to the side. I needed lingerie and a few nightgowns. But there was a dressing gown I simply couldn't resist. It's long and flowing and I thought I'd wear it when Moss arrives so he won't see how swollen my feet and legs are."

Jessica heard the anxiety in Billie's voice and sighed. "Dear child, I think you're making too much out of your appearance. Moss is not even going to notice how you look. You're going to be the mother of his child and that's what he's going to think of. I don't want you riling yourself up so that you can't enjoy your husband and the Christmas holidays."

"Are you sure, Jessica? I don't want him to have regrets." Her young voice was so full of hope and despair that Jessica found it hard to speak. "I'm sure, child. Run along now and dress for dinner."

Billie leaned over to hug the older woman. "I always feel so much better when I talk to you. I'll come back after dinner. I bought you two new mystery stories." She gave the older woman another light kiss and left the room.

There were tears in Jessica's eyes when she watched Billie leave the room. Billie was a Coleman now and she would have to accept the Colemans the way they were. They couldn't be changed—she had learned that hard and bitter lesson years ago. Billie was a fighter; she had that much going for her. How and when she was going to do her fighting would be what was important. Perhaps she was wrong not to confide in the young woman she had come to love. But how could she tell Billie that Seth hadn't come near her bed after the fourth month of pregnancy? How could she tell Billie about Seth's philandering over the years without making it sound like Moss would do the same thing? A wave of pity washed over her, not for Billie or herself, but for Seth and Moss. They were the losers. In the end, when it counted, she hoped that both men would realize that fact. She blessed herself quickly for her uncharitable thought. She *was* a Coleman after all.

Moss stepped off the train in Austin's depot, his duffel slung carelessly over his shoulder. "Pap!"

After the two men embraced, Moss pointed to his sleeve. "Take a look, Pap. Lieutenant commander."

"Good for you, boy. You might make admiral yet. You want admiral, I'll get you admiral!"

"Hell, no. Thad's the one who's going to make admiral the way he's going. No more string-pulling, Pap. I'm doing things on my own these days. Where's Mam and Billie? Anything wrong?" he asked as an afterthought.

"Your mother isn't feeling well, Moss. You need to know that."

"Pap, if that's another of your little tricks to get me stateside,

{ 135 }

forget it. Mam has you to look after her. Billie and Agnes can take up the slack. I've got a war to fight."

"Hrmmph! You're being overly dramatic, aren't you, son?"

"With you, Pap, everything has to be overstated before you get it through that head of yours."

"I knew you were going to say that," Seth grumbled good-naturedly. "What's important now is that you're home."

"Where's Billie?" Moss asked again.

"Back at Sunbridge. She's not up to par these days and you'll have to go easy on her. I hate to say it, but you didn't pick yourself a breeder when you picked that one. Pity we men can't try them out first. I had the same trouble with your mother. Seems like the finer bred they are, the harder time they have. Why, I've seen Mexican peasants give birth on the side of the road and go right back to work in the fields."

"What's wrong with Billie, Pap? Give it to me straight. Is the baby, okay?"

"Fine, fine, according to the doctor, anyway. But your little Yankee is having a hard time of it. Sick and pukey all the time. She tries to hide it but I can see it just as plain as the nose on your face. You got any fool ideas of picking up where you left off, just cancel them. You're not going to take chances with my grandson. You get my drift, boy?"

Moss stared at his father. "Is that your way of telling me I should take my biological needs to a cathouse, Pap?"

Seth grimaced. "The navy teach you to sass your pap, boy?"

"The nut doesn't fall far from the tree, Pap. You've got a strong way of talking yourself, if I remember."

"Damn well you remember. Just be nice to that little gal. She's carrying Riley Seth Coleman."

"I see you've accepted my preference for his name, with a little addition of your own." Moss laughed at the bright gleam in his father's eye. It was clear Seth couldn't wait for the baby to be born.

"C'mon, Carlo is waiting. Let's get the hell out of here. Once we're in the car I want you to tell me everything you've been doing. All of it. And who the hell's this Kingsley fella? Not letting him get the jump on you, are you?"

Moss felt as though he were swimming against the current as he talked to his father. What the hell was going on back at the house? Billie sounded fine in her letters, all seven of them each week. Jesus, he hadn't known there were so many ways to say the same thing over and over. Not that he didn't appreciate her daily letters. He did. He couldn't wait to see her. That's all he'd been thinking of for the past ten days. He had it all planned in his mind. He was going to rush her right off her feet and carry her up the wide circular stairway, and then, look out! A little bump in the middle wasn't going to make a bit of difference. There were ways to get around that.

"I've got it all planned, boy. We're going to ride the range like we used to do before you decided you wanted to fly planes. We'll roast a whole steer, have some people in so I can do a fair share of bragging, and then I'll tell you all about my new business ventures. Seven days, son, that's all we got this time around. I tried for a full two weeks but they balked. Seven was a gift."

Now. Tell him now, before he got up any more grand plans. "Pap, it isn't seven, it's four. I have to get back. I'm sorry as hell, but that's the way it is. Big things are in the wind and when they blow I want to be sure I'm there. If you're going to make a fuss, do it now. I don't want anything spoiling my leave with Billie."

"Boy, you haven't heard a word I said, have you? The little lady is in no condition to do much of anything. You're in drydock. Get it through your head. One of these days, that hot head of yours is going to get you into a lot of real trouble. Trust me. Tell me, I don't suppose you did any Christmas shopping for the ladies, did you?"

"Pap, Christmas shopping on an aircraft carrier?" Moss laughed.

"That's what I thought. Agnes did it all. I gave the lady a blank check and she bought out the stores. You're safe on that score."

"You two getting along?" Moss grinned.

"Like pigs take to the cornfield. We understand each other," Seth said generously. "You might say we have common objectives."

"I thought you would. How's Mam get along with her?"

"Now, son, you know your mother. If anything, she's too damn good, always looking for the best in people. How d'you think she's stood me all these years?"

A wry grin spread on Moss's face. "Sometimes, Pap, I've wondered. Hear anything from Amelia? I had a letter from her when I was in Hawaii but nothing since."

"Your sister has gotten herself married," Seth announced. "This time she's really gone and done it. Found herself an RAF pilot, a widower with a small son." He guffawed. "Imagine Amelia, harebrained and shiftless, being a mother. Glad it's not a Coleman she's raising. That little gal of yours has more sense in her little finger than your sister has in her whole head. And she marries a limey to boot."

Moss frowned. "Why're you so hard on her, Pap? Especially since you know she'd lay down her life for you if you asked her. What's her pilot like? How old is her stepson?"

Seth waved his hand through the air to cease all questions. "If there's something you want to know, you'll have to ask your mother. The details of your sister's life always either embarrass or bore me. If nothing else, your sister could have come home, given your mother the pleasure of planning the wedding and seeing her only daughter married. Selfish as she is, she does it half a world away."

"Pap, it isn't as though it's easy getting back and forth across the Atlantic. There is a war going on."

"Then she should have waited," Seth grumbled. "But your sister never waits for anything, as you well know." He sighed. "I suppose it's for the best, after all. Your mother isn't exactly up to planning weddings."

"What's ailing Mam?"

"Who knows? Doctors seem to think she just needs bed rest and there's something about her blood pressure. She's been in bed off and on. Mostly on, but it doesn't seem to be doing much good. Billie is good to her; I'll give her that. She spends a lot of time with your mother. They like each other."

That meant Seth didn't approve. Seth was likening Billie to Jessica and that was a definite fault in his eyes. The qualities Seth admired were strength and guts; Jessica had never had enough of those. Moss's eyes narrowed. "Why don't you like my wife, Pap? She's a wonderful girl and half the time I feel terrible about having married her. She deserves a lot better than the Colemans. We're too hard on our women. Jesus, Pap, if I find out you've made her unwelcome, I'll never forgive you."

"Calm down, son. You're going off half-cocked. It's nothing like that and you know it. It's just that she's always sick. She was sick the day she got off the train and she's been sickly ever since. She always looks like she's about to puke or faint or something. I never see her eat, but she must have put on ten pounds for every month she's been with us. Still pretty enough. But sickly, and you know I've got no patience with mewling females."

Sick. His Billie was sick and no one had told him. The car couldn't take him to the house quickly enough. He had to see for himself. From the beginning, Moss had had plaguing doubts about becoming involved with Billie. She was so young, so fresh and innocent. So trusting. And the two people she trusted most in the world—himself and Agnes—had betrayed her. Billie hadn't been ready for marriage, especially one where her husband preferred to be flying fighter planes. And he doubted she was ready to become a mother. It was like whelping a dog that hadn't come into her second season. The drain on her health and vitality could be devastating. Feeling guilty and worried, Moss sank into the plush seat of the limousine, only half listening to Seth as he explained in detail the new electronics division of Sunbridge. Who gave a damn if there was a radar installations contract pending with Washington when his own selfishness and Agnes's greed had caused Billie's suffering?

Billie stood beneath the front portico watching the long black Packard come up the tree-lined drive. She huddled in her thick sweater, her heart pounding so fiercely she thought it could be heard miles away. She was dizzy with anticipation. Tears burned her eyes when Moss leaped from the car before it came to a full stop. At that moment she would have given anything if she could have run to him, light and slim and girlish, just the way he'd left her.

Moss's shock beat at his brain. Lord, this couldn't be Billie! What had he done to her? The long dress she was wearing couldn't disguise her solid thickness. There would be no picking her up and carrying her up the long staircase. She looked puffy and ill. The old man hadn't been exaggerating.

Billie smiled and held out her arms. She had to trust that Jessica was right. Moss would swoop down on her and . . . and . . .

"Billie!" His arms were out but almost as if they were holding her at a distance. Her own outstretched arms dropped instantly to her side. He leaned over and kissed her full on the lips. A hurried public kiss. Billie kept smiling as she reached for his hand to walk indoors with him.

He'd been expecting so much. Wanted so much. Four days in the sack and then off into the wild blue yonder. Now it looked like he would get calluses on his ass from riding the range with Seth. Four days in the saddle could kill a man if he wasn't used to it. His eyes dropped down to Billie's hand clutching his. It seemed like a lot of flesh to him. The ring on

{ 139 }

her left hand was cutting into her finger. The long slender hands he remembered were now thick and swollen like over-stuffed sausages. Jesus! It was his fault. She looked like this because of him. He had to talk to the doctor; Seth said he came nearly every day. What if something went wrong? "How do you feel, Billie?" It was a goddamn stupid question, but he had to say something.

"Actually, I feel better than I look," Billie lied brightly. "The doctor is keeping his eye on me."

At a loss for words, Moss drew Billie to him. "I'm sorry, Billie, that you have to go through this while I'm not here to be with you." A waterfall of guilt poured over and through him.

"Let's not talk about that. We have seven whole days to be together. I want to hear everything and I have so much to tell you. But first, why don't you run up and see your mother? She's been waiting for days and days to see you."

Moss smiled at Billie. It was a meaningless, empty smile, she thought, but somewhere in his eyes had been relief. Relief that he could escape her? When Moss charged up the stairs to visit with Jessica, Billie turned to find Seth standing in the open doorway, the winter sun making a brilliant backdrop that threw him into shadow. She couldn't see his eyes but she felt them, hard and appraising. She was a disappointment, both to him and his son. And there was the mortal sin, being unworthy of his son.

Before Moss was home two hours he seemed to have fallen easily into his old routines at Sunbridge. He'd cast off his uniform for boots, plaid flannel shirt, and tight cord trousers. The few minutes he'd spent with Jessica had ended with her promise to come downstairs for supper. Billie waited for him downstairs in the cozy little den off the dining room. A fire had been lit and was hissing pleasantly. When he finally found her, he was wearing a rugged sheepskin jacket. Kissing her perfunctorily, he announced he was going out for a short ride with Pap and would be back after lunch.

"You'll be okay, won't you?" he asked politely.

Why shouldn't she be okay? She'd been okay all this time at Sunbridge without him, hadn't she? Why should now be any different? "You go on with your father. I'll have you all to myself after you get back." She tried for a brave and under-standing smile that wasn't quite up to par. Moss's blue eyes studied her seriously and she knew he was about to say that riding with Seth would wait. Then his father appeared in the doorway.

"There you are, son. Grease your tail; we want to get back before the sun goes down. These old bones don't take to the cold like they used to."

"You go along. I'll be here when you get back," Billie said with more enthusiasm than she felt. She wanted Moss here with her, sitting beside her, touching her. His homecoming was like a dream. She still could hardly believe he was really here.

He kissed her again, a lingering caress on her mouth. "I won't be long, Billie. And you could use the time to get yourself all gussied up for me." He was gone.

Gussied up! What did he think? That she'd just rolled out of bed this morning and lumbered out under the portico to meet him? She *was* gussied up! Hairdo, makeup, new dress . . . Tears flowed down her plump cheeks. Of course he couldn't know about the painful preparations she'd made. She looked like a baby whale and her hair was too short. He didn't like it or else he'd have mentioned it. The baby moved within her; she imagined she could feel one tiny foot land a solid kick. "Not you, too!" she cried miserably.

Jessica appeared for dinner as she'd promised. Although she looked a bit wan and her usual sleek hairdo was a bit askew, her joy at having her son home for Christmas had put a bloom in her cheeks. In honor of Moss's arrival (or so she said, but Billie thought it was more to keep her own hostess gown from looking out of place), Jessica was wearing a long, simply tailored dress with a delicate ruching of antique lace at the cuffs and a diamond brooch at the neck. It was violet, one of Billie's favorite shades, and although the style was a bit dated the velvet was still soft and lustrous.

Moss hovered near his mother's side, offering her a small glass of sherry. "Not for me, thank you, dear, but perhaps Billie could do with a drop."

Before Moss could ask Billie, Seth interjected, "Might improve her appetite! Little gal eats like a bird, mealtimes certainly can't account for..." His eyes flicked over Billie in embarrassment.

Billie flushed uneasily, feeling the color swim to the roots of her hair. Moss said, "Billie, what's this I hear about your finicky appetite? Don't you know you're supposed to be eating for two?"

At that moment, Agnes made her entrance in the doorway. "Like Seth says, she only nibbles at the table. Maybe she's got a hoard of chocolates under her bed." Her remark was softened by her presenting her cheek to Moss and welcoming him home. "I was in town when you arrived. Last-minute shopping. You look fit, Moss, but then you always do."

If Moss had been startled by the change in Billie's appearance, he was astounded by Agnes. The only term that came to his mind was *chic*. Very, very chic. Sunbridge certainly agreed with the old girl. Only Moss wasn't so sure "old girl" fit this new Agnes Ames. She'd done something with her hair—it was upswept to reveal a still youthful, graceful neck and over her forehead tumbled risqué little curls. And hadn't she lost a few pounds, or was it only the slim, obviously expensive, silk dress she was wearing, long enough to be tasteful but short enough to show an elegant curve of leg? And what had she done with those sensible shoes she'd always worn? These open-toed high heels didn't belong to the Agnes he'd known in Philadelphia.

"You're the one who's fit, Agnes. You're stunning!"

Billie lowered her eyes but not before Jessica saw the pain in them. Moss should be complimenting his wife, telling her how beautiful she was to him as she carried their child. "Shouldn't we go into dinner, dear?" she asked Seth. "Tita must have everything ready to serve."

"Billie hasn't had her sherry," Seth countered, preferring to remain here in the living room, enjoying the drama taking place. He avoided his wife's glance. Let Aggie have her moment of glory, he thought. Moss was right; she was a stunning woman. He couldn't wait for Christmas morning when she opened his gift.

Moss handed Billie a tiny cordial glass of sherry and sat down beside her, his arm on the back of the sofa behind her. "Having a rough time of it, honey? You never said in your letters."

"I'm exhibiting every classic symptom of pregnancy and then some." Billie tried for lightness. Moss would find self-pity unbearable. "I've missed you so much," she whispered when he leaned over to kiss her cheek. The baby suddenly fluttered and she quickly placed her hand over her middle. "This child has a kick like a mule!"

Tenderly, Moss's hand followed Billie's and a look of wonderment came into his eyes. "Riley Seth Coleman, you're giving your mommy a hard time. You're going to deserve that slap the doctor puts on your bottom." Heads together, Billie cuddled against her husband, craving this tender support and love.

"Hurry up with that sherry, Billie. You heard what Jessica said. Tita has everything ready and Moss could use a good meal under his ribs." Seth broke the moment. His expression was intense, as though he were silently trying to convey a message to Moss.

"There's no romance about you, Pap." Moss laughed uneasily, taking his arm from around Billie and helping her to her feet. "You're right about the meal, though. Sea rations and powdered eggs were never my favorites."

Billie could have wept (tears came so easily these days). Why did there have to be so many people about? Why couldn't she have a minute alone with her husband?

"Why don't you ladies go into the dining room?" Seth suggested, hanging back with Moss. "Did you forget what I told you this morning?" he hissed as the others exited. "I don't want anyone taking chances with my grandson, not even you! Don't think for a minute I didn't know you were trading yourself off when you had yourself reassigned. A bargain is a bargain, son, and a Coleman stands by his word."

"Moss, Seth, where are you two?" Jessica's voice carried through the hall. "Come in here and eat."

After dinner, when they had all congregated once again in the spacious living room, Seth tried to spirit Moss away into the study but Jessica wouldn't allow it. "Now, Seth, don't be greedy with Moss's company. We still haven't heard how he got his hamburger."

"Meatball, Mam, and I'm proud to say there are five of them on my fuselage. I don't know whether you know it, but the Big E saw action in the Solomon Islands after Guadalcanal." Moss sat beside Billie, taking her hand in his.

"Kingsley was the guy who made marks that day," Moss told them. "He was on a predawn strike force and was the first to sight a Japanese transport, but he was reaching the point of no return—that's when you've got just barely enough fuel to get back to mother, I mean the carrier. Anyway, he didn't get a chance to do any shooting. He was ordered back to the ship, but the positions he gave were good enough to blast the Japs to the bottom. Tough break for Thad."

"Hrmmph!" Seth punctuated. "Watch your step, son. This Yankee seems eager to me and likely to get ahead of you."

"So you said." Moss's tone was sour. "Pap, when I talk about Thad it's like I'm talking about myself. That's how proud I am of him. He's a good man, isn't he, Billie? Like Billie says, she danced with him at our wedding."

"Where's he from, this Yankee? Who's his family? What do they do?"

"Pap, I'm not Amelia out on her first date. You don't have to put my friends through the inquisition. Don't forget, I'm a big boy. Billie'll tell you, won't you, honey?"

Billie didn't like Moss putting her on the firing line with Seth. Besides, it was ridiculous to think that anything she could say would convince Seth of anything. After all, she was only "that little gal" to the patriarch. Agnes seemed to be the only woman whose opinion counted.

Jessica decided to retire early. The excitement of Moss's homecoming had proved to be a strain. "It's wonderful to have you home, Moss. I wish it were for good." There was a sadness in her eyes that went beyond worry for a soldier son at war.

Moss clasped Jessica's hand to his chest and leaned down to kiss her powdery cheek. "Someday it will be, Mam. Everything will be the way it used to be, only better. Have a good night and I'll come in to see you in the morning."

"I'll go up with you, Jessica," Billie offered, her gaze swinging to Moss. Surely after a few minutes he would follow.

After helping Jessica into her nightgown and tucking her into bed, Billie went to her room and gratefully removed her clothes. It was ironic that just months before she would have cheerfully died for a pair of silk stockings and now that they were a part of her daily wardrobe, she couldn't wait for evening to take them off. The garters cut into her thighs and her toes always felt squashed.

She ran a tub for a quick bath and donned one of the new nightgowns she'd purchased, topping it off with its matching peignoir of fine pale blue lace. Fondly she remembered sleeping nude with Moss or, at most, wearing one of his undershirts. The clinging cotton knit would never fit over her burgeoning belly now. She whipped a brush through her hair until it crackled and applied just a touch of cologne to her throat, wrists, and between her breasts. Then she waited for Moss. And waited. And waited.

The bedside clock read two-thirty—she must have fallen

asleep. She remembered putting her head down on her pillow for just a minute. The lights were still on and she was chilled from sleeping in the cool room uncovered. Where was Moss?

Going to the door, she opened it, peering into a darkened hallway. There were no lights coming from downstairs. The house had been locked and closed for the night. Everyone had gone to bed. Where was Moss? Why hadn't he come to bed? Her attention focused on the room next to hers. Moss had moved into it when he'd started college, abandoning his boyhood room in the far wing. Not believing that he could be there, Billie tiptoed to the door, tapped softly, and then turned the knob. A shaft of light came from within. Moss was asleep on the single bed, book in hand, bedside lamp still burning.

Billie sank back against the wall, her hand pressed against her mouth to keep the cries from escaping. A hunger welled in her breast, coming from so deep within her that it brought actual pain in her need for him. Didn't he care how lonely she was, had been all this time without him? Closing the door, she stumbled back to her bed and flung herself across it. Disappointment was a physical ache. She was cast off, ugly and undesirable. All she wanted was to be beside him, be held in his arms, feel close to him. She wanted to feel loved, feel his body beside her, touch him, have him press tender kisses to her lips. Desolate, abandoned, forgotten, Billie clutched her pillow and silenced her sobs.

{{{{{{{{{ CHAPTER TEN }}}}}}}}}

When Billie dragged herself downstairs the next morning she bore the badges of sleeplessness beneath her eyes. Moss had already left his room when she peeped in, so she hoped to find him waiting for her downstairs. Tonight was Christmas Eve, her first Christmas with her husband, but the disappointment of the night before had cast a pall over the occasion. Moss's rejection burned, but she was determined to face him as though nothing had happened. As though her heart weren't broken.

The dining room was empty except for Tita, who was fussing at the serving board with dishes and trays. "Good morning, Tita. Where is everyone this morning?"

Tita knew that "everyone" meant Moss. Poor Señora Billie. "Your mother is in Señor Coleman's study calling the florist about something and Señora Jessica will stay upstairs until the party this evening. Señor Moss left early this morning with his father. They took the plane over to Corpus Christi, but they say they will be back in time for dinner."

"I'd almost forgotten about the party," Billie said, struggling to keep her voice steady. "What time did my husband leave?"

"Very early—perhaps he didn't want to wake you, señora. ... ." Tita avoided Billie's glance.

"Who'll be here tonight?" Billie asked, swallowing her vitamin capsules. She would have liked nothing more than to spend a quiet holiday with Moss, alone, with tender little touches and sweet caresses and whispers that promised more wonderful Christmases to come. Would she ever be alone with Moss again?

"Just the family for dinner and later a few friends drop in, nothing big, very simple," Tita said. "Everyone goes home early," she added reassuringly.

"Is there anything I can do to help? Back home, Mother and I used to bake cookies and—make ..." Her words faltered. Those days seemed a lifetime ago.

"You can see if Señora Jessica has last-minute wrapping to do, and maybe you can have lunch with her. Then you make yourself pretty for the party, *sí*?"

Pretty. As though she'd ever be pretty again. "*Sí*," Billie answered listlessly.

Billie took a lunch tray up to Jessica's room and they ate together. Afterward, she took a long bath and lay down for a nap. Outside the window, the wild Texas wind howled, pushing against the house, finding cracks and chinks in the siding to whistle through. Twilight came so early this time of year, daylight deepening to a dark gray and then quickly to blackness. There were no streetlamps, of course, no uptown buzz of last-minute Christmas shoppers and endless holiday music. All that was forty miles away, in Austin. Billie's sense of abandonment and isolation increased as the day waned. She refused to think about the strong winds, which could affect Moss's flying home from Corpus Christi. She refused to think about anything at all as she lay on her bed and closed her eyes.

* * *

Moss followed Seth into the house, bringing with him a burst of frigid air. His wide-brimmed Stetson was glazed with frost, as was the sheepskin collar of his leather bombardier jacket, and there was a frown of frustration on his brow. Seth suggested a brandy in the study.

"Pap, that trip to Corpus Christi was unnecessary and you know it," he said, watching his father splash cognac into a snifter.

"Nonsense, no amount of attention to business is unnecessary. Can't let the men think I don't take an interest—they'd take advantage. Besides, with this dang war, it's hard to get help."

"The hell with the war," Moss muttered. "And you've still got the same old cowpokes driving that cattle as you always did. It's Christmas, Pap, a hell of a time to make an unexpected visit and take the men away from their families."

Seth's expression soured. "Don't go soft on me, boy. Those men have a job to do and I'm here to see they do it. Cattle still got to be fed and watered, don't they? If you hadn't run off to play soldier, you'd be here to help me."

The cognac slid down Moss's throat and warmed his belly. "I'm going up to change for dinner," he announced. His thoughts were on Billie. He wanted to see her. . . . There was an uneasy stirring in his loins.

"You've got plenty of time to change. I wanted to ask you what you thought of an idea I had. . . ."

"Not now, Pap. I'm tired and it was a hair-raising trip home. That wind must be blowing at thirty knots."

"We could've stayed in Corpus Christi," Seth muttered. "You were the one hot to get back here."

Moss drained his snifter and placed it on the table beside his chair. He was more than familiar with Seth's tug on his time and attention. But things had changed. Now it was more than a mother and sister he wanted to come home to; it was a young wife with a baby on the way. "You would've liked that, wouldn't you, Pap? Me and you staying over in Corpus."

"Damn right. Nothin goin' on here but a lot of women's foolishness. Parties, Christmas trees, bah!"

"Same old Scrooge." Moss laughed. "Remember the Christmas we were all supposed to go skiing and you sent Mam and Amelia on ahead of us and something came up so we never got there? I thought Mam's heart would break. They came rushing home here soon as they could, but by then the holidays were over and I was on my way back to school. For the life of me, Pap, I'll never understand how Mam put up with you all these years." Actually, Moss was thinking more about Amelia's disappointments than about his mother's. Amelia would've walked through fire for Seth if he'd just whistled. He never had. There were times when Moss felt guilty about the attention and affection their father showered on him. If Amelia wasn't such a good person, it would have created profound jealousy. But Moss knew her love for him was almost as great as her need for Seth's love.

"Jess puts up with me the same way that little Yankee gal will put up with you," Seth told him. "Have another drink."

"No more, Pap. I'm going upstairs to my wife. You just reminded me how hard we Colemans are on our women."

"Remember what I said, boy. Keep your pants zipped. I don't want anything going wrong for my grandson."

Wearily, Moss left the study and lifted himself up the long staircase, his boots noiseless on the thick carpeting. First he'd go see Jessica and then Billie. He worried about both of them—neither looked well. Jessica was tired and wan and Billie was bloated and sick. Poor Billie. She should be wearing pretty dresses and going to dances. Right now she should be enrolled in Penn State and looking forward to Christmas vacation instead of teetering around on swollen feet, balancing a pregnant belly. And then to be uprooted and sent all the way here to Texas, away from everything familiar . . . Christ! It was a wonder she didn't hate him.

Jessica was sleeping soundly when Moss peered in and he quietly closed the door so as not to disturb her. He worried about his mother but it was a concern that was somehow free of responsibility. With Billie, it was different.

When he opened Billie's door he saw that the curtains had been drawn and she was on the bed, lying on her side, a pillow propped between her knees to take the strain from her back. As he came nearer, he could see her face, full and round and still so pretty. Her mouth was soft and gentle but there was a pucker between her brows. Had he put it there? A stray blond curl rested against her cheek, accentuating the unhealthy flush. As his hand reached out to touch it, to smooth it away, his heart reached out for her.

Billie's eyes opened at his touch and he was gratified by

the slow, sleepy smile she bestowed on him. No, she didn't hate him, and somehow that wrenched his conscience. So young, so pretty, so very pregnant. And all for a debt, a payoff for his freedom.

Slipping out of his boots, he climbed onto the high bed beside her, taking her into his arms. She rested her head on his shoulder, throwing her arm over his chest. He could feel the heat from her body, the press of her breasts against his side, fuller and more womanly than he remembered. The intrusion of her rounded girth lay between them. He could smell the freshness of her hair, feel its softness against his lips. If he closed his eyes, he could almost believe this was the same Billie he'd met in Philadelphia—golden and pretty, fresh and unspoiled.

Billie lifted her chin, nuzzling his neck and kissing his jaw, her hands moving over him passionately, encouragingly. "I won't make love to you, Billie. I don't want to hurt you or the baby," he told her, softening his rejection with a kiss.

"*This* is loving," she whispered, hiding her disappointment. Pregnancy had changed her needs; physical lovemaking was no longer one of them. But it would have been nice to know he still wanted her. Perhaps he still did and it really was only his concern for her that held him back. Her hand slipped to his waist and then smoothed over his hip to his thighs. "Touch me, Moss. Touch my breast," she said, gratified by the signal of desire beneath her exploring hand.

"Billie," he murmured, his lips lost in her hair, "don't do this. Just let me hold you. That's all I want." Pap's warning was pounding in his brain.

"Your body is saying other things, Moss." She worked his belt and fumbled with the zipper. "There are so many ways to make love—you taught me yourself. Don't you remember?" His breath caught in his throat as her fingers made contact with his naked flesh. "You want me to, don't you, Moss? You want me to touch you like this. Don't you?" Her voice was deep and seductive and her lips were nuzzling his chin and intruding into the warmth beneath his collar. "Touch me. Touch me here." She leaned into him, disregarding the child who lay between them, sliding his hand down the firm globe of her belly to the place where her thighs met.

Moss's determinations and resolutions were fading quickly. She was right; there were many ways of making love and he would explore them all. Her body was exciting him; different, yet the same. She was fuller, warmer, strangely exotic. . . . Let Pap be damned!

Agnes, Jessica, and Seth waited around the Christmas tree for Moss and Billie. Agnes nervously fingered her strand of almost good pearls, and Jessica desperately attempted to keep a conversation going. Both women were all too aware of Seth's glowering anger. "What's keeping those two?" he asked impatiently. "That boy knows I like to sit down to dinner at exactly six o'clock. We'll hardly have time to eat before our friends start arriving!" He was drinking, not sipping, corn whiskey and he paced with agitation, leaning more heavily than usual on his cane.

"Seth, the children will be down. They just want to spend some time together, that's all," Jessica said soothingly. Despite her husband's annoyance she was happy for Billie. That's all the child needed, her husband's attention and comfort.

Agnes was not so charitable. Her fears ran along the same vein as Seth's. She should have said something to Billie, warned her of the possible danger to the baby, but she never thought that Moss would be romantically inclined in the face of Billie's full-blown pregnancy.

"Aggie," Seth growled, "you go upstairs and get that daughter of yours. Now!"

"That's not necessary, Pap," Moss said smoothly as he led Billie into the living room. "Here's our little mother-to-be, the hope of the Coleman clan." The sharpness of his glance covered the distance between himself and his father. Seth read it correctly. Moss was warning Pap that he'd better be careful how his wife was treated. Consideration and respect, and nothing less would do.

Billie was entirely unaware of the others' emotions. Her cheeks were flushed pink and there was a softness in her hazel eyes like that of a contented cat. A cat who'd spent the night on the back fence with her mate.

Seth turned away, slapping his glass down on an end table with an angry clatter. Moss wore the grin of a little boy.

Jessica sighed, rubbing her temples. Years of practice told her she must be the one to ease the situation if they were to have a pleasant dinner. "Moss, dear, we were waiting for you and Billie so we could each open one present from one another before we go in to eat. This is Christmas. Let's not be glum." Her last statement was for Seth.

"Holy bejesus, Jess! We'll hardly have time to swallow our beans before the Richardsons get here and you know I hate to rush when I eat. It sticks in a lump and takes me two days to get rid of it."

"Moss, why don't you give Billie her present?" Jessica said, ignoring her husband's complaints. "Billie, you go sit near the tree. I want Moss to use my camera to take pictures of us all." A disgruntled snort erupted from Seth. "You look so pretty tonight, Billie. Is that one of the new dresses you bought in Austin?"

Billie turned gracefully, modeling her long full dress. It was dark navy georgette with a square white sailor collar trimmed in red. "I was thinking if I had to be a navy wife, I should look the part," she told Jessica brightly.

"She looks terrific, doesn't she, Mam?" Moss said proudly, disregarding another snort from Seth.

For the next few minutes torn wrapping paper littered the living room. Billie squealed with pleasure when she opened Moss's present. A Chinese silk wrapper and tiny matching heeled slippers. Laughing, she slipped it over her shoulders and brought the front edges together. "I'll save it for after the baby," she announced, demonstrating how the protuberance of her belly prevented it from closing. Only last night she would have been overcome with self-consciousness and embarrassment about her size. But since this afternoon and Moss's ardent loving, she was accepting the changes in herself because he could. *That* was a gift more precious and valuable than any other.

For Jessica there was a carton from England, from Amelia, and inside was a delicate bone china tea service and a letter.

Seth received his usual box of cigars and bottle of bourbon and Moss had brought him an ornamental bridle for old Nessie. Seth presented Jessica with a $2,000 voucher in her name for her favorite charity, the March of Dimes. It was a tradition that had begun several years ago, after Seth had complained that buying a present for Jessica was harder than roping a wild steer in a blind canyon. Seth handed Agnes a long, slim box carefully wrapped in bright paper. He stood by while she fumbled with the ribbon. "For Christ's sake, Aggie, just rip it open. My beans are gettin' cold!"

It was a jeweler's box and inside was a twenty-four-inch

strand of perfectly matched pearls. Agnes's hands trembled when she lifted them out of their nest.

"Don't go saying you can't accept them, Aggie. Can't have the grandmother of my first grandchild going around wearing dimestore jewelry. And since you're so partial to pearls I thought you should have them."

Billie looked from the gleaming rope of her mother's gift to Jessica, who attempted a smile. The old bastard, thought Billie. She was very glad that she'd bought the antique silver picture frame to give to Jessica. It had a place for a portrait of herself and Moss, and one that waited to be filled with one of the baby. Certainly it could never compensate for Seth's thoughtlessness, but it was an acknowledgment that Jessica would be the baby's grandmother, too.

Agnes was overwhelmed by Seth's generosity, but her poise and polish made it appear that she was merely accepting what was due her. That seemed to rattle Seth. "Put them on, Aggie! I told you my beans are getting cold. What're you waiting for?"

A slow smile touched Agnes's lips. "I'm not so certain I like the idea of you thinking about my neck, Seth," she told him sharply.

"Take it easy, Aggie. If I ever want your neck on a chopping block, I'll give you fair notice. Put them on, dammit, and let's eat!"

The pearls slid over Agnes's head and rested on the cranberry velvet of her cocktail dress like twenty-four inches of smiling teeth.

That night, after the traditional Christmas Eve dinner, after the friends had gone home and all the presents had been opened, Moss slept in Billie's bed, holding her, caressing her, and allowing the drinks he'd consumed to overpower Seth's warning again. This was his wife and she was offering herself to him, consoling him for the time he'd gone without a woman, being the essence of womanhood when she welcomed his flesh into hers.

Christmas morning, when the first rays of daylight invaded the room, Moss awakened to the sound of Billie's pitiful retching in the adjoining bath. Hastily, he grabbed up his clothes and escaped to his room. Christ! What if he'd hurt her last night? What if it was all too much for her? He should have listened to Pap.

Two hours later, at the breakfast table, Billie was pale and weak, yet bravely making the best of it. But Moss was unable to look into her shadow-rimmed eyes any longer. He made the announcement that he had checked with San Diego, and he was ordered back at once. Billie's fork clattered onto her dish. Seth was appalled by Moss's statement, which he didn't believe for one second. He was leaving because of *her*! Billie glanced up at her father-in-law. His eyes hated her.

On February fourth, Billie began her labor. A private ambulance was dispatched on Seth's excited phone call. Billie was trundled into the back of the vehicle and a nurse held her hand. Agnes and Seth followed the ambulance in the chauffeur-driven Packard. Jessica watched the ambulance and Packard leave, her rosary clutched tightly in her hand. At that moment she didn't know whom she'd feel sorrier for, Billie or Seth. Billie, if the baby was a girl, Seth, if he should be disappointed.

Billie had fourteen hours of agony. Until the moment the mask came down over Billie's perspiring face she prayed for death, anything to take away the relentless pain. . . .

When Billie opened her eyes the first person she saw was Seth Coleman. He stared down at her accusingly. Her mother stood next to him with a judgmental look on her face. So, she had delivered a girl! Jessica would be pleased. Moss would be . . . Moss would be disappointed. She had failed. She wasn't a Coleman yet. Not yet, Seth's eyes told her. Should she apologize? They were waiting for her to say something, probably to ask about the baby. Instead she closed her eyes and slept. Deeply.

Later, on the ride back to Sunbridge, Agnes realized that she had never seen Seth so angry, so controlled. She understood perfectly. Perhaps too perfectly. Her own position—and Billie's too, of course—was in jeopardy until there was a Coleman heir. Good God, if something happened to Moss, Billie and she could be shipped back to Philadelphia without a moment's notice or a backward glance.

Striving for a light tone, Agnes said, "First pregnancies are usually hard on a young girl. Billie is young and healthy. Living at Sunbridge will put the bloom back in her cheeks. She'll be right as rain in a month. In three months she'll be ready to try again."

Seth hardly acknowledged Agnes's words. A damn baby girl, for God's sake! Moss was going to be fit to be tied. It should have been a boy; he'd depended on it being a boy. It was part of the bargain. Seth sank lower into the backseat of the Packard and gritted his teeth. That little gal Moss had taken for a wife had no more spunk and grit than Jessica. Sure, he'd hit pay dirt with Moss, but Jessica had failed him after that, first producing Amelia, then drying up completely and forever. Agnes had said something about three months and they could try again. That would be around the beginning of May. Three months to arrange for Billie and Moss to be together again.

When Jessica heard the news that her first grandchild was a girl, she stared down at the rosary in her hands. A girl, a little girl, just like her Amelia. Seth must be in a rage because this was something over which he had no control. She almost cried with relief that the child wasn't a boy. Seth's possessiveness could be a little boy's undoing. She threw her rosary beads angrily onto the bed. It was one of the few violent outbursts she'd ever experienced, and she was surprised at how good, how right it felt. Perhaps if she'd given vent to her anger all these years, she wouldn't have these terrible headaches and her heart wouldn't thump so madly in her breast.

Moss climbed from the cockpit of the Texas Ranger. As was his custom, he patted the plane fondly, the way a man might touch his woman. Less than a week before he'd fought in the battle of Rennell Island, the last of the Guadalcanal campaign. The heat of the victory still ran in his blood.

Two more meatballs would be added to the eight already on Moss's fuselage. He'd be asked to command his own squadron, to train his men, instill them with confidence. Well, he was ready. He'd had the best teachers, known the best men. He'd seen battle and smelled its hell, known victory and felt its elation.

The flight deck officer was running toward him. "Coleman, the chaplain wants to see you. Pronto!" It was in such contradiction to his train of thought that Moss's belly immediately constricted. Something was wrong, very wrong. Gut fear propelled his feet, his mind racing as fast as he ran. Seth? Billie? Jessica? But no way, no matter what it was, would he leave the Big E. He was being assigned to command his own squadron, things were turning up for him, things he wanted, needed. He wasn't going home until this was over, one way or the other, whether he walked through the door of Sunbridge under his own steam or was carried in in a box.

His salute was snappy, his words crisply spoken. "Lieutenant Moss Coleman reporting, sir."

"At ease, Lieutenant." The chaplain smiled. Freckled hands extended to give Moss the slip of paper from the radio room.

Moss read the message, a grin stretching across his face. A baby girl, Margaret Jessica Coleman. February fourth. Four pounds, three ounces. Mother and daughter both fine. Jesus, he was a father! Two months early! Billie was fine. His sigh of relief sounded loud in his ears.

A knock sounded on the office door and Captain Hardison stepped in, extending his hand to Moss. "Congratulations, Coleman. I was in the radio room when the message came through." He reached into his breast pocket and withdrew three cylinders, fondling them reverently before extending one to the chaplain and one to Moss. "I filched these from Admiral Halsey's private stock when we were in Pearl. If you tell anyone, I'll clip your wings, and as for you, Father, you will keep to the confidentiality of confession. Agreed? Pure Havana—I've been saving them for a special occasion. Think of me when you smoke it, Lieutenant."

Moss saluted. "I'll do that, sir." It wasn't until he was back in his own quarters with the cigar clamped between his teeth that he took a second look at the radio message. A girl! What the hell, a baby was a baby. There'd still be time for boys. Pap was probably belly up over the disappointment. He took a satisfying pull on the cigar, blue smoke ringing his head, then almost laughed. Agnes had been so certain that the baby would be a boy. "You were wrong, you old buzzard," he said aloud. He was the littlest bit disgruntled about it himself, but his delight over what he imagined was Agnes's chagrin was compensation. "Aggie, old girl, you've got to learn we Colemans are a slippery bunch. Very slippery indeed."

Billie returned to Sunbridge ten days after the birth of her daughter. Dr. Ward's dire warnings against another pregnancy too soon had darkened her day. She hadn't even considered having another child, suffering another nine months, swelling and vomiting and aching her way through another year. Seth was hell-bent on having a grandson. But boy or girl, it didn't matter to Moss, did it? Maggie was a beautiful baby, a little too small from being born prematurely, but she was healthy enough to be allowed to go home. Still, Billie hadn't liked the expression on the doctor's face or the technical language he'd used. Toxemia, low birth weight, breech presentation—it was all too much to understand but it left her with the feeling that whatever had gone wrong was her own fault. She still wasn't a Coleman woman, to have her children on the side of the road and run back to work, and perhaps she never would be. Dr. Ward's words made her afraid. At the same time, he had presented a challenge.

A private ambulance brought Billie and Maggie the forty miles out from Austin and she walked to the front door under her own power. When she reached out for Maggie, the nurse Seth had hired shook her head and cradled the baby protectively in her arms.

"I want to take Maggie upstairs and present her to her grandmother," Billie explained. If she spoke as though Maggie had only one grandmother, it was what she was feeling. Jessica's phone conversations twice a day to the hospital had been loving and her inquiries about Maggie sincere and enthusiastic. Now Billie wanted to proudly take Maggie up to Jessica's room and be gratified by grandmotherly croonings.

"I'll take the baby now," Billie said more forcefully, meeting the nurse's stare.

Agnes, who had followed the ambulance in the family automobile, came forward. "Don't be ridiculous, Billie. For all you know, Jessica is sound asleep. You're behaving like a child. The nurse has her instructions and you're not to interfere." For a moment, Agnes thought Billie would stand her ground. A warning bell went off in Agnes's head: Billie might very well become difficult and totally unlike the respectful, obedient daughter she'd always been. Until she'd met Moss, Agnes qualified. Before Billie could argue, Agnes touched her arm solicitously.

"There will be plenty of time to spend with the baby, Billie. You're still not completely recovered from the whole ordeal. Until you get your strength back, why don't you just rely upon me to know what's best."

Agnes's gentle caring penetrated Billie's reserve and she felt herself slipping back into the old rhythms of following her mother's directions. She was tired and still sore and cried easily. Dr. Ward said it was natural for a woman to feel depressed after the birth of a child. And it was just easier to have someone else make the decisions.

Settled back in her room, Billie rested in bed. She'd written Moss about the baby, describing Maggie's shock of nearly black hair and telling him that it was already obvious her eyes would be the same clear light blue as his. But what else could she tell Moss about their daughter when she hardly saw her? Little Margaret Jessica Coleman was at the other end of the house in her pretty little nursery with her own nurse in attendance. On Dr. Ward's suggestion, probably orders issued from Seth, Maggie was to be bottle-fed. The doctor's words—"You're hardly strong enough, Mrs. Coleman"—echoed in her head. Something else in which she was lacking. She felt fine now, even if a little tired, and her breasts beneath the agonizing breast binder were heavy with milk.

Reaching into her bedside table, Billie withdrew the stationery she'd received from Agnes at Christmas. Her name was engraved at the top: Mrs. Moss Coleman. Tears threatened. Whatever had happened to Billie Ames? She felt as though she'd been swallowed whole and was being digested as permanently and efficiently as Seth's favorite beans.

The bedroom door opened and Agnes came into Billie's room. "Darling, are you writing to Moss? That's good. Seth and I were worried about your lackadaisical attitude these past few days. Now that you're on the mend your life is going to be just wonderful. Aren't you ever so grateful that there is a nurse for Maggie? Why, when I had you I would have cut off my right arm for just a *little* help. Babies are so draining and they do prevent one from regaining one's strength. I also think it was very wise of Dr. Ward to start Maggie on bottles. There's nothing more loathsome for a woman than pulling out her breast for a baby to guzzle. Seth agrees.

"Billie, you are so lucky. I do hope you appreciate all of the help the Colemans are giving you. If we were back in Philadelphia, we'd both be worn to a frazzle. Now, with all of these tedious chores taken off your hands, you can concentrate on regaining your strength and getting back to normal. You never know—Moss could get leave, just like that." With this she snapped her fingers and then, in a rare moment of affection, bent over and kissed Billie on the cheek.

"We're going to have such wonderful times, Billie. As soon as you're on your feet, I'll take you to all the clubs and organizations Seth feels we should belong to. I've made some lovely friends and everyone is dying to meet you. You have to do it, darling, for Jessica's sake. That's what the Coleman women do, you know. *We* do the social scene while the men harvest the money. It's such a wonderful tradition."

"Mother, have you seen Maggie?"

"Of course I have. Everyone has seen the ... the little darling. Why, I peeked into the nursery just moments ago and she was sleeping soundly. The nurse is preparing her bottle right now. Canned milk and Karo syrup. Jessica is waiting in her room to be allowed to feed her. The nurse felt it would be better if you stayed here in your room. Just for a few more days. You have to take things slow at first. Trays will be sent up."

"Mother, I'm not an invalid. All I did was have a baby. Millions of women have babies. Why can't I go downstairs to dinner? Why do I have to have a tray? Is Seth so upset he can't look at me?" she said bitterly. "I know I spoiled his grand plans by having a girl instead of a boy."

Agnes stiffened. "Now that's enough of that kind of talk. I don't ever want to hear anything like that again. You're a Coleman now and it's time you were properly appreciative. It's the stairs, Billie. You can't keep going up and down. Not for a while yet. Those are Dr. Ward's orders. Seth had nothing to do with that, for heaven's sake. How could you think such a thing?"

Billie leaned back in the chair. She had forgotten the steps. They had been a chore to climb. So what if she had to stay up here for another week or so—at least she could walk down the hall to see Maggie. She could read to Jessica, and they could talk for hours about the baby and the delivery. She could write to Moss every day and tell him of Maggie's progress. As soon as possible she would have a picture taken and send it along. Moss could carry it in his wallet and show his friends. But would he? Seth would never brag about a daughter; of that she was sure. Would Moss? She had to admit she didn't know.

"I think I'll take a nap and then write to Moss. I'm rather tired, Mother." It was a dismissal and Agnes was grateful. They didn't have much to say to each other.

An hour later Billie realized she didn't need sleep. She settled herself in the chair by the window, her writing pad on her knee. It struck her suddenly how alone she was. Maggie was being taken care of. Agnes was off doing only God knew what—plowing the south forty, for all she knew. Her husband, dear, sweet, wonderful Moss, was off fighting a war to make the world safe for her and Maggie.

Billie sat for a long time, staring at the blank pad on her knees. In the end she wrote a trite, newsy little letter that told none of her true feelings. What would Moss think of her if she said she didn't care for his father? How could she tell him of the look in his father's eyes when she'd come out of the anesthetic? Moss didn't need or want to hear that sort of thing.

Little Maggie, as we call her, is doing fine. Nurse Jenkins seems to think she's a bit ahead of herself, gobbling down six bottles a day. She sleeps constantly, as do all babies. I rarely hear her cry because the nursery is down at the end of the hall, and anyway I think Nurse Jenkins picks her up as soon as she even whimpers. She does go through an exorbitant amount of didies. Tita is going to have her hands full with laundry. Mother said your father will get someone in to do Maggie's laundry. Isn't that generous of him?

I labored for almost fifteen hours, but I'm fine now, and pounds lighter. When you see me next I plan to look like the girl you left behind. The only difference will be that that girl is now a young mother. I hope you're pleased with the name we gave her.

The war news hasn't improved. I listen to it every chance I get, and I read the papers cover to cover every day. Please, Moss, take care of yourself, and when you have time, think of Maggie and me because we're here loving you.

How I treasure those few days we had at Christmas. If only it could have been longer. I'm not complaining; it's just that I miss you so.

Your mother sends her love. She's been talking about Amelia a lot of late. Before I went to the hospital we spent one entire afternoon looking at baby pictures of you and Amelia. She really does miss your sister. I wish I could meet her. Your mother seems to think that we would get on well together.

Darling Moss, I must close for now. I want to check on Maggie and it's almost time for dinner. I thought I would have mine with your mother this evening on my first night home. I guess it is my home now that Maggie's here, but in the beginning I rather felt like a visitor. Having Maggie seems to make me permanent, if you know what I mean.

All my love to you, Moss. Please write when you can.

Love, Billie

Billie sealed the letter and put an airmail stamp on the envelope. She wondered when Moss would get it. There had been no mail from him for over two weeks. Perhaps tomorrow. I'll say an extra prayer, she thought, and couldn't help wondering if Seth had heard from his son. She had shared her letters with him and Jessica, but Seth had not shown her the same courtesy. She hadn't wanted to make an issue of it and so had remained quiet, but it seemed so unfair. Didn't he know how worried and upset she was? And whom was she fooling about being permanent and belonging? At best she was merely tolerated. In a sense the baby did make a difference, but Maggie was a girl. Seth Coleman wanted a grandson.

Doctor's orders or not, she was going to take a shower and wash her hair. What harm could it do? And she would feel so much cleaner and better than with a sponge bath and talcum powder. She'd lock the bedroom door and the one to the bathroom. Who would know? Who would care, really?

The thick steak staring up at Billie made her gulp. Jessica's light salad and small dessert of Jello-O was more appealing. Billie picked guiltily, knowing she should be grateful for the meat. Back in Philadelphia her friends would have given anything for a steak like this one. Tita removed the heavy dinner almost intact. Jessica smiled as she poured the coffee from a handsome silver urn.

"Now tell me, child, how bad was it?"

"Bad. But it's over now."

"Billie, giving birth is the most wonderful experience in the world. We've been so fortunate. True, there is pain, but it's the most easily forgotten kind. Once you see that little pink or blue bundle, nothing else matters. Don't you agree?"

Billie knew what she was supposed to say. But to forget fourteen long hours of the most excruciating misery known to woman! And that pink bundle. Perhaps if she had been able to hold Maggie after the delivery, she might feel as Jessica did, but it had been three days before Maggie had been brought to her because of the baby's low birth weight. Still, pleasing Jessica and being agreeable was so much easier than telling the truth. Besides, Jessica didn't want to hear unpleasant facts. She was living her life within the four walls of this room, sheltered from unpleasantness and stress. Seth had said Jessica was to remain calm at all costs. So she forced herself to meet Jessica's eyes and took a deep breath.

"Yes," she lied.

"She's beautiful, Billie," Jessica went on enthusiastically. "So healthy-looking, despite how little she is, and all that hair! I'm sure Moss is delighted. Seth said he sent word to the *Enterprise*. I expect we'll be hearing from Moss any day now. I pray that we do every day. At least you'll never have to worry about Maggie going off to war. Good girls always stay near their mothers."

Billie sipped her coffee. Good girls? Did that mean she didn't consider Amelia to be a good girl?

"In England, Jessica, the women are doing their bit. I've been reading about it. They're so brave. The whole thing is just so terrible. While I was in the hospital I read—" Billie bit her tongue. What she had read would be considered upsetting to the frail Jessica. A young woman had been driving an ambulance with four wounded men inside and they'd been bombed right off the road. Only bits and pieces of the bodies were found. No, that surely would upset Jessica, with Amelia in England. Maggie was the only safe topic of conversation, or the weather. Mentioning Agnes always brought a tightening of Jessica's lips.

"I just wrote Moss a letter telling him all about Maggie," Billie said. "That reminds me. Can you recommend a good photographer to come and take her picture? I want to send it to Moss."

"Seth has already taken care of that, Billie. A photographer will come out when Maggie is christened next week."

"Christened? Next week? I suppose I'll be up to it, but I'm not sure about any of my clothes fitting me. My goodness, so soon?"

"Billie, there's nothing to fret about. Seth and Agnes will take care of everything. Besides, the mother doesn't go to the church. It's not going to be an event. A simple christening with some pictures taken. A sit-down dinner for a few of our closest friends. That's all there is to it. Maggie will of course wear the same christening dress that Moss and Amelia wore. I was very careful about preserving it when I packed it away. The laundress will see that it is cleaned and each tiny ruffle ironed to perfection. You don't have to concern yourself about these details."

But I want to! Billie almost screamed. She couldn't go to the church? It was unthinkable. She was going to miss her own baby's christening? Well, we'll just see about that!

"Billie, what is it? What's wrong?" Jessica asked anxiously.

With great effort, Billie forced herself to speak quietly. "I would like to do these things. I want to go to the church to see Maggie christened. She's my first child. How can I write Moss about it if I'm not there?"

"Darling child, this is the way we do things here. You're going to have to get used to it. You're a Coleman now and you have to accept our ways. That's why Moss sent you to us. I think you're overly tired and it *is* your first day at home. Tomorrow you'll realize that Seth is more than capable of handling all these matters. Your mother is helping—or will help, if she's needed. Moss expects it."

And that was the last word.

Billie held her tears in check when she bent down to kiss Jessica good night. "I'll go by the nursery and check on Maggie before I turn in for the evening."

Jessica hated to do it and she practically bit her tongue to make the words come out right. "Why don't you wait for morning, Billie. I'm sure the nurse has settled Maggie for the night and you might wake her. Routine. Nurses always have such strict routines."

"Is that the same as telling me the nurse won't allow me in the nursery to see my own baby?" Billie asked in a trembling voice.

"I'm afraid so, Billie. If the door is closed, it stays closed."

Jessica ached to gather Billie close to her, to pat her head and tell her everything would be fine. Lately, though, she'd begun to have the feeling she wouldn't always be here to comfort Billie. Mollycoddling, as Seth called it. The sooner Billie learned and accepted that things were done the "Coleman way," the better it would be for her. There was little sense in spurring the child into rebellion. Jessica drew her rosary from her dressing gown pocket, leaned her head back against the chair, and closed her eyes. There were cruel lessons that Billie would learn, the same lessons she'd had to learn herself. And for what? To end up a woman old before her time, sitting alone in her room with every unfought and unfinished battle still tearing at her heart. No, it would be easier in the long run if Billie became a true Coleman: hard, greedy, and selfish. Otherwise she'd have to run away, just as Amelia did. Just as she was doing herself.

Billie fled the room. Her eyes went down the endless hallway to the nursery door. It was closed. Her shoulders slumped as she entered her own room and locked the door behind her. She wasn't used to closed doors; she hated them. Tears rolled down her cheeks as she picked up the letter to Moss and held it close to her heart. It didn't bring him any closer.

Maggie was three months old the day Seth entered Sunbridge by the kitchen door, his weathered face wreathed in smiles. He'd just come from the Cattlemen's Club.

"You look like someone just handed you their prize bull," Agnes said as she poured herself a cup of coffee. "Would you like a cup? I just sent Tita up with tea for Jessica."

"My news is a damn sight better than getting a prize bull. I just got a call from Washington: the *Enterprise* is coming into Pearl for repairs. My boy is safe and sound and we might be able to get some calls through and talk to him. They're due into Pearl on the eighth of May; that's four days away, Aggie. I'm going up to tell Jessica."

Agnes stared after Seth's retreating back. It was awesome how the Colemans got everything their way, but things had to be handled delicately, quietly. Billie was getting her back up these days about the smallest things. If she were to suspect for one minute that another pregnancy was being planned by her father-in-law and her mother, there was no telling what her reaction would be.

Billie would be delighted to go to Hawaii to see her husband, though. And when she returned, with any luck she'd be carrying the Coleman heir. And luck *would* be on their side. How could anything be simpler than letting nature take its course?

PART II

{{{{{{{ CHAPTER ELEVEN }}}}}}}

*Agnes stared out the multipaned window in her bedroom, sa-*voring the seemingly limitless expanse of Sunbridge. For months now she'd considered the homestead, as Seth called it, her own.

She had sailed into her duties with a capability that had stunned Seth. At first she'd merely been efficient, making the household revolve around him and his activities. She could tell he liked the way she did things and she anticipated his every need. Often, she wondered how close she'd come to spending the rest of her life wasting away in Philadelphia, becoming older and dowdier caring for a small house and boarders. The thought made her shiver with revulsion.

Seth found Agnes amenable and smart and often invited her along to luncheons at the Cattlemen's Club. The day he'd leaned across the table and asked her opinion on a matter, in full view and hearing of his friends and their wives, she'd enjoyed their astonishment. Seth Coleman had never been known to ask a woman the time of day, much less her opinion! That day had marked Agnes's total acceptance into Austin society. All she had to do now was sit back and reap the rewards. But no matter how efficient she was or how dependent Seth had become upon her, she accepted reality. She was dispensable. At least until Billie produced a male heir. And what better place to get the ball rolling than the paradise of Hawaii? Romance and baby making went hand in hand. Moss would be more than agreeable, especially once he saw this new, ripe Billie, more than a girl, just a shade less than a woman. How appealing! The urge to smack her lips was overwhelming.

A rolling tumbleweed danced across the front lawn. Agnes frowned. Now where had that come from? She pressed her face against the window to see where the offensive weed had landed and made a mental note to remind the gardener to search it out in the morning. Her eyes strayed heavenward to the early spring sky. Even the first stars of evening seemed bigger and brighter, the moon more silvery and round. Perhaps it was true that everything in Texas was bigger than life and better than anywhere else. She, for one, certainly believed it.

A muted cry filtered down the hall and was instantly hushed. The baby. Agnes's lips thinned to a hard line. Maggie Coleman. Thank the Lord for nurses and nannies. Billie would be able to go off to Hawaii and not have a care in the world. Money was such a marvelous thing.

A second, more piercing yowl shuddered down the hall. Agnes gave her head a little shake and left her room. Seth would be waiting for her in his study, and she'd be willing to bet that the man hadn't poured his own bourbon but was waiting for her to do the honors. It was now a ritual she rather enjoyed, feeling a certain little warm spurt of power in being the one to please him.

A smirk played around Seth's mouth as he watched Agnes walk toward him with his evening drink. The woman amazed him. Bourbon and branch water. He'd been dumbfounded the first time he'd seen her pour and swallow the beverage as if it were Coca-Cola. And she was probably the only woman in Texas who didn't mind his cigar smoke. Liked it, she'd said when he caught himself apologizing. A thick Havana cigar found its way to his mouth. He clipped the end and lit up. Old Aggie never gasped or sputtered or dabbed at her eyes. Once he'd tested her and had blown smoke directly at her. She'd sniffed and smiled and passed his test. And she knew it.

Right now, he sensed there was a bee buzzing around in Aggie's bonnet. He could almost hear the droning. He thought he knew what was on her mind, but so far, except for the day Maggie was born, it had remained unspoken. He decided to play her little game, hear her out, see how she'd handle him. He always enjoyed how Aggie went about things. Every day she learned something new, some new kind of maneuver, some devious little trick to get what she wanted. It pleased him that he was making her work for what he would have given her anyway. She was going to be rocked back on her hind end when she found out he had Billie's ticket to Hawaii in his desk drawer.

Seth downed his drink in one gulp and held out his glass for a refill. Agnes stared at it a moment and then shook her head. "That was a double I gave you. You know the doctor said one drink and one drink only. If you want another, you'll have to get it for yourself. I refuse to be a party to your destroying your health." Seth knew she meant it. He clamped his teeth down on his cigar and almost bit off the end. Women!

"There's tumbleweed in the front yard again."

"For Christ's sake, Aggie, this is Texas. Tumbleweeds are all over the place. If it bothers you that much, I'll speak to the gardener in the morning."

"I've already mentioned it to him," Agnes lied. She was in charge of the house and that included the front lawn as well.

"Did your daughter get a letter from my son today? Tita said she did. I waited all through lunch for Billie to mention it and when she didn't I thought maybe Tita was mistaken."

"I really don't know if Billie received a letter, Seth. I'll check with her when I go upstairs." Damn Billie. And damn that Tita, too. If she ever got the opportunity to fire her, she would. The woman knew too much about family business.

"Billie looks well," Agnes began, "don't you think? Dr. Ward has given her a clean bill of health and the go-ahead to resume all her activities." Agnes met Seth's speculative stare unblinkingly. "I was a little concerned for her during her pregnancy." She led into the question and let it lie there.

"Well?" Seth demanded impatiently. "Just how concerned are you for her now?" Damn woman, she liked to play games as much as he did.

"Oh, I'm not concerned at all. Why should I be? Nature takes care of itself, I always say. Why, just look how she's bloomed. She's not the young girl who first came to Sunbridge. There's something different. Perhaps it's maturity. She's more of a woman, if you know what I mean."

"Damn right I do," Seth said dryly. "I was thinking the same thing myself. 'Course, I never knew Billie when she wasn't feeling sick, but right now I'd say I could almost see why my son married her."

Agnes ignored the left-handed compliment. "The baby is gaining rapidly, especially for a premature birth. Now that she's on a rigid schedule she's eating and sleeping better. Nurse is very pleased. It's so nice to know that Billie doesn't have to tax her strength with middle-of-the-night feedings and all that goes with a new baby. And little Maggie is just remarkable."

"She's a Coleman, isn't she?" Seth said gruffly.

"Moss is going to be so pleased when he sees what motherhood has done for Billie. It would be so nice if they could get together. Christmas was almost a farce, you know. I'd hate to think that Moss could only remember what Billie looked like then. A pity he can't see her." Agnes drained the last of her bourbon. She might need another before this conversation was over.

"C'mon, Aggie, pour me another drink. What can it hurt? You're going to have another. How can you sit there and drink it in front of me?"

Aggie. It was said with affection. She could hear the tone, feel it. "All right, but if you tell that fool doctor, I'll deny it."

Seth winked conspiratorially and maneuvered the cigar from one side of his mouth to the other. He liked it when he had her on the run. So much for her worrying about destroying his health.

When she handed him the refill, Seth removed the soggy cigar from his lips. He swirled the amber liquid in his glass, staring at it as if mesmerized. Agnes watched him, hardly daring to breathe. She had his habits down pat, knew what he was going to say before he said it. In the end she always let him think it was his idea.

"Aggie, do you think the girl is up to a trip to Hawaii? It's barely three months, you know. Jessica never mended this quickly."

"Billie comes from hearty peasant stock. On her father's side," she added hastily. "I'm sure she's well enough. We can check with the doctor and Billie herself. Seth, how marvelous of you to think of this. Billie will be forever in your debt if you can arrange it. You can, can't you?" she asked anxiously.

"For my boy, anything. Billie, too," he added hastily. Agnes understood. She held up her glass and Seth did likewise.

"What shall we drink to?" Seth asked.

Agnes pretended to ponder the question. "What else but love?"

Seth almost choked on an inch of wet tobacco. "To love."

"To love," Agnes said, swallowing the remainder of her drink. For one wild, crazy moment she wondered if Seth were going to throw his glass into the fireplace and smash it to smithereens. She wished he would, so she could do the same. Instead she set her glass firmly on the little coaster on the table.

"How long do you think it will take you to make the arrangements?"

Seth thought about the airline ticket in his desk drawer. "Five days. Take the girl shopping. Get her the best. Get something spiffy, Aggie. Moss always liked spiffy things."

Agnes hated to ask but she forced the words from her mouth. "How much should we spend?"

"As much as it takes." Agnes nodded. Silk and satin. Sheer gossamer nighties, silk underwear. Frilly, lacy, frothy unmentionables. A daring low-cut gown for dancing. Surely the Officers' Club would have dancing on the weekend. Officers always had the best. Some French perfume for wickedness. Moss was a sniffer. Scent was important if worn discreetly. Billie was going to be ecstatic. "Don't stint, and I suggest you start out first thing in the morning. In case you need alterations."

"Right after breakfast," Agnes said briskly. "I think it's time for me to go up and say good night to Jessica and check on Maggie. I'll stop by Billie's room and tell her, unless you want to tell her yourself."

"You do it. You're the gal's mother. I think I'm going to turn in myself. I plan to ride the range tomorrow. Old Nessie's been missing me. Five days, Agnes. Make sure the gal is ready."

"She'll be ready," Agnes said firmly. "And Seth, no more liquor. We bent the rules a little tonight, but this is the last time. You really have to start taking care of yourself."

Seth mumbled something unintelligible as Agnes left the room. Later, when she thought about it, she thought he'd said, "Until you want something else." She snorted.

Agnes's idea of saying good night to Jessica was a light wave in her direction as she walked past her lighted room. When she passed the nursery she put her finger to her lips to show she understood little Maggie was sleeping. Seth didn't need to know everything. She rapped quietly on Billie's door and opened it at the same time. Her daughter was sitting at her little cherrywood desk, writing beneath a gooseneck lamp. "Billie, can I talk to you?"

"Of course, Mother. Is anything wrong?"

"On the contrary, everything is wonderful. I have a wonderful surprise for you. Seth just told me this very evening. Minutes ago, in fact, and I came right up to tell you. You're going to Hawaii to see Moss. Isn't that wonderful? Don't ask me how Seth did it, but he's arranging the entire thing. Five days, Billie, and you'll see Moss. Tomorrow we're going shopping!"

Billie leaped up from the desk. "Truly, Mother? I can't believe it. Does Moss know? How? When? Five days. Good

Lord, Mother, what about Maggie? I don't think I can be ready in five days. Oh, Mother, I'm so glad the doctor said I was fit. It will be all right, won't it?"

Agnes preened. "Darling child, it's all been taken care of. When Seth says he has friends in high places, he means high places. We just have to be thankful that he's able to do all this for you. Moss is going to be so surprised. Darling, you are not to worry about Maggie. She has a nurse. Remember, now, you're a Coleman. You can go off and not worry. I'll be here to look after things. Be sure, though, to take some pictures of little Maggie to show Moss. Start thinking of all the gorgeous things you can buy to dazzle your husband. We really have to buy some wickedly expensive perfume to drive him out of his mind. Men have to be driven to the brink every so often to keep them in line." Agnes was almost babbling. All she could think of was the shopping trip and what she could buy for herself—and the ultimate outcome of the Hawaiian visit.

"Mother, does Moss know I'm coming?" Billie asked excitedly.

"I'm not sure. I'm sure Seth will get word to him within the next day or so. He has to know you're coming so he can arrange his schedule. Seth and I want both of you to have a marvelous time to make up for the Christmas visit. Seth will take care of things. Finish your letter and then get ready for bed. I think we should leave right after breakfast. Ask Jessica if there's anything we can bring her. Good night, Billie." Agnes leaned over to plant a dry kiss on Billie's forehead.

When the door closed behind Agnes, Billie threw herself on the bed and curled into a ball with the pillow clutched against her chest. Tears of sheer happiness burned her eyes. How generous of Seth. How wonderful of Seth. For the first time in her young life she was beginning to understand what power and money could do. It was going to be so wonderful. A second honeymoon. In Hawaii. The excitement was almost more than she could bear. She hugged the pillow tighter. New clothes. If she had anything to say about it, she wouldn't be wearing much more than a towel while she was with Moss. How long? Her mother hadn't said how long her visit was to be. It didn't matter. She would make the most of the time. Wicked perfume and a towel. She smiled as she dabbed at her eyes with the corner of the pillowcase. She was going to see her husband. She had never been happier in her life.

When Billie tripped down the hall to the nursery she felt light-headed. She rapped softly and peeked in the door. The nurse in her starched white uniform put her finger to her lips. Billie nodded and advanced on tiptoe into the room. The tiny pink bundle lay peacefully in the cradle that had belonged first to Moss and then to Amelia. One tiny, plump fist was being sucked on. Billie smiled.

The desire to hold her daughter was so strong that Billie leaned over the cradle. "Now, Mrs. Coleman, you know the rules," the nurse said in a harsh whisper. "When baby is sleeping we do not disturb her. Gas, colic, diarrhea, any of those things can result. Sleeping babies need their sleep." The nurse's voice was stern yet not unkind. Secretly she often felt sorry for the young, wealthy mothers who missed so much when they had nurses take care of their babies.

"Could I speak with you outside for a minute, Miss Jenkins?" Billie whispered. The gray-haired woman followed Billie into the hallway, leaving the door ajar. She was a good nurse.

Quickly Billie explained the situation, and the nurse said, "Mrs. Coleman, go to your husband. He needs you more than Maggie does right now. All that bundle in there needs is warm, loving arms and competent care. I can see to that. But your husband needs *you*. Maggie will be fine. I've been nursing babies for thirty years. I nursed Amelia and your husband, you know. I know Moss would want you to come to him."

"It's just that I'm her mother, Miss Jenkins. I should be feeding her and changing her. I should be rocking her to sleep. Don't misunderstand; I want to go, but I'm torn. I feel I should stay here with my baby. I know everything you're saying is true. Maggie won't know whose arms are holding her as long as they're warm and loving. *But I'll know.*"

The nurse walked her back to her room and patted her comfortingly on the shoulder. "Trust me, Mrs. Coleman. I'll take care of Maggie as if she were my own child."

Billie nodded and watched the older woman walk back down the hallway. The woman had an ample bosom for Maggie to snuggle against. She hoped that the starchy stiffness of the white uniform didn't chafe the tiny face.

Before retiring for the night, Billie walked across the hall to Jessica's room. Her mother-in-law lay propped up in bed with her glasses perched on her nose, her head at an awkward angle, sound asleep. Billie removed the glasses and laid them on the night table, along with a new murder mystery. She turned off the bedside lamp and tiptoed from the room. She would bring Jessica a new book, perhaps two, from the city tomorrow. Maybe she would even buy her a small sack of licorice. Jessica loved candy. Billie was sorry that she couldn't share the news with Jessica. Living upstairs the way she did now, the former mistress of Sunbridge was the last to hear of any of the doings in the house.

But Jessica seemed happy in her little haven, thought Billie, where every need was met and she lacked for nothing. Her prayer beads, her endless supply of mystery novels, her small secret hoards of candy, and her writing implements were all she seemed to need these days. And, of course, her twice-daily visits to the nursery when she got to hold the new infant for a few minutes. Someday, Billie was going to try to figure out how her mother-in-law could be so happy shut up on the second floor. Someday, but not now. She purposely pushed away the worrisome thought that maybe she wouldn't like the answer.

Back to her room to finish the letter to Moss. Dear, wonderful Moss. He was going to be so surprised when he saw her. How ugly she had looked at Christmas! Now she'd knock his eyes right out of their sockets. It was going to be a honeymoon fit for a princess. Hawaii.

Billie finished the letter and crawled into bed. It would probably arrive after she did. She smiled to herself as she hugged her pillow to her cheeks, pretending it was Moss. The misgivings she'd felt about leaving Maggie and the ache in her chest when she'd stared down at her little daughter were gone now. She thought only of her husband and of the time they would have together.

Thad Kingsley bellowed into the buzzing wardroom: "Hey, Captain Marvel, you've got a call coming in. The radio room says it's your father and the captain has given you clearance for the call. Move it, Coleman!"

Moss looked up, startled. Thad never raised his voice. A call from home? Mam? Christ, they'd only docked in Hawaii that afternoon and he wasn't even officially detached from the ship. Something must have happened to Mam. He didn't need Captain Marvel's magic word to do a disappearing act. He skidded to a stop in the radio room and reached for the phone. "Pap? What's wrong?" Moss shouted into the receiver.

"Moss? That you, boy?"

Moss's stomach settled down. There was too much exhilaration in the old man's voice. "Christ, Pap, if you got through to me just to ask how the weather is, I'll shoot old Nessie when I get home."

"You touch that old nag and I'll turn the gun on you!" Seth's voice was jovial. "Everything is fine here, real fine. Listen, I found a way to send that little Yankee gal you married over to see you. She's leaving in a few days. I'll be getting back to you with more information, but I just wanted you to know your little wife is fit as a fiddle and hungry to see you. Take care of yourself, boy."

The wireless operator grinned up at Moss. Some guys had all the luck.

"Pap? Pap, you there?" He looked at the radio operator, who shrugged and tapped the instruments.

"Hope your call was finished, sir. The signal's been terminated."

Leave it to Pap to drop the bomb, Moss thought with annoyance. He wished the old man would quit manipulating his life. Fit as a fiddle. Billie coming here! The first charge of excitement plotted its course. Now how in the living hell had Pap pulled this one off? Memories flooded. Fit as a fiddle. But he already knew that from Billie's letters. Then the dawn began to creep over the horizon and he saw the light. If Mohammed couldn't come to the mountain, Pap had found a way to ship the mountain. And when Mohammed sent it home it had better be pregnant. This time with a son.

"The old bastard!"

"Did you say something, sir?" the radio man asked.

"No, nothing. It's just that there are some advantages to this war after all. My wife is coming to Hawaii!" Moss pushed his cap to the back of his head and returned to the wardroom. Billie was coming here; damn the reasons, she was coming. Despite it being Seth's idea, the thought pleased Moss immensely.

Moss returned to the wardroom, bellowed *"Shaazz-zaaammm!"* at the top of his lungs, made a lunging leap into the air, and spun into the bulkhead.

"This, gentlemen," Thad announced, "is the navy's secret weapon. The expression of pure euphoric bliss worn by Captain Marvel can only mean he's next in line for Halsey's job. Come on, Coleman, spit it out so we can all hit the chow line."

"Billie's coming . . . my wife," he explained to the others. Hoots of approval and boos of envy resounded.

Thad grinned and clapped Moss on the back. "You lucky devil! Someday I want you to tell me how your old man does it."

Moss grinned. "He says, 'Shazam!' Didn't you know I'm a chip off the old block?"

There was no envy in Thad Kingsley or the other officers. How could you resent a guy because his wife was coming to see him? Besides, there wasn't a harder worker or better pilot than Moss Coleman.

"That was fast work, even for your Pap," Kingsley told Moss. "When's Billie coming? Where will you stay?"

"I've no idea. I'm certain Pap will arrange everything, but I spoke with him only for a few minutes. He said he'd get back to me. Knowing Pap, Billie will arrive with a list of instructions a mile long. All I have to do is wait it out. Christ, Thad, Billie is coming here, all the way to Hawaii!" He laughed. "When I met her she'd never been out of Philadelphia and now she's traveling halfway around the world to be with me. And from the looks of things the Big E will be in dry dock for a month at least."

"Billie will love Hawaii. You'll put in your day at the airfield and the nights are your own. Don't screw up, Coleman."

"What the hell is that supposed to mean?" Moss demanded.

"It means whatever the hell you want it to mean. I was with you last time we laid over in Hawaii and I know where you spent your nights and weekends. Try to control your greedy appetites. And I wouldn't take Billie sight-seeing—she might get a look at that little cutey you found yourself on the other side of the island."

"If you saw me on the other side of the island, you were there for the same reason."

"With one slight difference, my friend. I'm not married," Thad drawled, imitating Moss's accent.

Moss squinted past his cigarette smoke. "When I'm in Texas I'm married. When I'm not with Billie, I'm just ole Moss Coleman. Period. Don't go preaching at me, Thad."

"I'm not preaching. I'm telling you a fact. Remember, I met that little girl you married and I always thought she was too young for you. Don't make her grow up the hard way."

"Enough, Kingsley," Moss snarled.

"You're right. It's none of my business. I'm hungry. See you later."

Moss watched his long-legged friend stride across the wardroom. For a few moments his anger roiled, but then better sense prevailed. Thad hardly ever offered advice. Or was it a warning? He couldn't think about that now. Billie was coming to Hawaii and he'd have her to himself for over a month. He felt himself stiffening inside his uniform. He didn't need food. What he needed was a cold shower to tide him over until he could beg a Jeep and drive to the other side of the island. It would be more than a week before Billie arrived.

The five days allotted Billie flew by on eagle's wings. Agnes and Seth both were at their wits' end with Billie's wide mood swings. She would be wildly exhilarated one minute and depressed the next that she was leaving Maggie in strange hands. Soothing words of comfort were offered by her mother, while Seth made no pretense about his displeasure, telling Billie over and over of the lengths to which he had gone to secure permission for her travel plans. In the end she left Sunbridge with a smile on her lips, an ache in her heart, and tears in her eyes.

The Coleman luggage consisted of a trunk and four heavy travel bags jammed full of costly dresses, frilly nightwear, and enticing underwear that was more lace than cloth. One bag was full of nothing but shoes. Another held her nighties and her underwear and stockings, all silk. She had almost choked when the matronly salesgirl had asked demurely if there would be anything else, as though a five-thousand-dollar purchase of clothing that couldn't be worn outside the house was an everyday occurrence. They had bought little dresses, as Agnes called them, by the dozen. Summery, demure, sometimes sultry little numbers that exposed even as they covered up. A must, Agnes had said with authority. Later, in the quiet of her room, Billie had tried to tally her purchases in her head and almost fainted. Who in their right mind paid $9,000 for clothing for a trip to Hawaii. Agnes knew that Seth wouldn't blink an eye. But then again, it was Agnes who was writing out the checks these days.

When the chauffeur-driven car drove out of Sunbridge's long, circular driveway, Billie turned to look back. Once before she had seen that smug look on her mother's face—on the night Agnes had come home early from her graduation party and found her and Moss in their compromising position. How odd that she should now remember that look on her mother's face. A year ago she had thought it was disapproval.

It was to Jessica, standing in the upstairs window, that Billie waved good-bye.

"I think this calls for a drink, don't you, Agnes? Fetch me a triple Scotch and don't mess it up with water or ice."

"Why don't I just bring the bottle," Agnes called over her shoulder as she made her way into the house. She couldn't recall a time when she'd felt more proud of herself. Maybe Seth thought he'd pulled off a coup, but she knew better. Without her help he wouldn't have gotten to step one. They understood each other so well.

"Moss, I don't believe what you're telling me," Thad said. "It will be unforgivable of you not to pick up Billie—there must be a way," he muttered, running his fingers through his sandy hair.

"Try telling that to Captain Davis," Moss snarled. "The good captain doesn't approve of what he calls asshole saddle jockeys who have friends in high places. You're going to have to fill in for me, Thad. Billie will understand once you explain it to her. I'm giving you the day off. Take care of my wife for me till I can get to wherever Pap has her staying. I'll bet you a month's salary it's a house up in the hills."

"When it comes to your old man, I'm not putting money down on any kind of a bet, but you owe me for this one," Thad said, and grinned. "Okay, I'll stand in for you."

Moss laughed. "See that's all you do. I'd appreciate it if you would take my gear with you. The captain is allowing me to be off base five evenings a week but I have to be here full-time on weekends. He's going out of his way to show me I'm not a favorite of the Navy Department. It's okay. I'm not sweating it. Billie will understand. You're a good friend, Thad."

There were a hundred other things he would rather be doing than standing in for Moss with his wife. Secretly, he agreed with Captain Davis. Favoritism at this time was not a good morale booster for the others. The other guys had sweethearts and wives behind in the States. But he realized that Moss had had nothing to do with his wife's coming to Hawaii. The guy did what was expected of him and then some, and he did it well. He was a damn good pilot and the Texas Ranger had seen more action than most of the others. Thad stowed Moss's gear in the back of the Jeep and headed out of the base.

An hour later he was shading his eyes from the golden

sunshine to get a better look at the pretty young woman standing at the top of the airline's portable stairway. One hand was holding on to a wide-brimmed picture hat and the other was trying to hold down the hem of her skirt. Good legs. Damn good legs. This wasn't the same Billie Coleman he had met months ago. Thad sucked in his breath and stared a little harder.

Billie crossed the tarmac, her hands still keeping her hat and skirt from the clutches of the playful breeze that was whipping about the airfield. Her eyes were anxious as they searched for Moss. The minute she spotted Thad she smiled. Wherever Thad Kingsley was, Moss would be close behind. But there was no sign of him. The smile stayed in place when Thad took her by the arm and escorted her toward the car. "It's nice to see you again, Billie. Moss had duty and couldn't be relieved. I'm to take you to wherever you're staying and he'll join you around six. I've got his gear in the Jeep. We'll have to wait a few minutes till your luggage gets here. Do you have much?"

Billie hid her disappointment well. "A trunk and four bags. I don't think you're going to get it all in the Jeep if you have Moss's things, too." She was a navy wife and had to get used to these wartime changes in plans. Six o'clock was only three hours away.

"We'll manage. There's no way I can commandeer another vehicle today. This one was wheeled and dealed, so don't ask questions." Thad grinned. "Where are you staying?"

Billie withdrew a slip of paper from her purse. "Mr. Coleman said it's high up in the hills," she said. "Supposedly there's a cook and a gardener and it's very private. I think Mr. Coleman said it was the main house on a macadamia plantation. Do you think you can find it?" she asked anxiously.

"Didn't Moss tell you? I have a trace of bloodhound in me. I'll find it, Billie, and have you all set by the time your husband gets off duty."

"How is it you're off duty and Moss isn't?" Billie asked as she settled herself in the Jeep. Thad stared at Billie's legs. He'd always been a leg man and an open admirer of Betty Grable. From now on the long-legged movie star was going to be relegated to the rumble seat.

Thad waited till one of the ground crew secured Billie's baggage in the back of the Jeep. "Because Moss is my superior and he gave me the day off. *His* superior is not as generous as your husband. Moss thought you would be more comfortable with me, since we've met before, and he trusted me to explain the situation. I know you're disappointed but it can't be helped. This is the navy."

Billie smiled, her whole face lighting up. "Six o'clock will give me time to unpack and take a bath. Perhaps it's best this way. When you get back to the base, tell Moss I'll be waiting."

"I'll be sure to do that. Now, let's have another look at that address." Thad scrutinized the tiny square of paper and then drew a crumpled map from his flight coverall. "Okay, I know where you're going. May I say, Mrs. Coleman, that your father-in-law has exquisite taste." He smiled to show there was no jealousy in his statement. Billie thought she had never seen a more spellbinding smile. She liked Thad Kingsley.

Thad whipped the Jeep through the gates and headed toward the north shore. He drove effortlessly, forsaking the Wahiawa turnoff for a route through Kunia. The road was narrow, running alongside the Waianae Mountains and through endless fields of pineapple and sugarcane.

Thad expertly guided the car through Haleiwa, but instead of using the bridge to the north he opted to go left, past the harbor, so Billie could see the surf. The Jeep came to a stop. "Take a good look, Mrs. Coleman."

Billie's gasp of pure pleasure was all that Thad needed to hear. He knew he had chosen the right route for Billie's first look at Hawaii's famous surf. The waves were breaking clean, eight to ten feet high. Native Hawaiians were scattered all along the shore stretching out nets for fish. Children were gathering shells to sell for a pittance to the military men

"It's unbelievable," Billie said breathlessly. "I've only read about Hawaii. Seeing it is something else entirely. It's gorgeous."

"Mrs. Coleman," Thad teased, "you ain't seen nothing yet. This is just a teaser."

"I didn't think there was water so blue. It's like a giant jewel."

"That it is. Come along now, I have to get you to your house."

Thad drove steadily for forty-five minutes. When he took a second quick look at his rumpled map he was relieved to see he hadn't missed the entrance. Lush hibiscus and a monstrous banyan tree, like a giant umbrella, shrouded the time-worn iron gates at the entrance to Ester Kamali's estate, where Billie was to stay. The snakelike drive eventually widened and became circular, edged on both sides by regal palms standing sentinel. Billie's eyes widened. The house was long, low, and sprawling, with the sparkling Pacific below as a backdrop. Thad felt his breath hiss between his teeth. It was probably the most beautiful house he had ever seen.

"Are we allowed to walk on the grass?" Billie whispered. "It looks like a velvet carpet. Doesn't it, Thad?"

"It looks like soft green fur to me," Thad whispered back.

"Why are we whispering?" Billie asked. Thad shrugged.

Banks and mounds of scarlet hibiscus blinded Billie as they tripped across the emerald meadow. "What's that smell?" Billie demanded, wrinkling her nose.

"Plumeria. That's what the island girls make the leis with. Sometimes they use orchids, but mainly plumeria because of its strong scent. It lasts forever, or so it seems. The maids in the local hotels hang strands of it in the bathroom showers for the guests."

"What a charming custom." Billie sighed. "This has got to be the closest thing to paradise I've ever seen. Of course," she said, laughing, "I'm not a world traveler. I only have Philadelphia and Texas to compare this with."

"I'm sure you and Moss are going to be very happy here. You have the Pacific at your back door and this gorgeous garden at your front. The house is a work of art. You go ahead and ring the bell. I'll bring the luggage and then I have to hightail it back to the base."

A tiny woman attired in a bright red muumuu opened the door. Her smile was warm, welcoming. Her eyes sparkled like black stars in the small round face. "You dat same *wahine* Missy Kamali say is here?" At Billie's perplexed look the little woman frowned. "You *haole* lady from far, I t'ink." At a loss, Billie smiled and motioned behind her for Thad to hurry. The luggage should convince the housekeeper she had a right to be here. "No *pilikia*, no *pilikia*," the little woman muttered, her face wreathed in a wide smile.

Thad grinned. "She's saying there's no trouble. *Pilikia* means trouble. That's one of the first words you learn over here."

"Ass awri," the woman said, motioning them inside.

"She's telling us it's okay. In other words, she's been expecting you. I hate to leave you like this but you'll manage. I've got to get back to the base. You do want your husband here on time, right?" Billie nodded.

Thad pointed to the luggage and made a motion asking where it should be taken.

"Dat humbug question? What'sa matah you. Phillip carry for *wahine*."

"That settles it." Thad grinned and smacked his hands together. "I think you're in good care. Give my regards to Phillip, whoever he may be. Welcome to Hawaii, Billie," Thad said, and bent to kiss her cheek.

"Thanks for everything, Thad. Don't worry. I'll manage here. Hurry—I don't want you to be late or get in trouble because of me."

Thad's step was jaunty as he sprinted across the velvety lawn. At the last second before leaping into the Jeep, he picked a lush hibiscus bloom and stuck it between his teeth. He drove at breakneck speed down the winding road with the colorful flower in his mouth. A native trudging along the road turned to stare in amazement. Thad laid the red bloom on the seat and started to whistle. Billie Coleman was one hell of a looker. Moss might be wise to keep her here in this lush island hideaway.

{{{{{{{{{ CHAPTER TWELVE }}}}}}}}

The hilltop house opened its arms to Billie. It was low, sprawling, yet not overlarge, and it gave her a cozy feeling of coolness and light, so different from Sunbridge, with its heavy leather furniture and somber colors. In this house, the first she would share alone with Moss, every room opened to the outside. The French doors leading to the patio were sheltered from sun and rain by the sloping overhang of the tiled roof. Beautiful gardens were part of every view and seemed to come indoors to blend with the light bamboo furniture and the vivid greens and whites of the walls. Graceful paddle fans were centered on every ceiling, creating a pleasant breeze. And the tang of the sea far below seemed to fill each room.

Shown to the larger of the two bedrooms, Billie was wel-

comed by the scented sea breeze that billowed the sheer curtains hanging in the patio doorway. The carpet underfoot was egg-shell white, bringing into relief the dark tones of native mahogany furnishings. The bed, headboard, and upholstered chairs were covered with fabric of pale blue flowers scattered over a deeper blue background. Here, too, a paddle fan beat the air in a slow, hypnotic rhythm. The pudgy dark-skinned house-keeper moved unhurriedly as she unpacked Billie's bags, fingering the garments admiringly before hanging them in the louver-doored closet or laying them in sachet-scented drawers. Unwilling to break the spell this house was casting upon her, Billie silently crossed the room to find a tiled bath complete with tub, shower, and expanses of mirrors. Towels and accessories of palest blue complemented the eggshell fixtures and ceramic. This was indeed the loveliest house she'd ever seen and she was already wishing she could spend the rest of her life here with Moss.

After partaking of a light meal of fruit, cheese, coarse bread, and a cool, exotic fruit punch, Billie occupied herself by taking a shower and washing her hair. She primped for Moss's arrival, dabbing perfume between her breasts and behind her ears. From her closet she chose the intriguing Chinese dressing gown Moss had given her for Christmas. It was difficult to believe that the front edges once had barely met over her stomach. Now it fit perfectly and the tight sash accentuated her tiny waist. Nurse Jenkins's firming exercises had worked wonders.

Time was heavy on her hands. She walked the perimeter of the grounds surrounding the house. She arranged her toiletries in the bathroom and on the dressing table. She waited for Moss.

She explored the efficient and surprisingly modern kitchen and waited for Moss.

The minute hand on her slim gold watch hardly seemed to be moving. Again and again she shook her wrist, but she knew it was keeping perfect time. At last, weary from her trip, she fell across the bed and promised herself she would only close her eyes for a minute while she waited for Moss.

Driving up the steep hill road, Moss cursed the time. Captain Davis was a man without a heart. It was already almost nine o'clock and twilight was deepening to that purple shade peculiar to Hawaii. And half an hour ago he'd taken the wrong turn and had had to double back. Pulling into the drive, he was greeted by dim lights shining through the patio doors. Billie was in there, waiting. His pulses beat a rapid tattoo and his blood was heated in anticipation. When he'd asked Thad how she was, his friend had merely winked and smiled slyly. "Moss, you've got one hell of a surprise waiting for you!" Now what the hell did that mean? And was he going to like it?

Pulling the keys out of the ignition and stuffing them in his pocket, he carried his ditty bag to the front door. He decided to try the knob rather than clang the cowbells that hung from the eave. The door was open and the house was quiet. Not even a radio was playing. He followed the lights through the living room and into the bedroom. There, on the bed, lay Billie, one arm thrown over her head, knees bent, lovely face serene and composed in sleep. His eyes traveled the length of her from her slim ankles up her coltish legs to the width of her hips and the fullness of her breasts. Her waist was nipped, her belly flat. This was the Billie he'd married. Or was it? On closer examination, there was a new, angular quality to her face, the limbs seemed more elegant, slimmer, graceful. Had she done something to her hair? It was lighter, paler, sun-streaked, blonder than he remembered. And it had grown since Christmas, falling lustrously against her cheek. So this was the surprise Thad had hinted at. Billie was all grown up into a beautiful woman, riper, lusher. A slow smile grew on his face as he undid his tie and worked the buttons of his shirt.

Billie thought she was dreaming. She felt herself taken into strong, warm arms, felt herself nestled against a broad deep chest. She didn't want to awaken from this dream, so vivid, so languorously delicious. She felt his eyes upon her, heard him inhale her fragrance as he curled her beneath him. Her arms enfolded him, stroking his back, falling lower to his naked haunches where her palms smoothed over the curve of his buttocks. She heard her name.

"Moss!" she murmured, pulling herself from her dream and deeper into his embrace. "Oh, Moss! I've missed you so." She heard her voice, deep and throaty with desire. For months now she'd wanted him this way, dreaming about this moment every night, waking in a sheen of sweat, emptiness at her center. Now he was here, truly here, and she was in his arms and he was loving her.

The Chinese silk robe fell open under his commanding fingers and when he captured her breast, its pink nipple rose to greet him and bring him delight. Slowly he teased her ear with his tongue, following the pulse points to her neck and throat. He wanted her, urgently, but he would take her slowly, deepening their pleasure. His hands traced the contours of her body, following its curves, caressing its hollows. He explored the recesses of her mouth and the silkiness of her thighs. This was his Billie, his wife, as familiar to him as the back of his own hand and yet, somehow, new territory to be charted.

Her emotions were charged, more finely tuned than he remembered, and when she closed her hand over the proof of his desire she communicated her own demands.

She hurried him with her kisses, excited him with soft mewlings and murmurs, undulated beneath his caresses. She wanted him now, desperately. She felt she would erupt with a wildness too long contained. There would be time later for luxuriating in his arms, to have his hands soothe this fever, to have his lips take possession of her inch by inch. But now she needed completion.

Her thighs opened, her back arched, and he became a part of her. In the white heat of her passion she entrapped him, feeling him stroke within her, locking her legs behind his to take him deeply inside her where the warmth was building.

For the next week and a half, Billie thought she'd died and gone to heaven. Long evenings with Moss, lying in his arms. Midnight swims in the little cove at the bottom of the hill. Quiet dinners on the lanai, looking up at the stars. Two nights ago Moss had invited Thad for supper and she'd repressed her giggles when her enthusiastic husband had thrown broad hints that it was time for his friend to leave. Moss liked to be alone with her, to have her to himself. It seemed he couldn't get enough of her and this pleased her, because it was exactly how she felt about him. Hawaii was the the first time they'd been alone since their marriage. No Agnes, no Seth or Jessica, no one, just the two of them.

On the last morning before he had to leave for his weekend duty, she lay beside Moss, hearing his light breathing and feeling his warmth. Her lazy gaze drifted over to the miniature traveling clock stitched with Sunbridge cowhide. The time was five-ten. She had to wake Moss in another five minutes if he was to make the long drive back to the base. She stored the memory of how Moss looked the way a squirrel stores nuts for the winter. How dear, how beautiful, how wonderful he looked! There was a certain boyish charm in his dark tousled hair, but the rest of this exciting person was all man. Her man. She relished the peacefulness a moment longer before she rolled to his side of the bed. At the precise moment the minute hand on the clock reached three, Billie smacked Moss on the rump, let out a war whoop, and leaped from under the sheets.

"What the hell!" Moss bellowed as he fought with the covers. "A goddamn air raid at this time of the morning!" Seeing Billie laughing, he fell back against the covers. "If you ever do that again, I'll turn you over my knee."

"Is that a threat or a promise?"

"All you have to do is test me, Mrs. Coleman."

"Some other time, Mr. Coleman. Right now you have to hit the shower. You'd better hurry or you'll be late. Oh, Moss, I wish you didn't have to go. It's such a long time till you get back."

"Come here, Billie."

Billie practically ran to the bed and threw herself in Moss's arms. "Oh, Moss, I love you so. This is all so perfect. This place, this house, everything is just so wonderful. I want to share every minute with you. The hours we have together are so few. I'm not complaining. It sounds like I am but I'm not. I understand. There are so many couples who don't have what we do. I love you so. I guess that's the reason."

"I know you do, you little vixen. What do you think? Do we have time for a quickie?"

"Depends on what your definition of 'quick' is." Billie giggled and tugged on Moss's chest hairs. "Why don't we take a shower together? I'll wash your back and you wash mine. . . ."

"And I'll tickle your fancy and you'll tickle mine." Moss laughed, finding her suggestion exciting. He loved her skin when it was wet and slick with soap, yielding beneath the exploring press of his fingers, each curve and swell of her exquisite figure offering itself to him. He lifted the pale curtain of hair that fell across her face to kiss her. Her eyes shone with expectation and pleasure, her mouth was soft, her lips parted to allow him entrance. His arms closed around her, pulling her close, her nearness already affecting his desires. "Billie," he murmured, "if you don't go in and turn on the shower, we'll never get there at all."

Billie stood on the balcony, wrapped in a pale blue towel, her body still flushed and tingling from Moss's lovemaking. She shaded her eyes from the early-morning sun on the horizon. The military Jeep was a dot on the winding mountain road when she crept back into bed. Delicious memories of their total communion brought a smile to her lips as she drifted into a deep sleep.

Billie was walking along the private beach when she heard the Jeep coming up the road. She slipped into her beach sandals and raced around to the front of the house. "Thad!" she called in disappointment.

"Hey, I'm sorry I'm not the man, but he did send me. I can go back. I come bearing gifts, however, so think hard before you make any rash decisions." Thad grinned.

"Gifts! What kind of gifts? Why did Moss send you? Why didn't he wait till this evening to bring it? Not that I don't want to see you. I crave company that speaks the king's English. Tell me quick, before I explode."

Thad reached behind him in the Jeep and withdrew two cans filled with gasoline. "Moss said there was a Ford in the garage with no gas. Now you have gas. When you have gas you can drive. Drive, as in sightsee. Diamond Head. Waikiki. All kinds of great places."

"How wonderful of Moss. How did he get the gasoline?"

"You don't want to know," Thad said, reaching down to take his shoes off."I brought my bathing trunks for a quick swim before I head back. How much trouble would it be for you to get me a nice cold beer? Is it okay if I change in the cabana out back?"

"Of course. Go along and I'll fetch the beer. The water is crystal clear today. Hardly any whitecaps at all. I swear, Thad, I have never seen bluer water or bluer sky. It's as though they're married to each other. I'll never forget this vacation. Everything is so marvelous. I'm so glad Mr. Coleman knew Miss Kamali and arranged this for Moss and me. I don't know how I can ever hope to repay him."

"I don't think he wants payment of any kind. He wants both of you to be happy. Accept it, Billie, and enjoy the time you have," Thad said gently.

"Of course, you're right. Don't just stand there—move, sailor. This is the navy, and navy men do not stand around in their bare feet."

"Aye-aye, ma'am."

Billie uncapped a frosty bottle of beer from the icebox and placed it on a tray with some crackers and two wedges of cheese. Something was wrong. Thad was too up. His grin a little too wide. He was a shade too nervous. It had to do with Moss; of that she was sure.

"What do you think, Billie, could I pass for King Neptune?" Thad asked as he walked from the ocean brandishing a piece of driftwood.

Billie pretended to ponder the question. She took in his tall, lanky form and his dripping hair. He was thin, but not skinny. Muscular in the right places, denoting a whipcord strength. A honey-colored tan made him appear heavier than he really was. She liked the leanness of him. But more than anything she liked his dry, droll sense of humor and his ready smile.

"Okay, don't answer that. Ummm, this beer is good. You sure know how to treat a guest, Mrs. Coleman. Cheese and crackers, too."

"What's wrong?" Billie asked bluntly, the concern in her hazel eyes letting Thad know she was asking about Moss.

"Moss showed up late for training class this morning. He's been restricted to base for three days after this weekend," Thad replied just as bluntly.

"Oh, no!"

"Oh, yes. That's why I brought the gas. You're going to be pretty much on your own. I can come for you or meet you in Waikiki after hours and show you around a little if you want. It's the best we can do, Billie."

We. He had said "we." That meant Moss approved. Damn navy. Didn't they care that she was here and her husband couldn't see her? Then she remembered the early-morning hour in the hot, steamy shower. It would be a long time before she forgot this morning. A warm flush crept up her neck and settled on her cheeks. Thad pretended not to see and slugged away at his beer.

"Three days in addition to his weekend duty is a long time. He'll be here only one day and then he has to report back for the next weekend. It's awful, Thad."

"It's better than nothing. Learn to enjoy what you have, and you'll do fine."

"I never thought of it like that. Thank you, Thad. Of course you're right."

"I'm always right," Thad muttered under his breath. "What say, Mrs. Coleman, that I race you out to the first coral reef? First one back with a one-pound chunk wins."

"Wins what?" Billie laughed.

"Another beer, what else?"

The swim to the coral reef was effortless, with neither finding a pound chunk of coral. Then the lanky New Englander and the girl from Philadelphia frolicked like playful porpoises in the sparkling Pacific. There was no one to notice the darkening of Thad's eyes when he looked at Billie. And of course, the slight trembling of his hands could be blamed on the cool water. When he touched Billie's shoulder to tell her it was time to swim back he couldn't understand how his hand could feel so scorched. He shook his head to clear his thoughts and lashed out against the water. When he reached the shore he was gasping for breath. Billie was still some distance away, swimming slowly toward shore. He dried off with a thick towel. Anything to keep moving. A glass of lemonade and another beer for himself were held aloft as Billie swished into shore on a mini-wave. He had to get out of there.

"Billie, I'm going to dress. I have to get back. Think about what you want to do."

"All right. But first I have to dry off. I can't think when I'm wet."

He would have cut off his right arm at the elbow, he thought, to be able to touch her. "The sun will dry you," he said gruffly.

Thad returned fully dressed. "I'm going to pour this gas in the tank of the Ford and start up the engine to make sure it's okay. What did you decide?"

Billie trotted after Thad. "I'd like to do some sight-seeing, if you have the time. Thad, really, I don't want you to give up any plans for me. I can just as easily settle in here with a good book. Miss Kamali has a fully stocked library. But if you can really manage it, I'd like a firsthand view of Diamond Head and perhaps make a trip to Hana Drive."

"Hana Drive is in Maui. I don't know if I can get you there or not. I'll have to work on that one and check it out with Moss. You can't do it in one day. We would have to stay overnight. Diamond Head and Waikiki will be more than enough for one day. I'll draw you a little map and show you where to meet me. I can get off duty tomorrow at three."

"I appreciate it, Thad. Tell Moss . . . tell him . . . tell him I said it was worth it. He'll understand."

"I'll tell him. You'd better put something on over your suit or you're going to get a sunburn. This sun is different from Texas and Philadelphia sun."

"I will. Thanks for driving out. I'll see you tomorrow."

Thad didn't look back, nor did he glance in his rearview mirror. There was no point.

Moss caught up to Thad in the dining hall. "How did Billie take the news?"

"Like a trouper. She sent a message. Said to tell you it was worth it. She said you would understand."

A devilish grin split Moss's features. "At the time I thought so myself. Now, with three days' restriction, I'm not so sure. What did she say about the gas?"

"She's driving down tomorrow. I said I would meet her and show her around. I think you'll agree that you want her to start back before dark on that road."

"Absolutely. Thanks, Thad. Listen, I have an idea. I want to see if I can get a message to my old man. I want him to ship me two longhorn steers. I'm going to throw a Texas barbecue that will make a Hawaiian luau look like a grade school picnic. The Kamali pit is big enough. We might have to extend it a little or do up the second one on the beach, but it will be worth it. What do you think?"

Thad's mouth dropped open. Just like that he was going to have his father ship two steers for a barbecue. The damn fool would pull it off, too. "Listen, Coleman, if you can pull this one off, I'm right there with you. I could sink my teeth into some good Texas beef. How you going to explain it all to the captain? Two Texas longhorns turning on a spit aren't going to go unnoticed and they sure as hell can't pass for the traditional pig."

"Once it's a fact, who's going to say anything? If Pap can swing it, they'll be coming in from on high. So high, Captain Davis is only going to congratulate me. Talk to Billie about it tomorrow and if you have any spare time, work on the guest list. Hell, invite everyone. Tell Billie to buy herself something real colorful so she makes a big splash. I want Davis to eat his heart out."

He won't be the only one, Thad thought glumly. "I'll work on it. When are you planning this event?"

"Shindig. We call it a shindig in Texas. Just as soon as I get through to Pap. Hell, he might as well send all the fixings, too, as long a he's going to all this trouble. It will give him something to do. The man does like a challenge."

"Chip off the old block, or is it a nick in the old leather?"

Moss shrugged and grinned as he left the dining hall. He'd invite the brass, of course. Some of the enlisted men. Music and local girls doing the hula. Christ, Pap was going to go up in smoke. He told himself he was doing it for Billie so that she would have a wonderful memory of her visit to the island. Billie would love it. The perfect little hostess, and she'd sure impress the brass.

When the call came, Agnes picked up the phone. She quickly roused Seth from his desk. "It's Moss. Good Lord, you don't suppose something went wrong, do you?"

"Of course not. My son does not screw up. Moss? How are you, boy?" Seth said with forced heartiness. He listened for a moment and then laughed. "For a minute I thought you were going to ask for the impossible. Cleaned and dressed. I understand. Fixings? I'll take care of it. Three days, four at the most. You're right, boy. Billie won't ever forget this. Imagine, a Texas barbecue in Hawaii! Don't worry, boy. I'll take care of you. That's what fathers are for. I'll tell your mother. Leave it to me. Take care of yourself, son." He hung up and turned to Agnes.

"Now if that don't beat all. The boy wants two longhorns." There was pride in his voice. Agnes wrinkled her nose. Barbecues were so messy. Everyone ate with their fingers and wore checkered bibs and drank beer. "Fixings. He wants the works. Aggie, get out your pencil and let's get to work. We want to do the boy up proud."

"Seth, how are you going to get all . . . get it over there?"

"Don't you go worrying your head about things like that, Aggie. I got my ways. Moss must want it for a special reason and that's good enough for me. Hell, woman, I'd try moving the earth if the boy wanted it. Start writing."

"Seth, what is this going to cost?" Agnes gasped.

"Cost? You mean money? Not a cent. It's our beef. All the fixings come from the ranch. I might have to plunk out a little for the kegs." Seth favored Agnes with a heavy-lidded look. "I'll call in a few favors. You wash my hand and I wash yours, that kind of thing. Does your silence mean you don't approve?" For some reason Agnes's reply was important to Seth.

"On the contrary. I know you have friends in high places." Her voice was a shade short of being apologetic. She was going to have to get used to Seth and the way he did things.

Seth fiddled with a long fragrant cigar, rolling it back and forth between his fingers. "Aggie, who do you thinks supplies all the grade-A choice beef to the military? Not just here in the States, but all over the world?"

"I never thought much about it. Coleman beef, is that what you're saying?"

Seth nodded and clamped his teeth down hard on his cigar. "Now, if I was to get myself into a flap over something and shipped late or not at all, some five-star is going to get upset. You don't mess with the brass's dinner parties. You get my point?"

"Perfectly. I'll get on this right away. You said three days, possibly four. Which is it?"

"Make it four. We don't want to appear too eager. Coleman beef ships out on the first. That will give me three days of palavering."

Palavering. These Texans had a language all their own, just as they had a style all their own. More and more, she decided, she liked their flamboyance. She couldn't help wondering at what point she would consider herself a hundred percent Texan. Soon, she thought. Just as soon as Billie produced a male heir to the Coleman fortune.

The vintage Ford had its assorted shimmies and shakes. Billie drove carefully. Every so often she was forced to pull over to the side of the road till the engine quieted down. She would have to mention it to Thad.

The day was exquisitely beautiful, the sky so blue it made Billie gasp and long for at least one little cottonball cloud. The scarlet hibiscus along both sides of the road was so vibrant and colorful it made her eyes water. She wished she were an artist so she could capture the rich colors of the foliage and the cerulean ocean.

With several quick looks at the map Thad had made for her, Billie managed to arrive at their appointed meeting place without getting lost. She drove down Kalakau, the main street in Waikiki. She was conscious immediately of the smell of plumeria that scented the warm trade winds. Cottage after cottage was almost obscured by thick, lush foliage and red hibiscus. Billie parked the car and stepped outside to wait for Thad.

He arrived five minutes later, followed by a horde of children all demanding pennies. Dutifully he emptied his pockets. Billie combed through her change purse. How beautiful they were, these children of another culture. She thought of her little Maggie back home, who was so pale compared with these children. Their warm, molasses-colored skin enhanced pearly white teeth that shone in perpetual smiles.

Thad signaled the oldest and tallest boy. He brandished a silver quarter and told him to watch missy's car till they got back. He handed over the quarter and promised another on their return.

"I think it will be better if we go in the Jeep. How are you today, Billie?"

"I'm fine. How's Moss?" Surely he had sent a message. Thad was probably embarrassed to deliver it. Men!

"Cranky," Thad replied shortly. Billie waited. Thad steered the Jeep away from the curb and concentrated on retracing his route. "I'm taking you to Diamond Head first. Actually, you would have seen it if you were sitting on the right side of the plane when you came into Hawaii. But seeing it from the air and in person are two different things. Get prepared."

There was a pause and then he went on. "Moss asked me to talk to you about something." Quickly he explained about the Texas barbecue and the call to Seth. "It's all arranged. Moss picked the date and I'm to make up the guest list. He wants you to buy some colorful island wear to dazzle everyone with."

She couldn't help herself. "Was that all he said?"

Thad bit his tongue. "Yep."

"Did you give him my message?"

"Yep."

"Well, what did he say?"

"Nothing. He grinned." Billie smiled. Thad grimaced as he swung the Jeep onto Diamond Head Road. "Get ready now. I boned up on this last night just for your benefit. Diamond Head is seven hundred and sixty feet tall. The natives call it *Leahi*, because it looks like the sloping face and brow of an *ahi*, which is a yellowfin tuna. We're going to go inside the crater. I hope you're impressed, Billie."

"I am, I am. Tell me more." Billie giggled at the serious look on Thad's face. Imagine studying up so he could be sure she got all the facts!

"We could actually drive inside, but I think we'll leave the Jeep and walk. Supposedly we're going to get all kinds of breathtaking views once we climb to the top. I understand they have picnics and luaus on special occasions."

"Why do they call it Diamond Head?"

"I know the answer. Just let me think a minute. . . . Because," he drawled, "nineteenth-century sailors found crystals that resembled diamonds. They were actually calcite. But the nickname 'Diamond Head' stuck. Now that's all I know."

"I'm so impressed that you would do this for me, Thad. Truly, I appreciate it. I know Moss is grateful to you, too. If we're going to hike it, let's go before I change my mind. I am not at my best in high places." Billie looked at him and grinned. "Swear to me that I won't have to go near the edge of anything and that you'll protect me," she said teasingly.

With my life, Thad thought, but he merely nodded and cupped her elbow. He didn't like what he was feeling. Why in the hell had he agreed to Moss's request to show Billie around? Christ, what kind of man was he to lust—and by God, he was lusting—after his best friend's wife? There were plenty of women in his life. Why did this particular one have such a hold on him?

The view of Honolulu from the awesome crater was beautiful. She would treasure this sight forever. If only Moss were at her side drinking in the splendrous beauty, she thought, instead of Thad. Then, when they were old, sitting in their respective rocking chairs, they could reminisce about this moment. . . .

"I think I've had enough," she said. "Thank you for bringing me. I can't wait to tell the others back at the ranch how beautiful this is. Thad, you're awfully quiet. Is something wrong?"

Wrong? What could be wrong? I want to kiss you. I want to hold you. I want to share this moment with you. "I was thinking," he said, "about how much easier it's going to be going down than it was coming up. Would you like to take in the sights at Waikiki? I boned up on that, too. There isn't too much to see except for two big hotels. Quite grand, I understand. Or maybe you just want to go back to the house." He had to get away from her before he made a damn fool of himself. He could plead a headache, a stomachache. Anything. The only problem was, she would never believe it.

"Thad, if you don't mind, I think I'd like to go back. Could we do the hotel bit another day? I am rather tired from that climb and I still have the drive back to the house. Would you mind taking a look at the engine? The car shimmies and shakes something frightful. Twice I had to pull over, it was making so much noise."

That was something positive he could do. He hoped his relief didn't show too much. Damn Moss Coleman to hell. "Sure thing. Careful, now, that you don't trip."

Thirty minutes later, Thad raised his head from under the hood of the Ford. "I can't find a thing wrong. I'm no expert, but I'd say the knocking you hear is because the car hasn't been driven for a long time. It probably needs a complete overhaul, but it should get you back okay. Oil and water are all right. Just take it easy and don't speed. I don't think you'll have a problem."

"I'm sure I won't." Billie reached up on her tiptoes and planted a light kiss on Thad's cheek. "That's for being so nice and taking pity on a lonely lady. What a wonderful friend you are to Moss. Don't worry about me. I'll be fine." She waved airily as she turned the car around and headed back. It wasn't till she was halfway home that she realized Thad hadn't said anything about taking her out for the next two days. She shrugged. It was a lot to ask of anyone. Why would he want to spend his free time taking a married woman around the island?

She would have to make up her mind to amuse herself. Then when Moss did get back it would be twice as good.

The rusty Ford seemed to be working out its kinks as Billie drove along the mountain range. Jessica was going to be so enthralled when she sat down to tell her about her visit to Hawaii. Jess would want to know the "exact" of everything. The exact shade of the hibiscus, the exact feel of the velvety lawn, and how it could be so soft when it was so near the ocean. She made a mental note to find out. Jessica would want to know about Diamond Head and all about the climb and the breathtaking view. And she would certainly want specifics on Moss's friend, Thad. It would be the Pacific with its glorious colors that Billie was going to have difficulty describing. How did one describe one of God's greater perfections? The foaming curling whitewater and the fifteen-foot waves. "Breathtaking" was the best she could come up with at the moment.

Someday she would tell Maggie about this wondrous trip, too. She would save all her mementoes and bring them out to show the little girl, when she was old enough to understand.

The iron gates and the ancient banyan tree came into view.

Billie climbed from the car and opened the monstrous gates to the estate. She drove the car through and then secured the gates for the night. Again, as she walked around to the back of the house, she was assaulted with the scent of the ever-blooming plumeria. But she was getting used to it. It reminded her of honeysuckle, back in Philadelphia, but was sweeter, more heady somehow. And much more beautiful. Night-blooming cereus dotted the walkway down to the beach. Billie tossed her bag on the coral and slipped off her shoes. She walked carefully, not wanting to cut her feet. The warm trade winds were almost as gentle as her touch with little Maggie. Tears burned her eyes and she dabbed at them furiously, ashamed of herself. Maggie was being cared for by an expert nurse and didn't miss her. Jess showered her with love on the two short visits she was allotted each day. But she shouldn't be thinking of Maggie and Jess. Texas was practically half a world away. She could almost hear Seth's repeated reminder ringing in her ears that she wasn't to bother her head about such things.

Billie sat on the beach and stayed for a long time, her thoughts everywhere and nowhere. She stared out across the ocean and wondered if it met the Atlantic at some point. In her wildest dreams she never thought she would be sitting on a private beach in Hawaii. Alone.

The trade winds died down. She'd been hardly aware of the shift from the southwest. A niggling worm of thought attacked her mind. Pregnancy. The thought of Maggie had prompted it, she was sure. She was healthy, fit. On her last visit, the doctor had given her a clean bill of health and patted her on the back. However, he had also repeated that it would not be wise to contemplate pregnancy again. He had told her in his gentle manner that he had felt duty bound to inform Seth and her mother of her condition. Condition? she had queried. But stubbornly the doctor had only kept repeating his warning: she had a child now, why endanger her health again? She had listened solemnly, not overly concerned at the time. Moss was so far away. By the time she saw him again, whatever was wrong would certainly have mended. Women had babies every day of the week. She was young, healthy, and fit as a fiddle. Those were the doctor's exact words.

Moss had taken no precautions and she hadn't cared at the time. Did she care now? Moss had taken it for granted that things were all right. How could she tell him that she was less than perfect? Babies were a part of marriage. She couldn't tell him. Wouldn't tell him. In the whole world she wanted nothing more than to be perfect for her dashing young husband. She would take her chances.

Billie's teeth chattered with another abrupt change in the wind. Kona winds, bringing humidity and rain. It was late. She should be getting back to the house. She needed a shower to wash off the salt spray. Or maybe a long hot soak with some of the scandalous bath oil Agnes had insisted she buy. Then she might try out the piano in the living room. It had been so long since she'd played. It would soothe her so that she could fall asleep in quick order. She wondered what Moss was doing. She wondered if he ached for her the way she ached for him.

Billie contented herself over the next two and a half days by learning a few Hawaiian words, with Phillip's help. She learned that *kamaaina* meant "longtime island resident" and referred to Ester Kamali. *Mahalo* meant "thank you." *Ono* meant "tastes good!" (She said that over and over as she devoured twelve mangoes!) *Wahine* was "woman" and *wikiwiki* was "to do something quickly." Before the servant walked back to his quarters, he told her she was *nani*, which meant "beautiful." Billie smiled. The words weren't all that difficult to pronounce and sounded so lovely. When Moss arrived she would show him what she'd learned and practice on him.

Moss drove the Jeep carefully up the hill road, already anticipating the feel of Billie in his arms. She'd be there, waiting for him, ready for him. He smiled, biting down on the slim, ivory-tipped cigarillos he'd come to favor. He had deserved being restricted to base, he knew, but it had been rough duty when he'd tossed and turned all night long, waking to find himself alone instead of lying beside his wife. Damn, a man could get used to the nicer things in life.

Before he'd left the base, it had seemed as if Thad were avoiding him for some reason. He mentally shrugged. Maybe old Thad was more discreet and understanding than he'd thought and hadn't wanted to intrude on him and Billie. Still, it bothered him somewhat that when he'd suggested Thad keep Billie company, his friend had suddenly been busy with other obligations. Of course, though Billie certainly excited *him*, she was not exciting to be with. Perhaps that would come later, when she'd had more time to mature. But now, Billie posed no challenge; there was no aura of danger or mystery about her. He supposed most men felt that way about their wives and that was how it should be. A wife was steady and secure, predictable and safe. That was why men didn't marry girls like Lola, who worked at Holli Loki's on the other side of the island. Lola was never safe or predictable and she ran around with dangerous men, but Lola was exciting. And she showed him more interesting things than baby pictures of an infant he'd never seen.

Maggie. Now where the hell had Billie come up with that name? One of these days he'd have to ask her. Undoubtedly, she'd tell him it was after the author of *Gone with the Wind*, Billie's favorite book. Christ, there was no figuring women! Seth probably wouldn't have cared if Billie had named the baby Pepsi-Cola. Pap had no trouble keeping his priorities straight and the hoped-for grandson was most likely the only reason the old man had moved heaven and earth to send Billie to Hawaii. Pap had done his share and the rest was up to Moss. Making her pregnant with Riley Seth Coleman would be Moss's pleasure.

There couldn't be anything wrong with Billie, could there? She was the picture of health; she positively bloomed with it. Jessica's letter to Moss, arriving just about the same time as Billie herself, must have been written out of maternal concern. Still, his mother's words nagged at him. She had said that she'd talked with Dr. Ward one afternoon when he'd looked in on her for one of her headaches. He had warned against another pregnancy for Billie. Now what the hell was that supposed to mean? And if there was any truth to it, why wouldn't Billie have said something herself?

As he did with everything else that threatened his plans, Moss stowed this puzzle away on the back shelf of his mind. Billie was a big girl now—she was a mother herself—and it was nobody's damn business but Billie's and his! Moss began to whistle as the hilltop house came into view. Vaguely, he wondered if his son would have his dark hair.

CHAPTER THIRTEEN

Thad Kingsley stood just off the runway, smoking a cigarette.
It was forbidden, but there wasn't anyone around of importance
to report him. He took a deep drag and then crushed the butt
out with the heel of his flight boot. He bent over to pocket the
incriminating evidence and then looked overhead. A plane bearing the medical insignia of the Red Cross was about to land.
The pilot touched down with ease. Thad felt like clappng. The
guy, whoever he was, was loose as a goose.

Medical supplies? Usually they came by land in supply
trucks. Curiosity got the better of him and he stood around
until the bays opened. Two figures in army fatigues hopped
out. The taller of the two advanced to one of the ground crew
and held out his manifest. Thad watched as the sailor scratched
his head and then shook it. Thad inched a little closer, in time
to hear the big corporal say, "We got this delivery for some
guy named Coleman, stationed here. Look, don't give me any
of this crap that you don't know who the guy is. He's some
goddamn admiral, is who he is. If I told you where this stuff
came from, you'd know he was an admiral. What say we get
the lead out and tell Admiral Coleman his personal Red Cross
plane full of food is here." There was distaste on the man's
face.

"I'm telling you, I know every admiral on this base and we
ain't got no Coleman. We got a Coleman who's a second looey.
You want I should get him?"

"You better get somebody before this stuff goes bad. And
get more ice. My orders say a medical vehicle is to meet this
plane and take the contents to . . . an undisclosed destination.
This is all bullshit, sailor. Somebody's screwing around. I just
deliver. Go get this Coleman or get that truck, but do something."

"I don't have orders to do that," the sailor complained. "And
we don't have an Admiral Coleman. So, you do whatever the

hell you damn please. I go off duty in another three minutes."

"Where's this Coleman who's a second looey hang out? The one who ain't an admiral."

"In that building over there. He's a flight instructor. I'm officially off duty now. No more questions. Solve your own damn problems."

"Close those goddamn bays till I figure out what the hell to do with this stuff," the tall man shouted to his partner. "This heat will melt what ice is in there and whose ass do you think will be in a sling then?"

Thad stifled a laugh and turned his head.

"I need this. I really need this," the corporal grumbled as he loped toward the building. Thad could have told him that Moss had taken his class down to the far end of the airstrip, but he didn't. This was the best show he'd seen since joining the navy.

Two hours later, every admiral, captain, and commander on the base, it seemed, was on the airstrip to claim the contents of the Red Cross plane. "You got the password, you get the contents," the belligerent corporal said tartly. "No password, the stuff rots on the plane. You see who signed this manifest?" Thad felt a bubble of laughter rumble in his chest at the awed looks.

Moss Coleman led his weary band of students down the airstrip. His eyes took in the scene and the Red Cross plane. Next to it was a van with the same insignia. He took a deep breath and started to whistle "Deep in the Heart of Texas."

"That's good enough for me. Sign here," the corporal bellowed in Moss's direction. "If that guy's an admiral, I'll eat the entire contents of this plane," Thad heard him mutter.

Moss signed his name with a flourish. He turned and addressed the assembled brass. "Sirs, you're all invited to a Texas barbecue at my house in the hills. I've taken the liberty of posting a small map and directions on the flight bulletin board." He favored Thad with a heavy-lidded wink and ordered his flight group to about-face.

"Who the hell *is* that guy?" demanded a three-star with a forty-five-inch waist.

"Beats the hell out of me," a commander said shortly. "All I know is I saw the signature on the manifest and I am not about to ask one question. I'm going to the barbecue and that's all I know. Maybe we'll all be mentioned in *Stars and Stripes* if we play our cards right."

Thad had all he could do to keep a straight face. He walked over to the Red Cross truck, handed the driver a map, and bent through the window to give him Moss's instructions.

The burly corporal stared at Thad a minute. "You son of a bitch, you been standing here for three hours and you knew all along whose stuff this was and where it was supposed to go and you never said a word. You navy punks stink. Why didn't you say something?"

"I didn't know the password and I can't whistle. Would you have believed me?"

"Guess not. This stuff is like gold. Okay, sorry I blew up at you, but I still think you navy guys stink."

"Oh, yeah?" Thad growled. "Buzz off, buddy. And I out-rank you, so lets not bring it to a test. Move it! Corporal!"

"Yes sir!" the corporal said, smartly saluting. The minute Thad's back was turned the smart salute was minus four fingers.

Billie watched the hectic preparations for the barbecue. She could tell that Moss was irritated to the point where he was going to do or say something hurtful to the slow-moving Phillip. "Yes sir, Mr. Moss, sir, *wikiwiki*. Cow is big difference from pig. Pig is easy to roast. Cow much meat. Much more heavier. You have two cows. Much work. No help. You bring more help we move *wikiwiki*."

"Steer. It's a steer," Moss said in exasperation. "More help is on the way. Let's get this spit going and we can set up the other one on the beach. I don't see what the big problem is. Roasting a pig is the same principle as a steer. The only difference is you put an apple in the pig's mouth. You want an apple in this steer's mouth, you have my permission."

"Apple too small. Maybe pineapple. Stupid you no want luau. In Hawaii you have luau. We not make"—he searched his mind for the words Moss had repeated over and over to him—"Tukas barkut."

"Texas barbecue." Moss grimaced. Billie giggled behind her hand. Secretly she had to agree with Phillip. A luau would have been so much simpler.

It was three o'clock in the morning and Billie was tired. All she wanted to do was go to bed and sleep in Moss's arms. But Moss, she knew, had no thoughts of sleep. He was going to supervise until it was time to leave for the base at five-thirty. How he could devote all his attention and energy to this ridiculous cookout was beyond her. Phillip was literally falling asleep on his feet, but Moss would show him no mercy. Once the pit was just right and the steer secure on the spit, Moss stood back to view his handiwork. "Pap would be proud of me," Moss said with a clap of his hands. "Now all we have to do is get the other pit ready and then sit back. Billie, you took care of all the other food, didn't you? Ice is coming first thing in the morning—I want that beer to be ice cold. Who's shucking the corn? What about the sauce? Are you sure that gal in the kitchen knows what to do with it?"

"Trust me, darling. Everything is under control," Billie said wearily.

"Did you get yourself a colorful muumuu?"

"I didn't have the time. Don't worry. I have something to wear."

"Billie, I told you to get a muumuu. Or rather I told Thad to tell you. I wanted you to wear something bright and colorful with a hibiscus behind your ear. You've been lying around the house for days. How much trouble would it have been for you to go down to one of the shops in Waikiki and get one? Goddamn it, Billie, was that too much to ask?"

Billie felt like a whipped dog. Moss had never, ever spoken to her like this before. "I'm . . . I'm sorry, Moss. I didn't think it was all that important. I brought all these new clothes with me that I've never worn. They're so much prettier . . . than a baggy muumuu." Her shoulders slumped. "I'm sorry, Moss. I'll get one this morning."

Moss swung around. "You can't go anywhere today. You have to stay here and keep your eye on things. I don't want you to even think of leaving."

"All right, Moss. I'm sorry. Please, don't be angry. I don't want us to argue. Our time is so short and I don't want anything to spoil it."

Moss's eyes softened. "I'm sorry, too. It's just that you've always tried to please me. I rarely, if ever, tell you to do anything. I thought you would understand that it was important to me to have you wear a muumuu. I plan on having some pictures taken to send on to Pap and Mam. All the guys from the squadron are wearing floral shirts. Most of the brass is coming in island dress. You're going to stick out like a sore thumb. The hostess standing out like a sore thumb is not something I wanted, Billie. Pap and Mam are going to be disappointed.

"Well, it's too late now, so let's forget it. Old Phillip here looks like he's about wrung out, so you're going to have to help me with the beach pit. You can do that, can't you?"

At that point, Billie would have done anything to bring a smile to her husband's face.

When Moss left the house at five-thirty, Billie was exhausted. Both longhorns were turning slowly on the spits. The tender beef would be ready for serving by ten o'clock that night. Wet sand and salt covered every inch of her skin. Her blond curls were matted and caked with salt spray. She sank to the sand and cried. Moss had only pecked her on the cheek. It was the kind of kiss, she thought, a man would give his mistress as he exited her apartment so no trace of perfume would stay with him. She felt wretched. Angry tears scalded her eyes. Moss hadn't even responded when she'd said she loved him and warned him to drive carefully. He'd nodded curtly and climbed into the Jeep. He was angry with her. How could she have been so stupid?

Angry and frustrated, Billie kicked off her sandals and ran into the ocean. She struck out, beating at the waves as though they were the enemy. By the time she swam back to shore she could feel the tension finally leaving her shoulders.

Imperceptibly the slim shoulders squared. Moss wanted her attired in a muumuu. Moss would find her attired in a muumuu. Somehow, some way, she would find one. She shivered in the cool early-morning air. A smile touched her lips when she saw Phillip dozing on the lanai side of the house. She dried off and went in search of the housekeeper. When there was no answer to her quiet knock, she opened the door and stepped in. Again she squared her shoulders. She needed a little Coleman guts to do what she had to do. Gently she shook the plump woman's shoulder. "Wake up, Rosa. I need your help. Big *pilikia*," she said. "I need your help. You have to get up. Come, please. I know it's early, but it's going to be a busy day." The plump woman glared at her and smiled at the same time. "Please, Rosa," Billie pleaded.

Rosa rolled over, the bed springs creaking with her weight. "You wake me when sun high," she muttered, pulling the sheet over her head.

"Rosa, you don't understand. You have to get up, *wikiwiki*. Now. I need a muumuu. It's so important to me. I'll have to try to make one somehow. Is there a sewing machine here someplace?" Billie was so frustrated she wanted to stomp her feet and wail like a banshee. How *could* this woman sleep like this? How could she lie there and refuse to help her? Her happiness depended on getting a muumuu.

Phillip, perhaps he could help. Billie raced back to the lanai to rouse Rosa's husband. She hated to wake the old man after he'd worked all night with Moss, but she had no other choice. She shook him awake, none too gently. A full fifteen minutes later Billie had Phillip's less-than-interested attention. At least his eyes were open, she told herself. Quickly she explained her problem. Phillip snorted. "You tell she look like Queen Kamamalu. She get up and do what you say. Is only way. But you no mention word tattoo. She want. You listen good."

"Yes, yes. I understand. Don't say anything about a tattoo. Tell her she looks like Queen Kamamalu. That's it? That's all I have to do?" But Phillip was already asleep.

Billie rolled the queen's name over and over on her tongue. She had to look up the famous lady in Miss Kamali's library. Queen Kamamalu, Queen Kamamalu, Queen Kamamalu, she repeated to herself as she sprinted down the right wing of the house where Rosa slept. "Rosa, I had to come back and tell you something." Billie's voice was a bare whisper. "I simply couldn't let another day go by without telling you that I think you look just like Queen . . . Queen Kamamalu. You really do." Childishly she crossed her fingers for the little white lie she was being forced to tell. Maybe it wasn't a lie at all. She uncrossed her fingers.

Rosa rolled over and sat upright. "You think so, Missy Billie? Nobody believe but Phillip. Need tattoo here and here and here," Rosa said, jabbing at herself. "Queen Kamamalu much tattoo. Phillip say no."

Billie grimaced. "Husbands, Phillip, loco." Billie pointed to her head. She would do anything, say anything to get the housekeeper moving.

"You smart *wahine*. Smart *haole wahine*." Rosa smiled as she struggled from the bed.

"Now this is my problem. I need a muumuu," Billie said, enunciating each word carefully. "I thought maybe we could make one, or at least try to put together something. Is there a sewing machine here?" At Rosa's perplexed look, Billie made motions with her fingers as though she were threading a needle and then weaving it in and out of the hem of her shorts. Rosa smiled and said, "No. No sew. No ricky-ticky sew."

Tears of frustration gathered in Billie's eyes. "I need a muumuu, Rosa. My *kane*, my *ipo* won't like me." She felt stupid when she made kissing motions with her lips to show Rosa how serious the situation was. Billie never knew if it was the words that meant man and sweetheart or her tears that finally moved the housekeeper from her bed.

"Come duh udder room." Billie followed Rosa down the hall to what must have been Ester Kamali's bedroom. Rosa stood at moment as though undecided. A second glance at Billie's tear-filled eyes seemed to convince her to open the door. Billie advanced and then backed up a step. She knew this had to be the most beautiful room she had ever seen. Everything was pearl white or a light moss green, even the wicker. Splashes of yellow as golden as sunshine added just the right touch. Billie drew in her breath. It was a woman's room. She didn't know why, but she had the feeling no man had ever set foot across the threshold. It was too perfect. It smelled new, never used. Billie raised her hands palms up to show she didn't understand.

"Missy Ester's *ipo* died. No marry udder man, ever."

Ester Kamali's sweetheart died. How sad. Billie felt as if she were trespassing. The feeling was so strong she turned to leave, the tears running down her cheeks. Here she was worried about a simple thing like a muumuu and her kind, unseen hostess had lost her sweetheart. Rosa moved quickly and drew Billie back into the room. "Missy Ester go way. Not come back many, many years. No udder man for missy. You come."

Dabbing at her tear-streaked face, Billie followed Rosa into a small dressing room off the bedroom, watching as she reached up to one of the shelves for a porcelain jar and withdrew a small brass key. "You see, *wikiwiki*." Rosa blessed herself and dropped to her knees before a large wicker chest beneath the last shelf. Honey-colored hands were gentle with the mounds of tissue paper that lay inside, then they probed the depths of the chest. Rosa seemed to know what she was searching for by touch rather than sight. When her plump hands found it, she withdrew and held up a rainbow of multicolored silk. "For you, Missy Billie. No udder *wahine* wear. Missy Ester say hokay."

Billie was speechless. She was selfish enough to want to reach out for the dress but woman enough to know what the beautiful silk had meant to Ester Kamali. Tears welled in her eyes again. She shook her head at Rosa and backed off a step.

"You take. You wear. Missy Ester want you *kane* see you in her dress. You take. Is hokay. Is much hokay. Take."

Almost without intending to, Billie reached out for the vi-

{ 205 }

brant silk. It was just what Moss would have expected her to buy for herself. She held the flowing gown to her shoulders. Rosa's jet-black eyes glowed with pleasure. "Rosa, are you sure?" Billie wanted the dress more than anything in the world. She'd do anything to be able to wear it. Anything to erase Moss's displeasure. "I'll take care of it. I promise. I won't go near food. I won't even take a drink while I'm wearing it."

Rosa frowned. What *was* the *wahine* talking about? When Billie smiled, Rosa relaxed. "Missy Ester much happy that the dress make *wahine* happy."

Billie carried the silk gown back to her room and laid it on the bed. Moss was going to be pleased. She knew he wouldn't ask questions. He would simply accept the fact that she had somehow found a way to do as he wished.

Billie showered and washed and set her hair. She let the warm shower run, creating steam in the bathroom so that the silk, hung from a scented, padded hanger, would be free of wrinkles. There was no way she was going to lay an iron to this gorgeous creation.

When she made her way to the kitchen, Rosa and Phillip, along with assorted cousins, nephews, and nieces, were busily preparing food for the barbecue. The food that had arrived on the medical transport was off to one side. Rosa and a bubbly niece were making Hawaiian dishes that would be served separately. Already there were huge platters of *lau lau*, a mixture of fish, pork, and taro leaves wrapped and steamed in a Ti leaf. Billie selected one and popped it in her mouth. "Delicious." She laughed and took a second. Baking *ulu* and *opihi* were sending off delicious aromas. This would be the first time Billie would taste breadfruit and limpets. There were small pots of purple *poi*, made from crushed taro root. Billie wrinkled her nose. The young girls laughed as they dipped their fingers in the *poi* and licked them. Even if it was the traditional Hawaiian dish, Billie decided to pass on it. Instead her eyes were drawn to the containers of barbecue sauce and huge sacks of corn. She had a feeling she was going to be the one to shuck the yellow ears. Phillip made motions to her to indicate the beer kegs were on ice. That was good. The two cases of bourbon would go out on the terrace, where Moss was going to set up a bar. Two gunnysacks full of Idaho baking potatoes were being inspected by Phillip. He had his instructions as to baking them on the beach, next to the steers. "Much time left for totes."

"Potatoes," Billie corrected him.

"What I said, totes."

Butter was being iced and salt by the pound was being poured into heavy ceramic shakers. Cartons of heavy paper napkins were opened and a child of ten or so was busily folding them into intricate squares. From what she could see there were at least six red-and-white-checkered tablecloths. Seth did all this! she thought in amazement. Surely he'd forgotten something. Billie poked and pried into the cartons and sacks. Her eyes were wide when she extracted two full boxes of toothpicks and three one-pound cans of peppermint candies. For indigestion, she supposed. She rummaged more and found cabbage for coleslaw and six graters. God! Dressing was in the icebox in gallon jars. All this food, all the way from Texas. It was unbelievable. When her search was finished she had to admit that there was no fault to be found. Seth had thought of everything, right down to the huge cans of baked beans.

"Phillip, if you or one of the boys will carry the corn out to the monkeypod tree, I'll clean it. I'll need a basket or something to put it in." She had barely finished speaking when a tall youth hefted one of the sacks and slung a wicker basket over his shoulder. He favored her with a dazzling smile as he motioned for her to go ahead of him.

Billie crossed the terrace and smiled at a cherub brigade as they deftly ran thread through plumeria blossoms for welcome leis. Moss had thought of everything, too. It might be a Texas barbecue, but he was deferring in small ways to the beautiful Hawaiian customs.

As Billie sat under the tree shucking the corn she realized how far away from home she really was. The ripe yellow silk lay like a carpet at her feet and the lime-green leaves piled up. The lemony-colored corn was beautiful, the kernels in perfect rows. It was a pity she wouldn't be able to taste it. She was already regretting the promise she'd made not to eat while wearing Ester Kamali's dress. After the guests had gone she would take the dress off and eat some of the leftovers.

Two hours later, Billie massaged her neck and turned the balance of the shucking over to one of the boys. He wrinkled his nose at the pile of corn but fell to his task at a sharp command from his Uncle Phillip. Time to see how the sourdough bread was coming along.

Satisfied with the flour-strewn kitchen and dark mutterings from Rosa, Billie made a hasty retreat to the beach, where she went for a long solitary walk. At first her thoughts were lazy and dream-filled, but they intensified as the swells from the ocean whipped onto the sandy shore. All this commotion, all this fuss, all this trouble for a barbecue: what was Moss thinking of? And Seth, sending all the food from half a world away? She didn't think she would ever understand the Colemans. Moss's attitude and his sharp words to her this morning had hurt. Deeply. Secretly, Billie admitted to herself that she was jealous of the evening's plans. Why wasn't Moss satisfied just being with her? The two of them. The days were to be treasured now. She guessed the *Enterprise* was about ready to leave. Repairs were ahead of schedule. Who knew when they would see each other again? Learn to enjoy what you have, Thad had said. She must keep that in mind at all times.

This party was going to go into the early hours of the morning. Moss had to be back on base for his weekend restriction. That meant the cleaning-up chores after the party would fall to her and Rosa.

Billie sighed as she looked out across the waves. She should be delirious with happiness. Here she was in an island paradise with the man she loved with all her heart, a beautiful gown to wear for the evening, and she was feeling sorry for herself. Top brass, beautiful women . . . the party atmosphere should be intoxicating. Why did she feel so miserable, so let down? Was it fatigue from having worked through the night at Moss's side? No, she'd been up all night on many occasions and hadn't felt like this. Soul weary? Perhaps. Disappointed? More true than not. Was it too much to expect to spend every moment possible with her husband?

In just a few hours Moss would be home. At least they would have some time alone before their guests arrived. Unless of course Moss took it into his head to supervise every little detail. She would go to her room and take the bobby pins out of her hair. Maybe she could fix herself a glass of lemonade and sit in the sun on the balcony. A good book or magazine would help her wile away the time. But before she did anything she had to check both barbecue pits and make a second inspection of conditions in the kitchen. It was almost laughable. What did she know about roasting steers?

Phillip clucked his tongue and made clapping sounds with his hands to show his disapproval as Billie picked up the smoking banyan leaves. She fared no better when she peeked into the kitchen. It looked like utter chaos to her. There were pans and platters of food everywhere. Flour and something that looked like a pot of melting glue stood on the chrome kitchen table. Later, she must ask what it was.

The ornamental clock on the desk in the living room chimed six o'clock. Billie checked the gold circle on her wrist. Five minutes past. She was resetting her watch when she heard the Jeep coming up the road. She ran to the wide double doors and flung them open. Her excited welcome died in her throat. In the Jeep with Moss sat Thad Kingsley and three other friends. She forced a smile to her lips and walked out to the driveway. "Look, honey," said Moss. "I brought help. Come on in, guys, and Billie will fix you a drink. I want to check out the pits. Phillip is a grand old guy, but he isn't up on longhorn beef. Did you check on things during the day, Billie?"

How excited he was. How happy he looked. This was all so important to him. How could she even think of spoiling things? She was so glad now that she had accepted Miss Kamali's dress. "Yes, Moss, I did. Everything looked fine to me. Don't even consider going into the kitchen. Rosa will box your ears."

Thad and the others laughed. Moss loped toward the beach and Billie led the way to the outside terrace. She offered drinks and made small talk.

Twenty minutes later Moss was back and mixing his own drink. He settled down near his friends and conversation ran to the events of the day. Billie looked from one man to the other. Only Thad's eyes met hers in silent apology. She excused herself and knew no one was aware that she was leaving, except possibly Thad.

Billie filled the tub for a long, leisurely soak. She added a liberal dose of bath salts and watched the water foam. It was almost as frothy as the Pacific. She wouldn't cry, she just wouldn't. Sometimes this new married life stunned her. Moss probably didn't even remember that he had been sharp with her this morning. He was probably unaware how hurt she had been. It was time to shake this depression, time to get dressed and join Moss and his friends. Their guests would be arriving shortly.

When Billie made her entrance an hour later on the lanai all five officers jumped to their feet, but it was to Moss that Billie's eyes went. There was approval and pride in his glance and smile. The long sarong-like gown displayed her smooth tan shoulders and high rounded breasts, the side slit skirt allowing peek-a-boo glimpses of an elegant length of leg.

"You look lovely, Billie," Thad said sincerely. The other three pilots echoed Thad's approval. Moss kissed her lightly on the cheek and put his arm around her shoulder. Billie wanted to lean into him, to snuggle against him, but she held her emotions in check. She smiled warmly and settled herself on one of the wicker chairs. The silk crept up around her ankles, exposing a scandalously sexy high-heeled shoe that was nothing more than straps. Thad Kingsley swallowed hard. He had never seen anything so provocative as that gently swinging foot.

"I think I'll take a walk to the beach and check out your longhorns," he said. "If I were you, Coleman, I'd get the lead out and get dressed. You are the host and the brass should be arriving any minute now."

"Good thinking. I won't be long. Billie, refill the guys' drinks."

"We can do it, Moss. Let your wife rest. We enjoy sitting here looking at her."

"Suit yourself. I told you guys to bring dates."

"Surely you jest. When I party I party. All the way. You can't let go with the top brass milling about. Don't worry about us. We're here to eat all that beef you've been jawing about."

Moss shrugged. The guys were right. Jesus, Billie was going to knock the socks right off the brass. And their wives were going to do some double takes. He'd never seen her look so beautiful. The guys were impressed. Thad had looked like a fish out of water for a minute. The party was going to be a success. He could *feel* it.

By nine-thirty the last guest had arrived. Moss drew Billie aside as they surveyed the scene on the terraces and lanai. "Did you ever notice that all generals' and admirals' wives are old and wrinkled? Look at that one over there." Billie looked in the direction Moss was discreetly pointing. The woman's face was leathery and wrinkled, and the skin on her neck hung in unattractive folds. "So help me, if you ever get to looking like that, I'll divorce you."

"Are you going to be an admiral someday, Moss?" Billie teased, enjoying the few moments of intimacy.

"Not me, but Thad is. I'd bet Sunbridge on it."

Billie giggled. "Do you think he'll have a wife like one of these women?"

"God, I hope not. Thad's pretty selective. What kind of shoes is the general's wife wearing?" Moss asked curiously.

Billie peered straight ahead in the yellow lantern light. She giggled again. "Serviceable. Maybe she has a foot problem. But we're being unkind."

"The hell you say, Mrs. Coleman. That lady is a living, breathing bitch. She controls the officers' wives with an iron hand. The general doesn't make a move until he checks with her. It's common knowledge on the base. I'm glad you aren't staying there, Billie." Moss's arms tightened protectively around his wife's shoulders. This time, Billie leaned against him and whispered. He bent down to hear and grinned. "I'll take you up on that later. We better start to circulate, honey. Phillip is going to start carving soon and we have to head the line. I'll meet you on the lanai in, say, twenty minutes."

Billie maneuvered through the milling crowds, stopping to speak to one person and then another. The party was a success.

The moment Phillip's relatives struck the first chord of "Deep in the Heart of Texas" on their ukuleles, Billie made her way to the lanai to meet Moss.

Moss held up both hands as a signal for quiet. *"Hele mai ai!"* he shouted. "Come and eat!"

The small orchestra split up, half going to the area beneath the monkeypod tree and the other half to the beach. They strummed softly while native girls in their grass skirts swayed to the music. More than one man's eyes was on the girls instead of his beef. Billie felt smug. Moss had eyes for no one save herself.

"We'll have to do this again sometime, old buddy," Thad said with a slight slur to his words.

"The next time you can do it." Moss grinned. "What do you New Englanders do for a bash?"

"We have fish fries. And chowders. Stick-to-your-ribs chowder. Did I tell you you are the most beautiful woman here?" Thad said gallantly to Billie as he tried for a low, sweeping bow.

"Three times," Moss said, grinning. "You're getting crocked, Thad."

"Yeaaahhh. Billie, would you play the piano for me? That tinny music is getting to me. I have a yen for some good old U.S. of A. music. Old man, can your wife play me a couple of tunes?" Thad asked Moss.

"I don't see why not. It's up to Billie. Billie?"

"Of course. What would you like to hear?"

"Something with some beat. Something with heart. A little

honky-tonk, maybe some boogie-woogie. Is that a tall order?"

"Not too tall. I think I can manage. Come along, Lieutenant."

Billie settled herself at the keyboard. She flexed her fingers and tested out the keys. The baby grand was a magnificent instrument.

Billie was lost in the music, unaware of Thad's intent gaze as he leaned over the piano. She finished the last chord of "When the Lights Come On Again All Over the World" and swung into "The White Cliffs of Dover." "Harbor Lights" followed and then "Always."

"Slide over, Billie," Thad ordered. Billie obeyed and was stunned when Thad ran his long fingers the length of the keyboard. "Let's have a duet. Name your choice."

"I didn't know you played, Thad."

"There's a lot of things you don't know about me. Come on, let's tickle these ivories."

Billie laughed. "Name it, Lieutenant, and I'll keep up with you."

When the last guest had left, Moss took stock. "It was a roaring success, honey. We really did ourselves up proud. Mac took some great pictures. I'm not even going to try to get them developed over here. I'll send them straight on to Pap. Listen, honey, Thad, Mac, and Jack have to get back. If they take the Jeep, I won't have any way to get to the base in the morning, so I'm going along with them. I'll be back Monday night."

"Moss, it's only three A.M. You cold get a few hours' sleep and drive the Ford in the morning." If he left now, she wouldn't see him for another three days. "Moss, please."

"It's best this way, honey. By the time I get back, I can shower and change and write to Pap. He's going to want to know how things went. I'll see you Monday night. By the way, Mrs. Coleman, did I tell you how beautiful you looked this evening? Hey, are those tears? Billie, Coleman women don't cry over something as silly as this. Come on now, give me a smile." Billie's effort was hardly more than a grimace, but it seemed to satisfy Moss.

"Come on, you flight jockeys, move it! Who's almost sober?"

"I am," Thad said quietly. "Haven't had a drink in hours. I'll drive. Moss, if you don't want to drive the Ford down in the morning, I'll take it now and you can take the Jeep. You look done in. Why don't you catch a few hours' sleep?"

Moss shook his head. "We'll do it my way."

Billie's eyes thanked Thad for what he was trying to do for her. "Good night, gentlemen," she said quietly. "Thad, drive carefully. Moss, I'll see you on Monday." Without another word, she turned and headed for the bedroom, tears spilling down her cheeks. She'd been so sure Moss would stay.

Thad wanted to push his fist through Moss's smiling face. The ride back to the base was silent, heavy with emotions and confused loyalties. Moss was his friend, his best friend, Thad reminded himself. He would try never to forget it.

{{{{{{{{ CHAPTER FOURTEEN }}}}}}}}

Billie's Hawaiian honeymoon seemed to have ended. After the barbecue it was only rarely that she and Moss spent an evening alone together. They'd broken the ice; now it was their turn to accept social invitations, and Moss frequently entertained at the Officers' Club, just outside the base.

"It's important to me, Billie," he'd say when she complained. "It's not like I'm asking you to do anything but *be* there. All the arrangements are handled by the club."

"But I want to be *here*, alone with you, not with twenty other people. And I'm so much younger than the other wives, we've got very little in common."

"I don't like it when you whine, Billie. I don't like it at all. Promotions aren't handed out on merit alone. Not even in wartime. You're my wife and a Coleman. You've lived at Sunbridge long enough to see how things are done and I expect you to do them. Now get dressed."

"I could almost understand it if you were planning a career in the service, Moss, but you're not. Why is it so important to you?"

"Because I want to go as far as I can. I want to be up there where the decisions are made. There's no telling how long this war will last and I want to have some say in it. I've got some ideas of my own but no one will listen to them if I'm still just a flight jockey. Now do you understand?"

"Not quite. I really don't see why it should involve me. Thad doesn't have a wife to entertain for him and he's certainly not wanting for promotions."

It stuck in Moss's craw that Thad had been promoted to full lieutenant. His friend seemed to be fulfilling Pap's prophecy: "Watch out, boy, or that Yankee'll get ahead of you."

Billie was immediately sorry for what she'd said and meekly went to the bedroom to change. At least her expensive wardrobe was being put to good use. There was the Coleman image to preserve. Later, Moss would smooth her ruffled feathers with a gentle kiss and an approving whistle. And if there was one thing Billie desperately needed, it was her husband's approval.

Moss wasn't certain he liked the new assertiveness in his wife. In many ways he wanted her to be more independent, because it would mean greater freedom and fewer responsibilities for him. Yet he never really wanted her to change from that pleasant, acquiescent girl he'd met in Philadelphia. He rather liked being the one in control, and he considered Billie's occasional balkiness unattractive. Things were so much nicer when he could tell her not to bother her pretty little head about something and she would listen. This new Billie seemed to demand answers, and often he wasn't prepared to give them.

What Billie had said concerning Thad's promotion was niggling at him—perhaps she was closer to the truth of the matter than he was. It was possible that Billie's arrival in Hawaii had created jealousy among the other officers, reminding everyone he was a Coleman and had received special treatment. Then, too, perhaps the barbecue hadn't been that great an idea. Billie's instincts had been correct again. Settling back with his drink, Moss made a decision. Everyone had met the little wife . . . now it was time for her to go back stateside.

Billie stood under the shower spray wishing she had time for a bath instead. A nice long bath, fragrant with perfumed salts and a delicate powdering afterward. Then it would be so nice to crawl into bed beside Moss and make love to him. She wrinkled her nose in disappointment. Their social engagements usually ended late and Moss had to leave for the base so early; they had little time alone together. At least not for slow, luxurious arousals and falling asleep in each other's arms. Their lovemaking had become as hurried and demanding as everything else in their lives.

She lathered her arms, her neck, and her breasts, which were feeling heavier and more sensitive than usual, a sensation she remembered from her pregnancy with Maggie.

A little stab of remorse sent her thoughts to the baby she'd left back in Texas. It had been almost two months since she'd seen her daughter. Counting on her fingers, Billie realized that she'd left for Hawaii seven weeks ago. Seven weeks and no menstrual period. The thought was so devastating she felt light-headed, and suddenly Dr. Ward's warnings flashed through her brain. No, it wasn't possible. It was all the activity, all the swimming. Gingerly, she pressed her fingers into her breasts, feeling their tenderness. Missing a period didn't necessarily mean pregnancy and this was the way her breasts usually felt at the onset of her monthlies.

Hurriedly, she finished washing and rinsed off. Moss was waiting for her and she could practically feel his impatience. She wondered, not for the first time since arriving in Hawaii, if she should tell him what Dr. Ward had said about becoming pregnant again. Yet, as always before, it was something she couldn't bring herself to share with him. It would cause him worry and he had enough on his mind. Deep inside, she knew the real reason she wouldn't confide in Moss was that she didn't want him to think she was lacking in any way. She was ashamed of her inadequacies, even though this one was something over which she had no control. Besides, Agnes was well aware of the doctor's warnings and if there was anything to really be concerned about, her own mother would have said something. Wouldn't she?

By the time Billie stepped out of the bedroom, dressed in a white linen evening suit and high-heeled strapped slippers, Moss had come to the decision that his wife's return to the States was imperative, even if he had to fabricate the reasons for her leaving. "Billie," he said with a grin, eyeing the way the white linen skirt hugged her hips and thighs, "you're a knockout! Maybe you're right and we should stay home tonight."

Billie stepped into his arms, raking her fingers through the dark hair at the back of his neck. His thighs pressed enticingly against her own and his lips found the hollows of her throat. As her desires heightened, her questions subsided. This was her husband and he loved her and didn't want to share her with anyone tonight. When his mouth captured hers and she heard him emit a low groan of passion, tears of love and gratitude made crystalline paths down her cheeks.

* * *

Less than a week later, Moss arrived home early. Billie immediately knew something was terribly wrong. "What are you doing home?" she asked, dreading the answer.

"Billie, love, I can't stay. I've just come to pick up my things. I've got to get right back, but I wanted to see you before I left."

"Left? Where are you going?" There'd been so little time, so little time. Already she ached with missing him.

"I can't tell you that, Billie. You understand. I've already gotten through to Pap and he's making arrangements for you to go back stateside."

"Why can't I stay here and wait for you?"

"Now, Billie, love, don't look at me that way. Why would you want to stay here? I don't know when I'll be getting back and you do have our daughter to think about. I can't leave you all alone here in Hawaii. It just isn't possible. I'd never have a minute's rest!"

Billie sank into Moss's arms, too shocked for tears. "I've got to know where you're going. I've got to know when I'll see you again."

"Chin up, Billie. You knew this would happen. Pap knew it, too, when he sent you out here. It's out of my hands. Come here," he said softly. He tucked his chin on the top of her head so she wouldn't see the lies in his eyes. The Big E was still in dock.

Billie melted into his embrace. With her head against his chest, she could hear the wild thumping of his heart. She had to be brave; it was the least she could do for the man she loved, who was about to go off again to war.

Moss's hands trembled slightly as he caressed Billie's soft golden hair. She smelled so good, felt so good. He was a cad for what he was doing and he knew it. But hell, he was making a sacrifice, too! "Honey, I have to go. Take care of yourself and write to me. Every day, long letters. Tell me about Maggie and what's going on at Sunbridge. It makes me feel so close to you. Give my love to Pap and Mam. Tell them I'll write."

"Moss, I love you so much. I can't bear this."

He placed a finger against her quivering lips. "Shhh. Smile, Billie. Smile for me—it's how I want to remember you."

Billie felt beaten and bruised. . . . Would she ever be whole again? She helped him pack his ditty bag and saw him out to the Jeep. "I love you, Moss," she told him, leaning into his embrace.

"I know you do, honey. I know you do."

The following afternoon, Billie Coleman left Hawaii. She was pregnant with her second child.

Billie was welcomed back to Sunbridge by an aroused household in nightclothes. Too tired to respond in detail to questions, Billie issued a terse report on Moss and his well-being to her mother and Seth, then headed straight for her room. They were just going to have to wait until she felt up to the lengthy discussion they wanted. For now she wanted to see her daughter, to hold her and feel the soft downy head against her cheek. And then she wanted to sleep. For as long as possible.

"What the hell was *that* all about, Aggie?" Seth demanded. Agnes tried to hide her amusement at Seth's sleeping attire. She hadn't known they still made nightshirts these days. Red flannel, and with the seam split over his rump. She was going to have to speak to Tita about that. "Doesn't the girl know I've been waiting all day like a heifer in a mud slide for news of my son?"

"She gave you the highlights, Seth. She's tired. It's possible that our objective has been accomplished and Billie is feeling it even at this early stage. Patience. Tomorrow is another day. Moss is well and that's what is important. Go to bed now and we'll talk in the morning."

Dismissed. By God, Aggie was dismissing him like a kid. Seth bristled, but one look at Agnes's eyes told him he would get no further. Honey always worked better than vinegar, or so Agnes was fond of telling him.

Billie tiptoed down the long hallway to the nursery. The nurse was up from her narrow bed along the wall immediately. She brushed back her gray hair and sighed when she saw Billie. A weary smile crossed Billie's face when she peered down at the sleeping baby. She looked like Moss. At least she had his nose. Billie's chin, but Moss's nose.

A long arm shot out when Billie bent to pick up the sleeping baby. Billie straightened and locked eyes with the woman. "Go back to sleep, Nurse. I'm going to pick up my daughter and hold her. And then I'm going to sit in your rocking chair and rock her. If you don't like what I'm about to do, I suggest you pack your bags and leave now. The chauffeur is probably still awake because he just drove me here from the airport. Decide now. I'm very tired and I want to hold my baby."

"This is not good for the baby. She's colicky and needs her sleep. I never allow my charges to be awakened in the middle of the night." Her words were firmly said, but her eyes looked away first and her step was slow when she waddled back to the nursery bed. She had never been discharged from a position yet. This, she thought, was no time to start.

The downy head was soft against Billie's cheek. How sweet and clean Maggie smelled. How good she felt. It was almost as good as holding Moss next to her in a warm bed. Maggie squirmed and let out a large belch. "Just like your daddy." Billie smiled as she carried the sleeping baby to the rocking chair.

Billie rocked the old chair gently as she murmured an account of her trip to the islands to the sleeping baby. An hour later, when she could barely hold her eyes open, Billie nuzzled her face in the baby's neck, reveling in the scent and feel. Her own flesh and blood. Hers and Moss's.

Billie stood over the crib a good five minutes watching the sleeping child. Then she walked over to the nurse's bed. "Maggie is fine. She burped once, very loud, as a matter of fact. I didn't smother her. I didn't fall asleep while I rocked her. She's in a sound sleep and will no doubt sleep through the night. Good night."

"I'm going to have to speak to Mr. Coleman about this, Mrs. Coleman. He placed me in sole charge of Maggie."

Billie spun around and walked back to the bed. "I wouldn't do that if I were you, Miss Jenkins. Not if you want to continue to work here. The choice, however, is entirely up to you."

The nurse stared at Billie. Secretly she wanted to applaud the young mother. Hawaii must have been good for her. Maybe she'd give that old man a run for his money yet. She nodded.

Billie dragged herself back to her room and stripped off her clothes. Too tired to look for a nightgown, she slipped beneath the sheets naked. She was used to sleeping "in the buff," as Moss called it. In fact, she rather liked the satiny feel of the sheets against her skin. She was asleep as soon as her head touched the pillow.

The inquisition began over the dinner table the following evening.

"How did the boy look? Is he all right? Where is he now? You should have stayed longer. Don't tell me you came back because of Maggie."

Billie stared across the width of the table at her father-in-law. "Moss is fine. He looks wonderful. I don't know where he is. The navy didn't confide in me. Thad is with him. So are the others."

"What did you do while he was off duty? My God, girl, don't you understand I want to know everything about my son?"

Billie scooped out the soft mush of her baked potato, added a glob of sour cream, and then stirred it into a thick paste. Not because she wanted to eat it, but just to have something to do with her hands. "We talked about Maggie a lot. We took long walks on the beach. We went swimming early in the morning and late at night. When Moss was restricted, Thad Kingsley took me sight-seeing. I didn't have all that much time with Moss. In fact, if you want, I could total up the hours. I doubt that they would come to a full week."

Agnes broke a piece of bread and then crumbled it in her fingers. She had never heard such a resentful tone in her daughter's voice. She glanced at Seth.

Seth pierced his daughter-in-law with his bright gaze. "Why did Kingsley have to take you sight-seeing? Why didn't Moss take you? I know he doesn't like that piss-assed business, but it was your first visit. Just how thick are those two?"

"I told you, Seth, Moss was restricted. Thad was good enough to take me around to see the sights. Moss asked him to do it. He's very nice. He's Moss's best friend. They depend on each other."

"How was the barbecue?"

"The barbecue was a huge success. Practically everyone was there. Officers and their wives, some enlisted men, and a few Hawaiian civilians who worked on the base. Thad took pictures and Moss said he was going to send the film on to you to have developed. It lasted till three in the morning. A crew from the mess took the leftover beef back to the base. I think they made hash out of it. At least that's what Thad said."

"Did he send a letter? Did he give you a message for me?" Seth demanded. Billie stared into Seth's bright, hopeful gaze.

"He said to tell you he loved you and Mam very much and his next meatball was for you."

Agnes laid down her fork and reached for her water glass. Her eyes met Billie's. She recognized the lie and nodded approvingly. Billie's shoulders squared imperceptibly at the satisfied look on her father-in-law's face.

Billie excused herself and left the table. She wanted to spend some time with Jessica. The brief hour after luncheon hardly counted. She'd been appalled at the change in her mother-in-law on her return. *Feeble* was the only word she could come up with. Billie knew little or nothing about it, but she could sense that Jessica was dying. There was a lost look in the sunken, hollow eyes and a vagueness to her words that made Billie ache.

Jessica was napping, her rosary clutched in her hand. Prayer seemed to give her comfort even if she got the words mixed up. *He* knew what she was saying and thinking. *He* understood.

Billie stood at the window looking out at an arthritic-looking oak on the lawn. It was older than Jessica and would live many more years, dutifully giving shade in the summer and firewood when the limbs were trimmed. What more could a person ask of a tree? And what was expected from this frail creature in her high-necked dimity nightdress? Nothing. Her life was over. Dutiful fifteen-minute visits by Agnes and Seth. And the nurse, at Billie's firm-eyed insistence, would bring the baby every day.

Jessica woke just as Billie turned around. She smiled. "How are you, Billie? Did I fall asleep again? Lately I can't seem to stay awake. Forgive me, child. Please, sit down and tell me more about your trip. Would you mind terribly starting from the beginning? I fear I forgot most of what you told me earlier. But Billie, before you start, did you send off my letter to Amelia?"

"Yes, I did. I posted it right after lunch. Get comfortable and I'll tell you everything, right down to the beautiful monkeypod tree in the yard." Billie settled herself comfortably in a high wingback chair. An hour into her monologue Jessica's eyelids closed. Billie continued to speak for a few more minutes. Then, satisfied that Maggie's grandmother was soundly sleeping, Billie tiptoed about the room, turning off the lamps. She tilted the lamp shade on the night table so the light wouldn't bother Jessica and bent over to kiss the dry, wrinkled cheek.

Billie closed the door and went across the hall to her own room, thinking about the letter to Amelia she had included with Jessica's. After three pages of doings in Sunbridge and news of her father and Moss, Billie had thrown caution to the winds and written that, in her opinion, Jessica was dying. "If there's any way," Billie had written, "please try to come home. We all understand the war is making things impossible, but if need be I'm sure that your father will intervene and help you." She had signed it "Billie."

Billie woke slowly and knew there was something wrong. It was early in the morning, a month to the day after her return from Hawaii. It took barely two minutes for her sleep-filled brain to register that she was going to be sick. She bolted from the bed and raced for the bathroom. Her knuckles were as white as the rim of the basin she was gripping.

Agnes and Seth, on their way down the hall to a sunrise breakfast, heard the sounds from Billie's half-opened door. Their eyes locked, but neither missed a step.

Billie looked at her wretched reflection in the bathroom mirror. Her face was the color of a week-old mushroom. When she fell back against the pillows, she knew she didn't need a calendar to tell her what was wrong. She was pregnant. Somehow she had known. It must have happened the day Moss had been late back to the base.

Billie buried her face in the pillow and wept. Eight more months of misery. "Oh, Moss," she cried.

It was midmorning when Billie made her first attempt to get up. Her head reeled sickeningly. She swallowed hard and managed to get to her feet. By the time she had showered and dressed, she felt slightly better. Some tea and toast would help and then she would place a call to the doctor. He was going to be shocked that she'd ignored his advice. And right now she wished she had paid more attention.

When Billie's feet touched the bottom of the steps she looked up to see her mother walking across the wide central hallway. She was alone, which was odd because lately she and Seth were like each other's shadow. "Where's Seth?" she blurted.

"Out riding—why do you ask?" Agnes said sharply.

"No reason. Mother, join me for some tea. I want to talk to you. If you aren't too busy, that is."

"My, aren't we feisty this morning. Are you all right, Billie? Is there something bothering you? Can I help?"

Her mother's solicitousness prompted Billie to link arms with her. It had been a long time since there had been any closeness between the two of them. Since before she met Moss.

The tea was warm and spicy. Agnes stirred sugar into her cup and waited expectantly. "It's about Jessica, Mother. I'm sure you must know she doesn't have long. Will you ask Seth to see if he can get Amelia back home? I wrote to her but haven't heard anything. It could be months before she ever gets my letter and Jessica doesn't have months, Mother. Seth has powerful friends. It will be awful if Amelia doesn't get here in time."

Agnes felt confused. This wasn't what she'd expected to hear. This wasn't what she *wanted* to hear. Surely Jessica wasn't as bad off as Billie thought. Seth didn't seem overly concerned. "Darling," she said, "Jessica is ailing but she's nowhere near the end. The doctor's been most encouraging lately. I admit Jessica had a setback after you left for Hawaii, but she's on the mend now. If I do as you ask, Seth will think we're busybodies—he won't thank us; I can tell you that."

Billie's back stiffened. "Does that mean you won't speak to him?" Agnes nodded. "Then I'll speak to him myself."

"Billie, do you have any idea of what you're asking? We're at war. England is an exploding powderkeg. I doubt very much anyone can come home to the States now."

"We have to try. Mother, don't you care?"

"Of course I care. But you're asking the impossible. I don't think Seth's influential friends can help him in this."

"I don't see why not. Seth's influential friends helped him send a Red Cross plane full of food to Hawaii," Billie said bitterly. "This is a little more serious and a lot more important. It's a question of Jessica seeing her daughter before she dies."

"All right, Billie. I'll speak to Seth. But I can tell you right now that he's not going to be able to do anything. There's a war going on over there."

"There's going to be a war going on right here if someone doesn't do something," Billie snapped. "Excuse me, Mother. I have a phone call to make and then I want to read to Jessica for a while. You know, it wouldn't hurt you to really take some time when you visit with her. Now that you're the mistress of Sunbridge, I would have thought . . . well, never mind, Mother. I'll talk with you later."

Her little Billie was making demands! She never thought she would live to see the day. Agnes diddled with the spoon in her cup, clinking it against the edge. She would tactfully lead Seth into a conversation concerning his daughter and see what developed. Jessica wasn't dying. Or was she? Men had a way of not seeing what was right in front of their noses. This was something she was going to have to check out herself. Before she spoke to Seth.

Billie watched her mother's performance later in the day. Jessica made the effort and rallied for a short time for Agnes's benefit, appearing alert and aware of what was going on about her. It wasn't until Agnes left that the frail old woman collapsed against the pillows.

Billie ran to her. "Jess, are you all right? Should I call the doctor? Lie quiet and let me get your medicine. Why? Why did you exert yourself like that?"

Jessica lay quietly for a long time, the transparent eyelids closed. When she finally did speak it was with an effort. Billie had to strain to hear the words. "It's expected, Billie. Your mother has grit. I admire that. I never had grit. Seth admires that in women. I couldn't let your mother see me at less than my best. Yes, child, it has cost me but it was something I had to do. Give me my medicine and I'll sleep. Why don't you go in to Maggie now. Spend time with your daughter, Billie. Don't make the same mistakes I made. Love her, Billie."

"I will. Swallow this down and I'll be back later to check on you."

"Bless you, child. I think sometimes you're more like my own daughter than a daughter-in-law."

"No one can ever take a daughter's place," Billie said softly. Jessica was already asleep, an unhealthy blue tinge on her lips.

Dinner that evening was strained. Billie ate with her eyes lowered, volunteering nothing to the conversation. She was about to excuse herself to take her dessert and coffee with Jessica, when Seth fixed her with his steely gaze.

"Aggie here tells me *you* think Amelia should be brought home. She tells me you think Jess isn't long for this world. Now where would a slip of a girl like you get an idea like that?"

Billie swallowed past the lump in her throat. "From Jessica," she replied coolly.

Seth grimaced. "I'm the first to admit that Jess looks a mite peaked, but the Grim Reaper's a far piece down the road. I can't be asking my friends for favor upon favor. How is that going to look?"

Billie stood up. "I imagine it's going to look the same way it looked when you sent two longhorn steers to Hawaii for a barbecue to impress some top brass. Excuse me, Mother, Seth."

"You wanted backbone, you just saw backbone. I'd give this some real serious thought, Seth," Agnes said softly. "Some real serious thought."

"Spunk, Aggie. I wanted to see spunk. There's a world of difference between backbone and spunk. Like Rhode Island compared to Texas, if you get what I mean."

Agnes sat up a little straighter in her chair. "I'm afraid, Mr. Coleman, that you're going to have to settle for backbone. Personally, I wouldn't have it any other way." Agnes tossed down her napkin. Seth was reminded of another time when she had done exactly the same thing. He watched her ramrod-straight back exit the dining room.

Tita asked permission to remove his dinner plate. "Fetch me a coffee and a brandy and I'll drink it here at the table," he ordered.

Bring Amelia home, he thought speculatively. Go to the top and ask for another favor. Too soon. Much too soon. Go straight to the Red Cross. Possible. That damn fool doctor hadn't indicated that Jessica was seriously ailing, but the girl sounded so positive. Too damn positive. He felt guilty for a few seconds. He should have spent more time these past weeks with Jess. Up there all alone, of course she would feel badly. Make more of her illness than there was. When you didn't have anything to do with your time but pray for all the sinners of the world, your mind was sure to come up with all kinds of terrible thoughts. Death was so goddamn terrible. It was also inconvenient as hell. For those left behind.

He made a mental note to get a letter off to the Red Cross asking them to help grease the wheels for Amelia. He'd write the damn letter himself. His daughter probably wouldn't even want to come home. All this damn fuss because of that little Yankee gal. All he'd wanted was a little spunk, a little grit, some starch to the girl. Well, he wasn't giving in; he was compromising. It was important that everyone understand that. He'd make damn sure they all understood, and the first person he was going to inform was Moss. He'd write him a long letter this evening. Spell things out a little.

He was in a foul mood now. The girl could do that to him without even trying. Sometimes when he just looked at her he would get angry. He could literally feel his blood pressure shoot up. Times like now. Then he remembered the sounds he and Agnes had heard coming from her room this very morning. His mood lightened and he started to whistle. He called for a cigar and another shot of brandy.

* * *

The moment Billie stepped into the wide front hallway she knew something was different. An unnatural stillness seemed to permeate the very air. She found herself taking a long deep breath and holding it. What? Who? Maggie? Jessica? Never Seth or Agnes.

Billie released her indrawn breath with an explosive sound. *She knew.* She didn't need anyone to tell her Jessica was no longer a member of this earth. She knew.

She put her parcels and packages down on a cowhide-covered bench. There were two new mystery novels and a monstrous sack of licorice for Jessica. Jessica. Billie sat down with a thump on the cowhide seat, unmindful that the packages toppled to the floor. She didn't want to go upstairs. She didn't want to walk into that room where Jessica would be lying. Somebody should be about. Agnes, Seth, Tita . . . or were they all locked away in their rooms, telling themselves that Jessica just looked a little peaked?

Amelia! Amelia could never get here in time. Moss. Moss might not get the news for days, possibly weeks. The ground would be cold, the rains would come, and it would be all over.

The climb up the wide circular stairway was the longest she could remember. Her grip on the mahogany banister was like a vise that opened and closed. The empty bed, the coverlet and sheet tossed back as though Jessica had gone to the bathroom, brought a wild look to Billie's eyes.

Maggie! Billie's step quickened. But Maggie was lying in her crib gurgling happily. The nurse was knitting in the rocker. Her eyes met Billie's.

"I'm so sorry, Mrs. Coleman. I know how fond you were of the elder Mrs. Coleman. They called me right away but there was nothing anyone could do. It was peaceful and quick. It was Tita who found her. Mr. Coleman was out on the range. Your mother was at a meeting. The doctor has been and gone." Billie nodded miserably. "I don't know if this will give you any consolation, but when I took Maggie in after her noon feeding Mrs. Coleman asked if I would lay the baby in her arms. I was right there. She stared at Maggie for a long time and kept saying over and over that she reminded her of Amelia. Before I took her away, she was calling Maggie Amelia and saying she was sorry. I think she knew she was dying. When her daughter arrives, perhaps you'll want to tell her."

"Yes. Yes, I'll do that. Thank you for telling me. I know

it will mean a lot to Amelia."

Billie leaned over the crib, reached down for a colorful red rattle, and shook it gently. Maggie gurgled and kicked her feet. Billie reached out her arms. "Come to Mama." The nurse watched as Billie picked up her daughter and held her fiercely against her breast. "I'm going to try not to be like Jessica. . . . I don't want to die alone," Billie whispered against the baby's warm, soft head. When the baby started to whimper, Billie kissed her and laid her back in the crib.

"Where are the others, Nurse?"

"Your mother and Mr. Coleman are in the study. Tita and someone from her family are cleaning . . . what I mean is, they're getting . . ."

"I know."

Seth was standing next to the fireplace, in his hand a squat glass filled to the brim with bourbon. Her mother was sitting in Seth's chair. It didn't look right to Billie. She felt they should be doing something.

"Have you tried to reach Amelia?" was Billie's first question. When no one answered she tried again. "What about Moss?"

Seth turned to face Billie. There was a blank look on his face. "Not yet. I decided to wait until the *Enterprise* puts into port somewhere. I don't want him flying missions with . . . Later, he'll be told later. When the time is right."

"Amelia?"

"I wrote a letter to the Red Cross some time ago. I haven't heard."

Billie stiffened from head to toe. "That isn't good enough, Seth. You have to do something now."

"There's nothing to do. She could never get here in time for the funeral even if she left for home yesterday."

"I can't accept that. You have to try. If you won't, then I will."

"Billie, please. Can't you see that Seth . . ."

Billie clenched her hands into rock-hard fists. "Stay out of this, mother. Seth, I'm going to call the Red Cross myself. With or without your permission. You may be right about Moss, but Amelia is different."

"Billie, wait."

"Let her go, Aggie. She won't get very far. If she wants to strangle herself in red tape, let her," Seth said wearily.

"Shouldn't we be calling people, Seth?" Agnes asked hesitantly.

"No. We're going to have a private mass. It will be just us. She'll be buried here at Sunbridge. We'll put a notice in the paper next week."

"If you don't need me, Seth, I think I'll take a walk."

"You go along, Aggie. I'm fine. Tend to that daughter of yours."

It was two o'clock in the morning when the Red Cross returned her call. Billie picked up the receiver on the first ring.

"We found her. Now the problem is getting her on a plane. It's important but not top priority. I have to be honest and tell you I doubt that we can get her there in time, but we're going to do our very best."

"I'm so grateful. We all are. And if there's any other news, will you call me?"

"Of course. We're only too glad to help. I'm sorry we can't do more."

Should she wake Seth and tell him? Billie wondered. No. He wouldn't thank her for disturbing his sleep.

"Billie?" It was a soft whisper.

"Mother! What are you doing up at this hour?"

"I've been sitting in the kitchen waiting for you to get your call. I'm proud of you, Billie. I think it was wonderful of you to stand up to Seth and do what you did. I would like to think you would do the same for me. For the first time, perhaps, I have become aware of my own mortality. Now, why don't you join me in the kitchen for some hot chocolate? I've been keeping it on the back of the stove for you."

"I'd like that, Mother. There's something I want to talk to you about."

"Like back in Philadelphia. I miss those times, Billie."

"You're always so busy, Mother."

"Yes, I know. Sunbridge is so wonderful and heady. Perhaps I adapted too quickly. I'm sorry about Jessica, Billie. Really I am. I know how much you cared for her."

"How is Seth taking this?" Billie asked coolly.

"He was shocked. He is shocked," Agnes corrected herself. "He's had a long and loving life with Jessica and now it's come to an end. I'm sure, Billie, he would have tried to get through to Amelia once the initial shock wore off. He's very concerned

{ 227 }

about Moss, about not telling him. That's a terrible decision to carry around."

"And he's making me a party to it. How can I write to Moss and not let on? I think it's awful. I understand, but I still think it's awful. Moss *should* be told."

"It does place you in a rather awkward position. I'll speak to Seth later on. As I said, Billie, he's in shock now. He may look at things differently tomorrow."

"I hope so. I won't lie to Moss and I won't evade. My God, Jessica is his mother . . . was his mother. You know what I mean."

"Finish your chocolate and go to bed, Billie. It's late. Tomorrow is going to be very trying."

Agnes sat at the kitchen table for a long time. She drank cup after cup of coffee and it was bitter on her tongue. Billie hadn't yet mentioned a word about her pregnancy. How long did she intend to keep it a secret? By Agnes's best calculations it was already almost three months. The child would be born sometime in February. Agnes blanched. Maggie would celebrate her first birthday in February. This would be physically trying for a healthy woman, one who hadn't had complications during her first pregnancy. Agnes swallowed her coffee as though she were trying to push down her guilt. What was done was done. She hoped Billie would announce her news soon. Seth would feel so much better.

The small private service Seth had arranged for Jessica seemed to include half of Texas. And the other half sent flowers and telegrams and notes of condolence. Answering the door and the telephone kept Billie on the run.

Billie had never really dealt with the finality of death before. Her father and grandparents had died when she was too young to realize what was happening. Jessica had become a second mother to her, a more sympathetic and understanding one than Agnes, and Billie had come to love the woman dearly. She felt the need to creep off somewhere and grieve. Instead, she'd been asked to tend the door and the telephone.

Jessica was laid out in the front parlor in a huge bronze-and-oak casket, dressed in a pale blue lace gown and tiny satin bedroom slippers. Whoever had coiffed her hair had parted it on the wrong side. No one seemed to notice but Billie. Agnes thought the whole idea of having an open casket at home an archaic and heathenish practice. In Philadelphia things were done with a shade more taste. And wasn't that what funeral homes were for?

Jessica was buried on a sunny meadow hillock in the midst of a crowd of strangers. Billie had had no idea a funeral would be such an exhausting experience. The people here had come out of respect for Seth, business acquaintances and friends of his for the most part; the people who'd known and loved Jessica seemed very few. Billie shed her tears and placed a single white rose from Jessica's garden on the casket, whispering prayers through her grief. Poor Jessica. So alone. Moss and Amelia should have been here, Jessica's own children, her own flesh and blood. Even little Maggie should have been here, but the notion had been quickly vetoed by both Agnes and Seth.

Seth stepped forward, his thick gray hair waving aristocratically on his head, hat held respectfully in hand. He leaned on his silver-handled cane, his voice rumbling from deep in his chest. "Jessica Riley Coleman was a fine woman. We're burying her at Sunbridge because this was her home. It's where she belongs. Jess always knew what was expected of her. She was a good wife and a loving mother. She gave me a fine son, the best. And a daughter," he added as an afterthought. "We'll mourn her but we'll never forget her."

It was short, quickly said, and it summed up the total of Jessica's life. Seth put on his broad-brimmed Stetson and led the procession of mourners away from the grave. The Colemans never looked back. What was done was done.

{{{{{{{{{ CHAPTER FIFTEEN }}}}}}}}}

The day after the funeral everything was back on schedule. Jessica wasn't missed at breakfast, of course, because for months she'd been taking most of her meals in her room. Even the living room bore no trace of her last hours there; not a petal from the hundreds of flowers remained.

Agnes sat at the table opening the early mail. Her dark hair was upswept, its severity broken only by a few artistically placed curls over her brow. For the first time Billie noticed the slightest graying near the temples. "Please finish your breakfast, dear," Agnes said distractedly as she opened another letter. "There's so much to do today and I need the table cleared."

"Why do you open all of Seth's mail? Do you even open letters from Moss and see them before I do?"

"What a question, Billie! Of course I don't read Moss's letters. What are you thinking of?"

"Do I see every letter Moss writes Seth?" Billie persisted. "Or only the ones Seth thinks I should see? Why do you insist that I share my letters with him? Doesn't anyone around here think Moss and I are entitled to our privacy?"

Both Agnes and Billie were shocked to hear Seth's voice. "Colemans have no secrets from one another, little gal. Agnes, what's wrong with this youngster of yours? Ever since she's come back from Hawaii she acts like she's got a burr under her saddle."

Agnes's eyes went from Billie to Seth as though trying to communicate something. "Billie feels Jessica's death deeply, Seth. Emotions run high in young mothers."

Before Billie's very eyes Seth's anger abated and his pomposity seemed to deflate. "That's all right, gal," he said forgivingly.

Billie bristled. Why should *she* be forgiven? She'd done nothing except ask a few direct questions.

"What are your plans for the day, dear?" Agnes was asking, busy again with the mail, sorting business letters from notes of condolence.

"Oh, I thought I'd go into town. You won't be needing the car, will you, Mother? There're a few things I thought I'd look at in Balden's Department Store."

It was on the tip of Agnes's tongue to argue that it was improper to be seen window-shopping the very day after burying a family member, but her eyes slid to Billie and she held her tongue. Billie was lying or, at the least, not telling the complete truth. Agnes knew her daughter very well indeed. "How late do you think you'll be? Planning on having lunch in town? Perhaps you'd like me to come with you?"

"No, I'll probably be home for lunch. You've already said you've so much to do today, I don't want to bite into your time, Mother."

So, Agnes thought with satisfaction as she slit another envelope, Billie was going into town for nothing in particular.

She'd be home in time for lunch at one o'clock and she didn't want anyone with her. Agnes's heart was thumping. Billie was going to see Dr. Ward.

Less than an hour later, just after the car left the portico, Agnes whipped up the phone receiver and dialed Dr. Ward's number. "Hello, this is Mrs. Ames. Can you tell me what time my daughter's appointment is? I seem to have forgotten. . . . Yes, Mrs. Moss Coleman. I think she mentioned an appointment. . . . Ten o'clock? . . . No, that will be quite all right. I simply wanted to know if I should expect her home for lunch."

Dr. Ward's receptionist looked up and smiled when Billie entered the office. Mrs. Moss Coleman certainly dressed up the office in her crisp lemon-yellow dress and sparkling spectator pumps. Quite a difference from the young girl who had first visited the doctor in a loose-fitting cotton jumper and flat heels. Mrs. Coleman had developed her own style, one that would take thousands of dollars to imitate. The receptionist sighed. Some women had all the luck!

Billie was nervous and out of sorts. She knew she was pregnant. This trip would only confirm it.

After the examination she joined Dr. Ward in his office and faced his concern. "I'm disappointed, Billie. I really didn't want you to get pregnant again so quickly, if at all. I feel remiss in not emphasizing this sufficiently after Maggie was born. It isn't good, Billie, and I feel we should talk about a clinical abortion. You're endangering your health."

All of a sudden he was calling her Billie. Did all doctors assume a familiarity when they had bad news to deliver? "Are you trying to frighten me? Surely you aren't serious."

"I'm quite serious. Listen carefully. You didn't carry Maggie to full term because you became toxic. Toxemia. She was a breech birth and you had a very difficult time of it. The birth left you with a prolapsed uterus and it's quite likely you won't carry this child past the fifth month. Miscarriages are dangerous. Very dangerous. The possibilities for infection and childbirth fever are quite high and I don't think I would be serving your best interests if I didn't advise a clinical abortion."

"If I'm careful and don't gain too much weight and stay off my feet—would that help?" Her lower lip was quivering and her fingers played with a stray thread on her glove.

Adam Ward's heart went out to Billie. It was such a difficult decision. Her husband was fighting a war and her father-in-law was exerting tremendous pressure for a Coleman heir. She was playing out of her league. He himself was mighty sick of Seth Coleman's demands. If he weren't the head of gynecology and obstetrics at Memorial Hospital and more than aware that the Coleman patriarch could just as easily donate his money to other institutions, he never would have put himself under the old man's thumb. A single tear slipped down Billie's cheek and Adam Ward was tempted to lean over and wipe it away. She was so young and inexperienced, despite this new gloss of sophistication.

"Billie, you're facing a difficult decision. But it's against my best advice to continue this pregnancy. Don't let personal issues or religion enter. We're talking about your life. You have a husband and a daughter to consider. Let me call in a consulting doctor. You'll feel better and so will I."

"That's not necessary. I trust your opinion. But, as you say, in the end it's my decision only. I have to think—this isn't something I can answer right now."

"You can't wait too long, Billie. Another three weeks and that's it."

"I have to think! Don't push me! I can't think straight right now. I have Jessica on my mind, Maggie is cutting a tooth, and I haven't heard from Moss in almost a month. How could I keep something like this from Moss? I couldn't. I want to know how he feels. And Seth would never forgive me. I have to think! I have to think!"

"Billie, I want to remind you that this matter would be strictly between you and me. I won't discuss this with anyone, not even your father-in-law. *Especially* not your father-in-law."

"I understand, and I thank you. . . . I haven't mentioned this pregnancy myself." She looked up at him with gratitude and now it seemed perfectly acceptable that he call her Billie. He understood and right now it was so important to have someone in whom she could confide.

Settled in the back of the Coleman limousine, Billie watched the countryside flash past. Abortion. The word lay heavy on her mind . . . a vague, shadowy image of dark hallways and mortal sin gleaned from whispered conversations. Abortion. Hesitantly her hand went to her stomach, where another life grew. This little life that beat within her was not an unreal mystery, as Maggie had been before she was born. The same force that had created Maggie had created this little one, and Billie could already imagine the child in her arms and the sweetness she would find when she nuzzled its cheek. This unborn had a face very similar to that of the child she'd already birthed. To abort it, to kill this child, would be like killing Maggie.

She'd almost decided against the abortion when other arguments flooded her thoughts. According to the doctor there was every chance she would miscarry—and her own life would be at risk. Fear reached out with clutching fingers. She'd never considered her own death, never thought it a possibility. When death finally came it wouldn't be for *her*, but for the old woman she would become, a person so far removed from her that she could face that thought without fear and emotion. At least she always could before now. She wanted to *live*, for Moss, for Maggie, for herself. She wouldn't be robbed of what was rightfully hers! Years with Moss, years of watching Maggie grow. Yet as she thought again of abortion, she imagined she heard the cry of her unborn child.

Sunbridge was coming into view and Carlos stopped the Packard beneath the portico. Billie leaped out and ran for the door. She didn't stop until she'd climbed the stairs and burst through the nursery door. Even the stern Miss Jenkins didn't protest when Billie lifted the sleeping Maggie from her crib and cradled her to her breast.

"Seth, I'd like to talk to you," Billie said firmly.

"Talk away," Seth said gruffly as he pored over his open ledger. Billie knew it was a ploy. Agnes handled the books.

"Are you going to call the Red Cross so they can get word to Moss about his mother's death?" There, she couldn't be more blunt. It was out in the open.

"In good time. I don't want Moss endangered. When he gets into port."

"I'm sorry, Seth. I don't agree. I will not be a party to this deception. If Moss is man enough to fight a war, he's certainly man enough to handle his mother's death. And he will handle it. You cannot keep this from him. I doubt that he would forgive you. I can't write to him and not mention it—what will he think of me?"

"That's not important."

"Well, I think it's very important. You're asking me to lie to my husband. I won't do it."

Seth swiveled around in his leather chair. He wrapped his burly arms behind his head and fixed his gaze on his son's wife. "You don't know the boy the way I know him."

"Moss is no longer a boy. He's a man and my husband. I insist," Billie said coldly.

"Insist all you want, little gal, but my decision stands. Moss could do any damn fool thing. His timing could be off. Anything." His voice sounded desperate to Billie and she pressed her advantage.

"You're going to look rather foolish, then. I sent a telegram to the Red Cross an hour ago. I want you to trust me when I tell you Moss will handle this. I know my husband."

"You went ahead after I expressly told you not to do anything?" Seth bellowed.

Billie's heart pumped furiously. He wouldn't intimidate her. He would not. She owed Jessica that much. "Yes, damn it, I did. I'd do it again, too."

"By God, if you weren't Moss's wife, I'd boot your tail out of here."

"Don't let that stop you. I can be packed and out of here in less than an hour. Decide now, Seth."

"You had no right."

"I had every right. I'm his wife."

"I'm not going to forget this."

"I plan to forget it. It's done. It's past. We have to go on from here. How we do it is up to you."

"Where you getting all this grit lately, little gal?"

"From you," Billie said shortly. "It rubs off. I can't say that I like it entirely. How about you?"

Seth snorted. "Go on, leave me to my misery. See if you can't stir up some other trouble to torment me. I'm an old man. Leave me be." Seth sounded downright pitiful.

"A *cantankerous* old man," Billie said.

"Out!" Seth thundered.

Billie was achingly alert for any return word from Moss. Every time the phone rang her heart leaped. She believed she had been right to send news of Jessica's death, but Seth's fears had become her own. What if Moss's grief for his mother clouded his thinking, dimmed his reflexes? What if . . . What if . . .

At the dinner table Seth pointedly ignored Billie's presence, directing his conversation, if any, completely to Agnes. Watching from beneath lowered lids, Billie was amazed to notice how fidgety her mother was.

Over coffee and dessert, Agnes looped her precious rope of pearls around her thin fingers and blurted, "I received a telegram from New York this afternoon, Seth. It was from your daughter. She's arriving in Austin tomorrow morning and asked that the car be sent to the airport."

Seth's coffee cup clattered in its saucer and he threw his napkin onto the table. "Her mother's gone and buried! What the hell good does she think coming to Sunbridge will do? She ran off and left her mother and now she comes crawling back."

"Seth, please try to be reasonable," Agnes said. "What could I do? You weren't here. I couldn't take it upon myself to cable New York and discourage your daughter from coming to Sunbridge. You couldn't be reached. I didn't know what to do. . . ."

"I'm not blaming you, Aggie. It's that damn fool girl. She's been a thorn in my side since the day she was born and I sure as hell don't need her here now! I suppose she's coming with that husband of hers."

"There was no mention. But I don't imagine a British officer could have gotten enough leave during wartime to come to the States."

"Well, what the hell did she say, Aggie? Where's that telegram?"

"It was read to me over the phone, Seth. It simply said she was in New York, had managed to secure a flight to Austin, and asked for the car to meet her at the airport."

Seth stood up from the table, leaning heavily on his cane. "I can tell you this, Aggie. I never wanted to lay eyes on that girl again! She's been willful her entire life, getting herself into one scrape after another! When she lived at home I teetered on the edge of embarrassment because I never knew what she'd do next. Whatever it was she did, I knew I wasn't going to like it. And I don't like this! Why the hell can't she just stay away? I'm too old and too damn tired to put up with her pranks."

"Seth, she's a married woman with a young son—"

"That's not her son! That boy belongs to some limey! She didn't even have the sense to marry an American, for God's sake. That boy's not of my flesh and he's not of hers, either." With that closing statement, he left the dining room.

"I can't believe this," Billie gasped. "Amelia is his own daughter. And you, Mother, you defended yourself. Not Amelia! How could you be so cruel? Did you actually consider sending her a cable telling her to say away?"

Agnes's eyes glittered and her mouth formed a bitter line.

"I certainly did consider it and if I'd thought it wouldn't backfire on me, I would have. What you don't seem to understand, Billie, is that not *all* fathers love their children, at least not all of their children. Amelia has been a great disappointment to Seth and he can't find it in his heart to forgive her. And Seth's relationship with his daughter is none of our concern. Sometimes, Billie, you can be quite stupid, and you fail to remember where your bread is buttered."

"And just what does that mean?"

"Simply said, dear, I am concerned about Amelia coming home because Seth is quite vulnerable now since Jessica's death; a reconciliation between him and his daughter could have devastating results on your position here at Sunbridge, should anything happen to Moss. Never forget for one moment that blood is thicker than water. Even Maggie could quite easily be discarded if Amelia should ever have a son of her own. There's a lot at stake, Billie, and I wish you'd stop being so naive."

Billie sat back in her chair feeling as though the wind had been kicked out of her. "I never knew you to be so crafty and calculating, Mother. I never knew. . . ."

"What you never knew," Agnes said coldly, "was how I scraped and scratched to give you a good life, to put you on a level where a daughter of mine belonged. Just how far did you think your father's insurance policy and the little bit your grandmother left would go? And that house—you never knew there was a second mortgage on it, did you? And when you were about to go off to college, where did you think the tuition was coming from? From me, Billie, from me! I was prepared to go to work to pay for your education and you call me cruel? No, dear, you are the one who is cruel, taking all I ever had to give with never a thought for me. This is our one chance at security, Billie, and if you're too stupid to see it, I'm not!"

The next afternoon Billie watched for the limousine. Seth and Agnes had left the house, and Billie was determined that Amelia would receive the welcome to Sunbridge she deserved as Jessica's daughter.

The sound of tires on the cinder drive brought Billie once again to the window. Carlos brought the limo to a halt and sprinted around to the other side to open the back door. A tall, slim young woman with hair as dark as Moss's stepped out. She was wearing a travel-rumpled suit in somber grays and black. Amelia stood for a long moment staring at the double front door with a strange expression on her face, as if she expected it to fly open and reveal a fire-breathing dragon. A dragon, Billie thought, that would be carrying a silver-handled cane.

Amelia then looked up to Jessica's window. Her shoulders slumped beneath an invisible weight. It was only when a little boy hardly three years old came to her side that she smiled.

Billie opened the door and wrapped the trembling, fine-boned young woman in her arms, crooning words of sympathy, much as Jessica had embraced her that first morning at the Austin train station.

The child clung to Amelia's skirt, blond hair ruffling over his worried brow, coffee-bean eyes gleaming. "Rand, darling, this is your aunt Billie." Amelia dried her eyes and lifted the boy in her arms. "He's so tired, poor darling. It was such an exhausting trip, but I couldn't leave him in England with any peace of mind. Things are hell over there. It isn't even safe in the country outside London."

"Why don't we take Rand up to the nursery and settle him in? A nice warm bath, something to eat, and a nap is all he needs. He's a beautiful child, Amelia."

"Yes, he is. The image of Geoffrey."

Nurse Jenkins welcomed Amelia home. "Rand is my son, Miss Jenkins. There was an edge of defiance to Amelia's voice, as though she were well prepared to face opposition.

Rand tugged his mother's skirt until he was allowed to peek into the crib at little Maggie, who was sleeping peacefully and sucking her thumb.

"She's a beautiful baby, Billie," Amelia said. "With that dark hair there's no doubt she's a Coleman. She's the picture of Moss, isn't she?"

"That's one of the reasons I love her so much." Billie beamed. "Why don't we see if Rand will stay with me so you can go freshen up? Carlos is taking your luggage up to your old room and I suppose Rand can sleep in the nursery with Maggie."

Amelia's shoulders squared. "Rand will sleep in my room. There's been enough of separating the children from their parents in this house."

"Whatever you say, Amelia. Of course Rand will stay in with you," Billie said reassuringly. "After all, this is your home. You can do as you like."

Amelia took Billie's suggestion and left Rand with her while she went to freshen up. A tub was run while the little boy explored the nursery, investigating Maggie's collection of stuffed animals and issuing a cry of delight when he spied a jack-in-the-box on the shelf. "Mine! Mine!"

"No, that's not yours, young man," Miss Jenkins corrected. "That belongs to Margaret!"

"He must have one like it. Get it down for him, won't you? It reminds him of home."

"Mrs. Coleman, it isn't wise to spoil a child with everything he wants. If I'm to care for him, he must learn from the beginning what he may and may not have."

"You're not caring for him, Miss Jenkins. Rand will be staying with his mother during their visit. Now give him the jack-in-the-box and then get some fresh towels for his bath."

"Staying with his mother! Isn't that just like her to come and upset the household. I was nurse to both your husband and his sister. There was a selfish streak in her then and it's still there, I can see."

"Or is it you never quite gave Amelia the attention and care you gave Moss, because he, and not she, was the apple of Seth Coleman's eye? Now go get the towels."

Miss Jenkins sputtered away while Billie played with Rand as she got him ready for his bath. "You certainly know what you want, don't you?" Billie said, laughing as he reached for the toy, refusing to be separated from it.

"Listen," he said as he turned the crank to work the music box. Slowly, he worked toward the end of the song. "All around the mulberry bush . . . the monkey thought it all in fun—now watch, Aunt Billie," he said, holding up the box. "*Pop* goes the weasel!" Billie pretended to be surprised and laughed along with the child. He was a delight and his precise British accent, so like Amelia's—though she may have been born in Texas—pleased her. When Miss Jenkins returned with the towels, he splashed water at her and made a funny face. Amelia certainly had her hands full with young Master Nelson, but already he was like a ray of sunshine in the house.

An hour later little Rand Nelson had been fed and nestled down in Amelia's room for a nap. Billie sat with him until he closed his eyes and then she tiptoed quietly out of the room. She'd expected Amelia to come back and tend to her son. Where was she?

Billie found her sister-in-law sitting in Jessica's darkened bedroom. The draperies were drawn but a slim shaft of light slipped between their folds. "Amelia? What are you doing sitting in the dark? Rand is sound asleep."

"He's a wonder, isn't he, Billie? So like his father. Mother would have loved him—" Her voice broke off in a choked sob and she sank down on the edge of Jessica's bed.

"Oh, Amelia, I'm so sorry," Billie said, going to offer comfort. But Amelia's hands went up in immediate defense.

"No, no, don't touch me. I couldn't bear it. I'm afraid I'll fall apart at the first gesture of sympathy. I'm really a crybaby, you know."

"Anyone would cry. You've just lost your mother, your husband is still in England fighting a war. . . . You've got every right to cry," Billie said softly.

"Geoffrey was shot down over France last month," Amelia said through her sobs. "They saw his plane go down. It burst into flames. . . . He didn't have a chance."

Amelia's announcement was like a physical blow to Billie. She, too, was married to a pilot; she, too, had a husband fighting a war.

The women wept together, then Amelia stood up and moved across the room, taking Billie's now cold hand. "Don't worry about Moss. He's got the luck of the Colemans going for him. He'll come back to you safe and sound. You wait and see."

"You're a Coleman and you haven't been that lucky." Billie had thought about death, the danger of flying, the hell of fighting a war, but it had always seemed one step removed from her and Moss.

"I'm not *all* Coleman, not the way Moss is. Come downstairs with me. I think we both need a drink. At least I do. The hell with taking a bath. I'll do that later. Right now, I need to talk. What do you say?"

"We'll have the study to ourselves; your father is out somewhere. He doesn't spend much time at home since your mother died. I think it's his way of dealing with his grief."

"You think so, do you?" Amelia led the way downstairs. "I would say you're being quite generous, Billie. I'm sure the old man won't mind if I tipple a little of his bourbon. At least not any more than he minds anything else I do." She forced a smile.

Amelia and Billie sat in the dim cool of Seth's study for almost three hours, talking and sipping highballs. Two young women with common loves, Jessica and Moss, became friends.

"I loved him so much, my Geoff," Amelia was saying. "He was everything to me . . . friend, lover, husband. In many ways he made up for my being separated from Moss. And in more ways than I care to admit, he gave me the love and attention I never had from my father. Now he's gone and there's only Rand and me. I think the day I fully realized how much Geoff loved me was when he asked if I would adopt his son. That boy meant the world to him."

"Did Geoff have family left in England?"

"Oh, yes, quite a tightly knit family, in fact. So naturally, I'm the outsider now, except for Rand. Geoff was the oldest son, and he inherited the title and land, a very healthy estate, even by Texas standards. Now it all belongs to Rand." She laughed bitterly. "Can you imagine, that little boy up there is officially known as Lord Randolph Jamison Nelson, Earl of Wickham. Rand's net worth would make even my father squint. Of course, and thankfully, the estate is entirely in the hands of the family solicitors. I unabashedly admit I've no head for figures. Further proof I'm not a true Coleman."

"Then you won't be able to stay on in America, will you? Not if Rand has a heritage and tradition to return to."

"Thank God, no. We'll return to England in a few weeks, if the war permits. It was hell getting over here in the first place. Lord only knows how or when we'll get back, but get there we will." Her blue eyes, so like Moss's, flashed with confidence.

"When I heard you were coming back to Sunbridge I thought you wanted to mourn for a while, where memories of your mother are the strongest."

"You are only partly right," Amelia said quietly before she drained her glass. "Actually, I came back to get an abortion."

Billie was uncertain that she'd heard correctly. "An . . . an abortion? I . . . I don't understand. Why, when you've just told me how much you loved Geoffrey? How could you think of destroying his child?"

"It's the only way. I have Rand to consider. Billie, the responsibility of raising Rand on my own is overwhelming. Rand is Geoff's child, the child he entrusted to me, and if I'm to keep him, I'll have to fight tooth and nail. Geoff's family is taking legal action for custody of Rand. I can't allow that to happen. Rand is my son, not legally yet, but where money and influence play a part, I won't stand a chance. That's a little lesson I learned at my father's knee. Those who have, get.

Those who don't, get the shaft.

"I can't be strong and take on the vultures if I'm burdened with a pregnancy and another child. I'd be too vulnerable, too weak. Geoff loved me, he entrusted Rand to me, and I won't betray that trust."

She lifted her gaze and looked directly at Billie. "You're not saying anything, Billie; I've shocked you, haven't I? Are you all right? You look a little pale."

"No, no, I'm fine—at least I think I am. Amelia," she blurted, "I'm pregnant, too, and the doctor wants me to have a clinical abortion." Quickly, Billie told of her last visit to Adam Ward.

"You haven't said anything to Pap, have you? You already know by now that the sun rises and sets on Moss as far as he's concerned. I hate to say it, Billie, but my father would gladly risk your health and life if it meant he would have a grandson. It's all he's talked about since Moss was old enough to marry."

"I know. Even little Maggie doesn't count for anything."

"How well I know. And I suppose he had quite a lot to say about my coming home with Rand." Billie's embarrassed flush told Amelia all she needed to know. "Have you decided what you're going to do?"

"No. I suppose I'm feeling guilty because I really don't want to go through another pregnancy—not now, anyway. Also, as the doctor said, I could lose this baby without doing anything at all. It's risky." Billie's anguish was evident. "If anything should ever happen to Moss and I had gone through with the abortion, I'd never forgive myself. I don't know what to do."

This time Amelia comforted Billie. She wrapped her arms around her. "You'll do what you have to do, Billie. You'll think it out and come to a decision and it'll be *your* decision. I'll be here for you, but I promise I won't try to sway you one way or the other."

Seth's angry voice suddenly filled the room. "You gals having a sorority meeting in my study? And helping yourselves to my best bourbon, I see. You've got a whole house to yourselves—this room is off limits!"

"Hello, Pap, it's nice to know you're glad to see me. Still your lovable old self, I see. It's delightful to be welcomed back to home and hearth."

"Don't you go getting snotty with me, daughter. You don't have your mother around to cover for you anymore," he growled.

{241}

"Pour me one of those. Just how long do you intend to stay?"

"As long as I have to, Pap," Amelia said, lifting the bourbon bottle. "Three fingers or four?"

"Three, for starters. Christ, you look like something the cat dragged in. Don't tell me that's the latest style in London."

"Oh, you mean my clothes. No, they're not the latest style, but then widow's weeds were made for utility, not fashion."

Seth took a drink, walked around to the chair behind his desk, and sat down heavily. "That fool pilot you married bought it, did he? How's he listed? Killed in action or only missing?"

"Killed. His wingman saw him go down. It was over France."

"I hope he left you well off. The day you married that limey my responsibility to you was over. Jess left you a tidy sum. If you ever get your hands on it, that is."

"I didn't come home for what Mam left me and you know it, Pap. Any lawyer can make sure I get what's coming to me."

"Only God himself can see you get what's coming to you, Amelia. I can't say I'm glad you've come back, because I'm not and I won't be a hypocrite. I can feel my stomach going sour already. What'd you do with that stepson of yours? Left him where he belongs, I hope."

"Rand is upstairs in my room taking a nap. Which reminds me, I should go up and look in on him.

"Poor little tyke, he's really done in," she said to Billie, who was watching this confrontation with amazement.

"Amelia!" Seth called just as she was about to step through the door. "It's just as well your husband was killed. He spared you the humiliation of having him walk out on you!"

For an instant Billie thought Amelia would crumple to the floor and fragment into a thousand pieces. But she caught at the door frame and steadied herself. "You should know, Pap. Didn't Mother do you the same favor?" And then she was gone, leaving Billie to stare in shock, her heart thumping madly in her breast. When she again dared to glance at Seth, she found him smiling and unruffled. He took a sip of his drink.

"What are you looking at, little gal? I can see you're shocked by this little scene you just witnessed. You shouldn't be. You knew there was no love lost between Amelia and me. Now that Jess is gone, so's the pretense. We don't even have to be nice to each other for her sake.

"Which reminds me, little gal, I can't help wondering what Amelia's limey was thinking about when he let himself get shot down. Problems at home? Responsibilities? Bad news?

I'm warning you, if anything happens to my boy because you sent word of Jessica's death, you'll be the sorriest person alive. You'll think what you just saw between my daughter and me was a family picnic. Understand? I don't cotton to being crossed. I don't care who it is. And you, little gal, would be nobody if anything happened to Moss."

{{{{{{{{{ CHAPTER SIXTEEN }}}}}}}}}

Agnes, taking her cue from Seth, practically ignored Amelia's presence, but Billie could see that her mother was impressed with the Nelson family title. "If your husband was a lord, doesn't that make you a lady?" Agnes asked innocently.

"Ask my father, Mrs. Ames; he'll tell you he doubts anything in this world could make me a lady."

Agnes pretended not to hear her and looked at young Rand just as he dropped a forkful of peas onto his lap. "Really, Amelia, must that child eat at the table with us? He's far too young to have proper manners."

"When Maggie is three years old I intend to bring her to the table for informal family dinners," Billie said. "Really, Mother, one would think we never lived in Philadelphia and ate at the kitchen table every night, except for Sundays if we had company. Would you really like to consign Rand to eating dinner every night with old sourpuss Jenkins?"

"Supper!" Seth corrected. "Here in Texas, dinner is served at noon and anytime you eat after that it's supper."

"Well, supper, then. Besides, the way people carry on here Rand is a welcome relief at the table."

"None of my doing," Seth protested. "Look here, gal, you're not picking up that tone of voice from Amelia, are you? Moss wouldn't like it. I can tell you that. My boy never liked an ox in a ditch."

At Billie's questioning glance, Amelia explained. "That's Texan for trouble, Billie."

Agnes fidgeted with her rope of pearls. She wished Amelia

would go back to England, and quickly. She didn't like having Seth so upset and ornery all the time. It made him difficult and, worse, suspicious of everyone and everything. She had to watch her attitude toward his daughter. To be too friendly and accepting would turn Seth against her, but to be too indifferent might arouse his family loyalty. She wished she knew when Billie was going to announce her pregnancy. What was she waiting for? Did she want to tell Moss first and wait for his response?

"Billie, dear," asked Agnes, "could you give me Dr. Ward's phone number? I thought I'd make an appointment with him."

"It's in the phone book beside the phone, Mother," Billie answered, pushing food around on her plate. Instinctively, she knew it wasn't the response Agnes wanted.

"Yes, of course, how silly of me."

"Something wrong with you, Aggie?" Seth looked concerned.

"No, it's nothing. I just thought I'd have a checkup. Have you seen Dr. Ward lately, Billie? Isn't it time? Maggie is nearly six months old now and I know Dr. Ward takes a special interest in you."

"'Specially since the Colemans built him that fancy new wing at the hospital," Seth interjected.

"Yes, Seth, especially. Well, have you, Billie?" Agnes waited, watching her daughter, watching for the lie, praying for the truth.

"As a matter of fact, I have seen him. Everything is fine."

Agnes's hands nervously played with her pearls. Not a lie, but not the truth, either.

"Billie, I'm going into town tomorrow afternoon. Care to come with me?" Amelia stepped in. Agnes was like a vulture about to pick bones. The woman had taken Jessica's place, running the house at Sunbridge as though it were her own, as thought it were her right.

"Yes, I'd like that. I haven't been in since you came. We could go shopping. Will we take Rand with us?"

"No, not this time. I'll leave him with Miss Jenkins."

At the sound of the nurse's name, Rand dropped his fork onto his plate and roared.

"That's Rand's interpretation of Miss Jenkins—a real dragon," said Billie. "Right, Rand?"

"Sourpuss!" Rand said and laughed, tossing his bright blond head.

"You'll stay with Miss Jenkins when Aunt Billie and I go into town, won't you? That's a good boy. Mum'll bring you something nice."

Rand nodded his head. "Maggie, too. Maggie cries a lot, Mum. Bring Maggie a present."

Amelia and Billie laughed, but Agnes shook her head in disapproval. "That's hardly teaching the child proper manners. Sourpuss indeed! That's quite disrespectful. You should be careful, Billie, that it doesn't rub off on Maggie."

"Oh, Rand gets on with Miss Jenkins well enough, Mrs. Ames. It's just that he calls them the way he sees them. Even Pap would approve of that!" Amelia leaned over and kissed Rand's cheek, her sleek dark hair in dramatic contrast with his towhead curls. "Drink your milk, Rand darling, then Aunt Billie and I will take you upstairs so we can decide what we're going to do tomorrow and what kind of nice present we can bring for you and Maggie."

Upstairs in Billie's room, Amelia reclined on the chaise longue and sipped coffee from the cup she'd brought up. Rand was occupied in the nursery with Maggie. "I was serious about going into Austin tomorrow, Billie. I hope you will come with me."

"Love to. They should be showing some of the new fall clothes now and I thought I'd like to shop for some wools. It's been so long since I've sat at a sewing machine and I find I miss it. Your mother always told me I was welcome to use hers."

"I'm not going in to shop, Billie," Amelia said ominously. The gaze she directed at Billie was unflinchingly severe. "I've made contact with a few people I used to know and the arrangements have all been made for the abortion. We'll have Carlos take us into Austin and from there we'll use a taxi. My mind's made up and I'm going through with it. It's the only answer, for me and for Rand."

"Amelia, surely there are other considerations, other solutions. . . ."

"No, there are not! I received a cable from New York this afternoon. From a lawyer hired by Geoff's brothers. They're threatening legal action because I took Rand out of England."

"But he's your son! You have a right to take him anywhere you want!"

"Yes, he's my son in my heart, but the adoption hadn't gone through before Geoff was killed. I'm going to have a fight on my hands. I'd already contacted a lawyer in London. His best advice was to stay here at Sunbridge, or at least in Texas, for as long as I can. With the war in Europe and bad communication between here and there, it's the only way to delay action. I can't lose him, Billie, I just can't! I love him so much. Every time I look at him I see Geoff. And I promised, I swore before God and Geoff that I would always be here for Rand and I won't go back on that now.

"Geoff hadn't had the happiest of childhoods, despite the advantages of wealth and title." She laughed. "Geoff said I was Rand's hope of growing up happy and normal. Me! Amelia 'Never Does Anything Right' Coleman Nelson, a young boy's salvation: I'd sacrifice anything, Billie, to live up to the promise I made to Geoff. Please, help me."

The soft light from the lamp cast half of Amelia's face into shadow. Her shining cap of dark hair was sleekly molded to her head and knotted at the nape of her neck. The style lent her a severity that made her plea all the more poignant. Billie didn't want to help. It was contradictory to all her beliefs, and yet she herself was being forced to face the issue.

"You're backing off from me, Billie. I can see your principles are offended. Forget I asked. Forget I even told you anything about it. No hard feelings, just look after Rand while I'm gone tomorrow."

"Where are you going? Who's the doctor?"

Amelia's laughter was almost a shriek. "Billie, surely you can't be serious. Abortion is illegal, or did you forget? No doctor—no good doctor, anyway—would touch me. This is a connection I made through some not very respectable friends I used to have. Only clinical abortions, like the one Dr. Ward wants you to have, are performed in sterile hospitals."

Visions darker than creeping black cats walked through Billie's imagination. Stories of back alleys and butcher knives and knitting needles, stories whispered in the back of the girls' gym at school. "Amelia! You can't. It isn't safe!"

"I can and I will. Just you watch me." Her hand went to her middle, patting her stomach. "You know what's in here, Billie? A dream. That's all it is, a dream. But it's not for me and I want to forget it before it becomes a nightmare. Do you know how frightened I am? I'm scared to death of letting Geoff down. I've never done anything right in my entire life except love Geoff and Rand. I'm really quite selfish, you know. Very selfish. Ask anyone who knows me. Ask my father.

"I must do this. I want to do this!"

"I'll come with you," said Billie. "You need someone. I don't like it, I admit, but if you need me, I'm here. Moss wouldn't have it any other way. I won't sit in judgment of you, Amelia. I simply want to be your friend."

"Oh, Billie!" Amelia cried, clasping Billie's hands. "You are my friend. You're more. You're my sister!"

The next afternoon Billie and Amelia drove into Austin. They gave Carlos instructions to meet them at five o'clock in front of the Coleman Building, then waited until he pulled away before hailing a cab. Amelia sat stiff and silent in the backseat while Billie gave the address to the driver.

"You sure that's the address, miss?" the driver said, chewing on a cigar stub. "You don't look like the kind of ladies to go into that neighborhood."

"That's the address," Billie answered, her tone barring further comment. Amelia sat beside her, staring straight ahead, her cold pale hands clutched in her lap.

When the taxi came to a halt, Billie looked doubtfully out at the sleazy honky-tonks and littered sidewalks. "This is the place," Amelia said tonelessly. They paid the fare and stepped out.

"You want I should wait for you?"

"No, driver, thank you," Billie said, glancing around nervously. Men loitered on street corners; loud music with a Mexican flavor blared from the Loco Saloon; ragged children and hollow-eyed women walked aimlessly down the street. "Amelia, are you sure you have the right address?"

"This is it," she said, looking at a ramshackle doorway. "Let's get this the hell over with. Come on."

Billie had never been in such a place. The dark hallway smelled of burned garlic, mustiness, and garbage. Radios, each tuned to a different station, created a muffled cacophony. On the third floor, Amelia rapped sharply on a scarred door.

The door opened a crack and a pair of snapping dark eyes peered out suspiciously. When Amelia extended a crisp hundred-dollar bill, the door opened to admit them. A man in a dirty white shirt that strained across his vast belly called out in Spanish. A woman stepped into the room. Billie heard the locks being snapped behind her and knew a sense of panic.

"This is my friend," Amelia was explaining. "She's here to see I get home."

The woman shook her head and grumbled something to the man. "You were to come alone," he growled.

"No one said anything about coming alone. I need my friend with me."

The woman began sputtering and the man shouted at her. "You have all the money?" he said to Amelia. "Two hundred dollars?"

"Yes. My friend will give you the other hundred when everything is over."

"Your friend will wait here."

"No. She comes with me. Or I go somewhere else."

Again the woman began chattering. *"Silencio!"* the man raged. Billie was feeling weak-kneed and her hands were icy, despite the warm day.

"Okay. Go in there with Maria. She take care of everything. First I see the money."

"Show him the money," Amelia instructed. "Dammit, Billie, do what I say! Show him the money!"

Billie fumbled with her purse, extracting the bill and showing it to the man, who appeared satisfied. She replaced it in the zippered compartment quickly, as though it were burning her fingers.

Maria stepped aside to allow them into the adjoining room. It was empty except for a kitchen table and a single chair. Just beyond, Billie could see a filthy toilet. Newspapers covered the long windows that faced the back of the building. Voices shouted at one another from the other side of the wall. Maria was wearing an apron made of oilcloth. It was the same pattern that had once covered the Ameses' kitchen table in Philadelphia. A jumble of impressions penetrated her awareness like short punches to the brain.

She could feel Amelia's cold trembling hand in her own as she stood beside the table on which Amelia was lying, legs spread, teeth biting into her lips to keep from crying out. Maria was working between her legs. The pattern of her oilcloth apron swam before Billie's eyes, making her stomach heave. Suddenly there was the smell of blood and the sound of something dropping and spattering into the chipped enamel dishpan on the floor near Maria's feet. Billie's eyes reluctantly lowered to the floor. Dark red clots of blood and tissue swam in the pan. It was done. The small nebulous life Amelia had carried had been scraped and torn from her womb.

The cracked and filthy floor threatened to rise up and engulf

Billie. It had been so quick, so callously done. She felt as though her own insides had been ripped. There was a burning at her center, demanding she turn her focus inward. The small life that clung there could not survive without her. It could be torn from its haven and discarded just as easily as the contents of Maria's dishpan. That it would occur in a sterile operating room and she would be anesthetized made no difference. She was a mother and it was her child, and without her it would never breathe or cry or be hungry.

Billie had come to her decision. Her unborn child's life would depend on God, not the surgeon's knife.

Amelia's hands gripped hers, her teeth were chattering, and tears rivered down her cheeks. "Billie! Billie! God, what have I done!"

Later that night, after Billie had visited to the nursery to kiss Maggie good night, she stopped by Amelia's room.

"Amelia?" Billie whispered into the darkened room. "Are you sleeping?" She moved quietly across the carpet to the bed, careful not to disturb Rand, who was asleep in the little trundle bed on the far side of the room. "Amelia!"

"Billie. Billie, I'm so sick."

She touched Amelia's forehead. "You're burning up!"

"And I'm bleeding. Badly."

Billie clicked on the bedside lamp. Amelia was pale and white-lipped. "I'm calling Dr. Ward—"

"Billie, no! You can't. . . ."

"What will we do? You're sick!"

"It'll pass, I promise, it'll pass."

"No. No, it won't. Something went wrong this afternoon." She lifted the bedcovers and pulled at Amelia's nightgown. A spreading red stain darkened the pink cotton. "You are bleeding, worse than you probably know. I'm calling the doctor. . . ."

Amelia's hand gripped her wrist. "You can't You can't! I can't let anyone know. I can't take that chance! I've got Rand to think of. . . . Geoff's family would use this against me if they knew. And Pap is just mean enough to tell them if he thought it would hurt me."

"Seth's a mean old codger, but he'd never . . ."

"Look at me, Billie. Look at me and never say never. No, you can't, and I can't let you call Dr. Ward."

"All right, then, let me call someone else. Anyone. What if I drove you into Austin myself? You could go to the emergency room. No one would have to know."

Amelia's head sank into her pillow, rocking back and forth in denial.

"Amelia, you said you have Rand to think of. You could die from loss of blood, from infection. Think of Rand!"

"All right. You take me into the hospital. Not Memorial. Clinton General, on the other side of town."

Billie struggled with the Coleman family Packard through the dead of night. The ribbon of highway stretched out before the headlights like a long, narrow tongue. Amelia sat beside her, head thrown back against the seat, beads of perspiration glistening on her brow. The clock on the dash read twelve-thirty. As far as she knew, no one realized they'd left the house. But in the morning there would be explanations to be made, lies to be told, guilt to be hidden. She wouldn't think about that now. She had to keep her mind on the driving. This limousine was too long, too wide, and she was having difficulty judging distances. Her eyes kept going to the odometer. Twenty miles, thirty, thirty-five. Nearly an hour had passed. Amelia was quiet now, too quiet and too pale.

The lights of the city glimmered before her and traffic increased. The main avenue leading to the hospital was blocked by street lights, all of them red. "Hold on, Amelia, just a few more minutes," she promised, praying fervently all the while.

Things happened quickly when she pulled up to the emergency entrance of Clinton General. Amelia was placed on a stretcher and wheeled away. Then a nurse in a crisply starched uniform came to interview Billie.

"Patient's name?"

"Am . . . Amy Nelson."

"How long has the patient been bleeding and do you know the reason?"

"I don't know. . . . I don't know. . . . Where's the doctor? I want to see the doctor," Billie demanded.

"The doctor is with her now, but the patient is too ill to answer his questions."

Billie's eyes swiveled around the sterile waiting room. She didn't know what to say: how much should she tell?

"And your name?" the nurse was asking.

"Willa. Willa Ames." The misinformation came easily to her lips. "I'm a friend."

"Miss Ames." The nurse's eyes darted to Billie's wedding

ring. "*Mrs.* Ames, we already know that there's vaginal bleeding. We need to know if Miss Nelson is pregnant. Is she?"

Billie shook her head.

"Has she miscarried, do you know? Has she had an abortion? You must tell me. It could mean your friend's life."

"No, she hasn't miscarried" was all Billie would say. The other was just too horrible to admit. Visions of that chipped enamel dishpan turned revoltingly in her head.

"Then she's had an abortion. Correct? Do you know her family? Someone we can contact?"

"No! She has no one. Only me."

The nurse stood, her white uniform rustling stiffly. "Wait here, Mrs. Ames. I'll speak to the doctor."

Billie waited and waited and waited, each moment bringing new doubts and anguish. The minutes ticked by and then the hours. Seven o'clock. Daylight was streaming in through the wide glass doors. People milled about, white uniforms rushed from room to room, and there was still no word of Amelia.

At seven-thirty, Billie knew Sunbridge would be stirring. Rand would awaken and look for his mother. Agnes would soon go down to breakfast and wonder where her daughter was. Carlos would go out to the garage and find the car missing. Resolutely, Billie went to the pay phone and dialed the number. Thankfully, it was Agnes who answered. "Billie? Where are you? Aren't you upstairs?"

"No, Mother, I'm not. Don't ask any questions. Have Miss Jenkins look after Rand. Tell Carlos that Amelia and I took the car last night and I'll have it back soon."

"Amelia? Is Amelia with you? What do you mean you'll have the car back soon? Isn't Amelia coming with you? Billie, I demand to know what this is all about!" Something was wrong, terribly wrong; she could hear it in Billie's voice. "Billie, are you all right? Where are you?"

Billie sighed. There was no avoiding an explanation. "Mother, I'm at the hospital with Amelia. That migrane headache she had last night became worse during the night and she passed out."

"I don't believe you. Not for an instant. Billie, have you done something foolish? I know you're pregnant, Billie. Tell me, are you all right?"

"I'm fine. And so is my baby. Don't ask questions, Mother." There was an unmistakable threat in her tone. "As long as you know I'm pregnant then you should also know that Dr. Ward

{ 251 }

doesn't think I should go through with this pregnancy."

"Billy! What are you saying?" There was real fear in Agnes's voice now.

"What I'm saying, Mother, is that you are to cover for Amelia and me. You're not to let Seth know where we are or why. Take care of the children. I'll be back with the car as soon as I can. Don't let me down, Mother, and I won't let you down. Do we understand each other?"

Agnes's mouth gaped open. Could this really be her daughter talking to her this way? Issuing thinly veiled threats? Billie would never do anything to harm her child, would she? Yet something told Agnes this was a new and different Billie.

"Come home as soon as you can, Billie," she said softly. "I'll take care of everything here."

"Good for you, Mother. Good for you."

At a quarter to nine Billie was pacing the small waiting room on the second floor. Her eyes kept flying to the clock every thirty seconds. What were they *doing* to Amelia? Why wasn't anyone telling her anything?

"Mrs. Ames?" a woman's voice called. "Mrs. Ames?"

"Yes, here." Billie stood anxiously.

"The doctor would like to speak to you about Miss Nelson. Come this way, please."

Billie fell into step behind the nurse, her heels clicking on the tiled floor. She was shown into a cubicle. A young man in a white coat spoke. "Are you Mrs. Ames? I'm Dr. Garvey. I'm afraid we've had to perform an emergency surgery on your friend." At Billie's look of alarm he added quickly, "She's fine now. Her uterus was perforated, rather badly, and we had to perform a hysterectomy. Do you know what that is, Mrs. Ames? We've had to remove her uterus. Whoever performed the abortion was a butcher. You got her here just in time. She was hemorrhaging. Now we've got to be on the lookout for infection."

Billie's face had whitened during his recital and her lips were pale blue. "Mrs. Ames—here, sit down. I know this has been a shock."

"Will she be all right?" Billie managed to murmur.

"We expect so. Shame, though, in so young a woman. It would have been her first child, correct?"

"When can I see her?"

"She's in recovery now. Fortunately, she was conscious and able to sign the permission form; otherwise we'd have lost time attempting to get in touch with a blood relation."

"She has no one, anyway, only me. When can I see her?"

Dr. Garvey checked his watch. "About forty-five minutes. Why don't you go up to the third floor and I'll have someone get you when she wakes up. . . . Mrs. Ames, is there anything I can do for you?"

Billie raised her hand defensively, staving off the doctor's attentions. "No, I'm fine. Really. Third floor, you say?"

When Billie was finally admitted to see Amelia she had difficulty swallowing past the lump in her throat. Amelia was whiter than the pillow on which she lay, her lips dry and parched, her eyes lusterless and hollow.

"Billie." She could speak only in a kind of croaking whisper. "I know what you're thinking. It's no less than I deserve. Rand . . . please, take care of Rand for me." Her outstretched hand was cold and pale in Billie's.

"My God, what have they done to you?" The sympathy and compassion in her overflowed in salty rivulets down her cheeks.

"Don't cry for me, Billie, please don't. . . ."

Amelia turned her head away, her bloodless lips moving. "Go home, now," she said in a choked voice. "Take care of Rand. What's done is done. . . . There's no crying over spilt milk. Didn't I tell you I never do anything right? Go home."

There was nothing more Billie could do or say. She would go home and make excuses for Amelia's absence and look after the children. The children. Her hand went protectively to her stomach and she imagined she could feel the nebulous life of her unborn child beating there. It was safe, secure, and, most important now, wanted. Amelia's child would have been its crib mate. . . .

Billie's feet tapped a rapid tattoo on the tiled floor as she headed straight for the pay phone near the elevator. She fished in her pocket for a nickel to call Dr. Ward and tell him her decision.

Back at Sunbridge, Billie was numb to everything, including Seth's rage. "What does this gal of yours mean, Aggie?" he bellowed. "Where is that daughter of mine? And why did she leave that youngster here with us?" Agnes had no answer for him. "Damn fool troublemaker," he grumbled. "Never could trust her and never will. Goes off with friends and leaves that boy here. Friends! Miscreants is more the truth!" He glared at Billie. "When the hell is she coming back? I want to know when to wear my boots so I can kick her the hell out of my life!"

Agnes looked worriedly at Billie, who stayed silent. "Seth, Amelia needs a little time to herself right now. The boy is no problem—Billie is looking after him. Amelia won't be gone more than a week." She glanced at Billie for confirmation.

"And let me tell you one thing, little gal," Seth said, moving heavily on his cane toward Billie, "the next time you help yourself to the car without my say-so you'll hear it from me. What's gotten into you since Amelia's come home? I used to credit you with a *little sense!*"

"I suppose pregnant women do silly things," Billie said, hardly able to keep from sneering.

"What's this? Aggie, what's she saying?"

"I think she's telling you she's pregnant," Agnes cooed. "Billie, when can we expect our new arrival?"

"Maggie should have a little sister or brother for her birthday present."

"You mean a brother, don't you, little gal?" Seth countered sharply, yet he could not suppress a smile. "*This* one will be a son!"

The days trickled into weeks, the weeks into months. Billie and Amelia's friendship strengthened. Amelia's deft fingers crocheted and knitted little sweaters and baby blankets as she eagerly anticipated the birth of Billie's child. Her belief that nothing would go amiss, despite Dr. Ward's warning, was a comfort and pleasure to Billie. Amelia's concern was almost parental and, in Moss's absence, even husbandly. When Billie began to hemorrhage in her sixth month and she was confined to bed, it was Amelia who cared for her. She did it with such loving willingness that it brought tears to Billie's eyes. She was doing it for Billie, but for Moss, too, her adored brother. Little Rand was installed in the nursery with a nanny who catered to his every whim. Maggie thrived and grew like a healthy weed.

Moss's letters were infrequent and sparse. He was alive; that was about all they knew. Each of them lived in fear of the day a delivery would come by way of Western Union.

Billie lay in her half doze, her drowsy thoughts on her husband. Where was he now? What was he doing? Was he thinking of her?

"Being half-awake is better than being asleep," Amelia said

cheerfully as she poked her head in the doorway to check on her charge. "Time for tea, if you'd like. Rand and Maggie are napping, so it's just you and me, kid," she teased, doing her best impression of Humphrey Bogart.

Billie laughed, delighted. "Sounds good to me. I was dozing and thinking of Moss. It helps me to think of him and sometimes I have beautiful dreams! Do you think I'm sleeping too much?"

"As a matter of fact, I do. I know it's boring for you all alone in this big bed. Three months of complete bedrest is enough to drive anyone nuts. But I think I have a solution for keeping you happy, sane, and busy. Let me get the tea and we'll talk."

Tea trays were a creative process with Amelia. She always fixed them so prettily, delighting in the British custom. This afternoon the tray held a slim vase with two budding yellow roses, a white linen napkin embroidered with spring flowers, a simple white plate holding tiny sandwiches of melted cheese, and Jessica's best English bone china teapot. Fragile porcelain cups and saucers and tiny silver spoons nestled beside blueberry muffins.

As soon as they were settled Amelia came right to the point. "I've been thinking, Billie. I'm going to have to go to court when I get back to England and as you know, court appearances are just that: an appearance, almost like being on stage. Judgments are made on the weight of appearances. We've talked so much about your design studies and how much you loved them. I've seen what you've done with some of your maternity clothes and I've seen the things you've made for Maggie. They're gorgeous, Billie. Would you consider designing some clothes for me? Proper things, stylish but sedate. Something that conveys my responsibility and worthiness to be Rand's mother. This is important to me, Billie, very important."

"Amelia, I'm not a professional. I'm overwhelmed that you should ask. And I admit to being suspicious! Are you just looking for ways to keep me busy so I don't languish here alone in this room?"

"Hell no, gal!" Amelia did her best impression of Seth and made Billie laugh. "Seriously, I'd like you to do it."

"Don't forget I'm fresh out of school and what little I learned from Mrs. Evans back in Philadelphia I've probably forgotten. Why me? You could go to the best designers in New York or even have someone come here."

"I know all about those designers, but you see, Billie, I

want something that's perfectly me, Amelia Coleman Nelson. You know the real me, Billie. You really wouldn't have to do the actual sewing; there are seamstresses right here in Austin. You thought about pursuing a career in design, didn't you?"

"Yes, but Mother wanted me to become a teacher. Instead I married Moss and here I am. I can't even begin to think of a career—I want to be a wife and mother. Maybe later."

"Billie, later never comes. Something always gets in the way. This is the ideal time for you, while you're confined to bed. I'll help. Let's go back to the time when you hadn't met Moss. What were you going to do? What did you *want* to do?"

"I wanted to design fabrics, explore colors and shapes. Mrs. Evans, my home economics teacher, said she saw potential in me and worked with me after class. Before she married and had a family she worked for Oleg Cassini and she promised to head me in the right direction. I was even accepted to the Fashion Institute in New York, but when Mother got wind of it those plans changed. Perhaps Mrs. Evans was just being kind."

"Kind my foot. Don't forget, I've seen what you can do and from what I hear, acceptance into the Fashion Institute is no mean feat. Why was someone like your Mrs. Evans teaching school?"

"Mr. Evans thought life in New York too glamorous, so they moved to Philadelphia. She wanted her marriage more than a career. I do, too."

"Billie, it wouldn't hurt to lay some groundwork. Let me type up a letter to your teacher asking for the names and contacts she promised. You don't have to use them now, but we'll start a portfolio for you. When and if the time comes, you'll have everything at your fingertips. It won't hurt, Billie. I don't want to see you end up the way my mother did, wasting away here at Sunbridge, dying for lack of attention."

Billie didn't have the heart to tell Amelia those people could very well be dead by the time she got around to thinking about a career. But Amelia was right; it couldn't hurt, and if it would please her: "Okay."

"Oh, Billie, I'm so excited! I think it's wonderful. Moss will be so proud of you."

Billie's eyes widened. "Do you think so?"

"I know so. Moss likes interesting, exciting people. Billie, you're a Coleman now and Colemans always amount to something, or haven't you heard?" This last was said with an edge of bitterness. "Do you want to spend your life doing charity work and going to club meetings? Just remember my mother and her empty life once we children were gone."

Billie grinned. "You're making more sense all the time. Let's do it!"

Satisfied, Amelia leaned back in the chair and propped her feet on Billie's bed. "Talk to me. Tell me what you want to do when the time is right," she encouraged in the big sister voice Billie loved.

"Someday I want to work with silks and satins and brocades, but there's too much for me to learn before I can go into that. I'd start off with cotton. It's such a wonderful fabric, simple and clean and comfortable. No other fabric has those qualities. You always have to be aware of texture and weight if you want to combine it with another fabric for contrast. If I were designing something right now in cotton, I'd begin with the natural colors, wheat and ivory and oatmeal, and I'd add white for a catalyst.

"Later, I'll show you a design I did on cotton in high school. It's impressionistic bouquets of flowers in lines of black, white, and purple . . . sort of like a floating island. That was my first thought when I finished it and when I showed it to Mrs. Evans she said the same thing. She wanted me to do some work with batik, calico, and foulard, but they all seemed to call for stripes and I'm really not that fond of them so I went on to something else. There's so much more I need to learn."

"Tell me where to get the books, whatever it is you need. I'll ask Mrs. Evans to send me a list when I write her. You'll read them, won't you?"

"Of course! You're right, Amelia. It'll give me something to do and it's something that interests me."

"And you'll design some things for me?"

"I'll try. Designing a dress isn't as simple as it sounds. For you, I think it has to be soft yet have the body and substance of good construction and fabric. Nothing heavy, nothing stiff."

"I love it already."

"A kind of casual elegance." Billie narrowed her eyes as she measured Amelia's slim frame. "Maybe a suit skirt with asymmetrical pleating. A jacket in cotton or twill. Something you can wear with a hat. A dress with pure clean lines, maybe in a wool crepe. What would you think of a full tunic . . . ease and width, but we can control it with a belt. It would be different and you could carry it off with your height. I'll know more when I see and study some of the clothes you have. We can do a few mix-and-match outfits so it will look as though you have more. I like doing that; it's a challenge. What are your favorite colors?"

"All of them." Amelia laughed.

"Me too. Someday I want to create my own palette of colors as well as fabric designs. I have them all in my head. I've even given them names—the colors, I mean. I want to use them in silk, when I've learned more."

"What kind of colors? What sort of names?"

Billie laughed aloud. "Promise you won't laugh?"

"Cross my heart and hope to die."

"Blink Pink, Choke Cherry, Sherry Flip, Cocktail Fuchsia, Turquoise Icing. I could go on. If I ever do work in silk, I plan to use those names."

"Billie, I'm so impressed. It seems the Colemans got themselves a heifer with brains. Someday you'll put them to good use. My prediction, Mrs. Coleman, is that one day you'll be right up there at the top of the heap and not because you're Mrs. Moss Coleman but because your Billie Ames Coleman."

Billie wanted to cry. It had been so long since anyone paid her a sincere compliment. For the first time since coming to Sunbridge, she felt worthy of being a Coleman. The feeling was fragile and tenuous and she would treasure it and hold it close. Almost like a secret that only she and Amelia knew.

"I have an idea," said Amelia one Sunday after breakfast. "Why don't I read you the funny papers? What would you like, the Katzenjammer Kids or Tillie the Toiler?"

Billie sighed. "Neither. I'm too distracted over the patterns and construction for the wool suit I designed for you. I keep wondering if, when Mrs. Parker finishes the basting, it will live up to the design. The proof will be in the pudding."

"Don't worry, Billie. Mrs. Parker comes tomorrow for the first fitting and you'll see for yourself. Let's talk about something else. I don't like to see you this agitated."

"All right," Billie agreed, her mind refusing to leave her anxieties behind, struggling for something else to talk about. "How are things going downstairs with your father? Did you two make peace yet?"

"Surely you jest. No, we've not made peace and we won't, not in this lifetime, anyway. My father doesn't like me. He's never liked me and he'll never like me. As for love, the only thing Seth ever loved or will love is Moss and his horse, Nessie. You have to accept that. I have. Now if you don't want the funnies, how about one of Mam's mysteries? I saw one that looked like it would curdle our blood. Okay?" She scrambled out of her chair and went in search of the book.

Billie leaned back against the pillows and sighed. After the baby was born, Amelia and Rand would be leaving for England. Billie knew she was staying on at Sunbridge only out of concern for her; soon Amelia would need to return to face the inevitable lawsuit and her fight to legally adopt Rand. Billie would miss her, miss her terribly. Amelia cheered her up, bolstered her worries with a strength that seemed to know no bounds. She'd even fought with Seth for her—and won.

After the doctor had ordered Billie to bed for the balance of her pregnancy, Seth had stormed about Sunbridge like a rooster with no hens in sight. One disappointment was enough: no way was he going to lose a second chance at a grandson. A white-clad, stiffly starched replica of Miss Jenkins showed up in Billie's room.

Amelia took command. "Don't move," she said to the nurse. "Don't unpack and don't do a thing for Billie until this is straightened out." She turned to Billie. "I'm going to settle that old man, once and for all. He's not going to get away with this—unless of course you want the nurse." Amelia waited, holding her breath for Billie's answer. It was a negative shake of the head. Billie would feel so helpless and smothered by routine. The nurse pursed her lips and Billie could almost read her mind. These rich people never knew what they wanted. . . .

Sounds of the verbal go-round wafted up the circular staircase. Billie tried to distract herself by working a crossword puzzle, not very successfully.

"Don't speak to me like I'm one of your riffraff friends," Seth thundered at his daughter.

"Friend? Friend! You've never been a father to me, so how could you be a friend, riffraff or otherwise? And don't think you're going to throw me off the subject. If you want to talk about the relationship we never had, fine, but some other time. I want to talk about Billie. The doctor himself said she didn't need a nurse, that I could take care of her. I intend to do just that—did you hear me, Pap? I'm taking care of her. I already wrote Moss about it and so did Billie. Don't interfere. Because if you do, I'll snatch Billie right out of here. Chew on that one for a while. Now you get that goddamn nurse out of here and don't you ever pull something like that again. Not while I'm here. And just for the record, I'm staying until Billie delivers and is on her feet. Do we understand each another, Pap?"

"You always were a cantankerous little bitch," Seth snarled. "Your mam coddled you too much. I knew it would come to no good. Why couldn't you turn out like Moss? Jesus God, the things I've had to live with!"

"That's not the way I remember it, Pap. Every time Mam tried to coddle me, you slapped her away. You never approved of anything I did—my school work, my athletic ability, my friends, my driving, my music. You didn't approve of me at birth, so why I ever expected more is beyond me. But I kept hoping, trying to be what you wanted. Mam tried in her own way to tell me, but I never understood. I'm a female, and with you that counts for nothing. Not Mam, not me, not Billie, either. That little baby lying upstairs—is *she* going to have to pay the price the way I did? And this new baby, what will you do if it's a girl? Ignore it, too? And your son, the one who is so perfect, is he going to learn from you? Is he going to do to Billie what you did to Mam? God help us all."

"That's enough, Amelia."

"It's not nearly enough. It will never be enough. I won't let you take over Billie's life. Not while I'm here I won't."

Amelia's voice had risen to a high-pitched shriek. Billie imagined Seth backing off a step and Amelia advancing on him. "I'm young, I'm healthy," Amelia went on. "I've got guts and I have grit, not to mention spunk. You're an old man. You lost your wife, the only friend you ever had. You're going to dodder soon. Moss is gone. All you have left is your horse and Billie. The odds are a little more even now, Pap. Stacked in my favor, if you will."

"Get out of my sight! I couldn't stand looking at you the day you were born and I still can't stand the sight of you. If there's anything to be thankful for, it's that your mother isn't here to see how you turned out. She's probably turning over in her grave right now."

"You don't know and you never knew a thing about Mam. Don't bring her into this." There was a second's pause and then Amelia said, "If you think Mam didn't know about your carousing and those tramps you picked up in the city, you're wrong. She knew. She knew and she didn't care. I heard her praying one day. She actually prayed you would continue so you would leave her alone. What do you think of that, Pap?"

"You should have been drowned the day you were born. Get out of my sight."

The hatred in Seth's voice stayed in the air, drifted through the house. Then, Amelia's voice finally broke the silence, cool but threatening.

"Tell the nurse to leave. Now."

"If that's what it takes for you to leave my sight, all right. Send her down."

"Fetch her yourself. You hired her, now you can fire her."

"No-good tramp," Seth muttered as he made his way up the stairway.

Amelia told Billie what had happened next. The minute Seth was out of sight, she'd run to the kitchen and into Tita's arms. "My God, did you hear the things I just said? Was I wrong, Tita? Would Mam have been angry?"

"Your mother loved you very much. At the end, you were all she talked about." Tita had patted Amelia reassuringly. "You take this tea up to Miss Billie. The two of you can have a tea party, like you used to do when you were little. See how nice I fixed the tray? The cinnamon rolls are fresh, look."

It was a wonderful tea party. Their guests were Maggie, in her high chair, Rand, and Rand's little toy cat, Sally Dearest. No one paid any attention when he fed half his roll to Sally. As if by mutual consent, both women had pretended the sharp words with Amelia's father had never happened. But Billie would be a long time forgetting the murderous look in Seth's eyes when he'd arrived in her room to escort the nurse downstairs and back to town. And whenever she thought of that awful scene, she ached for Amelia. Moss had never told her those things. Did he understand how deeply Amelia had been hurt all the time they were growing up together? He loved his sister—that much she knew—and Amelia adored Moss.

Susan Amelia Coleman was born on a rainy day in February, almost exactly one year after Maggie's birth. Things happened suddenly, too quickly for Billie to be transported to Memorial Hospital in Austin. Tita and Amelia acted as midwives. Agnes sat near the head of the bed holding Billie's hand and wiping her brow, waiting for the arrival of the child who would secure their place at Sunbridge. When the child presented herself and her sex was declared, Agnes quietly left the room to solemnly announce the birth to Seth, who paced the upstairs hall. The instant he knew he had a second granddaughter, he stomped downstairs, threw on a cracked yellow poncho, and left the house, his face more thunderous than the storm outside.

Amelia was the first to hold the tiny infant. Exhausted, Billie lay back on the bed and watched the woman she'd come to love as a sister gaze down at her newborn daughter. The softness of Amelia's touch as she fingered the light damp curls brought tears to Billie's eyes. Amelia should be holding her own child, a child that could never be.

Dr. Ward arrived thirty-five minutes after the birth, examined mother and baby, and pronounced both healthy. Billie beamed. Doctors didn't know everything after all.

Amelia wept with joy when Billie asked her to be Susan's godmother. "I already love her as though she were my own," Amelia sobbed. "Thank you, Billie."

Seth managed to absent himself from Susan's christening, saying he had business in Corpus Christi.

When Moss received the news of Susan's birth he let out a whoop and threw his arms around Thad. "Son of a gun, it's another girl! Billie named her after my sister. What do you think of that?"

"I think it's great. What do you think?" Thad said quietly.

Moss frowned. "For sure I thought it would be a boy. I think everyone did. But as long as Susy is healthy, that's what counts. My sister is going to be the godmother—I like that. Did I tell you the doctor put Billie in bed for the last three months? Amelia took care of her all by herself. Billie says she was waited on hand and foot, and doesn't know what she would have done without her. That's my sister. We Colemans always come through in the end. Amelia's a great person."

"You didn't tell me Billie was having trouble." Thad's tone was accusing. "Three months is a long time to spend in bed. Billie isn't the invalid type."

"I know. It must have been rough on her. I could have sworn I told you, but I guess I had other things on my mind. Billie is okay and that's all that matters. Maggie is crawling around. Christ, I can hardly believe it!"

"It went all right with Billie this time, but if it happens again, she might not be so lucky. Just remember that you're responsible for Billie. You, Coleman, no one else."

Moss watched his friend walk away. Jesus, what was *that* all about? Well, with Thad in a snit over something there would be no gin rummy tonight. Good time to write to Billie.

In his quarters, Moss got out paper and pen. He hated writing letters. Except to Pap, but that was different. Pap was a man and they had things in common. Things that interested them both.

Darling Billie,

I just received the news about our newest daughter. Congratulations, honey! I'm pleased as punch that both you and Susan are fine. I was a little worried when you said you had to stay in bed. It's a good thing Amelia was there to care for you. Thank her for me. I knew you would like my sister. She's aces with me. Don't tell her I said that—her head is big enough.

I think of Mam often. It's wonderful of you to have Amelia take fresh flowers to the cemetery every day. I'll do it myself when I get back.

Tell Pap I have four more meatballs to my credit. He'll like knowing that.

Thad was just here and I told him about Susan. He said to congratulate you. He's such a hell of a nice guy. He sure was impressed with you. He thinks you're the most beautiful girl he's ever seen. He told that to one of the other guys, not to me. But I knew it.

I miss you, Billie. I think of our time in Hawaii. It was memorable. When you write to me again, send pictures of the girls.

Love, Moss

Billie's strength returned only slowly, much to her dismay. Frequent naps, good food, plenty of fresh air and sunshine, were the cure-alls, Amelia said. Billie obeyed and spent her recuperation waiting for the mailman and writing long, detailed letters to Moss.

When Susan was four months old, Amelia announced that is was time for her to leave. Her solicitor had prepared the case and she had to take Rand back home. Both young women clung to each other and cried. "I understand, Amelia. I'll always be grateful to you for what you've done for me."

"I'm going to miss you, you damn Yankee. And I'm going

to miss that little tyke in the nursery. Promise that you'll send pictures every month. I want to see her grow. Don't miss even one month. Promise now."

"I promise. Oh, Amelia, what will I do without you? I've come to depend on you too much."

"It's time you took over the reins. The doctor says you're back to normal—I wouldn't leave if I had a moment's doubt. It's time, Billie. Pap is going to heave a sigh of relief when I'm gone. I really think I've outstayed my welcome, if you could call it that! Be sure to write Moss and tell him I love him and to take care of himself. You're a wonderful person, Billie, and don't you ever let anyone say different."

Two days later Amelia was gone. Billie and Tita saw her off in the huge Packard. Rand clutched Sally Dearest in one chubby hand and waved good-bye with the other, his face full of smiles.

"I don't know why your father isn't here, Amelia," said Billie. "Something must have happened."

Amelia's eyes were bright with unshed tears. "Darling Billie, the eternal optimist. If you ever discover the *real* reason, let me know. Meantime, I won't hold my breath. Kiss Susan again for me. I miss her already and I'm not even out of the drive."

"I'll do that. Take care, Amelia, and be certain to write. I hope things work out with Geoff's family. Keep your chin up—after all, your lawyers seem quite optimistic."

"Yes, I know. But oh, if only Rand hadn't inherited his father's title, we'd be able to stay here."

"I wish they'd agreed to wait until it's safe to return there. I'm so frightened when I hear of the bombings. Those damn Germans . . ."

"Shhh. We'll be all right, Billie, I promise you. After all, I've got little Susan to come back to, and that's exactly what I intend to do. Take care of her, Billie, and take care of yourself." She gave Billie one last hug.

"And you take care of yourself and Rand. You're going to have one hell of a time getting back to England. Keep in touch."

"Don't worry, really. The Nelsons want Rand back. With them pulling the strings, getting back into England will be a piece of cake. I promise."

"Good-bye, Rand, be sure to take good care of Mommy for me, won't you?" Billie said. "Good-bye, Sally Dearest." She gave the cat a pat on the head.

The little boy nodded solemnly. "I'm almost four, Aunt Billie. I'll take care of us both."

Blinded with tears, Billie raced back to the house as soon as the Packard rounded the curve of the drive. She picked Susan up from her crib and kissed the downy head, as she'd promised Amelia. Tears of loneliness and loss streamed down her cheeks. The infant in her arms brought no comfort. Amelia, in the few months since Susan's birth, had been more of a mother than she. Billie hugged Susan closer and waited for the rush of maternal warmth to seize her. Susan's protests shrilled through the nursery.

{{{{{{{{ CHAPTER SEVENTEEN }}}}}}}}

Thad Kingsley leaned into the Enterprise *sick bay. Moss was* sleeping quietly in the right-hand bunk. The shelf over his bed held the portrait of Billie holding Maggie and little Susan. It was a familiar sight, yet it always came as a shock to Thad that Billie was the mother of two children. She was hardly past girlhood herself. It was November; soon Maggie would be two years old and blond-haired Susan would have passed her first birthday. It was unbelievable that a year and a half had passed since he'd seen Billie in Hawaii. Unbelievable that he'd never stopped thinking about her since.

The *Enterprise* fighter squadrons had been involved in night raids on the Philippines. It was after one of those raids that Moss had not returned to the carrier with his group. Radio contact with the "Texas Ranger" had been lost. Thad had stood with the warrant officer on the captain's lookout, peering through binoculars in the murky early-morning sky. He'd thought about the letter he might have to write to Billie and felt physically sick.

Scanning, watching, listening for one of the Big E's own. Finally: "Aircraft sighted, sir," the warrant officer had relayed to the captain. "Thirty degrees off bow, one o'clock. Stand by for identification." After a moment: "Identification positive, sir. Wildcat, listing to starboard. She's ours, sir. She's ours!"

Then a shout from Moss's squadron—the Texas Ranger was in sight! Flying like a wounded bird, it had made a less than perfect landing, but no man had faulted him for that. Moss has been rushed to sick bay and emergency surgery. He had taken shrapnel deep into the flesh and bone of his shoulder. Lacerations of face and neck, chipped collarbone and tissue damage. There was suspected nerve damage, which would be evaluated in San Diego.

Later, word was that when Moss had come to from the anesthesia, the first thing he'd said was "How's the Texas Ranger?"

Thad laughed to himself over his friend's concern for his plane. He loved this guy like a brother. Not that he approved of everything Moss did, but the pluses far outnumbered the minuses. With everything Moss had, with Billie and two beautiful daughters, with the backdrop of Sunbridge and all the wealth, it still wasn't enough for Moss. He was a bastard, bigger than life in all he did and all he was; so big that nothing less than a war was enough for him.

Thad decided against waking him and was just turning to leave when he heard a hoarse croak. "Thad?"

"Hey, buddy, you're awake. I've been here a couple of times but you looked like Sleeping Beauty. How do you feel?"

"Like mushrooms should be growing on the back of my throat. What happened?"

"Don't you remember?"

Moss nodded. "I remember. But I don't remember how I got back to the ship."

"On your own. And twenty minutes late at that, Coleman. I wouldn't be surprised if they put you on report!"

"How bad's the plane?"

"It's not being pushed over the side, if that's what you mean. I hear you're leaving us."

Moss shifted, or tried to, and scowled at Thad. "Like hell! This is just temporary; all I need is a week or so and I'll be good as new!"

"Afraid not, Moss. It's San Diego for you. Just think, San Diego and Billie. You both deserve the rest. You'll see your daughters for the first time. What more could a guy want?"

"How long? Did they say?"

"Jesus, Moss, I'm no doctor. All I know is they suspect some kind of nerve damage and they want San Diego to check you out. They don't have the facilities in Pearl. You don't want to take chances with that arm, do you? Sometimes, Coleman, you have to bend with the wind."

"I didn't even see that bastard come at me. He came out of nowhere. I had a bad feeling about that cloud cover. I could smell that slant-eyed son of a bitch."

"It *was* a little busy up there."

"The others get back okay?"

"Everyone's okay. Listen, fella, I've gotta get back to the wardroom. Try to sleep. You leave the Big E tomorrow at oh five hundred. Go to sleep and dream about them." Thad pointed to the photo over the bunk.

"Who put that there?"

"Your buddy, John Cuomo. He's always flying your wing tip, isn't he? He'd thought it'd cheer you up."

"Sure," Moss said tonelessly. He closed his eyes dutifully, but it wasn't Billie's pretty face he saw. It was the zero, coming out of the clouds at him. Over and over he played the scene in his head. He couldn't have handled it any other way. Now he was going to be in dry dock for a while. But not for the duration, by God. His bunk on the Big E would be waiting for him.

Seth Coleman hung up the phone, hands shaking, face drawn. Agnes waited, knowing that the message was about Moss. Her mind spun as she looked around the living room. She couldn't give all this up. There was no way she was going to give all this up! She forced herself to a calmness she didn't feel. Her voice was pitched low and full of concern. "What's wrong?"

"Those yellow sons of bitches got Moss." Agnes's heart thumped painfully in her chest. "They busted up his shoulder. Moss is being transferred to a San Diego hospital. We're going, Aggie. All of us. Tell Billie. Even the babies. The nurse and nanny, too."

Agnes heaved a silent sigh of relief. Alive. The man was too damn arrogant to die. Thank the good Lord.

"Do you know what I wish, Aggie?"

"What?"

"I'd like to blast the lily-livered yellow weasels right off the face of this earth. One of these days some smartass in Washington is finally going to say enough is enough and blow them to smithereens. They could have killed my boy, Agnes. He came *that* close."

"It's not going to last forever, Seth. Try looking on the bright side of things. You're going to see Moss soon. I think it's wonderful that we can all go to welcome him back to the States. Billie will be so pleased."

"How's her health?" Seth asked bluntly.

"Good. Why do you ask?"

"Because I have a feeling if the girl doesn't get herself pregnant now, she might not get another chance. It's that simple, Aggie. I want a grandson. And it damn well better be a boy this time around. You're the girl's mother. If I were you, I'd make sure she understands she might not get another chance to give Moss a son. Plain and clear, Aggie. Don't talk around it. If you aren't up to it, I'll do it."

"Seth! I'll handle it. This is woman talk. I know you're upset right now. Let things be. I take it you're going to make all the arrangements."

"I always do. We'll rent a big house with lots of bedrooms and lots of privacy. Why the hell did it have to be Moss? Why couldn't it have been one of the others, like that Kingsley?" Seth said viciously.

"Seth! You should be ashamed of yourself. How would you like it if one of their parents said the same thing about your son?"

"I'd expect it. I'm no hypocrite, Aggie. If it has to be them or Moss, I want it to be them. Not Moss. Never my son."

Billie dialed the operator and rattled off Amelia's number. Her anger rose to volcanic proportions when she thought of how Seth had insisted Amelia didn't need to know about Moss being wounded. "Save your time, little gal, and my money and forget it," he'd said in his usual voice, as loud as a freight train pulling into the Philadelphia yard. His unruly gray eyebrows had shot up when she'd picked up the receiver in defiance and then he'd stomped back into his study and slammed the door shut. But this was one time she couldn't care less about Seth's disapproval. Amelia had a right to know and a furtive phone call from the upstairs hall would not do, not this time.

"We'll ring you back, ma'am, when we get your call through. Will the wire be free? It may be a while."

"I'll be here and the wire will be kept free." Billie replaced the heavy black receiver and stood looking at it for a moment.

Billie settled herself in the living room, trying to focus on the fashion magazines she had carried down from her room for just this purpose. The minutes hung in the air; the quiet of the house accented the ticking of the clock on the mantel.

Four hours later the call came through. Billie picked up the receiver on the second ring. The operator's voice was clear, but Amelia's sounded scratchy and very far away. Billie pressed the phone tightly to her ear and spoke directly into the mouthpiece in a loud voice.

"I can barely hear you, Billie. What's wrong? Did something happen to Pap?"

Billie heard the anxiety in Amelia's voice, the concern for Seth. Her eyes went to the study door and then slid away. "No. He's fine! It's Moss, Amelia. He's got himself a shoulder wound. I thought you should know. We have every reason to believe he'll be fine. I wanted you to know."

"Is there anything I can do? Do you need me? Tell me the truth."

"It's just as I said. A wound. I'm fine, Amelia. Everyone is fine. How are you?"

"As good as can be expected. Have you gotten any mail from me?"

"Not recently."

"I wrote you a letter about the court case. It was a killer, Billie. A night didn't go by that I didn't cry myself to sleep. In the end, I had to flash the Coleman name and money. I hated to do it, but when it looked like I might lose, I brought it out. I had to prove to the courts I didn't need Rand's inheritance. Fortunately, his uncles couldn't prove the same. And of course they sliced me to pieces when they attacked my past and reputation. Whoever said the past is forever a part of the future must have been involved in a custody battle."

"Did you win, Amelia? That's what I want to know."

"Yes, thank the Lord, but it was a fight every step of the way. You'd be proud, Billie. I didn't lose my temper once, not in front of the judges, anyway. I behaved like the lady my mother brought me up to be. In the clothes you designed for me I was the picture of confidence even though inside I was dying. I did everything you said; I followed every shred of advice you gave me. I'll never be able to thank you, Billie. Left to my own devices, I would have gone off half-cocked and blown the whole thing."

"I'm so happy for you, Amelia. I prayed it would work out for you."

"It was your positive attitude and confidence that helped

me, Billie. When I think of that awful abortion and all I went through, I couldn't let those greedy vermin get Rand. I just couldn't. As Moss would say, it's a whole new ball game. I have to be a mother now and that means I must behave like one. A *good* one, do you know what I mean, Billie?"

"You can do it, Amelia. How's Rand?"

"Poor little tyke, he doesn't know half of what was going on, thank goodness. He's well. Really fine. That child loves me, Billie. Really loves me. When I think how close I came to losing him . . . Rand's uncles would have stopped at nothing and that would have included creating a doubt that my pregnancy was a direct result of my promiscuousness. Not that I ever was. At least not since I met Rand's father. It's been a hard thing to carry, Billie; you know what I'm talking about. But I couldn't have saved Rand if I hadn't done what I did. That boy means all to me, Billie, and he just thinks I'm his whole world."

There was such awe and emotion in the tinny voice coming over the wire that Billie was moved to tears. "Of course he loves you, Amelia. You're his mother!"

"I think we're about to be cut off, Billie," Amelia said hastily after a series of sharp clicks and static. "Give my love to Moss when you write. Take care of yourself and give Susan a squeeze for me. A letter is on the way. Write back."

The connection was broken before Billie could say good-bye.

Billie was pouring herself a glass of sherry to celebrate Amelia's victory when Seth came up behind her. "I heard the phone ring. What did the tramp have to say?"

"Tramp?"

"Amelia."

"Oh, you mean your daughter. Not much, Seth."

"You talked for a long time."

"Actually, Seth, I was doing more listening than talking."

"What did she tell you to tell me? What'd she say about Moss?"

"She told me to give Moss her love. Excuse me, Seth. I want to check the children."

Billie climbed the stairs, holding her back stiff and erect to hide the trembling she was feeling. She'd held her own there for a few minutes, anyway, and she owed Amelia that brief defense. Thank God things had gone well for her. Always it had been in the back of Billie's mind that Amelia might have sacrificed her own child for nothing. Now she would enjoy waiting for Amelia's letter, knowing it would have only good news. Good for you, Amelia. Good for you.

Amelia's letter arrived three days later, just before the Coleman entourage left Sunbridge for the Austin train station to begin their trip to San Diego and Moss. Seth and Agnes rode in the limousine while Billie, the children and the nurse rode in a separate car.

Billie carried the letter in her purse to read during the trip. It felt thick, a lot of news, Billie thought happily. The postmark was dated more than two months before. With the war, she realized, she was lucky to have received it at all.

Leaning back into the comfort of her seat, the children quieted by the motion of the moving car, Billie slit open the envelope. She had already heard the news about the trial, but there was more:

I've moved from London to a little village in the northeast. Billingford. London is torn to hell, thanks to Hitler, and each day we were forced to stay in the city filled me with dread. The nightly air raids and sirens frightened Rand. Fresh milk and eggs and all the other things young children need were difficult to get. Now there's fresh milk. I actually milk our one and only cow each day. Rand hasn't quite gotten the knack of pulling her teats, but he tries. We have a few chickens and fresh eggs daily. Meat is scarce. Rand, bless his little heart, will eat anything as long as we sit down together to eat. We take long walks, play ball, and I'm teaching him his letters and numbers. He seems to excel in arithmetic. Billie, can you believe I'm doing all this? I never knew how to cook and I never paid any attention in school, yet here I am, solely responsible for this child. I am taking it very seriously because I came so close to losing him. I can't ever allow that to happen again. Those dastardly uncles of his are not about to give up. I know they fell back to regroup and will have another go at me as soon as they can. My adoption of Rand won't be final for at least a year and with this damn war, it could take longer.

How are things in Texas? Is Pap still riding you hard?

You're going to have to learn to speak up and say what you mean. Don't worry about offending him; the ignorant can't be insulted.

Write and tell me about the children. They must be growing like weeds. I know Rand is. Children are wonderful. They blossom before our eyes and thrive on love and affection. We must be certain our children know how much we care for them. We must never stop telling them how we love them. If you're laughing at me, Billie, I can't help myself. I'm so overcome with all these new emotions.

I want to hear the latest news of Moss. He hardly ever writes me. How is he? Where is he? Do you know? Send him all my love when you write and tell him of my victory. Moss was always my champion and I love him dearly. How lucky the big galoot was to have found you. Tell him I said so.

I must sign off for now. I promised to play croquet with Rand and he's standing here with the clubs waiting so patiently with Sally Dearest under his arm. Take care, dear Billie.

All our love,
Amelia and Rand

Billie wanted to weep. Instead, she pressed the letter to her heart. Amelia was happy. Only one indirect mention of Seth. . . . Billie sighed. Some things in life simply could not be changed.

The entourage arrived in San Diego on a bright, blustery day. Moss was going to be confined to the hospital for at least two more weeks. Then he would spend his thirty-day recuperation in the rented house that stood high above the bay.

In its own way, the rambling, Spanish-style house was almost as luxurious as the one Seth had rented for Billie in Hawaii. The manicured lawns were magnificent, she thought. There was a tennis court and a heated pool, certainly a plus for anyone interested in swimming and tennis. She wasn't. Moss wouldn't be, either. There were servants, of course. Billie marveled at how easily she'd accepted having her needs catered to.

After settling the children and Agnes in the big house, Seth and Billie paid a first visit to the hospital. For the first time

Billie didn't hang back, but ran ahead of Seth to Moss's room and to his arms. His eyes met Seth's stormy gaze in silent apology.

"Billie, Pap," Moss said, "this is so wonderful! A visit from the two most important people in my life. It's so good to see you." And then he whispered against Billie's soft hair, "You feel wonderful, Mrs. Coleman."

It was what Billie needed to hear. Confident that Moss was all right and wanted her, she relinquished her position to Seth. Her eyes glowed brightly as she watched Seth's clumsy efforts to embrace his son, cumbersome cast and all.

"I hope you gave those yellow bastards what for for doing this to you," Seth growled, his grip on Moss's good shoulder fiercely tight. Moss didn't flinch.

"He came at me from my blind side from out of cloud cover. He got me before I could do a thing. They got him—my wingman saw to that. He took over when he saw I was hit. He's one hell of a guy, Pap. They don't make them any better."

Seth bridled. Of course they did. *His son* was the best. There would never be anyone even as good as Moss, much less better. Why did Moss always make light of his accomplishments? By God, he'd taught him better than that!

"They tell me you're okay, boy. Lucky, they said. Time to make another donation to the church."

Billie bit the inside of her cheek. It would be better if the old man *went* to church. She prayed constantly. Jessica had, too. Living proof of the power of their prayers was her husband smiling up at her right now. He winked and grinned. There were some things money couldn't buy.

"You'd better make it sizable, Pap. I still have a war to fight. I'm going back just as soon as they say I'm fit. No tricks. I mean it, Pap. I didn't come this far to quit now because of this little scratch."

"Little scratch! Little scratch!"

"They rebuilt it good as new, Pap. I might not be able to swing a pitchfork for a while, but I sure as hell can fly a plane. And I intend to fly, Pap."

"I know, boy. I know. You'll be able to come home with us soon. We're all settled in, the lot of us. Agnes, the nanny, the nurse, your children."

Billie noticed her father-in-law had difficulty saying the word *children*.

"I can't wait to see the girls. Some of those pictures were

terrific. Thad has two of them in his plane. Hell, all the guys do. I passed them around. None of the guys are married but me. I wanted to share my family a little. I hope you don't mind, Billie."

"Of course not. I think it's wonderful of you."

Seth snorted.

Trouble. Trouble between Billie and Pap. Moss knew the old man well enough to know that there was trouble, and then there was *big* trouble. He felt removed from the situation. Billie and Pap would handle it. He wasn't going to get involved. There was too much going on in his world to think about some petty domestic problem. After all, wasn't that why he insisted Agnes make her home with them? She was supposed to be handling all of this. And where the hell was Agnes?

"How's your mother, Billie?"

"She's fine. She wanted to give your father and me some time alone with you. She'll come tomorrow or the next day. Oh, Moss, I can't wait for you to see the girls. They've gotten so big. Maggie is talking already."

Another snort from Seth. He helped himself to a plug of tobacco. So, Moss thought, it was *big* trouble. Seth only chawed when things were out of hand. Okay, but he still wasn't going to worry about it. "They aren't even going to know who I am," he grumbled.

"Darling, they will! Every day I hold class and show them pictures of you. I talk about you and read them your letters over and over. Maggie will know. She actually asks questions. Can you believe it? She's a little confused between a bird and an airplane. I thought you would be able to explain that to her."

"Have you heard from Amelia?"

"I had a letter the day before we left. I brought it along so you could read it."

"Amelia's okay . . . a bit feisty at times, right, Pap?" Moss said, hoping to draw his father into the conversation. He didn't fail to notice that the smile left Billie's face at the question. So Amelia was the big trouble. He should have known. Pap was like a bronc with a burr under his saddle.

"So, Pap, how's things at the ranch? Any new colts? How many head of cattle did you ship this month?"

Seth shifted his chaw. He looked like he wanted to spit but didn't know where. He spoke out of the corner of his mouth. "I could have used you this past month, boy. Heaviest month yet. The army is after me for more, more, and then some more. Six new colts in the past three months. Nessie is ailing. Breaks my heart. That old gal has carried me a lot of miles. The vet is telling me I'd be doing her a favor if I put her down. Can't do it. She's gonna have to die of old age, same as the rest of us."

Billie listened to the tenderness in Seth's voice as he spoke of his horse. She'd never heard him speak like that about his wife. And Billie doubted he ever had in all their life together. Her features hardened. So, Moss thought, Amelia was at the center of the trouble, but there was more. Much more.

"You look tired, boy. I think we'll go along and come back tomorrow. We don't want you overdoing. Take a nap. Get your strength back. Come on, girl, let's let the boy sleep."

Billie stiffened. "No, Seth, I think I'll stay. If Moss wants to sleep, I'll read a novel. I brought one with me." Billie refused to meet Seth's eyes as she rummaged in her bag for the book she'd thought to bring at the last minute.

Seth glowered and shifted his chaw a second time. "How will you get home? Do you even know the address?"

"Of course I know the address . . . and the phone number. You go along. I'll find my way back. Taxis looked plentiful outside."

"What about the girls?"

"What about them?" Billie asked quietly. "You've seen to their every need. There isn't a thing I can do for them that Miss Jenkins can't. Mother is there to take up the slack. Don't wait dinner for me, Seth. I'll catch something here or filch something from Moss's dinner tray."

Seth all but snarled. "Dinner? That's hours away. How long are you planning on staying here?"

Billie laughed, to Moss's delight. "Until the nurse or my husband throws me out. Don't worry about me, Seth."

"I'm not worried. I think it's a damn fool thing to be doing. Using valuable gasoline for a second trip when I'm going now. Damn foolishness!" Billie smiled again but said nothing. She settled herself in the only chair by Moss's bed.

"I believe I will sleep," Moss said, feigning tiredness. He appeared to be asleep in seconds.

"Women!" Seth snorted. He shifted from one foot to the other. When he saw that his son was asleep, he turned and left without another word.

Moss cracked open one eye and grinned at Billie. She giggled. "Is the old boy gone?" She nodded. "Then come here, Mrs. Coleman, and welcome me home properly."

He didn't have to ask twice. Billie was on the side of the bed in a second, her arms around her husband, offering her lips, making up for all the months of longing. Her fingers raked through his thick dark hair; her breasts swelled beneath his caresses. He was home, here in her arms. Once he saw how much she needed him, once he held his daughters for the first time, war, hell, or heaven could never separate them again. Now that she had him, she would keep him.

His family was lined up on the verandah when Moss climbed from the ambulance with the aid of a corpsman: his father, Agnes, Billie, and his two children.

He saw it all in a flash but it was to Maggie and Susan that his eyes went. A lump rose in his throat as he climbed the dozen steps to the porch. How beautiful they were! His own flesh-and-blood family. Remarkable. "Hello, everybody, I'm home," he said spiritedly.

Billie watched the kaleidoscope of emotions on her husband's face and decided that the months of agony and misery and the difficult births had all been worth it. The love on Moss's face touched her soul. She bent low and whispered to Maggie. The child tugged harder on her mother's dress and then stepped forward. She lowered her dark head and peered at her father from beneath incredibly long lashes. Billie held her breath.

"Hello, Pap."

Moss stared at his daughter. He could feel something burn his eyelids. He was about to reach out to Maggie when Seth finally maneuvered his way between Billie and the little girl. He slapped his son on his back and drew him forward.

The precious moment was shattered. Billie wanted to cry. Instead, she hugged Susan closer. Agnes looked away. Moss turned and looked down at Maggie, who was once again sucking on her fist. The burning sensation behind his eyelids was gone. He knew he'd lost something in that moment, and still his eyes lingered on the little girl.

"We waited lunch, Moss," Agnes said cheerfully. "Sirloin tips with fresh mushrooms. I seem to recall it's one of your favorites. And the cook made a lemon meringue pie just for you."

"Sounds great. I'd like a nice cold beer, if possible. It's

been so long since I've had a beer I've forgotten what it tastes like."

"I'll get it for you, Moss," said Billie, "but you'll have to hold Susan. Would you mind? She doesn't wiggle and I don't think she'll hurt your shoulder."

"The boy doesn't want to hold a squealing baby," Seth said sourly.

"Sure I do, Pap. I want to hold both my girls. Come here, Maggie, and sit next to me. Let me get settled, Billie, and then hand me Susan."

Billie's eyes were so grateful—and full of something Moss didn't want to think about. He looked away. It was goddamn sinful the way his wife looked at him. And he loved it.

Susan let out an ear-splitting shriek when Billie tried to transfer her to her father. She grabbed at her mother and kicked out with her foot.

Seth's bellow of outrage could be heard all over the house. He stepped forward, yanked the shrieking Susan from Billie's arms, and thundered for the nurse. "Children belong in their rooms with their nannies. I told you this wasn't a good idea, but did you listen to me? Jess would never have pulled a damn fool stunt like this. The boy needs peace and quiet, not screaming, yelling brats."

"Pap, it's okay. Susan has never seen me. What do you expect? I don't mind. How do you expect me to get to know my children if you keep them penned up in a nursery?"

"You have plenty of time. You just got home," Seth said gruffly.

Billie stood staring from her husband to her father-in-law. What to do? Moss looked tired and he wanted a beer. He wanted *her* to get the beer. In the end she took Maggie's hand and led her from the room. She handed both children over to the nurse, raced to the kitchen, uncapped the beer, and reached for a glass. She double-timed back to the living room and just caught Seth handing his son a beer and a glass. She stood foolishly in the doorway. When Moss looked up, she smiled tightly. "I thought I would join you."

The girl was learning, Agnes thought as she excused herself to see about lunch.

"Good girl. Come sit here by me and rub my back. Remember that massage you gave me on the beach in Hawaii? I want one just like that."

"The atmosphere isn't quite right," Billie said, laughing as she filled her glass.

"I thought you didn't like beer. When did this start?"

"When your father beat me to the refrigerator. Waste not, want not. You'll probably have to finish it."

Seth glowered at Billie and settled himself directly across from Moss. "I want to hear everything you've been doing. Don't leave a thing out. Billie, why don't you help your mother in the kitchen?"

Billie locked eyes with her father-in-law. "What could I possibly do? There's a cook, a maid, and a young girl to serve. Mother herself is probably in the way. She's merely checking on things. You go ahead and talk. I'll just sit here."

Moss's hand tightened imperceptibly on hers. Billie glowed.

After Moss had climbed the stairs for a nap, Agnes suggested she and Billie go for a walk. "It's such a beautiful day and the girls are napping. Neither of us is needed here."

"Moss might wake and want something."

"That's why we have servants, Billie. We won't be gone long. I would like to talk to you."

"All right, Mother, but no more than thirty minutes. I want to be with Moss when he wakes."

"Thirty minutes will be fine. People tell me this is the best time of year to be in San Diego. It's beautiful, don't you think?"

"Yes, Mother, it is. What did you want to talk about?"

Agnes frowned and then decided on bluntness. "Billie, child, I know you've had a harrowing time with your last two pregnancies, but I think you had best give some serious thought to having another child as soon as possible. I know this is none of my affair, but you are my daughter. The next time Moss might not be so lucky. If . . . if he . . . What I mean is, if something happens, you won't have that piece of Moss that can only be yours with a son. The girls . . . well, they're girls. I'm sure you know what I'm talking about. You have to give it serious thought, my dear. A son, Billie. You need a son. Moss needs a son. We both know how disappointed he was when the girls were born."

"No, Mother, I didn't know he was disappointed. He never said any such thing to me." Billie stopped walking. She faced her mother.

"Darling, a husband doesn't say something like that to his wife. Think how inferior you would have felt. . . . But, darling, surely you knew, felt his disappointment."

"No, Mother, I never knew or felt anything like that. Did Moss say something to you?"

"Not to *me*, Billie."

Agnes looked away at the stricken look on her daughter's face. "Darling, don't you think Moss looks remarkably well for what he went through? If that shell had been a little higher or more to the left, you would be a widow, Billie. That's what the navy doctors told Seth. I'm sure Moss didn't want to worry you and that's why he's making light of his injury."

Billie felt as if her knees were going to buckle under her. They were coming at her from all sides. Seth with his deviousness, Agnes with her blunt information, Moss with his omissions. Didn't any of them care about her? Her jaw tightened. "I think this is far enough, Mother. I want to go back and wait for Moss to wake up. The girls will be awake soon. He might enjoy seeing Susan get her bath."

"I think you're absolutely right, Billie. It will do Moss a world of good to see his daughters and get to know them. They're so dainty and wispy. If you had had a boy, he would want to rough and tumble on the floor with him and he wouldn't be able to do that with his shoulder injury."

Billie was tight-lipped all the way back to the house. Her mother had the finesse of a buzz saw. It must have something to do with her spending so much time with Seth. She was beginning to sound like him, act like him. God forbid, she was even swaggering like him!

Billie settled herself in a comfortable chaise longue across the room from where Moss was sleeping peacefully, his good arm flung back on the pillow. It must be hard for him to sleep like that, Billie thought. He had always liked to sleep scrunched up into a ball on his side. The same side as his bad shoulder.

Her thoughts were chaotic. Her mother had voiced aloud what she herself had been thinking. In fact, it was all she had been able to think of from the moment Seth had told her her husband had been wounded. She *needed* a son. She wanted a son. For Moss, yes. But for herself, too. She wanted that piece of Moss that would only come with a son. It was a shame that girl babies couldn't give that same feeling. It wasn't fair, but it was a fact. Good Lord, whatever would she do without Moss? Would she be able to survive? Physically, yes. Emotionally . . . she had her doubts. But if she had that small bundle that was part of Moss, she would make it.

Marriage certainly hadn't changed much in her life, she thought with a grimace. Agnes had controlled everything she did up until the day she'd married Moss—and she hadn't relinquished that hold yet. If anything, her mother had even more control because of her alliance with Seth. Her very existence was in their hands. Moss, dear, sweet Moss, trusted them to take care of her and that was exactly what they were doing.

A horrible realization dawned. If anything happened to Moss and Seth died, Agnes would be in total control—unless Billie had a son. The son would inherit, but she, Billie, would be the dowager queen. She would be in control of her son and safeguard everything until he came of age. She could see to it that Maggie and Susan received their rightful share. Gamblers had a phrase for it—an ace in the hole. The ticket to everything. She *needed* a son. It was that simple.

Perhaps it was time to become a little selfish. Or, to put it another way, perhaps it was time to grow up and face reality, with the rest of the Colemans.

Moss woke, feeling vaguely disoriented. He gazed about the strange room. So many rooms lately, places where he'd slept, none of them secure and familiar. He suddenly yearned for his old room at Sunbridge, for old, familiar things, for things that he could hold and feel, that would give him a sense of his past and offer a promise for his future. A muted sound from down the hall brought a grin to his face. He had something better: he had two little girls, his own flesh and blood!

He noticed Billie sleeping on the chaise. She was beautiful. He lay quietly and watched her for a long time. She was so young to be the mother of two children. Twenty years old, not even old enough to graduate college or to vote, and here she was a wife and a mother. She hadn't fooled him with her letters that made light of what she'd endured with the pregnancies. He'd seen her that Christmas when she'd been carrying Maggie, swollen and worn and frightened. He decided he wouldn't put Billie through that again, no matter what Pap said or wanted. Two little girls were enough for him and if it didn't suit Pap, too damn bad.

It was time for Billie to enjoy life. Time for her to enjoy the girls and watch them grow. Maybe later, when the war was over, they'd take time out of their lives to try for a son. He was confident his luck would hold—the war hadn't gotten him so far and it would never get him. He was too smart, too quick.

He was a Coleman: Death was nowhere on his horizon. There would be time for a son. He would think of Billie now. Two children in two years was more than enough to ask of any woman.

Billie wasn't the same girl he'd met in Philadelphia and married. He could see it and feel it. He recognized she was growing up. She wasn't a girl any longer, but a beautiful, desirable woman. She was learning every day. She'd stood up to Seth. And, when she really became Billie Coleman, a woman in her own right, she would be formidable. He smiled. Billie. Dear, loving Billie.

Carefully, Moss inched himself from the bed. First stop, the nursery. He stood in the doorway for a few minutes watching the girls. Maggie was building a stack of blocks and he held his breath while one chubby hand added another and another. His eyes were drawn to Susan, playing quietly with a stuffed teddy, mangling its ear with her two bottom teeth. She looked up curiously from her playpen and Moss watched her apprehensively. Would she scream again? But evidently she felt safe behind the bars. Moss grinned because she looked so much like a fat little monkey in a cage.

Miss Jenkins was not present, and the grandmotherly nanny followed Moss's suggestion that she leave him alone with his daughters.

Maggie's brightly colored tower of blocks toppled to the floor. Maneuvering her plump little bottom and getting up on her haunches, the rosy-cheeked, dark-haired toddler looked around for nanny. But there was only Moss. She pointed a pudgy little finger at him and said seriously, "You did that, Pap."

Moss threw back his dark head that was so like Maggie's and laughed. By God, if someone had to be blamed, why not him? "I'll tell you what," he said, hunkering down, "I'll build you a castle. Would you like that, Maggie?"

The toddler jabbered like a magpie as Moss added block upon block. "Susy wants out. Get Susy, Pap!"

"Is that allowed? Would nanny like that?"

Maggie hung her head, her cheeks flushing just like her mother's. "No."

"Good. Then let's do it."

"Nurse will holler," Maggie warned precociously.

"Pap will take care of things. I think Susy wants to build with blocks, too. We can pretend she's the princess."

"Who am I, Pap?"

"You're the queen, Maggie darling."

Maggie pondered her father's words. "The queen is bigger!" She stretched her pink arms upward. "So big!"

"I think you mean better, don't you? Yes, the queen is bigger and better." Moss was grinning. Sibling rivalry already. "But just a shade better. Princesses are important, too."

"Yes! Get Susy!"

"I thought you'd see it my way." Moss took it slow and easy bending over his youngest daughter. He hesitated before touching her, afraid she'd begin to cry and upset Maggie, too. When his little girl wrapped her sweet arms around his neck and squealed not with fright but with delightful anticipation, Moss felt his heart melt.

Billie woke an hour later to laughter. She listened for a moment. The booming laugh came again, unmistakably Moss's. He must be with the children, she thought, and tiptoed down the hall. At the door to the nursery she clapped her hand to her mouth to prevent her own laughter from shattering the moment. Moss was sitting on the floor with Susan between his legs. She was busy peeling the paper from Maggie's crayons, and Maggie was drawing squiggly lines on his shoulder cast, telling him it was her name, Mommy's name, and Grandmam's name.

"Where's my name?" Moss complained. "Don't you know how to spell Pap?"

Maggie considered the question for a moment. Then she brightened. Her eyes flashed with mischief and a sudden girlish giggle erupted from her pouting mouth as she grabbed a deep purple crayon and drew a long bold line. Sitting back on her heels, she added another flourish and proudly announced, "Pap!"

It was Billie who insisted, despite Seth's objection, that Moss retire early. Her husband's face was ashen when he climbed the stairs to their rooms. He didn't object when Billie helped him undress, and he was asleep almost before his head touched the pillow.

Billie was satisfied just to have Moss here, in their bed. As long as he was near, within touching distance, she could be happy.

There would be other days, other nights. Clearly, her indestructible husband had overdone it today. It was the strain of coming home, dealing with the pain, playing with the girls—

and of being torn between his loyalties to his wife and to his father. But she would always remember this afternoon when her husband and their babies had shared wonderful hours together. If a son had been there, would it have been different?

She leaned over and brushed her lips across his brow. Quietly she undressed and climbed into bed beside him. How good it felt—and how lonely and empty her bed had been without him all these months.

It worried her that Moss was so eager to get himself back into the action. If only, just once, Moss would want her more than he wanted anything else. Why couldn't she and the girls be enough? As she turned toward him and slipped her arm around his waist to nestle close, she knew her decision was a good one. If his wife and daughters weren't quite enough, a son would be. A son.

{{{{{{{{{ CHAPTER EIGHTEEN }}}}}}}}}

The days in San Diego passed swiftly and smoothly. They were busy—Billie saw to that. Overnight, she had seemed to take charge. Family breakfast on the terrace included the girls. Then some time for play in the nursery, with Billie watching from the sidelines. After that, an hour or so for Moss to read the papers and maybe for a casual talk over a second cup of coffee. Lunch was on the terrace, too, and then the girls went down for their naps and Moss left for his physical therapy session at the naval hospital. When he came home from the hospital he was always exhausted and she made sure he had at least an hour of rest. Billie generously shared Moss with Seth at dinner and for an hour afterward. Then he was hers. If Seth didn't like the arrangements, he kept his opinions to himself.

One warm evening, as a gentle breeze stirred the lace curtains at the French doors and Billie and Moss lay quietly together listening to soft music on the radio, Billie said, "I want another baby, Moss."

She felt him tense. "Just like that? No. No more. Not now."

"Just like that," Billie repeated. She traced a long, delicate line down his chest and stopped just short of the rough patch of hair at the base of his stomach. "Look at me, Moss. Do I look sick? I'm young; I'm healthy. I take care of myself. And I'll do what the doctors say—I always do. Susan arrived safely and almost exactly on time. This baby will, too."

"You make it sound like it's already a fact." Moss pretended to glower. He was a man after all, and flattered that this beautiful young woman wanted to bear him yet another child.

"Isn't it?"

"No, Billie, it isn't. I don't want you taking chances. You've got to be strong for the two children we already have. When the war is over and I'm here with you, that's the time to think of another child. Unless, of course, you've got your doubts about my coming out of this one in one piece." His gaze was sharp, keen, piercing Billie.

"I don't think that at all. I know nothing will happen to you. That's another reason—I want to have a son for you when you return. Please, Moss. Darling?"

"Billie, I never willingly refuse you anything, but I think we should wait. The girls are wonderful, they're beautiful and charming, and they are more than I ever imagined daughters could be. I don't need a son."

Lie. Lie through your teeth, Coleman. Make it sound like the truth. Need. Want. There was a difference. He had said he didn't need a son. Change it, Coleman, before it's too late.

"I don't want a son right now, Billie," he said. "I'm content with Maggie and Susy."

Diversion. That's how some battles were won. "Billie, have you written Thad lately?"

It took Billie a moment to adjust to the sudden change in the conversation. "No, I haven't. Do you want me to write to him?"

"I think it might be a good idea. He only gets mail from his mother. He likes you, Billie, and I know he'd appreciate it. You could give him all the lowdown about how the girls are growing. When I tell it, it sounds like bragging."

Well, if he could do an about-face in the conversation, so could she. "Lieutenant, how would you like me to make love to you, Billie Coleman style?" The finger that traced the length of his torso insidiously invaded private property.

"Is there a difference from the Moss Coleman style?" he

asked, shifting to present himself to her hands and lips.

"Considerable . . . however, I'm not certain you're up to it," Billie teased as she nibbled his ear.

"I'm up to it and you know it!" He seized her hand and pressed it against him.

"Darned if you aren't!" She laughed, a soft, womanly sound, deep and husky with the knowledge of the pleasure to come. It was a sound that ripened his interest, that made him ache to caress her body and to lose himself in her. "If you promise me you won't go away, I'll be right back."

"In this condition? Where would I go? Billie, don't forget to—"

"Use the diaphragm," she finished for him. After Moss had been released from the naval hospital, he'd talked intimately with her about taking measures to prevent another pregnancy and made her promise to see a doctor in San Diego. He'd been so concerned, so sincere, that she could not deny him. She would use the diaphragm tonight, but she would also remove it whenever she felt like, even too early. She didn't think of herself as devious; she was just giving the odds a little boost. If it was meant to be, she would conceive another child. Her conscience didn't prick her, but her image in the bathroom mirror was bitter.

When Billie slipped beneath the silken sheets against Moss's warm, vital body, her face was warm and glowing. "Are you ready, Lieutenant Coleman?"

"Mrs. Coleman, when I see you like this, I'm always ready." The timbre of his voice sent a tingling ripple down her spine.

"No more talking, Lieutenant. I want you to just lie there. You're not to do a thing, understand?"

"Aye-aye, ma'am." His hands reached for the ashen fall of silky hair that fell about her face. He held it to one side and found her mouth with his own.

Billie let all thoughts evaporate. She was a woman, receptive only to loving sensations—the way her thighs felt between his hard, muscular ones; the way the tips of her breasts brushed against his furred chest. Her fingers found the planes and hollows of his body, knowing them more intimately than she knew her own. And as she traced moist patterns with her lips from the base of his throat to the flatness of his belly, she was attuned to his intake of breath, the little gasp of desire that quickened her pulses with a sense of her female power. She seduced him with her hands, her lips, the motions of her body upon him. And when she straddled him and took him into herself, there was victory in her cries of pleasure.

Billie lived in a dream world, surrounded by her children and her husband. It was an idyll, something she'd craved and needed and had never had. Even Seth smiled at her these days, and Agnes was complimentary about everything Billie did. Billie's sense of security grew, and she looked forward to Christmas. This year there would be two perfect little girls under the Christmas tree and Moss would be there, with that look of love and admiration in his eyes.

On the afternoon of December 31 Moss came bounding into the house on La Cienega Boulevard. His face was beaming with excitement. His summer-blue eyes twinkled.

"Look!" he told Billie, opening his jacket. She saw that the last of the bandages and the brace had been removed. "Good as new, fit as a fiddle. I leave to rejoin my squadron on the fifth!"

Before she could say a word, Moss took her into his arms and buried his lips in her smoke-blond hair. "Be happy for me, Billie. It's what I want. What I need."

And what of her needs? she thought. What of them? And the children? She was beginning to understand that if she forced Moss to make a choice, he wouldn't choose her.

"I'm going to tell Pap. Better batten down the hatches. He's not going to like this." He left her as quickly as he'd embraced her and hurried away to face Seth.

Agnes found Billie in the hallway on the bottom step of the stairs, elbows on knees, head in hands. "Billie? What's wrong?"

"Moss. He's going back to his squadron. He's telling Seth now."

Billie heard the hiss of her indrawn breath. "And what about you, Billie?" she asked. "What about us? All of us, including the children?" There was a desperate edge to Agnes's voice that she didn't try to disguise. Her long, brightly painted fingers played with her rope of pearls. The taffeta slip beneath her light woolen suit rustled pleasantly as she sat beside her daughter. "Do you remember our little talk? And do your remember how Seth treated Amelia, his own flesh and blood?..."

"That's enough, Mother! I don't want to hear any more. And as for our little talk, I'm doing the best I can. And this time it's for *me*, Mother, for me! Because *I* want a son. Everyone else be damned!"

Billie stood, leaving Agnes sitting alone on the stairs, and went into the living room. When she returned she carried a decanter of cognac and two snifters. Back straight, expression solemn, she climbed the stairs without a glance or a word to her watchful mother.

Outside her bedroom door, Billie shook back her hair and lifted the corners of her mouth into a smile, then burst into the room. "Hi, darling. I battened down the hatches but I didn't hear a sound. How's your father taking the news?"

"How else?" Moss said bitterly. "He's never understood what was important to me. He's furious and refuses to go out with us tonight. What've you got there?"

"Oh, I thought you needed someone to celebrate with. And I couldn't think of anyone better than myself. I want you to be happy, darling, and I'm happy for you."

Moss's expression softened. "You're quite a woman, Mrs. Coleman. Did I ever tell you that?"

"Not in those words. I didn't bring any ice—do you need ice?"

Moss laughed. "And ruin twenty-year-old cognac? C'mon, let's pour us a drink and celebrate a new year." He never noticed Billie locking the door behind her.

Billie lay beside Moss, her head fuzzy from the cognac, and felt his hands trail lazily over her body. "My wife, my beautiful wife," he was murmuring against her ear as his fingers worked the front buttons of her blouse. He'd drunk too much, taken two glasses to one of hers, and she knew that his judgment had evaporated in his excitement over being allowed to rejoin his squadron. It was exactly as she wanted it. Men had their war machines for battle; women had their own bodies. Hard steel or soft flesh, strength or passion. In the end it was the same, and always for the same selfish reasons.

Slowly, almost lazily, they undressed each other, lips kissing and moistening newly bared skin. It was late afternoon and dusky shadows hovered outside the lace-covered windows. Rosy light invaded the room, warming the color of their bodies and splashing intriguing designs on the walls and bedclothes. Billie curled toward him, one hand exploring his rock-hard chest, one leg resting lightly against his. Moss hovered over her, his liquor-scented breath pleasantly fanning her cheek. One bold finger charted her face, stroking her golden brow, following the slender turn of her nose, the downy prominence of her cheekbone and the yielding softness of her rosy mouth. He nibbled her lower lip, smiling when her mouth trembled. Her hazel eyes were sultry and alive, open to welcome him into their silvery depths.

He caressed her tenderly, tracing the tender hollow of her shoulder, the globes of her firm, coral-crested breasts. The nipples hardened and rose beneath his palms. His hands moved lower, to her narrow waist, the round curve of her hip, the soft flesh of her belly, the enticing golden down, and the warm valley.

Her eyes closed then, and she moved against his fingers, whispering in delighted encouragement when his mouth followed where his hands had been, finding her satiny contours. It was her murmur of delight that heightened his passion and left him trembling. The tide of his emotions was sweeping him into a sea of sensation. He was exhilarated by the cognac, by the power of bringing this woman such pleasure, and by the knowledge that he would soon be returning to his squadron. All of life was his and it pounded through his veins in a rhythmic rush that made all things sweeter. Life. Love. Passion.

He covered her body with his own, his mouth finding hers as he pressed into her and felt himself enveloped in warm, pulsing flesh that welcomed him.

Billie offered her mouth to his, tasting herself mingled with the cognac. Deeper and deeper he penetrated, slowly, languorously, until she completely surrounded him, taking him inside her, tasting, kissing, until there was no sensation beyond him. Moss, only Moss, within her, surrounding her, becoming her. Moss, filling her life, touching her heart, becoming her world and her universe. She did not exist outside of this moment. She needed, she wanted, she took. And gave. What had begun as a calculation was ending as a glorious gift, shared between them.

They fit each other. Her rhythms perfectly matched his own, her flesh and bones supported him, melted into him, comfortable, yielding in ever-deepening, ever-quickening undulations. Flesh swallowed flesh and became one, again and again, deeper and deeper, caressing with each stroke, possessing with rippling waves until there was nothing except those two parts of themselves that merged and joined and bonded, lifting them together in a path to the sun.

The Texas Ranger soared into the endless sky, away from Moss's squadron and back to the Big E. Something had jimmied in his instrument panel and his Wildcat was having difficulty maintaining altitude. The mechanics would have the Ranger right in no time. Moss banked to port and read his compass heading, exhilarated by the unhampered freedom of flight, by the satisfaction of a job well done. In late January, he'd been involved in strikes on Formosa and Okinawa. February had seen the first air strikes on Tokyo, and now it was March and the Big E and her men and machines were supporting the occupation of Iwo Jima.

There was a vibration in the fuselage, a shudder beneath his feet. He was steadily losing altitude! He attempted to make voice contact with his squadron, but the frequencies in his headset seemed jammed. Again he tried. Nothing.

Swallowing panic, Moss pulled back on the stick, feeling the Ranger attempt a response yet continue on her downward course. Her engine spit, then coughed. Emergency procedure drilled through his brain, but he wouldn't admit he needed to use it. Like death, it had always seemed only a remote possibility. The Ranger was spiraling down, about to roll into a tailspin. Moss tried to regain mastery of the fighter plane, all the while attempting to make radio contact with either the *Enterprise* or his squadron. The panel lights dimmed and then failed altogether. The prop was slowing before his eyes. If the Ranger went into a tailspin, a safe bailout would be impossible. The prop was making lazy windmills. Desperately he worked the rubber pedals, feeling them stiff, unresponsive. Useless. He'd heard an old flight chief talk about setting a Wildcat down on her ailerons and elevator, but the Ranger had gone dead in the air and was plunging from seven thousand feet to the hungry sea below.

Never bail out below a thousand feet! It was a precaution he reiterated several times a day in training. Yet he knew he must be below that when in a single explosive motion he hurled back the canopy, climbed to his feet, jammed the stick full forward, and pulled the ripcord of his chute. The dead Ranger dropped from under him; the parachute fluttered and opened and snatched him upward.

The sea felt like a concrete wall when he hit, but he managed to release the snap hooks that held his chute. The sea engulfed him and he went deep into its blackness. But when he struggled upward and broke the surface, he was free of the entangling silk.

He took huge gulps of air and pulled the toggles on his Mae West. One side filled at once; the other hung limp. Treading water, Moss laboriously blew up the lifesaving jacket. It was then that he noticed blood ribboning into the water beneath him. He must have torn his leg when the chute yanked him from the cockpit. Blood drew sharks, which were numerous in these waters. He must get himself out of the sea!

Reaching around, he zipped the pararaft out of its envelope and pulled the inflation toggle. It responded, whuffing into shape. Encumbered by the Mae West, he struggled aboard, lifting his torn leg into the raft. He could feel panic closing in on him, but he recognized it for what it was and held himself in rigid control.

Bobbing along on the waves with nauseating regularity, Moss watched the sky and waited. The long night descended. He prayed for morning and waited.

When the sun finally broke the horizon it was a hot, angry, crimson ball that rouged the cumulus puffs. His salt-caked face and the exposed skin at wrists and ankles began to burn. And still he watched the sky. He concentrated on guarding against despair.

He checked his watch and gratefully found it still working. He noted the time. If he fell asleep, it would seem only minutes but in reality it would be hours. He took a position fix on the sun. The wind seemed constant and he was drifting in a northwesterly direction, away from the last-known position of the *Enterprise*. Moss's equipment consisted of a sturdy bladed knife sewn into a sheath on the leg of his flight suit and a .45-caliber automatic pistol in a holster on the web belt around his waist. He worried that the pistol would be useless, but when he test-fired it the satisfying recoil sprang up his arm to the elbow. At least he wasn't completely defenseless.

He was parched and ravenously hungry. Before shielding his face from the sun by hunkering down into the protective shadow of his life vest, he checked his leg wound. A satisfactory clot of blood had created a scab. At least he wouldn't bleed to death.

The sun was only thirty degrees above the level of the sea when Moss awakened. Late afternoon. He cursed himself for having fallen asleep. Precious hours had been wasted; he should have been on the lookout for a passing ship. He squinted into the distance, blinked, and squinted again. Was it his imagination or was that a ship coming out of due west? The sun was blinding him and he was light-headed with hunger, panic, and thirst, but he would swear on his life it was a ship. As the sun sank behind it, its silhouette began to appear. A superstructure, a smokestack, a gun mount. It was a destroyer and it was heading straight for him.

Throwing himself onto his belly and reaching into the water, Moss paddled himself forward, attempting to close the distance between him and the ship. Rescue was imminent. He stood in the raft, balancing himself on widespread legs, waving his white cotton undershirt. With a whoop of excitement he saw the white water boil behind the stern, saw the bow make a course correction. It was coming for him! A sheer solid wall of steel rising and falling with the ocean's swell. Moss resumed paddling. A rope ladder was flung down to him. He grabbed it solidly with both hands and hoisted himself to safety. The prayer in his heart had been answered. A wide grin split his face—there was no beating the Coleman luck! He looked up, ready to shout howdy to his rescuers. His grin froze. The deck rail was lined with faces. All of them Japanese!

{{{{{{{{ CHAPTER NINETEEN }}}}}}}}

March had arrived at Sunbridge like the proverbial lion and was leaving like a lamb. Seth watched Billie's advancing pregnancy with a knowledgeable eye. This time it would be a boy, a grandson; he could feel it in his bones. Billie herself seemed pleased with the pregnancy. She was more confident, healthier. There was no nausea and sickness with this child as there had been with Maggie and Susan. Seth thought there was a peacefulness about Billie that had never been there before.

Agnes also watched her daughter. Although Billie was only beginning her fourth month, Agnes satisfied herself that the signs were there. Billie was carrying high and straight, instead of round and hippy as with the girls. It was definitely a boy this time. Seth would grunt whenever she mentioned it to him, but he believed every word.

Billie smiled. Neither of them could be one hundred percent certain. Only her. Billie Coleman would have her son.

Billie had announced her pregnancy only two weeks before, on the same day she'd written Moss telling him about their "little accident." She'd hugged the letter to her breast before she'd mailed it. By now, Moss would know another child was on the way and that she was certain it would be a boy.

As Billie settled down to write to Moss, she looked at the calendar as she did every day and crossed off the date. It was six weeks and three days since she'd heard from Moss. Even Seth hadn't had word. It worried her but it wasn't unusual. Often a pack of letters would arrive at once. Moss was fine; she felt it. If something had happened to him, she would know.

The bedside clock read 11:20 when Billie decided to go downstairs for a glass of warm milk. As she was crossing the wide, central hall the doorbell shrilled, startling her.

"Telegram for Mrs. Moss Coleman. Sign here." Billie's trembling hands reached for the yellow envelope. The delivery boy's face was a study in sympathy and pity. The return address was the War Department.

"Mother!" she screamed.

She experienced everything after that through waves of blackness, in slow motion. Agnes coming down the stairs. Seth stepping out of his study. She knew that in reality Agnes had flown down the stairs and Seth had exploded from his study.

Seth sat down on the cowhide-covered bench and stared at the rectangle of yellow paper. He seemed unable to move.

"Would you like me to open it, Seth?" Agnes asked quietly. He suddenly looked old and beaten. Two pairs of eyes watched as Agnes deftly slit the envelope. The words jumped off the page:

WE REGRET TO INFORM YOU LT. MOSS COLEMAN HAS BEEN LISTED AS MISSING IN ACTION.

Missing, not killed. Missing. Missing. It was all Billie had to hold on to.

"That's all it says." Agnes relinquished the telegram to Seth's shaking hands. She straightened and belted her blue chenille robe more tightly about her. "I'll make coffee. Follow me to the kitchen, both of you. We will not have hysteria. Moss is missing. It did not say he was wounded or dead, only missing. Until we know something definite we will carry on as before. Billie! Get hold of yourself! You have a baby to think of. We're going to have coffee and even some cake and we'll talk, all of us together. And then we'll all go to bed because that's all we can do."

"Those Jap bastards have him. They torture, they—"

"Not another word, Seth," Agnes said sharply. "I don't want you upsetting Billie. She's pregnant, or have you forgotten? We'll have no more of that kind of talk. And you, Billie, you have to believe that Moss is well and will come back. He promised he would come back and we must believe he will. Now, that's good enough for me and it has to be good enough for both of you." Billie nodded miserably as she dabbed at her eyes with the cuff of her dressing gown.

"All right, Aggie. Where the hell is that coffee you said you were making?"

"It's right here. What did I tell you about swearing in front of me? I know you're upset now but don't let it happen again. It has to perk. Five more minutes. Tita had the pot all ready for morning. I can't seem to find any cake, so we're having cornbread with butter. And some blackberry jam would be good."

Billie noticed the slight tremble in her mother's hands as she set the table. Busy. Always keep busy so you don't have to think. Agnes would keep busy and she and Seth would eat. They would chew and swallow. Then when Agnes dismissed them they would go to their respective rooms and cry like babies. Seth for his son, she for her husband, and Agnes for the good life.

They carried on; it was all they could do. Agnes prodded and poked at them to busy themselves. Her tongue was sharp and they obeyed.

Billie managed to fill her days with the girls and writing letters to Moss which she hid away in her lingerie drawer. It made no difference if she could mail them or not. It was something to do. She didn't cry; she didn't know why exactly. It had nothing to do with her mother, more with Moss's conviction that he would return. She hung on to that thought. It was the letters that arrived from Thad Kingsley that bolstered her sagging spirits. They arrived weekly and were full of nonsensical news that made her smile. He always mentioned Moss at the end, expressed certainty that he was safe somewhere and would manage to make it back home.

It never occurred to Billie to question how Thad's letters managed to be delivered weekly, with no in-between skips. He was fighting the same war as Moss, flying in the same squadron, serving on the same ship. It was enough that he wrote.

In a month's time Billie knew every member of the squadron and all about their personal lives. She knew about the girls they'd left behind and the pets they had grown up with. She learned about the inside of the planes and what made them fly. She learned Thad's middle name and what New England looked like in autumn. Her mouth watered for some Vermont maple syrup. The letters were long, written in a close, cramped style with many, many words to the page. Billie treasured the man's thoughtfulness. Someday, she would find a way to make it up to him. The comfort his letters gave her, the hope, could never be measured.

Seth stomped into the house late one afternoon, his shoulders bent and his face filled with misery. Billie's heart almost stopped. "What is it, Seth? Have you had word about Moss?" she asked anxiously.

Seth shook his head and wiped at his eyes with the back of his hand. "Nessie died."

"Your horse?" Billie said stupidly.

"Yes, my horse, Nessie. She died. Just now. I have to call the vet."

"If the horse is dead, why do you have to call the vet?"

"Because I do," Seth snarled. "Because I do."

It was as if the horse had been a flesh-and-blood person. It was almost more than Billie could bear.

Agnes's summary of the situation was simple: She and Billie didn't understand because they weren't born-and-bred Texans.

But Billie did understand. Nessie had been more important in Seth's life than his wife. There had been no tears for Jessica. She watched him make daily pilgrimages to the place where the horse was buried, and he always returned with red-rimmed eyes and a surly tongue. This, too, shall pass, Billie told herself. And it did. Seth, though, hovered over Billie after that. This child was his last hope—nothing must go wrong. It was all he had left. God help me, Billie thought, if this baby fools us all.

* * *

Moss was flung against the cold, damp bulkhead. The sea was rough tonight. He'd been blindfolded when they'd thrown him down here, but he could tell from the sounds of the engines and the slick sliding behind the steel wall that he was below the waterline in the hold of the Japanese transport ship. The hold was blacker than a cave and twice as cold. For mates he had several other Americans, a few Australians, and a rat.

Shortly after being rescued from the sea he'd been questioned mercilessly and then hoisted over to this passing transport. The poop had it that they were on their way to Japan. That had been eight days ago—he'd kept count by moving the end of his bootlace into successive holes and knotting the end. Once a day the forward hatch would open and uniformed soldiers, armed and at attention, would bring in a pail of water and rice balls for each of them, eight in all.

While Moss had been flying the Ranger, he'd thought of the Japanese as faceless robots of a corrupt government, enemies to the American way and all it stood for. Now the enemy had a face, yellow and flat and menacing, and he hated them, not just their government, not as a nation, but each and every one of them individually.

The prisoners' lives had become an eternity of blackness, of sensations of cold and filth. One marine, wounded on Iwo Jima, had died two days before. His body lay somewhere in the dark. One of the Aussies knew a bit of Japanese and had told the soldiers of the marine's death. Instead of removing the body, they'd merely withheld a rice portion, and tossed a dipper of precious water onto the metal plate floor. When an Australian infantryman had hauled himself to his feet and begun shouting at the Japs, he'd received a solid blow from a billy club as his reward. No one had spoken after that for a very long time.

Hours were endless, time meaningless; yet each day, after their one poor meal was served, Moss moved his bootlace into another eyelet. Now he was working on the holes in his left boot. He wondered if he would still be alive by the time he reached the top. He wondered if he wanted to be.

One cold gray dawn the transport ship's engines were cut and the ship rolled with the tide. The eight beaten, sick, half-starved prisoners came out on deck, into the fresh offshore wind, and saw that they were part of a larger group than they'd realized. There were sixty other prisoners. Word spread that they were all going ashore to a place named Muishi. Moss tried to remember his geography but he couldn't place it. Muishi, as it turned out, was a coal-mining camp deep in the hills of northern Japan.

Life became a living hell. Each dawn, shirtless, shoeless, the prisoners were herded into Muishi's coal mine, half walking, half crawling for almost two miles underground where the air was stale and noxious and the temperature dropped nearly thirty degrees. Each night they were herded out again, more dead than alive.

Nearly four hundred men slaved in the mines, working to their last breaths to dig and haul the coal from the earth for their Japanese masters. . . .

Food became an obsession in Muishi. The hard rice balls and an occasional watery stew and hard biscuits were hardly enough to keep the men alive.

The Japanese were ruthless and cruel taskmasters, but they respected religious ceremonies. So when the prisoners told their captors that it was the custom when a man died to leave food by the body and that the living smoked cigarettes and prayed and spoke praise of the dead, they were believed. And from then on, whenever a man died, the guards would provide bowls of rice, which they placed at his head, and a basket of fruit, which they rested by his feet. And cigarettes were given to the mourners.

In time, the prisoners' appetites faded; the mindless work anesthetized them; hope became a dim memory. But *home* was something shared by all, remembered by all, even though to each it was a different place and different people.

The desire to live strengthened in Moss. He wanted to see his children again, to hold his wife in his arms. Each day became a battle to hold on to his mental agility and to his toughness. And the only way he could do this was to hate, hate the enemy, hate the Japs. Hate.

Those who gave in to hopelessness soon died, believing the Japanese braggarts who insisted the war would last a hundred years. There was so little information coming from the outside that there were moments when Moss almost believed them, too. Those were the moments he nearly broke, nearly gave up. But he would remind himself he was a Coleman. Colemans never stopped fighting. Colemans were tougher than beef jerky and more stubborn than mules. He clung to his heritage and dreamed of his children. Maggie. Susan. The son that would never be if he gave in to despair. . . .

Early during the heat of August, Moss and the others noted that something was happening. Food became more plentiful, drinking water more available. No one was punished or beaten for being too sick to go down in the mine. Something was happening.

President Harry Truman had given the go-ahead. The ultimate weapon was dropped on Japan. On August 14, 1945, the Japanese government agreed to an unconditional surrender. Muishi was so far north that word didn't reach them until two weeks later.

On September 2, 1945, Japan surrendered formally aboard the USS *Missouri*. V-J Day. Victory over Japan. Moss and his fellow prisoners were brought aboard an Australian troop transport and into the arms of the victors.

Early that same day, as his missing father was being welcomed by the jaunty Australians, Riley Seth Coleman was delivered into his mother's arms. Billie had finally achieved her victory.

PART THREE

{{{{{{{{ CHAPTER TWENTY }}}}}}}}}

The land and the place known as Sunbridge had changed little in the fourteen years since Billie had first arrived from Philadelphia. The grazing lands were lush this year, thanks to plentiful rain, and the winter's tumbleweeds rolled silently along the miles of white rail fencing. The shrubbery surrounding the house was taller, but the rose garden was still perfectly tended, a living memorial to Jessica, now more than twelve years buried on the little hill behind the house. The house itself had mellowed to a softer hue, bleached by its years in the sun, now paler than the prairie rose.

But the seemingly unchangeable stability of Sunbridge halted at the front door. Inside, time had made its mark. Seth Coleman, righteous monarch, leaned more heavily on his cane and his shaggy mane of hair was more grizzled. But his tongue was just as sharp as ever, his watery blue eyes just as piercing. His only interest in life was his ten-year-old grandson, Riley. When Moss's look-alike wasn't flying, strapped to the seat beside his father, he was riding the hills with his grandfather. Riley had just given up his pony for a mare, a descendant of old Nessie, which Seth had given him.

Riley had been made a part of Sunbridge since the day he was born. As heir apparent to the Coleman throne, he was taught to love his heritage and was schooled with one aim: to someday take the reins of the Sunbridge empire. Riley was a lanky boy with soft, shining blue eyes and gently rounded cheeks. Despite the attention lavished upon him, he was unspoiled, a loving child who never demanded anything. Not that he had to demand anything; whatever he asked for was promptly given, whatever seemed to interest him was his—within the hour. But young Riley Coleman was a sensitive, responsible boy and his growing surplus of possessions alarmed him; he was beginning to learn to disguise his interests, to force his glance away from a new attraction. With his every wish anticipated, his every dream fulfilled, there was too much to see to, too much to care for. It overwhelmed him.

To Riley, it just wasn't right to own a complicated German-made camera and not know how to use it (he would have been more than satisfied with a Brownie Hawkeye, anyway), so he spent long, tiresome hours poring over the directions and studying books on photography, and what should have been fun became a chore.

Riley was just as conscientious in his personal relationships. He loved his sisters and took his role as brother to Maggie and Susan seriously. He knew just when to stop teasing and he could be counted on to keep secrets, any secret, especially Maggie's. With Billie, Riley was both boy and baby, warm and loving, seeking an extra little smile or a tender kiss at bedtime. With Grandmother Agnes, Riley was polite and always gentlemanly—although conversation was mostly limited to "Yes, ma'am," "No, ma'am," and "Thank you, ma'am." Agnes was satisfied.

But it was with Moss that Riley was all boy, all noise and vitality, whooping and hollering, rambunctious. It was with his father, too, that he shared his hopes and dreams, his hurts and wounds. He never cried, this Coleman child, because it was unmanly. The girls, though, who seemed more their mother's children than their father's, were permitted to wail or whimper at will.

Riley tried not to show favoritism, but Susan was his favorite sister. She didn't shriek and yell and call him names. She was soft and gentle, like Mam, and played beautiful music on the piano. Susan always did as she was told and no one ever needed to punish her.

Maggie, on the other hand, was willful and rebellious, and found more ways to get into trouble than he could ever dream. Sometimes he lay in bed at night and tried to figure out why Maggie was the way she was. There were times when he actually believed she hated him, hated everyone. She drank beer in the barn with the cowboys, and when Pap and Grandpap were off on the range or in town on business, she drove their cars around the ranch. She had ugly friends, friends who only wanted to be with her because she had money to spend and could steal wine and beer and cigarettes. Riley always included Maggie in his prayers. He should tell on her—he knew he should—but he didn't. He couldn't. He'd come upon Maggie one day in the new barn, where his horse was stabled. She was snuggled down in the sweet-smelling straw crying great, hard sobs. He'd never seen anyone cry that way and it bit at him, making him run away. Maggie would have felt terrible if she knew he'd seen her—she felt bad enough already. That was why he didn't tell her, or anyone. He'd seen her take boys into the barn, but so far he'd never said anything about that, either. The boys would come out smiling and furtive, but Maggie always looked surly and miserable. Someday, though, he was going to talk to Pap about Maggie. Pap would know what to do. Pap knew everything about everything, so the troubles of a thirteen-going-on-fourteen-year-old girl wouldn't stump him. Not Pap . . .

Tita and Carlos had been pensioned off with a generous monthly allotment and three acres of good Coleman land. Seth never ceased to be amazed at how generous Agnes was with his money. The elderly couple had been replaced with a spiffy buxom girl named Charlotte and her pockmarked brother, Miguel. They wore made-to-order uniforms, which Agnes ordered by the dozen. Trained by her, they were the perfect servants and, the most valuable of their attributes in Agnes's opinion, they recognized her position in the household and honored it. Sunbridge worked like a well-oiled clock. Things were in hand.

If anything could be said of Agnes Ames, it was that she had aged beautifully, thanks to the finest hairdressers, an expensive wardrobe, a weekly massage, manicure, pedicure, and facial, a careful diet, and exercises done secretly in her bedroom. A quiet little trip back east ("to visit with old friends") had taken her no nearer Philadelphia than New York City, where a plastic surgeon had removed the fatty pads around her eyes and tightened her jawline. Now nearer sixty than fifty, Agnes had achieved just the life she wanted. She was about to accept her second term as president of the prestigious Canterbury Club and had been sitting on the board of directors of Sunbridge Enterprises for the past six years. Agnes had come into her own and she ruled with a steel scepter. No one, not even Seth, questioned her. Agnes Ames always smiled right before she fell asleep.

Since returning from the Japanese prisoner-of-war camp, Moss's zest for living had never flagged. Acceding to Seth's demands, Moss had thrown himself into Sunbirdge activities: ranching, beef, corn, and oil. But always his greatest efforts were reserved for electronics, where his curiosity and firsthand knowledge of airplanes were put to best use. He and his personal team of researchers had patented a number of inventions that were adopted by the aircraft industry, including a high-range radio antenna and a method for pressurizing commercial aircraft cabins. His dream of building the biggest and most efficient aircraft factories would soon become a reality.

Moss worked and he played. He also drank more than was good for him, but he was still handsome and trim. And there were women. Billie was his wife, the mother of his children, and he loved her. But he had faced death many times during the war, then had endured a living death in the Japanese camp, and now he was going to savor and taste everything life had to offer. Life had so much to offer a man like him and he saw no reason whatever to deny himself.

The love of Moss's life was Riley. His son. His own chance for immortality. Maggie and Susan could never become as important a part of his life as Riley. Daughters were pretty, sweet, and they could flatter and charm their fathers. But a son was a projection of the man himself, both a whisper of the past and a statement for the future. Daughters grew up and married; other men became the focus of their lives. A man's son was his own forever, as much his own as a broken-in pair of boots or the money he earned.

Somewhere along the way—Moss wasn't exactly certain when—he had converted his childhood room into an office and shop that was kept strictly for his own private endeavors. He'd installed a couch in place of the single bed and more often than not, he worked long into the night and fell asleep there. It hadn't been his intention to abandon the bedroom he shared with Billie, but more and more of his clothes were finding their way downstairs and he had less and less occasion to climb the stairs to the room where his wife slept. It hadn't been planned; it had just happened, and Billie had voiced no objection.

It was to his business, his ambitions, and his friends that Moss was attentive. A week never passed that he didn't speak to Thad Kingsley on the phone. The bills had been enormous during the progression of Thad's career in the navy and his travels all over the world. Thad was a buddy, and whenever possible they got together. Now Thad was a rear admiral and commandant of Naval Air Operations, based in Corpus Christi, just a hop-skip-jump in the Sunbridge plane.

Moss confided in Thad, drank with him till the early-morning hours. It was Thad who made certain Moss was bedded down for the night. It was Thad who called Moss's private number the following day to check on his hangover. It was not unusual for the tall, lanky New Englander in his immaculate uniform to step from his own Piper Cub onto the dusty airstrip that ran two miles south of Sunbridge and come to the house for lunch or an afternoon drink that lasted through dinner. Then Thad and Moss would relive old times, hash over Moss's deep hatred for the Japanese, make plans for their futures.

Thad liked visiting Sunbridge, he liked seeing Billie, watching her from across the table, hearing the soft lyrical voice that had never really surrenderd the rounded sounds of the northeast to the flat drawl of Texas. He enjoyed Susan's gentle blondness—so like Billie's—marveled at Riley's charismatic charm, and watched Maggie's brunette beauty bloom like the darkest rose in Billie's garden.

Often lately, Billie hadn't been at home when Thad made his impromptu visits. Busy, Moss would say, Billie was always busy. Then, at Thad's inquiring glance, Moss would clarify. "Billie seems to have picked up where Mam left off. She belongs to all the little women's groups and she's active in the PTA, and, of course, there's Memorial Hospital in Austin. Pap expects it and she complies. Also, she's developed an interest in painting at this little studio. She's damn good, too, Thad. You should see the picture she did of Sunbridge for Pap this past Christmas. Pap said she finally did something worthwhile with her dabbling."

Billie added a delicious dab of perfume behind each ear. It was wickedly expensive and it always made her feel good. This morning she needed it. Perfume was hardly a substitute for her husband, but it would have to do.

She couldn't help letting her eyes stray to the mound of gifts piled on the chaise longue. Birthday gifts from her family and friends, presented to her the night before at a celebration at the Canterbury Club. Conspicuously absent was a gift from her husband. Unless, of course, you counted the bunch of wilted daisies lying on her dressing table. Charlotte had brought them up before the party and said Mr. Coleman had picked them himself. Picked them himself but couldn't be bothered to climb the stairs to present them. Angrily, Billie swept them off the glass-topped vanity.

Moss had danced with her once. He had even brought her a drink—the wrong kind. Then he had gone off to the bar to sit with Seth and the other ranchers.

When the party was over, Susan had helped her mother with her coat and Maggie had sneered when she'd seen tears in Billie's eyes.

"What did you expect, Mother? Did you really think Pap was going to sit here and pay attention to *us*?"

Yes, that was exactly what she'd thought. It was what she'd wanted. She had lain awake, alone, in the huge bed, waiting. Until dawn. She wanted her husband. She needed to have him beside her, needed to feel his touch and hear him whisper the old words. Even if they no longer held the same passion, she needed to hear them. She could always separate the lies from the truth later. . . .

Why *hadn't* he climbed the steps to their room? Her room now. Why hadn't he wanted her? Couldn't he see how she ached for him?

Where had it gone wrong? When had his clothes disappeared from the huge double closet? She couldn't remember exactly. Little by little, until one day only her clothes and shoes were behind the louvered doors. Why hadn't she seen it coming and done something? Was it too late now? Could marriages be mended the way ranch fences were? Was it worth it to try?

She had her own life now. A busy life, filled with busy things. Her clubs, shopping, the hairdresser, her classes at the studio. Billie sniffed.

Billie knew she was going to be late for breakfast. Lately it seemed she was always late. What did it matter? Moss only had coffee and it was usually on the run or in the backseat of the car. Agnes ate with Seth around sunrise, a habit she had begun on her arrival fourteen years before. Riley, Maggie, and Susan, in exclusive private schools in the city, returned only on weekends to Sunbridge and sometimes not even then.

The table was monstrously long. It was also empty. Billie sat down and pressed the little bell at her plate. "Coffee and toast. A three-minute egg," Billie said as an afterthought. "Where is everyone?"

"I don't know, madam. Would you like me to call your mother? I'm sure she knows where everyone is."

"No, Charlotte. And don't make the egg. I'm not in the mood for an egg."

"Very well, madam."

"And another day begins at Sunbridge." Billie sighed.

"I thought I'd find you here, Mother. I need some money. Fifty dollars." Maggie stood in the doorway, shoulders straight, back rigid. But her expression was sweet, her blue eyes mild and trusting, her gleaming cap of dark hair smoothed into place. Billie tried to deny the thought that whenever Maggie wanted something she donned the good-and-grateful-daughter pose like a cloak. Gone was the sullen rebellion, the tightness around the soft girlish mouth, the challenge in the eyes. Standing before her was a defenseless child with a need.

"I know it seems like a lot, Mother, but it's for books and there's this angora sweater in Kaplan's—" Maggie's words halted when Billie's face closed.

"I don't want to hear how I spend too much money!" Maggie said suddenly, her voice harsh. "Either say yes or no. I'm not in the mood for a lecture."

"I'm not in the mood to give you one," Billie said wearily.

Maggie's expression became a sneer. "Still smarting over Pap's ignoring you last night? I'd make him pay for that if I were you. I saw the pitying glances people gave you." When Billie turned her head, unable to defend herself, Maggie attacked again. "Well, are you going to give it to me or not?"

"You say you need it for books? And a sweater?" Billie knew it was a lie but was reluctant to delve for the truth. She knew she wouldn't like it. Anything was possible with Maggie, her poor hurting little girl. Her little girl who, more than anyone, missed Moss's attention. She was so like Amelia. The same hurt was there in Maggie, the same defiant rebellion. Billie forced her voice to express loving attention. "What color is the sweater, dear? Will it go with that new navy skirt I brought home for you last week? Why don't you sit with me while I have my coffee?"

Maggie knew there was no need to respond to the invitation—nor did she want to. She recognized this tender affection in her mother as surrender. The fifty dollars was as good as in her hand. "Can't. I'm meeting some of my friends. Well, are you going to give it to me?"

Billie was miffed and her hostility surfaced, but she overcame it. She wasn't up to an out-and-out fight with Maggie this morning.

Maggie accepted the money and stuffed it into her pocket. "I'm going to Galveston this weekend with Carol and her family. Tell me now if you're going to make a stink about it."

"And if I did decide to make a 'stink,' as you call it?"

"Then when I leave today I'll just go over to Carol's house and won't come home."

The challenge was there. Billie felt defeated but her motherly concern prompted her to try reasoning with Maggie. "Maggie, we have to talk. These friends of yours, I don't—"

"Forget it, Mother. You don't like anyone except that man you married, but the question is, does Pap like you? I think after last night the answer should be clear to you. You don't count, Mother. I don't count. Susan doesn't count. Only Riley matters. Riley and Grandpap. Go ahead and tell me it isn't true."

"Maggie . . ."

"Spare me, Mother. No more lectures. I'm up to here with words that don't mean a damn thing."

"Maggie, watch your language. You sound like a ranch hand. Why can't you—"

"Behave and act like a Coleman? Do you want to know something? I'm sick of the Colemans. I'm just plain sick to death of the whole lot of us. I didn't ask to be born into this stinking family. I can't wait till I can leave home and breathe some other kind of air. Air that Colemans don't own. God! They even own the damn air!"

"That's stupid," Billie said harshly. "Maggie, get control of yourself."

"Sure, everything I say is stupid. When did you ever hear me say anything that wasn't stupid? I'm no good. I'm ugly. I'm stupid. But I *am* a Coleman, so that makes me something, doesn't it, Mother?"

Billie's mouth opened and then closed, her brows drew together over the bridge of her nose, but her expression didn't begin to convey the hurt she was feeling for her child. "Maggie, how did all this begin? All I asked was what color sweater you were going to buy."

"And don't think I don't know why you handed over the money so easily. It's because you're afraid you'll have to come down to the police station again because I was caught shoplifting. I told you, that was all a mistake, but I don't care if you go ahead and tell Pap about it or not. So don't threaten me, Mother. You won't tell on me anyway, because you're like all the other parents—guilty. So don't ever help me again. See if I care!"

Maggie's arrow pierced the tender spot of Billie's confidence in herself as a mother. "Maggie, I mean it. I *want* that talk. . . ."

"All right, Mother, let's talk now." Maggie flopped down on one of the dining room chairs.

Almost fourteen years old and all that brightness wasted . . . so much hatred, so much hostility. Billie recognized that talking with Maggie now would only intensify her anger and would be more destructive than helpful. Would they ever reach an understanding? Why wasn't her love and attention enough for Maggie? Why was it Moss who should matter so much to the girl? "Not now, Maggie. I said this evening; it will give us time to cool down. We're both too angry and overwrought."

"It figures. It's never now. Always later. Funny thing is, later never comes. Did you ever notice that? Yes, I guess you have. Last night was your later, if you get my drift."

Billie glanced at her watch and looked at Maggie again, who was watching her knowingly. She could miss her art class today—she was already late—but she didn't want to miss it, didn't want to be here with a rebellious daughter who was beyond reason. And she didn't want to see Moss if he came in for lunch, either. Class was a refuge and she needed to be there. "Tonight, Maggie. Be here," she said firmly.

"You see, Mother, you didn't hear a word I said. I'm staying with the Lamberts and going to Galveston for the weekend. We can talk some other night. *If* you don't forget."

"Maggie! I didn't give you permission. . . ." But what was the use? Without another word, Billie picked up her purse and left the house.

Maggie ran to the window and watched her mother until she was out of sight. Her eyes ran and she didn't care. Maggie wasn't allowed at the Lamberts' house anymore. She'd been deemed unfit company for their precious daughter Carol since the two girls had been caught drunk with an empty six-pack of beer and the dregs of a bottle of Jack Daniel's. Maggie would never go to Galveston with them again. Carol was sorry but she was afraid to disobey her parents. And the only reasons the Lamberts hadn't told Moss and Billie was that Mr. Lambert had several real estate deals riding with Grandpap. They were intimidated by the Coleman power and money, too, of course. Still, word had spread among the parents of Maggie's other friends and invitations were few now and grudgingly given. No more Galveston, no more friends. But there were other ways of passing the weekend. A motel out on the highway with whoever picked her up. Two days spent with total strangers, men who weren't afraid of the Colemans. No questions. No answers. Then a two-hour soak in the bathtub to rid herself of the dirt. . . .

Riley skidded to a stop at the foot of the stairs. "Where to, Maggs?" he said, glancing at her overnight case.

"Galveston. Want to come along?"

"No. I'm going up in the new Piper Cub with Pap. How far is Galveston? Does Mam know you're going? Is it a secret?" Riley always asked what was or wasn't a secret.

"I told Mam. She doesn't care. I don't care if you don't come along. I didn't want you, anyway. Go on up in the new plane with Pap. I don't care. You stink, Riley. You and Susan both."

"What'd I do? All I did was ask if it was a secret. I think you're the one who stinks!" Seeing the dangerous glint in his sister's eye, Riley took off at a sprint.

Maggie stopped long enough to poke her head into the sunroom, where her sister was playing the piano. Everyone could do something. Riley could fly. Susan was terrific at the piano. Mother could paint *and* play the piano. No wonder Pap loved everybody except her. She was a nothing, a nobody. Susan's golden head was limned by the sunlight coming through the windows. So delicate, so pretty, so unlike her own harsh, dark looks. "You stink, too, you little snot!" Maggie yelled above the music.

Susan kept on playing, her long slender fingers racing over the scales. She'd heard this all before. Maggie hated everyone.

CHAPTER
{{{{{{{{ TWENTY-ONE }}}}}}}}

As Billie parked her little Italian sports car in the studio lot she could feel the tension in her shoulders. The scene with Maggie this morning had been a replay of many before, but she was still shaken. She had had to face the realization, one more time, of her ineffectiveness as a parent to her daughter.

Maggie needed Moss. They *all* needed Moss. But only Riley, bless his heart, could claim the prize of his father's attention.

Crossing the small dusty lot, Billie could already smell the turpentine and oil paints wafting through the open door. She loved coming here, facing the challenge of an empty canvas. Here among the paints and the easy camaraderie of the other students she could forget Sunbridge and her troubled marriage and family. Two hundred and fifty thousand acres and a twenty-room house, and she had to come here to find privacy and comfort.

The studio itself consisted of one large room with two skylights, a northern and southern. It was comfortable and it was beautiful, with canvases lined up against one long wall. Brilliant colors lived in this room. Comforting colors, exciting colors, somber colors, even dreary colors. The splendor of life, Billie thought as she hung up her short jacket and took her place. Today, only two other students were working. A third figure looked up at her approach and smiled, a great heart-warming smile whose intimacy seemed to encircle her. Jordan. Jordan Marsh was her teacher and her friend, tall and thin, with sandy hair—more brown than sand, really, with streaks of gray at the temples. When he smiled—and he was smiling now—he was almost handsome, showing off perfect teeth. She felt some of the tension leave her as she returned his smile. At least someone was glad to see her.

More tension dropped from her as she set about mixing pigments. Today she was going to finish a still life she had started earlier in the week. A single daisy in a small vase that resembled a child's pudgy hand. Riley's hand.

An hour into her work, Jordan came to stand behind her, watching her bold, sure strokes. "What's wrong, Billie?" he asked softly.

Billie turned on her stool and looked up at him. It had been so long since anyone had used that soft tone with her. She couldn't even remember the last time anyone had asked if she was all right. Asked as though they cared. Tears brimmed in her eyes. "I'm not sure, Jordan. Probably everything."

"Can I help? Do you want to talk? There's no point in continuing with this. Your colors are all wrong. The stem on that daisy looks like a dead snake."

"You're right, Jordan. I shouldn't be working today. I could use a cup of coffee, if you have one."

"I have a whole pot. Made it right before you arrived. Come

on, let's go back to my apartment. We can talk in private."

Billie had only been in Jordan's apartment once before, when he'd held a surprise luncheon to celebrate a private showing of his work. It was so nice, so private, and the best thing was he could simply walk into his studio at any time of the day or night, whenever he felt like working. He didn't have to go off somewhere like she did.

Jordan took her on a brief tour of his quarters. The rooms reflected his personality. Bold and bright living room, kitchen alive with hand-painted designs on all the cabinet doors. Natural hopsacking hung at the windows and were tied back with vivid scarlet sashing. It was just enough. The assortment of green plants and copper utensils completed the comforting, inviting atmosphere.

But it was the bedroom that Billie liked best. Jordan had done it all in earth tones. It was probably the most restful room she had ever seen. She wondered what it would be like to make love in that comfortable room . . . and promptly flushed.

"Hold that wicked thought, whatever it is!" Jordan said, smiling. Billie laughed, but the crimson stain stayed as they went back to the kitchen and talked over steaming cups filled to the brim with Louisiana coffee.

They chatted about an upcoming show for one of the other students. Then Jordan asked, "Now tell me, beautiful lady, what's wrong?"

"I'm sure I'm making more out of all of this than is necessary. I got up on the wrong side of the bed this morning," said Billie. "My father-in-law hosted a birthday party for me last night. It didn't turn out the way I wanted it to. I was disappointed, Jordan. The reasons aren't important."

"Yes, they are, Billie. They're important to you. Talking about it will bring it into perspective. Look at me, Billie. Where would I be today if I hadn't had someone to talk to, to help me when the bottle was killing me? I'd be in the gutter somewhere, trying to panhandle more money to buy more cheap wine. Someone cared enough to help me. Open up, girl. Share your problems. I know I don't come from your social circle, but I've knocked around, seen life, and I care enough to help you."

"What you are or where you came from has nothing to do with it, Jordan. I find it difficult to even admit there is a problem. Coleman's don't *have* problems. We aren't permitted. So we tend to ignore unpleasant things. We know that sooner or later they will go away." She took a deep breath. "But this is not going to go away."

Jordan was persistent. "Billie, you have to tell me what you're talking about—what isn't going to go away? Friends help one another. Don't shut me out now."

"I can't unload my problems on you just because I'm not strong enough to handle them."

"Have you tried? Or have you been coasting?"

"That's exactly what I've been doing," Billie said miserably. "I failed all the way down the line. I don't know where or how things went wrong. I can't give you a date or a time. Things more or less crept up on me. I feel as though there's a black cloud hovering over me and every day it gets lower and lower." Billie shook her head as though to clear her thoughts. "I think I might just be feeling sorry for myself," she said with forced cheerfulness.

"I don't believe you think that at all. You'd never've come back to my apartment if you weren't upset. How many times have I asked you back here? At least a hundred. You would never come, because it wasn't proper for a married lady to enter a man's apartment."

Billie laughed. He was so good for her. If she could still laugh, there must be hope.

Jordan leaned back on the wooden kitchen chair and watched Billie carefully. Didn't she know how he ached to fold her into his arms? Couldn't she feel the heat that emanated from him at the mere sight of her? Was he forever to be her teacher and no more?

"I don't think you can help me," she said, "but if you want to listen, I would like to talk."

Jordan rummaged in his smock pocket for his pipe—which he never smoked—and stuck it between his teeth. He nodded. He was ready to listen. Billie laughed again. "Someday you aren't going to be able to find that pipe and then where will you be?"

"Up the creek without a paddle." Jordan grinned. "It helps me concentrate. My security blanket, if you will. We all need one, you know."

"No, I didn't know that. I don't think I ever had something like that to comfort me. That is what you're talking about, isn't it, comfort?"

"In a manner of speaking. Start, Billie."

It poured out. Like a waterfall. Jordan sat without moving,

the pipe clenched between his teeth. He made no sudden moves, not wanting to break or disrupt Billie's flow. He didn't even nod.

And then she wound down, slowly, like a locomotive running out of steam. The flush was back on her cheeks. She had opened up, talked about things she hadn't known she remembered. . . . She didn't know if she felt better or worse.

Finally Jordan spoke. "That's a mighty heavy load you've been carrying around for years. But don't you feel a certain amount of relief now that you've opened up?"

Billie pondered. "Yes," she said quietly, "I do. But I still don't have the answers. What do you think, Jordan?"

"I think you have problems that only you can solve. I can't tell you what to do, Billie. You have to come to terms with things, make decisions and stick to them. You can't permit other people to control your life. Both of us know that.

"I will tell you one thing—and it's something I learned from experience, so I can share it with you. My problem was alcohol. It was destroying me. I had a love and it was, and is, art. I had to decide which was more important to me. There are days when I want a drink so bad I think I could kill for it. Then I look at one of my students and I know I can't even touch that bottle again. I was put on this earth for a reason. It's corny, but . . . Billie, I love you, you know."

"I rather thought you did." Billie smiled. Jordan looked a little surprised, and happy.

"Did it help to talk?" he said.

"I think so. I have a lot of thinking to do. I have to do something about Maggie before it's too late."

"Maybe. But wouldn't it be better to get to the root of things and work from there? I'm not saying Maggie isn't important, but until you resolve other things, I don't see how you can do much for her. And she'll recognize the desperation, anyway."

"I'm a coward, Jordan."

"Aren't we all."

"I could botch it all up."

"Then you'll have to live with that. But what's better, trying or doing nothing?"

"I have to think."

"Of course you do."

"I have strange feelings where you're concerned." She was

amazed at her calm, the feeling of easy candor she had with him.

"I rather thought you did." Jordan grinned.

"Time."

"Yes."

"The coffee was great. The talk was even better. I enjoyed sitting back here with you, but I think I should be out there painting. This might be a good time to work on my angry seascape."

"I'd say this is a perfect time."

"Time, Jordan. Give me time."

"All the time in the world. I'm not going anywhere."

On the return ride to Sunbridge Billie could feel her cheeks grow warm as she thought about her conversation. She'd handled his confession very well. Jordan was in love with her. Was that the same as loving? Still, it pleased her to know that an attractive, talented man like Jordan could feel something about her. Her self-esteem was pretty well trampled these days.

An affair with Jordan. It was something to think about. She wondered what it would be like to make love with him in his beautiful bedroom. Jordan was nothing like Moss. Jordan the man, the artist. Jordan the lover. And when it was over, because affairs were always over at some point, what would be left? Bitterness? Disappointment? Were the ashes of an affair as cold and hostile as the ashes of a neglected marriage?

As the miles spun on beneath the wheels of her car so did her thoughts. Before she reached home she knew without doubt that a woman didn't just fall into a man's arms, innocent and unaware. Not a married woman. It was a deliberate act, with eyes open, admissions made. Billie faced the fact that she needed a man to want her. She needed to be held, to hear the soft, wonderful promises of early love. She hungered for a kind word, a loving hand. But she also knew that in the end, she would be the one to break it off. Never again would she give herself as completely to a man as she had to Moss.

Billie parked her soldier-blue car beside Moss's racy Porsche. He was home. Before she made the decision to allow herself to fall into Jordan's arms, she'd try once more to talk to Moss. To get closer to him, to look for that little glimmer that would let her know he still wanted her and their marriage. Her steps faltered. It was really Moss she wanted; it was Moss she would always want. She still loved him beyond reason. How much of herself did that leave for Jordan? Would she lie in his arms and pretend he was Moss? Her heels tapped across the tiles in the front hall. Suddenly she wanted to see Moss, have him smile at her. After all these years, how could he still have this effect on her? Still make her pulses race and her arms ache to hold him? She must be a fool.

"Make me a gin and tonic, please, Charlotte, and bring it out on the terrace," Billie murmured distractedly. She wanted a little more time to think before approaching Moss. Get her lines down.

She had first discovered his unfaithfulness years before, but the pain was as fresh as if it had been yesterday. She'd been so wounded, so humiliated, she'd wanted to die. What was she lacking that had made him look elsewhere? The anger, when it came, had been brutal, eating at her like a cancer. She'd never really recovered.

It had been her decision, made in the solitary darkness of her bedroom, not to confront Moss. His infidelity was a passing thing, she promised herself. He would come back to her and their marriage would be as strong as ever. Sometimes affairs strengthened marriages. She would forgive . . . but she would never forget. That would be her punishment; she had to be at fault somewhere.

After the first time, Billie was aware of every one of her husband's indiscretions. Each time, he would return to her, as loving and kind as in the early days of their marriage. He would bring her expensive gifts, share her bed three times a week, whisper beautiful words in her ear. She endured because she loved her husband.

The gin and tonic was finished, and Billie set the glass down firmly. It was time to seek out her husband. She shoved trembling hands into the pockets of her jacket. It was all so ridiculous she wanted to cry.

"Mam? Look, Pap, Mam is here!" Riley exclaimed.

"Billie, what brings you down here? Is something wrong?" Moss asked.

"What could possibly be wrong in this paradise called Sunbridge?" Billie responded with forced cheerfulness. "Riley, I want to talk to your father for a few minutes. Why don't you go to the kitchen and ask Charlotte to make us some coffee."

Billie was alone with Moss. She looked at him through what she hoped were objective eyes. Still tall and rangy, more rugged-looking now, still so damned handsome. Hair thick, dark, a frosting of silver at the temples, and those blue eyes that could reach into her heart. But most remarkable about her husband was the power he exuded. Little wonder women found him so attractive. Even in this little room, amid a mess of papers and school pennants and trophies that he'd never removed, Moss was a powerful man. It was in the set of his shoulders beneath his finely knit sweater, in the tone of his voice and the light in his eyes.

She took a breath, knowing she must speak now before the moment and the will were gone. "Moss, what did you think of the party last night?"

"It was nice. Did you enjoy yourself? Pap went all out for you. I hope you thanked the old boy."

"Yes, it was nice. And yes, I thanked Seth. But it would've been nicer if you'd spent some time with me. After all, it was my birthday."

"Are you complaining?" Moss asked coolly, turning to face her.

"No— Yes, yes I am. I was embarrassed and I could see people were whispering. Why were they whispering, Moss?"

"How the hell should I know, Billie? You know I've never been much good at playing the attentive husband. I just don't know how."

"Perhaps you don't, but you're not stupid. I asked you why people were whispering."

"You're just imagining things." He turned back to his desk. At this point in any other conversation with him, Billie would have considered herself dismissed. Not this time.

"I asked you a question, Moss."

Moss's hairs prickled on the back of his neck. There was something going on here. This interrogation was unlike Billie. He turned to face her once again, all his attention focused on her now. The light from the window behind him fell on her face, making it golden and radiant, illuminating her hair and the clear sweep of her brow. She was beautiful, this wife of his, his Billie. She was also upset.

Warmth crept up from her neck to bloom on her cheeks. "I waited for you, Moss," she whispered. "I waited all night. I wanted you. Something's wrong, Moss. We seem to be losing each other and I don't know why and it frightens me."

Billie heard herself choke. Lord, she hadn't meant it to

sound as though she were begging. But wasn't that exactly what she was doing? Begging Moss to save her from falling into Jordan Marsh's arms?

"Billie, we're old married folks now. The honeymoon doesn't last forever. We're settled in. You know, old shoes."

"Moss, I don't want an old shoe. I didn't ever want to lose what we had. It's like dying. When was the last time you came to the room we used to share? Do you even remember? We need to talk, to communicate. We have children who need us, together. We were happy once. Tell me what's wrong. Tell me what I've done that you don't want me anymore."

She hadn't wanted it to pour out like this; she hadn't wanted to sound so lost, so desperate. Yet it had to be said and now was the time. Perhaps he didn't know how he'd hurt her.

"Billie, what's all this talk about communicating? You sound like one of those beatniks."

"And you sound like a man with something to hide. Is there someone else, Moss? Do you love her?"

"You're never here, Billie. You're always busy with your classes, the children, or whatever it is you women do. I have pressures, commitments. The ranch, the business. They're all taking their toll. Do you see this mess here?" he said, indicating the shelves and desk filled to overflowing with ledgers, charts, and blueprints. "I'm only one man. Pap is depending on me."

"I understand all that, but you could get someone to help you. Yes, I've been busy. It's the only way I can get through the days. What about the nights, Moss? I'm not busy at night, but you are. You haven't answered my question. Have you found someone else? If you have, tell me. We have to talk."

"We are talking. You just don't like what I'm saying." She knew. Christ, she knew and she had never said a word. That was like Billie. Ignore it and it would go away. He wondered if Agnes knew. "No, I haven't found anyone else. We're married, Billie. We'll always be married. You should know that. We have a commitment."

"If that's true, why don't we make love? You're a very virile man. We last made love two months ago and I had to hogtie you even then. I don't like this position you've placed me in. I don't like it at all." Some of the resolve had come back into Billie's voice. She spoke more firmly. "The fact that you aren't interested in making love with me can only mean one thing. You're involved somewhere else. We should be adult enough to discuss it."

"All the little nitty-gritty details, is that what you want to know? What color was the lace on her underwear? Was she exciting? Is that what you want to know?"

"Moss!" Billie said, shocked. "No. No, I don't want to know. All I want us to do is talk. About the children. Us. Our lives. Something's wrong. Can't you feel it? Can't you see that we've drifted so far apart that if we don't do something soon, it will be too late?"

"Billie, Billie." Moss sighed. "Where in the world do you get these notions? Nothing has changed. We've gotten older; the children are growing up. You have your interests and I have mine. That's the way marriage is. That's the way it was for my parents. I know you lost your father when you were young so you have nothing to compare to. Trust me, Billie. We're fine. Nothing is wrong. You're a romantic. You thought the honeymoon would last forever. Mam was sort of like that until Pap told her the way it was."

Billie suddenly felt smothered by self-doubt. The words stuck, hard and cutting, in her throat. "I'm afraid, Moss, that that isn't good enough for me. I want more. I want us to be a family, a united family. Maggie needs you. Don't you see what you're doing to her, have done to her? You're just like Seth and the way he treated Amelia. All you think about or care about is Riley—you should remember you have two other children. Maggie especially needs—"

"To be left alone," Moss finished for her. "You're right. She is like Amelia. She's a little wild and willful, but she'll settle down. The more we hound her, the worse she'll be. Believe me, I know what I'm talking about. Your problem is you worry too much, Billie. Relax, enjoy life a little."

"Like you do, Moss?" Her tone was bitter, accusing.

His gaze locked with hers. "Yes, like I do."

"All right, Moss, that's exactly what I'll do." Scalding tears of humiliation and frustration were about to escape down her cheeks. He was daring her to follow in his footsteps and have an affair! Only he didn't believe she had the guts to do it. Didn't believe in his heart that he could ever lose her. He was so certain that her emotional world began and ended with him, and the occasional crumbs he threw her.

Where had she gone wrong? Hadn't she loved enough? Hadn't she given enough? Billie shrank into herself. None of it made sense.

Moss went to Billie and lifted her chin with a tender hand.

"Billie, darling, don't look so defeated. We're all right, and we'll always be all right. You're my wife and you'll always belong to me. Don't you know that?"

Before she could shame herself by falling into his arms and begging for his love, his touch, Billie stepped back and turned away from Moss, her shoulders square, her head high, leaving the room that had become her husband's haven.

He sighed with weariness, just the way she sighed over Maggie. "Where are you going, Billie? I thought you said you wanted to talk.Come back here."

"I'm going to enjoy life, Moss, exactly as you suggested. I'm going to be just like you." She closed the door quietly behind her.

Moss sat silently, fighting the impulse to run after her. He always felt this way when he couldn't maintain complete control over the things and people that were his. But something told him that running after Billie would be useless, that she was too hurt, too wounded, and that it was his fault. He realized what it had cost her to come down here and to practically beg him to pay more attention to her, to the family. He was sorry for it but he hated to have demands placed on him. Billie had always given him enough room to spread his wings, to pursue his own interests. What had changed?

She sounded desperate. He guessed he *should* pay more attention to her, be more loving. Hell, he did love her, in his own way. Billie was probably the best thing that had ever happened to him. Because of Billie he had Riley, and God only knew how much he loved that boy.

Moss turned to face the clutter of his desk. As soon as he finished up here he'd go upstairs. A long, loving time with Billie would be just the ticket to get things back on an even keel. He would apologize. Billie was very forgiving. Maybe afterward they'd have dinner brought up to their room and have that long talk about Maggie. That would be good; that would clinch things with Billie and she'd be happy again.

There was a tap at the door and Riley peeked in, several books in his hand. "What've you got there, son?"

"Schoolwork. I thought you'd help me with this science project. The one who comes in with the best poster on how a pump works will get a prize. Will you help me, Pap?"

"A prize?" Moss said thoughtfully. "Have you got any ideas of what kind of pump you want to do?" He smiled, remembering the pump he'd designed when he was about Riley's age. The boy was a chip off the old block and Moss puffed with pride.

"I thought I'd show a windmill and how it takes energy from the wind to pump water for the cattle. How's that sound, Pap?"

Moss was already making room on his desk for Riley's books. "Sounds okay to me. But you're a Coleman, Riley. Why don't we show how oil is pumped from the ground?"

Riley dumped his books on the desk in the space Moss had cleared. He had wanted to do a windmill pumping water for cattle. Cows were nice and he loved animals. "Sounds good to me, Pap. We'll show an oil well."

"That's good, son. Whenever you do anything it should be something important. Oil is important. We use it for fuel and it heats our houses and flies our planes. . . ."

In her room, Billie kicked off her shoes and looked around at the result of the Coleman money. None of it made her happy. Not the satin drapes, the matching bedspread, the antique furniture, the closets filled with clothes. She'd be happy in a cozy two-room apartment if it meant she could lie in Moss's arms each night. That was the dream she'd concocted when she'd first met him, before she knew about the Colemans and their money and their power. Moss had made her think he was just a ranch hand, a dirt farmer, anything but what he really was. And damn her soul, she had loved him. She still loved him. Nothing would make her happier than to have him come to her now, this minute, to take her into his arms and love her.

The phone jingled musically on the bedstand. Once, twice, three times. Charlotte must be out of earshot. Billie picked it up and held the receiver to her ear. "Hello."

"Mrs. Coleman, please. This is Hester Eastland, from the Perret School."

"Yes, Mrs. Eastland, this is Mrs. Coleman. Is anything wrong?"

"We were wondering about Margaret, Mrs. Coleman. Is she feeling better? She hasn't been to school today."

"I should have called you, Mrs. Eastland. Maggie went away with Carol Lambert and her family to Galveston for the weekend. I'm terribly sorry I didn't notify you." Billie's temper rose. Damn Maggie! She hadn't said a word about not going to school. Billie had just assumed the Lamberts wouldn't be leaving until the end of the day. And that was another thing.

She'd intended to call Dottie Lambert and thank her for inviting Maggie along. Everything seemed to be getting out of hand; she was losing her grip on things because she was so wrapped up in her own misery.

"I don't understand, Mrs. Coleman. Carol Lambert is in school today. She brought some papers down to my office just a few minutes ago. Mrs. Coleman, don't you know where your daughter is?"

"I guess I don't. I thought she was going to school today, but she also said something about going shopping. I'm certain there's nothing to be alarmed about."

"Mrs. Coleman, as you know, Margaret has been a disciplinary problem in the past. I assure you, our only concern is for your daughter. However, if you're certain there's no problem . . ."

"There's no problem, Mrs. Eastland." She replaced the receiver, a sour grimace on her face. It was no good calling Susan at her school to see if she knew where Maggie was. And Riley would clamp his mouth shut out of loyalty, the way he always did. There was nothing she could do but wait. Then a thought occurred to her. She lifted the receiver again and dialed the Lamberts' phone number.

"Hello, Dottie? Billie Coleman." Something cautioned Billie to tread easily. It would never do to embarrass the woman. "I was wondering if when you're in Galveston you'd be doing any shopping. Moss is so fond of those homemade chocolates from that little shop in town."

"Why, I'd be glad to pick some up for you next time we get down there, but I don't know when it'll be. Zachary has been recovering from a nasty case of chicken pox. Lands alive! I can't remember when I last left this house! And all the poor boy is doing is scratching—I'm afraid he'll scar himself for life."

Billie listened impatiently to Dottie Lambert's dissertation, her mind racing. The Lamberts hadn't made any last-minute change in plans if Zachary had been down with the pox for more than a week. There had been no plans. Where *was* Maggie? Had she gone shopping? Why had she lied?

When Billie at last was able to extricate herself, she dropped onto the chaise to still the quaking of her knees. She was worried about her child, but it hadn't yet bloomed into fright. There were still several hours until dinner. Maggie would come home then. She would. She must.

A headache was building and would soon be a full-blown migraine. Then she'd be unable to cope with anything. Billie leaned back, yearning for sleep. Maggie would come home for dinner. . . .

CHAPTER {{{{{{{{ TWENTY-TWO }}}}}}}}

Rear Admiral Thaddeus Kingsley arrived Saturday morning for one of his impromptu visits just as the Colemans were finishing breakfast. Even Seth and Agnes were sitting down for a late cup of coffee. Maggie's chair was conspicuously vacant. Moss's family, all together breakfasting on the terrace on a warm June morning. The oldest child was missing and everyone behaved as though it didn't matter. Billie's head pounded fiercely. The huge Texas meal of steak and eggs and grits was congealing on her plate; the sight of it almost made her gag. She sipped her weak tea and lit a cigarette, not because she wanted to smoke but because it was something to do, a way to calm her fury.

Last night, when Maggie still hadn't returned home, Billie had told Moss after dinner about Mrs. Eastland's call from the school and the made-up Galveston story.

"What should we do?" Billie asked.

"What should we do? We wait. We simply wait. Perhaps you got it wrong, Billie. Perhaps you didn't understand Maggie and she was going over to some other friend's house."

"No, Moss, I didn't misunderstand. Maggie said she was going with the Lamberts to Galveston. She even threatened to go whether she had my approval or not. I called Dottie Lambert—Zachary has the chicken pox. There never were any plans for Galveston this weekend."

"What's goin' on in here?" Seth's voice demanded from the doorway of the living room, arriving, as usual, at the least opportune moment. "Moss, what's the matter with your wife? She's shaking like a dog shitting peach pits."

Billie turned on her father-in-law. "You may address your questions directly to me when I'm present, Seth. I do know

{ 323 }

how to speak for myself." Then, turning back to Moss: "I think we should call the police. I want to know where my daughter is!"

"Which daughter?" Seth growled. "Don't tell me. It's that Maggie. Just like Amelia, a thorn in a man's side. What's she done this time?"

Quickly, Moss outlined the situation for his father.

"And you say you called the Lamberts? What kind of fool are you, little gal? There's no call to go around making fools of us all. Calling the Lamberts and letting them know Maggie can't be trusted! That was a damn fool thing you did!" Seth pounded his cane onto the parquet floor. "And we won't be calling in the sheriff. Why, our name'd be spread through the county inside of twenty minutes. You're her mother. Why don't you know where she is?"

And so it had been settled. They would all wait until Maggie came home under her own steam. The evening had been endless for Billie and when Moss had come to her bedroom, suggesting he join her, she'd been so furious at his lack of concern for Maggie and for what she herself was feeling that she'd slammed the door in his face.

A picture of Maggie lying in a roadside ditch with her face battered was so vivid that Billie nearly choked on her cigarette. A savage burst of hatred for the Colemans turned her face crimson. She shouldn't be sitting here calmly at the breakfast table, knowing nothing. Where was Maggie? Where?

Moss was excited over Thad's arrival, and the two men embraced each other unashamedly. Thad was tanned and lean, with the same strong-featured good looks and the same quiet ways. It had been almost a year since Billie had seen him. Seth glowered sullenly but shook hands. Thad Kingsley, rear admiral. A power. And the talk was he would be vice admiral before long. Moss's long-range prediction that his friend would someday be head of the Pacific fleet was coming true and it was more than Seth could bear. He'd roared like an angry lion at each of Thad's promotions. He'd always compared his son with every other man he knew, and there were times when Thad had scored higher on Seth's invisible chalkboard. Billie took a certain pleasure in her father-in-law's dislike of Thad.

"Billie, it's impossible!" Thad exclaimed, bending over to kiss her cheek.

"What is?" she said.

"That you're more beautiful than when I saw you last. I'd

keep a tight rein on this little filly, if I were you, Moss. You know what they say—'Never older, only better.' Billie is living proof."

"Why do you think I keep her penned up at Sunbridge?" Moss joked. The merriment didn't reach his eyes. Billie noticed and so did Thad.

He turned his attention to the children. "Lord, Susan, you're growing prettier every time I see you. Have they booked you for Carnegie Hall yet?"

Susan blushed prettily and bit her lip. She liked Pap's friend. He was always nice and didn't demand kisses, like some of the other people who came to the house. She secretly believed he looked almost exactly like Gary Cooper.

"Where's Maggie?" Thad said.

"Maggie is off with friends this weekend," Seth said coolly.

Thad recognized the lie and his gaze locked with Billie's for an instant before he reached out his hand to Riley. "It's nice to see you again, Riley. How are things? Still going up with your father and taking over the controls?"

"Yes sir! Pap's got a new Piper Cub and she's a beauty. She's equipped with the new autopilot Pap designed and I'd like to show her to you, if you'd like."

"I'd like that very much, Riley." Thad smiled, then turned to Moss. "I take it you've brought that autopilot into production, Moss. Have any of the airlines picked up on it yet? Or do you save your best achievements for the navy?"

"What do you think? I worked long and hard on that project and only finished the designs the first of the year. The Pentagon is interested, but they think the price is too high. They'll come around, though, as long as Sunbridge Enterprises holds the patent."

Billie looked blankly from one man to the other, and her glance included her son. Autopilot? Is that what Moss had been working so furiously on all last year? And when it had been completed and declared a success, why hadn't he told her? Resentfully, she realized how little she knew about her husband—and how much of himself he shared with others.

The heir to Sunbridge and his sister were excused and Seth and Agnes made their apologies: "pressing business." Sunbridge operated on a seven-day-a-week schedule. Thad was left alone with Moss and Billie. Charlotte brought half a scallop-edged melon for Thad and fresh coffee for everyone.

Thad thought he had never felt such tension in his life. Not even on the Big E before a strike. Billie looked beautiful but brittle, as if she were about to disintegrate into a million pieces any second. Moss was strung as tight as bailing wire on the south forty. Trouble in paradise. Big trouble. "So, what's new?" he asked casually.

"Nothing," Moss grunted.

"What could be new at Sunbridge?" Billie said brightly. Too brightly.

"Why do I have the feeling I stepped into the middle of something?" Thad asked bluntly.

"I'm worred about Maggie," Billie said defiantly. There, it was out. Let Moss defend it now, in front of Thad. Let his good friend see what a fine, wonderful father he was to his oldest daughter.

Moss's features froze and then he laughed. "Mothers! Mam was just like Billie."

"Not quite," Billie said fiercely. "Not quite, Moss. Don't think for one minute that I'm going to end up like Jessica. I'm going inside and I'm calling all of Maggie's friends. I should have done it yesterday. I don't care if you and Seth like it or not. I want to know." Without another word, Billie rose from the table and entered the house through the French doors.

Thad stared after her for a second. "What was that all about?" he asked. "I thought your father said the girl was with friends."

"She is. Billie got it into her head the girl is off hanky-pankying or something. She's a mother, Thad. All women are like that with their kids."

"Isn't that what motherhood is all about? It's the way you are with your son and the way your father was with you. Why aren't you concerned?"

"Maggie is just like Amelia was. Nothing any of us could do or say could tame my sister. She was willful and determined to do what she wanted when she wanted. In the end, everything turned out fine. Maggie is just like her and it's nothing to get excited about."

When Billie returned to the terrace, her face was ashen. Thad jumped to his feet. "None of her friends know where she is. I've called half of Austin looking for her. Moss, we must call the police."

"Billie, get hold of yourself. If Maggie said she'd be back on Monday, she'll be back—and then you'll be standing there looking foolish. You're getting excited over nothing."

"Nothing! God only knows where she is or what she's doing.

My God, Moss, she's not even fourteen! I never told you this, Moss, but Maggie's been in trouble before. Last April I had to go to the police station in Austin to get her. She'd been caught shoplifting. Fortunately, I was able to smooth things over by paying for what she took. Before that, she was riding around with some boys and drinking. *That* time she got off with a reprimand from the juvenile officer. I didn't say anything to you because I couldn't bear to see the hateful looks on your face. And your father's."

Moss laughed. "Maggie must have been reading Amelia's diary. She did exactly the same thing. Wait till Pap hears this."

"I know I can depend on you to tell him," Billie said frigidly.

"What do you want to do, Billie?" Thad asked quietly. "Do you want to go look for her?"

"That's exactly what I want to do. I just can't sit here and do nothing."

"Moss? You going?" Thad said.

"And let that little snippet make an ass out of me, too? No, thanks." .

"I'll go with you."

Billie looked at Thad with grateful eyes, seeming not to hear Moss. "Let me get my purse and address book. My car is out front. I'll meet you there."

"This wasn't what I had in mind for the weekend," Moss grumbled.

"No, I don't suppose it was," said Thad. "What will you be doing while we're out looking for *your* daughter?"

"I'm going riding with Riley. I'll take him out and show him your plane. That kid's going to be an aviator. You mark my words. He's a great kid, Thad. Chip off the old block."

"Just what the world needs, another Moss Coleman," Thad said coldly. He picked up his seabag and went into the house.

Ten minutes later his navy whites were hanging in good order in the guest room and he was dressed in Sunbridge's official uniform: Levi's jeans and a shirt.

Billie was waiting by her car, her slender fingers playing with the key ring. She held them out to him and then quickly slipped into the passenger seat. Thad slid behind the wheel, gunned the powerful engine, and guided the sports car out of the drive and onto the main highway. "Direct me."

"Head toward Austin. I'm so grateful, Thad. I've been worried out of my mind and had no one to turn to. As much as I hate to do it, I think we should go to the sheriff's office first."

"I agree. Have you been having trouble with Maggie for very long?"

"I don't know if it's exactly trouble. Yes, I do know. She's always been a rebellious child. She's resentful of Riley and Susan and even of me. Perhaps resentful isn't the right word. Jealous. Jealous of anyone who has a claim on her father besides herself. She wants and needs Moss's attention so badly she'll do anything to get it. Moss, of course, is oblivious to it all. It breaks my heart . . . but I'm not entirely free of blame, either." She stopped a moment and her mouth tightened. "I let the Colemans dictate to me what kind of mother I should be to Maggie," she said bitterly. "They were wrong, Thad, and I was wrong."

"It's never too late, Billie," Thad murmured comfortingly. "Take things in hand now. Do the best you can. Caring is half the battle."

Billie turned sideways in her seat and looked at this quiet, solid man. It meant so much to her that he was her friend. "You've always been so good to me, Thad. Your caring means a lot. That's another thing I should have done, told you long before this."

"Friends don't have to be told, Billie." His eyes left the road for a moment, taking in the sight of her, a sight that warmed his heart. Even now, amid all her worry for Maggie, Billie was a beautiful, sensual woman. The slight breeze coming in through the cracked window stirred the spun-gold strands of her hair. Her face, once softly round with youth, had molded itself around her striking bone structure. There was a womanly warmth about her, but within still lived the innocence he'd seen when they'd first met in Philadelphia all those years ago. Clear hazel eyes faced him with unblinking sincerity.

"I'm so ashamed, Thad. I can't seem to get control of my own life, so I suppose it's not surprising that I've failed my children. The Colemans are like charged rockets aiming for the sky, but I fizzle out on the launch pad. The girls, too. I resent it bitterly, but I don't know what to do about it. Maybe there is nothing I can do."

"Yes, there is. When it's time for you to take action, you'll do it, like you are now. Don't be so hard on yourself, Billie. I won't allow it."

In the police station parking lot, Thad reached for Billie's hand. The silence in the small car thundered in Billie's ears. "I'm here with you," Thad said quietly.

Billie squeezed the strong fingers. "I know, and I'm glad."

Thad wanted to bring her close and whisper comforting words. He wanted to tell her that he'd always be there for her. . . .

"C'mon, Mrs. Coleman. Let's get our tails in there and do what has to be done."

Billie smiled. "I know you're just teasing, but please don't call me Mrs. Coleman. 'Billie' reminds me that we're friends just for ourselves, not because of Moss."

"Aye-aye, ma'am. C'mon, Billie."

Thad and Billie exited the police station an hour later. She hung her head in shame at all the questions, questions for which she had no answers. She leaned heavily on Thad's arm.

"They're right, Billie. It's really too soon to file a missing persons report. Maggie said she would be back Monday. She knows she has school, so it's very likely she'll be back to-morrow night. We'll both hold on to that thought. In the mean-time we'll ride around and go to all the places where you think she might be. At least we'll be doing something and you'll feel better."

"Thank you, Thad."

"For what?"

"For being my friend. I really don't have any friends. Did you know that? I mean real friends. Acquaintances are differ-ent. I have loads of those. But not one friend that I can confide in." Jordan didn't count, she told herself.

Thad's eyes were soft in the early-morning sun. She could feel the pull of the man as they walked back to the car. She wanted to fall into his arms and sob her heart out. But she couldn't subject him to herself and her problems. Thad deserved so much more.

It was late in the evening when Billie called a halt. "It's useless, Thad."

"At this point, I have to agree. Tomorrow is another day. We can start out early and hit every place you can think of that we didn't cover today. It might be a good idea to make a list."

Thad drove back to Sunbridge and parked the car facing out on the concrete apron. They sat quietly, each with his own thoughts. It was Thad who broke the silence. "Have you thought about what you're going to do or say once Maggie comes home? I think it's important that you have something concrete in your mind." He could see Billie shudder. It took all his reserve not to reach out to her.

"I think I can handle it, Thad. I'm all Maggie has. I'll be there, I'll do what I can. Maybe, when the time comes, I'll have some of the right words."

"I wouldn't be a mother for anything in the world," Thad said lightly.

But it wasn't his words that caught Billie's attention; it was the expression in his eyes as he looked at her. And as though a veil were being lifted, she saw behind the humor and the friendship to the tenderness and yearning hidden deep within him. It was a sudden revelation and she was moved to caress his cheek. What she had seen in his eyes made her heart leap. She felt like bursting into song. "When?" was all she could manage.

"That day on top of Diamond Head. Back in Philadelphia. When isn't important."

"It's important to me."

"Then you'll have to settle for forever." She held his hand and they sat for long minutes in silence. "It's late," Thad said finally. "We'd better go inside and report our progress."

"To whom? Do you really think there's one person inside that monstrous house who even cares?" Billie said bitterly.

"Look at me, Billie. You *can* handle this. You do have choices, options, whether you realize it or not. You're the only one who can decide what to do and when to do it. Tuck that thought away in your mental file cabinet. Now, I think I could use a drink. I deserve a drink. Move it, woman. I've had a hard day."

"When did you become such a tyrant?" Billie teased as they got out of the car.

"On the Big E, when I had to keep your old man in line." The moment the words were out, Thad regretted them. Billie smiled, but her eyes filled with pain and tears. It was more than Thad could bear. He turned abruptly and ran to the house.

The house was empty and silent, the way a house is when the inhabitants lead separate lives. Thad understood. Finally.

"It's goddamn pitiful," he muttered through clenched teeth.

"Did you say something, Thad?"

"I said I was thirsty."

"I'm fixing it as fast as I can. Sit down. Take your shoes off. I'll get us some sandwiches."

"A girl after my own heart." Billie smiled such a dazzling smile Thad felt like a kid on Christmas morning. Billie Coleman smiling, for him. What more could a man ask for or want? All of Billie Coleman.

The jukebox glowed eerily in the dark of Eddie & Arnie's Bar and seemed to throb with the rhythm of the country song whining through its speakers. A male tenor crooned a lonely lament from the spinning black disc. "Take a little time with me: . . ." Several couples swayed in each other's arms in a sensuous imitation of dancing.

Sipping his bourbon and branch water, the man glanced again at the girl sitting beside him at the bar. Thinking of her as a woman would have been ludicrous—he never considered a female a woman until she reached the age of thirty. Yet it was hard to place this one's age. She could have been anywhere between nine and twenty-nine. The revealing roundness to her chin and jaw and the smooth flesh of her upper arms could have belonged to a little girl. Yet there was a world of knowledge in those thickly mascaraed eyes and in the full lipsticked pout of her mouth.

When she'd come and sat down beside him, he'd been surprised. Even more surprised when the bartender had served her a drink. She hadn't spoken yet, but every move of her body told him she was very much aware of him. This, too, was surprising, considering there were other, much younger men in Eddie and Arnie's tonight. He wondered if she was waiting for someone. It was still early; the bar hadn't begun to fill with the usual Saturday-night crowd. Suddenly she drained her glass and asked him if he'd like to buy her another. For an instant he almost looked over his shoulder to be certain she was talking to him. Hell! He was forty-six years old and the father of three, and his waistline had disappeared a decade ago. It had been so long since something this young and vital had given him a "come hither" that he'd almost forgotten how to react. Almost.

Maggie perched on the barstool, her slim legs crossed in what she believed was an irresistible pose. The bracelets on her wrists jingled against one another as she reached for her pack of Pall Malls. The sleeveless black dress hugged her hips pleasantly and rode upward on her stockinged thighs, showing a long length of leg down to her high-heeled pumps. He liked her, she could tell. Just as she knew he was a traveling salesman. They were *all* traveling salesmen.

Someone dropped another nickel into the jukebox and a nice

slow song came on. She wished he'd ask her to dance. "I just love this song, don't you?" she said. She tamped her cigarette and put it between her lips, inviting him to light it for her

He struck a match and held it. Maggie gazed above the little flare directly into his eyes, the way she'd seen Joan Crawford do in the movies. Yes, there it was, the slight tremble of his hand, the sudden intake of breath. This was going to be easier than she thought.

"Huh?" he asked, clearly puzzled. "Oh, the song. I don't get to listen to music much."

"You come from around here?"

"No, this is just part of my route. I live in Oklahoma. But Austin is a nice city, little rough around the edges compared to New York or Los Angeles, but nice." He'd meant to impress her by mentioning how widely traveled he was, but she seemed more interested in her rum and Coke. "Are you waiting for someone? A boyfriend?" He wasn't springing another seventy-five cents for a drink just to prime her for some other joker.

"No. I just stumbled in for a quickie before heading home." Another line from a movie, Barbara Stanwyck, this time. She fixed her eyes on his face, willing him to ask the next question.

"You live alone?"

There it was. From here on in, things were going to be easy. As they conversed, Maggie leaned closer, intimately closer. Soon his arm would automatically go around her. She knew the younger men sitting at the other end of the bar were watching her. When she'd first come in they'd tried to strike up an acquaintance but she would have none of them. They were too young, too crass, and they frightened her a little. But a nice man like Fred, here, was somehow safe, reassuring. And besides, older men were so grateful to have a pretty young girl make a fuss over them. They knew how to be nice and attentive, and affectionate. Younger guy's only pawed and prodded and they didn't want to talk or anything; they only wanted to get down to business.

"You didn't tell me, Ruthie. Do you live alone?" Fred asked again.

"Not exactly, but my roommate's out of town this weekend. That's why I'm down here, 'cause it's so lonely in my apartment."

"I thought you said you came in before going home."

"I did. What I mean is, I didn't want to go home to a lonely apartment. Do you like to dance, Fred?"

{ 332 }

He seemed undecided for a moment, but then he stood and led her onto the small space in front of the jukebox. She walked into his arms and fit pleasantly into his embrace. He felt a little guilty about what he was contemplating. She felt even smaller in his arms than his sixteen-year-old daughter back home. Just how old was she, anyway?

Maggie laid her head against Fred's broad shoulder. His arms around her made her feel so safe and protected. And she liked the way he talked to her, as if he were really interested in what she had to say. As they danced, she told him lies about the kind of work she did. Tonight she was a shopgirl in Kaplan's Department Store. He told her about his work, selling hardware for boilers. It wouldn't have mattered to Maggie if he'd said he was Jack the Ripper; he was nice. Nice to talk to her, to dance with her. Nice.

Pap never talked business with her, not the way Fred was doing. Pap thought she was too young to know or to care, but she wasn't. She would have sat and listened for days if it meant that she could just have Pap smile down at her, like Fred was doing, or have him let her rest her head against his shoulder and make her feel safe.

The music stopped and Fred gave her a handful of change to select her favorite songs. Maggie chose indiscriminately. She didn't want to lose the moment, lose his rapt attention. Later, when he asked if he could take her home, she'd suggest a motel just down the road, saying she had a fussy landlady. That would be the part Maggie would like least, she felt sure— being with Fred with both of them naked and him rolling on top of her. But one or two more rum and Cokes and she'd hardly mind at all.

The neon sign outside the Morningside Motel glared in the darkness. "Hey, Ruthie, you know what motel spells backwards? Letom!" Fred seemed to think his joke very funny and he laughed uproariously as he walked her from his car to the room. He was drunk but not too drunk; Maggie knew by the way he kept pressing her hand against his crotch.

The room was like a thousand others: dark, dingy, and foul, but the bathroom was passably clean. Maybe someone had actually changed the sheets since last week. Maggie was feeling the effect of her four drinks and was beyond caring about the condition of the room anyway. All that mattered was that Fred was a nice man and he liked her.

Someone in the next room had a radio playing. Perry Como

was singing "Prisoner of Love." The song was melancholy, one of Maggie's least favorites, but Fred seemed to know it, because he hummed along while he urinated into the toilet. "You gotta use the john, Ruthie?" he called, peeking out into the room. Seeing she was already undressed and in bed, he muttered, "Guess not. You're a real nice girl, Ruthie. Real nice. I haven't met a nice girl like you in a long, long time."

Maggie squeezed her eyes shut, hoping he'd put out the light. She didn't want to see him naked, see his penis rigid and erect, ready to pierce her flesh. She didn't want to know if his stomach was flabby and his legs skinny. She wanted to pretend he was tall and handsome and wonderful.

Fred took her into his arms, feeling the delicacy of her bones, the youthful slimness of her hips. Again he found himself wondering just how old she was. Not old enough to have her backside spread a little or her hips widen. For a moment doubt crept into his mind, but her hands were playing over his chest and sliding down under the covers and there was no time to think.

His weight was pressing on her, making her legs spread wider than she thought possible. He was grinding himself into her, plunging deep inside her, hurting her, making her afraid. She hated this part. Hated being pressed into the smelly mattress. But she was afraid to protest, afraid to cry out as she'd done once before when she was with a man she'd thought was nice. That man had hit her, punched her, and then used her anyway, leaving her alone in the scary darkness where she'd cried and cried and cried. And the name that had always come to her lips was Pap.

Maggie bit into her lower lip to keep from crying out. From somewhere outside there were noises, men's voices. Fred didn't seem to hear until suddenly there was a sudden loud knocking at the door. She felt him stiffen, utter a low curse.

"Police! Open up!" came the command.

Fred padded to the door, a sheet wrapped around his midsection. "Hold your horses, I'm coming."

The door swung open and one of Austin's finest stood in the doorway looking beyond Fred's bulk into the dim room. "Identification, please, sir. Is this your wife?"

Fred was already turning back to dig through his pants pockets for his wallet. The pallor of his complexion spoke his embarrassment and fear. He wouldn't want anything like this to get back to his wife.

"Is this your wife, sir?" the officer repeated. "Can you present identification, ma'am?"

Maggie was dumbfounded. She clutched the sheet to her chin and held on to it like a lifeline.

"Mind if I turn on the light, sir?" the policeman said in mock affability. Maggie saw his eyes go to her again, studying her, taking in the smeared makeup, the black stains under her frightened eyes.

"What's this all about?" Fred demanded, fishing through his wallet for his driver's license.

"It's a crackdown, sir, on prostitution. It's a known fact that this place is frequented for illegal purposes. Is this your wife, sir?"

Fred's eyes swung to Maggie, his mouth agape. He'd never considered that she might have been a prostitute. There'd never been any question about an exchange of money. "No, no, she's just someone I met tonight," he stammered.

"Identification, miss?"

"I . . . I don't have any."

"No driver's license? Social Security card? Identification from your place of employment? Just how old are you, miss? What's your name and address?" Now, with the light fully illuminating Maggie's face, the officer could see the tears swimming in her eyes. He was becoming more suspicious about her age.

"No, nothing," she whispered, "unless you'll take my student membership card."

"Student membership!" Fred choked. "Listen here, officer, I just met her tonight. I didn't know how old she was. Not with that dress she was wearing and all that crap on her face. I didn't know!"

"Did she solicit you?" the officer asked. "Think carefully, sir. You could be facing charges for corrupting the morals of a minor."

Fred took a second to think, his face going paler by the moment. The effect of the alcohol was wearing off, leaving him to face reality. He had himself and his family to consider. "Damn right she solicited. Twenty bucks and I was fool enough to go along with it. Hey, you're not going to hold me or anything, are you?"

"Not if what you say is true. It's only the whores we haul in, not their customers."

Maggie wanted to die. She was ordered to get dressed. She

was going for a ride downtown. They were going to take her to jail!

"Just for the record, miss, your name, please."

"Maggie. Margaret Coleman. You can reach my father at the Sunbridge ranch. His name is Moss Coleman."

The officer looked blankly at Maggie. There was going to be hell to pay.

When the phone rang at 3:10 in the morning, Billie reached for it instantly. She'd been expecting the call. She felt calm and in control. It was about Maggie—she could feel it.

"Billie Coleman speaking."

"Mrs. Coleman, this is Sergeant Daley at police headquarters. We picked your daughter up a short while ago. I'd appreciate it if you would come down immediately."

"Is Maggie all right?"

"She's not hurt, Mrs. Coleman. We'll look after her until you get here."

"I'll be right there. Thank you, Sergeant."

Billie knocked quietly on Thad's door. She wasn't surprised to see that he, too was fully clothed. "I heard the phone ring. It's Maggie, isn't it?" Billie nodded. "I'm ready. Shouldn't we wake Moss and have him go with us?" Billie shrugged and shook her head.

The urge to throttle Moss was strong enough to make Thad clench his fists. The two went back a long way and God knows he'd been angry at his friend before, but this was different, because at the root of it was a thorough dislike of the man. Thad felt a flush of guilt and pain mix with his anger, but even more painful were the shadows of disappointment and futility he saw in Billie's eyes.

"Shouldn't you at least leave a note?" he asked.

"Why? I suppose this is how Maggie feels. The only family feeling you'll find at Sunbridge is family pride, and that's not quite the same thing." They were outside now, in the cool, fading darkness. Billie tossed Thad her car keys. "Take me to my daughter, please, Thad."

After a briefing by Sergeant Daley Billie and Thad were directed to a holding room. Before they even opened the door they could hear Maggie's sobs. Inside, at the far end of a long table, she sat, head in her arms, shoulders shaking.

"Maggie," Billie said, hands already reaching for her daughter. She still could not believe what Sgt. Daley had told her . . . her little girl picked up for prostitution. The man she'd been with hadn't been held, once he'd answered a few questions. When Maggie had identified herself, it was decided that the incident would be treated as a family matter and no charges were being brought.

Slowly, Maggie lifted her head. Her face was ravaged with tears and smeared makeup. The dress she was wearing was one Billie had never seen before, cheap, slinky tight, revealing. Her dark hair hung in her eyes. Billie gasped when she saw the pain in those eyes.

"Maggie, darling . . ." It was a cry from the heart. A sound torn from her throat. A mother's lament.

"Mother, I . . . I didn't want you to see me this way. I asked them to let me clean up, but they wouldn't. . . ." Maggie's voice choked off. Her eyes went to Thad, standing behind Billie.

"What's *he* doing here? Where's Pap? Why didn't you bring my father?" It was both an accusation and a plea. "Is Pap outside?"

"No, he's not. Thad drove me down here. . . ."

"Oh, I get it—Pap's not home or else he couldn't be bothered," Maggie said bitterly. "Can I go home now?"

"Yes. Maggie . . . is it true what the police officer said that you . . . you . . ."

"That I was in bed with a man old enough to be my father? It's true all right. But I never asked him for money. I never do!"

Billie swayed backward against Thad. Her hand itched to slap Maggie's rebellious face and at the same time her arms ached to hold her, to take away the pain. Where had her little girl gone? How had she come to this?

"Are you taking me home or aren't you?" Maggie demanded. "Or are you kicking me out?"

"Of course you're coming with us. Sunbridge is your home, Maggie. Poor Maggie." Billie almost wept. She took a step closer to her daughter, her arms extended, wanting to pull the child into her embrace, offer her safety, security.

"And I suppose you'll tell Pap all the tawdry details," Maggie said accusingly.

"No one is going to tell your father if you don't want them to," Billie whispered. She believed that was what Maggie needed to hear, that she didn't want Moss to know.

But Maggie's head sank down again on her arms and she

heaved great, shuddering sounds. Thad touched Billie's shoulder, prompting her to go to Maggie, and then he stood silently, his heart breaking for both, as he watched them embrace. Moss should be here, seeing this, hearing this. But he wasn't. The job had been left to a friend of the family. A friend who needed to be so much more.

CHAPTER TWENTY-THREE

Billie watched the raging storm outside her sitting room window. It was only ten o'clock in the morning, but the sky was midnight black. It was what Seth referred to as a real Texas storm, coming down from the Panhandle. Billie shivered and crossed her arms over her chest. She wasn't going to be able to go to the studio today. Rain and wind slammed against the window pane. Billie edged back a little, fearful that the glass would shatter. She could do a little reading, work on some needlepoint. Or she could go back to bed and try to sleep through the day. None of the ideas appealed to her. She could write to Thad, but what about? She wasn't in a chatty mood and there was no news.

Maybe she should make the bed. No, because then the timid little maid would think she'd done wrong and run to Agnes to plead her case. The rumpled bed would stay as it was.

She could reread some of Thad's letters. They arrived weekly and were just the right length, two and a half pages. He always asked about everyone and shared news he'd received of his hometown from his subscription to its weekly newspaper. She always went to the last paragraph first because it was about her. Sometimes it was whimsical, and at other times she could feel his heartache. Lately, he had been encouraging her to try her hand at textile design. He hadn't laughed like the rest of her family when she'd confided that for as long as she could remember that was what she'd wanted to do. Thad was special.

Tears burned at her eyes. She squeezed them shut to allay the stinging pain. When she opened them again her mother was standing in the room, looking as if she'd just stepped off a magazine cover. Billie hardly knew her anymore and that was just as well. Their views on things were so far apart they might have been living in different states.

"I brought us some coffee. With that wicked storm raging out there we're all housebound. I thought it would be nice if we had a little talk, the way we used to. We've all been so busy lately that we hardly see one another. We can't let that happen, Billie. We're a family."

Billie grimaced. Her mother was talking as if it were Billie's fault. She remembered one of Thad's letters about a visit to his hometown and family. He had made it sound so wonderful—the closeness of the family, the shared laughter. She had felt so envious. No wonder his face always wore a puzzled look when he saw the way things were at Sunbridge. "Thank you for the coffee, Mother. I can certainly use it," Billie said in a neutral tone. "I thought that last storm was bad, but this is horrendous. What are your plans for the day?"

"About the same as yours, I imagine. Seth says this storm will last well into midafternoon. By then all the roads will be flooded, so there's no point in thinking about anything but staying home. I have plenty to occupy me."

"Is there anything in particular you want to discuss, Mother? The children, Moss, Seth? My going to the studio every day?"

Agnes ignored Billie's tart tone. "As a matter of fact, now that you bring up the children, I couldn't help noticing how quiet Maggie was this past weekend when she came home from school."

A frown puckered Billie's brow. She didn't need anyone to tell her about Maggie's withdrawal. Maggie had been a different girl since she and Thad had had to pick her up from the police station: quiet, withdrawn, her usual sullenness turned to something deeper, more obscure. Billie didn't like to think about that night at the police station; it was something she wanted to bury. It was all part of the past now, she kept telling herself. Once she had taken Maggie to Dr. Ward for an examination and blood tests for venereal disease, from which Maggie had been found free, her sense of relief had been so overwhelming it was as if that night were part of an awful nightmare.

All through the summer and since school had started again, Maggie had spent inordinate amounts of time alone in her room, claiming to be working on a school project. But it didn't feel right to Billie and she had her doubts. She'd written to Thad about it; his advice had been simply to love her, to be there for her, and Billie had tried. But Maggie had not been receptive.

"I think it's high time you took that child in hand, Billie," Agnes was saying now. Heaven only knows when the tongues will cease to wag. Seth says we have to ignore the gossip, but I, for one, find it very difficult to do. You *are* her mother, Billie. You should do something!"

"Maggie also has a father and a grandfather, who ignore her."

"If you weren't so busy defending and protecting that child all the time, things wouldn't be this way. I found it reprehensible that you tried to keep it a secret, Maggie's being with that man in that sleazy motel. If you'd gone to Moss or Seth when it happened, the gossip could have been squelched there and then." Of course, that had been Seth's reaction, too. Moss had turned from Maggie in disgust and shot accusations at Billie.

Billie felt a tightness in her chest. "Funny how you're always quick to point out where I've been wrong, Mother. Seth and Moss are innocent in your eyes. But you're right. I am her mother and I'm going to do the best I can for her. I'll always be here for her, just the way you were for me," she finished bitterly.

"Feisty this morning, aren't we?" Agnes said blandly. "It must be this wretched storm. We're all out of kilter. Were you writing a letter? Did I come at an inopportune time? Thad, is it? You do correspond regularly, don't you? How does Moss feel about that?"

"Full of questions this morning, aren't we?" Billie mimicked. "Since when must I ask Moss's permission to write an old friend?"

"Feisty and testy." Agnes's eyebrows shot up. "Why are you so defensive?"

"Because I don't like the drift of your questions. I really don't owe you any explanations. Thad's always been a good friend and I plan to keep it that way."

"Yes, well, I suppose you could use a friend along about now," Agnes said offhandedly as she prowled Billie's room, touching objects and sniffing perfume bottles.

"If you've got something to say, Mother, come out with it."

"I didn't want to say anything, dear, but I think I should. You should have taken more interest in your husband. You never should have allowed him to move downstairs to that stuffy little room. I wonder if you know that Moss has been having...uh...I don't know quite how to say this, Billie."

"You mean am I aware that Moss has had affairs? Is that the word you're looking for, Mother?"

Agnes's face was pure shock. "You knew?"

"Contrary to what you may believe or have heard, Mother, the wife is not always the last to know. Yes, I knew."

"Does Moss know that?"

"Yes," Billie said shortly.

"And?"

"And what, Mother?"

"That's the beginning and the end of it? Did you talk it out? Did he promise to stop his..."

"Philandering? Now there, Mother, I *am* the last to know. My husband doesn't care to take me into his confidence when he makes decisions."

"His....past infidelities are one thing. All men go through that phase at some time or other. But I understand his current affair has been going on for close to three years. It could be serious, Billie."

Billie felt as if one of the packhorses in the barn had kicked her in the stomach. But she'd be damned if she'd let her mother know of her ignorance. "What do you propose I do, Mother?" Billie asked coolly.

"I must admit you've taken all of this rather well—I expected hysterics. Now, we have to map out a strategy. We cannot allow this to go on. The longer an affair goes on, the worse the marriage is. Now that's a pure, hard fact, Billie."

"Mother, strategy? Really! We're talking about my marriage. If Moss isn't interested in preserving it, why should I torture myself? I've come to terms with it."

Agnes reeled a little but recovered herself. "Surely you aren't thinking of divorce? What about the children, Billie? Moss would never let you have Riley. The girls, yes, but not Riley. He's your baby, your only son." Your only bargaining point, she wanted to add, but she held her tongue. "What *are* you going to do?"

"Not *do*, Mother, *did*," Billie lied. "Sauce for the goose is sauce for the gander."

"Billie Coleman!" Agnes said. "Are you telling me that you . . . that you . . . my very own daughter . . . No, I refuse to believe it. Not *you*!"

"Believe what you want, Mother."

"It's Thad Kingsley, isn't it?"

Billie looked her mother straight in the eye. "No, Mother, it isn't Thad Kingsley. Thad is too noble to take advantage of his friend's wife. I would have thought you'd realize that."

"Then who is it—I demand to know."

"Demand all you want, Mother. My privacy is my own."

"How ever do you keep a straight face when you see Alice Forbes at the club?" Agnes asked savagely. "Knowing she's been sleeping with your husband, doing the same things you did with him? . . . How can you bear it?"

"That's enough, Mother. I don't want to discuss this any further."

Alice Forbes, the girl in the photograph hanging in Moss's boyhood room. Billie felt sick to her stomach. Alice Forbes, playwright. Broadway playwright. Backed by Forbes money. Forbes money was right up there next to Coleman money. A real threat. Three years was a long time, almost an eternity. Did Thad know? It was suddenly important for her to know. As soon as her mother left she would call Thad and ask him. He would tell her the truth. Thad would never lie to her. Three years! A wife could possibly forgive, never forget, a one-night stand, a chance encounter where two people were caught up in a moment of passion. But three years? All the planning, all the lies, all the covering up.

Her sense of betrayal was so strong that she ordered her mother out of her room, actually pushed her through the doorway. She only felt safe and calm when she heard the tiny click of the lock shooting home.

A planned affair was when you slept in each other's arms. Overnight. An entire weekend. Vacations. Moss had gone to Europe not too long ago. Now that she thought about it, Alice had been absent from the last two club meetings. Alice and Moss in Europe. Tasting and exploring all the newness. Laughing and sharing as they made their way around the countryside.

Billie paced the room like a nervous filly. Angry tears rolled down her cheeks. Three hundred and sixty-five days a year for three years. What had she been doing on some of those days while her husband was making love to another woman? How many times during all those hours had they made love? You bastard, you miserable rotten bastard! she thought. How could you do this to me?

What did Alice have that she lacked? Was it Alice's money? Her profession? Was it their similar backgrounds? The shared childhood memories? Was her body better? Of course it was—Alice Forbes had no children. But she had given her husband a son. Alice Forbes could never say that, but she didn't need to. Alice Forbes wasn't insecure, plagued with a Seth or an Agnes. She was her own person. She had a career. She was interesting. A stunning-looking woman, more sophisticated than Billie, recognized in the entertainment world, a pleasing personality. She liked to ride horses. And she could pilot her own plane.

Billie cried till she was spent. She blew her nose lustily and then washed her face. The little address book that Riley had given her for Christmas last year was in her hand. This would be the first time she had ever called Thad at his office. Thad wouldn't lie.

"CO's office, secure line," a voice said briskly.

"I'd like to speak to Admiral Kingsley, please. This is Mrs.—this is Billie Coleman."

"Just a minute, ma'am, the admiral is on another line. Will you hold?"

"Yes."

Two minutes later Thad came on. "Billie, to what do I owe this pleasure?"

Billie cleared her throat and then apologized. "Thad, I have to ask you something. Are you aware of Moss's affair with Alice Forbes? The affair that's been going on for three years?"

Thad didn't know what he had expected, but this question was like a thunderbolt. How in the name of God could he answer? "Billie, that's not a fair question to ask me."

"I apologize, Thad. You just gave me your answer. You shouldn't always be so kind. People take advantage of you when you do that. Good-bye, Thad."

Billie dragged herself into the pretty bathroom that only she used. She looked at the floor-to-ceiling mirror without really seeing her reflection. The sight of the thick plum-colored towels hanging against the powder-blue tile was comforting, in a way. Moss had always rolled up his towel and tossed it either on the floor or in the tub. The toilet seat was down. He had been notorious for leaving it up all the time. The one bright yellow toothbrush in the holder looked particularly lonely. Without thinking, Billie opened the medicine cabinet and took out a new red toothbrush. She slipped it through one of the small openings. Two. As in couple. A small jar of Pond's Cold Cream, a bottle of Seconal, and some toothpaste were all that was in the cabinet. Billie's eyes lingered for a long time on the bottle of sleeping pills. She reached for it. It would be so easy. All she had to do was take a glass of water and swallow the pills. Lie down and go to sleep. No one would miss her until dinnertime. How many pills were in the bottle? She shook it and tried to count. Fourteen, she decided.

A vision of Seth at Jessica's funeral swam before her weary eyes. If she knew for certain that Moss would truly mourn her, it might be worth it to die. But the thought of him attending her funeral the way Seth had Jessica's made her dump the contents of the bottle into the toilet bowl. The sound of the flush was loud in the quiet, pretty room. She wouldn't end up like Jessica. The glass vial made a loud thump when she tossed it into the white wicker basket.

Billie's step was firm when she walked from the bathroom. The storm was still raging but it didn't seem as bad. The inky blackness was now a sooty gray. The rain was still coming down in great splashes against the window, but the wipers on her car were powerful. If she took the main highway to the studio, she might make it before serious flooding occurred. She threw on a bright yellow slicker with matching hat.

She wasn't going to Jordan Marsh's studio. She was going to Jordan Marsh.

CHAPTER
{{{{{{{{{ TWENTY-FOUR *}}}}}}}}*

Billie maneuvered her car along the rain-slicked highway, her mood and thoughts as threatening and oppressive as the thick gray clouds scudding above. Rain pelted the windshield. Matching the beat of her heart, the wipers beat a furious rhythm. "Shavers," Maggie called them when she was young. God, wasn't a girl of thirteen young? Or was it that since that June night in the police station she'd ceased thinking of Maggie as a child? The dreadful experience she'd seen on her daughter's face that night was that of an older, jaded woman. A woman who knew men's ways, as Agnes would have put it.

Billie drove the curves of the highway automatically, as though her car knew the way. Automatically. Autopilot. That's what Moss had been working on for this past year and he'd never mentioned it to her. Why? Did he think she was too stupid to comprehend? When they were first married he'd tell her not to worry her pretty little head about this or that. Then she'd found security in leaving the worrying to him, or so she'd thought.

Billie's foot pressed down on the accelerator, sending a sudden surge of power through the Italian-made engine. Even this damn car was one of Moss's choosing. *He* was the one who understood engineering and machines; *this* was the car she was to have. Billie regretted that she hadn't insisted on the Chevrolet she so admired. Italian sports cars were for women like Alice Forbes. Chevys were for the Billie Ameses of Philadelphia. Moss made every decision on every aspect of her life, even the aesthetic ones like choosing cars and travel plans, and even the vital ones concerning the children, like where they should go to school. She'd followed Moss's "suggestions" for so long that she hadn't even realized how long it had been since she'd made a choice of her own, a decision of her own, for herself.

Billie bit down on her lower lip and veered her car around the bend. Well, she was making one today in going to Jordan. And this was her own choice and it was entirely for herself.

When she pulled into the small parking lot adjacent to Jordan's studio, she was gratified to see his Oldsmobile parked near the door. No other cars were present; the storm had probably kept the other students away. For a long moment Billie sat in the shelter of the car, her hand gripping the steering wheel. It would be so easy to just restart the engine and leave. He'd never even know she'd come. She could forget it herself. Before she had time to reconsider, Billie swung open the door and stepped out into the rain, skipping across puddles as she made her way to his door.

"Jordan! It's me, Billie! Jordan?" She rapped on the glass pane.

"Billie? Billie, come in! You're drenched! I wasn't planning on holding class today; I thought the storm would keep my students away. At least the less devoted of them." He smiled, the warmth in his eyes chasing away the gloom of the day.

Billie stepped inside and let him help her off with her slicker; small puddles formed on the floor around her. "I didn't come for lessons, Jordan. I came to be with you." The words were out, but she was afraid to look into his face. Her hands groped for him blindly. She was in his arms. He felt so good. Smelled so good. The soft, well-worn shirt and faded jeans followed the lines of his body, making him accessible to her touch. His shoulder was against her cheek, his lips in her hair, and when he spoke her name with a sense of awe and wonder, she knew she'd been right in coming here. She was a wounded soul, pushing away thoughts of Moss's betrayals. Jordan could heal her.

Jordan tipped her face up to his with a gentle touch of his long, artistic fingers. When his lips met hers, his kiss was gentle, moving across her mouth slowly, meltingly. Then he pulled away, looking deeply into her eyes, and whispered, "Are you certain?"

Her answer was to step back into his embrace, holding to him tightly, offering her mouth again to the tenderness of his. She needed this, needed him. A great wrenching of her heart brought a sob to her lips. It had been so long since she'd been held this way, wanted this way. Even when Moss did come to their room, their lovemaking had become mechanical, a greedy self-serving act to satisfy themselves. An act. Gone was the spontaneity, the great yearning desire to give and share.

"Billie? What's wrong?" Jordan asked, searching her eyes for the answer.

"Only that I need you. So much," she told him truthfully. "I need to be loved, to be wanted."

"That's what I have to give you, Billie. Love. I want to make you feel my love."

Their clothes fell from their bodies like the petals of summer's first rose. His body felt strange and unfamiliar against her own. The stubble of beard on his chin was softer than Moss's. His touch was searching, tender. Moss's was sure and possessive, out of long years of charting her body and knowing it as well as he knew his own. Billie felt herself inwardly backing away from the intimacy Jordan offered. The very thing she so desperately wanted, this close loving affection, seemed unattainable and out of her reach. Memories intruded of that other man she had loved more than she loved herself. Moss.

{ 346 }

Jordan's lips traced lazy patterns along the sweep of her shoulders and down to her breasts. His effect on her was hypnotic, sensuous, and Billie willed herself to surrender to the moment and the man. She accepted his nearness, his touch, his kiss on the most intimate parts of herself. She accepted these things the way she would have taken food or warmth or air to breathe, because she needed them. And she did need them, to reaffirm herself as a woman.

Billie lay quietly in Jordan's arms, listening to the beat of his heart and to the lovely words he spoke. She was beautiful, desirable, loving, and warm. She was a beautiful lover. And yet it was Jordan himself who was all these things. They'd shared the most intimate act possible between two people. He'd brought her body to life beneath his hands and his lips. But it was her soul that was dying and however he tried he could not touch it.

Her body was satisfied, her ego fed, and yet misery lived in her core. There was no future with Jordan and she knew it. She had taken all he could give and she'd given nothing in return. With Moss, her greatest ecstasy had been losing herself in him, giving totally of herself and knowing that the offering was pleasing to the man she loved. She didn't love Jordan. She had nothing to give and taking wasn't enough.

"Will you come back to me, Billie?" Jordan whispered against her ear. "Was it good for you? As good as it was for me?"

"It was good," Billie murmured, wrapping her arms around him and nuzzling his jaw. "I'll come back."

Billie could never make up her mind about Sunday dinner at Sunbridge. With Agnes at the helm it resembled a Cecil B. DeMille production with Mickey Mouse overtones. The array of crystal, china, and silver was blinding. The maids were attired in bright pink uniforms with frilly white aprons and little starched caps. The children were always in attendance on Sunday night and then, after the large heavy meal, were driven by the chauffeur back to their respective schools. While the setting and the accoutrements were Hollywood style, the dinner participants and their moods were strictly Coleman. Seth ate like a ranch hand, talking with his mouth full, mostly about the ranch. Agnes did her best to look regal from her position at the foot of the table. She ate daintily, taking small bites of food and chewing each mouthful thirteen times. Moss and Riley jabbered and babbled nonstop. Maggie and Susan were quiet, depending on Billie to keep up their end of the conversation concerning school and their various activities.

Billie always took two aspirins at the end of the meal.

Something was off center this evening. Maggie was answering when she was spoken to but otherwise there was a blank vagueness about her that alarmed Billie. Was the child sick? Or was she getting ready to pull what Seth referred to as one of her aunt's stunts?

"Maggie, do you feel all right?" All conversation at the table stopped as the family listened to see what kind of story Maggie would come up with this time.

"I feel fine, Mother. Why do you ask?"

"You look a little flushed to me. Let me take your temperature after dinner."

"I don't have a fever, Mother. I feel fine. It's warm in here."

"We'll take the temperature anyway. I can't send you to school tomorrow if there's a chance you're coming down with something. The whole class could get it."

"Why aren't you eating your dinner?" Moss queried.

Maggie's head shot up. It had been a very long time since her father had asked her a direct question. Billie's throat constricted at the naked adoration on her daughter's face. She started eating immediately. "I guess my mind was on school and a test tomorrow," Maggie said between mouthfuls of food.

"Don't stuff your mouth. You're old enough to eat properly. And don't ever talk with your mouth full."

Billie's eyes narrowed and her left hand clenched into a tightly balled fist in her lap.

"I can't eat any more. Mother, may I be excused?" Maggie's tears were close to the surface, and Billie didn't dare take a chance on the girl's erupting into one of her screaming outbursts.

"Of course. Come along. I want to take your temperature anyway." Billie laid her napkin on the table. The glance she shot Moss was stormy.

"There's nothing wrong with the girl," Seth growled.

Billie stopped in midstride and turned. "I'll be the judge of what is or isn't wrong with my daughter. Don't interfere between my daughter and me, now or ever."

"Billie!" Agnes was aghast. "Now that wretched child has spoiled another dinner. You really are going to have to do something."

Billie's back stiffened. "The next time you feel compelled to blame someone for a spoiled dinner, try to blame the right person. My husband!" With a venomous look at Moss, Billie marched from the room with her head held high.

"That wife of yours is getting out of hand, Moss."

"That's enough, Pap. Billie's a mother. Mam was the same way." Agnes cringed inwardly at the accusing glance he directed at her.

Upstairs, Billie shook the thermometer. "You don't have a fever, but you don't look right, Maggie. You know your marks are good enough for you to take a day or so off. Maybe a bug is going around and we can nip it at the onset so you don't lose more time later. I really am worried, Maggie. Have you been sleeping?"

"Off and on. I have a lot on my mind. Mother . . . I . . ."

"Yes, Maggie? Whatever it is, do you want to talk about it?"

"Oh, never mind. Not tonight. Why don't you and I go shopping next weekend? I think I gained some weight. Too many late-night snacks with the girls after lights out."

The wan smile bothered Billie. "I'd like that, Maggie. Just the two of us. We'll go to all the big stores and get a whole new wardrobe. I think it's time you had some new clothes. You didn't want to go the last time, when I took Susan."

"I didn't need anything then. Why waste Pap's money? I told him he didn't have to give me such a generous allowance and that I was saving, but he didn't listen. I'm trying, Mam, but he—"

"Shhh, I know, honey. We're going to work it out. You let me worry about your father. If you feel all right, you'd better get your things together and get downstairs. I want you back at school before curfew."

Maggie picked up her weekend bag and a pile of books. "I'll see you on the weekend. I'm sorry about dinner. I never seem to do or say the right thing. I don't know why. I think there must be a devil in me somewhere. Grandpap says there is, anyway."

Billie could feel her temper rising again. "He said *that* to you?"

"It doesn't matter. Pap says it, too. I'm just like Aunt Amelia. Pap likes Aunt Amelia but he doesn't like me. You figure it out, Mam. I have to get going."

"If you don't feel well, call me. Promise, Maggie."

"I promise," Maggie called over her shoulder.

Susan and Riley ran in, kissed Billie quickly, and then ran out and down the stairs. Their clattering made Billie smile, but then the front door slammed behind them. Sunbridge was like a tomb again.

Billie sat down with a thump on her velvet-covered slipper chair. She kicked off her high heels and propped her feet on a hassock. Out of habit she reached for the packet of letters on the round cherrywood table. Reading Thad Kingsley's letters always made her feel better. Someday she was going to tell him how much they meant to her. She knew them by heart, but she still searched for the letter she wanted. The naval stationery was as crisp as fresh celery.

I can only try to imagine the heartache you are suffering over Maggie. You have to try to be strong, my dear. She's still a little girl in so many ways. She's not quite a young lady and yet she's not a baby. She's caught in that in-between time. I have to side with you when you say money, and by that I mean having too much, is not Maggie's problem. We both know what her problem is and until you can get Moss to see the light, both of you are going to be miserable. There are times when Moss needs to be hit over the head. His stubbornness can be overwhelming. In that respect Maggie does take after him. I feel that the constant comparisons to Amelia do not help matters. You asked for my opinion; otherwise I wouldn't comment or foist my thoughts on you. I have every faith that you will manage to pull things together. You have strength you haven't tapped yet. Trust me when I tell you it's there and to draw from it.

I would love to come to Sunbridge for a visit, but I don't think it would be wise under the circumstances. Moss drew the line on that last visit and I would feel very uncomfortable. He feels I betrayed him by going with you to look for Maggie. Moss doesn't take betrayal well. Our friendship is in jeopardy, as I'm sure you know. I also know that that's the main reason for your invitation, but I'm afraid, dear Billie, that it will have to come from Moss.

I would like to invite you and the girls to Corpus Christi for a weekend anytime you're free. I have a wonderful housekeeper and cook, and plenty of room. I have a monstrous fireplace. It's a nice place to sit and pretend. Fireplaces with blazing logs, the funny papers, and a cup of grog are for families. Oops, I almost forgot the dog! I have this mutt that wandered by one day and never left. I call him Solomon because he was wise enough to know that if he didn't do his business outside, he couldn't stay. We get along fine. He greets me when I get home and lies by my side all evening. Put him in the picture when you visualize my fireplace.

It's almost time for Solomon's nightly walk, so I'll close for now. Take care, Billie, and remember, if there's anything you need, anything at all, call. I'll always be here for you.

Warm regards,
Thad

Billie folded the letter and replaced it in the worn envelope. She must have read the letter three dozen times at the very least.

She was busily sketching in charcoal at her easel when Moss appeared in the doorway. Billie's eyes hardened. Let him see what she was doing. What did she care? She steeled herself for what he was going to say. He seemed ill at ease, which was strange for Moss. Always-in-control Moss. "Did you want something, Moss?"

"I can't seem to find—"

"Whatever it is, it isn't here. There's not one thing in this room that belongs to you. You saw to that. You're blocking the light."

"Billie . . . goddamn it, I want to talk to you."

Billie clenched her teeth so hard a shooting pain ran down the side of her neck and into her arm. "Why don't we make an appointment for later in the week—I think I might be able to squeeze you in then."

"I won't be here later in the week. I have to go up north for a week or so. I think we should talk now."

Alice Forbes was in New York. Everyone at the club assumed that rehearsals for her new play were getting under way.

Billie looked at the charcoal sketch. It had been giving her so much pleasure until Moss appeared. It was a sketch of Thad sitting in a deep armchair in front of his blazing fire with a sleeping Solomon at his side. She turned away and continued sketching, ignoring Moss completely.

"When I get back, we'll talk."

"If you happen to find yourself on Broadway, make sure you bring home a program for Susan. She saves them."

"I'll do that," Moss said harshly. "Good night, Billie." He waited in the hallway for a second to see if she would call out to him or run after him. She didn't. The pain he felt was like a knife slicing into his gizzard.

Billie continued sketching. This picture was therapy and it was giving her pleasure. It would bring a smile to Thad's face when he saw it.

It was midnight when Billie made the last touches on her drawing. The likeness of Thad was perfect. She hoped she had Solomon right. By two o'clock she had the drawing framed and packed in cardboard. Tomorrow, right after breakfast, she would put some of the Coleman money to good use. She would have the carton taken to the airport and put on the first flight to Corpus Christi. From there a private messenger service would deliver it personally to Thad at the naval air station.

For the first time in months, Billie slept soundly for the remainder of the night.

Ensign Calvin James accepted the package and signed for it. He marched smartly to the admiral's office and waited for clearance to enter. "Special delivery, sir."

"Anything special?" Thad asked curiously.

"It's from a Billie Coleman in Austin, Texas, sir."

"Don't stand there, James. Fetch it here."

He felt like a kid as he ripped at the cardboard carton and the heavy inner paper. When he drew out the framed charcoal drawing he didn't know whether to laugh or to cry. But Ensign James was standing at attention.

"Sir, you have a meeting in five minutes."

"When I get back I want this picture hanging right there where I can see it." Thad pointed to a wall across from his desk. He would have direct eye contact with the picture anytime he sat at his desk. By God, who would have thought Billie would do such a wonderful thing? He was going to call her. The hell with what Moss thought. Such thoughtfulness deserved a personal thank-you.

"Aye-aye, sir. I'll see to it right away." Ten minutes later everyone on the admiral's staff was admiring Billie Coleman's handiwork. "It does look like the old man, doesn't it?" James asked the staff. "But when did the old man get a dog?"

"Who the hell is Billie Coleman?"

"Some guy the admiral flew with during the war, probably," James answered. "Looks nifty. The old man will be pleased."

Billie Coleman's world was already teetering on its axis. It turned over and crashed around her the morning she went to wake Maggie for their promised shopping trip to Austin.

Maggie's bedclothes were tossed and rumpled, most of them at the foot of the girlishly draped canopy bed. Maggie herself was in her powder-pink bathroom leaning over the bowl, gagging and retching. An alarm, too poignantly familiar, sounded in Billie's head. All the signals were there. The sleepiness, the change from rebelliousness to quiet introspection, the thickening of Maggie's waistline despite her loss of appetite. Maggie didn't need a shopping trip into the city. She needed a doctor to confirm what Billie already knew: her daughter was pregnant.

Billie groped for the edge of Maggie's bed before she collapsed. How could this be? She'd taken Maggie to see Dr. Ward only days after discovering what Maggie had been doing. But then, of course, it would have been too soon to diagnose a pregnancy. That had been nearly four months earlier, back in June. Just when she was overcoming visions of her little girl in strange motel rooms with strange men, this had to come along. Just when it seemed she was making headway- with Maggie, getting closer to her, rekindling lost feelings of trust and love. Poor Maggie! Her life would never be the same. None of them would ever be the same. Forcing the numbness out of her legs, Billie stood in the doorway to the bathroom. "Why didn't you tell me, Maggie?"

"Mam . . ." Maggie tried to lift her head, her face a ghastly shade of green, her eyes sunken and miserable.

Billie dropped to her knees, cradling her child's head against her breast. "Why didn't you come to me? Why, Maggie?" Billie cried brokenly.

"Because you'd tell Pap and he already hates me!"

"He doesn't hate you, Maggie. But he has to know. Now, later? Does it really make a difference when he knows?"

"Send me away, Mam. Send me somewhere. There are

places. He doesn't have to know. Please, Mam. Help me!"

"Oh, Maggie, I wish it were that simple, but it isn't. How many periods have you missed?"

"Three."

"Oh, my God!"

"Mammmm!"

They sat on the cold bathroom floor, mother and daughter, two women. Billie brushed back Maggie's dark hair from her white brow and crooned soft words as her daughter retched.

"Don't fight it, darling. It only makes it worse."

God, what was she going to do with this child of hers? At that moment she felt as sick as her daughter. What would be best for Maggie? Her brain clicked and raced as she tried to second-guess the family's reaction. The word *abortion* loomed frighteningly in front of her. Never! Amelia was still too fresh in her mind. Moss had to be told. What would he say; what would he do? Tears filled her eyes. She had failed so miserably at everything. But to fail with one's own firstborn, that was unforgivable. Billie sighed wearily, knowing she was in for a storm of emotion from everyone in the house. Maggie herself would give her the most problems once she was on her feet.

"I feel a little better, Mother. I think I should go back to bed. I don't want to go shopping."

Billie had to shake her head to clear her thoughts. One minute the child was so close to her and now she had withdrawn again and was talking about shopping. Surely she realized the predicament she was in. Her whole life was at stake here. "I think that's a good idea. You get into bed and I'll ring for Charlotte to fetch some tea. Perhaps some dry toast and crackers. It's about the only thing that will stay in your stomach."

Billie waited till Maggie finished her tea before speaking. "What are we going to do, Maggie?"

"This is my problem. I'll take care of it."

"How will you do that, Maggie? Please, I want to know. I don't even know what to do at this point."

"That's your problem, Mother. You never seem to know what to do. You coast. I'll go away. I have some money I've been saving. If you know the right people, you can get an abortion. It's simple."

"No it isn't, Maggie. It's a terrible, horrible ordeal. That's not an easy answer. I need time to adjust and think."

Suddenly the little girl in Maggie came out as she clung to

her mother. For the moment all the girl's angry hostility and insecurity were shelved in her fear. "What's Pap going to say?" Billie ached at the tremble in her daughter's voice. Maggie didn't mind her knowing. She didn't mind her mother seeing her misery. Mothers accepted. That's what made them mothers. Maggie didn't care what she thought. In the end she was confident Billie could make it right.

"Maggie, I have no idea what he'll say. He's in New York. It does give us some breathing room to decide what we're going to do. Who's the father of this baby, Maggie?"

Maggie looked blank. "Father?"

"Yes, Maggie, father. Who is the father of your child?" Please, God, let her come up with a name. Don't let her . . .

Maggie sank back into the pillows. The old defiant look was back on her face. "I haven't the faintest idea, Mother."

"Maggie, I don't find that statement humorous at all."

"I wasn't trying to be humorous. All right, Mother, some guy I picked up. Steve something. I really don't remember. Maybe it was Earl. On the other hand it might have been Harry. Or Dick or John. Take your pick. What does it matter?"

"It matters a great deal."

"Face it, Mother. I'm a T.I.T."

"What's that?"

Maggie laughed, a short brittle sound. "For shame, Mother. Surely Grandpap or Pap told you."

Billie clenched her teeth. "What does it mean, Maggie? And how do you know your father and grandfather refer to you in that way?"

"Because Susan and Riley heard them talking and came and told me. That's how I know, Mother. Your precious Riley and Susan would never tell a lie. You really don't know, do you? Tramp in training, Mother. That's what it means. At least they won't be disappointed."

The blood drained from Billie's face. "Maggie, I swear to you, I didn't know. If I had . . ." She reached out and Maggie slapped her hand away.

"What would you have done, Mother? Let me tell you. You'd look away like you always do. Grandpap calls the shots around here and Pap backs him up. Would you have gone up against either of them for me? I don't think so, Mother. Your safe little world would have been disturbed. You know Pap is out there messing around. Grandpap did it, too."

The crack of Billie's hand on Maggie's face thundered in the quiet room.

"Do it again, Mother, on the other side. Maybe it will make you feel better. You can't hurt me. None of you can hurt me anymore. What did I say? The truth? Keep looking the other way, Mother. When Pap leaves you, what are you going to have left? Oh, I forgot, the Coleman money."

The pounding in Billie's head was no match for the pounding of her heart. She was going to be sick. Billie drew the heavy draperies and left the room. Maggie's eyes glared at her from the semidarkness.

The phone rang in the VIP suite of the Astor Hotel, and Moss reached out a reluctant arm as though to quiet an alarm. The shower was running as a background to a woman's sultry voice humming a tune from last night's Broadway musical. Awareness descended. It was 10:10 in New York; 8:10 at Sunbridge. He looked down at the messy bed and frowned. He hated wadded and twisted bedsheets. The phone continued to shrill. Moss came to terms with the fact that he'd have to answer it. Partying with Alice's friends until the wee hours of the morning and then two hours of bedroom calisthenics were not conducive to morning calls.

Moss heard Billie's tight, anxious voice just as Alice Forbes walked into the bedroom stark naked. Her body was always a shock to Moss. While her face was beautifully structured and feminine, her body was slim and lean to the point of boyishness. He was so accustomed to Billie's rounded body and soft, full breasts that he'd almost had difficulty achieving an erection the first time he'd taken Alice to bed. Almost. Now he appreciated those small, girlish breasts with their large brown areolas and those rack-thin hips that could undulate with such a greedy appetite.

"Darling, I know you're awake," Alice called out. "I have to leave for the theater. The second act still isn't right. Say you forgive me." Her hand flew to her mouth when she realized her lover was on the phone.

Moss's stomach lurched. Billie would have to be deaf not to have heard Alice. Jesus Christ! If Maggie was pregnant, why did she have to tell him at this hour of the morning? He couldn't change anything. "I can't come home now," he said, more coldly than he'd intended. "My business isn't finished yet. A few more days. You can handle things, can't you? Have a talk with Seth and your mother."

Trouble. He'd known the call was trouble the minute the phone had rung. It was Amelia all over again. Seth was going to go up in smoke.

Alice was dressed in minutes. She mouthed, "Billie?" When Moss nodded, her eyebrows shot up. She favored him with a conspiratorial grimace. Moss ignored her.

"I'll be home by the end of the week," he said. "We can discuss all of this then. It goes without saying the girl will have to have an abortion."

His daughter pregnant. At thirteen. Jesus! Where in the hell had Billie been all this time? How had she let this happen? He didn't need these problems right now. The girl was an alleycat. Seth had said it time and time again.

"That's enough, Billie! This is not something to discuss over the phone. The girl is pregnant and a few more days isn't going to make a difference. When I get back I'll have the name of a doctor *you* can take her to. I'll be home Friday night. Take a drink, Billie. You sound as though you need it. It isn't the end of the world. After all, the same thing happened to us."

Billie's gasp shrilled in his ears. "That was different," she said icily. "Your daughter doesn't know who the father is. What do you have to say to that?"

Moss stared at the phone in his hand. It took him a minute to realize Billie had hung up on him.

Moss didn't return on Friday as promised. "Unfinished business," he told Seth on the phone. He did, however, have the name of a doctor for Billie.

Sunbridge was as quiet as a mausoleum when Moss let himself in late Sunday afternoon. Thoughts and memories had haunted him since Billie's phone call: Maggie as a baby, growing up, her first real party. How in the hell had his lovely little girl gotten herself into this mess? Where had Billie been while it was happening? Where had he been?

Moss knew what a man's return to his castle should be like: his pretty wife running lightly to the front door to welcome and embrace him, children gathering around, clamoring for his attention. Daddy's home, he thought dourly, and there's no one here who gives a damn except Riley.

Billie heard Moss's step in the hallway. Her shoulders tensed but she continued sketching on the pad in her lap. The sun coming through the living room window had felt warm and good a moment ago.

Moss loomed in the doorway. "I'm here," he announced bluntly. "I don't suppose you can stop to make me a drink?"

"I suppose." Billie attempted to keep her voice level. Laying aside her charcoals, she crossed the room to the bar, stopping to dutifully kiss Moss's cheek. Moss's senses reeled unexpectedly at the familiar scent of her perfume.

Billie felt the charge leap between them. Would she never conquer these feelings she·had for him? Even after all these years and so many disappointments, she still wanted him as a man. It had little to do with her need of him as a husband; this was something more instinctive.

Moss accepted his drink, waiting for Billie to speak. Instead she seemed about to go back to her sketchbook. This irritated him, though he realized he was being unreasonable. Unreasonable to expect her to pretend she'd never heard Alice's voice in his hotel room. Unreasonable to wish she'd come to him in this silent house and welcome him into her arms and her bed. Groping for words, he asked, "Did you call that doctor for Maggie?"

Billie turned and stared at him levelly, her soft hazel eyes sharpening. "No, I did not. And I won't."

Moss sighed. "All right, if you're going to be stubborn about it, I'll call him myself."

"No, you won't. There won't be any doctor. Except one who will deliver our grandchild safely. I've had time to think, more time than I need." Her gaze accused him. "Maggie is a child in years but certainly not in experience. She'll have to live with the consequences of her actions. She's pregnant and she'll have this baby. Abortion is against the law and she knows it. To have us condone it, help her get one, wouldn't be good for Maggie. God only knows what she'd get herself into next time. Where will it all stop? I won't have any part of it, Moss. She's not even fourteen years old, and she'll have to live with it the rest of her life. I'd rather she live with having the baby than destroying it. In other words, Moss, two wrongs don't make a right."

"You shouldn't foist something on her just because your own principles will be affronted."

"And whose principles will you foist on her, Moss? She's

only a child and someone must give her the direction she's seeking." Billie knew she was right. Her code of ethics, her principles, might be right only for herself, but they were the only ones she had to offer Maggie.

"She is too young to be saddled with a kid, Billie. I am thinking of Maggie, whether you believe it or not."

"Things go wrong with abortions. I . . . I know someone . . ." Billie stopped, remembering her promise to Amelia. "Maggie won't be saddled with anything if she doesn't want to be. There's time enough to decide what to do with the baby. There are perfectly respectable adoption agencies."

"Just get that out of your head, Billie. This baby is part Coleman, and we don't put Colemans out like unwanted kittens. Stick by this decision and you'll be the one to live with the consequences. If you'd been more of a mother to Maggie, this never would have happened."

Billie's face was frozen and passive, her shoulders square and back stiff. He'd done and said his worst, and she was still standing. There was no glistening of tears. Moss experienced a sudden rush of admiration for her.

"*I* am not stuck with anything. We are. Maggie is a product of us and our failing marriage." There, she'd said the words she could barely admit to herself. "It's only a matter of time before the situation between us ruins Susan and finally Riley. If we fail now, Moss, it's all been for nothing. We'll count for nothing. I won't allow that to happen. Somehow, somewhere, we lost our lives. I want it back, Moss. All of it."

Moss seemed to deflate. He'd been expecting a confrontation, but not this. "What exactly are you saying, Billie? You know I'll give you anything in my power."

"I want a commitment from you, to your children and our marriage. I want us to be a family. I demand it."

"You do, don't you?" There was wonder in his voice.

"Yes, I do. And I believe that somewhere down deep, you want it, too."

"And what do the children want? Maggie, for instance. What does she say about the abortion?"

"At first she wanted to be rid of it, pretend it never happened. She's so young, Moss, she has no conception of the child she carries. But when I told her you wanted her to have an abortion, she became hostile and changed her mind. Now she wants to keep the baby. Moss, I don't know what's right or wrong. All that matters to me is Maggie and her future. Your daughter says she wants to have this child. What do you think, Moss? How do you read it?"

Moss shrugged. "She's almost a woman and I suppose she's changeable. . . ."

"Don't you ever look beneath the surface? Don't you see that she will go against anything you suggest? And why? Because it's the only damn way she knows to get your attention. Go against Pap and he'll always notice. Agree and he can forget you even exist. But this is too serious to play games with."

Moss gulped the last of his drink. "Billie, I'm tired. I have to think. Can't we talk about this after dinner? I'll come up to your room and we'll talk, just like the old days." He sent her a charming grin.

"We never talked in the old days. You talked and I listened. This time it's going to be different."

"C'mon, Billie, let me off the hook for a few hours, won't you?"

"No, Moss. We'll finish this conversation. I've never made demands on you, and perhaps I was wrong. But I'm telling you now, if you don't go along with me on this, on making us a family, I'll leave you. I'll take the children and leave. I want you to be a father. I want you to be a husband. I want a family, Moss, and I want it now."

"Just like that? No looking back? No accusations and re-criminations? Forget everything and start over?"

Billie's eyes locked with his. "Just like that."

"All right, Billie, you've got it."

"Your sworn word, Moss."

"My sworn word. Billie . . . I . . ."

"Please, Moss, let's just leave it at that. . . ."

She'd won, and yet her victory seemed hollow. Was this really what she wanted? This bargain, like a business deal?

"No, Billie, you've had your say and I want mine. You're my wife and I know I've let you down. I've been a heel but you've let me get away with it. I thought it didn't matter to you, that you didn't care. Do you know how much it means to me to know you care?" His voice was soft; his summer-blue eyes softened. She saw his arms open to her and felt herself move into them. But just for an instant, she imagined it was Thad's mouth seeking hers and the beating of his heart she felt against her breast. Billie hurled the image away. *This* was her husband, the father of her children, the man she'd promised to love for a lifetime, and God help her, there was a part of her that loved him still—a very old and tired part.

Moss's arms held his wife; his mouth touched hers tenderly, making unspoken promises. He felt her tremble for an instant before she lifted her face to his and he realized the old power he still had over her. It was a good feeling, this sense of possessiveness, a celebration of his prowess. A recommitment to his family wouldn't be so bad. He liked the idea of a family.

{{{{{{{{{ CHAPTER TWENTY-FIVE }}}}}}}}}

At times Billie felt as though she'd created her own hell. Moss was living up to his promise to commit himself as a husband and a father, but somehow it wasn't working. He was loving, attentive, and seemed to have foresaken his extramarital activities, but still there was an unrest within Billie. At night, lying in his arms, listening to his soft breathing, feeling the afterglow of his expert lovemaking, she fought against the growing restlessness and bitterness. This was what she wanted, wasn't it? To have Moss as her husband again? To have his love and his attention? She should be sitting on top of the world. But she wasn't; she was dissatisfied. Only this time she was dissatisfied with herself.

Moss had his work and had thrown himself into it with renewed fervor, as though to compensate for the quiet domestic life he was living. He talked about his plans for building a new enterprise that he called Coleman Aviation and the difficulties of procuring the proper licensing from the federal government. Billie made every attempt to listen, to appear interested, but it never came from her heart. She was envious of Moss's energy and ability to get a job done, to have meaningful work. She herself had no such outlet.

Billie had given up her art classes when she'd told Jordan Marsh it was over between them. He had accepted her decision with humiliating calm and she had had to wonder when he himself would have called an end to the affair. It had been difficult to pursue her craft on her own, without a teacher to criticize her work. Billie began to create a workshop out of one of the outbuildings behind the house, but it seemed to her that she was directing more effort to the project than to her art itself. Day after day she struggled with her decision to commit herself to home and family.

Maggie didn't make things any easier. As her pregnancy progressed she became more sullen and withdrawn, seeming to resent her mother and father's new, delicate relationship. It never mattered whom or what Maggie hated; she just did. She hated green beans. She hated the soft yellow they'd decided upon for the nursery. She hated babies.

Susan suffered gossip at school, where Maggie's pregnancy was common knowledge. Riley fell prey to Maggie's jealous scorn when at home on the weekends. When Amelia arranged for her talented goddaughter to study at the London Conservatory of Music, the family decided that Susan would be better off in England. Riley would just have to keep out of Maggie's way.

Seth and Agnes, who had become as much a team as peanut butter and jelly, Abbott and Costello, went about with sour expressions. They had completely disapproved of Billie's decision to continue with the pregnancy. They had been forced to face down the disgrace of one of their clan and had been made vulnerable to the many enemies of their power, real and imagined.

Billie juggled all these delicate and uneasy relationships and pretended to believe it would all work out in the end. She refused to admit, most of all to herself, that perhaps she'd been wrong. As Maggie's belly grew so did Billie's discontent.

Maggie's daughter was born during an early spring storm just a few minutes after midnight in the nursery at Sunbridge. Billie, cloaked in a sterile gown, was the first to hold the new infant. A surge of love and protectiveness rushed through her as she cradled the small bundle of life next to her heart. Sawyer Amelia Coleman looked up into the clear hazel eyes of her grandmother and perfected a bonding that would last a lifetime. Billie's finger trailed along the baby's delicate cheek. It had all been worth it. All the indecision, the pain, the pretending. Any price was worth this tiny infant's life.

Hours later, when Maggie lay in an exhausted sleep, Moss quietly tapped on the nursery door and entered. His eyes were full of something Billie couldn't identify. He walked over to the cradle to stare down at his first grandchild. Carefully, Billie lifted the infant and placed her in Moss's arms. His hands were trembling as he accepted the offering.

"She's beautiful." His voice was husky.

"Yes, she is," Billie murmured. "You're holding part of us, Moss. Us. This little girl was birthed by Maggie but she's ours, too. She'll always be ours. Another Coleman for Sunbridge."

"Billie, so much has happened to us. I don't know why or how and I'm more than willing to take the blame. Seeing you here like this, holding the baby, makes me realize how much of our lives I've missed. I should have been here with you when Maggie was born. And Susan and Riley. I should have been—I even wanted to be—but I had this crazy idea in my head that other things were more important. I was a fool, Billie, a damned fool."

Moss had uttered the words she had so longed for. His emotions were genuine—of that she was certain—but she felt no triumph, only sorrow. Sorrow for all the time lost, for the wasted passion, for the loosening of their bond. So many years she'd lived her own life just on the perimeter of his. They were married, they shared three children and now this precious, precious first grandchild, and this was the first and only time he truly mourned all that had been lost between them.

His eyes were moist and glowing, a silent pleading in their depths, and Billie's heart opened to him, to this man whom she'd sworn to love forever, this man of so many complexities. He leaned over the baby's head, his mouth finding hers in a tender kiss. Overwhelming emotions were released from Billie's soul as she allowed her lips to cling to his. "I love you, Moss. I love you," she whispered. And it was true. Or was it only the dream she loved, the home, the family, the unity and belonging? Whatever it was, Moss was an intrinsic part of that dream.

She'd learned many new things since those halcyon days when she was a girl and madly in love with her navy flyer, and she'd changed her opinions hundreds of times. But one fact was undeniable: she never wanted to be without him. She did love him and knew she always would. She'd learned that love had many faces, both beautiful and ugly, but one truth always remained. She loved him.

He tenderly touched his lips to the baby's downy brow before settling her down in her cradle. His fingers, warm and large, found Billie's hand and drew her to him. Arms about each other, they quietly let themselves out of the nursery and moved as one down the long wide hallway of Sunbridge to the silence and dimness of their room.

Billie's heart was tripping beneath her breast. Every sense was attuned to him, to his every touch and action. Some of her girlhood passion and excitement was stirring, blending with the patience and maturity of a woman. When he closed the door behind them she stepped easily into his arms, holding him close, the full length of her body pressed against him, her lips finding the opening at the neck of his shirt and nuzzling in the crisp dark hairs of his chest. She reveled in the scent of him, clean and faintly spicy, but was sharply aware of the deeper male scent beneath. His hands were in her hair, stroking. His lips were tracing concentric little circles near her temples. It felt so good to be held this way, close against him, almost a part of him. And his tenderness was unhurried. He would woo her, court her, and only when she wished it would he take her. Somewhere in her mind's eye she saw again the little kiss he'd placed on the baby's head. Sweet, loving. That was the way he was kissing her now. She was aware of his protectiveness and possession and it awakened long-dormant memories of the first time they'd made love in her girlhood bedroom back in Philadelphia. He'd been the master then, her teacher and guide, and his concern for her pleasure and regard for her inexperience had endeared him to her forever. That was how he was touching her now, as though she were a delicate flower that would bruise and wither with an indiscriminate touch.

The kisses that he was tracing along her neck sent delicious little quivers down her spine. The hunger in his voice when she touched the tip of her tongue to the base of his throat echoed within her. Expectation plucked at her nerve endings and heated her blood.

It was a familiar ritual, yet there was much to discover as well. As her hands caressed the smooth of his back, those muscles and planes to which she'd become accustomed were no less intriguing than they'd been the first time. Her pelvis undulated in a dance, pressing against his stomach and loins with a hungry need of its own. He was her husband and his body was even more familiar to her than her own, but there was an exhilaration in this knowledge. Although the room was dimmed, curtained and shaded against the approaching dawn, her mind's eye saw him clearly, knowing the hair patterns of his body, where the skin was smooth and white, delicately sensitive to her touch. There was assurance in this familiarity, certainty and comfort. The time for newness and timid exploration was behind her. There was no bashful experimentation to bring pleasure as there'd been with Jordan; this was the security of a well-traveled path, the route finely drawn on the chart of their lovemaking, and the reward was well known and joyfully anticipated. This was Moss; this was her husband, the man who shared her life.

His possession of her was tender, loving, making the exchange of pleasure between them sweet and unhurried, while beneath the surface ran a current of dizzying sexuality. As her garments fell away beneath his hands so did her defenses. Was this the way it was to be, then? A new beginning? Starting with the birth of their first grandchild? How fitting, Billie thought. She felt her hostility peel away, leaving her clean and pink and fresh. She *could* love again, she *could* give of herself; and with that thought she turned in his arms as he eased her down upon the bed, placing herself above him.

He wanted her, there was the physical evidence between them, pressing against her thigh. She caressed him with soft, loving fingers, thinking how through the years his male organ had been expressly shared by both of them, almost becoming a third party in their lovemaking. It never ceased to fascinate her, tempt her touch and invoke her kiss. It was her barometer of herself as a woman together with the glow in Moss's eyes and the sounds from his lips.

He helped her mount, holding her firmly by the hips, directing her movements. He fit into her smoothly, snugly, as she slowly descended the length of him, bringing herself tightly against him. His hands were on her breasts, teasing and enticing, drifting upward to caress her lovely face and trace the line of her jaw. She turned her face into the palm of his hand, breathing the scent of herself mingled with his own, feeling the tips of his fingers softly touch her lips.

"Come here to me, Billie, my Billie," he whispered, pulling her downward to meet his kiss. It was then, when she felt the moistness on his cheeks, that she realized she was crying. Her tears mingled with his and the hungry fulfillment of their bodies was secondary to the needs of their hearts. Overwhelming emotions engulfed her, drawing her body closer to his in an effort to touch his soul. Was it to be? This dream against which she'd hardened her heart? Was this love rediscovered? Was she at long last a part of Moss, the most precious part?

She heard her name upon his lips, saw the expression of love in his eyes. Her inner being reached out with long tender fingers, groping through the years of disappointment and darkness, to find him. Her soul seemed to feel him close, so close, closer than a breath away. But before she could reach him he was gone and only loneliness and emptiness were there to greet her. Before she could cry her grief her body commanded her back to an awareness of the here and now, driving to climax.

When it was over she lay weeping in his arms, hiding herself from him, curving her back and drawing herself inward.

Moss kissed her tear-wet cheeks and cradled her, sighing deeply with satisfaction. He was sated, she knew, and so should she be. Her body had demanded and received. But what of her soul? What was wrong with her? She choked upon her own sobs. Why wasn't it enough that he was her husband, that he cared for her, even loved her? Why must she demand something that perhaps he could never give? What part of her must demand that he also understand her?

"Billie, my own Billie," he was saying as he turned her in his embrace. She saw the tears that still glittered in his eyes as dawn streaked through the curtains. "Don't cry, sweetheart," he soothed. "It was wonderful for me, too. No one could ever love me the way you do."

But do I, Moss? she wondered. Do I really love you? And if I do, what becomes of me?

Maggie would have nothing at all to do with the baby. As soon as the doctor gave his permission, she was out riding at every opportunity and Seth complained that she would ruin the best mounts on the ranch with her carelessness. Her surliness and talent for mischief seemed inexhaustible.

Billie's gentle prompting was met with a stubborn denial. "I never wanted that baby. *You* wanted me to have it. You take care of it! I don't even want to know it breathes the same air I do!"

The entire Coleman family was at its wits' end and looked to Billie for a solution. They'd already faced down the worst of the gossip and the baby presented no problem. The problem was Maggie.

The solution of how best to help Maggie came about in a conversation with Thad. There was, he said, a very private, very good school in Vermont that operated with a limited enrollment, and although it wasn't mentioned in their brochures, they were known to help emotionally disturbed children.

Billie balked at the term Thad used but had to admit that he was being charitable. Seth and Agnes had far more dire adjectives to describe their granddaughter. Besides, she had to admit Maggie had problems, and she couldn't allow words and labels to stand in the way of what was best for her child. Still . . . Vermont?

"I can't just send her so far away, Thad! Certainly she needs schooling and, I'll admit, psychological help, but surely a family is important, too!"

"Contact the school, Billie. I'm certain they'll take her. And as far as a family goes, she can board there and on free weekends she can go to the country to my cousins. They've raised four kids of their own, and hell, it's worth a try, isn't it? What other ideas do you have?"

Billie had to admit she was at a loss. She wanted what was best for Maggie and there was the baby to consider. Maggie needed help.

Before mentioning the plan to Moss, Billie checked it out with the school and waited to hear whether or not Thad's cousins would agree. When she was met with approval from all sides, Billie breathed a sigh of relief and went to Moss with the proposal. He heard only "very exclusive, very private, and very expensive." Emotionally disturbed children were something other people had. Maggie was going north for the best education money could buy.

"I'll never forget this and I'll never forgive you, either of you!" Maggie shouted as the car taking her to the airport pulled away from Sunbridge. Billie's heart ached. Her last sight of Maggie, with red-rimmed eyes and teeth bared, was what she took to bed each night. To her lonely bed. Moss's promise, it seemed, had departed with Maggie. Once again he threw himself into his work, spending long hours away from home. Often, when he crept into their room in the wee hours of the morning, Billie could detect a faint aura of very feminine, very sophisticated perfume. With Maggie gone, Moss obviously considered the family problems solved.

Billie tried to tell herself it really didn't matter. But it did, terribly, and she seemed to spend her days swallowing a dry, hard lump that had become lodged in her throat. What was it she did want? Since the night of Sawyer's birth when she and Moss had made love, she had come to the realization that sexual gratification wasn't enough. Loving wasn't enough. There was supposed to be more—there *had* to be more—but for the life of her she couldn't put a name to it. Even her anger was gone; only a sense of bleakness remained.

Billie's invitation list to the opening of her studio—which was to take place today—was small and select. Two of Jordan Marsh's students with whom she'd kept in touch, Thad, and the family.

For weeks carpenters, painters, and delivery men had thrown Sunbridge into chaos, and the old carriage house was now ready for occupancy. Huge windows and skylights let in blinding amounts of light. Canvases and easels were set up to take advantage of the light at different times of the day. Boxes of paint, brushes, and pallettes were stacked neatly on sweet-smelling cedar shelves. A soft, downy sofa that opened to a bed took up one wall; a small refrigerator, an equally small stove, and a thickly padded rocking chair lined the other. Green plants in tubs stood in all the corners. And Billie had told the carpenters to section off a small room, right next to the sparkling new bathroom, for Sawyer's nursery. That way, any sound the infant might make would carry to Billie no matter where she was working.

Now Billie held Sawyer up on her shoulder. She was a round, cuddly baby, big for six months, the doctor said. She was bright-eyed and alert, gurgling constantly, to Billie's delight. Soft music played in the background as Billie walked about her new domain. She was excited about her new venture—she was reaching out for something.

Seth and Moss were the first to arrive. Billie handed the baby over to Moss, who reached for her unwillingly. Agnes arrived a few minutes later with Riley and the servants from the kitchen. Billie smiled when she overheard Agnes discussing their cleaning schedule. Never would one of her mother's servants take a cloth or broom to this private place. She would clean it herself. This was hers and she wasn't about to share it with anyone but Sawyer.

The coffee was gone, the Danish finished, and Riley had been driven back to the school. The two students lingered a moment or two longer and then departed behind Agnes. Seth limped off and Moss waited a moment longer. "I think this is wonderful for you, Billie. You should have done it sooner," he said. "I don't know much about art, but I can tell that you've improved since you went into the city to that commercial studio. I'm proud of you, Billie."

Billie scrutinized Moss's features for some sign that he was mocking her for doing something on her own. When she read the sincerity she had to smile. A year ago, even six months ago, she would have wept in sheer rapture at her husband's approving words. She felt pleased, but she felt more ecstatic at taking Sawyer from her husband's arms.

"I've got to get back to the office. I'm sorry Thad didn't make it. He must have gotten caught up in something. The navy isn't all that concerned about personal lives. I'd really like to see the old boy again. We've kind of lost touch. I'm glad that you've kept up your correspondence with him. Thad is one in a million."

Billie nuzzled Sawyer's neck. "One in a million," she repeated.

Moss looked around. Suddenly he didn't want to leave. He didn't belong in this place that was his wife's, yet he didn't want to leave. His eyes swept around the room, settling on the sofa bed. He'd be damned if he would depart this place without leaving his mark. The studio would become *theirs* instead of hers. "Billie, I want to make love to you," he said huskily, his hand reaching to touch the soft blond fluff of curls that fell against her neck.

Billie raised her head and at the same time gave Sawyer a slight pinch. The infant wailed on cue. "I'm sorry, darling. Sawyer needs to be fed and changed. Later, in our room. I'll wait for you."

Billie loved her new studio. It was the one place at Sunbridge that was hers alone. She wouldn't share it with anyone, not even Moss. She wanted no memories of him here.

"How long can it take to feed a baby? Can't you prop up the bottle?"

"I wish it were that simple, darling," Billie said sweetly. "However, Sawyer is now eating food that has to be warmed and then she takes a bottle that also has to be warmed. Then she needs to be changed from the skin out. The little love is a messy eater. At least an hour. If you want to wait." She made it sound like the question it wasn't.

"I can't wait. I have a board meeting. Good-bye, Billie. I'll be late this evening."

"All right," Billie called over her shoulder.

Moss stormed out to the garage.

Billie cooed to the baby. "It was necessary, sweetie. Forgive your grandmother." Sawyer gurgled as Billie placed her in the new crib. She wound up a colorful musical toy and within minutes the baby was sleeping soundly.

Now she was alone in her own place, organized and decorated by herself. It was what she wanted, the way she wanted it. It was hers. All hers!

The cigarette she lighted gave her something to do with her hands as she walked around the studio. Today was for looking and enjoying. Tomorrow she would get down to work. She was standing by the huge north window when she saw the plane flying low overhead. She knew who it was instantly. Thad would never forget. Now her perfect little place was complete. She watched the plane circle and then come in low, landing perfectly. She quickly checked Sawyer and then changed her shoes. If she ran like the wind, she could get to Thad before he took off in search of a ride to the main house.

As she ran across the field, her hair billowing out behind her, she kept saying over and over to herself, Oh, God, what am I doing? She didn't care.

At first he didn't see her and then the sound of his name circled around him like an exaltation of larks. He turned and watched Billie run to him. Then he was running toward her. "Billie!"

Billie skidded to a stop two feet from Thad. He pulled up short and both of them burst out laughing.

"Thad! I'm so glad to see you. I thought you weren't going to make it. I waited and waited. Now the day is complete. They're all gone. All except Sawyer and she's sleeping. Where were you? Why are you late? I'm so glad to see you. I've missed you." She was babbling but was unable to stop herself. How wonderful he looked. So fit and . . . and so . . . ready.

"Billie! I'm sorry I'm late. Last-minute check of the plane turned up a small defect. I was out on the field and couldn't get to a phone. I'm sorry. You know I wouldn't have missed your unveiling for anything. How are you? You look beautiful. You always look beautiful. How's the baby? How do you like being a grandmother?" Jesus, he was babbling just the way she was. He wanted to reach out, to take her in his arms. But it wasn't the time and it sure as hell wasn't the place.

"I'm so glad to see you. So damn glad." Billie laughed as she linked her arm in his. "Hurry, I want you to see Sawyer. She's sleeping. I left her alone for these few minutes. I shouldn't have done that. Run, Thad." Laughing like two children, they raced back to the studio.

"Billie, this is wonderful! It's so sunny with all the windows. Now I can picture you here working. I'm glad you invited me."

"You ain't seen nothing yet, Admiral," Billie said, drawing him into the little mininursery. She stood back proudly as Thad stared down at the pink-cheeked baby. "Well, what do you think?"

"What do I think? I think she's the most gorgeous thing I've ever seen, next to her grandmother, that is. Is she as perfect as she looks?"

"Admiral! Surely you jest. Would a Coleman be anything but perfect?" Billie teased. "Yes, she's a good baby. She's gaining weight rapidly and sleeps through the night. I just love her, Thad."

"I wouldn't have known if you hadn't told me," Thad teased back. "Have you heard from Maggie?"

"No. But I write and I send pictures of Sawyer almost every week. I tell her everything. I called a week ago. She sounded fine. She hasn't forgiven me or her father, but we're living with it. The school mails out a progress report at the end of every week. It's not exactly glowing, but her teachers seem to have a positive outlook. Now, tell me about you. I'll make some coffee. I saved some Danish in case."

"In case of what?"

"In case you made it after all. Did I tell you how happy I am that you made it?"

"Yes. But tell me again."

Billie laughed as she measured coffee into the percolator. "I'm so glad you could come. I've missed you, Thad. I think of you more often than is good for me. How's Solomon?"

"Ask a man about his dog and you have his heart. He's fine. His owner isn't all that well. I think of *you* more often than is good for me. I have to be honest with you, Billie. I wasn't going to come today. I was going to call you and say good-bye. Then I realized how cowardly that would be, so I hopped in the plane. I have new orders. I'm leaving tomorrow."

The cup Billie was holding fell and shattered on the new tile. "You're leaving? Where? Why? No, I'm sorry. I have no right to ask that. For how long?"

"I don't know for how long. It's the Pacific. My guess is at least three years."

"Three years! That sounds like forever. Oh, Thad!"

She cared. Jesus, she sounded as though she really cared. There were tears in her eyes. "It's only thirty-six months, or one thousand ninety-five days if you're counting. Who's counting?" He couldn't stand the stricken look on her face. He had to get things back on an even keel. "How are things with Moss?"

Billie drew in a deep breath. "Things are . . . things are . . . what they are. What I mean is, I try too hard. Moss doesn't try hard enough. It's what it is . . . for now. Moss will be sorry he missed you. He was saying this morning that it's been too long since you've seen each another. He's so busy, Thad. Really he is. He's home at night but he works in his office."

"And what about you, Billie?" Thad hoped his voice didn't sound as anxious as he felt.

"I think I'm content. I have my painting and Sawyer. Did I tell you? Of course I did—I'm working on some textile designs."

"I think it's wonderful, Billie. Would you like me to send you some silks when I get to the Orient? I'm to be stationed in Japan."

"Would you do that?"

"It would be my pleasure. As long as you're happy, that's all that matters."

Billie didn't respond right away. "Happy, Thad? I feel as though I'm on hold for the moment. I don't know if that makes sense to you or not, but it's as though I'm marking time, waiting for something or . . . you understand."

Or someone, Thad thought.

Why couldn't they say what was on both their minds? Why wasn't he telling her how he felt about her? Because, he answered himself, Billie was another man's wife—his best friend's wife.

"You'll keep in touch?" Billie asked. It was a plea.

"Of course. The Colemans are part of my life." That was a safe statement.

"What are you thinking now, this very second?" Billie's eyes were bright.

"About that time we were standing in the cavern at Diamond Head. What made you ask me that question?"

"I was thinking that one thousand ninety-five days is a very long time for two . . . for two friends to be separated. I've never been to the Orient. I'd like to see Hong Kong, Japan, the Philippines."

Thad tensed. "When?"

Billie's clear hazel eyes met his gaze honestly. "When?" she whispered. "When I need you most."

When Sawyer was eighteen months old, Moss came to the realization that Billie no longer lived and breathed solely for him. Days went by when she didn't enter Sunbridge at all but ate and slept in her studio. Once, unable to comprehend what was happening, he had tiptoed out of the house and gone down to the studio. He had stood in the dark and drizzling rain watching his wife play with his granddaughter. He could have gone in. He could have stormed in. Billie's rich laugher as she tussled with Sawyer on the thick carpeting brought a lump to his throat. He was losing her in so many little ways. He knew he had no one to blame but himself. A blanket of self-pity covered him as he stood watching. He didn't belong in the studio. He knew if he knocked on the door or simply walked in, Billie would smile but it wouldn't reach her eyes. The laughter would stop and a tenseness would take over. Billie's eyes would send silent questions: What do you want? Why are you here? She would say, "Moss, how nice to see you." She would be polite. They would be like two strangers.

His children were settled now and gave him no anxiety. It was Billie who was the thorn in his rose garden. This new Billie, who had ideas and opinions of her own and didn't hesitate to speak them. She had to be the youngest, the most beautiful, most caring grandmother he had ever seen. The love and devotion she showered on Sawyer should be his.

They should be doing things, going places, sharing. Instead, they were leading separate lives. Maybe Thad had the right idea after all. Bachelorhood couldn't be all that bad.

Back in his office, Moss delved into his paperwork. Two hours later he knew another trip to Europe was necessary. The sooner the better, and it was business that had to be handled personally.

Suddenly, Moss sat up straight. Maybe, just maybe he could work it so that his business trip coincided with Billie's tour of the Orient, make all the arrangements in advance for her to accompany him, then persuade her to drop her plans in favor of his. She'd discussed her trip with him and he had agreed she could go, although he'd known she would go regardless of what he said. Billie had been writing and making calls halfway across the world, setting up appointments and meetings that, she said, would add to her knowledge and further her career; whatever the hell *that* was! Now he could head her crazy ambitions off at the pass and offer her something far more suitable: togetherness.

A few calls produced two confirmed reservations on a flight to England, with return passage on an Italian ocean liner. A cruise home was just the ticket. What could be more romantic? Billie would love it. It would be a second honeymoon. Or was it their third? A month. A month for the two of them to see Europe. Billie would be ecstatic. He would tell her at dinner tomorrow night in front of Agnes and Seth. Riley would be there, too, since it was Friday and he'd be home from school for the weekend. Three allies.

Moss got up and poured himself a drink. Life had certainly changed since his marriage. Time was slipping through his fingers. He couldn't let Billie drift further away from him. He had to do something to bring things back to the way they were. The trip abroad could do it. He just had to stand firm.

Why? Why was he putting himself through this hassle? Things weren't uncomfortable. Billie shared his bed willingly. She never complained. What really bothered him? The studio? The baby? She still loved him; he could feel it. Sense it in the way she looked at him. He could hear it when they made love. It was all there, all the right things. There just wasn't enough of it. Billie was holding back, not giving one hundred percent to him anymore. A wife was supposed to give her *all* to the marriage, like Mom had. Blame? Fault? His? Every married couple had differences. Every married couple had trouble with their children.

Moss poured himself another drink and walked over to the French doors. He threw them open and squinted to look down across the back lawn to Billie's studio. There were lights blazing through the expanse of glass. Sawyer's bedroom was lit. It was almost the child's bedtime. Would Billie come back to the house or would she sleep in the studio? He'd been keeping track. Four nights out of seven she slept at the studio.

He could walk out, cross the lawn, knock on the door, and say he'd come down to watch Sawyer get ready for bed. It would be acceptable. Or he could carry down two drinks and offer to share a nightcap. Or he could go down there and kick the damn door in. Excuses. He needed an excuse to go there. He was an intruder, an interloper. His money was paying for it. He had rights.

The light went out in the nursery. His eyes narrowed. "The hell with it." He closed the French doors and locked them for the night. His eyes fell on the phone. Why the hell not? He dialed a number from his memory. "Alice? If you aren't busy, I'd like to come over. Yes, too long. Business, the children. I read the reviews. You must be very pleased. I can be there in thirty minutes." He listened for a second and then laughed. He hadn't laughed like that since the last time he'd been with Alice Forbes. "You got yourself a deal." There was a grimace on his face as he drew the drapes across the French doors, shutting out the blazing lights in Billie's studio.

Billie kissed Riley and then hugged him. The boy grinned and suffered the motherly embrace. How tall he was, Billie thought. He was a handsome youth. He looked so much like Moss, it was uncanny.

"How are things at school?" Billie asked.

"Great, Mam. Got an A this morning in my English test. I left my folder on the hall table, if you want to take a look at it. Pap has to sign some papers. How's everyone?"

"We're all fine. Sawyer had a big day and she's asleep already. Tomorrow you can play with her. But I have to warn you, she's got a wicked left hook." Riley laughed.

"I had a letter from Maggie and one from Susan this week. They seem to be doing all right. I'm going to answer both of them over the weekend."

"See that you do." She was so pleased that this son of hers thought enough of his sisters to write them. What was even more surprising was that Maggie kept up a steady correspondence with him. Susan, too, but her letters took longer to arrive. Her children did love one another. Neither Susan nor Riley judged Maggie. They accepted. Why couldn't adults do the same? Oh, no, they had to hang labels, make judgments, dole out punishments. She hated conditional love. Children were wise in so many ways.

"What's for dinner? I'm starved."

"I don't think I've ever seen you when you aren't starved," Billie teased.

"Mam, I missed lunch and only had oatmeal for breakfast. I could eat a side of beef myself right now."

"I think we're having prime rib. Your grandfather insisted. Blackberry pie for dessert. What do you think of that?"

"I can't wait. Where's Pap?"

"Someone call me?" Moss wrapped his son in both arms.

Dinner on Friday nights was always pleasant. Everyone, it seemed, put more effort into being pleasant. Early on, Billie had realized it was for Riley's benefit. Seth talked nonstop about the ranch and the business. Riley devoured every word and ate steadily. Moss never took his eyes off the boy. Agnes presided at the foot of the table with a little bell at her plate to summon the maid.

The atmosphere was a little different today, more electric somehow. Something was brewing; Billie could tell. Moss was moving his fork around on his plate, but he wasn't eating. He, like all the Coleman men, adored prime rib. The others were acting normally. It was Moss who was going to drop a bombshell. How well she knew this husband of hers. There was nothing to do but wait. He would bring it up over dessert or coffee.

Just as the new dark-eyed maid started to pour the coffee, Moss leaned back in his chair and reached inside his jacket pocket. He withdrew a folder and handed it across the table to Billie. "What do you think of that, honey?"

Billie frowned. She reached for the thick packet and opened it. Her eyes widened. She could feel her back start to stiffen. She was trapped; it was a familiar feeling. She slid the papers back into the packet.

"Well, what is it? Don't keep us in suspense, little gal!" Seth bellowed.

"Mam, what is it? Pap looks as though he just won a prize. Tell us!" Riley shouted. For a moment he forgot his second piece of blackberry pie.

"It appears to be two tickets to Europe." Billie said in tight, clipped tones.

"Moss! How wonderful!" Agnes trilled excitedly.

"Mam, you'll get to see Susan and Aunt Amelia. Aren't you excited?" Riley demanded.

"You don't look very pleased, gal," Seth growled. "Your husband went to a lot of trouble to do this. The least you could do is show you're happy."

Billie ignored everyone at the table. "Moss, you should have asked me before you did this. The thought is wonderful, but I can't go to Europe now and you know it. I've made plans to go to the Orient. We spoke about this several times and you said it was all right with you. Now you go ahead and arrange all this without consulting me. I'm sorry."

Seth scowled. "Sorry about what? You cancel your plans and go with your husband, the way a wife should. That's what you're going to do. Moss, settle this wife of yours."

Moss seethed. It was happening again. It was slipping out of his grasp. His plan wasn't going to work.

"It would be wonderful, Billie," he said. "We could tour Europe, get to see Susan and Amelia. You could go to the woolen mills over there. A second honeymoon, Billie."

Billie could feel herself begin to cringe as everyone at the table waited for her reply. Second honeymoon indeed. She'd been the one to hang up Moss's suit this morning and she'd been the one to take his shirt and underwear to the hamper. The faint scent of Alice Forbes's perfume still clung to his clothes. A second honeymoon. It was too ludicrous for words.

"I'm sorry, Moss. I've already made my reservations. You know I'm not interested in the woolen mills. My interest, if you paid attention to what I've been talking about, is in Oriental art. I'm sorry, Moss, but I can't make it. Perhaps when I get back from the Orient we can make plans to go sometime again in the future. Now, if you'll excuse me, I want to check on Sawyer."

"I'll be a son of a bitch!" Seth shouted as he struggled up from the table. "She's got you by the short hairs, boy. Reel her in and take hold. What's going on here? What's this garbage about going to the Orient? This is the first I've heard about it. Cut her off at the pass. Take away her money and she'll step into line. You only have to do it once and then they know who's boss."

"I can't do that," Moss said stiffly.

"And why the hell not?" Seth thundered.

"Because she told you the truth. She did talk to me about the trip to the Orient. *I* said she could go." This had to be an all-time low for him. Christ, he was eating crow in front of the old man, his mother-in-law, and his son. His eyes went to Agnes, who was twirling her pearls nervously. What the hell was *she* worried about?

Agnes excused herself with a remark to Riley to be sure to finish his milk. Moss headed for his office. Riley looked around the empty table. Sometimes Sunbridge could be so lonely. Maybe next week he would bring a friend home with him. His pal David would like the ranch. But first he would explain that his grandfather was a cranky man. And his grandmother wasn't the cookie-baking kind of grandmother the other kids talked about. He gulped down the remainder of his milk and left the table.

Billie lay quietly in the narrow bed, aware of Sawyer's light breathing in the next room. She wasn't fooling herself for a minute. She had choices and she had options. She was capable of making a decision. She had reinforced her commitment to Moss and she would honor it. She loved Moss. She would always love him. But now it was a different kind of love. The breathtaking grand passion was gone. The closeness and the intimacy of early marriage were gone. All that remained were biological needs that required exercising from time to time. And the commitment to each other. To do what? To live in the same house. To unite when the need arose in regard to the children. The name of the game was pretend. Pretend she didn't know about Alice Forbes. Pretend she never smelled perfume or saw lipstick on her husband's shirt. Pretend she didn't mind if he went off to Europe. Pretend that he cared about her work.

Billie stared into the darkness. How could she be so wide awake so late at night? She tried to make out the objects on the dresser across the room. For some reason it seemed important that she know exactly what was on the dresser. Over and over she told herself Moss was the father of her children. Over and over she told herself she loved him. It wasn't supposed to be like this. Her marriage was supposed to be the ultimate fairy tale with the ultimate fairy tale ending where both the prince and princess lived happily ever after. But reality didn't hold with fairy tales.

All the words had been said. All the tears had been shed. Reality was being wise enough to know when something was finished.

The churchlike silence in the house the following morning grated on Billie's nerves. If it wasn't for Sawyer's gurgles and cries of delight, she knew she would have screamed.

The young girl who helped out with Sawyer was waiting patiently by the front door for her charge. She enjoyed the pony cart ride in the morning almost as much as Sawyer did.

"Be sure to strap Sawyer in tightly and only keep her out for an hour," Billie said. "It looks as though it might rain. When you bring her back, give her a cookie and some milk and then fetch her over to my studio. Now, Sawyer, you be a good girl for Nancy, and later you and I will build a big castle with the blocks Grandma Agnes gave you." Sawyer reached out chubby hands and arms for a hug and a kiss.

"Solly good girl."

Billie laughed. "Yes, darling, you are. You're the best girl in the whole world. Now say Sawyer. Saw-yur."

"Solly." The little girl giggled.

Billie laughed, which had been Sawyer's intention. "Go along, then, Solly, and have a good time."

"'Bye, Grandma." Sawyer waved.

As soon as the door closed behind her, Billie headed down the hall to Moss's workroom. She made excuses to herself as she started to rummage through his desk. In the early hours of the morning she had awakened and made a pact with herself. If Moss was being truthful when he'd said this was to be a honeymoon trip, she would cancel her plans for the Orient. If, on the other hand, the trip was for business and he was taking her along for his own reasons, it was another story. She felt like a thief and looked over her shoulder constantly to see if Seth or Agnes was watching her from the doorway. Damn, she should have locked the door. What if one of the maids came to clean? A second look told her Moss's workroom was like her studio. No one from the house staff touched it. When she found the packet of papers, she smiled to herself. Under the blotter of course. Her hands trembled slightly as she withdrew the airline and cruise tickets. She laid them aside as she flipped through the other papers looking for Moss's itinerary. It only took one quick glance to tell her all she needed to know. The second honeymoon was a farce. With all Moss had outlined for himself in the way of business meetings, she would be lucky to meet up with him at dockside for the return trip home.

Perhaps the honeymoon was to take place aboard ship? But

she was making excuses again. She was settling for less than she wanted. Moss had specifically said they would "tour Europe." Those had been his exact words. Billie looked again at the typed itinerary. Every hour of every day seemed to be accounted for. Nowhere did it mention her or Susan and Amelia.

Billie sat down with a thump. Moss's chair swiveled slightly with her abrupt move. As long as she was snooping, she might as well see what else she could find. In the bottom drawer behind a box of cigars and a bottle of Kentucky bourbon she found a packet of letters addressed to Moss at a post office box number, all bearing a New York postmark.

Billie shifted the packet from one hand to the other. The letters represented a part of Moss's life. She knew she had no right to read them, regardless of what was going on between Moss and her. She was afraid to read them. Her thoughts were confused. They were married, and yet they weren't married. Not if Moss could do the things he had been doing. What about you? a niggling voice demanded. What about Jordan Marsh, and what about all those feelings you have for Thad? Shame rushed through her. Her eyes lingered on the top of the pile. The date burned her eyes. The letter was only a week old.

Billie replaced the letters and closed the drawer. The packet containing the tickets went back beneath the blotter. She felt dirty. Guilt and shame made her clamp her hands to her burning cheeks.

The walk back to her bedroom was slow, torturous. How could she have snooped and pried like that? Because, the niggling voice said, you were willing to give up your career plans, you were willing to sacrifice again, as you always do. You were willing to put your husband first. Now you see what his priorities are.

He's the father of my children. I married him for better or worse, Billie reminded herself over and over. What about you? the pesky inner voice questioned. What about what you want? What about your feelings? What about your life? Martyrs finish last in this life.

In her room Billie paced the floor to an unheard drum. Her hands were clenched into tight fists in the pockets of her paint smock. The hands unclenched and her stiff spine relaxed. "No more!" she said coldly to her reflection in the mirror. "No more!"

She twirled around and shouted to the empty room, "No more!" She would survive because she was a survivor. That much the Colemans had taught her.

A week later Moss left for Europe by way of Dallas and New York. Seth clawed at him with bony arms and hands, thumping him on the back and warning him to take care of himself. Agnes smiled and accepted the dutiful peck on the cheek that Moss never failed to give. Billie grimaced. Some things never changed. She was always last. This time she found it amusing.

"Billie, I'm sorry you aren't coming with me. We could have done Europe up in style. Susan will be disappointed. So will Amelia."

Moss was trying to lay guilt on her shoulders. She forced a smile and turned slightly to offer her cheek the way her mother had. "Give them both my love. Tell them I wrote a long letter and mailed it yesterday," she said. "Enjoy yourself, Moss."

"Enjoy myself? How can I do that without you there?" Moss waited. She could still change her mind at the last second and say she would go. He hadn't turned in her ticket. How still and unnatural she looked. Christ, she was starting to act like her mother. Giving him her cheek to kiss. Saying inane words that meant nothing. And that smile on her face was as false as the masks he used to wear on Halloween.

It was on the tip of Billie's tongue to say he'd never had trouble enjoying himself before without her along, but she held her tongue. Go already, go! her mind screeched. I don't want to hear the lies anymore. Just go!

"I'll see you when I get back, Billie. Pap, take care of my girl," Moss said. He wrapped his muscular arms about his father a second time. Seth growled something unintelligible and then Moss climbed into the car. Then he was gone. Billie sighed with relief.

Two weeks later Billie left for Hong Kong. Except that she had to leave Riley and Sawyer, she was ecstatic.

Going through customs in Hong Kong, showing her passport, and having her luggage searched pleased Billie. She was handling it all by herself. She had studied up on the currency and felt confident enough to transact some simple shopping. Red, green, and blue bills that reminded her of Monopoly money were tucked into the zippered compartment of her hand-bag. Her letter of credit from the Coleman's bank in Austin gave her a sense of security.

There were hordes of people and no smiles in the airport. But Billie's smile didn't diminish as she motioned for a porter to take her bags. He nodded and bowed somewhat stiffly. Billie realized he was quite old and was appalled as he lifted her heavy luggage onto a cart to take to the taxi area. She'd have to give him a generous tip. When she was safely inside the taxi she handed the porter a five-dollar Hong Kong coin and watched his face for some kind of expression. When his features remained inscrutable, she hurriedly dug out another coin and offered it. The man nodded but still he didn't smile. How tired he looked, how weary. Billie knew it would take many five-dollar coins to make this man smile. Impulsively, she reached out to grab his arm. "Here," she said, handing him a fistful of coins. The man bowed again and stepped back from the taxi. She knew that she had been foolish, even that she had probably insulted him, but when she thought of the smile on his wife's face that evening, she felt justified.

"Peninsula Hotel on the Kowloon side," Billie told the driver.

The driver shook his head. "You want red-and-silver taxi for Kowloon side. I only drive Hong Kong side. You get out."

"What?"

"You get out and take red-and-silver taxi. They go Kowloon side."

"Will you help me with my bags?"

"I just drive taxi Hong Kong side."

"I'll pay you," Billie said in a panicky voice. Her first problem. She searched the milling crowds for some sign of her porter.

"For five dollars American I will help you."

Fifteen minutes later Billie was installed in a new cab that was indeed silver and red. Her luggage was stowed in the trunk and the driver leaned in the window. "How you pay, Hong Kong dollars or American?"

"What would you prefer?" Billie asked in her best busi-nesslike voice.

"Twenty American dollars to drive you to Kowloon side. You pay toll in Hong Kong dollars."

"All right. Tell me something. How much do you charge to drive one of your countrymen to the Kowloon side?"

"Four dollars Hong Kong," the driver said as he pulled away

from the curb. He narrowly missed a tourist bus. Billie shuddered at the near mishap and decided to forget that she had been taken. Tomorrow she would practice up on the art of haggling. Now she was too tired. All she wanted was a warm bath and a nice clean bed.

Rolls Royces lined the circular drive to the hotel and two boy pages in crease-free white uniforms flanked the entrance to the opulent lobby. Tomorrow, Billie decided, she would admire it all.

Billie woke instantly, completely aware of where she was. Kowloon. Her first full day in Hong Kong. She was alone to do as she pleased. She could get up or she could stay in bed. She could bathe and dress and go to the dining room, or she could have room service. Brunch. That's what she would have. She would dillydally now, take a long luxurious bath, work out the kinks from all the sitting on the airplane. Then a long, leisurely brunch before business.

Billie clapped her hands childishly and bounced on the bed. She was truly in Hong Kong!

Billie stood uncertainly in the wide central lobby of the hotel. Should she go outside to order the taxi or ask at the desk?

The majordomo looked at her from top to bottom, she thought. "May I help you, madam?" he said.

"I'd like to go to the central district."

"Would you like to take a taxi, or would you rather take the Star Ferry?"

Billie looked at her watch. "I think I'd like the ferry."

"Then may I suggest a taxi to the ferry?"

Outside, Billie watched in amazement as a taxi rolled to the foot of the steps. As far as she could tell, the man hadn't made a signal, had uttered no word. One of the white-uniformed pages took Billie's arm, escorted her down the steps, and held open the taxi door. Billie smiled at the boy and was rewarded with a solemn dark-eyed stare. He nodded slightly as he shut the door.

"Star Ferry, please," Billie said, leaning back on the seat.

Once there, Billie paid the fare and followed throngs of people down the wooden ramp to the ferry. She slid to the end of a long slatted bench so she could have a view of the harbor. She was busily snapping pictures of the colorful sampans before the ferry left the pier. She snapped an entire roll of film and was changing the camera when the ferry came to a stop. For a brief moment Billie panicked. She was alone, half a world away from Texas. Then excitement took over. Up the ramp she went like all the other ferry travelers. She tried to blend in with her black suit and white blouse. No one, she noticed, paid her the least bit of attention.

A wizened man held out his hand and smiled a wide, tooth- less grin. "Missie want rickshaw ride? One dollar American!" Billie stared at the old man and then brought up her camera. She laughed when the man brought his hand up to cover his face. "Picture is two dollars American."

"All right." Billie laughed. "But only because you're the first person in this land who has smiled at me." She aimed the camera and took three shots of the man. First he smiled, then he tipped his raggedy straw hat. Lastly, he propped his foot up on the rickshaw and threw out his arms. "A ham, too," she said. "You'd be a hit on Broadway."

"You take rickshaw ride wherever. Wiggly wiggly."

"What does that mean?"

"That means I go where you want to go. Roads go wiggly wiggly. Taxis not go wiggly wiggly."

"Cloth Lane. Will you take me there?"

"I take for one dollar American. Pay now. Pay picture now."

Billie handed over the money. The man pocketed the bills in baggy black trousers that were the Chinese uniform. He wore only thin black slippers that looked like ballet shoes on his bony feet. How in the world, Billie wondered, could this old man who weighed no more than eighty pounds drag the heavy rickshaw with her sitting in it? He trotted off, his head bent and his back bowed.

The ride was pleasant, but Billy felt guilty that the little man was pulling her on foot. Once she got her bearings, she would walk the crowded, congested streets and drink in the sights on her own. In spite of herself she laughed. She knew, just knew, he made more money having his picture taken than he did hauling people around.

"Cloth Lane," the old man called over his shoulder. "You get out now."

Billie reached into her bag and handed the man two bills. She was amazed to see him snort and look at her with disgust. Her brain whirled as she tried to compute the currency. A two- dollar tip seemed more than fair.

"Money for nothing is not good. You not do again. You lose face if you do this."

"You don't accept tips?" Billie asked incredulously.

"No money for nothing. Smart lady not do this again." Billie debated whether she should hold her hand out for her money, but then he stuffed the currency into his baggy pants.

She laughed. "I won't do it again."

The rickshaw driver waved his hands to show he was finished with her and all women. He muttered to himself as he turned his cart around to look for another fare back to his stand.

Billie was on Cloth Lane. All manner of fabric shops lined the narrow street. Hundreds of colorful banners and metal signs, all lettered in Chinese, hung overhead. They blocked the sunlight. In the end she was forced to work her way down one side of the street and up the other until she found the specific shops she wanted.

When Billie returned to the hotel from her day's outing, she lay down across the bed. She missed dinner and slept through the night. The succeeding days were jammed full of shopping, appointments, and sight-seeing. She stored her treasures in a large trunk she bought to ship everything home. She sent out postcards and wrote letters to Maggie, Susan, and Riley.

On her fifth day Billie felt confident enough to haggle over prices, to the shopkeepers' delight. She set prices in her mind and wouldn't budge a penny. Twice she walked out of a shop only to have the owner come after her and give her the object she wanted at what she considered a fair price. She bought a camera for Thad that the shopkeeper said was idiot-proof. For some reason Thad always had his thumb or finger in every picture he took. For Moss she bought a pure silk robe and one almost identical, except for the color of the dragon on the back, for Seth. For Agnes a string of lavender jade whose price made Billie's eyes boggle. For the children, toys and trinkets of every size and shape filled the trunk to overflowing. She had to buy another one just for her silks and brocades. Hong Kong was marvelous. The only thing she regretted was that she had no one to share her experiences. The urge to turn to someone and say "Look at that!" or "What do you think of this?" was overwhelming. Instead, she talked to the shopkeepers, asked questions, and smiled.

By the eighth day she had eaten in six of the finest restaurants in Asia, taken the Kowloon-Canton Railway, and ridden the

Peak-Tram 30 kilometers to a height of 397 meters above sea level. By the eleventh day, she had explored every shop on Nathan Road, learned to drink Lushan Yun Wu Tea with gusto, and seen a Dragon Boat Festival with a yellow Dragon Boat that belched fire. Truly she was making it on her own.

Billie's time was almost up—only five days remained to her visit—and she still hadn't received permission from the government house to travel to Zhejiang on the east coast of China. The silks coming out of the famous Silk City were described as clear as water, beautiful as poetry, like clouds in the sky and flowers on earth. After she had come so far, it would be a shame to miss the mulberry trees and silk experts of Zhejiang Province.

A long, leisurely soak in the tub, with room service for dinner, was a must, Billie decided wearily. Her busy schedule was finally catching up with her. As she slid down into the steamy water, she wondered how Moss was faring on his trip to Europe and if he had gotten to see Amelia and Susan. She rather doubted it.

CHAPTER {{{{{{{{{ TWENTY-SEVEN }}}}}}}}}

*Billie was sitting down to her exquisitely appointed room ser-*vice dinner in her new crimson silk robe when the phone buzzed to life.

"Thad! Is that you? Where are you?"

Thad laughed. "I'm here at the Peninsula. Where else does a person stay when he comes to Hong Kong? You're traveling in high places, lady. This is the home away from home for kings, queens, divas, grand dukes, heads of states, captains of industry, and C.I.A. agents."

"How wonderful. When did you get here? How long are you staying? Why are you here?"

"Your last letter reached me in Japan. That's just a hop, skip, and a jump from here when one has a government plane at his disposal. I'm here for two days. I came to see you. It's that simple. How are you, Billie?"

"Oh, Thad, this is all so marvelous. I can't believe I'm here. I have managed to get around on my own. I missed having someone to share it with, though. I'm so glad you're here."

"Have you had dinner?"

Billie looked at the table with its array of fine china, silver, exquisite crystal. "No," she lied.

"Good. We'll have dinner here in the hotel, at Gaddi's. I'm sure you've tried it out by now, but I happen to think it's the finest restaurant in all of Asia."

"I'd like that very much. How much time do I have?"

"Ten minutes." Thad laughed. God, he felt good.

"I'll meet you in the lobby in ten minutes." Billie giggled. The new green silk off-the-shoulder gown with the slit on the side would be perfect. The jade earrings she'd bought on Nathan Road just this morning would set it off to perfection. Makeup and perfume would only take a minute. Her nails were freshly manicured. She could make it. Ten minutes to meet Thad. Billie never moved so fast in her life. Stockings, bra. The gown slithered down over her body. The feeling was so luxurious Billie gasped. Her heart leaped and fluttered at the thought of seeing Thad and spending the evening with him. Dear Thad. She had so much to tell him. Thad's being here was the consolation prize if the government wouldn't allow her to make the trip to the east coast of China.

Billie brushed her hair into place and picked up the seeded pearl bag that completed her outfit. The mirror told her she looked great. She felt wonderful. She hadn't felt this good since the day Thad had come to her studio. A year was so long. And the years kept slipping by.

When Billie stepped from the lift, Thad drew in his breath. Someone must have written a song about the way he felt. Billie had grown more beautiful over the years. His throat was dry. Christ, he hoped he'd be able to talk. This shouldn't be happening to him. He was no kid.

Their eyes locked across the wide golden room. The smile Billie gave him was radiant and spoke eloquently of many things. Thad was seeing Billie Coleman on her own in one of the most glamorous cities in the world. Hong Kong and Billie Coleman. The other guests were staring at her, too. There was a ring of heat around Thad's neck that was bent on choking him. Did she notice? Was she aware of how he felt? How could she look at him and not see what was mirrored in his face and eyes? Billie was no fool. Billie was a woman and he was a man. Adults. And it didn't mean a damn thing. She wasn't free. She was Moss's wife. He had to remember that. They were two old friends meeting for dinner. It was all he would allow.

Navy whites, tall and lean. Billie was aware of the man coming toward her. Lord, she was going to turn her ankle in the scandalous high-heeled shoes and make a fool of herself. What would he think? Who cared? How wonderful he looked. How dashingly handsome. Every woman there was eyeing him as he held out his arms. How right he looked. How good it felt to be taken into his arms in public this way. A kiss on the cheek was acceptable in this hotel lobby, where everyone waited for romance and wonderful things to happen. He smelled the same. Dear God, he was Thad.

"You look beautiful," Thad said, smiling down at her.

"I was going to say you're the handsomest man in this room, Admiral Kingsley. How are you, Thad?"

"You don't really want to know, do you?" Thad asked in a low tone."

"Yes, I want to know," Billie whispered.

"Why don't we just say I'm fine for the moment and let it go at that. How are you, Billie?"

"You don't really want to know, do you?"

"There are some things a man needs to know and some he doesn't. I seriously doubt that I could handle your answer right now. Let's go to dinner. I reserved a table."

Billie had no time or desire to appreciate the exquisite setting of the restaurant. She had eyes only for Thad. They talked of inane things while they sipped the finest wine the hotel had to offer. She hardly heard Thad order her for: *Emince de vilaille* in a sauce of *beurre maître d'hotel*, which, Thad told her, translated as sliced chicken in a lemony butter sauce. Later she could barely remember if she ate it, much less how it tasted. She was also unaware of the five waiters it took to serve their one table. It was only when Thad inquired after Moss that Billie forced herself to awareness.

"He's in Europe." She resented her husband's intrusion into this wonderful evening. "He flew over and is sailing back. I haven't heard anything from anyone, so I imagine those are still his plans. I hope he managed to see Susan and Amelia. It was a business trip. What about you, Thad? When are you going to tell me about your promotion?"

Thad dogged the question with one of his own. "How long will you be staying here?"

"I have a few more days and then it's back to Sunbridge. I miss Sawyer."

Not Moss, not her husband. Billie would have said if she missed him. No, it was the baby she missed. Thad smiled. "What do you think I could get for these four gold stars over here?"

Billie laughed. "Not much. If they were jade, you might come out with a few dollars—if you haggled first. I'm an expert. Tell me what you want. I can get it at a fair price and no one loses face."

It was midnight when Billie and Thad left the restaurant. "Would you like to go for a walk?"

Not wanting the night to end, Billie agreed. What did she care if she had to trip five miles in spike-heeled shoes? She could get twenty blisters and never be able to wear shoes again and she wouldn't care. She was with Thad.

"I've missed you, Billie. I can't tell you how I look forward to your letters. I told you, didn't I, that I managed to bring Solomon with me to Japan."

"Yes, you did. How does he like it?" Why were they talking about his dog? Why couldn't they talk about themselves? The two of them. If only she could look ahead into the future. Was Thad in her future anywhere?

Thad walked Billie to her door, kissed her again on the cheek, cautioned her to lock the door. They made arrangements to meet in the lobby for breakfast at eight and spend the day together.

When Thad heard the snick of the lock, he leaned against the wall outside Billie's room, fighting with himself not to knock on the door. When he finally forced his feet to take him to the lift, he started back down the hallway twice, only to return to the lift. Inside his room his hand went to the telephone four times in as many minutes.

He was brushing his teeth when his phone rang. He swallowed the glob of toothpaste and dropped his toothbrush in the bathtub on his sprint to catch the phone before it could ring a second time. "Hullo" was the best he could do with the minty toothpaste stuck to his teeth and tongue.

"Thad, did I wake you? I'm sorry. I just called to say good night and to thank you for a marvelous evening."

"I wasn't asleep." Christ, as though he would ever sleep again. "It was my pleasure, Billie. I enjoyed it as much as you did. I hope we can do it again tomorrow evening."

"I'd like that. I'll see you at breakfast, then. Sleep well."

Billie's hand was trembling so badly when she replaced the receiver that she had to clench both hands together. He should have said something. Made some overture. She'd certainly given him every opportunity. Short of throwing herself at him, what could she have done? Now she would never be able to sleep. True to her thought, she lay awake all night staring up at the high ceiling and listening to the bedside radio play the same songs over and over. She watched the sun come up through her window.

Thad dressed in casual civilian clothes the following morning. All night long he'd planned his day with Billie. He was more than familiar with Hong Kong, having spent a month of R&R at the famous hotel nicknamed the Pen, after the war. He'd enjoyed every incredible minute. Now he could share some of his memories with Billie. An entire day and evening with her.

After a light breakfast of tea and croissants he asked her to help him pick up gifts for his relatives back in Vermont. Billie was better at selecting gifts than he was, and she was indeed an expert negotiator.

Then they took a light picnic lunch to do some sightseeing in the New Territories. Thad showed her the Ching Chung Koon and Miu Fat Monastery, two of the most photogenic stops in the New Territories. From there they visited the market towns of Tai Po, Faning, and Yuen Long. The Amah Rock, Thad said, was a must and he proceeded to tell Billie the story.

"Legend has it that a fisherman's wife, with a baby strapped to her back, always went to that particular spot to watch for her husband's return. When she was told that her husband had perished during a certain trip, she refused to believe it. After a year of waiting and watching, the gods took pity on her and, with a lightning bolt, transported her and the child to her husband, leaving a stone monument to her fidelity."

"What a beautiful story. It really does look like a madonna and child." Not for all the tea in China would Billie tell Thad she had been here just a week ago and read up on the legend. Seeing it with him was like seeing it for the first time. Now she could share; now she could talk about what she liked and didn't like. Thad made all the difference in the world.

"I wonder if a man could be capable of being so faithful," Billie said sadly.

Thad turned and looked down at Billie. He reached for her hand. "Some men are," he said softly. Billie squeezed his hand slightly.

"Next stop, the Ten Thousand Buddha Monastery. This will be a first for me. They built this around 1950," Thad said, reading the brochure.

It was a beautiful, warm, close day for Billie. She couldn't ever remember feeling so good or so comfortable with another human being. If only...if...if... From time to time she found Thad watching her with a peculiar glint in his eye. She would smile and he would smile back. Once he put his arm around her and pointed out something. Billie found herself leaning into his hold.

"Today reminds me of the day we spent in Hawaii," she said. "Remember Diamond Head?"

"I remember," Thad said quietly. "I've often wondered if you ever thought about it."

Billie let her gaze meet Thad's. "It was a long time ago. So much has happened to both of us. That day and several others are memories I treasure. Thad...I think...I think we should talk."

"Not here. Not now." God, it was what he had been hoping for all these years. But not in this foreign land, where their lives weren't real. The pulse hammered in his temple.

It had been a mistake to say anything, Billie thought. What must he think of her? "I'm sorry, Thad. Forget I said anything. The worst thing we can do is talk about it. Please, forgive me. I didn't mean to put you on the spot."

"Billie...I..."

"Thad, please. Why don't we leave now. I think I've had enough of monasteries to last me for a long time. Why don't we go back and have some tea. I could really use some tea, couldn't you? Yes, that's exactly what we should do."

Thad turned to reach for Billie's arm, but she was too fast. She had swiveled and was all but running for the tour bus. When he caught up to her she smiled brilliantly and started to chatter about what they had seen so far. He'd fouled up and the moment was gone.

He took his cue from Billie and they chattered all the way back to the Peninsula Hotel. They parted at the elevator, promising to meet for dinner at eight o'clock.

Thad paced his room for over an hour. He had never felt so hopeless in his entire life. Why couldn't he say what he felt? Why couldn't he take what he wanted? What Billie wanted, too? "Right? Wrong? Who gives a good goddamn," he snarled as he smacked one fist into the other. Pain shot up his arm. It was so simple: you reached out and, if you were lucky, there was a hand reaching for yours. He knew Billie would meet him halfway, at least halfway. Nothing and no one seemed to matter except Billie and being free to tell her of his love.

His career had been, after all, a poor substitute for the one woman he could love. After all those wasted years, nothing mattered. The chance to become fleet commander of the Pacific loomed within his reach. It was something he'd worked toward, something to take the place of Billie. Honor, reputation, dedication—empty, empty, empty words. Right, wrong, Billie, Moss. It was all so confusing, so painful. It was a sad state of affairs when all a man had was a dog to call his own. A dog and a career. It wasn't enough and it had never been enough. It was all so meaningless without Billie.

The knowledge of what he was prepared to do was making him light-headed. He sat down on the edge of the bed with a thump. The hell with everything, with everyone. The years were precious now. Reach out!

Billie picked through the gowns and dresses, some still wrapped in the stiff rice paper in which the shops had delivered them. She wanted to wear something bright and mood-lifting, and finally chose a muted tangerine silk with slim sleeves and a mandarin collar. Gold earrings and a wide gold bracelet heightened the effect, and at the last minute she added a large topaz ring that almost obscured her wedding band.

Billie paced her room, feeling nervous and edgy, her thoughts filled with Thad. She realized how much she had shared with him over the years, how much of her time had been spent thinking of him, how important he had become to her emotionally. But now, she had to confront the knowledge that she wanted him physically as well as emotionally. It was something she had long denied.

Thad was already in the lobby when she stepped from the lift. He joined her immediately and Billie noticed a determined set to his jaw. His eyes held hers. A warm flush crept over her when he eyed her approvingly and tucked her hand into the crook of his arm.

Dinner was at the Chesa, a delightful Swiss restaurant that was a reproduction of an Alpine inn. Billie admired the hand-painted fabric used for the curtains and tablecloths and immediately recognized a painted bride's hope chest as being like one she'd seen as a young girl in Philadelphia.

"The cuisine is authentic," Thad assured her. "I've been to Switzerland for skiing and always come home with a few extra pounds around my middle."

"It's comforting somehow to think of you with a paunch," Billie teased lightly. "I never knew you had to be careful about your weight."

"There's lots of things you don't know about me, Billie," he said flatly, without any attempt to return her light banter. Something was different about Thad tonight, she thought. Something brooding.

They were shown to an intimate table that was quietly lit by a candle surrounded with freshly cut flowers. Billie would have liked something nearer the center of the room, where their conversation would be more guarded and the long looks he was giving her would be impossible. It didn't matter, she told herself. Nothing mattered except that there was tension between them and she was the cause of it. She struggled with the conversation, determined to say the right things in exactly the right tone. Thad, she noticed, was on his third drink, which was rare. He was about to signal the waiter again when Billie reached across the table and took his hand. "Don't, Thad. This isn't like you. We'd better talk."

Thad shook his head. "Not here, Billie. Later. I'm sorry I'm acting like such a boor. Forgive me."

"There's nothing to forgive. We'll talk later." Throughout dinner Thad seemed more himself, but neither of them really enjoyed the meal. They were both thinking about "later."

He watched her all through dinner, vacillating. But he had to take a chance, he had to reach out. She was so beautiful, this woman he had watched grow from a girl into this soft loving creature. She seemed to turn her face toward him the way a flower followed the sun. There was a new sharpness to her chin and jaw, the soft round contours of girlhood gone. All those years were gone, all those years of knowing she belonged to another man. But the real betrayal was knowing that she craved tenderness and love and was denied. That was killing him. He had so much to give, endless abounding love.

Billie was aware of Thad watching her. At times there seemed to be a hard glint in those dark, watchful eyes, and at others there was that golden light she'd seen when he'd seen Sawyer for the first time. Sawyer! Good Lord, here she was a grandmother, contemplating . . . contemplating what? Having an affair with Thad? Yearning for that gentle attention and tenderness she knew he had to give? What was it she wanted exactly?

Dinner over, Thad took her walking through the ornamental gardens across from their hotel. To suggest a quiet drink in his hotel room would be like putting out a fire with gasoline. Billie walked beside him, their shoulders touching, their fingertips brushing against one another. Suddenly Billie stopped and turned to Thad. "If you take me in your arms and hold me, I think I'll explode into a million pieces. And if you don't, I think my heart will break. Which shall it be?"

"I've always been good at putting the pieces together," he whispered hoarsely.

She slipped easily into his arms and rested her head against his shoulder. She felt so good, so right. This was not the first time he'd held her in his arms, but it was the first time he could feel her heart beating a staccato rhythm in tune with his own.

"Billie, Billie," he murmured, liking the feel of her name on his lips, the name he spoke only in his dreams.

She lifted her face to find his eyes, looking for answers to the questions her heart was asking. The moonlight caught that lovely oval and reflected the yearnings Thad found in his own heart. She was so appealing, this woman he loved. If he could never have another moment with her, he would remember this one—a moment out of all eternity and she was all that was appealing, this woman he loved. If he could never have another moment with her, he would remember this one—a moment out of all eternity that was theirs alone.

He found his voice, felt it rumble and tremble in his chest. "Darling, how long can we go on this way? I know you care for me—it's there in your eyes, in your voice when you speak my name. What's keeping us apart when we need each other so desperately?" Suddenly he panicked. Had he said too much? Would she reject him? Had he ruined what little they shared?

Billie lifted her hand and pressed tender fingers against his lips, stilling his words, fobidding any further declarations. Gently, sweetly, she rested her head against his chest and her words were spoken so softly that for a moment he thought he'd only imagined them. "Love me, Thad. Take me. I want to belong to you."

They found their way back to the hotel, clinging together like two children afraid to be lost to each other, fingers touching, hands holding, never losing contact with each other.

In Billie's room, surrounded by the dim glow from the little lamp on the bedside table, Thad's touch became more intimate, more demanding, hungrier, as he helped her out of her dress and smoothed the gentle planes of her shoulders and back. His breath was warm on her skin, his lips tender as they tasted each hollow and curve beneath his fingers. He lifted her face to his, kissing her eyelids, the curve of her mouth, lingering there and taking possession as he had only dared to do in his dreams.

Her hands were suddenly urgent on his clothing; she wanted to be closer to his flesh, wanted him totally. This was right, she knew; the rightness of it was singing through her veins. Thad knew it, too; she could feel it in his response, hear it in his voice as he whispered her name.

Lying beside him on the bed, close, so close she could feel each beat of his heart. Billie offered herself with love. It seemed as though she had been waiting her entire life for this moment, to hear him declare his love for her.

"I love you, Billie. I love you," he cried again and again, the words echoing from the chambers of his soul.

She needed to hear those words. She wanted Thad body and soul, complete with every kind of love he could express. And always, always, she gave all that she could in response. Her love was in the touch of her hand and in the softness of her kiss; it was there in the tremblings of her flesh and the yielding of her body. She welcomed him, this man who was so much a part of her life—more, a part of her being. Thad had shared with her, knew her joys and sorrows, her hidden thoughts and secret longings. But this was a new Thad, a different Thad; he was her lover, exciting her passions, lifting her desires, making their love everything she could ever want it to be. She knew she could spend the rest of her life exploring the wonders of this man who could love so softly, so unselfishly.

"I love you." They breathed the words together and moved in unison, each striving to give, to share, to make the other complete.

Thad poised himself above her, gazing down; her lovely

face seemed to hold an illumination of its own from the love-light within her. He kissed her mouth, the pink roses of her breasts, then began to move in command of her passions, still watching her until he became unaware of anything except the driving demands of his body and the welcoming heat of hers.

When he lay beside her, holding her tightly in his embrace, tears were burning his cheeks and he didn't know whether they were Billie's or his own.

It was late, almost midnight, when the telephone rang and brought the world back. Billie reached for the receiver. "Yes?"

Thad watched her face turn ashen and saw her white-knuckled grip on the phone. He waited, painfully aware that something terrible must have happened. Her body, which only a few moments ago had been warm and yielding, was now rigid and tense. "What is it, Billie? What's wrong?" he asked when she'd hung up. He had to ask twice before she turned to him.

"That was my mother. There was an air crash in Spain. There's every reason to believe Moss was on that plane, but he's not listed among the survivors. Seth suffered a stroke at the news. I have to leave."

Thad sprang into action. There was no time now to speculate on the cruelty of fate that this should happen now, when they were together, sated with their lovemaking and unburdened of their need to share and know each other's love. "Pack. I can fly you to Japan and from there you can get a commercial flight to the states. By this time tomorrow you'll be home. I've got to call the airport and have them ready my plane. Billie, will you be all right until I get back?"

"Yes. Do what you have to do. I'll call the desk and have them take charge of my trunks and ship them on later. Go along, darling, hurry, the children are going to need me. Especially Riley. Dear God, Riley!"

There were no trumpets to herald Billie's return to Sunbridge. Numb legs carried her through the massive oak doors and into the ominously silent house.

All the long journey home questions had pounded at her. Was Moss alive? Did the children know? Should she fly directly to Spain? How was Seth? God forbid, had anyone been callous enough to tell Riley before she could be with him?

The taxi driver who'd brought her from the airport placed

her carry-on luggage near the foot of the stairs and Billie quickly stuffed several large bills into his hand. She had been lucky to have found a cab to bring her all the way from the airport. After he'd tipped his hat and let himself out of the house, Billie's heels clicked impatiently on the hard tiles of the foyer and she shouted, "Motherrr!"

It was several moments before Agnes appeared from the back of the house. "Billie! I'm so glad you're home. Why didn't you call to have the car meet you?"

"That's not important. The plane was early. Has there been any word?"

"No news since I spoke to you. I have everyone working on it. Moss's name appears on the passenger list, but aside from that, we don't know anything. If the Spaniards are as haphazard as the Mexicans who work for us," Agnes said disapprovingly, "I imagine it's mass confusion over there. Perhaps later today . . ." Her voice trailed off and Billie looked at her sharply.

"How is Seth?"

"Resting comfortably. There's not much to be done, according to the doctors. He refuses to go to the hospital. I think you should go up and see him. Now."

"Later, Mother. The children?" She held her breath.

"They know nothing. It seemed senseless until we have confirmation."

Billie breathed a sigh of relief. At least she could be grateful for that. "Mother, had Seth heard from Moss while he was in Europe? How do we even know he was on that flight?"

"We don't! Moss called Seth several times and supposedly his last stop was Spain and from there he was flying home. I'm afraid we have to brace ourselves for the worst, Billie."

"Mother, exactly what did Moss say to Seth when he called? Did he give an outline of his itinerary?"

"Only that he was flying home via Spain and that he expected to stay over in New York for a few days before coming home." Agnes's eyes glittered with speculation. "I think you should go up and see Seth right now. He's very weak, Billie. The will seems to have gone out of him, and the doctor refuses to give us a prognosis. What's wrong with you? What happened in Hong Kong? You're different, somehow," Agnes accused. "It's as if you don't care about what's become of Moss."

"Don't be ridiculous. Of course I care. But this is no time

for me to fall apart. You go and see Seth. Tell him I'm home and I'll take care of things. Tell him I'll be up when I . . . when I do what I have to do."

Agnes stared at her daughter but obeyed her. It was something to do. Much as she disliked the sickroom and Seth's frail dependence upon her, it was better than being here with this strange Billie.

When Agnes was out of sight, Billie headed straight for Moss's study. She swallowed hard and opened Moss's private drawer where he kept his address book. Her hands fumbled with bourbon flasks and the box of cigars. The packet of letters was still there. Without hesitation, she read the top envelope and noted the postmark. A few days before Moss had left for Europe. She settled herself, opened the letter, and read it. Her face showed no emotion when she folded the perfumed stationery and replaced it in the pretty envelope. She slid the drawer shut with her knee, picked up the phone, and dialed.

The voice at the other end of the line was warm with sleep— or was it lax with drink? Billie didn't know and she didn't care. Her words were cold and full of venom. "You son of a bitch! Couldn't you at least call your father when you returned to the States? Or when you changed your travel plans? The plane you were supposed to be on has crashed. You are not listed among the survivors. Haven't you heard it on the news? Or have you been too busy? Seth's had a stroke, Moss; he's desperately ill!"

Billie listened a minute, then said, "Personally, I don't care much what you do. Your father might, however. Good-bye, Moss."

Billie's breath exploded in a loud *swoosh*. Something deep inside her had told her that Moss couldn't be dead. She would have known, would have felt something. Billie leaned back in Moss's chair, hands pressed to her temples. She loved Thad; she knew she did. It was a mature love, a woman's love. But would the girl in her ever stop loving Moss? Even now, there was a part of her that mourned this betrayal and grieved for her broken dreams.

Slowly, Billie reached for the phone. A migraine was hitting like a lightning bolt. She rang for the overseas operator. "Thad? I'm home. . . . I'm fine. Really I am. I just have a headache. I haven't seen Seth yet; Mother says he's resting but that his condition is serious. Moss is alive. I've just spoken to him.

He flew back to New York early. Fortunately, Mother was less than her usual take-charge self and didn't tell the children. Thank God for that. All the way home I was terribly worried about Riley. You know the way he adores Moss.... You're not to worry about me. We'll all be fine and I'll write in a few days. Thank you again for getting me to Tokyo. And Thad? Thank you for Hong Kong; I'll never forget it. Never."

At the silence from the other end of the line, Billie squeezed her eyes shut against the engulfing pain. She felt Thad reaching for her across the thousands of miles that separated them, tender fingers of love stretching over the distance. She knew he was waiting for her to say something more, but she also knew this was a luxury she must deny herself. She loved Thad deeply, but all the long way home on the plane she had grieved for Moss, the man who was her husband and the father of her children. Regardless of everything, even her love for Thad, Billie knew without a doubt that Moss was still a part of her life and always would be.

Thad's voice was a deep rumble of choked emotions that tore at Billie's heart. "Good-bye, Billie," he murmured. "I'll see you when I get back to the States."

"Yes, Thad. I'm counting on it. Good-bye." When she heard the connection break, Billie added with a tear in her voice, "Good-bye, darling Thad."

Billie climbed the stairs to Seth's room with difficulty. In the end she was forced to plant both feet on each step as she pulled herself to the top. The adrenaline that had raged through her, making her shake with unexpended energy, was gone. She was exhausted.

How fitting, Billie thought, that Seth should be confined to the same bed that had held Jessica prisoner for so long. It was almost divine justice. She walked into the room and stood near the bed, waiting for Seth to recognize her. Suddenly, Seth had become a very old, very frail man, a pathetic invalid. Agnes, who had been sitting with Seth, eyed Billie as if to agree with her daughter's observations. Then she quickly retreated, glad to be gone from the sickroom. Agnes poised outside the door, listening to Billie speak, marveling at her cool tone. There was authority there.

"Seth? It's Billie. I've just arrived home."

"Why'd you bother to come back?" he slurred. He was

difficult to understand, but there was no mistaking the resentment in those glittering hard eyes. "You should've been with your husband!"

Billie understood. What Seth really meant was that she should have been the one to die. "I didn't come to argue with you. I came to tell you that Moss is alive. He's in New York."

Seth shook his head in disbelief, his lower lip began to tremble, and a tear formed in his eyes. "You're lyin' to me, gal."

"Someday, Seth, you're going to call me by my given name and speak to me with the respect I deserve." She snapped up the phone from the bedstand and dialed the operator, giving her the New York number. "Your father would like to hear your voice," she said coolly when Moss answered.

Seth clenched the receiver in his hand with surprising strength. Billie helped him position it close to his ear. The raw emotion on Seth's face and the disbelief in his trembling voice was terrible in a man to whom emotion meant weakness.

"Son?" she heard him choke through his tears.

Billie stumbled from the room. Hearing Moss's voice again had knocked the wind out of her sails. She nearly bumped into Agnes, who asked, "Is it true? Really?"

"It's true. Believe it."

"Was he with that woman? Again?" Agnes persisted.

"Yes, he was with 'that woman.' Don't start on me, Mother. I don't want to hear how if I was a better wife, Moss wouldn't be the bastard he is. I'm not responsible for his actions, and hard as it is to believe, I am not accountable for his infidelities. Now I want to see Sawyer. Is she in the nursery?"

"Poor Seth." Agnes wrung her hands.

"That's right, Mother, poor Seth. All you've ever worried about was that I'd somehow fall out of favor and deprive you of the Coleman dynasty with all its prestige and power. Well, save your pity for yourself, Mother. Seth is not going to recover from this stroke and I know exactly who is going to take care of him from sunrise to sunset. You've bought yourself that honor, Mother, with all your little betrayals of me and the children and your self-serving alliance with Seth. Before long, Mother, you'll be looking for a little pity for yourself."

Billie turned and headed toward the nursery.

Rain drove against the Cadillac limousine windows and beat upon the roof. The distant crack of thunder reminded Moss of rifle fire. He was glad not to be driving today; it would have been impossible to keep his mind on the road. A jagged streak of lightning zipped overhead, making him shudder. A good old Texas rainstorm, bigger than life, punishing the open plains. Pap hated storms. The old man complained that they made the cattle skittish, but Moss knew storms were one of Pap's secret vulnerabilities. The other was himself.

Pap was getting old. He used to be tough and able to take anything in his stride. Oh, Billie had told him how Seth had grieved when his plane had gone down during the war and they hadn't known if he was alive or dead. But this time the old man had caved in. A stroke. Good God, a stroke! And it was all his fault. One lousy phone call and all this could have been averted. All of it. But he'd canceled the last of his plans because Alice had had some free time between plays and hadn't wanted to spend it alone. He'd whipped through Amelia's London house yelling good-bye to his sister and Susan. Susan had smiled limply and walked away as though to say she'd expected him to miss the recital she was giving at the London Conservatory of Music. Damn it, how could he have been so selfish? Alice Forbes would have waited; she always had. Just like Billie always waited. Billie. In a way, it was all Billie's fault. Her and her selfishness. If she'd traveled with him as he'd planned, there would have been no rush to get back to the States.

It suddenly occurred to him, for the very first time, that he could have been on that plane, that he and Billie could have been killed. The thought was horrible. But then he amended it. No, they wouldn't have been on that plane, because Billie would have insisted on staying in London for Susan's recital. Yes, he nodded, it was all Billie's fault. Her selfishness, her sudden attempt at independence, had driven him straight into Alice Forbes's arms.

It seemed a lifetime since Billie had called him in New York. How had she known he was there in Alice's apartment? Or had she just been doing a kindness by calling Alice to tell her about the plane crash in Spain? Would they have cried together? Tried to give solace to each other? The thought cheered him.

Before Moss climbed from the limousine he whispered a prayer. He didn't know exactly what to expect or how serious Seth's condition was. He knew in that instant he would gladly have gone down in that plane if Seth could have been spared.

Pap had to know he'd give his life for him. By God, he'd make Pap know and understand. They were father and son, and that counted. By God, it counted!

"Pap!" Riley called excitedly. The boy threw his arms around Moss and smothered him with a hug. As always, Moss was amazed at how tall and muscular the boy was. Chip off the old block.

"How's your grandfather?"

"Cranky." Riley grinned. "He doesn't like being kept in bed, but he can't move his left arm or leg. Grandmam says he's coming along. You'll make him feel better, Pap. He's been waiting for you ever since Mam told him you weren't on that plane."

Moss studied his son, looking for a judgment in his clear blue eyes. How much did he know? Would Billie be so cruel?

Riley seemed to read the questions in his father's eyes. "I'm glad you weren't on that plane, Pap. Real glad. Grandmam told me that was why Grandpap had his stroke, 'cause he was so worried about you. He loves you a lot, Pap, and so do I," Riley said shyly. He was unused to professing his feelings toward his father. It was something both of them understood and accepted.

"What else did your grandmother tell you?" Moss asked casually. "How's your mother?" If either one of them had told Riley more than was necessary, there'd be hell to pay. He would not allow them to deprecate him in his son's eyes.

"That's all Grandmam said, that it was all a big mistake and that I should just forget about it and try to help Mam as much as I could. Mam doesn't need me, Pap. She's taking care of everything. But Pap, Mam's different. She's not the same anymore. I can tell. I think she got real scared hearing about the plane and thinking you were on it. She's different."

Moss's heart pounded. "How's that Riley?"

"She...she's keeping herself busy, answering the telephone and taking care of Grandpap. She lets the nanny take care of Sawyer all the time, and she hasn't even been out to her studio since I came home yesterday afternoon. That's not like her, Pap. She smiles but she isn't really smiling. Do you know what I mean?"

"I think so. Where is she now?"

"I think she's reading the paper to Grandpap. I was up there, too, but I got hungry. Do you want something?"

"I could use a sandwich and a cold beer, if you think you can make it."

"Pap, I'm not a little kid anymore. D'you want me to bring it up or will you eat in the kitchen with me? Grandmam gets upset if we carry food about the house. Bugs."

"I'll be down to join you. You go along. Don't open the beer or it'll go flat."

Moss climbed the stairs slowly. Normally he took them two at a time, but today it seemed he could barely make one foot follow the other. He dreaded this first meeting with his father. Billie, too. Riley had said she was reading the paper to Seth. That meant the old man wasn't too badly off, didn't it? Drawing a deep breath, Moss strode into his father's bedroom.

Billie lifted her eyes from the newspaper she'd been reading Seth and turned to face Moss, her voice trailing off in mid-sentence. Sensing another presence in the room, Seth opened his eyes. A lopsided grin stretched across his face; his right arm reached to the prodigal son. In an instant, Moss had grasped his father's hand and was huddled over the bed.

Billie turned her head so as not to witness Moss weeping in Seth's arms. Her lip curled with disgust, as much for herself as for Seth's blind acceptance. What right had she now to hurl accusations, when she was just as guilty as Moss in betraying their marriage and the commitment to their family? She glanced at her husband kneeling at his father's side. For all his tears and grief she knew he would never change. He would continue living his life exactly as he wanted, as it pleased him. And if she herself were to do the same, where would that leave all of them; the children, the family?

Quietly, she laid the newspaper at the foot of the bed and walked from the room on lifeless limbs, knowing she was embarking on a lonely voyage. Her life was here at Sunbridge and she was doomed to it.

CHAPTER
{{{{{{{{{ TWENTY-EIGHT }}}}}}}}}

Things at Sunbridge changed quickly after Seth's stroke. With the doctor's permission, Seth was moved downstairs and the study was converted to a hospital-workroom. File cabinets, a desk, a high bed with removable sides, and a tray of medicines were the new and prominent furnishings. All the leather furniture and heavy draperies were removed to the cavernous attic to gather dust. In the far corner of the room stood a gleaming wheelchair with a dustcover. Seth refused to use it.

Agnes reveled in her new responsibilities. While she "checked" with Seth and Moss pretended to oversee her activities and decisions, they all knew it was barely more than a courtesy. Agnes Ames was now totally in control of Sunbridge and loved every minute of it. She loved hearing the respect and admiration in people's voices when they proclaimed that they didn't know what Seth would ever do without her. She loved attending board meetings and issuing Seth's orders as though they were hers alone, or altering Seth's instructions to suit herself. Agnes loved power and for the first time in her life she held it—and guarded it closely. What she didn't love were Seth's demands on her and her time. When Seth demanded a cup of coffee, he wanted Agnes to bring it to him. A servant would not do. He liked having the paper read to him, and this she did resentfully. She was at his beck and call twenty-four hours a day, whenever he banged on the wall with his cane, and she hated it. But this was the price for her new position—so with a smile plastered on her face, she tended his bidding and tried to focus on the rewards her efforts brought her.

But it wasn't enough. . . . Late at night in the privacy of her room, in total darkness, she wished for the old man's death and for the guts to change her name to Coleman. If only she could have those two things, she would be the happiest woman on earth. Power and money. That's what it always came down to.

Six weeks after Seth's stroke, Agnes was sitting in his room, her well-coiffed head bent over a stack of papers. Her shoulders were tense, her writing small and cramped, not her usual flowing style. She could feel Seth's eyes on her back and knew he was trying to figure out something for her to do—some nasty errand to take her away from the things she loved doing, like balancing the ledgers for Sunbridge Enterprises. The total at the end of the columns always brought a smile to her face. She did love totals. Her own bank books, she reflected, were so full and round that she sometimes had trouble grasping the number of zeros. Once it had actually made her dizzy—dizzy with delight. One day she would pack her bags and take off for a trip around the world. The whole world with no clocks, no time schedules.

At the sound of her name, Agnes pressed harder on the pencil she was using and broke the point. The tiny piece of lead skittered across the table. Ulcers. She could feel them beginning to form in the pit of her stomach. That cantankerous old man lying there with his damnable silver-handled cane was giving her ulcers. She turned, a pleasant smile on her face. "Yes, Seth, what can I do for you?"

"You can talk to me, is what you can do. I'm sick of looking at your back. I'm damn sick of this radio, and I'm even sicker of this bed. What's going on? Is Riley coming home today? When was the last time you saw that son of mine and what was he doing? Where's your daughter? Locked up in that piss-ass place she calls a studio? Why hasn't anyone brought Sawyer in to see me? For God's sake, Aggie, I thought you had things in hand. This is all too much for you, I can see." Seth fixed his watery gaze on Agnes and defied her to answer him.

Too much? She hated it when he made statements like that. He could still cut her out, change things right out from under her. He still had the power. As the days wore on it was getting harder and harder to be pleasant to this cranky old man. "I could move the desk around so you wouldn't be looking at my back. Would you like that?" Agnes asked agreeably.

"No, damn it. Why don't you get me a drink?"

"Because you are forbidden to have alcohol. And don't think for one minute that if a nurse is brought in she would give it to you. It's for your own good. Blame your doctor, not me.

Riley will be home this evening, to answer your question. I have not seen Moss for three days. I think he went to Arizona. At least that's what the cook said. Your son doesn't see fit to confide in me these days. My daughter is in the studio, as you well know. Sawyer is with her companion. If you like, I'll have her brought down, but she's about as cranky as you are today. Her nanny said she had an earache. She whines and cries when her ears hurt. Now, what else can we talk about? Would you like some tea or coffee?"

Seth snorted. He should have known better than to ask Agnes anything. She always had an answer. "How're thing going? How was our profit on that last shipment of beef?"

Agnes beamed. "Splendid!" Seth believed her. Few things could make Aggie smile, but money was at the top of the list.

It took more than a year of intensive physical therapy for Seth's speech to return almost to normal. Now, when he was tired or cross, his mouth would droop and he had difficulty swallowing his saliva. Agnes considered this distasteful and made every effort not to be in his presence when it occurred. But by the end of the second year the cranky old man had made enough progress to slide in and out of his wheelchair. "Get goin', Aggie," he'd demand. "I want to see my spread!"

Agnes hated it. She would push Seth around the grounds, detesting her old ally, detesting what had become of her life. The damnable chair was motorized, but the old man refused to utilize it, preferring Agnes's "devotion" to duty.

Nine long years passed. At first, Agnes didn't really notice Moss taking control of some bookkeeping chores, discussing certain business decisions. She was even relieved to have some of the burden lifted. Gradually, though, she realized that Moss had taken almost complete control, and that she was spending more and more time at Seth's beck and call. She didn't like it. Not one bit! She had given her all for the Coleman family. When was it going to be *her* turn to reap her reward—to travel?

It was September 2, 1966, Riley's twenty-first birthday. Hard to believe, Agnes thought, that almost a quarter of a century had passed since she'd first come to Sunbridge. She prepared to leave early for the country club to check on the decorations and the menu. Seth had instructed her to make this evening as perfect as possible—as if she would do anything less. Riley Seth Coleman was her insurance policy against a cold, bleak, unfriendly world . . . and she never forgot it.

Moss and Riley were to take Seth and his wheelchair in the big car; Billie and Sawyer were to go alone in Billie's car. Maggie, if she got off in time from New York, would arrive at the club straight from the airport. Agnes sniffed. *If* she arrived, she would no doubt spoil the party altogether. Maggie hadn't changed, not really. Although a woman now and working in the historical art department of some minor New York museum, she still had that bitter, childish pout about her mouth, and those same hostilities glowered from the back of her eyes. Agnes didn't like Maggie; she never had. Maggie was a threat, stirring up old feuds and buried feelings. As far as her grandmother was concerned, she had absolutely nothing to recommend her.

It was Agnes's responsibility to carry all of Riley's birthday presents to the country club. The young man was certainly going to be surprised when he opened the little box from his grandfather, which contained the keys to a new Porsche sports car. Moss's gift was the title to a Piper Cub single-engine airplane. Agnes couldn't help wondering what Billie was giving her son. How could she possibly outdo a car and an airplane? Agnes herself hadn't even tried; she'd gotten him a subscription to an aeronautical magazine. Then, at the last minute, she'd bought him a leather billfold and stuck a crisp one-hundred-dollar bill inside.

Another week and Billie's last chick would leave the nest to return to college. Now only Sawyer remained. Agnes made a promise to herself, as she checked the flower arrangements on each table, to try to repair her relationship with Billie. Now that the family was dwindling, there was no reason for them to lead such separate lives.

This little shindig, as Seth called it, was setting him back close to twenty-five thousand dollars. She secretly thought it was rather cheap, considering that two bands and a cocktail hour were part of the flat package the club offered. Shrimp flown in from the Gulf of Mexico, lobsters delivered from Maine just hours ago, and Coleman beef would serve the five hundred or so guests. A real Texas shindig.

Just thinking about it made Agnes wince. What would she be able to eat? she wondered. Her ulcers were spoiling her life. She practically lived on gruel these days. And all because of that damnable, cranky, demanding old man called Seth

Coleman. Once Riley went back to college, she was going to do some serious thinking. She still had a lot of years left, and it looked as though Seth did, too. She knew in her gut that ten more years of waiting on Seth would drive her into the grave. She wasn't getting any younger, while he was the same miserable, cantankerous old man he'd always been.

Susan Coleman hung her dress in the closet exactly one inch from the garments hanging on either side. The neat closet always pleased her. Everything should be neat and tidy. Her life was like that in many ways, she reflected. It seemed to make things easier when everything was in its proper place and well ordered.

Auntie Amelia and Rand were forever taking her to task about it. "Let up once in a while, Suse," Rand teased. "You're becoming so . . . so sterile." She'd been offended by his choice of words, but she hadn't argued. What was the point? It was her life and she would do as she pleased. Then Auntie Amelia had told her that the lack of passion in her life was affecting her work. That had hurt; any criticism of her music hurt. But she had smiled and placated her much-loved Aunt with promises to relax a little.

Susan glanced at the little clock on her beside table. It was nearly time to call Riley and wish him a happy birthday. She was almost sorry now that she hadn't attended his party, but it would have cut several weeks out of her life, weeks away from her music and from Peter—and Jerome, too, of course. Besides, she disliked traveling.

Susan tied the belt of her dressing gown with precision. This particular shade of ice blue flattered her fair complexion and cool blond prettiness. She preened before the pier glass, straightening the belt so that the knot was correctly centered and the ends were the same length.

A steady hand with short-clipped nails reached for the phone to place the call. Thirty minutes, she was told—not enough time to go downstairs and brew a pot of coffee and not enough time for a leisurely soak in the tub.

Susan frowned, resenting this loss of precious time; she didn't like it when things did not go according to plan. But she should have realized that it was still a part of the business day in Texas and that transatlantic calls would take time. Thank goodness she'd placed the call person to person. If Riley wasn't home, there'd be no danger of having to speak to anyone else

{ 408 }

in the family. Except for Mam none of the others would really want to talk to her anyway, but she would do what was expected, regardless.

Her eyes were drawn to the telephone again, this time her thoughts on Peter Gillette. She'd left the handsome assistant conductor of the London Symphony Orchestra only two hours ago. He was probably home by now. Home, with his wife and two children. A familiar throb of misery touched her at the thought. Only when she was with him, held fast in his embrace, lying beside him, was she able to forget he was a married man.

She'd never known that passion could be so wild and uncontrolled. Peter had shown her and Susan had been a willing pupil. She loved him, desperately, but his wife would never agree to a divorce and his celebrity would thrust the affair into the spotlight. The thought of a public scandal frightened her.

Everything about Peter was wild and exciting and cluttered. He was cluttered with a wife and children and disorganization. He lived for nothing but his music and love, he had told her. Of this Susan had no doubt, but surely there was more to life. Without her, he would forget to have his hair cut and would appear before an audience of thousands in shirts with frayed cuffs. These were the obligations of a wife, and while she took a certain small pleasure in looking after him, she hardly wanted to elect herself as Peter Gillette's caretaker.

They had so much in common; if only he wasn't so . . . She grappled for the word. Used. Yes, that was it, he was used, shopworn. Love—at least the love in her life—should be fresh and shining, untarnished. She'd suffered enough messiness during her early years at Sunbridge to last her a lifetime: Pap's infidelities, Maggie's pregnancy. . . . How could she consider getting involved with Peter, who would have to fight for a divorce, even endanger his career, in order to marry her? How much better, how much tidier, it would be if she had fallen in love with Jerome de Moray instead.

Jerome, concert violinist of genius talent. She'd met him last year during a tour of Italy and Austria, and he'd recently come to London to further his studies. Young, inexperienced, and terribly in love with her. Jerome was exactly the kind of man she wished Peter could be. Peter claimed Jerome's talent was adequate, but Susan knew he was jealous. Jerome was a classical virtuoso, and her talent combined with his could lead them to paths of glory in the music world. It seem like a storybook marriage, glamorous and romantic. No loss of reputation, no newspaper scandal; everything would be tidy and neat. If only she loved him.

Shy, beautiful Jerome, cloistered by his wealthy family and his love of music. She didn't think he'd ever been to bed with a woman; his violin was his mistress.

If love took courage, Susan thought wearily, she didn't have it. Loving a man like Peter took courage; loving a man like Jerome took compassion. One would cause tumult and disorder; the other would fit into her life as though he'd always been there. She sighed. One of these days she would have to make a decision, and she knew she would choose safety.

The telephone near her elbow shrilled. Quickly she snapped it up. "Riley! Happy Birthday!"

Billie laid aside her escritoire and began to reread what she had written to Thad. Time was growing short and she still had to apply her makeup. She would finish the letter after Riley's party. Thad would want to know how it went. She'd have some news of Maggie, too.

Billie met her gaze in the bathroom mirror. She didn't look all that different, only older. Thankfully, her figure was still slim, and her skin was clear—although she was using more makeup these days. Lord, where had all the years gone?

Billie rummaged in her work cabinet for Riley's going-away present. She hoped he would like the gift: she'd toiled over it for months. Her special present for her son, a painting of Sunbridge with portraits of all the family members looming over the spacious spread. It had been painstakingly rendered on blocked silk, and she'd spent hours selecting just the right frame. Riley would have a reminder of home to take with him. It had been painted with love and it would be given with love. It was small, no larger than an eight-by-ten photograph. The package was flat and easy to carry. Doubt assailed her as she walked back to the main house to see if Sawyer was ready to leave. What if he didn't like it? What if Moss and Seth deprecated her efforts? Her shoulders straightened. She would live with it, the way she lived with everything lately.

Secretly, Billie was glad that Riley was leaving. She had little to say about any decision that had to do with him. The young man lived a charmed life. Approval and admiration came easily to him, as did friendships and distinction. Inwardly, she believed that Moss's obsessive love could be Riley's undoing. She could see the burden her son carried trying to live up to the Coleman ideal.

In some respects the boy was different from the two powerful elder Coleman men. Riley had always returned love and affection. He'd been a wonderful brother to Maggie and Susan, never letting a week go by without writing them even when they didn't respond.

Once, late in the afternoon, Riley had come into the studio to talk with her. When he'd seen what she was doing, he'd appeared stunned and said quite openly that he'd had no idea she was so talented. His praise and approval had made her feel wonderful. Then he'd told her he feared he would disappoint his father and confided that he had terrible nightmares about it. She'd offered to intervene with Moss, but Riley had been adamant and confessed that he knew things would be different when he went off to school. He'd grinned and put his arms around her. "Thanks for not telling on me," he'd said softly. On that day, for those few minutes, Billie and her son had been close.

Sawyer was waiting by the front door, her gift for Riley in her hand. She hugged her grandmother and turned about to show off her first long dress.

Billie beamed down at the child and tousled her glossy chestnut curls. "You look so pretty, I'm going to have to keep my eye on you or some young man will steal you away. Right from under my nose!" She laughed. "I'm ready. Are you?"

"Grand, do you think Maggie will come? You said she promised." Billie saw the unspoken questions in Sawyer's hazel eyes, eyes that were so like her own.

"Do you want her to be there?" Billie asked.

Sawyer shrugged, pretending indifference. "It's just that I wish I knew her better. Maggie is such a mystery, just like my Nancy Drew books—you never know what's going to happen next with her."

"And Maggie is a book you'd like to read, is that it? Sawyer, darling, I've tried to explain Maggie to you and there are no more words left. I'm counting on her being there. She and Riley have a good relationship, and I don't think she'll miss his twenty-first birthday. I know she cares for you, darling, and of course she'll want to see you, but don't go getting your hopes up and expecting grand things from her."

"Am I like her?" Sawyer asked shyly.

No, darling, Billie wanted to say, you're nothing like Maggie. You're the sunshine and Maggie is the shadow. But Billie knew instinctively that Sawyer needed to connect, to belong, even in the most intangible way. "Yes," she lied, "you're very much like your mother. You have her curly hair and her talents for riding and swimming. And I think you'll be as tall as she is when you're full-grown.

"Now we'd best hurry, darling, or we'll be late."

As Billie drove along the highway with the fidgety but silent Sawyer beside her, she struggled with her ambiguous feelings toward Maggie. She remembered how she'd felt when Maggie had finished school in Vermont and returned to Sunbridge. Sawyer was almost four years old and Billie had feared the mother-daughter reunion. But her fears had proved groundless. To Maggie, Sawyer was just another insignificance of Sunbridge, a long-forgotten cry from a cradle in the nursery. At the time, Sawyer's love for Billie was so total that it made no difference to her how she'd come into this wide, beautiful world; the open-hearted, smiling girl won friends on her own merit, and her personality was so pleasing, her character so far above reproach, that everyone welcomed her eagerly into their midsts. But Sawyer was older now, and more susceptible to rejection. If Maggie ever built her hopes and then dashed them mercilessly, it would create a wound from which the child might never recover. Billie knew what rejection could do to a grown woman, much less a child. Moss had seen to that.

Moss. Her husband. She should have ended it all years ago. Why had she persisted in the fight to hold on to something that couldn't be saved? She had come to hate the word *commitment*. *Her* commitment, *her* sacrifices. Living as they did was a farce—she in her studio and Moss in the house or off somewhere near Alice Forbes or someone like her for weeks or months at a time. At least there was some sort of comfort in knowing that Moss couldn't be any more faithful to Alice than he was to his wife.

It seemed the only thing they had in common was the growth of their respective careers and interests. Moss's aviation company had grown to huge proportions; because of the growing conflict in Southeast Asia, fighter and transport planes were needed, and Coleman Aviation was being underwritten by government contracts to provide them. Once again Moss was sitting in the catbird seat, raking in the profits. The Colemans had the Midas touch; their timing was impeccable.

To Billie's surprise, the balance sheets showed her to be quite successful in her own right. Nearly four years ago, her small studio had been no more than a haven; it had provided solitude and a place to work. Then one day, quite by chance, one of the abstracts she'd given to a local art gallery on commission had interested a leading textile manufacturer. That interest had inspired Billie to forge ahead and establish herself as a designer. She'd unearthed the folio Amelia had compiled for her so very long ago, then made countless long-distance calls, to initiate the contacts and set up appointments prior to taking her first business trip back to New York.

That first trip had been an education. Gradually Billie had learned how to sell herself. Each item of her wardrobe—all "Billie" originals—had been tailored to complement the image projected by each of the companies with which she'd had appointments.

Those had been terrible days, Billie reflected, filled with self-doubt and anxiety. Pounding the pavement, braving rejection, waiting for hours at times in reception areas, only to discover that her appointments had been forgotten or would not be honored.

At her fifth interview with a leading textile manufacturer, Billie's vibrant designs had been enthusiastically received, and she had returned to Texas with orders for one-of-a-kind "Billie" designs. The contract had been small, but it had been a start, all she'd really needed to validate herself as a designer. Now nearly four years later, her work could no longer be considered a hobby; it was a business with deadlines and decisions. Table linens and bedcovers bloomed with her original designs, as did wall coverings and even her latest venture—silk scarves and needlework kits. Her signature was a bold, black *Billie* and was even a registered trademark. It gave her enormous pleasure to see that copies of her imagination and handiwork were carried by the prestigious Neiman Marcus and other leading department stores. Her original oils were in demand for gallery showings. The art and textile design world seemed to be at her feet. Billie still wondered what she had done to justify this success. How much was luck and how much was talent? Once she'd become established, it had been revealed that she was one of *the* Colemans of Texas. How much had that added to the interest she generated from leading manufacturers and designers?

In the end, she reminded herself of the early days—how

hard she'd worked, how persistently she had pounded the pavement. She was a word-of-mouth success and it had been hard-earned. Now she was Billie. Plain and simple. In her circle of work and interests no last name was needed. To the outside world she was an artist, a success. To the family, she was merely eccentric, holing herself away in her studio, preferring her own company to theirs—the original sin.

This was the part of the flight to Sunbridge Thad liked best—the last ten minutes before his descent. Looking down on the Coleman empire from on high gave a man a sharper perspective. Things looked smaller, less intimidating.

It was difficult to believe nine years had passed since his trip to Hong Kong. Nine years since he had held Billie in his arms. It felt as though he had put himself on hold, only to pick up right where he'd left off.

He was free now, unencumbered by his seven-year marriage, a marriage that Billie had encouraged him to consider. "Make a life for yourself, Thad. Don't wait for me. Love and be loved," she had told him. Somehow he had allowed her to convince him.

It hadn't been easy to find someone who could ease the hurt, but eventually Kate Harrington had entered his life. They'd been buddies, playing golf, competing at tennis, taking Solomon for long walks, in an easy, comfortable relationship that made no demands on either of them. He smiled to himself when he remembered his less-than-romantic proposal of marriage, her easygoing, laughing acceptance.

But the marriage had failed. He'd underestimated Kate's love for him, thinking she felt as he did, comfortable and easy, more companions than lovers, more steady and caring than passionate. He'd been stunned by her sexual demands and had obligingly tried to satisfy her, but he'd been unable to give her the love—the desire and the passion—that he still felt for Billie. It had been two years since Kate had divorced him.

The divorce had hurt, and even though he had come to terms with it, put it into perspective, the hurt would always be there, more distant and less poignant, but still there.

The sound of the Cessna's landing gear being released sounded like thunder in Thad's ears. A few more minutes and he'd be there. Sunbridge. Suddenly his shoulders felt lighter. Billie. Riley's twenty-first birthday. Billie.

Sawyer's eyes sparkled when she saw the decorations and the number of people attending Riley's party. The club was closed for all other activities, but it appeared all the members were in attendance anyway. Billie foced a smile onto her face and began to lead Sawyer through the crowd toward the family table. Should she put her present on the long table with all the others and hope it wasn't lost in the shuffle, she wondered, or should she keep it with her? In the end Sawyer made the decision. She bounded up to Riley and dragged him back with her to Billie. "Will you promise to open Grand's and my present last? They're the best. You'll see. Will you, Riley?"

"You bet I will, cricket. Let's see, yours has the purple bow and Mam's has purple paper. I'll remember. What's in it, Mam?" He grinned, shaking the box with curiosity.

"It's a secret," Sawyer chirped. "This is better than Christmas, isn't it, Riley? Did you ever get this many presents at Christmas?"

"No, squirt, I never did." Riley smiled brilliantly, the smile that warmed Billie's heart and reminded her so much of Moss when she'd first met him—when she'd first loved him. "I'm going to need help getting all these to the car when it's time to go home. Will you help me?"

"You bet!" Sawyer quickly agreed, looking up at him adoringly. Billie realized that Sawyer had the same warmth and charm that drew people to Riley. Charisma, they now called it. She knew that she herself had never possessed such magnetism, and she was proud of these two offspring of hers.

"Have you seen your grandmother?" Billie asked Riley.

"Yes. I believe she's over there somewhere with Pap." He indicated a crowd of people near the bandstand. "Mam, I want the first dance. Promise?"

"Promise. Sawyer, you don't have to stay here with the old folks. I see Arlene, Susy, and Patty over there with Cynthia. They're probably waiting for you. Don't get stains on your dress or get into any trouble."

"Grand!" Sawyer protested, embarrassed by her grandmother's admonition in front of Riley.

Riley laughed and put his arm about his mother, escorting her to the family table. "I think half of Texas is here," he said. "Pap does know how to throw a shindig."

"That he does. You should have seen the one he threw in

Hawaii. It would have curled your hair."

Riley grinned. "Mam, I've heard that story so many times I could give it to you verbatim."

Billie found herself grimacing. "I think you should start playing the guest of honor and begin to circulate. Mother is here and we can talk for a bit. It's your party, Riley. Enjoy it."

Riley kissed her on the cheek and disappeared into the crowd as Billie took a seat next to Agnes.

"You outdid yourself, Mother," she said tartly.

"Do you think so? I've had so many compliments and Seth is more than pleased. Moss said it's the most colorful affair the club has had in a long time. Riley is delighted."

"You can feel proud, Mother. This party will be a smash. Riley will have something to remember."

And then she saw him, on the other side of the room. How could she not have known he was here? How could she not have felt his presence? No one had told her. She should have been warned. Of course he would come for something so important. He'd always been fond of Riley.

Agnes's eyes narrowed as she watched her daughter, and she tried to focus on the person Billie was staring at across the room. Something was going on—she could feel the tremor that was building in her daughter. "Billie, are you all right? What's the matter? What's wrong?"

Without taking her eyes from the far end of the room, Billie answered her mother. "On the contrary, Mother, everything is fine. Wonderful, as a matter of fact. Excuse me, Mother. I see someone I know."

Thad Kingsley, dressed in impeccable navy blues, was searching the crowded room for some sign of Billie when he saw her coming toward him. Her eyes were as bright as stars and her smile was warm and welcoming. Billie. His Billie.

"Thad! How wonderful of you to come. No one told me. I'm so glad to see you."

Thad could feel the trembling in her body when he bent down to kiss her cheek. His hands were gentle on her shoulders and he was stunned when he felt the trembling subside beneath his touch.

"Billie, you're the loveliest woman here. Do you realize I haven't seen you for almost ten years? I should have written I was coming, but I wasn't sure I could make it. I didn't want to disappoint you. Besides, I love surprises. Do you?"

"You know I do. Have you spoken to Riley and Moss?"

"I've spoken to everyone in this damn room. I think the only person I missed is Agnes. Sawyer gave me a hug and called me Uncle Thad. I liked that. Is Maggie here?"

Why were they talking about family? Surely he had other things to say. "We'll clear the decks and then I can have you all to myself," Billie said boldly as she led him over to the family table, where Agnes was sitting with one of her numerous club friends.

"Mother, you remember Thad."

"Mrs. Ames, how nice to see you again," Thad said, holding out his hand. "It's been a long time."

Agnes froze in her chair. She wanted to tell Billie to wipe that silly smile off her face. When in the name of God had she last smiled like that? When had her eyes been this bright? Somebody should be handling this. She couldn't do everything.

"Admiral, how nice to see you. Yes, it has been a long time. Moss didn't tell me you were coming."

"Don't blame Moss, Mrs. Ames. I let it hang in the air. I wasn't certain I could make it, but I did."

"So I see," Agnes said tartly. "Moss is over there." She pointed to a knot of club members.

"I've already spoken to Moss and Seth. Riley and Sawyer, too. Now I'm going to steal Billie away for a while and take her for a walk. All these civilians make me nervous."

"I'll see you later, Mother," Billie trilled as she tightened her grip on Thad's arm.

Agnes watched them leave, then moved jerkily across the room to Moss and whispered in his ear. She was rewarded with a dark look as he excused himself from the cluster of people with whom he'd been talking.

"Why are you so upset, Agnes?"

"Don't you realize how this looks? Moss, I've never pried, but the fact that you and Billie aren't exactly lovebirds is no secret. I wouldn't be a bit surprised if she wasn't trying to give you a dose of your own medicine, if you know what I mean." She glanced meaningfully at Alice Forbes. "I told you it was a mistake to invite that woman."

"Agnes, I could hardly *not* invite her; she is a member of the club and everyone else was asked to come." Moss sighed. "Where did they go?" he asked.

"Outside, I believe."

Moss weaved his way through the throng of guests to the

verandah. There was no sign of Billie or a navy uniform.

"So this is where you are. Too many people inside for you, darling?" Alice Forbes asked playfully as she came up behind him. "My, my, aren't we glowering this evening? Looking for the little woman? I saw her going down toward the tennis courts with a tall, handsome admiral. . . . Darling, are you upset? I can't believe it! How long did you think the little lady was going to sit and wait for you to play husband?" She linked her arm through his and smiled up at him seductively. "Now come back inside and enjoy your son's party."

Moss looked at her as if he'd never seen her before, then slowly took his arm away. "You go in. I'll be in in a minute." Alice bit down hard on her lower lip. Surely he didn't still love that little snippet? No, Moss didn't love anyone but his father, his son, and himself. Immediately she felt better. She and Moss were two of a kind—in fact, the only difference between them was biological.

Moss sat down on one of the verandah chairs and lit a cigar. Thad Kingsley and Billie! His mind raced back over the years. . . . Why in the goddamn hell hadn't he seen it? All those letters, all those visits, all those phone calls. His gut churned and the smoke from the Havana made his eyes water.

Something—an instinct, perhaps—told him nothing had gone awry. Thad was too honorable; Billie was too honest. She would never betray her husband, certainly not with his best friend. They were old friends enjoying each other's company, nothing more.

He stubbed out the cigar in a tall urn and went back indoors. This was Riley's party and no one was going to spoil it.

CHAPTER
{{{{{{{{{ TWENTY-NINE }}}}}}}}}

The moon was full and shining brightly as Thad and Billie strolled arm in arm. Thad was intensely aware of her; her presence filled his senses. She was a heartbeat away, just beside him, beneath his touch. He felt like he was home again.

"It's so good to be with you again, Thad," Billie said, breaking the silence. "I was so sorry to hear about your divorce. I didn't quite know what to do, so I did nothing."

Thad flinched. "It's over now and we're each making new lives for ourselves. So many times I wanted to come here, to see you, to touch you, but I couldn't. I've missed you, Billie. Do you realize how long it's been since we've seen each other?" Thad groped for the words. "I tried to make a new life for myself with Kate, but it didn't work. It wasn't her fault. She's the one who told me I was a one-woman man and she's right. Do you know how long it's been?" he asked intently.

"Almost to the hour," she whispered, not daring to test her voice.

He laughed, a self-mocking, scornful sound. "We're so good, we two. We haven't seen each other for ten years, yet it seems like yesterday. Nothing's changed for me. I took your advice and it didn't work. So, here I am. Can we pick up where we left off?"

"We can work at it, Thad. We have been good people, and for too long. I was writing to you when it was time to leave for the party to tell you I'd come to a decision: I'm going to tell Moss I want a divorce. I can take care of Sawyer and myself. My business is coming along fine; we don't need the Colemans for anything."

Thad's heart leaped in his chest. Divorce. After all this time. "Are you certain, Billie? It's what you want?"

"It's what I want. The way things stand now in my life I'm just going through the motions. It's for me, Thad. What I want for me." She saw the love and relief in his face. He still loved her, wanted her, but he didn't want her to suffer the pain of a divorce merely on his account. If Billie reached out for what she wanted herself, she'd find him waiting.

"I really shouldn't be telling you this, since I haven't mentioned anything to Moss. With Riley's birthday and going back to college, it didn't seem right to spoil things. But I think it's time I started thinking of myself and what I want."

"Good for you, Billie. If I can help, if there's anything I can..."

"You'll be the first I call on." Billie laughed. "Wish me luck, won't you?" She reached out to touch his lapel, and his hand covered hers in a warm clasp. This was exactly the way it should be, she thought. He was there and he loved her, and he didn't need words to tell her. But she knew, without doubt, that when the time came to hear it, to know it, to have it said, he would speak his heart.

Thad's eyes misted. He was thankful for the darkness. "I want what's best for you, Billie. What makes you happy. Be sure in your heart, Billie. Be sure it's what you want."

Billie's eyes lifted, meeting his. There was a world of tenderness there, bridging the distance between them, waiting to be called upon, needing to be given freely and without reproach. "You're always kind to me, Thad. It's time for me to do this. And once I do, I'll be free and open to all life has to offer." She drew her eyes away from his, careful not to say too much, to promise too much. But there was joy in her heart and she could feel it emanating from Thad.

"Now that I've unburdened myself I think it's time to get back to the party before we're missed. Thad . . . I'm so happy you're here. I feel whole again."

"I love being here," he murmured in return. It was the closest they dared speak of love.

Four pairs of eyes were glued to the doorway as Thad and Billie walked back into the room. Seth glowered at them, angry and suspicious. Moss looked almost benign; his smile welcomed them, his best friend and wife, loyal to him and to all the Colemans. Agnes was worried. Did everyone see what she was seeing? Riley saw his mother enter the room with the man he called Uncle Thad. There was kindness and acceptance in Riley's smile. Mam deserved to be happy, and if Uncle Thad was the guy who could do it, more power to the both of them. "Go for it, Mam," he muttered. When they smiled at him from across the room, he gestured for them to join him. He felt no disloyalty to his father, only admiration for Billie. Moss had it all. Why shouldn't Mam have what she wanted?

They had just joined him when Riley noticed that Sawyer was staring at the front entrance. Maggie had arrived.

She looked wonderful; her sleek black silk suit was perfectly tailored to her neat shapely figure, her dark hair was stylishly pouffed à la Jacqueline Kennedy, and she even sported the tiniest of evening hats—barely more than a circlet of fabric to match her suit. Her eyes found him, centering on him as she drifted across the room. Beside him, Sawyer fidgeted expectantly. Please, Maggie, Riley implored silently, just smile at Sawyer; even a smile will make her day.

"Happy birthday, Riley." She kissed his cheek. "You're finally getting out from under the Colemans. Good for you!

This is a night I wouldn't have missed for the world." Then, turning, she looked at Sawyer. "You're taller," she said.

Unable to hide her joy that Maggie had noticed she'd grown, Sawyer pressed further. "Do you like my dress, Maggie? It's special for Riley's birthday."

Maggie's eyes flicked quickly over Sawyer's first long dress. "You don't even have to tell me who picked it out for you," she said, glancing at Billie. "It shows in each little ribbon and bow. When I get back to New York, I'll send you something *really* nice." Smoothly, with barely a breath between statements, she turned to Thad. "Is that a new stripe I see on your sleeve? Congratulations," she said brightly, offering him her cheek for his kiss.

Billie's joy at seeing Maggie again was spoiled by the sudden expression of hurt on Sawyer's face; she put her arm around the child's shoulder. "Hello, Maggie," she said quietly.

"Mother," Maggie greeted, almost as an afterthought, leaning to kiss the air near Billie's cheek. It wasn't until Moss turned and saw her that Maggie's eyes came to life. It was always like this, Billie thought. Maggie standing as though poised for flight, cheeks flushed, eyes hopeful, waiting for Moss's attention. She watched as Moss merely nodded and then turned back to his conversation. There it was—the sudden deadening of the eyes, the tiny bitter line around the mouth that so many mistook for sullenness. Now, Billie knew from experience, Maggie would snap at the first person who dared speak to her. Unfortunately, Agnes put herself on the firing line.

"Maggie! I wondered if you'd make it! It was getting so late."

"I told you I'd be here," Maggie snapped. "Not getting senile in your old age, are you, Grandmother?"

Agnes deflated like a punctured balloon. But she was at least partly responsible for some of Maggie's genes and quickly retorted, "I see you're still an admirer of Jackie Kennedy. They say imitation is the sincerest form of flattery. But really, Maggie, for someone who professes such sophistication, can't you develop a style of your own? Lucky for us that it wasn't Bess Truman you'd met at the White House!"

"Very good, Grandmother." Maggie barely smiled. "Now let's see, who was first lady when you were my age? Dolly Madison, wasn't it?"

"That's enough, Maggie," Billie interrupted. "I think you

look lovely. You always do. When next I come to New York, will you take me shopping?"

"Sure. Next time. Riley, why don't you go get me a drink? Scotch," she said pointedly, aware that all the others were drinking wine. "Make it a double, won't you?" When she noticed Billie's disapproval, she attacked. "You'll never guess who I ran into as I came in the door. Alice Forbes. I had no idea she was down from New York, did you, Mother?"

Thad broke in before Billie could answer. "That's a terrific band Agnes hired and I haven't danced in years. What do you say, Billie? Are your feet insured?"

Billie glanced at Sawyer, unwilling to leave her, but the child was already looking around for her friends. As though Sawyer were on the same wavelength, she said, "You go and dance with Uncle Thad, Grand. I see Arlene waving to me. Can I go?"

"I've got a better idea," Maggie trilled. "You stay here with Grand and *I'll* dance with Uncle Thad."

"It will be my pleasure, Maggie," Thad said uncertainly.

Maggie's eyes gleamed, challenging Billie. See, Maggie seemed to be saying, anyone can take your men away from you. Alice Forbes, your own daughter, anyone!

The party was in full swing when Riley looked around in awe at the turnout of people for his birthday. He would have preferred a simple family dinner with everyone in attendance. But that was being foolish; Pap would never allow his only son's twenty-first birthday to pass unnoticed. All this—the people, the food, the free-flowing drinks, a full orchestra— was an indication that society considered him a man today. Well, he wasn't certain he was comfortable with the role; he liked being a son, grandson, and brother.

Where was Maggie? He'd seen her a moment ago. Summer-blue eyes so like his father's scanned the room and he saw his sister at the bar. He began to weave his way to her side, stopping just long enough to smile, shake hands, thank people for coming. He was nearly there when Moss appeared from a knot of people and tried to draw him into the little crowd.

"In a minute, Pap. I just spotted Maggie and I don't want to lose her."

"C'mon, boy, this bash is for you. You can always find Maggie later if she doesn't get skunked and take off. And if she does, it's no loss."

Riley met his father's burning gaze, knowing he would

embarrass Moss if he didn't obey. Moss's friends were standing and waiting to see what the "chip off the old block" would do. But before the guest of honor could make a move one way or the other, Maggie was in his arms. "Congratulations, brother! Twenty-one . . . it's a landmark."

Relieved, Riley returned her embrace, murmuring, "Thanks, sis. Things were about to get sticky."

"Yeah," Maggie said softly. Poor Riley. She'd seen Moss deliberately put Riley in the position of having to choose up sides. It wasn't fair. She looked over her shoulder and saw her father glowering at her. Well, he wasn't talking to anyone now, and sooner or later he was going to have to acknowledge her.

"Pap, it's nice to see you," she said, and reached out to touch his arm.

Deftly, he reached up to straighten a tie that didn't need straightening. "Glad you could come," he said indifferently.

You bastard, Maggie thought angrily. She turned back to her brother. "I'll see you later, Riley. I want to talk to Mam and Uncle Thad. Doesn't Uncle Thad look terrific? He *always* looks terrific."

Riley gave Maggie a bone-crushing hug and another kiss. "I'll catch up with you later. Don't you dare leave until this is all over. I want your promise, Maggie."

"You have it," she said with false gaiety. "Enjoy yourself. This is your party." She waved once and was gone.

Riley was aware that Moss had hurt Maggie deeply. His eyes locked with his father's, and Moss could sense the disapproval. For a brief moment he was ashamed of himself. Then the liquor in his bloodsteam took over and with a wide smile he proudly displayed his son to his circle of friends.

Billie Ames Coleman filed for divorce on the first day of October, twenty-four years after marrying Moss. She joined Seth and Agnes at dinner to inform them of her action. Moss was out of town on business, but Billie decided to make the announcement anyway. Seth picked up his cane and swiped at the flower arrangement in the center of the table, scattering bits of crystal, flower petals, and emerald leaves. "Over my dead body!" he bellowed.

"If you want to drop dead over a divorce, that's your affair," Billie said coolly. "Personally, I think it's a little foolish. Why should you care? You never liked me from the moment I arrived here. You can no longer control my life. I'm forty-two years

{423}

old and I want what's left of my life for myself. Accept it, Seth, because in the end that's all you can do. Sawyer will go with me. You'll finally have your son to yourself. He's always been yours anyway. I never for one moment felt as though he were mine. You did that to me. You made me feel like that. Now you can have him."

"There will be no divorce in this family!" Seth thundered.

"There will be a divorce. Count on it, Seth. I filed for it this very morning."

"Then you'll damn well unfile it."

"No!"

"Yes!"

"You can't intimidate me anymore, Seth. I've had enough!"

"Billie!" Agnes's voice came out in a tired squeak. "What are you saying?"

"Mother, my mind is made up. I wanted to tell Moss first, in private, but he's never here, and I can't defer my plans for his convenience any longer. Save your breath. You can't talk me out of it. As far as I'm concerned the subject is closed."

"Little gal," Seth bellowed, "I'm telling you for the last time, there will be *no divorce in this family.*"

"Mother, the dinner was excellent. Enjoy your coffee, both of you. I'll be in my studio if you need me."

Outside in the cool, brisk air, Billie drew a deep breath. Seth had reacted exactly as she'd thought he would.

Inside the house Seth continued to rave at Agnes. "I'll boot her tail right out of here if you don't put a stop to all of this nonsense, Aggie!"

"Frankly, Seth, I don't think she cares. Perhaps you didn't listen, but Billie is prepared to leave Sunbridge. She's not a young girl anymore. I think we may have to accept it and go on from there. If you want me to leave . . ." Agnes let her words hang.

"Now don't go off half-cocked, Aggie. No one is going anywhere. Moss will smooth things over. So he hasn't paid too much attention to her lately and the little gal is miffed. Men are like that. I'll see to it that he does what's expected. You get that daughter of yours back in line, Aggie, and I'll make it worth your while."

"In what way?" Agnes asked lazily. It always paid to know these things in advance.

Seth pretended not to hear. "I will not tolerate a divorce in this family. I might be an old man, but I still control things around here. Moss will do what's expected. How does ten thousand sound?"

"It sounds fine, but I don't think there's anything I can do. I'm prepared to leave, if that's what you want. With my daughter gone I doubt that you would want me around."

"Stop talking drivel, Aggie. We both know I need you. You belong here at Sunbridge, just like that little gal. Riley is going to be mighty torn up about this."

"I don't think so. I rather think he's been expecting it. I know I have. Moss, too, when you get right down to it. You're the only one who is surprised. Things haven't been right for a long time."

"Since when are things ever right between two married people? You were married once. Was it ever right for you?"

"There were moments," Agnes hedged. "You can't make a life on moments, Seth."

"The hell you say! Moss will make it right or I'll know the reason why. Well, do we have a deal or not?"

"What if I fail to convince Billie?"

"You want it up front—is that what you're trying to say?"

"In a manner of speaking."

"Write yourself out a check. If the little gal doesn't step back into line, you give half of it back. Agreed? . . . Now what's wrong? You don't look as if you cotton to all of this."

"I don't, but money is money. It's agreed."

"What will make you perk up? A bonus? I know you love bonuses. Tack on another five if you convince her to drop this foolishness." This time Agnes did smile. Three more zeroes. No matter what the outcome, she couldn't lose.

Billie waited for Moss to come to the studio. The letter she'd left on his desk would surely let him know the situation was urgent. He was due back sometime around seven o'clock. Unless, of course . . .

No, she refused to worry. She would let nothing dim this wonderful excitement—she felt like a child on Christmas. Thad was her Christmas. She'd been so empty without him in her life these past years. It was fate that he should come to Riley's party. How was it possible he could still look the same, feel the same? He had tried to establish a little for himself by marrying and she was proud of him for that, but she was glad— oh, so glad—that he still loved her, had never stopped loving her. It was selfish, she knew, but she didn't care. The bond between them was stronger than ever. Soon, soon all those years of waiting and longing would come to an end. Whatever life might bring, they would face it together.

Moss tossed his briefcase on his desk and flopped down on his swivel chair. Christ he was tired. He hated Washington and all those damn officials who thought they knew what they were talking about. He goddamn well knew how to build planes—why couldn't those smartasses let him do what he did best? Why did they forever have to stick their noses in? He was going to have to talk to Pap about this.

Moss took his briefcase off the desk and noticed the square white envelope underneath. He opened it and read the short note from Billie.

Two minutes later, Billie let him into her cozy studio. She got right to the point. "I'd like a divorce, Moss. I was going to tell you earlier, but you were out of town. I told your father and my mother at dinner this evening. I filed this morning."

He'd known in his gut it was something bad. Somehow, though, he'd never thought of this. "Is it Thad Kingsley?"

"No, it isn't. Moss, we have nothing between us anymore. I don't want either of us to blame the other. It's over."

Over. She was saying it was over. She'd also said it wasn't because of Thad Kingsley. Billie never lied. God, a divorce. Pap must have taken the roof off with that one. "Why a divorce if you have no plans or there isn't anyone else?" How casual his tone was—almost as though he didn't care. But he did care; the threat of losing her made him want her more.

"I want to be free to do what I want. I want to be on my own. I want to see who Billie Coleman is. Can you understand that, Moss?"

"No. I know who you are. So do you. This is rather stupid, isn't it, Billie?"

"I was hoping you wouldn't take that attitude, Moss. I don't want to dredge up old hurts, old wounds. This is what I want and it's what I intend to have."

"I don't want a divorce," Moss said harshly.

"But I do. I mean to go through with it, Moss. I'm not going to back down."

"Are you trying to get back at me for all the hurt—"

"No! God, Moss, it's been so long since you've seen me for the person I am that you don't know me at all. I want this for me."

"What did my father say?"

"What you would expect. He said there would be no divorce in this family. I stood up to him . . . and I can stand up to you, too."

"Why don't we think about this for a while? I have to admit I wasn't expecting it. I need time to adjust to come to terms with it."

"Take all the time in the world. As I said, I already filed. I just wanted you to hear it from me and not your father."

"Billie, Billie . . . where did we go wrong? We had so much. How did it come to this?" Moss sighed wearily. He needed this. He really needed this along with everything else going wrong right now. Jesus, he was gong to have Pap on his neck, too.

"I don't know, Moss. I know I tried. But I'm too weary to keep batting my head against a stone wall."

"You are blaming me. I can hear it in your voice. You said *you* tried. You didn't say *we* tried. I did, too, damn it!"

"Not hard enough. We wouldn't be a divided family if *you'd* tried hard as *I* did. None of us has anything. Can't you see that?"

"Yes, I do blame you. I wanted this family united. I wanted you to feel as I did. You promised and you broke that promise. The one thing, the only thing I ever wanted you didn't give me. My family. Now, I don't need it anymore. I don't need you, either, Moss."

Moss stared at her. "Did you hear what you just said?" he said slowly. "Did you hear yourself?"

Billie walked over to the door and opened it. "I heard it; I also lived it. It's late, Moss. You'd better get back to the house. I'm tired."

Moss hated the sound of the bolt shooting home. He stood outside, a cigarette dangling from his lips. He stood there for a long time after the lights went off. How could it be over? It would be over when he said it was over. And he wasn't ready. He knew how to fight—and fight he would, for what was his.

Riley was glad the Thanksgiving holiday was over; he'd missed being at home with the family for the traditional dinner. But he'd had work to do, important work. He stared out his dormitory window at the effects of last night's snowstorm. It was going to be tough protest-marching against the military draft in weather like this. He hoped the media would still turn out to cover the event. Anne Marie Wolosky had said they would, and she always seemed to know how something was going down.

"It must be twenty degrees below zero out there," Riley muttered to his roommate, Mike O'Neil. "We're going to freeze out butts off out there."

"I know. I've got my long johns and two pairs of socks. Relax, Coleman, it's only for a couple of hours. We'll survive. This snowstorm is old hat to the news media and we'll give them something else to write about. It's worth the frostbite."

Vietnam, that unholy altercation on the other side of the world. Not many called it a war, but they would, Riley knew. It was still being called a "police action," Riley thought as he put the finishing touches to the placard he would carry: BRING 'EM HOME!!!

"It has its message." Mike grinned. "What d'you think of mine?"

Riley craned his neck to see the sign Mike was waving: I'M NOT GOING!!! "Is that your final word, O'Neil?"

"Damn right."

"Let's get going. The others are waiting and I don't want to have to hoof it over to the administration building. Creature of comfort that I am, I prefer to be warm until we get there."

The demonstration on the campus of Kent State University promised to be one of the largest launched yet; the media would have to carry it.

The march began peacefully enough and would have remained so if some rookie cop hadn't swung his billy club in frustration at the "rich asshole kids who had nothing better to do." Mike O'Neil took the blow on his left shoulder. The sound of his buddy's shoulder cracking drove Riley into a frenzy. He whipped about in the swirling snow and brought his sign down on the cop's right hand, knocking the club to the snow. Sara Fitz picked it up and brandished it in the air at the cop's partner. Riley shoved Sara out of the way and leaped on the cop, swinging wildly. A cameraman zoomed in on Riley's angry face as he pummeled the cop for all the world to see. All hell broke loose.

Mike O'Neil, his face contorted in pain, was handcuffed and shoved into a police car next to Riley.

"His shoulder's broken. Take his cuffs off," Riley pleaded. "We aren't going anywhere. Give him a break. Can't you see he's in agony?"

"Shut up and don't let me hear another word out of you. You're all scum. Draft dodgers are all scum."

"Think whatever you like, but please take the cuffs off him. Look at his shoulder if you don't believe me." For an answer, the officer laughed derisively.

"Save your breath, Riley," Mike muttered. "Look, if I pass out, don't hold it against me."

Riley stared at his friend. There was a bluish tinge around his lips and his face was ashen. The police wagon was warm.

"I'm not going to ask you again. Take these cuffs off my friend. Please."

"Shut up!"

Riley's brain whirled. Sometimes there just wasn't any other way. "My grandfather isn't going to like this," he murmured. The officer had to strain to hear him. "Neither is my father. When they get upset, a lot of other people get upset. Like police commissioners."

"I'm real scared." The officer grinned maliciously. These punks were all alike.

"You should be. My name's Coleman"—Riley paused— "just like the mayor's."

"Bellamy, check that kid's wallet," the driver said over his shoulder. Bellamy yanked Riley's wallet out of his back pocket.

"That's what it says. Riley Coleman." The police wagon ground to a halt and slid fifteen feet in the snow. "Should I take off the kid's cuffs?"

"Hell, yes, take them off. We don't need the department coming down on our necks. I've got a wife and kids to support."

"Take it easy," Riley warned. "Watch out for that shoulder. Jesus, can't you see it's broken?"

"Kid gloves, Bellamy. Wipe his nose, too."

"Good for you, officer," Riley snarled. "You okay, Mike?"

"Better . . ." There was a slight pause, then Mike slumped back against the seat, unconscious.

"He's passed out. You happy now?" Riley cried. "Let's get him to a hospital. Move it!"

"Get his cuffs off, too, Bellamy. Christ! I wish I were in Florida!"

"Oh, no, you don't. My cuffs stay on. You already read me my rights and arrested me. You're stuck with me. My buddy is something else. You get him to a hospital, and then you can book me. That's what you do, isn't it?"

"Then your grandpappy and your old daddy are going to

spring you. Get the hell out of this car. We'll take your buddy to the hospital."

"You pitch me out of this car and it's the last thing you'll ever do. . . . You're wasting time."

"He's right. This guy is still out. He don't look too good," Bellamy said coldly. "We can worry about this punk later."

An hour later, with the aid of a snow truck leading the way, the police wagon pulled into the emergency entrance of the hospital. Riley was pulled out of the wagon and a gurney with two white-clad figures rushed to help Mike.

"Riley!" It was Sara. Riley noticed she had a knot the size of a lemon over her left eye. "What happened?"

"Mike's got a busted shoulder. Anyone else hurt?"

"Devon has a fractured windpipe. Some cop caught him smack in the throat. He's in surgery. Betsy is having her arm set; it's broken in two places. Calvin is getting sewed up right now. He got a big gash in his cheek; his nose got tipped up a little, too. Those cops really came out swinging. We didn't start it—remember that."

"Hey, I was there, remember? Jeez, I hope Mike is all right. He didn't look good to me. These nerds handcuffed him."

Sara shifted the ice pack she was holding and sidled closer to Riley. "There must be a hundred reporters in the lobby. They're waiting for one of us to talk to them. Beats me what they're all doing out in this storm. I can't believe this happened. It was supposed to be peaceful. We all agreed that there was to be no violence, no matter what."

"It's hard not to fight back when someone is cracking your bones," Riley said bitterly. "Peaceful—bullshit! Who's going to do the talking?"

"I think you should. It will go a long way for our cause. Riley Seth Coleman of *the* Colemans. You game?"

A vision of Seth and Moss watching the evening news flashed before his eyes. And then another vision of his buddy's blue lips and ashen face swam before him. Sara was waiting. But it was the picture of his mother that decided him. "Okay, I'll do it. Give me a rundown on what happened after they shoved us in the police wagon." Riley listened intently as Sarah ran through the course of events. His agile brain sifted, collated, and filed the events in chronological order. He was prepared.

"The cops aren't going to want you to talk to the press. We might have to create a scene for you. All the reporters are at the front of the hospital. We're in emergency and that's at the back. They're going to want to take you straight to the police station."

"Hell, they wanted to boot me out of the car when I told them the mayor was my grandfather. When the press gets hold of the fact that I'm one of the Colemans of Texas, it's really gonna hit the fan. I had to do it," Riley said defensively. "They cuffed Mike and he couldn't stand the pain. They can't hold me for too long. Let me know as soon as possible how the others are. Deal?"

"You got it. I think Saul is our best bet. He's a charmer with the ladies. He's got a broken hand no one is paying attention to. Look at him—he's making a date with that student nurse. I'll have him get her to pass the word to the press. You stand tight and don't let them take you out of here till the press comes around back. Fight if you have to."

"Make it snappy. Here come those two cops now. How long do you think I can stall? I'm under arrest, in case you forgot." He watched as Sara hurried away to speak with Saul.

"Okay, Coleman, let's go, so your daddy can get some nice lawyer out of his nice warm bed to spring you."

"I'm not going anywhere till I know how my buddy is." Out of the corner of his eye he noticed the blond student nurse sprint down the hallway. All he needed was a few more minutes. Sara was sauntering over with Saul.

Riley held his one-man press conference in handcuffs on the steps of the emergency entrance. It was aired on the six o'clock news. The eleven o'clock news made it nationwide.

It was five o'clock when Agnes finally relented and allowed the servants to leave (now that the children were gone the live-in help had been replaced with dailies who left after dinner). However, Agnes had no intention of slaving away in the kitchen: she'd ordered all manner of food prepared when the snow had started to fall heavily.

"I think we'll all have trays in front of the fire," she said brightly. "The cook make a monstrous pot of black bean soup and we can have ham sandwiches. It's only fair, Seth. The help want to get home to their own families and the roads will close in another hour. Moss doesn't mind, and I called down to the studio to ask Billie to join us. Good hot soup is the best thing to eat on a day like this."

"The girl won't be able to find her way," Seth growled.

"For heaven's sake, Seth, the studio is only at the back end of the yard. I assume what you mean is you don't want her here since she filed for divorce. If that's the case, say so. I'll call her and tell her not to come."

"Tell who not to come where?" Moss demanded as he walked into the room, heading straight for the bar.

"I asked Billie to join us for soup and sandwiches." Her tone was defensive, something she hated.

"You letting this divorce throw you, Pap?" Moss asked sardonically. Agnes watched through narrowed eyes as Moss drained his double bourbon and poured another. If he kept this up, there would be an unholy row sooner or later. Better to call Billie and tell her to stay in the studio.

"You're damn right it's going to throw me. Colemans don't divorce. You slipped up, boy. I'm disappointed. Who ever heard of such a thing? Divorcing and socializing at the same time. How come she didn't up and leave like she said she was gonna do? How come our hospitality is good enough for her, but you aren't? Tell me that, boy."

"Leave it, Pap. Billie and I will handle our own affairs. That studio is hers. Sawyer is more comfortable here than in some apartment in town."

"The girl's in school all week. And when she is home on the weekends, she's off with her friends. Some logic," the old man snorted.

Hoping to divert the showdown she felt was coming, Agnes offered to turn on the television for the evening news. As she settled herself in her own soft, down-cushioned chair, Billie walked into the room, her head held high. There were two bright spots of color in her cheeks. "Billie!"

"Can I get you a drink, Billie?"

"Thank you, Moss. I'd love a glass of sherry."

"Seth says it's wicked out there. He was afraid you would get lost trying to find your way to the house," Agnes said nervously.

"Don't you mean Seth was hoping I *would* get lost? This house is lit up like a Christmas tree—all I had to do was walk a straight line. My feet are wet, though. You won't mind if I sit by the fire, will you?" She looked directly at Seth, who nodded curtly, not bothering to answer.

"Darling, I'll just run upstairs, and get you a pair of slippers. I don't want you catching cold. Pneumonia is nothing to sneeze at. Sorry about the pun," Agnes said, forcing a smile to her lips.

The fire hissed and crackled. Billie moved from the hearth and settled herself next to the snack table Agnes had set up by her chair. Soup and crackers and a cup of coffee would do it for her. She was dipping her spoon into the soup when her son's image flashed on the screen.

"What the hell is Riley doing on television?" Seth bellowed.

"That is Riley!" Moss said with his sandwich halfway to his mouth.

"For heaven's sake, it is Riley," Agnes murmured nervously.

Billie watched as the scene was played out on the small screen.

Five minutes later they all knew what Riley was doing on television. In a fit of anger Seth tossed his soup, the bowl, and his sandwich into the roaring fire. Moss's face was as stormy as the weather outside. Agnes sat slumped in her chair. Billie calmly finished her soup, then excused herself and went back to the studio, silently applauding her son. If he truly believed in what he was doing—and she felt he did—then more power to him.

She wasn't out the door when the phone started to ring. The Colemans were going to have their hands full. Poor Moss. What a blow to his pride.

When the eleven o'clock news went off the air, Agnes called Billie on the studio phone. "Seth was furious, absolutely livid. Moss called Riley a draft dodger and said he was shirking his duty. Seth and Moss went at it tooth and nail. I wish you could have heard them, Billie. I was so appalled I had to leave the room. What's come over everyone? I simply can't understand all of this. My grandson in handcuffs! He's free now. Seth called the family lawyer, but Riley wouldn't leave unless the others were freed, too. Wasn't that nice of him? He's at the hospital now, waiting to see how his friend Mike is."

Billie sighed. That was so like Riley. "Mother, what do you think?"

"I don't know what to think. I guess I have to admire Riley, standing up for what he believes in. But national television! We had to take the phone off the hook. Moss is downstairs as drunk as the proverbial skunk. Why did you leave, Billie? You're Riley's mother."

"I'm only Riley's mother when it's convenient for the others. What good could I have done? I'm on Riley's side. You don't think for one minute either Seth or Moss wanted to hear that,

{ 433 }

do you? Mother, I don't want Riley going to Vietnam. I couldn't go through all that again. I almost lost a husband to the other war. I don't want to lose a son. I don't care what they call him as long as he's safe. Why was Seth so angry? He doesn't want him to go, either."

"For embarrassing all of us by being interviewed in hand-cuffs. At least that's what I got out of it. When Seth gets in a rage like that it's difficult to tell what he's really angry at. He was raving at Moss when I came upstairs. Why do these things have to happen to us?" Agnes lamented.

Billie couldn't help herself. "Because, Mother, we're Colemans. We're news."

"If that's the best answer you can come up with, Billie, I'll ring off. Good night, dear."

"Good night, Mother."

Riley Coleman didn't go home that weekend or the next. He didn't leave the campus until he was certain Mike was well enough to fly east for a special operation. He managed with the aid of his friends to successfully avoid phone calls from his father and grandfather. He just didn't want to hear all the words, all the harangues he knew would be forthcoming. His mother was a different story; she understood. When he'd called her at the studio she'd told him to take it easy, not to worry about his father and grandfather. He sighed. At least she hadn't thought it necessary for him to leave school and rush home to defend his actions. Christmas would be time enough. By then everyone would have a cool head. He was counting on it.

{{{{{{{{{ CHAPTER THIRTY }}}}}}}}

The Christmas season at Sunbridge that year was dismal. The house was beautifully decorated, but it was Billie's studio that held the spirit of Christmas. Sawyer and Billie made handsome homemade decorations and hung them on a fragrant tree. They popped corn and hung stockings. Colorful gift-wrapped packages were everywhere. Pine cones burned merrily in the fireplace and gave off a tantalizing aroma as Billie and Sawyer drank hot chocolate in front of the fire. This place, this converted carriage house, was more of a home to Billie than Sunbridge ever was.

Lately, Billie knew, Sunbridge was divided. Agnes was finding one excuse after another to visit the studio. Seth was harder to get along with than ever. Moss acted the part of an outraged father—how dare his son associate with radicals . . . act less than a Coleman?

Billie could almost feel sorry for all of them. Seth, Agnes, and Moss were all unhappy. Riley was unhappy, too. Only she seemed to be moving in a straight line, taking things as they came.

It was three days before Christmas. Sawyer had finished her decorations by ten o'clock and was now in bed. When the doorbell shrilled, Billie ran to answer it before Sawyer awakened.

"Riley!" She embraced him in a warm hug. How good he felt. How good he smelled. Billie shivered as she pulled him into the studio and closed the door. "Take off your jacket and sit by the fire. Would you like some hot chocolate? With marshmallows?"

"Do you have some?"

"It's the only way Sawyer will drink it. Me too, for that matter. I'll just be a minute. Add another log."

Billie's hands trembled as she set the tray with cups and a plate of cookies from the big house. This was an unheard-of event. Riley never came to the studio first. He was evidently dreading the confrontation with his father as much as she was.

She waited until Riley had almost finished his chocolate before she asked about Mike.

"He's going to be okay. They're thinking of a bone transplant. He's back east now. I'm going to call him on Christmas Day to see how things are progressing. Mam, I had to do what I did. I'd do it again."

"I know that, Riley."

"Pap isn't going to understand. I've been avoiding him. I wasn't going to come home for Christmas, but I couldn't do that to you and Sawyer. I really wanted to go to New York to see how Mike is doing."

"It's time you stood up to both your father and grandfather. We can only hope they listen."

"Call Pap, Mam. Ask him to come down here now and talk. I sort of feel that this is neutral ground."

"Are you sure, Riley?"

"I'm sure."

"Do you want to talk to him on the phone?"

"No," Riley said shortly.

Moss picked up the phone on the second ring. "Moss, it's Billie. Riley is here. He'd like you to come down.... I can't do that. Riley wants you to come here.... I can't believe you're saying that, Moss. I didn't even know he was here till he rang the bell." Billie listened a moment, then hung up.

"He's angry. With both of us. He's not taking the divorce well, and I believe he's regarding this visit of yours here as betrayal. We'll wait awhile to see if he comes down. How about some more chocolate?"

"I'd like that, thanks. Mam...tell me—how do *you* feel about having a draft dodger for a son?"

Billie thought for a moment. "I think there are worse things in life. I think Vietnam is a senseless war, and the mother in me wants you safe."

"Mam, it has nothing to do with my personal safety. I don't believe in Vietnam. Our guys are being slaughtered over there. For what?"

The doorbell pealed, and both Billie and Riley jumped. Billie drew a deep breath and went to open the door.

There was no joyful reunion between Moss and Riley. Both looked to Billie as if they were squaring off to do battle. Billie's eyes were drawn to her son. The moment she saw the anguish in him, she realized that Riley would do whatever his father wanted.

"I'm disappointed, Riley," Moss said bluntly. "Let's not talk around and up and down this thing. What you did was wrong. It was sinful. I never shirked my duty. I never turned my back on my country. This country has been damn good to the Colemans and don't you ever forget it!"

"Pap, will you at least try to understand? Will you listen?"

"Not if you're going to give me that same old crap you gave those newspaper people. That hurt, boy. Your granddaddy almost had another stroke over that little performance."

"It wasn't a performance. It was the way I felt and the way the others feel. I still feel that way. We don't belong in Vietnam. And if you tell me we do, I'll tell you you just want to sell more planes to the government."

"That's enough, Riley."

"No, it isn't. I'm not afraid, if that's what you're thinking. I'm not a coward."

"That's the way it looks from where I'm sitting. That's the way other decent folks are looking at it. Jesus, in handcuffs yet. I had to do some fancy talking to get around that one. You *are* going to stop this, aren't you?"

Riley stared at his father. What had he expected? Love, understanding? Just like that his father expected him to stop—to restructure his thinking to the Coleman point of view. Out of the corner of his eye, he could see his mother wringing her hands as she followed the one-sided conversation.

Instead of answering his father directly, Riley turned to gather up his jacket. "Do you know what I wish, Pap? I wish I'd never been born a Coleman." Without another word, he left the studio.

Moss sat down in Billie's chair and dropped his head into hands. Billie wanted to go to him, but she stood firm.

"You were hard on him. Too hard, Moss. Why can't you try to understand?"

"Is that what you think, that I don't understand? I understand. He's afraid. Don't tell me you didn't think it for a minute or two yourself."

"Riley isn't a liar. If he says he isn't afraid, then he isn't afraid. He simply doesn't believe in Vietnam."

"Billie, he burned his draft card! Do you know what that means? Stop thinking like a mother for a minute."

"Moss, I *am* his mother and I'm simply trying to understand our son."

"You're condoning all of this, aren't you?" Moss exploded.

"I'm trying to understand! If you take that to mean I'm condoning it, then, yes, I am."

"Well, I'll never understand it, not in a million years. My son!" Moss said bitterly.

"Our son," Billie corrected Moss. "Why don't you go up to the house and talk to him? Talk to him like a father, not like the head of Coleman Enterprises. Don't spoil what you have with your son."

"Like I spoiled everything else. Isn't that what you were going to say next?"

Billie sighed. "Leave it, Moss. This isn't the time to air grievances."

But Moss wasn't to be deterred. "You remind me of Riley

now. Both of you; the girls, too. All you've ever done was bitch and gripe about the Colemans and the money. But not one of you ever turned your back on it."

"That's unfair, Moss. I never wanted the money. All I wanted was you."

"You had me."

"I never had you, Moss. You always belonged to someone else— Look, I'm very tired, Moss. It's late, and I would like you to leave."

"We'll talk again, Billie."

"It won't do any good."

"Nevertheless, I'll be back. I want us to have a nice Christmas."

"What makes this Christmas different from all the others? You never seemed concerned before. It's too late. Don't you understand? I'm going through with the divorce. Please, go to Riley—he needs to talk to you. You need to talk to him."

When the door closed, Billie wanted to cry. She sat in front of the fire, watching the flames shoot up the chimney. So many years had gone by. So much had happened. Her youth was gone; her children were grown. Her marriage was over—*by her choice*.

Perhaps this divorce action she'd initiated was a mistake. She shook her head, trying to clear her thoughts. What did she really want? What would make her happy? Moss's undying love? A bitter laugh escaped her. She bent over and tossed another log into the fire, then shifted her position on the comfortable sofa and curled her legs under her.

Love . . . that beautiful, intangible, fragile emotion. Where had it gone? It was still within her, she knew, but so deeply buried that resurrecting it would only cause more heartbreak and pain. No. Her marriage was over. Part of her would always love Moss. Part of her would forever cherish the dream. That's what she would mourn and grieve for—the loss of the dream. But it was her turn now.

Billie stirred and woke. For a moment she felt disoriented, then she remembered turning off the lamp next to the sofa where she'd been resting and realized she'd fallen asleep. The fire had become smoldering ashes. She shivered and wrapped her colorful afghan more tightly around her.

It was an hour or so till dawn, she surmised without looking at her watch—officially Christmas Eve. Thad always called on Christmas Eve or Christmas Day. This year it would be such a relief to talk to him. She had so much to tell him.

Christmas. A day to rejoice. If only there was something to rejoice about. Sawyer, of course. But little else. Billie sighed. Soon, after the first of the year, all of this would be behind her. She would move into the city and start her new life.

Shivering in the early-morning dawn, Billie tossed the afghan aside and added several birch logs to the fire. She sprinkled the fire with fragrant pine cones and then crept back to her nest on the couch.

Yes, one more week and she would be on her own for the first time in her entire life. Better make that two weeks, she amended, or even a month—apartments might not be all that easy to find. One more month. That sounded about right.

Moss raked his fingers through his hair as he stared at his son. "I can't believe all this nonsense you've been spouting to me for the past two hours. I send you off to school hoping to give you the best education possible and what the hell do you do? You turn into a goddamn radical....I expected more, Riley, a hell of a lot more," Moss said, taking a deep breath. Jesus, was he getting through to this kid? Was he absorbing what he was hearing, or was he being polite? "Well, Riley, what do you have to say for yourself? Are you going to force me to yank you out of that college and send you someplace where you can't get into trouble? Someplace like Notre Dame?"

Riley could feel his gaze drift. He'd heard it all before, perhaps not in those exact words, but he'd played and replayed his father's response over and over in his mind for weeks now, and he was tired. Tired of fighting, tired of making excuses, and damn sick and tired of being a Coleman, whatever the hell that meant.

"Riley, I'm talking to you. Are you going to answer me?... I want you to stop this foolishness and start acting like a man. We're all going to put this behind us and start fresh. You are not to ever shame us this way again. Do we understand each other, Riley?"

"Yes, Pap. Can I go to sleep now? It's almost morning."

"All right, Riley, go to sleep. We're going to have to go through this one more time with your grandfather and then we're going to lay it to rest. Are we in agreement?"

Riley's gut churned, but he nodded and tried to respond when his father put his arms around him. Something was missing. He wondered if it was Moss's love. By day's end he would know.

It was shortly after two in the morning when Riley crept downstairs and placed his presents beneath the huge spruce tree in the living room. He laid Maggie's and Susan's gifts on the side for Mam to take care of, propped up the notes he had written to everyone on the mantel, and then left Sunbridge. He walked to the main road and hitched a ride for Dallas. No sense going into Austin. The old man would only alert the airlines and have him yanked off and returned to the bosom of the family. He managed, with the aid of a friendly trucker, to get within a mile of the Dallas airport and from there he took a flight to New York under an assumed name.

Riley did two things that day. He visited his friend Mike and offered him all the encouragement he could. Then he called Thad Kingsley and talked for two hours.

Riley stood on the corner of Thirty-fourth Street and Seventh Avenue, his eyes searching the deserted streets for a taxi. He huddled into his sheepskin jacket and jammed his hands into his pockets, wishing he had thought to bring gloves. This was probably the first time in his life he was somewhere other than Sunbridge on Christmas morning. But that was another life, a long time ago.

A cab snaked to the curb. "Merry Christmas," the driver greeted him. "You're in luck—this is my last trip before signing off duty. If you're going uptown, that is."

"That's where I'm going." Riley rattled off Maggie's address and settled back on the cracked leather seat. He was grateful for the steamy warmth of the cab. "Merry Christmas," he said as an afterthought.

The cabbie made good time, gauging each successive traffic light perfectly. The streets were nearly deserted, only a few pedestrians coming from or going to church. The desolation was contagious and Riley slumped down in the seat.

Ten minutes later he was admitted into Maggie's apartment building by the doorman, and after a quick call to the penthouse apartment, he was permitted to take the elevator. She was waiting for him and as he stepped off the elevator he was in her arms. He could feel the trembling in her slim body . . . or was it his own?

"Come in. You must be freezing. Coffee's brewing. We'll

go into the den. I made a fire. When you called earlier I couldn't believe you were here, actually here in New York. Here, give me your jacket. What's wrong, Riley? Why aren't you at Sunbridge? Would you rather coffee or a drink? You look awful and I'm talking too much and asking too many questions. Sit. I'll be right back."

Riley slumped into the oversized sofa and looked around at the spacious apartment. In the far corner stood a Christmas tree, a giant evergreen trimmed from top to bottom with sparkling ornaments. Presents were stacked beneath the tree, and even from here he would tell which ones were from Sawyer. His throat tightened at the sight. Maggie alone, opening her presents by herself. How many years, when he'd been happy and involved with the family on Christmas mornings, had Maggie been alone?

"Here we are—coffee, juice, muffins, and bottle of brandy to go with the eggnog. I think we should toast the holiday. Whatever the reason, I'm glad you're here, Riley. I can't tell you how I've been dreading this day."

"Why don't you turn on the lights so I can see how that creation of yours looks.... My God, it's beautiful," he said as the giant tree came to life.

"Just like home, huh?" Maggie said proudly. "Let me tell you, it was no mean feat getting that tree up here. I don't even want to think about taking it down."

"What are you doing here in the city on Christmas? I always thought you went to Saint Moritz for the holidays. I called you before I remembered that."

"I don't think I actually ever said I went there. I alluded to it. So now you know my secret. I hole up for the holidays and cry my eyes out. I make myself a turkey dinner and I open my presents and then I cry some more. Then I make a few drinks, get blitzed, and go to bed. What do you think of that?"

"Not a whole hell of a lot. You could have come home, been with us. Mam always said something was missing when you weren't there. She missed Susan, too, but at least Suse always called on Christmas Day. You never did." There was no accusation in Riley's tone, only sadness.

"Could I, Riley? Could I really have gone home? I never belonged there and I don't belong there now. I'd be a guest. This is okay for me; it's the way I handle things. Listen, can you stay for the day? Have dinner with me? We can open my presents and I can tell you what I sent you and the others at

Sunbridge. We can have our own family day."

Riley nodded. He wouldn't spoil this day for Maggie for anything in the world. Later, he would talk to her about his decision. For now, he had to find the strength he needed to deal with sad Maggie and this particular Christmas. "That's a sweet offer, Maggie. You've got yourself a deal. With one stipulation. We don't talk about the Colemans or Sunbridge or Texas. . . ."

Maggie laughed, a sound of pure delight. "Or Mam or Pap or Sawyer or Suse or Seth and Agnes. Doesn't leave much, little brother. They're our lives."

"Not right now," Riley said firmly. "This is our time. Can you really cook?"

"Damn right I can cook. Come with me. I want to show you something." Riley followed Maggie to a large kitchen containing every modern appliance. On a butcher-block cutting table stood a monstrous turkey with its legs trussed together. "Fully stuffed, little brother. Wild rice and chestnuts. These," she said, pointing to a bowl, "are fresh cranberries. These are yams and will end up with marshmallow, butter, and brown sugar. This is fresh asparagus, greenhouse variety. We're having mince, pumpkin, and apple pie; take your choice. I baked them last night. Candy canes are on the tree, one for each of us. Did I forget anything?"

Riley's face showed his awe . . . and something else besides. "Damn you, Riley," Maggie cried, "don't you dare pity me! This is the only way I know to get through the holidays."

Riley took his sister into his arms. "Hey, this is me. I don't think I've ever judged you. I'm not judging you now. In fact, I think I'm one hell of a lucky guy to be here right now. Just think—I could be back at Sunbridge listening to Seth squawk about how he doesn't need another flannel shirt and hearing Agnes squeal over her latest piece of jewelry. . . . Sorry, I broke my stipulation."

"Listen, let's go sit in front of the fire. I want to hear all about what you do. This is some fancy pad, must cost a fortune in rent."

"The price is right."

"Maggie, where are your friends?"

"Here, there, yonder. Who knows? I usually start talking about going away around Thanksgiving. They all think I'm in Saint Moritz, too. This is what I want and it's my choice."

"We Colemans make strange choices, I'm discovering. By

any chance did you happen to catch my television debut? Don't tell me you didn't see it. The whole world saw it, according to Grandpap."

"God, Riley, I couldn't believe it was you! Handcuffs. That must have set Pap back a pace or two."

"Yeah, he thought I was crazy."

"Not me. I was rooting for you all the way. That took guts. I don't know if I could have done it."

"Are you telling me this doesn't take guts?" Riley waved his arm to indicate the empty apartment. "You've got more guts than me, Maggie, than all of us."

They drank coffee while Maggie finished preparing the turkey. They talked about everything and anything, each careful not to say anything that would wound the other.

"You can set the table and I'll get dressed, okay?"

"Just tell me where everything is and I'll pitch in and do my share."

"Right there in that cabinet. That holiday tablecloth is a 'Billie' original, by the way," she called over her shoulder.

When she returned a few minutes later, Riley gave an appreciative whistle.

"What do you call those things you're wearing?" he demanded.

"Hostess pajamas. It's for entertaining at home. Mam sent it to me for my birthday. It's probably the most beautiful thing I own."

"Mam's talented, isn't she?"

"Yes, she is. I don't think she knows just how talented herself. I couldn't touch this outfit for less than five hundred dollars even if I could find it in a store."

"Are you serious?"

"Yup. Mam has it. This is what she calls Blink Pink. It makes me feel good to wear it.

"C'mon, let's guess what's in all these presents. I counted them. There's twenty-six altogether. There isn't one from you," Maggie said pointedly.

"Yes, there is, but it's back at Sunbridge. Mam'll send it on. When I left I didn't . . ." Riley flushed.

"You didn't know you were coming here. I don't care, Riley. I'm just glad you did come. You go first. Guess what I sent you."

Riley kicked off his boots and squatted down beside Maggie. "A shirt. A tie. A new wallet."

"Wrong. It's my turn. This is from Sawyer. I'll bet it's a new hairbrush. She told me she had twenty-seven dollars to do her Christmas shopping and she had to buy seven presents."

"What did you send Sawyer?"

"I have a friend who's an art dealer. I had him get me a set of lithographs of planes from the *Kitty Hawk* to modern jets. I had them framed and sent. You know how crazy Sawyer is about flying and planes. Just like you and Pap. I hope she likes them. And I sent her a couple of books on aviation. And there's a sweater and new slippers and a few other odds and ends. She's growing up, she's not interested in dolls any longer."

"The Cricket will go up in smoke when she opens them. But then she'd love a lump of coal if you sent it to her, Maggie."

Maggie avoided Riley's eyes. "This package is from Sawyer too. It's probably a picture of her standing next to one of Pap's planes. She told me about it in her last letter. She was tickled when Pap took her to the factory one day. This one is from Mam and Pap. I think it's some kind of fur. It's your turn to guess about my present."

"Pajamas, socks, sweater."

"Wrong. My turn again. This is from Susan. She always sends me a wool sweater." The bell timer in the kitchen rang, interrupting Maggie's guessing game.

The hours flew by as Maggie and Riley talked and played, trying to guess what each gaily wrapped gift contained. Occasionally Maggie would take time out to check on the turkey. Finally, she returned from the kitchen in triumph.

"It's time. Get your appetite ready. You can pour the wine and I'll carry everything into the dining room. You carve. Do you think we should have some pictures of this event?"

"Sure. Get one of me carving. I never did it before."

"Well, you're the only man in the house, so you won't have any competition." In the kitchen, with the door closed, Maggie's shoulders slumped. All this forced gaiety on both their parts. It was wrong, all of it. Riley belonged at Sunbridge with the rest of the family. Something was on his mind—this was no casual visit. There was a kind of desperation in his eyes, as though he were clinging to her. For Riley, she would play the game, say the right things, act the way he wanted her to act. It was the one thing in life she had learned to do well.

An hour later Riley loosened his belt. "I'm stuffed. I don't think I ever ate this much. Keep talking, Maggie, or I'll fall asleep."

"You won't have the chance. We have to clean up and do dishes."

"That's women's work."

"Tough. You eat, you work."

Maggie cleared the table and Riley wrapped the leftovers and put them in the mammoth refrigerator. Maggie washed and dried the exquisite china and crystal, not trusting it to the dishwasher. He was enjoying himself; he was glad he'd decided to come here, not just for himself, but for Maggie, too.

"Riley, would you like to take a walk down Fifth Avenue to look at the Christmas decorations?" Maggie asked as she hung up her apron.

"No, I want to see you open your presents. That's the best part of Christmas. You and I are probably the oldest two kids I know." Maggie laughed and settled down by the tree. She was so pretty, this sister of his. So troubled. How often, he wondered, did anyone but himself see the vulnerability in her eyes.

"I'll open and you clean up the paper, okay?"

"Deal."

"Ah, I told you. A hairbrush!"

Riley watched as Maggie carefully stacked Sawyer's presents in a neat pile. The lynx coat from Mam and Pap was left in the box and carelessly pushed aside as well as Susan's blue wool sweater. He showed no surprise when Seth's emerald bracelet and Agnes's satin robe weren't removed from the tissue paper. A sparkling cocktail ring with more diamonds than he could count was placed beside Sawyer's gifts. He did not question the giver.

"Give up?"

"Yep."

"I sent you a liftime supply of Tootsie Rolls."

Riley burst into laughter. "I also sent you a lifetime subscription to *Reader's Digest*."

"Maggie, you didn't!"

"Yes, and I also sent the required tie, socks, shirt, sweater, and pajamas. Now, what'd you get me?"

Riley was laughing so hard the tears rolled down his cheeks. "A fifty pound box of M&M candies and lifetime membership in *National Geographic*."

Maggie began to giggle and then joined Riley on the floor laughing, rolling into each other's arms at the ridiculousness of their gifts. When the joy ebbed out of them the laughter became tears of poignant sadness. So many Christmases they'd missed sharing with each other. So many years distance between them. Thank God they hadn't lost each other, especially not now, when everything else seemed to be changing or gone. "Let me get some wine. We both need a little fortification," Maggie said softly, wiping the tears from her eyes.

"Yes, it's time we talked about why I'm really here," Riley said hoarsely, clearing his throat, choking past the lump of raw emotion that seemed to be stuck there.

Maggie curled herself into a ball in the corner of the sofa and listened intently as Riley talked.

"That's it. I just picked up and left. No one knows I'm here. What do you think, Maggie?"

"The sister in me says don't do it. I'm scared, Riley. But part of me says go ahead." That's the part that wants revenge on Pap, she thought, hating herself. The ultimate revenge for years without loving and sharing. Anything to spite Pap. "Do it, Riley," she said, hardly believing the words she heard coming from her mouth. "Do it."

Riley's enormous faith in human nature shone in his eyes. Because he himself was so good-hearted, so trustworthy, he could never see any meanness in others. Maggie was his sister and she loved him as he loved her. It was what he'd wanted to hear. "I'll do it. Quick, before anyone or anything can change my mind."

At that moment, a little piece of Maggie Coleman shriveled up and died. Then Riley grinned and her heart turned over. She felt as though she were saying good-bye, and it scared her. "Riley, dear heart, are you certain you want to do this?"

"Now you sound like Mam." Riley frowned. "You can't have it both ways, Maggie. Either you think I'm doing the right thing or you don't."

Maggie took a swallow of her wine. "Let's not bring Mam into this, okay? It's better to leave all of that alone."

"No, Maggie, we can't leave it alone. I never understood why you always give Mam a hard time. My God, Maggie, she loves you heart and soul."

"Well, she shouldn't," Maggie snapped. "She has no right. We were never close, Riley. She was never a mother to me. Someone else always did for me." There was bitterness in Maggie's voice. "When I got pregnant with Sawyer, that's when Mam decided to become a mother, but then it was too late. I was the only one never to have anyone. Mam had her art and she thought she had Pap. Pap had his work, his father, and his son. And you, Riley—you got it all, and there wasn't anything left for Susan or me."

"And you don't hate me?" Riley asked, tormented.

"I love you, Riley. I know I'm filled with resentment. I tried to fight the only way I knew how. I became pregnant and had a child and I was sent away. Now that child lives at Sunbridge getting everything I never had. She belongs there and I never did. What's the use?... Why are we talking about this?"

"You have to talk, Maggie. I want to leave here knowing you're all right."

"I'm all right. I can live with it. Suse is the lucky one. Everything falls into place for her."

"No, Maggie, you're wrong. Susan missed out, too."

At least she never had to worry about rejection. She has what she wants, her music and Aunt Amelia, who dotes on her the way Pap dotes on you."

"Maggie, I'm younger than you and Suse, but I could see that Susan was just as scared as you, only her fears took a different turn. Suse never had the guts to be a Coleman, to stand there with egg on her face and stare the world down. She doesn't want to be sullied... and we Colemans are certainly mucked up, aren't we?"

"We certainly are, brother mine, we certainly are."

"What say we drink this wine and get a buzz on? Let's forget about Sunbridge, Pap, and the whole damn state of Texas."

"I'll drink to that," Maggie said, clinking her glass against Riley's.

At eight o'clock in the morning on the day after Christmas, Riley Coleman enlisted in the United States Navy.

Billie heard the news from Thad two days after Christmas. "Thad, why didn't you stop him?" she cried. Not waiting for an answer, she rushed on. "Why? Why did he do it? He didn't even spend Christmas with us!"

Billie's sobs tore at Thad's heart. "The boy did it because his father expected it of him. He's not a coward, Billie. Don't ever, for one minute, think that about your son. I know that boy. I'm sorry he felt he had to enlist this way, but I'm not sorry he chose the navy. Only the navy would have satisfied his father. I'll do my best to look after him. He's a man now, Billie. We have to let him act like one."

"Did you speak to Moss yet?"

"No. I called you first. I knew you would be in the studio. I'm going to call him now when I hang up. Riley wanted it this way. You first and then his father. He told me to break it to you easy and to tell you he loved you and not to be angry."

"I am angry. Not with him, but with Moss. Oh, Thad, what's going to happen now?"

"Riley is going to distinguish himself like his father did. At least that would be my guess. It's done, Billie. I'm sorry I didn't call you as soon as I knew, he specifically wanted me to call today. You understand, don't you?"

"I'm not blaming you, Thad. I'm sorry Riley had to place you in this position."

"I'm not sorry. I'm glad he came to me instead of some stranger. I'll call you over the weekend. Take care, Billie."

Billie threw herself on the couch in front of the fire and wept. Riley, Riley, how could you do this? Dear God, keep him safe. Don't let anything happen to my son. Thad would watch over him. Thad would keep him safe, if it was at all possible.

Billie sat up and wiped her eyes. Crying wasn't going to help. Things had to be done.

The trek to the main house in the deep snow left her exhausted. She stormed through the front door, not bothering to remove her snow-caked boots, and strode into the library where Moss, Seth, and Agnes were talking excitedly. "It's your fault, the two of you!" she cried. A long, trembling finger shot out and jabbed at Moss's chest. "It's your fault, and you know it. I'll never forgive you, Moss. Why couldn't you just leave it alone? The boy would have come to his senses sooner or later. Damn you!"

"Hold on there, missy," Seth bellowed. "None of us like what the boy did, but we're gonna live with it. I have a call in to Washington right now."

Billie turned and caught the glittering look in Moss's eyes. Surely he didn't approve of what Seth was doing? Or did he? "Moss, don't allow this. Riley did what he thought you wanted. You must let him go through with it."

"Stateside, we'll keep him stateside. That's all Pap is going to do, Billie," Moss said in a resigned tone.

"It won't work! Riley is going to do what you did. He feels he has to prove himself to you. Forget your call, Seth, and leave the boy alone."

"Don't interfere, little gal. You don't belong to this family anymore. That divorce action you started ended any rights you have here at Sunbridge," Seth said harshly.

"How dare you! Riley is my son, too!"

"Go back to the studio, Billie," Moss said wearily. "We'll handle this. We'll do what's best for the boy."

"Will you, now. Well, we'll just see about that. I'm calling Thad. I won't have either of you interfering in Riley's life. You've already done enough harm."

"Pap is right, Billie. You have no say anymore. Go play with your paints and brushes."

"I always knew you were a bastard, but I didn't know you were cruel, too. God forgive you, Moss, because I won't!"

CHAPTER
{{{{{{{{{ THIRTY-ONE }}}}}}}}}

"It's settled, Moss."

It was a week after Billie's confrontation with her husband, and Seth had sent Agnes to fetch Moss to the sunroom. Alone with his father, Moss knew there was no need for pretense. "How? Where?"

"The day the boy leaves the Oceanic Naval Air Station in Virginia he'll be on his way to that speck in the Pacific."

Moss's eyes widened. "Guam?"

"What better place? There's no way the boy will ever find out either of us had a thing to do with this."

"And Thad?" How bitter his friend's name sounded these days.

"Your friend will do as he's told. He's a military man. He's used to obeying orders."

Moss frowned as he paced the spacious sunroom. "Riley isn't going to like this."

"Trust me, Moss. The boy will be flying, but he'll be piloting weather planes . . . or an occasional search and rescue flight—he'll like that. The thing is, he'll be safe, and as long as he's flying he'll accept his orders. The Naval Air Station in Agana is just the place for our boy."

"For some reason, Pap, I'm not reassured," Moss muttered. "I can feel a snafu coming up somewhere.

"Where's Kingsley now?" Seth barked.

Caught off guard, Moss had to admit he didn't know.

"It could be important. Agnes will know." Seth banged his cane on the floor and bellowed Agnes's name until she came hurrying into the sunroom.

"Seth, must you shout? I placed a bell right near your chair. All you have to do is ring it."

"I told you I feel like a cow when I use that damn bell. You're supposed to anticipate my needs," the old man said sourly.

"I do. You're just too cantankerous to realize it. What is it you want?"

"Do you have an address for that Yankee admiral?"

"He's on Sunbridge's Christmas card list. Do you want it?"

"Why do you think I asked you about it? Yes, I want it. Right now."

Agnes was back in five minutes with a leather address book. "Would you like me to write it down?"

"It would help, Agnes," Seth drawled.

"Hmmmn, Commander Fleet Air Western Pacific. Atsugi, Japan."

"Jesus," Moss said in awe. "The old boy is right up there, isn't he? Japan is a stone's throw from Guam in case you didn't know it, Pap."

"Moss, you're worse than a pregnant widow. Relax. Kingsley isn't going to interfere. Now let's just roll with this till the boy is on his way."

"And Billie?"

"As far as I'm concerned that little gal is no longer a Coleman. I don't owe her any explanations. If you're wise, you'll take the same attitude. In fact, I'd suggest you close in, Moss, or I might just yank the rug from under you."

Moss lit a cigarette to avoid looking into his father's eyes. Even though the blue-gray cloud of smoke made Seth's eyes water, he had to smile. He recognized the ploy—and knew he was still in control.

Back in his workroom Moss lit another cigarette. What did he know about Guam? Not much, really. He'd spent a day and a half in Guam once. It was green—that much he remembered—and humid, like Florida in midsummer. He recalled that the people were pleasant, always smiling. Riley could do worse. In the end he wasn't going to have much choice but to go along with things. At least the boy would be safe. He wouldn't be going to Vietnam.

At the thought of Billie Moss groaned aloud. Jesus, where was it all going to end? He ached for the old days, his younger days, when he didn't have to account to anyone or anyplace. Of late, the feeling that his world was coming down around him was getting stronger. He felt helpless, and he hated it.

His feelings were so mixed with regard to Billie. Should he try to palaver, to negotiate—risk making a fool of himself? They'd been apart for so long. This new Billie with her emancipated thinking was someone he no longer knew. Did he want to put forth the effort to try to make things work again? He didn't know. He didn't want to know, not now, not when his mind was full of Riley.

Three weeks later, Billie Coleman moved out of Sunbridge to take an overly large apartment in downtown Austin. It was a penthouse with two skylights and an outdoor balcony, and it was just what Billie had wanted. She'd signed a three-year lease and made arrangements to move her work materials and her personal belongings into the apartment within the week. Everything would be new, right down to Sawyer's bedroom furniture. Moss had been very generous with what he'd called her "going-away check." Whatever she wants, he'd told his lawyer; give her whatever she wants. Keep her happy, but drag out the divorce. Maybe, just maybe, she would come to her senses.

Work was going well. She had two orders for her designs and the promise of a third if she could fulfill her first commitments on time. She hadn't been this self-confident since the day she'd married Moss, and she reveled in the feeling. She was Billie Coleman, textile designer; she was also solely responsible for her granddaughter, a responsibility she had every intention of fulfilling. She was in charge of her life and would see to it that only good things came her way.

It was a new beginning.

Lieutenant Riley Seth Coleman left Oceanic Naval Air Station in Virginia on the same day his mother moved out of Sunbridge. For Riley it was a new beginning, too. Guam! The old man would have a bird when he found out. Unless of course he was behind the written orders. Riley didn't think that was likely, though, and in the end he'd let it go. He and Adam Noble were going to Guam to fly P-3 weather planes and a few search and rescue flights. At least these planes had Coleman instrumentation in them—some of them were no doubt Coleman planes. That would give both his grandfather and father a kick.

He admitted to Adam Noble on the long flight to Guam that it wasn't what he wanted. The folks would be happy, though. What could go wrong flying a weather plane?

"I want to know what we're going to do with our free time," Adam said. "I hear they roll up the roads at five P.M. I don't think Guam is in the social book of records."

Riley grimaced. "We might like it. We aren't going to be all that far from Tokyo. Hawaii will only be five hours away. We have to look at the bright side of things. I brought plenty of books for the long hot nights."

"Good for you, Coleman. While you're reading I plan to explore and meet some of the locals. I've heard the girls are beautiful."

"And well protected." Riley laughed. "You're liable to have a duenna after you. Give it some thought. Besides, we're not supposed to mess around. You know that."

Adam's blue eyes sparkled. "I never forced a girl to do anything she didn't want to do. I think I can handle these sloe-eyed beauties."

"And their mamas," Riley reminded him. "You're a long way from the San Fernando Valley, Adam, and they play by their rules over there."

Ten days after setting foot on Guam Riley realized he disliked the humid island. The verdant foliage and lush tropical blooms made him homesick for sagebrush and rolling farmland. The rain depressed him. It seemed as though the skies opened hourly and warm, wet waterfalls cascaded down from the heavens. The roads steamed and the vapor rose to make him sweat like a Trojan. He itched. He perspired. He hated.

"C'mon, Coleman," Adam said one Sunday afternoon. "You're coming with me. I got you a date with a sweet thing, and if I have to boot your tail all the way to Barragada, I'll do it."

"Dust off, Adam. I'm staying here. I have some letters to

write. It would do you good to write home, too—the CO had a letter from your mama last week wanting to know if you were alive or dead."

"I'll write her tonight if you come with me this afternoon."

"Adam, I don't want to go. Tell the girl I got sick unexpectedly."

"Aren't you interested that I'm in love? This girl is different. I mean it, Riley, I'm in love. She loves me, too. I'm going to talk to the CO tomorrow about marriage."

"I don't believe it," Riley said in awe.

"I'm serious. Her parents aren't crazy about me, though. They're Chomorra, and I don't think they like Americans. I'm trying to win them over. Nita—that's her name—got you a date with a friend of hers, Otami. But that's not the main reason I want you to come along; I really want you to meet Nita. Will you do it?"

Riley sighed heavily. "All right, let me just slick down my hair and get some clean clothes."

An hour later, Adam swung the borrowed car into a rutted driveway that was overgrown with weeds.

A quonset hut was off to the left. Everywhere there were pots of flowers, some in bloom, others getting ready to bud. It was so colorful, so rich, Riley wanted to reach out and pluck one of the blossoms. His first thought was that the unseen Nita came from a poor family. Clean, neat, but poor. A dog barked and circled his feet. He bent down to scratch the animal behind his ears.

"If you say 'Good girl, Bo,' she'll be your friend for life," Adam said knowingly. "Here come the girls. Mine is the one on the left. Isn't she beautiful? That's Otami on the right."

Riley's cap was off in an instant. The vision walking toward him had to be the most beautiful creature he'd ever seen. Even her name was beautiful. Introductions were made. Riley shifted from one foot to the other, trying not to take deep breaths. Adam and Nita had already forgotten about him, intent on each other.

"*Hafa-adai*, Lieutenant," Otami said shyly. She was welcoming him to Guam, where the day begins. "Would you like to go for a walk?"

Walk? She wanted to walk with him. "Yes, I'd like that." He felt suddenly tongue-tied in her presence, too warm under the collar. Every word, every thought, had to be monitored so he didn't babble like an idiot.

{ 453 }

"Come along then, Lieutenant. Nita can't leave the house until her parents return from a Christening, but we can go for a short walk, and by the time we return, her parents will be home. I can show you a little of the village. You're in Ordat, by the way."

As she spoke, he listened to her voice, wishing she'd go on forever. Her musical, lyrical way of speaking intrigued him. Her accent was soft—at times the way she strung her words together seemed awkward to his ear—but the effect was foreign and exotic, and he loved it.

She was small and slim, the top of her head barely reaching his shoulder, but her figure was womanly; all the curves were in the right places. She wore a simple cotton dress, fashionably short above the knees, and on her narrow feet were flat-heeled black shoes. Her long straight black hair was knotted at the top of her head, and long feathery tendrils escaped here and there. In the sunlight the mass of ebony glinted with shimmering blue lights, and it looked incredibly soft.

"Do you live with Nita and her family?" Riley asked.

"No. We attend university together. I live down the road with my uncle. He was quite ill for a time and my parents wanted someone from the family to stay with him. At the same time they didn't want my studies interrupted, so I attend university part-time. I'll be going back to Tokyo when the term ends."

Riley missed her already. "That's not too far away."

"To me it is." She smiled. "I miss my parents and my friends. Where do you live, Lieutenant?"

"Texas. Near Austin."

"Do you miss Texas?"

Riley nodded. "Very much. I can understand your missing your home, but we have to make the most of it. We can always go home. Home will always be there. Please, call me Riley."

"Only if you call me Otami. You haven't said my name even once."

"Otami." He said the name almost to himself, liking the way it felt on his tongue, liking the sound of it in his ears. "What are you studying at the university?"

"Advanced English courses. I've done some translating for a publisher in Japan, but I'm mostly interested in journalism. My father owns a newspaper in Tokyo and I am hoping to work with him someday." She smiled. "Japanese fathers are very protective of their children. I think he would rather have me sheltered from the world. Naturally, he believes that one day I will marry and bless him with grandchildren."

"Will you?" He was panicked at the thought that there might already be someone who had spoken for her.

"Will I what? Marry or have children? Yes, I suppose I will." She turned up her chin to face him, her gaze almost a tangible touch to his face.

"Is there anyone special right now?"

Her smile was sunny and more than a little mysterious. "There may be, Riley. There just may be. Tell me about your family. Is your father the typical indulgent American father?"

Riley threw back his head and laughed. "If you ever met him, you'd eat your words. My grandfather would make you swallow them. There are some who'd say I've been indulged, but I've paid a hefty price." He thought of how hard he'd tried to please Moss and be worthy of all that love. "My mother is different, though. She loves just for the sake of loving, expecting little in return."

"As a mother should be," Otami agreed. "As my own mother is. It's wonderful to have two such people to care for you."

"Remarkable. Your hair is beautiful and your eyes are like black coffee." He half expected her to turn away or even to giggle. But Otami lifted her chin and stared up at him, pleasure coloring her cheeks and glowing in her eyes.

"And yours are like the skies of summer," she told him simply, truthfully. "My favorite time of the year."

"You didn't tell me if there was someone special," Riley said bluntly. He had to know.

"No. Do you have a special girl?"

"No." Until now, he thought. This girl was special from the top of her shiny head to the tip of her toes. There was a certain stillness about her—it was a trait he coveted. He himself always seemed to be churning and stewing about something.

"How do you like Ordat?" Otami smiled.

"Not as much as I like you," he said brazenly, wondering if he'd spoken too soon. Would she turn and run from him? Had he been too impetuous? She made a movement; he tensed. Suddenly she slipped her hand into his. It was small and soft and cool.

"Will you see me again? After today?"

"If it is what you would like."

"When?"

"Whenever you would like. My uncle is doing nicely now

and I don't have to spend as much time with him. You must come to our house, though. I cannot meet you here again; it is not really proper. My uncle would be displeased. He is a nice man, a fair man, but I must be honest. He does not like Americans, for what they did to Hiroshima."

"My father doesn't like the Japanese, for what they did to Pearl Harbor. During the war he was a prisoner and he's never forgotten."

"It is regretful, is it not? We must all live with one another in a world that seems at times too small. My father believes old wounds and old hurts must be put aside. Life goes on and we all endure, doing the best we can."

"Your father is a wise man," Riley said sincerely. "And he has a very beautiful daughter."

Riley lay awake for a long time that night. Was there such a thing as love at first sight? Was it in fact love? Or was it that this beautiful girl with the beautiful name was different from the other girls he knew? She was shy, but yet she wasn't shy, at least not when it counted. She was sweet and natural. She listened, she smiled, and she interjected her thoughts and opinions in a soft, melodious voice. And she wanted to see him again! He was in love. But if his father found out, he could ruin everything—get him sent home, away from this beautiful creature.

Well, I'm not going to allow that to happen, Riley thought. Not this time.

He'd have to keep this part of his life secret. Riley lay staring at the ceiling, his hands under his head.

Secrecy. He was good at that.

In the months that followed, Billie sensed a change in her son. A new kind of maturity, an empathy, came through his letters. Perhaps what he had needed was to get away from Sunbridge, away from Moss and Seth, even from her. It was as though he'd found himself, was seeing himself through someone else's eyes. She wondered about those eyes. Did they belong to a woman? Perhaps. Riley never said. She satisfied herself with being glad for him.

Her textile designs were in demand and she had licensed them through a very prestigious agency. Billie was happy in her work, happy with her quiet life. The only fly in the ointment was the divorce. The Coleman lawyers were doing everything, pulling every trick in their books, to delay a court action. Billie didn't think that Moss even cared any longer, although he called her once a week. He'd even taken her to dinner once or twice—to discuss the problems Coleman Aviation was having with the government.

She remembered her horror when he'd explained how they had demanded he step up production or lose the contracts altogether.

"And you're letting them do that to you?" she had cried. "Moss, our son flies planes manufactured in *your* company, and you're telling me they're not safe!"

"Take it easy, Billie. That's not what I said at all. The planes are safe enough; it's the instrumentation I'm worried about. There're some bugs that still have to be worked out, but the government won't allow the time for it. If I force their hand, they may give those contracts to someone who's not as conscientious as we are."

Billie had seen the pain in Moss's face, and she'd had to respect his judgment. Still, every time she thought of Riley and other men like him, her blood ran cold.

She'd thought of writing all this to Thad but felt it would be disloyal somehow. Besides, contact between them had dwindled. They still wrote, but there were longer and longer periods between letters. The last time she'd written had been to tell him that Susan and Amelia had come to the States for a concert tour, which had been very successful. Susan was a lovely young woman—blond and shining with serious eyes. Billie had been hopeful that they would stay in Texas for a time, wanting a chance to become reunited with her daughter. But Susan had been eager to return to Europe, where, it seemed, there was a particular young violinist who had put the glow in her eyes. Also, Susan hadn't wanted to stay at Sunbridge any longer than absolutely necessary; she'd been quick to perceive Seth's disapproval of her beloved Aunt Amelia and would have no one, absolutely no one, mistreat her.

Billie had conveyed their parting scene at the airport to Thad, since he was the only person besides herself who knew of Amelia's tragedy. At the last moment Amelia had thrown her arms around Billie, thanking her over and over again for allowing Susan to stay in England with her. . . .

"You'll never know how much she means to me," Amelia wept, "or how much I love you for sharing your daughter with

{ 457 }

me. Now, it seems, we're both about to lose her. This affair with her violinist seems serious. Our little Susan is a woman grown."

"You were better for her than I could ever have been," Billie found herself confessing. "Here in Texas it would have been second-rate music teachers and living down Maggie's reputation. I heard someone say once that our children are only loaned to us, that they're not ours to keep. I just relinquished her a little early, Amelia, and into the most loving arms she could ever know."

"I do love her, you know," Amelia said, brushing a tear from her eye. "In most ways I've been a lucky woman. I've had Susan and a loving stepson. I've told Moss he should write to Rand and invite him over for a tour of Coleman Aviation. They'd like each other and they have so much in common. Rand loves anything that flies and he's quite a genius with computers and physics and all that rubbish. He asks for you often, Billie. He's never forgotten your kindness to him when we came to Sunbridge for Mam's funeral." Amelia's eyes told Billie she would never forget it, either. "Oh, look at me, gushing and crying like an old woman! I suppose I'm not looking forward to the prospect of being alone once Susan flies the nest. I should have listened to you years ago and married again, but it seemed so pointless, since I could never bear another child. My wanton ways have caught up with me. I envy you, having Sawyer. I've always suspected you refused to allow Maggie to have an abortion because of what happened to me. You were right. I can't bear to think of this world being denied our bright-eyed little Sawyer. How is it you always make the right decisions?"

"I don't, Amelia. Don't ever think that. I've hardly ever been in control of my own life. But that's all changing now, and I'm glad for it. You don't suppose Susan will run off with her young man, do you? Moss and I would like to meet him."

"No, I don't think our daughter will deprive herself of a wonderful wedding with all the trimmings. Don't worry about her, Billie. She's making all the right choices. I suppose when next I see you it will be at the wedding."

"At the wedding, then," Billie agreed, and hugged Amelia tightly. "It will be nice for Sawyer to visit London. She's never been abroad."

The flight announcement came over the loudspeaker and Amelia reached for her carry-on luggage and turned toward the gate. "San Francisco, here we come!" she said gaily. "Send Riley my love; next time you see my brother give him a good swift kick with my compliments, won't you?"

"I'll do just that." Billie laughed and waved to Susan, who turned and blew a kiss to her.

"After San Francisco we're headed for New York," Amelia called. "Why don't you think about coming up and joining us?"

"I'll do just that!" Another wave, another kiss on the wind, and they were gone.

Riley Seth Coleman was in love. When he looked into Otami's beautiful eyes, he saw himself as he wanted to be: tender, gentle, manly. Otami's love for him was quite different from any he'd ever known, unselfish and undemanding. Theirs was a sharing, two faces shining toward the future, certain of endless happiness and togetherness.

Wonderful days and nights raced into weeks and months. They had committed to each other and wanted to spend the rest of their lives together. Riley proposed marriage to Otami four months after meeting her.

Dark eyes sparkled with tears. "I thought you would never ask me."

"Will you? Marry me?" Riley held his breath, waiting for her answer.

"We will have to face many problems, my love and I," Otami whispered. "The military will frown upon our marrying and may not give us permission."

Riley gathered her into his arms and buried his lips in the soft wealth of her hair. They sat entwined in each other's arms and watched the moonlight on the rolling surf.

He knew what she said about the military was true, but he had already determined that nothing, no one, would stand in their way if she would have him. "Don't worry about a thing," he reassured her. "I think I've got that base covered. I have this friend—I call him uncle—and he'll go to bat for me. It's your uncle that concerns me."

"He will not give his permission. I will have to go against him and my family."

Riley took another deep breath. He couldn't make her marry him; either she wanted him more than anything or anyone else, or she didn't. He waited, willing her to give him the answer he needed.

"I love you, Riley, with all my heart, for all my life. How

could I say anything but yes? Yes, I will marry you."

Riley touched Otami's chin and tilted her face upward to his. He kissed her deeply, little shock waves tripping through his veins at the thought that such happiness could be his. Otami was like an Oriental work of art, finely turned and created with beauty. So many times he had thought he'd be unable to control himself, that he must take her and make her his own. But always he remembered her words. "Lovers with true hearts," she had said, "bring honor to each other and their love. My body aches for you, Riley; my soul reaches for yours. But to claim a right that is not ours would dishonor us both. Please, try to understand." Now she would be his wife and welcome him into the garden of her desires, where they would find each other as lovers with true hearts.

"Otami," he whispered huskily against her cheek, "my heart has been yours from the moment I first saw you. You're my life. Remember that always. It may not be easy for you in the days to come. What will your uncle do?"

"He will cease speaking to me and then banish me from his house. I will no longer be his niece. My parents will be told and they, too, will lose face. If I marry you, I will bring disgrace upon them. It does not matter, Riley. I must live my own life and know my own heart. I can live with anything as long as I have you. In time, perhaps, my family will come to understand and approve. It has been known to happen." She smiled.

"I don't plan on informing my family—not right away, at least. Unlike your family, I'm afraid, they would insist on being involved. I can't see them disowning me, but I can guarantee a lot of grief. I'd rather do without their interference; there's time for that later. We'll have enough to contend with. I love you, Otami. There are no words . . ."

"No words are needed. Don't you understand, Riley? I know how you feel because it is how I feel. I will be whatever you want. I will do whatever you want me to do. We will have children and they will be raised in their father's way, in their father's religion."

Otami saw the frown on Riley's face. "Have I said something wrong?" she asked, touching his mouth with her long, cool fingers.

"Wrong? Never wrong," Riley reassured her. "I've never had anyone love me as you do, Otami. All my life people, my family, have given me things. Ponies, cars . . . airplanes, for God's sake! The only person who gave of herself to me was my mother, and then it was only what they permitted her to give. When I think back, I realize that for all their talk about family and closeness we were never a family in the true sense of the word. Everyone had a separate life, solitary ambitions. I don't know why and I suppose there were times when I wondered about it, but I don't do that anymore. You're my life now, Otami, and I want to keep it that way."

Riley gathered Otami close to him, resting his cheek on the glossy curve of her head, and looked out over the water. This was enough for him, he told himself, being here with the woman he loved and knowing she loved him in return. It had to be enough.

CHAPTER THIRTY-TWO

{{{{{{{{{{   *}}}}}}}}}*

Maggie Coleman heaved a sigh of relief when she affixed the last stamp of approval to the pile of paperwork littering her desk in Sandor Locke's prestigious art gallery. The remainder of the work requiring her attention would just have to wait. She needed a few minutes' break from sorting out the multitude of applications from artists, both well known and obscure, seeking a showing at the gallery. Each day it seemed she was busier and busier, with barely enough time to snatch a quick cup of coffee for lunch. She liked being busy; it gave her less time to think. Lately, however, she was beginning to wonder if she'd made the right choice in leaving her position at the museum to become the personal assistant to Sandor Locke. Working in this Fifth Avenue gallery was a plum of a job, and she knew she was envied by everyone on the staff. Sandor himself was the biggest, juiciest plum of all, and she had him right where she wanted him. The question she postponed facing was, What was it she wanted to do with him? It was the same old question that had plagued her entire life. Fight for what you want—kick, scratch, connive, manipulate, and do anything necessary to reach your goal—and then, when it was in your hand, you looked at it and realized it wasn't the goal you wanted but the challenge of reaching it. Maggie supposed it had something to do with being a Coleman. She didn't like living like this, but it was the only way she knew. "Go where the money is" was Seth's philosophy. Another of his ditties was "It's not *what* you know, it's *who* you know." How right he was. She'd dropped a few words here, a thought there, and Sandor Locke had come to her offering her the position at twice the salary she'd earned at the museum. She wished now that someone had told her ten-hour work days were part of the job.

Maggie leaned back in her chair and stretched her arms over her head, appreciating her newly decorated office, one of her first demands of Sandor. It was the perfect backdrop for her own striking brunette looks. The soft, plush earth tones were selected with care to show off the vibrant jewel colors she wore. The eggshell chair set off her glossy dark hair and honey-colored skin. If she owed anything to Billie it was her flair for fashion and her sense of color and balance; from Moss, his summer-blue eyes and ambition. Damn, why was it every time she tried to relax and enjoy her success thoughts of Sunbridge and the family would crop up? She should be over that hurtful stage of life. She was a woman now, with her own sense of worth. Sunbridge was behind her. She didn't live there anymore and hadn't lived there for years and years. Whenever she did go back, which was rare, she was a visitor.

It was a damn good thing she'd escaped, Maggie assured herself. Or had she been driven out? She felt the familiar dampness on her eyelashes. A visitor. She had to use the doorbell. She possessed no keys to the house. If only she had a key, perhaps she would feel as though she belonged there. Riley belonged there. Was that why she'd encouraged him to join the service? Because she was jealous that he belonged to Sunbridge and she didn't? Even though the letters she received from Riley expressed contentment it still niggles the back of Maggie's brain that she'd advised him to join the Navy more out of her own purposes than for her brother's welfare.

Regardless of how successful she became, no matter how high she climbed, it still wasn't enough. Something was missing. The sense of belonging, the sense of sharing in the closeness of a family. When was she going to accept that it was never there for her and put it all behind her? "The day I die," she muttered as she dabbed at misty eyes.

Deciding work was preferable to dwelling on memories, Maggie attacked the pile of applications with a vengeance. She sorted, appraised, and considered the stack of rejections grow-ing compared to the number of acceptances. Opening a folder of photographs of an artist's work, she was faced with an electric geometric design. Exactly what Sandor wanted to bal-ance the primitives he intended to display in early spring. It would be the height of the art season, and from these examples of geometrics and linears the showing would propel the artist's career into importance. She flipped through the photographs, appreciating the artist's sense of color and scale. But it was when several examples of textiles fell under her view that she turned back to the name on the application. Billie Coleman. Mam's agent had sent the folio and application without any idea that she was now employed by Sandor Locke and that a showing would rest on her own decision. A sense of power coursed through Maggie. She realized all too well that she could lift her mother out of the designer class and move her into the front-running category of accepted artists. "Well, Mam, paybacks are a bitch." The brilliant-hued designs were tossed onto the rejection pile. Maggie stared at it for a moment, the colors rioting in her head, her conscience pricking. Then, be-fore she could entertain reconsideration, she grabbed the folio and shoved it to the bottom of the stack. No, she couldn't allow Mam's work to hang for weeks in Sandor's gallery. Having to be faced each day with Billie's exhibition would create too strong a flow of memories. Maggie knew she was just not that strong emotionally.

She was raw enough now and she had to fall back and regroup and think things through again. Just last week she'd been lunching with Sandor when Moss walked into the restau-rant with Alice Forbes on his arm. Her initial response had been shock, and then the hatred settled in and she had glowered across the room at Alice Forbes with such intensity it was a small wonder the woman hadn't felt it as though it were a tangible thing and turned to face her.

It was then, when she'd looked back across the table at the slim, fastidious Sandor, that she realized he was actually her father in disguise. Charming, distinguished, and sophisticated, Seth would have called Sandor "slick." Even Agnes would have seen through to the cruelty beneath his layer of cosmo-politan charm. Sandor Locke, patron of the arts, wealthy, knowledgeable, and married. She herself was the Alice Forbes in Sandor's life and she didn't like it.

"Seen a ghost, Maggie?" Sandor asked perceptively.

"My father, Moss Coleman." She indicated the table where Moss and Alice were sitting.

"And the lady?" he persisted, clearly amused by Maggie's discomfort.

"Alice Forbes, the playwright. My father and she were childhood friends back in Texas."

"She is also an embarrassment I take it." Sandor refused to allow the subject to drop. There seemed to be more here than met the eye.

"Not to me, she isn't. She's just one in a long line of many. Only she's lasted longer. It's my mother who should be embarrassed."

"Do I detect an edge of bitterness, Maggie darling?" he said smoothly.

"Damn right I'm bitter. If my mother hadn't been so lily-livered she would have put an end to my father's philandering years ago and he would have been home where he belonged, being the kind of father he should have been."

"Why, Maggie, do you realize that in those few words you've told me more about yourself than you have in our entire relationship? This has been quite revealing."

Maggie's eyes glowed with fury. "Has it, Sandor? I didn't think there was much you didn't know about philandering husbands—being one yourself, I mean." She allowed her statement to settle on him, enjoying the fact that for once the suave, sophisticated Sandor Locke seemed to be at a loss for words. It was more than apparent he wasn't used to candor, especially where it concerned himself. "Thank you for lunch, Sandor. Can we leave now? I've an enormous amount of work waiting for me at the gallery."

"Certainly." Sandor peeled greenery from beneath a gold money clip, his brain whirring like a computer, sifting and storing facts. Maggie has said Texas. Coleman. Moss Coleman. Beef, oil, land, aviation, electronics, wealth, and power. Maggie was one of *the* Colemans. How interesting. He stored the information in his brain, knowing someday he might have to pull it out and look at it all again.

Leaning his elegant form against the frame of Maggie's office door, Sandor Locke quietly observed her as she rifled through the paperwork on her desk. She was going through an emotional turmoil; he could see it on her face. He knew she was so caught up in her thoughts she wouldn't have noticed him if he'd perched on the end of her desk. The yearning and regret in the summer-blue eyes startled him. He'd never quite seen that expression before now. Poor little lost black sheep. He was puzzled when he watched her shuffle a particular folio. Three times now she'd tossed it into a stack of others only to remove it. The sadness, the deep yearning, was replaced with bitter coldness when the particular folio was finally pushed to the bottom and covered with others. His eyebrows rose. This was Maggie's department, and she was very good at what she did. He wasn't about to ask questions and interfere.

Maggie Colman, and her flair and style, was a definite asset for the Locke Gallery. It was a lucky day when he'd heard she was interested in coming to work for him. He'd become quite fond of Maggie. She was an exciting woman and very attractive, with her honey skin and night-black hair, and more, she possessed a wit and natural charm that made her welcome into exclusive social circles. When she'd casually mentioned over cocktails one day that she was looking for a new apartment, he had come back with the offer to let her use the penthouse of the Locke Building while the owner was in Europe. At least that was the story he had told her. It was really his own apartment, which he reserved for private moments away from his wife and children. It was a wise man who didn't tell Maggie Coleman everything. It wasn't at all difficult for him to recognize certain traits in her that he possessed himself. She was sly, calculating, and manipulative. It wouldn't surprise him in the least if she'd known all along that the apartment was his. They had been enjoying their affair for almost a month when she had asked for a two-year lease. He had laughed. "Your rent is free. Why do you need a lease?"

"Because, Sandor, you're just like me. One day you'll wake up and say, 'This is the day I have to unload Maggie.' I'm not saying you'll do it; I'm saying you could. I need a little edge, that's all. And that doesn't mean you move in with me, either. You can visit."

He visited her on a regular basis and gave her an open lease. She could stay for as long as she liked.

"Maggie, darling, take a break. I want to talk to you for a moment," he said from the doorway.

Maggie lifted her head, and immediately the pain and longing disappeared from her lovely face and she welcomed him with a bright smile. "I'd love a break, Sandor, but really, I'm swamped." She indicated the work on her desk.

"Dinner?" Sandor prompted.

"I was sort of planning an evening at home." Maggie continued sorting through papers. "Wash my hair and all that, you know."

"Maggie, I want to see you." There was not a plea in his tone but rather a command.

"All right, Sandor," Maggie complied. "Tell you what. You bring dinner and I'll cook it. We can lounge all evening with some wine and good music. Would you like that?"

Sandor's eyes narrowed in annoyance. He didn't like Maggie's knack for turning his demands into something she condescended, waiving the privileges of his rank and assuming a superior air. Back Maggie Coleman into a corner and she'd have you believe being there had been her intention all along. "I didn't know you could cook, Maggie."

She laughed. "I can broil or boil. Take your choice."

"Steaks?"

"You're talking to a Texas girl, so make sure you bring all the fixings. Shoo now. I want to finish this."

Sandor felt his pressure rise. She had dismissed him. He was no longer in her thoughts or worthy of her consideration; it was as though he didn't exist. No woman had ever treated him the way Maggie did, and by God, he was putting out for her. Anything she wanted he gave. Money, an apartment, a penthouse apartment, travel, gifts; hell, he even pleased her in bed, satisfying her hungry appetites each time she clamored for more. He was the perfect friend, boss, and lover. What more did she want? Something he couldn't give her. Whatever it was Maggie yearned for, it wasn't in his power to give. Poor little black sheep.

It was two weeks later when Maggie shuffled through her mail. A letter from Sawyer. The childish handwriting reminded her of her own years ago. She squinted at the sprawling letters with the exaggerated loops. Just like her own. They should have been sisters; Sawyer was much more Billie's daughter than she would ever be her own. Sawyer was at Sunbridge enjoying all the things she herself could never have again. Maggie knew she shouldn't be jealous, but she was. It was more than jealousy, it went deeper than that. It was all mingled with shame and disappointment and rejection.

Dear Maggie,
   Grandmam told me to write you. We are coming to

{ 466 }

New York City next month. Grandmam is doing business. Do you think we could have lunch or go to the movies together? I would like that and so would Grand.

I love the Barbie doll you sent me. Grand has made me so many outfits for her that the other kids don't have. It was nice of you to send me the doll. How did you know I wanted one?

My friend Marjorie is so jealous that I'm going to New York. I wasn't jealous when she went to California. It's not good to be jealous because you cry at night. I like to go to sleep thinking about nice things.

My pencil needs a new point so I have to end this letter.

I love you, Maggie, with all my heart. I hope you love me a little bit, too. Grand says you do. Will you tell me that someday?

Love,
Sawyer

Maggie scrunched the letter into a ball. She opened it, reread it, and felt the tears begin. Dammit! Every time she was getting herself together she had another blow below the belt. The tears came then, great, ugly, choking sobs. When at last she lay on the sofa, spent of emotion, she folded the letter into a neat little square and slipped it into the pocket of her robe.

She reached for the phone. "Sandor, Maggie here. I'm glad I caught you in. Listen, I've some vacation coming. If the invitation is still open do you still want me to go to Europe with you?" She listened a moment. "I was hoping you'd say that. You will take care of the tickets and all those nasty little details? It's only a month away, but already I can see Paris and feel the excitement."

{{{{{{{{{ CHAPTER }}}}}}}}} THIRTY-THREE

Bittersweet memories attacked Thad as he settled back in the taxi on his way to the airport. He supposed he was getting old to have weddings affect him this way. Or was it that he felt guilty for betraying Billie and Moss this way by being a party to Riley's secret marriage? Secret to everyone in Texas, that was. He'd done his best to discourage Riley, but the young man would have none of it. So Thad had done some checking on Otami. Family background, reputation, everything was impeccable. If anything, Otami and her family were as wealthy—and even more respectable—than the Colemans. One way or another, Thad knew, Riley would have found some way to marry the girl he loved.

Inwardly he felt he'd done the right thing in securing permission for Riley and Otami to marry. One only had to look at them to know they were made for each other. Only once before had he seen the kind of love that shone in Riley's eyes. It had been in Billie's eyes the day she'd married Moss.

And it had been in Otami's eyes today, as she'd married Riley in an entirely different kind of ceremony—two of them, in fact. First the Catholic service, where Otami had been the picture of innocent loveliness in her white dress; and then, later, a traditional Buddhist ceremony, where she had worn a kimono of bright red silk to denote her joy. Thad shook his head as he recalled those two beautiful faces bearing their undisguised love. That's what it was all about, he knew—finding that kind of love. He had found it years ago with Billie, and despite all odds that love had survived.

"I think our wedding is over, Mrs. Coleman." Riley grinned as the last of his friends piled into the car that was returning to NAS. "We have to thank the Santos again and tell them how wonderful everything was. It was wonderful, wasn't it?"

"It wasn't just wonderful, Riley. It was perfect. I hope you have no regrets about your family. Your uncle Thad is an amazing person. He's very fond of you," Otami said quietly.

Riley looked down at his new bride and noted the sparkle in her eyes. He knew he would kill to protect this fragile young woman. His wife. Jesus! Was she having regrets? Was she worried about the old uncle and her parents back in Japan? Maybe Thad could do something there. He'd have to give that some thought. "No regrets. Never regrets. You're my life now. Uncle Thad is one in a million. When the time comes, if I can't make it right back home, he will. It's you I'm worried about. I hope the day never comes when you have second thoughts about marrying me. Families are important. Very important. One day you and I will have our own family."

"Riley, from this day on, I don't want either of us to talk about having regrets. If we're to discuss family, let us do it in loving ways. One day they will see how right this is and then they will be happy for us. Perhaps not for a long time, but it will be all right as long as we have each other. Can we agree to that?"

"Anything you want. By the way, now that the car is gone, how are we going to get to the farmhouse you rented?"

"We could walk. It's not far." Otami giggled.

"Are you sure you want to stay there? It's not too late to make arrangements for Hawaii," Riley said anxiously.

"Darling, this farmhouse is perfect. Wait until you see the way I fixed it up. Nita helped me. When you see it you'll know Hawaii cannot compare to it. On our first anniversary you can take me to Hawaii. I don't want to stay in an impersonal hotel and I don't want the long plane ride. I want to spend every hour of every day of your leave with you. I want to make breakfast for you with my dishes. I want you to dry them when I wash them. I want you to sleep in my bed, under the sheets that I embroidered. I want to hear you say what a marvel I am. I painted, hung drapes, scoured, and cleaned. I hung my painting from Hong Kong, and Nita's brother drilled holes and we hung ferns all over the place. We did such a fantastic job you aren't going to recognize the place. It's where we belong for now," Otami said shyly.

Riley was overwhelmed. She had done all this for him. All she wanted was him. Hawaii with all the glitz and glitter didn't appeal to this precious person who was his wife. Ten days of togetherness. Paradise.

It was Nita's youngest brother who finally found a truck in running order to transport the newlyweds to the farmhouse. Riley and Otami took one look at it and burst out laughing.

"It runs," Carlos smirked. "I lease it for a dollar a year. The springs are gone and the brakes are so-so."

Riley stood back to get a better look at the truck. Once it had been white. It wasn't the rust, nicks, or scratches that concerned him. In the bed of the truck there were two metal chairs with what looked like thirty-three coats of paint on them. Each was tied to the metal sides with stout rope. "I'm game if you are." Otami nodded as she gathered up the skirt of her long white gown and, with the help of her new husband and Carlos, settled herself on one of the chairs. Riley, in his crisp navy whites, settled himself on the other chair. "I think this is where we hold on for dear life and pray that we get to the farm. You'd think the owner would provide seat belts."

"Carlos, you will take our picture, please," Otami said seriously as she sat primly with her hands folded in her lap. "For our children one day." She grinned at Riley.

"Absolutely."

The truck backed out of the rutted driveway and careened down the road. Riley shouted to be heard over the rattling. "Always remember that I love you!"

"I will remember!" Otami shouted back as the truck screeched around the corner.

Eight houses up from the San Juan deBautiste Church, Carlos swung into a long driveway. A wooden sign tacked to a banyan tree read RILEY AND OTAMI COLEMAN.

"What happened to the jungle?" Riley asked in awe.

"You are pleased. Then it was worth it. Carlos and his brothers cut it back, and now the house can be seen from the road. It was important that our friends be able to find us. We have a lawn now. See, over there, that's a fern patch. Farther down in the back is a bamboo bed. I will show it to you tomorrow. There is a wonderful place there, a glade of sorts that would be perfect for lovemaking."

Riley laughed. "I thought you were shy."

"I wanted you to think that. I am really bold and brazen and I plan to devour you one hour from now."

Carlos handed over the key to Riley with a flourish. "You might need transportation," he said briskly. "It's only a short walk back to my house. Call on the padre if you need anything; he's at the bottom of the hill."

Trying desperately to keep a straight face, Otami thanked Carlos for the use of the truck. If she had anything to do with it, the truck would remain in the same position for the entire ten-day honeymoon. Riley winked at her. So, they thought alike. Good. But then, she had known that almost from the first day.

"What do you think, Mr. Coleman?" Otami said with her hands on her hips. "Carlos and Frank painted the house. See how it gleams. We were unsure of the maroon trim, but it makes the house noticeable from the road now that it's been cleared."

It was a small concrete house with a flat roof. Riley considered it trim and neat. By Texas standards it would have accommodated little more than a tractor or a horse and one groom. It suited him perfectly. It looked right and it felt right. Otami had known, bless her heart.

Riley reached down for Otami's hand and together they walked to the carport with its concrete overhead roof. Colorful blooms in bright clay pots hung from the beams. "We will eat breakfast here. And lunch and dinner, if you like. You will be in charge of carrying in the cushions if it rains."

"Ordering me about already, are you?"

"Yes. It is to be a fifty-fifty relationship. You will do what I tell you." Otami giggled. "You said your favorite colors were yellow and green, and I paid attention when it was time to stitch the pillows. Can you smell the new paint on the table and chairs?"

"I can hardly notice. You are the marvel in marvelous, Mrs. Coleman. It's time for me to carry you over the threshold. We want this to be right from the beginning."

"It is right. Can't you feel it?" Otami asked as she snuggled against Riley's chest.

"This is going to be tricky." Riley grinned. "If I'm holding you, how can I open the door?" Otami squirmed in his arms and leaned down to open the door. "It's stuck."

"Aha, so you aren't perfect after all," Riley chortled. "You should have had the presence of mind to rub soap on the sides of the door. Or oil. Or better yet, installed a screen door. Now I have to set you down and try to open this door. Is it locked?"

"No one locks doors here. It must be the humidity that makes it stick. I am so sorry. I spoiled the moment."

"Shhh," Riley said, laying a finger on her lips. "I was teasing. You haven't spoiled anything. I'll have this door opened in a second and we can get back on track."

Twenty minutes later the door was still stuck. Riley was huffing and puffing and sweat was running down his face. "It looks like you're going to have to climb through the bathroom window. You're tiny enough. I'll remove the louvers and push you through."

"And what happens if I can't get the door open from the inside," Otami asked anxiously.

"Then I'll blow a hole in the damn house. Or drive that ridiculous truck through the front window. Don't worry. I'll get in."

An hour later, Otami, with her gown tied in a knot about her waist, was standing on the kitchen counter removing the glass louvers. She poked and jabbed at the screen until it fell out. Riley climbed in the kitchen window and they both collapsed on the counter laughing and giggling. "I can't believe that Carlos varnished the door and then closed it. This is going to be the only way in and out until I can pry it open."

"We aren't going anywhere."

"That's true. The hell with the door. When we're old and gray we can tell our children and grandchildren that instead of me carrying you over the threshold I was forced to push you through a tiny bathroom window. Two more pounds, Mrs. Coleman, and you wouldn't have made it. But we're alone. We're finally alone."

"I know. Isn't it wonderful?"

"It's beautiful, Otami," Riley said, looking around his new home.

"It is beautiful," Otami agreed. "Nita and her brothers helped with the painting and scraping. I did the decorating. It wasn't all that difficult, since there are only four rooms. Cleaning the dirt and mildew was the worst. The house had been vacant for too long. Can you imagine, Riley, it only costs one hundred and twenty-five dollars a month. We must pay the electric bill. I looked and looked until I found what you could afford to pay on your salary. I know how to be economical."

Riley grinned. "That's exactly what I need, an economical wife. Why do you keep looking out the window? Surely you aren't expecting company, or are you?"

Otami frowned. "Something must be wrong. It always happens at this time of day. It was my last surprise for you."

"You mean there's more?"

"Yes, one more thing." Otami leaned over the kitchen sink to look through the window. "Ahhh, here it is. Come quick!"

Riley leaned over the sink and stared out into the twilight. "I'll be damned," he said. "Don't tell me you have something to do with this?"

Otami laughed helplessly. "His name is Pete and every morning he brings that bull he's leading to the field behind our house. Then he comes back in the evening to take it somewhere else. I couldn't wait for you to see it. I thought it would remind you of Texas and your steers. It's an old bull and it can barely walk, as you can see. But it is the same color as the pictures you showed me of your cows. Some days, it wanders down onto our lawn; that is why the grass is cropped so close. This will be another memory for us to hold close."

"You are a piece of work, Mrs. Coleman. How could you keep that a secret?"

"It was easy. Don't you see, Riley? This was all meant to be. Everything fell into place; everything worked out for us. It was not wrong for us to marry. This place is perfect for us. This will be our beginning roots, the start of our memories. Tell me I did right. Tell me this was meant to be. I need you to tell me, Riley."

There was a lump in Riley's throat. "It's right. It was right from the minute we met. We both know that. I'll be telling you that every hour of the day. You'll get tired of hearing it."

"Never!" Otami cried.

"Are there any more surprises you haven't told me about?"

"The bull was the last one."

Riley grinned and looked around him. It was time to explore his new home.

He was standing at one end of a long room divided by a bar that separated the living room from the kitchen. The appliances were old but sparkling clean. Chrisp white curtains fluttered in the warm breeze at the louvered windows. White wicker furniture boasted colorful yellow-and-lime-colored padding that complemented green-and-gold flecks in the new tile floor. Otami's Hong Kong picture set off one stark white wall to perfection.

"I put that up there for you by myself," Otami said, pointing to a brass butterfly near the front door. "The hook is for your navy cap. I bought it at the Ginger Jar—it is my wedding present to you."

Riley drew her close to him, overcome. "Thank you," he whispered against her sweet-smelling hair.

Silvery moonlight penetrated the lacy curtains, illuminating the farmhouse bedroom, chasing away the deepest shadows. Otami lay with her head nestled in the hollow of Riley's shoulder, her face, like his, betraying a sublime satisfaction. They had made love, shared love, brought to each other the best they had to give; it had been like opening a doorway to heaven.

Otami moved against him, her dark almond eyes opening slowly as she reached up to caress his cheek. She felt the tremor that rippled through him. "My Riley, my husband, did I please you?"

"Your husband is pleased." Riley sighed, drawing her closer, pressing his lips against her brow. His fingers slid through her long black hair. This woman, with her small high breasts and soft yielding thighs, fit him like a glove, as though she had been made for him. And he knew beyond doubt that it would always be this way between them, a sweet offering of love and amazement, because what they brought to each other was more than physical; it was the touching of souls.

Blissful, euphoric days followed. The communion between Riley and Otami was so complete neither felt the need for anything or anyone. Their lovemaking was wondrous and spontaneous. Shared, enjoyed . . . perfect.

On the third day of their honeymoon, Riley armed himself with a screwdriver, a spatula, and a hammer and finally managed to pry open the front door of the farmhouse. "I think, Mrs. Coleman, that it is time we explored this beautiful little island. What do you say? Why don't we take a picnic lunch and start out after breakfast and explore till we're tired."

"Where would you like to go? Guam is only thirty miles in length, twelve miles in width, and four miles wide at its narrowest point. I learned that on the second day of my arrival," Otami said proudly.

"I can do better than that. I," he said loftily, "have a brochure on the island. I also have all the poop from fellow officers. While you're making the pancakes I'll tell you exactly what we're going to do. While you pack our lunch I'll take a shower. Is that fair?"

"No. But I am a good, obedient, Japanese housewife and will do as I'm told. Until such time as I don't like your orders and then I will resign. How do you like that, Mr. Coleman?"

"As long as you warm the syrup and melt the butter for the pancakes, you can do whatever you want. You can even walk on my back."

"No, thank you. I am a modern Japanese. I will just cook and clean and make love to you."

"Well said," Riley beamed. "Now, let's see. We can take a drive through the Nimitz Hill area and get a panoramic view of the natural harbor. He'll be able to see the Glass Breakwater. My C.D. tables told me it was named after Captain Henry Glass, who claimed Guam as a possession of the United States. I think that's a must. I'd like to see it, wouldn't you?"

"Absolutely," Otami cooed in his ear as she set his plate of pancakes in front of him along with the melted butter and warm syrup.

"Do that again." Riley grinned.

"Do what?"

"Nuzzle my ear." Riley groaned as Otami willingly obeyed.

"What are you crossing out?" she asked a moment later.

Riley was flustered. "I—I didn't think you'd want to go to Nimitz Beach Park. I'm not sure I want to go there, either. It was the battle site of the American invasion in 1944. Why don't we leave it for last."

"All right, Riley. But I think you should see it. It will be something for you to talk about with your father later on."

"You're serious, aren't you."

"Yes. You aren't going to be able to hide from your father forever. Sooner or later you will talk. This will be common ground, something he can relate to."

"You always know just what to say and when to say it. In a way, I am hiding out. Why couldn't I say the words? Why did you have to say it for me?"

"Because I'm me and you're you." Otami smiled and the tricky moment passed. "Would you like a slice of mango?"

"Nope, I'm full."

Otami set about clearing the table. "Where else are we going?"

"To Fort Soledad Vista Point. According to this guide we'll be able to see Umatac—the place Magellan is said to have visited in 1521. We might want to tell our kids about it someday. History, you know."

"If we do all that you've said so far, it will be time for lunch. Where will we picnic?"

"Another cup of coffee, Otami. Quick, you aren't anticipating my needs. Two sugars."

"Two sugars, is it? I think I might like a second cup myself. I'll sit here till you fix it."

"I get the point." Riley laughed, jumping up to pour the coffee. "How about this place?" Riley asked, pointing to a map. "It's called Yigo. The CO was telling me there's talk about building a memorial park on the spot to commemorate the half a million Japanese and American soldiers—and civilians as well as Pacific Islanders—who lost their lives during World War Two in the Pacific conflict. They plan to erect a monument on the sight that will symbolize the determination of the United States and Japan to promote friendship and world harmony. Supposedly it will be a figure praying for eternal peace."

Otami's expression was as solemn as Riley's. "I think that you and I are the two perfect people to visit that sight. I will pray that it comes to pass and is built."

"Something else to talk to Pap about someday. I think that will be enough for one day. Provided that truck will get us back and forth. Wear good shoes, Otami, in case we have to hoof it. I wonder if there's gas in the tank."

"Of course there's gas. Who's going to do the dishes?"

"Not me, I have to take a shower and shave. Guess it's your turn."

"I have a better idea. I'll wait until you're finished and then you can dry as I wash. This marriage is fifty-fifty, remember."

"Okay, okay."

"When we come back from exploring, would you like to make love down in the glade where all the wild ferns grow? We can make a bed of them. We can even bathe in the pond."

"It's a puddle, not a pond. If you do the dishes, I'll meet you there."

The rickety truck proved to be a horror. Otami prayed and constantly blessed herself, to Riley's delight. The day flew by. The picnic lunch was quickly devoured, and before they knew it, it was time to head back to the farmhouse.

"There's a bottle of champagne in the refrigerator for us." Otami smiled. "My uncle sent it. While he could not participate in our wedding or give his blessing, he did what he could. He is a fine old gentleman and he loves me dearly. It is his way of wishing us well without losing face. We must drink the toast he wanted. I will prepare it for us."

Riley waited until Otami returned with a tray and two glasses. He took his glass from the tray and handed Otami hers. "I think we should have a flowery toast, something meaningful and different, but I can't for the life of me think of a thing. Why don't we drink to our new life, yours and mine? To love and understanding. May our new life be filled with humor, beautiful music, and wondrous words. To us."

"To us," Otami said softly. "Always us."

The *fanuchanan*, or rainy season, came and went. The *fanumnangan*, or dry season, set in, and Riley's two years in Guam were almost up. He'd come to love his new island home and dreaded the day he'd be ordered to leave. Otami had settled into the little farmhouse as though she'd been born there. She continued with her studies at the university and often, late at night, Riley would find her bent over the long, narrow kitchen table with its butterfly cloth, studying. The moment she spotted him, however, she'd run to his arms. Riley had never been happier in his life. This was paradise. This was home. He hoped he'd never have to leave.

But as always, with something so fragile as perfection, snafus are bound to happen.

When Riley's tour of duty in Guam was up, new orders sent him to Atsugi, Japan, and from there to Vietnam. Immediately, he was flying night missions over the Mai Cong Delta in Coleman aircraft.

When Thad Kingsley looked at the postmark on Riley's letter, he paled. Jesus, how had the kid ended up in Vietnam? He was supposed to remain in Guam—forever and ever, if necessary. What had gone wrong? He read the letter.

Dear Uncle Thad,

I know this letter is going to come as a surprise to you. I'm here! God, I hate it. I know that I'm capable of killing to get out of here. I am killing. Every day I kill. I try not to think about it, but sooner or later I have to take count and it makes me sick. I didn't know it was possible to be so piss-assed scared, but I am. I don't mind telling you I have had to fight with myself to keep from writing to Pap to get me out of here.

Otami went back to Japan. I haven't heard from her for a long time. She was going to see if her parents would welcome her back. She was worried about it; I could tell from the sound of her letter. The main reason she went back instead of staying in Guam to wait for me is she's pregnant. Jesus, Uncle Thad, she's going to have my baby all by herself. She needs her family. You have their address. Will you check on things and see how it's all going? If Otami's parents refuse to accept her back into the family, see what you can do for her. You might have to intervene and do some business with my bank back in Texas. Otami has all the papers. Do what you can.

I hate this place. I don't know why I'm here. No one else seems to know, either. How did this happen? Who's responsible? The only thing that makes it all bearable is that I'm flying Coleman planes. I feel safe in them.

Give Otami a kiss for me if you see her soon and tell her how much I love her. Take care of her for me, Uncle Thad.

All my best,
Riley

Thad felt out of his depth. He hated Vietnam almost as much as Riley did. His gut churned and he knew his new ulcer was going to start acting up.

Maybe it was time to put in a call to Moss. He'd call Billie later; right now Riley needed his father's reassurance. He could be tactful, casually mention the boy, and see what developed in the conversation. He also had to get in touch with Otami and see what was going on. He'd have to go to Tokyo—this was too important to trust to a phone call. For Riley Coleman—for Billie's son—he would do anything he could.

Thad didn't sleep that night at all. At first light, he called Sunbridge and was told that Mr. Moss Coleman was away on a business trip and would be back in three days. By midafternoon he was in Tokyo and at the address Riley had sent him. He rang the bell and a trim maid in a silk kimono opened the gate for him. "Yes?"

"I'd like to see Otami. Tell her Admiral Kingsley is here."

"You come inside house, sir. Missy Otami is in garden. I fetch her."

Thad stood with his hat in his hands. He didn't know much about Japanese furniture or houses, but this place looked fit for a king. Wealth, the kind the Colemans were used to, was right here. Perhaps more.

The naked fear in Otami's eyes was more than Thad could bear. He quickly rushed to assure her that nothing was wrong, then kissed her. "That was from Riley."

"You have heard from him? Tell me. Is he well? How is he? I have had no word for many weeks now."

Thad handed her Riley's letter and watched as her hungry eyes devoured each word once and then again. She folded the letter carefully and handed it back to Thad. "Thank you so much for coming here. I know Riley was very worried about my family. They opened their arms to me. I am most fortunate that they love me as they do. You are to tell Riley that I do not need Coleman money. My family would be dishonored if they could not take care of me, their daughter. Riley will understand. I must accept, for the misery I caused them in the beginning."

"I'm happy that everything has worked out for you. Riley will be relieved."

"I've written him many letters explaining things to him. Soon he should receive them. Perhaps all at one time."

Or not at all, Thad felt like saying. The Vietnamese had a knack for knocking out mail planes. "If you want to write a letter, I'll take it back with me to Atsugi and put it on the next flight. Riley will have it by tomorrow night. Would you care to have dinner with me?"

"Admiral Kingsley!" Otami said, clearly shocked. "You must dine with my family. My father would be most upset if he found out you were here and did not honor us for dinner. My mother has a passion for American film stars and will want to . . . how do you say . . . pump you for inside information. Say you will dine with us."

"I'd like that very much. I want to meet your family."

"Good. I have met Riley's family. By that I mean you. Now it is your turn to meet my family. I would be very honored."

"Otami, when is the baby due?"

Otami laughed. "Any day now. My mother is much concerned. My father is also concerned, but he pretends that he isn't. Men are strong and brave. This is women's business. It will be the first grandchild for my parents. We are all nervous. Me especially. I wish Riley were here. My mother says it will be a boy. My father wishes for a girl that will look like me." Otami shrugged to show she couldn't fathom this kind of thinking. "I am praying for a son for Riley. But a daughter will be nice, too." She smiled impishly.

"Twins," Thad said inanely. Otami giggled.

Dinner was served Western style for Thad's benefit. He appreciated it and said so.

"We wish to make our daughter's uncle welcome. We could do no less for you, Admiral. I must admit that Yankee bean soup is not something I would want to eat every day." Shadaharu Hasegawa said with a twinkle in his eye.

"It's not a favorite of mine, either." Thad grinned. Both men laughed. Thad sucked in his stomach, waiting for what he knew was coming next.

"Come, we will have a cigar. In the garden. The women will have tea and then we can talk some more. My daughter will pester me if I keep you to myself. Go, go," he said, making shooing motions with his hands to his tiny wife and daughter. He rolled his eyes and said in an indulgent tone, "I promise you, my wife, that you can discuss film stars with Admiral Kingsley later if he is amenable." Thad nodded and the tiny woman squealed with pleasure. Otami put her arms around her mother and left the room. "Women, they are fond of films."

Uncertain of what his response should be, Thad merely agreed.

When the cigars had been lighted, Mr. Hasegawa spoke. "Now that we are out of earshot of the women we must talk of the young man, Riley, and his family."

"Mr. Hasegawa, I am not a blood relation to Riley. I am a family friend, but I love the boy as though he were my own son. I'm not sure I should be discussing his family with you. Not that I don't want to, but I did promise Riley and must honor that promise. I hope you understand."

Shadaharu Hasegawa nodded wearily. He contemplated the tip of his glowing cigar. "There is so much these days that I do not understand. I am not progressive, my wife says. My daughter says I must learn modern Western ways if I am to survive. The old ways, our culture, suddenly is not enough for the young people. I have many more daughters. Eight in all." He grimaced. "Do you know what nine women can do to one man who treasures the old ways?"

Thad grinned. How pitiful this rolypoly man looked. How woebegone—until you looked at his shrewd eyes. "I think I have some idea of what you are talking about. I'm very relieved that you welcomed Otami back into the family. I came here today to be sure she was well taken care of. On Riley's request, of course."

"Tell me of this young man. My daughter goes on for hours, but she is a young woman in love. I must know of the family this young man comes from."

"The Colemans are a fine old family. Very well respected. They're good people, Mr. Hasegawa. Your daughter married into a fine old family. They're wealthy, if that's important. Riley has a trust fund that will keep him and his family well off for all his life. You need have no worry on that score."

"I am well off, too. I can provide for my daughter and the baby." Mr. Hasegawa bristled.

"I'm sure you can. You will recall I said 'if it's important.' I don't think that Riley or Otami has given much thought to money. I mentioned it in case you were . . . were wondering."

"I was. There is no use pretending I wasn't. Why doesn't the young man want his family to know about his marriage to my daughter?"

He'd dreaded the question and searched his mind for just the right words. "I think—now understand, Mr. Hasegawa, it is merely my opinion—I think Riley was afraid that his father would spoil things for him. I must tell you that I agree—I think his father would have spoiled things. It is to your credit that you were wise enough to welcome back your daughter rather than lose her."

Mr. Hasegawa snorted and then puffed on his cigar. "My wife, that tiny porcelain doll, told me, as did my other daughters, that if I did not welcome Otami back, they were all going to America to seek careers in the films. What could I do? I, too, learn from the young. I know I must be progressive to survive. Also, I cannot, I simply cannot, stand all the chirping and chattering when I do not go along with their plans and ideas."

"You're a remarkable man, Mr. Hasegawa. You have a fine family. It is a wise man who knows when to . . ."

"Buckle under to the pressure of his womenfolk. I believe it is an ancient Chinese proverb, is it not?"

Thad laughed and puffed on his cigar.

"It would not be a wise idea, then, to get in touch with the Coleman family?"

"No, Mr. Hasegawa, it would not be a good idea. Not at this time. In the end it must be Riley and Otami's decision. Not yours. I'm sorry if that offends you, but that is the way I see it."

"My daughter tells me her husband has great respect for you. I can see why. You have told me what you wanted to tell me, what you think I needed to know. No more. I respect that, Admiral Kingsley. I will go along with their wishes. My daughter will always have a home with her family. It would dishonor us all if I left her to fend for herself—particularly now. The Colemans are not to be notified of the birth?"

"Only if Riley gives his permission. Otherwise, you must honor his wishes. You will have one consolation, though. You will have this child all to yourselves."

"It doesn't seem fair. To deprive one's family of a child. There is a grandfather, Otami tells me."

"No, it isn't fair. But it isn't up to either of us to judge or make decisions. All we can do is be here for them if needed."

"You are a wise man, Admiral. You must come to my house again so that we can get to know each other better. You will want to see the infant when it is born."

"I'd like that very much. I would be honored."

"My house is yours. You will come and go as you see fit. Anytime you wish. Now, I'm afraid we must return and you will tell my girls stories of the film stars. I beg of you, do not make them too glamorous."

Thad laughed. "I think I can handle that."

"Admiral, do you think you could tell them that Clark Gable is not as handsome in real life as he is on the screen?"

"I think I can tell them he has a wart on his nose that is covered with makeup. Is that all right?"

Shadaharu Hasegawa puffed contentedly on his cigar. "That would be quite wonderful, if you don't mind the little white lie."

"Who said it was a lie? Every man in the world believes it." Thad laughed as he followed his host back into the house.

Four days later Thad received a phone call from the *Tokyo Sun Times*. He was told it was a person-to-person call from Shadaharu Hasegawa. The excitement in Otami's father's voice could only mean good news. "A boy child!"

"Congratulations, Mr. Hasegawa. Give Otami my love. I'll get word to Riley."

"Thank you, Admiral. You will come to my house next week. Please."

"Thank you. Will Sunday be all right?"

"We will all look forward to your visit. Good-bye, Admiral Kingsley."

Thad ached with the feelings he had to suppress. This was the kind of news a person liked to deliver. Billie would be so delighted. Moss would be ecstatic—until he found out the mother of his grandchild was Japanese. This was news he would have to keep to himself.

Riley landed his plane and headed straight for his quarters. Sleep was what he needed. Sleep and dreams of Otami. He was halfway across the compound when his CO handed him a slip of paper. A boy! "Mother and son doing fine. Everything under control." The message was signed by Fleet Admiral

Thaddeus Kingsley. He'd known he could count on Uncle Thad.

A son. A boy to carouse with. To just look at, not smother. It was all so right.

His conscience pricked him for a moment. He should write to Sunbridge. Someday. Someday far away. For now he was going to sleep off his all-night air strike and dream of his wife and new son.

A month later the first picture of his new son arrived. Riley Shadaharu Coleman. Seven and one-half pounds. Twenty inches long.

It was two o'clock in the morning when Riley met his flight buddies on the makeshift runway for their nightly strikes. He lovingly touched the wingtip and offered up his daily prayer. "Let me come back to my wife and son," he whispered softly. "Coleman Aviation, don't fail me now."

An hour into the air strike Riley's plane started to lose altitude. Fear rose in his throat, threatening to choke off his air supply. Jesus, not here, not over this godforsaken country no one's ever heard about. Not for something no one understood. God, not now! Riley screamed. The plane banked and Riley's feet danced on the pedals. He was too low; he could never bail out. Red lights glowed, reminding him of eerie Halloween eyes. His last conscious thought before he crashed into the mountain ridge was that Riley Shadaharu had his grandfather Coleman's nose.

The Navy Department was only too willing to have Thad travel to Texas to break the news of Riley's death. He personally got on the phone and begged Washington to hold up notifying Otami until he could notify the Colemans. Irregular, they said, but because of their own snafus they were willing to make any and all concessions.

The moment Billie opened the door to her Austin apartment and saw Thad in full dress uniform she knew. She took a deep breath. Thad poured her a drink, which she declined. "Tell me everything you know." It was a while later when she finally asked, "Why can't I cry?"

"You're in shock, Billie. Come with me. I can't leave you here. I have to go to Sunbridge. Moss is going to need you. So is Seth."

"Yes, yes, you're right. Let me get a sweater. You're right.

They're going to need me. Did I thank you, Thad, for coming? I did, didn't I?"

"Several times. I thought you would rather hear it from me than the War Department."

"Do you know what happened?"

"They were flying low strikes. Riley's plane started to lose altitude. He crashed into a ridge. That's all we know."

"Moss won't be able to accept this. Neither will Seth. Was it a Coleman plane?" she asked in a hushed whisper.

"They were all Coleman planes," Thad said softly.

CHAPTER
{{{{{{{{{   THIRTY-FOUR   }}}}}}}}}

The scene at Sunbridge set Thad's teeth on edge. Threats, insults, and recriminations flew thick and fast. Seth bellowed and snorted like a frostbitten dragon. Moss downed half a bottle of brandy in two gulps. Agnes flopped down on a chair and fingered her strand of pearls, her eyes never leaving the raging Seth.

"Don't interfere, you said. That's what you said, gal. Your exact words, don't interfere. Now he's dead. Riley is dead. My only grandson. It's your fault!" he shouted, pointing a clawlike hand at Billie.

"But you did interfere. You had him sent to Guam to fly weather missions. You can't blame me for my own son's death. What kind of man are you? If you had left things alone, he might still be alive. Oh, no, you and Moss, the pair of you, you had to get right in there and do what you always do. Pull strings, make threats, bribe people, to get what you want. Now look what's happened. My son is gone. I have no son. Why couldn't you leave him alone?" Billie cried brokenly.

"You don't even belong here. What are you doing here, anyway? Who asked you to come here? Get her out of here, Moss. I can't stand to look at her face."

"That's enough, Pap," Moss thundered. "Thad, what happened? I want it straight."

"Riley was flying in low, one of his nightly strikes. The

plane started to lose altitude and he couldn't bail out. He went into a ridge and the plane exploded. It's all we know, Moss."

"It was a Coleman plane?"

Thad had to strain to hear the question. "Yes, Moss, the whole squadron flies Coleman planes. You know that as well as I do."

"There was some kind of foul-up!" Moss cried. "Riley was supposed to stay in Guam for the rest of his tour. He was already in Vietnam when we found out. He was supposed to be rotated back day after tomorrow. Jesus. Two days! I can't believe it."

Billie stood up. "Moss, you've had enough to drink. Why don't we all go into the kitchen and have some coffee."

"Coffee! Get this stupid woman out of here," Seth roared. "I mean it, Moss. My grandson is dead and she wants to make coffee. Agnes, you raised one hell of a woman here. I never heard anything so stupid in my life."

"Shut up, Seth," Agnes said angrily. "One more word out of you and I swear I'll gag you personally. Coffee is something we all need. You will either keep a civil tongue in your head or you'll be wheeled to your room. Do we understand each other, Seth?"

"Don't tell me to shut up, Aggie. This is my house."

Thad, Moss, and Billie followed Agnes into the kitchen. Seth wiped at his eyes with the sleeve of his flannel shirt and spun his chair about. He'd be goddamned if he'd go out there and have coffee. In the end he wheeled his chair closer to the door so that he could hear the low voices coming from the kitchen. Billie was weeping, but Agnes seemed to be in control. As always. It was time to rid himself of both of them. Who needed them now? He certainly didn't. Everything was over. What was the point in going on?

Billie held herself in rigid control. Things had to be done, calls had to be made. Maggie, Susan, Sawyer. She had to do it, break the news. It took several tries before she could dial Maggie's New York number correctly. Her daughter's breathless voice came over the receiver on the fourth ring. "Maggie . . ." Now that she was actually hearing her voice, Billie was unable to continue. Some part of her was denying Riley's death, some part of her believed if she did not say the words, it would not become reality. "Maggie, oh, Maggie!"

A bolt of alarm electrified Maggie as she clenched the phone to her ear. "Mam? What's wrong? Did something happen to

Pap? Mam, are you there? Answer me!"

Moss took the phone from Billie's shaking hand and, with all the control he could muster, spoke. "Maggie. Riley was killed. We've only just got word. Mam can't talk, but we wanted you to know."

Maggie bit down so hard on her lip she could taste the blood. The pain, the rage, couldn't be stifled. Dear God in heaven, Riley couldn't be dead. He couldn't! She needed to lash out, to hurt in return. "He was flying one of your planes, wasn't he, Pap?" She broke the connection.

Helplessly, Maggie looked around her apartment, the place where she had encouraged her brother to enlist in the service in order to spite Moss, remembering that awful lonely Christmas they'd spent together. Now there would never be another Christmas.

Madness spurred her forward, to the desk, where she searched frantically for the packet of photographs she and Riley had taken that night. When she couldn't lay her hands on them immediately, she upended the desk. The pictures slid from their envelope onto the carpet. Maggie dropped to her knees and scrambled for them, tears streaming down her cheeks as she clutched them to her chest.

"No, no, no!" she cried aloud. "Not Riley, never Riley! Me! It should have been me! Dear God, I wish it had been me!"

Thad felt emotionally bruised and battered as he climbed into the cockpit of his plane for the return flight to California. He hated leaving Billie, but there was nothing he could do. How wrong they had been to think that Seth and Moss would need her. Feeling like an outcast, she had crept from the house with him like a thief in the night. When they'd said their good-byes there had been no tears. The tears would come later.

Otami stared at Thad, containing her grief. "He never saw his son," she whispered brokenly. "He never got to do all the things a father wants to do with his son. Do you think, Admiral Kingsley, that he thought of them, the things he would do when little Riley grew up?"

"I'm sure he did, Otami. I notified the Colemans. I didn't mention you or the baby."

"It is . . . was Riley's wish that they not know. We must honor that wish. My parents are away. My mother went with my father on a business trip. They will not return for another month."

"I can notify them. You shouldn't be alone now. They would want to be here with you."

"Admiral Kingsley, I am not alone. I will never be alone. You forget, I have Riley's son. I will be fine. You are not to worry about me. I knew that this might happen someday. I am not prepared, but I must accept it."

Thad gathered the girl close to him. "Cry. It will make you feel better."

"I cannot do that. Perhaps someday. I must go to the baby now. It is time for him to nurse. Thank you for coming. Would you like to stay for dinner?" At Thad's negative nod, Otami turned and left the room.

When Thad left, he knew he wouldn't be back—not for a long time. The Hasegawas would do all that was necessary. He would only be a grim reminder of Riley and that was the one thing they didn't need. Life had to go on. . . .

Billie handled her grief in several ways. She painted and worked obsessively. She spent time with Sawyer, sometimes talking for hours, and Sawyer told her little things she had never known about her son. What gave her the greatest comfort were her long letters to Thad and his equally long replies. There had even been one hour-long phone call from Tokyo that she would always treasure. Thad's concern was almost more than she could bear. In the end, however, she had been the one to comfort him. She never knew where her strength came from, but she was coping, handling things to the best of her ability. She was going to survive.

Moss Coleman cradled the phone on his shoulder as he waited for his party to come on the line. His voice, when he identified himself, was cold and harsh. "I think it's a hell of a note when a father has to beg the United States Navy to return his dead son's belongings. I've written six letters, sent three telegrams, and I've had no word. There must be some paper shuffler or pencil pusher who knows what's going on. I'm not getting off this phone till I get the answers I want."

"One moment, sir. I think Major Henry is the person you want to speak with. He's on another line. Will you hold?"

"I'm holding. I've been holding for two months now," Moss snarled. "Of course I'll wait."

{ 487 }

Five minutes later the phone crackled to life. "Major Henry here."

Moss ran through his speech a second time.

"Mr. Coleman, your son's effects were sent to his wife. Those are the rules. I can't change them, even for you."

"Wife! What wife? My son wasn't married. You idiots must have Riley mixed up with someone else. Just like his orders were mixed up. My son would be alive today except for that screw-up. What do you have to say to that, Major Henry?"

"I don't know anything about your son's orders, but I do know that the lieutenant was married for almost two years to a Japanese girl while he was stationed in Guam. His personal belongings and his military insurance were forwarded to his wife. There is also a minor dependent, a son. This information came to us after your son's death. It was included in his record. . . . Mr. Coleman, are you still there? . . . Mr. Coleman?"

Moss stared down at his desk. "Yes, I'm here, Major. I didn't know about the marriage. Even his mother didn't know."

"I'm sorry about that, Mr. Coleman. Sometimes these young men get antsy when they're so far from home. Everything was in order."

"Yes, Major, I'm sure it was. My son never did anything halfway. Could you tell me who this girl is and where she lives?"

The major gave him the address of Otami's parents. "I'm sorry for any inconvenience that this may have caused you, Mr. Coleman. And you have my deepest sympathy, sir."

Moss's vision blurred as he stared at Riley's picture on his desk. How could the boy have done such a despicable thing . . . married a Japanese, when he knew how his father felt about them? His fist banged the desk so hard that Riley's picture fell and glass shattered all over the polished floor. What the hell had happened to "like father like son"? Where had he gone wrong? A Jap! A goddamn Jap!

Major Henry had said there was a son living in Japan. Well, by God, no grandson of his was going to grow up in that hellhole, living on rice and picking in garbage cans! He'd go there and bring back the boy. Raise him here at Sunbridge. This was Riley's flesh and blood. He could learn to live with the rest of it. And a new baby in the house might be just what Billie needed. Moss smiled grimly. For Riley's baby son she would come back. He'd make book on it.

Moss left the following morning for San Francisco. From

San Francisco he caught a Pan Am flight to Guam, and from there he flew to Tokyo.

After checking into a hotel, Moss headed straight for a bar and downed three stiff drinks in quick succession. The liquor didn't help to steady his nerves. He hated this land and he hated every Japanese that walked the earth.

The doorman at the hotel flagged down a cab for him. Moss showed him the address and the driver's eyebrows shot up. "Yes, sir," he said in polite, stilted English.

"You understand English?" Moss barked.

"Yes, sir, I studied at UCLA for four years. Is there something you wish to know about Japan?" he asked politely.

"I know all there is to know about Japan. I don't want to know any more. How far is that address from here?"

"Not too far. Perhaps fifteen minutes, depending on traffic."

In spite of himself Moss couldn't help but ask, "If you studied at UCLA, what are you doing driving a taxi?"

"Japan is a poor country. It is difficult to make ends meet when you have a family to support. I have three sons to educate and that takes much money. It is not a dishonorable profession. Is this your first visit to Japan?"

"No. I was here once before. This will be my last visit," Moss replied harshly.

From time to time the driver looked into the rearview mirror at the brooding American face. He'd never seen such misery in a human being before. He concentrated on his driving, leaving Moss to his dark thoughts.

"Why are you stopping?"

"This is the address you wanted. See, the numbers are on the gate. You must ring the bell and someone will admit you. I bring many customers here."

"Customers? Is it a brothel? It looks like a goddamn palace."

"I beg your pardon, sir. I understand your words, but what makes you think that this is a brothel? It is the home of Mr. Shadaharu Hasegawa. Mr. Hasegawa owns three newspapers in Tokyo. This is his city home. Did you make a mistake in the address?"

"No, this is the address." Moss paid the man in American currency and knew the tip was outrageous, but he had no desire to quibble over price. He felt uncertain now as he stood outside the palatial house. Hasegawa was the right name. He jabbed at the bell with a blunt finger. The gate swung open and Moss walked through. He turned at the sound of the well-oiled hinges closing the gate: he was locked in. His forehead was beaded with perspiration as he waited in one of the most luxurious houses he had ever seen. This was no ricky-ticky rice paper shack. There was money here.

It was like a parade. First came a rolypoly man followed by a miniature little woman who must be the rolypoly man's wife. Behind them were eight young women.

Once they were all lined up, they bowed on a cue from the round man. "Welcome to my home, Mr. Coleman. Please, you will follow me and I will introduce you to my family." There was nothing for Moss to do but obey. This was not what he'd expected.

Mr. Hasegawa motioned for Otami to step forward. "This is my oldest daughter, your son's wife."

"Under what law?" Moss demanded cruelly.

"American law," Mr. Hasegawa said, enunciating carefully. "A legal marriage. There are certificates, if you wish to view them."

"I wish."

The Japanese man clapped his hands and a young servant appeared. He spoke quietly and the girl minced her way from the room, her head bowed, her hands clasped in front of her. She returned minutes later with a number of papers in a manila folder, and Moss scrutinized each of them.

It was all real.

"You wish to see your grandson?"

Moss nodded. He hated himself for staring at the girl, Otami, who was trying hard not to stare herself. Again, Mr. Hasegawa clapped his hands and this time merely nodded. The little maid returned minutes later with a fat cherub of a baby. Mr. Hasegawa indicated that Moss could step forward to view the infant. "I believe, as does my daughter, that the child has your nose. It is most remarkable."

Moss felt his throat constrict. Riley's son. He could see the resemblance in this placid, sleeping baby. It was enough. "I want to take the child back to Texas," he said coolly.

In the blink of an eye Otami stepped between her child and Moss. She said nothing, but her eyes implored her father.

"That is impossible, Mr. Coleman. The child belongs here with his mother and family. It was your son's wish."

"What do you know of my son's wishes? Don't think for one minute I'm going to buy that hogwash. That child is a Coleman. He belongs in Texas. Not here! Never here!"

"That is impossible. The child needs his mother. He will lack for nothing here. I believe I can match your income, if that is what's worrying you. Please, you will not insult us by offering to buy the child. That was your next move, was it not?"

Moss blustered, "You don't buy humans." But in his heart he knew that that was exactly what he had been going to say. "I'll go to court," he threatened.

"Your American courts have no jurisdiction here in Japan.....Please, it is not our desire to have trouble with Riley's family. We can all contribute to the child. You and your wife will be welcome in my house at any time. My daughter will be your daughter. It is fair and just."

"I don't want your damn daughter. I want my grandson. I won't leave here without him."

Otami stepped forward. "Mr. Coleman, Riley and I spoke of this many times. It was his wish that the child remain with me. When his time was up in the navy, he had planned to make his home here in Japan. I am speaking the truth to you. It is what Riley wanted."

"What you made him want. How did you do it? What tricks did you use to snare my son? Riley would never agree to any of this!"

"If what you say is true, then why am I here with my son, and why didn't you know of our marriage and our son? I assume the navy informed you. Riley himself did not want anyone in Texas to know. It is true, Mr. Coleman. And I did not trick your son. I fell in love with him and he fell in love with me. And our baby—Riley and I discussed this— our baby is named after Riley and my father. He is Riley Shadaharu Coleman."

It was the last bitter straw for Moss. Not to have his grandchild named after him. A damn Japanese name that he couldn't even pronounce.

Mr. Hasegawa stepped closer to Moss. "Please, Mr. Coleman, do not bring dishonor on yourself in front of my family. In my newspapers every day we have one reporter or another writing about ugly Americans. For all our sakes, do not act in this manner. You must accept the situation. Our home is yours whenever you wish."

"Go to hell," Moss barked, then he turned on his heel and left the house. There had to be a way. If necessary, he could kidnap the kid. Then he looked at the iron gates and knew it for the idle threat it was. He was beaten. He'd lost not only the battle, but the war as well.

He had nothing to do but think for eighteen hours on the long flight home. In the end he decided to keep the news of Riley Shadaharu to himself. No one would ever know of his humiliation. Not as long as he was alive, anyway.

When Moss returned to the United States he was a man driven by grief and rage. Besieged by the loss of his beloved son, he turned to the bourbon as though it were an old friend. Beset with rage over the humiliation he had suffered at the hands of the Hasegawas, he immersed himself in his work. He knew that he could have his grandson if he was willing to compromise; a basic kindness and acceptance would reward him with the only piece of Riley that was left in this world. But he hated and feared the Japanese; and he would not have anything to do with the child unless all ties to his mother's heritage had been severed.

Billie was aware of Moss's turmoil and tried to comfort him; she believed he was blaming himself and his aircraft for Riley's death. Moss never bothered to enlighten her. His reasoning was simple, at least in his opinion: he knew that if he told her, Billie would rush to Japan to embrace that child. And he did not want her to have what he denied himself—the comfort of loving Riley's son. He knew he was selfish. It was something he'd always known. It was something he could live with.

Seth watched what was left of his world crumble about him. A week after his son's return from Japan, he suffered two small strokes back to back that left him virtually incapacitated and entirely dependent upon Agnes. His speech was now slurred, but the timbre of his voice hadn't changed—he ranted and raved, cursed and cajoled her. He thought nothing of waking her in the middle of the night for a drink of water. He resented her because she was alive and well and could function on her own. He hated his deformity and made her pay for it by tormenting and ridiculing her in any way he could.

In the privacy of her room, Agnes broke down and cried. A victim of her own making, she could do no more than look after his health by day and plot his death by night.

That spring, Agnes made up her mind that she was going to get out from under one way or another. On the first truly warm day when the windows could be opened, she put her plan into action. "We're going for a ride today, Seth. It's time you got some fresh air. You're absolutely shriveling up to nothing. I insist."

"Insist all you please. I ain't going nowhere. Get it through your head, Aggie, that I'm confined to this room and that's where you and I are going to stay. Fetch me some coffee and read me a paper."

"Not today. Today the doctor said you were to go outdoors. It's an order, Seth. He said if you don't do as he says, he's discharging you as his patient."

"I'd like to see him try. I'll cut off all endowments to his fancy hospital and where will that leave him? No ride."

Seth watched Agnes out of the corner of his eye. She was taking his refusal just a little too well. She must be up to something. He'd have to pay close attention to see what it was.

With Agnes's diligent care and the doctor's daily visits, Seth began gradually to show signs of improvement. Each day, Agnes offered to take Seth for a ride in the country. The day he finally accepted, she stared at him with a stupid look on her face. "Well, don't stand there—get someone to come and help me into the car."

Agnes shifted from one foot to the other, her hands twisting at the pearls at her neck. "Are you sure? Why do you want to go today? What made you change your mind?"

"That damn fool doctor, that's who. He wants me in his office to give me some kind of newfangled test. That's where we're going. Don't get any ideas about stopping off at department stores. We're going to his office and then we're coming home. You got that, Agnes?"

"Yes, Seth, I have it. . . . You could have given me some notice, you know. The chauffeur isn't here this morning. Moss forgot some papers and wanted them brought into the office. And don't think for a minute that I'll drive you."

"That's exactly what I think, old woman," Seth demanded contrarily. "Now go get yourself ready. I don't want to be ashamed of you. How a woman can let herself go the way you have is beyond me. Have you no pride?"

"I have pride, Seth. Make no mistake about it. I'll just be a few minutes." Agnes turned and left the room, her back taller and straighter than Seth had seen it in a long time.

Up in her room, Agnes picked up the house phone and called the garage. "I want you to go into town and pick up Mr.

Coleman's prescription at the pharmacy," she told the voice at the other end. "Take the ranch truck and leave the limousine." Her eyes darted to the clock. "I'll need that prescription before noon, so you'll have to hurry."

When she replaced the receiver in the cradle she sank onto the edge of her bed, facing the window where she could observe the driveway. Within a few moments she saw the dark blue ranch truck churning up the dust. Quieting her pounding heart, Agnes picked up her coat and walked down the stairs.

As she helped Seth into his coat and wheeled him down the ramp they'd erected over the front stairs, Agnes felt the perspiration break out on her upper lip. Hearing her quick shallow gasps, Seth tormented, "Gettin' old, hey, Aggie? You can be replaced. Yes, indeed, that's what I'm thinkin' of doin', Aggie. Put you out to pasture, is what I'll do. Or maybe I'll just put you out!" He cackled gleefully, spitefully. Agnes's hands tightened on the wheelchair grips. She pushed him as far as the garage, then steered him toward the side door.

"Whatcha doin', you crazy old woman? You can't get this contraption through there. Go inside and open the big door and get me in that way."

Silently, deliberately, Agnes squeezed the chair through the side door, struggling with it between the fleet of automobiles. "Damn fool woman, it's easier to heft me in the backseat from out there!" He jabbed a finger toward the outside.

"Shut up, Seth. We'll do this my way or not at all. Now are you going to complain the day away, or are you going to help me?" She swung his arm over her shoulder and lifted; Seth obliged by swinging himself into the Cadillac.

"Fold that contraption and put it back here with me," he snarled. "Damn fool woman does everything ass-backward." Scowling, Seth reached into his breast pocket for his cigars, bit off the tip, and proceeded to light up. "C'mon, hurry up. We ain't got all day!" he scolded between puffs.

Agnes pretended not to hear. Her movements were slow and deliberate as she closed the door and sat behind the wheel to start the engine. The Cadillac roared to life. "You just sit tight, Seth. There's something I have to get from the house. I'll be right back."

"For crissake, Aggie, turn off the engine while you're gone, or at least open the big door!" His gaze narrowed when he saw her remove the automatic garage door opener from over the sun visor. "Aggie, I said shut the damn engine off!"

"I'll be right back, Seth. Sit tight. You're in no position to give orders."

"The hell you say!" Seth roared. "Shut that damn engine off! Open the door, either one! What the hell are you tryin' to do?" With surprising strength and agility, Seth lumbered forward and reached over the seat, grabbing Agnes by the back of her head, his clawlike fingers digging into her scalp before locking on her hair.

She struggled, trying to pull herself free. His strength was terrible, so unexpected. Agnes gasped for breath; Seth's voice roared in her ears. Her feet shifted, searching for purchase to brace herself against his assault. He was shaking her by the hairs of her head, pushing her backward and forward. Agnes's elbow accidentally struck the gearshift, tripping the transmission into drive. The Cadillac shot forward, crashing into the back wall, destroying the shelves mounted there and sending their contents shattering to the concrete floor. A spare container of gasoline puddled out of its bent and cracked container.

"Look what you've done, you stupid bitch!" Seth yelled. "What are you trying to do, kill us both?"

The words sent a chill up Agnes's spine. The gasoline, Seth's lit cigar. Quickly she turned off the ignition, and the engine died. "Your cigar! Where's your cigar?" she cried. She scrambled from the car and fell to her knees, searching.

"For crissake, Aggie, find that damn thing. It must have rolled out when you started your hysterics."

The oily smell of gasoline stung her nostrils as it puddled and rivered under the front end of the car. There it was! She reached for the smoldering object—a second too late.

"You've done it this time, Aggie!" Seth bellowed. It was the very last thing she would ever hear.

The funeral was small and private. Neither Billie nor Moss could face a large, curious crowd. Amelia could not come home for the funeral and neither could Susan. Concert bookings. Maggie had other plans. Only Billie, Moss, and Sawyer attended. Agnes was laid to rest in the family cemetery beside Jessica. Seth, as he had requested, was buried in an unmarked grave beside his old horse, Nessie. In the small cemetery stood a marker in memory of Riley Seth Coleman. They had never found enough of her son to bring him home. It was the first time Billie had seen the white marble plaque, and she gave in to her grief. Moss stood dry-eyed, staring off into the distance.

PART IV

PART IV

All the partings, all the eternal separations, and all of them without a single good-bye. Riley, Seth, Agnes. Even a grandson, a poor substitute for Riley and one that Moss doubted he could have ever come to love and proudly show off to the world, was lost to him because of uncompromising prejudice and ignorant pride. Maggie and Susan counted among the losses, their lives twisting and turning them away from Sunbridge. Amelia, her life in Europe—time and change had separated sister from brother. And second only to Riley was the loss of Billie. Even though the divorce had not been finalized at the time of Seth's funeral, he had lost her.

Moss and Billie had been drawn together in mutual grief. He had pleaded with her to move back to Sunbridge, to give their marriage another chance. Recognizing her own need for continuity in her life and wanting to share these black times with someone who was also touched with the same grief, Billie had complied. The divorce had been put on hold. Resuming a marriage whose ashes were long cold was difficult at best, if not impossible, but loyalty to the past and what they had shared prompted Billie's return.

At first it seemed it might work. Moss was making every attempt to mold himself into the husband she'd always wished he would be. In a very carefully worded letter to Thad, she stated her reasons for abandoning the divorce. Only one phrase had leaped out at Thad from the pages. "We need each other." Thad had written to wish them well. Billie knew there was little else he could have said. There was nothing he could do.

Before the first anniversary of Riley's death, Billie realized her move back to Sunbridge wasn't going to work. She wasn't enough for Moss, who ghosted about the house shrouded in grief for his son. He thwarted her every attempt at closeness, preferring to lock himself in his workroom with his aeronautics schematics, his memories, and a bottle. He had already dissolved Coleman Aviation; he wanted no part of building government-contracted planes and instrumentation. Moss claimed that it was their fault Riley had died; but he knew that it was his fault for not standing up to them. And that was what tore him apart. He emerged from his workroom with haunted eyes, and an aged weariness slumped his shoulders.

Billie ached for him, but there was nothing she could do to help. Sharing his bed provided only a momentary respite. Billie realized that Moss was punishing himself and everyone else. But he needed her, and even if her own wants and desires went unfulfilled, she remained at Sunbridge, working by day in her studio and sleeping by night in the lonely bedroom on the second floor of the great empty house.

There were days when the loneliness was so intense that she believed it was insane to stay. Yet she realized that she had a commitment to Moss . . . and to the past. And yes, it was a kind of loving, too, but it was not *love*.

Air-mailed letters, phone conversations, unspoken wishes and devotions: these were her love; Thad was her love. She knew she had only to whisper the words and he would come flying into her arms. It was the one thing she would never ask.

Before two years had passed, Billie was convinced that Moss no longer wanted her at Sunbridge. He had set up a New York office, and he had not been back to Texas in over six weeks. Sawyer was away at school most of the time. The house was lonely, empty.

She decided to return to Austin, hungry for the stimulation of city life, for the sound of another voice. When she called Moss in New York to tell him she was moving back to her old apartment, his only reaction was surprise that she'd kept the lease for two years. His final words were "I'll miss you, Billie, but I suppose it's for the best."

Work was Billie's salvation. Designs spilled from her canvas, and most of them were accepted by textile manufacturers. Her sense of self grew along with her business, but Billie never pushed herself: she wanted to enjoy her accomplishments.

Billie's social sphere was expanding and she wondered how she had managed by herself for so many years. The university art department had pleaded with her to teach several classes each week, and in order to lecture on textile design, Billie was forced to learn more about it herself.

When a major manufacturer of bed linens and tableware seduced Billie into copyrighting designs especially for them, she had to hire an assistant. Judy Wood, a very capable young artist, was put in charge of this new endeavor. Designs by *Billie* was a runaway success; Billie Coleman had arrived.

She and Moss were now legally separated—on the advice of Moss's old family lawyer. Billie no longer thought in terms of legally divorcing herself from Moss. There seemed little point to it—she was already free, in body and in spirit. Perhaps deep inside her she may have harbored the secret hope that things might someday be mended between herself and Moss. For whatever reason, she couldn't take the action that would untie that final knot. Moss was a part of her—and always would be.

CHAPTER
{{{{{{{{{ **THIRTY-SIX** *}}}}}}}}*

Billie hung the last of the Christmas cards on the narrow garland she'd strung near the fireplace. One of them caught her eye. MERRY CHRISTMAS AND A HAPPY 1979! The sight made her knees want to buckle when it suddenly struck her that soon it would be ten years since her son had lost his life somewhere in Vietnam. Where had that time gone? What had filled her days? The ache in her heart was still as raw as it had been the day she'd been told Riley was dead. How had she lived through it? Ten years of missing his face, his sudden smile, his love.

Often, more often than she liked to admit, she believed Riley had only been loaned to her and Moss. Conceiving her son had been a contrivance, a deliberate, desperate move to preserve her marriage, to secure Moss's love, and, shamefully, even to secure her own and Agnes's position at Sunbridge. Perhaps Riley was never meant to be; perhaps she had somehow forced the heavens into giving her a son.

"Billie? Darling? What is it?" Thad's voice, filled with concern, reached out for her. This was the first Christmas they were spending together in Austin, flying in the face of convention. Usually, especially during the holidays, Billie would meet him somewhere.

"I just happened to notice this card and realized it will soon be ten years since Riley was killed. Sometimes it just reaches up and smashes me in the face. It's funny, isn't it? I mean, I don't mark the day Maggie left home, or Susan. And I have to think to remember the day Seth and my mother were killed. Only Riley."

Thad moved across the room to take her into his arms. She nestled her head familiarly against his shoulder.

"It's only natural, Billie," he soothed. "Riley was your son and he's lost to you. Seth and Agnes were old. You know your daughters live in this world with you. You can hear their voices, reach out and touch them. The heart always yearns for what it can never have. Don't you know that?"

"I know in my head," she told him. "Knowing it here"— she thumped her breast—"is something else entirely. . . . Why don't you make us that toddy now? I get maudlin when I start thinking like this and I don't want to spoil Christmas for you."

He kissed her lightly on the cheek and released her. As he prepared their drinks, Thad recalled how often over the past ten years he'd ached to tell Billie that Riley had left the legacy of a son, a piece of himself to hold and to love; he knew it would bring her such joy. But Otami would not release him from his promise of secrecy. Thad had explained that Billie didn't know she had a grandchild, that Moss had never told her of his trip to Japan. For years he'd begged her to reconsider her decision. But Otami believed it was her duty to uphold her dead husband's wishes in the matter and had refused to give her consent.

And if Thad broke that promise and told Billie now, after so many years, would she hate him for having kept the knowledge to himself? Would she ever understand his allegiance to Riley and Otami? Thad shook his head. He couldn't take the risk; losing Billie now, after all these years, was unthinkable.

Billie curled against Thad as they stretched out before the fire, silently watching the flames flicker, burning away the darkness in the room. Her head rested against his chest; she could hear his heart beating beneath her cheek. They were so comfortable with each other, she thought, yet there was passion, too. His hands played in her hair, brushing the sensitive skin at the back of her neck. Emotions were building within her and she knew that soon he would kiss her lovingly, tenderly, and together they would reach out for each other and share their love.

As though reading her thoughts, she felt him move beside her, pressing his lips close to her ear. "I like being your lover, Billie Coleman," he whispered seductively.

"Lover," she answered. "I like that word. I like what it means. Somehow, though, I never think of myself as that. It always seemed to fit other people, other women." He knew she was thinking about Alice Forbes.

"You are my lover, Billie. We share so much, even though we're apart for so much of the year."

Billie sighed. "Yes, I know. I wonder sometimes how you can be so understanding, so patient."

"I love you, Billie. I've always loved you; it's that simple."

Billie's eyes filled with tears. "Hearing those words means so much to me, even at my age." She struggled for a laugh. "Moss never said them, you know. I would tell him I loved him and Moss would always reply, 'I know,' as though my loving him were inevitable and deserved. Such simple words and yet they mean so much." She turned in his arms, embracing him, pressing herself against him. "I love you, Thad. And I want you. I always want you."

Thad's mouth lowered to hers, drawing a deep, loving kiss. Her admissions of love never ceased to touch him; her whispered invitation to make love to her excited him. He captured her mouth with his own, entering to feel the velvet of it. He began the ritual of their lovemaking, feeling and knowing the freshness she brought each time they were together this way. He would never have enough of her; he would never tire of this woman who gave herself so willingly, so gently. Theirs was a finely tuned passion, giving and receiving, enjoying and delighting. He could almost feel her body vibrate with expectancy when he caressed her breasts and possessed them with his lips. When his hand strayed between her thighs she moved against him and he could hear the response to his own passion in the catch of her breath and the deep sound that came from her throat.

"I love the way you touch me," she confessed huskily, her own hands reaching for him, drawing him closer, wanting to share this pleasure with him.

Her body was delicious, her responses exquisite, but it was the gleam of love pouring from her eyes and the pleasure he saw there that evoked his own climax. Billie, his beautiful, loving Billie.

They lay together, legs entwined, basking in the afterglow

of their lovemaking, warmed by the heat of the fire that bronzed their skin and reflected in their eyes. He soothed and stroked her, enjoying the fullness of her breasts and the smoothness of her skin. In his eyes she was every bit as beautiful as she'd been that day in Hawaii on Diamond Head. Even more beautiful now, he amended, because now the light in her eyes was for him and she brought with her love all the sensitivity and maturity of a woman. "You're a beautiful lover, Billie," he breathed. "I never want to be away from you. I want to spend the rest of my life enjoying what we have now, this minute."

Billie turned in his arms and kissed him fully, sweetly. If only all of life could be this way, she thought, if only everything were so simple. I love you and you love me and all's right with the world. But the scars on her heart reminded her it wasn't so. Life could be bitter and jealous, taking happiness and joy and obliterating them. Perhaps it was maturity—or experience—but Billie had long ago learned not to take even the smallest joy for granted.

Billie stood at the kitchen sink rinsing the last of the breakfast dishes, a smile playing about her mouth. Thad had made feeble excuses to leave the apartment early, murmuring something about finding authentic plum pudding for Christmas dinner. Billie knew that when he returned, his arms would be full of gaily wrapped packages, which he would unsuccessfully attempt to sneak under the tree.

When the phone rang, she quickly wiped her hands and ran into the living room to answer it. It was her office manager, Judy Wood, wishing her a merry Christmas and assuring her that things were battened down at the office until after the holiday.

Billie sank down at her desk, smiling back at a photograph of Sawyer in riding clothes atop her stallion, Menghis. How she loved this bright granddaughter who was so like herself. Sawyer was to arrive in time for dinner tonight, and Billie had to admit that she could hardly wait to see her and hear all about what Sawyer was doing in college.

"Give the family my love" had been Judy's parting words. Sawyer and Thad were her family. Her daughters had been invited for the holidays, but they'd declined. She knew that the trip from Europe would be impossible for Susan and her husband, Jerome—who were to appear together in concert during the holidays—but she was disappointed that even after all these years Maggie still refused to share even the smallest part of her life with her parents. Billie knew that Maggie resented Moss's attitude both to her husband, Cranston Tanner, and to her son, Coleman Tanner. Even Billie was surprised when Moss had accepted the news of his first grandson so blandly, refusing to acknowledge the boy beyond a cash gift for his birthday and at Christmas. It was cruel to Maggie and Billie couldn't blame her daughter for being offended. And for some reason Moss and Cranston, who was a successful attorney and wealthy in his own right, were constantly at each other's throat whenever they chanced to be together. This was the first real Christmas Billie would be spending with Thad, here in Austin, and she was glad there would be no tension, no frustration.

The downstairs buzzer shattered Billie's reverie. Thinking it was Thad, she ran to the panel beside the front door and pushed the button to allow him into the building. Two minutes later she threw open the front door, ready to rush into his arms. But it wasn't Thad.

"Paul McDermott! How nice of you to stop by."

"Hello, Billie. . . ."

"Come in. Can I get you a cup of coffee? You look frozen."

"Sounds nice. . . . Have I come at an inconvenient time?"

Billie was gracious but bewildered. She and the Coleman family doctor had hardly ever been on social terms. "Not at all. . . . I can hardly remember the last time I saw you, Paul. Wasn't it just before the accident in the garage?" Paul had been Seth's doctor.

"About then. I didn't have office hours today and I thought I'd come over. There's something I want to talk to you about." He accepted the proffered mug of steaming coffee, sipped it, then placed it on the table near his elbow. "Billie, there's something I thought you'd want to know. I'm aware that you and Moss no longer live together, but I also know that my coming here was required. I don't feel as though I'm breaking Moss's confidence by telling you this, since he didn't specifically ask me not to. . . ." His jowly face seemed clouded and his words were halting. "Billie, this will be Moss's last Christmas. He's dying, Billie. Leukemia. And he refuses treatment. I stopped by Sunbridge today to check on him. He belongs in a hospital, but he won't hear of it. Is there a chance that the two of you can put aside your differences? . . . He needs someone, Billie. He needs you!"

Billie's mouth dropped open. The coffee mug trembled in her hand and the world seemed to sway under her feet. She'd heard the words, they'd registered, and now every fiber in her being was denying them. It was a long moment, a very long moment. Something inside her was railing against this betrayal. Ridiculous that she should feel this way, but she knew it was what she was feeling: betrayed. It was something she had become accustomed to dealing with in her life. Agnes, Seth, Moss, Maggie, and even Riley in his own way. "How . . . how long has Moss known?" she managed to ask. "You said he refuses treatment. Surely he knows how serious this is." Again the drum was beating inside her head. Moss knew something like this about himself, something so critical, and he had not told her.

Paul McDermott marveled at Billie's control. He'd always admired this shy, unassuming woman. "Moss has known for about six months. He came to me with complaints about his health and the tests have confirmed my suspicions. I've only recently learned that he's kept this from you. He's been alone for too long and he's been throwing himself into his work. He always has, I know, but this time it's almost with a vengeance. I don't think he ever recovered from Riley's death. He claims he has work to finish and it's quite important to him. Hospitals, tubes, medication, would prevent him from completing it, or so he says. Somehow, Billie, I believe him. I've seen men afraid of death and doctors, but that's not the case with Moss. It's as though he's resigned to it and simply must go on with his work."

"Yes, that would be typical of Moss. Do you think he'll finish it? His work, I mean."

Paul McDermott shrugged. "I have no knowledge of what he's working on, and if you're asking me how long he has . . ." The words trailed off. "Three months, six, a year? I have no way of knowing, Billie. No one does, really."

"Paul, how do I let Moss know you've told me?" Her voice sounded dry and raspy.

"I can't say for sure. I've had a long talk with him and at times I had the impression that he might tell you himself. And then again, maybe not. That's why I took it upon myself. At this point I don't know what he's feeling. I thought you'd be the best one to handle it. Can you, Billie?"

She nodded. "I'm trying." Then she said with more confidence, "Yes, I can handle it. It must have been terrible for Moss. He must have felt so alone."

"He is alone, Billie, but I knew he could count on you." McDermott was relieved. He'd known Moss for a very long time, and as a rule he didn't like to become emotionally involved with his patients.

Billie could only sit there dumbstruck. If only the doctor's voice weren't so kind. If only he would say something else, other words that didn't knife through her this way. "You should be getting home, Paul. It's the holiday season and you should be with your family." Family. A mother and a father. A husband and a wife. Children. Grandchildren. Family.

When Thad arrived back at Billie's apartment from his impromptu shopping spree, he found her sitting quietly in front of a long-dead fire, staring into the cold, blackened hearth. She was so still that for a moment he thought she'd fallen asleep, but there was something about the rigid set of her shoulders and the pallor of her skin that alarmed him. "Billie?" he said softly, dumping his armful of presents onto the sofa. "Billie, what's happened?" Alarms began blaring in his skull, and a dull, creeping sensation was prickling the back of his neck.

Billie kept her eyes averted. She didn't want to look into that beloved face and see the touches of gray near his temples, reminders of how much time had passed since she'd first known she loved him, evidence of how much time she had wasted. Most of all, she didn't think she could bear the expression in his eyes when she told him about Moss and the decision she'd come to during the past few hours, a decision that would break his heart.

He sat down beside her, immediately taking her into his arms. "Thinking about Riley?" he asked quietly, sympathy for her grief making his voice husky.

Billie shook her head. "No, I'm thinking about Moss." Suddenly she turned, wrapping him in her embrace. "Darling, I must tell you something, but first I want to tell you that I love you. I'll always love you. I need for you to know that, without a doubt. I need for you to believe in me."

Thad's apprehensions intensified. He accepted her embrace, feeling as though it would be the last time he would ever hold her in his arms, and listened while she told him of Paul

McDermott's visit and his news about Moss. With each word, Thad's heart sank lower and lower. He wished he didn't love her so much, so that he could argue with her, fight her, beat her if necessary, to make her see what she was doing to the both of them, to their love.

"I don't know if he'll have me," Billie was saying, "but I know I have to try. Can you understand, Thad?"

He buried his lips in her hair, inhaling the fragrance of her shampoo. "I can only try to understand. Yes, dammit, I *do* understand, but I don't want to! I don't want to share you again! I want you for myself, Billie. Dammit, I've waited too long as it is and I don't want to wait any longer!" In anger and frustration, he tore himself from her arms and paced the room in his long-legged stride, running his long fingers through his hair. "Don't look at me that way, Billie. Yes, I'm angry— hell, I'm mad! I think I could almost hate you right this minute. You're asking me to be noble again and I don't want to be. I wish I didn't care about Moss or the years I've known him and loved him. I wish he were dead already and this was over and done with." Thad's face crumpled with anguish. "I love you, damn you, and you're taking yourself away from me!"

Billie ran to him, forcing her arms around him, giving him what comfort she could. He hadn't said anything she hadn't already told herself. All the hateful things; all the things she didn't mean. She felt Thad relent, felt his arms opening to her, and he held her for a long time. Then he left her arms and moved toward the door. She choked back a sob. He was leaving, then, leaving her with a broken heart. She wanted to cry out that he shouldn't leave her, not ever.

Thad stopped short of the door, standing before the desk, his eyes, like her own, immediately drawn to Sawyer's picture. He picked up the phone and dialed, waiting a long moment before someone answered.

"Hello! Moss? Thad here. Listen, I found I was able to make it to this great state of Texas for a good old-fashioned Christmas. I stopped by to see Billie and we were just thinking how good Sunbridge would look to us right now. Have you got your tree up?...Then we'll just have to come and decorate it for you!"

Billie sank down onto the sofa, burying her face in her hands, tears streaming from her eyes. Thad. Dear Thad.

"Yes, Sawyer is coming to spend Christmas with Billie;

she's coming in later this afternoon. . . . Just a minute, I'll ask her." Covering the receiver with his hand, Thad spoke to her. "Moss said his chauffeur is already in town and if we'd like, he can stay to pick Sawyer up at the airport. He sounds as though he's glad to have us come, Billie. We can leave now or we can wait for Sawyer."

Unable to meet his glance, Billie said simply, "Tell him to have Ephraim meet Sawyer. We can be at Sunbridge in a little over an hour, if he'd like. Ask him to have the heat turned on in my old studio."

There. It was so simple. Who ever said you can't go home again?

Sawyer Coleman, with the aid of the chauffeur, slid and skidded down the incline to Billie's studio. Laughing and giggling, she scooped up snow and tossed it at the stern man carrying her baggage. Her own shopping bags, filled with brightly wrapped packages, were scattered all about the lawn. "It's Christmas, Ephraim. Smile," she teased, then set about gathering up her damp packages and shoving them helter-skelter into her shopping bags. She could tell Ephraim felt that at twenty-one one should be more grown-up. Ha! Well, her grandmother loved a good snowball fight; she wouldn't have to coax her too hard.

"Grand! I'm home! Merry Christmas!"

"Sawyer! I was so worried. Was the plane late?"

"There's a storm out there." Young arms reached out and the embrace was warm, tender, and full of love. "You look wonderful, Grand. I bet you got some new accounts. But what's that sad look in your eyes? You always said a smile had to reach the eyes to count. I want to hear all about it."

Billie laughed. "And so you shall. All in good time. You are as gorgeous as ever. It must be all those carrots and string beans I made you eat when you were little."

Sawyer turned. "Thank you, Ephraim. I'm sorry about the snow. I'm just happy to be home. Being here at Sunbridge is such a surprise and it's something I always used to do when I was little. It wasn't fair to you. Forgive me."

Billie watched the stern chauffeur melt and smile at her granddaughter. Even the staunchest diehard responded to Sawyer's beautiful smile. When the door closed behind him, Billie questioned her. "What was that all about?"

"I felt like a snowball fight," Sawyer gurgled. "What do you say, Grand?"

"Sounds good to me. Let me get my boots and parka." How wonderful this child could make her feel. She could almost forget.... Almost.

Billie stopped in the hallway to take a long look at her granddaughter. Tall and slim, with honey-colored hair that fell to her shoulders in soft waves. For a minute Billie saw her as a little girl again, tucking her hair into a powder-blue parka with white lamb's wool around the edges. Those years, would they always haunt her? "I don't know which is bluer," Billie said affectionately, "your eyes or the parka. You should wear blue more often."

Sawyer preened for her grandmother. "Got my first semester marks ahead of schedule. Fourth in my class. I'm almost a certified aeronautical engineer. What do you think of that?"

"I think it's wonderful.... Sawyer, I want you to find the time to make your grandfather talk to you. I want him to know what you've done and how well you've done. It's important."

Sawyer sobered instantly. So, that was the reason for the sadness in her grandmother's eyes. She should have known. "I'll try. We have so much in common, but he simply isn't interested."

"He will be now. I think he's looking forward to your visit. You have to make him talk. Use every trick you know."

"I will, I will. Why are you so tense? Unwind. Come on, this snowball fight is just what we both need to get rid of all of our hostilities for a little while."

They rolled and tumbled in the carpet of white for what seemed like hours. They threw snowballs and pelted each other with great handfuls of the soft flakes. They laughed and shrieked until they were breathless.

Standing at the top of the hill with his cap pushed back on his head, Thad Kingsley watched the women with a wide grin on his face. "Hey," he called, "can you use another body?"

"Thad!" The cry of pure delight was almost more than Thad could bear, especially after the difficult hours he'd just spent with Moss.

"Uncle Thad!" How wonderful the young voice sounded, so much like Billie's had years ago.

"Well?"

"If you think you can handle us, come on," Sawyer cried happily.

Thirty minutes later Thad's impeccable navy blues were covered with snow. His shiny black shoes were crusted with ice, and he complained that his feet were frozen and his ears were frostbitten.

"Let's hear it for womanhood!" Sawyer shouted.

"Yaaah!" Thad croaked hoarsely. "Now can we go in?"

"I was just getting warmed up," Billie teased. "I know I could last out here at least another two minutes. Had enough, Sawyer?"

"Yeah. I'm hungry. Why don't we call Grandpap to come down for something to eat?"

"Call him," Billie said, trying to shake the snow from her parka. "Better yet, since you love the cold, why don't you go up to the house and invite him in person?" She glanced at Thad for confirmation.

"Do that, Sawyer," he agreed. "I just left him a little while ago and I know he was going back into his workroom. Tear the old boy away, if you can."

Billie linked her arm in Thad's and they headed for the studio. "It's going to be a wonderful Christmas. I don't know if Moss will cooperate, but I sure as hell am going to try. *We're* going to try."

Thad frowned. "I just spent two hours with him and he didn't say a word to me, just wanted to talk about old times. If he knows about us, Billie, he didn't say anything. Something tells me he'll be glad for the company this Christmas."

Billie stood for a moment, looking up into Thad's face. "Have I ever told you I think you're wonderful?" she asked softly, watching the love flow into his eyes.

"You're pretty wonderful yourself, darling, and I love you, very much." Billie was aware of Thad's trembling hands and the moistness in his eyes. She pretended not to see. "You never took your suitcase up to the big house; it's still in the car. You'd better get out of that wet uniform. You can use the bathroom and I'll change in my room."

Billie and Thad were just getting the fireplace going when Sawyer bounded into the studio. "Hot toddies coming up!" she called gaily, heading directly for the kitchen to heat the water. "Grandpap said he already had something to eat but that he'd come down later for a drink. We'll all be together. Won't that be nice?"

"Yes, it will be very nice."

"Almost like a family again." Sawyer smiled brightly.

If there was one word in the English language Billie hated, it was "almost." In many ways, it summed up her life. Everything was almost. Almost married. Almost divorced. Almost loved. Moss was almost dead. God, she hated that word.

"I want to unpack and see if I can dry off my Christmas presents," Sawyer said. "You don't mind, do you, Grand?"

"Of course not. You go along. Thad and I will sit here before the fire and pretend that that little bit of snow invigorated us."

"Speak for yourself, woman," Thad teased. "If you could have gone on for another two minutes, I could have topped you at three."

"I have news for you both." Sawyer laughed. "I couldn't have stood that cold air for one more minute."

"What can I do?" Thad asked the minute Sawyer's door closed.

"Be there if he needs you. Be the friend you've always been."

"Moss was supposed to live forever," Thad said in a choked voice.

"I know. That's what we all thought. I don't think Moss was ever aware of his own mortality. Even now I don't know if he comprehends what's going on. Why?" Billie cried in a strangled voice.

"It's his time. It's going to happen to all of us."

"To us, yes. To Moss, never. I'm having trouble accepting it. I hope and pray that I'll do the right things, say the right words."

Billie's brokenhearted words tore at Thad. He should be comforting her. "Look at us. We're acting as though it's over. Moss would never want a wake. We have to accept it because there is nothing else we can do."

"He never came out of it after Riley died. Not even the death of his father affected him as intensely. That's when he sold Coleman Aviation and devoted himself to what I call his dream plane. It's all he's done for the past years. He blames himself for Riley's death.

"I remember when he returned from Japan after Riley had been killed. It was as if he'd simply caved in. I've often wondered what happened. I thought he went to see you. I never asked because I thought it was a private matter between the two of you. Can you tell me now what he spoke of and why he felt the need to go all the way to Japan to see you?"

Thad thought he was going to swallow his tongue. He knew someday this was going to come up. Still, he wasn't prepared for it. Should he lie? Should he tell the truth? Which was worse? He didn't know. She was looking at him so strangely, waiting for his answer. "He needed comforting. The kind of comforting one man can give another." Would she hear the lie in his voice?

Billie stared at Thad for a long time. The words didn't ring true, but this wasn't the time to press the issue. Let it lie. Don't raise old ghosts. Someday . . .

After a sketchy meal of canned soup and grilled cheese sandwiches, Sawyer, Billie, and Thad settled down in front of the fire, Christmas carols playing softly on the radio. At the sound of a light tapping on the door, Billie opened it to admit Moss. He looked much the same, thinner perhaps, a little more gray in the dark hair. The awkwardness of the moment was saved by Sawyer, who leaped up from her position on the floor and hid her hands behind her back. "Now don't look, Grandpap. I'm making you something for Christmas and it isn't finished yet. Close your eyes until I can hide it in my room."

Thad and Billie laughed aloud. "What's so funny?" Moss asked.

"We've seen what she's making. I hope you remember it's the thought that counts. Sawyer is definitely not a needle-woman."

"I heard that!" the girl protested. "But I do make extremely good toddies. Would you like one, Grandpap?"

"I could use one after that cold walk from the big house. . . . Say, Sawyer, would you come up to the house in the morning? There's something on my drawing board I'd like to show you."

"I'll be there at first light, Grandpap. I've been itching to get into that workroom of yours for years now."

Sawyer's statement seemed to please him; a broad grin struck his face. "Your grandmother has told me about your grade point averages in college. I'm proud of you, Sawyer. I have to be honest and say I never thought you'd stick it through. Aeronautics is hardly a profession for a woman."

"I'm not just any woman, Grandpap. I'm a Coleman woman."

"Yes, you are. And I'm proud."

Unable to contain herself, Sawyer spontaneously hugged

her grandfather. "I've waited a long time to hear you say that. I did what you always said and gave it my best shot."

"Well, it was a hell of a shot. We'll talk in the morning. Now I want your grandmother to tell me how her business is going." He turned to Billie. What was that she saw in his eyes? Was it regret? "That damn housekeeper of mine went out and bought bedsheets, all of them with your signature on them. Christ, all those flowers and Chinese pagodas. When I complained, she asked me if I'd prefer Mickey Mouse or Snoopy."

After a pleasant evening filled with laughter and reverie, Moss said he had to be getting back to the house if he was to get up in time for Sawyer's break-of-dawn visit.

"I'll go easy on you, Grandpap. How's ten o'clock?"

"Perfect. We'll rap in the morning. Isn't that what you youngsters say when you want to talk?"

"Right on, Grandpap." Sawyer laughed.

"You picked up some savvy along the way, too, I see."

"Along with my grit and spunk. Grand said I had to have those qualities or I couldn't be a Coleman."

"Well, you got them. Now if you'll excuse me, Billie, I have some work I want to finish before retiring. Thad, there's something I'd like to show you, if you have the time."

"My time is yours."

When the door closed behind them, Sawyer rushed to her grandmother and hugged her. "Did you hear what he said? I can hardly believe my ears. He wasn't putting me on, was he?"

Billie swallowed hard. "Yes . . . yes, I heard. Isn't it wonderful?"

"He's going to show me his dream plane, isn't he?"

"It doesn't pay to second-guess your grandfather. Just when you think you have him figured out, he does something completely out of character."

"What you mean is he throws you a curve and then you're back at square one. . . . You still love him, don't you, Grand?" It was said so casually, so softly, that Billie was taken off guard.

"I'll always love Moss." It was true, she realized. A part of her would always love the dynamic man she married. But that didn't mean she could never love anyone else, experience the kind of mutual giving and sharing that came later in life, when one was old enough to understand and appreciate it. Enduring love.

"I always loved Grandpap," Sawyer said quietly. "He was

all things to me. I know he had no use for girls. Riley was his life. Riley tried to explain him to me one day. I didn't understand what he was saying then, but I do now. It wasn't that Grandpap didn't love me or my mother, Aunt Susan, too. He never let his thinking go beyond a male heir. He couldn't conceive that any of us could contribute. That's what it's all about, Grand, contributing. Grandpap Seth used to say that women belonged in the house taking care of their men. There's something beautiful about that. I, for one, would never dispute the fact that men are stronger—physically, I mean. When it counts, though, we're the stronger ones. Look at the way you handled Riley's death. Grandmam's, too. You grieved, but you didn't fall to pieces. You grew and made a life for yourself despite everything that went on here. I used to hear you cry at night, Grand, when Grandpap had socked it to you in one way or another. Uncle Thad loves you, you know."

How like Sawyer to talk about one thing and then get to the heart of the real matter without a break in the conversation. "Yes, I know," Billie replied. "He's a wonderful person. He's been a magnificent friend, and I don't know what I would have done without his support at times. I'll always be grateful."

"Grateful is all right. Love is something else. It's there. If you want it, don't be afraid to reach out for it."

"If the time is ever right, I just might do that. . . . Isn't all of this a bit heavy for this time of night?"

"Okay, now tell me what you want me to do. I'm all yours till the end of January."

"Christmas has to be as special as we can make it. Christmas Eve dinner and Christmas brunch are all yours. Someone has to fetch a tree and it has to be set up and decorated. There's still shopping to do. . . . Look, I don't think either of us wants to go to bed, so why don't we make some lists?"

The two women were on their second pot of hot chocolate when the phone rang. They looked at each other. "Answer it," Billie said nervously. Who would be calling the studio at a quarter to six in the morning?

"Of course I'm awake. Isn't everyone?" Sawyer said cheerfully into the phone. "I'll be there in two minutes.

"Grandpap. He's waiting for me," Sawyer called over her shoulder. Billie smiled at the blue streak zipping up the parka, catapulting through the doorway.

Outside her grandfather's workroom, Sawyer wet her lips, pinched her cheeks, and brushed impatiently at her long hair.

Here we go, she thought. Taking a deep breath, she crossed her fingers and tapped softly on the door.

"Come in. You said two minutes. It's—"

"Three. I lost a boot coming up the hill in the snow." Sawyer held her foot aloft to show the soaking-wet sock.

Moss nodded. "Don't ever let little things stand in your way. Take your socks off and sit over there by the heater."

Sawyer obeyed. Her eyes were hungry, devouring the room that had been forbidden for so long. She loved it, loved every drawing, every scrap of paper, and every pencil in the room. "Can I look around?" Moss nodded.

He watched keenly as Sawyer walked from one wall to the other, finally standing next to him at his drawing board. "Is it done?" she asked in awe.

"Almost."

"When?"

"Things are slowing me down. I've been working day and night for some time now. I just don't know."

"Do you have a deadline?"

"A personal one," Moss replied wryly.

"What can I do?"

"I'm not sure yet. Let's sit down and talk."

CHAPTER
{{{{{{{{{ THIRTY-SEVEN }}}}}}}}}

It was noon when Thad sauntered downstairs and quietly turned the knob on the door of Moss's workroom. He smiled. Moss was leaning back in a deep chair and Sawyer was sitting at his feet with one boot on and one foot bare. They were deep in conversation. Thad closed the door softly and dressed for outdoors. Billie would want to know about this. He couldn't wait to tell her.

"It's something I've prayed for for a long time," she said, smiling. "But it does leave me with a problem." Quickly she showed Thad the lists they'd each made. "Sawyer was going to fetch a tree this morning—get it up and decorated."

Thad took the lists from Billie's hands. "Well, why don't

the two of us take care of all of this together?" he asked. "We could go out now to chop down a tree and drag it back to the house and trim it."

"Oh, Thad, that'd be wonderful!... Would you like to take the sleigh? There's one in the big barn. Seth always kept it for the big storms. I imagine it's rusty, but if we oiled it, we could get it to slide. What do you think?"

"I think that's a marvelous idea. The big barn, you say?" Billie nodded. "I'll get a saw and rope and meet you there. Dress warmly. It looks like it's going to snow again."

There was something festive, something inspiring, about choosing and cutting down a Christmas tree, and Billie enjoyed the outing in the horse-drawn sleigh. Snuggled with Thad beneath a thick lap robe, she was aware of his body warmth and his powerful presence. Dear Thad. What would she do without him in her life—her one-man emotional support system? She needed him so, especially now. She felt so confused, so... vulnerable.

"How about that one over there?" Thad asked. "The blue spruce? It's an eight-footer easy."

"You're the man with the saw. The ceilings at Sunbridge are twelve feet high. It's perfectly shaped," Billie said, climbing from the sleigh.

"I'll loop this rope around the middle of the tree, and when I say pull, you pull. But stand clear. I'm going to tie this end of the rope to the back of the sleigh, so you're going to be pulling slack. Can you do it?"

"Certainly," Billie bristled. "I've helped cut down trees for years. I'm no novice at this. It's you Yankees that can't get your act together."

"I'll remember you said that. Hold fast now. I'm going to start sawing."

It was totally unexpected. The minute the monstrous tree hit the ground, Billie herself slid down the side of the sleigh and collapsed in tears. Thad stood by helplessly as sobs racked her body. Then he dropped to his knees and pulled her close to his chest. "Go ahead and cry, Billie. Get it all out."

"Oh, Thad, what am I to do? I don't know if I can see this through. If I had gone ahead and divorced Moss, I wouldn't have to... I wouldn't..."

"Yes, you would. You'd be the first one on the scene and we both know it."

"I'm so mixed up. I was beginning to get my life in order

{ 517 }

and thinking about starting the divorce proceedings again. Moss didn't need me. Months went by when we didn't see or speak to each other. When I think about it, I get so sick—all those years, Thad! My God, all those years."

Thad stroked her hair and listened. He felt helpless, out of his depth.

"All these years you've been there when I needed you," Billie said, weeping quietly now. "You never took advantage of my situation. You never made demands. How has your love for me endured all these years?"

"I don't know. I just know that my feelings have never wavered, never faltered. They have endured and will continue to endure. . . . In a way it seems heartless to be talking about love now when Moss . . . what I mean is, I feel so disloyal."

"I want you to understand about my commitment to Moss."

"Shhh," Thad said, laying his finger on her lips. "I understand. You don't have to explain anything to me. It isn't necessary. . . . Did anyone ever tell you you're a mess when you cry?"

"I seem to recall you saying that to me at one time or another. Forgive me for breaking down like this. I'm glad it happened here, away from the house. Isn't it funny . . . I don't mind you seeing me like this, but I don't want anyone else to see how vulnerable I am."

"I don't know if this has anything to do with anything, but I once read somewhere that Freud agonized all his life over the meaning of the word love. When he lay dying, someone asked him for his definition of love, and his answer was 'Love is letting the other person see your vulnerability.' I think I have to go along with his answer."

Billie smiled through her tears. "How like you to have the right words. Someday I'll let you know if it was the right answer."

"If you're done bawling, let's get this tree home," Thad said hoarsely.

It was going to be all right.

It was a very special Christmas. Moss closed the door to his workroom and joined them all in the great living room with the huge sparkling tree. He made every effort to join in the holiday spirit. Thad watched as his friend's eyes traveled from Billie to Sawyer and back to Billie. In the end, these two women, whom he had neglected, had discounted all his life, were going to help him fulfill his dream. How ironic that it had come to this. When he shook hands with Moss the day after Christmas, he knew he would never see him again. At the last moment Moss reached out both arms and drew his friend close. "Hey, you damn Yankee, I don't think I ever thanked you for being my friend. A guy couldn't ask for a better friend. We go back a long time. Look, if . . . ahh, what I mean . . ."

"I'll take care of her," Thad said in a choked voice.

Moss's eyes were full of unasked questions. Thad nodded. Moss sighed wearily. "Does Billie know?" Thad nodded a second time, unable to trust his voice. "Take care of yourself, Thad."

Thad could feel his throat constrict. Tears trickled down his cheeks. He made no move to wipe them away. Neither man seemed willing to let go of the other. "You too. If there's anything I can do . . . if there's anything you want . . . an arm, a leg, a kidney, send out a call."

"How about your heart? That was always special. You always had heart, Thad."

"It's yours."

"Get out of here before you have me blubbering like baby." One last bone-crushing hug and the door was closed behind Thad. Tears streaming down his cheeks as he stood outside in the freezing cold. He fished for a handkerchief to wipe his eyes and blow his nose. Then turned smartly, eyes dry, and gave a stiff salute to the closed door.

From his position behind the lace curtain on the door, Moss's salute was just as snappy.

Sawyer closed herself in Moss's workroom, allowing her grandfather and grandmother the time they needed to be alone. The blueprints in front of her blurred. How was it all going to end? She wished she knew. For now, she had to make a pretense of working until it was time to leave for the airport. Aunt Amelia and Rand were coming for a post-Christmas visit. Sawyer was excited; it had been ages since she'd seen them. Rand had to be a handsome devil. His pictures in his RAF uniform made her mouth water. Maybe it was time to start thinking about a man in her life. . . .

Minutes later, Sawyer slipped quietly out the side door of the workroom and left the house.

* * *

Billie sat on the sofa with Moss. Neither seemed sure of what to say. Moss took the initiative. "I would have told you. I'm sorry that Paul got to you first. I suppose I was trying to find the right time and the right words. I know now there is no right time and no right words. I need you, Billie. You and Sawyer. I can't do it alone. Maybe if I had more time, more strength, I could pull it off, but I'm no fool. This is one dream you're going to have to finish for me. There's not another soul in this world I'd trust to do this for me."

Billie reached for Moss's hand. She nodded. "Tell me what to do, what you want of me."

"I explained the intricacies of it all to Sawyer. She understands. The girl has a head on her shoulders. I never knew that. There's a lot of things I never knew. A lot of regrets, Billie. If I had done this . . . if I had said that . . . this is where I am now. There's so little time."

"Treatment?"

"No. It's too late for that. I need a clear head for what has to be done. Sawyer says she's free till the end of January and has even agreed not to return to school if I need her. Time now, Billie, is my enemy. I have to do this. I have to succeed. I'm realistic enough to know I may not make my deadline, and that's why I want your promise, yours and Sawyer's, that you'll finish it up for me."

"I promise. You look tired, Moss. Why don't you rest for a while? Amelia will be here soon and you're going to want to spend some time with her. Lay here on the sofa. I promise to wake you when they get here. I'll get a blanket."

Moss lay back on the sofa pillows, a grimace of pain stretching across his face. Billie returned with a colorful afghan Jessica had made and covered him. "Billie, I'm sorry."

There was no use pretending she didn't know what he was talking about. The time for pretense was gone. "I know you are, Moss. Sleep now."

"Billie . . ."

"Yes, Moss."

"I really am sorry. Somewhere I got off the track and couldn't get back on. Forgive me."

"There's nothing to forgive, Moss. It's past now. History, you always said. I have to be honest . . . I do forgive you; but I can't forget." She bent over and kissed his cheek. Through her tears she could see his pain-filled eyes.

"You'll make it, won't you, Billie?"

"You can count on it, Moss," she whispered as she brushed the hair back from her husband's forehead.

"What are you thinking, Billie? Not feeling pity for me, are you?" Moss asked after several quiet moments, watching Billie stare out into space.

"No, not pity. I was just thinking how this is really the first time you've ever talked with me this way. It's the first time you've come to me for help. After all these years."

"I always knew you were there for me, Billie. I always knew I could count on you from the first day we were married."

Billie turned her head, her eyes searching his. Her fingers had already found his hand and she willed some of her strength to pour into him. "In many ways, Moss, today is my wedding day. This is the day of commitment. We've shared something together, you and I. I've always loved you, Moss; I love you now, and if I could, I'd live it all again, even the bad times." Billie swallowed past the lump in her throat. Tears coursed down her cheeks.

"And Thad? You love him, don't you?"

Billie nodded. "Yes, Moss, I do. But there's one thing he can never give me, one thing that I need. My dream, Moss. Only you can give me that. The home, the family . . . our children. It's all I've ever wanted and it's what I still want." She was crying now, trembling with the force of her sobs. Moss took her into his arms, sharing her tears, grieving for the past.

"I don't deserve what you're doing for me, Billie. I've never deserved you. I knew it then and I know it now. I'll confess something to you, Billie. Whenever I would think about dying I always knew I wanted it to happen while I was in your arms." His lips brushed her cheek and their tears mingled.

Sawyer Coleman dug her hands deep into the pockets of her ranch mink jacket, a gift from Moss. The holiday atmosphere of Austin's airport was gone, leaving only a few disgruntled, weary travelers who kept their eyes on the clock and their ears tuned for flight announcements.

Pan American's flight 691 had landed and the passengers were deplaning. Aunt Amelia had said she and Rand would clear customs in New York when they changed flights for Austin. Sawyer watched now as a column of passengers made their way up the long carpeted ramp to the main terminal, struggling with their carry-on luggage as they maneuvered to the escalator. She spotted Aunt Amelia and Rand almost immediately and waved. Her mouth felt dry and she could feel a warm flush on her cheeks as Rand scooped her into his arms. "Little Sawyer, all grown up," he teased with a glint in his deep brown eyes.

"Sawyer, you gorgeous creature!" Amelia trilled. "Didn't I tell you she was beautiful?" she said to Rand. "Now unhand that girl so she can give me a proper kiss."

"You should have said ravishing," Rand corrected Amelia as he released Sawyer. "You were only a tad when I saw you last. Let's see, you must be all of eighteen or so. Am I correct?"

Sawyer bristled. "I'm past twenty-one, if you must know." She kissed Amelia soundly on the cheek and offered her own cheek to Rand, who turned her around and kissed her full on the mouth. Sawyer gasped, half in delight and half in annoyance.

"Pretty girls are my downfall."

"He's telling you the truth, Sawyer. Beware of him, he has a young woman hiding behind every pole and bush. My son is very handsome; he looks like Robert Redford, don't you think?"

It was Rand's turn to look uncomfortable and Sawyer pressed her advantage. "Oh, I don't know, Aunt Amelia. Perhaps, in a certain light."

"Why does one simple statement make me sound as though I've a wart on the end of my nose?" Rand asked coolly. Brazen, a little brash, but oh, so feminine. She was beautiful and she could blush so prettily. Aunt Billie had described Sawyer as being independent as hell and he had to agree as he met her level gaze and the slightly insolent curve of her smile.

"You said it, not I," Sawyer bantered lightly. "Look, the baggage is starting to come up. Get it together and I'll get a porter. My car is out front."

"Isn't she a darling child, Rand?" Amelia prompted as she and Rand walked to the baggage area. "I can't believe she's twenty-two, or soon will be. That's old enough to be married. Brainy, too. Runs in the Coleman family. Billie did an amazing job of raising her. Almost as good as I did with you," she said fondly.

"She's not a child, Mother. Those aren't the eyes of a child," Rand said knowledgeably.

"She'll always be a child to me, as will you, here in my heart. Sawyer is the last of the Colemans, and from what Billie tells me, she's taken Riley's place in many ways with her grandfather."

Amelia settled herself in the backseat of Billie's Mercedes while Rand slipped in beside Sawyer. Checking for traffic, Sawyer gunned the engine and the luxurious sedan growled to life as it spewed snow and ice in its wake. Rand closed his eyes in mock horror. Amelia smiled. This grandniece of hers was just what Rand needed. Wait till she told Billie.

"Where did you learn to drive?" Rand demanded as Sawyer narrowedly missed a snow plow and a pickup truck stuck on the side of the road.

"Actually, I taught myself. I do better flying. Don't tell me you're nervous driving with me."

"Nervous? Petrified would be more like it," Rand said through clenched teeth.

The heavy car ground to a halt, narrowly missing a snow-bank, its tires spinning on an ice patch. Sawyer clenched the wheel in her gloved hands. She turned slightly to face Rand. "The way I see it, Rand, you have two choices. You can either walk the rest of the way to Sunbridge or you can sit there quietly. Make your choice."

"How far is it to Sunbridge?" Rand asked.

Sawyer burst out laughing. "Forty miles, the way the crow flies. That tender English skin of yours will freeze right up. What's it going to be?"

Rand threw up his hands. The laughter was there, the tone was half-teasing, but the eyes were something else. She would have booted his tail out of the car. Goddamn it, where had this one been all his life? Growing up. He decided he liked the finished product. "Drive."

The rearview mirror told Sawyer her aunt approved. Why was her heart beating so fast and why was her mouth so dry? This man was having an effect on her she didn't like. He was too damn handsome, too damn knowing, too damn observant. It was obvious she wasn't what he'd expected, just as he wasn't quite what she had expected. She wasn't in the market for a fling or any kind of a relationship. She had things to do and she was totally committed to Billie and Moss. Whatever feelings she was experiencing for this man would only clutter things up. Besides, he probably thought she was too young for him.

Most of the trip was made in silence. Amelia dozed occasionally in the corner of the warm car. Rand sat with his arms crossed against his chest, a grim look on his face. Finally he spoke. "You have a pilot's license?"

Sawyer nodded. "I will also soon have a degree in aeronautical engineering."

Rand's eyes glowed. It was obvious he approved of what he saw, what he heard. "Shall we call a truce?" he asked, smiling.

Sawyer looked over at him. "What you see is what you get. Don't interfere in my life. Don't for one minute think I can't cut it because I'm a woman." She paused. "Truce."

Amelia smiled contentedly. She'd known all along these two would like each other. These little spats, these little declarations and assertions, were all part of getting acquainted. If there was one person she knew in this world, it was Rand, and Rand's eyes were telling her something was happening to him.

The crunch of tires on the hard-packed snow alerted Billie that Sawyer was back from the airport. She felt suddenly old and brittle when she got up from the comfortable chair. She checked on Moss, then went to the foyer to meet the new arrivals, careful to close the door behind her. Moss needed his rest and from now on she would see that he got it.

"Amelia, how wonderful you look!"

Amelia wrapped her arms around Billie and hugged her. "This is where we both lie to each other and say how neither of us has changed."

"It's not a lie. You look the same, but older."

"How's that for flattery?" Amelia laughed. "You remember Rand?"

Billie held out her hand to the tall, handsome young man standing beside Sawyer. "It's been a long time. The last time I saw you, you were clutching Sally Dearest for dear life."

Sawyer hooted with laughter. "Sally Dearest? Who or what was Sally Dearest?"

Rand threw back his head and laughed. It was a pleasant sound and Billie liked him instantly. "Sally Dearest was my cat when I was three years old. She died when I was twelve."

"That's sad." Sawyer gurgled.

"They've been baiting each other all the way from the airport," Amelia said happily. Billie grinned. Amelia was already matchmaking. Sawyer, too, had a gleam in her eye. The look on Rand's face was appreciative.

"How's Moss?" Amelia asked anxiously.

Billie shook her head. "Not too well. He's sleeping right now. Let's go into the library. I had fire going a while ago and we can replenish it."

"I'm going to take Rand to the workroom to show him the plane. If Grandpap wants me, that's where I'll be."

Settled in the library alone with Amelia, Billie handed her a glass of sherry. "That's quite a young man you've raised, Amelia. You're very good with children. Rand and then Susan."

"I think it was simply that they were good children to begin with." She laughed lightly. "I know how difficult it must have been for you to turn Susan over to me that way."

"There was little else to do at the time, considering the mess Maggie had created. We all felt it would be better for Susan, although I must admit, I never dreamed she would take to you and England like a duck to water. I'm proud of her, Amelia. She's made quite a name for herself and she seems very happily married. Even if we're not close as some mothers and daughters, that doesn't mean I can't admire her. And I always had Sawyer. It was like having a second chance."

"She's wonderful. But then, she always was. And she certainly enjoys all the beauty in this family. No, I take that back. You still lay claim to quite a bit of it yourself, Billie. When I look at Sawyer I see you thirty years ago. She's as much like you as Rand is like his father. Spitting image."

"Then I can see why you fell head over heels in love with Rand's father. Such wonderful blond good looks. He must be thirty-five, thirty-six?"

"He's thirty-eight and please don't remind me! The plastic surgeons tell me I've only one more face lift left in this lifetime! God, I wish I had your skin."

Billie laughed and refilled Amelia's glass. The conversation became serious. "I have something to tell you, Amelia. You're going to have to be strong. It's Moss. He has leukemia. There's not much time left."

It took several minutes of disbelief and intense questioning before Amelia seemed to accept the truth. "I can't believe it," she cried. "Not Moss. He's all I have left, Billie." Hard sobs tore at her body.

"That's not true. You've Rand and Susan and me. We've still got one other. Amelia, you must be strong. Don't make this any harder for Moss than it already is. Promise me you'll get hold of yourself." She gathered the woman into her arms, comforting her. Poor Amelia. Poor, lonely Amelia. Throughout her life Moss's love and approval had always been there for her, steadying her.

"You know, Billie"—Amelia blew her nose and wiped her eyes—"when things were roughest when I was growing up here at Sunbridge under Pap's disapproving eyes, it was always Moss I could go to with my troubles. He stood up to Pap for me, protected me. And even when I made a shambles of my life, I always knew I could count on him to love me."

"I know, I know," Billie soothed.

"When I see him, he'll know I've been told. He'll see it. There's no way I can hide it."

"I'm not asking you to hide your feelings, Amelia. Of course you should let Moss know how much you love him, how much you'll miss him. Tell him how much he's meant to your life. You're his sister, the two of you have shared the same beginnings and memories. All I'm asking of you is that you accept his decision to refuse treatment. Allow him his dignity. Don't press him, Amelia. Think of his suffering before you think of your own."

Amelia squeezed Billie's hand. "Of course you're right. You know me so well. When you told me that he was refusing treatment I'd already decided that I was going to force him to go to a hospital. Now I'll simply let him know I'll always be here if he needs me."

"He'll need you, Amelia. He'll always need you."

The days that followed were intense and frenzied. Moss's eyes followed Billie constantly. He'd never in all the years they'd been married paid this much attention to her. Now his unwavering gaze was direct and speculative. She sensed he was assessing, gauging, measuring, and *liking* what he saw. While this pleased her, it didn't mean half of what she'd thought it would. She no longer *needed* his approval; but it was nice to know it was there. How ironic.

It was the evening of the last full day of Amelia and Rand's visit. Arm in arm, Sawyer and Rand burst into the sunroom, where Billie, Amelia, and Moss were deep in conversation. "If there are no objections," Sawyer interrupted, "Rand is taking me to dinner in town. Auntie Amelia, it's all right with you, isn't it?"

Amelia nodded agreeably. "Go along. But"—she held

up a warning finger—"our flight leaves at seven in the morning, so try and get back before then. It's a long ride to the airport."

"We'll bloody well be back by then," Rand replied. "After dinner this child insists we dance the night away. Texas style." He grimaced. "She's taking me to a place called Dirty Nellie's." Rand looked at Billie. "Will I come out alive?"

"Good question." Billie laughed. "Trust Sawyer."

When the couple left the sunroom, Moss turned to Billie and Amelia with a strange look on his face. "Isn't he a little old for Sawyer?"

Amelia's jaw dropped. Billie blinked. "Old?" she echoed. "Moss, they're only going out to dinner. Rand is leaving in the morning. I wouldn't worry."

"Rand has scores of young women fawning over him back home." Amelia smiled. "Don't rattle yourself over this little harmless dinner."

Moss snorted. "Women are supposed to be astute where romance is concerned. Why haven't either of you picked up on Rand's feelings for Sawyer? I certainly saw it. Or does it take a man to recognize the symptoms?" he asked irritably. "Take him home tomorrow, Amelia, and don't bring him back until this project is finished. Sawyer has things to do now and I don't want her distracted."

Billie's gaze flew to Amelia. "We'll deal with it, Moss," Amelia said briskly. "They're sensible adults, and Sawyer knows what's at stake. . . . Why don't you relax and take a small nap. Billie, I could use some help in packing. This way, if everything is done, all we'll have to do is hop out of bed, dress, and be on our way."

Moss nodded and closed his eyes. Christ, how he hated these forced naps his body demanded of him. So little time and he had to sleep five times a day. He was half-aware of Billie and Amelia leaving the room. Once he tried to open his heavy lids. He loved to see Billie walk, that charming, crooked little walk that made her rear end sway from side to side. But he was just too tired. He would make a point of watching her tomorrow.

Sawyer was uneasy. Had it been a mistake to spend this last evening alone with Rand? Perhaps she should have said she was busy. But she wanted to be with him, wanted to sit across from him and feel those dark eyes warm her. It was just as well he was leaving in the morning. But these last few hours tonight were hers.

Rand's capable square hand reached for Sawyer's across the tabletop. His golden handsomeness was illuminated by the tapered candles and the reflected light of the chandeliers. "I've always loved England, and no matter where I was I couldn't wait to return. This time it's different. I don't want to go back. You're quite a girl, Sawyer Coleman, and I think—no, I know that if I stayed I would . . . Do you believe I can't get the words out?"

Sawyer tried for a good-natured smile. "I'm sorry you're leaving. We just got to know each other. I've enjoyed the time we spent together in my grandfather's workroom."

"I'm more than a little in love with you, Sawyer. We've both skirted around it, but Christ, I'm leaving tomorrow."

"I know. I know. I can't get involved. I have a commitment to my grandparents. What kind of person would I be if I turned my back on my responsibilities?"

"I'm not asking you to do that."

"Listen to me, Rand," Sawyer said, leaning over the table, both hands clasped in his. "I'm one of those people who can only do one thing at a time. This project has top proprity. If I slip or deviate even a little, I won't be able to get back on track. It wouldn't be fair to you, either. By now you must know I don't do things halfway. It's one hundred percent or not at all."

Rand nodded. "For a while I thought it was my age. What you're telling me is it's chin up and all that English rubbish. I thought you wild-west characters didn't deny your feelings."

"I'm not denying my feelings. I'm saying I can't act on them. I want you to come back. I know you promised my grandmother you would come if she needed you. I'd like to think that holds for me, too." Rand's answer was in his eyes. Sawyer swallowed hard and squeezed his hand.

"Grand has taken on quite a challenge seeing that Pap's plane gets off the ground. I just hope and pray we haven't bitten off more than we can chew. Oh, Rand, it's simply horrible, but I don't think he'll ever see his dream become a reality. Every day takes its toll on him. I'm sure you've noticed. I can see the day-to-day changes in him and it breaks my heart. I have to stay here and do what I can."

"Moss's dream has been shared by many others. There's been talk of a slant-wing craft for as long as I can remember."

I want to go on record right now, Sawyer: That specification we've been fighting over the past few days isn't going to work." Rand reached for a pen out of his breast pocket and made scratches on the back of the menu.

"I think this design has a good chance, Sawyer. Other oblique-winged craft have been tried, but as far as I know, no one has tried cantilevering the wing span, as you want to do."

Rand scratched a detailed design, one that had become very familiar to Sawyer over the past two weeks. The craft was a long needle-nose design with a single wing positioned above the fuselage. For operation at low speeds or takeoff and landings, the wing would be positioned conventionally, at right angles to the craft. For flight at higher speeds, the wing pivoted at an oblique angle of up to sixty degrees with the fore and aft centerline of the fuselage, reducing drag and promising greater speed and range without an increase in fuel consumption.

"Damn you, that cantilevering will work!" Sawyer cried. "I had the best engineers working on it. Why are you being so stubborn? You haven't been able to give me one good, justifiable reason except gut instinct that it won't work. That isn't good enough. I deal in facts and figures. I thought intuition was a female trait."

Rand held up his hand. "Okay, okay, you win. The specification stays. What I think Moss is really on to is the unusual composite material. Strong and lightweight. The foam core he's developed is revolutionary. He's quite a man, your grandfather. I wish I'd known him better all these years."

Sawyer felt momentarily drained. Arguing with Rand over something so important made her feel terrible. She was right; she *had* to be right. Every engineer in the plant said so. Yet she trusted Rand's opinions and knew he wasn't just trying to be difficult. "There's not a chance in hell that that plane could go down. I'd stake my life on it," Sawyer said forcefully.

"It won't be your life, Sawyer; it will be the life of the test pilot."

"I'll take that responsibility."

"Taking responsibility is one thing; living with the result is something else entirely."

"Damn you, Rand, don't keep doing this to me. You can't shake my confidence. Pap trusts me and so do all the other engineers."

"They don't love you the way I do," Rand murmured.

There was a pause. Then Sawyer said quietly, "This isn't supposed to happen."

"The one thing you can't count on in this world is emotion."

"Maybe you can't count on it, but you can control it," Sawyer countered desperately.

"I hope you do better at it than I'm doing."

"I won't let *anything* interfere or stop me. Accept that, Rand."

"I have. Why do you think I'm leaving tomorrow? But I'll be back. Now *that's* something you can count on."

Sawyer nodded miserably. The tears glistening on her lashes tore at Rand. "Shall we order?" she said with false bravado. "I'm starving!"

"I'll bet you are, you little savage." He laughed, trying for levity. "You're always hungry."

"Don't blame me," she chided, looking up at him with mischief in her eyes. "If I can't nourish my soul, then my stomach takes precedence."

"Sometimes, Sawyer, I think you need a good spanking just to remind you to behave like a lady. And watch those devilish eyes. I just might change my mind about leaving tomorrow."

CHAPTER
{{{{{{{{{ THIRTY-EIGHT }}}}}}}}}

The long days of winter were upon them. Moss's workroom was cramped and on the dark side of the house, so Billie demanded that he move everything out to her studio, where the sun could shine through the glass doors and there was enough space for the technical engineers and designers in Moss's employ to move about freely. Moss's oblique-winged aircraft was becoming a reality. Manufacture of component parts and the construction of the plane itself had been under way in one of the old Coleman Aviation hangars since early last summer. All systems were go.

Billie set aside her own business, completing only the work for which she was already under contract. Now she spent her days and many of her evenings working beside Moss, answering the telephone, setting up schedules, and doing general dogwork. The studio was also ideal because of the proximity of the bedroom. In the big house the bedrooms were far removed from the workroom, and Moss could not be persuaded to leave his work and lie down. Here, with the work proceeding just outside the door, Billie could more easily cajole him into taking a nap. The little kitchen in the studio became a central hub from which delicious aromas of freshly brewed coffee, soups, stews, and snacks could tempt Moss's appetite. So much activity, so much work, yet nothing could forestall the ravages of the disease attacking his body. By will alone, Moss presented himself each day to his men, never allowing his optimism to flag. He worked them hard, praised them often, and was genuinely grateful for their energy and loyalty. It was when he was alone with Billie that he allowed his doubts to show. "You'll see it's finished, won't you, Billie?" he would plead. And always she would promise.

One afternoon in early May, Moss went into the bedroom without prompting. Billie called the crew chief over, worry darkening her eyes. "I think you and the men should make an early day of it, Joe. Things aren't good with Moss."

"We'll leave as soon as we clear up a little, Billie. He's been looking bad all week." The burly man shook his head, already grieving. "Don't you think you should get him to a hospital or something?"

"No, Joe. He doesn't want that. Dr. McDermott comes out every other day to check on him and keep him comfortable. He told me just yesterday that Moss was already in renal failure. It won't be long now."

"Go to him, Billie. I'll take care of things out here and before we leave I'll take the phone off the hook so he won't be disturbed."

"Thanks, Joe." Her eyes were already wandering to the closed bedroom door. "Tell the men thanks for everything and I think they should take the next few days off. I'll keep in touch."

For the next three days Billie remained at Moss's side. He was no longer able to get out of bed and he made feeble jokes about being as weak as a kitten. Paul McDermott had told Billie what to expect and wanted to send out a nurse to help her. Billie rejected the offer. "I'll let you know if I need help. Right now, I'm certain I can manage."

{ 531 }

"I wish you'd let me put him in the hospital. He's in no condition to object. It would make it easier on everyone."

"Perhaps on everyone else, but not on Moss, and he's the only one who counts now."

Moss lay in Billie's bed, late-afternoon sun filtering through the draperies. Dark shadows stained his cheeks beneath his eyes. He'd lost a great deal of weight during the past months, but he was still handsome, and fire and purpose burned in those summer-blue eyes. Billie sat in her chair quietly while he slept, studying his face, committing it to memory. Death stalked outside the door and neither prayer nor denial would chase it away.

"Billie . . ." The sound of her name in the quiet of the room startled her. His voice seemed stronger, some of the old vitality singing in it. "Billie, come and lie down beside me." It was a question; it was a plea.

She settled herself on the bed beside him, resting her head against his shoulder, her arm wrapped around his middle, holding him. "This is a hell of a way to say good-bye, isn't it? I hate leaving you, Billie. These past months have shown me what we could have had all these years. If only I'd allowed you into my life."

"Shhh. You don't have to say these things. I already know them. There's so little I don't know, darling."

"Am I? Am I your darling?"

"You're my first love, Moss. You know what they say, don't you? First love, last love."

He nodded his head, not trusting his voice. After a moment: "But there are other loves, Billie. Different loves, and that's what I want for you. I know what you and Thad mean to each other and I want you both to be happy. I've been a bitter, foolish man, and I'm so sorry."

"There's no forgiveness needed, Moss. I'm so glad we've had this time together, this time to know each other and rediscover the reasons we ever loved each other."

Long moments. Eternities. "Billie?" Moss whispered. "I'm afraid. I don't know what's waiting for me . . . there."

Billie bit her lips, wincing back tears, choking back sobs. She stroked his cheeks, pretending not to feel the moistness beneath her fingers. "Don't be afraid, Moss. Have faith. There are so many whom we know, whom we've loved, waiting to help you, to meet you."

"Do you believe that?" His breathing was labored; he couldn't seem to catch his breath. "Tell me."

"I believe, darling. I believe one day I'll see Riley again. And Seth and my mother. All those who have gone before, waiting."

Moss nodded, accepting her faith as his own. Quietly, he repeated each of the names, always coming back to Riley. "Pray for me, Billie. Pap always had a lot to say about a good woman's prayers."

Again silence. Moss's breathing became rhythmical, long and deep, skittering quickly to short, shallow breaths, and then becoming long and deep again. Even as she held him she sensed the life force leaving him. His eyes fluttered; it was as though he were pulling himself back for one last moment.

"I love you, Billie, with all my heart."

"I know you do, Moss. I know."

They were the last words he ever spoke to her. Words she would remember for the rest of her days. Words that should have been spoken so many years ago. At last he had said them.

Dudley Abramson, the Coleman family lawyer, had to be almost as old as Moses, Billie thought as she watched him make a production out of opening his briefcase. His bony fingers clawed at the stiff crackling papers, finally separating them in the order he wanted. Small eyes crowned by bushy snow-white brows scanned the room. Wills were his favorite legal transaction. He loved watching greedy faces, disappointed faces, faces lit up with genuine surprise. This assemblage would offer no surprises. Moss Coleman's will was cut and dried; there would be nothing to contest. He felt a little disappointed. Still, a will was a will, and he'd best get on with it and put all of them out of their misery. He cleared his rattly throat and took a swipe at his few thinning hairs.

"Are we all gathered here today, all those I sent letters to?" He ran down the list: Billie, Maggie, and Susan; then after a second, Sawyer. He could feel Maggie's tension and bristled. Everyone knew that Sawyer Coleman was Maggie's illegitimate daughter. He sniffed. They weren't going to like this one bit. No sir, not one little bit. He felt better. His voice, when he continued, was still reedy and thin, but feisty somehow, as if daring one of them to object. He glossed over the sound mind bit and got to the heart of the matter. He read off the small bequests and token gifts, then paused for a dramatic effect, pushed his wire-frame glasses higher on his bony nose, and proceeded. "To my daughter Maggie, the sum of ten thousand dollars. A like amount of ten thousand dollars to my daughter Susan. The balance of my estate to my wife, Billie."

"That's it, ladies and gentlemen. Are there any questions?" He always liked this part, because there were always questions. He leaned back in the leather swivel chair and waited.

Maggie could feel her insides start to churn. She had hoped that things would go right today. She should have known better, she thought bitterly. How dare he? To be sloughed off with ten thousand dollars was more than she could bear. Was that what she was worth in her father's eyes? All those years, all those tears, all that hate . . . for what? For ten thousand dollars and the opportunity to visit her father's grave whenever she felt like it. Goddamn you, Mam, how could you have let him do this to me? All that talk you used to give me was just talk. You never cared, because if you had, you wouldn't have allowed this to happen. Well, from here on it's war. One of us is going to get bloodied and it isn't going to be me.

Billie watched the slight hand movement of Maggie's husband as he nudged her to get up and speak. Maggie shrugged off his hand. "Yes, I do have a question. What exactly does that mean? The statement that all the estate goes to mother? Does that mean we have to wait for her to die before Susan and I can inherit our share? If so, I don't think it's fair and I don't like it one bit. What about you, Susan?"

Susan flushed. "It doesn't seem fair to me. Maggie and I certainly deserve more than ten thousand dollars. That doesn't go very far these days. I don't like being dependent on my mother. Can't she distribute it to us if she wants?" Her husband wasn't going to like this. He'd been counting on a really large settlement to start his own music academy. "It's not fair," she repeated loudly.

"Fair or not, it's what your father wanted." He couldn't help but wonder which of the two girls would bring up the matter of contesting the will. The older one, Maggie, probably. She'd always been a handful and that husband of hers looked as though he had his own ideas. The old lawyer leaned over the desk when he saw Maggie turn to face her mother. Sawyer moved to stand protectively behind her grandmother's chair. So, the lines had already been drawn. Susan turned, too, and half rose out of her chair. It was Maggie who spoke.

"Well, Mother, are you going to let this ridiculous will stand or are you going to make some serious distributions? What about my son, Coleman? This isn't right and you know it." And then so cruelly that Billie bit down on her lip: "How is your will going to read? All of the estate to Sawyer? Why aren't you saying something, Mother? I want to know now. I want my share now. I don't want to have to wait for you to die and then fight with my own daughter over what should be mine. All my life I've been cheated. You know it, Mother!" Maggie's voice was a shrill scream.

Susan nodded her head and narrowed her eyes. How in the world was she going to explain this to her husband? she wondered frantically. What could you do with ten thousand dollars? Jerome needed ten times that much to get his music academy under way. How could Pap cheat her this way? It had to be Mam's fault. Pap was ill and didn't know what he was doing. Mam could have seen to it that the money was distributed fairly. Now she was going to have to get involved in a nasty suit; she could see it in Maggie's eyes. Why couldn't she just get her inheritance and walk away? Oh, no, that was too simple. Fight, choose up sides, go against her mother. It was disgusting. Well, this was one time she wasn't going to back off and take a wait-and-see attitude. She would fight with Maggie. By God, she was entitled. Someone was going to have to pay and it might as well be Mam.

"I agree with everything Maggie said," she cried angrily. "It should be divided evenly and I want mine now, too!"

Billie thought her head was going to explode. It was Sawyer's firm grip on her shoulders that calmed her. Billie's back stiffened. "No. Your father made this will and it will stand as is. If you need—"

"Need?" Maggie screeched. "*Need?* And then after you review our needs, our requests, you'll make the final decision. . . . You'll dole it out to us in dibs and dabs, is that it? Well, I don't want it that way."

"I don't, either," Susan said petulantly.

"You both have husbands to take care of you. Perhaps it's time you tried earning a living. Make something of your life."

"Stuff it, Mother. I'm entitled and so is Susan. Is that your final word?"

Billie drew a deep breath. "Yes, it's my final word. It's what your father wanted. What do you think he would do if he could see the way you're acting? Both of you should be ashamed of yourselves."

"It's so easy to be shame free when you're sitting on millions and millions of dollars, isn't it, Mother? Well, that isn't good enough. You had best revise your thinking or I'll engage a lawyer of my own. Susan?" Susan nodded agreement.

"Hold on a minute here," Billie protested. "There's something you must understand. First of all, I'm not sitting on millions and millions, as you put it. Your father was up to his neck in debt." She waited for the realization to sink in.

"That's impossible!" Maggie protested. "You're lying!"

"No, Maggie, I'm not. You both know that your father was in the midst of seeing his dream come true with his plane. Dreams cost money, lots of money."

"Pap built planes before and it only made him richer," Susan countered.

"That's true, but that was when the government subsidized him. This time Moss wanted no governmental interference. This time he was going it alone. Because of his health, he practically shut down every other enterprise. Sunbridge no longer provides beef for the military, and in truth, I doubt that there's fifty head of cattle left on the ranch. He poured everything into this plane and I'm not even certain there's enough to see the project through."

"So don't see the project through. What can you know about planes, anyway?" Maggie said rudely. "Take my advice and get out from under. Pap's dead and buried. Sell what you've got to the government and let them handle it from there. At least we won't be paupered by it."

"I promised your father and it's a promise I intend to keep."

Billie felt as though her innards were shriveling up. She thought she had prepared herself to explain things to Maggie and Susan. But they would never understand. And telling Maggie now about Moss's last, bedside bequest to her would not be a good idea. The Sunbridge house and ranch were to go to Maggie—but only after Billie had completely financed the project; if necessary, however, she was to place Sunbridge on the auction block. "Do your damnedest, Billie, to see that Maggie gets it," Moss had said. "But if your back is to the wall and you have to sell or mortgage, then do it." Would Maggie accept and understand the stipulation? Right now, Billie just didn't have the stomach to find out. Such naked hatred on both her children's faces. Hatred that was directed at her, not Moss. Dear God, what do I do now? she cried to herself. Her shoulders slumped in defeat. It was the slight pressure Sawyer exerted that made Billie sit up straight and look her daughters in the eye. "Do you hear me?" she said quietly, firmly. "I intend to honor that promise."

"If I may interject . . ." Dudley Abramson cleared his throat importantly. "If anyone here intends to contest this will, I will testify that Mr. Coleman knew of his illness almost two years ago. That was the main reason he did what he could to delay a divorce. He wanted to be certain your mother was his legal heir under the law of the state, not merely a beneficiary named to his estate. And if I might say"—his hawk eyes impaled Maggie and Susan—"it seems he was quite right in doing so. Since your mother and father were never divorced, your claims to the estate cannot take precedence over hers. And if it will comfort you, it is in my knowledge that the Coleman assets have been greatly reduced to less than a third of what they once were."

"And that's supposed to be a comfort? Mother"—Maggie turned her wrath on Billie—"you simply cannot proceed with this foolishness! Damn the plane. I, for one, cannot allow you to squander the rest of Pap's estate on something so ridiculous."

"Maggie, you heard Mr. Abramson. You and Susan have been given your share; the rest is mine to do with as I please. And I please to continue your father's work to its completion."

"Oh, no, you won't, Mother." Maggie jumped from her chair and towered over Billie. Susan seemed horrified by this aggression. "I happen to know a little something about the law. Susan and I have every right to protect the inheritance we can expect to inherit from *you*! We won't allow you to squander what's left."

Sawyer stared at Maggie in disbelief. This was her mother! The sudden urge to throttle her was so intense she bit into her lip. She'd never witnessed such hatred. Any leftover childish yearning for her mother evaporated at that moment. It was her and Grand against Maggie and Susan. She'd fight them both until there wasn't a breath left in her body. She was a Coleman, and by God, she was going to act like one.

Maggie and Susan were as good as their word. Four weeks later the Coleman assets were frozen by court order. Billie took the news badly. Sawyer tried to bolster her by showing her a list of names and banking institutions she planned to go to for financing.

Billie tried to swallow past the lump in her throat. Sawyer stood in front of her dressed in a tailored business suit with a light cashmere coat over her shoulders. Each hand gripped a briefcase. She was going out to make Moss's dream come true. Her travels would take her from one end of the world to the other. How young she looked. How vulnerable. "I should be coming with you," Billie said anxiously. "You can't do this alone. We need more help, Sawyer."

Sawyer set the cases down and put her hands on her grandmother's shoulders. "Look at me. We can do this; we'll find private investors. I have all the letters, all the specifications, and I know what I'm talking about. If you've lost faith in me, now's the time to say so."

"It's nothing like that, Sawyer. It's just that it's so much to ask of you. Promise me you're going to take it one step at a time."

"I promise. You take care of yourself and I'll call over the weekend. Don't wish me luck. Say a few prayers." Billie nodded.

While Sawyer was winging her way to California, Billie was placing a call to Thad. She almost fainted with relief when his voice came over the wire. "Thad . . . Sawyer left this morning. I need my one-man support system. Can you come?"

"Give me a day to clear the decks and I'll be on your doorstep before you know it. Are you all right?" The genuine concern in Thad's voice brought tears to Billie's eyes.

"I need you, Thad. I need someone besides Sawyer to tell me I can do this. I've never had such an awesome responsibility before. I'm beginning to doubt myself."

"Well, don't. Stop right now and start thinking positively. Lay in some supplies and begin cooking up a storm." He rattled off a list of things he wanted to eat. "Real American food. Go easy on the rice and make lots and lots of spuds."

Billie laughed. Already she felt better. Dear God, thank you for creating such a wonderful human being. "Thad, I can hardly wait to see you."

"The feeling is mutual. Keep busy and I'll be there before you know it."

Billie was sure the entire airport could tell how happy she was to see her old and dear friend. Her love. Thad's presence was her magic elixir, her security blanket, her safety net.

He held out his arms and Billie melted into them, her head resting against the rough navy wool. "I'm so glad you could come. So very glad," Billie whispered.

"I'm all yours. I've always been yours," Thad said huskily against her hair.

Billie raised her head to stare up at Thad, oblivious to the milling inbound and outbound passengers. Airports were places for good-byes and hellos. No one paid them the slightest bit of attention. They had more privacy here than at a secluded restaurant behind a wooden trellis and a potted plant.

"Let's get a drink, Thad. There's a small cocktail lounge to the left. I want to sit and look at you."

"I'm all for that, but you stole my line. I want to sit and look at you."

"Good. Then let's sit and look at each other. You look wonderful. You never seem to change, Thad."

"She can lie with a straight face, too." Thad grinned. "Okay, what'll it be?" he asked once they'd been seated and the waitress had approached.

"Whiskey sour."

"I'll have a double bourbon on the rocks."

"Was it difficult to get the time off, Thad? I should have given you more notice, but I panicked. I'm so glad you're here. I need your stability and your good common sense. Tell me I'm doing the right thing."

"You're referring to the plane, of course." Billie nodded. "Of course you're doing the right thing. You're honoring your commitment to your husband and to his dream. It's right, Billie."

"If it's so right, why are you, Sawyer, and I the only ones who think so? Maggie and Susan are Moss's children and they aren't looking at it that way. They won't even speak to me. All they want is the money."

Thad's next words caught Billie off guard. "The mother in you should recognize that that's all they have left of their father. They're both hurt, sore and bruised. It's the last thing they can do to get even—not with you, Billie, but with Moss—for all those hurts, all those slights, the lack of the love they both wanted. Maggie especially. I think Susan is just going along with Maggie because she thinks it's the thing to do. Greed is a powerful motivator. To destroy or prevent Moss's dream is all they really want. At least that's my opinion."

"I never wanted it to end like this. I tried to talk to the girls, but it did no good. Maggie was so cruel. Susan was . . . she just looked at me with a blank stare and didn't say anything. She was actually mute. Without Maggie behind her she's lost.

I didn't want to divide us. Maggie was unbelievably cruel to Sawyer when the girl stood up for me."

"How are things going?"

"Sawyer has taken to the road to see if she can get financial help. The men helped her, the crew Moss hand-picked to work on this project. Right now morale is low. Wages haven't been paid. I've gone through all the cash I could get my hands on before the court freeze. I've even used up Mother's inheritance. Amelia has helped out, but that's a drop in the bucket. We're talking dollars when we need millions. It doesn't look as though the courts are going to be in any hurry to speed things up, either. Maggie managed to get herself one terrific lawyer. He can make his reputation on this case. The longer it's dragged out, the more publicity he gets."

"There's no deadline, is there?"

"Not a date with a red circle on a calendar, if that's what you mean. But how long will those men continue to work without pay? Costs are mounting every day. Coleman credit is topnotch, but Moss was Coleman Aviation; I'm unproven, and investors and banks have little faith in me. I don't know where to turn."

"I have some money. It will just be another drop in the bucket, but if we keep filling that bucket with drops, sooner or later it will fill up."

"Thad, I can't let you do that. The money goes out faster than it comes in. And if the courts decide in favor of Maggie and Susan, this will all have been for nothing. . . . I'll never be able to complete Moss's dream. Never."

"Do you have a dollar-and-cents figure of what it will take to get this project into the air?"

Billie laughed bitterly. "I have it in every language and in every color. It's all back at the house. Will seeing it make a difference?"

"It might. Drink up and let's get out of here." There had to be a way. Thad's mind clicked away as he paid the check and guided Billie to the baggage area.

His luggage in tow, Thad and Billie left the airport and returned to Sunbridge. Within an hour Thad was settled in Moss's workroom, poring over ledgers and specifications. When he was finished he put on his cap and jacket. "Let's go out to the hangar and have a look-see." Billie obliged. Thad would know what to do.

It was a little after six in the evening when Billie and Thad returned once again to Sunbridge. She fixed them both some scrambled eggs, toast, and coffee, then sat down at the kitchen table to talk.

"Well, what do you think?" she asked anxiously.

Thad's brow was furrowed. "There might be a way. I'm just not sure." With long, thin fingers he raked through his sparse hair, seemingly lost in thought.

Billie sensed some inner conflict, something tearing at Thad. Unsure of what she should do or say, she carried the dishes to the sink and started to wash them. When she'd finished, Thad was still sitting hunched over the table, wearing the same intense look on his face.

"Thad? Is something wrong? You don't look right. Please tell me what it is."

Thad's tormented eyes lifted to meet Billie's worried gaze. He didn't know what to do, what to say. By tomorrow, he could be in Japan talking to Otami's father. Shadaharu Hasegawa had the money to help Billie. If Thad presented the case properly, there was every possibility that Moss's dream could come true. But in order to do that, he would have to break his promise and tell Billie about Riley's marriage . . . and his son. All the years of silence . . . what would Billie say when she found out she had a grandson? How would she feel? Thad groaned aloud.

"Thad, what is it? Are you ill?" Billie asked in concern.

"Make us some more coffee, Billie. Then I want you to sit down. I have something to tell you."

Billie sat silently at the table, listening intently, not touching her coffee. When Thad finished she had to wet her lips twice and force the words from her throat. "A grandson? Riley had a son and Moss didn't tell me? Oh, Thad, why didn't you tell me? What must that girl think of me? Of Moss? Riley . . . poor Riley."

"He loved Otami very much, Billie. And she loved him. It was what he wanted. He made me swear that I wouldn't confide in either of you. I had to do it, Billie. For Riley. Please, tell me you understand."

Billie's gazed eyes stared at Thad. "It seems so unreal. How could Moss not have told me? A grandson . . . Riley's son. So many years lost to all of us. Do you think Riley's wife will see me? The boy, too?"

"Of course. Billie, you have to understand that Otami would have made some overture to you sooner or later, or convinced

Riley to do so. Unfortunately, the boy was killed before he could release her from her promise to keep the marriage secret. The Japanese are a very honorable people, and Otami was duty-bound to honor her husband's wishes. She's a wonderful girl, Billie. You'll love her."

"I'm sure I will. It's Moss's not telling me that I'm having trouble with," Billie said wretchedly. "How could he keep that from me, Thad? Even when he was dying he didn't tell me. We'd come to terms with so many things in our lives. That was the time for him to tell me, for him to be honest. I don't understand. I'll never to able to forgive him if I don't understand."

"I can tell you Otami's side of it. Moss never chose to tell me about his visit to Japan. Otami's father wanted me to know, in case questions ever came up later."

"Tell me what happened, Thad."

Thad squirmed in his chair, dreading what he was going to have to say. "Moss went to Japan believing Otami was some sort of tart who'd gotten her hooks into Riley. I think he had a vision of her living in a rice paddy with the baby strapped to her back. When he arrived, he must have been shocked. The family home is equal, if not superior, to Sunbridge. Well, anyway, Moss made a mistake of demanding the child—he made all manner of threats."

"Oh, my God!" cried Billie.

"I understand from several letters I received from Otami that her father was frightened for his family. He hired guards to protect her and the boy. He wasn't sure what Moss would do."

"Thad, I have to go to Japan. Should we call first? Will they welcome us?"

"With open arms, Billie."

"Make arrangements, please, Thad. I'll go upstairs and pack. And Thad, we can't ask them for financing for this plane. It wouldn't be right. They might think that was the only reason we're making the trip, and it isn't. We'll find our financing some other way."

Thad poured himself a drink and picked up the phone. Inside of thirty minutes he had confirmed reservations to Tokyo via San Francisco, Hawaii, and Guam. He leaned back in the swivel chair, debating whether or not to call Otami. Would a surprise be best, or should he do the decent thing and call? The decent thing, of course.

Otami's voice was just as sweet as ever. "Uncle Thad, how nice of you to call. Are you planning on coming for a visit? My family would be honored. My father constantly asks about you."

"Yes, Otami, I am coming for a visit. I want to bring Riley's mother with me. It was necessary to tell her about you and your son. I will explain later, but I had no other choice. I hope you will forgive me."

"There is nothing to forgive. I'm sure you did what you believed was right. We will understand."

"We'll be there in less than twenty-four hours. Otami, Riley's mother needs you."

"Uncle Thad, I, too, need Riley's mother. More than you know. My son will be told and I will arrange for him to take time off from school. Is it not strange that Riley loves airplanes?"

"Not so strange, Otami. Preordained, I should think."

{{{{{{{{ CHAPTER THIRTY-NINE }}}}}}}}

Billie and Thad walked through Guam's new airport. Thad looked around, hardly believing his eyes. "This rivals anything we have in the States. You should have seen it in the old days."

"So much marble," Billie said, looking around.

"Come along, Billie. The commander at the Naval Air Station has arranged for a car. I'm going to take you around Guam and show you where your son lived and was happy. I owe that to you. We only have a few hours, but the island is small. Can you handle it?"

"I can handle it."

As Thad drove the car along Marine Drive he and Billie oohed and aahed. "Ten years makes one hell of a difference. I understand that Guam is now *the* Japanese honeymoon resort. There's a shopping center in Agana now. When Riley was here there were tiny little stores and I assume he did most of his shopping at the commissary. Things are so different."

"It rather looks like Hawaii. Where are we going first, Thad?"

"I want to show you the church where Riley was married and the little house he lived in with Otami."

As the navy car ate up the miles Billie craned her neck, not wanting to miss seeing anything her son might have lived with. After a short while, Thad slowed the car and turned. "The church on the right is where Riley was married. It's open, if you'd like to go in. They had it decorated that day with plumeria and orchids. It was beautiful. Otami has pictures of the wedding. I'm sure she'll share them with you."

"No, Thad, I don't want to go in. It's enough that I see it. San Juan deBautiste Church," Billie said softly. "What a lovely name."

"Start counting now. The little house where Riley and Otami lived can be seen from the road. Eight buildings including the dental clinic."

Billie drew in her breath. Why this was so important, she didn't know. A piece of her son's life. The last piece. "There it is!" Tears misted Billie's eyes as she stared at the small stucco house that was painted white with what looked like burgundy trim. A spanking new yellow Suzuki pickup truck stood in the driveway. "I wonder who lives here now," Billie whispered hoarsely.

"The sign on the tree says Deo. Riley and Otami had a sign, too. It said Riley and Otami Coleman. Rather like the plaque at Sunbridge. I know one thing, though."

"What's that?" Billie asked, dabbing at her eyes.

"If the people living here now are one-tenth as happy as Riley and Otami were, they've got all there is to have in life. Have you seen enough?"

"It's all so beautiful." Billie's eyes misted over again. "I'm so glad you brought me here, Thad. Thank you."

"I have to be honest. I did it as much for myself as for you." Billie's smile was wan. "I know."

"Back to the airport. If we burn rubber, we'll just make it."

It was cold and blustery when Thad and Billie descended the portable stairway on the Continental jet. The minute Billie's feet touched solid ground, her shoulders slumped. Jet lag had finally caught up with her. Try as she would, she could barely keep her eyes open. Customs and baggage, and then she could check into the hotel and take a shower. She'd need some good strong coffee before she could even think about going to see her daughter-in-law. Her heart was pumping furiously. She couldn't help but wonder whether it was from bone weariness or wild anticipation.

Thad's face showed his concern as he ushered Billie through customs. "If you're half as tired as you look, you have to feel the way I do. I think we should go to the hotel and get some sleep. It's early and we have plenty of time. Otami will certainly understand. You look done in, Billie."

"I am. I agree. We both need sleep. A few hours, anyway. I can't believe I'm really here and that I'm going to see my daughter-in-law and grandson in a short while. It's so overwhelming, I don't think I'm over the shock. Do you think they'll like me, Thad?" Billie asked anxiously. "I'm not like Moss. I don't ever want them to think I am. But I have to try to explain to them why he acted the way he did. It's all right to do that, isn't it?"

"Of course it is. Otami and her family are wonderful people. They'll understand. They bear no malice toward you and I'm sure there was none for Moss. Be yourself, Billie. That's the best advice I can give you."

"I brought Riley's baby pictures," Billie blurted. "As a matter of fact I brought all his pictures for Otami to see. And I . . . I brought his baseball mitt and his ball that Hank Aaron autographed. The Japanese have a great love of baseball. As a matter of fact I just recently read an article about the Tokyo Yomiuri Giants. They're known for their hitting and fielding. I read the article, I don't know why. At least I'll have something to talk about with my grandson."

Thad raised startled eyes to meet Billie's tired gaze. "I'm sure you will. Most Japanese boys grow up playing baseball."

"Hopefully I'm going to be able to show you Mount Fuji before we leave. In all my visits to this wonderful city I've only seen it twice myself. It's quite awesome. The clouds are usually too low to see the snow peak. For you, Billie, I have a feeling the cloud cover will lift."

Billie forced a smile. She had never in her life been so exhausted. "How long are we going to be here? I never thought to ask."

"Five days. It was the best I could do. Enough time for you to get acquainted with Riley's family. I'm sure that Otami will want to show you her beloved city. It's a far cry from Texas. Ten million people live in Tokyo."

One eye was drooping sleepily. Thad smiled at the valiant effort Billie was putting forth. "I would like to shop on the

Ginza," she said, yawning. "Sawyer will be so impressed with me."

"I think Sawyer will be more impressed if you tell her you got up the nerve to take a ride on the Shinkansen Super Express. It is called the bullet train and supposedly it's the speediest in the world, traveling one hundred thirty miles per hour. Her technical mind will want to know everything, so it might be wise if we got some brochures for her."

"That sounds good to me, Thad." An instant later Billie was asleep.

Thad shifted his weight slightly so that Billie's nodding head would rest comfortably against his shoulder. He spent the remainder of the long ride from Narita to Tokyo rehearsing what he was going to say to Otami's father. Billie was caught up in emotionalism and rightly so. It would rest with him to bring up the matter of the plane and what had to be done. A pity Sawyer wasn't here. The fact that he had a good rapport with the Japanese would certainly help. He didn't think he would have to talk too long or too loud to get his point across. Riley's grandfather would understand what was happening. The man would listen, tilt his head to the side, and then say, How can I help? How much do you need? And that would be the end of it.

Thad shook Billie's shoulder gently. "Wake up, Billie, we're at the hotel."

Billie was too groggy to appreciate the beauty of the Asian hotel as she followed Thad and the diminutive Oriental carrying their bags. She needed sleep and she wanted to be at her best when she met Otami and her grandson.

"Here's your room, Billie. I'm down the hall in fifteen-oh-eight. Sleep now and ring my room when you wake." He kissed her lightly on the cheek and walked on down the hall, leaving Billie to herself. She immediately took off her coat, drew the draperies, and crawled into bed fully clothed.

She slept deeply and soundly for twelve hours, hardly disturbing the bright blue covers.

While Billie slept, Thad headed for the Virgo dining room with its French cuisine and panoramic view of Tokyo. While he ate he rehearsed the talk he was going to have with Otami's father, rejected some ideas and expanded on others. Finally satisfied, he gulped his tea, paid the bill, and left the restaurant.

Once Thad was outside, his step was springy, his bearing

more military. When things were going right, it was easier to stand tall. It was easier to do a lot of things. Simple everyday living was a delight; anything beyond that a bonus.

Mr. Hasegawa welcomed Thad in the Western manner. They shook hands and then bowed to each other.

"Welcome, Thaddeus. It has been a long time since you honored me with a visit. My daughter and wife are in a state of delirium that Mrs. Coleman is here. After all these years we thought it would never come to pass. My sorrow was yours at the news of Mr. Coleman's death. On many occasions my family prayed that he would one day return and make my grandson his. We wanted to share our good fortune with him. I know it was your sorrow, also. Tell me, quickly, do you bring news of the film stars for my wife? She has called me twice already today to see if you had been in touch. She is particularly taken with . . . one moment, I wrote down the name. Aah, here it is: Tom Selleck. Yes, Tom Selleck. Do you know much about this film star?"

"He's the eighties heartthrob. I think I can give her a few highlights. How is the boy?"

"Young Riley makes me more proud each day. I believe he follows in his father's footsteps. He thinks of nothing but planes and flying. We have our own jet and he is forever begging to go with me. Unfortunately, I like to keep my feet on the ground as much as possible. It is the miracle of progress. Sit down, Thaddeus, and we will have some Scotch and one of those fine Havana cigars you brought on your last visit. Then we will talk. I wish to know how all this came about."

Thad waited until the room was blue gray with smoke and the Scotch bottle was nearly empty before he began his speech. It all came out neatly, slow and easy.

"So . . . Mrs. Coleman needs my help. That is clear. Tell me what you want me to do. I will need at least a week with my bankers. Is my presence in America essential?" the old man asked anxiously.

"Only if you wish to be there."

They talked for hours, these two old friends. When the room became too foul with cigar smoke they adjourned to another. They talked of the old days, his daughters, and his grandchildren. Moss Coleman's dream would be backed by Hasegawa money. How ironic, Thad thought, that this beautiful human being whom Moss Coleman had detested was going to make his last dream a reality.

"I don't know how to thank you for your generosity. The return on your investment will be substantial. I guarantee it."

Hasegawa waved his hand to negate Thad's words. "Sometimes, Thaddeus, a man's dreams are all he has. When they are not fulfilled it is most sad. I, for one, never had much use for people who had the power to shatter a man's dreams. We are to build, to create, to finish. If one cannot do it, then it is up to another to carry on. I do this for Moss Coleman, for his son, whom he loved with all his heart, and for my grandson, whom I love with all my heart. Cannot we say that finally the East has met the West and let it go at that?"

"Very well said," Thad replied with a catch in his throat. "I think it's time for me to return to the hotel. Mrs. Coleman might wake and she is most anxious to see her family."

"Regardless of the time, you are to bring her immediately. She must not wait one minute longer than she must meet her family. Are they not wonderful words?" Shadaharu Hasegawa asked with a twinkle in his eye. "Your promise, Thaddeus."

"Yes. Until later, old friend."

"Until later." Hands were shaken and bows were made.

It was done.

When Billie woke, she lay for long moments thinking about where she was and why she was here in this strange land so far from Sunbridge and Moss's dream. When her eyes became accustomed to the darkness around her, she reached toward the bedside lamp and turned it on. The digital watch, Japanese-made, read 5:05. The sun would be up soon. She lay still a few moments longer, rested now and in control. She'd shower, dress, apply her makeup, and then call Thad. They could have coffee in the hotel dining room and then make an appearance at her daughter-in-law's home. At a respectable hour. The Japanese were very particular about the social amenities, or so she had read.

On her way to the bathroom thoughts of Moss skittered through her mind. Later she would have to sort them all out. Betrayal wasn't something to take lightly. She would get her perspective and deal with it all sometime soon. Nothing was going to mar this visit if she could help it.

The stinging shower woke Billie completely. She wrapped herself in one of the hotel's plum-colored bath sheets and applied makeup sparingly but deftly.

She called Thad and they agreed to meet in twenty minutes. He sounded wide awake—he'd probably been up for hours, Billie reflected, waiting for her to wake and call him.

Billie shook out the mauve silk dress and hung it in the bathroom to smoothe away the wrinkles. She could dry her hair in five minutes, then dress and be ready to leave.

"Do I look all right, Thad? Am I too dressy or do you think I should wear a suit? I brought one. I don't want to look overdone but more done, if you know what I mean," Billie babbled.

"Believe me, you look fine. Beautiful, in fact. The dress is perfect. Now stop worrying. If you keep frowning like that you're going to get wrinkles, and then what will you do?" Thad said lightly.

Billie stopped in midstride. "But Thad, I already have a few wrinkles."

"Do you? I hadn't noticed. To me you look the way you did when I first met you. I'm the one who's aged. You want wrinkles, you can have all of mine. I'll gladly share."

"I really hadn't noticed," Billie said seriously as she peered closely at Thad's face. She laughed nervously and Thad joined in. "I'll tell you what. You keep yours and I'll keep mine and then we can both forget about them. I need coffee, Thad. I'm too nervous to eat, though."

Ninety minutes later the huge iron gate opened to admit Billie and Thad. They were ushered into the house and immediately taken to a formal sitting room where Otami, her parents, and two of her sisters waited. There were greetings and introductions all around. Billie stood rooted to the floor, unable to move in Otami's direction. A vision of Jessica Coleman holding out her arms to welcome her so long ago flashed before her. A radiant smile and outstretched arms were all Otami needed. She forgot the Japanese way for a moment and ran to Billie. Tears burned Billie's eyes as she wrapped her arms around Otami. Was it Otami trembling or was it Billie herself? Was that Otami's heart pounding or her own? Did it matter?

"Please forgive me, Mother Coleman. I have prayed for this moment for so long and now that it is here I am so overcome I have forgotten my manners. Welcome to my home. Riley is on his way from school and will join us within the hour. We wish, my family and I, that you and Uncle Thad will join us for breakfast."

"There is nothing to forgive. It is I who must ask forgiveness for my husband and myself. I didn't know. I would never . . . I didn't know, Otami."

"I know that, Mother Coleman. You're here now and that's all that matters. After breakfast you and I and Riley will talk of your son and my son." Impulsively, Otami threw her arms around Billie a second time and this time wept openly with happiness. Billie drew her close and kept her arm around Otami's waist as they made their way to a formal dining room whose table was set Western style.

"In your honor, Mrs. Coleman, we will breakfast in the American manner. My cook is preparing eggs Benedict, pancakes with Vermont maple syrup. Real maple syrup, Thad." Mr. Hasegawa chuckled.

"You are indeed a man after my own heart. Are you serving that awful green tea or are we having coffee?"

"For you, nothing but the best. I believe it is called Crock of Nuts ŏr some other ridiculous name."

Otami laughed. "Father, it is Chock Full o' Nuts. Riley taught me to drink coffee, and when I returned home I had my father import the coffee for us. We drink it all the time. My father is teasing you, Uncle Thad, as you well know." Her words were directed to Thad but her gaze never left Billie.

"All these females I surround myself with are outnumbering me. Now, before my wife goes up in a puff of smoke, we will talk of the American film stars and what is going on in tissue town."

"Tinsel town, Father. It is Mother's only vice. She is perfect in every other way." Otami smiled. "She has an obsession with the film stars," she explained to Billie. "Uncle Thad keeps us abreast of what is going on in Hollywood. He sends magazines and pictures and movie reviews. My mother does not speak English but she can understand when Uncle Thad talks of the stars."

Billie laughed. "Thad, you never told me. What else haven't you told me?" Instantly she was sorry for the words, even though her tone was light and teasing.

Billie and Otami had eyes only for each other. It was as though neither could get her fill of the other. Thad droned on about Tom Selleck and Kenny Rogers, and both Otami and Billie grinned conspiratorially when Thad started to describe the endowments of Jacqueline Bisset and Dolly Parton. Caught up in the moment, Thad was unaware of the silence at the table and flushed sheepishly when his host clapped his hands loudly. Otami giggled and Billie lowered her eyes so Thad wouldn't see the laughter in them.

Breakfast progressed slowly. They started with juice and fruit, then followed with toast and small muffins. Coffee was liberally poured by a small girl dressed in a sky-blue kimono. The eggs Benedict were perfect and Billie ate heartily, while Thad did justice to the buckwheat pancakes with maple syrup. Without looking at her watch, Billie knew the hour was almost up. Her grandson should be arriving shortly. She took a deep breath and looked at Otami.

"It is understandable for you to be anxious about meeting Riley. He is anxious, too. He tries so hard to be all things to all of us. He is very much like his father, as you will see. He did inherit one thing from my family and that is his love of the entertainment business. He adores American music. He will be here soon, Mother Coleman. We are finally a family. It is all I ever wanted for my son and now it has come to pass. My father, who is wise in so many ways, thought this would happen someday. You were so right, my honorable father."

"Do you hear that, Thad? She called me her honorable father. I can't remember the last time she did that. We are joking, Mrs. Coleman, to put you at your ease. I see we are not succeeding. We understand. Otami, take Mrs. Coleman into the library and I will send Riley to you when he arrives."

Billie's eyes shone with relief. It wasn't that she didn't want to meet her grandson in front of the entire family, but she needed to get herself and her emotions under control.

Otami linked her arm through Billie's and led her to her father's library. "This room has many chairs for our Western visitors. My father thought you would be more comfortable here. We have so much to talk about. So many years to compare. I want to share what Riley and I had with you. In his heart he would want me to do this."

"Why have you never remarried, Otami?"

"There is only room in my heart to love one man. Riley is dead, but his son is alive. He is never far from me. I am content. But to answer your question, I could never find anyone I could love the way I loved Riley," Otami said softly. "Tell me, Mother Coleman, will you be able to marry another?"

"Yes, Otami."

"Would I be forward in asking if Uncle Thad is the person you would consider sharing your heart with?"

"You wouldn't be forward at all. Yes, Thad is the person I would share my heart with. I think I've been sharing it for years."

"We will share all these things later, if you are agreeable. There is so much I want to know. There is so much I want to share with you. I think all my life—and I mean that part of my life with Riley and afterward—I thought your family would not welcome me. I never got beyond the welcome part, but I wanted you to love me. I wanted all of Riley's family to love me. In his own way I think Riley was trying to tell me this wouldn't be possible and that's why he made me agree not to get in touch with you. He didn't want me to be hurt."

Oh, damn you, Moss. Damn you. Billie reached out her hand to Otami. She would neither defend nor chastise her husband's memory. It was history. This was now. This beautiful woman would have to decide for herself what was real and what was true.

Otami's grip on Billie's hand tightened when the knock sounded on the library door. "My son is here to meet his grandmother at last."

Billie took a deep breath and stood next to Otami. Through her blurred vision she watched Riley's likeness walk toward her. Incredible dark eyes drank in the sight of her as his arms shot out and Billie found herself in her grandson's embrace. She rested her cheek on the top of his dark head and squeezed the tears back from her eyes. When young Riley released her he was embarrassed, as any ten-year old would be by the sudden display of his emotions. Clear, intelligent eyes, not the same summer blue as his father's but a dark, deep ebony, shone up at her.

"Hello, Grandmam." He smiled but kept his arm around her to steady her. "Welcome to our home. My mother and I have waited a long time for this day."

"And then you nearly crush the breath from her!" Otami said sternly. "Apologize."

"But Mother, that's what you said Father used to do to you. You said his father did it to his mother. I wanted to welcome Grandmam Texas-style. I didn't mean to offend you," Riley said anxiously, his eyes on his frowning mother.

"You didn't. I loved every minute of it, and yes, Otami, Riley was right. It is an exuberant Texas custom. I want you to be yourself; otherwise we'll never get to know each other."

"We have the advantage, Grandmam. Mama has told me

all about you and the Coleman ranch, and Texas and American airplanes. I intend to be an aeronautical engineer."

"My granddaughter, Sawyer, is doing the same thing. You would make some team." Billie laughed. "I brought pictures. Actually, I brought several family albums for you and your mother to see. We can have prints made from any of the pictures you might care to have. There's one in particular of your father on his first pony. Perhaps that isn't quite true; he was falling off the pony when I snapped the picture."

Otami laughed delightedly. "Riley used to tell me that the horse hadn't been born that could throw him."

"Not quite true. Riley tended to exaggerate when it came to horses. He was more at home around planes. In all fairness to Riley, he more or less slid off the pony. But he was thrown more times than I can remember, and he always got right back on. His grandfather insisted. Your father always tried to do what was expected of him."

"Until he met me," Otami said sadly.

"No, no, no, you must never say that. You must not even think such a thing," Billie said, moving closer to Otami and putting her arms around her. "Riley loved you and it was inevitable that he marry you. It's just that he was unwilling to take even the slightest chance that his family might . . . might not see things his way. I regret his decision, but I understand it. As my father-in-law, my husband, and my son used to say, it's history now. What we have now are our memories. Some of them aren't too pleasant and others will be with us for the rest of our lives. However, one cannot live on memories. I have my philosophy where memories are concerned."

"What are they, Grandmam?" Riley asked curiously.

"Memories have a place in all our lives. They dull and they fade with time, and that's as it should be. Only cowards live on memories day after day because they're afraid to reach out for life." At Riley's solemn nod, Billie glanced at Otami's stricken face. "No, no, Otami, I didn't mean you."

"But it's true. My family has been telling me that for years. My son manages to tell me that at least once a day when he is home. I never thought of it in terms of cowardice before. You must not be sorry for your words, because they are true. Do you see my son shake his head? At last he has an ally. You are of one thought. Even my father chastises me from time to time." A beautiful smile lightened her serious features. "I promise to work on it."

"We'll hold you to it, Mama. Between the two of us, Grandmam, perhaps we can convince my mother that there is a world outside the gates of this house."

"Then there is no hope for me." Otami sighed.

"Ah, but there is. Now we can go to America and see where my father lived. You promised me that if Father's side of the family ever recognized us, you would take me to Texas. A promise, Mama, that must now be honored."

"We haven't been invited, Riley. Where are your manners?"

"But of course you're invited. Anytime. I would love to have your entire family come to Sunbridge. Riley, you will have so much in common with my granddaughter. She'll share the Coleman dream with you. A dream that you'll understand and perhaps want to work on. Later, we can discuss what's going on back in Texas. I brought something for you, Riley. It's in a package by the front door. Will you fetch it?"

Riley loped off to do his grandmother's bidding. Otami raised questioning eyes to Billie.

"I . . . I brought Riley's baseball and mitt for young Riley. The family albums are in the package, also. At the last minute I stuck in Riley's baseball cap. Was it a mistake, do you think?"

"Never. My son doesn't have much from his father. The few belongings that were returned to me by the navy were . . . what I mean is, he will appreciate these things because they are from his father's boyhood and his home."

Riley returned carrying the package, his gaze anxious as Billie unwrapped the string and held out the contents of the box: "I think you should have these things. There are others at Sunbridge that you might . . . that you . . ."

Riley looked down into the box and dropped to his knees. His touch was gentle as he lifted out the worn mitt and the ball. The little league cap went onto his shiny black head immediately. The baseball was brought lovingly to his cheek. "Was this the way my father smelled?" he asked, handing the hat to Billie, who sniffed obligingly. She nodded, a lump settling in her throat.

"It's right and fitting that you have what belonged to your father. I don't think this is the time to discuss it, but you and your mother also are entitled to Riley's inheritance. I'll have to have my lawyers work on that. I didn't know about you and your mother until a few days ago."

"Do you think Uncle Thad would like to field a few balls, Grandmam?"

"I think so. Why don't you go ask him? Your mother and I have a lot of talking to do."

Riley bent over to kiss his mother and Billie. His dark eyes lingered on Billie's face for a long time. "My father looked like you."

"Yes, he did a little. But he had a lot of Coleman in him, too. He was a wonderful man, Riley. He was a father for you to be proud of."

"Thank you for the gifts. I'll treasure them always."

Otami turned to Billie. "That was most kind of you. I often regretted I had nothing to give the boy but a few old clothes that were returned to me. You have made my son very happy and that makes me happy. I promise you I will give serious thought to the discussion on memories."

"You aren't offended?"

"No. You spoke the truth. It took courage for you to do that. Now, can we look at the photographs you brought along? I would like to see the comparison to my son." Billie nodded as she lifted the albums from the bottom of the carton she had brought from Texas.

The pictures were shared with Otami and then with Riley and Thad, and yet again with Otami's parents. When Billie looked at her watch it was late afternoon.

Wonderful, meaningful days passed with Billie and her new family. Riley insisted on a tour of the university and Otami made sure that a walk down the Ginza at dawn was as memorable as Billie knew it would be. Kabuki drama was Mr. Hasegawa's contribution. It was an experience Billie knew she would never forget.

It was agreed that Otami and Riley would journey to Texas as soon as the school semester ended in a month's time.

The entire Hasegawa family saw Thad and Billie off at the airport. Minutes before boarding, on Thad's advice, Mr. Hasegawa pressed an envelope into Billie's hand. "For the dream," the old man whispered as he kissed her lightly on the cheek and then bowed low. Billie swallowed hard and nodded, unsure of what he meant. One last, long look at her daughter-in-law and grandson and she was ushered through the turnstile.

"What do you suppose Mr. Hasegawa meant when he said this envelope was for the dream?" Billie asked Thad as she buckled her seat belt.

A smug look settled on Thad's face. "Why don't you open it and see?"

Billie slit the envelope with her nail and pulled out the contents. Her face drained of all color as she looked at the oblong pieces of paper. All checks drawn on the Tokyo bank. Blank except for a signature. A square of crackly, cream-colored paper was enclosed and Billie unfolded it with trembling hands. Dabbing at her eyes, she thrust the paper at Thad. "Please, read it to me."

My dear Mrs. Coleman:

It is unbearable to me that your husband's dream be shattered for lack of financing. You and your family will honor my family if you will accept our help in this endeavor. My only request is that you allow our grandson to share in the fulfillment of his grandfather's dream.

May good fortune smile upon you always.

With much affection and understanding, I remain,

Shadaharu Hasegawa

Billie blew her nose lustily. "I can't believe this. Thad, I didn't want you to ask him, to even discuss it. What must the man think?"

"What he thinks is obvious if you read this letter. I've known the man for years, Billie. I knew he would want to help. If you'll notice, there are no legal papers, no strings, no terms. He trusts you. He wants to do this. Accept it, Billie, in the spirit it's meant. He would die of shame, and I mean that literally, if you refuse."

"But Thad, blank checks? What does that mean? How are we to know what is too much? How can I just fill in amounts?"

"As much as it takes. It's that simple. Or, if you prefer it another way, unlimited funds."

"What if things go wrong again and the money goes down the drain like the last time?"

"It won't happen, Billie. But if it should, there will be another batch of checks. It's done."

"The man never laid eyes on me until five days ago and he's giving me carte blanche with his money. Thad, it isn't done."

"I beg to differ. And the man knows you better than you think. I told you we've been friends for years. Allow him the honor of helping you. He wants to do it."

{556}

"I'll never get over this. I didn't know there were people like that in this world."

"If the situation were reversed, what would you do?"

Billie laughed, a delightful sound that sent shivers up Thad's spine. "I'd do the same, I guess. Thank you, Thad. I think I'm glad that you didn't listen to me. I have a lot of thinking to do. What do you think of young Riley? He's such a marvelous young man. So like Riley in many ways and yet he has the Eastern culture that makes him what he is. My Amerasian grandson. So much has happened to me in these last days."

"Why don't we both try to get some sleep? You're going to be one busy lady when you get back to Texas, and I have to get back to the navy before they send out a search party for me."

"That's one of your better ideas. I'm still waiting for your best one yet."

"It's coming. Count on it."

"I will."

{{{{{{{{{ CHAPTER FORTY }}}}}}}}}

The months flew by with Sawyer and Billie at the helm of Moss's dream.

Otami and young Riley settled into Sunbridge as though they'd been born to the place. There wasn't a nook or cranny that Otami didn't explore. Her dark eyes took on life and she smiled constantly. Her husband's home. She was finally seeing what he had spoken of so often. She was feeling what he felt, loving what he loved. The sadness was gone and was replaced with optimism.

Eight months after Otami and Riley's arrival, the project hit one snag after another. Money seemed to evaporate into thin air. When the phone shrilled at Billie's elbow, she had a feeling it was going to be more bad news. She wasn't disappointed.

"I could tell you this at home," Sawyer said tightly, "but I didn't want to upset Otami. I know you'll take it all in stride, Grand. We blew it. We were so damn close and we blew it. We're ninety-one million dollars down."

"Ninety-one million down! Does that mean . . ." Billie's voice was full of awe and fear.

"That's exactly what it means. This plane doesn't just eat money; it gobbles it up. I spoke to Grandpap's advisers, and if you're agreeable, we want to take this project to Japan. Mr. Hasegawa insists he can find financial backing for us over there. It's the only way, Grand."

"What went wrong?" Billie asked grimly. "Give me a reason, something to chew on."

"We didn't trim enough weight. We're not meeting specifications for fuel consumption. I knew it. I'm losing control, Grand. We have to go on the road with this. Otherwise we lose everything, and I, for one, don't want that to happen. Give me a yes or a no."

Billie felt light-headed as her granddaughter waited for her answer. Otami's puzzled face was staring at her. "Go for it, Sawyer. You have my approval. Just give Otami and me enough time to get packed."

The laughter in the background made Billie raise her eyebrows. "Grand, Riley just told me his grandfather has things under control. The hangar will be ready, the engineers and crew ready for work. All we have to do is pack our duffel bags and blow this place."

"Are you taking the entire project team?" Billie asked hesitantly.

"Only those who don't fight me every step of the way. I've been right all the way down the line, Grand. I'm not being cocky. You have to believe that." The desperate tone in Sawyer's voice made Billie's thoughts race back in time to hear Moss's hoarse whisper: *Give Sawyer her head, Billie. Stand behind her and give her all your encouragement. She can do it. If she makes a mistake, and she will, she won't make it a second time. Promise me.*

"Darling, I do believe you," Billie replied warmly. "Do what you have to do. If at all possible, we want to keep this in the family. The Hasegawas are family. If it isn't possible, have Riley's grandfather bring in whoever he thinks can help us."

The relief in Sawyer's voice made Billie feel faint. "You are the grand in grandmother," Sawyer cried exuberantly.

After she'd hung up, Billie quickly explained the situation to Otami, who listened, nodding. "Riley spoke to me of this just last week," she said. "He wanted to talk to you about it and so did I, but I know nothing of airplanes. . . . It is only money, Mother Coleman. My father will see to it that the plane stays in the family, our family."

"But to start over! So much money, so much time. I didn't know . . . I had no idea . . ."

"Dreams don't just happen, Mother Coleman; they are created. Your God's creation took six days. This will take just a little longer. When are we leaving?" she asked.

"Day after tomorrow. Is that too soon?"

"I am already packed."

"I have to call Thad and tell him."

"He knows. I think he and my father have had their heads together. Neither man wanted to suggest . . . what I'm saying is . . ."

"It had to come from Sawyer. She had to admit she needed help, the kind of help the men aren't giving her. I suppose it's natural that they resent her. I have so much faith in that girl. Moss would never have turned this over to her if he didn't think she was more than capable."

"We're a shoo-in." Otami giggled.

Billie hugged her daughter-in-law. "My world is right-side up now. Do you feel it, Otami?"

"Yes, I do. This is right."

"I know. I feel it here. Did they say anything about a deadline?" Billie asked anxiously. "Investors and governments always talk of deadlines. You can . . . you can lose everything on a deadline. They're going to start from square one and . . . is there going to be some kind of deadline?"

"I don't know."

"If there is, we aren't going to worry about it. Sawyer will handle it. She's so young, Otami."

"Only in numbered years. In here," Otami said, pointing to her heart, "she is ageless. Her grandfather would not have entrusted his dream to a child."

Eleven months after moving into the Hasegawa household Billie felt more at home than she had ever felt at Sunbridge. She was glad now that she would soon be able to turn Sunbridge over to Maggie. Any monies she might have realized from the sale of the valuable property would have gone unnoticed in this war of megadollars. It would be better for Maggie, better for everyone.

It was late and for some reason she couldn't sleep. No doubt Thad's impending arrival had something to do with it. Billie decided that a stroll in the Hasegawa garden would settle her nerves.

How beautiful this was, so far removed from cactus and sagebrush. Everything was of the dwarf variety, even the statuary. The sparkling ponds and scaled-down bridges were so pleasing to her eye that Billie sat down on an iron bench to look around her. For some reason she suddenly felt Moss's presence. Nervously, she raised her eyes upward. "She's doing it," Billie whispered. "This was the only way. Soon, Moss, your dream will take wing and then it will all be over and you can rest in peace."

From his place in eternity he had interfered again. Now she was openly jittery. Things were going well—everyone said so. Six more weeks, two months at the most, and the plane would be ready to test. Sawyer seemed confident. Riley was openly jubilant.

She should be walking off some of her uneasiness. A stroll through the beautiful garden might ease her jumpy nerves. If Thad were here, she would be fine. Her reason for living . . . Thad.

Billie's stroll took her around the garden to the back level of the Hasegawa house. Sawyer's windows were open and Billie could see her silhouette in the dimness of the room. She looked as though she were talking on the phone. At this hour! Billie walked over slowly, taking the time to smell a bloom or pick a budding flower from the round, manicured beds.

How easily Sawyer had adapted to this new environment. To the men at the plant she wasn't an American female with a know-it-all attitude; she was just another worker in a grease-stained coverall and billed cap. She listened to them and they listened to her. There was no fight for control, no manipulating for power, none of the double-dealing so rampant back in the States. This was a joint effort and each man carried his share. At the end of the long work day they bowed to one another and returned to their families. Many returned after the dinner hour to rehash the day's events one last time and set up for the following morning so things would move along faster. It was dedication of the first order.

"Rand, I'm telling you, it will work," Sawyer was saying.

"I managed to shave off another two hundred pounds. I feel you're wrong. This plane has to go with a maximum T-O weight. I'm that close. Stop being so damn pigheaded and listen to me. I know what I'm doing.

"Let's talk about something else for a moment. I miss you. I really do. Did you get my last letter? . . . What do you mean *I'm* a piece of work? That's American slang. It *was* a compliment, wasn't it?"

Billie tapped on the windowsill. Sawyer motioned her to walk around to the sliding doors. She kept on with her conversation while her grandmother settled herself in the one comfortable chair in the room. She hugged the sound of her granddaughter's happy voice to her heart. Sawyer might not know it, but there was that special tone in her voice that only lovers used. The sparkle in her eyes was something Billie recognized from her own youth and could still see in the mirror when Thad was about to make an appearance.

"I need a test pilot. Do you think I should advertise in the *New York Times*?" The mock horror on Sawyer's face made Billie laugh. "You! I never thought of you, Rand. . . . The hell you say. You bloody Englishmen are touchy, aren't you? Listen, if you want to take a shot at it, the job is yours. How soon can you be here? . . . No good. What about day after tomorrow? . . . Me, set you up! How could you even think such a thing? I'd never trade on our friendship. I'll take you to dinner. . . . You're on. Good night, Rand."

"Did you set him up, Sawyer?" Billie asked.

Sawyer grimaced. "Sort of. Look, Grand, he's the best in the business. We need the best. He knows this plane's design as well as I do. Aside from a minor point or two we agree on everything. He trusts me. He wouldn't agree to test this baby if he didn't trust me. Right, Grand?"

"Right."

"If I'm so right, why do I feel so . . . so . . . uneasy?"

"Could it be because you care for him more than you'll admit? Is it possible that the things you're arguing about are more important than you think? He's laying his life on the line to test this plane for you. That's trust of the first order. You have to be sure, Sawyer."

"I am sure, Grand. But so many things could still go wrong. I could go over this six ways to Sunday and some piddly little thing could go wrong and Rand's life could hang in the balance."

"It's up to you to see that nothing goes wrong."

"It's such a terrible responsibility. Sometimes, Grand, I feel as though I'm a hundred years old. I'm glad Rand is coming. I need to know who I am again, for a little while. I do care for him, Grand, maybe too much. We write, you know, and talk every so often. He rings me on the telly. Isn't that quaint?"

"About as quaint as talking on the horn. Isn't that what your generation says?" Sawyer laughed.

"Thad is coming in a day or so," Billie volunteered. "Maybe even tomorrow if things go right."

"When are you two getting married?"

"Just as soon as this plane gets airborne. We're going to Hong Kong, and when it's right we'll, as you say, tie the knot."

"I'm so happy for you. You've been a brick through all this. Grandpap sure picked himself a winner when he picked you."

"I always thought so." Billie laughed. "Time for bed. You have an early day and I need my beauty sleep."

The following two months were the happiest Billie had ever known. She was drawn into the Hasegawa family and basked in their loving acceptance of her. Thad drew on his leave and visited for days at a time, making her happiness total and complete.

Otami and Billie watched the romance between Rand and Sawyer blossom. It was obvious to anyone who cared to observe that the young girl that the commitment to her grandfather's dream came first. Rand appeared to understand . . . for now.

They were all seated around the Hasegawa dining room table having cake and coffee. The test flight, Sawyer had just said, was scheduled for March 31, the last day of the last month granted them by their investors to come up with a marketable product. Rand was scowling. Sawyer looked gloomy, and Riley sat with his hands propping up his face. The elder Hasegawa let his glance stray to the young people and then to Billie. He clearly wanted to know what the problem was.

Suddenly Rand spoke. "I'm telling you, Sawyer, a sixty-degree angle on the wing sweep is too steep. Either you bring it back to fifty-five degrees or you get yourself another test pilot. There're a lot of things I'll do for you, but killing myself isn't one of them."

"I'm telling you sixty degrees was one of Grandpap's original specifications," Sawyer argued heatedly. "I've lived with this plane for two solid years. I know what I'm doing. The others agree. You're the only dissenter."

"Maybe I'm the only dissenter because I'm the only one who's going to fly that bird. I want to come back in one piece. Fifty-five degrees!"

"No! We'll lose efficiency."

"Yes!"

Sawyer got up and walked around the table till she was facing Rand. "Do you think for one minute that I'd let you fly the dream if I had one iota of doubt?... Well, you bloody Englishman? Answer me—but before you do, you should know something else: I love you. Now think long and hard before you give me your answer."

Billie's eyes widened. She'd never seen Sawyer so adamant. Otami was busy picking at her nails and Shadaharu was staring intently at a spot on the immaculate linen tablecloth. Only Riley stared at the couple.

Rand's brain clicked, reeling off the plane's specifications. Twice he frowned. Sawyer's penetrating, demanding gaze forced him to make an immediate decision. The niggling doubt would have to be shelved. He'd go over it again on the drawing board and then inch by inch in the hangar. Sawyer wasn't stubborn just for the sake of being stubborn. She'd made a believer of him on more than one occasion. Her gaze was clear and steady, defiant. He nodded. He was rewarded with a bone-crushing hug.

"You aren't humoring me, are you? You know I'm right. I haven't taken a chance or a gamble yet. I would never play with your life, Rand, not for anything. Tell me you trust me, that you trust what I've done," Sawyer demanded passionately.

Rand nodded again, unable to speak. His tongue was so thick he had trouble swallowing. Neither noticed as the others got up from the table. It was Sawyer who later ran into the hall to call them all back to the dining room.

Sawyer stood next to Rand, her eyes apologetic. "Mr. Hasegawa, the plane won't be ready March thirty-first. We need an extra day, possibly two. What will that mean to your people?"

How like Sawyer not to apologize. They'd all given it their best shot and failed to come in on schedule. One day, two, what difference could it make? A lot, according to the investors. Their contract gave them until the last day in March to prove themselves . . . or lose everything. And a contract was a contract. If April first arrived before the project's completion the contracts would be in breach.

"I can't ask more of the men than they've given. To come so far, so close, and not be able—"

"Grandfather, do something," Riley cried. "Make it right."

The elder Hasegawa placed a gentle hand on his grandson's shoulder. "It is out of my hands, my grandson."

"I don't believe that, Father. There must be something. You have always been the perfect father with the perfect solution for everything. It can't all have been for nothing. We can't lose now," Otami cried as she clutched at her father. "Please, think of something."

"We need an extra day in March. Just twenty-four hours. That's all," Riley cried childishly.

"Enough! I will look into the matter but can make no promises," the Japanese said formally as he withdrew from the room.

"Why do I feel as though I've failed?" Sawyer cried brokenly.

"You didn't fail. Things got in the way. You did magnificently," Rand said loyally. The others chorused their agreement. "Come along, back to the hangar. We have work to do. No one went home tonight. The crew is sleeping in three-hour shifts."

Billie sat down with a thump and buried her face in her hands. Surely they couldn't lose now. Otami put her arms around Billie's shoulders. Riley sat across from her. "Grandfather will find a way. I know he will."

"My father is a remarkable man, Mother Coleman. If it is humanly possible to make this right, he will. He will feel he must do it for our honor. We must all think positively."

Billie nodded.

They worked like Trojans for the remaining days. Thad arrived to offer his help and input. Billie rarely saw him and when she did he was so tired she could do no more than kiss his cheek and cover him with a blanket while he slept his allotted shift. Everything was the dream now. Nothing else mattered.

March 31 arrived all too soon. Sawyer was gaunt and red-eyed. Rand, at her side, looked no better. Everyone seemed to move in slow motion, Billie thought as she entered the hangar to seek out Sawyer. "Will you make it?"

"No. We need another two shifts. I did everything by the

book. We didn't allow for the human element. . . . Grandpap didn't tell me that. Eighteen hours, that's all. My God, Grand, I can't believe it."

At six o'clock that evening Shadaharu Hasegawa entered the hangar, a smile on his face. He closeted himself with Riley and Sawyer in her makeshift office for eight minutes, and when they emerged Sawyer's red eyes were sparkling as she waved an airy arm in Billie's direction. It was going to be all right.

"Thank you, God," Billie whispered. "Thank you."

The time was one hour past dawn. The calendar said it was April 1, but Riley's grandfather had proclaimed an extra day in the month of march. The Hasegawa newspapers in Tokyo carried the date of March 32, and newspapers didn't lie.

It seemed the world watched Moss Coleman's dream that day. Present were the Hasegawa family, the entire crew, Sawyer, Billie, and Thad. The media stood in a roped-off area ready to record the progress of the slant-winged silver bird.

Sawyer in her greasy coverall and visored cap stared into the sun. She ran half the distance to the runway and gave Rand a thumbs-up salute. Rand blew her a kiss and climbed into the cockpit.

As the plane started its glide down the runway, Billie blessed herself and whispered, "Rest easy, Moss. In a few minutes it will be history."

Strong arms enveloped her and she leaned back against Thad's chest. "Remember your promise," he said close to her ear. "Win or lose, fly or not, we get married tomorrow."

"I've been dreaming about my promise for a lifetime," she told him.

The dull roar of the engines exploded in the air as Rand taxied onto the far end of the runway. Billie stood in the circle of Thad's arms, fingers crossed, eyes lifted heavenward. "In just a few minutes we'll know."

"Do you mean we'll know if it was all worth it?"

"No. Everything, every joy, every tear, has been worth it for my whole life to bring me here with you today."

He kissed her cheek, holding fast to this woman whom he had loved for the whole of his life.

Billie turned to face Thad, her hazel eyes smiling into his. Overhead, Rand was airborne and holding steady. "Sometimes, Thad, I see questions in your eyes. Don't you know that some loves are for yesterday and others are forever?"

The light from her smile obliterated the shadows in his heart. "That's how I love you, Billie. Yesterday and forever."

{{{{{{{{ CHAPTER FORTY-ONE }}}}}}}}

Maggie Coleman caught a glimpse of her reflection in the pier glass. The image staring back at her made her gasp. She looked like a bag lady without the shopping bags. Her hand went to her hair and then to her cheek. What day was it? She had to stop and think, to try to calculate the month as well as the day.

How long ago had it been since her husband had left her? A year, six months? She didn't know and didn't care. She didn't feel his loss, would never feel it. It was over.

Pap's dream, that was over, too. The silver bird had flown beautifully off into the wild blue yonder with Rand at the controls. Sawyer must have convinced him to test the plane. Hate rushed through her veins at the knowledge that Sawyer had been the one responsible for making Pap's dream come true. Mam had called her excitedly from Japan, expecting Maggie to rejoice with her. Despite everything—the court injunctions and legal blockades to prevent Mam from squandering everything on that damn plane—she still expected her daughters to share in the glory. The lady certainly knew how to dish out the guilt.

Everyone was gone now. Pap was gone, Mam was gone, Sawyer was gone, her husband was gone. Coleman was away at military school, and she only saw him at Christmas and for the last two weeks in August. Stolen from her; everything in her life that should have been hers had been stolen from her. It hurt, and she had cried—for days, for weeks, for months. She was still crying, still trying to bandage her wounds, but there wasn't a Band-Aid large enough to ease the monstrous pain that attacked her twenty hours out of every day. The years, where had they gone? How had she lived through them?

Maggie's vision blurred momentarily as she looked around frantically for the vodka bottle. The clear liquid always made things better, or at least dulled the pain so that it didn't hurt quite so much.

There it was, on the night table, right next to the letter from old Dudley Abramson that had been sitting unopened for several days. She filled the tumbler to the rim and stared at the stark white envelope for a long moment before tossing it into the wastebasket. She didn't need his advice, or his criticism! She didn't care what he had to say. "You just wasted a stamp, you old buzzard," she said aloud.

A few minutes later she fished in the wastebasket and withdrew the letter. Maybe she should open it and see what it said. She was practically sober; she could handle it. She took a deep breath, ripped the envelope open, and stared with unbelieving eyes at the three pieces of paper in her hand. It was the key taped to the deed to Sunbridge that made her sink to the bed. The letter itself was short:

Dear Mrs. Tanner:

As per your parents' instructions, I am forwarding to you a fully executed deed to Sunbridge. The key is taped to the deed. Sunbridge now legally belongs to you.

I would like to take this time to remind you the taxes were due the first of April.

If there is anything the firm can do for you, please feel free to call upon us.

Yours truly,
Dudley Abramson

Maggie's hands were shaking so badly she could barely get her father's letter out of the unsealed envelope. It was handwritten, a jerky, uneven scrawl. The date on the single sheet of paper showed it had been written a week before his death.

Dear Maggie,

I can't go to that unknown place that awaits all of us until I do this one last thing. I hope and pray the time comes when Mr. Abramson will feel confident enough to forward this, my last word, to you. Your mother and I have spoken at great length about my intention of deeding Sunbridge to you. She has promised that if at all possible, she will not put Sunbridge up for auction but will turn it over to you. If, for some reason, it does have to be sold, I wanted you to know of my intentions. Our lives are full of uncertainties these days, but we must not dwell on them; we must all move forward, you most of all, Maggie.

Soul-searching has become a necessary pastime these last weeks. Old hurts can never be rectified. The ache in me for what I missed is more painful than the illness controlling my body. Forgiveness is something I have always taken for granted. I find it impossible to believe you will forgive me, but your mother assures me you will. I truly regret, dear Maggie, that I was so blind to your needs. I will carry that regret with me to eternity.

Only you, Maggie, can fill Sunbridge with love, life, humor, beautiful music, and wondrous words, because you care. Bring your son here, Maggie, and make a new life for yourself. I know a Higher Being will allow me to watch over you here in this place we call Sunbridge. Trust me, Maggie. You are part of my life, my love, my daughter. Be happy.

Pap

Maggie threw herself on the bed and howled. The huge four-poster rocked with the force of her sobs. When her release was complete she wiped her face with the corner of the bedspread. Her smile, when it came, was as radiant as the first golden sun of summer.

Four hours later Maggie Coleman Tanner was Texas bound. She was going home.

The key clenched in her hand was all the proof she needed that this wasn't all some kind of dream.

The rental car ground to a stop and Maggie was out in an instant. There it was. Home. What a wonderful, glorious word.

The key slid into the lock. She turned the handle and the door swung open. The first thing her tired eyes saw was the four-peg hatrack holding three Stetsons. Seth, Pap, Riley. She knew in her heart that the last peg had been ordained for her son, Coleman. His Stetson would hang there just as soon as that military school could send him here.

Home to Sunbridge.

TEXAS HEAT

In memory of Lucy Baker Koval, mother, grandmother, and friend.

ACKNOWLEDGMENT

It's true what they say about Texans; their hearts are as big as their wonderful state.

You invited me into your homes; you shared your lives, your families, your victories, and your secrets with me. Your warm hospitality, delightful humor, and unending assistance was greatly appreciated. My special time with you will always be remembered.

My sincere thanks to Eve and Houston Daniels; Helen and Rufus Abrams, Sharon and Mike Glazer and all those Texans who said, "Howdy, ma'am, welcome to Texas." Without all of you *Texas Rich* and *Texas Heat* would still be in outline form. I couldn't have done it without your inspiration.

Fern Michaels

{{{{{{{{{ PROLOGUE }}}}}}}}}

Sawyer Coleman watched the patterns the lazy California sun created on her cluttered desk. It had been weeks now since she'd seen the shiny cherrywood surface. Papers were strewn into haphazard piles, pencils with broken points, pens with chewed tops, all signs of overwork and frustration. She really should hire an assistant, someone to help with the load, but no one had ever satisfied her and she loathed having to check and recheck someone else's work. She had admitted to herself a long time ago that she was a workaholic, but lately she seemed to meet herself coming and going.

Heaving a sigh, Sawyer ran her long, manicured fingers through her wealth of golden-blond hair. There was no getting away from it; the work had to be done, and she was the best one for the job. Coleman Aviation was a family-held enterprise, a leader in manufacturing and designing small private jet planes, and she was the only one with the background and education to handle the growing company.

There were those about her, in the outer offices, who said Sawyer was too dedicated, too persnickety. She'd just heard that one the other day. Persnickety, for God's sake. The only thing she was certain of was that it wasn't complimentary.

Sawyer rummaged in her top drawer for cigarettes and lit one. She rarely smoked, usually only in tense situations

1

or as a ploy to stall for time. She was doing both now. Stalling because she didn't want to look at the invitation a second time, and tense because she hadn't heard from Rand in over two weeks. That alone was enough to make her itchy. Add that to Maggie's invitation and she could become a basket case within the hour.

Mother Maggie. Maggie, mistress of Sunbridge. Maggie the man-eater. Maggie, her own mother. Sawyer grimaced.

She was up and out of her chair, smoothing the soft gray flannel skirt over her trim hips. At the window she fixed her gaze on the bright ball in the sky. Aztec gold, she thought inanely as she puffed furiously on the cigarette she didn't want. The invitation was for a command appearance, a return to Sunbridge to watch Maggie preen. But there was more to it. Maggie needed the family's approval to take the helm. Bad girl Maggie returns to the scene of her crime but is forgiven. Sawyer laughed and choked on the cigarette smoke, sputtering until tears came to her eyes.

Grand would probably call soon, by tomorrow the latest. Then the others. And Rand, she thought with sudden hope, yes, Rand would call. Long-distance relationships were hell, overseas relationships even worse.

Damn, now her whole day was ruined. Why couldn't Maggie have sent the invitation and her chatty little bull-crap letter to the apartment instead of the office? Communication with Maggie shouldn't be so upsetting after all these years, but it was. She wished she had a hide too thick for Maggie to penetrate. What she did have was a sore, bruised heart that would never heal.

Family reunions should be outlawed. There was no way she could escape the invitation. She'd just have to put a good face on it. Seeing young Riley again would be worth a confrontation with Maggie. And to see Rand and spend time with him, she'd travel to Africa if necessary.

Rand. Her life, her love. Without Rand in her life, there would be nothing but endless days of work and endless nights alone. It was time to think about settling down, time to think seriously about marriage. Just the thought excited her and made her feel warm all over. Her work could be done just as well in London.

Quickly, before she could change her mind, she scrawled a note of acceptance to the July fourth bash. Later, when it was all over, the family would all say what a good sport Sawyer was. Good old Sawyer. Sawyer didn't bleed red blood like everyone else. Sawyer just hurt and ached inside, but the wounds didn't show.

Having Rand to herself would make up for everything. Just his smile would drive Maggie from her thoughts. Rand was all she needed, now and forever.

{{{{{{{{ CHAPTER ONE }}}}}}}}

Today would be one of Sunbridge's finest hours. Tomorrow's newspapers would carry each detail, right down to what the waitresses were wearing. When Sunbridge had a party, it was news, but when Sunbridge hosted a Texas-style barbecue, it was even bigger news. The family would come, and an impressive showing of some of Texas's most influential people. Maggie Coleman Tanner's smile widened. Funny the way she always personified Sunbridge, as though it were a living entity. In some ways it was. Sunbridge had been her past, and now it would be her future.

Maggie's eyes, blue as the winter sky, took in the flurry of activity below the bedroom balcony. Servants, caterers, waitresses—a whole passel of them, as old Seth would say—were getting *her* first barbecue under way. The fatted calf, the return of the prodigal child, Maggie thought. She herself was the prodigal, but could a prize longhorn steer qualify as a fatted calf?

She had ordered red-and-white checkered picnic cloths and matching napkins from Neiman Marcus by the dozens. She also vaguely recalled ordering two hundred wicker bread baskets that went for forty bucks a shot. Lobster flown in from Maine, shrimp, crab, and beef, all the accoutrements of a successful bash. The theme might be "country," but there wasn't anything provincial about her guests' tastes. It would be her way of showing them all that she was one of them, that the years she'd lived in New York hadn't been spent under a rock. She'd traveled in sophisticated circles where conversations centered on the theater, the stock market, and the new exhibit at the Guggenheim—conversations in the abstract. Here in Texas, the topics were more to the point—money, oil, beef, and more money, and not necessarily in that order. The crystal wineglasses winked up at her in the bright sunlight, reminding her that while Texans liked to pretend a "down-home" style of living, they were all smart enough and rich enough to know Baccarat from Cristal d'Arques.

Old Grandpap was probably turning over in his grave. His idea of a barbecue was beer on tap and red beans and rice, his patronizing attempt at being a "common man who made good." No one would have dared criticize if he'd chosen to serve good bourbon in paper cups; Seth Coleman was too important and influential to offend. On a whim, he could make or break a man and his fortunes, and there was no telling when the old codger would take it into his head to lead you to ruin just for the hell of it.

Things were different now. Old Seth was dead and buried and Maggie was mistress of Sunbridge. This party was just a way of driving that point home. Home. God, it felt wonderful to be back at Sunbridge. No, that was wrong. It felt wonderful to finally *belong* at Sunbridge.

All her invitations had been accepted; everyone would be here—half of Texas, not that she gave a damn about them, and the family.

Maggie leaned over the railing. This party was costing a fortune and she wasn't even truly certain why she was throwing it. What was she trying to prove, and to whom? Living here, holding the deed, that was the real proof of who was the owner of Sunbridge. Why did she feel this need to flaunt her ownership? Or was it really because she needed to show the world that she'd finally won her father's approval, that Pap had thought enough of her in the end to leave his beloved Sunbridge to her, and to no one else? By God, Sunbridge was her birthright! Sawyer had taken it away from her. Her daughter had lived at Sunbridge almost her entire life, while she, Maggie, had been banished. Now Sawyer would be returning as a guest in Maggie's home. That had to be some kind of divine justice.

Maggie stared off into the distance at the softly rising knoll overlooking the front of the house. All the white cross-fencing and rich golden meadows belonged to Sunbridge. A possessive heat blazed in her. This was Coleman land, her land, and it was alive again because she was home again. She could feel the power of this place. Two hundred and fifty thousand acres of prime land, Coleman land, and she would make it grow and prosper and flourish. She could almost understand what had kept old Seth going all those years. It was Sunbridge, the vigor of the land beating through his veins. His authority had gone unchallenged; he'd been supreme ruler, the invincible force that had built it and loved it and mastered it. Seth, meanest old man who ever took a breath, mean enough to depose his own grandchild. Sunbridge had been meant to go from Seth to his son Moss and then to his grandson Riley. Her sister Susan and she were insignificant females, worthless to him. "Do you see me now, old man?" she said, focusing on the gently sloping knoll where he was buried. "I'm here now, where I belong, where I've always belonged."

Coleman Tanner, Maggie's son, walked on cat's feet
to stand behind his mother. He knew he could wait there
for an hour and she wouldn't be aware of him until she
turned and actually saw him. It was only Sunbridge, this
place, that interested her. All her talk of his belonging,
of hanging his Stetson on the peg near the front door
beside those of his great-grandfather, grandfather, and
uncle, was just bullshit. The hat was dumb, just like everything else in Texas. When he did wear it, it was only to
humor her. Half the time he didn't know where it was,
but somehow his mother always managed to find it and
hang it on its appropriate peg.

Coleman was never certain if he should intrude upon
his mother when she was alone like this. "Alone" wasn't
quite the word to describe these moods of hers, when she
seemed to close herself in with her thoughts. Insulated
would be closer to the truth—insulated against everything
outside herself, including her own son. When he was
younger, it used to hurt and wound him; now it only made
him mad. At school, the other boys would comment on
how beautiful she was—gleaming dark hair worn just
above her shoulders, falling softly around her face to contrast sharply with her crystal blue eyes. He'd even seen
some of his instructors watching her slim figure when they
thought no one was looking. And there was no smile like
his mother's smile—open, bright, and genuine. When
she laughed, her eyes would sparkle and the corners of
her mouth would turn up and crinkle. She was beautiful
—Coleman had always thought her so—but none of
that beauty belonged to him. She was a stranger, and it
had been so long since she'd smiled for him, really for
him.

Coleman wasn't certain what Maggie was thinking
about, but he did know her thoughts weren't on him. She
hadn't even been available to pick him up from the airport
when he'd returned from school three days ago. Some
anonymous chauffeur had met him promptly upon his
arrival, instead. She'd explained by saying she'd lost all

track of time, what with planning the party and everything. On and on she'd explained, and he'd let her. He liked it when she got flustered and tried to apologize for something she thought she'd done wrong. That meant he could usually get what he wanted out of her without hardly trying.

Cole was growing and, in time, promised to be taller than any of the Colemans, thanks to his father. His eyes and nose were Cranston Tanner's, the father he rarely saw, but his strong chin and square white teeth and wide, generous smile came from his mother's side of the family. Maybe his feet, too, but no one seemed certain. A size-thirteen shoe at the age of sixteen was something no one wanted to discuss. He wore his light brown hair close to the head, in a military butch, and he thought it made him look like a boiled owl. But his mother said he looked just like the pictures of her father when he had finished boot camp.

Cole wondered when he'd gain weight. Lean instead of slim, they'd put him on a bodybuilding regimen at school, but so far it didn't seem to be working, no matter how much he busted his hump. He did it because it was required of him, just like he did everything at that rotten school. He hated it, hated the regimentation, the other boys, the uniform, the instructors, and the pomp and circumstance, yet he excelled in everything. Once, the major had told his mother he was the nearest to a perfect student he'd ever seen.

Maggie had done her motherly duty and smiled and sort of hugged him. But she didn't really give a damn, Cole thought. She was just concerned with appearances. Get rid of the kid, pay the duty calls and the bills, and then turn on the mother act for vacations. Like now. Fourth of July. Barbecue time. A real Sunbridge shindig, she was calling it. He'd heard about them for years, but he'd never attended one. He wasn't sure he wanted to be here now. He felt like an intruder. This would never be his.

He was expected to dress Western; that's what Maggie

called it. Western-cut jeans and shirts and boots that
pinched his toes. That pissed him off. Wearing a military
uniform ten months of the year was bad enough, and now
he had to wear another costume. Nothing made him feel
like himself, not the uniform or this dude ranch crap. He
wanted to pick out his own clothes, like his Brooks Brothers tassled loafers and the other designer things that hung
in his closet, things he seldom got to wear.

"For someone who's about to throw the biggest party
in Texas, you look worried, Mother," Coleman said suddenly.

Maggie whirled. "Coleman! You startled me. . . . And
how many times have I asked you to call me Mam? You
used to, when you were a little boy."

She was jabbing at him. It was always like this; he saw
it as her way of keeping him at a distance. Never answer
a question directly; never say what you were thinking.
Instead, launch the attack. But why was he the enemy?

"It's probably hereditary. You insist on calling me Coleman, when you know that Cole is the name I prefer. I've
told you enough times." Coleman's voice was deep, and
always shocked Maggie these days. Somehow it didn't go
with his gangling youth.

"Touché. It's just that you *are* a Coleman, and I don't
want either of us, or anyone else for that matter, to forget
it."

"How could *you* forget? It's all you ever talk about or
think about. I know you'll take back the Coleman name
when the divorce becomes final. Don't worry about it,
Mother. Everyone knows who we are; changing your name
isn't going to prove a thing." Coleman's voice was accusing; a smirk twitched at the corner of his mouth.

Maggie appraised her son. He was a Coleman—not in
looks, but certainly in his ability to cut straight through
to the quick. She knew he was reminding her of her alcohol dependency, of her failures as a mother, and saying
that nothing, neither Sunbridge nor changing her name,
would ever erase those facts. He was a boy, she reminded

herself. What did he know? She grimaced. At his age
she'd been older than Methuselah and more knowing. At
his age she'd already given birth to Sawyer, who had
reaped all the benefits she and her son had been denied.
Until now. Things were going to be very different with
her in charge. Somehow she had to make Coleman understand, make him see that this was where his roots were.

"This is where I belong, son, and so do you. Sunbridge
was built for the Colemans."

"Maybe for you, Mother, but not for me. My name is
Tanner and it always will be. This is just a place, not a
way of life—not my life, anyway." There was anger in
his gray eyes, carefully restrained bitterness in his tone.
"I don't like Texas and this hokey cowboy crap. I don't
like the clothes you make me wear and that stupid hat. I
don't want to be here; I want to go to Europe."

"You want to do *what*?" Maggie shrilled.

Cole snorted, his fine brows arching upward. "I thought
as much. Don't you *ever* read the notices they send from
school? My French class is going to Europe till the end
of August. I signed up and even paid the deposit."

Maggie turned back to the balcony to hide her confusion. For a long moment she watched the activity taking
place below. Vaguely, she remembered something about
a trip. But she hadn't given her permission; of that she
was certain. Why did he have to bring this up now, when
she was preoccupied with her family and herself? Her
eyes narrowed. Was it possible there was more of Pap in
her son than she realized? This sudden announcement in
the midst of an argument was like something her father
would have pulled. If she gave Coleman her permission
to go to Europe, he'd be perfectly behaved at her party,
showing family and friends their close, loving relationship. He'd be the perfect son and grandson, warm to
Amelia and charming to Susan. He'd pretend to be Sawyer's adoring half brother. But if she didn't play his game,
this cranky, selfish son of hers would show his true colors.

It wasn't fair! Why couldn't she make him see that all

this was for him, too, to make him a part of the family, to lay his birthright at his feet? This was her party—she'd chosen the Fourth of July weekend for the barbecue to symbolize her freedom from the past, her own independence. She couldn't allow a sixteen-year-old boy to spoil it for her. She turned to face Coleman, watching him, knowing he was waiting her out, confident he would win, as always. Not this time, she thought. There were new rules now. "Why don't I take this matter under consideration and let you know my decision *after* the party?"

Coleman bristled. He hadn't expected this, and he understood perfectly. Behave, act the perfect son, and maybe, just maybe, she'd give him permission for the trip. He didn't like it, but he was caught, trapped, and he would have to play the game by her rules. He nodded, giving his agreement, and knew he was dismissed when his mother's eyes returned to the scene below.

Coleman left the room, closing the door behind him. She'd have her way—for the time being, at least. But if she thought she'd keep him here at Sunbridge, trapped under her thumb and exchanging the excitement of a trip to Europe for "down-home" living, sweating horses, and ignorant Texans, she had another think coming.

She wanted him to belong to Sunbridge. He'd never belonged anywhere except military school. He used to feel ashamed that his parents had no time for him, that they didn't want him around, until he'd realized the other boys had almost identical problems. Once his adviser had convinced him he could become a man, a real soldier, without his parents, he'd felt better. "Be independent; heft that gun, soldier. You're ten years old now. Act like a man."

After that, Coleman didn't cry into his pillow at night when his shoulder hurt from carrying the heavy rifle. He'd suffered the black-and-blue marks from the rifle's kick during target practice without a whimper. He'd worked himself up in rank, becoming one of the youngest platoon leaders, forcing himself and his men to do extra marches, score higher marks, achieve more awards.

By the time he was twelve, he'd been promoted twice. Rank, he discovered early on, carried untold privileges, and he'd learned to use each and every one to his own advantage. He knew how to wheel and deal, to hustle the lower classmen and strike fear into the skinny little boys with their glasses and protruding teeth. Coleman liked power. At the end of the term he was acknowledged as the undisputed head of E Wing, Zone five. Now, how was it going to look if he didn't go on this European trip because his mommy said no?

When Cole closed the door behind him, Maggie's shoulders slumped. She couldn't allow him to ruin things for her, but she couldn't give in to him, either. He was still a child, looking to her for direction and challenging her at the same time. Coleman was so different from her younger brother, Riley. At sixteen, Riley had been warm and caring, his gentle, unspoiled nature and charismatic charm attracting people to him. Anyone who knew Riley loved him. He'd been all the things her son wasn't and probably never would be.

Maggie didn't need anyone to tell her where she'd failed Coleman. Caught up in her own life, her own despairs, she'd never really been there for him. How could she have handled a small boy's problems when she hadn't been able to cope with her own? And her marriage to Cranston had been on a downhill slide for the past seven years. She'd hung on, telling herself that she had to keep the family together for Coleman's sake. In truth, she'd hung on so long because there was nowhere else to go, no one else to go to. *That* Maggie Coleman Tanner hadn't liked herself very much, and her low self-esteem had only added to her fears of being alone. As long as Cranston hadn't made any moves to end their marriage, neither had she. But at last her self-loathing had spilled over onto Cranston, and after she'd started drinking too much as well, he'd left her.

Maggie shook her head as though to clear it. She didn't

want to think about all that now, not today. She'd come
a long way from that desperate, unhappy woman. She
was still uncertain about this new person she wanted to
become, but she'd taken long strides. Pap leaving Sunbridge to her had done that—given her a kind of assurance
that she did belong somewhere, that she was loved, that
she hadn't been overlooked by the one person who'd been
more important to her than any other. Pap. All her life
she'd wanted his approval, his love. She'd been such a
mixed-up kid and then such a hostile, mixed-up woman.
But she was determined to change all that, and now, for
the first time, she felt success was within her grasp. No,
she wouldn't think about Coleman now; she wouldn't let
anything spoil this day.

The colorful Japanese lanterns strung around the front
yard were perfect. They wound in and out of Grandmam
Jessica's rose garden and down toward the long, winding
drive. They'd be lighted at dusk, just as the guests began
to arrive. That's when the orchestra would begin to play,
and later on, when the food was served, the piano player
would pound out Scott Joplin tunes in accompaniment to
a banjo. Billie would probably choke when she saw the
ice sculpture of a rearing stallion where champagne would
cascade through transparent tubes. Maggie shrugged.
Tacky, of course, but expected. It would keep Austin
buzzing for weeks.

The hot July sun beat down with merciless intensity,
and she was glad she'd chosen the colorful striped tent
awnings that sprawled across the lawns. It all looked so
gay. Funny how something as banal as acres of yellow-
and-white canvas could make her feel so good. The surprise of the evening would be the special fireworks that
would be displayed over the pond behind the house. Even
Coleman would approve of the millions of starbursts that
would light up Sunbridge at midnight.

A stray breeze caressed Maggie's shoulder. Soon it
would be time to dress for the family's arrival. She planned
to wear one of her mother's original designs, a Christmas

gift. She loved the filmy rainbow creation and had been saving it for a special occasion. Wait till Mam saw her. Billie's eyes would light and she'd smile that warm, loving smile.

When Maggie had first gotten the idea for this party, she'd never realized it would become so important to her. For weeks now she'd lived with only one thought—the reunion. Even Coleman's homecoming had taken second place to the business of preparing Sunbridge for today. She'd had to send a chauffeur to the airport to meet Coleman instead of driving in herself; then she'd been late getting home from town and had missed his arrival. When she had at last returned home, he'd waved lazily in her general direction and gone back to reading his book. She did go up and hug him, but he'd been stiff and unyielding, punishing her for her oversight. She'd made a mental note to work harder at her relationship with Coleman; but he resisted her so, and rejection still came hard to Maggie.

Perhaps young Riley would be a steadying influence on Coleman. She was eager to see her brother's son. Not long ago she would have had to admit that she wanted him here to assuage the guilt she felt over her brother's death. But now she knew she wanted to share some part of Sunbridge with Riley. He was her nephew and a member of the family.

She remembered the day Billie had called to tell her Otami had been killed in an automobile accident in Tokyo. All the old guilt had come rushing back then, until she'd literally been sick to her stomach. First Riley and then his lovely Japanese wife. Only young Riley was left. His Japanese grandparents had taught Maggie something about unselfishness and generosity. Immersed as they were in their grief, it would have been understandable for them to keep Riley all to themselves. Instead, they wanted him to come to America to take his place as a Coleman, to become a part of his heritage. Wisely, they realized they wouldn't live forever. What would become of their pre-

cious grandson after they'd gone? "For as long as he needs
to be there," Billie had said. It was more than all right
with Maggie. The last time she'd seen the boy, she'd seen
how much he resembled his father. And she'd been terribly
flattered that Billie would trust her to care for Riley, the
only child of her only son.

A sudden breeze, stronger and different in character
from before, chilled Maggie. Nothing, not even an act of
God or nature, was going to spoil this party. She looked
to the sky, still crystal-blue, only a rare puffy white cloud
scudding across the horizon.

Maggie was feeling restless; and the confrontation with
Coleman hadn't helped. She glanced at her watch; it was
still too early to dress. On a sudden impulse, she kicked
off her high-heeled sandals and ran through the house and
outside, heading for the stables in search of Lotus, her
favorite mare.

Lotus nickered in anticipation of a run when she recognized Maggie. Maggie bridled the roan and led her to
the mounting post. She hiked up her skirt, straddled
Lotus's satiny back, dug her bare heels into the mare's
flanks, and was off. A startled groom stared after her,
then shrugged. Lotus needed a run.

Maggie took Lotus at a fast canter, following the white
cross-fencing circumventing the back corrals and pastures, taking the full circuit until they approached the
knoll overlooking the front acres of Sunbridge. Lotus knew
her way, head held erect with confidence, obeying the
urgings of her mistress.

Once upon the knoll, Maggie slid from Lotus's back.
First it was her grandmother Jessica she visited. Then it
was Seth, and then Agnes. Pap was always last. The best
was always saved for last.

While Lotus cropped the fresh green grass, Maggie
went to Jessica's headstone, reaching out to follow the
deeply chiseled letters of her name. She'd never really
known her grandmother; Jessica had died when Maggie
was only an infant, but Billie had often mentioned what

a kind and gentle soul she'd been. Seth would grumpily agree with Billie, then add his own interpretation. "Timid is what she was, no grit!" Seth, cantankerous old man who'd ruled Sunbridge with an iron hand. Dead now, but never forgotten. Maggie grimaced when she looked to the left of his tombstone. Nessie, Seth's first horse, and then Nessie II and then Nessie III. It was obscene that three horses should rest in the family cemetery, but Seth would have it no other way, and no one else seemed to mind. Maggie had no fond memories of any of them—not Jessica, whom she'd never known; not Seth, who had condemned and banished her; not Agnes, who'd been a flesh-and-blood buzz saw with no one else's interests at heart but her own. Yet each of them had shaped Sunbridge, Maggie knew; each had left an indelible mark.

Pap. Tears pricked her eyes as she dropped to her knees. Idly, she picked at a weed and tossed it onto Seth's grave. Her father, her own Pap, was the real reason she came here. Here she talked and visited and felt more welcome in his presence than she ever had when he was alive. There were times when she'd spend hours here talking to her father, working things through in her mind. It was Pap's last act that had turned her life around; he'd given Sunbridge to her.

"Listen, Pap," she said, "this is my day. I think I'm finally going to make it. Giving me Sunbridge made me back up and take a second look at Maggie Coleman Tanner. Did I tell you I'm taking our name back when my divorce comes through? Well, I am. And about this shindig today, I don't know where the idea came from, but I think it's one of my best. The whole family is coming and I'm sure they'll all be trooping by here, so keep an eye out for them.

"And I'd appreciate it if you'd accept young Riley. He is one of us, you know, and I think you also know by now that life's too short to waste on old grudges and stupid prejudice. Riley loved Otami and together they had this wonderful boy. You cheated us all, especially Mam, when you didn't tell us you knew Riley had a wife and son. Wherever you are, be kind and gentle in your thoughts of all of us, especially Riley. You know I'm still carrying this guilt around with me. I could have stopped my brother from running off to join the navy, but I encouraged him because I knew it would hurt you. I should have stopped him, but I didn't. You didn't do a lot of things, either. Maybe I can make up for it now, just the way you tried to do by leaving me Sunbridge. I know, you always thought I was a rebel, freethinking and independent. Well, I'm not. I'm so damned insecure I get sick inside. How come you never knew that?

"Hey, Pap, do me a favor, will you? Tell my brother I'm going to make things right for his son. The way you did for me. I love you, Pap. Tell Riley I love him, too."

Maggie, her eyes glistening, brought her hand to her lips and then gently touched the tombstone.

{{{{{{{ CHAPTER TWO }}}}}}}

Home to Sunbridge. Billie rested her head against the back of the seat, her soft hazel eyes half closed against the sun's glare. She watched Thad at the wheel as he handled a bend in the road. Driving an automobile was as natural to him as flying a plane; both were done with an economy of movement and the same enjoyment. She could see the sharp bridge of his nose and his gentle gray eyes, eyes that were always ready to brighten with laughter or reveal the depths of his love. The first time she'd met him, so long ago in Philadelphia, she'd thought his eyes were his nicest feature, softening his chiseled, craggy features and echoing his smile.

Thad Kingsley hadn't changed much over the years. His mellow gold hair was paled with gray now, but he still had that same burnished tan. He carried his height with dignity and he was still military fit and trim. Despite the fact that he was a world traveler, his voice still carried the hint of a crisp New England accent, the vowels slightly flat. Now that he was again living in his home state of Vermont, his accent had deepened, become more a part of him.

When she'd first told Thad of Maggie's phone call inviting them to this Fourth of July party, he'd grinned and said, "When do we leave?" Just like that. No matter what he was doing, Thad would stop on a dime to do something that was important to her. Dear Thad. God, what if she hadn't opened her eyes in time and listened to her heart? What would have become of her?

A rolling tumbleweed skittered across the road. Billie noticed Thad didn't bother to brake. The weed was out of sight by the time the rental car sailed down the road.

Texas. Land of the rich and powerful. She realized now she'd never liked it, not really. She'd never belonged. It was too vast, too high-powered for her. She liked living in Vermont in the two-hundred-year-old farmhouse they'd modernized with a hot tub, a spanking new kitchen, and a greenhouse. The guest cottage had been converted into a studio for her, but she found she was using it less and less these days. Licensing out her trademark name of *Billie* had brought her all the money she could ever hope to need. She enjoyed being sought after to design a special pattern or fabric for one of her rich, famous clients. Sometimes she obliged and sometimes she didn't. It all depended upon what Thad was doing and how much free time he had. They were a unit, a twosome. She loved her life and wouldn't change it for all the Sunbridges in the world. Billie Coleman Kingsley had found her place in this world and the one person she wanted to share it with, Thad.

"We're almost there," he said softly, breaking the silence. He removed his hand from the wheel and placed it on her silken leg. "You can handle it, can't you, Billie?"

She heard the anxiety in her husband's voice. "Thad, I can handle anything, even those nine puppies of Duchess's we left behind. This is a visit. Of course there are memories here for me, but that's exactly what they are— memories—and they belong to the past. Promise me you won't worry about me."

"I promise." He patted her leg reassuringly, then put his hand back on the wheel. "Are you worried that Maggie is up to something?" he asked.

"I admit it crossed my mind, but it's not fair to Maggie, is it? Why do we always expect people to remain the same and never change? We all change, don't we, Thad?"

He took his eyes off the road for a moment to grin at her. "Not you, Billie. You're still the same girl I met at the USO dance in Philadelphia. You're still the angel on my Christmas tree."

Billie flushed beneath the intimacy of his voice. "Life changes all of us, and that includes Maggie. I think she just wants to see us all under the same roof and wants us all to know she's happy at last. How could I deny her this visit? I'm her mother. Even if—and I don't believe it's the case—even if Maggie had an ulterior motive and I knew about it, I'd still have come. She asked us. She didn't manipulate or demand; it was a hopeful invitation. I wanted to come for Maggie. It's been a long while since I've seen her. We talk on the phone, but that's hardly the same thing."

"The gathering of the clan. I like the idea. Families are important," Thad said quietly.

"My one regret, darling, is that I couldn't give you children. If only I'd been stronger, reached out for what I knew I wanted sooner, there might have been time for us."

"And I've told you a hundred times, having children

was never important to me." He reached for her hand and squeezed. "You've always shared your children with me, and in a large way, I feel Sawyer belongs to us. As long as I have you, that's what's important. You promised you weren't going to mention that ever again."

"And I meant it. If this invitation hadn't come up, I'd have stuck to my word. This is quite a family, the Colemans. Of course there will be outsiders, like Amelia's husband—" Billie threw her hands into her lap. "You see what I'm doing? I'm just like these Texans; I guess it's become ingrained after living with Seth for all those years. I'm decreeing who belongs and who doesn't. Old Seth always called you that 'Yankee cracker,' warning Moss to 'Watch out, boy, or that Yankee'll get the better of you.'

"I worry about young Riley, Thad. I know how Sunbridge can devour a life. I know how it can suck out the fine things like loyalty and courage and devotion. This is a demanding place, taking the best and spitting out anything that doesn't measure up."

"Don't forget Sawyer. She was born and raised at Sunbridge, and it hasn't done her any harm."

"That's because I was older and wiser then with my own children when I took Sawyer into my care. I was strong for her; I protected her and saw to it that her values weren't confused."

Thad was silent for a moment. They'd had this conversation before, and Billie had mentioned that she was nervous about Sawyer coming to Sunbridge. Maggie and her daughter had been apart for too many years; the hurts and wounds ran too deep, Billie said. He wondered if Sawyer would have accepted the invitation if she weren't bringing young Riley in from Japan.

As if reading his mind, Billie said, "In many ways Sawyer and Riley are alike. Two little orphans coming home to Sunbridge. Sawyer was terribly shaken by Otami's death. They'd become very good friends, you know. There was no time to prepare for what happened, if it's ever possible to prepare for a death. One second Otami was alive and the next she was gone. A drunk driver and a life is gone, one we all treasured." Billie wiped her eyes.

Thad could feel a lump in his own throat. When the news of Otami's death reached them in Vermont, Billie had wanted to fly to Japan immediately. But when he'd called the Hasegawas, they'd urged him to stay in Vermont and to allow them to handle their grief in private. Thad had understood and tried to make Billie understand.

"I wouldn't worry too much about Sawyer, Billie. That young woman is doing just fine. She's successful, charming, and beautiful, and your granddaughter. And she's in love."

Billie was silent for a long time, her thoughts on the family. She *was* worried about Sawyer. Thad was wrong. For all her sophistication and intelligence, Sawyer was as vulnerable as a child, still believing that everyone was going to live happily ever after. There had been very few disappointments and little unhappiness in Sawyer's life.

"Billie? Did you hear me?" Thad broke into her thoughts. "I said not to worry about Sawyer."

"I heard. And I'm not worried about her business capabilities; she more than proved herself as an aeronautical engineer. I don't know what's actually bothering me. Perhaps I'm being foolish, but I can't help it."

Thad laughed. "Hey, listen, I'll never ignore your intuition again. When you said Duchess was going to have her puppies on Monday night and then woke me at three in the morning to tell me mother and all nine daughters were doing fine, you made a believer out of me! If things look like they might turn sticky between Sawyer and Maggie, I'll just remind them who I am."

"And who's that?"

"Fleet Admiral Thaddeus Kingsley, Retired, now farmer and horse breeder."

Billie giggled. "That should certainly impress them. Aren't you going to tell them that the politicals in Vermont want you to run for Congress next time around?"

"Naah, that sounds too much like bragging. People who live in Texas don't care about Vermont, unless of course their maple syrup is slow in arriving. Let's not mention it."

"I won't, but I think it's wonderful. The United States Congress!" Not for the world would Billie let Thad know the idea scared the daylights out of her. She didn't want to live in a Washington fishbowl. And she didn't want her husband compromising his principles, as she knew most politicians were forced to do eventually. But if it was what Thad wanted, she'd back him all the way.

Thad was saved from replying. "We're here."

Billie raised her eyes. There it was, the high wooden arch with the name Sunbridge emblazoned on it. Miles of white fencing stretched into the distance; tall oak trees arched over the winding drive; and behind them was an expanse of bright green lawn dotted with sprinklers pulsing rhythmically.

Billie always felt as though she were traveling through a tunnel of dappled green. The drive ahead of them sparkled with reflected sunshine, and when they made the final turn, the house came into view.

Thad braked the car, as much for himself as for Billie. Both of them sat for a moment, still captivated, still awed after all these years, at the sight of Sunbridge.

Sitting upon a gently sloping rise, the great house basked beneath the blue Texas sky and was caressed by the sun. Billie had once thought that only here, in this place, could the sun seem so warm and golden. In Vermont, she'd learned the same sun was warmer, even more golden.

The house was a three-story brick of the palest pink, flanked by two wings that were also three stories, but set back from the main body. This expanse of prairie rose was accented by white columns that supported the roof of a sweeping veranda. A multipaned fan light crested the huge double front door, and the design was replicated in miniature over each window on the top floor. Ornamental topiary trees and crape myrtle hugged the foundation, and

surrounding the house was a magnificent rose garden
complete with trellises and statuary.

"In the old days, Thad, this was called 'a spread'—at
least that's what Seth called it. I can still hear him boast-
ing, 'Two hundred and fifty thousand acres of prime land!'"

Thad laughed. "I can almost hear the old bastard. And
to think that he built this all himself—the son of an itin-
erant sharecropper, a boy with no education, only good
sense and a talent for ruthlessness."

"Sunbridge," Billie said softly. "It's the perfect name
for it. Even Jessica told me she was amazed by Seth's
poetic turn of thought when he named it. He always said
he felt as though he could reach up and touch the sun
from here. I never felt that way, but I'm sure Maggie
does."

Thad reached over and slid the back of his hand down
Billie's silky cheek. "What say we get this show on the
road, Mrs. Kingsley?"

"Sounds good to me!" Thad could always make the
darkest moment bright again. God, she loved him.

Maggie stood beneath the portico, waiting. She'd felt
lightheaded from the moment she'd heard the sound of a
car coming up the drive. Who would arrive first? She
strained to make out the passengers. Mam! And Thad!
Thank God.

The car had almost come to a stop when she realized
Coleman wasn't beside her. She'd called out to him on
her way down the stairs, but he hadn't followed her. No
matter—there'd be time for Coleman later. Mam was here!
Mam had come to visit her at Sunbridge.

Billie was out of the car and up the steps, her arms
outstretched. Thad watched from his position inside the
car. He reached for one of their bags. It was all right;
everything was going to be all right.

"Mam, you're stunning! The most beautiful mother in
all Texas. Did you design that silk dress yourself?"

Billie nodded shyly as she noticed Maggie's silk lounging outfit. "Didn't I give that to you for Christmas? Let's see . . . how many years ago?"

Maggie laughed. "I don't deal in those kinds of numbers anymore. You're right, though; this is one of yours. I'd bet the rent that everyone in the family will be wearing a Billie Original today."

"You look wonderful, Maggie. You look happy."

"I am, Mam, really happy. Come inside. Coleman—he wants to be called Cole—will be down in a minute. Thad, come along. You must be thirsty."

Billie approached the door. Everything was the same. The ethereal grace of Jessica's rose garden and the feminine sweep of the pink clematis vine softened the heavy, masculine-looking oak doors, made them seem more welcoming. Inside would be the same, Billie suspected; Maggie wouldn't have changed a thing. Shining oaken floors, massive beams studding the first-floor ceilings, thick dark Oriental carpets, and man-sized leather furniture. It all bore Seth's stamp; Jessica's influence was nowhere apparent on the first floor of the house. Only outside and in the bedrooms could her whimsical and very feminine hand be felt. Billie imagined for a second that she could smell Seth's cigar smoke. The great house of Sunbridge, Coleman domain. No, nothing had changed, and she doubted it ever would.

Maggie embraced Thad affectionately. The tall man smiled down at her. Amazing how coming home to a pile of stone and brick could affect a person, he thought, how a true sense of belonging could bring out the best. "Just point me in the right direction," he said, indicating the piece of luggage, "and I'll be back before you know it."

"Top of the stairs, second door to the left," Maggie said easily. "And if you see Cole up there, tell him it's time for him to come downstairs. Someone will see to bringing the rest of your things upstairs and parking the car down by the garages."

Billie felt her breath explode in a loud sigh. She turned to look at her daughter.

Maggie flinched. "Mam, you didn't think I'd put you and Thad in your and Pap's old bedroom, did you?"

"I . . . I wasn't sure," Billie answered hesitantly. It was exactly what she'd thought.

As though reading her mind, Maggie tilted her head and smiled shyly. "Friends, Mam?"

Billie wrapped her arms around her daughter. "Always and forever, darling."

"We've had some rough times, and some things can never be fixed. Someday I want to sit down and talk. Maybe to apologize, maybe to try and explain . . ."

"It isn't necessary, Maggie. All I've ever wanted was for you to be happy. That's all any mother really wants for her children. Sometimes we make mistakes along the way, but if the intentions are good, somehow they right themselves in the end."

Maggie's eyes were bright with unshed tears. "I'm being selfish; you've had a long trip and must want to freshen up, too. I'll be out on the patio. I hope that scamp Cole didn't run off on me. He says he doesn't like parties."

Billie laughed. "I can remember a party or two that his mother managed to wriggle out of."

Maggie grimaced after Billie left the room. Where the hell was Cole, anyway? She wanted to show him off, but she was still worried that he'd do something to embarrass her. Billie's reminder of how often she'd refused to attend family events was grim. She crossed her fingers. The boy would behave; she'd see to it. She decided the kitchen with its array of tempting food was the logical place to look for him.

"Martha, have you seen Cole?" she asked the buxom cook, who looked up from chopping vegetables.

"No, Mrs. Tanner, he hasn't been in here."

"I thought he might be in here filching a Coke or something."

It was on the tip of Martha's tongue to suggest that Cole might be found outside filching beer, but it wasn't her place.

"Well, if he comes in here, please tell him I want to see him."

"I'll do that, Mrs. Tanner."

A worm of apprehension crawled around in Maggie's innards. What was Cole up to? He knew how important this party was to her.

When Maggie finally found her son on the rear patio, she had to stifle a laugh. She had to admit he looked a bit ridiculous in his Western outfit. The jeans Cole had purchased were too crisp, too new, and the bright plaid shirt, which should have had a pointed spread-wing collar, instead had a typical Ivy League button-down over the black string tie. "Cole, your grandmother and Thad are here. They went upstairs to freshen up. I'd like it if you came into the living room to welcome them."

Cole looked up from his magazine and stared for a moment at his mother. "Righty-o, Mam," he drawled.

"And don't be a wise-ass. I know you can behave like a gentleman. I pay that school enough to teach you manners, so practice them."

"It's a bit hard to act a gentleman in this getup," Cole retorted. "You think I'll fit in with all the other cow-pokes?"

"Stop it, Cole. Get into the house; Mam'll be down in a minute. Don't screw up. I mean it."

Cole threw down his magazine, obeying his mother. He liked it when she used slang to get her point across. That meant he was getting to her.

Billie felt a sense of exhilaration as she linked her arm in Thad's to walk down the long, winding staircase. This was someone else's house now; she and Thad were visitors. They could leave anytime they wanted.

"You aren't sweating this at all, are you?" Thad grinned.

"Not in the least. I'm looking forward to seeing my children. I was just thinking that Sunbridge has no hold over us anymore. I'm all right, really."

"I can see that. I hope you're looking forward to our trip when this visit ends."

Billie's eyes brimmed and Thad was immediately sorry he'd brought up the subject of Japan. "I am looking forward to seeing the Hasegawas again. Otami is with Riley now, and that's all she ever wanted. As for young Riley coming here to Sunbridge, the Hasegawas' unselfishness amazes me."

"It didn't surprise me. Shadaharu was wise to give Riley the choice."

"Feel better?" Maggie called from the bottom of the stairs.

"Much better." Cole was standing beside Maggie, and Billie swallowed a giggle at the vision her grandson presented. A cartoon cowboy all decked out for a Saturday night. She knew Thad was reacting the same way—she could feel the tremble of laughter in his arm.

"You've grown, Cole, and you're so handsome! But then, I suppose all grandparents say things like that." Billie wrapped the boy in her embrace. She kissed him and leaned back, her hands on his shoulders. "Yes, very handsome." She beamed. "So much like your father."

Cole laughed, but the humor never reached his eyes. "What you're saying, Grand, is you have to look to find the Coleman in me."

"There's better than Colemans in this world, dear. But you *do* have your grandfather's smile and jaw."

"The world isn't big on jaws. It's the rest that counts," the boy joked.

"You're home, and that's what matters," Thad interjected. "Besides, a fella can get a bit overwhelmed by all these Colemans. At least you can keep your grandmother and me company. You know our veins don't pump Coleman oil. It takes good old Yankee blood to crank our machinery."

"Home to Sunbridge," said Maggie. "This is the first time Cole has been here for more than a long weekend. Remember, Mam, how hard you said it was when you first came here?"

"I certainly do. Your mother's right, Cole. It's overpowering at first, but you won't let it get the better of you."

"I'm sure you're right, Grand."

"Say, why don't you and I go find something cool to drink?" Thad said to Cole. "Perhaps your mother and Grand would like to talk before the others arrive."

"I'm with you." Cole clumped out behind Thad, his stiff new Western boots creaking.

Billie couldn't help herself and began to giggle. Maggie frowned and then laughed, too. "Mam, he hates dressing like that, and he just doesn't know how to put it all together. I'm the first to admit he makes himself look ridiculous."

"Then why?"

"When in Rome, right?"

"But the boy looks so unhappy."

"For a few hours it won't hurt him. If he'd let me help him select his clothes and had taken the time to break in his boots, he wouldn't look like a sore thumb."

"Poor Coleman." Billie sighed. "Perhaps when Riley gets here, they can commiserate with each other. Being half-Japanese in Texas is being another sore thumb."

"Don't worry about him, Mam," Maggie said. "I'll be backing that kid up all the way. And don't underestimate the people here in Texas. Attitudes have come a long way in the forty years since you first arrived. Besides, Riley's last name is Coleman. If that doesn't turn the trick, nothing will."

"I'm sure you're right, Maggie. But I can't help worrying about the boy. He's leaving everything he knows." Her hazel eyes were touched with grief. "When a boy is sixteen years old, he should know where he belongs."

"He will," said Maggie. "He'll know he belongs here in his father's house. I've had Riley's old room made up. I even went up to the attic and got down all of his stuff— you know, his camera and books and all those little treasures from when we were kids. They belong to Riley's son, don't they, Mam?"

"Maggie, it's wonderful of you to do that for your nephew."

Maggie flushed. "Can you believe I found those old Flash Gordon sheets and the Lone Ranger blankets? I made up the bed myself."

"I think of our Riley almost every day," Billie said quietly.

"So do I. Especially since I'm back here at Sunbridge. Mam, why wasn't a grave marker put up on the knoll for Riley? I know his body was never recovered from the plane crash, but why not a memorial stone?"

"That was your father's doing. He couldn't bear it."

"When the time is right, I'm going to talk to young Riley about it. Something should be done, don't you think?"

"I think that when the time's right, you'll know what to do. Whatever you decide, you can count on me."

"Otami, too? A memorial stone, I mean."

Billie's brows shot upward. This certainly was a new Maggie, with this sense of family. "Perhaps. But Riley might not want to stay at Sunbridge. You must prepare yourself for that, Maggie."

"As sure as I'm standing here, the boy will stay. I feel it in my bones."

"Perhaps. Come along, dear. Let's go find Cole and Thad. I could use something cool to drink myself. What time do you expect the others?"

"Within the hour. Isn't it wonderful? All of us under the same roof; all of us back at Sunbridge after so long."

The sound of a car pulling up the drive and a blaring horn saved Billie from further reply. Who else could it be but Amelia, returning to Sunbridge with fanfare. Billie stood back as Maggie raced for the door and out to the portico.

"Auntie Amelia! And this must be Cary! Welcome, welcome to Sunbridge."

Billie, standing in the shadow of the doorway, registered shock that she immediately concealed. Cary Assante, Amelia's new husband, was young, quite young in fact—

at least twenty years younger than Amelia. . . . Billie disliked what she was thinking and stepped out the door, her arms open.

"Billie! How wonderful to see you again. I really snagged a winner, didn't I? Admit it!" Amelia whispered in Billie's ear as the women embraced.

"He has my vote." Billie laughed to see her sister-in-law and best friend so animated with happiness. When Amelia had become widowed during the Second World War, she'd only been a few years older than Billie. Amelia had spent a good portion of her life alone, but now she had Cary. "I'm happy for you, Amelia," Billie murmured sincerely. "And you look wonderful!"

"I should!" Amelia said with her usual candor. "I've had everything lifted that could be lifted. I've more tucks than the good friar himself!"

Billie thought of her own wrinkles. The laugh lines around her eyes, the tiny brackets at the sides of her mouth, the deeper grooves in her forehead. For a time she'd toyed with the idea of a nip and a tuck herself, but as long as Thad loved her the way she was and pink light bulbs in the bedroom could work their magic, all was right with the world.

Amelia squared her shoulders imperceptibly, something she found herself doing whenever a younger woman was in Cary's presence. Maggie looked gorgeous, alive and vital. Just like Cary.

Cary Assante was movie star material. Slightly taller than medium height, lean and chiseled; something animal and hungry in those sparkling dark eyes. He was magnetic, handsome in a rough, virile way. His shoulders broad, like those of a boxer, back straight, light gray trousers hugging muscular thighs. His Italian heritage was visible in his sable-black hair and in his skin, which accepted a healthy tan. He had the look of a hawk, hungry and alert, but when he smiled, his expression was genuine and friendly, and it was obvious that he was quite comfortable with his good looks.

When they all moved to the shady back patio, Billie

found herself observing Cary while introductions were being made to Thad and Cole. He was carefully put together, she decided. His thick dark hair was meticulously barbered and windblown to exactly the right degree. His tan—earned no doubt, on the tennis courts beneath the California sun—was also exactly right, neither too leathery nor too blushingly pink. Everything about him seemed carefully designed for natural elegance—his Lauren shirt, Cerruti jacket, Italian shoes, and the solid gold Rolex winking on his furred arm from beneath his sleeve. Everything he wore had obviously been selected for him by Amelia; at least it was obvious to Billie, who was so familiar with Amelia's tastes.

The introductions completed, Cary approached Billie. His voice was a light baritone with shades of a New York accent, easy to listen to. He smelled awfully good, too. "I've been eager to meet you and your family. Amelia speaks of you all so often, especially you, Billie. I have to admit, I'm jealous, since I've no family of my own."

"None at all?"

"Not that I know of. I was raised on the charity of New York City in a Catholic orphanage. But," he added lightly, holding up a finger, "don't feel sorry for me. I survived, and some of my friends from those days did, too. In fact, they're still with me in business."

"What do you think of Texas? Have you ever been here before?" Billie asked. She really had to buy some of his cologne for Thad.

"I like it. And no, I've never been before, except for a week or so a few months back. I've been considering a parcel of land this side of Austin for a housing development. No, actually, it's much more than that. It's kind of an inner city outside the city." He laughed. "Townhouses, condominiums, and single-family homes, complete with shopping center and some light industry."

"Here in Texas?" asked Maggie, who had overheard.

"Yes, outside of Austin," Cary repeated. Maggie relaxed instantly: no city lights would be seen from Sunbridge. "Amelia agrees it could be a good idea. I'm going to look into it. This party will give me an opportunity to talk to some of the locals and see what they think of the idea."

Billie tried not to show her dismay. Something as large as what Cary was talking about would require a great deal of money and expertise, not to mention luck.

"You wouldn't believe this man," said Amelia. "He reminds me of Moss; he has a finger in lots of pies, all of them exciting!" There was an uneasy silence as Amelia looked from one face to the other. "Cary, perhaps you'd better tell them, right now, that you didn't marry me for my money."

Amelia had caught everyone off guard, but it was so typical of her that Billie almost laughed. "Amelia, no one—" Her eyes were drawn to Cary, who had moved closer to his wife.

"That's what I call letting it all hang out." He put his arm around Amelia's slim shoulders. "No, I didn't marry Amelia for her money; in fact, I'm not certain this lady isn't a gold digger herself. But I took my chances because I love her." He sighed dramatically. "So if there's anyone to be concerned about here, I guess it's me."

"What he means," Amelia said, smiling mischievously, "is that he's worth about ten times more than any of us here. At least at last count."

Billie sighed with relief and Amelia felt better immediately. It was important to her that Billie like Cary. "There's a difference in our ages, but Cary says it isn't important. What's important is the here and now, and the devil take the rest."

"Amelia makes *me* feel young," Cary said, grinning, as if that explained everything. "And now that we've gotten that out of the way, what do you say about something cold for a parched throat? It's a throwback to the old days when I didn't have two nickels to rub together. I talk about money and my mouth goes dry."

They were all on the back patio sipping drinks, and none of them heard the car come up the drive. "Well, hello, everyone!"

"Susan!" Maggie cried exuberantly, jumping up to embrace her sister. "Suse, I'm so glad to see you. Almost everyone is here now."

Cary, who had never met Suse or her husband, Jerome, was standing now and walking toward them, his hand outstretched. Amelia followed quickly behind her husband. Susan, who had lived with her in London as a girl was like a daughter to her, was only a year or two younger than Cary. Amelia felt it in every step she took. Yet she embraced her niece with genuine affection, her laughter real, her blue eyes sparkling. The introductions were made, and Amelia felt herself stiffen when Cary kissed Susan. But he immediately turned back to her and slipped an arm around her shoulder. He kissed her teasingly, lightly, below her ear. "I think I can detect a faint resemblance."

Amelia let out her breath in a sigh. With Cary's arms around her, everything was all right. He was behaving the loving, dutiful husband. Now, why had she thought such a thing? she wondered. Cary was always affectionate, always demonstratively loving. She mustn't allow herself to bristle like that. He was so in tune with her, he noticed any change almost immediately. But she could have been mother to all of them . . . including Cary, the man she adored.

{{{{{{{ CHAPTER THREE }}}}}}}

Billie had recently visited with Susan in New York, so there was no urgency to push through the rush of kisses and hugs and fond hellos, promises to meet more often, and latest travel gossip.

When they'd all settled down again, Maggie said, "You look weary, Suse." Her tone was fond and caring. It was true; Susan's normally fair, blond prettiness now seemed wan and pale, and her light eyes were rimmed with circles not even Estée Lauder could hide.

"She always looks that way after a tour." Jerome's voice sounded slightly harsh, as if he were annoyed at Susan's fragility.

Billie frowned and Maggie could feel something building inside herself. Susan looked more than tired; she appeared ill. "Well, I have just the remedy, Suse," said Maggie. "You sit between Mam and Amelia, and they'll pamper and pet you, and I'll get you whatever your heart desires. Name it—cold drink, something to eat?"

"Anything, as long as it's cold. Do you mind if I kick off my shoes?" Susan felt like crying.

"This is home, Suse," Maggie called over her shoulder. Then all the women gasped when they saw how swollen Susan's feet were.

"It's flying," Jerome interjected quickly. "Lots of people's feet swell from sitting too long."

"You should never take your shoes off on the plane," Amelia advised. "You'll never get them on again."

"You fly first-class," Billie said with concern. "Can't you reserve a bulkhead seat? Ask the stewardess for several pillows and prop your feet up."

As Jerome spoke with Thad and Cary, it seemed to Maggie that he was forcing his smile, pretending a joviality he didn't feel. In the past few years Jerome de Moray had lost his robust, youthful appearance to a kind of overfed middle age. He wasn't fat, only threatening to become so. His clothing seemed one size too small, and his once boyishly pink cheeks now seemed florid. His sherry colored eyes had kept their intelligence, but his easy smile now seemed pinched and forced, as though his shoes were too tight.

Amelia reached out and patted Susan's knee. "Darling, don't you think it's time to cut back on these grueling tours?"

Jerome, standing across the patio, answered for his wife. "Not at all, Amelia. Susan always gets tired, but she recovers soon enough. She's such a perfectionist, you know. Every detail, every reservation, is arranged by her. Do you know she personally irons my shirts when we're on the road?"

Amelia snorted. She'd never cared for Jerome, and now that his early promise had faded—if one was to believe the critics—he was hanging on to Susan for dear life. Susan was the talent; Susan was the box office draw. Cary quickly moved to Amelia's side and pulled her up from the chaise. "They're playing our song." He laughed lightly. "Let's show everyone that fancy dance step we learned in New York." Cary led her to the open floor and whispered, "You were about to put your foot in it, my darling."

As Amelia fell into step beside her husband, Coleman raised the volume on the stereo. The music blared as they took center stage on the patio amid hoots of approval and applause.

After five minutes, Amelia collapsed onto the chair

beside Billie, her face flushed. Cole wanted Cary to teach him the step and began to ape his movements. Amelia laughed as she watched them. "I hope you're the only one to see how frazzled that left me, Billie. I'm not as young as I used to be. My heart's going like a trip-hammer."

"Cary relieved a bad moment. I saw it coming but didn't know what to do."

"The man can read my mind. Jerome and I have had several arguments in the past about Susan. Cary was avoiding a scene. He never fails me." Amelia lowered her eyes, then looked back up at Billie. "You see, I'm doing it again, trying to justify my marriage to Cary, always pointing out how wonderful he is. I don't know why I do it! Or is it myself I'm defending?"

"Why don't you just be you and let Cary be himself? I like him, Amelia. The man's in love with you; any fool can see it. Enjoy it; don't let old ghosts ruin this for you."

"We do make our own hell, don't we. We make so many mistakes along the way. But I'm not wrong about Susan. She looks ill, doesn't she, Billie? It's not my imagination."

Billie glanced at her younger daughter, seeing again the tired dark circles under her eyes, the yellow pallor, the puffiness around her ankles and fingers. "No, I'm afraid you're not. We should have a talk with her later on."

"Easier said than done. Jerome isn't about to let his bird out of her cage. Over the years he's become an abso-lute dictator. I thought I liked him once, but that was when he was a young, blossoming virtuoso. I put down his temper and eccentricities to his being a genius. Now I think he's just spoiled and selfish. Oh, how I wish I'd been able to convince Susan that Peter Gillette was the man she needed, and not Jerome. But Susan and her 'tidy' life couldn't bear up under the scandal of Peter leaving his wife and children for her. I tried to tell her it'd blow over in a matter of time, but she was so afraid, she jumped for Jerome as though he were a lifeline." Amelia sighed, a frown creasing her brow. "I worry about her, Billie."

"I know you do, but let's not worry now and spoil Maggie's wonderful party. It's getting late, isn't it?" She glanced at her watch. "Sawyer and Riley should have been here by now. Rand, too."

"The plane was probably delayed. Rand was going to wait for them at the airport so they could all drive out together."

The tall, wheat-blond-haired man lounged in his chair at the airport bar, drawing appreciative glances from passing females. Unabashed, he stared back at them, making his own assessments: too short, too tall, too skinny or fat, too much makeup. He disliked the kind of frizzled hair that seemed to be all the rage these days, or hair that was cut boyishly short. By the time he'd finished his second Bombay gin, he'd warded off one flagrant flirtation and had taken two more subtle ones under consideration before smiling his gleaming white smile that echoed in his coffee-brown eyes.

Rand Nelson hated airports and train stations almost as much as he hated to be kept waiting. He'd been waiting nearly three hours now for the flight from Japan via San Francisco. Even from this distance, his keen gaze could read the green-screened monitor declaring the two-hour delay from San Francisco. In two hours he could consume four more drinks and probably smoke an entire pack of cigarettes. He considered calling Sunbridge to alert them of the delay.

In some ways he was already regretting this trip. At the age of forty-three, he was old enough to know what he wanted and didn't want in his life. Mostly, he realized, he wanted life to go smoothly. Perhaps he'd remained a bachelor too long; perhaps he was too set in his ways. Rand wished he could pinpoint the time and place when he'd realized he'd achieved all of his major goals. He enjoyed his successes, savored each of them, but some instinct told him it was time to start winding down, time to stop and smell the roses. Bulging bank accounts, fingers in pies that didn't require his personal involvement, had allowed him to think about the pursuit of pleasure, doing something creative or having the choice of doing nothing at all.

The Bombay gin slid down his throat, crisp and icy. He'd learned to like his drinks American, that is, with ice and served in frosted glasses. There wasn't much of the Englishman in him. He supposed having Amelia for a mother and almost constant world travel had erased his tastes for warm beer and warmer liquor and endless days of London weather. Lord Randolph Jamison Nelson, Earl of Wickham, was a name and title that had little to do with the man; it was a name listed in the peerage and would be as long as there was an England, but it said nothing about himself.

Sawyer. Her name brought a vision of sunshine and energy and the sound of a girlish voice softened with a Texan accent. Slim, lovely, bright, intelligent, and only twenty-six years old. She was on the brink of discovering her abilities, of putting her education and her unique position as head of Coleman Aviation into effect. Her instincts for business were as sharp as her grandfather's and great-grandfather's had been before her; with little more than legal advice, she'd been successful in licensing the most innovative, lightweight personal aircraft in aviation history—and keeping the copyrights intact for Coleman Aviation to boot. Sawyer was hooked on achievement, and nothing would keep her from testing her abilities. The trouble had nothing to do with Sawyer's ambitions and success; in fact, he admired her for making the most of her talents. But he'd had enough of high-powered business deals. What would become of Sawyer and him if they married? He wanted to wind down, and she was just coming into her prime. Age was just a number, but they were two people at opposite ends of a rope.

Sawyer had been in Japan and it had been almost two months since he'd seen her, time enough for Rand to think, to really face the fact that while he loved Sawyer Coleman, he was not in love with her. He hated to think of himself as capricious, and in his heart he knew he wasn't, but time had a way of changing people, often against their will. His time with Sawyer had been wonderful. They'd had so much in common, working on designs and specifications for her grandfather's aircraft. Common goals, loving the same people, seeing things the same way. But the goals had been won, and loving the same people and being involved in the same family wasn't enough. Now Sawyer had new goals to conquer, and she would embrace them the way she embraced all of life—with humor and gusto and a sense of adventure.

Rand ordered a fresh drink and lit the last cigarette in the pack. The minutes on the clock over the bar ticked away. Soon the plane from San Francisco would arrive. Soon he'd have to look into Sawyer's crystal-gray eyes. What would she see in his own?

Perhaps Sawyer would argue that he was "dropping out," but Rand knew he wasn't. He simply wanted time to himself, to reap the rewards of his hard work. There were things he'd always dreamed about but could never find the time to indulge: fishing, hunting, and yes, even planting that garden and watching it come to fruit. Books, pleasure trips, refurbishing the four antique automobiles he'd collected. But most of all he wanted time for the people he loved, those involving relationships he'd been unable to develop as he'd run from one airport to the other.

Rand stubbed out his cigarette and paid his bar tab. His tip was overgenerous. If Sawyer had been here, she would have computed the bill and stuck the overage in his breast pocket. Sawyer did things by the book. Rebelliously, Rand placed another dollar on the table. A weary waitress working a dull shift on the Fourth of July needed a little extra. She'd probably missed her family barbecue in order to work today. All Texans went to a barbecue on the Fourth.

Crossing the terminal, he passed a monitor. The blinking words "at the gate" meant Sawyer's plane was in and she and Riley would be deplaning. His step quickened and he straightened his tie. Then he smoothed his tousled thatch of wheat-gold hair. If only he were happy to see her again, if only he didn't feel like a first-class rat. Worse, a coward.

She was beautiful, tall and slim as a fashion model. Men turned for a second appreciative glance; women envied her graceful, long-legged stride. Those incredibly long, shapely legs were bringing her closer and closer. Rand hardly noticed the tall young man beside her. This was Sawyer: brilliant gray eyes, clear pink skin, and generous smile that lit her surroundings. Bright and fresh, her skirt barely wrinkled, every sleek blond hair in place despite the intolerably long trip from Tokyo.

Sawyer stepped into his arms; her soft lips found his. He responded lightly, wishing his heart would stop its furious pounding, wishing she wouldn't look at him with such open-hearted love.

"I missed you, Rand. We have a lot of time to make up," she whispered, then drew back and looked into his eyes. Whatever she saw there seemed to satisfy her. "Riley!" she said. "We're almost forgetting you!"

"You must have grown a foot since I saw you last, Riley," Rand said, stretching out his hand.

"He's cropping out at six feet and still growing; what do you think of that?" Sawyer beamed like a proud mother.

"It's uncanny how much like your father you are. You're even built like him."

"I could hardly believe it myself." Sawyer laughed. "He was just a little twerp when we saw him last, and now look at him! There's a picture at Sunbridge of Grandpap and Riley when he was this age. I'm going to hang a picture of you right beside them. I'm embarrassing you, Riley. I'm sorry."

"It's okay." Riley smiled. "I'm used to you by now. I weigh in at one sixty; she usually mentions that next," he said to Rand. "How are you, sir? It's been a while."

"Too long." Rand clasped the boy's hand. "I was awfully sorry to hear about your mother, Riley. This must be a difficult time for you."

"Thank you, sir." The grief was there, clouding the clear nutmeg-colored eyes, but the chin was firm, the voice steady.

Sawyer took a playful swipe at her cousin. "I can't wait till Grand sees you! She's going to flip out. You were a plump little sushi roll when she saw you last!"

"Come on, let's get your baggage," Rand said. "Have you been embarrassing this lad all the way from Tokyo?"

"I don't mind." Riley smiled. "Which way to the baggage area?"

Riley followed behind Sawyer and Rand, glad to be in the company of people as tall as himself. It had been getting difficult in Japan. Towering over almost everyone else brought attention to himself, and at the age of sixteen going on seventeen, being conspicuous was the last thing Riley wanted. He was tall like his father, and had become the butt of much good-natured ribbing. It always pleased him when comparisons were made to his father, and he took pride in the resemblance. He'd inherited his strong profile and well-defined nose from his great-grandfather Seth; and he knew his smile and thick crop of fine black hair, which bore a tendency to wave, also came from his American background. Only his eyes revealed his Oriental heritage. Because of his height and build, people often mistook him for Hawaiian. Sawyer told him not to fight it when his ancestry was mistaken. "Eventually, people accept you for *who* you are, not *what* you are," she'd said. "People who matter, anyway."

On the ride to Sunbridge, Sawyer carried much of the conversation, telling Rand about the business meetings she'd had in Tokyo and their fruitful outcome. There was a tenseness in Rand's shoulders; Riley could see that his eyes never left the road to smile at Sawyer's jokes. And even though he laughed, there was something hollow in the sound. Sawyer was trying too hard to be amusing, reaching over too frequently to smooth Rand's hand or rub her palm against his cheek.

By the time they reached the turnoff for Sunbridge, Riley could feel the tension in his own shoulders. Sunbridge, an ancestral home. His father's roots were here. But were his? He hoped it hadn't been a mistake to come here. What if he was viewed as a burden? Perhaps Maggie had just been doing what she thought was her duty. Maybe resembling his father as he did would make everyone uncomfortable. He wished he knew. Traveling halfway around the world to come to Sunbridge had been difficult, especially since it meant leaving his mother's family. His Japanese grandfather would be terribly disappointed in him if his stay in America wasn't a success. "Knowing only one side of your ancestors is knowing only one-half of yourself," the old one had counseled.

The "old one." Riley smiled to himself. It was the name Grandpa Hasegawa preferred. It denoted wisdom and respect in the traditional Japanese manner. Japanese . . . American . . . who was he?

He looked American, from the top of his billed baseball cap to his scuffed Adidas. Sawyer had assured him it was all right to travel in jeans. The button-down plaid shirt was his own attempt at dressing up. The cap had belonged to his father, and it was never off his head, except when he ate and slept.

Riley couldn't wait to meet his cousin Cole. They'd eat American pizza, hot dogs, tacos, and burritos. For starters. Listening to rock music was his second-favorite pastime. Maybe he and Cole could go to a rock concert together. He could almost picture them walking through the crowd looking for chicks. All American boys were after chicks. Riley frowned. Girls shouldn't be called "chicks," but he was going to have to adapt. A girl was a girl in any language, and the universal response was always a smile. Sawyer told him he had a smile that would knock girls dead. He grinned to himself.

Sunbridge land. Rolling green hills, crisp and clean and

sharp, as though painted on canvas. He particularly liked the tumbleweeds and remembered the way he'd chased them across the lawn on his last visit.

He wasn't visiting now. He was to make this his home, the old one had said. He'd always known he'd come back here someday, but he hadn't expected it so soon. If his mother hadn't been killed, he'd still be in Japan attending the university. This is what she would have wanted for him, the old one had said. The old man had cried at the airport, his stoic Japanese resolve abandoning him. Riley had shed tears of his own, but not until he'd gone to the restroom on the plane. He missed Tokyo already; he missed the old one.

Sawyer leaned over the back seat. "So, what do you think? Has Texas changed?"

"It looks the same to me, just as beautiful. I always expect to see men on horseback come galloping along."

Sawyer laughed. "They only do that in the movies. Another mile or so and we'll be there. A bit anxious, eh?"

"A little," Riley admitted.

"The one thing you can count on, Riley, is that Sunbridge will never change. Perhaps some new paint, the trees get bigger, the animals get fatter, but aside from that, everything stays the same. I feel as though I'm coming home. For such a long time this was my home. I can't imagine how you must feel."

"I want to belong," Riley said simply.

"You do. This was your father's home. If he hadn't died, this place would have gone to him and to you as his son. We talked about that on the plane. Just because Maggie holds the deed doesn't mean a thing. Sunbridge is as much yours as it is Maggie's and Cole's. Maggie herself will tell you the same thing, I'm sure."

"They may consider me an intruder."

"I'm sure that will never happen, but if it does, Grand will make it right. You belong here. Accept it, Riley."

"Yes ma'am," Riley said, saluting smartly.

"Hew do you feel about coming to Sunbridge, Rand?" Sawyer asked a trifle anxiously.

"I've always loved Sunbridge, ever since I was a tad and Amelia brought me here for the first time, during the war. It's a grand place."

"I know...."

"I can see the arch," Riley said, breaking the awkward moment.

"That means we're home," Sawyer said airily. Homecomings were so important to everyone, for different reasons.

When they climbed from the car in the wide, circular driveway, Sawyer found herself brushing shoulders with Rand. He was so silent—the kind of silence that trembles. How absurd! she thought. Rand was the most together person she knew. He didn't have a nerve in his body. But she did give him a second look before she threw her arm around Riley's shoulder.

This was her mother's house now. Not Sunbridge, not their home. Maggie's home. Sawyer couldn't help but wonder how Riley was going to fit in. For all her brave, reassuring talk, she wasn't certain. Maggie had loved her brother, and if things went right, she would love young Riley, too. For Maggie's own reasons.

Riley's smile and dark good looks were certainly charming everyone else. The baseball cap was clutched fiercely between his hands. A pity the boy didn't know he had nothing to fear. At least from the Coleman women. The envy and dislike in young Cole's eyes might give the boy a spot of trouble later on, but that was to be expected. Boys were always rivals in one way or another.

Maggie took center stage, calling for quiet. "I think we're all here now. I'm so happy you could come here today. It's kind of a momentous holiday. Freedom and independence, that kind of thing. It's been such a long time since we were all gathered under the same roof. If we can, let's put the past behind us and move closer to making this the kind of family we should be. It's what I want, and I think all of you want the same thing. For any of you who don't know, Riley is going to be staying with us here at Sunbridge for as long as he wants. This is his home as well as mine. Sunbridge belongs to all of us. This is home."

Cole stood up and clapped his hands. "Bravo, Mother. Very well said." Maggie flushed with embarrassment. "Cole," she said apologetically, "doesn't understand what Sunbridge is all about. He's going to learn, though. This summer he's going to ride the range and do all the things Pap and my brother used to do. He's going to learn what Sunbridge is all about. Riley, too."

Cole sputtered. "You promised. . . . You lied to me . . ."

"That's enough, Cole," Maggie said quietly.

"Why? So you can pretend to all these people, this wonderful family of yours, that you're the grande dame of Sunbridge? You had no intention of considering my trip to Europe! You had this summer all planned out for me. For him, too," Cole said, jerking his head in Riley's direction.

"I said that's enough, Cole," Maggie said, coldly this time.

"Stuff this party, Mother. I'll be in my room," Cole said, stalking off and turning his ankle just as he walked through the doorway.

Maggie's eyes spun around the assembled guests. To apologize for her son or not . . . Everyone had family problems. Her gaze locked with Rand's. The rosy circles on her cheeks stood out starkly.

Billie let her breath out in a soft sigh. She was standing beside Riley. Her hand went protectively to his arm. She wanted to say something comforting but couldn't find the words. It was Riley himself who saved the moment.

"Aunt Maggie, which horse will I have? And if I'm to ride the range, how many days will it take for my blisters to heal?"

Maggie laughed, a light sound of relief. "About a good two weeks. For starters, I think you can ride Lotus. She's fairly gentle and she likes an apple for any ride over thirty minutes. Later, you can ride Stormy. Your father's riding gear is in his closet. From the looks of you, it'll just fit."

Rand glanced over at Sawyer, who was still staring at

the doorway through which Cole had stumbled. He knew her feelings for Maggie were unresolved. It was never easy being abandoned. Sawyer was quite sensitive on the subject of her mother. He found himself gulping his drink. Knowing this, how could he be such a heel? How could he add to her hurt?

There was a knock on Cole's door and Riley was standing in the open doorway. "They sent me up to find you," he explained. "I'm glad to meet you. I wanted to see you the last time I was here, but it just wasn't possible."

"I lived with it," Cole said sarcastically. His cousin stood head and shoulders above him had made him feel all of four years old. "I could live with it if you left right now. I don't understand why you're here to begin with."

Riley took a step backward as though he'd been dealt a physical blow. He'd never encountered such rudeness; it would never have been allowed in his grandfather's house. But the old man had cautioned him not to bring shame on their family, and the boy answered quietly, "This was my father's home. I never knew him; Sunbridge is as close to him as I can get. I'd like to know how he grew up here in Texas. I'd like to experience it for myself."

"Well, I don't want to be here, and I sure as hell don't want to live with some Japanese orphan. Don't go getting any ideas we're going to be buddies and that I'm going to ride the old south forty to help you chase down your father's ghost."

Riley bristled. "I won't ask you for anything. I didn't come here to freeload, if that's what you're thinking. I can earn my keep."

"Oh, yeah, and what're you going to do? Ride the range, herd cattle, mend fences, muck the barn?"

"If I have to," Riley said sharply. "You don't have to like me, Cole"—there was an inner core of strength in his voice—"but I'm not going to let you walk all over me just because I'm a guest in your mother's house. I can handle myself."

"Look how impressed I am. I was on the boxing team

at school. You're just what we need around here, a smart-ass with a black belt in karate."

Riley laughed. "Is that the same thing as being a wise-ass?"

Cole didn't laugh; he knew Riley was mocking him. Cole turned his back and took two steps away, the hackles on the back of his neck warning him that Riley could pound him to a pulp. He was ready for anything, ready to fight if Riley made a move. "Dumb Jap prick!"

Cole turned suddenly, expecting Riley's onslaught, but he found himself alone and facing an empty doorway. Cole swept his arm over the top of his dresser, finding small satisfaction in the tinkle of broken glass.

{{{{{{{{ CHAPTER FOUR }}}}}}}}

Maggie presided over the long, linen-draped table. If she noticed the vacant place beside hers, she gave no indication. Coleman's presence, she decided, was almost incidental to this gathering. Smiling, she rose to offer a welcoming toast. "To our family, each one of us!"

The chorus of enthusiastic responses pleased Maggie. "Wait," she said, holding up her hand. "We have another toast. To Sunbridge!" This time the responses were more subdued. Only Riley beamed from ear to ear, and it was his echoing toast that could be clearly heard.

In deference to the huge Texas-style barbecue that would be offered later that evening when the other guests arrived, Maggie's luncheon menu was purposely light: salad in aspic, which she noticed the men refused, baked lemon sole fillets, and asparagus tips. For the heartier appetite, a rich fish chowder was served, complete with thick slices of French bread and crumbled bacon. And, for dessert, coffee, pie and ice cream.

"Still watching your weight, Susan?" Maggie asked as she dug into her apple pie.

"In a way. At our age it's difficult to take it off. Besides, I'm looking forward to those barbecued ribs."

Jerome, mining his way through a second piece of pie with double ice cream, glanced at his wife. "I don't want you to overdo tonight. Remember your diet." Then, looking around at the others, he said, "Susan has to be careful. It's critically important how she looks onstage. She's been admired for her angelic, ethereal appearance when she sits before the piano. One bulge and it's all ruined."

"Susan has always been a disciplined person," Billie said. "I quite admire you, darling. And as for your figure, you have nothing to worry about. Whatever do you do when you want to binge? What's your secret?"

"I look at Jerome, Mam," Susan said coolly. An uneasy silence shrouded the table.

"I think you need a good, long rest, Susan," said Amelia. "You're looking a bit peaked," she added bluntly.

"There's nothing wrong with Susan," Jerome said sharply. "It was the trip, coming off the tour and getting ready for the next one. Susan is fine."

Thad whispered to Billie, "Methinks he doth protest too much. Follow your instincts, darling. She's your daughter."

"I'll talk with her later, Thad. She looks miserable enough now; I don't want to add to it."

There was a lump growing in Susan's throat. All her family was here, and if there was ever a time to make an announcement, this was it. Damn Jerome and his career. Damn the tour and damn the critics. First she looked at Amelia, and then at Billie, who nodded slightly to show she understood. Susan had something to say, and this was as good a time as any to say it.

The knife was in Susan's hand before she could think, and she was tapping lightly on her water glass. "Listen, everybody, I have an announcement." She carefully avoided looking at her husband.

"Susan! We've discussed this," Jerome hissed at her across the table. "Not now, for God's sake!"

"Now!" she said. "Everybody..." She took a deep breath. "Everybody, I'm pregnant! Isn't it wonderful?"

Maggie was off her chair and took her sister into her embrace. "Suse! How wonderful! I'm so happy for you! This calls for another toast!"

"There hasn't been a baby in the family since Coleman." Billie laughed. "When is this wonderful new addition to arrive?"

"In time for my birthday. February." Susan was brightening before Billie's eyes. Already there was more color in her cheeks, and her eyes were glowing.

"That's if all goes well," Jerome said.

"Why shouldn't it?" Amelia asked. "Our Susan's a strong, healthy woman. Or is there something you're not telling us, Jerome?"

He was saved from having to reply by Sawyer, who had left her place at the table and stood behind Susan's chair. "If you're in the market for a godmother, I volunteer. How lucky you are, Susan! So very lucky." She squeezed Susan in a hug.

Rand's pulses were pounding. The naked want on Sawyer's face saddened him and terrified him at the same time. They'd talked of this, of marriage and children. Sawyer should have children, lots of them. She'd be a wonderful mother. But what of himself? He just couldn't see himself at fifty with toddlers climbing on his knee. He knew Sawyer was looking at him, willing him to share her secret smile, to give her some sign that one day the two of them would achieve this miracle. When Rand refused to meet her eyes, Sawyer dropped her head, silky blond hair hiding her face.

Susan patted Sawyer's hand and looked directly at Jerome. "Don't say another word, but I'm going to have another scoop of ice cream." There was a challenge in her eyes, determination in the set of her mouth. There, it was out in the open. She'd told her family and they were delighted. Until this very moment, with Jerome's badgering, she hadn't been certain herself that she wanted this baby. But now her family knew, and they were happy for her.

Servants were clearing the table, bringing out an array of cordials: Courvoisier for the men, Grand Marnier for the women. Bowls of fruits and boards of cheeses replaced pie plates and ice cream salvers.

Billie followed Riley's gaze as it rested first on one face, then another. It hurt to look at the boy. Her heart ached for her dead son. Seeing Riley, now a young man, recalled so many old torments. It was uncanny how much he resembled his father, her son who had died so young. Hardly fifteen, but already he was as tall as his father had been at twenty. Maggie was right: the worn jeans and favorite shirts and perhaps even the boots that had been stored away because no one could bear to dispose of them would fit the boy now. If Riley chose to wear them. And Billie knew what his decision would be. She hoped she'd be gone from here before then. Grief, it seemed, held to no time clock.

Maggie clutched Billie's hand as they walked back to the house to rest for a while and change before the guests began to arrive. "I'm scared as hell about tonight, Mam. I don't know if I can pull this off."

"You'll do fine, Maggie. Stop worrying and just enjoy your guests. Everything's under control, and you have your entire family here to back you up."

Maggie slipped her arm around Billie's shoulder and squeezed. The deep sable tones in her hair contrasted with Billie's blondness. "I know, and I appreciate it, believe me. It's just that I'm afraid to make a fool of myself. Sunbridge is home now; it's important to me to be accepted by my neighbors."

Billie laughed merrily. "I'd hardly call the governor

and his wife neighbors, but I know what you mean. As we were driving out today, I saw how developed Crystal City has become. I remember when it was Crystal Crossroads, with nothing but a general store and a gas station. Now, it seems, culture has arrived. Boutiques and bookshops, and didn't I see an art gallery and gift shop?"

"You did. And a hair salon and haberdashers. You name it, we've got it. Most of the shops and businesses have been opened by bored matrons from the country club. Their clientele consists mainly of one another, but I'd say they're thriving, giving Neiman-Marcus a run for its money."

"It's been almost a year since you're out here, Maggie. Have you joined the club and made friends?"

"I've joined the country club, but I don't know if I've made friends. Oh, I play tennis and even some golf, and I'm a member of the Cattleman's Association, but I don't really know if they accept me."

"I felt the same way when I lived here with your father. They're a closed unit, and while they smile on the outside, I guess you have to be one of them to know what's going on inside. I wasn't born here, Maggie; you were. You're more like them than you know—you belong here. Besides, you're not lacking in social skills. I remember some of the clippings from the social columns describing the parties you threw when you lived in New York with Cranston. And even before that, you were director of Sandor Locke's art gallery as well as his unofficial hostess. I should think that New York crowd would be much more critical than people here in Texas. You've always been a success, Maggie; things won't change now."

"I hope you're right, Mam. This is a first for me." Maggie opened the door to the house and allowed Billie to step through. "I didn't get one refusal, but I can't fool myself. I know why they're coming and so do you. They want another look at all of us, Amelia, Susan, you."

"Perhaps you're right, but we'll present the united front you want. Stop worrying. As you said, no one refused your invitation, not even the governor!"

"They want to eat my food and drink my liquor! They're all freeloaders who live from one party to the next!"

Billie giggled. "Seth used to say almost the same thing. ... And Maggie, I noticed that you aren't drinking at all. I'm proud of you, believe me."

"I do, Mam. I need a clear head for my future, and I won't clutter it up with booze and pills. I don't want to be dependent on anything except my own resources. I have Cole and Riley to think of now. It's a new Maggie."

"And I like her," Billie said. "I always liked the old Maggie, too."

"For a while I didn't know that, Mam. I wasn't certain anyone liked the old Maggie, not even myself."

"Maggie, Sawyer doesn't—"

"Not now, Mam. Not today. I'm not so sure this new me is strong enough to tackle that old skeleton. Let me take it one step at a time."

"All right, Maggie. But it won't go away, you know. Sooner or later you and Sawyer will have to resolve your feelings."

"I know. I'm doing my best. I'll try, really."

"You know, just for a minute you looked like Moss," Billie said quietly. "That same haunted expression used to come into his eyes when he was forced to make a promise he had no intention of keeping. I'm sorry, Maggie. I don't want to press you."

Billie shivered and a sudden prickle of goose bumps broke out on her arms. "Come away from the door, Mam; we're standing in a draft." Then, in a lighter tone, "Guess what I'm wearing tonight."

Billie laughed. "The honeysuckle-patterned beaded gown?"

"Exactly. It'll knock everyone's eyes out. Everyone will know you designed the fabric especially for me. Amelia said she bought a new Adolfo, and Susan told me she's wearing the two-piece watered silk you sent her for Christmas. I didn't get a chance to ask Sawyer."

"Whatever she wears, she'll be stunning. Are you planning on a receiving line, Maggie?"

"Absolutely. All the Coleman women will be lined up to let 'em get a first-crack look at us. What're you planning to wear?"

"Well, since you insist they're coming to gawk, I just might wear my birthday suit! That should set them back on their heels!"

Cary stepped out of the shower and into the thickly carpeted bedroom, a scanty towel wrapped around his hard, lean middle. With another towel he was drying his obstinately wavy black hair.

"Are you finished with the bathroom?" asked Amelia. "How come you always get to use the shower first?"

"Because I don't stay in there for two hours and you do." Cary quipped, moving closer to plant a kiss on the side of her neck. Lovingly he took his wife's hand and held it, oblivious to the network of blue veins and the faint brown splotches. He only felt the softness and the affectionate pressure she returned.

"Mmmm. You smell so good." Amelia relished the feel of his lips against her skin and his fresh soapy scent. Beads of water clung to his shoulders and glistened in the thick mat of his chest hair.

Cary recognized the expression in Amelia's eyes and the heated quality of her voice. "I'll give you a nickel if you yank off this towel," he murmured intimately. "And two bits if you follow through."

Amelia resisted the intoxicating invitation and quelled her pulse-thumping reaction with a laugh. "Make it a dollar and you might have a deal." She moved away from him, carrying the impression of his touch with her. She didn't want him to see how much his overtures pleased her, how hungry she was for him. "But first I'll have my shower, and it's going to take me time to redo my makeup...." She paused thoughtfully. "On second thought, make that ten bucks."

"Sweetheart, you could appear at this shindig wearing a J.C. Penney towel, and you'd still be the best-looking broad here."

"No, thank you, I'd rather wear the dress I brought especially for this occasion." She stepped over to him and presented her back for him to undo her zipper. "Cary darling, what did you think of the clan?" His answer was important to her and Cary knew it, too, so he chose his words carefully.

"It's a family I'd like to belong to."

"You do. You married me."

"I mean, I'd like to have been born into it."

"No, you wouldn't. Trust me. You think we were always like we are now. Well, you're wrong." Her tone lowered, old regrets coloring her voice. "Cary, people did awful things to one another in this house." Then, wanting to be on firmer ground, she asked, "What did you think of Billie?"

"She's terrific. Her admiral is an okay guy, too."

Cary's streetwise vernacular never bothered Amelia. In fact, she enjoyed being called a "good-looking broad." She'd known others with more refined speech and manners who hadn't half the honesty and character of Cary. She sucked in her breath when he dropped the skimpy towel around his middle and stepped into silky bikini briefs. She blinked and looked at her watch meaningfully.

Cary grinned. "You had your chance."

Amelia escaped temptation by flying into the bathroom. Chances. Maybe that's what her life really was, just one chance after another. Susan's announcement had come as a shock. Cary was only a few years older than Susan. Did he compare ages? If it hadn't occurred to him already, it soon would that she, Amelia, was almost like a grandmother to Susan's baby. Grandmothers, those little shrunken women with rosy cheeks and sparkling white aprons to match their hair. She didn't fill the bill and neither did Billie. But there was a new breed of grandmother these days: taller, slimmer women who hid their age with the help of Clairol, belly suctions, and face lifts.

Stepping up to the bathroom mirror, Amelia studied herself. She was a network of fine scar lines almost invisible to the naked eye. But she knew where each and every line was. Time and gravity, those two ancient enemies to be warded off at all cost. Especially now, especially since Cary.

A rigid regimen of diet and exercise, torment and torture, was worth every deprivation, every sore muscle, if it meant having Cary. She lifted her arm and looked into the mirror over her shoulder. No trace of a wrinkle or loose, crinkly skin. She could wear a sleeveless dress without a worry. For the time being, at least. Sooner or later it was going to catch up with her, and then what? Cary wouldn't want her then. Amelia peered closer into the glass. Behind the visage of a smooth-skinned, wide-eyed, almost beautiful woman, she saw a Disney version of an old hag crooning in a cracked and wicked voice, "Mirror, mirror on the wall..."

Upon reentering the bedroom after her shower, Amelia found Cary struggling with the string tie he was attempting to thread through a silver clasp. "Damn it, I'm going to look as stupid in this getup as that kid did this afternoon. What's his name, Cole?"

After Amelia came to his rescue and fastened the tie, he stepped back and struck a pose by shoving his thumbs into his belt. "What d'you think? Will I pass muster?" His Western-cut pants fit him like a glove, hugging his thighs and falling to exactly the correct spot over his boots.

Amelia pretended to ponder. Would he pass muster! Every female with a hormone left in her body would be after him tonight, and some of these Texan ladies were like barracuda in open water. "You'll do," she said offhandedly. "I only hope I won't have to defend your honor later on tonight."

Cary's brows rose slightly. There was an angry, feral glitter in his dark eyes. "What's that supposed to mean?

You make me sound like a fox in a chicken coop!" It annoyed him when Amelia said things like this. Christ, didn't she know he loved her? She was everything he wanted in a woman: smart, classy, affectionate, and open-hearted. Women were strange. Why couldn't they just accept things, accept the truth and go on from there? Why did they always have to look for problems? He knew exactly what he wanted and that's why he'd married her.

It hadn't been easy kicking and clawing his way to where he was now. Growing up in an orphanage, barely making it through high school and having no way of going on to college. He'd been street-bred and street-raised. Life had been tough, but he'd never forgotten his debts. He'd started out driving rich people's cars cross-country, making contacts and eventually going into the limousine and rental car business. By the age of twenty-nine he'd made his first million in real estate, but long before that he'd been sending monthly checks to St. Anthony's Orphanage in downtown Chicago. He was a hustler and didn't have a lot of class or polish like these Colemans, but he could hold his head up. Self-made. From what Amelia had told him, her old man had been self-made. That said a lot for a man and his character. Class could be bought and the polish would come later.

Having a seven-figure bank balance and another ten million on paper didn't make Cary feel rich, compared to these Colemans. He couldn't imagine, considering his humble beginnings, what it would be like to live like this, to be so damned important that a governor would drop everything to attend a Fourth of July picnic. Strange, this life of the Texas rich—but something he could take to like a duck to water. Cary's financial success had come from making the right deals, being in the right place at the right time. Luck. Relationships and friendships had never entered into it. Cold, impersonal phone calls, listening to the advice of brokers, and having a nose for money had been the extent of his involvement. Now Cary found himself wanting to belong in Texas, and that feeling was strong. Amelia could guide him, introduce him, set him on the right course. He'd mingle with people who weren't overwhelmed by his wealth, play a friendly game of golf, and be welcomed for himself, not just because someone wanted to talk a deal.

"You're deep in thought." Amelia glanced at her husband's reflection in the vanity mirror. "I didn't mean to offend you, really I didn't. You're a city boy; you've no idea how little chance a fox actually has if there are enough chickens in the coop. And there'll be enough chickens here tonight. I can't blame you because you're so damned attractive, so don't blame me if I'm a little jealous and insecure. I worry that you might regret marrying me. But if I were ten years younger, darling, the shoe would be on the other foot." She meant to convey teasing humor; instead her tone came across as bitter.

"If I ever regret marrying you, you'll be the first to know. I don't like it when you talk like this. I thought we agreed you weren't going to keep harping on this damned age business."

Amelia blew him a kiss and returned to her mascara.

"And there's something I don't understand. How come men wear plaid shirts and sport coats and the women wear gowns and jewels?"

"Because you're in Texas; that's the way we do things. The way the women dress is how the men are measured. Get it?"

Cary digested the information and nodded. "Makes sense, if you're a Texan. How much did that gown you're wearing cost?"

"You don't want to know. Besides, it was before I married you."

"I'm serious, Amelia. How much?"

"You are serious, aren't you?... Four thousand."

"For one dress!"

"For one itty-bitty dress," Amelia drawled. "You don't want me looking tacky, do you?"

"God forbid!"

"I know how you can spend your evening. Get together with Rand. He has quite an eye for jewelry. Between the two of you, you can calculate the cost of what the women are wearing. It'll blow your mind."

"You have five minutes, Amelia," he told her, looking at his watch.

"God! I'll never be ready in time! Hurry—help me with these snaps and hooks." When he'd finished his struggle with the tiny hooks and even tinier eyes, she turned to face him. "Well, what do you think?"

"I think you're going to outshine everyone else," he said, approval lighting his eyes. Her cocktail-length dress was made of some silky sapphire-blue material that rustled softly and shone like satin. Cut high in the front with bell-shaped sleeves, it was nearly backless, revealing the graceful sweep of her back and flawless light olive skin. Cary realized it was the cut and fabric, rather than any ornamentation, that lent the dress its elegance. He especially approved of the way it revealed Amelia's shapely legs and trim ankles, showcasing her sexy high-heeled sandals. "Honey, you're a knockout." He whistled. "Wear that perfume that drives me nuts."

Amelia promptly spritzed herself with Van Cleef & Arpels' "First." Sapphire and diamond earrings and a simple matching brooch worn high on the left shoulder was all the jewelry this dress demanded. Cary sniffed with delight and put his arms around her from behind. She loved it when he groaned with pleasure and nibbled behind her ear. It was a good thing he didn't ask how much the perfume cost.

{{{{{{{{ CHAPTER FIVE }}}}}}}}

Austin society arrived in Mercedes-Benzes, Rolls Royces, stretch limos, Ford Rangers, and pickup trucks. They came to see the Coleman women and weren't disappointed. An hour into the party and Maggie's eyes were sparkling.

She'd been accepted. Oh, she'd seen the little huddles, could imagine what all the whispering was about, but she didn't care. She'd pulled it off—with the help of her family. On her own it would have taken years. But with this one magnificent master stroke, Austin was hers. You didn't offend a Coleman.

Maggie beamed and bustled about. In December when the society reporters rehashed the year's social events, Maggie knew this affair would be number one on the list. She felt wonderful—until she saw Cole draped over a chair on the back patio. He'd been drinking. God, if he threw up, it could ruin everything. For a moment she panicked; then she saw Rand walking toward her. If she could get his assistance, she just might be able to avoid a scene. But before she could wind her way through the knots of people, Rand was out of sight. As she neared Cole she saw that Riley was already there. His left arm was braced against the stone wall while his right arm held her son up. He was laughing and Cole was snarling.

"Darlings," Maggie cooed, coming up quickly behind Riley, "I think both of you should go indoors and get something to eat or some coffee."

58

"I'll second that," Rand said firmly. Maggie whirled, relief shining from her eyes. "If you can do some fancy footwork and a little chitchat, I think I can get Cole into the house without too much of a stir. Riley will help me."

"I don't need any help from you or any slant-eyed Jap," said Cole.

"If there's one thing I can't stand, it's a drunk. A nasty drunk is worse," Maggie said coldly. "This is unforgivable, Coleman." To Riley she added, "He didn't mean what he said. You can see he's not himself."

"It's all right, Aunt Maggie. I think I got to him before anyone saw what was happening."

Maggie was rainbow bright as she danced her way around the clusters of guests, stopping to chat first with one group, then another. Out of the corner of her eye she watched Rand's progress. As soon as it was possible, she darted through the wide French doors and headed for the kitchen to join them. She was disgusted and ashamed of her son, doubly ashamed of his cruel remark to Riley.

"Cole's a bit young to be hitting the sauce," Rand said coolly.

"It's my fault. I should have kept an eye on him. He was angry... is angry with me.... I was so busy...."

"Don't defend him, Maggie. He's old enough to know better. There's nothing worse than a mean drunk. A mean sixteen-year-old drunk is something I don't even want to discuss. I think it's time to get him into the bathroom. Grab him, Riley."

Maggie watched in dismay as Rand and Riley literally dragged her son into the bathroom. The familiar sounds that filtered through the door made her wince. She'd been on that end more times than she cared to remember.

She paced the kitchen uncertainly, feeling down. Her son needed her, yet she should also be with her guests, circulating. Her hand was on the doorknob when Rand opened it.

"Go back to the party, Maggie. I'll get him to bed. I'll let you know when he's tucked in."

"I should be... How could this... I feel..."

"Guilty? Look, the kid is drunk. He's sick. It's not the end of the world. We'll get him to bed and tomorrow will be soon enough to deal with it. Trust me, Maggie."

"Go ahead, Aunt Maggie. We can handle it," Riley said.

"If you're sure... Thank you, Rand," Maggie said, standing on tiptoe to kiss his cheek. For one startled moment she stared deeply into his eyes. It was Maggie who looked away first.

Forty minutes later, Rand sought her out as she stood in a family group. "We stuck him under the shower and put him to bed; he's sound asleep. He's going to have a big head tomorrow, but he'll survive."

"I'm grateful, Rand. It could have been disastrous. What can I do to thank you?"

Riley didn't flinch when Sawyer's nails bit into his arm. He could feel the trembling in her body. There was something wrong. "Dance with me," he said abruptly.

"Nice try, Riley. I'm not in the mood to dance. What I need is a drink, maybe two or even three."

"Make it one. I've had enough drunks for one night."

"That's what I like, an opinionated male," Sawyer said bitterly as she headed for the bar. Riley came up behind her in time to hear her order a double Scotch straight up. Damn Cole Tanner.

When the last shower of fireworks lit the heavens and the final strain of "Deep in the Heart of Texas" filled the air, Maggie loosed a sigh of relief. It was three-forty-five in the morning, and as far as she could tell, not a single guest had left. This, then, was the closing signal. Unless, of course, she wanted to serve a champagne breakfast at dawn. Tiredly, she toyed with the idea. It would be a massive undertaking.

"Don't even think it," Amelia whispered, coming up behind her. "I've danced my feet off and it's time for bed. Just start saying good night and they'll leave. Pap used to stand up and say, 'That's it folks, party's over!' It was a real smash, Maggie; you did yourself proud."

Maggie turned eagerly to Amelia, warming to her aunt's affection. "I couldn't have done it without all of you. I know that now. Hell, I knew it from the beginning." She smiled wearily. "By the way, that's some guy you got there. I like him, Aunt Amelia."

"So do I, and I thought we were going to dispense with that aunt routine."

"Habit. I'll try and remember. So, how does your husband like all of us?"

"What's not to like? He adores us, all of us. If you want the truth, I think this little shindig blew his socks off. To him a barbecue is hot dogs and hamburgers on a grill in the backyard. Six guests, tops. He'll get used to us Texans. I think he's serious about wanting to buy that property he was talking about. High middle-income housing. Something like that."

"If he is serious and wants to look into it, why don't you both stay on here until he makes up his mind. God knows there's plenty of room. You could see more of the boys, and Cary might be a good influence on them. Think about it. Uh-oh, they're getting ready to leave. Once Orwell Snyder puts on his Stetson, that means he's going home. Come, we have to smile and play the game."

That's exactly what it was—a game. Winners and losers. And tonight, for the first time, Maggie was a winner.

When the massive oak doors closed for the last time, the weary Coleman family followed one another up the long, circular staircase.

"This house needs an elevator," Susan complained. Her husband shot her an angry look and leaped up the steps two at a time. Susan held on to the rail, each step torture for her aching, swollen feet.

Billie, walking behind her, kept silent. She knew Jerome wouldn't appreciate interference from her or anyone else. Then, as she waited for Thad to open the bedroom door, she pretended not to see the hunger in Sawyer's eyes as Rand said good night and left her standing outside his bedroom door.

Come home to Sunbridge and all its problems, Billie thought wearily. Welcome home.

Maggie stopped to chat a moment with Sawyer, then looked in on Riley. She let the boy hug her and kiss her soundly on the cheek. "It was a great party, Aunt Maggie. I'm glad I was here to help celebrate."

"This is your home, Riley, for as long as you want. Remember that."

"Thank you, Aunt Maggie. Get some rest; you look tired."

"I am, but I don't think I'll be able to sleep. I think I'll have a cup of tea and maybe unwind all by myself. Sleep well."

Maggie had had no intention of having a cup of tea, but once she mentioned it, the idea sounded good. She fussed with the kettle and found the tea bags in the canister on the kitchen counter.

She carried her cup outside to the front lawn, glad of the cool, early-morning air and the silence. Carefully she picked her way through the party debris. Tomorrow the caterers would clean up, but now there was just quiet and solitude. She was sitting with her feet propped, heels kicked off, when she realized she wasn't alone.

"Too much party?"

"Rand! I thought you'd be sound asleep by now."

"I never sleep when I have things on my mind."

"I'm like that, too. This party was so important to me, and now that it's over I have to unwind. I thought tea would help. I don't drink anymore."

"I noticed. Maybe one of these days I'll go on the wagon myself."

"How long are you staying?" Maggie asked quickly. She had no desire to discuss her abstinence from alcohol; it was a private thing.

Rand shrugged. Maggie shrugged back. Colemans didn't limit their invitations; he knew he could stay a month and be welcome. She settled back in her chair.

"I don't know which I like best, the sound of the crickets at night or the early-morning chirping of the birds," she said, sipping her tea. "The birds, I suppose, because their chirping means the beginning of a new day. I'm into new beginnings."

Maggie's words startled Rand. This soft-spoken, almost humble person wasn't the Maggie he had avoided in the past. "I can understand that," he replied, so softly Maggie had to strain to hear him. "I'm more or less in a winding-down process myself. So, I suppose that's a new beginning of sorts. I'll have to adjust my life and go on from there."

"Sort of getting your house in order, that kind of thing?"

Rand laughed. "I guess you could say that. Tonight convinced me that I want to sit back now and enjoy my life. I'm not getting any younger—that's for certain."

"None of us are. It's amazing where life has taken us. Good things, bad things, things that are so meaningless in the end and yet so crucial at the time. Do you suppose this is a time to mend fences, to ride into the future without regard for the past?"

"For some of us. But there are always fences that are impossible to mend, words said that can't be taken back, only be forgiven." Guiltily he thought of Sawyer. He should be upstairs right now, this minute, making love to her. She had expected it—he read it in her eyes. "That's what hurts, that's when you have to be strong—do what must be done, say what must be said, and suffer the consequences...." Rand smiled. "Early-morning philosophies always sound so profound," he mused. "I wonder why. Perhaps because the early hour simply lends an air of profoundness to very ordinary observations."

Maggie leaned her head back, eyes closed, thinking about what he'd said.

"You should go to bed, Maggie. In an hour or so the sun will be completely up."

"That's okay by me. The dark and I don't get along. I sleep with a night-light, and if you ever tell anyone, I'll deny it."

Rand laughed, a genuine sound of amusement; it made him realize that he hadn't laughed in some time. "I can top that. I have this raggedy old cat that goes everywhere with me. It has a permanent niche in my suitcase, and I can tell you I've gotten some pretty curious looks when I go through customs. Still, where I go, she goes."

"Sally Dearest?" Maggie asked in amazement.

"You remembered?"

"Remember? When we were little I would have killed to get that cat away from you. It was so broken in, so ugly, so incredibly..."

"Dirty and mended. It was my security blanket. I guess in some ways we never give those things up; we only trade them in for other things. Still, old Sally Dearest was a comfort."

"I wouldn't know about comfort. I was never permitted to take anything to bed with me. I wasn't allowed to suck my thumb or anything children do to settle themselves down. We went to bed cold turkey, and we slept or we didn't, but we went to bed. Nurse was a bitch."

'You survived," Rand said softly. He lifted his glass to get the last ice cube and started crunching on it. Maggie liked the sound.

"If you want to call it surviving," she said. "God! I'd never want to go through that again. Youth isn't all it's cracked up to be."

"It's good you understand that, Maggie. I think you're due for a round of battles. Cole is a very unhappy young man."

"I know. What I don't know is how much of his unhappiness is my responsibility, or what I can do about it. We'll work it out," Maggie said confidently. "We have to."

"I hope so."

"You're doubtful?"

"I am. Perhaps Riley being here isn't such a good idea. Cole already resents him. Riley will do his part; family and friendships are important to him. But Cole feels intruded upon; that's evident. That kind of bitterness is personal, Maggie, and has nothing to do with prejudice. I have the feeling your guts are going to be churning from time to time. But if you listen to your heart, if you're fair with both boys, I think you'll be able to handle it. That's the key word, Maggie. Fair."

"You're probably right, Rand," Maggie said quietly. Already, she knew she preferred Riley, although she loved Coleman because he was her child. A finger of guilt touched her. No, she thought, shaking her head, that was just being honest. Who wouldn't prefer the open genuineness and affection of Riley to the darker, troubled, guarded Cole?

Rand turned to look over his shoulder toward the east. "It's been a long time since I've seen the sun come up," he said softly.

"Well, you're in the right place. There's nothing to compare to sunrise in Texas, unless, of course, it's the sunset."

Rand laughed again, turning to Maggie, finding the reflection of his own amusement in her eyes. "Spoken like a true Texan," he said. "Let's enjoy the peace and quiet, Maggie. It won't be long before everyone is up and about and the circus begins again."

While Rand slid down in the chair to rest his head against its back, Maggie craned her neck in the direction of the house. Her eyes widened when she scanned the upper windows. Most glowed with light. Sawyer was outlined against the sheer curtains. Maggie's heart thumped in her chest at the realization of having been observed without her knowing. A shadow passed before Riley's window. He, too, was awake.

Rand, questioning Maggie's silence, opened his eyes and followed her gaze. He recognized Sawyer's slim form at the window. He could feel her staring at him, could feel her confusion and her silent accusation. It was his fault she was up there alone. They hadn't seen each other in over two months—he should be there with her, not out here sharing this sunrise with her mother.

Billie lay restlessly beside Thad in the big, oversize bed. Overtired, she told herself. But she knew it was this house, Sunbridge, that was making her restless. She wished now Maggie had put Thad and her in the studio behind the house. Even with the dust and the mildew, the studio would have been preferable to sleeping here. She'd spent more than half her life beneath this roof, had known her greatest happinesses and greatest sorrows here. But she'd never belonged here.

Her hand reached out to smooth the flatness of Thad's belly. Softly curling hairs grazed her palm and she felt him move beside her. He wasn't sleeping, either. He'd seen how nervous she'd been when they were getting ready for bed and had sensitively known that she feared he would want to make love to her, here, in this house, where she'd spent so many years with Moss.

"We're both tired, darling," he'd murmured as she'd nestled her head onto his shoulder. "Let me hold you until you fall asleep." His lips had brushed her temple as he'd taken her into his arms.

Until that moment she hadn't known how anxious she'd been about sharing a bed with Thad in this house. Thad was too special, their love too cherished, to taint with memories of Sunbridge.

Billie snuggled down further, wrapping her arm around him. If she just lay here, quietly, and tried to relax, surely sleep would come.

The voice was intimate and cunning when she heard it whispering in her ear. "You fell asleep first," Amelia replied playfully.

"But I'm not sleeping now," Cary said, sliding closer to her, his warm, knowing hands gliding the length of her body.

Amelia wrapped her arms around his neck, pulling him down to her to find the warmth of his mouth. "I love making love at dawn," she murmured, her voice languid with desire.

"I love it any time of the day or night." Cary nibbled her lower lip, teasing the tip of his tongue along the sensitive inner flesh.

"Don't talk about it; do it!" Amelia slid her hands over

the muscular smoothness of his back, squeezing her fingers between their bodies, searching for him, knowing that his arousal would come hard and swift from the pressure that was already throbbing against her thigh.

He felt her touch and she was satisfied by the sound of his indrawn breath. His kisses grew heated; his hands searched the hollows of her offered body.

"How much time do we have before this house starts jumping?" he asked, smiling at the familiar response of her arching back as his fingers slipped softly between her legs.

"Never enough," came her breathless answer as she surrendered to the sweet abandon to which only Cary could bring her.

Billie snapped the latch of her Gucci carry-on bag and tried not to listen to Susan and Jerome squabbling in the room across the hall—the room she had shared with Moss. It had heard many such arguments and seen much unhappiness.

Thad was stuffing his shaving gear into his bag as quickly as he could so he and Billie could escape this place. No way were they going to stay for four days! One night and he'd had enough of Sunbridge for a year. Anxiously he watched Billie out of the corner of his eye, knowing she couldn't help but hear Susan and Jerome.

Billie saw Thad watching her, and their eyes met. "Perhaps if I knock on the door and tell them we're leaving, they'll stop." Suddenly, she dropped onto the bed, her head lowered, hands over her ears. "Oh, Thad, I thought I'd never have to hear the word abortion in connection with one of my children again. I only hope no one else can hear them."

"If you knock on the door, they'll stop—but only pick up where they left off once we're gone. You know, Billie, I never really had an opinion about Jerome until yesterday. The guy's an out-and-out bastard."

Billie shook her head. "I didn't know. All this time I thought Susan and Jerome were so well suited for each other. They seemed to share so much. But if they can't agree on becoming parents...there must be chasms of differences between them. Now I know why Susan blurted out the news of her pregnancy yesterday. She thought once it was out in the open, Jerome would never dare push the issue. But it seems he has it all figured out. Thad, I have to talk to her."

"Darling, play it by ear. If we miss this plane, we'll catch another. Don't worry about time schedules; you and Susan are more important."

Billie flashed him a smile of gratitude. There were times she thought it would be enough just to have Thad love her; his understanding her was a bonus not many women enjoyed.

The sounds of the argument continued, and as Thad and Billie finished their packing, they couldn't help but listen.

"Damn you, Susan, you agreed you wouldn't tell anyone! You said you'd think about an abortion. We can't have a baby ruin our lives. Why weren't you more careful? I can't forgive you for this."

"Then don't. I never agreed to an abortion. You did all the talking, Jerome. You made all the decisions. This is my life, my body, my child."

"It's my child, too, and I don't want it. What about the tour? Do you just expect me to cancel because you're pregnant and aren't supposed to fly so often? It isn't done that way and you know it. Copenhagen is very important to me. I wouldn't put it past you to have done this deliberately."

"Copenhagen is important to *you*, not me! What's important to me is this baby. But I'll compromise. I'll tour for another three months; I'll be in my fifth month then. Take it or leave it."

"Three months doesn't cover Copenhagen," Jerome said angrily. "If you're going to do it, do all of it or nothing."

"If that's the way you feel, then it's nothing. You can leave today if you want. I can stay here with Maggie, I'm sure."

"We don't need a baby; we don't want one. What's going to happen when it arrives? Are you planning to retire? What about me?"

"You always want to know how something affects you. What about *me*? You may not want this baby, but I do. I'm getting older. I never thought I'd become pregnant. I didn't plan this; it just happened—and I'm *glad* it happened! It's not the end of the world."

"I've heard enough, Thad," Billie said. "It's time to leave."

"Are you certain?"

"Certain." She smiled weakly. "From what I've heard, Susan is handling herself admirably. She knows what she wants and she'll fight for it. I'm proud of her."

Thad was relieved. "Okay. Just give me a chance to get these bags downstairs and then say good-bye to Susan. We can work on the hugs and kisses with the others downstairs."

Billie walked across the hall and knocked softly on the door, calling her daughter's name. Susan swung the door open, her eyes filled with tears, and fell into her mother's arms sobbing. Billie cradled the blond head to her breast. "Do what's best for yourself, Susan. Make your decision and stick with it. I gave you our itinerary for the next month; after that, you can get in touch with me in Vermont. Our home is yours if you ever need it."

"Mam..." Susan gulped. "I never meant for you to know. I didn't want anyone to know. I never thought Jerome could be so selfish...so cruel."

"Darling, all our idols topple from time to time. We just learn to live with it and to forgive them. Now, dry your eyes. Thad and I are ready to leave."

Maggie stood on the front portico, a lump in her throat. It was hard to have her mother leave her. Always before, she had done the leaving...or the running away. She felt a stab of regret for all that had been forever lost—until Billie stopped in midstride and ran back to her, throwing her arms around her daughter.

"This is what you've always wanted, Maggie; now work to keep it. I know it's going to be all right; if I wasn't certain, I wouldn't leave." It was a lie, but a small one. If Maggie could take comfort from it, she could be forgiven. "Seth used to say this is the time to fish or cut bait. Last night was a magnificent beginning for you. Use it."

"I'll make it, Mam," Maggie whispered fiercely.

"I know you will. Take care of yourself and the boys."

"Tell the Hasegawas I'll take care of Riley, not to worry. And Mam. Tell them thank you, for me."

Maggie's eyes lingered on the winding driveway long after the car had disappeared.

"I never did care for good-byes myself." Rand's voice was loud in the quiet morning.

Maggie whirled around, annoyed that someone had seen her at such a private moment. "Haven't you been to bed yet?"

"No, and from the looks of you, I don't think you have, either."

"Since I'm still wearing my dress from last night, I wouldn't exactly call your observation astute. I'm going up now to shower and change. Do you think you're up to riding with the boys? I heard you make plans yesterday afternoon."

"Yes. But I don't know if Cole will remember. By the way, I looked in on him and he's still sleeping."

Maggie winced. "Don't wait for him, Rand. Go with Riley. Cole will be a wet hornet when he does haul himself out of his bed. Did you have anything to eat?"

"No, not yet. I noticed the buffet in the dining room. Very English." He smiled in approval. "All that's missing is the kippers and kidney pie. I'll shower first and then get something. Maybe by that time Riley will be down."

"He's already in the barn. He said his good-byes to Mam and Thad and ran off. I think he was afraid he'd cry if he stayed to watch them leave."

Rand climbed the stairs to his room. He knew Sawyer was up. She'd never have missed kissing her grandmother good-bye. He found himself lightening his step as he passed her room and then hating himself for it. Damn it, what kind of coward was he?

Once in his own room, he stripped and turned on the shower full blast. The steam rose and misted invitingly. He was already behind the frosted glass shower door when Sawyer opened his bedroom door and closed it softly behind her.

She waited a moment, feeling the strength seep slowly out of her. Nervously she touched the door latch, about to step back into the hall. Then, before she could change her mind, she pressed it, locking the door securely.

Whatever was wrong with Rand was going to be settled now. She'd waited long enough. It was difficult to ignore what she was thinking, what Rand was making her think by avoiding her, by his indifference. It would be so easy just to step beneath the needle-sharp spray and press herself into his arms. She loved the feel of his body against hers, loved it when they showered together, wet and slick with water and soap, touching, kissing, yielding. It had been so long, too long, and she *needed* him. Last night he'd begged off, saying he was tired. But he hadn't been too tired to stay with Maggie, and he'd still been with her when Grand and Thad had pulled out of the drive.

Sawyer didn't like what she was thinking. And she feared what she was feeling. Don't think, she told herself. Act!

Trembling fingers fumbled with the belt of her terry robe. Prickles rose on her skin in the warm room when her nightie dropped to the floor. If he just holds me, it'll be all right, she thought nervously. Rand will make it right. Over and over she whispered the words to herself, working up the confidence to open the bathroom door and step into the clouds of steam.

She could just make out his form behind the clouded glass. The sound of rushing water filled her ears, echoing the desperate rush of her need for him.

Rand stood beneath the invigorating spray, trying to purge the effects of a night without sleep and the haunting image of Sawyer's face. The water was hot, almost too hot; he could feel the slope of his shoulders and his buttocks reddening from the heat. Punishing, but good; one kind of pain to mask another.

Silently, the shower door opened, and he felt her before he saw her. She stood almost as tall as he did, long-legged, slim, water beading on her shoulders and the fullness of her breasts. Venus dawning from the sea. It was the expression on her face, her hopeful smile, the deep yearning in her eyes, that paralyzed him.

Her movements were slow and fluid when she reached for him, pressing herself against him, drawing him into her embrace and searching for his kiss. Her body was impatient in its demands; her pelvis danced a sensuous rhythm; her thighs clung to his. His skin was clean, fresh; rivulets of water entered her mouth as her tongue licked near the base of his throat. She enticed him closer with the firm press of her fingers on his haunches, pulling him closer, inviting him with almost imperceptible gyrations of her hips. If she was aware that his arms did not hold her, that his lips did not return her kiss, she did not show it.

Sawyer felt the panic swell in her throat. There was an emptiness within her that only he could fill; yet his arms hung limply at his sides, his mouth did not respond to pressure. Boldly, she clutched at him, demanding he answer her caresses, appealing to his senses, refusing to accept his denial. She found herself falling to her knees, wrapping her arms around his legs, finding him with her mouth, almost crying with frustration when she realized that her urgings were futile. He was hardly aroused; he did not want her; she could not make him want her.

Rand's hands were clutched at his side. He wanted so much to reach for her, to soothe her, to explain; but how could he without encouraging her? If he released his rigid control for even one instant, he would lose his resolve. To use her, to make love to her when he did not love her, would be more unkind.

A low groan of misery escaped him. He raised his head,

unable to look down into her face. Even squeezing his eyes shut could not prevent the tears that ran down his cheeks to mingle with the shower spray.

Blindly Sawyer struggled with the shower door, throwing her weight against it, forcing it open. With an almost frenzied desperation she fought against the scream that was building in her as she skidded across the slick bathroom tiles. She needed to get away from him, to hide, to find oblivion.

Stumbling, stopping only long enough to jam her arms into her robe and wrap the thick terry cloth tightly around her body, she flew back to the privacy of her room.

Water that hadn't been absorbed by her robe ran in rivulets down her legs and puddled at her feet. Her hair was wet, dripping onto her shoulders and face, but she was oblivious to it all.

Rand, Rand! she cried to herself. Why? What has changed? What changed you? It can't be over between us. I won't let it be over.

Sawyer sank onto the bench in front of the old-fashioned dressing table, unable to meet her eyes in the mirror, afraid of what she would see. She'd sensed this change in Rand, had refused to admit it. She'd closed her eyes to his indifference, shut her ears to his excuses. But no longer.

Premonitions. Dread. Fear of losing someone you love, someone you want to love you. It was a familiar story to Sawyer. It was being a child again, writing letters to Maggie and waiting days by the mailbox for answers that never arrived. It was always feeling sore and bruised and heartsick.

She looked up, and a bitter smile met her reflection in the mirror. Well, she'd been forced to accept the situation as a child, but she wasn't a child anymore. This was one situation she refused to accept! If nothing else, she would find out why Rand had changed.

Sawyer glanced around the room. This wasn't hers; she'd grown up in the studio out behind the house. There she'd had a room that was her own. All her things were

there, her childhood things. That was where she wanted
to be. This impersonal room Maggie had assigned her
made her feel like a guest, as though Sunbridge hadn't
been her home, her past, almost her entire life.

She made up her mind in an instant, shedding her damp
robe to change into a worn pair of jeans and a blue denim
shirt. In scuffed riding boots, comfortable as a pair of old
slippers, and with her hair pulled back into a ponytail,
she felt more like her old self, the self that hadn't been
humiliated in a shower with Rand. The self that still
believed Rand loved her.

{{{{{{{{ CHAPTER SIX }}}}}}}}

Amelia tripped into the dining room, Cary behind her.
Her eyes sparkled and her cheeks were rosy. It was obvious
to everyone that she had just made love, very satisfactory
love. She smiled warmly at Susan and Jerome. Riley was
already seated at the table, digging into a plate of ham
and eggs and sipping from a monstrous glass of orange
juice. Cole was nowhere in sight.

"Good morning, everyone," Cary said genially as he
filled his plate. "Are Texas mornings always this beautiful?"

Susan shrugged. Jerome merely burrowed deeper into
himself. "I think so," Riley responded shyly. "When I was
here before, it was springtime, but it was gorgeous."

"You could have asked me, Cary," Amelia said with a
pout.

"And listen to a dissertation on Texas weather? Don't

forget we have things to do this morning."

Susan's head shot up. "Are you going out, Aunt Amelia?" she asked anxiously.

"As a matter of fact, I am. I think we'll be gone till later in the day."

"Could we talk after you get back?"

Amelia hesitated. She was not in the mood to be a mother hen to Susan today; she wanted to concentrate on Cary. "I'll see, sweetie. Perhaps before dinner, okay?"

"Sure...."

As Susan went back to toying listlessly with the scrambled eggs on her plate, Cary stared at her sympathetically. She looked awful—tired, bloated, and unhappy. Apparently, pregnancy did not agree with her.

Jerome got up from the table, his plate empty, and finished off the last of his coffee. "Ready, Susan?" he asked.

"No, I'm not. I think I'll have another cup of coffee."

"No, you won't. Caffeine makes you nervous and you won't be able to practice later."

"I wasn't going to practice later. I'm on vacation—or did you forget? Besides, I don't feel well."

"You'll feel better if you practice," Jerome said.

Cary stopped with his fork halfway to his mouth. He didn't like Jerome, he decided. The man was a bully, he'd always hated bullies. If he didn't watch it, Jerome could ruin his entire day. Then, out of the corner of his eye, he could see Amelia warning him to stay out of their argument.

Jerome saw the silent exchange between Amelia and Cary, and sensed his argument with Susan could result in a family confrontation. Without another word, he turned on his heel and stomped from the room.

"Susan," Amelia chuckled, "you never told me Jerome was so testy in the mornings."

Susan's eyes brimmed. "Aunt Amelia, there are a lot of things I haven't told you about Jerome. I do need to talk to you."

"Yes, yes, of course you do. I promise we'll be back

before dinner." With a bright smile, Amelia patted Cary's hand and stood up. "No time for another cup, darling. We're late as it is."

Hurriedly she bent down and kissed Susan's cheek. "Cheer up, darling. All men are bears when they wake up in the morning. This, too, shall pass," she said lightly, and left the room clinging happily to her husband's arm.

A wayward tear splashed into Susan's coffee cup and she rose in disgust. Mam was gone, Amelia was off with her new husband, and she was alone. She supposed she could talk to Maggie or Sawyer...or she could try to solve her problems herself. Sighing, she stood up and headed back to her room. Whoever would have thought having a baby could destroy a marriage and a career?

How forceful could she be? she wondered. She'd never really been tested. As long as she'd done what Jerome wanted, things had gone smoothly. But for the first time in her life, she was tired of doing what Jerome wanted. Tired of traveling, tired of playing the same music over and over, tired of doing laundry in hotel rooms. She wanted a home. And a child. What was wrong with wanting to take a year or so off to have a baby? It was time to feel life, to nurture it, to have someone to love and love her unconditionally.

Susan entered their bedroom and slammed the door behind her, looking at her husband in surprise. "What are you doing, Jerome?"

"What you should be doing. We're leaving. We have commitments, and I won't allow you to cancel them on a whim."

"A baby isn't a whim, Jerome. We have a week. You promised. I need this week. Why are you being so awful about this? I don't like it!"

"You know I never liked this place. You told me you didn't like it, either. I don't understand why all of a sudden you want to stay here. Music and I, we're your life. Aren't we?"

Susan stared at her husband until he looked away. "It's

the only home there is, for now. I can rest here. I'm very run-down."

"It's not my fault you don't take your vitamins," Jerome snapped.

"It's not just a question of vitamins. We're always eating on the run; the food is either overcooked or underdone. And I don't get enough sleep. All we do is travel and work. I can't keep it up. You have to understand."

"What I understand is you should have gone for an abortion the first thing. That's what I wanted. That's what's *best for us*."

"For you, maybe, but not for me! I told you I don't want any part of an abortion. I couldn't live with myself. Listen to me, Jerome—I will never, ever get an abortion!"

Jerome's stomach tightened into a knot. He was so angry he could barely force out the words. "You're ruining me! Deliberately! You're putting an unborn baby before me. You don't love me. You never loved me!"

Susan sank onto the edge of the bed. Maybe he was right. Maybe she never really loved him. She felt confused. Then suddenly she realized Jerome always did this to her—made her feel guilty just to get his way. Well, not this time. She was a Coleman, by God, and all the Colemans had grit! "Exactly what is it you want from me, Jerome?" she asked, an edge of steel in her voice.

"Get an abortion. We'll finish the tour. We'll take it easy next year. I promise you we'll take that trip to the Greek islands you've always wanted. I don't think that's too much to ask."

"Are you interested in hearing what I want? Or what I feel is good for me and our baby? Let me tell you. I'll finish off the tour, and if Maggie will have me, I'm coming back to Sunbridge to have our baby. I'm going to take two years off. You can continue on your own. You can go back to England or you can come home here to Sunbridge. That, Jerome, is my one and only offer. And whether we leave today or at the end of the week is not going to change my mind. Either you take it or you leave it."

Jerome's brain was clicking away like an overworked computer. Once he had Susan away from here, he was sure he could get her to do whatever he wanted. And he wanted Copenhagen. "It's a deal. But I want to leave today. This evening. We can take the Concorde back. What do you say?"

What difference did it make, really? Susan thought tiredly. She'd be back in three months anyway. Pray God, Maggie would agree.

Cole swung his legs over the side of the bed and immediately fell backward. His head throbbed, his heart pounded, and bile rose in his throat. He knew he had to make it to the bathroom but couldn't move. He rolled over and retched on the dark brown carpet. He groaned. Why in the hell had he messed with beer? He could have gotten high on a joint without a hangover. One thing he knew, he'd never make a drunk.

Had he made an ass of himself last night? Evidently, or he wouldn't be feeling this way now. Memories of Rand and Riley floated around his buzzing head. He remembered Rand sticking him in the shower after he'd puked his guts up, while Riley had looked on. Goody-two-shoes Riley. Already he hated the little Jap and he'd only been here a day.

Cole's head continued to throb. There was something he'd planned on doing this morning. If only he could think. He wondered why his mother hadn't come in to check on him. She'd probably had a flying fit last night. Maybe she'd peeked in while he was asleep. He didn't really care one way or the other.

A quiet knock sounded on the door. Cole ignored it. The knock sounded a second time. It wasn't his mother; she'd have walked right in. When the knock sounded a third time, Cole rolled over and yelled, "Come in!" wincing at the sound of his own voice.

Riley poked his head in the door. "Are you going riding, Cole?"

"Not today I'm not. And don't count on me for future days. I hate horses.".

Riley blinked. How could a Texan not like to ride? "Can I get you some aspirin or a glass of water?"

"No, thanks. Get out of here. I've got things I have to do today."

"Cole, your mother sent me up here to get you. I wouldn't have bothered you because I—"

"Knew I was drunk last night. Well, this morning I'm sick. I don't care if my mother wants me or not. Tell her I'm still sleeping. That way you can be the conquering hero just like your old man."

Riley bristled. "What's that supposed to mean?"

"It means whatever you want it to mean. Why are you here, anyway? How long are you staying? Who invited you?"

"My grandfather and our grandmother talked it over, and Aunt Maggie sent the official invitation. I'm to stay here as long as I want. This was my father's home, too." He wanted to say more, but decided against it; Cole was sick and angry enough without a fight.

"And I'll just bet you can't wait to get your share, right?"

"My share of what?"

"Don't play dumb, little Jap boy. This place. Sunbridge. Well, the deed is in my mother's name, and when she buys it, I get this place. The first thing I'll do is sell it."

"Cole, I don't need a share of anything. I'm here because I never got a chance to know my father. That's the only reason."

"Sure, sure," Cole muttered as he struggled to his feet. Immediately, he grabbed hold of the bedpost. "I thought I told you to get out of here!"

"I'm going. I hope you feel better later on," Riley said, closing the door behind him.

What was he going to tell Aunt Maggie? Riley asked himself as he walked quietly down the hall. A lie was a lie no matter how you looked at it. Maybe he could stall by going back to his room for a while. He grinned. It would be worth it just to look in the floor-length mirror again. Every stitch of clothing he had on was his father's, right down to the Jockey shorts. Everything had been preserved in plastic bags and cardboard boxes—he'd seen the cartons in his closet, all bearing his grandmother's handwriting—then they'd been taken out, laundered, and placed in sweet-smelling drawers. He'd repacked his own things and piled his suitcases on top of the shelf. From now on he was going to wear only his father's things.

Riley returned to his room and sat down at his father's desk, rubbing his cheek on his shoulder. The checkered shirt gave off an aroma of cleanliness . . . and something. The same scent that lingered on the baseball hat his grandmother had brought to Japan on her first trip.

This room that had belonged to his father was so different from his room back in Tokyo. There the furniture had been Eastern, light and airy. Here the furniture was heavy Western style. He could see traces of the boy in the man's room. The shelves in the closet held treasures he would go through when he felt the time was right. He could envision himself sitting here at the desk, using the same goosenecked lamp, poring over the same books, maybe even using some of his father's pencils; there were enough of them in the drawer.

He wanted to charge outside and explore and investigate. On the long plane trip with Sawyer he'd fantasized about doing all kinds of things with Cole; they'd be friends, inseparable buddies. Sixteen was almost grown-up. There would be girls and they'd date, and then in the confines of their rooms they'd talk about those dates.

It wasn't going to happen. Fantasies? Not really. The reality of his situation had hit him the moment he'd been introduced to Cole. Cole Tanner was his cousin, but he was pure trouble. And right now, trouble was something he didn't want to deal with.

Sighing, Riley stood up and took a last look at himself

in the mirror. He couldn't delay going downstairs any longer. Aunt Maggie had sent him to get Cole, and he'd have to tell her something. He was relieved to see Cole when he rounded the corner of the hallway. He didn't hurry his step and wasn't surprised when his cousin didn't wait for him.

Riley knew his aunt Maggie thought they were together when she appeared at the foot of the stairs and watched them come down. Neither boy did anything to make her think differently.

"There you are. I was beginning to think you were going to sleep all day." She was talking to Cole, but she turned to Riley. "Ken has your horse ready to be saddled. You might as well learn from scratch. Cole will join you soon. I want to have a cup of coffee with him first.

"Feeling a bit under the weather, are we?" Maggie said indulgently after Riley had left.

"Come off it, Mother. I'm suffering from a hangover and we both know it. Cheerfulness isn't going to help my pounding head or my sour stomach. And let's set the record straight right now: I'm not going riding, with or without my cousin. I'd appreciate it if you wouldn't keep shoving him at me."

Maggie took a deep breath. Obviously it was going to be one of those mornings. "Look, Cole, you and I have quite a few things to discuss, and now is as good a time as any. That's an order."

The minute Martha had poured Cole's orange juice and left, Maggie started in. "I'm very disappointed in you, Cole. I expected more from you last night. You knew how important that party was to me. How could you do that? You're only a child!"

"I seem to recall someone saying you'd already had a baby at my age, Mother," Cole drawled insolently.

Maggie flinched but refused to take the bait. "Cole, we have to talk. I don't like what's happening here. I want us to be a family. We have things that need discussing."

"Like the way you said you'd think about allowing me

to make the trip? That was just lip service, wasn't it. You never had any intention of letting me go. Admit it!"

"I admit it," Maggie said through clenched teeth. "I want you here at Sunbridge. You aren't going back to military school, either. In the fall you'll go to school right here. I'm sorry to hit you with all this when you aren't feeling up to par, but it's necessary."

"No it isn't. You like jabbing me and you know it. Why is Riley here? You never did give me a straight answer to that. Don't get any ideas that we're going to be best buddies, because it won't work."

Maggie set her coffee cup precisely in the center of her saucer. "I was hoping it would work. I was hoping you'd try because it's important to me. Are you jealous of Riley, Cole?"

Cole snorted. "Me? Jealous of a Jap? Come on, Mother."

"I can't force you to like him, but I can insist you be civil. And I do insist," she added sharply.

"Or what? You already said I can't go on the trip. You said I'm going to the local schoolhouse, so what's left?"

"Why are you being so difficult? Why can't you meet me halfway? Why do we always end up at each other's throats?"

"Why is it always *my* fault? *You're* the one who seems to have problems with relationships," he snapped.

"I'm getting very tired of you throwing up my past. I'm trying to get along with you. I've made my mistakes and I'm living with them. I don't want the same thing to happen to you."

"The nut doesn't fall far from the tree. Is that what you're saying?"

"No, that's what you're saying. I'm trying to prevent you from making my mistakes, and your attitude isn't helping."

"If you'd leveled with me from the beginning, we wouldn't be having this discussion."

"Would you have listened? Would you?" When Cole shrugged, Maggie continued, "As for Riley, he has as much right to be here as you and I. If his father had lived, *he* would have inherited Sunbridge."

"Second best, eh, Mater?"

"Stop it, Cole! You're not funny. Right now, you could take a few lessons in manners from your cousin."

"I knew that was coming. He's tall and handsome! I'm a head shorter and skinny. He looks good in his father's clothes, and I look like a clown dressed up for Halloween. Well, you can't make me into something I'm not, Mother."

"I'm not trying to make you into anything. I'm trying to give you a decent home so you can put down roots. It's important, Cole. Before, you were at school during the year and a guest in an apartment in New York for holidays. That wasn't home. *This* is home!"

"*Your* home, Mother. It's just a house to me. The apartment was fine. I liked New York."

"Well, I didn't."

"That's the bottom line, isn't it. It's what you want. It's always what you want. You and Dad didn't even tell me you were getting a divorce. I had to hear it from my counselor at school."

"I wanted to tell you. Your father did, too. But your counselor thought it would be best coming from him. And unfortunately, we listened to bad advice. I'm sorry about that, but I can't undo it."

"I called Dad this morning."

"You *what*?"

Cole laughed. "I thought that would get a rise out of you. I called Dad this morning. He'll be here this weekend. He said he was planning on coming next week as a surprise, but he'd move it up to this weekend because he's free." Cole savored the look on his mother's face, for a moment, then moved in for the kill. "He said I could come and live with him in New York if I wanted."

Maggie managed to gather her composure. She reached for her coffee cup with trembling hands, gripping it around the middle, but she didn't drink. "I have sole custody of you, Cole," she said evenly. "You cannot go to New York unless I agree. I do not agree. Do you understand?"

"Dad's a lawyer. He said he'd work it out with you."

"There's nothing to work out. You're staying here."

Cole jumped up from the table. "You can't make me into your brother or your father! That's what you're trying to do. You wanted to see me in a military school so I'd wear a uniform like Grandpap did. You constantly try to find a resemblance to him in me. Now you want me to play cowpoke like your brother. You want to use me to make yourself feel better."

"That's not true!"

"Isn't it? Then why is Riley here? You could have said no when Grand asked you if he could come. You're using him, too."

Maggie brought the coffee cup to her lips. The boy's words bothered her.

"No, Cole, you're wrong."

"No, Mother, I'm right."

"I won't argue the point. Now that you've told me of your father's visit, we'll wait till he gets here to discuss it. Meantime, you will do as I say—when I say it. I know you don't feel up to riding, but they can use some help in the barn; so if I were you," Maggie said, her voice firm but not unkind, "I'd get moving and get your chores done."

Cole stared at her, mouth agape. He was about to protest, then thought better of it. He'd keep a list to present to his father. His father would understand; his father would take care of everything.

When Cole had stomped angrily out of the dining room, Maggie crumpled. Suddenly a firm hand was placed on her shoulder, and she started in surprise. "Rand!"

"I thought you handled all that very well. I'm sorry I eavesdropped, but when I heard the discussion, I didn't want to come in and interrupt."

"That's all right. I guess you can see I have a problem on my hands."

"Yes, you do. Perhaps when the boy's father arrives, you can work something out."

Maggie laughed bitterly. "That's not likely to happen.

Cranston didn't give me an argument over Cole. He simply wanted nothing to do with him. He was happy to give me sole custody of the boy. We're in the middle of divorce proceedings. For Cole to go to him . . . It did upset me."

"He's no different from most kids. He'll play both ends against the middle if he can get away with it."

"I don't understand. I've given him everything. The finest schools, the best clothes, an adequate allowance. Wonderful vacations. What more does he want?"

"That's not exactly the question here. What he did want before—what he needed—was a family, but he was sent off to school. Admit it, Maggie. You weren't the most attentive mother. I'm not trying to be insulting; believe me. Now you suddenly want a family. Cole is confused and he's angry. He sees Riley as an intruder, an interloper. Somehow you're going to have to work it out. Hopefully, Cranston will help. Parents always want what's best for their children."

Maggie let loose another sardonic laugh. "Time was I would have called that a bold-faced lie. I have a lot to learn, Rand. I'm still deep in the woods, but I see a patch of light."

"That patch will get bigger and brighter. Just keep your eyes open."

Maggie laughed. "I always do."

Rand bit into a piece of toast. She was beautiful when she laughed.

Sawyer loved the sweet smell of hay and the pungent odor coming from the barn. Of everything on Sunbridge, this was her favorite spot. It was a large milk-white barn with apple-red trim. From here she could see the studio with its southern exposure and vast skylights. It looked so neat and tidy, so empty, its inhabitants long gone. Even some of the memories were gone. If only time could stand still, just for a little while. Time to capture the memories and make them a part of oneself, so that just by closing one's eyes they could be relived.

Her eyes traveled lovingly to the gentle slope she had rolled down so many times to the house called Sunbridge. It was beautiful in the late-morning sunshine. Prairie pink, with the golden globe casting it in shades of light mauve and dusty rose. The windows winked at her like diamonds. There were secrets behind those panes of glass, secrets both joyful and painful, even shameful. Rand was behind one of those windows. What was he thinking?

She was startled by a noise behind her. "Cole, I didn't know you were here."

"I'm not here because I want to be, that's for sure," he said sourly. "Our mother seems to think I need the discipline of cleaning out this smelly place. Riley is going riding with Rand, if you're looking for him."

Sawyer studied her half brother for a few moments, wondering how much, if anything, they had in common. She hardly knew him, but so far there'd been nothing to indicate he could be even remotely likable. "I used to do exactly what you're doing, almost every day, as a matter of fact." She smiled. "It's necessary for their comfort and health, and in time you get used to it. I love horses."

"I don't. I don't like to ride, and we have stablehands. Mother is just being nasty this morning."

"Oh, why is that?" Sawyer asked nonchalantly; she couldn't help herself.

"I disgraced myself last night. I drank too much beer and it went to my head. Rand and Riley rescued me and Mother observed and is meting out the punishment. She's also more than a little ticked that I called my father in New York."

"Isn't that permitted?" Sawyer asked curiously.

Cole squinted into the bright sunlight. "Under normal conditions she usually doesn't care, but this time I asked him if I could live with him in New York. He's coming here this weekend. Mother was a tad upset," Cole said, smiling viciously.

"I had the feeling you liked it here. I know that we don't know each other very well, but it isn't because I didn't try. I want you to know that."

Cole looked at his sister. He liked her, he decided. He'd always liked her short, on-the-mark letters—and she always sent the keenest presents. "I know," he replied slowly. "I never had the opportunity to either like or dislike this place. This land was taboo when I was growing up. I wanted to come here, but Mother always wanted to go someplace else. You know what I'm talking about."

Sawyer grinned. "Poor little rich boy. The kids used to call us poor little rich girls; Maggie, too. I had my share of cruelty. I was illegitimate. The names used to hurt. . . . I know how you feel, Cole, if that's any help."

Cole didn't answer, but Sawyer decided he wasn't being difficult or remote; it was just that he was a boy, and he was hurting. "Listen, I have some hostility I have to work off," she said. "If you get another pitchfork, I'll help. I was going riding, but I can do that anytime. We can bitch to each other about what a hellish job this is. What d'ya say?"

Cole smiled. "Wait here. I'll get the other fork."

It was Cole's intention to let his sister do the bulk of the work, but when he saw her attack the job as if she meant business, he couldn't do less. They worked, sweating and grunting with exertion, in a companionable silence. When Sawyer declared it was time to take a break, they both fell back into a mound of straw.

"I'm out of shape," Sawyer gasped.

"I'm hung over," Cole grunted.

Sawyer burst out laughing. "I bet that really threw Maggie into a fit."

"It sure did. She's got herself convinced that I'm into drugs, booze, and whatever else is out there. It was the only way I knew to handle that damn party. She wanted to show me off as one of the Colemans. But I'm not really a Coleman; I'm a Tanner. Then Riley showed up," Cole blurted, surprising himself. He rarely confided in anyone like this.

"Ah, that must have been a little hard to take."

Cole leaned on his elbow, a piece of straw stuck between his teeth. "About as hard for me to take as it is for you to see Rand cozying up to my mother."

"Among other things, you're a smart-ass, too," Sawyer said coolly.

"They're having breakfast together this morning."

"Are you deliberately trying to hurt me?" Sawyer asked.

"Probably," Cole replied. "She's your mother, too. Whatever she's done to you, she's doing to me in a different way. Our mother is a bitch."

"And you and I are the good children, and she's out to destroy us. Is that what you're thinking?"

Cole flushed. "I didn't say that. But she falls a little short of being the perfect mother. Surely you noticed."

"I've noticed. I didn't know that it carried over to you, though. I'm sorry about that. You see, I had Grand. You didn't even have that."

Cole jumped up. "Don't feel sorry for me."

Sawyer noticed Cole's white-knuckled grip on the pitchfork. "No way, kid," she said lightly. "You're going to have to grow up the way the rest of us did and make the best of it. Let me give you one little piece of advice, though. Colemans don't snivel, and they don't buckle under. In public, that is. Since you're half Tanner, you're going to have to make your own decisions." Sawyer stood up. "Let's get back to work before I cool down and have to work up another sweat." Sawyer put her arm around her brother and then clapped him on his thin shoulder. Cole responded by leaning into her a little. Sawyer felt pleased.

An hour later Cole leaned on his pitchfork and said, "Hey, I'm sorry about that crack I made about Mother and Rand."

Sawyer turned, but didn't break her rhythm. "Was what you said true?"

"Yeah."

"Then there's no reason to be sorry. I'll handle it."

She would, too, Cole thought. He was sorry now that he'd missed getting to know her all these years. He sensed

that she would work double time at being his sister. But
he also knew she would make him meet her halfway. And
she would be a friend, too. The thought pleased him.

"So tell me, what do you think of Riley?"

Cole shrugged noncommittally.

Sawyer paused in her work. "He's a nice kid, Cole.
You could make all the difference to him on his visit here."

Cole shrugged again.

{{{{{{{{ CHAPTER SEVEN }}}}}}}}

Cary was glad of Amelia's company. He enjoyed doing
things with his wife. She made everything sound interesting and somehow or other managed to find a challenge
in whatever she did. Right now, she was better than any
tour guide, pointing out landmarks and property lines,
quoting the cost of fencing, and estimating the manpower
hours needed to run a ranch, even a small one.

The fields were rolling pastureland. It was a beautiful
Texas day, clear skies with only a cottonball or two dotting
the porcelain blue that matched Amelia's dress. "Have
you ever seen clearer skies or breathed cleaner air?"
Amelia asked, drawing deeply into her lungs.

"I can't say that I have. This is country. I expected to
see more houses. How big would you say this . . . spread
is?"

"This is Santo land on the right. Mr. Santo is a Tex-
Mex who started out when Pap did. I'd say he's got around
seventy thousand acres. One of his sons has a house back

in there. You just can't see it from the road."

"The main house looks big," Cary said, craning his neck.

"Oh, it is. It's a Mexican villa type. All one floor. It's gorgeous."

"As beautiful as Sunbridge?"

"In its own way, yes. The Santos are nice people. I think you'll find most Texans are nice. Shrewd businessmen, though."

"There you go, reading my mind again."

Amelia shrugged. It was true. She always seemed to be able to anticipate his next question, especially if she was really paying attention and it was a one-on-one conversation. She squirmed around in her seat so she could study Cary's profile. Strong, chiseled. Firm. She liked that. She sighed deeply, and Cary glanced at her.

"What's on for this evening, or are we just staying home with the family?" he asked.

"What do you say to a night in Crystal City? A little wining, a little dining—we have to watch our waistlines— a little dancing, and then a great deal of lovemaking later on."

"I'd be a fool to turn down an offer like that. Crystal City it is. Would you like to invite the others, or is this strictly a twosome?"

There it was. Amelia knew Cary was just being generous; he was like that. But she only wanted to be with him. She certainly didn't want to share him with her family. "If you think I'll bore you for a long evening, then we can invite the entire household," she said lightly.

Cary cursed inwardly. He'd screwed up again. Now she was going to sulk all night unless he could cajole her out of it. It occurred to him suddenly that he had been doing a lot of that lately.

"Well, here we are. This is the tract I was telling you about."

Looking at it, Amelia estimated the parcel to be just under two square miles. Out here, with Austin's skyline visible in the distance, the land was flat and uninterrupted.

"You see," Cary was saying, "the highway leads right into the city, so there'll be no difficulty with access. Of course, we're hoping that the offices and light industry space, as well as the shopping mall, will take care of jobs for those living right here."

Amelia raised her eyebrows. "You'll need more than a few square miles for that."

"That's what's so beautiful about the plan. We begin construction at the heart of the project and spread outward. There are fifteen available square miles here, on both sides of the highway and out there"—he pointed— "beyond that slight ridge. We'll be buying out several homeowners. Many of them, in fact. But then we're also thinking of incorporating the existing homes and small ranches into the project. That'll give us an even wider scope in the future."

"Then it's decided you're going to throw in with the developers?"

"I'd like to. Of course, I wouldn't decide anything without you. We'd have to live here, at least until things got under way. That's a decision for the two of us to make."

"You know, I believe some of this land belongs to Jake Baker. It hasn't seen a plow or a steer in a good number of years. Good drainage, though. Pap always said look at the ditch first." She laughed. "Jake's an old horse trader. His land won't come cheap."

"Let's take a walk over to the ridge. We can get a better perspective from there."

She looked down at her four-hundred-dollar Ralph Lauren crocodile shoes and winced as he took her arm and led her into the field. The thorny bush and dried grasses snagged her nylons and she kept a wary eye out for snakes and prairie dog holes. Being from the city, Cary assumed that empty land was just that—devoid of life. He never considered the insect and other life that dwelt on any open stretch of country land.

"You realize I don't know a hell of a lot about building and architecture. In fact, it's safe to say I know nothing. I can learn, though," he said positively. "Sewers, electricity, building permits, union workers, the whole bag. But I have a feeling about this, Amelia. The minute Johnston and Alphin brought me out here, I knew this dream could become a reality. I knew I wanted to be a part of it, more than an investor. And long after I'm gone, it'll still be here, some part of me."

"Can you afford it?"

"If I can't, there's always the bank. I think I could swing it; I know how to deal."

"Cary, I can always throw in with you."

"No, you can't. This is our project, but my money. We've gone all through this, babe. All I want is for you to point me in the right direction. Alphin says a deal like this has to be finessed, and it doesn't hurt having a wife who comes from around these parts. He knows what he's talking about, honey. He's a good ol' boy from North Carolina and he understands people. He says this is too near the heart of the farmland; ranchers might think they're being crowded. No one likes change, not when it affects them personally."

"Your man seems to know how people think, all right. Even though most of our neighbors are well-to-do and like to think of themselves as progressive, they have roots planted in this country. You just might meet up with some opposition. What about Johnston? What does he say?"

Cary grinned. "He takes Alphin's word to heart, just like I do. But if there's one thing Johnston knows about, it's building. He's creative, knows the best materials, the top-of-the-grade contractors. He was the one who came up with the idea of this 'inner city outside the city' idea. He nixed the idea for tract houses, saying that a certain amount of exclusiveness would be more acceptable to the local powers."

"He's right, you know. But first you have to get the land, and that's going to be tricky. Texans don't part with land if they can help it; they might lease it, but they won't sell."

"Hell, Amelia, that isn't going to do me any good."

"You'd quibble over a ninety-nine-year lease with an option to buy?"

A slow smile lifted the corners of his mouth. To Amelia he looked just like a cat who'd swallowed a canary—she could almost imagine him smacking his lips. "Of course, things could get a little sticky, me being an outsider, I mean."

"And that's where I can do you the most good. Amelia Coleman Assante, returned to the heartland!" she said. "We'll entertain, join clubs, become a part of the local politics. And you can do it, darling. You love a challenge. You'll have them eating out of your hand."

Cary was becoming more excited about the project; his dark eyes shone with the thrill of the challenge. "Johnston says customization is the key. Everything tailored and first-quality. He says there's money out here and Alphin agrees. 'Don't judge a man by the age of his truck or the green of his grass,'" Cary drawled, doing his impersonation of Alphin's soft Carolinian accent. "'That ol' boy'll be sittin' on more than he wants you or Uncle Sam to know about.'"

Amelia laughed. "Stick with them, darling, and you won't go wrong."

"And you're right about joining clubs and making friends. I know what it means to be an outsider. I know all about closed shops and being the only dago in a school full of Irish. You have to earn the right to belong. And by God, Amelia, I want to belong to this place."

"Okay, then let's go talk to Jake Baker and see what he says. Let's see if he remembers Seth Coleman's little black-haired girl and the fact that Pap bought my first pony from him."

"Sounds good." He was already leading her back to the car.

"Customized, eh?" Amelia mused. "Ask me what I'd

want in a house, Cary. I've got hundreds of ideas."

"Okay, I'm asking."

"A gorgeous kitchen. Out-of-this-world bathrooms. I'm big on bathrooms. Room-size dressing rooms. Hot tub, Jacuzzi. Fireplaces. Solid oak floors. Curving stairways. One in the front of the house and one off the kitchen. Adequate servants' quarters. Swimming pool built like a grotto. Designer landscaping so the house looks as if it's been there for years. Ironwork, grills, that sort of thing; decorative, of course. But Cary, I have to admit it's such a colossal undertaking that it frightens me. Building houses is one thing, but planning a city and all the things you were talking about last night makes me nervous. It's going to take millions!"

"Amelia, look at me. Do you believe I can do it?"

"Of course I do. But remember, though I might come from money, I wasn't one of the ones who did the making. I think it's natural for me to be a little nervous."

Cary sighed. He wanted Amelia to have faith in him. He'd been doing a little worrying last night himself. The contacts he'd made at Maggie's barbecue would come in handy later, but it was going to take more than just contacts, and he knew it. "Financing, I think, isn't going to be too much of a problem. Banks love the building industry."

"What you're saying is every man has a selling price."

"That's right. With some men it's harder to find than with others. Everyone has a price."

Without stopping to think, she said, "My father and brother didn't have a price."

"Yes they did. You just don't know what it was. Or if you do know, you don't want to think about it."

Amelia didn't like the conversation and was sorry she'd blurted out her opinion. She'd never really argued with Cary before. Hesitantly, she asked, "And what's your price?"

"It's there. It never pays to let a woman know all a man's secrets."

"That's my line—or I should say that's a woman's line.

Women are supposed to be mysterious, never letting their lover know everything."

"What don't I know about you, Amelia?" Cary asked, his voice serious.

"Not a damn thing. I've been an open book with you. Unfortunately or fortunately, as the case may be, I am neither mysterious nor secretive. What you see is what you got. Now you're going to get me in a snit until I figure out what your price is."

"I wouldn't lose any sleep over it, darling. It may never show up till I'm eighty years old."

God! If he were eighty, she'd be... "My shoes are getting ruined, Cary. I can wait in the car if you want to explore a little more."

"I think I've seen enough. I know what I want, and the next thing to do is see about getting it. After we see Jake Baker, we'll go back to Sunbridge and I'll start setting up my appointments."

"I could do that for you," Amelia said. If he was going to spend hours on the phone, what was she going to do?

"This is man's work, baby. You did your share at the party when you paved the way for me. I can handle it from here."

"Don't need me anymore, eh?"

Cary turned the key in the ignition. "I'll always need you, Amelia. I can't imagine what my life would be without you. I was serious when I said until death do us part. Don't you know how much meaning you give to my life? Hell, I was only a rich drifter when we met. A hustler. You turned me around. I'll never forget that. We're a team, we belong together, and don't you ever forget it."

Amelia beamed. She forgot about the mud caked on her shoes. She forgot about the phone calls that would take Cary away from her for a little while.

After working in the stables cleaning stalls, Sawyer and Cole rewarded their efforts by taking a long ride through the back hills. They purloined a picnic lunch from a kitchen in amazingly good order, considering the amount of activity that had taken place there the night before.

Sawyer led Cole along her favorite riding paths, skirting the scrupulously fed and watered lawn, taking him into the low-rising hills far out of sight of the house and sound of occasional trucks on the highway. Off in the distance, they'd seen Rand and Riley returning from their morning's ride, and Sawyer watched them until they were out of sight. She felt the distance between Rand and herself was much greater than the mile or more of Sunbridge acreage that separated them now. She flushed when she remembered how she'd tried to seduce him earlier that morning. Why wouldn't he talk to her, tell her what was wrong?

When Sawyer and Cole returned to the house, they turned their mounts over to a groom. "I'm for a shower," she said, "and you don't smell so hot yourself. C'mon, I'll race you!"

Cole ran close on her heels. He had the slim, loosely jointed body of a natural athlete, and he moved with grace.

"Nice going!" she called over her shoulder. "C'mon, don't stop now!"

Rand, sitting on the back patio, heard Sawyer's familiar laugh, and when he turned, he saw her running ahead of Cole toward the house. The sun shot her hair full of golden lights, and her long, slim legs ate up the distance. He'd never thought there was much resemblance between Sawyer and her half brother, but now he noticed the same agility, the same loose stride, slim hips, and coltish legs. He found himself smiling.

When they'd rounded the side of the house and were no longer in view, Rand laid his head against the back of his redwood armchair. Seeing Sawyer running across the lawn with Cole was another reminder of how young she was. So wonderfully young. But he knew her youth wouldn't protect her from the pain he was inflicting. He must talk to her, explain. But what explanation could a man offer a woman who loved him and thought she was loved in return?

He laughed, a bitter, tight sound. That was just the trouble: he did love Sawyer. He simply did not love her enough.

She was young, resilient; she'd forget him. She deserved the best life had to offer—a family, children to mother, the right to fulfill her ambitions and build her career without a disenchanted husband who wanted a quieter, simpler life. She should not have to sacrifice anything for him.

Rand sat lost in his thoughts for a very long time, grateful that no one came out to the patio to interrupt the silence. He liked it out here amid the huge redwood tubs, which held shrubs and bright red and yellow flowers. Maggie had seen to every comfort. Intimate groupings of brightly cushioned furnishings invited leisure and conversation. Less than a step away on the dull gray flagstones was a portable bar, well stocked with cold drinks and snacks, with a television and telephone on top. The pool nearby was perfect for cooling off, although he'd been too lazy to indulge when he'd returned from his ride with Riley.

There were stirrings in the house now—voices, footsteps. Rand glanced at his watch: almost the cocktail hour. His stomach churned in rejection of the idea, anticipating the inevitable confrontation with Sawyer. Suddenly memories of their times together, their shared experiences, came flooding back. He pushed them away, refusing to be drawn into the intimacy they created.

"Hello, I thought I'd find you out here," Sawyer said lightly as she leaned over to kiss his cheek. "Can I get you something to drink?"

"If you're buying, I could use a Coke."

"And what kind of day did you have?" Sawyer asked cheerfully as she walked over to the portable bar.

"Lazy. What did you do?"

"I got to know Cole a little. I helped him clean the barn and we went riding. He seems to be a nice enough kid who has a few problems, but then don't we all?" She handed Rand his soda in a frosty glass and sat down in the chair opposite his. "What did you think of my step-brother?"

"I'm the last person you should be asking. He managed to tie one on last night, and Riley and I had to dry him out. He's a bit young for that sort of thing. Other than that, I can't say I know the boy at all. Riley, now, is something different. I spent quite a lot of time with him last year when we were in Japan, and he's what a young man is all about."

Sawyer could hear the clipped British formality in Rand's voice, a sure sign of his disapproval. Defensively, she replied, "It was probably the only way Cole could get through Maggie's party. You have to admit it was over-whelming."

"The boy could have caused quite a scene, and this party was very important to Maggie. He should have had enough consideration for his mother to behave."

"You sound like a stern father."

"God forbid! That's the one role in life I'm not cut out for. I suppose it is easy to preach about other people's children."

"Yes, I guess so. Isn't it exciting, though, that Susan is going to have a baby?" Sawyer said dreamily. "A baby at Sunbridge again. I was the last one."

"That's right. Cole wasn't born here, was he?"

"No, in New York. I don't think he regards Sunbridge the way the rest of us do. Sometimes I think we're all obsessed with this pile of bricks."

"It's a beautiful place. I can't deny that," Rand said, bringing his glass to his lips.

Sawyer noticed, not for the first time, that he was having trouble meeting her gaze. "What's wrong, Rand? Did I do or say something that offended you? You've been avoiding me since we got here. Even as far back as Easter I sensed something was wrong. Have you had a change of heart?" There, the dreaded question was out. She held her breath, locking her gaze with Rand's.

"Sawyer, there's no easy way to say this. It won't work for us. We're worlds apart in just about everything. You're young and you have your whole career ahead of you. I'm so much older than you. You deserve children. I don't want children. I . . . I don't think I even want to get married."

Sawyer could feel the heat on her face. The sick feeling in her stomach was crawling up to her chest and throat. She wanted to cry, could feel the tears welling up in her eyes. She should be saying something, but she couldn't seem to think straight. "Don't I have anything to say about all of this?" Sawyer whispered in a choked voice. "The children, marriage, our ages?"

"No."

That one word, so dreaded, so quietly said, destroyed her. This was final; she could read it in the pain in his eyes, in the set of his jaw. Sawyer stood up, her glass shattering on the flagstones unnoticed. She jammed her hands into her pockets so he wouldn't see how they trembled. "I love you, Rand. I thought you loved me."

"And you had every right to think so." He stood to face her; his hands reached to steady her, to soothe her. "I love you, Sawyer. You're a beautiful, wonderful person. But I'm not in love with you. It . . . it just wouldn't work for us. Believe me, I never wanted to hurt you—"

"Is there anyone else?" she blurted, unable to stop herself.

He seemed startled that she should ask, even offended. "No, of course there isn't. I'm so sorry. You know I wouldn't hurt you for the world."

Sawyer clapped her hands over her ears and squeezed her eyes shut. She wanted to kick, to scream, No, I don't know any such thing! You just ripped my heart out and you say you wouldn't hurt me for the world. You're my world, Rand, you! But she bit back the words, swallowed the screams. Colemans don't snivel and they don't buckle under. Isn't that what she'd said to Cole only hours ago? Well, she was a Coleman . . . and right now she wanted to throw herself at this man who had just crushed her world, beg him to take back the words.

Cole stood in the doorway. He'd heard part of the

conversation, and now he saw the expression on Sawyer's face, in her eyes. Without thinking, he ran out to the patio, seized Sawyer by the arm, and dragged her into the house. The first open door led into Seth's old study, a small room occupied by a large desk and several worn leather armchairs.

"You can cry now," he told her. "I'll never tell."

Sawyer sank down behind the huge oak desk beside Coleman. She hid her great heaving sobs from the world, accepting only the solace Cole offered with his presence and hesitant comforting pats. He dug in his pocket to offer her his handkerchief.

A long time later she blew her nose lustily. Look-alike eyes met in understanding. "He'll change his mind," she said. "He loves me. You'll see. He loves me."

}}}}}}}} CHAPTER EIGHT }}}}}}}}}

The Texas sky was dark, the usual puffy white clouds now a dark blue blanket shrouding Sunbridge. Rand stood on the wide front portico overlooking the old rose garden and tree-lined drive, his hands jammed tightly in his pockets. There was a storm brewing; winds from the southeast were churning tree limbs and rattling the shutters. He should have left Sunbridge by now, but he'd wanted to stay because of Sawyer. Once he'd told her it was over between them, he felt it only fair to be around in case she needed to talk. He'd had enough of avoiding, of running away, and he'd wanted to see for himself that Sawyer would be all right.

Instead, it had been Sawyer who had avoided him, occupying herself with Cole and Riley; but Rand had often felt her watching him, listening to his conversations with others. He'd known she was waiting for him to approach her, to say something crazy had gotten into him and beg her to forgive him. Yesterday she'd left Sunbridge, her eyes dark with questions and hurt. He knew all it would take was one phone call from him and Sawyer would return. He could make her world right again. . . . But no, this was best, for both of them.

A sudden driving wind buffeted through the portico, forcing him backward into the shelter of the doorway. The air was thick with humidity, strong with the smell of oncoming rain. The slender stalks in the rose garden bent before the wind; petals swirled upward like confetti. The storm was welcome; it gave him something to think about besides Sawyer and what he'd done. He could find shelter from the rain inside the fortress walls of Sunbridge, but what he really needed was safety from his own emotions.

It was darker now; the arthritic old trees bent beneath the onslaught. He searched the slate-gray sky, having heard tales of the merciless twisters that could plague this part of Texas.

He turned around and looked up at the house. No lamplight shone from the front windows. Susan and Jerome had left Sunbridge days ago, but Amelia and Cary were still here, out promoting their land deal. Riley and Cole were probably in the barn, which left only Maggie and the servants in the house.

Rand went inside and pushed the door closed against the wind. It was darker in the foyer than it was outside. Not a single light shone, and the bleakness increased his anxiety. "Maggie! Maggie!" he called, moving to the interior of the house, switching on lamps as he went.

At the bottom of the stairs he called upward, "Maggie, you up there? It's really blowing up out there; we're in for a real Texas storm!"

He fumbled for the wall switch, and the magnificent center mahogany staircase appeared. The thick Navajopatterned carpet runner silenced his footfalls as he mounted the steps. Maybe it was the oncoming storm, but something had him thinking too much, remembering too much. He tried to shrug off all his thoughts, thoughts of Sawyer, Cole, Maggie. . . . He'd been concerned about Maggie since she'd told him Cole had invited Cranston to Sunbridge. He wondered how she'd handle seeing Cranston again here, in her own home. He liked Maggie—probably more than he should.

Suddenly he decided to finish his packing and leave, storm or no storm, right away. He wanted out of Sunbridge, away from Maggie and her son, now, before Cranston arrived. He didn't belong here.

"Can't wait to leave, is that it?" Maggie queried as she swept down the hallway, only to back up at the sound of Rand's suitcase snapping shut. "By the way, thanks for lighting the house."

"No problem, I assure you," he said, his voice gruff.

"Is anything wrong, Rand?" she asked uneasily.

"Not at all. I just thought I'd leave a bit early. Who knows what'll happen to the flights or how long this storm will last."

Maggie's face showed alarm. "Surely you aren't thinking of driving to the airport now. Have you ever seen one of our storms?"

"Yes, I was thinking of leaving now, and no, I've never had the pleasure. Don't tell me you're concerned for my safety." He'd said it sarcastically, yet he realized that her answer was important to him. Right now, he needed someone to care about him.

"Of course I'm concerned," she answered seriously, searching his face with her eyes. "Rand, it's raining now, the proverbial buckets. I doubt if you'd get as far as Crystal City before the road washed out. I was going to suggest you call the airline and reschedule your flight till tomorrow or even next week. You aren't in a hurry to get back to England, are you?"

"Won't it be a little awkward when your husband arrives?" he said stiffly. "Amelia and Cary are hardly ever here. I'd just be in the way."

"In whose way? Certainly not mine. I don't care if Cranston never comes. Once he gets here it'll be one problem after another. Unfortunately, I have to deal with it this time: Cole's future is at stake." She gave him a tight little smile. "Cranston doesn't want Cole to come and live with him, not really, except for the fact that it would hurt me. He's just using the boy. Your being here might even ease the situation a little."

"No, thank you, Maggie. I don't like playing middle-man in a domestic situation."

"I wasn't trying to use you for that, Rand, really I wasn't. It's just that . . . that . . ." Maggie looked down at her shoes, and Rand almost expected her to scuff them in the carpet. "You see," she began again, "Cranston has always been able to intimidate me. Everything that happened between us has always been my fault, according to him. Most of it was, I suppose, but not all of it. Maybe it's just the way I react around some men. My father and grandfather always intimidated me, and now when I look back, I think it was one of the reasons I was drawn to Cranston. I thought I had something to prove. If Cranston could accept me, love me even, then it might mean that my father and grandfather could respect and love me, too."

"And what about me, Maggie? Do I intimidate you?"

She laughed. "Not at all. I'm quite comfortable with you. I'm sorry you're leaving; I could have used a friend while Cranston is here. And I'm even sorrier that you seem unhappy."

"You know something went wrong between Sawyer and me, don't you? You're just too polite and well-mannered to ask."

"I wasn't prying, Rand. Sawyer is your business."

"In a way, she's yours, too."

"No, not really. We may be mother and daughter, but we're two very different people."

"It might have helped her to talk to another woman."

Maggie flinched at Rand's words. She'd tried to

approach Sawyer but hadn't been able to face her daughter's hostility. How was she to explain that to Rand when she couldn't explain it to herself? "A—a friendship has to be earned. It's never been that way between Sawyer and me.... Well, I have things to do. Let me know if you'll be here for dinner, won't you?"

She was gone, down the hall and around the corner to the stairs. She'd caught him off guard with her candor. It was something he'd never been led to expect from Maggie. The *old* Maggie, he corrected himself. He decided he liked this Maggie. And he especially liked the scent of her perfume. Hell, maybe he would stay until after dinner.

Rand managed to kill time by reading seventy-seven pages of a novel whose title he later couldn't remember. He hoped no one ever quizzed him on the contents.

A drumroll sounded overhead, followed by a second, a third, and then a loud crash. Jagged streaks of lightning tore across the sky, piercing his room with a blaze of light. Another ominous collision in the sky and the room went dark. The power was out. Faintly, he could hear Maggie's voice calling from downstairs for everyone to stay still and she would be up with candles.

"Sort of like Halloween, isn't it?" Maggie smiled as she entered his room, a candle in one hand and a hurricane lamp in the other. "The boys are downstairs. We have a generator, but I don't know the first thing about it. Would you mind taking a look? We could be without power until tomorrow. This is a bad one." Maggie nodded toward the window. "We should have dressed for the occasion. I wish I'd thought of it earlier. The boys might have had some fun. They look so glum. No television, no stereo, just plain old conversation or reading by lamplight."

"I imagine we'll all survive," Rand said. He was standing too close to Maggie, drinking in the scent of her, seeing the softness of her hands and wanting to touch them. He backed up until she was bathed in pale yellow light. It was true; a woman looked beautiful in candlelight. At least this woman did.

"There are so many shadows here, so many dark corners. Susan and I used to hide and play games up here. I always found Susan."

"Susan couldn't find you. Is that it? You must have been aces at the game."

"Susan didn't like to play games," Maggie said thoughtfully. "She preferred to read or color in her books."

"I remember Susan as a child," Rand smiled. "She was like a little sister to me, too. She was always more interested in her studies than in games. I think of those days often."

"I never think about them," Maggie said firmly.

"Maybe you should. Maybe it would help you understand your own son a little better."

They were standing at the top of the stairs. Everywhere there were candles in decorative holders, hurricane lamps, and a flashlight or two casting light upward.

Maggie turned around until she was just inches from Rand. "Why do I get the feeling you can't make up your mind if you like me or not? Does it have something to do with Sawyer?"

"Maggie, you're wrong. I do like you. Too much. I know exactly where you've been and where it is you want to go. I've been down that road myself a time or two." He paused, then added almost brusquely, "Don't analyze. One thing has nothing to do with the other."

Maggie searched his eyes for a long moment, then smiled and turned away, starting down the stairs. Rand followed close behind. "Dinner is by candlelight," she said cheerfully. "I suppose the boys will think it's eerie and will complain about not being able to see their food, but I think it's romantic."

"What time do you expect Cranston?"

"He should have been here by now. It's possible his plane didn't land," Maggie said blithely. "We're certainly not waiting dinner for him."

"I don't mind waiting."

Maggie smiled. "But I do. The boys are hungry and so am I. The cook can fix a plate for Cranston if he arrives.

. . . You notice I said 'if.' He's notorious for saying one thing and then doing another. He used to promise to take Cole to ball games and then wouldn't show up. Once he was supposed to take him to the circus, and Cole was so excited he threw up. Cranston didn't show up that time, either." Maggie turned and actually bumped into Rand. "My husband was and probably still is the consummate bastard. He was cruel in lots of little ways. But I was no better. I baited him, and I think we fed off each other's hatred. I know where mine came from, but I never knew what ate at Cranston. The only thing I truly regret is that he wasn't a better father to Cole."

"Were you a good mother to the boy?"

Maggie hesitated. "I could have been better. I made my share of mistakes, but I love Cole. I'm not sure Cranston ever did. He has our pictures on his desk at the office. Isn't that funny? A picture of the little woman holding her son's hand is supposed to instill comfort and confidence in clients. What that client doesn't see or know about are all the other women, the ones who make him feel young again. If I sound bitter, it's probably because I am, a little. Cranston used me and I can't even hate him because I used him, too. . . . End of true confessions. I hope you're hungry. Prime rib and roast potatoes."

Rand laughed. "It's always prime rib. Don't you Texans ever make lamb chops?"

"Bite your tongue. This is a cattle ranch. Lamb and pork are dirty words out here. When we want pork or lamb, we go to Crystal City."

Maggie did her best to keep the conversation lively during dinner. Occasionally Riley lifted his eyes and contributed. Cole was sullen as usual, chewing his food noisily and slurping his water.

"Did you call the airport?" Cole asked suddenly.

"The lines are down. You know the phones are the first to go during a storm like this. Rand is going to look at the generator after dinner, so we'll have television, at least. We can see just how bad things are. It's more than possible your father's plane didn't land."

Cole scowled and stuffed an entire buttered roll into his mouth. Maggie tried not to notice and concentrated instead on Riley, who was eating quietly but steadily.

"Did you have a good day, Riley?" she asked. "Aside from a sore bottom, I mean."

"Very good, Aunt Maggie. When I was here before, I was too young to go riding alone. I've always wanted to see just how far Sunbridge goes. So far I've only covered about half of it."

"Are you homesick?" Rand asked. He noticed that Cole stopped chewing long enough to hear Riley's answer.

"Not at all. I do miss Sawyer, though. She's been a good friend to me." His voice was quiet, but his eyes bored into Rand. "She promised to write to me."

His sister said she'd write to *him*, thought Cole.

Maggie looked up, first at Rand and then at Cole. She could feel her heart start to pound. There was going to be trouble here in a minute. "Tomorrow," she said quickly, "if this storm is over, there's going to be tons of work to do. We might even have to hire on some extra help to clean up."

"When do you think the power will be back on?" Riley asked.

"A day, two at the most." In the awkward silence that followed, Maggie willed Cole to say something, anything, to show he was part of the group, that he belonged. Riley was trying, at least; so was Rand. Her son, on the other hand, had chosen to maintain a stubborn silence. Why? She sighed wearily.

"What's for dessert?" Rand asked heartily.

"Apple pie, I think. Martha made some this morning. Ice cream. She makes that, too."

Rand laughed. "Top that off with some good Colombian coffee and you have an order."

"Me, too," Riley seconded.

"None for me," Cole said as he tossed his napkin on

the table. He didn't excuse himself, merely pushed back
his chair and left the room as dessert was being served.
Riley's eyes fell to his plate. Rand wanted to run after the
boy and shake him till his teeth rattled. He half expected
Maggie to go after her son, but she didn't. Instead, she
looked at Riley and smiled.

"You're certainly going to have a long letter to write
home," she said, watching as Riley made short work of
his pie. "The party, the storm, seeing Billie and Thad and
all the others. Where did Sawyer go? Do you know?"

Riley flushed. He'd promised Sawyer not to tell Rand,
but how was he to lie to Aunt Maggie? He was searching
for the words when Rand himself came to the rescue.

"She said something earlier about going back to California to finish up some business. Are you concerned,
Maggie?"

"No, just curious. . . . Another piece of pie, Riley?" she
asked cheerfully.

"No thanks, Aunt Maggie. I want to go out for baseball
in September, so I have to watch my weight. If you don't
mind, though, I'd like to take a look at the generator."
He pushed his chair back and stood up. "I know where
it is. Finish your dessert."

"He's such a nice boy," Maggie said after a moment's
pause. "I hope some of him rubs off on Cole, but I'm not
expecting miracles." She smiled brightly. "So, what did
you think of the pie?"

"Probably the best I've had since I was here last. That's
a beautiful dress you're wearing. What do you call the
color?"

"Wineberry. It's a Billie Original."

"There's no reason to sound defensive."

"Was I? Sounding defensive, I mean. I didn't mean to.
For a long time I wouldn't wear the things Mam designed
for me. Now I wear what I have to death. By the way,
what do you think of Thad going into politics?"

"My personal opinion is he's too honest for it. The
leeches and parasites who'll make it possible will chew
him up and spit him out. Billie's the one I pity."

"But do you think he could make it?" Maggie asked.

"With his record, chances are he will. But I'm not sure, from talking to him, that it's what he wants. Billie mentioned the word governor to me in a very shaky voice. I think she's worried."

"Just how deep will the opposition dig into Thad and Mam's background?" Maggie asked sharply.

Rand hesitated. "To the bare bone."

"That's what I thought."

In that instant, the lights came back on and Rand was able to see the anguish in Maggie's eyes. "It's something else for you to worry about now, isn't it?" he asked, his voice soft.

"Yes. My life can't stand up to a microscopic examination. A bare bones investigation will harm Thad. Mam, too. They don't deserve that. Thad's a great guy, the greatest in my opinion. I'd put him right up there with Pap. They were best buddies, you know." Maggie leaned her elbows on the table and cupped her chin in her hands. Rand thought her skin looked like satin in the bright light. "Isn't it funny how we go through life never thinking our past is going to catch up to us? When it does, it usually cripples us. God! I don't want to be the reason Thad doesn't make it if he decides to run for office. I couldn't bear it if Mam had to defend me in public."

"Did you talk to her about it?" Rand asked gently, seeing Maggie's eyes glisten with unshed tears.

"How could I? This place was like a madhouse, and then they left so quickly. I'm sure they must have discussed it. What will I do if Thad's career in politics is ruined because of me?"

"Vermont is far away, Maggie, and that was so long ago."

She laughed, a bitter sound. "He could be in Guam and they'd still sling mud. That's what politics is all about. Mam is news and so are the Colemans. And my drinking and outrageous behavior wasn't that long ago. Enemies have long memories."

"The elections aren't until next year. I wouldn't start

losing sleep over it now. A lot can happen in a year and a half. The best advice I can give you is to wait."

"What else can I do? I can't turn back the clock."

Suddenly Rand tilted his head to one side, listening. "Has the rain let up? Let's take a look at the telly and see how much damage has been done. I just might be able to make the airport after all." Rand couldn't have said why, but he was pleased to see the look of disappointment on Maggie's face as they left the dining room.

Riley called to them from the hallway. "It works!"

"And there was light!" Maggie called gaily.

"Did you have any trouble?" Rand asked.

"No. I simply turned the switch. Anyone could have done it."

"Easy or not, we have power and that's what's important. Now, let's see what the weathermen have to say. Rand is eager to leave us."

Every TV station they tuned in had preempted regular programming to give a report on the storm. According to one, the airport in Austin had been closed down for four hours. It was open now, but all flights were delayed. Disgruntled passengers were shown mumbling and muttering about their time schedules. Flooding on the roads was lessening. Rain was needed, "but this is ridiculous," chortled a weatherman from his dry control room. Trees were down, blocking the highways, but maintenance and power workers were out in full force. Electricity would be restored by noon tomorrow.

Maggie looked at Rand expectantly. "You're leaving." It was a statement.

Rand nodded. "Riley, would you give me a hand?" The boy nodded without enthusiasm.

"I'll have your car brought around front. I'm sorry you're leaving, Rand. I hope you'll come back over the holidays. Consider this your invitation."

"I'll think about it. It'll be nice to see the boys again and to spend the holidays with my mother and Cary."

"I'll get your bags," Riley said. "Is your jacket upstairs?"

"No, it's in the hallway. Thanks, Riley."

"Do you suppose he thinks I'm getting infirm, or has he been counting my gray hairs?" Rand asked lightly.

"Truthfully, I think he just wants to be rid of you. He's confused right now. He adores Sawyer, has from the first moment. So in a way you're his enemy now. There's a lot about Riley I don't know. There was a righteous streak in my brother—perhaps I should say it was a keen sense of justice. I think Riley's the same." She reached up to kiss his cheek lightly, then smiled. "Keep in touch, Rand."

{{{{{{{{ CHAPTER NINE }}}}}}}}

As Cole was looking out the parlor window to watch Rand leave, he noticed a white Cadillac powering up the drive. It could only be his father!

He rushed past the dining room, where he could hear Riley and Maggie talking, and stole out of the house to greet Cranston beneath the shelter of the portico. He waited for the car's engine to stop before rushing around the front of the car to greet his father. "Hi, Dad. I was afraid you wouldn't make it because of the storm."

Cranston climbed from the car. He was a tall man, lean as a reed and tanned from his recent trip to Florida. "I almost didn't make it," he said offhandedly, leaning once again into the Eldorado to retrieve a garment bag, which he unceremoniously handed to his son. "Goddamned power lines are down. I thought we'd have to reroute back to Atlanta." Casually he tossed Cole the keys. "Get my luggage out of the trunk and bring it into the house."

Cole's face mirrored his disappointment. This was hardly the greeting he'd been expecting. He took a deep breath. "Dad, I told Mother I want to live with you in New York."

"Oh, you did, did you? I believe I told you not to say anything until I'd had a chance to talk with her. What did she say?"

"She wants me to stay here. She'll probably raise a stink, but you can handle her, can't you, Dad?"

"Like I said, Coleman, this is between your mother and me. Where is she? Did you have dinner yet? I'm hungry as a bear."

Coleman watched him go into the house before retrieving the luggage from the trunk. He didn't like the way his father had said, "This is between your mother and me." That meant only one thing—his father was going to use him as leverage to get something else he wanted. Still, he had come all the way from New York. That meant something, didn't it?

Maggie was midway up the stairs when the front door opened behind her. She turned to find Cranston standing there, looking up at her. "So, you made it after all. I'll call Cole."

"I've seen him. He's outside getting my luggage." Cranston Tanner found himself looking at his soon-to-be ex-wife with incredulity. Surely this wasn't Maggie—not this healthy, vital woman staring down at him? "You look wonderful, Maggie."

She laughed. "You expected otherwise?" Damn right he'd expected otherwise. She knew him so well, this husband of hers. He'd hoped to find a broken-down old sot, an unfit mother unable to concentrate on anything but the next drink. That would have completed his fantasy.

"You always were a beautiful woman," he said. "Sunbridge obviously agrees with you. I haven't seen you looking this lovely in years."

"Thank you, Cranston. Now I'll show you to your

room so you can freshen up. Then you can have dinner if you haven't already eaten. Cook is keeping a plate warm for you."

For a tall man, Cranston moved with quickness and grace. With only a few steps he was on a level with Maggie. Close up, he decided she looked even better. He was about to lean over and kiss her when she moved slightly to avoid him. For a moment his eyes, the color of an overcast sky, narrowed. Then he caught the light, drifting scent of her perfume, one he'd always liked and usually purchased for her at Christmas. Maggie. His wife. His soon-to-be ex-wife.

"You really are stunning, Maggie. I approve."

Maggie murmured her thanks for his compliments, but she found herself resenting his mellow, intimate tone and decided not to compliment him in return. He was well aware of the elegant picture he created in his custom-made summer suit and his handmade Italian shoes. Flawless. Handsome. Brilliant.

Cranston knew he'd been rebuffed and smarted as he walked alongside his wife up the long, curving staircase. "How's Cole been?" he asked for want of anything else to say.

"He sulks, something he does very well these days. I think we should have a talk before we bring Cole into this. That is, if you're interested in his welfare, Cranston, truly interested. But if this is just another of your triyearly visits..."

"Still haven't lost your capacity for cruelty, I see," Cranston snapped. "Besides, it hasn't been three years since I've seen the boy; it's only been—"

"Two years and eight months if you're counting," Maggie said sweetly. "Cole has been counting. What you call cruelty, I call concern for Cole. And another thing, Cranston, spare me any of your courtroom melodramatics. It won't work any longer."

Cranston's eyebrows shot upward. Apparently things were very different here. After a moment, as he followed her down the long second-floor hallway, he remarked on how much Cole had grown.

"Did you tell him that?" Maggie asked pointedly. She stopped in front of one of the closed doors. "I'm putting you in Grandmother Jessica's old room. I think you'll find it comfortable."

Cranston paced the large bedroom that had once been Jessica's. He found it too feminine for his taste, but it would do for now. Taking off his jacket, he threw himself across the bed, unmindful of the smudges his shoes made on the white bedspread. If Maggie noticed, she said nothing. "I don't think I've ever been in this room before," he told her.

"That's right, but then you've only been to Sunbridge twice before. Once for a day and a half and once for six hours."

"I didn't know you were counting, Maggie." He grinned, a studied, charming gesture. Maggie knew it for what it was but felt a pang in her chest in spite of herself.

"How long are you staying this time?" she asked.

"As long as it takes to make a decision about what's best for Cole. At least through Sunday."

Maggie laughed, a bitter, sardonic sound. "I see *you* haven't changed. Time limits, conditions, you name it. We're talking about our son, Cranston. What if we don't resolve this by Sunday? Will you still leave?"

"Of course. I have pretrial arrangements and appointments for Monday."

"Of course." He was better-looking than the last time she'd seen him. Perhaps it was the deep, golden tan. She surprised herself by blurting, "Are you seeing anyone in particular these days?"

Cranston's mouth tightened imperceptibly. "Not really. Dinner, the theater, that sort of thing."

"Does that mean you're celibate?"

"Well, well, some things never change, do they, Maggie? Go right for the throat."

"Wrong," Maggie said breezily. "Actually, Cranston, I couldn't care less what you do or who you see. But your

life-style has a direct bearing on Cole. Besides, I want to
be sure nothing stands in the way of our divorce. All the
agreements still hold, right?"

"There is one difference. Cole said he wants to come
and live with me. I know you have custody of the boy,
but we have to do what's best for him. Why the hell you
took him out of that military school is beyond me. You
didn't even consult me."

"Why should I?" Maggie flared. "You weren't intersted.
You're his father, but all you've really done for him is
send a support check every six months. And you don't
even see to that personally—someone from the account-
ing department at the firm does it."

"The school was doing wonders for Cole," Cranston
said as if he hadn't heard her. "He's an expert marksman.
His grades are way above average. His deportment is
excellent. He's under close supervision. He's not on drugs.
Face it, Maggie: you made a mistake by taking him out.
He wants to go back to the academy or to a private school
in New York."

Maggie's heart fluttered. She could feel the first stirrings of panic. "Cole needs a home, a sense of family. He
doesn't need strict rules and regimentation. I'm sorry I
ever listened to you and enrolled him in the first place."

"Come off it, Maggie! You didn't want to be bothered,
either. He was cramping our style. Every chance you got
you sent him off somewhere. Now all of a sudden you
have motherhood running in your veins, and you think
you're going to make him live in this godforsaken shrine
to your father. I think that's sick!"

Maggie flinched. "It's what's important for Cole *now*!"
She took a deep breath. "And I refuse to let you draw
me into some discussion only a lawyer can win. If you
want to talk about Cole, fine. If not, I'll leave you to
whatever it is you want to do.

"By the way," she added, "my nephew, Riley, is here.
Please be civil and don't allow your prejudices to get in
the way."

Cranston blinked in surprise. This definitely was not

the Maggie he once knew. Something about her reminded
him of Billie—the same iron fist in a velvet glove. He got
up from the bed and began to prowl the room.

"Okay, let's talk. Cole called me and asked me to come
here. He told me that he wanted to live with me in New
York. I told him I'd think about it and would discuss it
with you. I didn't promise him anything. But what are
you going to do, Maggie—force him to stay here? He said
he hates this place."

Maggie sat on a soft green slipper chair and crossed
her legs. "Cole is just angry because I took him out of
school. He wanted to go off this summer on a trip to
Europe with his friends, with little or no supervision. I
said no. I think it's time he put down roots, and Sunbridge
is as good a place as any. It's my home now, and it's his
home. Trust me when I tell you this is what's best for
him."

"Best for him or best for you?"

"For him, of course! A sixteen-year-old doesn't belong
in a New York City apartment with no supervision. Cole
has some problems, and I think this is the place to work
them out. No child likes upheaval, but he'll come around
if you back me up. Right now, Cole doesn't like either of
us, Cranston, and if we let him, he'll play us against each
other. I don't want that to happen—and I'm going to need
your help to prevent it."

"I have to talk to Cole. I'll make my decision after I
hear what he has to say."

"I'll fight you, Cranston. All the way. You gave me
sole custody. You can't rip him away from me now. You
don't want Cole; admit it. What you want is to get back
at me."

"Now you're talking like a child. Why would I want
to get back at you?"

"Because I left you before you left me. I walked out
on you and took Cole with me. You didn't care about us.
All you cared about was how it was going to look to your
partners and friends. You had to make explanations, tell

lies. And you cooked up some pretty wild stories—I know because they filtered back to me. I didn't bother to defend myself at the time because I was afraid of you. But I'm not afraid of you any longer."

"The Coleman grit. It's awesome, I have to agree. You're on your own turf here. I can see how you'd get cocky."

"Damn you, Cranston! I'm doing my best to turn my life around and make something of it. I also want to help Cole, and I won't stand by and see you ruin him. Now, that's all I'm going to say about it. I don't think I'll join you in the dining room after all. I'll send Cole in my place. I think it's time you saw your son."

"I do, too. I guess I'll see you at breakfast."

"Only if you're downstairs at seven sharp. Otherwise, you'll have to wait till lunch. I have things to do."

"Mistress of Sunbridge." Cranston laughed.

Maggie pretended not to hear as she left the room, but she could feel her cheeks grow warm. He made it sound like a dirty title from a grade B movie.

When she reached her own room, the first thing she did was lock the door. Then she let the tears come. Lonesome tears, which rolled down her cheeks and onto the wineberry dress, spotting the delicate fabric. She should have worn a suit of armor for her meeting with Cranston, she reflected bitterly. Battles always left the wounded and bloodied.

She began to pace restlessly, trying to think. Cranston could do her in with legal mumbo jumbo. He was the boy's father. He could say he was busy trying to earn a living to support his wife in the style to which she'd become accustomed. Juries loved to sink their teeth into anything even remotely scandalous or sensational. Her past was going to rear up and slap her smack in the face—not once, but twice, when Thad's opponents got a crack at her.

It occurred to Maggie suddenly that she had no close friend, no confidant. If ever there was a time to confide in someone . . . Without thinking, she picked up the phone, dialed the airport, and had Rand paged. Ten minutes later she heard his anxious voice on the phone.

"Rand, it's Maggie. I need a friend."

"I'm all yours. I've another two hours before my plane leaves, and even then it's doubtful I'll get off before morning."

Rand smiled as he listened to Maggie talk. Suddenly, the airport seemed less lonely. They spoke for nearly the entire two hours, and he never once looked at his watch. He doubted he would have heard if they'd announced his departure. But it really didn't matter: there would be other planes.

It was Maggie who reminded him the two hours were nearly up. "Lord, Rand, I don't know what got into me."

"You said you needed a friend. We're friends. Don't make it complicated."

"I feel as though I've gone through my entire life without someone I could turn to. Thanks, Rand. Perhaps I can return the favor one day. See you over the holidays."

Rand listened to the dial tone for a few moments, then, very gently, replaced the receiver.

{{{{{{{{ CHAPTER TEN }}}}}}}}

Maggie sat in her favorite lounge chair on Sunbridge's back patio soaking up the late-August sun. It felt good, warming her to the core. It wasn't often she felt warm these days; Cole's hostility had been arctic since Cranston's visit just after the Fourth of July.

Nothing had been settled by the time he left, and he'd returned to New York alone. Maggie knew then that he hadn't really wanted the boy; if he had, neither heaven nor hell would have prevented him. But Cole could not be convinced. Meanwhile, she had to suffer their son's petulant antagonisms.

Aside from that, however, things had progressed nicely for Maggie. The Fourth of July bash had given her entrée into several social circles, mainly the country club set in and around Crystal City. Her calendar was filled with tennis and luncheon dates, and she often reciprocated with informal picnics at Sunbridge. Last week she'd held a cocktail hour and sit-down dinner for twenty in honor of Jamison Royce, an artist of acclaim whom she'd known back in New York. Her ability to bring new and interesting people to the Crystal City set guaranteed her success.

Amelia and Cary were busy with Cary's project, but not too busy to decorate most of Maggie's shindigs with their special kind of West Coast glamour. Maggie's new-found status also brought another benefit—Riley was making friends with the younger set. Cole, of course, was an entirely different matter. Maggie felt a frown wrinkling her brow when she thought of her son and purposefully smoothed the lines with her fingertips. She felt drowsy sitting here frying in her own fat, and she didn't want to think about anything unpleasant, including Cranston's impending return visit to Sunbridge sometime tomorrow.

Cole appeared out of nowhere, a talent he seemed intent on developing; obviously he enjoyed the way it unnerved his mother. He plopped down at the foot of her chaise, the all-too-familiar scowl on his young face. Maggie squinted through the sunlight at him, noting he was dressed in snowy white ducks and a striped jersey that seemed to accentuate his slimness.

"So, Mother, did you hear from my father? Have you two come to a decision?"

"You already know my decision, Cole." Wearily

Maggie laid her head back and closed her eyes again. "Your dad will be here sometime tomorrow. Monday is the last day for school registration; I'd like to settle this once and for all before then. . . . Cole, why aren't you down at the corral with the others? Don't tell me Riley didn't invite you, because I heard him myself. There's at least a dozen kids down there setting up for tonight's barn dance and they're having the time of their lives. Don't you like to have fun?"

"Not that kind of fun. Riley's a fag."

"The others don't seem to think so. I think he's adapted very nicely, and he certainly has gone out of his way to make friends. You're the one who refuses to get involved, Cole. Personally, I think you're a glutton for punishment. Or is it that you want to embarrass me and Riley?"

"If you say so, Mother," he replied insolently. "Are they all staying for dinner?"

"They're having an afternoon cookout. Then they'll go home and be back for the dance tonight. I told Martha not to fuss with my lunch; a sandwich will do me. I thought you'd be with the others. . . . I'm really sorry you've been so unhappy this summer, Cole. I was hoping you'd meet me halfway."

"Look, Mother, I don't want to go to this yokel school. Did you get a look at those kids? The girls especially!"

"Of course I did. They look like kids anywhere, and that includes your fancy military academy."

"They're all a bunch of faggots. I don't like them; can't you understand that? I don't fit in with them, and I don't want to. I don't belong here."

Maggie sighed. "At least make an appearance down at the barn. Sunbridge is your home, Cole, and you're the host. Do the proper thing."

"Riley's doing it for me. He's the one they like, not me. And don't tell me it's my fault, 'cause I don't want to hear it. Besides, I don't care. I got one over on old Riley this morning, didn't I?"

"How?"

"With that letter I got from Sawyer, that's how. Riley hasn't heard from her in weeks, but I have. He pretends it doesn't bother him, but I know it does and I'm glad."

Maggie hadn't realized Cole was hearing from Sawyer, and she was instantly curious. There were questions she wanted to ask about her daughter, things she wanted to know, but when she saw the look of smug satisfaction on Cole's face, she decided not to play into his hands. "Are you or aren't you going down to the corral?"

"All right, have it your way. But I don't understand why you're doing this to me. I hate it here. I hate everything about Sunbridge. Why are you making me stay?" His voice had risen to an agonized pitch somewhere between the frustration of a boy and the rage of a man.

Maggie's face drained of all color; she was speechless. She'd once cried those words—but in reverse. Light years ago she'd howled, *"Why are you sending me away? I belong here. Don't make me go! Why are you doing this to me?"*

Cole stared at his mother. He'd never seen that look on her face before and it frightened him. She seemed about to shatter into a thousand pieces. "I'm going, I'm going! Forget I said anything. Just forget it." He turned and began to run toward the corral, where Riley and the other kids were cooking hot dogs. He knew he'd hit a nerve, a very sensitive and painful nerve. It exhilarated him to have such power over her, and at the same time it frightened him to realize that his mother could be so easily destroyed.

"Hey! There's Cole! Just in time for lunch!" called one of the boys, enjoying the titters of laughter from the others.

"Where've you been, Cole?" one of the girls demanded, brushing her hands off on the seat of her jeans. "We've just hung the last paper streamer in the barn, everything's ready for tonight, and you didn't do a thing to help us." She giggled. "Maybe you shouldn't come to the dance tonight, even if it is your party."

"Cole had something to do for Aunt Maggie," Riley said quickly. "Otherwise he'd've been hanging from the rafters like the rest of us. Who gets the first hot dog?"

Cole bristled; he didn't need Riley to defend him and lie for him. "I didn't have—"

"Hey!" someone shouted from the barn. "Look what I found! Let's have a tug-o'-war! Guys against the girls!"

"No fair! No fair!" the girls complained. "It's even-steven or nothing!"

Sides were chosen, weight estimated and evenly distributed on both sides. Cole was encouraged to join and instinctively chose to pull opposite Riley. Riley was the tallest of the boys and he also had the prettiest girl beside him—if you didn't care about her braces, that was.

Cole grabbed his end of the rope and dug his heels into the soft ground. He felt the hardness of his muscles in his thighs, the tension and rigidity across his shoulders. This wasn't a game; it was personal. He clenched his teeth and pulled, surprising himself with his strength. Sawyer had been right; all the work he'd been doing this summer was the same as bodybuilding.

"Pull, Cole, pull! I think we've got 'em," the yell went up.

"That's what—you think," came from the other side, grunting. "C'mon, Riley, pull! Use those—muscles. You're—the anchorman."

"And his anchor's in his ass!" Cole shouted. He gave the rope a vicious yank, straining so hard he thought he tasted blood. His leg muscles shivered, his hands grew slick with sweat and threatened to slip, a pain tormented the back of his neck, and there was a freight train pounding through his head. But he kept his eyes focused on Riley, groaned and grunted and held his ground. He was the first man on his side of the rope, Riley the last on his. Inch by inch Cole's grip closed the distance between them; step by step Riley's team fought defeat. They were giving way; they were losing. If it killed him, Cole was determined to see Riley go down.

Cole's hands were still frozen around the rope when his teammates were laughing and clapping him on the back. "We did it! We won!" A tiny girl named Marcy kissed Cole on the cheek. "That's for winning." Cole blushed.

Riley dusted himself off and grinned as he held out his hand. "That was great, Cole. I guess you're right about where my muscles are. Hefting that pitchfork all summer really built you up!"

Cole looked pointedly at his cousin's outstretched hand. Then he smirked and walked away.

Embarrassed, Riley flushed and jammed his hands into his pockets. "Hey, Riley, lean down here," Marcy said.

"Why?"

"'Cause I want to kiss a loser. Don't pay any attention to Cole. He ruined Grace's party, too, by being a jerk. Ignore him," she said, planting a wet kiss on Riley's cheek.

Riley shrugged. Cole wasn't a jerk. He wasn't sure what Cole really was, but he wasn't a jerk.

Feeling cocky and smug, Cole sauntered back to the house. His mother was nowhere in sight. He flopped down on the chaise she'd been in and pulled Sawyer's letter from his hip pocket.

It was a long letter, but only a single sheet of paper. Typed. Cole grinned. Sawyer would never make it in the office pool: the letter was full of typos and crossouts. But what mattered was that she'd taken the time out of her busy schedule to drop *him* a note. He'd already rehearsed several versions of his response, but he wouldn't actually write till he heard his parents' decision regarding school.

Hello, little brother,

Bet this surprises you. Surprises me, since letter writing isn't one of the things I do best. I meant to write sooner, but work is keeping me pretty busy and I had some other things to take care of, too— you know, wounded pride, sore heart, tearful recriminations . . . If you're interested, and I know you are, I'm not any better but I'm not any worse.

Right now, I'm staying with an old college buddy, Adam Jarvis. He's a great guy—kind, gentle, considerate, and he wipes my tears when they get out of hand. He's a cartoonist. I think he's a genius.

We live on the upper east side. His apartment is a mess, but I pretend not to notice. What it needs is a good dose of Billie to fix it up.

I hope things are going well for you. How's your back? Not broken yet, I bet. Try not to be bitter, and take some advice from me; anger only eats you alive. I don't want to have to worry about you.

Christmas isn't that far away. Perhaps Maggie will invite me for the holidays. Or, if possible, you might want to wangle an invitation out of me to come to New York after Christmas. Riley's welcome, too, if you can tear him away from the ranch. You guys would have a ball.

Well, it's time for me to get to work. I got up early this morning to write this and I have an 8 A.M. appointment with an eye doctor. Guess I need new reading glasses. Things get blurry every so often. Adam says my tear ducts have dried up. He's probably right.

I know you must be very busy, but if you get a chance, drop me a line—and remember what I said about Christmas.

Say hi to Maggie and tell Riley I'll probably write him tomorrow. I'm giving you my phone number in case you ever want to call me.

Take care,
Sawyer.

Cole stared at the scrawled signature for a long time. Up till now it hadn't mattered that he had a sister. Now it was different. He had to remember to tell her about the tug-of-war. She'd laugh. He could almost see her eyes crinkle up and then the thick fringe of her lashes would glisten.

He read the letter a second time. Christmas in New York sounded great. Better than here. Maybe he could make a deal with his parents. If they decided he'd have to stay here, and he was sure that was the way it was going to be, then he'd simply make the deal for Christmas. Or he'd threaten to run away. That always put the fear of God into a parent.

Maggie slithered into a cornflower-blue lounging gown shot through with silver threads. The high mandarin collar brought the color close to her gently tanned face and cloud of dark hair, while the short capped shoulders exposed her gracefully rounded arms. Two side slits from the ankle to above the knee softened the line of an otherwise severely straight skirt. The outfit looked as though it had been made for her, and it had.

She knew Cranston would approve of the way she looked tonight. Glamour, that's what he expected and demanded, glitter and glitz, all the things that had nothing to do with reality and living.

Cranston didn't know Maggie Coleman Tanner anymore, she reflected wryly. He didn't know that she was different now, inside as well as outside. But tonight was her chance to show him that he wasn't dealing with the old Maggie, that Cole was important to her and that she'd fight for him if she had to. With all the Coleman money and the Coleman legal firm behind her, she could put up a pretty impressive fight. She hoped it wouldn't come to that.

She patted a stray strand of hair into place. Pearls? Why not. Her grandmother Agnes's matched strand would be perfect. She put them on and admired her reflection in the mirror. Yes, Cranston would be impressed. He knew real from imitation—and this time, she was real. More real than he was.

She twirled around until she was dizzy. "Hey, look at me now!" she cried to the empty room. Then, just for a moment, she felt foolish. She didn't have to prove anything to anyone. She didn't have to impress anyone, either.

The old Maggie did things like that.

Still, she didn't remove the pearls or the cornflower-blue dress. They were part of her. They, too, were Maggie Coleman Tanner.

As Cranston maneuvered his car down the long, tree-lined drive to Sunbridge, he was thinking about Maggie. Since his last visit, he'd done little but think of Maggie. She'd blossomed somehow, grown beautiful, more mature and elegant, more confident; desirable traits in a woman, definite assets in a wife. Even her attitudes seemed different, so different, in fact, that he'd been forced to reassess his decision to divorce her. At first he'd thought that she'd somehow manufactured all the changes. But in the weeks since his last visit, he'd decided that Maggie Coleman Tanner of Sunbridge might be a valuable asset indeed. With the Coleman money behind him, Maggie to perk up his dinner parties, and Sunbridge at his disposal for holiday weekend entertaining, he should have no trouble succeeding in his plan to buy out the other partners in his firm and reign as undisputed head of a law dynasty. He smiled at the image of himself playing lord of the manor—on a part-time basis, of course.

Cranston dug around in his briefcase for his tobacco pouch, then stuck a pipe, a gift from a grateful client, in his mouth and proceeded to puff thoughtfully. Just how hard would it be to get Maggie back? he wondered. Probably not too hard—you simply had to know your adversary. And Maggie was his adversary . . . for the moment.

Two weeks at Sunbridge ought to just about do it. Yes, he thought, amused, Greece could wait. It was time he got to know his wife and son. And by tonight, if he played his cards right, he wouldn't be sleeping alone.

Martha, the Mexican housekeeper, opened the door wide for him. She beamed a smile and ushered him into the wide foyer. His eyes went immediately to the Stetsons lined up on the hall hat rack. He grinned at the baseball cap on the last peg. He knew it didn't belong to his son. The Japanese kid—Japs were big on baseball.

"You finally made it."

Maggie walked into the foyer, looking beautiful and smelling wonderful. Cranston opened his arms in welcome, ready for her to step into his embrace and curl herself against him. Instead, she kept a formal distance between them, looking just a bit smug as she ushered him into the library. It annoyed him.

"Steven will take your bags upstairs later," she said graciously. "You look well, Cranston. Winning your case agreed with you, I take it."

"It's important to win," Cranston replied, his voice brittle. "I was prepared."

Maggie smiled again. "So, it isn't true, then, that old adage: it doesn't matter if you win or lose, it's how you play the game that counts?"

"I told you I was prepared. I knew I would win. You can't go off half-cocked in the courtroom. Substantiated facts and a sympathetic judge. It's a winning combination."

Maggie grimaced. "Can I get you a drink?"

"What are you having?"

"Ginger ale."

"Then I'll have the same. It must have been hard for you to give up liquor."

Maggie looked at her husband. "Yes, it was hard. I'm getting my life in order, Cranston, slowly but surely. I'm proud of myself because I did it on my own. Every day I tell myself I'm an alcoholic. I'll make it."

Maggie's sincere little speech somehow irritated Cranston. "I'm sure you will," he said curtly. "How's Cole?"

"Antsy. He really believes you're going to take him back to New York. Now that Sawyer is there, there's more incentive for him to want to go. I'd like you to talk to him as soon as possible. Tomorrow is the last day for registration at Crystal City High. I had to make a concession, too. Private school for both boys at this point is something I feel won't work. I want them to relate to all kids, not the chosen few who can afford expensive priv~te schools. What do you think?"

"I'm willing to go along with you on the public school. For a semester. If it doesn't work out, we'll go on from there." Always concede a little, he reminded himself, so that when the time comes, they'll remember you were fair. He'd won more than one case that way.

Maggie felt relieved but somehow suspicious. "What happens after the first semester?" she asked. "Are you going to take him? Fight me for custody?"

"That's a long way off. Why worry about something that may never come to pass? We can deal with it when the time comes."

"In the meantime you'll find a way to get an edge on me. I know you, Cranston. Let's spell it out now. I don't want any surprises later on. Cole thinks you'd be willing to take him. Now we both know that's wishful thinking. I'm willing to give up child support but still allow you fair visitation rights."

"Mother Maggie. Whoever would have thought you'd become a lioness defending her cub."

"I just want what's best for him."

"That's what you say."

"Stop talking like a lawyer. If you want legalese, I'll call Dudley Abramson and you two can go at it. In the meantime, the boy stays here till it's settled. I mean it, Cranston."

"I know you do," Cranston said, holding out his glass for a refill. "This time add a little whiskey. How's Cole getting on with your nephew?" he asked.

"They aren't. And it's Cole's fault. He's sulky, insolent, disrespectful, and a general pain in the butt."

"Why haven't you done something about it?"

"I'm trying. But he needs a father—and he needs to know we're united where he's concerned. I really need your help, Cranston."

"I'll talk to him. Where is he?"

"He's probably lurking somewhere trying to figure a way to devil Riley. He's jealous, and I don't know what to do about it."

"Send the kid back to Japan."

"I can't do that. I won't do it. Riley has every right to be here. Besides, Riley isn't the source of Cole's problem. *We* are his problem."

"All right, so we'll work on it." Cranston saw Maggie watching him speculatively and he knew she was trying to figure out if he had an ulterior motive. Or was she thinking of the good days in the early part of their marriage?

"Are you seeing anyone?" he asked abruptly.

Maggie laughed, a delightful sound that sent shivers up Cranston's arms. "No. I don't have the time right now to get involved in any kind of a relationship. Besides, I like things the way they are, for the present."

"What about Rand? Now, don't jump down my throat," he said when Maggie opened her mouth to protest. "Cole mentioned it to me and he was upset."

"Upset about what? That Rand and Riley had to dry him out? Your son got drunk at the barbecue and made an ass out of himself. He just likes to twist the truth and the blame. That's the kind of thing I'm talking about, Cranston."

"Cole said Rand broke off his long-standing relationship with Sawyer. He also said Rand was cozying up to you."

"I hate that expression. We just talked, about everything and nothing. I didn't know about Sawyer until after Rand left. I had nothing to do with Rand's decision—and I was not the reason they broke up."

"If you were, it'd be damn shameful. Mother steals daughter's boyfriend. There's probably cause for a suit there somewhere."

"Stuff it, Cranston. Rand and Sawyer are adults."

"I told Cole you were probably trying to patch things up between them rather than break them up. Of course the boy didn't buy my explanation. He said Sawyer left early, and that you didn't try to stop her. Still jealous of her, eh?"

"No! Cole sees what he wants to see. He had no right to make assumptions and then run to you with them. You're doing the same thing. Admit it, Cranston. You think I'm having an affair with Rand."

"I never admit to anything."

"Well, that's your problem; it always was a thorn for me. . . . Don't get up," Maggie said coolly. "I'll see where Cole is."

Cranston watched his wife's retreating back. So, tonight he would sleep alone. He'd been a little premature in his estimate. It would take a few days. At the most.

In the falling dusk Cole and Riley faced each other at opposite sides of the tennis court. Cole thwacked the ball viciously, sending Riley running for it out of bounds. He'd seen his father arrive and now felt as if he were going into an emotional tailspin. One moment, he was certain his father would put his mother in her place and take him back to New York. The next, he saw his father for what he was and knew he'd be left behind with his mother. At Sunbridge.

The tennis ball sailed back over the net, but instead of hitting it with the racket, Cole caught it and pitched it back to Riley with a snap of his arm.

"You've got a wicked curve ball," Riley panted after leaping up to catch it. "If you'd been on the mound, that would've been a strike."

Cole hunched over and positioned himself for Riley's serve.

"Are you going out for the baseball team? You should. The competition will be stiff, but I bet you could make varsity if you wanted."

"You make it sound like it's definite that I'm not going to New York," Cole snapped. "Do you know something I don't know?"

"No. I just thought . . . even if you go to a new school, you should consider going out for baseball if they have a team. You're good," Riley said sincerely.

"Sports aren't my thing."

"What is your thing? You have to start somewhere. You're a natural."

"Look, why don't you mind your own business?" Cole said angrily. "You must know by now that you and I aren't going to make it as friends or cousins. So why don't you just buzz on out of here and let me alone?" He watched Riley's retreating back, then called out, "I got a letter from Sawyer yesterday."

"I got one today," Riley called back over his shoulder.

"I got one today," Cole mimicked. "Well, she's *my* sister!" Angrily he threw a tennis ball in Riley's direction—and almost hit his father.

"I've been looking all over for you," Cranston said, neatly catching the ball. "Hey, good throw. Who knows, you might be Yankee material."

"Not good enough for your Orioles, huh?" Cole shot back. "Mother told me that you always had a secret desire to play for them. I'm a Mets fan myself."

"They're losers. Never align yourself with losers or you might become one." He noticed Cole was getting taller, broader across the shoulders. The suntan seemed to take some of the narrowness from his face, Cranston thought. There was an improvement here, a noticeable one. Maybe Maggie was right—maybe Sunbridge was best for Cole right now.

"They've come from behind before. They did win the pennant once. They aren't going to do it this year, but they might get a shot at it next time."

"Nope, they're losers," Cranston said coolly. "Take my word for it."

"That's your opinion. It doesn't necessarily have to be mine." Cole paused, then asked belligerently, "Did you and Mother decide?"

Cranston's eyes narrowed at his son's tone of voice.

"Yes. You're going to Crystal City High the first semester. We'll evaluate the situation again in February. Be ready at nine tomorrow. I'll be taking you to the school to register."

Watching the expression on Cole's face, Cranston softened a little. He found himself searching for just the right thing to say to his son. "This was not a rash decision on our part, Cole. Your mother has been to the school and talked to the principal. There are some very qualified teachers there if you're interested in learning. Their sports program is enviable, too. Your mother has taken the trouble to arrange a car pool so you won't have to take the bus. I know this doesn't fit in with the plans you had, but you have a lot of years to make plans.

"Your mother said Riley registered himself several weeks ago. He wanted to sign up for several extracurricular activities. It wouldn't have hurt you to sign up at the same time."

Cole snorted. "I'm not Riley and I'm not interested in computers and baseball."

"Just what the hell are you interested in, Cole?" Cranston asked, exasperated.

"Nothing around here, that's for sure. I'll go to Crystal City High, but don't expect any great things from me. I'll put in my time."

"Your grades had better reflect that time, young man."

"Aren't you a little late with this parental concern?"

"Look, I don't have to take any of your bullshit, Cole. I demand your respect and I'll settle for nothing less."

Cole turned till he was facing his father, fixing him with a level stare. "Mother always taught me that respect has to be earned." He turned away and walked toward the house.

By the time Cranston rejoined Maggie, he was scowling. He felt as though he'd just lost the most important case of his career.

"Maggie, if you don't mind, I have a few notes to go over and some letters to sign. I tried to clear the decks before I left, but ended up filling my briefcase. Can you have the cook send me up a pot of coffee, and then I'm going to make it an early night. Have Cole ready by eight-thirty tomorrow morning."

"All right," she said, feeling strangely disappointed; she'd been looking forward to spending the evening with Cranston now that they'd agreed about Cole. "Would you like a sandwich, some cookies or fruit?"

"No, coffee's fine. See you in the morning, Maggie."

"Good night, Cranston."

Maggie spent the rest of the evening curled in a chair, sipping tea and reading a mystery novel. At ten-thirty she was just closing her book when Riley walked in, looking flushed and happy. "Did you have a nice evening?"

"Yes, I did. I'm not late, am I? I asked Cole to come along, but he didn't want to go. I guess he was waiting for his father."

"Cole will be going to Crystal City High with you. His father told him this evening."

Riley rolled his baseball cap in his hands, his short black hair standing up in little spikes on his head. "I hope he goes out for baseball. Aunt Maggie, he has a curve ball that'll knock your eye out."

"Really! I didn't know that. Cole never seemed interested in sports. I know he played tennis and golf at the military academy, but that was mandatory. He did some canoeing too, but I didn't—"

"He's good. Better than me. I don't mean that I'm that good, but I think I might make the team. Cole wouldn't have any competition at all. All the kids asked about him tonight. I explained about his father arriving. . . ."

"Riley, you don't have to make excuses for my son. And don't ever for one minute think you don't belong here. You do." She smiled at him. "I saw that you got a letter from your grandfather today. How is he? Are things all right back home?"

"They miss me. The old one writes short letters, but he says what he has to say. Two of my cousins had girl babies. He grumbled. He asked me if I was going to come home over your Christmas holiday. We'll be off for three weeks. I don't know what to do."

"You don't have to make a decision right away. What I can do is make a reservation for you to make sure you have a flight. It can always be canceled later on if you decide not to go. The holidays are bad for travel from here to any foreign country. Christmas, unfortunately, is the worst. I have the school calendar, and I can do it tomorrow if you want."

"Yes, please. I will explain all that to my grandfather. He has never been to America."

Maggie laughed. "Then why don't we invite him? Mam and Thad would surely come for the holidays if they knew your grandfather would be here."

"I don't think he would come. It's such a long trip. It would be nice, though."

"We'll give it a try. Everyone likes to be invited, even if they have to turn down the invitation. I'll do it first thing tomorrow."

"Thanks, Aunt Maggie," Riley said, and gave her a bone-crushing hug. He kissed her soundly on the cheek before he took the hall steps three at a time. Such long legs, thought Maggie, just like his father. She touched her cheek gently with the tips of her fingers. Her own son had never kissed her or hugged her like that. Never, not even when he was little. How much she'd missed in her life! She sighed. How much she could never recapture.

Impulsively, Maggie looked at the phone and calculated the time difference in England; it would be four-thirty in the morning there. She frowned. Perhaps she could pretend she'd miscalculated . . . Before she could think about what she was doing, she dialed the operator and placed a call to Rand.

A sleep-filled voice came alive when the nasal twang of the operator announced an overseas call from Texas.

"Maggie! Good Lord, what's wrong?"

"I woke you. I'm sorry. I confused the time. There's

nothing wrong. I simply wanted to talk to a friend."

"Well, I am that—a friend, I mean. You're sure nothing is wrong?" Rand asked anxiously.

"Absolutely nothing is wrong," Maggie assured him. "I lost track of time. I'm sorry I woke you. How are you, Rand?" How stupid that sounded! "I enjoyed that funny little card you sent. It made me smile all day."

"That was my intention. I didn't mean it. . . . What I mean is, you didn't have to feel . . . your letter, I enjoyed it, too." No reason to tell her he'd read it at least a dozen times.

"One of these days I'll write you another one," Maggie said, feeling shy. "Have you seen Susan lately?"

"Two weeks ago, and she looked terrible. Ill, very ill. Jerome said it was the heat, but I think it's more than that. I was thinking of calling you and telling you to get in touch with her. If Amelia were here, she'd have her in bed. . . . Sorry I don't have better news."

"That's all right. Overseas calls are usually sad or full of news— I don't know why I said that, Rand. Possibly something from when I was a child and a call came in from overseas and Mam always got upset. . . . Cranston is here," she blurted.

So, Rand thought, that was the problem. "Will he be taking Cole back with him?" he asked in what he hoped was a neutral tone.

"No. We agreed that Cole will go with Riley to Crystal City High for at least one semester. Cole, of course, isn't happy about it, but it's settled. Cranston will be here for two weeks. It's his vacation and he plans to spend some time with Cole."

"Does Cole plan on spending any time with him?"

"Very funny. We're all going to try. . . . How are things in England?" Maggie asked.

"Very merry as usual. That's a joke. Listen, I'm glad you called. I've been thinking of you the past few days. I didn't know if I should answer your letter or not. There were no questions to answer and I didn't want to presume.

I'll be leaving this afternoon on a business trip. I'll drop you a line."

"I'd like that. You know, Riley mentioned tonight that his grandfather would like him to return to Japan for Christmas. I suggested inviting him to Sunbridge, and Riley seemed to like the idea. I thought I'd invite the whole family again. Please try and make it."

"I'll do my best."

"I'll look forward to it and the letter you're going to write to me." She laughed. "I'd better hang up now so you can get back to sleep."

Rand wanted to tell her not to hang up. There was so much he wanted to tell her. So much. He took a deep breath—and said, "Thanks for calling. I'll write. Take care of yourself, and if you do call Susan, make it sound like it was your idea."

"I'll do that. Have a safe trip."

Maggie replaced the receiver. Neither of them had actually said good-bye, she realized.

"Boyfriend?" Cranston asked, coming up behind her.

"Friend." Maggie smiled.

"That's not what your eyes say."

"It really doesn't make a difference, does it? We're being divorced. What are you doing down here, anyway? You said you were turning in for the night."

"Huffy, aren't we? I brought the coffeepot back to the kitchen. I'm an excellent guest. I like to be invited back."

"Good night, Cranston," Maggie snapped as she set about turning off the lights. "I'm going up now myself. Sleep well."

"I'd sleep better if you joined me," he said boldly.

"If that's an invitation, I'm afraid I'll have to decline. You see, the only thing we have left in common now is our son."

"We could try."

"Not tonight we couldn't."

Cranston laughed, a sound that was deep and hoarse. It made Maggie shiver.

Back in her room, she looked at the shiny brass lock on the door. Without hesitation, she turned the latch.

Rand's voice had sounded so clear, she thought as she hung the cornflower-blue silk on a padded, scented hanger. Almost as though he were talking from the next town. And so ... so warm. Was Rand the reason she'd locked her bedroom door? she wondered. Earlier, she'd looked forward to spending the evening with Cranston. If she hadn't called Rand, she might have accepted Cranston's invitation. It had been a long time since she'd had sex. And years since she'd made love. For a while she hadn't known the difference.

Maggie looked at the tiny bedside clock. It was still early; she rarely fell asleep before two or three. She could write some letters, maybe drop a note to Sawyer. Tomorrow she could get her New York address from the boys. Or Susan—should she write or call? Rand had made her illness sound serious. Maybe she should wait and talk to Amelia. There was still time; she and Cary weren't home yet.

Quickly, Maggie penned off a short note asking Amelia to stop by if she wasn't too tired. Then she stood by her door, listening, before she opened it. She felt sneaky and ridiculous. This was her house! Boldly, she walked down the hallway past Cranston's door. No trace of light showed on the hall carpet. Riley's and Cole's rooms were dark, too. When she reached Amelia and Cary's room, she stuffed the small piece of paper between the door handle and the jamb.

Then, on an impulse, Maggie crossed the hall to the darkened nursery. She switched on the light and looked around.

Nothing had changed. The crib, the cradle, and the single bed were still there, all freshly made-up. The rocking horse with the plumed tail stood in the corner, its black eyes staring at the wall. She had the crazy urge to get on it and rock till she was dizzy. The padded rocking chair with its scarlet cushions looked so inviting. She should have sat in that chair and rocked Sawyer. Someone else had done that—Mam and the nurse. Angrily, Maggie marched over to the chair and sat down. Her arms were empty. It was too late.

The toy box with its hand-painted clowns drew her like a magnet. She propped up the lid and stared down at the contents. There was her own Raggedy Ann doll, well worn, well loved. She looked up; Nancy Drew, the Hardy boys, and Cherry Ames marched across the bookshelves, old favorites she'd read over and over again. Maggie's eyes filled with tears. So long ago! Roots. Beginnings. Memories. Most of them were good, especially the ones from this room. Only when she'd moved down the hall had the memories turned sour.

It was several minutes before Maggie realized she wasn't going to find what she was looking for in this room. There had been another child here once, but there was no trace of her now. Sawyer's childhood possessions were locked away in Mam's studio, inaccessible and remote. Just like Sawyer herself.

{{{{{{{{ CHAPTER ELEVEN }}}}}}}}

As Maggie approached her room, she noticed Amelia still in her evening clothes with her arm raised to knock on the door. Maggie wondered how a woman her age could look so vital at midnight.

"What's wrong? I read your note. Cary is asleep on

his feet. Dancing in pointed shoes isn't the treat for him it is for me. Poor dear, what he puts up with. Tell me, what is it?"

"Rand called earlier," Maggie lied, unwilling to admit to something that might be misinterpreted and cause trouble. "He said he saw Susan and she was very ill. He said if you were there, you'd have her in bed. You don't seem the type, or at least you never did, to overreact. I take it Susan is very sick but continuing with the tour."

"Jerome will drive that girl into the ground to get what he wants. He's a nothing without her. I think he knows it, too. He's trying to get as much mileage out of her as he can on this tour." Amelia sighed. "I don't know what we can do, if anything. Certainly we can call. Jerome will get on the phone and say Susan is resting or Susan is sleeping or Susan is shopping. She never gets my messages. I think he even screens her mail. She called me once so upset she could hardly talk—said everyone was ignoring her and so on. I tried explaining, but she wouldn't believe me. She said Jerome would never do anything like that because he loved her. Well, my dear, if *that's* love, it's sick."

"I didn't know that," Maggie said softly.

"There's a lot you don't know. About all of us. I don't mean that to be unkind, but there was a time when you—"

"I know, Aunt Amelia. Things are different now. I was going to wait up a little longer and call around seven or eight Susan's time. What do you think?"

"I think it's a good idea, but if Jerome answers, I don't know how far you'll get. I'll be glad to wait it out with you. Why don't I go down and get us some tea and crackers or something."

"I have a better idea. That's a Galanos you're wearing. Why don't you change and I'll get the tea and crackers."

"A hen party, I love it." Amelia giggled.

"Chicks, Aunt Amelia," Maggie said, smiling. "We're not old enough to be hens."

"Chicks it is. By the way, is the big C here? I saw the rental car in the driveway."

"Yes, Cranston is here. He arrived this evening. He's going to be here for two weeks. At least that's what he says now. Go change. We can talk later."

First Amelia checked on Cary, who was tucked between the satin sheets on their bed, snoring lightly. How handsome he looked! And he was all hers, every goddamn inch of him. Then she removed her gown, draped it over the back of a chair, and quickly changed into a frothy creation of champagne-colored silk with a matching robe. Later, she would remove the carefully applied makeup. No point in frightening Maggie if she didn't have to.

"I'd kill for that creation," Maggie said in awe when the two women had settled in for a cozy talk.

"I almost did." Amelia laughed. "I had to fight this buxom woman from Austin who was six sizes bigger. She said she would diet to get into it. It's a six."

Maggie smiled. This was so nice—she and Amelia, sitting here late at night, sipping tea and talking like equals. Family. "You know, Aunt Amelia, I was always jealous of you and Susan and your close relationship."

"I'm sorry about that. Listen, could we forgo that aunt business? It makes me feel old."

How like Amelia not to go into some long song and dance about it being the best thing at the time, Maggie thought. "How are things going in the building business?" she asked.

"The building hasn't started yet. Cary is such a stickler about everything. Then there's the financing. We're talking millions here. He bit off a good-size chunk and he's doing a lot of chewing. I think we might turn him into a Texan yet."

"You really love him, don't you?"

"Heart and soul, Maggie. Not too long ago I was thinking to myself that all the little affairs, the relationships, the one-night stands—and we've all had them—they were nothing more than exercises for this one grand love. They

always say you'll know when you're in love. I remember
the way I used to ask my mother, and all she'd do was
smile and say, 'You'll know.' She was right. I take it the
grand moment hasn't yet arrived for you."

Maggie grimaced. "Not yet, and time is really flying
by."

"Tell me about it. I just had my last face-lift. No more
nips and tucks. This is it. I don't think I really mind
growing old; it's just that I have this miserable skin that
tends to wrinkle. When I was twenty-nine I must have
looked like I was forty. It's hereditary."

"Don't tell me that," Maggie said, fingering her cheek.

"Not to worry. You got your skin from Billie. We're
talking flawless here."

"I know. There are so many things I'm grateful to her
for. One of these days I'm going to sit down and tell her.
The time just never seems right."

"What do you hear from Sawyer?" Amelia asked pointedly.

"Nothing. Both boys have heard from her. I know she's
in New York, but that's about it."

"She must have been devastated when Rand broke it
off. She was so in love with him, it made me want to cry.
At the time I thought to myself, no woman should ever
allow herself to love a man that way. And look at me—
I'm worse than she is. But Sawyer does have youth on
her side. I'm sure she'll bounce back. On the other hand,
I'd just shrivel up and die if Cary left me. This is between
you and me, Maggie. If you ever say a word, I'll deny
it."

Maggie replenished her tea. "What we talk about is
between us. It will never go any further. Tell me, what
are you doing while Cary is out there beating the bushes?
You're never home."

"I run interference for him. He really respects my opinion. I'm the idea person. So far, it's working out great.
Don't get the notion that Cary can't make a decision or
that he needs my ideas because he doesn't have any of

his own. It's just that we really share everything. A duo, a matched set, a union—call it what you like. I never thought I could be so happy." She leaned back and took a sip of her tea. "Now, enough about me. I've hardly seen you these past weeks."

"I've been busy, too," Maggie said. "If I'm not on this committee, I'm on the next one. I try to get in a set of tennis every day and play golf once a week at least. I've been doing the standard volunteer work that Mam did for a while and sort of carved my own niche. I'm pretty interested right now in a gallery that's set to open soon in Crystal City. The curator is a friend of a friend. He even offered me a job. I said I might be interested on a part-time basis. I want to be here when the boys get home from school. It's all busy work, Amelia, but I'm content."

"You look content, and that's what matters. This is none of my business, but I'm asking anyway. Is there any chance you and Cranston might get together again?"

"I don't think so. Cranston and I have drifted apart. We aren't enemies or anything like that. In fact, right now, we're both working to cement some kind of relationship with Cole."

"Your mother?"

"We're friends. I couldn't want or ask for more."

"Rand?"

Maggie hesitated. "He's a friend."

"And none of my business, right?"

"For now," Maggie said quietly.

"He's my son."

"I know."

"I wouldn't want to see him hurt. I think he's hurting right now."

"I know that," Maggie said, bringing the teacup to her lips. "Are you telling me you're one of those people with long memories?"

"Not at all. I know how precious love—real love—can be. More so when one has the nerve to reach out for it. All I'm saying is each of us does what we have to do for our own personal happiness. Because we're the ones who have to live with that happiness. If it's at someone else's expense, we have to live with that, too."

"Gotcha. That was a nice little sermonette. I enjoyed it." Maggie smiled.

"I rather thought you would. I should have spiked this tea. I'm wide awake. How much longer before we can call Susan?"

Maggie looked at her watch. "At least another twenty minutes. Something's bothering you, isn't it? I've noticed you've been squirming in that chair since you sat down. Do you want to talk about it?"

"Yes. No. Oh, I don't know. I haven't even said anything to Cary yet."

"Come on, Amelia, what you say here isn't going any further. We settled that a while ago."

Amelia paused for a long moment, then took a deep breath and blurted, "My mother's house is for sale!"

"Really!"

"I want to buy it."

"Why? Are you going to settle back here?"

Amelia set her teacup down and leaned toward Maggie. "I don't know if you can understand this, but my father sold that house from under my mother. She wanted to keep it so she could take Moss and me there to learn about her side of the family, the way her family did things. My father wouldn't permit it. He said she didn't need anything but Sunbridge, especially not another house. It was his way of making sure she stayed under his thumb. It almost broke her heart. We used to talk about it. I probably know that house as well as you know this one. I know where every stick of furniture was. Of course, everything was sold off long ago, but I remember it all. In fact, Mam and I made drawings of the whole house. I think they're probably still up in the attic with my old school things. I could redo it."

"Why?" Maggie asked. "Will you live there?"

"Why? Why did you want to come back here? I know

it sounds silly, since I grew up here at Sunbridge. If Mam couldn't have it, maybe I can. Who knows what I would do with it? Look at it, walk through it. Maybe Cary would want to live in it. I didn't say I was definitely going to buy it," Amelia said defensively. "I just said it was for sale. Cary won't be needing me as much once the building gets under way. They don't like women hanging around construction sites. It would give me something to do. Something Mam would have wanted."

"Then you should do it," Maggie said. "I'm for whatever makes you happy. How much is it?"

"I called," Amelia said in a hushed voice.

"How much?" Maggie whispered.

"One million six in an area that's not exactly what it used to be. The surrounding acres are what's driving the price up."

"God! Are you prepared to..."

"Yeah.... I'd liquidate everything to get that house."

"Are you telling me that's all you have?"

"I'm talking about liquidity. Don't forget I'd have to refurbish. It would cost a fortune. I have it; that's no problem."

"The way I see it, Amelia, you have to ask yourself what it's worth to you. Look, if you need some—"

"Maggie! I have more than enough. Cary could buy it for me if I didn't have it, which I do. It's just ... What I mean is, I don't... Hell, I don't know what I mean."

Maggie remained silent. This was a side of Amelia she'd never seen. Now she could understand the deep friendship between her mother and this woman.

"What would you do, Maggie?"

"I'd go for it. Life's too short. If it's going to make you happy, then that's the way to go."

"But I don't know if it will. That's a lot of money. What if I can't handle it?"

"Amelia, I don't think there's anything in this life you can't handle. If it doesn't work, bail out. Resell it. It's that simple."

"I'm not going to rush into it, but on the other hand,

what if someone snatches it out from under me?"

"Take an option. Put down some money till you've thought it through and talked it over with Cary. That's what you're really worried about, right?"

"A little. He's a wonderful person, and sentimental in his own way. But I don't think he'll understand the price tag or what it will cost to refurbish."

"If it's what you want, I think he'll agree."

"Maybe you're right. I'll talk to him about it tomorrow. God, it must be time to call Susan by now."

Maggie tossed and turned all night long. The telephone conversation with Susan had done nothing to reassure her. Jerome had been reluctant to call his wife to the phone, but Amelia had insisted. Susan had sounded weary, as if even a telephone conversation was too much for her, although she'd tried to reassure Amelia and her sister that she was feeling fine.

"Someone's not telling the truth here, and I know it isn't Rand," Amelia had said bitterly after they'd hung up. "I'm worried, Maggie, really worried. I know Susan, and I didn't like the way she sounded. And Jerome saying she was just tired doesn't make sense. It's first thing in the morning over there, for God's sake; she's just had a night's sleep! Another thing—Susan was always a chirpy little bird in the morning; she said it was the best part of the day for her. I don't like it, not at all."

Maggie hadn't liked it, either. She worried over her sister all night long and still felt uneasy the next morning, as the lacy lavender shadows of a pale pink dawn followed her over the footpath to the cemetery on the knoll. When her feet grew wet and slippery from the dew, she bent down to remove her sandals and noticed for the first time that someone had walked the path earlier.

She stopped and looked around, slightly irritated that someone was intruding on what she considered to be her private place. Who from Sunbridge would be out this early? And why the cemetery? She walked softly on her bare feet, not afraid, only curious; she couldn't imagine anything bad happening in this peaceful, tranquil place.

As she came closer to the knoll where the Coleman family rested, her sense of unease increased. She could hear a voice, indistinct and hurried. She crept even closer, careful to make no sound. Something seemed to warn her to remain out of sight. A splash of color, vibrant purple in the pale light, drew her eyes like a magnet. Amelia!

Maggie felt an enormous sense of relief. Of course it would be Amelia; who else would care enough to come to this place? As she debated whether to wait or leave, her aunt's voice carried clearly to her on the fresh, clean air of a beautiful new day. . . .

"I think it's a wise move on my part, Mam. I suppose I'm not being exactly honest with everyone when I tell them I'm buying your old homestead because of you. It's too late for you. Maybe it isn't too late for me. Maybe, maybe, maybe. I'm going to buy that damn house, and I'm going to fix it up just the way it was when you lived in it. Hell, Mam, maybe I'll even live in it myself with Cary. God, I wish you were here. There's so many things I'd like to talk over with you. This awful insecurity. Who would ever believe I live in mortal fear that Cary will leave me?"

"I would," Maggie whispered to the quiet around her.

"You know, Mam, I'm so much older than he is. One of these days he's going to take a good hard look at me and realize just how old I am. If you only knew how much I love this man. I think I could kill for him. . . .

"Did you ever have the feeling that when things are so good, something bad is going to happen? That's exactly how I feel right now. I know something is going to go wrong. It's too perfect. I'm too happy. I wouldn't want to live if Cary left me. I couldn't face the emptiness. Is that how you felt? Is that why you curled up inside yourself? But it wouldn't take me twenty-five years to die, Mam," Amelia whispered. "I know quicker ways."

Maggie turned away, blinded by her tears. She had no right to stand here and listen. She felt like a criminal as she tried to back up the narrow footpath. A sudden purple movement made her dart into the bushes and crouch down. From her position in the shrubbery she had a clear view of Amelia standing by the gravestones. She didn't know whether to laugh or cry when she saw Amelia thumb her nose in the direction of Seth's grave.

Moments later, Amelia's pedicured feet passed by. Maggie waited for what seemed like a long time before she stood up. She made sure there was no sign of Amelia in her purple dress, then stepped onto the footpath.

Cary was just emerging from the shower when Amelia walked into the room. "So, you weren't kidnapped after all. Watching the sun come up?"

"More or less. I was at the cemetery. It seemed like the thing to do when I woke up." Amelia smiled warily.

"You don't have to be defensive with me, Amelia. You don't even have to explain. I thought you were downstairs on the patio watching the sun come up. . . . Is there anything bothering you, hon?"

Amelia sat on the edge of the bed watching her husband dress. She loved the way he kind of took a little hop and then zipped his pants. He grinned, and she grinned back, then took a deep breath. "I want to talk to you about something. I want your opinion and your advice. I suppose that's what I was looking for at the cemetery, but it was kind of a one-sided conversation. I guess I wanted to talk it out in my mind first. . . . Am I making sense?"

"Absolutely. What is it?" Cary asked, sitting down on the bed next to his wife.

"I want to buy a house."

Cary threw his hands up in the air. "So what's the problem?"

"It's not just any house. It's the house that my mother grew up in. I told you how Pap sold it out from under her. I found out it's for sale and I want to buy it. I want to be sure I'm buying it for the right reasons."

"Seems to me that if it was your mother's house, that's reason enough. Buy it."

"You don't mind?"

"Amelia, whatever makes you happy makes me happy. If you don't know that by now, you never will."

"I'll have to renovate. There's probably a lot of work to be done. The price is high, but then all real estate these days is high. I have the money; that's not the problem."

"Then what is the problem?"

"I'm not sure. I don't know anything about real estate. Maybe you won't even like the house. I have diagrams and a picture up in the attic. If I do decide to buy it, I want it to be exactly the way it was when Mam lived there. I thought it would give me something to do when you're out on the construction site."

"I like the idea. Home is wherever you are, babe. You know that. And don't worry about what you know and don't know. Who the hell ever thought I'd go into the building business? Go for it."

"The price is one million six."

"Steep. If you want it, get it."

"No. Do you still think I can do it?"

"Hell, yes. Just don't pay cash. Take as big a mortgage as you can get. It'll be one hell of a tax write-off."

"Mortgage? I was going to pay cash."

"Never pay cash. Always use someone else's money. How do you think I got where I am? You're going to have to palaver a little."

"Oh, yeah." Amelia grinned. "Seems like I just said that to you not too long ago."

"I took your advice. Now it's your turn. Go to whoever owns the house now, make an offer, then go to the bank. I wish I could go with you, but you know my schedule today. If you need me, call."

"I will. . . . You know, Amelia, I feel as though I belong. Almost. Thanks to you, everyone has taken a real interest and no one has screwed me. I don't expect they will, either. A handshake is good enough. You did all that for me."

"That's what I'm here for."

"Oh, lady, you are so wrong. This is what you're here for."

Amelia giggled as Cary's busy hands fumbled with the ties of her dress. "You're going to be late," she warned.

"Who cares? I'm the boss, remember? This is more important. You come first, honey. Remember that."

Amelia sighed, growing languid now in his embrace.

"Now let's do what we do best."

When he held her like this, close against him, his hands urgent and demanding, taking possession of her before warming and slowing to tender caresses, Amelia's heart pounded with an answering passion. She could be young again in Cary's embrace, young and breathless and just a touch innocent. There was nothing to think about except his need, nothing to fill her world except this man. She loved him, needed him more than she wanted him to know. She wanted to satisfy him, to pleasure him, for only in his pleasure would she find her own.

Cary felt his wife yield to his embrace and offer herself to his hands and lips. He wondered at the miracle of her, at the way she instinctively knew what caress would heighten his desire, at the way she was always accessible to him, never holding back her favors. She was an experienced lover, knowledgeable of her own body, of what would make her respond and bring her satisfaction. Yet there was something fragile and innocent about her, too, and she always brought a freshness to their lovemaking that excited him and made him anticipate being locked in her embrace the next time. She imbued him with a sense of his own manhood, made him know and feel his own power; but most of all, Amelia made him know that he was loved, unconditionally, forever. That, more than anything, coming from a background where love, if given at all, was given in very small measures, made him completely hers.

Cary rolled onto his back, bringing her with him, putting her in the female-superior position they both enjoyed. Her knees gripped his hips as she rode him, her hands braced against his broad chest to push herself backward and take him deep inside herself. He steadied her movements by gripping her buttocks, supporting her with his pelvis, and measuring his movements to hers. Soon he felt the initial tremblings that told him she was near her climax. He watched her face, saw her close her eyes and throw her head back, an expression of sheer joy illuminating her features. That he could bring this woman such rapture, this woman he loved so well, brought him a special kind of satisfaction, a certain desire and passion. Just as he was aware of her body closing tightly around his, as her undulations deepened and a kittenish sound began to rise in her throat, he rolled her to the side, following after, his hips still imprisoned between her thighs, He buried himself deep within her, mimicking the rhythmical movements she had made while astride.

Amelia clung to Cary, following him with her body, answering him with her soul. That she could satisfy this man was a joy beyond joy, and at the moment they shared their climax she laughed—a soft, deep sound of triumph.

Maggie was uneasy about several things this morning as she sipped her coffee at the breakfast table. First of all, there'd been that ludicrous conversation with Jerome and Susan; and secondly there was Amelia. Each time she pondered one, the other seemed to break into her thoughts.

Amelia. . . . Maggie knew her aunt dearly loved Cary Assante, but she was also aware of the difference in their ages. At the moment, it seemed Carry was also very much in love with his wife; but how long would that last? Forever? Was anything forever?

Cranston was the first one down, looking fit in a striped blue cotton knit pullover and casual white duck pants that hugged the lean length of his thighs. He helped himself to breakfast from an array of food laid out on the sideboard, then took a seat across from Maggie and poured himself coffee from the electric percolator.

"Nothing like life in the country, is there?" he asked enthusiastically. "Maggie, darling, why don't we all go on a picnic today? We can leave as soon as Coleman and I get back from registering him at the high school."

Maggie looked across the table, hardly believing her ears. "A picnic? I didn't know you liked picnics. I don't believe we ever went on one together. Or did we?"

"No, we didn't. We should have. There's a lot of things we should have done, Maggie. Maybe it's not too late to start. I'm here now; I have all the time in the world. Why don't we try getting to know each other again? It might make things easier between us. For Cole's sake," he added casually.

"Thank you for not throwing blame on me, Cranston," Maggie said softly. "I wasn't much of a wife, I know." She hesitated. "I'm not sure about the picnic, though. I have two meetings and a luncheon scheduled for today. I gave my word. People expect me. I can't just—"

Cranston leaned across the table. "Cancel them, Maggie," he said, his voice husky.

Again Maggie hesitated. A picnic might be fun. There was no denying Cranston could be pretty persuasive when he wanted to be. Right now, his handsomeness, the tone of his voice, the vulnerability he was displaying, made it hard to believe they'd been so unhappy together. All the past hurts, the destruction they'd heaped upon one another, seemed so far away. . . .

"Okay, you've got yourself a date," she said, getting up from the table. "Just let me make a few phone calls and have Martha arrange a picnic basket for us. It should all be done by the time you come back with Cole."

Cranston rewarded her with a boyish smile, one she hadn't seen in what seemed like a hundred years.

When Cranston returned from Crystal City he found Maggie waiting for him, dressed in hip-hugging jeans and a loose-fitting sky-blue shirt, which she'd tied in a knot at her slender waist to expose a small patch of sun-darkened belly. Cranston drew in his breath. In a pair of scuffed sneakers with rolled-down socks and a bouncy ponytail, she looked about sixteen.

"Where's Cole?" Maggie asked, looking behind Cranston for their son.

"He said picnics didn't exactly turn him on, so I dropped him off at some kid's house to go swimming."

"Whose house?" Maggie demanded. "Don't you know who it was?"

"Mike something or other. Hey, don't get so worked up," Cranston said soothingly. "I'd like to think I was the main attraction at this picnic."

Maggie forced herself to relax. There could be other picnics with the three of them and after all, if she and Cranston got to know each other better this time, wouldn't that eventually benefit Cole? "You won't be the main attraction once you smell Martha's fried chicken," she laughed gaily.

Cranston felt the tension leave his shoulders. Not for anything did he want Maggie to know that he'd lied to Cole about this picnic in order to have her all to himself. "Do you have a spot in mind?" he asked as he led Maggie out the door and relieved her of the picnic basket.

"I know a beautiful spot. Susan, Riley, and I used to play there when we were little. We'd carry out play dishes and Riley would carry the picnic basket, and we'd stay there for hours."

"So, you did have some good times here, after all," Cranston said smoothly.

"Of course I had some good times," she said defensively. "It just so happens that the bad outweighed the good." She smiled. "You should have seen Riley trying to carry the basket. We had to tie a string on it so he could pull it. . . . I miss him, and there are times when I feel so guilty." The moment the words were out Maggie regretted them. Cranston was not someone she wanted to confide in.

"Why in the world should you feel guilty about Riley?" he asked. "He was killed during wartime. Is that why you brought young Riley here?"

Maggie shrugged evasively. "I'm alive. I'm going on a picnic with a handsome man. Riley won't even be able to go on a picnic or play ball with his son. I feel bad about that. And no, that's not why I brought Riley here. The boy has every right, Cranston. All of this," she said, waving her hand, "would be his if his father hadn't died. I can't forget that and I won't. I thought Cole and Riley would become friends since they're cousins and the same age. Unfortunately, Cole is prejudiced, much like you, Cranston. But Riley is doing well on his own. He's got all sorts of friends and"—she grinned—"he's already beating the girls off with a stick. The children have accepted him more readily than they've accepted Cole. But it's Cole's fault. He simply isn't interested. He doesn't even seem interested in girls. Academically, though, I think they're going to be neck and neck." Maggie pointed down a small incline. "So, what do you think?"

Cranston peered over the small ridge to gaze down where his wife was pointing. "Looks like a glade of some sort."

"It is. There's a small spring-fed pond that makes the ferns and bushes grow. There're some pines on the other side. It smells so good. All pungent and woodsy. Susan used to fall asleep on the fern fronds. We'd make little pallets. First the pine needles, then the ferns. Do you want to?" Maggie asked eagerly with a peculiar light in her eyes.

"Why the hell not!" Cranston shouted as he slid down the embankment, Maggie right behind.

They worked in companionable silence arranging their fragrant pallets. Maggie knew Cranston was having fun in spite of himself. It was probably the first time he'd actually put his penknife to use. She felt like a kid herself.

"I think mine's a little neater," she said when they'd finished, "and I didn't have a knife. But I'm experienced.

You have to be careful the way you break off a fern frond.
Yours will do, but you left too much end on the frond;
it's going to prick you. I'll spread the cloth and you can
take out the goodies. Martha always outdoes herself for
picnics."

"She must have; this basket was a bastard to carry. I
have a crick in my neck."

"Don't complain, Cranston; just enjoy. I think both of
us have forgotten how to do that. I'm getting on track
now, and you should, too."

"What's that supposed to mean?" Cranston demanded.

"It means whatever you want it to mean. For me it
meant time to stop and relax, take stock of myself. The
only person who can make you miserable is yourself. The
only person who can make you a workaholic or an alcoholic is yourself. In the end we all have to pay our dues.
I'm lucky—I woke up in time to realize I didn't like my
life. I was existing. I wasn't living."

Cranston bit into a crisp chicken leg and chewed
thoughtfully as he listened to his wife. An hour later he'd
learned more about her than he'd known in all the years
they'd been married.

"And another thing," Maggie said, pointing her chicken
leg in his direction. "I know why you're here. I know
why you came the first time, too. Even if Cole hadn't
called, you'd have found a way to get to me. There was
a lot of hatred there, on both sides, when I left. You were
going to try and get custody of Cole so it would look good
on the divorce decree. And Cole played right into your
hands. I also know that you have the opportunity right
now to buy out the other partners in your firm, and that
you're considering it. It'd be a real coup for you. . . . Ah,
I was right. I can see it in your face." Maggie shook her
head. "What happened to your courtroom poker face?"

"I left it in New York," Cranston said shortly.

"I left a lot of things in New York, too. This is a new
life for me. As I said, I'm on track now. There's a lot I
still have to do. I know now there are some things I can

never make right again and I—I'll have to live with that."

Cranston leaned back with his head cupped in his clasped hands. "Neither of us worked at the marriage. I'm willing to take my share of the blame. How in the hell did we ever manage to have a child?"

"If you want the details, I can give them to you." Maggie laughed, then busied herself repacking the hamper. "Between the two of us we almost destroyed Cole, you know. The fact that we can talk now and actually be civil to each other is a big step." She stopped for a moment. "I can't even believe you're here. When was the last time you actually took a vacation?"

"Maybe ten years. I can't even remember."

"Was it all worth it?"

"Right now I'd have to say yes. Yesterday I probably would have said no. I am what I am, Maggie. The firm is my life. Maybe it shouldn't be, but it is."

"And if you do buy out the others and the firm becomes yours, what then?"

Cranston shrugged. "King of the heap. Come here and lie next to me."

Despite herself and her better intentions, Maggie allowed Cranston to pull her down beside him and cradle her head against his shoulder. And even though it felt so right, so easy, to be here beside him this way, she still felt uneasy, as if she were being taken in somehow. "I'm not sure this is such a good idea, Cranston," she forced herself to say, her voice light, a shade breathless. "We're being divorced, remember? By the way, when is the court date?"

"The first week in January sometime. I forget the exact date. Are you telling me," Cranston asked as he propped himself up on one arm, "that you don't feel anything, anything at all?"

"I won't let you manipulate me. If and when I want to go to bed with you, it'll be because it's what I want, not what you manipulated me into doing." She moved away from him a little. "Now, about the divorce. We have to discuss Cole. I don't want you just walking in here and snatching him away from me."

Instantly Cranston lost all his amorous thoughts. "Cole is old enough to make his own decisions," he said sourly. "A judge will talk to him, and it'll pretty much be what the boy wants."

"Damn you, Cranston, that's not good enough! You gave up custody. What'll it take for you to keep it that way?"

"Absolutely nothing. Cole is the one who is unhappy. Look, Maggie, I don't like to take potshots at you, but you were an unfit mother. A drunken, unfit mother. Judges pay attention to things like that."

"And what does that say for you? You wanted out so bad, you signed away your rights to your son to a drunken, unfit mother."

"What that would mean in a courtroom is Coleman money intimidated and paid off. Next question?"

"You son of a bitch! Tell me you wouldn't do that to Cole and me."

"We all do what we have to do. Those are your words, Maggie. I'm just repeating them."

"Money, that's it, isn't it?" Maggie cried. "You need money to buy the firm. Using all of yours, paying bank loans, will strap you. Now, let's see, where can you get money at no interest? Who'd be sucker enough to go for a deal like that?"

"There's probably one or two people walking around who might go for a deal like that," Cranston said smoothly. "Your mother, for instance. Isn't Thad going to run for office? I know some very influential people. You could come out smelling like a lily. On the other hand..."

"You bastard!"

"Is that the same as son of a bitch?" Cranston laughed.

"And to think I almost made love to you. You're vile and disgusting."

"You're wonderful, exciting, and I feel as if there's an electric current running through me. Forget all this bullshit

and make love with me," Cranston said, pulling her back
into his arms.

Maggie struggled. Cranston's heart was beating so fast,
she thought he would collapse—or was it her own heart?
It had been so long since she'd been with a man. Her
struggles increased, then grew weaker as Cranston's arms
pinned her to him.

She knew exactly what she was responding to—this
was passion, not love. This was frustration, even desire,
but it was not love. Over and over she repeated this to
herself, issuing warnings that were overridden by the feel
of his body pressing into hers, by the heat of his hands
as he fumbled with the buttons on her blouse.

"Don't fight me, Maggie. You know you want it as
much as I do. We were always good together; we can be
good again." He was breathing into her ear; there was a
desperate edge to his voice.

Maggie's fingers dug into the flesh of Cranston's back.
What he was saying wasn't true. They weren't always
good together. There had been times when he'd rejected
her, refused her, played nasty little games to punish her.
But there had been times when he'd deemed her "worthy,"
times when her self-esteem had almost equalled his; those
times had been good, very, very good. "Don't do this,
Cranston," she pleaded. "I don't want it; I don't want
you!"

"Yes, you do. You know you do." Suddenly he ripped
her shirt apart, popping the buttons, revealing her breasts.
"Look at yourself. Look at the way your body wants me
to touch it, to kiss it, like this..." He lowered his head
and took one pouting nipple into his mouth, running his
tongue over the hard nub, biting it lightly. "I can feel the
heat coming off you, Maggie." His hand slipped between
her legs, rising upward along the inside of her thigh.
"You're already wet for me, aren't you? You were always
wet for me, Maggie, and it always drove me crazy." He
was gasping the words against her mouth, claiming her
lips, invading the soft recesses with his tongue. "Show

me how wet you are, Maggs. Show me," he demanded, working the zipper of her jeans, exposing her flesh to the filtered sunlight dappling through the trees.

Fireworks shot off inside Maggie's brain. Her mind was telling her one thing while her body demanded another. Against her will she was helping him, kicking her legs free of jeans and underpants. He laughed with satisfaction to find her wet and ready for him.

"You're no good, Cranston," she breathed, "no damn good. But I want you, good God, I want you!"

"What do you want, Maggie?" he teased. "Show me. Tell me!"

"This!" She wriggled beneath him, finding him with her hand, touching the hardness of him. "Don't tease me. Don't do this to me," she nearly cried, her voice a choked sob. "Take me now, for God's sake, take me now!"

When it was over, Maggie lay in Cranston's arms. He could be gentle now; the first chaotic rush of passion was over; they had both gotten what they wanted. Tears blurred Maggie's eyes. It shouldn't have happened; she never should have placed herself in this situation. She was ashamed of herself, ashamed of the need she had revealed to him. Another weapon, another triumph for Cranston.

"Why so quiet, Maggs?" he asked, nuzzling her ear. "Wasn't it good for you? It was wonderful for me."

Maggie remained silent.

"Don't be sorry, Maggs," he whispered, as though reading her thoughts. "It was inevitable. We haven't gotten over each other. You know it and so do I. This is the way it should have been all along. I can't tell you how sorry I am for the bastard I was to you. To you and to Cole. I don't know how you'll ever forgive me, but I'm begging you to try. Please try, Maggs, please."

A rush of emotions rebounded through Maggie. How long she had waited to hear those words. How much she needed to hear them. Cranston continued to purr in her ear. She listened, she dreamed...*Family!*

{{{{{{{{{ CHAPTER TWELVE }}}}}}}}}

The loft in midtown Manhattan was a work of art, thanks to its renovator, Adam Jarvis. He was a political cartoonist whose biting satire caused Washington to gasp as often as it cackled in glee. He was successful, semisatisfied with his life, and in love with his loft. When he'd purchased it years ago for an outrageous sum of money, he'd spent weekends renovating, and it was now pretty much what he wanted—open space, skylights, lush green plants, colorful furniture with brilliant cushions, shiny oak floors that were almost like mirrors. Probably the only thing it lacked was a woman's touch, and at times he wasn't sure even a woman could improve it, except to lend her presence to the vast openness. Four thousand square feet of space was a lot for one person. His only companion until Sawyer had arrived was a female cat with a ferocious appetite, named Marble. Probably, he was the only political cartoonist in the United States to walk a cat on a leash and carry a poop scoop.

Work wasn't going well today. It hadn't been going really well since Sawyer moved in. It wasn't that she bothered him; it was that she was so desperately unhappy and there was nothing he could do to ease her pain.

She arrived, this old high school chum and college buddy, in the middle of the night, tear streaks on her cheeks and lips quivering. She'd cried a lot that night and he'd held her like a father holding a daughter, but there were no words, no comfort he could give her.

He'd suggested she move in, and she'd agreed. Room-
mates only, though, she'd said. She'd insisted on paying
her share of the expenses. And she did, to the penny. She
didn't tidy up after him and he liked that. She didn't
interfere in any way with his work schedule. Once she'd
transferred to the Coleman New York office, she was up
and out of the loft by seven in the morning; most times
she didn't come home till eight or nine in the evening,
taking her meals in restaurants if she ate at all. He noticed
a weight loss and debated whether or not to speak to her
about it. He personally liked to see a little meat on a
woman's bones. Probably because he himself was so tall
and rangy. He ate like a horse and never gained an ounce.
Sawyer always said he looked like a string bean with curly
red hair.

Sawyer. He'd adored her when he'd first met her and
had fallen shamelessly in love with her soon after. Friends,
she'd said. She had things to do and places to go. Relationships only got in the way of her goals. The years had
gone by, and Adam remained a bachelor—by choice. He'd
never been able to get Sawyer out of his thoughts. Time
and distance had dimmed his memory a little, but he'd
continued to love her. He loved her now. It was that
simple. Only he couldn't tell her. She needed a friend,
not some lovesick cartoonist.

The blank paper on the drawing board stared at him.
For a moment he felt frightened. What if he was losing
it? What if Sawyer and her pain consumed him to the
point where he couldn't work? He stirred uneasily. Maybe
he should water his plants or make something to eat. Hell,
he could even put the dishes in the dishwasher. That's
exactly what he should do, since the sink was filled to
overflowing.

He got up and headed for the kitchen, his cat-green
eyes peering across the dim space to where Sawyer was
sitting writing a letter. She wrote a lot of letters these
days. The only personal mail she received was from the
boys in Texas and her grandmother in Vermont.

The Coleman clan was something he didn't like to think about. He was from Texas himself; he knew a thing or two about clans. His own family was so goddamn normal, it was disgusting. When he'd first met Sawyer, he used to wish the Jarvis family had a scandal, too, so he and Sawyer could be branded together. He'd been a staunch, feisty defender of Sawyer's parentage; he'd even squired her to dance recitals and plays, generally making an ass of himself. Oh, how he'd suffered at Sawyer's hands. God, how he loved her.

When the last glass had been added to the dishwasher, Adam filled the soap dispenser and turned it on. Jesus, the thing sounded like a jet cutting back on its engine power.

Sawyer came up behind him and tweaked his ear. "Susy homemaker," she said fondly. "You got any apples?"

"Do I have any apples? Do I have any apples? Do I look like a supermarket? The answer is no. I have some oranges, though. Good, juicy ones. Real orange. No pits. I'll peel it for you." Christ, how could he not have apples? Sawyer loved apples. "Wait a minute. I have some apple juice. No good, huh? Shit!"

"I'll take the orange. For God's sake, what's wrong with you?" Sawyer asked, noticing his agitation.

"Wrong? Nothing." His hands were busily peeling the orange. He offered it to her as though it were a prize. "It's not a good orange unless the juice trickles down your chin," he said inanely.

"I know. If the pulp doesn't stick in your front teeth, it's worth shit, right? That's what you always used to tell me at school. Remember the time Mrs. Snyder sent you out of class for picking your teeth?"

"You remember that?"

"I remember everything. Sometimes I feel as though my head is so full it'll burst. . . . I don't want you looking like that at me. I'm not worth it," Sawyer said flatly. "Forget it, Adam."

Adam's heart pounded. Christ, was he that transparent? "Nick Deitrick was right. You are ugly. I wasn't sure until now."

"You aren't exactly a prince, you know," Sawyer said lightly. "Nick never knew which end was up."

Adam grinned. "You always were a bitch."

"That's true. But you were never a bastard." She shook her head and turned away. "I'm sorry. I am grateful, Adam. I had no right coming to you with my problems and just moving in. I can leave if you—"

"Did I complain? You aren't bothering me. I'm worried about you, Sawyer. Listen, I'm ahead on the strip," he lied. "Why don't we take off a few days and get some sun. Florida, California, wherever. You could use a break. You're killing yourself. Take a look in the mirror."

"I can't take the time off. Besides, work is the best thing for me right now. I mean it, Adam, if I'm cramping your style—"

"You're not. I told you I was between ladies at the moment. A hiatus, if you will."

"Okay." Sawyer noticed the relief in his eyes. "You having trouble with the strip today?"

"Sort of. I have days when nothing I do seems right. I must have gone through a ream of paper already."

"When all else fails, take a potshot at Reagan. Your fans'll love it. By the way, did I tell you Cole is now a fan of yours? He said you're sharp." She yawned. "I think I'll turn in now. I'll wash the towels tomorrow; it's my turn."

"Damn right it's your turn. I had to call Bloomie's to order more this morning."

"Tell me you didn't do that!"

"Have I ever lied to you? I had thirty-six towels when you moved in here. There are thirty-six towels in the laundry room. All of them dirty. You're the one who uses a towel for her hair, one for her body, and one for her face."

"You went into the laundry room and counted the dirty towels and didn't wash them? You didn't wash them, but you counted them! That's disgusting!"

"It's your turn," Adam said loftily.

"How many did you order?"

"Three dozen."

"You're nuts."

"I know. Go to bed. I just got an idea."

"Thanks for the orange and the conversation."

"Anytime. Sleep well."

In her room, Sawyer threw the letter she'd written to her grandmother into her handbag; she'd mail it on the way to the office in the morning. Then she undressed, throwing her clothes on a chair, and sat down wearily.

It was time for bed. Time for sleep. She was so tired; always so tired. It seemed a lifetime since she'd left Sunbridge like a thief in the night. For so long afterward she'd hoped, even prayed, that Rand would come after her. But he hadn't, and now nothing seemed worthwhile. Not even her job, which she loved. She was just going through the motions of living, unable to take pleasure in anything. Rand was all she thought about.

Humiliation and rejection. She fed on humiliation and rejection, knowing she would never be able to help herself: the need she felt could never be filled. But it didn't really matter now. Nothing mattered.

Tears of self-pity rolled down her cheeks. She made no move to stop them or wipe them away. Crying always made her sleep. Tomorrow she would simply wear her dark glasses. There wouldn't be anyone at the office to notice except the janitor. If only there were some way she could fill this aching void inside her. Would the time ever come when she could put all of this behind her and start a new life? Would she ever be whole again?

The satiny quilt caressed her bare shoulders as she snuggled beneath it. The loft creaked and then settled into quietness.

Two hours later, Adam checked on Sawyer. She was sleeping soundly, her hand cupped on her cheek. He went into the laundry room and started the washing machine

filled with towels. He waited through the cycle, then tossed
the load into the dryer. He drank three cups of coffee
while he waited for the towels to dry. He folded three
fluffy yellow towels and laid them gently at the foot of
Sawyer's bed. The last thing he did before going to bed
was write a note to himself to call Gristedes and order
apples.   *

Maggie lay beside Cranston in Jessica's high bed. He
was breathing lightly and felt warm beside her. She marveled at how quietly he slept while she tossed and turned
restlessly. In the mornings, Cranston's side of the bed was
smooth and unruffled, while hers looked as though a flock
of chickens had been scratching and nesting.

Cranston's vacation was almost over. Day after tomorrow he would leave. She'd heard him speaking on the
telephone, making arrangements with the office to ready
his caseload and begin making appointments. Two weeks.
A time of renewal, Maggie had tried to convince herself.
A time to make a fresh start with Cranston, for them to
get to know each other again; hopefully, to like each other.
And it had almost worked.

Cranston had been saying all the right things at all the
right times. She had responded to his mesmerizing eyes
and his softly spoken words. Wanting and needing to
believe, to trust. Oh, yes, she had to admit to herself that
her needs for husband and family were very real. Husband, security, identity—they all meant the same thing.
The divorce proceedings could be stopped at any time,
or so Cranston said. He'd made it sound so tempting.

She looked over at him, resisting an impulse to brush
the lock of hair off his forehead. She'd come so close to
falling in love with him all over again. He'd as much as
told her she could have it all—dutiful husband, full-time
son, the entire ball of wax—if only she agreed to move
back to New York with him, give up living at Sunbridge,
turn her back on everything she loved, everything she'd
fought for her entire life. Oh, and one thing more. Cran-

ston's law firm. For a cool three million dollars it could be all his. All she had to do was supply the three million.

Maggie was a big girl now; she'd learned the rules of the game. The money didn't bother her. But Cranston did. If she went back to New York with him, she would soon become just another of his possessions, like his town car and his sailboat. There was every danger he would devour her again, as he had once before—telling her how to dress, what to say, how to behave, making her doubt herself, always feeling his disapproving eye. He would use her, and he'd use Cole if she allowed it.

Reaching across the pillow, Maggie gentled the stray lock of hair that gave Cranston such a boyish look. She supposed that all along, despite her bravado and heroic attempts to straighten out her life, she had secretly wanted the security of being Cranston's wife, to erase the rejection, to have a second chance at having a family, of belonging to her own little family. Yet despite his smooth words and heated passions these past two weeks, he had made no mention of love, of growing old together, of sharing. Things Maggie wanted, things Billie had found with Thad. With Cranston, Maggie would have an agreement, a contract. This for that. Whatever he wanted.

The mattress shifted slightly as Maggie swung her legs over the side. This wasn't what *she* wanted. She didn't want to be an extension of her husband; she wanted to belong to herself, to be admired for herself and loved for herself. It might even be exciting to see what else might be in store for Maggie Coleman Tanner on her own terms. If Cranston wanted her, he'd have to take her on those terms.

Maggie bent over slightly as her foot traced a pattern on the floor, searching for her slippers. When she felt herself drawn backward into Cranston's arms, she didn't struggle against it. It would be a very nice way to say good-bye.

{{{{{{{{ CHAPTER THIRTEEN }}}}}}}}

There was a true October chill in the air as Amelia made her way to the lawyer's office. She stood outside the old building, in deep thought. Was she doing the right thing? She hoped so. It felt right.

She took a look around at the brilliant foliage. Everything was so lush, so radiant; it reminded her of autumns she'd spent in the North Country of England. Texas wasn't usually this blessed in October. More often, the long, hot, dry summers forced the trees and grasses to suffer a premature death. But this year summer seemed to have vanished quickly, bringing warm sunny days and brisk, cool evenings. It was going to be so nice lingering in the house with a fire blazing merrily in the hearth. Maybe once in a while Cary could take time off from his project to join her for a picnic-style lunch in front of the fireplace. And in the winter evenings, they could curl up there together and sip sherry, talking quietly, sharing ideas and business decisions. She could almost see him sitting there with her, the glow from the fire highlighting his classic Roman features and throwing shots of gold into his wavy dark hair. He'd look at her with those falcon's eyes, and she would read his desire there, hear him laugh softly as she went into his arms to be crushed against his chest. The daydream was so strong, so forceful, Amelia's heart began thumping. Determinedly, she pushed open the door to the Abramson building. The old house would be hers.

An hour and twenty minutes later, Amelia pulled her silver Porsche into the driveway of her new house. Hers. Signed, sealed, and delivered. She tried to swallow past the lump in her throat. Mam's house.

"This is for you, Mam," she said, fitting the key into the old lock. She wondered if it was a lie.

It was an incredibly old house, well over a hundred years old. Nearly thirty acres surrounded it, a major reason the price had been so steep. The structure itself looked incongruous out here in the hill country of Texas; it would have seemed much more at home in a small seaport in Maine overlooking the harbor. Three stories high, with a widow's walk cresting the sloping mansard roof ... Amelia had always thought it looked like something out of *Peter Pan*. Clapboard walls and brick walks and drive. Sixteen rooms in all, every one of them holding a hundred layers of paint, even the beautiful chestnut woodwork. Only the front door and the staircase spiraling through the center of the house seemed to have escaped the painters' merciless brushes. Amelia had already decided she would save what she could of the original structure and decor, and remodel what she couldn't. Her efforts would be a tribute to Jessica and would ultimately create a home for Cary and herself.

The briefcase she'd brought with her contained drawings and diagrams of what she planned to bring to life here. What a celebration she and Cary would have when it was all finished! Dinner by candlelight in front of a fire. Champagne, pheasant under glass—Cary had always said he wanted to eat pheasant under glass—the works. Cary would smile in awe over the miracle she created and then they'd make love and live happily ever after.

For a moment she felt frightened. Was it possible she'd bitten off more than she could chew. She opened her briefcase and took out a yellow pad, fresh and unwrinkled, and a pencil with a sharp point. Ready to make notes, she chewed thoughtfully on the end of the eraser. She decided to make a list of everything to be done, beginning with the kitchen, then the library, front parlor, and so on through the house. Purposefully she made her way to the door behind the stairs.

Hours later, when she'd finished her inspection, Amelia felt depressed. This was supposed to be fun, a lark of sorts. Her list was monstrously long. The previous owners had done a lot of work, modernizing most of the house. Thank God they'd at least left the wainscoting in the library and front parlor. And the chestnut staircase— that, too, was beautiful. Hand-carved. She knew from her mother that the post at the bottom end of the landing unscrewed. Jessica had often told her she hid things in the little hidey-hole

Amelia caressed the antique wood, wondering if the previous owners had been aware of the secret. Her touch was gentle as she twisted the carved pineapple. She didn't expect to find anything and sure enough, the little cavity was empty. Yielding to her curiosity, she walked up thirteen steps to the landing and twisted the second pineapple, then hesitated a moment before putting her hand into the small space. Her eyes widened when she withdrew a brass ring, tarnished and black, and a small piece of yellowed paper with brown edges, obviously ripped from a notebook. Little shavings of the paper fell away as Amelia carefully unfolded the note and read its contents.

Her eyes filled with tears that slowly rolled down her cheeks. Her father had written this little note to her mother over sixty years ago. It was short and to the point, just like Seth himself.

To the prettiest girl in all Texas,
    Some day, Jess, I'll give you a ring full of dia-monds. I'll build you the biggest, fanciest house in all of Texas. I ain't much for writing but you can take these words for true. If your finger gets green from this ring, keep it in your pocket to remind you of me and my promise.

                                        Seth Coleman

So much for promises. Amelia swiped at her tears with the back of her dusty hand, leaving streaks down her cheeks. He'd made good on his promise to her mother. He had given her a ring full of diamonds. And Sunbridge was the biggest, fanciest house in this part of Texas. It might have its equal in size, but she knew there was none better. The only problem was, Sunbridge hadn't been built for Jessica; it had been built for Seth himself. Jessica had just resided in it. But she'd saved the ring and the note in her secret place.

Angry now at what she'd found, Amelia whirled about. There was no one to scream or yell at. Her mouth was grim, her teeth clenched, when she returned the brass ring and note to the empty cavity. Not for the world would she ever open it again.

She turned to the light switch on the landing, then peered over the banister railing at the chandelier. Most of the crystals were gone. It must have been magnificent in its day, she thought.

Jessica had once told her it had been installed when she'd been about seven, during the Christmas holidays. When it was turned on, she'd said, she gasped in awe because it looked as if someone had taken a big blanket full of diamonds and flung them into the air. Amelia decided this was one project she personally would undertake. She made a note on her yellow pad: cleaning the crystals.

She looked at her watch. It was getting late. The house would be dark soon, and there was no power. Tomorrow the electric company, the phone company, and the furnace company were coming to turn everything on.

Tomorrow she would go up into the attic. Who knew what treasures she would find? She loved attics. Susan and Rand used to play in the attic back in England. God, that was so many years ago. Numbers made her itchy. Always numbers.

Halloween arrived. Maggie scurried between the new art gallery, her Red Cross work, and all her various meetings. Having an eye for detail and decoration had put her

at the top of the list of volunteers. Somehow—she wasn't
sure how—she'd ended up being the chairperson for
Crystal City High's October dance festival committee.
Both boys had dates for the dance. As far as she knew,
it was the first boy-girl date for either of them. In a way
she was pleased about being on the committee, since it
was Cole who'd asked her to help out. He certainly seemed
different these days, almost as though he were coming
around.

The day before the dance, Maggie sat at the dining
room table in front of a pile of papers and lists stacked
next to boxes of paper pumpkins and crinkly witches, all
of which had to be organized, folded up, and then tied.
As she worked, she reflected that she should have recruited
some of the girls from the boys' classes; but they were
always so busy with after-school activities. She really
could use some help.

"Could you use some help?"

Maggie looked up in stunned surprise. Cole stood
watching her from the dining room doorway. "As a matter
of fact, I could. Actually, I could use about six pairs of
hands."

"All I have are two, but they're all yours," Cole said,
sitting down next to his mother. "Just tell me what to do."

Mother and son worked together amicably for a while.
Maggie noticed that Cole had a good eye for color, and
his nimble fingers sorted through the piles and stacks of
papers. Within minutes, it seemed, things were organized.

"Who's going to decorate the gym tomorrow?" Cole
asked.

Maggie laughed. "You're looking at her. When I was
put on this committee I had three helpers. I'm what's
left."

Cole was silent for a few seconds. "I'll help you. Standing on a ladder isn't one of the things you do best. I'll
see about getting out of my first class. I'm carrying an A
average so far, so I don't think it'll be a problem." His
voice was gruff, as if he were afraid she might reject his
offering.

"I'd like that if you can manage it," Maggie said softly. "And you're right; hanging streamers from a ladder isn't one of the things I do best." She waited for him to make some sort of snide remark. When he didn't, she smiled at him. He grimaced and she laughed.

It wasn't togetherness, but it would do for now.

Susan's eyes popped open the moment the alarm sounded. She felt awful. Why did she have to get up? This baby she carried in her was taking its toll—in more ways than one. It seemed that all she and Jerome did these days was fight and bicker. She knew she was beginning to hate him; she certainly hated the music he insisted they play. Wincing, she shifted her position, quietly, so as not to wake Jerome. She didn't want to have to talk to him if she could help it.

Oh, how she wished she were back in Sunbridge with her family! The brief visit in July had fortified her somehow, enabled her to continue with Jerome and this damnable tour a little while longer. But she should have stayed behind. Maggie would have let her stay till she was feeling better.

Susan dangled her legs from the bed, wanting to cry at the sight of her swollen ankles. She dreaded looking at her hands, knowing she might not be able to play the piano if they were puffy and pink. Jerome would get the ice water immediately. Good old Jerome, he would get the last ounce out of her if it killed her.

She decided to take a shower, then eat some crackers and take her medication. Maybe after that she'd place a call to Rand. Let Jerome squawk.

She hobbled to the bathroom, her swollen feet protesting at every step. The pipes groaned as she turned on the water, yielding little more than a trickle, which irritated her. She didn't need this. A towel wrapped around her, she made her way to the dresser. The cellophane crackled as she removed it. For some reason crackers always settled her stomach in the morning. She took her vitamin and three other pills, and was sitting with the phone in her lap when Jerome woke.

"What are you doing, Susan?" His voice was light, almost indifferent. But he had to fight with himself not to get up and rip the phone from her hands.

"I'm going to call Rand. Do you have any objections?" Susan asked coldly.

"Why don't you wait till later, until you're more awake and things are settled."

"I'm settled and I'm awake. I've taken my shower, eaten my crackers, and taken my pills. What I haven't done and what I have no intention of doing is polishing your shoes, packing your bags, or going to the store for fresh rolls for you. I'm not even going to practice today. I'm going to sit right here with my feet up. I might even read a trashy magazine instead of music scores. I'm fed up. Do you hear me? Fed up!"

"You can't give in to these little aches and pains. You have to keep going."

"No, Jerome, *you* have to keep going. I don't! I'm quitting right now. I can't bear the thought of sitting at a piano for five or six hours. Even the doctor said I should be resting with my feet up. Now I suppose you're going to tell me he doesn't know what he's talking about, that you know more than he does."

"I know *you*. That's what's important. You can't do this to us. We've come too far, worked too hard—"

"I've certainly worked too hard—and I've had it! If you don't have the guts to cancel the rest of the tour, I'll do it. Or, go it alone."

"Susan, look at me. We only have five more performances. You can do it. I know you can. We'll cut out practice today. I can see that your legs and feet are swollen." Jerome's insides churned. He had to find a way to keep Susan going. He took a deep breath and fished around the tiny refrigerator for some milk to soothe his stomach. When there was none to be had, he waved his hands about like a maniac. "You know I need milk! You were supposed to get it yesterday. A lousy container of milk and you couldn't even do that for me."

"Yesterday my physical condition was worse than it is today," she replied tightly. "You had me practicing for five hours. The concert lasted three. You had me laced into a maternity corset that almost suffocated me. All because you didn't want people saying I looked like a cow." Her voice grew shrill. "That's what you said, Jerome, a *cow*! I had hardly anything to eat because you said it would fog up my head. If the stage manager hadn't given me a banana, I would have fainted on stage. And when we got back here, all the shops were closed. Where was I supposed to get your milk? It's *your* stomach—*you* get the goddamn milk!"

"Calm down or they'll throw us out of here," Jerome said, hugging his stomach.

"That's the best thing that could happen to us. To me especially. No more, Jerome. This is it. I'm calling Rand."

"And what's Rand going to do for you?"

"Something. I don't know. Just shut up, Jerome, and leave me alone. Don't get any funny ideas about trying to stop me, either. Because if you do, I'll go to the lobby and make the call from there."

"Please, Susan, don't do this," Jerome begged. "You know how important this tour is to me. I'm just as sick as you. We can't cancel out now. People are depending on us."

"If you're as ill as you say, then you shouldn't be continuing this tour, either. I have a baby to think of. I'm sorry now I let you talk me into leaving Sunbridge."

Jerome wept, but Susan ignored him as she placed her call to England. The moment Rand's voice came over the wire, she felt better. "I need your help, Rand. Jerome and I are in Germany at the moment.... Yes, but I want to go home, back to Texas.... Yes, now. Will you call Maggie and ask her if I can stay at Sunbridge? I haven't heard from her or Amelia for so long I don't think they remember who I am. Will you do that for me, Rand?" Susan listened to Rand for a few moments. Her eyes narrowed as she stared at her husband. "I really don't know if I can make it to the airport.... Well, I suppose it wouldn't matter if I left my luggage. . . . Right. I'll wait for your call."

Jerome stared at his wife. For the first time in his life he was afraid.

"You bastard," she hissed. "You black-hearted bastard. Why didn't you tell me my sister and Aunt Amelia called me? I didn't believe Amelia that one time when she tried to explain—I couldn't believe it of you! Where are my letters? Rand called, too. He wrote *three* letters. I want them. They're from *my* family. You had no right to keep them from me! It would have made all the difference in the world. I needed their support. You took that away from me and didn't give anything back. Don't come near me, Jerome, because I'll smash this phone in your face. How could you! How dare you! You would have worked me to death just to finish this tour so you would look good. You don't care about me or the baby. You know what, Jerome? We don't care about you, either."

Jerome's helplessness exploded in rage. He slammed about the tiny hotel efficiency suite, sending hairbrushes, perfume bottles, and sheet music crashing into furniture and walls. He cursed in every language he knew, and still she sat passively on the edge of the bed, the hard, black telephone receiver clenched in her fist.

His fists clenched, he stared at her, eyes brimming with fury. She was ruining him, this bitch. Ruining his career, ruining his future. And for what? A squalling brat that would interfere in their lives, suck the energy out of their work. He hovered over her, arm raised. He wanted to hit her, destroy her the way she was destroying him.

"Don't do it, Jerome," she warned in an icy tone. "If there's breath left in my body, I'll see to it you enjoy the comforts of a German jail. And how will that look in the press releases?"

Jerome's fist fell to his side.

"On second thought, Jerome," Susan was saying, no hint of remorse or even of pity in her eyes, "I'll help you pack." Jerome stormed out of the suite, the door shuddering on its hinges behind him.

* * *

The transatlantic calls came in one after the other. First Billie, then Maggie and Amelia. Of course she could come to Sunbridge, Maggie cried happily. The nursery was there and waiting. She could stay as long as she liked, forever if she wanted.

"Are you sure you're well enough to make the trip?"

"Rand is going to meet me in England and bring me home. He's got it all planned. I'll stay on a few days and get a good checkup and then we'll head for Sunbridge. Maggie, I am so grateful, I don't know what to say."

"Then don't say anything," Maggie said in a choked voice. "This place needs a baby. This place needs you, Susan. You've been gone too long. Everything will be ready. I'll make an appointment with a good g-y-n man for you the day after you get here. I can't wait to see you!"

"Sure you don't mind that Rand is coming along?"

"Of course not. He was coming for Christmas anyway. The more the merrier. I'm worried, though. Is Jerome going to cause you any trouble? He'll let you go, won't he?"

"I'd like to see him try and stop me. I'm not bothering with luggage. Rand said something about a wing and a prayer."

"I can shop for you. I know your size. That's the least of your problems. You're sure you're okay?"

"Now I am. I may have regrets later, but I have to think about the baby. Today I just blew up."

"Take care of yourself, Suse. We'll be waiting. We love you."

"I know, and I love all of you," Susan said softly. "I'll see you in a few days. Thanks, Maggie."

She was just checking her purse to be sure she had her passport when the phone rang. It was Rand.

"If you get to the airport in the next forty-five minutes, there's a reservation in your name."

"I can make it. I'm dressed. I'm not sure if I have

enough money on me, though. Enough for taxi fare, but that's about it. Jerome handles the money."

"Just get to the damn airport. The ticket is prepaid. Once you get here, everything'll be fine. Hurry now."

"I will. Thanks, Rand. I'll see you in a few hours."

Suddenly Susan felt guilty. It didn't seem right to just walk out on Jerome like this. Everything had happened so quickly. She laid his passport and the tour schedule on the dresser next to his keys. Quickly she penned off a small note.

> Jerome,
>   I'm sorry it's ending this way, but I must think of the life we both created. I'll be at Sunbridge if you want to get in touch. Take care of yourself and don't lose your passport.
>
>   Susan.

Ninety minutes later Susan was airborne. When she landed in England hours later, Rand's was the first face she saw. She literally fell into his arms.

Rand sat with his arm around Susan's shoulders on the ride to his house. He had to do something for her before he took her to Sunbridge. Amelia and Maggie would worry themselves sick over her. It was all he could do to keep the shock from his own face. Rest, some good food, some fresh air, and maybe, just maybe, she'd be ready to travel in ten days or so.

Then it would be back to Sunbridge. Back to Maggie. And Amelia and Cary and the boys. His heart soared.

Cole stood beside the empty bleachers watching the Crystal City High School in practice, their short skirts swinging about their slim thighs, their sweaters bouncing with each leap and jump. Kelly Jensen was one classy chick. Captain of the freshman squad, she was one of the most popular girls in school. All the boys had the hots for her, including him. Even Riley lost his cool when Kelly was around.

Watching Kelly was only a side benefit. Cole's real purpose in coming to the athletic field was to watch Riley being put through his paces as right guard for the junior varsity team. He squinted into the sun, looking for the familiar number sixty-four, bold green numbers on a white jersey. Even from here Riley looked intimidating: tall, broad, long powerful legs pumping him across the distance as he took down the opposing tackle to enable the quarterback to get off a clean pass. The coach blew his whistle; the play was ended. Saturday was a big game for Crystal City and excitement was running high.

"Good play, Coleman!" Some of the other boys jostled Riley's shoulder pads. Ass slapping was for the pro teams.

"All right! Hit the showers! Practice tomorrow after school, films tomorrow night! Show you guys what you'll be up against when you play Edison. Who's number one?" the coach shouted.

"Mustangs! Mustangs!" came the hoarse, masculine cries of the team.

"Who's number one?"

"Mustangs!"

Cole's eyes narrowed as he watched Riley walk off the field, Coach Hamrah's arm on his shoulder, heads close together. Then he returned his attention to Kelly, who was waiting near the gate for Riley. Cole spat the bitter taste from his mouth. If Riley's last name weren't Coleman and if he weren't a part of Sunbridge, no girl would even give him a second look. Especially not Kelly, a bluenose who probably didn't even know the last name of her family's Mexican housekeeper. Cole spat again; still the bitter taste lingered. Just went to show what the right name and the right contacts could do for a guy, he thought contemptuously.

That Cole had recourse to the same name and contacts was a reality he ignored.

At the gate leading onto the field, just within earshot,

Kelly was playing up to Riley. "A bunch of kids are going over to Patti's house tonight. Her father got a copy of *E. T.* from the film studio. Did you ever see it?"

Riley shook his head, a faint blush staining his cheeks.

"Want to come with me? They're going to show it right after dinner; it'll be an early night, I promise."

"I don't know, Kelly. I've got that English paper to do by next Tuesday and I'm behind."

"What if I said I'd help you with it on Sunday?" Kelly coaxed. "Mine's done; I've got plenty of time. I could even go to the library for you while you're at films tomorrow. That would save some time, wouldn't it?"

"Yeah"—Riley grinned—"it would. But I can't ask you to do that for me."

"You're not asking; I'm offering. My mom and I can come by Sunbridge right after dinner, say about six-thirty? You'll be home before ten. I promise. Say you'll come, Riley, please?"

Cole thought he was going to throw up. Kelly Jensen begging up to nobody Riley Coleman. Couldn't she see that he wasn't one of them? Cole didn't even want to wait around to hear Riley agree to go to the film. Patti hadn't asked him to come, and she was supposed to be his friend.

Walking beneath the bleachers so Riley wouldn't see him, Cole went back to his moped. His mother had bought one for each of the boys, since taking the school bus wasn't always practical when there were after-school activities. He was astride and backing up when Gina Higgins hopped on behind him. "Take me home, Cole. I've got a date tonight."

"I've got better things to do than drive you around. Where's your bike?"

"Got a flat and it'll be dark soon. C'mon, Cole, don't be a pain."

"Get off, Gina. I'm not taking you anywhere." He knew where Gina would be tonight—at Patti's, probably with Dan Carroll, another hotshot football player. "I told you I've got something to do."

Reluctantly Gina climbed off the back of the moped, her pretty face in a pout. "What have you got to do? Watch your soon-to-be all-star cousin? I saw you watching him. He'll make all-star, you know, just like Danny. Next year, Riley will probably make squad captain. Must make you feel like shit."

Cole burned rubber as he throttled down.

"It shows, you know!" she yelled as he made a U-turn. "Everybody knows you're jealous, Cole. Why don't you just cool it and give us all a break?"

He heard what she said. Everything true. He hated her. He hated all of them!

Thirty minutes later with still a mile to go, Riley slowed his moped beside Gina. "What are you doing walking this road in the dark?"

"Your cousin refused to give me a ride. He's a jerk."

"Just like that? For no reason? Put the helmet on or you don't ride with me," he ordered.

Gina snapped the chin strap. "It was my own fault. I told him he was jealous of you and that you were going to be captain of the squad next year. Guess he didn't want to hear that. I think I may have mentioned you were going to be all-star."

Riley groaned. "Please, Gina, I have enough problems with him as it is. I wish you hadn't said that."

"I'm sorry, Riley. He gets my goat, though. He's always hanging around—sneaking, really. I think he likes Kelly. You know something else? I think Kelly likes you. We were talking at practice yesterday about the homecoming dance. She doesn't have a date, in case you're interested. I'm not sure, but I think she's waiting for you to ask her."

"Me! Do you think she would go with me?" Riley asked incredulously.

"I think so. Why don't you ask her? Look, I'm sorry about Cole. I was niggling him. I'll apologize tomorrow. But I still think he's a smart-ass. How can you stand him?"

"He's different; you have to know him," Riley said

defensively as they pulled into Gina's driveway.

"Sure, sure." Gina grinned as she handed back the helmet. "Don't forget to ask Kelly. Promise?"

"Okay, I promise, but if she turns me down, it's your hide I'm coming after."

"Danny will protect me." Gina giggled. "See you, Riley."

When Riley entered Sunbridge by the back door, Cole was just finishing his warmed-up dinner. Maggie was perched on a stool trying to make conversation.

"Sorry I'm late, Aunt Maggie."

"I was getting worried. Did you stop off somewhere? Your dinner is in the oven. Martha had prayer meeting this evening, so I'm chief cook and bottle washer."

Riley glanced at Cole. He quickly averted his eyes, but Maggie saw the look. "I had to drop Gina off. She missed the bus and her bike had a flat." He knew he sounded defensive. He always did when he was around Cole.

"Gina's a nice girl. I know her parents well. What in the world happened to her hair?"

"She was on the summer swim team and the chlorine in the pool turned it all colors," Riley said as he removed his dinner from the oven. "Boy, am I hungry."

Maggie didn't bother pouring Riley a glass of milk. She set the pitcher in front of him and knew he would drink it all. His father always had an enormous appetite. She noticed that Cole stayed on his stool staring at Riley as he wolfed down his chicken and pan-fried potatoes.

"Is either of you going to the homecoming dance?" Maggie asked lightly, trying to draw her son into the conversation. Cole shrugged. Riley grinned as he attacked his blackberry pie.

"I'm going to ask someone to the dance tonight," he said. "Maybe she'll go and maybe not. I thought I'd try. If she says no, I'll go stag. This is real good pie, Aunt Maggie."

"Martha will be glad to hear that. I think she cooks

just for you two boys. Don't keep us in suspense, Riley. Who are you going to ask?" Maggie asked, leaning over the counter to smile at her nephew.

Riley wiped his mouth and laid down his fork. "Kelly Jensen," he said firmly, his eyes on his cousin.

"Ha!" Cole laughed. "Fat chance."

"The way I look at it"—Riley grinned—"is I'll know firsthand what rejection from a girl feels like. It'll be an experience for me. I know what rejection is, but this is different. Who are you going to ask, Cole?"

"I'm not going, and they don't allow stags at homecoming."

For a moment Riley's face fell. Cole was doing it again. Trying to make him feel unwanted, like an outsider. The boy's spine straightened. He'd had about enough of Cole Tanner. "I guess going stag is okay if you're on the football team," he said firmly. "The only reason you aren't going is because you can't get a date. You've made an ass of yourself with every girl in school. Tell Aunt Maggie why I was late. Go ahead—tell her!"

"Shut up!" Cole said, jumping off the chair.

"I don't have to shut up. I live here, too." Riley looked directly at his aunt. "Gina asked Cole for a ride and he refused. I had to take her home."

Maggie's eyes widened. She'd never heard the boys go at it before. Riley was usually quiet, defensive, and, if anything, inclined to stick up for Cole no matter what. She wasn't sure she liked this openness. Where would it lead—to fights, punching, downright war?

"How could you do such a thing, Cole?" she asked. "Gina's parents are my friends. What happened to good manners?"

"You just take his word for it, just like that! You don't bother to ask me if it's true or not. Some mother!" Cole slammed from the kitchen, the door banging against his heels.

Maggie was off the chair in a second. She sprinted through the door and grabbed Cole by the ear, literally dragging him back into the kitchen. "Now, we can settle this one of two ways. Either you tell me the truth—or I will call Gina's parents and get the truth."

Riley wanted to fall through the floor. Cole's face flushed crimson, but he stood defiantly trying to jerk free of his mother. Maggie waited.

"I lied, Aunt Maggie. I thought you would be angry if I was late for dinner again."

Maggie's heart turned over. She knew Riley was lying and she knew Cole expected him to lie. Cole said nothing, just stood there smiling impudently. With a sigh, Maggie let go of him and turned away.

"Go to your room, Cole."

"Yes, ma'am," Cole said with a sneer.

When the door closed behind him, Maggie placed a gentle hand on Riley's shoulder. "I wish you hadn't lied for him. You don't have to, Riley. He has to make it on his own or he'll never be a worthwhile human being. You must have been particularly fed up with him this evening to say what you did."

"I was and I'm sorry. I'm nervous about asking Kelly. What will I say if she turns me down? I never asked a girl for a date before."

"It's not easy for a girl, either. Most times, girls have to sit and wait for a guy to call. They get all frazzled that the wrong one will call, and then there are excuses to make—and girls do make excuses. Not out of meanness or anything like that. It's more like trying to save the boy embarrassment. Girls are sensitive, for the most part."

"I'm going to see her tonight. We're going over to Patti's house to watch a movie." Riley's cheeks reddened. "I don't know if I'll have the courage."

"Then why don't you call her? It'll be easier over the phone. Trust me," Maggie urged.

"Then I'd better call her now, before she leaves to come pick me up. Jeez, I hope I'm doing the right thing. Kelly's one of the most popular girls in school. She's captain of the freshman cheerleaders and she's on the honor roll. She'll probably make National Honor Society in her junior year."

"I know." Maggie grinned. "But she's still a girl. Those are things she does. It's not who she is, Riley. Go ahead—call her from here. Do you want me to leave?"

"Heck no. Stay here. I need all the support I can get. If I get tongue-tied, just take the phone from me and tell her it's a wrong number."

Maggie's heart pumped furiously as she watched her nephew dial Kelly Jensen's number. A movement at the door made her turn. Cole, standing outside listening.

"This is Riley Coleman. Can I speak to Kelly, please?" Riley took a deep breath and rolled his eyes back in his head.

"Kelly? . . . Hi, it's Riley. I'm calling because I . . . I was wondering if you would like to go to—to the homecoming dance with me. Of course, if you're busy or have a date . . ." Out of the corner of his eye he could see Maggie shake her head no. He groaned inside, then his eyes widened as he listened to Kelly's reply. "You will?! That's yes? Yes, you'll go with me? It was just hard to hear for a second. My aunt is rattling the dishes . . . Okay! Great! Yeah, see you later. . . . Yeah."

Maggie laughed. "See! It wasn't all that bad." She rattled dishes to make her point. "Do you like this girl, Riley?"

"Me and every guy in school. She's nice, but she hasn't dated one particular guy. She goes to all the parties and . . . Aunt Maggie, I'm sorry about Cole."

"I'll talk to Cole after I clean up here. You'd better get ready if you're going out tonight."

Riley hugged his aunt and grabbed an apple and a bag of potato chips off the kitchen counter. He was almost to the swinging kitchen door when he returned for two bottles of Coke.

"Bottomless pit." Maggie sighed as she attacked the dishwasher. When she finished in the kitchen, she made a phone call.

"Gina, this is Mrs. Tanner." The silence on the other

end warned her to be careful. "Gina, I want to apologize for Cole. I'm sorry he left you to get home on your own." She felt awful taking such an approach to the situation, but she had to know for sure what had happened.

"It's okay, Mrs. Tanner. Riley picked me up and brought me home. I guess Cole was a little mad at me. I was needling him."

"That's still no excuse. I'm sure Cole will apologize tomorrow."

"It's no big thing, Mrs. Tanner. Don't make a big deal out of it for Cole. We all have bad days."

"It's nice of you to be so forgiving. Give my regards to yours parents."

"I'll do that. Good night, Mrs. Tanner."

Maggie marched upstairs, tromped down the hall, and entered Cole's room without knocking. "I want to talk to you."

"About what?"

"I want to know why you let Riley lie for you this evening. Why couldn't you be man enough to stand up and tell the truth. I called Gina myself and she confirmed it.

"Gina is a big mouth. What difference does it make. She made me mad. If I was going to go out of my way to take her home, the least she could do was to be appreciative. All she did was needle me."

"About what? What could she needle you about that would make you leave her by herself when it was getting dark?"

Cole could feel the blood rush to his head. He actually felt lightheaded. Through tight lips he snarled, "She was giving me the business about being a gun-toting, military snot. Stand straight, aim, fire, that kind of crap. She made me mad."

Maggie listened to her son. She felt he was lying, but what could she do? She couldn't force him to tell her the truth. All she could do was try to understand and be there for him if and when he decided to confide in her. She sighed. "All right. Good night, Cole. Lights out by eleven."

Cole pounded his fist into his pillow. He was enraged that his mother had called Gina, humiliated that Riley should have tried to cover for him, and even a little scared by the tone of his mother's voice when she'd said good night. It was as though she'd dismissed him, didn't care about him, maybe even wished he weren't her son.

"Damn it!" he exploded. "Why can't anyone ever take *my* side? She's supposed to be *my* mother, not his!"

{{{{{{{{ CHAPTER FOURTEEN }}}}}}}}

"Texas! I never thought I'd be this glad to be here," Susan sighed wearily as she dropped down onto a banquette in the baggage area. "I feel about a hundred pounds lighter. I'm very grateful to you for bringing me home, Rand."

"My pleasure. I have a perfectly good reason to visit Sunbridge and see Amelia again. I miss her. You're very fortunate to have a place to come home to, Susan."

"Yes, I know." Susan smiled at her cousin. "I loved living in England with you and Aunt Amelia. I never could have pursued my music in Texas the way I did there. But I suppose, in many ways, Sunbridge is home. And I'm looking forward to putting myself under Aunt Amelia's wing."

Rand laughed. "In a few weeks' time I'll remind you you said that. After you've had enough coddling and pampering and you begin to complain the way you always did when you were a child."

"Aren't we all children? Even you, Rand, all grown-up and terribly capable. You've lived an exciting life, successful in business, heir to a fortune and huge estate; you were even an officer in the RAF. Quite diversified, quite accomplished. Tell me that you don't become a small boy again around your mother. It's almost impossible not to. When I was here in July with Mam and Aunt Amelia, I felt as though I were twelve years old again."

"And now there's even Maggie to pet and watch over you. Spoiled thing," Rand teased.

"Maggie's been wonderful about all this. She made me feel so wanted. You know, we weren't always close, but we managed to keep in touch. She's had more than her share to cope with over the years. All of us have, in one way or another."

"And now Maggie is a part of Sunbridge. Or is it the other way 'round?" Rand said quietly.

"Maggie is right where she wants to be. I think—and this is my personal opinion—that it would take an act of God to get Maggie away from Sunbridge. Don't you?"

"Yes. It's as though she were meant for it."

"She was. Is. When you and I closed up the flat in London yesterday, I didn't feel anything. It was just five small rooms and an overworked piano. Half the furniture wasn't mine. Just walls. Perhaps it was my fault. Maybe I should have tried to make the place homier. But Jerome and I were rarely there, and it seemed such a terrible effort. We did get all my things, didn't we?"

"Every last stitch. All that's left belongs to Jerome."

"He'll go back eventually. If for no other reason than to auction the piano. But my point is, Maggie could never pack up and leave Sunbridge the way I left my apartment. I think it would kill her. She had to leave once. It must have ripped her heart out. But she's happy now, and that's what matters."

"Our baggage is here," Rand said abruptly. "I'll have a porter take it to the curb. You wait with it till I pick up the rental car. Are you certain you'll be all right? Are you warm enough?"

"I'm fine, Rand. Really. I can manage. Stop hovering. You're reminding me of how awful I must look."

"Little mother, you're a beauty." Rand winked and offered her a dashing smile.

"And you're a pretty liar." She giggled. As they followed the porter, with Susan straggling behind, she was amused by the admiring glances Rand received. His height and imposing good looks always caught feminine eyes. And Susan knew Rand's attractiveness was more than skin deep. He was a genuinely nice person, kind and considerate; she knew how bad he must have felt to break it off with Sawyer. The breakup of a relationship could be devastating. She knew.

"This way, Susan." Rand came back and took her arm. "We'll have you home in no time."

"Does it look good to you?" Rand asked as he pulled the car beneath the shelter of the portico.

Susan sighed. "It looks beautiful!"

"Then let's get a move on and make you part of that wonderful household. Maggie's probably chewing her nails and Amelia is wearing out her shoes pacing the hallway. Go ahead. I'll bring in the baggage and park the car."

Susan's steps were light when she climbed the stairs leading to the portico. Maggie burst through the door and hugged her sister while her eyes searched the car for Rand.

"Come inside," she said. "It's chilly out here. You look exhausted. Tea. Some good sugar cookies and an afghan. Soft music and a nap."

"Maggie! I'm not an invalid. I'm pregnant. But I'll take all those things for now because I am tired. Tomorrow, though, will be different."

"One day at a time. I made a doctor's appointment for you on Friday."

Maggie was readying the tea tray under Martha's supervision when Rand walked into the kitchen. The spoon clattered against the sugar bowl Maggie was holding. How handsome he was! "Rand, it's good to see you. Thank you so much for bringing Suse home. What did the doctor say?"

"That she's to stay off her feet, get plenty of rest, fresh air, and good food, nothing fattening. She's dangerously close to miscarrying" Rand stepped closer to her. "I'm so glad to see you, Maggie."

"I ... I ... wasn't expecting ... I thought I would have ... Christmas is when you were coming back. What I mean ..."

"I'm confusing things for you is what you're trying to say?"

"In a way." Maggie could feel herself drifting toward him, the sugar bowl still clasped in her hands. Her pulses were hammering so loud she was sure he could hear them. "We had this humongous pumpkin for Halloween," she said inanely.

"Really."

"Martha and I carved it. We toasted the pits."

"Amazing."

"This is difficult for me.... You see ..."

"It isn't easy for me, either."

"This wasn't supposed to happen."

"It usually works that way."

"Mam wouldn't ... approve."

"I know."

"There's Sawyer. I don't know if I can handle that."

"I don't know if I can, either."

"I missed you after you left."

"I thought of little else but you," Rand said, taking the sugar bowl from Maggie's hands. He set it on the tray and picked the tray up. "Our patient's tea is getting cold. We have three whole days to discuss what we have to discuss."

"Three days? That's not very long."

"A lot can happen in three days. In some cases it's almost an eternity. It's seventy-two hours."

"Seventy-two hours sounds better than three days,"

Maggie mumbled as she followed Rand into the study, where Susan lay propped up on the sofa.

"I'm letting you wait on me today, but that's it," Susan said, reaching for her teacup. "Oh, Maggie, it feels so good to be home. I know you're anxious to hear what happened, but I can't go through that right now. I don't know if I'll ever be able to talk about it."

"You're home now, Susan. There are no demands, no restrictions, no orders to be followed. All you have to do is take care of yourself and your baby. I'll do the rest."

"What did Mam say?"

"She wants you to call her, and if you need her, she'll be glad to fly down."

"I don't think that's necessary. Christmas will be soon enough. She's so happy up there with Thad. I don't want her worrying about me."

"That's exactly what I told her, but you know Mam. Later, after you nap, you can call and reassure her."

"Where's Aunt Amelia? I thought she'd be waiting for me."

Maggie met Rand's glance. How was she to tell her sister that Amelia was never home, that she had other things now to occupy her time? This was going to present a problem, one *she'd* have to deal with.

"When do you think Aunt Amelia will be home?" This time there was an edge to Susan's voice.

"Probably around dinnertime," Rand said soothingly. "This is a good chance for you to nap so you'll be fresh when she gets here. She's been working long days, or so Maggie tells me."

Rand added another log to the fire while Maggie covered Susan with the afghan. "Sleep, little Susie," Maggie whispered as she bent to kiss the wan cheek. Then she and Rand quietly left the study.

"Would you like some lunch, Rand?" Maggie said when they were in the foyer.

"No. I would like to take a walk to clear my head and maybe get rid of a little of this jet lag. Want to join me?"

"I should stay here with.... All right. I guess I owe you the treat of showing off our Texas foliage. Most of it is gone now and—" Maggie stopped, realizing that if she didn't watch it she'd soon be babbling like an idiot. "I need a jacket, though. Wait."

Wait. As though he had anything else to do. As though there might be anything else he'd *rather* do than wait and take a walk with Maggie.

"I'm ready," Maggie said, buttoning a dove-gray suede jacket. A brilliant scarlet scarf that boasted the name Billie at the end was thrown carelessly around her neck. Rand thought she was beautiful.

"How are the boys?" he asked as they left the house.

"At each other's throats most of the time."

"What happened with Cranston?"

"We agreed to agree. I have Cole until the next semester. Then Cranston will reevaluate the situation."

"What about your divorce?"

"January. Nothing has changed. We both tried to... oh, patch it up, I suppose, but it was for all the wrong reasons. Once you realize that, things go forward. I think Cranston and I can be friends now."

"Is that what you want?"

"For a while I didn't think so. I thought a lot about family and the commitment we both have to Cole, but now... yes, it's what I want. It's such a relief to say those words out loud."

"How's Amelia doing, and the great inner city?"

Maggie laughed. "The great inner city is coming along beautifully. Everything is under control. Cary is happy and tired when he gets home at night. I think that annoys Amelia a little. There isn't much time for partying during the week, but they make up for it on the weekend. To be honest, I rarely see them. I stopped by the house Amelia is renovating; you heard about that, didn't you?"

"Her mother's old house. Yes, she seemed quite excited about it."

"She's doing a wonderful job and spending a fortune. She's doing most of the work on the inside herself and contractors are working outside. I think they finished up this week. She wanted all outside work done before the bad weather set in. It's amazing, Rand. She gets up at five in the morning, has breakfast with Cary, and then goes straight to the house. I don't know if I could be that dedicated."

"Look, there's an old log," she said, striding ahead. "Why don't we sit down for a while. The sun is warm."

Rand stared after her, watching her long-legged stride in low-heeled boots beneath a wide, circular skirt. Fashionable, he thought. Always fashionable.

Maggie patted the space next to her on the old tree. "Tell me what you've been doing since you left."

"Getting along. Marking time. Waiting for Christmas."

"You just said the same thing three different ways." Maggie laughed.

"I did, didn't I?"

"What will you do when you go back?"

"Get along. Mark time. Wait for Christmas."

"Why go back?"

"That was the deal."

"What if I said the deal could be changed?" Maggie said hesitantly.

"I'd still go back. I think we both need more time."

Maggie picked at a piece of loose bark with her fingernail. "I suppose that is best. The family . . ."

"Will that make a difference to you?"

"Of course it will make a difference. Mam will . . . Mam won't approve. Cole . . . God only knows what he will think, do, or say. He's become very close to Sawyer. Which brings us to my daughter. I haven't heard from her since she left? Have you?"

"No, I haven't."

"Why are we talking like this?" Maggie asked in a hushed voice.

"Because we're two people who are drawn to each other. We're also adults and know that other people can get hurt by our actions."

"There was a time in my life when I would have plunged

in regardless of the consequences. I don't think I can do that now," Maggie whispered.

"It's Sawyer, isn't it?"

"Of course, it's Sawyer. It's Mam, too. And myself most of all."

"It's over between Sawyer and me."

"You know that and I know that, but I'm sure Sawyer still has feelings for you. Very strong feelings. She loved you, Rand, heart and soul. I know it hasn't been easy for her. Once in a while Cole will drop something. Mam is worried about her."

"Sawyer is twenty-six years old. People do live when a relationship ends. First they grieve, then they get angry, then they accept it."

"You sound very knowledgeable. Have you been through it yourself?"

"In my own way. Only I was doing my grieving before the relationship with Sawyer was over. While I was coming to terms with the fact that I didn't want the same things Sawyer wanted. There was anger and finally acceptance."

"I think that's the way it was with Mam and Pap."

"So what do we do?"

"I don't know. I do know I'm very attracted to you. When Cranston was here I found myself comparing him to you. When you said you'd write, I started watching the mail. I had to fight with myself to keep from calling you. I don't want anyone to be hurt. I know that sounds strange coming from me, but it's the way I feel."

"What about us?"

"It would be kind of hard to have a secret affair. That's what you're talking about, isn't it? I've lived in the shade too long, Rand. I want everything out in the bright light. I want the sun to smile down on me. I want to be happy with my choices. . . . I think we should both think about this some more."

Rand laughed. "Ever practical Maggie. If that's what you want, so be it."

Maggie smiled, then stood up and stretched. "I think

we should be getting back. Why don't you take the car and see the house Amelia is working on? I know she'd be pleased to show it off to you."

"Sounds like a good idea. What will you do?"

"Watch Suse sleep so she sees me first thing when she wakes up."

"Mother Maggie."

Maggie laughed. "Sometimes I surprise even myself. As soon as I knew she was coming, I had all her things brought down from the attic. The old canopy bed and her little dressing table. I thought she'd like that."

"Home. There's no place like it."

"You make it sound like you never had one."

"Not like here. During the war we were shuffled from pillar to post, and half the time we lost most of our things. There was no permanence to anything then. The house I live in now is just a house. It has no character. There are no memories. It's a place to sleep."

Maggie's eyes twinkled. "There's always room for one more at Sunbridge. You can call this home."

"You'd run like hell if I moved in bag and baggage."

"Right now I would. Who knows what I'll do later? It's something for both of us to think about."

On the walk back to Sunbridge, Rand held Maggie's hand. When they were almost to the back garden, he stopped. "I think I'm falling in love with you, Maggie. I want you to be aware of that."

Maggie raised her eyes. They brimmed with tears. "I'm aware."

"And?" It was a tortured question.

Maggie shook her head. "Not now. I need time. Please understand."

"I have all the time in the world. I can wait. And I will."

"No one ever said that to me before." Maggie's smile was as golden as the last rays of the sun.

"I left the keys in the car, so if you give me directions, I'll go on over to Amelia's and see how she's doing."

* * *

Maggie took off her boots outside the study door, then walked softly inside and had a peek at Susan's peacefully sleeping face. The tea in the pot was still lukewarm, but she barely tasted it as she watched Susan sleep and thought about what had just happened.

It was out in the open now. She'd known it would be— from the moment she'd first heard his voice on the phone telling her he was bringing Susan back. How was she to handle this? The woman in her wanted to wait until everyone slept, to go to him in a froth of lace and silk, to stand in the moonlight in his room. The mother in her told her she would regret such actions. The daughter in her insisted it was her life to do as she pleased.

This would be no brief fling, no casual affair.

Rand, following Maggie's directions, turned onto the road leading to Amelia's new project. My, my, he found himself thinking, the Assantes are certainly hot for real estate. He wondered at Amelia's sudden need for a project, an interest. She'd always been keen on people, had forever been surrounded by interesting personalities. Now, married to Cary and supposedly still enthralled with newly wedded bliss, she'd adopted some sort of massive undertaking. Why?

The dark gray slate tiled mansard roof came into sight in the distance. The house stood alone, a sentinel guarding the expanse of surrounding land. Scaffolding climbed the clapboard exterior; men crawled about, scraping and painting what had been a dull yellow to a soft dove gray. The gingerbread fretwork was coming alive with a fresh coat of white.

Rand gave a low whistle as he looked through the windshield. This place must have cost a pretty penny, and obviously the restorations involved were mind-boggling. The house did have character, though; he'd give it that much.

"Rand! You devil! How good it is to see you," Amelia cried as she wrapped her arms around him. "When did you get in? How was the trip? Is Susan all right? Lord, you get more handsome each time I see you, or is it only a mother's pride? . . . Well, say something."

"Susan is fine—or will be, I'm sure. We got in a few hours ago. We had a smooth trip. And I'm no devil, but you're right; I'm handsome. How's it going?"

"Look around you and tell me what you think."

"I see one hell of a big mess. Why didn't you just buy a new house?"

"Oh, Rand, I thought you'd understand," Amelia said, disappointed. "I used to talk about this house to you when you were little. Don't you remember?"

"Of course I do. It's just that it looks like such a monstrous job. You must be spending a fortune. Are you planning on living here, or are you fixing it up as a shrine?"

Amelia's eyes clouded. Rand somehow had an uncanny knack of zeroing in on things. "I like shrines. I might live here, and then I might not. Does it make a difference?"

"Not to me it doesn't, but I should think it would to you. What's the bottom line?"

"It keeps me busy. It was Mam's house, and I think it should be preserved."

"Let me ask you something, Mother. If you lived out-of-state and you came back to Texas, and this house and Sunbridge were both available to you, which would you choose to live in?"

"I don't feel like playing games, Rand. Come along. I want to show you what I've done. It's marvelous what the right people can do."

Rand followed Amelia from room to room, listening while she droned on about what had been done to date and what still was in the works.

"It'll be fit for a king when I'm finished."

"What about the queen?" Rand asked seriously.

Amelia laughed. "Wait till you see the chandelier. The crystals are coming from Bavaria. They promised delivery in December. Mam was always partial to this particular chandelier. She said it was like a fairyland when it was lighted."

"What's your target date for completion?"

"Spring of next year, I think. I'm not rushing it."

In that one instant Rand felt sorry for Amelia. In all the years since she'd taken him under her wing, he'd never pitied her. He felt confused and saddened. "If Cary doesn't want to live here," he said, his voice purposely light, "you have a tenant waiting and ready to move in."

"I think Cary will like it. When I first started the project, I would call him and he'd come by and we'd have a picnic lunch, but he's too busy now. He's out on the site and I can't bother him."

"You must get lonely all day here by yourself."

"Not at all. The workmen are here and we chat and have lunch around the same time. We're a congenial group." Amelia laughed.

"I understand Cary's project is quite an undertaking. You must be very proud of him."

"I am. You can't imagine how well he's doing. He loves it. The men like and respect him, even the *real* Texans—you know, the older ones."

"Cary's a nice chap. What's not to like?"

"I was worried in the beginning that you two might not hit it off. I mean, he is younger than I."

"Mother, if you're happy, then I'm happy." He hesitated. "I would hope you'd feel the same about me."

Amelia looked away. "Have you heard from Sawyer?" she asked pointedly.

"No. I didn't expect to. Have you?"

"No. Rand, you never told me what happened, and I never asked. I'd like to know so I don't say the wrong thing at the wrong time."

He sighed. "It wasn't working. Sawyer deserves to have a family; she's young and full of life. I'm winding down and she should be revving up. So I had to let her go."

"That sounds like the flipside of my situation with Cary," Amelia said thoughtfully.

"You're wrong. Cary loves you madly and you love him. Sawyer and I never had that, not really. It just wouldn't have worked. Believe me, Mother, I wish it could have."

"Enough. I'm sorry I brought up the subject. It's just that everyone is so sorry for Sawyer, and they think you dumped her." Amelia grimaced. "I hate that word."

"When it comes right down to it, Mother, it's no one's business but Sawyer's and mine."

"I understand you're returning for Christmas. Sawyer won't come if you do."

"Is that your way of telling me to stay away?" Rand asked.

"No. It's my way of telling you you've deprived Sawyer of her home. Everyone wants to go home for the holidays. Think about that."

Rand nodded his head slightly. Then he kissed her and left without another word. Amelia watched him from the window. The moment his car turned at the corner, her shoulders slumped. She sat down on the window seat and brought her knees up to her chin.

She didn't need another problem right now. And Rand and Maggie would be the worst kind of problem. Did he think she was blind? Wanting and denial were worse, in her book, than all the sins in the world.

Trying to shake off Rand's visit wouldn't be easy. Tonight was going to be an at-home evening. When Cary had finally returned her calls, he'd told her not to expect him till after ten. She had two choices: she could either stay here and read a book or go home and pretend it didn't matter that Cary would be late.

Pretend. That's what her life was all about these days. If she hadn't asked her husband, she wouldn't have known his plans, would have spent the entire evening anticipating his arrival.

The lights were on now. The place looked messy, as if the job would never get done. But it would. She'd see to it, even if she had to spend money like a madwoman. Often the workmen looked at her as if she were crazy when she gave an order to rip something out that had twenty or thirty years of life left to it. Cary said he understood, but she also knew he looked in her ledger almost every day, keeping a running account of the money she spent.

The workers began to troop out one after another, calling good night over their shoulders. Home to families who waited for them. It was dinnertime, and here she was, all alone, in an empty house.

Damn it, she was lonely! What she wanted to do more than anything in the world right now was drive to Cary's construction site. She'd hoped that her husband would ask her to work in the trailer office answering the phone and ordering supplies. But he'd said it wouldn't look good if his wife worked on the site. As if she cared what anyone thought! But she didn't dare oppose Cary. He was happy having her here, puttering around, where he could find her at a moment's notice.

She'd felt restless these past few days, not in tune with herself. She wondered if it had anything to do with Susan's and Rand's return. Reminders of her age. She didn't want to have to stay cooped up at Sunbridge and hover over Susan, even though she loved her dearly. Fussing and fretting over Susan and worrying about Rand's possible affair with Maggie was simply not what she had in mind for herself. God, why did she feel so depressed?

Maybe she should lock up and go home. By the time she reached Sunbridge, dinner would be over and the kitchen cleaned up. The boys would be studying in their rooms. Rand, Maggie, and Susan would probably be in the study talking over after-dinner coffee. She'd say her hellos, give the proper hugs, then go upstairs. A long warm bath, a sexy gown, a drink, and she'd be ready for Cary. She could even call Billie; that always gave her a lift. And if Susan was still up afterward, she would visit with her.

When Amelia walked through the wide front doors of Sunbridge, her eyes, as always, went to the hat rack in the foyer. The sight of Riley's baseball cap always seemed so incongruous beside the Stetsons. But it brought a smile to her lips. Change.

The sound of subdued conversation and the soft clink of silver echoed out to the wide center hall. Taking a deep breath, she headed for the study. Susan lay propped up on the couch with an afghan covering her stomach and legs.

Immediately Amelia's heart went out to this girl who was like a daughter to her. She dropped to her knees, one hand fondly patting Susan's stomach as she pretended not to see the tears in Susan's eyes. Always before she'd been able to make things better for her niece. Not this time.

"Darling, how nice it is to see you. Under the weather, are we?" she said cheerfully. "Well, we'll have you right as rain in a week or so. All this Texas air has to be good for something. I'm glad you're here, sweetie. Imagine, a baby at Sunbridge," she said, turning to face Maggie. "It's been years since a child's footsteps echoed in this old place. Since Sawyer. What a dear child she was! So good and yet so mischievous. Billie did try to keep her to the studio, but she liked to come here and run about, especially up and down the steps. To look at her now, you'd find it hard to believe she was such a precocious toddler. Smart! My dear, that child has brains she hasn't used yet." When she saw Maggie flinch, she stood up, planted a kiss on Susan's brow, and said, "Well, I'm off to my avocado bath and thirty minutes in the Jacuzzi. Rand, tell Susan about my house. I'll fill you in on the details later. I'm going to call Billie. Does anyone want me to deliver any messages?"

Maggie felt as though a stone had lodged in her throat. She shook her head. Rand managed to mutter something about sending his regards, and Susan said to send her love. Amelia smiled at everyone and bustled out.

For a few moments, all was silence. Damn you, Mother, Rand seethed, seeing the stricken look on Maggie's face.

Susan, who was oblivious of the drama being played

out before her, spoke first. "If you don't mind," she said, sighing wearily, "I think I'll turn in."

Rand held out a stiff arm. "Grab hold."

Susan bounced to her feet and laughed. "This baby has had one tough life so far. A jolt or two now isn't going to matter. Good night to both of you." She kissed Maggie soundly and held on to her a moment longer than necessary. "Thanks for having me, Maggie. I don't know what I would have done without you. And Rand, thanks again. I know I'm repeating myself, but I am so grateful. I actually feel safe. Now isn't that a sad state of affairs?"

"Sleep well, Susan. I'm going to be right behind you. I have some letters to get out. Rand, why don't you lock up and turn off the lights?" Maggie said, averting her eyes as she hurried to follow Susan up the stairs.

Rand sat downstairs for a long time. Amelia's words echoed in his brain . . . and he knew he could never find it in himself to forgive her.

The ritual Amelia went through after her bath was long and tedious. First, she applied scented lotion to her entire body, then she powdered it with the same feathery scent. She creamed her face, oiled her eyelids and earlobes, and waited ten minutes. She applied light makeup, knowing the peach-colored light bulbs she'd placed in all the lamps would make her look dewy and fresh. She blow-dried her hair, gave it a few twirls with the curling iron, and then fluffed it out with her fingers. She added tiny gold-and-diamond earrings to her ears, a gift from Cary on her last birthday. The turquoise silk nightgown slithered over her body, making light swishing sounds. The side slit in the gown showed off a generous expanse of satiny leg as she fished around in the closet for matching high-heeled mules.

The bedside clock read 9:45; time to call Billie.

"Is anything wrong?" were Billie's first words.

"Wrong? At Sunbridge? Surely you jest! I just thought I'd call and see how the sap is running in Vermont."

"Thad says it's fine. How are you? How's the house

going? You said you were going to write and tell me all the things you did. I've been waiting for a letter."

"You shouldn't believe a promise like that. It's so much easier to pick up the phone and call. I think I'll be done by spring. I want your promise that you and Thad will come to my housewarming."

"Complete with gift." Billie laughed.

"How's Thad? Any more news on whether he's going to run for office?"

"The committee is doing its best to talk him into it. I don't say anything. It has to be Thad's decision."

"Susan is here, you know. She looks ghastly, Billie."

"I spoke to her today. She sounded tired. Maggie said she thought rest and fresh air would do it. We'll see what the doctor says. I feel better about her being in the States, but I am sorry about Jerome. Coleman marriages certainly seem volatile. I'm so glad you're staying at Sunbridge."

"I'm not here much of the time, but I'll do what I can. I tend to think Susan and Maggie will draw closer now."

Billie listened to her old friend. There was something different about Amelia's voice. It sounded strained, and the vibrancy she'd always associated with Amelia was missing. Her heart fluttered wildly. Something had happened and no one was telling her. "How's Cary doing with his project?"

"Wonderfully. I hardly ever see him, but then, I'm busy myself. We seem to meet up in the bedroom, which is all right with me. He's working seven days a week, poor darling."

"I'm eager to see it. Thad was asking me about it just the other day. He's very interested. Men love that sort of thing."

"*It*, as you put it, isn't much to see at this stage. The land's been cleared and there's a bunch of trailers used as on-site offices. Some slabs and foundations have been installed. And oh, yes, I mustn't forget about sewer and water, gas and electricity lines. Everything is underground, you know. There are even provisions for a cable

TV system. It's all very exciting," Amelia said listlessly. "We're just praying the weather holds."

"Amelia, is anything wrong? You sound funny."

Amelia closed her eyes, clutching the receiver. How could she admit, even to Billie, that she was afraid her young husband was losing interest? Suddenly she blurted, "I think something's going on between Rand and Maggie. He's here now; he brought Susan home. I'm beginning to understand why Sawyer left the way she did after the breakup, poor dear."

Billie settled back in her chair, concerned. She'd never heard this vein of bitterness in Amelia's voice before, and certainly not in connection with Rand.

"Billie? Are you there?" Amelia asked shrilly. "Didn't you hear what I said? I think there's something going on between Maggie and Rand!"

"I heard you, Amelia. Perhaps there is something between Rand and Maggie; perhaps it goes even deeper than friendship. Now I'll tell you what I said to Sawyer when she confided her suspicions. Knowing Rand, I'm pretty sure his relationship with Sawyer was already over before the Fourth of July. Second, she has nothing to base those suspicions on except seeing Rand and Maggie talking on the lawn after the party. And finally," Billie said sternly, "I think her bitterness toward Maggie is childish and unfounded."

Amelia bristled. "Perhaps you approve, but I don't. Something like this could tear the family apart, and we've had enough of that already. I more or less let Rand know how I feel. If he wants to end his relationship with Sawyer, that's certainly his prerogative. But he doesn't have to throw Maggie in her face." She sighed. "Oh, I don't know what to think, Billie. I don't know how far it's gone or if it's just getting off the ground. I am staying here in Maggie's house, so unless I'm prepared to leave, I have to be careful what I say."

"Good thinking, Amelia."

Amelia gasped. "You seem quite approving."

"I really don't know what to think. I'm terribly confused, and my better sense tells me to keep out of it. I
don't know the reasons Rand and Sawyer ended their
relationship. I thought they would marry. It must have
been more one-sided than we thought. But I do know
Maggie well enough to say she wouldn't deliberately set
out to hurt Sawyer. I can't believe that."

"Rand is my son, but he's a man and he goes after
what he wants. And I can't hold my feelings in; I'd hate
it if it was done to me. I can feel Sawyer's pain. I can
feel it!"

"I know," Billie whispered. "I was in that same place
once myself."

"What should we do?"

"Nothing. They have to work it out for themselves.
I've had a few letters from Sawyer since July. None of
them really said anything, but I can read between the
lines. I'm worried sick. She's such a child, really. Her life
has been . . . well, charmed, one might say."

"Charmed? How could you say that?" Amelia asked
hotly. "She was a child born of a child and rejected by
her child-mother. It would have been better if she'd never
been born. You never should have insisted Maggie go
through with that pregnancy. Why did you?"

"Why? Because of you, Amelia. Because of that terrible botched-up abortion that left you unable to have
another child. I believed abortion was wrong then and I
still do. And if Maggie had had an abortion, we wouldn't
have Sawyer today, would we? And perhaps we wouldn't
have Cole, either." Silence on the other end of the line.
Suddenly Billie was ashamed of herself. "Amelia, forgive
me. I had no right. What's wrong? It isn't just Sawyer
and Rand. I don't believe I've ever known you to be bitter,
and yet that's what I'm hearing in your voice. What is
it?"

"Nothing. I'm just edgy these days. And there's nothing to forgive, really. I shouldn't have said what I did."
Amelia swallowed against the tears that always seemed

so close to the surface these days. "Isn't there something we can do for Sawyer?"

"Thad suggested I go to New York on one pretense or another. But Sawyer would see right through my motives. She knows I'm here for her if she needs me. I have to think of Maggie, too. What do you suppose she's feeling?"

"Maggie's fighting it. I know she is," Amelia said. "But she isn't strong, Billie. She's looking for something in her life. For a while there, I thought she and Cranston were going to patch things up, but I guess it didn't work out. . . ." She sighed. "You're right, Billie. Let's leave it alone for now. Besides, Rand will be gone in a few days. I know he has to get back to England. He's selling out the estate, or most of it. Did you know that? He leaves day after tomorrow."

Days, Billie was thinking. So much could happen in three days. She reflected on her time in Hong Kong with Thad years ago. You could fall in love in minutes; you could commit your entire life to that love in days. Other people could be destroyed by that love and commitment in an instant. Where had she and Thad found the strength to deny themselves? Tears glistened in Billie's eyes at the knowledge of all the time wasted, time they could have had loving each other, being there for each other. Was that really what she wanted for Maggie? And in the end, would it really make any difference to Sawyer? It wouldn't make Rand love her again.

"Billie? . . . Billie, are you there? Can you hear me?"

"I hear you, dear. Keep an eye on Susan for me. You're so good at that. I'll never forget the way you took care of me when I was pregnant with Suse. If it weren't for you, Susan might never have been born. Thad and I want to know when you and Cary are going to come visit us here in Vermont."

"One of these days. Probably when I'm old and gray. It's so cold in Vermont, and it's all I can do to anticipate a Texas winter. I'm not looking forward to it."

Billie laughed. "Our winters are bitter, but then it's a

matter of who you spend them with. Thad's back is a wonderful place to warm cold feet."

"Bless you, Billie, for even admitting your feet get cold. I thought I was the only one."

It was eleven-ten when Cary walked into the bedroom. He grinned at Amelia and then groaned. "You're the best thing I've seen all day. And you smell good, too."

Amelia's heart soared. "Are you hungry? Can I get you a drink?"

Cary leered at her, his dark, expressive brows lowering over that hawklike gaze. "What I want from you doesn't come from the kitchen or the bar. This is going to be the shortest shower on record. Strip down, baby. I'll be right back."

Amelia found herself laughing happily. "That's the best offer you've made since yesterday." She did as he'd told her. The silky sheets felt cool against her naked skin. But that was only temporary.

Amelia rolled over onto her side, her face buried in her pillow, Cary sleeping soundly beside her. She didn't care that the pillowcase was making creases in her face or that if she didn't make herself sleep she'd be a wreck in the morning. All she cared about at the moment was that Cary had fallen asleep almost in the middle of their lovemaking. Her brain told her how exhausted he was; demon Vanity was telling her that she wasn't exciting enough to keep him awake.

Before anyone had come down to the breakfast table, Maggie sat there in her usual place addressing an envelope. She hummed as she picked up her engagement book and leafed through it. Lord, she was spreading herself thin. An accident about to happen, Riley liked to tease. She was keeping the three weekdays before Thanksgiving free in order to oversee preparations for the big day. The football game, the family dinner, the homecoming dance

for the boys the following night. The expected letdown
when it was all over. Then the official beginning of the
Christmas shopping season.

A thrill ran through her at just the thought of Christmas.
Presents, family, belonging. She wanted this year to be
the most festive ever, even outdoing Billie's efforts when
she'd lived here.

Her eyes dropped to the envelope she was addressing
to Sawyer. She'd tried several times to call Sawyer at her
office. Each time she'd been put on hold, then was told
Sawyer was out of the office and wouldn't return until
late: was there a message? Well, Sawyer couldn't ignore
a letter.

Dear Sawyer,

I tried calling your office today, but your secretary said you wouldn't be back till quite late. As
you know, I'm not much of a letter writer, but I
thought I'd take a crack at it since you didn't return
any of my other phone calls.

Obviously, you're upset with me—more so than
any time in the past. I think we should have talked
this out months ago. I'm sorry now we didn't.

The boys tell me you're staying with Adam
Jarvis. I'm glad. I know what a good friend he's
always been. Why don't you bring him home with
you for Thanksgiving? (I don't want to make this
an official invitation because this is your home and
I want you to come anytime you feel like it. The
door is always open to you.)

Christmas this year promises to be a huge success. Everyone will be here. I'm sure the boys have
told you Susan is already here. She's looking much
better these days. We're all sort of hoping for a boy,
but no one's saying it aloud!

I've told both Riley and Cole they can return to
New York with you the day after Christmas, assuming you come. At first Riley was going to go back
to Japan, then he decided against it. I wrote his

grandfather inviting him here, but he said he was too old and too set in his ways to make the trip. He also said he understood Riley's vacation was too short for a trip of that length.

I want you to know how grateful I am for the interest you've taken in Cole. It's made all the difference in the world to him. I wish he and Riley got on better, but they don't. I'm working on it!

I'm enclosing my Thanksgiving menu to entice you and Adam. Please try to make it. My Christmas menu is also enclosed. I only added one thing to it from our old traditional menu—plum pudding. Rand said he's partial to it.

I hope you aren't working too hard, Sawyer. New York is the place to be at this time of year. Enjoy yourself and get in touch even if it's just to say hello.

                                    Love,
                                    Maggie

Maggie carried the letter out to the mailbox. The air was cold and damp, and the thin sweater she'd wrapped around her shoulders for the walk down the drive wasn't much protection. But there was also a chill inside her. She felt awful about mentioning Rand to Sawyer in her letter. But she'd had to let her know he was going to be here. Sawyer had to make up her own mind.

Maggie leaned against the mailbox, unconscious of the cold, biting wind. How alone Sawyer must be feeling! How empty. Her heart went out to her daughter; she didn't want to see her hurt. Perhaps in time she'd forget about Rand, find someone else to love. What hope was there for Rand and herself otherwise? Any relationship between them would tear this family apart.

Abruptly Maggie turned and began to run back to the house as though a demon were at her heels. The cold air filled her lungs; her heart pounded. But she couldn't escape the words ricocheting in her head. *What about me? What about me?*

* * *

"Hey, I'm home! Anyone here?" Sawyer called as she bolted the door behind her. "Guess what. I took off early to cook dinner. Spaghetti and meatballs. I hope you're hungry. I bought all the stuff on my way home.... Anyone here?" she called a second time.

Adam groaned. Not ten minutes ago he'd finished a triple-decker sandwich with a side bowl of Franco American something or other. He looked down at the dimples and crevices on the House Speaker's face. The man just wasn't coming alive. Maybe it was the nose, or the hair. ... The hell with it. "I'm here. Did I hear you say you were going to cook? The peanut butter and jelly princess of Austin, Texas?!"

"Come see for yourself." Sawyer sailed her hat in the general direction of a chair. She flung her coat over another chair and sent her shoes and handbag in different directions.

Adam poked around the mesh bag. "Ahhh, jarred spaghetti sauce! Is this the one with savory herbs and spices that I'll recognize as being better than my grandmother's?"

"Same one. Of course, I'm going to add a few things to it to make it even better. I do know how to cook. It's just not one of my favorite pastimes."

"What is your favorite pastime?"

"Making love."

Adam stared at her. "What happened to you today?"

"I don't know. It started this morning when I put on my funky watermelon-colored hat. People stared at me. It was one of those contagious things. They smiled and I smiled. Strange for New York, eh?"

"Very strange. You should wear it every day if it has this effect on you. How long till dinner?" he asked, trying to look hungry.

"An hour, hour and a half at the most. I know you must be starved. I'll hurry."

"No, don't hurry. Why don't we have a drink while

the sauce bubbles, or doesn't it have to bubble since it's from a jar?"

Sawyer peered at Adam's face. "You've eaten, haven't you?"

"A little of this and a little of that. Mostly I picked and nibbled. By ten o'clock I could probably eat a nine-course meal. You could put that time to good use by cleaning the bathroom. It's your turn."

"I was going to do it tomorrow."

"That's what you said last week. Once you do the meatballs, you know the rest takes care of itself. I'll do the tub and shower if you do the sink and the floor. I'll flip you for the john."

"No, you won't. I can handle all of it. Go back to your drawing board. Dinner will be at ten and I get to take the first shower in the clean bathroom."

"Wipe down the damn walls, will you?"

"Go, go, go." Sawyer made shooing motions out of the kitchen.

Adam settled himself in front of the drawing board, and within seconds the paper sprang to life. As he worked, his characters took on distinct personalities, and the little quote he finally thought up to give to the House Speaker in the bubble made him chortle. A few more bold strokes, his name scrawled at the bottom, and he'd finished for the day.

"Bathroom's done!" Sawyer called. "I'm going to take a shower. Drain the spaghetti when the timer goes off. We can dine when you pour the wine."

Adam's stomach rumbled. He wasn't hungry. But he would do justice to this culinary endeavor if it killed him.

Sawyer joined him later wearing a flowing tangerine-colored caftan and high-heeled slipers with fluffy pom-poms. She'd applied a light dusting of powder to her face and added some perfume. Adam approved—oh, yes, he approved.

She played the perfect hostess that evening—waited on Adam as if he were the love of her life, inquired if the food was done properly, saw that his wineglass was filled, and kept her dinner conversation lively. He tried to ignore the strain he saw in her blue eyes.

"The least I can do is clean up. Take the wine bottle into the den and put on some good music. I'm too stuffed to do anything but crash out. You outdid yourself tonight, my dear," Adam said in his best W. C. Fields voice.

"What rest of the wine? We drank it all. You drank most of it."

"Guilty as charged. We'll simply have to crack open another bottle. Get out of my way while I clean up." In sixty seconds Adam had the dishes in the sink, the condiments back in the cabinet, and the lid on the spaghetti pot. He whisked the bread crumbs onto the floor, explaining that Marble would clean them up later. By the time he'd placed the bowl of fruit back in the center of the table, Sawyer had uncorked a second bottle of wine.

"Ah, if only this was Dom Perignon." Adam sighed.

"You're half-buzzed now. Riunite will be just fine. You're lucky it isn't Ripple."

"I cut my teeth on Ripple. So did you. Don't go getting fancy on me." Adam grinned.

"We did have fun in those days, didn't we?"

"Things haven't changed all that much," Adam said as he put his arm around her shoulder. "You're you and I'm me. We grew up a little. Supposedly, we're responsible adults now. Know what? Sometimes I want to be a kid again."

Sawyer turned. "What you want, what we all want at some point in our lives, is yesterday. To go back and relive the important times. That's what I'd like to do."

Adam grew serious. "You're talking about Rand, aren't you? Why do you keep torturing yourself? You said it was over."

"I didn't say that. I did, actually.... What I mean is that's what Rand said. I know he doesn't mean it. It's the age difference. When I see him at Christmas, I think we can patch it up. I know I'm going to try. Whatever I did to upset him will have faded and we'll be able to talk and straighten it out."

"What if it doesn't work?" Adam asked quietly.

"It has to work! I can't see myself going on without him. He loves me; I know he does. We...we just have a problem, and we're going to work it out."

"Maggie?"

Sawyer's face colored. "I'm ashamed of myself, Adam. How could I have thought such a thing just because I saw Rand and Maggie talking? *Talking*, for God's sake! I know I've always said Maggie was a man-eater, but I was just blowing off steam. Sometimes she made me so mad I couldn't think of anything horrible enough to say about her. I must've been crazy to think she set out to snatch Rand from me. Maggie just wouldn't do anything like that!"

"Well said, well said."

"For God's sake, she's my mother! Besides, Rand is too decent, too much of a gentleman, to do anything so ...so..."

"Shitful?"

"Yes, damn it, yes!"

"Hey! Cool down. I'm agreeing with you." He poured from the bottle a second time. By now his eyes were glassy and he had to keep blinking in order to focus.

"I have it all planned. I know exactly what I'm going to say," Sawyer told him, her voice slurring a bit. "I'll make sure it's at just the right time. I've rehearsed it a hundred different times. It really is true, that old saying ...if you want something bad enough, you can get it if you keep trying."

"Sawyer, I don't want to see you set yourself up for another disappointment."

"Don't look at me that way! There's pity in your eyes!" Suddenly, she covered her face with her hands; her sobs came in great choking heaves.

"No, no, there's not," Adam said, alarmed. He crept closer to her, taking her into his arms. "My heart is breaking for you, Sawyer, but that's not the same thing as pity, is it?"

She buried her face in the crook of his neck. He could feel her body shuddering, shaking with the force of her sobs racking through her delicate bones and heating her flesh. Too much wine, too little control, and Sawyer was fragmenting into tiny shards, each of them stabbing his heart.

He held her for a long time. When at last it seemed her tears were exhausted, he carried her to bed as though she were a child. She felt so light, almost weightless; he wondered how many meals she'd skipped, how much weight she'd lost. Could a person truly die of a broken heart?

He placed her gently on her bed and pulled the comforter up around her shoulders. She was so still, so silent, he thought she was asleep. Just as he was about to leave, she reached for his hand. "Don't leave me, Adam. Please. I don't think I can bear to be alone. Hold me. Just hold me."

Adam lay down beside her, cradling her in his arms. She pressed her face into his shoulder; he could feel her warm breath on his neck. "I'll hold you, honey. Forever, if I have to. Sleep, try to sleep."

"You're good, Adam, so good."

Through the night he held her, calming her night tortures when she stirred and soothing the little sobs that erupted without warning.

He loved her. And if she couldn't love him in return, then it would have to be enough that she needed him.

{{{{{{{{{ CHAPTER FIFTEEN }}}}}}}}}

When Adam awoke in Sawyer's bed next morning, she was already up and moving around. He cracked an eyelid open and followed her progress across the loft to the bathroom. He heard the rush of water and the now familiar rattle of the aspirin bottle.

Adam lay quietly, trying not to think of the interminable night through which he'd held her, soothed her, his own heart breaking with the futility of it all. He'd calmed tears shed for another man when all the while he wanted her for himself.

When the shower stopped, he burrowed a little deeper into the covers. Sawyer came back into her room and selected several items from her closet. Back in the bathroom the blow-dryer whined. He could get up, he thought, see to it that she had some breakfast—but he wasn't certain what kind of reception he'd receive. The last thing he wanted was for Sawyer to be shy and ashamed of having needed his comfort during the night. Would she be embarrassed that she'd bared her soul to him? That the bravado she'd been trying to exhibit had crumbled into a thousand pieces, leaving her so vulnerable?

Adam's eyes snapped shut. Sawyer was on the move again. The scent of her perfume trailed behind her, seeming to settle near the bed. When the scent localized, he knew she was staring down at him; he could hear her breathing. "Sleep well, dragon slayer," she whispered as she kissed him on the mouth. "Thank you."

When the door to the loft closed, he brought his finger to his lips.

Today was a work day, Adam tried to convince himself, not that he had any ideas. He didn't feel like working. He didn't want to work. What he wanted to do was impose on an old friend who was a practicing psychiatrist and talk to him about Sawyer. Six-thirty in the morning wasn't too early. Nick would grumble and complain, but he'd come through. That's what friends were for.

"What do you mean you're still sleeping?" Adam asked with mock indignation. "You told me and everyone else you know that you run through Central Park at six in the morning. Five miles!"

"So I lied. I run around the apartment at seven o'clock. Same thing." The sleepy voice groaned. "It's a sin to call someone this early."

"I need to talk to you, Nick. It's important. How about stopping by before the office and I'll make us some breakfast."

Nick's voice was suddenly brisk, almost professional. "What's wrong? You sound okay. This won't be for free, you know."

"It's Sawyer. She needs some help."

"If she needs help, why isn't she calling me instead of you? She'd at least have the decency to wait till seven thirty. You can't save the world and everyone in it, Adam. When are you going to get that through your head?"

"The same time you do. Who do you think you're kidding? I know how you spend your free time. You're the biggest savior of all. We have to try."

"You're a pain in my butt, Jarvis. I want eggs Benedict, fresh-squeezed orange juice, and a side order of home fries. Real ones."

"If I do that, I don't want a bill."

"Fine. Swear to me you'll send a hundred fifty dollars to the YMCA Children's Camp Fund."

"You son of a bitch, is that how much you get an hour?" Adam squawked.

"Someone has to pay for my Park Avenue address. I'll see you in forty-five minutes."

"Eggs Benedict and home fries, my ass!" Adam fumed as he stormed around the kitchen. He was just rinsing the last vestiges of shaving cream from his face when Nick Deitrick banged on his door.

Nick was round, a one-size-fits-all type body type. He had a trusting, compassionate gaze, pink cheeks, and a winsome smile that endeared him to his patients. No one who wanted to remain his friend ever referred to his encroaching male pattern baldness.

"At least you could have put out the ketchup to kill the taste," he grumbled. "What did you fry these eggs in, and why are they brown like this? I never saw eggs this color."

"The butter burned. I never said I was a cook. How are the fries?"

"Don't ask. Talk while I eat. I can do two things at the same time, unlike some people I know."

Nick studied his friend as he talked. The man looked terrible, like the life was being drained out of him. And Nick knew why.

"Sawyer's been here since July, as you know," Adam said, running his fingers distractedly through his hair. "She was pretty heavy into a relationship with this English dude. He used to be an RAF jet pilot and he tested the Coleman Aviation plane. You remember that?" Nick nodded. "She had herself convinced they were going to get married. Over the Fourth this guy, Rand, broke it off with her and she came here. There's another problem. It's possible that Sawyer's mother, Maggie, and this guy Rand might have something going. When Sawyer first came here, that's what she thought; now she's convinced it's not true, or at least she *says* she is. I'm worried about her. She looks like a ghost. She's lost weight; she works sixteen hours a day; she gets these headaches all the time.

She doesn't seem able to throw off her depression. Last night she told me that she's going back to Texas for Christmas and Rand will be there. She's convinced she's going to make things right between them."

Nick chewed his toast and swallowed his coffee. "Aside from playing big brother in all of this, what's your interest?"

"I love her, Nick. You've always known that."

Nick nodded. "What Sawyer is going through is normal and natural. Everyone has a time clock for grief, and she is grieving, you know. Depression is usually triggered by a loss of some kind: a mate, a lover, a job. When you have to face a loss, you feel lost. Sawyer was pulled up short, stopped in her tracks. The thread of continuity in her life snapped. Are you following me? Sawyer's life wasn't ever smooth to begin with; you've told me the story."

"But this isn't like Sawyer," Adam protested. "She should be coming out of it a little. Instead, she's planning and scheming ways to get Rand back. She won't let go."

"And of course you want her to let go so you can step in," Nick said quietly.

Adam leaned across the table. "Yes, that would be nice, but I don't bank on it. Sawyer had plenty of opportunities to have me if she wanted me; she didn't, and I'd be a fool to think she would now."

"But you're hoping."

Adam stood up abruptly, toppling his chair backward. "Yes, dammit, I'm hoping!" he cried, slamming his fist on the table in an uncharacteristic display of rage. "But I'm afraid for her. I know she's on the ragged edge, and she's basing everything on Christmas. What if it doesn't work out? What happens to her then? What if she wasn't off base about something going on between this dude and her mother?"

"I could reel off a lot of medical jargon, but I won't. Sawyer's loss is challenged. It was forceful, unexpected, and right now she probably can't imagine her life without Rand. In her depression she's mourning the loss of that someone who gave meaning to her life. She should be searching for a replacement so she can build on her loss. But before she can do that, she has to accept the end of the relationship.... I should be talking to her, not you," Nick grumbled.

"Are you saying it's okay for her to go back home over Christmas and try again? That maybe it'll show her the relationship is really over so she can go on from there?"

Nick shrugged. "Like I said, I should be talking to her, not you."

Adam raked his fingers through his hair. "Look, Nick, I need to understand. I might be able to get through to her and even get her to go see you."

"Fine, but I suspect it won't be easy. It's hard to come to terms with a loss. Sawyer is probably thinking that to go on without Rand is being disloyal to her own ideals as well as to him. Silly? Incongruous?" Nick smiled. "Yeah, I know, but that's the way it is. Some people take longer than others. You can't measure love with a yardstick."

"What can I do to help?"

"Be her friend. Be there for her. Try to get her to seek professional help. It can shorten the grieving. Many of us need to be given permission to let go of the past."

"I appreciate this, Nick. I should have made you a decent breakfast."

"Forget it. Nick wiped his chin and swallowed the cold dregs of his coffee. He reached out with pudgy pink hands to grip Adam's long, slender fingers. "Sawyer is a survivor. Remember that."

"I'll try. Christmas is looming like a monster for me now. I was going to Vermont to ski, but now..."

"Go!" Nick was as concerned about Adam as Adam was about Sawyer. If his friend wasn't careful, he might end up in Sawyer's shoes, suffering the same kind of loss. He sighed. "And call me if there's anything I can do, will you?"

Adam smiled. "Thanks, Nick."

"Anytime. Don't forget about the YMCA."

"It's done."

* * *

Sawyer sat at her desk rubbing her eyes, trying to massage away her headache. It was only eight-ten and most of the staff was just straggling in. She'd made the coffee, picked up the Danish on her way to work, and was contemplating the rest of the day. In order to face it, she had to look back at the long, long night.

She had used Adam. Eagerly taken the comfort he'd offered and given nothing in return. But in truth, she'd do it all over again if it meant she could get through another long, lonely night. It was the nights that were impossible to bear, when memories and dreams chased sleep like the demons they were. She'd slept more last night than she had in months. And when she'd stirred, Adam was there to comfort her.

Adam. She loved him—in a special way. Was that what Rand meant when he'd said he loved her but wasn't in love with her? No, no, it was different with Rand. They'd been lovers; they'd shared something she had never shared with Adam. Maybe she *was* being selfish, using Adam this way, but she couldn't help it. Anything was better than this madness; anything was better than being alone with the emptiness and broken dreams.

Sawyer shuffled some papers on her desk, and a red-and-blue TWA ticket holder slid across her desk. She was supposed to go to Hong Kong at the end of the week! How could she have forgotten such an important trip?

Grandpap's fuel-efficient, small-scale jet plane, christened the *Coleman Condor* by Billie, was slowly but surely creeping toward full-scale production. It was an important project, one that could secure the Coleman family fortunes. So, even though Sawyer was primarily an aeronautical engineer, she had undertaken to see personally to every detail of its completion. In Hong Kong she would be supervising the purchase of quality fabric and the manufacture of the *Condor*'s luxury-detailed seats and overhead liners.

One glance at her appointment book told her she was going to be on the run up until it was time to board the plane. Three-and-a-half weeks in Hong Kong was a long time. Perhaps she should write the boys before she left— or, better yet, call them.

Sawyer asked for an outside line, and in seconds she heard Martha's voice telling her to hold on. When Cole's voice boomed over the wire, she slid the phone away from her ear. She'd forgotten how deep and loud the boy's voice was. "It's Sawyer, Cole. I'm sorry about calling so early, but I wanted you to know I'm going to Hong Kong in a few days. I'm behind on my letter writing. I didn't want you worrying about me or trying to call."

"Hong Kong! I wish I could go. Grandmam Billie said it's a wonderful place to visit."

"It is, but this is business. How about next summer? I can probably arrange my vacation to coincide with whenever you're free. Work on it. It'll give us both something to look forward to.

"What's going on at Sunbridge? How's school? Keeping your marks up? How's the football team doing?"

"School's okay. My grades are A's and the football team is undefeated. It's because of Riley," he said grudgingly. "I think he's going to make the all-stars."

"Does that bother you? The truth now."

"Sure it bothers me. He does everything great. The coach says he's a natural for football and any other sport, for that matter. I can't hack sports. He even snagged the best-looking girl, and she's captain of the cheerleading squad, for his date at the dance. Every guy in school has the hots for her. I don't know how he did it."

"By being nice, probably. He is a nice kid, and so are you. You guys could have made a great team. I wish you'd work on it, Cole. Jealousy is an awful thing to have to deal with."

"Mother is on my back all the time about it. By the way, Rand is here." He heard the deadly stillness come over the wire and wished he could cut his tongue out. "He brought Aunt Susan here. She's sick, or it's something about the baby. Mother says she looks awful," Cole babbled. "He's not staying. In fact, I think he's leaving tomorrow."

"It's okay, Cole. You don't have to make explanations to me. And you're right; it does hurt. I haven't heard from him at all."

"He's a bastard, if you want my opinion. He's on mother's tail no matter where she goes. I watch them. Aunt Amelia chewed him out the other day. I heard him tell that to Mother. Aunt Susan keeps watching them, too. Riley . . . well, it's hard to tell with Riley, but I think he stares at the two of them a lot." Another deadly silence.

"Listen, do you want me to say anything to him? Cole said desperately. "Give him a message or tell him about your trip?"

Sawyer could feel a sob building in her throat. She had to get off the phone. "No, no, don't say anything. I—I have to get back to work now, Cole. And you better get off to school before you're late. I'll send you a postcard from Hong Kong," she said hoarsely. "Take care of yourself."

"You, too. Goody-bye."

Cole looked at the telephone for a long time. His eyes spewed anger as he made his way to the dining room and saw his mother and Rand at the table, laughing and eating together like an old married couple.

"Cole! You're going to be late!" Maggie warned.

"I've got a study hall first period. Don't you care if I eat or not?"

"Of course I care. I thought you ate with Riley. He's gone."

"My plate is next to yours. Does it look like I. ate?" Cole asked snidely as he filled his plate with scrambled eggs. He jerked his head in Rand's direction. "What's he still doing here?" It pleased him to see Rand's lips tighten.

"What do you mean, what's he doing here? Rand brought Susan home."

"She's been home for two days and he's still here. Don't tell me—he's holding her hand. Oops, wrong again.

It's your hand he's holding," Cole said coldly. "Isn't that right, Mother?"

"That's enough! Apologize."

"To who for what?" Cole asked with his mouth full.

"To Rand."

"He doesn't deserve an apology. I don't think he belongs here. A few other people don't think he belongs here, either." He stood up abruptly. "Well, I have to get going so I don't miss my second class." At the doorway he turned and asked, "Just when *are* you leaving, Rand?"

Goddamn little monster, Rand thought. Sawyer's champion. But how could he blame Cole for trying to protect his sister?

"Soon," he said.

"How soon?" Cole shot back.

"Will tonight be quick enough for you?"

"No, but if that's the best you can do, then do it. We don't need you here, none of us."

Maggie got up from her chair, her face drained of all color. "I don't want to hear another word out of you, Cole. We'll discuss this tonight."

"Before or after the Earl of Wickham leaves?" Cole said before stamping from the room.

Maggie stood silent for a long time, her arms crossed over her chest, her chin raised in defiance. "Goddamn you, Rand. Why didn't you break it off with Sawyer when she was in California? Why here, where for some reason everyone believes it's my fault? My God, I can't even defend myself. Cole believes we're having an affair. He probably told Sawyer and Mam and anyone else who would listen. He's absolutely right; you have to leave— the sooner the better."

"I do want to have an affair with you. It's all I've been thinking about. Admit it—you've been thinking the same thing!" Accusation met accusation; Maggie stormed from the room and Rand felt like a dog.

Susan was holding on to the banister as she descended the stairs. She looked a little better; at least there was some life in her eyes. Rand met her halfway up.

"Late for breakfast again," she said. "I'm ravenous.
And I'm going to eat."

"Good girl. You'll be feeling better in no time at all.
Well, you better get along before Martha clears the sideboard. I've got some packing to do."

"Are you leaving so soon?"

"There are those among us who think I've overstayed
my welcome. Just out of curiosity, what do you think?"

Susan stared at this man she'd known practically all
her life. He was like a big brother, an uncle, almost a
father image. She loved him and was grateful for the many
kindnesses he'd done her over the years. She tried to
choose her words carefully. "I think, Rand, that you should
return to England, not because of what anyone thinks or
feels, but because this isn't the right time. Sawyer's one
of us. It always comes down to that in one way or another,
us versus them. Right now, you're one of them. We Colemans have a tendency to close ranks. You saw it happen
with Jerome. Maggie is vulnerable right now."

"And you think I'd take advantage of that, do you?"

"Not deliberately. Maggie can't keep her eyes off you.
I noticed you have trouble in that department yourself.
There's a ghost between you. For God's sake, Rand,
Sawyer is Maggie's daughter! You understand that, don't
you?"

"Only too well. What would happen, Susan, if I told
you I loved Maggie and she loved me? What would all
you Colemans do then?"

Susan shook her head slowly. "I don't know. I suppose
we'd have to wait and see. I know what Sawyer must be
going through. She loved you, Rand. She thought you
were going to marry her. Now, Sawyer is not a stupid
woman. She must have gotten that impression somehow.
You've hurt her terribly, Rand. Her Coleman pride pre-
vents her from letting you know just how much."

"Would you want me to marry Sawyer if I wasn't in
love with her?"

Susan's puffy eyes were cold now, heartless. "You made the decision. You didn't give her a chance. You just ripped out her guts and walked away." She brushed past him, then turned abruptly, almost losing her balance. "Can I ask you something, Rand?" He nodded. "Did Sawyer ever say the age difference bothered her?"

"No."

"Did she ever say she wanted children?"

"Not in so many words. All women want children."

"Did she ever say she could be just as happy with you without children?"

"In words to that effect," Rand said harshly. "If you're trying to make me feel guilty, you don't have to bother. I feel terrible."

"It wasn't a mutual ending. She didn't have anything to say about it. She didn't deserve that kind of treatment."

"You're right; she didn't. I'm not disagreeing with you. But I'm not apologizing, either."

"Maybe you should," Susan said softly, and turned away.

Up in his room, Rand flopped miserably on the bed. He lay for a long time with his hands laced behind his head, his thoughts racing. Right? Wrong? If he had it to do over again, would he do it any differently?

There had been a time in his life when people's opinions hadn't bothered him. Now that he was older, it was important to him what other people thought. Billie and Thad were at the top of the list. And Amelia. He didn't want them thinking he was a bastard. If something wasn't right, it wasn't right. Did he have to be miserable to make someone else happy? But then again, did he have the right to make someone else miserable?

Poor Sawyer, what had he done to her? The answer was so terrible, he rolled over on the bed. One clenched fist pounded the pillow. He'd destroyed her. He knew it as sure as he knew he had to take another breath. Beautiful, wonderful Sawyer. And he was itching and lusting for Maggie. Jesus.

Rand rolled back over and stared at the ceiling. There was no way he could make things right. What was done was done. He, Sawyer, and Maggie were going to have to live with it.

Her scent arrived before she did. Rand opened his eyes in surprise to see Maggie in front of the closed door.

"Are you leaving?" she asked in a strange voice.

"I didn't hear anyone asking me to stay. I'm some kind of bloody pariah now. Susan just laced into me coming up the stairs. Cole hates me and does his best to make it known. Riley can barely tolerate me. My own mother told me where to get off. You've pushed me away. And you want to know if I'm leaving? I'm sorry I came."

"I'm not. I felt so happy with you here. It's almost as though you belong."

"I don't belong here. Sawyer's ghost lives here."

Maggie's eyes spewed fire. Her lips trembled and she clenched her hands into white-knuckled fists. "It's always Sawyer. No matter what I do, no matter where I go, she's between me and whatever it is I want. I can't get away from her. I've always been jealous of her. She was given what should have been mine. If it had been mine from the beginning, I never would have become a roadside whore at the age of fourteen and she never would've been born!"

"Maggie, Maggie, you don't know what you're saying."

"Oh, don't I? Don't I?" She crossed the room and loomed over him. He was sitting on the edge of the bed now, alarmed at her sudden intrusion, overwhelmed by her fury. "She even had you, damn her, she even had you!" Enraged and provoked by his feeble attempt to soothe her, Maggie attacked, pummeling him with the heels of her hands, beating him in her madness; all the while, hot tears streamed down her face, heaving sobs erupted in her throat.

Rand caught her against him, throwing her onto the bed beside him, attempting to control her struggles with his weight. Bit by bit her fury passed, leaving her exhausted and miserable. He smoothed the silky dark hair back from her forehead, crooning to her, comforting her. "Cry, Maggie. Cry for the both of us."

She looked up at him, a curious little expression in her eyes, as though she were seeing him there for the first time. "I don't want to cry! I want to make love to you!" At the edge of her tone was a trace of desperation.

Rand covered her mouth with his own, pulling her body against his. Yes, yes, Maggie was thinking. Yes, make love to me now, while I'm still angry enough to go through with it, while I don't give a damn about anyone or anything except what I want.

As Maggie surrendered herself to Rand's loving, her wild thoughts scurried like mice in a maze. She told herself she wanted Rand; she even believed she loved him. She was Maggie; not Billie, who had made a career of self-sacrifice until her commitment to her family was completed. Life was too short to be so good and noble. Life was too empty and it was hard to be alone.

Alone. Alone. The word echoed in her brain. She focused on it, allowing all the rage, jealousy, and resentment to fall aside. Only the guilt remained. But it's only for now, Maggie told herself, only for this little while. She'd come into Rand's room blind with rage. She was maddened with herself that she was sending Rand away and out of her life, and yet, ridiculously, she was angry with him that he'd hurt Sawyer. Absurd, ludicrous, and even lunatic, but that's the way it was.

Rand was reveling in the feel of Maggie's arms clinging to him. This was what he'd been dreaming of for months. This was what had kept him awake and miserable all those long, lonely nights. To be with her, to hold her in his arms this way, to know she felt the same way about him. All the notes and letters, the telephone conversations, ways to get to know her. Seeing her here at Sunbridge, knowing her concern for family, all these things brought her closer to him. Even Cole, who never missed an opportunity to be difficult and unloving; Maggie loved the boy. Her devotion to Riley, her understanding with Susan, even the rage with which she'd first entered his room. All these things were a part of Maggie and he loved her.

In his arms he held a woman who had tested life and had come to know herself. She wasn't a child who believed love could overcome any obstacle. Experience and maturity, those were a part of Maggie, too. And now he wanted to become a part of her, to share with her, be understood by her and, in turn, to understand her. This Maggie, his Maggie.

His lips seemed to devour her, nipping gently at her throat and falling lower between her breasts. Eager fingers, greedy for the feel of his skin, lifted the bottom of his sweater, exploring the expanse of his back, the solidness of his muscles, the width of his shoulders. Fury still pounded through her blood. She wanted Rand in spite of herself, in spite of Sawyer's pain and what might be ahead of them.

Maggie became immersed in Rand's kisses, allowing his gentle, unhurried touch to calm her roiling emotions. Again and again his mouth came down on hers, sometimes softly and at other times with a sense of desperation, as though he believed she might slip through his arms like a vaporous dream. He seemed to sense that she wanted him to take her quickly, because he murmured, "Slow, Maggie, slow. I want it to last. Make it last."

His movements were unhurried and controlled, arousing her, allowing her to put everything behind her and to concentrate only on him. Her heart was beating randomly; all her senses awakened, responding to him, becoming acutely aware of his touch on the fullness of her breasts and of the heat that was generating at her center. He undressed her—slowly—unwrapping her as though she were a long-awaited gift, discovering her inch by inch and always smoothing or kissing her newly exposed skin.

When she lay naked upon his bed, he undressed himself beneath her heated gaze. Her eyes were drawn to the masculine slope of his shoulders, the flat of his belly, and the firm globes of his buttocks. Fine golden hairs furred his chest, and when he stepped closer, the light from the window revealed the integration of silver among the gold.

He lay down beside her and she moved easily into his arms, pressing herself against him. She nuzzled the delicate skin at the base of his neck, tickled her lips against his crisp chest fur, inhaled the spicy clean scent of his shower soap, aware of the presence of his own male scent beneath.

Rand's hands were in Maggie's hair, lifting the glossy black strands to his lips, stroking the nape of her neck and tracing patterns along her jaw. It was as though he were committing her to memory, as if his lips and fingers were branding her image in his brain. The kisses he traced along the curve of her neck sent little shivers of delight up her spine. Anticipation throbbed through her veins and warmed her center. It seemed an eternity that she wanted to know him this way, but it had only been a matter of months. Months, weeks, a lifetime. She'd tried to rid him from her thoughts and, failing that, had attempted to place him within the confines of friendship. She'd failed. Only now could she admit to herself that during Cranston's visit and their most intimate moments together, it had been Rand she'd wanted and needed. She'd tried to substitute, but nothing she'd dreamed or fantasized could have prepared her for this moment.

His hands traveled her body, lightly skimming her tingling flesh from the hollows beneath her breasts to her smooth haunches. He explored the curve of her hips and the softness of her belly to the firmness of her bottom. She shuddered beneath his hand when he leaned up on one elbow to follow this newly discovered path with moist kisses and gentle teasings of his tongue. It was as though she were rediscovering herself through this journey of hand and mouth. She reveled in his delight and in the growing, hungry need that burned through her loins.

Maggie was unable to lie still beneath his touch. His

caresses had inspired something in her, a need to share, a desire to give. In tender, sensuous patterns she stroked his flesh, beginning at the definition of his chest to the plane of his belly. She traced his hair patterns, following the lines that swirled upward over his breasts and downward over his middle to a darker, thicker patch surrounding his sex. He quivered when she kneaded the muscle of his inner thigh and moved upward to his groin. Her movements were teasing, enticing, affecting her as well as Rand until the throbbing in her veins became a roaring demand to have him for her own, to become a part of him and him a part of her. His mouth moved over her body with exquisite care, nipping, nibbling, heating her flesh.

"Now, Rand, now?" she whispered. It was a question; it was a demand.

"Now, Maggie, my Maggie." His voice was husky, filled with emotion. He wanted her, had wanted her these many months, but the emotion was deeper than being with her this way. He didn't merely want to couple with her; he wanted to fulfill her, to know her and become a part of her. When he placed himself between her open thighs, he looked down into her face, seeing there her kiss-bruised mouth, moist and pouting, the flush of passion staining her cheeks and spreading over her throat. But it was her eyes that held him, the color of a summer sky and glistening with tears. His heart reached out for hers as he kissed the crystal droplets that had fallen onto her cheeks. Her own heart, Maggie's heart, was only a breath away. And when she cried his name, it seemed their souls broke through an eternity of desolation to reach out, to touch. Loneliness and emptiness were banished, and it was with a boundless joy that she drew him inside her, the passage hot and wet, stroking with long, slow undulations.

He arched his back, holding himself above her, his loins pressed hard against hers, forcing himself to be still, struggling for control as he had not since his first sexual experience. That same boyish impatience flooded through him, but the man he had become knew the wisdom of waiting and relishing each sensation and sharing it with his partner. But Maggie refused to be still beneath him. Her hands raked his chest, teasing his nipples and pulling at the hair. Her hips moved, rocking her body beneath his, locking him against her, her sheath stroking and rippling around him until he yielded to her passions and her driving needs.

He thrust himself into her, seeking to relieve this pulsing ache she had created in him, unable to go deep enough or hard enough, until the fire spread from his loins to touch every part of him, and he surrendered to the blinding rapture and joyful knowledge that Maggie was just behind him, following closely, sharing in this glory.

Maggie became a part of him, suffering the same agony, seeking the same release. She followed the route he charted, heard the cries from his throat and reveled in the deep thrusts that filled her completely. She held herself to him, matching his movements, feeling herself floating beyond these delicious physical sensations to a place that was quiet and still, a place where he waited for her to touch her soul with his own. Her fingers dug into his flanks as she penetrated the last barrier before finding her own satisfaction, giving herself over to the warm waves of pleasure ebbing and flowing with each beat of her heart.

They held each other for a very long time, like two children hiding in the dark while they waited for the danger to pass. He rested his chin on the top of her head, smoothing the round of her shoulder and stroking the tender skin near her temples. She was crying. There were tears in his own eyes and a lump in his throat. He didn't need to ask why she was crying; words were unnecessary when two souls touched. They had done it, committed the very sin of which they were accused.

"Now, more than ever, I have to leave, Maggie." His voice was deep, ragged.

She nodded. "Yes, you must leave." She choked back the tears, swallowing hard, working her throat muscles until she could ask, "Will you come back, Rand? Will you?"

"That's up to you, Maggie, my Maggie," he said when he could speak. "Will you want me to come back? We've found something together, darling, something very, very precious. The question you must ask yourself is do we have any right to keep it?"

{{{{{{{{{ CHAPTER SIXTEEN }}}}}}}}}

The kaleidoscope of autumn's colors gave way to the drab browns of encroaching winter. Halloween passed with a lone jack-o'-lantern dotting the portico of Sunbridge. The early weeks of November rushed past accompanied by, according to the weather forecasters, the most severe weather in years.

The last football game of the season was played and won by Crystal City High, thanks to Riley's defending tackle and interception. The dance ended on a high note of frivolity. Maggie herself was one of the chaperones. Cole did not attend.

December found Maggie meeting herself coming and going. Texas, it seemed, went all out for Christmas. She was forever chasing from one meeting to another, freely lending her name and her expertise. She used her lunch hours to run to the Crystal City Post Office, where she rented a mailbox. At least every other day box 771 held an airmail letter from England. She sat in the parking lot, nibbling on crackers, while she read Rand's latest offering. She herself wrote almost every day—light, chatty, newsy letters full of the happenings of her life. Always she ended each letter with the hope that he would join all of them for the holidays. She said she counted the days, the hours, and sometimes the minutes.

Today she had to Christmas shop. She'd put it off too long already. She wanted mountains of gifts for everyone, and the biggest Christmas tree in all of Texas. And she meant to have it. This was a special Christmas.

Another few days and the boys would be out of school for the holidays. She'd made no definite plans yet. She didn't even know for sure who was coming for the holidays. Billie and Thad had agreed to come, subject to last-minute events at the farm. She'd been unable to reach Sawyer for confirmation. Cole and Riley claimed to be uncertain of Sawyer's plans. Rand hadn't definitely committed, either, but she was certain he would come because she wished for it every night.

She was so busy planning parties, luncheons, and tree trimmings, not to mention a private church service, she hardly had time to remember that her divorce from Cranston would become final soon after the New Year. She would deal with that on the second day of January, she told herself.

Maggie sat for a few moments holding Rand's letter to her breast, oblivious to the mink-clad woman who walked past the car. Amelia was tempted to tap on the window, but didn't. There was something clandestine about the way Maggie was sitting in the parking lot of the post office holding a paper close to her breast. Obviously she had a secret. It didn't surprise Amelia. And it didn't take any brains at all to figure out who the secret was.

Amelia completed her business at the post office and was leaving the building when she saw Maggie pull out of the parking lot. It was probably a good thing Maggie hadn't noticed her, she thought as she got into her car. She might have said something that could be taken wrong.

Amelia sighed as she pulled out of the parking lot. Life at Sunbridge was not what she'd thought it would be. There were so many undercurrents these days! Cole and

Riley were at each other's throats hourly. Susan wandered around the house with a vague, lost look in her eyes. Maggie was always flitting from this place to that. Even Cary seemed out of it. Business was consuming him; their lovemaking had dwindled to once a week on a Sunday morning—and even then only if she initiated it.

Every day this week she'd called and invited Cary to lunch. Every day he'd refused, nicely of course, saying he had to be on the site. She'd offered to bring a picnic basket in the car, but he'd vetoed that, saying the other workmen wouldn't appreciate it. They ate together, all the hard hats, with the bosses.

She was almost at the site now. Maybe she could stop and at least say hello. She could go into the trailer office, have a cup of coffee, and leave a note for her husband on his clipboard. He'd get a kick out of that. Or would he feel she was chasing him, not giving him breathing room? The hell with what he felt. This was what she wanted to do and she was going to do it.

The road leading to the construction site was a series of deep potholes, all of them filled with water. For miles all she could see was acres of mud and slabs of concrete. Here and there were trailers with wires hooked up to generators. Bulldozers, all manner of heavy-duty equipment, were at work.

She sat for a minute before she turned off the ignition, wondering if it all was going to work. Was Texas ready for Cary's dream? God, it was going to take ten years to complete. She could be dead by then. Cary would just be coming into his own, a handsome fiftyish widower. The thought was so terrible Amelia almost leaped from the car. Mud splashed up on the silvery mink. She cursed loudly and strongly. Then she laughed. She'd wear hip boots and slog through mud up to her waist if she could be near Cary. She'd eat out of a metal lunch box and wear a bright yellow hard hat. She might even give up her false eyelashes and fingernails if they got in the way.

Amelia drew in her breath when she opened the door

to the trailer office. The last time she'd seen it, it was
dirty and messy. Clutter everywhere. Some magical fairy
must have been at work, she decided. Now there were
tailored drapes on windows that just last month were practically solid grime. Green plants rested in wicker baskets
on the tables. The floor was clean and the lamps dusted.
There were piles of incoming and outgoing mail in wire
baskets on Cary's desk, next to a new computer/printer.
Amelia frowned. Cary hadn't said anything about a computer. The old black telephone was gone, too, replaced
by one of AT&T's newest consoles.

Amelia looked completely around her. She didn't
remember the walls being paneled. Or the aluminum-
framed pictures of different sections of the state of Texas.
Four chocolatey-colored chairs were scattered about the
long room, with not a trace of fuzz or dust on the deep-
welted corduroy. The bar, another new addition, was
stocked with expensive brands of liquor. She knew there'd
be a refrigerator behind it, filled with beer and soft drinks.
Clients? Hardly. Probably Cary and his partners. The union
men wouldn't be permitted to tramp in and out of this
office.

The last thing she checked was the tiny bathroom. It
had been newly carpeted in pink—pink!—and a wicker
basket with yellow-and-white daisies sat on the back of
the toilet. She peered into the bowl. It was clean. So was
the sink. Pretty paper towels in a stack. Hand towels? A
bottle of Avon hand lotion and little squares of what looked
like Cashmere Bouquet soap were piled neatly next to the
paper towels. Even the mirror and overhead light were
different.

Who had done all this? She wondered. Cary hadn't
said a word about it. For some reason, she felt annoyed—
and vaguely uneasy. She also felt hot.

She was turning down the portable heater when the
door opened and a pair of trim ankles in outrageously high
heels came into Amelia's view. She turned and stood erect:
"I thought this was set too high. Fires can happen with
these things," she said coolly.

"I suppose you're right. It gets very cold in here. Drafts from the door. Can I help you? First I have to take off my coat and scoot to the bathroom. I had to get lunch for the men. Chinese," she called over her shoulder.

Amelia blinked. Whoever she was, she had the closest thing to a perfect figure Amelia had ever seen. She also had good skin, and she was young. Very young. Twenty-five, tops. Perfection? Confection? The men must love coming in here, Amelia thought.

"I'm sorry to keep you waiting, but nature calls every so often," the young woman said blithely. She settled herself behind the desk, hiked up her clinging blue jersey skirt, and looked directly at Amelia. "Now, what can I do for you?"

"Perhaps you could tell me where my husband is."

"If you tell me his name, maybe I can. My name is Eileen Farrell."

"Cary Assante. I'm *Mrs.* Assante."

Eileen's deep brown eyes widened. "*You're* Mrs. Assante?"

"In the flesh," Amelia said coldly.

"Uh . . . hi! Cary didn't say you'd be stopping by. He's out on the site somewhere. We're supposed to have lunch at one o'clock, but they're late now. We'll probably have to put it in the microwave."

"There's a microwave here?" Amelia asked in surprise.

"I insisted. What with the cold weather and all. The men need something warm when they come in. It's over there behind the cartons. It was the only place to hook it up. Cary said it's a wonderful idea. Everyone seemed pleased."

Microwaves, bars, green plants, pink carpets in the bathroom, and this . . . this ball of fluff. Amelia wanted to gag.

"Tell Cary I was here," Amelia said, bringing the mink close to her neck. It tickled her chin. Any other time she would have smiled.

"I'll do that, Mrs. Assante. I love your coat. It must have cost a fortune. Someday I plan to get one."

"Make sure it's a Fischer if you do. If someone else is paying for it, that is."

Eileen giggled. "Oh, you mean if I get a rich husband or lover."

"Whatever. It was nice meeting you, Miss Farrell. By the way, how long have you been here?"

"Exactly a month tomorrow. You wouldn't believe what this place looked like when I took the job. The first thing I said to Mr. Assante was I couldn't work in such a messy place. He gave me some money and told me to fix it up. Everyone loves it. It's a pleasure to come to work now."

"I just bet you're worth every penny of your salary."

"Mr. Assante says I am. The others seem to agree. I finally got the hang of this computer. I'm the only one who knows how to work it. The Wang Company sent someone out here to train me."

"How much are you earning?"

"I guess it's okay to tell you, being you're Mrs. Assante and all. Four fifty a week."

"Dollars?" Amelia asked in amazement.

"Plus benefits," Eileen chirped. "Dental, eyeglass plan, major medical, as well as three weeks' vacation and twelve sick days. I snapped this right up."

"I would, too," Amelia snorted as the door closed behind her. So, nothing was new on the construction site. Well, Eileen Farrell was new, like a bright, shiny penny. Even her eyelashes were real, heavy-fringed and perfectly mascaraed. Soft brown naturally curly hair that she'd kill for. And she was young.

Amelia returned to her mother's house. She wasn't in the mood now for carpenters or paperhangers. She didn't want to see the workmen goof off and she didn't want to remind them that she was paying them by the hour.

A whole afternoon to get through. She knew she wouldn't accomplish anything—she'd just be waiting for the phone to ring. Cary would call her; that much she knew. He'd think something had happened. She never visited the trailer anymore—not since he'd told her it didn't look good to the other men. She didn't want to embarrass him, did she? Oh, no. She'd *never* do anything to cause Cary trouble.

Eileen Farrell. Who was she? The intricate wooden sign on her desk had read Design Consultant. Eileen Farrell, Design Consultant. But just what the hell did that mean? What did she design . . . and who did she consult with?

Amelia felt like smashing something—preferably a mirror, any mirror.

It was three o'clock when the phone rang. Amelia let it ring seven times before she answered. She made her voice sound breathless and impatient. "Yes?"

"Hi, babe, how's it going?"

"You really don't want to know. I'm handling it. How are things at the site?"

"Fouled up as usual. I'm sorry I wasn't here when you stopped by. You could have joined us for some Chinese. You didn't miss anything, though; it wasn't all that good."

"Poor baby," Amelia cooed. "I didn't know you had a microwave."

"Oh, sure. We got one when we fixed up this place. How'd you like it?"

"I thought you did a pretty good job."

"Hell, I didn't do it. The little gal Eileen did it. I just gave her the bucks and told her to go to town. It was a smart move the day Jacobsen brought her here and we hired her. Things sure are running smooth. We even got a computer with a printer. Damn fool thing scares me, but Eileen is a whiz with it."

"What does she design?" Amelia asked airily.

"Elevators. Best one in the business according to Jacobsen. And he's the best architect in Texas."

"Elevators are important," Amelia said stupidly.

"Damn right. You can't do anything without elevators." Amelia thought she could hear a giggle in the background.

"Gotta go, darling," she said with false lightness. "One

of the workmen is calling me. I'm glad you're getting hot meals for lunch these days; I do worry about you. See you tonight."

Cary hung up the phone and grinned at Eileen. "She's something, my wife."

"She sure is. I loved her coat."

"She must have twenty. All different colors and lengths. She's one classy lady."

"I could tell," Eileen said sweetly.

"Listen, Eileen, if Sherm Alphin calls, tell him I'll be in around six-thirty and not to leave till he hears from me."

"Mr. Assante, why don't you get a beeper? Each of you men should have one. It would make things so much simpler for you. I could have the phone company come out here and hook up a phone in the middle of the site and you guys could just call to your heart's content."

"Do you really think we should get those things?"

"I certainly do. I can make the arrangements and have them ready for you by the middle of next week."

"Do it," Cary said, clamping his hard hat on his head. "It occurs to me that you're doing the work of a secretary instead of what you're supposed to be doing."

"Mr. Jacobsen pays me extra for design work. I don't mind doing all of this. Besides, design consultants don't get benefits. Your package was what I needed. I'm only too glad to help out. The pay's good, too." Eileen grinned. "How else do you think I could get a mink coat like your wife's?"

"You could get some guy to guy it for you." Cary laughed as he closed the door behind him. Cute kid. Lots of savvy. He wondered if Jacobsen had a thing going with her.

Cary grinned as he made his way through the mud holes back to the work area. He understood the Eileen Farrells of this world; he, too, had had to claw his way off the bottom. It had to be harder for a woman. Inside of a month Eileen Farrell had taken over, and she was fast proving herself an indispensable member of his team. With right

clothes and the right connections, it would be clear sailing
for the little girl who'd come from a small town under the
x in Texas.

The really funny part of the whole thing was, she was
smart as a whip, and she had a brain like a calculator.
Beauty and brains. In a year probably she'd be asking for
a slice of the pie; he could almost guarantee it. And if she
got that far, he'd vote in her favor.

He had to remember to ask Amelia what she thought
of Eileen. Amelia knew women almost as well as he knew
men. He really respected her opinions. They'd compare
notes and then make a wager like they usually did. Half
the time Amelia won and half the time he won. Good
odds.

A week before Christmas a festive air settled over Sunbridge. Garlands of balsam decorated the stairway and
mantels. Mistletoe hung in open doorways. A monstrous
twelve-foot blue spruce waited in the corner for its
branches to settle in preparation of tree-trimming night.
Aromas of baked cookies and spice cake drifted about,
greeting each person who entered the house. Gaily
wrapped packages were propped on chairs and in corners
waiting to go under the tree. Fragrant pinecones burned
in the fireplace. At last, Christmas was about to arrive.

Sunbridge's guest list would be identical to the one for
Maggie's Fourth of July bash. She was pleased. Just this
morning she'd received a letter from Rand saying he would
definitely arrive Christmas Eve.

Since that morning in Rand's room, letters had gone
back and forth between England and the States on a daily
basis. Long letters, pouring out doubts, reaffirming affections, but always excluding the word "love" except in
closing. "Love, Maggie," she would write, or sometimes
"Love, your Maggie," remembering the way he had said
to her that morning, "Maggie, my Maggie."

Their favorite topics were each other—how one felt
about this, the other about that—and questions about the
way the family would either accept what they had come

to mean to each other or not. The "not" always caused the greatest alarm, the deepest distress.

The past few letters had broached the subject of Cranston and Cole and the wisdom of not allowing anything to interfere with Maggie's divorce. As a result, they'd decided they would have to remain "discreet." Logically—and because they both wanted it so desperately— discreet meant sacrifice. And since they'd promised each other to discreetly sacrifice their desires, there was no reason Rand shouldn't come to Sunbridge at Christmas. Logical, reasonable, adult—and so very, very dangerous. The day Maggie received Rand's confirming letter, the smile stayed on her lips all day.

Everyone would be home for dinner this evening. It seemed as though the Christmas spirit was drawing the family closer together, although in Cary and Amelia's case, the weather probably had more to do with it. As far as Maggie knew, the site was closed for a few days because of the last storm. Susan, pounds heavier but looking wonderful, was taking her meals downstairs now, along with the boys, who chatted and bantered. Even Cole was making an effort to be civil. He obviously wanted to very much be allowed to go to New York with his cousin the day after Christmas.

It was a heavy, cold-weather Texas meal. Beef stew cooked in the old iron pot for seven hours, savory and incomparable. There was corn bread and sourdough biscuits, along with asparagus and a green salad. Three meringue pies dotted the sideboard: banana cream, coconut custard, and lemon.

As Martha ladled out the stew, Maggie asked everyone at the table, "Have you finished your Christmas shopping?" The diners responded with sheepish looks, nods of agreement, and hoots of displeasure for the reminder.

"I finished yesterday. Now all I have to do is wrap." Maggie smiled victoriously. "I think I bought out the stores."

"I ordered through the catalogues," said Susan, "and everything arrived except one item. I plan to finish wrapping this evening." She sighed. "If I don't eat too much and fall asleep, that is."

"I'm done," Cary boasted. "Finished last week, as a matter of fact." No need to tell anyone he'd slipped Eileen his charge cards to do his shopping.

Amelia groaned. "I've been so busy with the house and all, I lost track of time. I've got the major portion to go. I'm hitting the stores tomorrow as soon as they open."

"I'm almost finished," Riley volunteered. "I'm waiting for something from home."

Cole looked up and around the table. "I didn't start yet."

"I hope everyone remembers everyone. Rand will be here, Mam and Thad, and Sawyer, although she hasn't said definitely that she's coming."

"Maggie, would you mind if we invited someone from the outside?" Cary asked.

"For dinner? The more the merrier. Who do you have in mind? Your friends, Sherm and Clara Alphin?"

"No, they'll be in North Carolina with their grandchildren. Not just for dinner, either. I was thinking of Christmas Eve and Christmas Day. The girl in our office, Eileen Farrell. She'll be alone in an empty condo with a plastic tree. This family is so informal, I thought it would be nice for her to be with a big family."

Maggie could feel Amelia's stillness and was afraid to look at her. The request surprised her, and there was no way she could refuse. "Of course. Sharing is what Christmas is all about. That means, of course, that I'm not done shopping. You said her name is Eileen? I'll pick up a few things, cologne, a scarf, a book, so she has presents to open. Shall I send her an invitation, or will you take care of it?"

"I've already asked her. I knew you'd say yes. You'll like her. Amelia thinks she's great. We'd be lost without her at the site, I can tell you that."

Riley looked from Cary to his aunt Amelia, who was sitting beside him. He could hear her grinding her teeth.

He went back to the asparagus he hated. Adults sure had a funny way of showing approval.

"She designs elevators and acts as a major domo of sorts," Amelia said breezily. "She's even gotten Cary and the others to wear a beeper. Now he can be paged anytime of the day or night."

"I'm impressed." Maggie laughed. "Where's she from, Cary?"

"Under the *x* in Texas," He laughed. "She went to some design school in New York. She knows her business, all right. Let me tell you what that little filly did."

Amelia sucked in her breath. She could feel Riley watching her. Filly? Is that what they said under the *x*?

There was a chorus of "What?" from around the table.

"She asked for a contract. I told you she's no fool. She knows this project is going to take almost ten years to completion. She wants to be sure she gets her share."

"Does she want a percentage, too?" Amelia asked, her voice cool and controlled.

"It came up in the discussion," Cary said vaguely.

"How much?" This time she didn't try to control her tone of voice.

"One percent, a half. No one decided. I'm not sure it's a good idea. I don't mind the contract."

"I thought all of the investors had to put in a certain amount of money. You did say that, didn't you?"

"Hell, yes."

"It would seem to me that if she's going to be given a percentage, you should take her off salary. You're paying her handsomely now. What was it you started out with, four fifty? It's up to seven hundred now, I believe. Elevator design pays extra."

Maggie met Susan's concerned glance across the table. Striving to keep her voice casual, she said carefully, "I thought the first thing you learned in business is you never, ever, under any circumstance, *give* anything away."

"Maggie's right," Susan said tightly. "Running an office and designing elevators hardly seems enough of a reason to give the woman a percentage. You ought to fire her and let Amelia run the office. She'd be a whiz."

"I offered," Amelia said coolly.

"I told you, Amelia, I didn't want you working out there. You have your own thing going with the house. You wouldn't have the time. It's not good for a husband and wife to work together. Look, since you all seem opposed to the percentage business, I'll vote it down. Maybe it wouldn't be a good idea for her to come for Christmas."

Amelia looked around the table. No one said anything. Maggie didn't reinforce the invitation. Susan looked glum, and the boys had no opinions. It was up to her, and she would have to be careful. "On the contrary, Cary, I think Eileen should come. She should get to know us. I'll buy her something special from both of us."

Maggie sighed with relief. Cary looked at his plate. Amelia had just bailed him out of a touchy situation, and he knew it. He'd never make that mistake again.

"Billie, I'm not sure we're going to make it to the airport," Thad said in a worried tone. "The Bronco will make it if the plows have been out, but I'm not sure the planes will be taking off. Call again."

Billie called and repeated the message. "United is still flying the friendly skies. Look, Thad, I'm not going to be upset if we can't get to Austin. I'd kind of like to have Christmas here with just you and the dogs. It seems we're always somewhere else at Christmastime. I can open my present here as well as there. You did get me a present, didn't you?" Billie teased.

"I thought you wanted to see Sawyer. And to see how Susan is progressing. And to check on the Maggie and Rand thing. Not to mention Riley and Cole."

"I do, I do, but I can do that after Christmas. After all, our safety is the most important thing. What d'ya say, let's stay home."

"Lady, did I ever tell you how happy you make me?"

Billie laughed. "I know now. Why didn't you just come out and say you didn't want to go? I'd've understood."

"It's not that I don't want to go; it's that I'd rather stay here. Our tree is up and I want both of us to enjoy it. *Us*, Billie."

"I only said I wanted to go because I thought you wanted to get away from all the politics and pressure up here. We could pretend we're gone, though. Let's just snuggle in. We have plenty of food; leave the Bronco in the garage. There won't be anyone driving by to see our lights, so we're safe. They all think we're going since we've been talking about it for the past month. Better yet, let's disconnect the phone."

"After you call your family."

"Let's do that right now."

"While you do that, I'm going up in the attic to get down my old sled. It's a Flexible Flyer, you know. I'm going to wax the runners tonight and pull you all over the farm tomorrow."

"Really, Thad!" Billie hugged her husband, love shining in her eyes.

"Well, maybe not all over the farm. You have put on a few pounds. We could take turns."

"Already you're wimping out. When you get tired pulling me, we can take a spin on the snowmobiles. I'm so glad we aren't going."

The relief on Billie's face was almost comical. Thad grimaced. "We must be getting out of sync here. Usually, I know what you're thinking and visa versa."

"It's the family, Thad. You know, you feel guilty. But I'm sure they won't even miss us. They'll toast us and then go on about their holiday activities."

"Aren't you being a little hard on them?"

"Not at all. That's the way it is. Go get your sled while I try to call Sawyer. I know she's avoiding me, but I'm going to try."

Adam Jarvis answered the phone. "Merry Christmas, Mrs. Kingsley."

"The same to you, Adam. Is Sawyer there?"

Adam's brief hesitation told Billie the girl was there but wasn't taking any calls. She couldn't call Adam a liar, and she wanted to thrash Sawyer within an inch of her life. Why was she being so stubborn? "Will you give her a message, Adam? Tell her Thad and I won't be going to Sunbridge for the holidays. We're having an awful storm here and we expect the planes will be grounded momentarily. Ask her if she'll call me back so I can wish her a Merry Christmas. Oh, and tell her I sent her gifts ahead to Sunbridge so I wouldn't have to carry them on the plane. Have a happy holiday, Adam."

"You too, Mrs. Kingsley."

Maggie was next on Billie's list. She had just explained the situation and heard Maggie squeal, "Oh, no, Mam, I was so counting on you and Thad! I understand—" when the phone went dead. Billie looked at the receiver in her hand and burst out laughing.

"We're cut off from the world," Billie yelled to Thad, who was up in the attic. "The phone just went dead."

"My God, do you mean it's really just you and me and the old Flex and the dogs?"

"You got it," Billie chortled. "Do you want me to make some popcorn?"

"Hell, no. Go put that lacy green thing on. We'll sit in front of the fire and I'll wax the runners on the sled."

"What are you going to put on?"

"Not my long johns, that's for sure. We haven't made love in front of the fire for a long time."

Billie sprinted up the stairs like a young girl. Life was so good, so wonderful! "Thank you, God," she whispered.

"You really put me on the spot, Sawyer. Your grandmother knew I was lying. I could tell by her voice. Why won't you talk to her?

"You know, I hate going off and leaving you here by yourself. Swear to me that you really are going to Sunbridge so I don't drive myself nuts worrying about you."

"I am going to Sunbridge. For Christmas Eve and Christmas Day. I plan on bringing the boys back with me for a few days. Rand, too, if he can make it."

Adam's heart turned over. Her eyes were too bright, her cheeks too flushed. She really believed what she was saying. "You didn't answer my question about your grandmother," he said gently.

"I didn't want to have to go into the whole thing. Grand understands. It won't be the same without her, but I'm glad she's with Thad. Now, there's a marriage made in heaven."

"She's concerned about you, Sawyer. It's cruel, what you're doing. Does Maggie know you're coming?"

"Of course. I was invited, remember?"

"Sawyer, what if things don't . . . what if . . ."

"You worry too much, Adam. Everything'g going to work out. I've played the game by the book. I didn't call, write, or pester. When Rand sees me and realizes what a mistake he's made, things'll be just fine. We're in love."

You mean *you're* in love! Adam wanted to shout. He knew what was going to happen to her, and it made his guts churn. But this time Sawyer would have to deal with it herself. He wasn't going to be there.

"I can't believe you're taking all that stuff!" Sawyer said in awe. "A man could go to war with less. Didn't you say you were staying only five days?"

"That's what I said, but that was before . . ."

"Before you invited Paula Zachary to join you. I took the call, remember?" She laughed.

"See this little thing? This is what I'm taking to Sunbridge. I know how to pack."

"Know-it-all." Adam sniffed. Secretly, he wondered if he'd packed too much, but he absolutely refused to do laundry while he was on vacation.

Sawyer grinned. "Who's picking you up? A taxi or a truck?"

"Actually, I hired a limo. Paula has quite a bit of stuff herself. Stop being so nosy. I've gotta go. The limo should be here any second now and I said I'd be downstairs."

"I'll carry your skis and your boots. Do you think you can manage the rest?"

"I'm gonna have to, since I'm not about to make two trips. You always were a big help—a pain in the ass, but a help nonetheless," Adam said fondly.

"I hope you have a good time. Think of me when you toast in the New Year."

"I always think of you. New Year's Eve isn't going to make a difference. Make sure you think of me. And I hope it goes the way you want. Say hello to your family. Merry Christmas, Sawyer," Adam said as he kissed her lightly on the cheek. "I left your gift under the tree."

"Yours is in the duffel bag. Don't break a leg now."

The limo pulled up to the curb, and there was the usual confusion as to what went where and Adam telling the driver the best way to go to pick up Paula. Sawyer rolled her eyes at him and grinned.

Then he was gone.

Sawyer walked around the loft, picking up one thing and laying it down, only to pick up something else. Adam's work area was clear, especially neat. The kitchen, too, was neat and tidy, the dishwasher emptied. No crumbs littered the floor. Marble, the cat, lay contentedly under the table.

There was nothing to do. The laundry had been done earlier, washed, dried, and folded. it would be dark soon; maybe she should turn on the tree lights. It was a gorgeous tree. Adam had trekked out to Long Island in a borrowed pickup and lugged the tree all the way back. It was beautiful when it came to life with hundreds of tiny lights. The decorations, Adam said, had been sent to him from Germany by a friend. Adam had so many friends. Thoughtful friends, who never forgot him. She thought about it for a while and decided Adam had a lot of friends because he was a friend. She couldn't even begin to imagine what she would do without him.

Gift. He'd said he left her gift under the tree. Actually,

there were two gifts bearing her name. One would be frivolous and the other, she knew, would be serious. She poked, rattled, and shook the gaily wrapped boxes. She could tell by the puckered Scotch tape that Adam had wrapped them both himself. Store gift wrap never puckered.

Adam hadn't said she couldn't open the gifts. After all, she would be leaving tomorrow and wouldn't be here for Christmas. She really should open them just in case he called while she was at Sunbridge.

Sawyer played a game with herself as darkness invaded the loft. First, with only the twinkling tree miniatures for light, she poured herself a glass of wine and toasted the holiday. Then she made a toast to her future happiness with Rand. She walked all around the tree, admiring it, sipping from her long-stemmed wineglass. There were a lot of gifts underneath. Two days ago the tree skirt had held nothing but a few pine needles. It smelled so good—Scotch pine was her favorite. Rand said he loved Scotch pine best, too. They always had blue spruce at Sunbridge.

Sawyer kept staring at the gifts. She turned on the small brass lamp atop the desk, then dropped to her knees and sorted through the presents: To Adam from Nick. To Adam from Blake. To Adam from George and Hugh. To Adam from the gang. To Adam from Mom and Dad. To Adam from Joan. To Adam from Steve, Bill, and Carmen. To Adam from Alice and Ed.

So many friends who thought enough of him to drop by with presents! Sawyer wondered if he'd bought presents for all these people. Her gifts, she noticed, were a little to the side. She finished her wine and poured another glass. On hands and knees she scrambled to the bookshelf in the corner, selected a Christmassy-sounding audio cassette and popped it into the player. Now it seemed like Christmas.

The oddly shaped box that didn't rattle was her first choice. Even as a kid she'd always gone for the biggest first, knowing full well the best was in the smallest package. Carefully she opened the box and stared down at her present. Her very own Cabbage Patch doll! The adoption papers read, Willow Carmena. Wait till Adam opened his duffel and found Willow Carmena's twin, Cornell Damian. She shrieked with laughter.

Spent, she leaned against the sofa and opened her other gift, the small one, the serious one. It was a book of poetry simply titled *New Beginning*. Sawyer turned the pages, pleased to see that the poetry was Adam's; she'd recognize it anywhere. Dear God, all the poems were for her. How much time and effort must have gone into this book! It was bound beautifully in rich Moroccan leather with her name embossed on the inside. As she leafed through the slim volume, a small card slipped out.

Merry Christmas, Sawyer,
    I didn't know what to get you for Christmas, but I wanted it to be special from me to you. I wanted to give you part of myself because you won't accept the whole of me. Enjoy my humble effort, and if you ever tell anyone I gave you this, I'll deny it.

All my love
Adam.

Sawyer wept, tears of sorrow, of anger, of remorse. If only they could be tears of happiness. "Oh, Adam," she sobbed, "I do love you, but not the way you want!"

{{{{{{{{ CHAPTER SEVENTEEN }}}}}}}

Riley woke suddenly from a horrible dream. Sweat soaked the sheet he'd wrapped tightly about him in sleep. His arms and legs flailed as he came to grips with the reality of a new day. The dream had been so real. He'd awakened from surgery; a nurse handed him a mirror. Heart pounding, he'd looked for the tiny sutures around his eyes that would make him as American as his father. There were no sutures and no Westernized eyes. If anything, his eyes were more lidded, more oblique than ever. He rolled over, burrowing deeper into the covers. Having his eyes Americanized was his dream and his nightmare.

Christmas Eve. One of the happiest days of the year in America. His room looked dim, grayish and dull. It had to be mid-morning. He leaped out of bed and whipped open the lacy curtains. Snow! Aunt Maggie said it always snowed at Sunbridge for Christmas. The overhead light went on and both lamps were lit. Riley dived into his clothes, gave his face a skimpy wash and his perfect white teeth an even skimpier cleaning. The fine stubble could wait till later. He wasn't hairy like Cole, and it made him self-conscious. Cole, he knew, *had* to shave every day, whereas Riley could do it once a week, and even then it wasn't necessary. His legs and chest were also free of the fine curly furring that bloomed on Cole. The girls teased him in the summer, but he'd accepted it good-naturedly, saying he'd just been waxed. And at least he had a deli-

cious—according to Kelly Jensen—full head of wavy
black hair. He grinned as he brushed it into place.

Sawyer was supposed to be here by noon. Rand was
to have arrived before breakfast, Aunt Maggie had said.
Tree trimming was set for late afternoon, fiveish or so
with cocktails, and then there was to be a six-course dinner followed by carols in the huge drawing room. Midnight
service in Crystal City and then gift opening. He could
hardly wait.

The breakfast table was full. He took his place amid
smiles and light teasing about being a sleepyhead and
slugabed. He grinned as he piled his plate with sausage
and eggs, then crunched on toast as he looked around the
table. Rand, fresh from an early flight, was busy buttering
a piece of toast. Aunt Amelia and Cary were bickering
about whether she should go out in the snow or not. Cole
had just finished gulping the rest of his orange juice and
now stood up, throwing his napkin onto the table. Riley
was relieved to hear his cousin say he was going into
Crystal City to finish up his last-minute shopping.

Suddenly, everyone was talking at once, and all the
conversation was directed at him. Everyone laughed and
he flushed.

"We'll back that all up and start over," Cary said kindly,
noting the boy's flushed face. "Amelia?"

"I was wondering, Riley, if you don't have plans for
the rest of the morning, would you come over to the house
and shovel the driveway? The weathermen are predicting
sleet later, and I'd like to salt down the steps and the
walkway. Cary has to go over to the site and check on
the gas lines and then pick up Miss Farrell."

"Sure I'll do it. I love the snow."

"Good, that's settled. Amelia is like a bee with one
wing this morning," Cary said fondly as he patted her on
the shoulder. "Susan, you're next."

"It's no big deal. I just wanted to know if you'd carry
my gifts downstairs. Some of them are rather large and
awkward. I'm not too graceful these days. Would you
mind?"

"I'll do it when I finish breakfast," Riley said cheerfully.

"I just wanted to remind you to call your grandfather later on, and I'd like to wish him a happy holiday," Maggie said. "I know it's not a holiday for him, but he is so aware of ours, I thought it would be nice."

"I won't forget. I was going to wait till about eight o'clock this evening. It'll be Christmas morning in Japan and the old one will just be rising. Did he send presents?" Riley asked anxiously.

Maggie laughed. "A truckload. It took United Parcel an hour just to unload. It took Steven another hour to carry the packages indoors. I'd say he didn't forget you or anyone at Sunbridge." There was an odd tremor in Maggie's voice. Riley suspected it had something to do with the fact that Rand was sitting next to her.

"The old one always played Santa Claus at his newspaper for Christmas," he said. "A lot of the employees were American. He got a kick out of it. He likes to exchange presents."

"Rand, how was—the weather in England when you left?" Susan asked nervously.

"Nasty." He hesitated. "I tried to call Jerome before I left, but the phone was disconnected."

Susan's heart thumped. Disconnected? Why? Despite the resentment she felt, regardless of his rejection of their child, Susan's feeling toward her husband were ambiguous. More than ever, she wanted someone to share this experience with—Maggie and Amelia simply weren't enough. A child should know its own father, and that father should provide a home for his family. Even if that father was Jerome, damn him.

"Well, I have to be going," Cary said, standing up and bending over to kiss Amelia on the cheek. "I should be back by mid-afternoon. Nice to see you again, Rand. Maggie, is there anything I can bring back from Crystal City for you?"

"No, it's all under control. Thanks for asking, though. Please, drive carefully; the roads are bad."

" 'Bye, darling, see you later," Amelia called gaily.

"You be careful driving, too. Don't forget, Eileen will be with me."

"Darling, how could any of us forget?" Amelia said coolly. "You've mentioned it at least a dozen times."

"Who's Eileen?" Rand asked after the door closed behind Cary.

"The girl who works in Cary's office," replied Maggie, glancing apprehensively at Amelia. "It seems she'll be alone for the holiday and Cary asked if she could spend Christmas with us."

"Excuse me, all," Amelia said stiffly. "I want to call down to the barn and have them bring up some rock salt. Riley, dress warmly and see if you can't find the snow shovel. It used to hang inside the cellarway. Is it still there, Maggie?"

"As far as I know. Drive slowly. We'll keep the fires burning and have a toddy ready for you when you get back. Is there any last-minute wrapping you want me to do?"

"No, I've got it all covered. You'll be busy enough entertaining Sawyer when she arrives." Amelia looked at her pointedly. "She's due soon, isn't she?"

"Around noon, I believe." Maggie smiled and hoped her breezy tone would drive the disapproving look from Amelia's face. "Have fun, you two! See you later."

Susan excused herself right after Amelia and Riley left. There was an awkward silence, and then Rand spoke.

"It appears we're alone," he said quietly. "You're acting like a cat on a hot griddle. In other words, sweet, you're feeling guilty."

"Am I?" Maggie whispered. "I guess it's because I am."

"For God's sake, Maggie. We went through all this. You told me just last week on the phone you were your own person and you were going to do what you wanted, and that included me. Have you changed your mind?"

"No... yes... oh, I don't know. I so wanted this

Christmas to be perfect. First, Mam can't make it. Amelia disapproves of us and is acting as though I stole her jewels. Susan is avoiding me. Cole refuses to do more than look at me, and when our eyes do meet, his are full of disgust. Riley is torn. Sawyer will be here soon. My God, I feel like a thief. Please, you have to try and understand."

"I do understand. I shouldn't have come. It was a mistake, Maggie. I don't like playing games."

"Neither do I," Maggie said, so quietly Rand had to strain to hear her.

"I think I'm in love with you, Maggie."

"Don't say that. Not now."

"It's Sawyer, isn't it? The rest you can handle."

"I'm not sure. You know how I feel. My God, yes, I want you. I've caused so much hurt in this family I can't cause any more. You have to understand my position."

"No thumbing your nose at them and happy ever after?" Rand asked quietly.

"Maybe I could come to England. . . . We . . . could . . ."

"Goddammit, Maggie, I'm not talking about some cheap affair. I'm talking about you and me. Us. Our lives."

"The others . . . they'll think . . ."

"Who the devil cares what they think? We have to think about what's best for us. They'll all come to accept it. Don't make this more difficult than it is now."

"I do care about the others. My son, Mam, Riley . . ."

"What about Sawyer?" Rand asked coldly. "That's what this is all about, you know. Admit it. Mother versus daughter. I'm in the middle."

Maggie's face closed. "That must make you feel pretty powerful. Two women in love with you."

"Sawyer is in love with an image. I wasn't sure till now that you care for me. Is the word love so hard to say?"

"For me it is. I never had any. I'm not even sure I know what love is. The concept of love, maybe. I do feel something for you I've never felt for anyone else. But you're wrong about Sawyer. Sawyer loves you with her whole heart. For Sawyer it was now and forever. That kind of love. How could you not have seen that?" Maggie asked angrily.

"I did see it, damn it. Don't jam home the guilt, Maggie. I was Sawyer's first love. That will always be special to her. I didn't love her enough. It has to be mutual or it doesn't work. You have to realize that I was a father image to Sawyer. I believe that in my heart. You have to believe it, too. You had the same kind of problem with your own father."

Tears burned Maggie's eyes. Sawyer, always Sawyer. "Could we just put all this on hold, get through Christmas, and then work it out?" she asked, swallowing hard. "I really can't deal with it today."

"Right now I feel if I don't take you in my arms, I won't be able to take another breath," Rand said hoarsely.

"Right now if I don't get up from this table, I will let you do exactly that, and then I'll end up hating both of us. This is the way it has to be ... for now. Forgive me," Maggie whispered as she ran from the room.

Only in her own room with the door closed behind her did she let go. Why me? Why is it always me? I didn't lead him on. I didn't set out to snatch him from Sawyer. It just happened. I'm sorry. I can't change feelings. Why do I have to be the one who has to give everything up? Why does Sawyer get it all?

Maggie watched as the snow swirled about the treetops. She'd seen enough Texas storms to know this one was just about over. The snow was fine, powdery, perfect for skiing. There must be at least six inches on the ground. The drifts on the north end of the house were up to the windows on the first floor. As a child she and Susan had jumped and played snow angel in them. How long ago that was!

Something churned inside Maggie. A need to confide, to talk, to seek answers to her problems. Susan was besieged with her own worries right now, and Amelia,

while loving, was disapproving. Mam? She could give it
a try.

Quickly, she dialed the familiar number in Vermont,
only to be told the power and telephone lines were out
due to the storm. Service would most likely be restored
by late afternoon. But that was too late. She needed to
talk *now*.

In the blink of an eye, Maggie had on wool slacks and
her heavy parka. She found her boots by the kitchen door
in the boot tray.

"If anyone asks where I am, you don't know," Maggie
told Martha as she pulled on her boots over heavy socks.
She almost laughed at the startled expression in the woman's eyes. "It's uphill most of the way. The drifts are on
this side. Look, it's almost stopped snowing." Before
leaving the kitchen, she plucked a bright red poinsettia
from a plant on the kitchen counter.

The gravestones looked desolate with their mantles of
snow. Mittened hands dug a hole in the snow. Already
the poinsettia was frozen; she propped it up with scoops
of snow. It looked like blood—her blood. "Merry Christmas, Pap," she said softly. "I think I'm just going to wing
this one."

Maggie returned the way she'd come. She placed her
boots neatly in the back door tray, hung her parka on the
wooden coatrack near the back door. Martha held out a
cup of coffee for her, which she accepted gratefully as
she made her way up the back stairway to the nursery.
She felt better. At least she was in control of her emotions
now. Fresh air had a way of clearing the head.

She didn't see him at first simply because she didn't
expect anyone to be in the room.

"That was a damn fool thing to do," Rand said coolly.

"Yes, I suppose it was," Maggie replied just as coolly.
"However, it was something I needed to do. I usually do
what I want. I'm all grown-up now."

"Being grown-up doesn't necessarily mean you always
make the right decisions. We need to talk, Maggie."

"No. Not now."

"When? Tomorrow, next week, next month, a year from now? When? Give me a time and a date."

"I can't do that. Don't pressure me, Rand. This isn't any easier for me than it is for you. I'm going to have to handle it my way, and you're going to have to handle it my way, too."

"You really mean it, don't you?" Rand asked incredulously.

"Yes, I do." Maggie's gaze was level, defying Rand to pursue the matter. When the door closed behind him, her shoulders slumped.

Her cheeks were as rosy as if she'd dusted them with crimson rouge. Biting wind or... Rand?

Rand marched downstairs to the beat of a drummer he'd never heard before. He headed straight for the study and the portable bar.

Susan looked up from the magazine she was reading. "A bit early, isn't it?" she asked gently.

"Early, late. What the hell difference does it make?"

"A lot, if you really care about Maggie. If she sees you hitting the sauce because you can't handle... whatever, she might—I'm not saying she will but she *might*—decide to take a drink herself."

Rand was a straight-up two-finger whiskey man. His hold on the bottle was tight, the knuckles stretched taut. He put the bottle back in the rack and picked up the newspaper.

Susan sighed. "Don't worry," she said. "I'm not going to lecture and preach. That's the one thing I don't do. I really believe I've become a fatalist."

Rand nodded absently. His innards were roiling. He glanced at his watch. Allowing two hours for bad weather, road conditions, and other acts of God, Sawyer should be arriving within the hour. He almost wished he were back in England.

"So, what did you get everyone for Christmas?" Susan asked.

Rand's teeth dug into his lower lip. "What you really want to know is what I got Maggie and Sawyer."

"You must have had a tough time selecting the gifts that would say something, yet say nothing. Men are always so conscientious that way. One gift for commitment and one for.... What's the word for discarded?"

"Knock it off, Susan. I've had about enough."

"I'm sorry. I don't know why I...Forget it.

"It's almost Christmas Eve. Peace on earth, goodwill to men, right?"

"If you say so." Rand sat down in the chair opposite Susan and picked up one of the newspapers from a nearby coffee table. "Have you decided on a name for the baby yet?" he asked idly.

"As a matter of fact, I have. If it's a boy, it's going to be called Moss. If it's a girl, it will be Jessica. What's the news in the paper?"

"It's full of peace on earth, goodwill to men. What else do you want to know?"

"Not a thing," Susan said, going back to her magazine.

It was three o'clock when Cole returned to the house, his arms laden with red-ribboned boxes. Amelia and Riley arrived fifteen minutes later, each going their separate way. Maggie was halfway down the stairs when the doorbell rang. Susan entered the foyer from the dining room, opened the door, and immediately squealed with delight.

"Sawyer!"

Maggie's stomach heaved as she forced a smile to her lips and continued down the stairs.

Mother and daughter locked glances for just an instant. "Merry Christmas, Sawyer."

"Merry Christmas, Maggie. Where shall I put all these?" Sawyer asked, indicating two huge shopping bags. "The other packages arrived, didn't they?"

"Yesterday. I took off the wrapping paper and string. They're in the hall closet."

"That was nice of you. Thanks. Where is everyone?"

Maggie waved her hands about. "We're having eggnog

shortly and then tree trimming. Come along into the study. Susan, where are you going?"

"Where I go every ten minutes, the bathroom. Merry Christmas, Sawyer."

As Sawyer hugged Susan, her eyes met Maggie's for the second time.

"I guess you know your grandmother won't be here for Christmas," Maggie said, leading the way into the study.

"I know. Christmas won't be the same without her."

"We're going to make the best of it. Rand's here. He got in early this morning. And Cary will be bringing his office girl." Maggie looked at her watch. "About now, as a matter of fact. We're a houseful."

Rand. In just a few seconds she would see him. Sawyer's mind suddenly went blank. All the rehearsed phrases, all the practiced smiles in the mirror, deserted her. She ached. Maggie looked so confident, so self-assured, that Sawyer's heart started to pound. If it was a fight Maggie wanted, a fight was what she would get. She set her jaw determinedly.

Out of the corner of her eye Maggie assessed her daughter, calculating the cost of her outfit with a practiced eye. Oscar de la Renta slacks fitted into knee-high Bally boots, both in the same shade of taupe. Autumn haze mink coat, styled with wide shoulders and wide leather belt. A matching hat that swallowed Sawyer's golden-blond hair. And at her neck a blazing red-orange silk scarf for that right touch of pizzazz. Chic and fashionable were the only words to describe her.

"Rand, darling!" Sawyer cried breathlessly. She ran to him, throwing her arms around him. She drew back immediately and stared into his eyes, frightened by what she saw. She kissed him lightly on the lips and linked her arm through his. "Come, sit here by me and tell me everything that's happened since July. I should strangle you for ignoring me these past..." There was a slight pause. "Weeks. Don't tell me you're still angry with me."

"I could never be angry with you, Sawyer," Rand said gently.

"Tell me I look lovely. You always tell me that," Sawyer teased. "I spent a fortune on this outfit and one for tomorrow. I want to dazzle you. Maggie always said when you're in love with a man, you have to dazzle him. Isn't that right, Maggie?"

Maggie forced a laugh. "I do seem to recall saying something like that. I think Mam was the one who said it to me, or maybe it was Aunt Amelia." She was too gorgeous for words, this daughter of hers. And somewhere between July and now, she'd learned how to fight. Maggie literally backed up a step. "What would you like to drink?"

"Same as Rand, two fingers of whiskey straight up. The things this man taught me, you wouldn't believe. Oh, darling, I'm so happy to see you! I have such wonderful plans for us. By the way, I'm taking the boys back to New York the day after Christmas. Please say you'll join us. I've arranged to take a week's vacation. We can celebrate the New Year together."

Rand glanced at Maggie, then turned away at the look in her eyes. Fortunately, he was saved from replying by the arrival of Cary and Eileen Farrell. Their entrance, directly behind Susan's, was exuberant and filled with Christmas cheer. He could feel Sawyer stiffen at his side as Maggie made the introductions.

"English nobility!" Eileen gushed. "What a Christmas this has turned out to be." Maggie watched with interest as Eileen settled herself beside Rand and immediately began conversing. Sawyer on one side, Eileen on the other; Susan and she directly opposite. Opposing generations.

"Where's my wife?" Cary asked enthusiastically.

"Upstairs. She just got in a few minutes before Sawyer. You have exactly thirty minutes to get back down here for drinks before tree trimming."

"Yes, ma'am." Cary grinned. "Take care of my girl here."

"You can count on it," Maggie said, and settled her gaze on Miss Farrell. She decided the woman was a man-chaser. It was obvious in the way she gushed over Rand, the familiarity with which she conducted the conversation, and the fact that she was all but ignoring her hostess. Eileen's attention automatically homed in on the male species, while her treatment of other women was apparently offhand and damn near condescending. Maggie bristled. Just what Sunbridge needed for the holidays, as if there weren't enough going on already.

Cary and Amelia made their entrance. Cary had changed from a business suit to casual light tan slacks, which fit with tailored perfection, and a White Stag ski sweater of softest mohair. But it was Amelia who came under Eileen's scrutiny, and Amelia knew it, had expected it. She'd deliberately elected to wear an understated little number by Nippon—a bright red silk shot through with silver threads, whose skirt swung easily with every step. The newly fashionable wide shoulders were emphasized in a long-sleeved shirt jacket that flattered her neck and hipline; its short skirt revealed one of Amelia's best assets, her long, gracefully turned legs.

Immediately, Eileen rose to her feet to cross the room, offering her hand in greeting. "Mrs. Assante, how nice to see you again."

"You remember Eileen, Amelia," Cary prompted.

"Of course." Amelia smiled congenially. "How could I forget? Merry Christmas, Eileen." She linked her arm once again through Cary's for much-needed moral support. Her dress and shoes cost more than half of Eileen's wardrobe, but it couldn't substitute for thick shoulder-length natural blond hair and a dewy complexion. Damn! She wished Billie were here. It was far from flattering to be an entire generation older than some of the women in the room and two generations older than the rest. "Cary, I'm going to offer your services as bartender. You don't mind, do you, Maggie? Cary makes the best hot toddies. Order up, everyone," she said with forced gaiety. "Cary is a specialist."

It seemed to Rand that Sawyer was at his heels for the entire afternoon. She was there when he lit the fire and again when he added more logs. It was to him that she handed each ornament to be hung on the tree, all the time chatting vivaciously, sharing memories of past Christmases. Susan and Rand also had memories in common: living in the townhouse on Halston Square, vacations in the country, the petty fights and arguments that all young people have. Amelia and Rand reminisced about wartime England and one particular Christmas when their pet dog had had puppies.

It seemed to Maggie that she was the only one without memories to share.

Cole and Riley joined in for the tree trimming, and together with Sawyer they made a happy threesome, joking and laughing and singing Christmas carols to records. Maggie couldn't remember ever seeing her son quite so happy. It was Sawyer who made the difference. Sawyer could give Cole something she couldn't. Was it that way with Rand, too?

They all shared a late dinner, carrying their plates into the living room to eat near the tree. Susan sat at the grand piano, striking familiar chords from Handel's "Messiah." They all chanted the "Hallelujah" chorus—Eileen, surprisingly, taking the high octave soprano. Cary divided his attention between Eileen and his wife, seemingly oblivious to the look in Amelia's eyes or the grim line of her mouth.

"Perhaps you'd like to go up and lie down for an hour or so, Mrs. Assante. You look tired," Eileen was heard to say.

"Do I?" Amelia challenged, her eyes burning coals of defiance. Eileen smiled and turned away quickly.

Maggie, witnessing this exchange, deftly interrupted when she saw Amelia's arm reach out to grasp the younger woman's shoulder. "We should all be thinking about getting into town for the midnight service, don't you think, Amelia? There's quite a few of us, so we'll have to arrange the cars. Why don't you and Cary take Riley and Susan in your car? Cole and I can take Rand and Sawyer, Eileen, and Martha in the station wagon."

She saw the relief in Amelia's eyes and realized her aunt was near the breaking point. However, Eileen was right: she did look tired; exhausted, as a matter of fact. Her sleek brunette hair had flopped forward onto her brow. She was pale, and the bright red of her silk dress made her skin look sallow. And Maggie knew Amelia's feet had to be killing her in those four-inch heels.

"The station wagon is behind all the others, Maggie," Sawyer said sweetly. "Why don't Rand and I take the boys, and you can use your own car to take Eileen and Martha."

"That sounds like a fine idea," Amelia said hurriedly. "I'll just run upstairs for my coat. Cary, why don't you come with me? I want you to wear something warmer." She could hear the edge of panic in her voice. If Maggie hadn't interrupted, she would have clawed Eileen's face to shreds. She had to get control of herself. She'd had too much to drink and too little to eat. Fear and jealousy had knotted her innards. Get control, she repeated over and over.

All the way to the church Maggie was silent. With one deft stroke Sawyer had succeeded in keeping Rand and both boys to herself while she, Maggie, rode to church with a housekeeper and a stranger.

Maggie's mood was much uplifted by the time she returned to Sunbridge. The church service had been lovely, the choir heavenly. Meeting and greeting friends and acquaintances; Rand maneuvering to sit beside her in church. The candlelight, the music, the whisper of softly falling snow outside the stained glass windows, peace on earth and goodwill.

She shed tears for those who were not there this Christmas and held Riley's hand tight, knowing his thoughts were on the father he'd never known and his beautiful mother, Otami.

Maggie tried not to think of Sawyer, who was sitting

on the far side of Rand, sharing a hymn book and helpfully turning the pages. When all their voices were uplifted in song, Maggie caught a glimpse of Sawyer's lovely face, radiant with the moment and with being so near to Rand. Her daughter, her own child. They'd been so far apart for so many years, but now there was Cole and Rand and Riley. How could two women share their men?

Maggie's eyes closed, a crystal tear shining on her cheek. What kind of woman was she to do this to Sawyer, to even entertain the thought of being in love with Rand? She'd had her chance at happiness when she'd married Cranston; shouldn't Sawyer have her chance? And Rand, what this must be doing to him. . . . Or was she allowing herself to be taken in again? Perhaps Rand had been a bachelor for so long that the idea of marriage was frightening to him. Perhaps he really loved Sawyer but was unable to commit himself. What if he was simply using her—Maggie—to drive a wedge between himself and Sawyer?

Maggie looked up at Rand, saw his finely chiseled profile, the gentle sweep of his brow, the soft blond hair that fell over his forehead. And then he turned, his chocolate-brown eyes meeting hers, and they were filled with a longing that told her of his love. For an instant she allowed herself to be filled with the meaning of his gaze, feeling her own emotions brim. No, Rand would never use her; he'd never use anyone to suit his own purposes. Not this man who had taken her in his arms and made love to her. The man who had whispered, "Maggie, my Maggie," and had touched her soul with his own. She could feel Rand still looking at her when she herself had turned away.

The Christmas mood prevailed during the drive back to Sunbridge. This time Riley and Cole had squeezed into the car with Maggie, Eileen, and Martha. Maggie knew it was a kind of conspiracy to leave Rand and Sawyer alone, but she didn't care. She trusted Rand, even if it meant she might be hurt. Her voice carried with the others as they sang all the way home.

* * *

"We draw lots to see who hands out the gifts," Maggie said gaily when they were once again around the Christmas tree at Sunbridge, warming themselves with hot chocolate and rum toddies. "Whoever gets the blank paper plays Santa."

Cary won the honor and beamed with pride. Amelia, Santa's helper, glowed beneath her husband's attention as he teased that she shouldn't look only for the presents labeled with her own name.

Eileen's eyes burned as she watched gift after gift happily bestowed. She was pleased but stunned that there were so many gifts for her. The Coleman family wasn't only rich; it was generous.

By the time the last present had been opened and admired by all, it was almost dawn. Eileen felt as if she were in the bargain basement of a huge department store. Stereos for the boys; someone had received a hand-tooled saddle—the Amerasian boy, she thought. Adidas sneakers replete with little calculators that measured distance, speed, calories burned. Jewelry galore. Cary had given his wife an expensive serpentine gold chain from which dangled an eye-bruising diamond. Perfume, designer clothes, silk scarves, and Gucci bags. Golf clubs and riding crops; Maggie's son got his own full-scale video game. Even Susan's unborn child received toys and cute little shirts and baby booties that made the momma-to-be squeal in delight.

"It always seems like such a letdown when all the presents are opened." Maggie smiled wearily. "Such wonderful presents."

"And now there's this mess to clean up." Riley yawned.

Eileen laughed. "All that fancy gift wrap and ribbon cost more than all my Christmases put together. I'll clean it up; it's the least I can do to thank you all for your lovely gifts. I never expected anything; being here was more than enough."

"It was our pleasure," Amelia said generously. "The vase you gave Cary and me is exquisite."

Eileen dropped to her knees and began to roll the papers together. Rand joined her. "Go on to bed, everyone. Eileen and I will have this mess cleaned in a minute."

"Rand!" Sawyer exclaimed. "Eileen is our guest; we can't have her doing chores. I'll do it. You go along to bed, Eileen," she said in a no-nonsense voice, actually grabbing Eileen's arm and lifting her to her feet.

"Yes, come along," Amelia said sweetly. "Leave it to the *family*. You, too, Maggie, you've had an exhausting day."

Maggie found herself with the rest of the clan as they climbed the stairs to their respective rooms. She knew what Amelia was doing, and there wasn't a damn thing she could do about it ... or wanted to do.

When they were alone in the living room, with only the light from the Christmas tree twinkling against the darkness, Sawyer turned to Rand and said softly, "I thought I'd never get you to myself. I've been waiting all day for this moment."

Rand wished her tone weren't so intimate, so seductive. He knew where this conversation was going to lead. On the way home from church Sawyer had tried to fill him with memories of things they'd done together, of what they'd been to each other. In the car he'd been able to head her off by inducing her to sing Christmas carols and talk about Riley and Cole. Now he was trapped ... and perhaps it was just as well.

"Thank you for the wonderful gift," she was saying. "I'm so pleased you remembered my passion for bracelets, but really, you were too extravagant. Do you know I wear the one you gave me for my birthday all the time? I love the earrings you gave Maggie. Do you think she'll wear four-leaf clovers? Are they significant somehow?"

Rand was tired; it had been a long and difficult day. His nerves were stretched to the breaking point, and he felt like a criminal, guilty and condemned. But where was the crime in loving Maggie? "Sawyer, you must listen to what I have to say. We're going to talk, and this time

you're going to listen and *hear*. I don't want to seem cruel,
but somewhere you've gotten the idea that we can just
pick up where we left off before the July holiday. It's not
that way and I'm sorry."

Sawyer rocked back on her heels, a tangle of ribbon
threaded between her still fingers. She tried to focus on
his face, saw the way the tree lights reflected in his hair.

"I care for you, Sawyer, very much, but what I feel
isn't love, at least not the kind of love your looking for.
I don't love you enough. I regret that."

"Stop!" Sawyer clamped her hands over her ears. "I
don't want to listen!"

He grasped her hands, pulling them away from her
ears, holding them tightly against his chest. "You've got
to listen! You're becoming obsessed with the idea that I'll
come around and find that I've loved you all along and
that I'll always love you. Don't do this to yourself, Sawyer, and for God's sake, don't do it to the rest of us!"

She seemed frozen in time, hearing but not believing,
incapable of believing. "You loved me once..." she began.

"Yes, and I still love you, but not the way you want."
He gentled his voice, loving her and pitying her at the
same time. She had to set him free, him and Maggie.

"Last time you said we were at opposite ends of life.
That you didn't want a family. You wanted to settle down
to a simpler life. All right, then, no children, no work,
just each other. I want only you, Rand. Nothing else means
anything, only you."

Rand was shaking his head, lost in the futility of it all.
"No, Sawyer. What I told you then was the truth; that's
how I feel about where I am in my life. But a simpler
truth is that I can't love you the way you need to be
loved. The way you *deserve* to be loved. Can you understand? It's not enough for you and it's not enough for
me."

She raised her eyes, holding him with her gaze. It was
as if she were delving into his head, demanding answers
for questions she couldn't ask. "It's not supposed to be

this way. I was so sure, so certain—" Her voice broke; a shuddering sob, silent and terrifying, shook her.

Rand wanted to reach out for her, to hold her against him, to give comfort where none could be found. "Don't do this, Sawyer; please don't do this."

"You said that before. Only you said not to do it to the rest of you. Who's that, Rand? Who else am I hurting besides myself?"

"I only meant that something like this could break the family in two. I know you don't want that."

"You know what I want. I guess I made a fool of myself again. I thought time and distance would've changed your mind. I know now I was wrong. But I need you to tell me something first." Sawyer choked back a sob. "I need to hear you say there's nothing between you and Maggie. Tell me you aren't having an affair with my mother." When there was no answer to her entreaty, her eyes filled with tears. "I think I could take anything but that. I can't believe you'd betray me like this."

"Sawyer, it's not a betrayal. Why won't you accept that what we had wasn't strong enough?"

There was a wild thing beating in Sawyer's breast. Words, all the wrong words. Adam had known. Even she had known. Hearing it again was like a death sentence, one she could not accept. "Apparently it wasn't, since you couldn't wait to jump into my mother's bed," she cried hoarsely. "My God! Doesn't she have any decency?"

"Sawyer, it wasn't like that. What can I say to make you understand?"

"Why don't you ask what will make me forgive you, because I understand all right, damn right I understand! I know what she is even if you don't. I'm sorry for you, Rand, terribly sorry." She fought her way to her feet, hampered by the empty boxes and cartons, the snarls of ribbons and acres of shredded paper. Only in the privacy of her room did she let the tears flow; quiet, hateful tears.

Rand sat with his head in his hands for a very long time. When the daylight, bright from the reflection of the snow, penetrated the draperies, he hefted himself to his feet and began to clear away the litter. He made four trips to the back service porch, where he piled the hefty sacks of trash neatly one on top of the other. He was hurting and he wanted to be comforted.

He wanted Maggie.

{{{{{{{{ CHAPTER EIGHTEEN }}}}}}}}

Christmas Day was the horror Rand dreaded. He thanked God untold times for the boys and for Eileen, who kept things going. Neighbors visited with traditional good cheer, and Riley and Cole's friends livened things up with a spontaneous party, dancing to records and making a pleasant din amid the silence. Sawyer joined the young people, her laughter strained and her face a bit too pink from Cary's hot toddies. Maggie, ever watchful, knew what must have happened. Amelia, knowing nothing but her jealousy of Eileen Farrell, stuck close to her husband. Susan lay down for a long afternoon nap and finally asked to have her dinner sent to her room. Only Cary, oblivious to everything except the holiday fun and the exuberance of the youngsters, enjoyed himself.

It was four o'clock in the morning the day after Christmas when Cole found Sawyer downstairs in the living room, her head buried in her arms as she lay facedown on one of the sofas. On the floor within reach was an empty decanter of Scotch and a toppled glass.

Cole knew an overwhelming sense of helplessness. What could he do to help her? All day she'd been too bright, like a bulb just before it burns out. She hadn't told him what was wrong, but it hadn't been hard to guess, seeing the distance she'd suddenly put between herself and Rand when she'd been falling all over him on Christmas Eve.

Right now he had to get her upstairs and into the shower. Somehow she had to be sober and fit to travel by seven in the morning. But he couldn't do it alone.

Riley woke at Cole's touch and sat up groggily. His first thought was something had happened to his grandfather. "Say again?"

"I said I need your help. Sawyer's downstairs and she's dead drunk. If we don't do something, neither one of us will be going to New York. Hustle your ass, Riley, and get downstairs. Do you know how to make coffee?"

"No, do you?"

"No, but she needs it to sober up."

"Hey, Cole, you know what you learned in school. Nothing sobers you up, not coffee or food or anything, only time!"

"That's exactly what we don't have. We've got to be leaving here in three hours! Now hustle!" he hissed. "We don't have to get her sober enough to drive, only to get her on her feet and moving."

Riley grabbed his terry robe and followed Cole down the stairs.

"Let's get her into the kitchen. You take one arm and I'll take the other. Between us we'll figure out how to work the percolator. She's so drunk it won't matter how it tastes."

"It might make her sick. That's what happened to you."

"Yeah, at least she'll puke up the booze in her stomach before it hits her bloodstream. I learned *that* in school, too. Meanwhile, you got any better ideas?" Cole snapped as he gently took Sawyer under the arm in a firm grip.

Sawyer was roused enough by the manhandling to mutter, "Let me alone. Let me sleep." Determinedly, they dragged her into the kitchen.

"It might help if you'd tell me what's going on," Riley said as he tried to hold Sawyer erect on the chair. "I've got a right to know."

"Yeah, I guess you do," Cole said grudgingly as he filled the electric percolator and dumped coffee into the strainer basket. "I think Rand's got something going with my mother. I'm pretty sure of it. The bottom line is he dumped Sawyer."

"That was in July. Why'd she get drunk now?"

"I think she thought they could patch it up. I just found her like this a little while ago. And if we both want to go to New York, we better fix her up quick."

For the next two hours both boys badgered, cajoled, and walked Sawyer around the kitchen. When her insides ripped loose, Cole held her head over the sink and Riley steadied her.

"I'm going to kill both of you for this," Sawyer sputtered as Cole doused her entire head in lukewarm water.

"You told me if I made an ass out of myself, I damn well better be ready to take the consequences. This is your consequence. We're gonna get you upstairs and you can change your clothes. You've got exactly forty-five minutes to get ready and be downstairs. You got that?"

"Miserable, rotten cretins. I'll lose you in New York. I'll starve you!"

"He's not worth it!" Cole cried vehemently.

"Just shut the hell up. I'm all right now. I can walk by myself. It wasn't necessary to wet my head."

"Wear a hat," Riley suggested.

"Riley, get your gear and stow it by the front door," Cole ordered. "The car will be out front by seven. I'm packed. Once we get her in her room, I'm going back to clean up the kitchen. Watch her."

"Who put you in charge?" Sawyer demanded. "You sound like a goddamn drill sergeant."

"When the first in command falters, the second in command takes over. So move it! And be quiet."

Riley opened Sawyer's door and shoved her inside. "I have to get my bags and get dressed. I'll be right back. Can you manage?"

"I can manage. I'll be ready. What are we doing about saying good-bye to my hostess?"

"I thought you said good-bye last night. I did. Aunt Maggie said she was sleeping in. I guess Cole did the same thing."

"You're right. I'm just a bit foggy. Do what you have to do."

Sawyer snapped the latch on her bag and looked around to see if she'd forgotten anything. She was bundling her damp hair into a knot on top of her head when the door opened. Maggie stood in the doorway.

"If you're here to gloat, do it quickly. It's almost time to leave," Sawyer said flatly. "I want you to know something before I leave because I won't ever be coming back. All those years when you were so rotten, I found excuses for you. I used to cry myself to sleep saying over and over, 'Tomorrow she'll write,' or 'Tomorrow she'll call.' You never did. You simply didn't give a damn. I feel sorry for Cole. At least I had Grand to care. And you know what, Maggie? You deserve to see all your chickens come home to roost. I hope I never have to see you again."

Maggie's insides crumbled. She listened and knew she deserved everything Sawyer said. But it didn't make it any more bearable. "I thought you had more guts, Sawyer," she said. "I'd hoped you were a fighter, a survivor like me. I was wrong. Good-bye."

Sawyer stared at the closed door. Guts. Be a fighter, a survivor like her. No thanks, Mother, not if it means being like you.

Cole raced up the stairs, taking them three at a time. As he rounded the corner of the wide upper hallway, he met Riley. "Where's Sawyer?"

"She's almost ready. She told me to get lost," Riley muttered.

"That's probably the best advice you'll ever get," Cole answered coldly.

"I've had enough of you, Cole! Get off my back. You want to start something, now's as good a time as any."

"I'm not afraid of you. I'll take you on, but some other time. First, I want to get away from this place."

Both boys eyeballed each other. Their day of reckoning was coming and they both knew it.

Maggie stood by her bedroom window watching the limo roar down the drive. She sank against the window, her brow cooled by the glass. How could things have gotten so messed up? She hadn't wanted an open confrontation with Sawyer; she had gone to her daughter's room to check on the boys and say her good-byes. It had been Sawyer who'd lashed out first. Maggie's hands formed into fists, the knuckles whitening. Why did she have to fight for everything she wanted? And why was she always the one to wear the black hat?

"They've gone, have they?"

Maggie swung around to see Rand standing in the open doorway. He looked terrible.

"Yes, they've gone," she replied. "And as usual I've made a mess of things. I got up to say good-bye to the boys and came face-to-face with Sawyer. She let me have it with both barrels."

"Were you surprised?"

"No, but I regret it. I've never had much of a relationship with Sawyer, but when she said she never wanted to see me again, that she'd never ever come back here to Sunbridge, it was like being hit over the head." She laughed, a bitter sound in the quiet room. "I've got a lousy track record, Rand, and it doesn't seem to be improving."

"What will you do?"

"I was just thinking about that. I was remembering the way they sent me to Vermont after Sawyer was born, and how I cried and cried and told Mam that I hated her and that I'd never love her again."

"And what did Billie do?"

"She said it wasn't important that her children love her. That she hadn't brought us into the world to fill a gap in her life. She brought us into the world because she loved us and that love carried a responsibility. And that's why she was sending me away from Sunbridge, because she loved me and it was for my own good."

"Do you believe that now?"

"Yes, without a doubt. But I can't seem to get over the hurt that I wasn't wanted here in the first place. That I could never seem to find my own niche here."

"You do belong at Sunbridge, Maggie. And you also belong here." He opened his arms to her and she walked into his embrace. He held her close, burying his face in the fragrance of her neck. "And I do love you, Maggie. Without doubt."

The ski lodge was toasty warm. Adam leaned back in his swivel chair by the fire. How was he going to tell Paula he had to leave? Just up and tell her, or take the coward's way out and fake a virus? She'd be fine on her own, and since everything was paid for, she could stay on. The hot coffee mug warmed his hands. His breakfast was lying heavily on his stomach. He was brooding, fighting off a feeling of impending doom. All was not right with his beloved Sawyer. He had to get back to New York.

"Paula," he said lazily, "how upset would you be if I cut out and returned to New York?"

"Work, stomach virus, or the truth? . . . You're worried about Sawyer. I'm sure I can manage. I am staying on here, right?"

Paula was a great girl. Fun, understanding, and no strings attached. Bedroom eyes smiled at him. "Go, you big goof. You'll only make both of us miserable if you stay. The shuttle leaves"—Paula looked down at the slim square on her wrist—"in forty-five minutes."

"You're a sport. I can be packed in five minutes."

"You never really unpacked, did you, Adam? Just pay

the bill, honey, and leave my airline ticket on the dresser."

"I should marry you is what I should do." Adam grinned.

"No way. You'd be drawing cartoons of me and hanging them in the bathroom after the first month. Why spoil a good thing? Enjoy yourself, because I'm going to have a ball."

"See you." Adam waved airily. Paula waved back. She *would* have a good time, the witch.

Sawyer herded the boys into the dingy freight elevator. "I know this looks rather weird, but when you see the loft, you're going to be surprised."

As soon as they walked through the front door, a horn blared. Confetti streamed from the top of the door sill. "Welcome home, gang!" Adam yelled at the top of his lungs.

"Adam! What are you doing here?"

"I got tired of sitting by the fire and drinking toddies. You must be Cole, and of course you're Riley," Adam said, extending his hands to both boys. "Are we going to have a ball. I've been dying to see New York ever since I moved here. I mean really see it. This slug"—he indicated Sawyer—"is just along for the ride. Come on, I'll show you where you're bunking. Then I'll show you some of my better work; we'll catch some news on TV—that's a must, because I make my living spoofing the politicos—and then we'll take off for one of my favorite eating places, the Back Porch. There's no place like New York for eating out. You guys are gonna beg to come back here."

The Texans took on the Big Apple with verve and determination. The hectic week started off with a visit to the most famous lady in the world, the Statue of Liberty, followed by Wall Street, the Twin Towers, the Village, and Chinatown's Mott Street. They breakfasted at Samantha's, lunched at the Four Seasons, dined at the Sign of the Dove, and managed to fit in Sloppy Louie's for the best fish in the world. Cole, who'd lived in New York most of his life, discovered places he had never known. Bloomingdale's, Saks Fifth Avenue, and St. Patrick's

Cathedral were followed by a trip to the Seventh Avenue garment district. The Museum of Natural History and the Modern Art Museum vied with a matinee of the Broadway show *Cats* and a screening of the latest Chuck Norris adventure.

"Someday I'm going to write a book about this town," Adam said during the hair-raising ride to Kennedy Airport in a cab being driven by a Lebanese camel jockey.

There were manly handshakes, boyish kisses and hugs. The memories of New York were something none of them would forget.

"By God, that was one of the best weeks I've ever had," Adam said happily on the ride back to the apartment.

"Adam, I don't think I can ever thank you for what you did this past week."

"Thank me? Hell, I should be thanking you. I really saw New York. I lived it; I loved it. I'll probably never do it again. I think the boys had a ball."

"They did. They really liked you, Adam. Texas is going to seem tame after this glorious visit." She paused thoughtfully. "I was surprised that Cole went to see his father yesterday. For some reason I thought Cole had scratched him off his list of people to know and love."

"New Year's Day, what do you expect? He probably felt it was something he had to do. He did seem a little subdued afterward, but he snapped out of it."

"Subdued? I thought he was like the cat that ate the canary. I know him. Something went on yesterday, and we probably won't know what it is until he's ready to tell us."

Back in the loft in front of the fire, Adam poured generously from the wine bottle. "Now, tell me, how are you? We've danced around it all week. It's time to talk."

Sawyer's voice was flat, almost a monotone. "I feel like I'm in a holding pattern over hell. Does that explain it?"

"It explains the way you feel; it doesn't tell me what happened," Adam said gently.

"There's not much to tell. Rand's having an affair with

Maggie. I asked him point-blank and he didn't deny it."
She laughed bitterly. "Then I got drunk, very drunk. Cole
found me early in the morning. That kid's okay, Adam,
he really is. Maggie screwed him up just like she screwed
me up. If there was a way I could take him away from
her, I would," Sawyer said grimly. "I've been thinking all
week of having a talk with Cranston. Maybe we could
strike up a deal."

"You'd go that far to get back at Maggie?" Adam asked
in awe.

"I'd go that far. Don't judge, Adam. Not until you've
walked in my shoes."

Marble, tired of warming herself by the fire, leaped
onto Sawyer's lap, knocking the wineglass out of her hand.
The cat immediately began licking the wine.

"Don't worry about it; she's been drunk before," Adam
laughed, and the tense moment was over.

"I'm not worried about the cat," Sawyer grumbled good-
naturedly. "What about my skirt?"

"Sponge it off. It's no big deal. That's the secret to
life, you know. You have to know what's important and
what isn't."

"You really can be a nag, Adam. However, I love you
dearly. I don't know how I could have made it through
the week without you."

"No thanks are necessary. Have some more wine. Do
you think Marble's whiskers are turning gray?"

"Probably. She's old, or hadn't you noticed? Speaking
of old, you should have seen the show Ms. Eileen Farrell
put on for my aunt Amelia. She had her hooks out for
Cary, but when she found out Rand was what she called
'nobility,' she homed in on him. Aunt Amelia is so jealous,
it oozes out of her pores. I had a few moments of feeling
sorry for her, but I was so wrapped up in my own problems, I forgot about it till this minute. Cary is such a good-
looking man. You know, I really believe he loves my aunt.
She adores him, but she's playing the same game we all
play, making her own hell. She's just waiting for the day
he wants firm flesh and nubile breasts."

"Did you ever think about talking to her? Maybe she needs an ear. We all do at one time or another."

"Not my ear. I'm young. I'm the enemy. Grand is the one she'll talk to if she ever needs a confidante. I think we should eat something; I'm getting woozy from all this wine."

"I'll cook if you clean up. I'm just as woozy, so you're taking a chance letting me cook. Of course, you don't know how to cook, so maybe you aren't taking a chance after all."

"You're not woozy; you're blitzed."

"So are you."

Sawyer giggled. "I know. Just make sandwiches."

"Fluffernutters okay with you? Those boys ate us out of house and home, and that's all that's left."

"Sounds good to me. Put a dab of jelly on mine."

"You got it," Adam muttered as he went into the kitchen.

Sawyer watched him for a moment, then rubbed her eyes. She could hardly focus. Wine never did this to her before, and she was getting another one of her headaches. Too much excitement. She'd rest up tomorrow or go into the office and think about taking a vacation.

The New Year began for Maggie with a mixture of joy and sadness. Joy because Rand was staying on at Sunbridge, sadness because of Sawyer.

They played a little game, Rand and Maggie. By day, they enjoyed riding in the frosty winter air and made the rounds of holiday parties with Susan or Amelia and Cary. By night, they made love and slept in each other's arms.

It had been decided that Rand should remain at Sunbridge until Cole and Riley returned from New York. If there was to be any flak, Rand wanted to be there for his share instead of leaving Maggie to face it alone. When they did return, the day after New Year's, neither of the boys seemed to have much to say, but their sympathies clearly lay with Sawyer.

For once the two boys seemed to be in agreement about something. At times Maggie thought they were engaged in a conspiracy against her, although she knew they still didn't get along. Even Riley had changed toward her. Before the trip he'd always asked her how her day had gone, was interested in the daily workings of Sunbridge. In return, he'd share his day with her, air his views, and discuss his plans. Now he had nothing to share and little to say. Cole was so openly hostile, Maggie avoided his company altogether. Something about his bearing, in the way he looked at her, told her he'd found a way to strike back. Only in her darkest hours did she think of Sawyer, and when she did, Cole was always there in her thoughts. The two of them allies, children against their mother.

Aside from Rand, the only bright spot on Maggie's horizon was her divorce from Cranston. She could hardly wait to put it behind her. Once she was a free woman, she and Rand could bring their feelings for each other out in the open. Then, and only then, would they be able to face the family together, firm in their right to be together. Disapproval for other reasons, such as loyalty to Sawyer, would simply have to be ignored. Besides, they loved each other and didn't need anyone else's approval.

Just after New Year's the phone at Sunbridge shrilled to life. Maggie caught it on the fourth ring, taking her coat and hat off at the same time. A cheerful voice told her Cranston Tanner was calling long distance. When he came on the line, Maggie took a deep breath and said cheerfully, "Happy New Year, Cranston." Then she waited.

"I've decided to sue for custody of Cole," he said abruptly, not bothering to return her greeting. "You can fight me, Maggie, but it won't do you any good. Of course, that puts the divorce on hold for now. You'll want time to see your lawyers and time to speak to Cole. In the end it will be what Cole wants, and he wants his father."

She'd been expecting it; she'd known Cole had been up to something when he'd returned from New York. "Why?" was all she said, all she could say.

"Because I'm getting married again and the boy deserves a family."

"You said you weren't seeing anyone," Maggie said hoarsely.

"That was in September. This is now. You could say I've found the love of my life. Cole will fit in nicely."

"You don't want him; you're just trying to get back at me for rejecting you. I thought we came to an understanding. You said the divorce would come off on schedule and we'd do what was best for Cole for the second semester."

"That's exactly what I'm doing. Cole can finish out the school year, then come here in June. This way he can spend as much time with Sawyer as he wants. I've spoken to Sawyer and she thinks it's a good idea."

"Sawyer! What right do you have to...Damn you, Cranston! Sawyer has nothing to do with this."

"Sawyer has everything to do with this. She's Cole's sister and probably the only person he really cares about. He came to visit me while he was in New York. He didn't tell you, did he?"

"No, he didn't, but I suspected. What did he tell you?"

"Enough so you'll never keep the boy. I'll win, Maggie. I always win. Look, I admire the fact that you've gotten your life together and stopped drinking. I'm glad that you're happy at Sunbridge. But you're no good for Cole. You never were. You weren't any good for Sawyer, either. You're not a mother. That about sums it up. Now, we can do it the easy way or the hard way."

"You can go to hell, Cranston."

"I expect I will someday. I'll probably see you there," Cranston replied smoothly. "Nice talking to you, Maggie. Give my love to Cole."

"You bastard!" Maggie screamed into the mouthpiece as she hung up.

"Who's a bastard?" Amelia asked. "God, I need a drink. Tonic water," she added hastily.

"Have what you want. Other people drinking doesn't bother me. That was Cranston. He's going to try to take

Cole away from me. He's getting married and he wants Cole to be able to see Sawyer as much as he wants. That girl has ruined my life. I can't even stand to hear her name anymore."

"You don't mean that. You're upset."

"Of course I'm upset, and you're right; I don't mean it. My bottom line is always Sawyer. I don't know how much more I can handle."

"You'll handle whatever is dished out. That's how you survive. According to Cary, God never gives us more than we can handle. Personally, I sometimes have trouble believing it, but there must be truth in it because we're both here kicking and scratching. Was going to bed with Rand worth all of this? That's what it's all about and you know it."

"Who I go to bed with is none of Cranston's business. If he's getting married, he's gone to bed with someone, too."

"What are you going to do?" Amelia asked curiously.

"Spend a sleepless night and call Dudley Abramson first thing in the morning. I can't believe Cranston could be this cruel. I'm going to call Sawyer and give her a piece of my mind, and then I'm going to talk to Cole."

Amelia finished her tonic water. She couldn't wait to get to her room so she could have a real drink. And think about the Christmas present Cary had given her. It had been delivered today, a gorgeous Persian rug, almost identical to the one her mother had said was in the library. The owner of the small store had delivered it himself, thrilled that it was going into such a beautiful house. She'd spent an hour with the little man, showing off her renovations. Then, something the carpet dealer had said burned in her brain till she couldn't take it anymore. "The young lady was very pleased with the carpet. She had the specifications all written down." Amelia had sent the workmen home early and locked up.

My God, how she'd gushed and trilled to Cary about his wonderful gift! And that damn Eileen had just sat there looking smug while she'd made a fool of herself. What angered Amelia more than anything else was Cary's play-acting, pretending that he'd trudged into the city and roamed and searched till he'd found the "perfect gift" for his beloved wife.

"I guess you'll want privacy for your call, so I'll toddle along upstairs," Amelia said, shaking off her thoughts. "I expect Cary early this evening. Hopefully, in time for dinner. What's on the menu? That's the first thing he asks."

"Beef stew and corn bread. Cherry pie. Martha made ice cream today. The boys seem to love it."

"Great." Cary would love it. "I'll see you at dinner-time." As as afterthought she called over her shoulder, "I wouldn't worry too much, Maggie. Things will work out for the best, or at least the way they're meant to. I'll see you in a little while."

Maggie waved absently, her mind already on the call to New York she was about to make. She dialed the oper-ator, gave her Sawyer's business number, and made the call person-to-person from Coleman Tanner. The moment Sawyer's voice came on the wire, Maggie cried, "How could you go behind my back to conspire with Cranston? That wasn't what I meant by guts. I won't have a chance in hell of keeping Cole now. My God, how could you?"

Sawyer tried to listen, but her head was pounding so, she could barely make out Maggie's words.

"I really don't want to get involved with you and Cran-ston, Maggie," she said. "Handle your own affairs. I thought I made that clear to you before I left."

"Well, let me make this clear to you right now. Cole is off-limits to you. Don't call him and don't write to him."

For several moments Sawyer stood there and listened to the dial tone, feeling as if she were going to be ill. If only she could get rid of this damn headache! Suddenly she gripped the edge of the desk and swayed.

Peter Andrews, on his way back from the water cooler, saw Sawyer sway. He quickened his step when he saw her loosen her grip on the desk. An instant later her knees buckled and she slid to the floor. He shouted for help. In twenty minutes Sawyer was on her way to the hospital. Peter personally undertook to notify Adam Jarvis and Sawyer's grandmother.

Amelia was on her way down to the library and the evening paper when the phone rang. Cary, of course. She'd known it even before she picked up the phone.

"Darling, I'm not going to make dinner. Keep something warm for me, will you? There're some things here I want to clean up tonight. Eileen's going to help me. I know we agreed to catch some television and lounge around this evening, but ... Amelia? You aren't angry, are you? I'll try to get out of here as soon as I can."

"No, of course I'm not angry. You're missing a good dinner, but I'll keep yours warm. Beef stew gets better the longer it sits. We have homemade ice cream and cherry pie."

"Oh, God, I can taste it now. Keep a light in the window. Love you."

"I love you, too," Amelia cried passionately. "The light will always be there for you. Drive carefully; the roads are slick." The connection was broken; Amelia looked at the receiver for a long time before she replaced it.

"The temperature must have dropped outside," Eileen complained. "I have all four heaters on, even the one in the bathroom. Are you sure you want to stay and finish this up, Cary?"

"You were the one who offered to stay."

"That was before the temperature dropped. I'm afraid my car is never going to start."

"So, I'll give you a jump. You should be wearing warmer clothes," Cary said, eyeing the thin jersey material of Eileen's dress. "This trailer is like a wind tunnel. Wool slacks and a heavy sweater would be more practical."

"Well, bring your chair around by me, then. We can

at least huddle. An hour, Cary, that's it. I've got the bids all sorted. I have three proposals on hand. Sherman looked at them today and made comments in the margins. Let's get to it so we can get out of here."

"You sound like you have a heavy date."

"I do, but not with the man I'd like to have a date with. I've been wanting to ask you since Christmas if Rand is still here. Is he involved with anyone?"

"I really don't know. For sure, I mean," Cary said truthfully.

"Maybe I'll give him a call tomorrow and see what his reaction is."

"By the way, that really was nice of you to get the carpet for me. I made six trips to Austin and made a dozen or so calls to Houston and Dallas looking for that damn thing. You really saved my hide and I appreciate it. How in the hell did you find it, anyway?"

"I started off with the yellow pages and went on from there. It was such an expensive item that all the shops I called were more than willing to help. Of course, when I told them who it was for, they were even more helpful. The Coleman name is very powerful in Texas."

"So I've found out. I wouldn't be where I am now, nor would you, if it wasn't for Amelia's help."

"You'd have found a way. You're a very talented man, Cary."

Cary's eyes were only inches from Eileen's. "No, I wouldn't. I couldn't have done any of this without Amelia. She believed in me and made me believe in myself. The most you can say for me is that I know what a hammer is." He paused, then said pointedly, "We're a team, Amelia and me." Imperceptibly Eileen moved her swivel chair. Her eyes were the first to lower. She understood.

They worked for over an hour without a break. Cary smiled when he closed the folders. "Done! Tomorrow you can zero in on the other stuff, and from there it's smooth sailing. At least now I can see some daylight. Thanks for staying, Eileen. Get your things and I'll turn off all the heaters and get the lights and lock up. I'll wait to see if your car starts."

Thirty minutes later Eileen's old Ford was still dead. "You probably need a new battery. Where the hell did you get this clunker anyway?"

"From a used car lot. I can't afford anything else."

"Jesus Christ, with what we pay you, how can you stand there and tell me you can't afford anything better?"

"Would you like to see my rent receipts? You know, it isn't easy being single and living alone. I barely make ends meet. I like to take a vacation at least once a year, so I have to save for that. I'm not a Coleman," she said coldly. "I'm just a working girl."

"Okay, okay. Maybe we can find a way to get you a company car. I suppose we could lease it, or I could cosign a loan. Get in the car. I'll drive you home."

"I can't afford the payments. I'll have to take a taxi tomorrow morning and that's going to cost me at least twenty dollars. I can't seem to win these days. Thanks for wanting to help, though."

"It's going to take at least ten minutes for the heater to warm up the truck. Damn, I should have called Amelia to tell her I was going to be late."

"I'll call her tomorrow and apologize. I'll tell her it's my fault and explain the situation."

Cary's heart raced. "For Christ's sake, don't do that! I'll handle it." He calculated the time it would take him to drop Eileen off and return to Sunbridge. He'd be lucky if he got in by ten-thirty. For the first time it occurred to him to wonder if Amelia was jealous of Eileen. He knew she had no cause, but even so....

"How bad are the roads?" Eileen shivered inside her cashmere coat.

"Icy. They'll be worse by morning. I'll pick you up. Have someone come to look at your car tomorrow. Tell them to bring a battery just in case. I'll talk to Sherman and Clara about you using one of their cars, at least until most of this bad weather is over. Then we'll see about getting you a loan. Maybe we can work something out with the company. But if it can't be written off, we can't do it. That's Sherman's rule of thumb."

"It's a good rule. Companies like yours need tax breaks. If getting me a car helps, I'm all for it."

It was half an hour's ride into the city of Austin. Eileen and Cary kept up a cheerful banter of office gossip and business all the way.

"Thanks, Cary."

"No problem. Spiffy building," Cary said, eyeing the doorman.

"A girl has to be safe. We have an elevator operator, too. It's a good security building. That's why I moved here. Most of my salary goes to pay for rent."

"How much?"

"Thirteen hundred a month. It's going co-op in six months. I'll have to move, since I can't afford to buy. Drive carefully."

"I'll pick you up at seven-thirty," he called before driving off.

Eileen let herself into the luxury apartment. It was like a layout in Bloomingdale's catalogue. Right down to the porcelain figurines. Soft gray and peach, easy on the eye and elegant. Amelia Assante would be hard-pressed to find anything wrong with this apartment.

Borrowing that old clunker of a car from a friend was going to pay off. Everything would pay off, sooner than she'd hoped. The company car would lead to a BMW, and soon the apartment would be picked up, too, as a corporation property. But she'd hold the title, of course. They needed her. That was the bottom line. Just like she needed their money. A trade-off. She'd certainly learned a lot since she'd started to work for the company.

Eileen's slender fingers plucked at the row of cassettes. She selected a Lionel Richie tape and popped it into the stereo. She stripped down and headed for the shower. She'd order dinner to be catered. One way or another she would find a way to put it on one of the men's expense accounts. She might have to put out a little tonight, but she'd get it back when it came time to buy the BMW. The man she was seeing tonight was a BMW dealer. Cost? Perhaps below cost.

You scratch my hand and I'll tickle yours. She giggled.

{{{{{{{{ CHAPTER NINETEEN }}}}}}}}

It was almost midnight before the duty station nurse would allow Adam into Sawyer's room. She seemed to be sleeping, but the squeak of the door alerted her to a presence in the dimly lit room. "Adam, is that you?" she asked wanly.

"Who else? I've been sitting outside for hours. Look at me; I'm a wreck—and you're the one who's in bed. How do you feel?" he asked anxiously.

"That holding pattern I'm in seems to have shifted a little, dropping me closer over the hellhole. Exhaustion, I guess. Don't worry, Adam. I'll be fine in a day or so. I can't believe they brought me to the hospital. All I need is a couple of days of rest and some of your greasy cooking."

Adam tried for a smile but failed. "The nurse said something about tests."

"I don't know. Standard hospital procedure, I'm sure. There's nothing wrong with me. I'm planning on leaving here tomorrow. They already did some tests."

"What kind of tests? For what?"

"Blood tests. They X-rayed my shoulder, my neck,

and my head. Seems I hit it when I fell. My mouth is so dry. Could you get me a drink?"

"Sure." Adam poured from a carafe and handed the glass to Sawyer, then watched as she reached out for the glass and missed, spilling the water over the sheet. "It was my fault. I'm sorry," he said soothingly.

"I guess I'm still groggy. They gave me a shot of something. It seems to be wearing off now a little. What time is it?"

"After midnight. I didn't want to leave until I was sure you were all right."

"What time did they bring me here?"

"This afternoon. Late, I think. I'm glad they did. Now they can check you out and put you on some good vitamins. I'll be back in the morning."

"You don't have to do that, Adam," Sawyer said sleepily. "I'll be leaving and can take a taxi back to the apartment."

"I'll call you, then. How's that?"

"That's fine . . ." Sawyer's voice trailed off. Adam stayed for a long time watching her. Her breathing was easy and she seemed to be in a deep sleep. A drugged sleep. He knew she'd sleep through the night, but still he didn't leave. It wasn't until the night nurse poked her head in the door and suggested he go home that he moved. She was right, of course. He couldn't do anything here.

At the nurse's station he stopped to talk. "Miss Coleman told me that she was scheduled for more tests tomorrow. What kind of tests?"

"Are you a member of the family?"

"She lives with me." At the nurse's blank look, Adam explained, "We cohabit. As in live together. I am the closest thing to a relative she has here in New York."

"We don't give out information to anyone but family. You aren't family," the charge nurse said in a no-nonsense voice.

"Look," he said, deciding to try another tack, "I'm the one who is going to be paying the bill. That makes me responsible. So, if I'm responsible, you can tell me what I want to know." He leaned over the desk and lowered his voice. "My mother doesn't approve of us living together, either, but it's the only thing I could think of to get her to marry me. I'm monogamous. But she's afraid because her parents didn't have a happy marriage." The nurse seemed to be relenting, so Adam drove home his advantage. "You look like you have a good head on your shoulders. Wouldn't you do the same thing if you were me? I'm in love with her. I can't lose her."

The nurse's stiffly starched uniform crackled as she moved back a step, closer to the rack that held the patients' charts. Adam watched in relief as she flipped through the charts arranged according to room number.

"Neurological testing," she said through tight lips. "Another urinalysis and additional blood tests."

"She already had a blood test. What are they looking for?"

"This is not a question-and-answer period, young man. I shouldn't have told you what I did. Now, if you want more information, you'll have to speak to doctor. I'm simply not at liberty to say anything else. It's late and your voice carries. We can't have you waking our patients. Call doctor tomorrow."

Adam looked at the plump starched nurse. Her iron-gray hair was like tiny corkscrews sticking out every which way from her white cap. Her eyes were round and serious, but oh, so wary. She was on the defensive now that she'd done something she knew was wrong. Probably she had never broken a rule in her life, until now. "You take good care of her, for me. I'll be back in the morning."

"I won't be here," the woman blurted.

"I'll be back in the evening, too. Thank you."

"Young man..."

"Yes?"

"It's routine when a patient has a blow to the head. Get a good night's sleep."

* * *

Marble hissed nastily when Adam sat down on the sofa and pulled the phone to his lap. She continued to hiss and spit, her claws digging at the sofa cushions. Adam swatted her on the rump and pushed her off the couch. "The other lady in my life is first right now. Eat that popcorn if you're so hungry," Adam muttered as he tossed fat fluffies on the carpet. Marble hissed again and walked away, her plumed tail straight in the air.

"Nick, it's Adam. Sorry about the late hour, but I have to talk to you."

"Late, early, what difference does it make when you're here to serve the masses? My time is yours as long as you pay for it. What's wrong?"

"Sawyer's in the hospital. She fainted and they're scheduling neurological tests for tomorrow. They took a blood test today and more are scheduled for tomorrow. I...That's all I know."

Nick's voice was suddenly professional, clipped and cool. "Was she hurt when she passed out? Did they take any X-rays?"

"Shoulder, neck, skull. She gets these blinding head-aches. I thought it was because of the stress and strain. Remember how I used to tell you she had the eye of an eagle? Well, she just got glasses. She really has to wear them. She complained one day that her vision blurs every so often. Put the migraine headaches, the glasses, and the fainting spell together, and there's room for worry."

"It's possible they found some abnormality and are doing more testing to be sure. On the other hand, it could be nothing. Both of us could speculate all night, but I'm not the attending physician. Be glad she's in the hospital where they can take care of her. If you like, I can stop in and see her tomorrow."

"Do that. Call me and let me know what you think, okay?"

"Will do. Take two aspirins and go to bed."

Sawyer didn't leave the hospital that day or the next. She made threatening noises to the doctor but in the end realized she was too weak and drained to do more than make a token effort. The results of her tests would take another day.

"I hate airports, Thad. They have such bad connotations for me. I have this feeling that something is terribly wrong. Adam didn't know anything really. I guess that's what's worrying me more than anything. Young girls don't land in the hospital for four days for a fainting spell. Sawyer is going to be angry with Adam for calling me, and she's going to be angry with me for calling Maggie."

"What I can't understand," Thad said as he packed down the tobacco in his pipe, "is why Maggie won't go to New York and meet you. She is Sawyer's mother, after all. I'm sorry, Billie, but that's something I will never understand if I live to be a hundred. Maggie has come so far, made so many changes in her life. Why can't she and Sawyer come to some kind of terms?"

"Who are we to say Maggie must do this and Maggie mustn't do that? Maggie and Sawyer have to work things out themselves. From what Amelia has told me, Christmas was a total disaster. Now I'm really glad we were snowbound."

"They're calling your flight, darling. Call me when you land and again after you see Sawyer. If you need me, call, any time of the day or night. Promise now."

"I promise." Billie kissed him soundly. "Say a little prayer on the way home that Sawyer is all right."

"I will, darling. Have a safe trip."

Billie was uneasy during the plane trip. The feeling stayed with her while she claimed her luggage and called Thad. It was still with her on the cab ride to Adam's loft. When there was no answer to her repeated ringing, she left her suitcase beside the door and hailed a cab for the hospital.

Billie's stomach churned as she made her way down the corridor to Sawyer's room.

Outside the door, she stood quietly for a moment trying

to compose herself. Sawyer was going to be upset that she'd made the trip, but she could talk her way out of that easily enough. What was going to be hard to explain was Adam's frantic phone call to her. And if Sawyer should ask, she would have to admit that she'd called Maggie. Of course, she wouldn't have to tell her how Maggie had reacted. Billie suspected there was more to the situation than met the eye. With a smile on her face, she pushed open the door to Sawyer's room.

"Grand, what are you doing here? . . . Adam called you, didn't he? I can see it in his face. He worries too much. We're waiting for the doctor to come in and discharge me; he's supposed to have all the reports from my tests. I've been burning the candle at both ends, and it finally caught up with me. I'm run-down, anemic probably. They'll give me megavitamins and send me home. You shouldn't have made the trip."

"I wanted to. It's nice to see you again, Adam. You haven't changed at all."

"Still as good-looking as ever, right?"

"I said you haven't changed." Billie forced a laugh. Something *was* wrong here; she could feel it.

"Perhaps I should go on to the loft. I did go there first and left my bag. You'll want privacy with the doctor."

"That's silly, Grand. Wait. You can certainly hear what the doctor has to say. We'll all go back to the loft together."

"Makes sense to me. I always said this chick had a head on her shoulders," Adam quipped.

"Beautiful head." Sawyer grinned. "Oh, here's the doctor." Sawyer made the necessary introductions. "Now tell me, Dr. Finley, how many vitamins do I have to take a day? I'm anemic, aren't I? Do I need B-twelve shots? . . . You look so serious. Don't tell me I have an inner ear problem; I used to get that when I was little."

Billie hadn't realized she was holding her breath until it escaped in a tortured sigh. Adam was squeezing and releasing his fists. He could feel it, too.

* * *

There was little in Susan's imagination that could compare with the dreariness of early January in Texas. All the life seemed to drain out of the land, leaving a poor imitation painted in indistinguishable shades of gray upon gray. And she fit perfectly into the landscape, gray and lifeless like an aging slug whose middle is too swollen for movement. She longed for a warm climate, blue skies, sunshine.

For as long as she could remember, she'd never been this lonely. First, it had been Mam and Pap and the rest of the family here at Sunbridge, and then Amelia and Rand, and finally Jerome. She'd never lived on her own or had the responsibility of making a life for herself. Even now she was under the protective umbrella of Sunbridge and the family. But it didn't relieve the loneliness.

Every day she wondered where Jerome was and what he was doing. She'd sent letters to the flat and to their agent, Theodore Lewis. All of them had been returned unopened. It was as though Jerome had dropped off the face of the earth. When she'd called Theodore, he'd been unwilling to give any information, although he'd expressed confidence that Jerome would soon come to his senses. "He'll turn up," Theodore had said. "Perhaps he just needs a little time to get accustomed to being a father." Eight months wasn't enough time?

Yes, sooner or later he'd turn up. Of that Susan was sure. He'd appear suddenly, like an apparition, after the baby was born and she was able to go back to work. He'd be filled with plans and schemes and probably have a tour schedule in his pocket.

She worked at her fingers, massaging them gently. How puffy they were. She'd tried just the other day to play the piano, but the finely tuned instrument hadn't responded. In the end she'd slammed down the lid. Maybe she'd never play again. Maybe she'd never do a lot of things again. Right now her top priority was staying well so she could play out her own private miracle of giving birth.

Susan patted her belly, pleased with the little ripples

that made her fingers jump. She wondered if her child would be a boy or a girl. It didn't matter. She would love it. And the child would love her back, unconditionally.

A walk on the portico would feel good now. She'd seen the workmen clear the snow away earlier; there would be no danger of her slipping and falling. Before she could change her mind and snuggle down into the comfortable chair, Susan slipped her arms into a down coat and added a woolen hat to her golden head.

"Suse, where are you going?" Maggie asked in alarm as she watched her sister maneuver awkwardly down the stairs.

"I need some fresh air. I thought I'd walk up and down the portico."

"Wait, I'll go with you. I don't want you falling. They always manage to leave little patches of ice."

"I'm dressed, so I'll wait for you outside." Already she could feel the perspiration beading her forehead.

Maggie joined her sister and they began to stroll, arm in arm. "I wonder what the temperature is today," Susan said. "Remember how we used to cup our hands to our mouths and blow out clouds of what we called venom?"

"I remember. I think I remember everything about our childhood. I went for analysis and the things I remembered shocked the psychologist so much, he suspended my visits till he could get a handle on it. I never went back. I learned that you have to help yourself first, and if you need someone for the rocky spots, then you consult a professional. How are you doing with your rocky spots?"

"I was thinking upstairs that I'm going to have to make a life for myself very soon. I'm going to have to find an apartment and a job. I screwed up, Maggie. Before I came here I didn't take my share from our bank accounts. There's nothing left except the trust fund Mam set up for me here."

"For God's sake, Suse, is that what's been making you look so glum? I have enough for both of us. That should be the least of your worries. You can stay here forever if you want. I love having you here. I can't wait for you to have the baby. Please, I want you to stay. I'll switch over some monies tomorrow. I can even do it today."

"Maggie, I can't. . . . It isn't right . . ."

"Of course it is. Don't even think about paying me back. I'm glad to help. Whatever's mine is yours. This is your home. Pap said I should fill it with sunshine. I don't want you to even think of leaving. Listen to me. Jerome might have cleaned out the bank accounts, but you can stop any further monies from Coleman Enterprises being sent to England. I'll do that for you. It will be funneled here to your bank account once we open it. It's not the end of the world. Your baby is going to be well provided for. That's what you're really worried about, isn't it?"

Susan nodded miserably. "I really thought she or he would be born a pauper dependent on your generosity."

"My God, Suse, why didn't you say something? We should have done some serious talking a while ago. I didn't want to intrude, because you seemed so out of it. Many nights I got as far as your door and then turned around and went back to my room because I thought you wouldn't want to be bothered."

"I thought you were too busy with Rand and the kids and everything. I didn't want to be an added burden." Susan dabbed at her eyes and sniffed. "I feel so alone."

"Well, you're not alone, so stop thinking like that. We both fouled up. We Colemans are good at that. For some reason we never get around to talking till it's too late. If we hadn't met like this this afternoon, you probably would've driven off one day and left me standing here wondering what I did to make you leave. We're going inside right now and talk. I have a lot I want to get off my chest, just like you do."

"What about Rand?"

"What about him? You're important to me, Suse. Rand will just have to manage to entertain himself while we do what we do best. Lord, how we used to jabber for hours on end. We're going to have a pot of tea and some cake, just you and me." Maggie squirmed under Susan's grateful gaze. How could she have been so insensitive to her sister? That was all going to change now.

Much later, the sisters walked hand in hand to dinner down the long stairway. Rand stood at the bottom. He was so handsome, Susan thought, but she was now seeing something she'd never seen in him before. A new awareness, a certain vitality that seemed to form a nimbus around him. It was a silly thought and she smiled. Rand didn't notice; he had eyes only for Maggie. She exerted a little pressure to her sister's hand, her seal of approval. Let them be happy if this is what they both want. Maggie responded with a tight squeeze of her own. It would be all right, she realized. Maggie had a grip on things.

Rand noticed the imperceptible change in Susan and smiled warmly. "I'm starved," he said, "but may I say the wait was worth it? You both look lovely."

"We know." Maggie grinned. "May we say you look quite dashing?"

"You may."

It was a wonderful dinner. Riley and Cole were drawn into the conversation when the talk switched to ice hockey. Maggie was stunned by her son's knowledge of the dangerous sport. She hadn't known he'd played goalie on his old school team.

When the boys returned to their rooms to study, the trio had coffee in front of the fire. Rand regaled Maggie with tales of Susan's young life in England. It was one of the most enjoyable evenings of Maggie's life.

It was after ten when Susan excused herself, saying her eyes would no longer stay open. At almost the same moment, the telephone rang. As Maggie went to answer it, Amelia and Cary opened the front door, a blast of cold air swirling about them. Susan wished everyone a good night and was halfway up the stairs before she heard Maggie's voice change.

Rand watched in alarm as the color drained from Maggie's face. Her grip on the telephone receiver was so tight, her knuckles looked iridescent.

"Thanks for calling me, Mam. I'll . . . What I'll do is . . .

I'll. . . . Yes, of course. . . . This is unreal. . . . I'll . . . call you tomorrow. No, no messages."

Amelia's voice was just short of shrill. "What's wrong? Did something happen to Thad? For God's sake, Maggie, *what is it*?"

Susan echoed Amelia's words. "Are you sure Mam is all right? *Maggieeeeee*!"

Maggie turned till she was facing the small group. She was trembling so badly, Rand jumped up and put his arms around her shoulders. She leaned gratefully into his hard body. "I . . . don't know quite how . . . how to say this except . . . except . . . Sawyer has an inoperable brain tumor." The silence around her brought tears to Maggie's eyes. "Sawyer is still in the hospital. They're calling in another team of neurosurgeons." Suddenly overwhelmed by guilt, she drew away from Rand and walked to the liquor cabinet. She gripped the gin bottle tightly. "I was going to go, you know, when Mam said Sawyer was in the hospital, but when . . . but when she left here, she said she never . . . never wanted to see me again."

The sight of Susan gripping her stomach brought Maggie to her senses. "We're . . . we're all going to handle this. Right now, I don't know how, but we will. Susan, go to bed. You need the rest. We're all in shock right now, so why don't we wait till tomorrow to . . . to talk about it."

"You're right, of course," Amelia said as she reached for Cary's hand. "It's my opinion that all doctors are quacks. They probably made a misdiagnosis and we're all . . . Billie wouldn't have called unless it was . . . Good night, everybody," she said in a small voice.

Maggie sat down on the love seat across from Rand. They watched each other for a long time.

"I think I know what you're thinking," Maggie said gently.

"I *know* what you're thinking," Rand said just as gently.

"It's too late.

"We have to try. My God, Maggie, what kind of people would we be if we didn't try?"

"I didn't say I didn't want to. Sawyer is the one who won't let us exorcise our guilt. That's what it is. Pity is an awful thing. I could never go to Sawyer out of pity. She'd see through it in a minute."

"She's alone," Rand said in a choked voice. "She has to go through this alone."

"She's not alone. Mam will always be there for her. Sawyer's staying with an old friend of hers. Adam has loved her since they were little kids. Rand, I feel so helpless. I can't even comfort you and you can't comfort me."

"Maggie, I'm in love with you. This is . . ."

"Going to change things. I understand that. I have to think, Rand. I'm going upstairs. The boys have to be told, but I think that can wait till tomorrow."

"Maggie!"

"Yes?"

"Did your mother say . . . did she say how long Sawyer has?"

"A year, possibly. They're not certain . . . less. Doctors tend to shy away from. . . . What they do is they won't commit. . . . A year. A goddamn lousy year."

The bolt shot home on Maggie's door. Long fingers raked through her hair. She felt itchy all over. The tears had stopped. Had she cried? She couldn't remember. She rummaged in the drawer for a cigarette. She lit it, puffed on it, crushed it out, only to light another. She paced the room with the cigarette clamped between her teeth.

When she was younger, when Pap was still alive, she'd prayed to God and the devil that Sawyer would die. The memory was so vivid, she raced for the bathroom and upchucked her dinner. Her hand trembled so badly, she could barely brush her teeth. "God, I didn't mean it!" She knew it for the lie it was.

Maggie dropped to her knees, her head resting on the edge of the tub. "I need your help. Please, show me what to do," she prayed.

A long time later, Maggie dragged herself from the bathroom. She dialed New York information for Adam's number, then called him without a thought as to the time.

Neither Adam nor Mam would be sleeping. Would any of them ever sleep again?

"Mam. Help me."

"Maggie, I wish I could. This is something you'll have to handle by yourself. I think I'm still in shock. Adam is." There was a little pause. "Adam is praying. I did that, too. I imagine you did the same."

"I did, but I tend to think He ignores me. Just like that, no warning. I can't accept that."

"It wasn't quite like that. Those migraine headaches Sawyer's had for the past few years, that was the onset." She recounted other maladies that Adam had repeated to her. "We mustn't come to any fast conclusions, Maggie. The doctors don't believe the tumor is malignant, but it is in a vital area which they usually consider inoperable. I told you, there's another team of neurosurgeons coming to see Sawyer. We'll have a better picture then. Go to bed, Maggie, and try to rest."

"Mam, how did you get through Riley's death?"

"One day at a time. Listen to me. Sawyer isn't dead. She's very much alive. Remember that. She still has time."

It was three o'clock in the morning when Maggie descended the attic stairs, a cardboard box in her hands. Her old diaries. Journals, Mam always called them. Little leather-bound books that covered five years of one's life. From her closet she removed the corrugated box she'd brought with her from New York. These were one-year journals, filled out in more detail. Only here in these pages had she been honest.

Maggie Coleman Tanner's life. In two cardboard boxes. It was going to take a lot of guts to read these. The first diary started on her eighth birthday. She smiled when she looked at the childish scrawl. She remembered sending Sawyer a diary on her tenth birthday—a handsome leather-bound journal with her initials embossed in gold.

Maggie sorted through the diaries, placing them in chronological order. She stared at them for a long time.

A person's life shouldn't look so neat. She shook her head
and went downstairs to perk a pot of coffee. She carried
the percolator and a fresh pack of cigarettes upstairs. The
last thing she did was put a note on her door telling everyone she was sleeping and not to waken her. Then she slid
the bolt home and settled herself down to read.

Maggie's life exploded before her very eyes, one page
at a time.

}}}}}}}}} CHAPTER TWENTY }}}}}}}}

When Maggie heard the sound of the garage door closing,
she steeled herself. Telling Riley and Cole about Sawyer
was going to be the hardest thing she'd ever done. Riley,
she knew, would remain calm on the surface. But she
couldn't even begin to imagine what Cole's reaction would
be. Should she wait till they got upstairs and talk to them
in their rooms, or should she call them into the study?

"I'll wait till they settle in," she decided aloud, uncon-
sciously wringing her hands.

Rand watched her as she paced the study. He knew
she was exhausted; she'd told him how she'd spent her
night and morning. Her eyes looked hollow and bruised,
her face pale and drawn. But there was beauty in her, and

an inner strength that would allow her to stand tall and
accept last night's phone call. He ached for her, wanted
to comfort her in some way, but he hurt so bad himself,
he couldn't make the effort.

"If it were me, I think I'd tell them in private," he said
quietly. He watched her a short while later as she climbed
the steps to the second floor.

Voices from the corridor outside the kitchen made him
turn. Amelia must have come through the kitchen, Susan
in her wake. Both women had cups of tea in their hands.
If he drank one more cup of tea, Rand thought, he would
float out the door. He greeted both women with a kiss on
the cheek, then poured himself a triple Scotch.

"I couldn't stay at the house another minute," Amelia
said. "Nothing went right today. I thought I was going to
crawl out of my skin. I tried to call Cary nine times, but
he was out on the site and couldn't be reached. I *needed*
to talk to him," Amelia said in a brittle voice. "I have to
call Billie. Maybe I should go to New York. Sawyer would
understand. She'd know I was making the trip for Billie.
But ... I'm not sure now. I don't know how to ... How in
the name of God are we supposed to act? Do we rally
'round, offer ... what? Sympathy? Pity?"

"I think you should do whatever feels right to you,"
Rand said, staring at the amber fluid in his glass.

"What are *you* going to do?" Amelia demanded. "How
are you handling this?"

"Very carefully. I'm taking it hour by hour. Look, I
did the right thing and I did it for the right reasons. You're
both going to have to accept that. Maggie wasn't in my
life when I broke it off with Sawyer. I'm sorry you've all
chosen up sides. I'm the bad guy now. I'd cut off my right
arm if it would help Sawyer."

Amelia leaned her head back wearily. "I know, Rand.
In a lot of ways Sawyer had more than most, but she also
had less of the things that really count. Billie isn't going
to be able to make this right for her. And she shouldn't
have to," Amelia said angrily. "From here on out it's
Maggie's job."

"Sawyer was supposed to be godmother to my baby," Susan said tearfully.

"What do you mean *was*?" Amelia asked. "She isn't dead, you know. Of course she's going to be the godmother if she's up to it. How could you even think of anything else?"

"It's such a shock. I guess I haven't fully accepted it yet," Susan said softly.

"And that's another thing. Stop whining, Susan. Other women have babies. Other women's husbands leave them. Face up to your responsibilities. Grow up!"

"Aren't you being a little hard on her?" Rand asked, his eyes wide.

"You're another one. Sometimes you make me so angry. You're sitting here riddled with guilt, not knowing what to do. You already did it. Now stand up to it and handle that guilt. Do what's best for Sawyer. And what's going to be best for Sawyer is that you not be here when Susan's baby is born. Go back to England."

"I'm not a kid anymore that you can order around. Why do I have to go back to England? What's done is done. I intend to work my tail off making Maggie see that I care for her. If that means I have to stay here, then I will. We will all deal with this situation the best way each of us knows how. I'm sorry you feel this way, Mother."

Tears pricked at Amelia's eyes. "Sawyer's needs will be different now. She needs the warmth, the caring, of a man who loves her. If only you hadn't been so rash. You could have put your life on hold for a year to see her through this. This betrayal, this blatant carrying on with Maggie. Just imagine what Sawyer must be going through, how she must be feeling."

"There isn't a day that goes by that I don't think about it; no one will let me forget! But I still wouldn't have done things differently. I don't love Sawyer. Would you stay with Cary if he didn't love you?"

Amelia flinched. "Of course not," she cried.

"Susan, would you stay with a man who didn't love you?"

Susan sniffed. "That's a strange question to ask me. I'm here for just that reason. I don't think any of us should say any more. We're all uptight and liable to say things we're going to regret later. Where's Maggie?"

"She went upstairs to tell the boys. If there was a way I could do it for her, I would. She's really hurting, Mother. You saw it at lunchtime, didn't you, Susan?"

"Yes. I wanted to cry for her, but it wouldn't have done any good. We'll talk when the time is right for Maggie. I think I'll go up to my room now and watch the news. It's time I took an interest in what's going on in the world. I'll see you at dinner."

"Now, what's really bothering you, Mother?"

Amelia sighed. "Aside from Sawyer, it's Cary. I told you I called him nine times and he didn't return my calls. He wears a beeper and there's a portable phone in the Bronco." She looked up at him defiantly. "Don't get the idea that I call and pester just for the sake of hearing his voice. In fact, I make it a practice not to bother him. But I really needed him today."

"So, what are you trying to say?"

"I don't think Eileen gave him my messages."

"I think you're off base, Mother. Surely, if that was her intention, she knows you would mention it to Cary this evening and ask him directly. What could she gain?"

"My husband. One of the other investors. She made a play for you over Christmas. Have you been in touch with her?"

"She called me one day and invited me for dinner, but I begged off. I don't need any Eileen Farrells in my life."

"I don't need an Eileen Farrell in my life, either," Amelia cried passionately. "God, she's so young. Sawyer is so young. I'm sorry, Rand. It's been a bad day. I think I'm going to go up and soak in a hot tub. If I'm not down by seven, check to see if I drowned."

"I'll do that. Do you want a copy of the evening paper?"

"No, thanks. I have enough problems without taking on the world. Relax, Rand, and don't let this string you out to the point where you do something foolish."

"I'll bear that in mind." Rand poured himself another drink. Then he settled down, his eyes fastened on the stairway, to await Maggie's return.

Both boys stared at Maggie in disbelief. "Is there anything you want to ask me? I don't pretend to have all the answers, but I can call Mam and find out."

There were tears in Riley's eyes. "It isn't fair!" he cried.

"No, it isn't fair at all. We all have to make the most of the time we have."

"Can we call her?" Riley asked in a quivering voice.

"Of course, but I'd give it a week or so. Why don't you write a letter first. What you put in that letter is going to be up to you, so be careful."

"I will. I'm going to write my grandfather. He's very fond of Sawyer. Excuse me, Aunt Maggie."

Maggie was left alone with her son. There had been no show of emotion on his face when she'd told him about Sawyer. There was none now. "Cole, I . . . wish I wasn't the one who had to tell you this. I know how much you've come to love Sawyer. I'm so sorry."

"Sorry, Mother? I find that a little hard to swallow. You've always hated Sawyer. Why should you be sorry now? Won't you dance on her grave when they bury her?"

Maggie's hand shot out. The bright red mark on the boy's face didn't make her apologize. Cole backed off a step. "This should fit right into your plans. You and Rand live happily ever after. Grand won't have Sawyer to fuss over anymore, only you and Aunt Susan. You'll be the queen bee, the great matriarch of Sunbridge. She'll haunt you, Mommy dearest, until the day you die. You fucked up," he said cruelly.

Maggie's hand shot out a second time. "If you ever— I repeat, ever—talk to me like that again, you'll wish you hadn't. We don't use words like that here. Remember that. I suggest you sit down and think about the coming

year and what you can do to make it better for your sister.
Dinner is at seven."

"I'm not hungry." Cole's hand was on his cheek.

"I don't care if you're hungry or not. Be at the table
and be civil. If not, you'll get more of the same, only next
time I won't hold back. Do we understand each other?"

"Perfectly," he sneered.

Outside in the hallway Maggie leaned against the wall.
She was trembling so badly, she had to wrap her arms
around her chest. She wouldn't cry. She couldn't lose
control now.

As she stood there trying to gather herself together
before going downstairs, the blinding whiteness from
the second-floor landing drew her. She looked out at the
mounds of snow extending into the distance as far as the
eye could see. She'd been happy here for such a short
while. Her heart told her that happiness would never
return. Mam's phone call had changed everything. Or was
it the hours she'd spent reading her diaries, looking into
her soul? What was that elusive thing called happiness?
Did it really exist? Was it waking up with a smile in a
place you loved, ready to take on the world? Was it tit-
illating bits and pieces of time that made the adrenaline
flow? Did it come from within or from outside? Was it
insulating yourself from everything and anything so you
didn't feel? She shook her head. If you didn't feel, you'd
be safe from pain, but then you wouldn't know happiness,
either. It was a package deal.

Tears rolled down Maggie's cheeks as she made her
way downstairs. She made no move to wipe them away.
Let the world see, for all she cared. The phoenix had
risen from the ashes; so would she. She'd fight.

Cole Tanner stood in the center of his room. He felt
disoriented. He should do something. Pound the walls,
stamp his feet, bellow out his rage. He jammed his shaking
hands into his jeans pockets.

Sawyer was going to die.

Not Maggie, not his father, not his aunts or Riley, but

Sawyer. How could that be? She was so healthy, always taking vitamins and exercising. She'd worked like a dog with him this summer in the barn. If you were sick, you couldn't work like that. She'd been fine in New York. She'd eaten as much as the rest of them, had trekked along for hours and never seemed to be the worse for it. She'd laughed and had a good time. He knew you could do all those things with a broken heart, but when you were sick you slowed down. You didn't laugh when you were sick. Not Sawyer. Anybody but Sawyer.

He was going to be alone again.

Anger rushed through him. It wasn't fair! Not to Sawyer and not to him. He didn't care about the others: his mother, his grandmother, or his father. What did they know about loneliness, not belonging?

He didn't care what his mother said. He picked up the phone and called Adam Jarvis. Adam's voice came on the line, the same voice he remembered, only stronger somehow. "Can I speak to Sawyer?"

"She went for a walk with your grandmother. I'm not sure when they'll be back. Cole, she's all right for now. She's trying to come to grips. She knows what the doctors told her, but she can't quite believe it. Do you know what I mean?"

"I suppose so. I wanted her to know that she could count on me if she needs me. I could drop out of this next semester and come to New York. My father would agree to that. My mother would have a fit, but I don't much care."

"Sawyer knows she can count on you, Cole. Right now, though, I think she has to learn to count on herself. I'll tell her you called and give her the message. Don't be hurt or surprised if she doesn't call you back for a while. And Cole?"

"Yes?"

"I'll take care of her. Trust me."

"Shit, I know that. Tell her . . . tell her that . . . Oh, shit."

"Kid, the word love isn't so hard to say. You have to

practice it and use it. I'll tell her for you."

"No, don't do that. I'll do it myself when she calls me. Just tell her I called."

"Cole, how did Riley take the news?"

"It was a blow. He loves her, too. He said he was going to his room to write to his grandfather. I think Sawyer and his grandfather were very close. Sawyer was good friends with his mother, too."

"Maggie?"

Cole's voice was cold, so brittle Adam thought he could hear the wire crackle in his ear. "Business as usual. Dinner's at seven. Nothing upsets the routine here. If you want to know if she's upset, I can't tell you."

Adam hesitated. "Rand?"

"That's one cool dude. It's in his eyes. I'd say—and this is only my opinion—he feels bad. He should for hurting Sawyer."

"Don't place blame, Cole. People do what they have to do even if we don't understand their reasons. Don't hate him; Sawyer doesn't. Take care of yourself. I'll tell Sawyer you called."

"Call me, Adam, even if Sawyer doesn't. Promise."

"I promise, kid. Hang tough."

Riley opened the door at the sound of a knock. He was stunned to see Cole standing in the doorway. "C'mon in." He made no move to wipe away the tears streaming down his cheeks. Both boys stared at each other. "I don't care if you see me crying. I don't care if you tell anyone, either," Riley said belligerently. "Here." He handed his cousin a wadded-up ball of toilet paper.

"Who'm I gonna tell? She's my sister. She's the only one who ever cared about me." Cole gulped. "What gets me is she didn't look sick to me. We had such a good time in New York. Now she's gonna die. I don't understand."

"I don't understand, either. I was talking to my mother fifteen minutes before she was killed. I feel like you do. I don't have anyone, either, but my grandfather, and he's very old. Here in the United States I have no one but the

Coleman family. I've been thinking about going back to Japan. That should make you happy."

"Finally realized you don't belong," Cole said coolly. "About time."

"That's not why. I'd never let you drive me out."

"I'd never stay someplace I wasn't wanted."

"When it's you doing the wanting, it doesn't bother me. *If* I do decide to go home," Riley said defiantly, "it won't be because of you."

"I didn't come in here to discuss that. I came to talk about Sawyer. We get out of school the end of May. I thought maybe she'd like to go on a trip or take a vacation. We could go for the whole summer. I don't know anything about brain tumors, how she'll feel or anything. Do you?"

"No. We could call up a doctor and ask. Your mother would probably know."

"I'm not asking my mother anything. Adam will know. He'll want to go, too. It'll be like Christmas. We could make all the plans and sort of spring it on her and Adam."

"Who's this supposed to help? Them or us?"

"Us, you jerk. Nothing can help Sawyer. We're just gonna be her support system. But we're gonna need a lot of money. How much do you have?"

"In the bank or on me?"

"You are a jerk. In the bank. We'll need money for tickets and money to rent some place. I've never been to Hawaii. Have you?"

"Only on a layover on the way here from Japan. I think I have thirty-three hundred in the bank, maybe less. The statement didn't come yet and I took out a lot for Christmas. I can get some money from my grandfather if you tell me how much we need. How much do you have?"

"You must be kidding. I have fifty-six dollars and no place to get any more. It's up to you if we pull this off."

"I knew there was a reason you came in here. I'm writing to my grandfather now. How much should I ask for?"

Cole sat down at Riley's desk and pulled out the calculator. "I've seen commercials on TV for flights to

Hawaii. They quoted a $599 ticket, so that's $2,396 for the four of us. Maybe we can rent a condo. That's the off season for tourism in Hawaii, so let's say $1,500 a week. If we stay a month, it will be $6,000. We have to eat and see the sights, take in the other islands. Probably $5,000 on top of that. Figure a total of $25,396. My mother will give me some money, and I can squeeze some from the old man. Not a lot, though, so don't count on it." Cole looked up anxiously. "Do you think your grandfather will send it?"

"When I tell the old one what it's for, he won't ask questions. What if we run short?"

"Then ask for a little more. If we don't use it all, you can send it back. Look, I'm sorry I can't contribute, but I can't draw on my trust fund till I'm twenty-one. You know how hard it is for me to get money out of my mother. If you don't want to go along with this, say so now."

"I think it's a good idea. Sawyer will approve of what she calls our ingenuity. Adam'll probably be glad we took care of the details. The money isn't the problem. It's me and you that's the problem."

"We'll call a truce. I don't get in your way and you don't get in mine. We managed at Christmas and we can do it again."

"Okay. Truce." Riley sighed. "Someday I hope you tell me what it is you have against me. I came here prepared to like you."

Cole snorted. "Fat chance."

"Right. And now that I've made you feel better, you can toddle off to your room and act like a man instead of a sixteen-year-old who thinks it's shameful to cry. When I hear from my grandfather, I'll let you know."

"You aren't throwing me out. I'm leaving on my own." Cole turned at the door. "By the way, I . . . I called Adam. He said Sawyer went for a walk with Grand. He'll call us and keep in touch. I thought you might want to know."

"Thanks for telling me."

"Drop dead," Cole muttered as he closed the door.

Riley sat with his chin cupped in his hand, staring at

the door for a long time. It was really the first time Cole had come into his room and stayed to talk. Maybe they were making progress of a sort. He wished there was something he could do for Cole. How lonely he must be.

It was late; the bedroom lamps cast dim shadows into the corners of Maggie's bedroom. The house was asleep except for the two of them.

Maggie lay in the crook of Rand's arm, wide awake. He, too, was awake, staring at the ceiling. He liked the pressure of Maggie's dark head on his shoulder, liked the feel of her body pressing against his. If this was wrong, why did it feel so right, so good? It was crazy, but he felt like he'd finally come home after a long, long journey. They nurtured each other, loved each other, and he didn't want to lose what they'd found together. But it wasn't going to be up to him. He knew Maggie was sending him away. This was their last night together; he'd return to England tomorrow.

He'd tried to explain to Maggie that what happened to Sawyer wasn't their fault. The tumor had been there, growing, long before last July. Their loving each other hadn't caused it.

"But our loving each other is causing this pain!" she'd cried.

She'd listened to his arguments but hadn't heard a word he'd said. When he'd finished baring his soul, she'd looked at him with tears in her eyes and told him she'd miss him terribly. That she felt as though she were giving up a part of herself.

Now she lay in his embrace, her fingers tracing patterns down the length of Rand's arm. "I know you don't understand. I don't understand, either. It feels right to me, so I have to do it. I'm an expert at giving up things; it comes easy to me. I learned at an early age that it was expected of me. They all expect me to give you up now. I don't have any choice. Maybe someday..." Her voice trailed off.

"Someday isn't good enough. What's been done is done.

I'm not sorry. Maggie, we can't let the past rule our lives. We have to deal with the future and with today the best we can. My going back to England isn't going to change things. I know Sawyer. She'll never come back here."

"I have to try. Somehow I—"

"It's too late, Maggie."

"We have to go on from here. It's something I have to do alone. If you're here, I won't be able to do what I have to do."

"What exactly are you going to do? What miracle are you going to perform to make things right? Tell me, Maggie, so I can understand."

"I don't know, Rand. When I returned to Sunbridge, I thought my fighting days were over. I know now those little skirmishes were only preliminaries for the biggest fight of my life. And I have to win this one, not just for me but for Sawyer as well."

Rand turned so he was facing Maggie, his face just inches from hers. "There are some things that can't be fixed, Maggie, things that are better left alone. You're going into a very volatile situation. You'll need me here for support."

"It's true; I do need you, my darling, and that's the reason I'm sending you away. I can't allow myself the luxury of depending on you when the going gets tough. I have to start off like Sawyer—alone. Please, Rand, don't make this any harder on me than it already is. Pap told me once that you have to take responsibility for your own actions. That's what I'm trying to do. We'll talk to each other from time to time. I'll write; hopefully, you'll write back. I want us to be friends."

"Maggie, I want to marry you."

Maggie turned away. How she'd longed to hear those words! For the first time in her life she was loved with an intensity she could return . . . and she had to give it up. What irony.

"I'll drive you to the airport in the morning."

"That's your answer—I'll drive you to the airport?" Rand asked incredulously.

"It's the only answer for now."

There were no arguments left. Rand gathered Maggie into his arms again and held her close. Memory after memory flashed before him. He tried to lock them in his mind for all the long, lonely months ahead. He knew Maggie was doing the same thing.

They slept in each other's arms, a light sleep full of dreams and promises.

Rand sat in the airport bar, an empty beer glass in his hand. He hadn't wanted the beer—any kind of drink, for that matter—but he couldn't sit and take up space without ordering.

He didn't like Kennedy Airport. It was too big. There were too many travelers, none of them smiling. And he'd never known it to fail yet: every damn time he hit Kennedy, his flight was delayed. This time, he had an hour to kill. An hour to think. If only he could forget.

A familiar scent teased Rand's nostrils. Sawyer's perfume. He looked around anxiously. He could almost feel her presence, yet he couldn't see her. He sniffed again. He wasn't imagining things—there she was! He'd been so deep in thought, he'd almost missed her. Billie was with her; they were walking from the lounge, their arms linked together. He left crumpled bills on the table and rushed out.

"Sawyer! Billie!"

Sawyer turned, her face alive and bright for a split second before it closed to blankness. Billie wore a startled expression. Neither spoke; neither greeted him.

"Hello," he said warmly. "What are you doing here?"

"I'm going back to Vermont," Billie replied. "Sawyer decided to wait with me. What are you doing here?"

"Going back to England. I'm sorry you couldn't make Christmas. We all missed you."

"We were snowed in." Billie lowered her eyes, made a show of rummaging through her purse, looking for something she knew wasn't there. Why didn't he go away and leave them alone? Surely he knew. Maggie would have told him.

"What time is your flight? Can I buy you both a drink? I have an hour to kill." He cringed at the casual use of the word kill. He wanted to bite his tongue.

"No, thanks. Grand has only a few minutes till boarding. Have a nice flight, Rand."

"It was nice seeing you, Rand," Billie said quietly.

Rand watched their backs as they walked away from him. Well, what in the hell had he expected?

He waited until Sawyer returned from the security gate. When she saw him, she tried to avoid him, but he blocked her path.

"I want to talk to you."

"I don't know why. You said everything there was to say at Christmastime. What makes today any different? I have to get home, Rand."

"That's a lie and we both know it. Come into the lounge and sit with me for a few minutes."

"Why?"

"Because I want to talk to you."

"I'm sorry, I have to go. I don't want a scene, but if you persist, I'll make one."

"Sawyer, don't hate me. Please."

"Hate? That word is probably right up there with love. Hand in hand, you know, like salt and pepper. When you're going to die—and don't pretend you don't know— that word takes on new meaning. There's only one person in this world I hate. And it isn't you."

"That's what I want to talk to you about. You have it all wrong. Why won't you listen?"

"Because I don't care. That means I'm not interested. Why won't *you* listen to me?"

She turned her back and started to walk away. This time he didn't stop her.

As Rand was flying toward the shores of England, Sawyer lay on her bed, collapsed in tears. She was glad to be alone, glad Adam wasn't there to comfort her. She cried not for herself but for what she'd done to Rand. She'd left without giving him a shred of understanding, taking victory in the fact that he'd left Sunbridge and wasn't with Maggie. She'd deliberately hurt him, wanted to stun him and force him to carry her bitterness away with him. She wanted to punish him because he didn't love her. Was what she had done to him loving?

Hours later she awoke with a nagging headache and tried to sit up. The loft was too quiet. Adam was probably out running, she decided. He'd stayed pretty close these past days trying to bolster her. Steady-as-a-rock Adam. Who could blame him if he had cabin fever? She'd been just as steady, accepting the doctor's prognosis like a real trooper. She knew she was still in shock—half believing, half disbelieving. Other people got brain tumors. Other people died. But God, she was only twenty-six. A year wasn't enough time!

If it was all you had, it had to be long enough.

She fluffed up the pillows behind her head, picked up the notepad and pencil on her night table. Resign her job at the office. Money? Her bank account was healthy enough, no worry on that score. Her insurance was paid up. She had to change the beneficiary now; Cole, of course. Billie would understand. She'd make a will. Her stock to Cole and Riley. Little by little she'd dispose of her things so that when the time came and Adam had to clean out her part of the loft, he'd only have to deal with her clothes. Neat and tidy. Now it was down to basics.

What did she want? To be loved. To be wanted and needed. She wanted to share and laugh and possibly cry, but for the right reasons.

The biggest challenge of her life. Late into the night, when Adam thought she was asleep, she'd lain thinking about her grandfather Moss. He hadn't whimpered and whined when he was told he had leukemia. He'd had a time limit, too, and had used that time to work toward his dream. She herself had carried out that dream with her grandmother's help. How could she do less? She was, after all, a Coleman.

Since there was nothing she could do about her own condition, she had to start thinking about Cole. He would be her number-one priority. Maggie had forbidden contact with her son, but at this point in time, what Maggie wanted or didn't want was of no interest to her. Like Moss, she would have to leave something behind, something Cole could sink his teeth into. Her dream. The only problem was, she didn't have a dream of her own. She made a note to make an appointment with Cranston. They would be allies. She, for the betterment of Cole; he, for his own reasons.

Now the pen flew over the yellow paper. She had to write Cole—Riley, too. She would put both letters in one envelope addressed to Riley; he'd see that his cousin got her letter.

All things considered, she felt she had a handle on everything. She'd make it if the others gave her space. Adam was trying. So was Grand. Poor Grand. First Riley and then Moss. There'd been such love and worry in her eyes at the airport, but she'd carried it off.

The day Sawyer mailed her letters to Riley, one arrived from Cole. She read it several times and then showed it to Adam, who laughed in delight. "By God, those kids are something. I say we should go for it."

"Me, too. Did you notice, Adam, that although Cole makes a point of saying it was all his idea, he gives financial credit to Riley? I told you the way the two of them sobered me up over Christmas. That was a joint effort, too. I'm pleased."

"And well you should be. I'll send the money back to Riley's grandfather," Adam said generously. "The kids will never have to know."

"No, no, no, you can't do that! Mr. Hasegawa would lose face. You can't ever return a gift to a Japanese. Besides, he'd give the world to Riley if he could. Money means nothing to them. If his generosity could make Riley and me happy, he'd clean out his bank accounts. He gave blank checks to my mother for my grandfather's plane. Blank checks! No, we're going to accept, but I think three months is too long. Let's go for six weeks and play the rest by ear. Agreed?"

"Sounds good to me. That means I have to get my work in ahead of schedule. I'm not going to have too much time to spend with you. What will you do?"

"Do? Do, you ask? Shop. As in shop. I'm going to run my credit cards to the limit. From here on in it's plastic all the way. Do you need anything? As long as I'm shopping, I can pick up whatever you want. Listen, Adam, we agreed, business as usual. Don't start pampering me now. Get your work done. Get it in so we can leave with free minds. Promise?"

"You got it. You want to rustle up something to eat while I shower? You didn't do the towels, did you?"

"Nope, but I will. It won't kill you to use the one you used yesterday."

"And the day before that and the day before that," Adam muttered on the way to the bathroom.

He stood under the shower spray, letting the water beat on his head. In the oblivion offered by the steam collecting on the shower door, he sank back against the tiles. Dry, heaving sobs racked him, the sound stifled by the pounding spray. Where would he find the strength to continue this charade? To go along with Sawyer as if everything were normal, as though they hadn't told him he was losing her forever? He was already grieving, already denying what he knew to be true. Even though she would never say the words he so desperately wanted to hear, he loved her. He couldn't think of a life without Sawyer. In the isolation of the shower he cried his grief, and for long after he remained there, struggling to regain his composure in order to face her again. He mustn't let his emotions show; he mustn't let her see his anguish. If he did, she would send him away, and he intended to share every waking moment with her for as long as they had.

* * *

Over breakfast Sawyer asked Adam's advice. "Grand told me about this place high in the hills in Hawaii that Seth arranged for her and Moss when he was on leave. A lady, Ester Kamali, owns it but doesn't live there. I wonder if she could somehow get in touch with the lady and ask if we could stay there. There's a caretaker and housekeeper, or at least there was. Grand said it was the nicest place in the world and one of the happiest times of her life. Once she told me in secret that she thought that was where she fell in love with Thad, only she didn't know it at the time. That's where I want to go. I'll call this morning and write to the boys so they can cancel any condos the travel agency wants to rent them. Grand has pictures. I'll tell her to send them so you can see what I'm talking about."

"I don't like to bring this up, but I have to." Adam bit into a piece of crunch toast. "Is it possible that Maggie can stop this trip? She does have sole custody of Cole now."

"I suppose anything is possible. Riley already has his grandfather's permission. I'm going to talk to Cranston. I don't think we have anything to worry about. Maggie won't interfere. If she does, we'll have to switch to plan B."

"Which is..."

"Whatever the boys come up with. You and I are only along for the ride."

"Then I won't worry about it.... This toast is good. I kind of thought you were going to cook something. You know, something I could sink my teeth into, like eggs or pancakes. Food."

"I don't have time. I have to do the laundry and go shopping. Maybe I'll stop by Cranston's office instead of waiting for an appointment. He'll see me because he'll think it has something to do with Maggie and Cole. As soon as those towels are in the wash, I'm calling Grand. Get to work, Jarvis. I don't want anything spoiling this trip, even if it is months away."

Sawyer called her grandmother. Billie's heart soared when she heard her granddaughter's request. "I'll get on it right away. I can't promise anything, Sawyer. It was so long ago. I'll call you back this evening."

When Billie hung up, she dug out her address book and scanned the numbers. At Sunbridge there were ledgers, journals, notebooks, all dusty now, full of names. Surely Ester Kamali would be listed there somewhere. She called Amelia.

Amelia said she'd drop everything and return to Sunbridge to get the information, then call back as soon as she had news. When Amelia hung up, she called Maggie, who agreed to go to the basement and search out old telephone bills. Thank God, nothing at Sunbridge was ever thrown away.

When Thad returned to the house at lunchtime, Billie told him what was going on. Thad looked at her in amazement and then laughed. "Billie, why didn't you call the house in Hawaii and ask to speak to whoever is there? It's possible Phillip and Rosa aren't there anymore, but someone should be. There's also the possibility that the place has been sold."

"Don't you remember, the telephone number was unlisted."

"Ah, now that you mention it, I do seem to recall having to carry the number in my hip pocket. That's one for your side. What will you do if you can't get the house?"

"Shhh," Billie said, placing a finger on his lips. "One way or another, we'll get that house for Sawyer. Trust me."

"I do. I do. Personally, I think what those two young boys are trying to do is just as wonderful."

Billie smiled wanly. "Not trying, Thad. They're doing it. By tonight, it will be a fact."

And so Ma Bell worked her magic, from New York City to Vermont to Texas, from the Pentagon to the Miramar Naval Air Station in San Diego, then on to Pearl Harbor and ending up in Hong Kong.

Amelia was on one extension and Maggie on the other

as they called Billie to give her the news. "We got it for you, Mam," Maggie said breathlessly. "I tried the number in Hawaii and it's been disconnected." There was awe in her voice when she said, "I had no idea Seth traveled in such high places. Amelia did some razzle-dazzling that would knock you off your feet."

"Billie, we have the number for you. Everything sounded positive. The house is empty, has been for years. Rosa and Phillip passed away. There's a grandson who looks in on things. Miss Kamali is living in Hong Kong and has never returned to the island." She repeated the number twice to be sure Billie had it right. "You should be able to place your call. It's tomorrow over there. Take a shot at it—and good luck."

"Mam, if there's anything I can do, call me," Maggie said.

"I'll do that, Maggie. Thanks again."

"I got it, I got it!" Billie said, dancing around Thad's chair. "Cross your fingers that Miss Kamali gives her okay. I'm going upstairs to make the call. This is going to be woman talk."

"Go ahead, darling. I'll sit here and smoke my pipe and remember the time we spent in Hawaii."

"Just don't fall asleep till I get back."

"What do you have in mind?" Thad leered.

"The same thing you do. Stay alert!"

Thad watched his wife run up the stairs, seeing the young girl he fell in love with. He thanked God again, as he did every day, for his good fortune. He packed his pipe, struck a match, and waited. He would always wait for Billie. Till the end of time, if necessary, and in eternity he'd be there with his hand in hers.

Billie's heart pounded furiously as she placed her call. She crossed her fingers and waited. Six rings, seven, and then a soft voice came on the line.

Billie introduced herself and waited to see if the woman would remember her.

"But of course I remember you. My housekeeper did

nothing but talk of you for months after you left. What can I do for you, Mrs. Coleman?"

"It's not Mrs. Coleman anymore. It's Mrs. Kingsley. My husband died several years ago." Billie quickly explained her problem. "Whatever the cost, I'll pay it. Please, Miss Kamali, whatever it takes, I'll do it."

"My hesitation has nothing to do with money, Mrs. Kingsley. The house has been closed up for many years. I don't know if it's fit to live in. One of the caretaker's grandsons is supposedly looking after it, but they get lazy, if you know what I mean."

"That's not important, Miss Kamali. I'd be glad to pay for repairs and to get it ready."

"Please, call me Ester. I feel as though I know you. May I call you Billie?"

"But of course." Suddenly Billie blurted out that she had worn the rainbow silk dress that had been packed in the chest.

Ester laughed. "Rosa told me. She said you looked beautiful in it. It made me happy knowing someone got to wear it. My beloved never got to see me in it."

"You've never been back to that beautiful house since you left?" Billie asked in awe.

"Never. My soul is there. I'll go there when it's time for me to die. For now, my heart is here in Hong Kong. I have a pleasant life with a man who loves me very much."

"And do you love him very much?" She had no right to ask, but she wanted to know about this faceless woman who could fill Sawyer's life with sunshine for a little while.

"There are some loves that are for yesterday and others forever. My love belongs to yesterday and so do I. For now, what I have is pleasant. I'm able to live quite happily, but there are too many shadows in my life for me to move on. But to give you an answer, of course you may have the use of my house. Your father-in-law was very kind to some members of my family years ago. I could never forget that. If you can manage to send someone to Hawaii to look things over and have the house opened, you have my blessing. There will be no discussion of monies. It will be my gift to your granddaughter, and I will pray for her and for you. I'll send you a set of keys tomorrow."

Tears streamed down Billie's cheeks. "I don't know what to say. You're the second-kindest person I've ever known. I can accept your generosity only if you allow my family to make any repairs the house may require. It would break my heart to see that lovely place fall into ruin. Please, say it's all right."

"I accept, but you must tell me who the *first*-kindest person in your life is." There was a smile in Ester's voice and Billie played to it.

"The person whose love for me is forever, my husband. Thank you, Ester. I'll stay in touch. Perhaps one day we'll meet."

"I'll look forward to that time. Good-bye, Billie. My prayers are with you and your granddaughter."

Now she had to call Sawyer and tell her everything was set. Then a quick call to Sunbridge.

Sawyer was delighted. "I'll tell the boys I know of a place. I know they'll be thrilled. Thanks, Grand."

"For what?"

"For coming through for me."

"All I did was make a few phone calls for you. Good night, darling. I'll talk to you later in the week."

The call to Sunbridge left Billie stunned. "Let me do it, Mam," Maggie pleaded. "Let me go to Hawaii and get the house ready. Sawyer doesn't need to know I'm the one who's doing it. Let her think the place is ready to move into. I'll make up some story about where I'm going for the boys. I *need* to do this, Mam. Please say yes."

"You're sure you can handle it? Sawyer and the boys are not to know; is that right?"

"I think it would be best, don't you?"

"For now, anyway. Maggie, what about your divorce and Susan and the new baby? When will you go?"

"The end of April, beginning of May. That would give

me plenty of time. There's not much I can do about the divorce. The lawyers are handling that for me. Cole is old enough to speak for himself. I'm hoping this time he's going to spend with Sawyer will open him up to life. What I do from here on in is going to have a direct bearing on his decision. I'm hoping for the best, but I'll be able to handle the worst. I'll be here for Suse when she has the baby and the christening. It'll all work out."

"I'm sure it will. Maggie . . ."

"Don't say it, Mam. Let me do this my way."

"Maggie, please, listen to me. I was going to ask you about Rand."

"I sent him home. I thought you knew."

"Yes, I knew he went back to England, but I didn't know you sent him back. Why? I thought you loved him. I thought he loved you."

"Yes. Yes. He does. I do. We do. Oh, Mam. . . . It was for the best."

"Who? For God's sake, Maggie, for whom is it best?"

"Everyone. Sawyer, Amelia. The boys. Suse, too."

"What about you?"

Maggie snorted. "Since when does it matter what I want?"

"It matters to me. Fight, Maggie. If Rand is what you want, then fight for him. Don't let Sawyer or anyone else take that from you. If it's right in your heart, then it's right for you."

Maggie's voice was suddenly lighter, buoyant. "Mam, do you know what you just said to me?"

"Of course I know. You deserve to be happy, Maggie. So does Rand; so does Sawyer. Each of you has to find the way to make that happen. It isn't too late for you and Rand. What was the last thing your father wrote to you, Maggie?"

Maggie recited the short, last letter Moss had written her. "Be happy. Those were his exact words. Mam, he said to be happy. Oh, my God, I sent Rand away. I was afraid to be happy. I'm still afraid. I love you, Mam,"

Maggie cried before she hung up the phone.

"And I love you, too, Maggie," Billie said softly as she replaced the phone. How important those words were! Everyone should say them at least once a day. Well, she was going to say them right now to the person who deserved them the most.

"Is this what you call staying alert?" Billie laughed at the sight of Thad dozing in the chair with three of Duchess's puppies snuggled against him. She dropped to her knees. "Are you going to tell me happiness is snuggling with a warm puppy?"

"They were just standing in till you got here. Did everything go all right?"

"Everything's fine. Come along, darling. I have plans for you, but first I want to tell you I love you with all my heart."

Thad stared down at his wife, at the invitation and promise in her eyes. "And I love you for now and forever."

"We make a good team, don't we?"

"The best," Thad said as he snuggled the puppies next to Duchess in her bed by the fire. "The very best."

Maggie lay propped up with a stack of lace-edged pillows behind her dark head, paper and pen in hand. Rand would think she was out of her mind. Maybe she was.

Dear Rand,

When you receive this letter, you will probably think me out of my mind. I feel like a yo-yo and so must you.

I made a mistake when I told you to go back to England. You made a mistake by doing what I asked. I thought I was sending you away for all the right reasons, but I was wrong. Mam made me see it. She said if we love each other, we should be together and happy. The rest will take care of itself.

I'll be here till the end of April, but I know you

may need some time to think. And I understand. I just want you to know that I love you, for all the *right* reasons.

Forgive my fear and my weakness. Be happy with me.

All my love,
Maggie

{{{{{{{{{ CHAPTER TWENTY-ONE }}}}}}}}

Jessica Margaret de Moray made her entrance into the world on February 14, Valentine's Day. She was golden-haired and pink-skinned, weighed six pounds, two ounces, and measured eighteen inches long. For Susan it was love at first sight. Maggie and Amelia crowed with delight when the pink bundle was held at the viewing window for their pleasure and first introduction. Cary beamed and cooed through the nursery window.

"A woman shouldn't have to go through this alone," Cary muttered to Amelia and Maggie on the ride back to Sunbridge.

"You're right; she shouldn't. But who the hell knows where that dog Jerome is? And he wouldn't have wanted to be here, anyway. Susan didn't ask for him once, but I knew what she was thinking. She felt deserted." Maggie brightened. "But she's not alone anymore, is she. Now she has little Jessica Margaret."

Cary laughed. "You don't really intend to call her that, do you? That's quite a mouthful for such a little thing."

"No, I guess not." Maggie sighed. "But I can't help reminding anyone who'll listen that Susan named her after

Grandmam Jessica and me. It's an honor, Cary, it really is. Don't you think so, Amelia?"

"Yes, I suppose." Amelia knew she was having a hard time coping with the birth of Susan's baby. It made her feel old, so old.... And Cary was taking this birth with such rejoicing. Did he want a child of his own? At forty-two, he certainly was young enough to become a father for the first time. But who'd give him that child? She certainly couldn't. No, it would have to be someone young, someone like Eileen.

Maggie was still jabbering. "I can't wait to shop for the baby. Lacy dresses, frilly bonnets. They make such beautiful toys these days—creative and progressive. Oh, and she must have an English coach carriage. You know, Amelia, like the ones those English nannies push around Hyde Park on sunny afternoons. The ones with the huge wheels. I'm going to telephone Harrod's first thing and have them send one over," she said happily. She couldn't help wondering, though, why the baby hadn't been placed in a bassinet beside the other infants after the viewing. The masked nurse had whisked little Jessie away as soon as the oohs and aahs were over.

The phone was ringing when Maggie and Amelia entered the house. Maggie caught it just before Martha. "Suse! What are you doing calling? Couldn't wait to hear the compliments over little Jessie? You should be resting."

She listened, her face going absolutely blank.

"What's wrong?" Cary asked, his arm going around Maggie for support.

"I've never heard of spina bifida. Operating on her when she was just born!" Maggie listened intently. "Suse, I'm coming back to the hospital to be with you. Yes, yes, I want to." She replaced the receiver and sat down on the bottom step of the staircase.

"Don't keep us in suspense, Maggie. What's wrong?" Amelia demanded.

"It's the baby. She was born with something wrong with her spine, a hole or something. Suse doesn't quite understand it yet. They're going to operate within the next few hours."

Amelia shook her head. "Will it never stop? Always one crisis after another. And Susan all alone except for us. She should have a husband by her side." Her eyes narrowed. "It's all Jerome's fault! If there's anything wrong with that child, he's to blame. Working Susan the way he did, fitting her into corsets so her pregnancy wouldn't show—"

"Amelia," Maggie implored wearily, "please don't go on this way. I know Jerome was hard on Suse, but I'm certain none of this was his doing, or Susan's, either. It just happened. Little Jessie will be fine; she has to be. Whatever you do, don't repeat any of this to Susan. She has enough to contend with. Do you understand?"

"Yes, of course we do, Maggie," Cary interjected. "You won't say any of this to Susan, will you, Amelia?" He spoke sternly, tightening his grasp on his wife's arm. "We'll all be very careful of what we say."

"All right, Cary!" Amelia pulled her arm away. "You don't have to speak to me as though I were some kind of witch ready to pounce on Susan." She flew up the stairs, brushing past Maggie, her slim-heeled Bally shoes noiseless on the thickly padded carpet runner.

"Now, what the hell has gotten into her?" Cary asked. "She's so damn irritable lately; everything I say seems to come out wrong. I didn't mean to be rough on her, but there's no telling what she'll do these days. I didn't want to take the chance that she'd face Susan with all sorts of accusations that wouldn't help the situation."

"I know, Cary," Maggie said quietly. "But remember that Amelia practically raised Susan, and she's never really liked Jerome. She's worried and so am I. I'm leaving again for the hospital. Do you think you'll be here to eat dinner with the boys? You could tell them about the baby and reassure them that everything will be all right. At least I pray it'll be all right."

Susan lay propped up in bed. The peach-colored bed

jacket seemed out of place against the starched white sheets. The room was bare of flowers and cards. Tomorrow it would be full.

"Here, blow," Maggie said, holding out a white handkerchief.

Susan blew her nose obligingly and dabbed at her eyes. "They're operating on her right now. The doctors assure me it's standard procedure for spina bifida. I didn't even know what it was till they told me. It originates in the first month of pregnancy. The vertebrae of the spinal cord are not formed correctly. That's why they have to operate right away. It's my fault. I knew I should have taken better care of myself. I shouldn't have let Jerome bully me the way he did."

"Suse, it's not your fault and the doctor will tell you so. Children are born all the time with defects. They're operating, so that will make it right, won't it?"

"There could be fluid in the brain. The doctor said they can treat and monitor the children and possibly they can grow into independent adults living full lives. But I know it won't happen. Why should I be one of the lucky ones?"

"You can't think like that," Maggie said sternly. "Your thoughts have to be positive. Your baby is alive and being taken care of. Other mothers aren't that lucky. Count your blessings."

"I am. I'm fortunate that the pediatrician recognized the disease and acted on it. This is one of the few hospitals that can treat it. I was listening, but he was talking so fast, I think I only caught half of it, and I was a little groggy. He said something about incontinence of bowel and bladder, paralysis of leg muscles, and lack of sensation. That's all I know."

"We'll find out all there is to know tomorrow," Maggie promised. "When the doctor comes back, you'll have to talk to him yourself and ask every question you can think of. It's going to be all right, Susan. Be glad you're here with your family. We'll all do what we can."

Susan held on to Maggie's hand until she dozed off.

An hour later the doctor entered the room. He was a tall man, dressed in operating green. He looked, Maggie thought, like a man who didn't smile enough. He was smiling now, though. How awesome, she thought, to hold the power of life and death in your hands. She looked at his long, slender fingers. What must he have thought when he sliced into that tiny back? She had to know, had to ask. "Please, Doctor, tell me, what did you think about when you started to operate?"

"I wasn't thinking. I was praying. I always pray when my scalpel makes the first incision. The baby came through just fine. She's sleeping now and will get some glucose in a little while. It's too early for me to say anything else at this time. So, for now I'd say the baby is resting." He smiled again, a smile that would warm any mother's heart.

Four hours later Susan woke, a look of alarm on her face. Maggie reached up to smooth the hair back from her brow. "Jessie came through the operation just fine. She's sleeping and probably getting glucose right now."

"He came in, the doctor, I mean?"

"Hours ago. I didn't want to wake you. He said he'll be in to see you tomorrow. I checked with the night nurse a while ago, and she said when you woke they'd wheel you down to see her. Suse, he said he prayed when he made the first incision. I thought you might want to know that."

"Thanks, Maggie. I couldn't have gotten through this without you."

"After you see the baby, try to get some sleep. It's what you need now." Maggie kissed Susan lightly and tasted the salt of her tears. "You can handle it," she whispered.

"Yes, I will. It's late. Go home. Call Mam."

"I already did, but I'll give her another call. See you tomorrow."

Cary felt as though he were tiptoeing around the bedroom when he was really making more noise than usual.

He knew Amelia was antsy, waiting for him to ask what was bothering her. Had she understood about his trip to New York? Damn, it couldn't have come at a worse time. Just last week she'd told him that in the next few days the carpet and draperies were going to be installed in the house and she'd have to be there. She was bound to think he'd planned this trip deliberately so she wouldn't be able to go with him.

Amelia had been acting strange these past few weeks. She'd taken the news of Sawyer's illness very badly. And tonight she'd curled into a ball on her side of the king-size bed. He'd had to be extra gentle with her, cajoling her into telling him what was wrong. She'd gulped and cried that suddenly, for the first time, she was aware of her own mortality. Think of little Jessie; think of Sawyer. It could happen to anyone—it could easily happen to her. Look how much older she was. He'd tried everything he knew to shake her out of it, but she'd been inconsolable. Now he had no choice but to go to sleep. He *had* to get up in the morning. It wouldn't make a difference if Amelia was late getting to her house.

When Cary woke the following morning, more tired than when he'd gone to bed, he saw Amelia lying on her back, staring at the ceiling. He knew she hadn't slept at all. He felt annoyed with her and then with himself that she could upset him like this. God knows he'd done his best. He'd shared every aspect of his life with her, and there weren't many men who did that.

Cary lay quietly for a few moments listening to Amelia's light breathing. God, he loved her. Of all the women he'd slept with in his life, she was the one he wanted to wake up next to. She always smiled and reached out to him. He knew he'd be grouchy and irritable all day if he didn't make the first move. He reached out, a sleepy smile on his face. "C'mere."

Amelia obligingly snuggled closer to him. She sighed deeply. This was where she belonged. "I'm sorry I was so . . ."

"Bitchy?"

Cary could feel the smile against his shoulder. "Yes, bitchy. I don't expect you to understand about this family. All I can do is tell you the way it is. Susan's baby . . ."

"Amelia, listen to me. I do understand. It gnaws at my gut about Sawyer. She hasn't even begun to taste what life has to offer. But neither of us can change things. If it was something simple like an organ transplant, I'd donate one of mine if it would make you happy. Susan's baby is alive. It could be worse, much worse. None of it is your fault. You can't shoulder it all."

"I'm not trying to. I'm trying to come to terms with it. Oh, Cary, I'm so afraid to die."

"Don't you think everyone feels like that? I do. Just the thought of leaving this earth and not having you with me makes me sick to my stomach. Now, I know men aren't supposed to say such things, but that's how I feel. You're my life, Amelia. I wouldn't be here now doing what I'm doing if it wasn't for you."

Amelia rolled over petulantly. "I don't want you to be grateful to me."

"Goddammit, Amelia. I am grateful. That's only a small part of it. Why are you fighting me? We never had a problem till we came back here. Maybe it was a mistake. Maybe I wasn't cut out to take on this project. I did it for you. For us."

Amelia stubbornly closed her ears to Cary's explanations. She'd heard it all before. Why wasn't he talking about Eileen? Eileen was what was bothering her. Couldn't he see it? If he understood her as well as he said he did, he should know what was bothering her.

"When are you leaving for New York?"

"Tomorrow morning." Cary sighed. He couldn't dally any longer or he'd be late for the office.

Amelia made no effort to get out of bed. So what if she was late? The contractor had a key to the house; he could let the workmen in. Cary was upset with her. She was upset with Cary. Where did they go from here?

She swung her legs over the bed, slipped into a lime-green robe and matching mules, then fluffed at her hair. "How busy are you going to be in New York?" she called through the open bathroom door.

"Pretty busy. My evenings should be free, though. At least part of them. Want to change your mind and hit Fifth Avenue?"

"No. I was thinking maybe I'd make the trip with you and go on to Vermont and see Billie. I guess I can delay things at the house. I could join you the last day and we could see a play or something. I don't want to interfere with your business." Warily she watched him to see his reaction. He appeared to be delighted.

"That's a great idea. Call Billie and tell her before I leave so I know you'll be happy today. You'll have to make a reservation, though. I can have Eileen do it for you."

"I'll do it. Yes, I think it's a great idea myself. I need a break. We could take Sawyer and Adam out to dinner if she's up to it. I'll pack your evening clothes."

"Good girl. Hey, maybe we could stay an extra day and make it a sort of fourth honeymoon."

Amelia giggled. Maybe they could get back on track.

On the way down the hall, both Amelia and Cary stopped at the nursery. Susan was cradling the baby, a dreamy look on her face. "She falls asleep and doesn't want to burp. I have to take her into the doctor's today. She's gorgeous. Don't you think so?"

Amelia blinked. All newborn babies looked like creatures from the unknown to her. Baby Jessica *was* different, though. She looked pink and perfect, her tiny lips puckered as though expecting more. The soft, downy fuzz on her head was standing on end. Cary laughed as he tried to smooth it down. "Porcupine hair."

"Have you had breakfast yet?" Amelia asked.

"Good heavens, no. Jessie comes first. I had to change her from the skin out. When she's ready to eat, she's ready. She's a slow eater and she takes forever to burp.

You go on. I'll be down in a little while."

Cary, who was by now quite late, gulped a quick cup of coffee and left. Amelia picked at some scrambled eggs and watched as Maggie devoured a stack of pancakes. "How can you eat like that and not gain an ounce?" she grumbled.

"I rarely eat lunch. Breakfast is the most important meal of the day. I gain; don't kid yourself. How's the house coming?"

"It's almost finished. Cary is going to New York tomorrow on business. I'm going to make the trip with him and go on up to Vermont to see your mother for a few days. I'll spend a few days with him on the return trip and do some shopping. I thought we'd take Sawyer out to dinner if she's up to it."

"That's a great idea. Mam is going to love having you. I think you're her best friend."

Amelia waited for some mention of Sawyer. When Maggie returned to her pancakes, Amelia set her coffee cup down. "Look, I know I'm out of line, but I have to know how you can be so . . . so completely—I don't even know what word to use—in regard to Sawyer."

Maggie pushed her plate away, the pancakes half-eaten. "Callous is probably the word you're looking for. You are out of line, but it's okay. We're family. I suppose I do appear that way to you. From long habit I've had to cover up my feelings. But I do have them—feelings, I mean. Right now I'm trying to figure out what I can do, if anything.

"There's something else I suppose I should tell you. I wrote to Rand and told him I made a mistake in sending him home. I love him, Amelia, and he loves me. Mam made me see that I have to reach out for whatever happiness I can get. And by God, I'm going to. Now, if you want to condemn me for that, it's okay. I understand."

Amelia mashed the egg on her plate. When she finally looked up at Maggie, her eyes were full of tears. "Your mother was right. You should be happy. I'm sorry if I indicated anything else. If I had my way, everyone in the world would be in love and happy as Billie and Thad. And Cary and me," she added as an afterthought.

"Sawyer?" Maggie hadn't meant her voice to be so hoarse, so whispery.

"I think I know Rand better than anyone on this earth. I know he wouldn't play you against Sawyer. His mind was made up long ago—last spring, in fact. I suppose we all thought . . . we all wanted the two of them to get married. But that wasn't what Rand wanted. Who are we to sit and judge? Every person walking this earth deserves to be happy."

"But you still don't approve of me, do you?"

Amelia buttered a piece of toast she had no intention of eating. "You remind me so much of myself in my younger days. Those days are behind me and they should be behind you, too. What I didn't approve of was your indifference to your mother. And your indifference to Sawyer now. My own mother died before I could make it up to her, all those awful, rebellious years. You at least had a chance to mend fences with Billie. What you do or don't do for Sawyer is something you're going to have to live with. No one can help you but yourself."

Maggie smiled. "That's honest, all right. I'm glad we had this little talk. I was beginning to wonder if you were avoiding me."

"In a way I was. I don't like to think about those long-ago days. I hate confrontations because I had so many of them in my life. There comes a time when you have to look everything square in the face and deal with it. Soul-searching is not for the weak."

"Tell me about it." Maggie smiled. "What do you think of little Jessie? Isn't she gorgeous? I love rocking her and giving her a water bottle."

"Another one. Between you and Susan, you're going to have one spoiled child on your hands."

"Susan is taking it all very well. The doctors have mapped out a routine for her, and she's to take Jessie in for treatment. I managed to get together some material for her to read. She's tough, Amelia. I didn't know that about Susan. And she means it when she says no one but her is going to take care of this baby. She wrote to Jerome, you know, right after the baby was born. She sent the letter in care of their old business manager. She said he had a right to know, and of course he does, but I'm a little concerned about what he might try to do."

"If you think Jerome is going to be interested in a baby with a birth defect, forget it. The divorce will go through and we'll never see Jerome again." It was brave talk and Amelia knew it for the lie it was. Sooner or later Jerome would show up and cause trouble. She could feel it in her bones.

Maggie sat at the table for a long time after Amelia had left. She herself had a busy schedule, but she couldn't seem to get herself together this morning, couldn't seem to stop thinking. Amelia and Cary, Cranston and Cole, Sawyer . . . Rand.

Why hadn't Rand called or written? Certainly enough time had gone by. On an impulse she pulled the phone to the table from the sideboard and placed a call to England. The phone rang fifteen times before she replaced the receiver.

Cary was so cheerful, Amelia could feel her teeth grind together. She wasn't looking forward to the plane ride or the layover at Kennedy Airport before she could get a flight to Vermont.

"Amelia, if you don't hurry, we're going to miss the plane. What's the problem?"

"My hair," Amelia said shortly. "I should have gotten it cut, but I didn't have the time."

"You look beautiful. Let's go. Eileen just pulled up in front of the house."

"Eileen?" Amelia's hairbrush paused in midair.

"Yes, Eileen. She's going to leave her car at the airport. Come on, we really have to hurry. I have your coat, and the bags are downstairs."

"Why is Eileen taking us to the airport?"

"Because she's going with us. Sherman thought it would be simpler if she came along and I didn't have to scrounge around for a temporary girl to take notes and then wait for the papers to be sent back here. Eileen's on top of things. I thought I told you."

Amelia seethed as she followed her husband down the stairs. She was going on to Vermont, and Cary was staying in New York. With Eileen! Her head started to pound, and she could feel the perspiration breaking out on her forehead.

The ride was filled with Eileen's gay chatter. She'd never been to New York, and there was so much she wanted to see, so many things she wanted to buy.

"I thought you were going along to work," Amelia said coolly.

"I am, but I get a lunch hour, and some of the stores are open in the evening. Cary promised me Saturday off."

Cary could feel the chill emanating from his wife. Jesus, surely she didn't. . . . That was exactly what she thought! Was that how much she trusted him? First he felt annoyed, and then angry. He'd asked her to come with him in the beginning, but the house was more important. Then it was going on to see Billie. Women! Well, let her stew for a while; it would do her good. Maybe then she'd realize how ridiculous she was being.

"Why don't you drop me off at the door," Amelia said. "I have to pick up my ticket. If you give me yours, Cary, I can check both of you in."

"Eileen, do you have the tickets?"

"In my bag. That's nice of you, Mrs. Assante. I might not be lucky in finding a parking spot and end up taking the shuttle. We're cutting it close. I was on time," she added apologetically.

"No one's blaming you. Amelia is at fault here," Cary said in a gruff voice.

"You didn't tell me we were being picked up. In fact, you didn't tell me a lot of things. I thought we were taking the limo to the airport. When Martin drives us, we don't have to worry about a parking space. You stay with Miss

Farrell. In case you don't make this flight, you can be together for the next one. If that happens, I'll leave your tickets with the reservation clerk. This is fine. Let me out here."

Cary hopped out of the car and ran around to open the door for Amelia. The look she gave him froze him in his tracks. Out of the corner of his eye he could see Eileen rummaging in her purse for something. She was smiling.

Amelia waited patiently in line till it was her turn. She handed over Cary and Eileen's tickets and waited for her own. "There seems to be a mistake here," the young girl said hesitantly. "Miss Farrell and Mr. Assante are sitting together. Preseating," she said by way of explanation. "You requested a seat in smoking. Do you want me to change the seats?"

"Absolutely not. Is the flight on time?"

"The plane's at the gate. In fact, they're boarding now. You don't have much time."

Amelia felt like kicking something. She looked around for some sign of her husband. "I don't think they're going to make it," she said tightly.

"You'll miss it if you don't hurry. The next flight is booked solid. I recommend you board and leave the other two tickets with the desk."

Amelia was the last passenger to board the plane. Behind her dark glasses, she cried all the way to New York. She was still crying when she boarded her flight to Vermont.

Cary and Eileen gathered up all their papers, stuffing them haphazardly into briefcases. Cary was in a hurry to get back to the hotel so he could make arrangements for an intimate in-room dinner with Amelia. They'd spend the evening together and tomorrow take in the Big Apple. He was as excited as a college kid on his second date.

Christ, he'd missed Amelia! He'd felt like a louse when they'd missed the plane. His phone calls to her over the next few days had been made on the run or when he was too exhausted to think straight. He didn't know why he'd bothered except that he couldn't let her think the worst. But she did; he could tell by her voice.

"I think I have everything, Cary," Eileen said hoarsely.

"We're going to get you back to the hotel and call a doctor. I can tell just by looking at you that you're running a fever. You should have stayed in bed today. All you're doing is sneezing and coughing. I wouldn't be surprised if you had pneumonia."

"Bronchitis maybe, but not pneumonia. I'll take some aspirin and I'll be fine. I hate it when you fuss over me," she said. Fuss, fuss, hold me! she wanted to shout. Tell me you'll take care of me.

"Someone has to take care of you. What the hell kind of employer would I be if I didn't? We're in a strange city. Make sure you take a good hot bath before you settle in. Amelia says that's a cure-all for colds."

"Amelia should know. Amelia is really knowledgeable, isn't she?"

"She certainly is. She knows something about everything. She can hold her own in any situation."

In the warm taxi Eileen managed to sit closer to Cary than necessary, pleading the chills. "Do you know what I want more than anything right now?"

"What? Don't tell me you want a company credit card." Cary laughed.

"That, too. No, I want a good hot toddy. I haven't had one in years. You know, the kind your mother makes for you when you're really sick. Not that I'm really sick."

"You're wrong. I can feel the heat from your body. You do have a fever and I'm calling the doctor. I have to make sure you're all right before I can enjoy my evening with Amelia. When I tell her how sick you are, she'll say I did the right thing."

"I wouldn't bet on it," Eileen muttered under her breath.

Eileen got out of the taxi on wobbly legs. She realized for the first time that she really was sick. Maybe a doctor wouldn't be such a bad idea. At least he'd give her an antibiotic, and she'd have the weekend to recuperate before the return flight on Monday. She wished there was someone who cared enough for her to sit and hold her hand. It was a hell of a way to spend time in New York.

Cary grabbed both briefcases and helped Eileen through the lobby to the elevator. "I'm taking you right to your suite. I'm not leaving till the doctor is on his way and you're in bed."

"Thanks, Cary. Your wife is one lucky lady."

"I keep telling her that, but she doesn't listen." Covertly his eyes dropped to his watch. Amelia's plane would get in in another thirty minutes. He would have to hurry to make all the arrangements in time. "Get in bed and I'll start making calls."

The desk clerk assured him a doctor would check on Miss Farrell in half an hour. He called room service for a hot toddy for Eileen and dinner for himself and Amelia for nine o'clock. Then he made two calls to Texas and one to the airport to check that Amelia's plane was on time. It was. At this time of day it would take a taxi about forty-five minutes to make it into the city; he might as well hang around and wait for the doctor. His last call was to the hotel florist. Roses and daisies would be delivered in abundance to room 1012. Amelia's favorite flowers.

When room service arrived, Cary tipped the waiter and carried the tray into Eileen's room. As she was taking her first sip, there was another knock on the door.

Cary ushered the doctor into Eileen's room and quietly withdrew to the sitting room. He was sipping at a Scotch and water when the phone rang. He picked it up on the third ring. "Hello." There was no response, and after a moment he hung up.

The doctor emerged ten minutes later. He was a round, pudgy man with a no-nonsense demeanor. "The young lady has a good case of bronchitis. I gave her a shot and left some antibiotics. She'll be asleep in a few minutes. I'd like you to get her a small vaporizer from the pharmacy; it will help her to breathe easier. She's to take the capsules four times a day. She'll be fine in a few days. I'll leave my bill at the desk. If you like, I can stop at the pharmacy and have them send up the vaporizer."

"I'd appreciate that," Cary said.

Cary waited around for another thirty minutes until the vaporizer arrived. He hooked it up on the dresser, checked Eileen again to be sure she was all right. He turned the lights off, leaving only the bathroom light on in case she woke and was disoriented. He made sure the water pitcher was full and placed a glass on the night table next to the packet of pills.

Now it was time for his wife. He could hardly wait.

Amelia ended her all-too-short visit to Billie after the second day and arrived at Kennedy International Airport late in the afternoon. She entered a cocktail lounge, trying to make up her mind whether to join Cary at the Hyatt Hotel or take the five-o'clock flight back to Texas. She knew she was being stubborn, even stupid. She trusted Cary; she really did. It was Eileen she didn't trust. Eileen would have to go before she would ever feel safe again.

"And what happens to all the Eileens after that?" Billie had asked her. "You can't insulate him from women, Amelia. If—and this is a big if, because I don't think Cary would ever stray—but if it does happen, you won't have anyone to blame but yourself. You'll be the one who drove him to it."

Billie was right, Amelia thought as she sipped at her brandy Alexander. But Billie hadn't seen Eileen Farrell. Even Thad's head would turn for a second look. Now, Thad was one man who would never stray; he might look, but he'd never touch. She hadn't known Cary for a lifetime the way Billie knew Thad.

Amelia ordered a second drink, glancing at the departure monitor from her seat at the bar. She had twenty minutes to make her flight to Austin, if that was what she wanted to do. She had the rest of the day to hail a taxi that would take her to the Hyatt. She gulped her drink, paid the check, and hurried to the check-in counter, where she was told there would be a ten-minute delay. Just enough time to call the Hyatt and leave a message for Cary. Let him eat his heart out.

Information gave her the number. She dropped coins into the slot, got the Hyatt, and asked for Cary Assante. The phone rang and rang. Finally she hung up and dialed the Hyatt a second time, this time asking for Eileen Farrell's room. The phone was picked up on the third ring, and she heard her husband say hello. Her gloved fingers felt numb when she replaced the receiver.

Her change purse yielded enough coins to make a third call. The message she left was brief: Mrs. Assante is returning to Austin.

Cary looked around at the beautiful flowers. His watch told him Amelia was two hours late. Somehow, in his gut, he knew she wouldn't be here. Suddenly he thought to call the desk and ask if there were any messages.

"Yes, sir, there is a message. The boy is on his way up to your room right now. We've been terribly busy, and couldn't get to it before now; I'm sorry."

Cary opened the door, tipped the bellhop, and read his message before he closed the door. It had been Amelia on Eileen's phone. He felt like crying.

At nine o'clock room service knocked on the door, and Cary didn't have the nerve to tell the man to take the food away. He watched as everything was carried in. How Amelia would have loved this, he thought. He reached for the magnum of champagne in its silver bucket. Why the hell not? Who cared?

Amelia Coleman Nelson Assante slept on the floor of her mother's house that night, wrapped in her sable coat. It was a deep, soundless sleep of defeat.

{{{{{{{ CHAPTER TWENTY-TWO }}}}}}}

Sunbridge took on an air of strain when Cary returned from New York. Amelia was civil as she listened to his account of the trip, didn't bat an eyelash when she heard how sick Eileen was— so sick, said Cary, that he wanted her to fill in at the office if she could find the time. Secretly, Amelia was pleased, and she agreed to help out until Eileen was able to return to work.

"All you have to do, darling, is answer the phone. Eileen can catch up on the other stuff when she's back on her feet."

Cary looked to miserable, so worn, that Amelia took pity on him . . . for the moment. Maybe he was telling the truth. Time would tell. But she had no intention of going upstairs and making love with him as if nothing had happened. She still felt too raw and bruised for that.

Forcing a smile to her lips, she said cheerfully, "Go to bed, darling. You look tired. I have some papers and bills to go over. After all, I was away for three days. And I promised Susan we'd have a talk. She wants some input from me on little Jessie. I think she's considering forming some kind of organization or starting a little club for parents of children with spina bifida."

Cary nodded like a schoolboy who was being punished for something he didn't understand. He went upstairs without another word.

Damn, she thought petulantly, he might have coaxed

her a little! How quick the was to accept her reasons why
she wasn't ready for bed. The truth of the matter was she
herself was so tired and strung out, she couldn't see
straight. If ever there was a time for a drink and a joint,
this was it. The den would be dark and as welcome as
her thoughts; she could hang out there till morning with
no one the wiser.

She couldn't ever remember feeling so awful, so alone.
This was her first serious rift with Cary since they'd been
married. Maybe she should tell him *exactly* how she felt.
Her fears might be foolish and unfounded, but they were
damaging her relationship nevertheless. Wouldn't it be
better to get everything out in the open?

Amelia lit the marijuana cigarette she'd purchased from
one of the young workmen.

Good weed, the young man had said. Pure Colombian.
Amelia dragged deeply on the joint and leaned back. She
could feel the tension leave her body almost immediately.
She felt almost giddy. . . . She giggled and wondered vaguely
if she had shut the study door, not that it mattered. She
was somewhere else now and enjoying every minute of
it.

It was five o'clock when Amelia came down off her
cloud. The room reeked of pot. She gulped her watered-
down drink and opened the window a good two inches.
Then she closed the door behind her and climbed the
steps. A shower and fresh clothes would make her feel
better. Today she was replacing Eileen Farrell.

Cary waited till after three for his wife to come to bed.
He'd refused to seek her out and beg for her favors, however—they were married, for Christ's sake! When he
finally heard her come into the room, he cracked one eye
open to look at the clock on the night stand. Jesus, it was
practically dawn. She went immediately into the shower.
Then, just as he'd decided to join her, he heard the snick
of the lock.

Two minutes after the alarm was turned off, Amelia
opened the bathroom door. Cary noticed that her makeup

was fresh but her eyes were lusterless. He felt rotten. They were going to be in real trouble if something wasn't done soon.

"Morning, babe," he said softly. "I missed you last night."

"I slept downstairs. I guess I dozed off. When I did wake, I thought I would disturb you, if I came up, so I finished out the night on the sofa."

"Alone?"

"In a manner of speaking. I smoked a joint and had a couple of drinks." Defiantly, she added, "I needed it."

"What about Susan and the work you had to do?"

Amelia turned to face her husband. "I changed my mind. I decided I wanted to be alone. Surely you can understand that. I'm going to have some breakfast, so anytime you're ready to leave, I'll be ready."

Cary blinked as the door closed behind his wife. By God, he thought, she's declared war! This room is the front, and I'm going to get caught in the cross fire if I don't take charge damn quick.

His shower was the shortest on record, the spray barely touching his body before he hopped out and dressed. Twice he nicked himself shaving and plastered bits of tissue over the bleeding spots. Now he not only felt like a war casualty; he looked like one, too.

Most mornings, Amelia filled his plate from the sideboard and buttered his toast. This morning, however, she remained seated, reading the *Crystal City Times* while she munched on an English muffin.

"What's new in Crystal City?" he asked heartily as he dug into his eggs.

"Not much. We're supposed to have a wet spring this year. The Cattleman's Association is meeting next week on some land bid. The Canterbury Club is sponsoring a St. Patrick's Day Dance. The tickets are a hundred dollars each."

"Buy a block of them."

"Why?" Amelia asked as she folded the paper in two. She passed it over to Cary, who ignored it.

"I'll give them to some of the workers. Don't you think it's a good idea?"

"No," Amelia said shortly. "Your workers won't be welcome at the Canterbury Club. You don't want to embarrass them, do you?"

"You just said the tickets were on sale for a hundred dollars each. Don't they want to sell them?"

"Of course they want to sell them, but to the right people. They don't want riffraff. I don't make the rules; I'm just telling you the way it is."

Cary put down his fork. "What you're telling me is some hardworking stiff who puts in fourteen hours a day to take care of his family and has dirt under his fingernails isn't going to be permitted to attend even if he has one of those expensive tickets." Cary's face was grim, his eyes cold and hard. "Will they be turned away at the door?"

"Of course not. They'll feel ill at ease. I seriously doubt if any of your men would even take the tickets, much less attend."

"Well, if that's the case, count me out. If some man who is out there busting his ass for me isn't good enough to go where I go, then I don't belong there, either. You make up your own mind, Amelia. I've had enough breakfast. I'm ready to leave."

"You're just being stubborn. You know how they do things here. I've certainly told you enough times. You even laughed."

"That was before I got involved. The next thing you'll be telling me is they burn crosses on lawns and go around in white sheets. Just because I married you doesn't make me one of you. I'm no different than those guys out there slogging away day after day. I've never asked anyone to do anything for me I wouldn't do myself. You knew that when you married me. I don't want to be a Coleman. You aren't a Coleman anymore, either."

Amelia bristled as she buttoned her coat. "Right now you're feeling guilty, so don't take it out on me, okay? If you don't want to go to the dance, don't go. I'll buy myself a ticket. I am on the board, after all. If you want to argue, let's argue about the issues. Don't go throwing some stupid dance into the ring to divert me. We're a little too old to play games."

"Guilty? Me? Come off it, Amelia. I told you the truth and I'm not going to go through that scene again. What you see is what you got. I've never lied to you, nor have I ever been unfaithful. And in your heart you know it. Whatever the hell your problem is, I hope you solve it before you bust up this marriage. Get the hell in the car, because I'm leaving."

Amelia's back stiffened. "Don't talk to me like I'm one of your workers. I'm your wife. I won't stand for it, Cary."

"If you're my wife, I wish to hell you'd act like it. I'm sick and tired of dancing around you, worrying about saying the right thing at the right time. You're the one who's screwing things up."

They rode to the construction site in silence. Cary glowered all the way. Amelia sat in a pitiful huddle, angry with herself and with Cary.

Cary's face lost none of its grimness as he set about turning on the heaters and the lights. He waved his arm vaguely in the direction of the coffee machine. "It'll warm up soon. Make some coffee. Some of the men come in from time to time and may want something to warm them up. Keep it filled. Do you know how to work the phone system?"

"I know how it works." She watched as his eyes looked up toward the fluorescent lights and then down at her hair. She felt a moment of panic. What was he seeing? She longed suddenly for the pale light bulbs in their bedroom. Go, her mind shrieked, so I can see what this is doing to me. God, go!

"I'll try to make it back for lunch," Cary told her. "Order something around one o'clock."

"I'll do that. Have a good day."

He hesitated a moment. "You have a good day, too. I'll see you later."

"I'll be here."

The second the door closed behind him, Amelia had her compact open. She angled it this way and that, hoping to see whatever it was Cary had seen. Damn, it was too small. She removed the huge square bathroom mirror and carried it out to her desk, then sat down and inspected herself.

She looked awful. Her makeup was garish; her dark hair cast unflattering shadows on her face, the roots showing at the part line. All she needed was a red nose and she could pass for a clown.

Wobbling on the swivel chair, Amelia reached up to lift the ceiling block. She unscrewed not one but two of the bright lights. Immediately she felt better. Now that the glare was gone, she might be able to get through the day. She looked into the mirror again. It was better now, but she'd lost something in those few minutes under the glaring light. She was getting old and it was eating her alive.

By mid-morning Amelia was bored to tears. She called her house, spoke to the workmen, and was assured that everything was progressing on schedule. She went over her paperwork, made a few calls, rescheduled delivery of the upstairs carpeting, and watered Eileen's plants. She read two chapters of a Herman Wouk novel, got bored, and put it back in her bag.

One o'clock came and went. She ordered hamburgers and French fries from a diner down the road. The smell made her nauseous. At two o'clock she poked through the files to see what kind of system Eileen used.

An hour later, Amelia Assante's world crumbled around her. She sat in stunned disbelief, staring at the papers in her hand. One was the deed to a co-op apartment in Eileen Farrell's name; the other was the certificate of ownership for a new Ford Mustang. When the phone rang, she answered it automatically. She even managed to record messages.

Her movements were awkward and clumsy as she

searched through the cabinets a second time. When she found what she was looking for, she sat down and fought her tears. The co-op had actually been purchased by Cary Assante, but a copy of a quitclaim deed said Cary had deeded the apartment to Eileen Farrell for the princely sum of one hundred dollars. The Mustang had been purchased outright; a photostat of the registration and bill of sale carried Cary's name.

At three-forty-five Amelia took the phone off the receiver and left the trailer. She drove home, packed her husband's bags, and brought them back to the office, placing them neatly by the door. She left the incriminating papers on the blue desk blotter. The receiver was still off the hook, pinging noisily. She replaced it and the light bulbs overhead.

She didn't look back. There were some things a person didn't need to see more than once.

Susan sat across the desk from Jessica's pediatrician. The metal plate on his desk read Ferris Armstrong, M.D. She liked him and the way he treated Jessie. He didn't mince words—he warned her what she was up against and what the future might hold for Jessie and herself. But he was always hopeful.

Now his cornflower-blue eyes twinkled when Jessie belched loudly. Susan flushed. "She hasn't learned her manners yet."

He laughed, stretched backward on his swivel chair, and propped his foot up on the desk. In the time Susan had been bringing Jessie to him, he'd come to like her and had learned he could drop his professional demeanor after the baby's examination and relax. He enjoyed talking with her. Lacing his long fingers behind his head, he studied the tips of his shoes down the length of his long legs. "Do you plan to stay here in Texas or return to England?" he asked.

"I'll be staying on. I'm living at Sunbridge with my sister, as I've told you, but I'm planning to find my own place. Actually, I own a house that was given to me years ago, but it's being rented. I might consider moving there. I want a yard for Jessie and room for her to grow. She will grow, won't she?"

"I've told you everything there is to know, and I've given you pamphlets and books and articles to read. You know I'm not holding anything back. What you must understand is that spina bifida affects each child differently. The prognosis for Jessie is excellent. Why would you think I was holding back? I know how precious Jessie is to you; I want what's best for her as well as you."

Susan sighed and relaxed in her chair. Jessie cuddled on her mother's shoulder. "I have no reason to think you're holding anything back. I just feel so lost sometimes, as though Jessie were the only baby in the world with this defect. My family tries to help, but they can't really share it with me."

Ferris Armstrong looked at Susan compassionately. She had told him of the breakup of her marriage, and without even knowing the details, he had developed a strong dislike for Jerome de Moray. Jessie needed a father and Susan needed a husband, someone to share her worries and help with the burden of raising a child.

"I've been in touch with some of the names you gave me, Dr. Armstrong—you know, other parents of spina bifida children. We're forming a group to help each other. You know, to seek out information, hold little gatherings, and just talk. It's already helped me and, I hope, some of the others. I want to start an organization here in this area."

Ferris smiled. "I approve. How far have you gotten?"

"Not very far. Just some ideas I've been kicking around. Jessie is only an infant, but you know the needs of other children, older children, like her. I was hoping you'd have some suggestions."

"You're taking on a handful. Once begun, it wouldn't be fair to drop such a thing midstream. Be careful; you could pull the rug out from under a lot of people who are already in a painful situation. An undertaking like this would require a strong commitment."

"I know. And that's why I've been doing a lot of thinking. I've consulted my sister and she's agreed to deed me a piece of land on Sunbridge property where I could build a camp. That seems to be what's needed. According to other parents I've talked with, our special children have little or no opportunity to experience things that normal children do because there aren't any facilities for them. But it's all in the thinking stage at this point. The only thing I'm certain of is that I want Jessie to live as full a life as possible and to be with other children. If I can help others while I'm helping her, so much the better."

"It's commendable," Ferris heard the excitement in his own voice. "It would take a good deal of money."

Susan frowned. "Unfortunately, that could be a problem. Do you have any kind of ballpark figure in mind?"

"Nothing under a hundred thousand, and that would just get it off the ground. But if you're campaigning, I'd be more than glad to make a donation when you're ready."

Susan was struck by his wide smile and realized that whenever she was with him she watched for it, allowed herself to be warmed by it. Ferris Armstrong loved his work and he loved the children; she could tell by the way he handled little Jessie. His hands were incredibly large, with long, sensitive fingers; he could hold Jessie's bottom in one palm. His blue eyes could be compassionate one second and stern the next and merry the second after that. She gauged him to be somewhere in his early forties, and once when she'd mentioned his family, he'd told her he didn't have one.

Single, attractive, and sensitive. The thought pleased Susan, and she felt herself flush. "I like you, Ferris Armstrong, M.D.," she blurted.

His eyes met hers, and for an instant there was a sense of tension and indecision between them. Then Jessie belched again and they both laughed.

"Raising money for your foundation shouldn't be much

of a problem," Ferris said after a moment, dropping his feet from the desk and fixing his gaze intently on Susan. "I heard you play when I was in Los Angeles three years ago. You were magnificent. I shouted with the rest of the audience at the end of the concert. Why don't you think about playing here? You certainly are a celebrity, and all of Texas would turn out to hear you, especially if they were spending tax-deductible dollars to do so. Give the proceeds to your foundation." He held up a hand. "Don't say no too quickly. A talent like yours shouldn't be hidden. Jessie might need a lot of things, but so does her mother. Think about it."

"I don't know if I have the time to spend practicing," Susan said doubtfully. "Hours and hours at the piano, hours Jessie will need me. But yes, of course, I'll think about it."

"Good. Now, I want to see Jessie next week. I'll give you a call over the weekend to let you know what I've come up with in the way of the suggestions you want. First, I want to talk to several physicians in the area and see what they think about an outdoor camp for children with special needs. Getting their input from the beginning would help to ensure their participation later. Get me?" He winked.

Susan found herself laughing again. "Gotcha! But I've got a better idea than having you call. Why don't you come to dinner on Saturday night? If you've no other plans," she added hastily. "I can show you the piece of land my sister is turning over to me."

Ferris quickly ran a mental check of his plans for Saturday. "I'm free as the breeze," he said cheerfully. "What time?"

"Early, while it's still daylight. If you come in the afternoon and the weather is nice, we can ride out on horseback."

"You've got a date." He made a few illegible squiggles on a notepad—for Susan's benefit; he knew he wasn't going to forget.

"I'll see you on Saturday, then. Thank you, Dr. Armstrong."

"Why don't you call me Ferris? I'll call you Susie."

"My family calls me Suse."

"I like Susie better."

Susan's heart fluttered all the way to the car. She'd never felt like this. Not even Jerome had made her heart flutter. Wait till she told Maggie.

"Sounds like a date to me," Maggie said, smiling. "Is he good-looking? Not that it matters, but it's the first thing women think about."

"Not terribly good-looking, but he has these incredible eyelashes. I like him, Maggie. I can't believe I had the nerve to ask him to dinner, though. I hope you don't mind. He's coming over early in the afternoon. Do you think you could watch Jessie while we go horseback riding?"

"Of course I don't mind, and of course I'll watch Jessie. I can't wait to see this man who can turn my sister into a weak-kneed mass of jelly! What shall we have for dinner? What do you think he likes?"

"Maggie, I hardly know him. But when in doubt, always go with prime rib and some fancy dessert, right? . . . Maybe I'm making too much of this. Here we are thinking this is actually a date, and it isn't. He's just coming to lend his expertise so Jessie can have a better life. It's true that I asked him because he interested me, if you know what I mean. But that doesn't mean he's reciprocating my feelings."

"Little Suse, listen to your sister Maggie. Men, especially doctors, don't go out of their way unless they're interested. Doctors simply don't have the time, and what time they do have they guard very jealously. That's my expert opinion."

"That's good enough for me. Oh, Maggie, I can't tell you what it means to be here! There was a time when I thought we were lost to each other."

"Yeah. Me, too," Maggie said softly.

Susan wrapped her arms around her sister. "Have you heard from Rand?"

"No," Maggie whispered. "I screwed up, Suse. Maybe someday I'll learn."

Susan could hear the hint of tears in Maggie's voice. "No, I refuse to believe that. I'm sure there's an explanation. Rand is always on the go; he might be traveling. You did send him away. He probably went off to the country to lick his wounds. He never has mail forwarded; it just piles up, sometimes for as long as two months. You could call him, you know."

"I've tried. No luck. Actually, I don't know which is worse—the fear that he will answer or the fear that he won't. No, a letter is best. I'll just have to wait it out. I still can't believe Mam told me to go for it. Does that surprise you?"

Susan thought about it. "No, not really. All Mam ever wanted was for us to be happy, to be a family. She made her mistakes just like we did—and she learned from them the way we're going to have to. Mam's one wise lady, Maggie. Her seal of approval can make you happy. So that's exactly what she gave you."

"I wish I called her before I sent Rand away. I didn't know. I expected her to choose up sides."

"You dope. She did. She picked you, if that's the way you want to think of it. You have to get it out of your head that it's you versus Sawyer. That's not the way it is."

"Go take care of your baby. I hear her crying," Maggie said, not unkindly. "I'll think about what you just said while I prepare a gastronomical delight for Saturday."

"I'm partial to peach cobbler, if that makes a difference."

"Cole likes it, too. Peach cobbler it is."

Peacefully nursing little Jessie in the old nursery, Susan had a clear view of the corridor. She watched in stunned amazement as her aunt Amelia stalked into the room she

shared with Cary. She continued to watch and puzzle over
her aunt's actions, when, approximately five minutes later,
two huge traveling bags were pushed into the hall by
Amelia's foot. An oversize plastic bag, the kind bowlers
and athletes used, was pitched down the hall ahead of the
suitcases. There was anger in Amelia's straight back, and
strange sounds seemed to be coming from her mouth.

Something was wrong. Susan could feel herself start
to tremble. She'd played out a scene much like this once
herself. Cary was leaving, Amelia was leaving, or they
were both leaving. Where were Maggie and the boys? She
looked at her watch: four o'clock, too early for the boys
to be home from school. Maggie was probably in the study
or out riding.

It was five-fifteen when Amelia once again stalked down
the hall to her room. This time Susan had a clear view of
her aunt's face. It looked old, beaten, and drawn. So, she
thought, it was Cary who was leaving. Did he even know?

Susan willed the small bundle in her arms to burp. It
took a while, but Jessie finally complied, and Susan sighed
with relief. She kissed the downy head, felt the baby's
diaper, and then laid her down to sleep. She rocked the
cradle a few times just for the pleasure of doing it, and
then closed the door halfway.

To knock or not to knock on Amelia's door. Susan put
her ear to the wood and heard the sound of hard, deep
sobbing. Maggie. She had to find Maggie.

Maggie was just coming up the steps, boots and riding
crop in her hand. When she saw Susan's wild eyes and
trembling lips she drew her sister into her room. "What
is it, Suse? What's wrong? It isn't Jessie, is it?" Maggie
asked in alarm.

"No, it's Amelia." Quickly, Susan recounted the scene
she'd seen played out for her. "She's in her room now,
sobbing."

"Do you think we should interfere? Amelia might want
to be alone. I mean, this is between her and Cary. She's
been real touchy lately. I knew something was wrong

when she came back from New York. Mam would know."

"Mam isn't here," Susan said curtly. "She's really hurting, Maggie."

Maggie licked her lips. "Okay, but I don't think she's going to appreciate this." She rapped softly on Amelia's door and then turned the knob. Amelia was lying on the bed, sobbing into her pillow, great hulking sobs that shook her slim shoulders. Susan and Maggie looked at each other helplessly for a moment. Then Susan climbed on the bed from the right side, Maggie from the left. It was Maggie who gently drew Amelia to her. She was stunned at how thin the woman was. "What can we do, Amelia?" Maggie asked soothingly.

"Nothing. I already did it. It's over. I've been such a fool. How all of you must have laughed at me."

"No one has ever laughed at you, Amelia. What did you do? If you've done something foolish, you're entitled. We're all fools at one time or another. Talk to us, Amelia. Perhaps we can help."

Amelia started slowly, haltingly. Then the words began to speed up, and soon she was like a runaway car down a steep hill.

Susan looked at Maggie and then at her aunt. She knew they were both thinking the same thing. "When we fuck up, we really fuck up."

Maggie burst into hysterical laughter. She'd never heard Susan say so much as "damn." "We sure do!" Amelia nodded miserably.

"Maybe you should talk to Cary one more time," Susan said softly, ever the peacemaker.

Amelia sat bolt upright on the bed. "Why? So I can listen to more lies? No, thanks. Tell me, what would you have done? When you'd had enough, didn't you leave Jerome? Maggie, when Cranston got to you, didn't you leave? What makes me different?"

"He'll come back; you know that," Maggie told her.

"I took his keys off his ring before I left. Don't let him in, Maggie. Promise me."

"I promise, if that's what you want. Look at us. We're all in the same boat and not a paddle among us." She hesitated. "What are you going to do, Amelia?"

"I'm going back to England on the first available plane. Susan, will you call and make me a reservation on the Concorde? Book me a flight to New York. I'll sit in the airport. This place," Amelia said, looking around, "has caused me nothing but grief my whole life. Why I thought it would be different now is beyond me. Maggie, you'll help me pack, won't you?"

"Of course, if that's what you really want. But what about your house? You've done so much work on it." She struggled for just the right words. "Sometimes, Amelia, when you do things in haste or hatred, they can't ever be made right. Do you know what I'm talking about?"

"I'm not an idiot, Maggie, just a fool. I know exactly what you're saying. You're even thinking of all the mistakes you made with Sawyer. But this is different. Cary was my life—I made him my life. I didn't leave room for anything else."

Maggie felt as if she'd been slapped in the face. She forced herself to speak calmly. "It's not too late. You could go back and talk to Cary. I mean really talk. This time listen to what he says. Don't just hear him, listen, Amelia."

"Is that what you'd do, Maggie?" Amelia asked tearfully as she threw her clothes into an open suitcase.

It took Maggie so long to answer that both Amelia and Susan stopped what they were doing to wait for her reply. "If I loved him with all my heart, yes. I wouldn't give up without a fight."

"Will you please *look* at me?" Amelia cried. "Do I look like I have any fight left? I'm an old woman. Eileen Farrell is just a name. There will always be Eileen Farrells. And each one will be younger as I get older."

Maggie bit down on her tongue. When she tasted her own blood, she grabbed Amelia by the arm. "You aren't running away from Cary or Eileen. You're running away from yourself. Admit it, Amelia. You're a Coleman and you're copping out. For shame. I thought you were tougher than that. We're all that's left. Fall back and regroup! Go talk to a shrink and get it all in perspective, but make sure you know the reason. It's you, Amelia."

"We're all that's left! You fool, we're all there ever was. Your mother wasn't a Coleman, only by marriage. We didn't have a choice. Maybe you are right." Amelia turned to look at Susan, who had just gotten off the phone. "What's the verdict, Suse?"

"There's a ten-o'clock flight to New York. You can pick up your ticket at the airport. I told them you would American Express it. You have a seat on tomorrow's Concorde flight."

Maggie's shoulders slumped. "How about some coffee? A sandwich or something."

"I'll take the coffee and a chicken sandwich." Amelia looked at herself in the dresser mirror. "I'm going to have to wear dark glasses," she muttered.

Maggie turned to stare at her aunt. "You only have to wear dark glasses if you want to wear them. The choice is yours. You have nothing to hide, Amelia."

"My age," Amelia whimpered. "I have to hide my age."

Susan crossed the room in three strides. Maggie held up her hand to stop her sister. "Then hide it. If you want to hide behind dark glasses to keep the boogeyman away, then you do it. I'll get the coffee." She made a motion for Susan to follow her. When the door closed behind her, Maggie sagged against it.

"You were a little hard on her, don't you think?"

"Maybe I wasn't hard enough. When you give up the fight, it's all over. You exist. But this is as much as we're going to interfere. Do you agree?" Susan nodded. "If Cary comes here, we don't know anything. Let's see what kind of man he really is. If he's what I think he is, he's going to sweat it out. He won't go after her the way she wants. And that's when we'll know who Amelia Coleman Nelson Assante really is."

"I feel so sorry for her. I never thought of her as old. For me she's never changed. I don't understand how that could be so important to her. So many things in life that are more important, yet she's only worried about her age."

"That house of her mother's was important to her. She actually used to light up a room when she came in at the end of the day. Cary was so proud of her. Where did that go? I can't believe that he got mixed up with that little snot Eileen. If he did, she engineered it. She had her claws out for Rand, too."

"I think, if you want my honest gut opinion, that Cary is a victim. I think there's an explanation for everything. He loved Amelia."

"Past tense?" Maggie asked.

"I haven't been as close to the situation as you. I've been busy with Jessie—and coming to terms with her disability. But I've accepted it now, so I can go on and do the best I can. No one can ask more of you than your best."

"Good girl, Suse. Come on, help me with the coffee. I don't think any of us are going to be hungry this evening. Didja ever notice how good we all are at stirring our food around the plates?"

"Yeah, I noticed. . . . She's going to be all right, isn't she, Maggie?"

"I don't know. It's going to hit her hard once she's back in England. If Cary is a no-show, I can't even imagine what she'll do. All we can do is be supportive. I'll call Mam after she leaves and give her the facts. I hate to burden her, though. It's time we left her alone. But I'm glad they're coming for the christening. Have you heard from Sawyer?"

"Not yet. I was going to call her this weekend. She'll come through."

Sawyer didn't come through. It was Maggie who held Jessica Margaret in her arms for the christening.

It was a private ceremony with just the family. Cole, dressed in a new suit, stood quietly next to his mother, watching the proceeding with narrowed eyes. Billie, Thad, and Riley sat at the front of the church. Ferris Armstrong stood in the back next to Cary Assante. Both men left quietly before the family started the walk back down the long center aisle.

Billie and Thad stayed for mid-afternoon dinner and caught an early-evening flight to New York.

There was no mention of Sawyer.

{{{{{{{{ CHAPTER TWENTY-THREE }}}}}}}}

Rand Nelson waved to his mother as she took off down the lane on her bicycle. The sight of her maneuvering the old one-speed made him smile, as usual. He still couldn't get used to having her here, with him. He'd been shocked and surprised a month ago when he'd received the call to pick her up at Heathrow Airport. She'd done little talking on the way back to the house, but what she had told him was enough to make him angry. Not with Cary, but with her. He'd tried to talk sense to her, and she'd listened politely, but he knew she hadn't really heard a word he'd said.

But she'd changed a great deal since then. She'd put on some weight. She was letting her hair color fade out. Her artificial nails and phony eyelashes were gone. She made no effort to coat her eyes with the makeup she used to buy by the pound; they looked wistful now, but alive. She was quite beautiful, possibly the prettiest woman he'd ever known.

For the first few weeks Amelia hovered close to the

phone and was outside, rain or shine, when the postman arrived. Eventually she'd given that up; these days she forgot to pick up the mail unless he reminded her. Once she'd had her old bicycle fixed, she'd begun to take long rides on the country lanes, sometimes asking him to join her. He could do more than relate to Amelia now: he could actually understand.

There'd been no phone calls from Texas for him, only that short letter from Maggie after the holidays. His guilt was so overpowering, he couldn't make himself pick up a pen or the telephone to make things right. In her own way Amelia was handling things better than he.

The only regular mail that arrived from Texas to Ribbonmaker Lane was from Susan. She wrote faithfully, every ten days or so. Rand never answered, and from Susan's letters, he learned that Amelia didn't respond, either. Once again he read the letter that had arrived today, enjoying the chatty, breezy tone.

Dear Amelia and Rand,
Spring has finally come to Texas. It's almost as beautiful as Jessie. Sometimes I put her out on the patio in her carriage for hours at a time. I've actually gotten Cole and Riley to baby-sit if I go out. Of course, they don't do it together. Some things never change!

Did you know the boys were taking Sawyer and Adam Jarvis to Hawaii for a summer vacation? They're going to be staying someplace high in the hills, at the house Mam stayed in when Pap was stationed at Pearl Harbor. It's where I was conceived! They're leaving in June and staying for about six weeks. Maggie is going in April to ready the house for them. No one knows that, so please don't mention it. It seems the place has been closed for years and years. I don't know how long she'll be there.

Sawyer didn't make it for the christening. Maggie took her place. She's so wonderful with the baby. I've enclosed some snapshots the boys took. Jessie's hair is starting to curl now into little ringlets. Cute, huh?

My attorney informed me yesterday that Jerome will

be here the early part of April. I'm dreading that. I suppose he can make all kinds of trouble, but I won't allow it. I don't even want him to see Jessie, but I suppose I have to let him. Of course he'll blame me for her disability.

I saw Cary in town one day last week. He looked so tired and drawn. He asked about you, Rand, said that he received your check and where the hell is your body? They could use you. That's a direct quote. Why don't you give him a call?

Cary tells me the progress they're making on his inner city is phenomenal. Some of the structures are actually up. I plan to take a look the next time I'm there. Ferris is impressed. Ferris is Ferris Armstrong, Jessie's doctor. I've been seeing him a little on a social basis. He's helping me organize a small group of parents with children like Jessie. He's very nice.

Well, that's my news for now. It would be nice to hear some news from England. I miss you both.

I send my love and Jessie's, too,

Susan

Rand watched Amelia pedal her bike up the lane. He waved the letter as she drew near. "Susan," he called loudly so he wouldn't have to see the disappointment on her face.

She hopped off the bike and adjusted the kickstand. "Be back in a minute," she told him. "I want to put this fish in the fridge."

It was a long time before Amelia joined him. Long enough to read the letter three more times. Maggie was going to Hawaii soon.

Amelia read the letter, folded it, and replaced it in the envelope with the bright red border. "Would you like rice or noodles with your fish?"

"Rice. What did you think of the baby's pictures?"

"She's adorable. She looks like Susan, thank God. One of us should write to her."

"Yes, one of us should," Rand said thoughtfully.

"I'm not much of a letter writer," Amelia said, sipping her tea.

"I'm worse."

"Then one of us should call," Amelia said tightly.

"Yes, I suppose you're right. One of these days."

"Yes, one of these days," Amelia said. They were like an old shoe and an old sock, she thought sourly. "We're having an early dinner this evening. I'm playing back-gammon with the Goodwins. Would you like to join us?"

"No, thanks. Do you want me to drop you off?"

"I'm quite capable of driving myself, but I'm going to bike it. Since you put that light on my bike, I can use it in the evening. Don't worry about me, Rand."

"It's that bike I'm worried about. It's prewar."

"Almost as old as me. It's holding up very well. Most things do over the long haul. Do you get my drift?"

Rand laughed. "I sure do. Do you?"

"You bet. Dinner in an hour. Is that all right with you?"

"Yes," Rand responded absently. Maggie in Hawaii.

Amelia pedaled her bike down the lane at five minutes of six. At five minutes past six Rand placed a call to Vermont. He talked to Billie for well over an hour. Actually, he did more listening than talking. Why was it, he wondered, that some people had the ability to make others feel wonderful and always, always, had the right words?

That night Rand slept deeply, peacefully, for the first time since he'd returned to England. It was only when he woke to a new day that he realized he hadn't needed half a bottle of whiskey to sleep. He felt like singing.

Her name was Valentine Mitchell and she was Maggie's attorney. She was thirtyish and tall, almost six feet. Crisp and neat in a gray flannel suit with a white silk blouse. There was a Mark Cross bag over her shoulder and she carried a Gucci briefcase in her hand. Her hair was short and wavy, complementing a sharp, suntanned face. Her eyes, Maggie noticed, were the color of bright new spring leaves just coming into bud.

"I know you must be surprised to see me here, but Mr. Abramson said he thought I was the best one to handle this case. I used to practice in New York before joining this firm. I was one of the legion of assistants to the Manhattan district attorney. I watched your husband in court many times. I've done nothing but work on this case for the past month. I think we can beat him."

"Think? That isn't good enough, Miss Mitchell. He's clever and he's hateful."

"Yes, think. A good lawyer never says he knows anything for certain. Trust me. Yes, Cranston is clever, and yes, he can be hateful. I've seen him when he lost a case. I never even knew he was married till Dudley told me."

Maggie giggled. "I never heard anyone call Mr. Abramson Dudley before. I always thought of him as being born old and everyone bowing down to him."

"Dudley likes young women. I'm his right hand, or so he says." The bright green eyes were bitter when she added, "And that hand has been very busy indeed."

"I see. I'm sorry."

"Don't be. I was one of these young women who believed Gloria Steinem when she said, 'Be a lawyer, don't marry one.' I bought it. I'd like to talk to your son. I want to hear exactly what it is you're prepared to give up and what you want to keep. I want to hear from the boy where he stands. I'm good with kids. I want you to trust me with your son, and I don't want you to interfere. Your case comes up in two weeks, so we don't have a lot of time."

Maggie looked into the leaf-green eyes. Something she saw there made her nod. "Whatever you want. Stay for dinner and you can talk to Cole afterward. My time is yours now."

"Good." The Gucci briefcase snapped open. Legal papers crackled.

Maggie's eyes dropped to Valentine's feet. Ferragamo shoes at three hundred dollars a pair. This was going to be one expensive divorce. "Shoot," Maggie said happily.

* * *

Dinner was more than pleasant. Maggie enjoyed every minute of it. Val, as she preferred to be called, regaled them with tales of her stint in the Manhattan prosecutor's office. The boys, in turn, talked about baseball and archery. Riley surprised his aunt and Cole, too, by bragging that Cole was the number-one archer on the school team. Cole could do no less than supply all of them with Riley's batting average. "His RBI is the best the school's ever had."

Maggie beamed.

They had coffee in the living room, after the boys had excused themselves to do homework.

"Cole, don't go anywhere. I need to talk to you. When do you think you'll finish your homework?" Val asked.

Cole's eyes swiveled to his mother and then returned to Val. "Forty-five minutes."

"Good, I'll be up then."

Maggie sipped at her coffee. "Just how well did you know my husband?"

Val grinned. "Very well. But I didn't go to bed with him. I know somebody who did, though. His name was Evan Lantzy."

Maggie sputtered her coffee all over the front of her blouse. "*What*?"

"Feel better about this case now?"

"My God! I never.... Who would..."

"Isn't it great? Once in a while I love to play dirty. Just tell me what you want, Maggie, and it's yours."

"Cole. That's all I want. Forget the rest. Are...are..."

"Yes. He has to know. Dudley and I discussed it. Regardless of what that old bird is, he does know law and he knows Cranston. We did a run-through on his past cases. Hey, he could destroy you in two minutes without Evan's affidavit. He's got enough on you to.... You know what I'm saying. You were married to him, so you know how dirty he can be. It's a game. All lawyers play games and make deals."

Maggie was still in shock. 'I don't know if Cole can

handle this. Are you sure he has to know?"

"Yes. That's why I'm going to be the one doing the telling and not you. As far as you're concerned, you never heard what I said. That kid can handle anything. I watched him during dinner. I told you; I'm good with kids, especially kids in trouble. I worked with them a lot in New York. Do you want to see Evan's affidavit?"

"No. God, no."

"It wasn't a one-night stand. It lasted quite a while. According to Evan, he was devastated. Right now, the man of the hour is a buyer for Saks Fifth Avenue. He buys children's outerwear. His name is Wade Holder."

Maggie shook her head. "It's so hard to believe. He told me he's getting married."

"He is. To a very nice woman, I might add. Dumb, but nice. She bakes cookies, is a hospital volunteer, and quite rich. We ran a check on her, too."

"Do you ever get sick of what you're doing?" Maggie asked curiously.

The bitterness was back in Val's voice. "Every day of my life."

"Why do you stay with it?"

"Because I bought the bullshit line that I could do it on my own. They told me I didn't need someone to take care of me; that I could do it myself. They're right. I can. I suppose it's a case of wanting versus needing. Men do business like this every day of the week. Everyone has to work in the gutter once in a while. You go home at night and take a bath. Some of it washes away."

"What happens when you can't wash it away anymore?"

Val laughed. "Then I'll get married and scrub my husband's back. Dirt doesn't seem to stick to a man like it does to a woman.

"While we're waiting for Cole to finish his homework, I have a pile of papers for you to sign. You won't even have to appear in court. I'll personally deliver your divorce papers."

It was nine-thirty when Valentine Mitchell walked out

of Cole's room and came down the wide circular staircase. The leaf-green eyes had tears in them.

"Remember what I told you before," she said to Maggie. "Don't ever let Cole know you know. If you do, you'll destroy him. He came through it. He'll be all right. Trust me."

Maggie did.

Maggie lay in her bag bed staring at the dark ceiling. A clap of thunder overhead made her jump. She must have been dozing a little. She was about to get up and close the window when she noticed her door opening.

"Mother?" It was a hoarse whisper from Cole.

"Yes. Are you sick, Cole?" Of course he was sick. Sick in his heart and sick in his soul.

"No. I can't sleep. I want to talk to you about something."

"Sure. Do you want to go downstairs and have some cocoa?"

"Yeah. Let's do that. I want some bright light. Did I wake you?"

"No. The thunder did," Maggie replied truthfully.

Sitting in the brightly lit kitchen, sipping cocoa, Maggie watched her son struggle for the right words. She wanted to help him, but remained silent.

"Do lawyers lie? I know Dad's a lawyer, but do they ever say things that . . . that . . . you know, they make up so their case is better than the other lawyer's?"

"That's pretty hard to do, Cole. They could get disbarred if anyone found out. Perjury is a very serious offense. Why are you asking? Are you worried about your father?"

"Father? No. What about that lady that was here tonight? The one who talked to me."

"What about her?"

"Would she lie?"

"She works for the biggest and best law firm in Austin.

They've been this family's attorneys since before I was born. No, I don't think she would lie. Why? What's the matter?"

"Everything they put down on those legal papers... They have to have real proof, right?"

"Yes, they do." God, she was sick to her stomach. How must her son feel?

"That's what I thought. I guess I'll be staying on here until it's time to go to college. Dad doesn't need me."

"I'm sorry. It's his loss, Cole. You have to believe that."

"I wanted him to like me. I wanted us to go to ball games and do things."

"I know. I used to want those things myself. My pap never had time for me, either. Mam tried, but I didn't give her a chance. I regret that now. I think your father loves you as much as he's capable of loving anyone."

"He hates me. He only tried to use me to get what he wants."

"No, Cole, you're wrong. It's me he hates. Not you. He used you and you used him. You have to accept that."

"He was going to use Sawyer, too, and make me use her. I hate that!" Cole cried, rubbing at his eyes with the back of his hand. "Sawyer's going to die and I can't do anything."

"That's not true. You're doing one hell of a thing by planning the trip to Hawaii. Mam was impressed when she told me all about it. I wish you had told me, Cole."

"I thought you wouldn't let me do it. I didn't care; I was going to do it anyway. But you said she was off-limits."

"We all say things when we're angry. I regretted it the moment I said it."

"Then I can go?"

"Of course you can go. I'll be cheering you every step of the way. You make this the best, the very best time of Sawyer's life."

"How sick is Sawyer going to get?"

"I don't know. Maybe God will be merciful and won't make her suffer."

"What are you going to do about her?"

Maggie sighed. "It's all I think about, Cole. I'm going to ... I'm going to try and make things right between us. I don't know if it will work, but I'm going to ... to go to New York.... I have to give her some time to adjust to this crisis in her life. I'll go before you leave for Hawaii."

"I want to know about Rand."

"Yes, I guess you do. It's very simple. I love him. I sent him away because I thought no one would understand. I didn't steal him or snatch him away from Sawyer. It just happened. When he came here for the Fourth of July, he told Sawyer that he wanted to break off their relationship. He felt he was too old for her.... He's a fine man. I'm sorry he let me send him away. After it was too late, after he was gone, Mam told me I made a mistake. Cole ... wait here. I want to show you something. Make some more cocoa till I get back."

Maggie raced up the stairs in her bare feet, her nightgown crunched above her knees. She pushed the small button in her desk and a secret door popped out. Her father's last letter lay there ready to be snatched up by her eager fingers. She slammed the drawer shut and loped down the hall, then took the steps two at a time. By the time she came back into the kitchen, she was breathless. If ever she was to get Cole, this was the time. She handed her father's letter to her son, and watched his eyes as he read. She could see his hands trembling much as hers were. When he finished, she folded it and put it back in the envelope.

"Keeping you here was the sunshine. Do you understand? Rand was going to make me happy. That's what it's all about."

"You let him go. You sent him away. Yet, you'd fight for me. Why?"

"You're my son. My flesh and blood. I had to fight for you, for myself as well as you. The love, the feeling, I have for Rand is different. I could send him away because it was best. I'm sorry. I'd give anything to undo some of the things I've done in my life, but some things can never be made right."

"I want to know about Sawyer."

"Cole, it's four o'clock in the morning."

"I want to know."

"All right."

They talked and talked and talked. When Martha walked into the kitchen at six o'clock, Maggie waved her away. At seven o'clock Maggie took Cole by the hand and led him upstairs. She settled him in the bright rust-colored chair in her room. "You aren't going to school today. I'll tell Riley not to wait for you. You're going to read these," she said, handing him her box of diaries. "It's time for you to know who I am. Don't come downstairs till you finish. I'm going riding now. I'll see you later."

Cole drew away from the box. "Mother, I don't think I want to read these."

"I don't want you to read them, either, but you have to if we're ever to be mother and son. I'll send up some breakfast."

Maggie slipped from Lotus's back and tethered her. She crept up to the grassy knoll, her face full of hope. "I think I'm on the way, Pap," she said, crunching down. "I couldn't have done it without you and your letter. In a little while we're going to know how much Coleman is in my son. I took a big chance, and I don't really know if my gamble is going to pay off. Maybe I blew it. Rest easy, Pap; I'll be back."

Lotus nickered softly and danced around in a circle, sensing her mistress's uneasiness. "Let's ride, Lotus." Maggie leaned low, crouched against the horse's silky mane. The animal's hooves pounding the ground sounded like thunder in Maggie's ears. She gave the horse her head.

Riley peered from the school bus window at the lone

rider thundering across the fields. He knew it was his aunt
Maggie. He also knew something was going on. Cole was
staying home . . . and not because he was sick.

It was one o'clock when Maggie climbed the stairs to
the second floor. Her heart hammered in her chest. What
would she see in her son's eyes? What would he say to
her? She opened the door and entered the room.

It was empty. The diaries were piled neatly in their
respective boxes. For a moment she thought she was
going to faint. She hadn't allowed herself to think, even
for a moment, that Cole would cut and run. He was her
son; he wouldn't do that. She ran into the hallway shouting his name.

"Psst, shhh!" Cole hissed loudly, almost as loudly as
his mother was shouting.

"Cole!" Maggie leaned against the door frame, her face
drained of all color. Cole was sitting in the rocking chair
giving Jessie a bottle of water.

"Jeez, I just got her to sleep."

Maggie literally slid down the door frame till she was
sitting on the floor. She waited.

Cole watched his mother for a few seconds. He knew
she was waiting for him to say something. "You're one
hell of a lady, Mam."

Maggie rolled her eyes back in her head. "Don't swear
in front of Jessie."

Cole grinned. "So, you're one heck of a lady. I was
trying to emphasize a point. Did you get it?"

"Yeahhh," Maggie drawled.

"Where'd you go?"

"Up on the knoll."

"Didja get any answers?"

"No. I just talk it out up there. The answers have to
come down here. Welcome to Sunbridge, Cole."

"You want to take this kid? She just wet my pants.
Aunt Susan said I didn't have to worry about her nappies.
That's her pants, right?"

"Yeah. Diapers. In England they call them nappies. Here, I'll take her."

Cole smiled. Maggie smiled back.

"I'm going to school," he said, heading out the door. "I have archery practice, and the coach kicks us off if we miss. I'll take the the moped. See you at supper."

"Shoot one for me," Maggie called.

"Shoot one what?"

"Arrow, you ninny. Go, go already."

Jessie's diaper secure, Maggie laid her on her stomach. Her fist went immediately to her mouth. God, she thought, I have a son. I have my son.

She walked to the window. The sun shining down on Sunbridge was warm and golden.

She watched from the window as Cole rolled his moped out to the driveway. She saw him look up and around. He, too, was noticing for the first time how bright it was.

Sunbridge.

A dusty pickup truck rattled down the road, its bed overloading the springs until the rear license plate was only inches from the ground. It bumped to a halt and the driver, Ben Simms, rolled down the window and peered up at the wooden arch proclaiming the name Sunbridge. Callused hands jammed his worn straw hat farther down onto his grizzled head. He turned to the young girl sitting beside him. "Looks like this is it. Mind your manners now, gal. We need this job."

She wanted to die, just die. At the last crossroads a ranch truck filled with workers had hooted and hollered as the Simms truck strained past them. And no wonder— they looked like a rerun of the *Beverly Hillbillies*. The only thing missing was Old Granny in her rocking chair.

"Luana, you hear me? We need this job and you well know it. Just sit there like the proper little lady you are and let me do the talkin'. When the missus talks to you, just smile and let her know you're willin' to work. Got that?"

"Yes, Pa."

Ben forced the truck in gear and turned into the drive. He glanced at his daughter and was satisfied when he saw her running a comb through her long, sandy-colored hair. Sprucing up, just like her ma. Spittin' image of her ma, too. Luana dropped her comb and sat with her hands in her lap just the way he liked. She was a good girl, he thought, not like her ma. Trixie had been a wild one till the day he'd married her, and then she'd settled down some. But when Luana was six years old she'd cut and run with a farmhand, and he hadn't seen or heard from her since.

"I think we'll like it here, don't you, Luana?" he said enthusiastically. "Look out there at those fields. Hear tell they raise a good strain of cattle out this way. You seen it, ain'tcha? The sun with the single bar? Stands for Sunbridge."

He squinted through the bug-spattered windshield, his wind-roughened features and square bristly chin strong and still beneath the brim of his hat. His caramel-colored eyes narrowed as they rode past outbuildings and stables and miles of white cross-fencing.

"This is some spread, ain't it, Luana?"

"Yes, Pa."

"That all you got to say? Yes, Pa; yes, Pa. You sound like a broken record."

"Yes, Pa." There was an insolent tone in the soft, girlish voice that drew Ben's attention. Saucerlike brown eyes, a color deeper and brighter than his own, continued staring out through the windshield. When she felt him looking at her, she dropped her thick, sooty lashes demurely.

"You know I don't like you wearing them short skirts," he growled, more for her lack of interest and insolence than for the skirt. He eyed her legs and the generous expanse of thigh. "What's these people gonna think, you dressed like that? Ain't no call for you to dress like some tramp. You sit in the truck while I talk business. Don't get out, you hear?"

"Pa, this skirt's the only one I got. Miz Halpern give it to me. You said it was all right; you said! There ain't no hem to let down."

Looked like her ma and had a mouth like her, too. Trixie always had an answer. In another year or two he was going to have his hands full if he didn't come down hard on her now. "Then you should've worn long pants. Sinful. It's a sin to show so much of yourself."

Luana snorted. She stared at her father, her eyes half-closed in the bright early-spring sunshine. She'd been practicing this expression from the cover of *True Confession's* magazine for weeks now; she couldn't wait to try it out on some real men. Pa was always saying this was trampy, that was trashy. Hell, yes. Pa was the tramp and she was the trash. But all that would change when she turned sixteen and got herself away from him and his preachin'. She'd head for the big city, and the first thing she'd buy was the brightest dress she could find and high-heeled shoes to match. She'd get fancy combs and do her hair up like in the magazines, and then she'd buy a whole bagful of Maybelline and go to town on her face. Big gold earrings and some bracelets, maybe even one for her ankle.

"You wearin' a brazzere, gal?" Ben said abruptly; breaking into her thoughts. "You know I don't like it when you're bouncin' around under your shirt. You're a good girl, and I want you to stay that way. You ain't gonna turn out like your ma."

"Yes, Pa. I'm wearin' one. Only it ain't my fault it's all stretched out. I need new duds. You keep sayin' you're gonna get me some, only you don't," Luana complained petulantly.

"We ain't been in one place long enough to put money aside for extras. We're clean and that's what counts, a lot more than fancy duds do. If the folks in town were right about them needin' help out here, we just might have that extra money right soon."

Luana rolled her eyes and slipped on her sunglasses. It was the same tired old story, all the same excuses. This place wasn't going to be any different from all the others.

They'd live in a shack for a few weeks and then they'd move on, mostly because Pa would run up bills and drink all his wages. But Pa was a good worker. Some of the time it wasn't even his drinking—it was when the women got a look at her that they were sent packing. But Pa never got mad about that. He'd say in his best Sunday preacher voice that God gave her her beauty, and she had to bear it and so did he. Then they'd read from Scripture. Every day it was the same thing. Maybe if they stayed here, she could go back to school. She was so far behind now, she didn't know if she could ever catch up. But she was a fast learner, and usually there was some boy who'd offer to help her as long as he could look down the front of her blouse.

Luana had learned early that boys wanted to look real bad. If you let them touch you, they'd give you just about anything you wanted. She'd managed to get three dollars off one boy just for letting him stick his hand down her blouse. She'd bought black mascara and a bag of M&M's from the dime store. She would've had ten dollars from that hunk who hung out by the trailer court in Pineville if his girlfriend hadn't come along. Maybe she was like her ma, she thought defiantly. So what? Pa couldn't give her the things she wanted; she had to find a way to get them for herself.

Luana squirmed in the cracked leather seat. Just thinking about all those things the boys wanted to do to her made her feel funny. She wondered what it would be like to really "do it." She'd had enough offers, but she was holding out. Being a virgin had its good points. She knew she was what men called a tease; boys called her that, too. Her breasts were big, full and ripe. She wanted to look like Dolly Parton. Her waist was tiny and her legs were long and slender. If she just had the right clothes, she knew she'd be a knockout.

The pickup bounced over the road. Ben could see his daughter's breasts jiggle with each bump. His lips tightened. Maybe it *was* time the girl had some new clothes—

clothes that fit. Other things, too. Living like gypsies, from pillar to post, wasn't good for Luana. His pretty little girl deserved better than he was giving her.

"I'll drive around the back," he said as he maneuvered the truck around the circular drive. "You stay inside. Keep the windows rolled up and don't go talkin' to no one."

"Good luck, Pa," Luana said softly, looking around her. Maybe her pa could get work here. The people in town had said something about putting up some cabins for crippled children. It might be fun to live in a nice place like this for a while.

Maggie and Susan talked to Ben Simms for a long time. Susan showed him the sketches of the buildings that were to go up. He looked at them carefully. "I can do it. I do good work, missus. You'll find no fault with anything I do."

"We plan to erect modular units, constructed at the factory and brought out here to the site. It would save a good deal of time. You'd be responsible for helping to lay in the foundations for the buildings and for building fences. I need a kind of jack-of-all-trades, Mr. Simms. Think you can fill the bill?" Susan had already decided to hire him. He looked capable and eager. The work she was offering was menial and the pay low. Most of the skilled laborers and construction workers in this area had already been snapped up by Cary.

"Yes, ma'am," he replied eagerly. "But I'll have to find a place to live. I have a daughter to take care of. She's fourteen and needs to go to school."

Maggie met Susan's gaze. Maggie nodded. "There's a small apartment all furnished over the garage. You could stay there. The school bus stops at the end of the road. Our boys take it."

"Boys! You got boys here? My girl is only fourteen. How old are your boys?" he asked anxiously.

"Sixteen. They're good boys, Mr. Simms," Maggie assured him. "You don't have anything to worry about."

"Boys that age are full of juices. I speak my mind,

missus. I'm a God-fearin' man who reads Scripture, and so does my daughter. If you say they're good boys, I'll take your word for it. About that apartment, now. If I take it, I'll work Saturdays for nothing. Is that fair?"

Susan and Maggie nodded. "When can you start?" Susan asked.

"All I got is out there in that truck. My daughter and our belongings. We can move right in. I can start to work this afternoon."

"That's just fine, Mr. Simms. Why don't you drive around to the garage. The door leading to the upstairs is open. It's probably dusty. I can send our housekeeper over to clean it up for you."

"No need for that. Luana is a good little housekeeper. Just like her ma used to be."

"After you're moved in, you come back here and we'll go into town and order your supplies," Susan told him. "Everything's been staked out."

"If we're going to town, do you think I could register my daughter for school?"

"Of course."

As they followed Ben Simms outside; Maggie and Susan smiled gleefully at each other. "God does work in mysterious ways, doesn't he?" Susan whispered, and both women giggled. Then they saw Luana Simms get out of the truck to help her father carry the cartons and bags up the stairs.

"That's Luana?" Maggie gaspped, gripping Susan's arm. "Didn't he say she was fourteen?"

"That's what he said," Susan said in awe. "More like fourteen going on thirty-four!"

"I never looked like that at fourteen." Maggie giggled. "I was pregnant, though. This smells like trouble to me, Susan. My God, wait till the boys see her at the bus stop tomorrow." She groaned. "You don't think she'd wear that skirt, do you?"

"God, I don't know."

"Maybe I'll wander over there after you two go to

town. You know, offer my help or something."

"Why do I have this feeling I've made a mistake?" Susan muttered.

"I'll give you my expert opinion a little later. If you're going into town with Mr. Simms, I'll have Martha stay with Jessie while I talk to the child."

"That one is no child. Trust me. I like Mr. Simms, though. I bet he gives me a good job." She shrugged. "And if it doesn't work out, we'll ask him to move on."

Maggie's face wore a dubious look. She'd never known Susan to make such a quick judgment before. Normally, she thought about things until you wanted to scream at her to make a decision. She didn't realize her fingers were crossed till one of them started to ache.

When Susan and Ben Simms left for town, Maggie knocked softly on the door of the garage apartment. A muffled voice told her to come in. Maggie drew in her breath and walked inside, not knowing quite what to expect.

Neither did Luana, it appeared. She'd been wiping the kitchen floor and stood up abruptly at the sight of Maggie, stopping only to put the soapy rag back in the bucket. She looked around for a towel; finding none, she wiped her hands on her short denim skirt. "Are you Miz Tanner?" she asked shyly.

"Yes. You must be Luana. I hope you and your father like this place. It's kind of small, but it does have two bedrooms."

"Ma'am, this is the grandest place. The grandest. We ain't never had anything this fine before. I don't know how to thank you."

Maggie stared at the girl, feeling as if she'd just been run over with a tractor by her vehemence.

Luana's chest heaved as she continued to talk at breakneck speed. "We ain't white trash, Miz Tanner. We're poor, but we're good folks. My ma, she run off when I was six. My pa says she was trash, but I don't believe that. She wanted fun and bright-colored clothes and perfume. Pa couldn't give it to her."

"Yes ... well ... I'm sure everything will be fine. Your father is going to be working for my sister...."

"You must be happy living in this swell place. I don't think I ever saw such a beautiful house." She pronounced it bee-yoo-tee-ful.

Maggie laughed. "Yes, I am happy here. Look, your father was concerned about the school. The bus stops right at the end of the road. It picks up my son and my nephew at seven-fifteen and gets back here around four in the afternoon. I think your father is going to register you this afternoon.... Is there anything you want to ask me?"

Luana tilted her head, and Maggie groaned inwardly. The ripe little mouth seemed to pout as the girl thought about what she'd just been asked. "No, I don't think so. I don't want you to worry about me breaking these nice dishes or making a mess. I know how to keep house and cook. I'll keep this place just spotless. You can come here anytime and check it over. How old is your son and nephew?"

Maggie was still working on the house check. "Sixteen," she said without thinking. Whoaaa, she thought. "Are you interested in boys?" she asked carefully.

Luana's voice was soft, without guile, almost shy. "No, not really. Boys seem to like me, though. Pa keeps a tight rein on me. I'm too young to date. I was just wondering how much older they were than me because they might not know where to direct me at school tomorrow."

"They'll know. Trust me," Maggie said flatly.

"What do the kids wear? Is it a fancy school?"

As compared to what? Maggie wanted to ask. She supposed it was fancy or would appear so to someone like Luana. "Neatness counts," she said.

"I'm clean and I'm neat. I don't have much, only hand-me-downs from people Pa worked for."

Maggie almost choked. Honey, she wanted to say, there

isn't going to be anyone looking at your clothes. "Well, if there's nothing more I can do, I'll be going back to the house. If you think of something, let me know. By the way, there's a washer and dryer in the back of the garage. Feel free to use them."

"Ma'am, do you mean that? Do you really mean that?"

"Of course I mean it. Why do you sound so surprised?"

"We ain't never lived anywhere where there was such fine things. I do the wash in the bathtub unless there's a Laundromat, but that's so expensive."

On the walk back to the house, Maggie couldn't make up her mind if her leg had been pulled or not. She puzzled over it all evening. When the boys left the table after dinner she casually mentioned Luana and asked both boys to watch out for her.

"Eighth grade! Mother!" Cole grimaced. "How's it going to look with us squiring an eighth-grade baby around?"

Riley grinned. "You're asking a lot, Aunt Maggie. We've got our images to consider."

"Nevertheless, you'll do as I ask, won't you?" Maggie said pointedly.

"Yes, ma'am, only we're not going to like it."

When the boys left the room, Maggie smiled at Susan. "Wait until they see this eighth-grade baby. At least it's only for one day, and I suppose that won't kill them."

The next morning Cole and Riley were crossing the yard to the garage, where they kept their mopeds. If they'd forgotten their promise to Maggie to look after the daughter of the hired help, they soon remembered. Luana Mae Simms had just stepped out of the long, deep early-morning shadows into the sunshine. The boys stopped in their tracks. Cole had seen girls like this in New York; Riley hadn't even known they existed.

The early-morning sunlight caught the sandy blond of Luana's hair and made it glint with gold. The breeze caught the ends and blew them about her face—not a pretty face, especially, but one that was still softly rounded with youth. Her mouth was full, her lips pouting and ripe, and her thickly lashed eyes were dark and smiling as though she alone knew a delicious secret. She wore faded jeans that hugged her thighs and delineated the globes of her backside. Her blouse was of simple oxford cloth and the first three buttons were open, revealing a suggestion of cleavage between her high round breasts. She walked across the driveway, the heels of her boots tapping on the concrete.

"Are you gonna take me to school?" she asked, looking at the mopeds and then back at the boys. "I ain't never rode on one of those."

"Yeah . . . well, you're supposed to take the school bus," Riley said. "If you need to know anything at school, just ask one of us." With sinking heart, he thought of Kelly Jensen. She wasn't going to like this one bit.

Luana stood in their path, her lower lip jutting out stubbornly. "But I don't know nobody on the school bus. Miz Tanner said you'd look out for me. Can't I ride with one of you?" Her speech was slow, almost indolent, and the boys found themselves waiting almost breathlessly for the next syllable.

Riley shook his head. "I don't think it's a good idea. It can get pretty cold riding on the back of a moped, and that little windbreaker you're carrying won't keep you warm."

"I won't mind," she insisted, turning her attention to Cole, who was standing there as though carved from granite. "You must be Miz Tanner's boy. Your mama said you were nice. I'm Luana. Luana Mae Simms."

Riley, watching Cole, thought he'd never seen such a sappy expression on anyone's face. He felt sort of stupid himself and almost dropped his books when Luana hooked her thumb into the waistline of her jeans and swung her windbreaker over her shoulder, one hip jutting forward, the thin fabric of her blouse straining over her breasts.

"Yes, I'm Mrs. Tanner's boy . . . er, son—I mean, I'm Cole."

"Nice te meetcha, Cole." She smiled, her full lips parting to reveal nice white teeth with very even edges. Her lips were pink, but Cole couldn't see any traces of lipstick.

"Are you from China?" Luana asked Riley.

"No, Japan. Look, Cole, we better get a move on. Luana, you'd better get down to the road or you'll miss the bus."

"I won't mind. Then maybe Cole here would take me to school on his motorbike."

"Moped," Cole corrected. "I'll ride you to the road so you don't miss the bus. Wait till I get 'er started and then hop on."

The mopeds rattled and sputtered to life. Luana straddled the seat behind Cole, her arms clamped around his waist, her full breasts pressing into his back, her strong thighs gripping his bottom. She lowered her head and buried it against his back as protection from the wind. He heard her giggle with delight as they sped down the drive, Riley close behind. When Cole turned out of the drive, the school bus was just coming up the road, but he spun out ahead of it and carried Luana all the way to school.

Riley didn't have to wonder why. Just the sight of Luana's neat little bottom bouncing and swaying on the back of Cole's moped gave him all the answers he'd ever need.

{{{{{{{{{ CHAPTER TWENTY-FOUR }}}}}}}}}

Spring settled over Sunbridge like a bright green cloak.
Maggie always thought it was her favorite time of year
... until she saw the golden foliage of autumn. For now,
the brilliant spring flowers in their neat, trim beds nodded
sociably to one another. New growth on the lush shrubbery gleamed like emeralds in the bright sunlight. Maggie
just *knew* the sun was brighter.

She walked onto the patio, letting the sun's warmth
caress her from the top of her head to the tip of her toes.
Her world was wonderful. Cole was back in her life. He
knew who she was and he still loved her. His gentleness
had stunned her. Her son.

The only thing missing in this perfect setting was Rand.
Twice more she'd tried to call him in the London apartment because Susan had said there was no phone in the
country house. Her shoulders twitched. She was going to
have to accept this rejection the way she had so many
others. A letter, three attempts to call, told her all she
need to know. Too much, too little, too late Maggie.

She should be thinking about going to New York to
see Sawyer. In fact, she should make a reservation today
and go next week. Spring in New York was almost as
wonderful as spring in Texas.

It was such a beautiful morning, she hated to go indoors.
The decision was taken out of her hands momentarily
when she heard a shrill argument wafting from the garage

apartment. Shamelessly she pushed her chair closer to the patio railing so she could hear. Her eyes widened.

"I won't have you acting like a slut. I told you, I warned you, what I'd do if I caught you hanky-pankin' with those boys. Now you bend over and take your punishment. Then we'll read Scripture."

Maggie didn't know which was louder, the sound of the belt whacking through the air or Luana's screams. "Pa, I didn't do nothin'! The boys was just bein' nice. Paaaaa," she wailed. "I was bein' polite because Miz Tanner is bein' so good to us."

"Your nice Miz Tanner is goin' to fire me if you keep on actin' like a slut. I ain't about to let that happen. You ain't goin' to turn out like your ma. You hear me, Luana?"

Maggie cringed. She could almost imagine the red welts on that round, voluptuous bottom. But this was none of her business. How Ben Simms raised his daughter had nothing to do with her. She realized suddenly that she was angry. Angry at Ben Simms for abusing his daughter because of his hatred for his wife.

She was worried about the boys and their open admiration for Luana. These days she could see and feel the tension between them. Just last night Riley had told her he'd asked Luana to go on a picnic with him. Luana, of course, had declined. Cole had smirked, but there'd been a look in his eye Maggie had recognized. He meant to ace his cousin out, if he could.

Maggie had made it her business to observe the girl for over a week now. As far as she could tell, Luana was a little snip, playing one boy against the other. She'd go to archery practice and watch Cole; then she'd go to the baseball diamond and cheer Riley on. In bad weather she rode the bus home. When it was nice outside, she'd hang around school, allowing herself just enough time to walk the three miles or hitch a ride. She'd career into the yard, and before long the smell of frying onions or garlic would sift through the kitchen screen door. Maggie often heard the faint rattle of dishes. Inside twenty minutes, the girl would have the beds made, the breakfast dishes done, laundry going in the machine, and dinner in the oven or on the stove. Then she'd take another few minutes to change her clothes and put on skimpy shorts or the denim miniskirt. By the time Cole and Riley rode their mopeds up the drive at five-thirty, she'd be sitting on the steps reading one of her schoolbooks—at least Maggie had thought it was a schoolbook at first. Cole had told her Luana kept a copy of *True Confessions* magazine folded up inside her schoolbook. At the time Maggie had grinned; she used to devour the pulps by the pound herself. The boys, of course, would head immediately for the garage and talk with Luana until the timer pinged from the kitchen window. Ben Simms walked up those steps promptly at five minutes past six. By that time, the boys were safely in their rooms doing their homework or washing up for dinner. The girl had it down to a science.

Luana's sobs were now shrieks of pain. "All right, Pa, I won't talk to them no more! You tell Miz Tanner they ain't good enough for me. Go ahead, you go and tell her! There goes your job and this swell place. Sometimes I hate you, Pa. Go ahead, hit me some more. I don't care no more! You keep telling me you want me to get book learning, but we move around so much I forget from place to place. Cole and Riley said they'd help me. What's wrong with that?"

Whack. Maggie flinched.

"Get the Good Book and we'll read."

Maggie listened as Ben Simms's voice droned on and on. Once in a while she could hear Luana as she responded to her father.

The following week Maggie made plans to go to New York. She also made it her business to cancel most of her charity work in order to hang around the house. She didn't know why until Wednesday, when she just happened to see Riley skirt the main road and roar across the field on his moped. He had a rider on the back, whom Maggie knew instantly was Luana.

Riley never cut school. And he certainly never cut baseball practice. She looked at her watch,—1:15. Where were they going?

For hours she paced Sunbridge like an expectant father. Finally, at five-fifteen, Maggie heard the roar of Riley's moped. She sighed heavily. Time for both of them to get back—Riley to his room, Luana to her frying onions.

On Friday, Luana left for school in a new dress, a brilliant red silky thing, and matching high-heeled shoes.

On Saturday, Maggie canceled her trip to New York and rescheduled it for the following week.

On Monday afternoon it was Cole who cut across the field with Luana on the back of his moped. On Wednesday, when Luana left for school, she was wearing Calvin Klein jeans and a LaCoste pullover.

That morning, as Maggie was brooding over what she'd seen, Susan joined her on the patio, a cup of coffee in hand. "What happened to good deeds lately? Why are you so antsy? What's going on you haven't told me?"

Maggie filled her in.

"You mean that little bitch is peddling her ass?" Susan asked outraged.

"It looks that way," Maggie said morosely. "I know one thing, though. Both boys think they're 'it' as far as Luana goes. I shudder to think what's going to happen when they find out they're at opposite ends of the rope."

"Does her father . . . Of course not. She'd be black and blue if he did. Maybe I should talk to him."

"No, Suse, don't do that." Maggie told her about the beating Luana had gotten from Ben Simms.

Susan sipped her coffee, nearly scalding her tongue. "Maggie, that man is an absolute powerhouse. He's already laid two foundations for the modular buildings, and his work is exact. Ferris is very impressed. Because of Ben Simms, we can expect to have the modules ready by Labor Day."

Labor day. That was five months away. A lot could happen in five months. Then Maggie remembered that the boys were leaving for Hawaii in June. Still, even two-and-a-half months was a long time. A girl could get pregnant in two-and-a-half months. Maybe she should have a talk with Luana.

At four o'clock on Saturday afternoon, Ben Simms knocked at the back door and asked for Susan.

"Missus, I have to go to town. I need to order some more supplies. I want to bring back a keg of nails so I have them first thing Monday morning. I'll be owing you two hours of time, but I'll make them up Monday. I need to buy some groceries at the supermarket, too. Luana tells me it's open till ten o'clock."

"That's fine, Mr. Simms. Have the lumberyard send me the bill. You can take off early whenever you want. Here's your pay, cash like you asked for."

Ben thanked her, tipped his hat. "I wonder if you'd give Miz Tanner a message for me."

"Surely, Mr. Simms."

"Tell her I was wrong with the boys. They're very respectful of Luana. I don't cotton to that one with the slanted eyes, but Luana says he's real good with numbers and she needs help. If the boys still have a mind to help her, they can come over after supper and work at the kitchen table. I'll be right there."

Luana watched her father as he headed for the bathroom. He'd told her to make a grocery list, and she had—a nice long one.

She hummed to herself as she stirred the onions in the pan. Pa would do just like he said—he'd get his keg of nails, the groceries, and load everything in the back of the truck. But after that, he'd stop at the roadside cafe and wouldn't be home till past midnight or maybe not till morning, if he found a woman. So she had six hours she could definitely count on, perhaps the entire night.

Her mind raced as she fried the last of the hamburger meat. She smiled, remembering the set of lacy black underwear she'd bought in Austin on Friday. Maybe she'd wear it tonight. . . .

The minute supper was over, Luana leaped up to do the dishes. She'd just finished wiping the last one dry when Ben stuck her grocery list into his pocket. "You be a good girl while I'm gone. Keep the door locked. Study your homework and read your Scripture because I'm going to ask you questions in the morning."

"Yes, Pa," Luana answered obediently. She was stunned when Ben handed her a twenty-dollar bill.

"Next week you buy yourself some new duds."

"Thanks, Pa." She perched on tiptoe and kissed Ben's cheek.

He reddened with pleasure. "Trixie'd always do that when I g've her something," Ben said and patted her cheek awkwardly. "You're all I got, gal."

"I know, Pa. Don't you go worryin' about me. Both of us is going to be all right from here on out. When words gets around what a good worker you are, jobs will be lining up from here to kingdom come. You watch. Maybe Miz Tanner will let us rent this place permanently."

"You like it here, do you, gal?"

"I really do, Pa. This is the first place that seems like home since Ma left. I keep it nice, don't I?"

"You do. You make me proud."

Luana kissed him again and obediently locked the door behind him. She didn't move till she heard the pickup truck drive out of the courtyard. Then she stripped and showered and powdered herself all over with talcum from the dime store. "Djer Kiss." It smelled nice and she liked the name because it had the word kiss in it.

Her fingers itched to touch the lacy black underwear. After she slipped it on, she looked into the big, round mirror over the chest of drawers. She had to hop on the bed for a full look. The silky black made her skin look whiter, and the bra pushed her breasts up and together, making them fuller. The little black bikini pants barely covered her where they should, but they made her legs look longer and slimmer.

She wobbled on the lumpy mattress and fell into a heap,

laughing, delighted with herself and her purchase. She pulled on the Calvin jeans and rummaged for a dark plaid blouse, worn but ironed. She didn't want the lacy bra to show through. The blouse was primly buttoned to the neck; her long, almost flaxen hair was pulled into a high ponytail. She tugged at a few loose ends near her ears and did the same with a light fringe of bangs. Her face was shiny clean—better not wear makeup around Miz Tanner. But she did curl her eyelashes.

Five minutes later Luana knocked timidly at the back door, waiting for Martha to answer. She wondered what time it was. Maybe by this time next week she'd have a watch.

"I'm here to see Riley and Cole, ma'am," she said politely when Martha answered the door. "I'll wait out here on the porch."

"Mrs. Tanner," Martha said into the intercom, "that little girl from across the way is here to see Riley and Cole."

"I'll be right down, Martha."

"Is something wrong, Luana?" Maggie asked when she reached the service porch.

"No, ma'am. Cole said maybe he'd help me with homework tonight if he wasn't doing anything."

Maggie stared at the girl, trying to see beneath the surface innocence. But when she remembered the way Ben Simms had whipped his daughter, sympathy overrode her suspicions. She knew it shouldn't, especially since both Riley and Cole were involved, but she felt she should take up the issue with them and not Luana.

Luana met Maggie's gaze, her eyes level and innocent. "Would you call Cole, Miz Tanner?" She asked gently. "Can I see how you used that gadget on the wall? They have something like that in school. Is it the same thing?"

"The intercom? Yes, I suppose so, but on a much smaller scale." Before Maggie realized what she was doing, she'd called Cole on the intercom. Within seconds, she heard his feet down the stairs.

"Hi, Cole. I came to see if you'd help me with my

homework," Luana cooed, her big brown eyes flashing, just the hint of a smile touching her full, youthful mouth.

Cole was staring at Luana as though she were Christie Brinkley, and it irritated Maggie. She wanted to shake him till his teeth rattled.

"It's okay with me," he agreed readily. "I wasn't doing anything tonight. Wait for me. I have to go get a book. I'll be right down."

Cole sprinted up the stairs. He could feel his Jockey shorts filling out. It had gotten to the point lately where he couldn't even think of Luana without a feeling of tension in his loins. She hadn't ever let him go all the way, but she'd taught him things he'd never learned from *Playboy*. Quickly he calculated the amount of money he had in his wallet, money he'd been saving for his trip to Hawaii with Sawyer. Fifty dollars ready cash. He wondered exactly what Luana would give him for fifty dollars.

Maggie watched Cole and Luana cross the courtyard to the apartment over the garage. She wanted to call her son back. Instead, she comforted herself with the knowledge that Ben Simms would be there; nothing would happen under his watchful eye.

"Gee, Cole, for a minute I thought your ma wasn't goin' to let you help me with my homework." Luana laughed. "There was sparks shootin' from her eyes like the Fourth of July. Does she always get jealous when her baby boy is gonna be with a girl?"

Cole bristled. "Cut it out. You don't have a mother, so you don't know how they are. And I'm not her baby boy."

"Are you a man, then, Cole?" They'd reached the door to the apartment on the far side of the garage. In the shadows Luana turned and pushed herself against him, looking up into his face. "Are you, Cole? Are you a man yet?"

"What do you think?" he growled, wrapping an arm around her waist and pulling her hard against him so she could feel his erection.

"I think you're impatient, that's what." She giggled,

sliding through the doorway and racing up the stairs.

Cole followed her neat Calvined bottom, reaching for her when she stopped at the top landing.

"Now, you be a good boy, hear?" she said coyly. "I don't want you gettin' all mad at me the way you did day before yesterday. It wasn't nice to leave me out there by my lonesome. I had to walk all the way home."

"I went back for you, but you'd already left. I didn't know which way you went."

Luana raised her brows, giving him the wide-eyed innocent expression that Cole knew was just another way of teasing him. There was nothing innocent about Luana.

"Well, never mind," she told him. "I managed to get back on my own. That's what matters, ain't it? I don't suppose I'm mad at you anymore."

She led him into the kitchen and saw him wrinkle his nose. The smell of fried onions lingered in the air. "It's my pa," she said quickly. "He likes them stinky old onions. Sometimes I think I'll never get the smell off me. Did I?" She pushed her palm under his nose, knowing that it held traces of "Djer Kiss." "Is it in my hair?" she asked, sliding up close and laying her head against his chest. She could feel his heart pounding as though it were going to burst.

"You smell good to me," he muttered.

"Well, I don't like how this kitchen smells, anyway. Let's go into my room; I want to show you this story I've been readin'. The boy in the picture looks just like you, Cole; that's why I bought the magazine."

He followed her into the sparsely furnished bedroom. On the narrow iron bedstead were several pairs of socks and the new pink blouse she'd worn to school the other day. Scattered about were schoolbooks and papers, and on the dresser was her hairbrush and a large bottle of shampoo.

Quickly, she reached beneath the mattress and brought out several magazines: *True Confessions*, *Secret Love*, *Intimate*. "My pa don't like me readin' these. He says they're dirty." She giggled. "Maybe they are, a little." She riffled through the pages. "Here, this is what I wanted to show you."

Cole sat down on the edge of her bed. He didn't want to look in magazines; he wanted to look under Luana's blouse. She stuck the picture under his nose.

"See, don't he have nice light hair like you? And don't he look a little like you around the mouth? And don't the girl look like me, even a little?"

Cole wasn't sure the boy in the photograph looked like him, although the girl did look something like Luana: long blond hair, full petulant lips, eyes half-closed. But it was what they were doing in the picture that quickened his pulses. The boy was leaning over the girl; he was shirtless, his bare back glistening with sweat. And the girl was lying on her back, one leg lifted to rest on the boy's shoulder, the other wrapped around his waist. Her panties were white, and it looked as though the boy were about to pull them down to see the origin of the darker shadow between her legs.

"Don't you think we look like these two? Don't you." Luana was saying. "Let's see if we do. I could tilt that mirror and we could see ourselves. Take your shirt off, Cole. I want to see." She stood and kicked off her sneakers and pulled down her Calvins. She watched for Cole's reaction to her lacy black underpants and was satisfied when she saw him staring at them. "I'll just tilt the mirror this way...." She flopped down on the bed and looked toward the wall. "Yes, that's right. I can see myself. Can you see, Cole?"

He had stripped to the waist; the room air felt chilly against his skin. In order to look into the mirror, he had to lean over Luana, his face very close to her breasts. He saw the playful look in her eyes and took his cue. "Your blouse has to be opened, like the girl in the picture." He undid the buttons, revealing her flesh inch by little inch.

"Cole! That girl don't have her blouse open all the way!"

"But you do. Here, put your leg up like she does. Is this the way?"

"Cole, don't you be naughty. We're only seein' if we look like the picture."

"You're prettier than the girl in the picture, Luana. And you have prettier underpants."

"You think so? Me, too. I got these underpants and bra for you, Cole, with the money you gave me last time. I like having nice things to wear for you."

"I like when you wear nice things, Luana." He felt himself become breathless. He was watching her small rounded belly as it moved with each breath. She was getting that look in her eyes that said she wouldn't mind if he touched her.

"Don't we look like the picture? Don't we, though? Look, Cole, look in the mirror!"

He dragged his gaze away from her to the glass on the wall. He found it strangely exciting to see himself there with Luana as though he were only an interested observer. He watched his hands graze over her skin, saw her wriggle beneath his touch. He pulled her bra straps over her shoulder and exposed her breasts. Still watching himself in the mirror, he touched her, seeing the palms of his hands graze over the stiff little nubs of her pink nipples. He saw her watching him, her eyes directed also to the mirror.

"Oooh. It's like being in the movies, ain't it?" She sighed.

This was like no movie Cole had ever seen. He'd only heard about them from the other boys at school. But this had to be better. This was Luana and her beautiful body, lying here with him. It was his own hands touching her, feeling her. He rolled her over onto her side and undid the hooks of her bra, freeing her breasts of their confinements. In the old barn Luana had allowed him to do this, but she'd never let him take all her clothes off. If he stripped her of her panties, she insisted on wearing her bra and blouse. And if it was her breasts she allowed him, then her jeans remained firmly in place. But tonight would be different.

"Cole! What are you doin'! That's not how it is in the picture!"

"You should see some of the pictures in my magazines, Luana. You're a whole lot prettier than any of the girls in those books, too. And they don't wear anything, nothing at all."

"Nothing! When are you gonna show me? I want to see those pictures."

"I'll show you, right now. Just keep looking in the mirror."

Luana turned her head toward the wall, watching him through the mirror. She lifted her hips to allow him to take off her underpants. When he lifted one of her legs and rubbed a knuckle against her, she squirmed and sighed. She liked it when Cole played with her. He wasn't afraid to see what was between a girl's legs, the way Riley was. Riley only wanted to play with her breasts, and sometimes he bored her. Other times he left her, nerves jangling and strung out tight, and she never felt better until she'd had a nice hot bath.

Cole was different. He let her see how much he liked to look at her. And he knew where to touch her, like now. He was making her feel all funny inside, and there was a heat growing at her center. She wanted to press herself against his hand, and she wanted him to kiss her nipples the way he liked to do at the old barn. But she was afraid she was losing control, and that would never do. She liked the power she held over Cole, and if she gave too much too soon, the money and pretty gifts would stop.

"Do I look like the girls in your magazines?" she asked, her voice hardly more than a whisper.

"Better than the girls in the magazines." Cole's voice was choked. He was mesmerized by the sight of her, by the excitement of being with a girl who was naked. He imagined Luana pressing herself against his hand, allowing him to open her with his fingers. The tension in his loins was becoming unbearable; his jeans were too tight, squeezing him. He explored her sweet pink-lined cleft, feeling her grow wet and warm. He found the place he knew she liked to be touched and then watched the reflection in the glass. Luana's hips began to move, rotating, her legs stretching out, spreading, hiding nothing from his touch or his view. Suddenly, she clamped her thighs shut, imprisoning his hand, squeezing it against her with contractions of her muscles. When the moment had passed, she looked up at him, her eyes languorous and glazed. "You do such nice things, Cole. Such nice things for Luana."

"Now do something nice for me," Cole said hoarsely. The rigidness in his loins was unbearable. He grasped her hand and drew it toward him, already anticipating relief.

"No, I can't!" She pulled her hand away as though it had been scorched. "I don't know what time it is!"

"I do. It's early, it's early." He searched again for her hand.

"No! I have to know exactly what time it is! My pa might come home. I'm always worried about the time, Cole, always!"

Cole glanced at his watch, a handsome gold Piaget. "It's not even nine o'clock."

"If I had a nice watch, I'd know what time it was." Luana smiled. "And I could be nice like you want me to be."

Cole got the message. He dug into his hip pocket. "Here's fifty dollars. Now you can be nice, can't you?"

She stuck the money under her pillow and reached for the belt on Cole's jeans. As her hand searched to free his sex from his jeans, she leaned over him and whispered, "I know how to be nice, Cole. Just you wait. I know how to be very, very nice."

Ben Simms was almost sober when he drove his pickup onto Sunbridge land. It would be light in another twenty minutes or so. Dawn. Sunday morning. He'd have to sleep an hour or so and go heavy on Scripture to cleanse himself of his animal lust. He was disgusted with himself for doing all the things a man does when he hasn't been with a woman for a couple of months. If a man ever does anything like that to Luana, he thought darkly, I'll kill him with my bare hands and ask questions later.

His stomach felt sour and his mouth tasted the way mouse fur smelled. For a moment he wondered guiltily if Luana realized he hadn't come home last night.

Then he told himself defensively that every man needed to go on a rip every so often. It might be sinful, but it proved he was a man.

He cut the engine of his truck and glided down the little rise leading to the garage. He stumbled out and tried the front door. Good, he nodded in satisfaction. Luana had locked it. He fished around for his key, jiggled it a little, and finally got the door open.

The place looked the same as when he'd left. The dishes from supper had been put away. Luana's schoolbooks, pencils, and notebooks were stacked neatly on the kitchen table. The small living room was neat and the television was off. He walked around the corner and peeked into Luana's room.

She was lying almost spread-eagle, the sheet and light blanket half-on and half-off. She looked like an angel in sleep, he thought. Then he saw black lace panties and a black shoulder strap, and his eyes widened. He walked boldly into the room, staring down at his daughter in her fancy underwear. One lone, shapely leg with a light feathering of pubic hair showing at the panty line made him draw in his breath. Suddenly Luana rolled over, her buttocks exposed, the sheet falling away from her breasts. Anger spilled out of him when one pink-tipped breast escaped its lacy prison.

Ben leaned over, reached for a hank of Luana's hair, and pulled her off the bed. All he saw was pink flesh. "Where did you get those sinful things?" he demanded.

"What sinful things?" Luana asked cursing inwardly for having been dumb enough to put the set back on after Cole had left. "What's wrong, Pa?"

"That underwear," Ben said through clenched teeth. "You cover yourself back up before I turn your flesh as black as what you're wearin'."

Luana hastily complied. "Miz Tanner give it to me,

Pa. She said it was just to sleep in. She said it cost sixty dollars but don't fit her no more. It's just to sleep in, Pa," Luana whined. "I wouldn't never wear this under clothes. Never, Pa, I swear it."

Ben looked down at his daughter's frigntened eyes. Luana never lied to him. If she said Miz Tanner give it to her, then she did. Just for sleeping.

"I don't want to see you in that outfit ever again. You ain't old enough for the likes of that. That's something your ma would have worn. Under her clothes," he said tightly.

"Well, I ain't like Ma. I just wore it to sleep like Miz Tanner said. You see for yourself, Pa." She smiled up at him, a sweet, innocent smile. "You want I should make you some breakfast, Pa?" she asked.

Sleep was out of the question—he was wide awake now. "Yeah, might as well. Make up a kettle of grits and some bacon and eggs. I'm gonna take a shower. The groceries are in the back of the truck. You can bring them up."

"Okay, Pa. I'll have it ready by the time you're done shaving. Are we going to church?"

"Not this Sunday. We'll read the Bible. It's just as good as going to church and neither one of us has Sunday clothes."

Luana sighed with relief. Every Sunday she asked the same question, and every Sunday she got the same answer. She knew her pa.

The bacon was fried just the way her father liked it, light brown and crisp. The eggs were scrambled in butter, not bacon grease. The kettle with the grits was sitting in the middle of the table on a pot holder. She'd even folded up a paper towel for a napkin and placed it under the fork. When she heard the bathroom door open, she knew she had a few seconds to run downstairs and snatch a few flowers from Miz Tanner's garden. She set them on the table in a water glass.

Ben walked into the kitchen and stood there a moment,

taking in the scene. No doubt about it, his daughter was one a man could be proud of. He felt more of a man today than he'd felt in a long time. Clean clothes, a shower, and a good meal made by someone who loved him.

Luana ate with her eyes downcast. From time to time she'd steal a look at her pa. He wasn't a bad-looking man. In fact, he was kind of handsome in a craggy sort of way. She wished he wasn't so God-fearing and straitlaced, but he'd always tried to provide for her.

Sunday brunch at Sunbridge was usually pleasant and drawn out, an opportunity for Riley and Cole to regale Maggie and Susan with the week's activities—sports, school events, what parties were coming up, school dances, and the eternal question, When are we going to get cars of our own?

This Sunday was different. There was an added dimension to the hostility between Riley and Cole, and Maggie knew it had to do with their competition for Luana. She felt responsible; she knew she should have intervened before this. But she'd been afraid her interference would somehow rock the wonderful new relationship she had with Cole.

Now she listened uneasily as Cole mentioned that he'd been with Luana, helping her with her homework. Riley, she noticed, nearly gagged on his food, his deep olive complexion reddening alarmingly. Another mouthful of milk and his fork clattered on his plate. "Last night? You didn't say anything about helping Luana before I left to go out with Kelly," he said angrily. "I've got to hand it to you, cuz; you really know how to get the jump on somebody."

Susan fidgeted and leaned over to check little Jessie, who lay in the bassinet beside her chair. She didn't like it when the boys argued, and she blamed herself for hiring Ben Simms and bringing Luana onto Sunbridge.

"How are her studies going?" Maggie asked Riley, trying to speak calmly.

"Okay," he said sullenly. "She's behind in her math and it isn't easy to catch up."

"Does she understand the basics—addition, subtraction?"

"More or less," Riley answered evasively. He knew he wasn't a very good liar. He hadn't spent fifteen minutes helping Luana with math. If there was anything to be taught, it was Luana doing the teaching.

"Cole, how's her English coming?" Maggie prodded.

"Fair. She still has a long way to go." He glanced at Riley and knew they were having much the same thoughts. But he was one up on his cousin, he thought with satisfaction. Last night had been something else. Luana had never let him go so far before, and every time he thought about how they'd looked together in the mirror over her dresser, he could feel the heat build in his body.

Maggie set her cup down. "I think it might be a good idea for Luana to have a certified tutor. In fact, I'll insist on it when I speak to her father."

"But then they'll have to pay, and they don't have the money," Riley said, a note of desperation in his voice.

Cole looked trapped. "Tutors are expensive. They don't have that kind of money."

Maggie looked from one boy to the other, disgusted. "How much money have you given Luana?" she asked sharply. "And why did you give it to her? Do you both think I'm blind? How much longer did you think you'd get away with it before Mr. Simms noticed the way you look at his daughter? And all those new clothes she's wearing. The man's not stupid." She took a deep breath. "I've seen *both* of you take her back to the old barn. I know you've been cutting school."

As if at some unheard signal, the boys pushed back their chairs and faced each other. Cole's arm shot out, but Riley blocked the blow.

"You stupid son of a bitch!" Cole hissed. "I knew you'd get caught. And you squealed to get the edge on me. I knew you Japs couldn't be trusted."

Maggie gasped and stood up. Susan quickly moved the baby's bassinet out of the way. Little Jessie began to cry.

Riley suddenly swiveled, striking a karate pose, one arm extended, the other held close to his chest. The sound that came from his throat was menacing and frightening. He straight-armed Cole and then spun around, catching his cousin's midsection with the heel of his foot. "I told you to lay off me and I mean it! You ever call me that again and I'll kill you!"

Suddenly Maggie looked up from the boys and saw a figure standing in the doorway. Ben Simms. How much had he heard?

As Cole rolled on the floor, Riley stood over him, daring his cousin to retaliate.

Simms crossed the room and reached for Riley. Sensing movement behind, Riley spun around, one arm stiff, the fingers splayed. Maggie thought he looked carved from stone. Deadly. Capable of killing. Something in his eyes stopped Ben Simms, and they stood facing each other, two figures frozen in time.

It was Maggie who finally moved, going to Cole and helping him to his feet. She sat him down in his chair, then spoke to Riley. "That's enough. Sit down. You boys are too rough on each other, and I won't have you fighting at the table." She hoped she was conveying to Simms that this was a family dispute, plain and simple.

"You wanted to talk to us, Mr. Simms?" she asked, turning to him with a gracious smile.

"Yes'm. I come over here to thank you for them clothes you gave my daughter and to ask you not to give her any more. Some of them things ain't suitable for a gal her age, especially some of them nightclothes."

Maggie stiffened. Then, after a long moment, she said, "All right, Mr. Simms, I won't give Luana any of my clothes."

"And I'd be real obliged if you'd keep these two boys away from her. Especially that one." He jerked his thumb in Riley's direction. "And I'm sad to say I don't think you own boy is any better. Luana's young, real young, and she ain't wise when it comes to boys. You know what I'm saying, Miz Tanner?"

She smiled grimly. "Yes, Mr. Simms. I know."

"I'm takin' you on your word, Miz Tanner. When I went into town last night, I didn't know a minute's peace leavin' Luana all by herself at home. If you don't bring those boys into line, Luana and me will have to move on."

Silence lay heavy in the room long after Ben Simms left. Then Maggie's anger erupted.

"I hope you're both satisfied. And I hope that poor man doesn't really know what's been going on here, or I feel sorry for Luana." She told the boys of the time she'd heard Ben beating his daughter. "I should have stopped it, I know, but it's hard to know where to draw the line. It isn't easy interfering between a father and daughter. Now I'm afraid for the girl and there's no one to blame but you. She's not blameless, but you both know the difference between right and wrong. From now on that girl is off-limits to both of you. Understand? Off-limits!"

She stalked out of the dining room, her thoughts rioting with images of Luana and Riley and Cole. She felt sorry for Luana, even sympathized with her. At Luana's age she hadn't been much different, a little girl searching for something. But sympathy only went so far—looking out for herself and the boys took precedence. And they're was no getting around it: Luana was a scavenger.

The thought made Maggie's blood run cold.

{{{{{{{{ CHAPTER TWENTY-FIVE }}}}}}}}

The first day of May was all an early spring day should be. The new grass was a tender green, the windswept sky a vital blue, and the air fragrant with Grandmam Jessica's early roses.

It was a perfect day for traveling. Maggie's bags were packed and ready to be put in the car. Cole joked that it looked like a mountain of Louis Vuitton. Despite her high spirits, however, Maggie dreaded her stopover in New York. Eight hours to see and talk to Sawyer before she went to Hawaii. Eight hours to try to set things right when a lifetime hadn't been enough.

She checked her purse. Airline tickets, travelers' checks, a full line of credit from the bank in case the cost of refurbishing the house was more than she anticipated. Car rental reservation, a map of the island, directions to the Kamali house. She had everything she needed. Everything except Rand. He came to mind suddenly, as he always did, when some foolish thing or word reminded her of him. She'd sent him away and hadn't returned. She couldn't even find it in her heart to blame him. How could he know, how could he trust, that she knew her own mind and now had the courage to follow her heart?

Maggie snapped her handbag shut and turned to Cole and Riley. "I'm not going to lecture you or beg you to behave while I'm gone. I trust you. Both of you. If you know what's right, you can't do wrong. Remember that. Don't bring shame on Sunbridge."

She embraced both boys, lingering a moment longer with Cole, looking deeply into his eyes. She smiled at what was reflected there and gave his shoulder a gentle squeeze. "I'll call after I see Sawyer. So stick around, okay?" She looked around at the gentle slope rising behind the house, at the fair expanse of lawn and the miles of white fencing creeping off into the distance. "I hate leaving here. I love it so."

"You'll be back before you know it," Susan said cheerfully. "Good luck, Maggie. But don't expect too much. Some things can never change."

Maggie smiled at her sister, then leaned in close. "C'mon, Jessie, give Aunt Maggie a big buss." The infant gurgled happily in Susan's arms. "Take care of things, Suse. So long, guys."

Cole watched the big limousine take his mother down the drive. She seemed to be taking something with her.

It was Susan who noticed Cole squinting up at the sky. "You still don't get it, do you? Maggie is the sunshine. She just took a little bit of it with her."

Adam Jarvis sprinted down the stairs to answer the bell. He looked through the peephole. "Oh, Jesus!" It was Maggie. He recognized her at once from the pictures Sawyer used to carry in her wallet. That had been many years ago, but there was no mistaking the shining dark hair and summer blue eyes, or the striking resemblance to Sawyer. He sighed deeply and opened the door. "Mrs. Tanner. I'm Adam Jarvis."

"Hello, Adam. I was hoping to see Sawyer. Is she at home?"

Adam hesitated. "Yes, she's up there. I was just on my way out to jog." He wavered as a thought struck him. "Mrs. Tanner . . . before you go up, could we go down to the corner and have a cup of coffee? There's something you should know."

Maggie walked beside Adam to the coffee shop, in reality a Jewish delicatessen complete with the tantalizing aromas of cured meats and garlic pickles. Adam found them a table and held the chair for her. Maggie was quite taken with him, aside from knowing how much Billie liked this young man. He was near Sawyer's age and she knew, already quite successful. Tall, broad-shouldered, good-looking, and with such an expression of tenderness in his eyes that she wondered how Sawyer was able to resist him. He loved Sawyer; Billie had said so, and now Maggie could see it for herself.

"I don't want to be there when you see Sawyer," Adam said abruptly after he'd ordered two coffees. "Okay, so I'm a coward, but she's been putting me through hell and I don't know how much more I can take." Those broad shoulders seemed to slump, his chin lowered to his chest. "I guess I'll take whatever she wants to dish out, won't I? It's no secret. I'm crazy about her."

Maggie stretched her hand over the table and touched Adam's. "Yes, it's pretty evident how you feel. Adam, I'm so sorry."

"I didn't drag you down here to get your sympathy, Mrs. Tanner."

"Maggie, please."

"Maggie, there's something you must know. Sawyer's going to be livid when she finds out I've told anyone, but that's a chance I have to take. She's had tests, more tests. We went to the Sloan-Kettering Institute, where they do a lot of experimental work. The group of doctors there have reached the conclusion that Sawyer's tumor might be operable. They give her a twenty percent chance of success."

Maggie's eyes brightened with joy and relief. "That's hope, real hope!"

"Not according to Sawyer. She refuses to have the surgery."

"Why? I can't believe—"

"I don't know why, and I don't much give a damn what her reasons are!" he exploded. All the worry and concern, all the defeat, everything he felt was there on his face, in the agonized tone of his voice. "She swore me to secrecy, but I had to tell someone. We've been arguing for days."

"This is stupid. I'll have to call her grandmother. If anyone can talk some sense into her, Mam can. When do they want to operate?"

"As soon as Sawyer will allow it. Fortunately, that thing in her head is growing slowly, but there's no doubt it will be fatal if she doesn't do something."

"You want me to talk to her?"

Adam nodded, his eyes glazing with tears. "I love her, Maggie. But she's so filled with resentments and hates, she wants to punish the world. It's almost as if she wants to die to get even with everyone who's ever hurt her. Does that make sense?"

"No," Maggie told him sadly. "But these things never do. C'mon, walk me back to the loft. Then you can go for your jog. I think I should see Sawyer alone."

Lugging the carry-on bag over her shoulder, Maggie climbed the stairs and let herself into the apartment. It was a beautiful loft. A loving place. She could feel it.

She walked around slowly until she found the dining area. Sawyer was at the table having coffee, dressed in a lavender sweat shirt and jeans. It was impossible to believe she wasn't in the best of health. Her golden hair was shining, her skin clear and luminescent in the sunlight streaming through the windows. She registered no surprise when she looked up and saw her mother.

"Slumming?"

"Hardly. This is a beautiful home you've made here with Adam."

"Why are you here? What do you want? Whatever it is, I'm all tapped out."

"Sawyer, I want to talk, about us."

"You're a little late, Mother." Sawyer was trembling so inside, she had to use both hands to hold her coffee cup.

"You aren't going to help me, are you?"

"You're right about that. I told you, it's too late."

"It's never too late. Look, Sawyer, I won't beg you. All I can do is ask that you *try* to understand. I'm sorry—"

"Sorry!" Sawyer laughed, a bitter sound that sent chills down Maggie's back. "Who's that supposed to make feel better? Me? You? Go get absolution somewhere else."

"Look, Sawyer, I can't undo what's past, but I want to try to... to at least have an understanding with you. The past is gone; the future isn't here yet—all we have is the present. Why can't we work on that?"

"For some reason that doesn't make me feel better. I'm going to die. I won't be in your life anymore. That shouldn't bother you. It never bothered you before. I hate you," Sawyer cried vehemently. "Don't you understand that?

"And you know something else? I'd have worked my butt off to get Cole away from you. You won that round, too. You always win, Maggie. You're a bitch—a living, breathing bitch. If someone has to die, it should be you."

Maggie flinched at the hatred in Sawyer's eyes and the venom dripping from her tongue. But she didn't turn away. "I thought the same thing," she said quietly. "That I should be the one to go. I did make life miserable for everyone. If you'd let me try to explain... maybe you could..."

"Forgive you? Never. I don't know a lot about motherhood, but I know this: either you're a mother or you aren't. You never even bothered to pretend."

"Everything you've said is true. Maybe I am a bitch. But as long as you want to fight in the gutter, let's tell it like it is, okay? I did hate you, but it was a crazy kind of hate all mixed up with love I didn't understand. For God's sake, I was only a child myself. What did I know about babies? You got it all. You got to live at Sunbridge; I was sent away. You had everything that should have been mine. You had Mam. You helped bring Pap's dream to life. I couldn't share any of that. You were loved, doted on. I was the outcast. Everything that should have been mine was given to you."

Sawyer's voice was filled with ice. "No good, Maggie. It's all bullshit. The only thing I ever wanted was you. You couldn't be bothered. What was your excuse when you were finally on your own?"

Maggie spread her hands. "It was too late. Mam filled my shoes. I had to live with that. There wasn't a day that I didn't think of you. Most of them I spent hating you; I admit that. I fed off that hatred for a long time, just the way you're doing now. I understand. Maybe, in some small way, I can help."

"I don't want your help. I don't want anything from you except to be left alone. You have it all now. Grand, Sunbridge, Rand, Cole. Even Riley thinks you're the best thing since peanut butter. They just don't know you. You said I was a thief, that I stole your life from you. What about you? You just walked in and took over. Man-eater Maggie. Get out of here and don't ever come back."

Maggie stood her ground. "If you're referring to Rand, let's get one thing straight right now. I didn't snatch him from you. If you want to be crude about it, he dumped you. And he had his own reasons for doing it, Sawyer— Rand and I were nothing more than friends at the time. Later on . . . yes. I did go to bed with him. Several times, as a matter of fact. The first time was out of anger, anger with you. I had your man, the one who dumped you. At the time I thought you had your whole life ahead of you, that one rejection wasn't going to kill you. I was still hating, you see, even then. But he made me take a good long look at my feelings. And when I did, I saw that I cared for him. But I didn't want the wrath of God coming down on me, so I sent him away. And that's the truth.

"You say you want honesty. You want truth, right? Okay. Well, now I'm going to give you some more. Mam said if Rand made me happy, I should go after him. She told me I deserved to be happy. I couldn't believe it at first. I love that man, Sawyer, but I sent him away because of you. Everything is always because of you. I'd cut off my right arm to keep you alive if I could. Rand loves me;

honest-to-God loves me. But I was willing to give him up. Hell, I did give him up. I wrote to him afterward, but he hasn't answered. That should make you happy. He doesn't want me either now. *I did not steal him from you.*"

"I loved him, too," Sawyer said through clenched teeth.

"Sometimes that isn't enough. Rand loved you, but in a different way. I tried to be jealous of that, but I understood. The commitment two people make has to be strong, unshakable. I never had it—and I flubbed up just when it was within my grasp." She smiled bitterly. "I always fail. Surely you've noticed that. Whatever I touch seems to wither and die. I couldn't be a mother to you because I knew I'd fail you. And that's the best, most honest explanation I can give you. Now that my guts are hanging out to dry, I have something I want to leave with you." Maggie tossed her carry-on bag across the floor to Sawyer.

"Whatever it is, I don't want it," Sawyer said flatly. "I don't want your garbage invading the place I live."

Maggie's eyes brimmed. "I can't say as I blame you. But don't be too quick to discard what's in that bag. It's my life. Up until last evening. You can make today's entry, any way you want. I have a plane to catch. If there's anything you need or want, call me."

"I'd die before I called you." The realization of what she'd just said made Sawyer bite down on her lip. She tasted her own blood. She could barely see Maggie through her tears, but she heard her voice before the door closed behind her.

"A twenty percent chance is better than no chance at all. You're a quitter. I used to be like that. You don't like me, don't want to be like me, yet you're doing just what I used to do—give up, don't fight. Blame everything on someone else. I said it before, and I'll say it again: You have no guts. You *say* you care about Cole; you *say* you care about Mam, but it's a lie. If you did care, you'd fight.

"Twenty percent. Some people don't even get that. I can't believe you'd use your own life to get back at me.

That's sick. You're trying to make us all guilty. Well, it won't work with me. If you need my help, you know where I am. Call me."

Sawyer screamed, "Didn't you hear me? I said I'd rather die than call you!"

"Then you probably will," Maggie said evenly.

"You bitch!" Sawyer screamed again. "You can't fix this. You can't go back and make it right!"

"It's taken me all my life to realize that. I'm glad you finally do. Good-bye, Sawyer."

"Go to hell!" Sawyer yelled. "Go to hell, goddamn you!"

"I'm already there," Maggie whispered to herself as she made her way down the narrow steps.

Sawyer paced the apartment, wishing Adam were there. Marble followed her, her tail swishing furiously as she tried to rub against Sawyer's leg.

The nerve, the gall, the unmitigated gall of Maggie. How dare she come here and...and... Why had she come? To offer help, to pity her. To tell her Rand didn't want her, either. Was that supposed to make them friends?

No guts. It was true; she had no guts. A fifteen to twenty percent chance for success. Why bother? An accident on the operating table wasn't her idea of the best way to end her life. Even worse, what if she lived through the operation but came out a vegetable? It could happen. Still, if the operation was a success, she might live to see Cole grow to manhood. Riley, too. Maybe someday she could fall in love again. She might even get the chance to dance on old Maggie's grave.

"Get away from me, cat. I'm trying to think, and I have enough trouble without you crawling up my—" Sawyer broke off as she saw the bag. She bent down to pick it up, surprised at the weight. She unzipped the nylon bag and looked inside. Diaries. Old Maggie was really pulling out all the stops now. Well, wasn't she going to be surprised when she found out they'd been burned.

Breathing heavily, Sawyer hefted the bag and carried

it to the fireplace. She was shaking the little books from the bag when Adam walked in.

"What are you doing?" he asked curiously.

"Burning Maggie's life. She must be out of her mind to think I'd want to read about her trashy life! Where are the matches?"

"We ran out," Adam lied. "Don't do it, Sawyer. If you don't want to read them, okay, but don't destroy them. I'll pack them up and mail them back."

Sawyer's foot kicked out, scattering the different-colored journals. She was pleased to see a fine dark ash settle all over them. "Go ahead. I have to leave now. I have an appointment with Nick."

Adam looked up at Sawyer from his crouched position, one of the coffee-colored books in his hand. Sawyer noticed his thumb tracing the word "Diary" on the cover. "I didn't know you were seeing Nick," he said softly. "I'm glad."

"I'll probably stop after this visit. I don't like opening old wounds. I'm going to die, so what's the point?"

"You have a choice. Twenty percent isn't great odds, but—"

"Fifteen to twenty percent is what the doctor said. No guarantees. I could end up a slobbering idiot. Will you let me live here then? Will you wipe the spittle from my chin? Will you spoon-feed me? Will you put diapers on me if I wet my pants? Will you be able to look in my eyes and see nothing?... Well?" Sawyer demanded cruelly. "Answer me, Adam."

"Yes."

"You're lying," she said, but she knew in her heart he wasn't. He would do all those things.

"Keep feeding on your hatred, Sawyer," he said. "Just don't direct it at me. Direct it where it belongs, at yourself. Go on, see Nick, try to fool him. Or try to help yourself if you have the guts."

"You sound just like my mother. What do any of you know about guts? Neither of you ever had a death sentence."

"That's true," Adam said, zipping the carry-on bag.

"But you're copping out. You have a choice, and I'm going to jam that choice down your throat every chance I get. There's a lot of things I don't like in this world, but the one thing I cannot stand, cannot tolerate, is a quitter. You've got all of us plugging for you. The best doctors, the best medical care, the best goddamn support system in the world. But you—you're in a cold secret place full of hate and darkness. This is your ultimate end: get Maggie where it hurts. Die. Make her pay. Make her live with it every day after you're gone. But there's a kicker here. If everything you say about Maggie is true, she really doesn't give a shit, does she? She wins, but what does she win, Sawyer? She has it all now. So you won't really be getting back at her, will you?" He turned away, dismissing her. "Now get out of here before I really get mad. Nick charges for missed appointments."

Adam picked up the phone when he heard the downstairs door slam shut. He was breathing as if he'd just run five miles.

"Nick? Adam. Listen..."

All the way to Hawaii, Maggie brooded about her meeting with Sawyer. By the time she disembarked from the L1011, she was a bundle of nerves, exhausted and drained of all emotion.

A rented Chevy station wagon was waiting for her, and she wasted no time settling herself behind the wheel. She turned on the engine and listened. It sounded tinny, kind of like a Ford sounded in the States. She tested the windshield wipers and horn, checked to see that the lights were where they were supposed to be. Automatic transmission. Everything seemed to be just fine.

According to the map, she should head for the north shore. She drove carefully, following the turnoff for a route through Kunia. The narrow road made her uneasy. It was very close to the Waianae Mountains and ran through endless fields of what looked like pineapple and sugarcane fields.

She was feeling more confident when she led the car through Haleiwa. She ignored the bridge to the north and turned left, past the harbor to the shore.

Maggie gasped in pure delight at her first glimpse of Hawaii's famous surf. The ocean was so blue it looked like a giant jewel. The waves were breaking clean, eight to ten feet high. Native Hawaiians were scattered all along the shore, stretching out fishing nets. Children were gathering shells, their honey-colored skin shimmering in the bright sunlight. It was so beautiful she wanted never to leave, but she had at least an hour's drive ahead of her.

She almost missed the turnoff. Lush hibiscus and a monstrous banyan tree, like a giant umbrella, shrouded the timeworn iron gates at the entrance to Ester Kamali's estate. The snakelike drive eventually widened and became circular, edged on both sides by regal palms standing sentinel. The house itself was long, low, and sprawling, and much in need of paint. But the sparkling Pacific was exquisite, a perfect backdrop. Maggie felt her breath hiss between her teeth.

She stopped the car and glanced down. The grass looked like dark green fur, recently trimmed. Impulsively, she kicked off her shoes and walked up to the house. She knocked on the door and then laughed, remembering no one lived here. She tripped back across the emerald meadow to get her purse, savoring the scent of plumeria.

Maggie slid the key in the lock, then panicked for a moment when it didn't turn. She tugged furiously, perspiration dotting her brow. When she heard the cooperative snick of rusty tumblers, she leaned against the wall in relief.

The hilltop house opened its arms to Maggie. It was large, yet not overlarge, and it gave her a cozy feeling of coolness and light. She worked busily, ripping off dust covers and dropping them in a heap in the middle of the floor. Every door opened to the outside. The French doors leading to the patio were sheltered from the sun and rain by the sloping overhang of a tiled roof. Beautiful gardens were part of every view and seemed to come indoors to blend with the light bamboo furniture and the vivid greens and whites of the walls. Graceful paddle fans were centered on every ceiling, creating a pleasant breeze. And the tang of the sea far below seemed to fill each room.

Maggie toured the house, removing dust covers as she went along. She felt refreshed by the scented sea breeze that billowed the sheer curtains when she opened the doors. The carpet in the bedroom was eggshell white, bringing into relief the dark tones of the native mahogany furnishings. The bed, headboard, and upholstered chairs were covered with a fabric of pale blue flowers scattered over a background of deeper blue. Here, too, a paddle fan beat the air in a slow, hypnotic rhythm.

She crossed to the bathroom to find a tiled bath complete with tub, shower, and expanse of mirrors. Dusty towels of the palest blue hung from the racks.

Everything was so beautiful. She tried the water faucet. Good, the water had been turned on.

As she made her way back to the car to drive it up to the garage, Maggie wondered how it was possible to have two such beautiful homes in a lifetime. She tugged at the garage door, but it wouldn't budge. It didn't matter, she decided; the car could stay in the driveway.

She carried in her bags and headed for the kitchen. In the refrigerator she found juice, eggs, a loaf of untouched bread, bacon, and a bowl of mangos. She wondered who her unknown benefactor was—probably the same person who had turned on the utilities and manicured the lawn.

She poured herself a glass of orange juice and toured the rooms again, this time paying careful attention to what had been done. All the rooms would have to be painted, draperies and carpets cleaned. Everything had to be washed and polished, and the outside would have to be scraped and painted. So many things would have to be supplied or replaced—cookware, bedding, appliances... Maggie sighed. Not today, though. Today was for savoring this paradise. A pity she wasn't going to be able to share it with Sawyer. But at least she'd be making everything perfect for her daughter. And then maybe, just maybe, Sawyer would rethink her decision. How could a person give up things like this in life? Perhaps the island would work some magic. She prayed it would.

Maggie fixed herself a light supper and spent the rest of the evening on the back lanai, drinking in the scent of the rich flowers. Jet lag claimed her at nine-thirty and she headed for bed.

She slept deeply and awoke at seven o'clock. She padded barefoot to the kitchen and made a cup of instant coffee, carrying it out to the back terrace to watch the graceful swell of the waves on the shoreline. In her whole life she'd never seen anything so beautiful. She could almost picture her mother and father here. How happy they must have been! And Thad—Thad was part of all this, too. Now she could talk to Mam about that time in her life.

When she'd had her fill of the Pacific jewel, Maggie reluctantly returned to the kitchen. Phone. She couldn't do anything without a phone. She picked up the white receiver and was rewarded with the buzz of the dial tone. Thank God. Now she could begin.

Twenty-one days later, the house was finished, inside and out. Maggie looked in her checkbook. She'd shelled out twenty-eight thousand dollars. But she didn't care; she would have spent three times that much.

The pantry was loaded with every staple available, the deep freeze filled with a side of beef. Maggie washed the crystal and dishes herself, piece by piece, then dried it all the same way. The only thing left for her to do was engage a housekeeper for the time the children would be here. One of the cleaning girls had said her aunt would be glad to take on the job.

Maggie walked through the rooms, delight written all over her face. Cole, Riley, Adam, and Sawyer were going to love this place. She opened a fresh bottle of wine and poured some into one of the fine crystal wineglasses she'd

just bought. She toasted her efforts. Then she called
Susan.

"It's done, Suse. I took pictures. Now I'm feeling at
loose ends with nothing to do and I'm beginning to worry
about the boys." Susan's silence alarmed Maggie.

"What's doing with Ben and Luana?" Maggie asked,
testing the waters.

"Everything's going fine," Susan said, satisfied she
could report truthfully. "The boys are behaving themselves—sort of an armed truce, if you know what I mean.
I haven't seen much of Luana, thank the Lord. I'd really
hate to lose Ben Simms at this stage of the game. Those
modular units that Ferris and I ordered are going to be
delivered by the end of the summer when all the foundation work is done. A representative from the company
came down to check on the work. He told me how lucky
I was to have such a conscientious man working for me.
Everything that should be level is level, and all the corners
are square."

"That's nice, Suse." Maggie hoped her voice conveyed
some kind of enthusiasm. "About Luana, though. Do you
know if Mr. Simms hired a tutor for her?"

"No," Susan confessed, "but he's joined the church,
and Luana goes to Bible class on Sunday. They both attend
services, of course. He . . . he asked if we'd rent out the
apartment to him when his work is done, but I told him
there would always be work at the camp as long as he
wanted it." Susan hesitated. "I hope that's okay, Maggie.
I really do need him. You know our funds are limited."

"I know, I know," Maggie said wearily. She was getting
a headache. "As long as Luana stays away from the boys
and they stay away from her."

"Trust me," Susan said.

"I do, but I get all queasy whenever I think about the
situation. I guess I'm not as much of a freethinker as I
thought."

"You're Maggie." Susan laughed. "I got a letter from
Aunt Amelia the other day. She says she's well and coming to terms with things, whatever that means. And didn't

I tell you Rand was in the country with her? That's where you should have mailed your letter, Maggs. Amelia said Rand was working too hard and holding long telephone conferences with his bankers and lawyers. Something about dissolving his interests in several companies without causing a run on the stock. I didn't understand what she meant. No other mention, Maggie. I'm sorry."

A long silence. Maggie squeezed her eyes shut to prevent the tears.

"Cary stopped by last week wanting to know if we'd heard from Amelia. Of course, I hadn't received her letter yet. He looked awful. I don't think he eats or sleeps. I can't believe Amelia is behaving so childishly, and I'm going to tell her that when I write."

"We all do what we have to," Maggie said softly.

"When do you plan to come home?"

"I think I'm going to stay on here another week or so and enjoy this place. Suse, it's so beautiful, it takes your breath away. First I'm just going to hang out on the beach. And then I might visit Diamond Head and take in Waikiki. I may even consider a side trip to Maui. I'll call you before I leave."

"I wish you weren't alone. I don't like being alone. That's why I'm so glad Ferris is in my life." Susan hesitated, then said shyly, "Maggie, he's asked me to marry him once I'm divorced."

"Oh, Suse! If it's what you want, I'm happy for you," Maggie said sincerely. "Any news on Jerome?"

"Nothing. But I really haven't tried. I guess I'm afraid to confront him. Remember how Rand used to say that I'd avoid nastiness and ugliness at any cost? Well, I suppose he's right."

"But what if it means losing Ferris? Are you willing to pay that kind of price?"

"No. But I don't have the stomach for making hundreds of calls to Europe to track him down. And our agent doesn't want to cooperate with me. He's a greedy bugger, and since I'm not making money for him, he has no use for me."

"You could always try Valentine Mitchell. She could set some bloodhounds on Jerome's trail. She's got the knack, all right."

"I suppose that would solve my problem. But I'm still worried about you, Maggie. Are you sure you don't mind being alone?"

"Suse, I've been alone most of my life. Sometimes you can be alone with yourself without being lonely." Before Susan could reply, Maggie said, "Kiss Jessie for me and tell the boys I love them and am counting on them."

"I will. Enjoy."

Maggie hung up the phone and stared morosely out the window. She ached to hear Rand's voice; her fingers itched to reach out and touch him. She pulled the phone closer and placed a call to England.

The phone rang and rang. There were tears in her eyes when she replaced the receiver. The tears stayed with her until she fell asleep in the blue bedroom.

Rand sat across from Amelia in the sunny breakfast nook. Outside the open window the daffodils and tulips were making a grand show against the verdant lawn. The rosebushes were in bud, their droopy little heads hinting at the color that would soon arrive if this dazzling May sunshine continued. The hedgerow bordering the path was already in need of a second trim, and the birds splashed in the puddles left by Amelia's early-morning watering.

Rand smiled at his mother. "I haven't seen you look this well in a long time. I'm trying to decide what you've done to yourself. I know you've put on some weight, but that's not what it is, exactly. Would you care to satisfy my curiousity?"

Amelia leaned across the table. "I think it's called coming to terms with oneself. You look rather well yourself. Maybe we're kidding ourselves, and it's really this clean fresh air and sleeping with the windows wide open."

"I'm leaving this afternoon," he said abruptly. "I'll drive to London and then take the Concorde to New York."

"I know. I'm glad for you, Rand."

"What about you, Mother? Are you ready to go back with me?"

"Do you want an answer this second?"

"Before noon; that's when I'm leaving. Be certain, though." Amelia nodded. "I'll clean up the dishes," he said. "Why don't you take a walk, do some thinking? I know you could be packed in ten minutes."

"Yes, I could, but it isn't time for me to go back. You do what's right for you. Are you going to Sunbridge?"

"No, Hawaii." Quickly, he filled Amelia in on his plans. "I don't know if she'll have me, but I'm going to give it another try. It feels right."

"Go for it," Amelia said forcefully.

"You know, I could set down in Austin and see Cary."

"No. I have to work out my own problems. I don't need or want you to run interference for me."

"Okay. I hope you know what you're doing."

"I hope so, too. You go along and have a good trip. Give Maggie my love."

"Before or after I give her mine?" Rand chuckled.

"Before. She won't be interested later."

For all her bright, savvy attitude, Rand knew Amelia had been hurting for a long time. When Cary hadn't followed her to England, some of the heart had gone out of her. She looked now, though, as if that heart were making a comeback. Her face smoothed out somehow, lost its tight, nervous look. She moved calmly, gracefully, as though she were seeing things from a new perspective. Out of the rat race, she was the Amelia he had loved since he was a toddler.

Long after Rand left, Amelia sat on the country porch, surrounded by early spring blooms. She'd lugged the crocks from the quarry and filled them herself with bright petunias, daisies, and pansies. From the high ceiling she'd hung clay pots filled with luxuriant ferns and grape-ivy. She sipped at her tea, her thoughts on Cary.

She'd been so sure he would come after her. For all of two weeks she'd been sure. Then, when she'd finally realized he wasn't going to follow her, she'd done some hard soul-searching. And in those first weeks without him, as she'd cleaned the country house and started her garden, she'd come to understand something that had evaded her all of her life: she didn't belong to anyone but herself. She realized she'd slavishly embraced all Cary's hopes and dreams as if they were hers, never bothering to find out what it was *she* wanted. The house she'd been renovating was one of her biggest, costliest mistakes. It was a decoy, something to make her feel needed, important. Something for her to suck on, like a pacifier, while her life line was otherwise occupied.

How was it possible for one person to be so unhappy, so unsatisfied, so filled with low self-esteem? She thought of all the surgery she'd had done to retain an illusion of youth. To compete. Now she knew she'd only been fooling herself.

Once she'd reconciled herself to the fact that Cary wasn't coming after her, she'd felt better. And she realized now that if he had, she might never have learned anything about herself. Billie had told her at their last meeting that she had to have faith in herself and who she was, or no one else would. "It comes from within," Billie had whispered. "You have to dig down, way down, and get rid of all the clutter and garbage. Do it, Amelia."

Amelia was almost ready now to go back and set her various houses in order. First she'd finish decorating her mother's house. It was a symbol of the past, and she should never have bought it—but she had, and this was one project she was going to complete. Then she'd move from Sunbridge; she had never been happy there. Why she'd thought Cary would make a difference was something she was still trying to come to terms with.

She'd loved him with her heart and soul. He'd loved her, too—she'd had enough love affairs in her life to know the difference between love and lust and passion.

Cary had seen into her soul, something she'd never allowed herself to do. She'd opened up, given of herself, because she loved him. And he hadn't abused that generosity. *She* was the one who'd destroyed it. She'd let

Cary see her soul, then hadn't trusted him to nurture it.

But things were different now. She'd changed. She felt rested for the first time in her life. The cares and pressures she'd imposed on herself had dropped away shortly after she'd arrived here, in this peaceful place. She'd learned she had no one to account to but herself. She was sleeping, thank God, although every night Cary made a guest appearance in her dreams. She welcomed her pillow at night and the familiarity with her subconscious. She was on the mend. Soon, another week or so, and she'd be ready to go back to Texas. And knew now, hoped really, that if she went back to Sunbridge, Cary wouldn't see the ten pounds—or was it twelve?—she'd put on or the fine networking of wrinkles that were coming back. He wouldn't see the natural gray streaks in her hair or the fact that she wasn't hiding behind a mask of makeup.

Amelia smiled, a genuine expression of contentment came from deep within. Even her eyes smiled. Her right index finger caressed the wide gold band on her finger, loving symbol of her marriage to a wonderful man. Now maybe she could make it work.

She looked at her watch. Rand should be in London by now. In four hours he'd touch down in New York, and then his life would really take on meaning. There was no envy in her. Rand deserved happiness, and if Maggie was the one to give it to him, so much the better. Soon it would be her turn.

If it wasn't too late.

{{{{{{{{ CHAPTER TWENTY-SIX }}}}}}}}

*This time Rand felt as though Kennedy Airport were wel-
coming him on this, the first leg of his journey.* Even the
expected delay, circling before they could land, didn't
annoy him. What did a few moments matter when he had
an entire lifetime ahead of him?

He took a taxi to town and got out on the corner of
Forty-first and Third. He paid the driver and turned around
to get his bearings. He couldn't believe his luck when a
block later he saw Sawyer swinging toward him. He
stopped in the middle of the sidewalk as people jostled
and cursed at him. Sawyer, too, stopped in her tracks, a
look of confusion on her face. She advanced a step as
though she intended to go by without acknowledging him;
then she stopped. "Hello, Rand," she said, her voice cool,
indifferent.

"Hello, Sawyer. I was heading for your apartment.
Where are you going?"

"To the market. Why were you looking for me?"

"To talk to you."

Sawyer stared at this man, whom she loved. Who once
claimed he loved her. How long ago that seemed now!
All the words had been said. What did he want—absolution like Maggie? "We can get a cup of coffee over
there." Sawyer pointed across the street to a sign that
claimed Mike served the best coffee in the state of New
York. It was a lie, of course; the coffee was rancid and

tasted as though the pot had never been cleaned. But neither of them noticed.

Rand removed his sunglasses. Sawyer kept hers on. Looking at him through the brown glass somehow made it bearable.

"I wanted to talk to you, face-to-face," he said. "I have something to tell you, and I wanted you to hear it from me."

"That's assuming I want to hear what you have to say. Obviously, you have me confused with someone who gives a damn."

Rand blinked. She sounded like she was talking about the weather or making casual conversation with one of her friends. "What I want you to know is I'm going to ask Maggie to marry me. I'm hoping she'll say yes."

"Why wouldn't she? She wins—the whole ball of wax. Why tell me? That's your business and Maggie's."

Rand wished he could see behind the dark glasses. He didn't want to hurt her. God, he'd never do that, not intentionally. He struggled to find the right words, knowing it was impossible. "Maggie sent me away. She said it was best. I was angry . . . much the way you were, I suppose. I know how much I must have hurt you. Sawyer, I'd do anything for you. You know that. And I do love you, but it isn't the same. Your feelings for me—"

"Were wasted time on my part. It should be obvious to you, as it is to me, that I lowered my standards. You fit right in there with the love of your life."

"Don't, Sawyer. Please don't . . ."

"Don't what, Rand? Why is everyone so concerned about how I feel? Breathing down my back, saying love is love and you and Maggie deserve to be happy. Now that I'm going to die, no one knows quite what to say. They all dance around it, trying to appease Maggie and me at the same time. My grandmother gave her seal of approval to your affair, and that's all that was needed. So you see, you really came here to make *you* feel better. Only I'm not interested in how *you* feel or how *Maggie* feels or how my *grandmother* feels. I have nothing to give any of you."

"I don't want anything, Sawyer. I just wanted you to hear it from me."

"Well, don't bother to invite me to the wedding. I might not be around."

Anger sparked in Rand's eyes. "I'm not going to pretend I don't know about your illness. I'm disappointed, though. I thought you had more guts than that. Maggie said you didn't, but I didn't believe her. Billie told Amelia about the operation you refuse to risk. How can you... just give up? Any kind of chance is better than none. Reach for the brass ring! You have nothing to lose and your whole life to gain." He reached across the table and removed the polished sunglasses. Then, speaking very slowly, deliberately, he said, "You're a taker, Sawyer. You don't know how to give."

It was almost dusk when Rand drove past the big banyan tree on Ester Kamali's estate. It was beautiful, breathtaking. The rental car took the last rise to the end of the drive. He felt himself trembling as he removed the keys from the ignition. The thought he'd been trying to avoid throughout the entire trip would no longer be denied. What if Maggie didn't want him? He hadn't heard from her since he'd left Sunbridge just after the first of the year. His nerves were jangling, spidery tingles creeping close to the surface of his skin. He walked across the soft green fur carpet to the house and rang the bell. When there was no answer, he tried the back of the house. On the terrace he saw a beach towel. He let his eyes travel down the path to the shimmering Pacific, where the huge ball of sun silhouetted a slim female figure scampering from the surf.

Maggie looked up, droplets of seawater dripping from her eyelashes and clouding her vision. Standing on the back lanai was a man. She hesitated, frightened. She rubbed her eyes. It couldn't be. Not here, not all this way.

Her throat closed; her heart leaped.

Rand stood mesmerized by the sight of Maggie, a sea nymph, a gift from the sea. She'd seen him. He waited.

Rand. Her eyes must be playing tricks on her. Rand. Her life. Her future. The figure moved. She took a step forward. "Rand!"

She flew into his arms, finding her happiness, her safety. "How, when?!.. I thought I'd never..."

"Shhh, I'm here."

"You've always been here," Maggie whispered. "I brought you with me, here." She pointed to her heart. "I take you everywhere I go."

"That's because I belong here, with you, and you belong here." He tapped his own chest.

"You came halfway around the world to find me?"

"I'll always find you, Maggie, I'll never let you go. I'll never let you send me away again." As if to make his words true, he slipped his arms around her waist, pulling her tighter against him.

"Let's go inside so I can change. We have so much to talk about."

"Yes, we do, Maggie, my Maggie."

The sound of his voice warmed her heart. They walked inside, Rand's arms still around her, holding her close. He said all the appropriate things about the house and prowled around until Maggie came out in a pair of cotton shorts and a T-shirt. Arm in arm they walked back to the lanai overlooking the sea. She fixed them drinks and took her place beside Rand on the glider. It creaked slightly as she nestled herself into the crook of his arm.

"Now let's talk," she said.

By the time Maggie and Rand finished talking, the early-morning sun had slanted over the island and glistened on the water like fairy dust. The air was already warm, with hardly a breeze, and the Pacific swelled and ebbed, foaming the shoreline. After a leisurely breakfast on the back lanai, they took a stroll along the sun-warmed beach.

"How do you feel about skinny-dipping?" Maggie teased.

"The same way you do." Rand laughed, already out of his shirt and working on his belt.

She was about to plunge into the surf when he seized her hand, pulling her tightly against him. He loved the feel of her, the delicate framework of her bones, her satiny-smooth skin that invited his touch and the caress of his lips. "Not yet, Maggie, not yet. First I want to show you how I love you."

She looked into his eyes, and it was like peering into his heart. Dark eyes that told her how much he wanted her, loved her, needed her in his life.

"I like beginning the day with you, Rand," she said softly. "Welcome home, welcome. I've missed you."

"And I've missed you, Maggie, my Maggie."

She could barely catch her breath; she was mesmerized by his eyes, drugged by the meaning she found in them. Her blood was racing through her veins, her flesh tingling and eager for his touch.

Rand traced her mouth with a delicate concentration, teasing the fullness of her lower lip with his tongue and claiming his kiss while his hands caressed the long, slender ridge of her spine and the swell of her bottom. Her knees lost their strength and he gently lowered her onto the pile of their discarded clothing. She opened her arms to him, holding him close, sighing with the simple pleasure of being with the man she loved. His hands possessed her, finding those places that intrigued his imagination, discovering those places that made her cry out with delight. She loved having his lean, warm body pressed against the length of hers once again. She realized the hollow ache that had plagued her since he left her, since she'd so foolishly sent him away. His hands covered her; his mouth moved slowly from her throat to the valley between her breasts and lower until he groaned, "Maggie, Maggie, I want you now!"

"Take me, Rand. I want you to take me," she whispered, her consciousness floating above waves of undulating heat as she took him into her ready flesh.

He held himself above her, supporting himself on his arms, his hips pressed hard against hers. He was fighting himself, denying his needs, holding himself back, struggling for self-control. He wanted it to be good for her; he wanted to satisfy her. But Maggie would not be still. She captured his buttocks, pulling him closer, deeper within her. Her legs lifted, her body opening to his.

"I love you, Maggie," he cried hoarsely, surrendering to the strokings of her sheath that surrounded and rippled around him. He saw her smile, joyous, victorious, the smile of a woman who knows she's bringing herself to the man she loves. He looked into her eyes, summer-blue, and he found himself drowning in her, reaching for her, finding her, and touching her. They joined, their hearts caressed, their souls met, and together they chorused their joy.

Sawyer greeted Amelia with outstretched arms. When her aunt had phoned from Kennedy Airport, she couldn't have been more surprised. Even more unexpected, however, was this change in her appearance. When Sawyer cried, "You look wonderful!" she meant it sincerely. There was a softer look about Amelia, as though someone had smoothed the hard edges. Her hair, salt-and-pepper now that she had let it grow in, was more flattering to her skin tones than the sable-brown that had come from a bottle; and she seemed to have fleshed out. More than anything, though, Amelia looked happy. Still stylish, still perfectly groomed, but happy.

"How was England? What made you decide to come back?" Sawyer asked, leading her aunt over to the comfortable sofa that faced the long, unadorned windows. Sawyer had removed the curtains and blinds in her desperate desire for light. Her eyesight was failing her, and she was determined to see everything as clearly as she could for as long as she could.

Amelia turned sideways to avoid the glaring brightness streaming through the windows. "I decided," she said firmly, "to fight. But first, if it isn't too late, I'm going to apologize. Your grandmother tells me it's never too late."

"Sometimes it is," Sawyer said somberly.

"Never," Amelia declared. "Look, darling, I want to talk to you, but I don't know what to say. I've made such a mess of my own life, I have no right to intrude on yours. . . . You—you look well." Then, remembering her new resolution, she said abruptly, "That's a lie; you don't look well at all. You look ill."

"That's because I am ill, Aunt Amelia. I can talk about it."

"I can't. I can't understand why you won't at least consider the operation. If it's because of Rand, let me tell you, no man is worth giving up your life for. I almost made that mistake. You can't give up. One chance in a million is better than no chance at all!"

"You look wonderful," Sawyer interrupted. "Really wonderful."

Amelia sniffed. "I thought you said your eyesight was failing."

"It is, but you're six inches away from me. I can see you clearly. You remind me of Grand now. I don't know, you look . . . womanly. Not so brittle. I don't mean that to sound unkind, but you were so thin and . . ."

"Hard-looking is what you're trying to say. I wanted to look like you. I wanted to be like you. The impossible dream. Or is that the American dream?"

Sawyer laughed hollowly. "No, I just saw on television the other day that the American dream was a Gold American Express Card, a Mercedes, and a Kirby vacuum cleaner."

Amelia laughed. "Where's Adam?" she asked. "And what is that!" She pointed to Marble, who was contentedly washing her face. "I hate cats. They slink and stare and see things the human eye can't see."

It was Sawyer's turn to laugh. "Adam went to the post

office," she said. "Marble's been a great companion. I talk to her and she doesn't ask questions or make demands."

"I told you the cat was an idiot. So are you if you don't give it your best shot. That's what life is. I know. Either you go for it or you don't. Either you win or lose. I can't get any plainer than that. I never thought of you as a loser, Sawyer."

Sawyer grimaced. "I've been called a lot of things lately. A quitter, no guts . . . Cole says I'm burned-out or a burn-out, something like that. There were other names, too, but no one has called me a loser yet."

"So make them eat their words," Amelia said bluntly. "That includes me, too. Don't let this awful thing beat you. You're a Coleman, and by God, it's time you started acting like one!"

"I'm so scared," Sawyer whimpered against Amelia's cheek. "I've been seeing a shrink. A friend of Adam's. In fact, I have an appointment in a little while. Adam usually walks me over there. To make sure I go."

"Is it helping?" Amelia asked, stroking Sawyer's hair.

"I suppose so. I talk. He listens. He doesn't make judgments. Today is the day I talk about Rand's visit. He met me on the street two weeks ago, if you can believe that. He was coming here to talk to me. He said a lot of things, too, things I didn't want to hear. Things I don't want to think about. I will today, though."

"Sawyer, look at me. Listen to what I say. There is every possibility the operation will be a success. *Think*. For God's sake, use that wonderful brain you have to see what's out there for you. Reach out. Fight with everything you have. How can you not want to see the first buds of spring or the first snowflakes of winter? I don't understand it. When it's time for me to go, I plan to kick and scratch all the way. How can you give up Cole and Riley? They love you. Your grandmother is eating herself alive because you won't fight. And what about Adam? That young man loves you. *Loves you*, Sawyer."

"It's my life," Sawyer said defensively.

"You belong to all of us. Even Maggie and Rand. Once you touch someone's life, they have a claim on you. Has Maggie been here?" Amelia asked suddenly.

"Yes. She dumped her garbage on me." At Amelia's perplexed look, she explained, "Her diaries. Seems she kept them from the time she was ten years old. Just the way I did. In fact, she gave me my first one. It's probably the only thing we have in common. We both write in diaries."

Amelia was dumbfounded. "Maggie actually gave you her diaries! I can't believe it."

"Well, she did. I threw them in the fireplace. I was going to burn them, but Adam rescued them. I don't know if he mailed them back or not."

Amelia found herself at a loss for words. She felt awe, relief, and something like pride that Maggie would bare her soul to her daughter. "Sawyer...do you have any idea, any idea at all, what it cost your mother to bring those diaries to you? Do yourself a favor and read them."

"I can't. I don't want her in my life. I don't want to be in hers. Rand told me he was on his way to ask her to marry him—said he wanted me to hear it from him. He told me that in some greasy restaurant. Then he left."

"How did you feel?"

"Numb. It was a terrible experience. I made it through, though. It took a lot of courage for him to tell me; I know that now. Nick—that's the shrink—made me ... What he did was help me see that you can't make someone love you. It's like Adam and me. He loves me. I love him, too, but not the way he loves me. Maybe someday. Rand couldn't wait for someday."

"Why should he wait, Sawyer? Life is too short. Surely you can see that. Don't begrudge his happiness or Maggie's. Don't hate."

"It's what I feed on now," Sawyer said honestly. "It's what keeps me going."

"Then you're lost. I'm just wasting my time. And I

don't have all that much left, so I have to put it to good use. Go to your shrink and play games. Wait till it's too late and blame everyone but yourself because you're going to die. I'm sorry if that hurts you, Sawyer, but that's the way it is." Amelia stood up. "I was going to stay overnight, but I don't think I will. You depress me. I need sunshine in my life and I'm going back to get it. You stay here with that crazy cat and wallow in your misery. I'm glad your grandmother can't see you. Good-bye, Sawyer."

Adam found her crying at the dining room table, Marble purring softly in her lap. "What happened?"

"Amelia stopped here on her way to Sunbridge. She let me have it with both barrels. It's closing in on me, Adam. They're all saying the same thing: that I'm a quitter, a loser, that I have no guts. Rand said I was a taker, that I don't know how to give. They're all disgusted with me. Instead of being supportive like you are, they come here to jab at me and leave. Fight, they tell me. What the hell am I fighting?" she cried suddenly. "Do you think I want to die? I don't. Honest to God, I don't. I'm scared out of my wits. I don't want to die on an operating table. I don't know what to do."

"For starters, you're going to wash your face and comb your hair. Then we're going to see Nick. You're going to talk this out if I have to force him to cancel all his other appointments. Go on now; do as I say."

While Sawyer was in the bathroom, Adam called Nick. "I'll pay. I want you to stick with her till she can't talk anymore. I don't care how long it takes."

"Be glad to do it. Do you think she's coming around?" Nick asked hopefully.

"I'm afraid to think. I'm hoping."

"I'm waiting for her now, so get moving."

Nick settled his soccer-ball body comfortably in an easy chair across from Sawyer. "Take off your sunglasses. I want to be able to look at you when we talk."

"The mirror of one's soul, is that it?"

"More or less. So, tell me what's been going on. You haven't been here for two weeks."

Sawyer spoke haltingly at first, and then she sped up, like a child on a downhill slide. Soon there was no stopping her. At one point she jumped up angrily and lashed out, "They have no right, no right at all!"

"Do you feel like smashing something, putting your foot through the wall?" Nick asked complacently.

"Huh?"

"Don't play games. You heard me. If that's what you want to do, do it. I told you, when you come to this office you can do whatever you want. If you want to cry, cry. If you want to scream and yell, do it. You want to smash something, be my guest. You will, however, clean up and replace when you're finished. Go ahead. I'm not stopping you."

"That's stupid," Sawyer said in disgust.

"Don't you think it's more stupid to hold the anger in and direct it at people who don't deserve it?"

"Of course. You're saying that's what I'm doing?"

"No. I asked you a question. You assumed that's what I meant. You already know the answer. I told you, Sawyer, no games are played here. Now, tell me about Rand."

Nick listened carefully to Sawyer's wild babblings, all the while sifting, collating, making neat little summaries in his head. In the beginning he'd made notes, but his scribbling seemed to bother Sawyer, so he'd opted for this "sit and chat" area, as he called it. She'd relaxed almost immediately.

"What, in particular, didn't you like about the meeting?"

"I didn't like his nerve. I don't owe him anything, even conversation. He assumed he could 'get through to me' where the others failed."

"Did he?"

"He hit some nerves. Yes. He made me think."

"Do you still hate him?"

"Hate Rand? Oh, no!" Sawyer cried passionately.

"You said he's going to marry your mother. Does that bother you?"

"Of course it bothers me! It's tearing me up inside. She tricked him."

"Does even one small part of you believe he could really love her? You told me he didn't love you enough to make that final commitment. Yet now he's ready to make that commitment to your mother. How do you explain that?"

Sawyer hedged. "He might care for her...a little. I told you, Maggie is a man-eater. She mesmerized him."

"But you said she sent him away. Sometimes people do that when they love too much because they can't handle it."

"Maggie can handle anything," Sawyer said bitterly.

"Even your illness? Is she handling that?"

"Of course. She came to see me, dumped her trash on me, and left." She hesitated a moment, then burst out defiantly, "It's *her* fault—all of this is her fault!"

Nick lit a cigarette, his third of the day. "You told me you didn't want to read her diaries, that Adam packed them up. You said her life was trash. Actually, I believe you used the word garbage."

"So what if I did? It's how I feel," Sawyer cried. "Why should I waste my time reading about *her* life?"

"You tell me. Why would it be a waste? Are you afraid of what you might see in those diaries?"

"Of course not," Sawyer blustered.

"If I asked you to read them, would you?"

"Probably not."

Nick stubbed out his cigarette. "I have to assume you're afraid."

"I'm not afraid. I'm petrified," Sawyer whispered.

"Tell me what you're petrified of."

Sawyer lit a cigarette with trembling hands. "There might be something in them that would...that I might not like. Maggie always comes out on top. She wouldn't have given me those diaries if they were going to hurt her. She wants to hurt me. That's why she gave them to me."

"That thing you think might be in those books, would it absolve Maggie?"

"Of course. It would make me take the rap. I told you, Maggie always wins. Didn't she finally get Sunbridge? She got Rand. Amelia and Susan are living there. My grandmother gave her permission, _gave her permission_," Sawyer shouted, "_to take Rand_!"

"If you read those diaries and your worst imaginings are true, then you won't have anyone to blame. That's what you're saying."

Sawyer pondered Nick's words. "I suppose ... in a manner of speaking, you're right."

"So now, at the most crucial time of your life, you need someone to blame. Your illness is the biggest crisis you've ever had to deal with. But you aren't dealing with it, are you?"

"I'm trying."

"Then why won't you go for the operation?"

"I told you, I'm petrified."

"I don't believe you."

"I really don't care. You all expect too much of me. I'm only human."

"Ah, you're only human. What does that make the rest of us, inhuman?"

"I didn't mean that."

"Then what the hell did you mean?"

"People are choosing up sides. When you do that, there's a winner and a loser."

"Which are you?"

Sawyer laughed hysterically. "I'm going to die and you ask me a stupid question like that! Of course I'm the loser."

"How did that happen, that you're the loser?"

"Maggie."

"Maggie has nothing to do with your illness. You lose

when you don't fight. If you decide to go ahead and have the operation and it's successful, what will happen then?"

"I don't know. Look, I don't want to talk about this anymore."

"I know you don't, but we're going to talk anyway. Now answer the question."

"Life will go on."

"Maggie and Rand will live happily ever after. Your grandmother and her husband will live happily ever after. Your aunt Amelia is going back to Texas to reconcile with her husband, and they'll live happily ever after. Your aunt Susan is going to get married again, and she and her new husband will live happily ever after. Cole and Riley are going off to college, two handsome studs with girls dropping at their feet. Who does that leave who isn't going to be happy?"

"Me," Sawyer cried. "Damn you, me! What about me? When do I get to be happy?"

"When you open yourself to it. You can't buy it; it isn't a commodity. You want to know something else I found out? You have to earn it. Take my old buddy Adam. He's unhappy—miserable, as a matter of fact. He'd die for you if it would make you happy. You know that, don't you?"

"Yes."

"Let's talk about something here for a minute." Nick handed her a piece of paper and a pencil. "I want you to list all the things in order of importance—now that's crucial—all the things you'll never see or do again if you don't go for this operation. I'm going out to the other office to call some of my patients who think I'm the greatest thing since sliced bread."

"You must be kidding."

"Do I look like I'm kidding?" He nodded as Sawyer reluctantly picked up the pencil. "When you're finished with that list, I want you to make another one on the back of it. Things you can do and will do; things you *want* to do if the operation is a success."

Nick closed the door behind him and immediately called Adam. "Look, I'm not promising anything. I think I have her on the run, though. Christ, for a minute there I thought she was going to wreck my office. I actually gave her permission, knowing you'd pay the bill." He grinned at the hysterical squawking on the other end of the line.

"I think the best thing for Sawyer was having Rand and Amelia talk to her. She's thinking, and that's the first step. I'm hopeful. Don't worry about her getting home. I'll put her in a cab. Just be there for her."

Nick waddled to the men's room and back to his secretary's desk, where he made several more phone calls. When he returned to his office, Sawyer was sitting with her feet propped up on the round table in the chat area. There were tear streaks on her cheeks, which he pretended not to see. He scanned both sides of the paper in front of him. "Good," he said briskly. He lit another cigarette and held the light for Sawyer.

"Is that it for today?" Sawyer asked through a perfect smoke ring.

"Not quite. Let's touch on the operation." He held up his hand to ward off her objection. "My talking about it isn't going to change anything. I want you to talk about it. I do understand more now, though. I called your doctor because I wanted to make sure I could explain anything in case you had some questions. You gave me permission, so wipe that look off your face. . . . Well?"

"Twenty percent odds aren't very good," she said in a tight voice. "Actually, the neurosurgeon said it was more like fifteen."

"When you buy it in a car accident, there aren't any odds at all. You live in one of the biggest cities in the world, with one of the highest crime rates. You could get killed in a grocery store. There aren't any odds there, either. Don't look at the numbers."

"You sound like the rest of them. It's easy for you to say, easy for you to be objective. It isn't easy for me. It's my life."

"I'm trying to give you perspective. I do know one thing, though. Your chances are better right now than they would be six months from now. The bottom line is, it has to be what you want, what you're willing to do. The reasons have to be the right ones. What your grandmother or I think isn't important. The right reasons, Sawyer. For you. For these," he said, waving the papers under her nose. "Do you want me to make a copy of them for you?"

"No," she replied, so faintly that Nick had to strain to hear her.

"What say I take you over to Jim McMullen's for a brew?"

"How about a rain check? I just want to go home and put my feet up. I have another one of those nasty headaches. I'd appreciate you flagging a cab for me, though."

Nick locked up the office, and they rode the elevator in silence. Outside, he hailed a checker and helped Sawyer climb in.

"The truth," she said hesitantly. "How did today go?"

Nick grinned. Sawyer thought he looked like a cherub. Or a munchkin. "You tell me. You know we shrinks don't answer questions. See you next week."

"Good night, Nick."

Sawyer leaned back for the ride downtown. She didn't know if she felt better or worse. But she did know one thing: she had a lot of thinking to do.

{{{{{{{{{ CHAPTER TWENTY-SEVEN }}}}}}}}}

Amelia fought her way to the baggage area in the airport
terminal. She'd never seen such crowds before. She
engaged a redcap, who got her a taxi. Amelia tipped him,
gave the driver the address of the Hilton Hotel, and leaned
back. God, she was exhausted.

Forty minutes later she checked into the Hilton and
accepted a copy of the *Crystal City Times*. All she wanted
was a long, hot bath and some sleep. It would be bliss to
hear or see Cary, but not now. One thing at a time.

The following day, as Amelia dried her hair in front of
the hotel mirror, she wondered if she was doing the right
thing by not going to Sunbridge. She planned to go to her
house first and follow through with her renovations, actually sleep there until the project was completed. It was
time to see something through to the end. Then, and only
then, would she call Cary.

It was noon when Amelia checked out of the Hilton
Hotel. A uniformed doorman tipped his hat to her, smiled,
and crooked his finger at a bellboy, who was standing at
attention. "Put the lady's bag in the cab." He smiled again
at Amelia, approvingly, and tipped his hat a second time.
Amelia smiled in return. Usually, she didn't notice hotel
personnel. She'd been too busy comparing herself to the
other guests. And another thing: She usually hired a limousine. Now she felt she didn't have to impress anyone

but herself. Anything with wheels would get her to where she wanted to go.

As the taxi driver pulled into the driveway, Amelia noticed it had been paved in her absence. The wide, circular front porch was finished, gleaming in the noon sunshine. The inside must be done, too, for she heard no hammering.

A little thrill coursed through her when she slipped the key into the new oiled lock and the solid oak door swished open. Slowly she walked from room to room. All the carpentry work was finished. The bathroom was remodeled, the carpeting laid. All she had to do was clean everything up, arrange the various *objets d'art*, and outfit the bedrooms. The furniture she'd ordered months ago was being held, as were the drapes. She'd made calls this morning to arrange delivery for tomorrow and the following day.

Amelia climbed the stairs a second time to change into her coveralls. Then she set to work with a vengeance, scrubbing and polishing till late in the evening.

A long, soothing bath made her feel drowsy. She spread her sable coat on the clean floor and slept like a newborn infant, her hand tucked under her cheek. When she woke in the morning, she couldn't remember if she'd dreamed or not.

At nine o'clock the rental car she'd ordered arrived, and Amelia immediately drove to a deli in Crystal City. Hot coffee in three containers and a bacon-and-egg sandwich to go would hold her till later. She also picked up a copy of the morning issue of the *Crystal City Times*. Back at the house, she ate breakfast and read her paper from cover to cover, rereading the local business page. There was a brief mention of Cary and his associates and the remarkable progress they'd made. But there were no pictures. Amelia looked longingly at the yellow wall phone. Not yet. Not till she was finished.

By three-thirty every window in the house was draped. By six o'clock all the downstairs furniture was in place.

She had only to dust, arrange her art objects, hang the pictures that were in the hall closet, vacuum. At eight o'clock everything was done. Amelia called the deli and had them deliver a pastrami on rye and two cups of coffee.

She bathed early, ate dinner, and slept, wrapped in her sable coat in the middle of the furnished living room.

Every night before he returned to his empty apartment, Cary drove through the silent streets trying to relax. And somehow—like tonight—he always found himself driving to Amelia's house. Why? he wondered. Why did he keep punishing himself? What was it he expected to find?

As usual, he slowed his car once he rounded the curve of the road. There it was, all by itself on thirty acres of ground. He pulled up to the curb and cut the engine. The house was dark and silent, as always. He sat for over twenty minutes staring at it. For some strange reason, he felt closer to Amelia than ever before. If only . . . if only . . .

He didn't notice the car in the driveway when he slipped the car into gear and drove away.

It rained the next day, great buckets that slapped at the newly draped windows. Amelia turned on the heat to chase away the chilly dampness. The upstairs furniture arrived at eleven-thirty. At twelve-thirty she backed the Mustang out of the driveway and headed for Crystal City's poshest department store. She bought bedding, towels, soap dishes, mattress covers, sheets, blankets, spreads. The last things she purchased were bathroom mats and drinking glasses for the four bathrooms. The trunk and backseat of the car were so full, she had to use her side-view mirror to drive. She stopped at the deli for more sandwiches, then continued on to the house.

She spent the next three hours dressing the beds and manicuring the bathrooms. She vacuumed a second time for lint, then replaced the sweeper in the upstairs closet.

It was done. All of it. She felt absolutely giddy with relief. She'd started from scratch and seen the whole thing through to the end.

Amelia ate a corned beef sandwich and munched on the deli pickle as if she were eating pheasant under glass. The coffee tasted good, so she opened the second Styrofoam cup and drank that, too. Then she wadded up her trash and carried it to a container in the garage.

Everything smelled so new. All the place needed was someone to move in. Amelia smiled when she sat back down at the kitchen table with her work papers in front of her. She used a purse minicalculator and worked for close to an hour. She'd spent a quarter of a million dollars renovating this house that had been her mother's. Added to that was the original cost of the house and land: 1.6 million dollars. Before leaving England, she'd instructed her bank to pay off the mortgage company in Austin. So she was now full owner of a house worth roughly 1.85 million dollars. She'd done the work, paid for it with her own money. It was all hers.

An hour later Amelia walked out onto the back porch. It was still raining, and she shivered inside her fuzzy robe. She secured the dead bolt on the door, then turned off the lights as she made her way to the living room, where she would again sleep wrapped in the sable coat. No way was she going to disturb the newly made beds upstairs. She was sound asleep when Cary drove past the house at eleven-fifteen.

Amelia stayed in the house for four more days, waiting for what she called perfect weather. She was getting sick of deli sandwiches and pickles, but she had no other choice. When she woke on the fifth day, she could feel that it was right. She checked outside: it was airless; not a leaf in the garden moved. All she had to do now was wait. She sat on the back porch eating her sandwiches, drinking her coffee, and reading snatches from a lusty romance novel that set her teeth on edge.

At twenty minutes before noon Amelia walked into the Liberman Insurance Agency and presented her homeowner's policy. "Cancel it and issue me a credit. I'll wait." The scurrying around amused her. When a Coleman canceled a policy of any kind, the whole town would know.

That was all right; she didn't care. When she left the office with the huge red CANCELED stamped across the face of the policy, she felt pleased. As of 12:01 she was uninsured.

She laughed as she got into her car. God, she felt good! To celebrate, she stopped at a steak house on the highway and ordered a T-bone, rare, a large country salad, a baked potato with butter and sour cream. Then she finished off her meal with blueberry cheesecake and coffee, left a generous tip, and returned to the house that was now hers—and uninsured.

Amelia sat on the back porch with coffee she'd heated in the microwave. It tasted awful, but she sipped at it complacently as she leafed through the romantic novel.

At seven o'clock, just as dusk was settling in, she took the gardening shears and walked across her perfect lawn to her perfect flower beds and neatly clipped exquisite perfect flowers, which she arranged in a perfectly cut crystal vase. She set them in the foyer on a cherrywood table that was a genuine, perfect antique. She returned the shears to the potting shed in the yard and resumed her seat on the back porch. The evening hadn't gotten cooler; it was still hot and airless. Deathly still.

It was ten-thirty when Amelia left her chair on the back porch. She entered the house, closed and locked the back door. She walked through the rooms, admiring her hand-iwork. Her mother would have been pleased. She walked upstairs, going from room to room. Everything was per-fect. She parted the draperies in the master bedroom and looked outside. She pulled the drapes in the bedroom, then did the same in the rest of the bedrooms. She didn't turn her head for a second look. On the landing of the stairway she turned off the night-light. She walked through the downstairs, turning on the magnificent chandelier for a better look. She loved it.

She picked up her sable coat, then debated a second. People would think she was crazy, carrying around a sable coat in this weather. She folded it neatly and laid it on the back of a beautiful morris chair she'd had custom-made. The chandelier twinkled and glistened before she turned it off. The only remaining light was in the foyer.

Amelia left the front door slightly ajar when she went out to the rental car. She threw her purse into the backseat and backed the car down the driveway with only the parking lights on. She opened the trunk and removed a filled kerosene can, stuffing the car keys into the pocket of her slacks so she could use both hands to carry the can. Inside the beautiful house, she hurried up the stairs, sprinkling the kerosene as she went. Then she turned and did the same thing downstairs until the can was empty. She placed it outside the front door and went back upstairs, digging in her pockets for matches. She lit little fires that blazed into big fires. The steps were burning behind her as she rushed down to light still more fires.

The house was blazing when she closed the door for the last time. With the kerosene can in one hand, four unused matches in the other, she walked down the drive. It would be a while before anyone noticed. The fire department would come ... maybe. She'd stand right where she was in case they did come. She'd tell them to let it burn ... to the ground.

It was almost midnight. She was free. The past was gone. Tomorrow would be a new day. Only the future remained. What she did with it would be up to her.

Amelia stood in the darkness and watched her house burn. She was officially broke now, by Coleman standards a pauper. She laughed, enjoying the feeling.

Damn, a car was coming down the road. Well, when the driver slowed and finally got out, she'd tell him the same thing. Let it burn to the ground.

Cary slowed his car and stared. Amelia's house was lit up like a Christmas tree. When he slammed the car into park, he realized the whole damn thing was blazing, a bright red-and-yellow conflagration against the dark Texas sky. "Holy Jesus!" he groaned, about to get back into the car to go for help.

A figure emerged from the shadows. "Let it burn."

"Amelia! Amelia, is that you?"

"Cary? Cary darling, what are you doing here?"

"I can't believe it's you." The house, the fire, everything was forgotten in that one instant as Cary reached out. Amelia. How good she felt. "My God, how I missed you. I thought you were never coming back. I prayed. Amelia, I prayed."

"Shhh. So did I. I'm free now. Look at me, Cary."

"You're the most beautiful creature on earth," he said as he gazed into her loving eyes. "Look at me! I've lost sixteen pounds and I look like hell. Life was hell, without you."

Amelia laughed, a young, girlish sound. "I guess beauty is in the eye of the beholder."

"In this beholder's eyes, anyway." Cary squeezed her tightly. He was never going to let her out of his sight again. Never. "Amelia, your house. What happened?"

"I finished it. I came back from England and finished it. I've never really finished anything I've started until tonight." Tears glazed her eyes, but they were not tears of regret. "I was using that house just like my mother did. As an escape, a place to hide. I made myself so busy trying to regain the past that I couldn't look ahead to the future, and I cheated myself and everyone else of the happiness of the present. I burned it down, Cary. It's an effigy to the ghosts of the past, and I don't need it anymore."

"We don't need anything, Amelia, only each other."

Someone had alerted the Crystal City Fire Department; Amelia heard the distant whine of sirens. Quickly, she explained about the insurance and paying off the house. "Don't let them fight it, Cary. I don't want anyone hurt, and there's nothing in there worth saving. Let it burn."

Dawn broke when the last engine pulled away from the ashes of what had once been Amelia's house. The firemen hadn't fought the fire but had stood in readiness to keep it from spreading.

"Let's go home," Cary said, nuzzling Amelia's hair.

"Hey, you did something different to yourself," he said in surprise. "I don't know what it is, exactly, but you look great. Fatten me up, okay? My clothes don't fit anymore."

Amelia laughed, a joyous sound that rivaled the music of the early-morning birds.

She was finally free. Free of the past, of the ghosts that had haunted her, of fear of the future. She was Amelia Assante now. She'd be Amelia Assante until the day she died.

When the intercom in the nursery buzzed, Susan leaned over and listened. "Miss Susan, Mr. de Moray is here. Will you see him?"

Susan's heart skipped a beat. Her eyes flew to the crib where Jessie was sleeping. "Did you let him in?"

"No, ma'am. He's standing on the porch."

"Good, let him stand there. Tell him I'll be down in a few minutes." She immediately called Valentine Mitchell, who chuckled when Susan explained the situation.

"Don't panic. I'll be right there. This saves us a lot of time and bother. Invite him in, by all means. Offer him a drink; be cordial. It'll be the last time he ever enjoys Sunbridge's hospitality."

Susan's heart refused to return to its natural beat. Her eyes were drawn again and again to the sleeping baby as she threw the infant's laundry back into a basket. Should she call Ferris or not? She decided to deal with it herself, with Valentine's help.

Susan opened the door and motioned for Jerome to enter. She led the way to the living room and offered him a drink. Jerome asked for a gin with a twist of lemon. With surprise, she realized she'd forgotten this was her husband's favorite drink.

"This is as hospitable as I'll get. Now, what do you want? Why did you come here?"

Jerome's eyes widened. "For you, of course. Now that you've had the baby, maybe we can get on with our lives."

Susan laughed hysterically. "You must be out of your

mind! I haven't heard from you in almost a year. You steal all my money, don't call or write, and suddenly you show up and expect me to welcome you back. Didn't you get my letters? Didn't you get the divorce papers?"

"No. I don't know what you're talking about."

Susan knew he was lying, and Jerome knew she knew; still he persisted. "I managed to get us a South American tour. The money is fabulous. Now that you have this motherhood thing out of your system, we can pick up where we left off."

Susan hooted. "You are out of your mind! I don't want anything to do with you. Do you realize you haven't even asked about our daughter? By the way, her name is Jessica Margaret."

Jerome blanched. He should have known he'd have to go through the baby to get to Susan. "I didn't forget; it was just that the pleasure of seeing you again drove it from my mind. Of course I want to see her. Our agent said she's crippled or something."

"Or something," Susan said coldly. "I noticed you mentioned a tour before Jessie, too. Well, forget it. I'm not interested. All I want is to be rid of you. Did you go through all the money you stole from me?"

"It was *our* money."

"Wrong, Jerome, most of it was *my* money, left to me by my father. It's all gone, right? That's why you're here. All I want from you is a divorce."

Jerome changed his tactics. "Look, Susan. I need you. If you want to bring the baby, that's okay. Get a nurse or something. We can take on the world, be really famous the way we were in Europe. You liked it—the applause and the recognition and the money. Admit it!"

"That was light-years ago. The only playing I do now is for charity to help our daughter. As a matter of fact, I'm giving a recital next week. This might surprise you, but we sold seven hundred and fifty tickets for one hundred dollars each. All of the monies will go to the spina bifida organization I've started here."

Jerome's eyes almost popped out of his head. Susan was talking about seventy-five thousand dollars! "You're giving it away to some . . . some . . ."

"Say it, Jerome. Spina bifida. Yes, I'm giving it away. In the fall I'm giving another recital in Austin. And another thing. I want you to hear this from me and not someone else: As soon as my divorce is final, I'm remarrying."

"Susan, please reconsider. I can't make it without you. I want us to stay married."

Susan's heart was beating normally now. She looked at the man she'd been married to for so long and felt only relief that she wouldn't ever have to see him again after today. "I have a baby now," she said calmly. "I have to put her first. Music will always be a part of my life, but it won't *be* my life. Jessie is. I'm sorry you won't be around to enjoy her. I can't believe you're not interested in your own child."

"She's crippled," Jerome said as if that explained everything. "But I love you," he said, grappling for something to say.

"That's really funny, Jerome. See how I'm laughing," Susan said coldly.

"You'll be sorry. I'll never give you a divorce. I can even sue for custody of that kid. Now what do you have to say?"

"She isn't going to say anything," Valentine Mitchell said as she laid her briefcase on a mahogany table. "I'm Valentine Mitchell, Susan's lawyer.'

A woman lawyer. It figured. "Well, Valentine Mitchell, Susan's lawyer," he said mockingly, "maybe you better tell *my wife* what my rights are."

"I suppose I could do that, but why don't I show you a few things I have in my briefcase. Maybe you'll want to rethink what you just said."

Jerome's eyes narrowed. Susan was folding and pleating the folds of her dress nervously. The only sound in the room was the lock of the Gucci briefcase snapping open.

"What we have here are signed affidavits from two banks. In this hand are canceled checks and bank drafts. In this third pile here are your joint accounts, which you had every legal right to use. This fourth pile, the long papers, are the divorce agreements."

"If you think I'm signing anything, you're crazy," he said contemptuously.

Valentine smiled, showing a perfect set of even white teeth. She looks like a barracuda, Jerome thought, suddenly afraid.

"I think you will," she replied. "Now, as I said, it was all right for you to withdraw the seven thousand eight hundred sixty-five dollars in your joint checking and savings. Also the stocks and bonds in both your names. I'm not concerned with those. But the authorities take a very dim view of forgery, both in England and here in the States. And you forged your wife's name on monies that were sent to her from her trust. You also requested some rather large advances, forged your wife's name to the letters and then to the drafts." She smiled at him. "You could get five to ten for that.

"Now here are the divorce papers," she continued, "and this other legal-looking sheaf of papers is also waiting for your signature. It says, in layman's terms, that you are giving Susan sole custody of Jessica Margaret de Moray. No alimony or child support is requested. I will give you—" Valentine looked at her watch "—exactly three minutes. At the end of those three minutes I'll call the sheriff, who, by the way, is my granddaddy." Valentine uncapped her silver pen and handed it to Jerome.

"You're railroading me!"

"I suppose you could say that. It's your choice. Prison life doesn't agree with anyone."

Jerome signed his name in a mean, narrow scrawl. He was seething with anger when he stared at Susan.

Valentine looked up from the papers. "What was that you just whispered? A threat? Tell me that wasn't a threat."

Jerome stalked to the door . . . then stopped and came back. Susan stared at him as he spoke, not believing a man could actually force words past tight lips and clenched teeth. "I don't have enough money to get back to England."

"I thought of that," Valentine said coolly. "Check into the airport. There's a People's Express leaving tomorrow. I prepaid a ticket for you. Good-bye, Mr. De Moray."

When the door closed behind him, Susan broke down and cried. "He didn't even want to see Jessie. He called her a cripple. How could I have loved such a person?"

"Everyone's entitled to one mistake. What did he say to you?"

"He said . . . he said . . . he made it sound like Jessie wasn't worth loving because of her handicap. *He's* the cripple, not her. She's different, and I love that little girl more than life itself!" Susan cried vehemently.

"Then that's all that's important. I understand you'll be getting married when the divorce is final. I hope you'll invite me to the wedding."

Susan smiled. "Of course. But it won't be right away. I want to be sure I'm doing the right thing. I don't want to make any more mistakes."

"Honey, Ferris Armstrong is no mistake. He's as good a person on the inside as he looks on the outside. You snagged yourself a real hunk this time. You Coleman ladies seem to have a knack for picking winners."

"Only after we go through hell with the losers. Thanks, Valentine."

"My pleasure. Listen, there aren't any more of you, are there?"

"No, I'm it. What do you think will happen to Jerome?"

"He'll go back to England and scout around for some nice lady who is musically inclined, and then go on from there. The Jeromes of this world always keep going. I'll get this on the court calendar, and you should be a free woman in thirty days."

Free. What a wonderful word. Just her and Jessie. Ferris too, if she wanted him.

And she was beginning to think that she wanted.

{{{{{{{{ CHAPTER TWENTY-EIGHT }}}}}}}}

Maggie and Rand returned to Sunbridge over the Memorial Day weekend. They were greeted with enthusiasm and hoots of pleasure, and Maggie basked in her family's joy at seeing her. It was Rand who announced that they would marry at the end of summer when the boys returned from Hawaii.

"We'll have just enough time to take you guys shopping for new clothes. Do you still want to stay in New York a few days before leaving?"

"Adam said it might be a good idea," Cole said. "The plane leaves New York on the twelfth of June."

"Has anyone heard from Sawyer or Mam?" Maggie asked anxiously.

"Not a word," Susan said. "I'm sorry, Maggie."

In the middle of her unpacking Maggie stopped, picked up the phone, and called Sawyer. "It's Maggie, Sawyer. How are you?"

"What difference does it make? Is there something you want?"

"Yes. I want to know how you are."

"I'm still alive. I'll be able to make the trip. Does that make you feel better or worse?"

"It doesn't make me feel anything. I'm numb. I want to know if you've changed your mind about the surgery."

"No. I haven't changed my mind."

"You're a fool."

"Like mother, like daughter. Right, *Mam*? So why don't you just get off my back?"

Maggie hesitated, trying to think of things to say. At least Sawyer wasn't hanging up on her. It was almost as though she wanted her to stay on, to bait her, to keep the verbal exchange going. "I wish I could, but I can't."

"It's too late. You're always too late, Maggie."

"I know," Maggie said, and Sawyer could hear the pain in her voice. "Nothing can ever be the same again. We aren't the same people we were back then. But I think we're wiser now. Why can't we come to terms, try to work things out? I'm willing."

"You should be. After all, it's easy to be forgiving when you're the one who screwed up. I'm the result of your screwup. You want me to forgive you; well, I can't. So why don't you just hang up and let me alone?"

"Why don't you hang up?"

"You called me, remember?" Sawyer said through clenched teeth.

"I want to see you before you leave for Hawaii. I'll come to New York with the boys. I won't stay. I just want to see you."

"Why?"

"Because I care how you're doing. Because I want to see you with my eyes."

"You want to play ghoul so you'll feel better is more like it. Well, I don't look so great, so save yourself the trouble," Sawyer said, her voice cracking.

"I'll be there with the boys. You can always tell me to leave. Will you let the boys see you act like that?"

"They know my feelings."

"I suppose they do, but they don't understand them. Not anymore. I don't think you have either of them mesmerized anymore. They know you're being selfish and acting like a fool."

"Let them tell me that."

Maggie sighed. "Sawyer, regardless of what you *think*,

you know I care. I want to help you if you'll let me."

"Don't you mean you want to help yourself? You can't help me. No one can help me."

"That's a damn lie!" Maggie screamed. Rand came running, and so did the boys. They stood helplessly in the doorway while Maggie ranted into the mouthpiece. "You're being stupid! Everyone wants to help you. Mam, Adam, Rand, all of us. Dr. Marlow is the best surgeon Sloan-Kettering has to offer and he will do his best for you. His best. Do you *hear*? Goddamn you, Sawyer, use your head and stop blaming everyone! You're really getting off on this phone call, aren't you? You like making us sweat. Admit it!" Maggie cried. "You like playing martyr. It must have been a real comedown for you after being pampered and coddled all those years. You're getting all the attention again, just like before. Let's all pity Sawyer. Look how noble she's being. She's going to die. Rally 'round, everyone. Coax Sawyer, plead with her, tell her how much she's loved and cared for. You make me sick. If I were Adam, I'd have booted your tail out of there a long time ago. You must make him sick, too."

"Get off this phone and don't call me again!" Sawyer screamed.

"No!" Maggie screamed back.

"Go to *hell*!"

"I've been there and back. It's not a nice place. Think about that. God will punish you for giving up. You're a Coleman."

"Shit on the Colemans!"

"We're only good enough when it's convenient for you. Is that it?"

"Hang up! Damn you, hang up!"

"No. You hang up on me." When Maggie heard the sound of crying at the other end of the line, she gently replaced the receiver. Tears streamed down her face, but she was smiling when she turned to face the trio at the door. "It isn't what you think. She wouldn't break the connection. She's starting to reach out."

"Mother, is she all right?" Cole asked fearfully.

"She's on the way. She's thinking, considering the odds. I don't know which way she'll go. Pray—that's my best advice."

While Maggie, Rand, and the boys shopped and packed, Sawyer took long walks in the park and saw Nick Deitrick every day. She paid two visits to the Sloan-Kettering Institute. She called her grandmother, and the gentle sorrow in Billie's voice was almost more than she could bear. Why didn't she rail her out the way Maggie and the others had done? "I want to come up there to talk with you, Grand," she begged.

"No, I'm sorry. You can't come here. I can't make decisions for you. It's not the operation anymore. It's Maggie. Don't confuse the two. I can't help you, darling. Only Maggie can help you. Don't be afraid. Make the first move . . . and call me again if I can help."

"She thinks I've forsaken her for Maggie," Billie said sadly after she'd hung up. "She really believes it, Thad."

"No she doesn't. She's just floundering. She has to struggle before she can accept what she needs most. You did the right thing. Poor darling, your heart is breaking. It'll be all right. I have a good feeling about it."

"If you told me it was light outside and I knew it was midnight, I'd believe you." Billie smiled wanly. "Let's go for a walk."

"With the dogs?"

Billie laughed. "All ten of them." She whistled, and they came from every corner, slipping and sliding on the kitchen tile, then lined up with unbelievable precision at the door.

"This is the way we're going to do it, gang," Thad told them. "I go first because I'm an admiral, and Billie goes next because she's an admiral's wife. You follow one at a time. There will be no cheating."

Billie looked over her shoulder at the dogs, who trotted in single file till they were on the road. Then Thad clapped his hands. "Disss-misssed!" The dogs scattered.

"We should take pictures of that. No one would believe it."

"It's just a question of authority. It's the tone, the rank, and my straight back."

"And the gumdrops you'll feed them when we get home."

Thad sniffed. "That's just a small part of it."

"So I'm Sawyer's authority figure. Is that it?"

"I knew I married you because you were bright."

"What about beautiful and charming?"

"That, too."

"You always make me feel better. It will be all right, won't it, Thad?"

"Yes, darling. Like I said, I have a feeling about it. But let's pray that someone up there is going to help us out."

On one of the shopping expeditions into Austin, Cole and Riley both picked out a gift for Luana—unbeknownst to each other, of course. Riley chose an exquisite bottle of perfume called Joy. Cole, more daring, bought a Gucci shoulder bag.

Cole didn't know what was worse: being with Luana for a few minutes of furtive kissing and hugging, or worshiping her from a distance. He'd obeyed the rules because he didn't want to see Luana get hurt. But he knew he was in love and wondered how he was going to get through the summer without seeing her. He imagined all the things he would buy her—native jewelry, a muumuu, a flower lei. He knew she liked him best, even though she hadn't said so. She'd cried when he'd told her he was going away for the summer. Then she'd asked offhandedly if Riley was going, too. He wished she weren't so nice to everyone. It gnawed at his gut.

Right now she was angry with him because he wouldn't risk going over to her apartment. But tonight was Saturday, date night. He was going to hang around the back porch like some ninny, hoping Luana would come out and sit with him on the steps. Maybe, just maybe, he'd take a chance, and if Ben Simms did go into town, he might . . .

When dinner was over, Riley left the table to get dressed for his date in town. "A cool chick," he told Rand, laughing. "She knows all about sports, and baseball is her favorite. She knows all about ground balls and sliders, and she says my curveball is the best she's ever seen."

"As compared to what?" Rand teased.

"As compared to an older brother who plays ball in the minors. I don't think I'll be too late, Aunt Maggie."

Maggie and Rand were going to the country club. Susan had a date with Ferris, and Ferris's mother had a date with Jessica. Cole was on his own.

In his room he could hear Riley whistling. He hated the sound. They'd both been fighting long and hard for Luana's affections, but Riley, not content to put all his eggs in one basket, kept dating—one girl after another. Evidently Riley wasn't as lovesick as he was. Cole hated what the feeling was doing to him. He *wanted* her. The other girls, even the ones who chased him—something he thought would never happen—didn't appeal to him at all. He knew the guys talked about Luana. Tease, trash, slut—they'd whispered all the worst names, and he'd heard them. But he knew in his gut that Luana was a virgin. Besides, she'd told him she was. And she was different with him. She didn't pretend the way she did in school. He knew how hard it was for her there. He hadn't belonged in the beginning, either.

Ever since he and Riley had gotten their own cars, though, things had changed. Luana seemed to prefer his Cougar convertible to Riley's Berlinetta. His mind raced as he tried to figure out a way to take Luana for a spin this evening. If he just happened to be out on the road leaving Sunbridge, and she just happened to be out there, too, he could pick her up. He could christen the Cougar. Jesus. He almost fainted with the thrill of excitement that rushed through him.

Riley had given up whistling; now the Oak Ridge Boys

were singing. Cole grimaced and stuck a Lionel Richie
tape in his player, turning up the volume. Luana liked
Lionel and Michael Jackson.

It was just starting to get dark when Cole heard the
Berlinetta roar out of the driveway. He looked out his
bedroom window and saw Luana sitting outside the apartment door, an open book on her lap. He craned his neck
to see if her father's truck was in the yard. It wasn't.

Quickly he finished dressing. Preppy tonight—a white
polo shirt, gray slacks, a navy-blue blazer, and topsiders.
He doused himself with Brut after-shave, then slicked his
hair back with both hands. He was ready. This was going
to be *the* night; he could feel it.

In the circular driveway Cole pretended not to see
Luana. He made sure, though, that she saw the way he
was dressed. Susan had just secured Jessica into her travel
seat and was about to climb behind the wheel. He walked
over nonchalantly and leaned in the car window.

"Wow!" Susan said, whistling. "Don't you look nice.
And you smell terrific." She grinned. "Big date?"

Cole knew their voices would carry to Luana. "Yeah,"
he drawled. "There's a party in town."

"You're going to have to fight the girls off with a stick,
looking the way you do. Remember now, don't drink and
drive."

"I won't, Aunt Susan. Did Mother and Rand leave
yet?"

"About five minutes ago. You have a good time. I'll
see you tomorrow."

Cole backed away from the car and stuffed his hands
into his pants pockets. That's what movie stars did to
show nonchalance. He was going to turn in a second now
and walk to his car, at which point he would notice Luana
for the first time. He turned, a look of pleased surprise
fixed on his face.

The look turned sour when he saw Luana was gone.
He sprinted upstairs and grabbed the big white gift box
with the red-and-green stripes, then raced down the back

steps, across the yard, and up the stairs to the apartment above the garage.

It was empty.

Cole tossed the Gucci box on the kitchen table next to Luana's books. Where the hell was she? She'd been here just minutes ago. He'd be dead meat if Ben Simms found him here. Maybe she'd gone for a walk. His pulses pounded in his ears on the way down the steps. By the time he climbed into the red sports car, he was in a near frenzy. He slammed it into reverse, then first, and was already in third when he tooled out of the yard onto the long stretch that would lead him to the main road.

Just outside the arch, Cole flicked on the high beams and screeched to a stop, his hand working fast as his left foot stomped on the clutch. There she was. He let the car idle as he pulled to the side of the road. The window slid down with a press of his index finger. "Want a lift?" he asked coolly.

"Where y'all goin'?"

"Party in town. Want to go?"

"I wasn't invited and I'm not dressed for a party," Luana said, pointing to her jeans and faded T-shirt. "If you have time, I could go to MacAllister's for a Coke."

"Sure, why not. Those parties never start to move till after ten anyway. Hop in."

"I do love this car, Cole," Luana cooed breathlessly as she hooked on her seat belt. Cole felt like groaning when he saw the way it mashed her breasts. He wanted to reach over and slide it between her breasts instead of over them.

"By the way," he said casually, "I left a present for you on your kitchen table. One minute you were there and the next you were gone."

"I didn't want to see you leave. Everyone from the big house was going out. I saw Riley leave. I felt jealous, so I decided to work it off by going for a walk. You didn't have to get me a present. It was nice of you, though. What is it?"

"When I drive you back home, you'll see it." Cole knew Luana was smiling in the darkness.

"I'm going to miss you guys when you leave. Just a few more days," she said softly.

"I'll send you a postcard, or I could write you a letter."

"That would be nice." She noticed there was a Michael Jackson tape playing, although it was hard to hear with the wind roaring in her ears.

"What are you going to do this summer?"

"Summer school, and I got a part-time job as a mother's helper for some six-year-old runt. The guidance counselor got it for me. The pay is three fifty an hour. I can use the money for school clothes in the fall."

"Too bad I won't be here to see them," Cole said morosely. "Your clothes, I mean. I'm leaving the end of August for prep school for my senior year, and then it's college."

"Riley, too?" Luana asked conversationally.

"Riley's going to Yale."

"You sound pleased. Are you going to Yale?"

"No, Notre Dame. Riley almost had a perfect SAT score. Fifteen ninety. I only scored thirteen hundred. Riley is Yale material." He wasn't going to tell her he actually felt proud of his cousin, even if he didn't like him.

"What are you going to do tonight?" he asked as one of McAllister's carhops brought them their Cokes.

"Read *The Red Badge of Courage* for a book report. It has to be in on Monday."

"You want to use mine? I got an A on it. I think I have it in my old papers from school."

"That'd be cheating," Luana said virtuously.

"Hey, I just asked. You don't have to use it. I thought maybe instead of going to the party, I could take you for a drive somewhere. Unless your father is coming home early," he added anxiously.

"No, he's out for the night. Okay, I'll use the report. Where do you want to go?"

"Hell, I don't know. We can't go to your place." He slapped at his head as though he just remembered something. "Hey, I know! There's an old line shack at the end of the north acreage. It's got an old couch, a stove, and some chairs, I think. And a hurricane lamp. No electricity or bathroom, though." He could feel his heart pounding.

"What'll we do there?" Luana asked innocently.

Cole grinned. "What do you think?"

"All the way?" Luana gasped.

"I have some rubbers. Come on, Luana, you're driving me crazy. You said you would when the time was right."

"My pa would kill me. You, too, if he ever found out."

"How's he gonna find out? I sure as hell won't tell him. That leaves you."

"He might be able to tell. My pa watches me like an eagle."

"Hawk," Cole corrected. He could almost feel her full, round breasts in his hands. "There's no way he'd be able to tell. Make up your mind; the girl's coming to take the tray."

Luana considered. "What am I gonna get out of this? The first time is supposed to hurt, and I'll have messy underwear. I've been saving myself. I know guys like you think that's corny, but I don't care. You're going away pretty soon. What am I supposed to do till you come back?"

"Wait for me. I won't hurt you. Maybe a little, but you'll forget it in a hurry. I have about two hundred dollars. Will that help you make up your mind?"

"Two hundred dollars! Well, sure, but there's something not right about taking money for . . . for . . ."

"You don't have to take it."

"I didn't say I wouldn't take it. I sure could use it. . . ." She thought it over for a few moments. "Okay, let's go to the line shack."

Cole's gut churned as he backed the Cougar out of the parking lot.

Forty-five minutes later Cole sat in the line shack staring at Luana. He handed her the two hundred dollars and she quickly slipped it into her hip pocket. Then he watched, fascinated, as she pulled her T-shirt over her head. He sucked in his breath. She was wearing a pink lacy bra that barely contained her breasts. A moment later the faded jeans slipped to the floor.

As Luana put her hands behind her back to unhook her bra, the strangest thing happened to Cole. First, his whole life flashed before him. Then a vision of his future crowded out his past. When he could see clearly again, the half-naked girl who stood before him no longer interested him. He wanted to tell her so, but the words wouldn't come.

Her breasts were free now, large and pink-tipped. There was no hunger on his lips to taste them. He continued to watch her as the bikini slid down. She was beautiful. She beckoned him with her eyes as she lowered herself to the old leather couch; her movements slow, sensual. Suddenly she squirmed and yelped as the sharp strips of aged leather cut into her skin. She jumped up, twisting and turning.

Even in the dim light from the hurricane lamp, Cole could see the thin slashes of blood. He walked over, bent down to feel the cracked leather. It cut his finger like a knife. He drew in his breath sharply and straightened up, cursing. "This was the worst idea I ever had. Get dressed," he said, sucking the blood from his finger. "I'll wait outside. Blow out the lamp before you leave."

Oh, shit, now he was going to want the two hundred dollars back. Just her damn luck. If her pa ever saw the marks on her back and ass, she was going to have some real tall explaining to do.

"Do you want the money back?" she said when she climbed into the car.

"No. You were willing. We made a deal."

"Why'd you change your mind?"

"Is it important for you to know?" Cole asked through clenched teeth.

"Well, sure it is. I thought you liked me. You been after me for a long time, and when I finally say yes, you tell me to put my clothes back on. You must be nuts, givin' me two hundred bucks for nothin'. Well, not for nothin', exactly. I did strip for you. But why'd you change your mind?"

Cole pressed his foot to the gas pedal. There were a lot of things he could tell her, but he decided to spare her, "I couldn't get it up," he said coolly, hoping she could hear him over the rush of the wind.

When Luana had absorbed what he'd said, she laughed. At Sunbridge she got out of the car, leaned over, and said quietly, "I know a lie when I hear one. You decided I wasn't good enough for you. I *saw* it in your eyes."

Cole looked away. "You better put something on those scratches," he said quietly. Luana backed away from the car, and he spun out, burning rubber.

She watched till she couldn't see the taillights any longer, then sprinted up the stairs and tore open Cole's present. A real Gucci bag! Excitedly, she fished for her two hundred dollars and put it inside. Then, slinging the brown strap over her shoulder, she walked about the kitchen, feeling like the richest woman in Texas. She forgot about putting something on her cuts. After she'd tucked her gift safely away, cut the Gucci box into small pieces and carried them down to the trash, she settled down to read *The Red Badge of Courage*.

It was after one in the morning when the high-beam headlights of the Berlinetta swooped around the circular drive, shining upward to Martha's room. On her way to the bathroom, the housekeeper stopped to look out the window, a habit of many years. She watched Riley climb from the car and noticed that the bright red Cougar was parked alongside. He was headed toward the house when she saw him turn.

Martha drew back a little into the darkness of her room and watched as Luana raced across the driveway. She nodded in satisfaction when she saw Riley shake his head and motion to the house. Luana took his arm and tried to pull him toward the garage. Riley resisted but allowed himself to be pulled as far as his car. Then he jerked free and leaned back against it, his hands jammed in his pockets. Martha strained to hear their conversation, but finally had to give up. Whispers didn't carry to the second floor.

The digital clock on her nightstand read 1:23 when she climbed into bed. If she'd had her way, she would have sent Ben Simms and his daughter packing five minutes after they'd arrived. She was almost asleep when she heard a door close. Riley. She opened one eye to look at the clock: 1:44. Two minutes later, she was asleep.

Cole, too, had seen the Berlinetta's lights sweep into the yard. Must have been a good party, he thought as he got up to go to the bathroom. On his way back to bed, he looked down into the courtyard, just in time to see Luana run across and grab Riley's arm. He stood by the window a long time, watching them. He felt pleased when Riley turned and went into the house. A few minutes later his cousin passed by, and he heard the sound of a door closing.

Cole nodded in satisfaction. They'd both obeyed the rules. Neither of them would bring shame on Sunbridge or the Coléman name.

*

Ben Simms climbed the stairs to the apartment, his arms loaded with the weekly groceries. The stove light was on, casting dim shadows over the neat kitchen. He put the groceries away, folded the bags neatly, and stuck them between the refrigerator and stove.

He walked wearily to his room. He'd had a few drinks, shot some pool, played some poker. The woman he'd been seeing, he was told, had gone to Maine to see a sick sister. There'd been no point in hanging around at two-thirty in the morning, and as a rule he didn't like dingy bars anyway. So he'd taken his bag of meat the bartender had kept in the refrigerator, slapped it in the back of the pickup, and driven home.

He tiptoed to the bathroom, relieved himself, washed and dried his face and hands. He opened the laundry hamper and was about to throw his clothes in when he noticed Luana's faded yellow shirt and threadbare jeans. He pulled them out and held them up to the bathroom light. They seemed to be crisscrossed with lines of blood. He stared at them for a long time, then, his teeth clamped together, he strode down the hall to his daughter's room. He threw open the door and turned on the light switch. Luana was lying naked on the bed but hastily pulled the covers over herself when the overhead light came on.

"What's the meaning of this, girl?" he demanded harshly, shoving the blood-streaked clothes close to her face. Half-asleep, Luana could only stare guiltily at the soiled clothing. "You better give me some quick answers."

"Pa, I didn't do nothin'. I swear I didn't."

"Git up, right now!" Ben thundered.

"Paaaa, I ain't got no clothes on."

"That's right; I'm yer pa. Now, get up and let me look at you."

Having Cole see her naked was fun. She'd wanted to see him stare bug-eyed at her bare breasts, wanted to see him swallow hard when he saw her without a stitch of clothes. Having her pa see her was sinful; she felt ashamed as she slipped out of bed. There was a look on his face, in his eyes, that made her feel sick. He reached for her, turning her around. "How'd you get those marks?"

"I don't know, Pa. I swear I don't!" Luana cried.

"Ye're lyin' to me, girl. I kin see it in yer face." He pulled her to him till he could feel her breasts against his own bare chest. "Ye're jest like yer ma," he said softly. "Jest like her."

Luana struggled. She didn't want to have him touch her, but suddenly his hands were all over her. The more she struggled, the more intense her father became. She found herself being dragged to the bed. She wanted to scream, to make someone hear what was going on, but she couldn't. Shame ripped through her at what she knew was about to happen.

Exactly eight hours after Riley entered the kitchen the night before, his life changed. It was 9:14 when four sheriff's cars roared into the Coleman driveway. Martha blessed herself and used the intercom to tell Maggie she was wanted downstairs right away.

"Rape!" Rand shouted, staring at Ben Simms in stunned disbelief. He was still in his robe and pajamas, his hair tousled from sleep. Maggie stood beside him, clutching his arm.

"Who was raped?" she asked hoarsely.

"My little gal, that's who," Simms said sharply. "If you want, you can go to the hospital and see for yourself."

"Who raped her? Who'd do such a thing?" Maggie tried to organize her thoughts. "Why is she in the hospital?"

"She was found wandering the main highway, Mrs. Tanner," said one of the sheriff's men. "Pretty badly beaten. The first aid squad was called and they took her straight to the hospital. She *said* she was raped, but there's no conclusive evidence yet, ma'am. They're doing tests on her now." He looked pointedly at Ben Simms.

Maggie felt Cole standing beside her. "Will she be all right?" she asked.

"Yes, ma'am. She's been roughed up, but she'll recover."

Cole's heart was thundering in his chest. He saw Riley, his face almost white, standing beside Rand.

"You got some gall askin' if my little gal will be all right!" Ben Simms cried. "She'll never be all right again! But she was able to talk to me when I got to the hospital. Wouldn't talk to nobody else, neither, not my gal. She knows her pa's the only one to help her. And she told me who did it to her. Told me clear and loud. It was that Jap kid, that's who it was!" Simms lunged for Riley. Two of the officers pulled him back.

"You're lying!" Maggie cried, and turned to Rand. "For God's sake, do something!"

"Deputy Pierson, ma'am," a tall young officer said politely. "Stand back, Mr. Simms. I'll handle this."

"Tell us what happened, Deputy," Rand said quietly. "But first I'd appreciate it if you'd remove Mr. Simms from this kitchen."

When Ben had been escorted away, Deputy Pierson turned back to Rand and Maggie. "Mrs. Tanner," he said soberly, "Luana Mae Simms has accused your nephew of beating and raping her."

"But it isn't true! Riley wouldn't do such a thing."

"Mr. Simms says the boy is violent. Is it true that Riley Coleman attacked him in your dining room when he tried to break up a fight between your son and your nephew?"

"No, Riley didn't attack him; he just didn't want the man to touch him. . . ."

"That's not what Mr. Simms says. Have there been any other acts of violence between your nephew and your son, Mrs. Tanner?"

"What does that have to do with Luana?" Maggie asked, wringing her hands.

Riley sagged against Rand. "I didn't touch her. I didn't do it. I swear I didn't. I talked to her for a couple of minutes when I got home, but I didn't touch her!"

"That's true, what the boy says," Martha interjected. The deputy took notes as she explained about being awakened by Riley's headlights. "I heard him come in. I heard the door close."

"Thank God, Martha. Thank God you heard."

Cole stepped forward. "I saw him come in. I heard him, too. I also saw Luana go back up the steps. I was watching from my window."

Cole moved back until he was standing next to Riley. Maggie saw her son's hand touch Riley's shoulder. Any other time she would have been pleased; now she was frightened out of her wits.

"I want to call our lawyer," she said, trying to speak calmly. "None of us will say one more word until she gets here."

"Please have your lawyer meet us at the Crystal City Sheriff's Office. I'm sorry, Mrs. Tanner, but we have to take the boy in for questioning."

Rand stepped forward. "Deputy Pierson, do you have to take Riley immediately? Why not let the lawyer come here? It would be much less disruptive to the family. How would you like a cup of coffee?" He turned to Martha without waiting for an answer. "Martha, how about some of that delicious coffee of yours. And would it be too much trouble to cook up some breakfast? We're all starving, and I'm sure the deputy and his men haven't eaten for hours."

Martha hurried to the stove. "Yes sir, Mr. Nelson, a nice mess of grits and ham with eggs on the side. How's that sound?"

Maggie smiled weakly as she headed for the study to call Valentine Mitchell. They'd take Riley to the sheriff's office eventually, but not before they gorged on Martha's biscuits and ham.

Two uniformed officers stood outside the kitchen door, their hands on their holsters. Everyone else was seated at the table in the breakfast nook waiting for Valentine Mitchell when Maggie excused herself again and returned to the study. This time she called Amelia.

"I need you and Cary," she said, then tersely explained what was going on.

As soon as she'd hung up, she called Ferris Armstrong. "Send Susan, please, Ferris. I want the family here."

Her last call was to Billie. Thad answered and when Maggie explained, Thad was comforting. "Has anyone thought about calling the boy's grandfather?"

"I thought about it, but I don't want to alarm him. He's elderly and not well. Will you do it, Thad?"

"Of course, as soon as I hang up. Stand tough, Maggie. Don't let some smooth-talking pickup jockey railroad the boy."

The ensuing hours were a nightmare.

When Valentine arrived, the police led Riley away. Cole watched in silence until the police car was out of sight; then he turned and kicked out at the kitchen chair, overturning it. Swearing savagely, he raced upstairs, nursing his injured foot. He ran straight to the bathroom and was violently sick. After he'd cleaned up and brushed his teeth, he went to his room and called Sawyer, explaining the situation in jerky sentences.

"I think you should come here," he said harshly. "Grand is on her way. We need everyone. I'm the next one they're going to haul in."

"Of course I'll come. I'll bring Adam with me. I don't know when we can get a flight, though."

"Charter one! If ever there was a time to use all that Coleman money everyone brags about, this is it."

"I'll be there, little brother," Sawyer promised. "Just hang on."

Cole hung up and made a second trip to the bathroom, retching till his stomach muscles ached.

It was after two when Luana was brought back to the house. The ambulance driver handed Deputy Pierson an envelope. He handed it to Maggie, who read what was inside and then passed it to Rand.

From her seat in the breakfast nook, Maggie could see the ambulance drivers helping Luana up the steps. She'd been raped; it was on paper now, a fact, not something Ben Simms made up.

By three o'clock the Cougar and the Berlinetta were impounded. Riley and Valentine were still at the sheriff's office. Maggie chewed off three of her fingernails.

CHAPTER TWENTY-NINE

Thad and Billie arrived at four-thirty that afternoon, Saw-
yer and Adam shortly after. The sheriff's deputies arrived
at six with a warrant for Cole's arrest. Cole's face was
grim and frightened when he kissed his mother and then
Sawyer. "I didn't do anything and neither did Riley. You've
got to believe us!"

"We do!" Maggie and Sawyer cried in unison, then
watched helplessly as he was led away.

Just after midnight Shadaharu Hasegawa arrived in a
limousine. He embraced Billie and Thad and bowed low
to the others. "Now, tell me."

The old Japanese gentleman listened as Thad explained
the situation. "My grandson would not bring dishonor on
his family," he said calmly. "And I do not believe my good
friends' other grandson would do such a thing. There is
a truth here beyond what we see. We must find it."

At around twelve-thirty Valentine Mitchell called with
a status report. Riley and Cole were to be brought into
court for arraignment in the morning.

"What's an arraignment?" Maggie asked Rand, who
had taken Valentine's call.

"She says it's to go before the court to see if there's
enough evidence to set bail and put the wheels in motion
for a trial. Valentine says not to worry; the boys will be
released to our custody. They're to appear in court at nine
o'clock tomorrow morning."

* * *

Appearing before the judge was a sobering experience for Riley and Cole. Up until then, everything that happened the day before had seemed like a bad dream. Now it was a reality. They had been accused; the grounds of suspicion had been weighed and found substantial. Both boys had been implicated, but only Riley had been charged with rape. Cole, they believed due to evidence found in his car, had aided and abetted the crime.

Riley was still dazed from his appearance before the judge when he entered the anteroom outside the court. The first person he saw was his grandfather. Tears sprang to his eyes. "Old One, I did nothing to disgrace our family."

Cole, who had entered the anteroom behind his cousin, felt a lump in his throat. His mother was crying; they were all crying except Thad and Rand. The old Japanese gentleman reached out his arms, and Riley, two heads taller, walked into them. Words were unnecessary.

"Where do we go from here, Valentine?" Rand asked in a muted voice.

"We wait," she answered, stuffing papers into her briefcase. "I want you to take the boys into Austin General Hospital for semen sampling. It would be easier on them if you didn't bring Maggie. We're waiting for the results of the slides made from cervical smears taken from Luana Simms. If we're lucky, the two tests won't compare and Riley and Cole will be off the hook. I'm not taking any chances, though; the test work will be done by two independent laboratories as well as the hospital. Tell Maggie that was Dudley's quick thinking, and thanks to the Coleman sway, we managed to get the D.A.'s office to agree."

"We'll leave in a while," Rand assured Valentine. He turned in time to see Cole walk out the front door, Riley following behind.

"Where're you going, Cole?" Riley asked.

Something in his tone caught Cole's curiosity. "What's it to ya?"

"Because I want to talk to you."

"So talk."

"Not here. Out back."

Cole shrugged and walked around to the back, Riley dogging his steps. From the way Riley was acting, Cole sensed there was going to be trouble. He wasn't surprised when Riley's arm shot out and turned him roughly around.

"You bastard," Riley hissed. "It was you who attacked Luana, because I know it wasn't me. You were the one, and you're going to let me take the rap! I heard the evidence this morning, and if no one else is asking you questions, I am. How did Luana's fingerprints get all over your car? How did her blood get there? She wouldn't let you into her pants, so you roughed her up and then raped her!"

"Hold it, Riley. That's not the whole story; you don't know what happened!"

"Don't I? I sure as hell do, and I'm not going down with you. Damned if I am!" The anger Riley had been struggling to control since early that morning erupted. Cole never saw the blow coming and took it full on the chin. Another kick from Riley's foot hit him square in the gut, bending him over double.

"Fight! Stand up and fight!" Riley shouted, already bracing himself against attack.

Cole lashed out, his knuckles grazing Riley's cheeks and then returning for a closer aim at his nose.

"Rand! Thad!" Billie shouted. "Stop them! Stop them!" They had all followed behind Rand when he'd hurried out after the boys. He'd sensed trouble coming, seen it in the bearing of Riley's shoulders, in the clenching of his fists as he'd followed Cole out the door.

Rand held Riley back; Thad kept Cole's arms pinned behind him. Blood was dripping from Riley's nose; Cole's lip was split and swelling.

"Let me go!" Cole struggled. "Let me go. I've gotta tell him something."

"Not now," Maggie said. "Just be quiet. There's been enough damage done." She reached into Riley's pocket for a handkerchief to wipe his nose.

"Let him speak," Mr. Hasegawa said firmly. "It's time we all knew what they know. Let us all hear, Cole. Riley, only a fool refuses to hear."

"Riley," Cole began, sputtering through his swollen mouth, "it isn't what you think. I didn't touch her. I met her on the road; she was hitching a ride." He looked guiltily at his mother. "Anyways, you know how it is with Luana. One thing led to another and I took her to that old line shack. But nothing happened! I didn't touch her. I told her to get dressed. I saw that her back was bleeding from the crackly split leather on that old couch in the line shack. *That's* how her blood got in my car. *That's* why her fingerprints were all over the place!"

Riley's shoulders relaxed. Rand felt the tension leave the boy's body.

"Believe me, Riley. I'm no more guilty than you are."

"I do believe you," Riley muttered. "And I know what it cost you to tell me all this in front of the family. I'm sorry, Cole."

"So it is East meets West," Mr. Hasegawa said sagely.

"Sir." Cole smiled shyly. "Just for once, could we make that West meets East? It'd be nice to get top billing."

Riley laughed, the first joyful sound they had heard in what seemed an eternity.

The following days were an agony of waiting. The tests had been taken on both boys. Ben Simms had packed up his daughter and their belongings and moved into town. What had happened to Luana was no secret, and Ben aired his hatred of the Colemans at every opportunity.

It was the old Japanese gentleman who put the man's actions into perspective. "There is no prouder man in the world than the man who can claim an injustice. Mr. Simms is pleased with the attention he is receiving, even for these few days, by being the center of a community's sympathy. And the more he cries and grieves his daughter's lost virtue, the more praise he will receive and the purer she is thought to have been. And for his grief, Mr. Simms receives praise from his neighbors for being the perfect father."

Sunbridge seethed with hostility, directed and misdirected. As Maggie tried to describe it to her mother, "It's like we're an accident waiting to happen. Everyone's temper is short. Everyone has an idea, but no one knows what to do about it."

"Darling, the 'accident' already happened," Billie said. "Thad and I both believe it's a question of money. Has Miss Mitchell come up with anything from the private detectives the firm hired?"

"Only that Simms is exactly what he is—a drifter who does handyman work and who goes to church, when he's in the mood, and who can recite the Bible from one end to the other. They've never, ever been in trouble. He has no record anywhere. Not so much as a traffic or parking ticket. The girl is behind in school, but that's because they move around so much. She's pretty big on reciting the Bible herself." She hesitated. "Valentine tells me the psychologist who is treating Luana told her, or sent her a report—I don't remember which—that said Cole forced Luana to have sex with him. But they aren't classifying Cole's actions as rape. Because"—Maggie drew in a deep breath—"he gave her things and money in return for... for her favors. But she's sticking to the rape story."

Billie sighed. "There isn't anything we can do, then?"

"Nothing. If we could just get to the girl, I think one of us could talk some sense into her. The last I heard, and that was in the *Crystal City Times* yesterday, was that Luana is being watched by some woman, a friend of Simms. I don't know if she's a housekeeper or what her function is, exactly," Maggie said dejectedly. "If only those tests would come in; I know the boys would be cleared."

"The press has been very unkind. If Seth were alive, this wouldn't have gotten off the ground."

"In those days *we* were the good guys. Today it's a whole new ball game. They're raking up all that old stuff on me. I just want to sit down and cry my eyes out. But I have to be strong and take everything they throw at us. I'm dreading the day the other side comes up with the dirt Valentine dug up on Cranston. If she has it, it's a matter of public record."

"No it isn't. Those records are sealed. That's one good thing about being a Coleman. Seth always had that agreement with the law firm. He paid handsomely to whoever it was in charge. I know that for a fact, Maggie," Billie added quietly.

"They're really out to get us, Mam. You must have noticed the phone hasn't rung once since you've been here for anything but crank calls. We're off everyone's list. It's hitting Cary hard. Some of the men actually walked off the job. The real big investors are nervous. If they decide to pull out, he loses everything."

"I know just the person to step in and help out." Billie grinned. "Riley's grandfather. He helped us once before; he'll do it again. Don't even think about it. As far as the workers go, all Cary has to do is up the wages and other men will come running from out-of-state." Billie hesitated, then asked, "Where is . . . everyone?"

Maggie knew who she meant. "Sawyer's down at the barn with the boys." She smiled. "Adam is over in your old studio, working up a storm. He decided to take on the state of Texas. The muckrakers may be getting in their shots, but he's retaliating. And the papers are printing his stuff. He's made quite a name for himself, and he does have some powerful friends in the media. *And* he's from Texas, a native son, so they have to pay attention. For now, it's our only plus. You went to bed early last night, so you didn't see the eleven-o'clock news. We made it— the wire services, the whole bit. We're news, Mam." She shook her head. "I can't believe this is happening to us."

"I can. The Colemans have always been news."

"Let's talk about something else," Maggie said. "More coffee?"

"Half a cup. I'm jittery enough without caffeine."

"How do you think Sawyer looks?"

"Like she's held together with spit and glue. Dry spit and old glue," Billie said sadly.

"We've had some fairly civil conversations," Maggie told her. "Of course, they had to do with the boys. It was a little awkward at first with Rand being here, and Adam and all. But I think we've managed to put those feelings aside for now. Maybe some good will come of all this."

"What do the three of them *do* down in the barn?" Billie asked curiously.

"Talk, I guess. I really don't know."

"They're up to something. Sawyer always was a planner, a master one at that."

"Maybe that's what we need, a plan. Action. This sitting around is driving me insane. We should be doing something."

"There's nothing to do. Drink your coffee, Maggie. I think I'm going to take a walk."

"To the cemetery?"

"Yes. Would you like to join me?"

"Yes. Yes, I would."

Sawyer stared at the boys. They stared back. Her head pounded, but she did her best to ignore the pain. From where she was sitting on a bale of hay, she could see them clearly. They looked so hopeful, so expectant. "Okay," she said, "let's go over it one more time. I know you've said it three hundred times. Humor me. Once more." She listened carefully. When they were finished, the only thing it seemed they were in agreement on was that Luana had been a virgin.

"If she was a virgin when you left her at home around ten, Cole, and when Riley left her at one-forty-five or so, that gives us some time to play with. Simms says he got home at three. That gives us one hour and fifteen minutes. Whoever it was had to have raped the girl in that span of time. Simms says—and this is just his word—that he didn't find out about Luana until the deputies came to take him to see Luana at the hospital. But he's lying; we all know that. We also know why. Big bucks. Right now, the only thing you have going for you is the hospital test. So, what we have here is one hour and fifteen minutes or five hours, give or take a few minutes."

"The cops have gone all over this," Cole muttered. "So have the lawyers."

"We're it, Sawyer," Riley groaned. "We can't prove we didn't do it. It looks like they can prove we did."

"Unless..." Sawyer let the word hang in the air. Both faces were so hopeful, she wanted to cry. "Unless, in that hour and fifteen minutes, or in that five hours, give or take a few minutes, Ben Simms raped his own daughter."

Cole's mouth dropped open. Riley's jaw dropped just as far as Cole's.

"Her own father!" Cole gasped.

"That's... that's..."

"The word you're looking for is incest," Sawyer said coldly. "Think about it. In all the years I lived at Sunbridge, we never, ever had anyone come on this land who didn't belong. Not up to the house, anyway. Somebody would have heard. The barn dogs would have barked. Strangers just don't pop up, even for a girl like Luana. She might have jerked your strings, but she'd never take the chance and invite someone from the outside here. There'd be a car, a moped, at the very least a bicycle, and I think we have to rule that out. We live twenty-five miles from town. Does either of you think she'd ask someone here?" At their negative nod, Sawyer continued, "That leaves Ben Simms committing the ultimate sin."

"It makes sense, but why didn't Miss Mitchell say something?"

"Think about it, Cole. Incest. You can't accuse a man of something like that. You can't even dance around it. Look, I'm not pretending to be a wizard or anything like that. I'm sure it's occurred to everyone, but no one wants to put it into words. If we did that, we'd open ourselves to the biggest lawsuit this state has ever seen. I think we should talk to Adam. I'm kind of tired, so why don't you guys go get him and bring him here. I'm going to flop down on that straw and see if this headache will go away."

The boys glanced at each other. "You stay with her, Cole, and I'll get him," Riley offered.

Cole nodded and lowered himself to the sweet-smelling straw. "It's worse, isn't it?" he asked Sawyer when Riley had left.

"Yeah. I don't think I would have made it to Hawaii. I was going to give it a hell of a try, though."

"You're nuts," Cole said, not unkindly. "What's happening to us can't even compare to what you're going through. You have to do something."

"Wave your magic wand and make me better," Sawyer said nastily.

"That's bullshit. Tell your surgeon to wave his magic scalpel and take your chances. That's what I would do."

"Well, you aren't me, little brother, so keep your opinions to yourself. If you're worried about me being around for the final verdict, forget it. I'll be here."

"I don't care about that. If I have to lose you, I want it to be the right way. I want to know you gave it everything you had."

Sawyer leaned up on one elbow, piercing Cole with her gaze. "And if I don't make it?"

Cole swallowed hard. "Like Miss Mitchell says, there aren't any guarantees. Not for me or Riley, and not for you. You aren't a gutless wonder, so stop acting like one."

Sawyer groaned. "I'm supposed to be in charge here."

"Well, shit, if you're in charge, act like it. Not just for Riley and me, but for yourself. You must be driving Adam fucking crazy."

Sawyer burst out laughing. "Where'd you learn to talk like that? Maggie would put soap in your mouth." Cole laughed, too, and then fell back into the hay. They were both laughing and throwing straw at each other when Riley and Adam walked into the barn.

"I wish you'd tell us what's so damn funny. We could

sure use a laugh or two," Adam said, smiling.

Sawyer leaned up on both elbows, straw sticking out of her hair and ears. When she spoke, her voice was solemn. "My brother here, this pip-squeak, says he'll put flowers on my grave if I die. He said he'd pray for me. This guy," she said, pointing to Riley, "said yesterday he'd stay with me through the entire operation. He has one small fear: he's paranoid about the sight of blood. I have decided to go ahead and have the operation. As soon as this is all wrapped up."

"No. Now," Cole said forcefully.

"Wrong. It's my decision. When this is over."

"I take it all back," Cole said coldly. "Now or forget it. We can hang on till this is over. You don't have the time."

"I'll think about it," Sawyer blustered.

Riley grimaced. "That's something I'd say. Tell us now, in front of Adam, so he can make the arrangements."

Sawyer struggled to get to her feet. It was getting worse; who was she kidding? How many more days could she take like the last few? "Okay," she said, swaying dizzily.

"You get a free ride for this one," Adam said, scooping her into his arms. Cole noticed that his eyes were wet. Shit, he didn't care. He felt like he'd just climbed the tallest mountain in the world.

"Did they tell you what I came up with?" Sawyer asked sleepily.

"Don't think about that now."

"Don't tell me what to do, Adam. I can still think for myself. While you're making the arrangements, I want to talk to this family. Get them all together around the dining room table."

"You're a real pain, you know that?"

"Yeah, I know. Just humor me and then I'm all yours."

"Do you mean that?"

"For God's sake, of course I mean it! When we get to the house, get me one of those green pills and a shot of brandy. C'mon," she squawked, "what's the delay here?"

"Just shut up and enjoy the ride," Adam said. Cole grinned. Riley punched him playfully on the shoulder in return.

Maggie and Billie ran out to the driveway as they saw Adam carrying Sawyer up the walk. "What's the matter?" Maggie gasped. Billie immediately put her hand on Sawyer's forehead.

"She wants a meeting," Adam said. "You boys explain while I get the pill and the brandy. She wants Cary and Amelia here, too."

Ninety minutes later the entire Coleman family was assembled at the dining room table. "You're on, Sarah," Adam called to Sawyer, who was in the kitchen. "This better be a performance worthy of Bernhardt."

"I have something to say to all of you," Sawyer announced." She paused a moment to marshal her strength. "We find ourselves involved in not one but two crises. I'm the first, Cole and Riley the second. Each is equally important. I could literally die. Their lives could be ruined. In my eyes, that's the same thing." Again she paused, this time for effect. "I've agreed to have the operation. At the insistence of Cole and Riley, I'm leaving this afternoon for Sloan-Kettering. Now, if I'm willing to put my head on the block, I want all of your necks on the same block. I want you—us—to accuse Ben Simms of raping his daughter. I think we all know that's exactly what happened. So put it on the line, just like I am. If I can do it, so can you." She looked around fuzzily, blinked to regain her vision. But it wasn't working; the faces were still blurry. Her heart fluttered wildly as she gripped the edge of the table and spoke. "Maggie? Grand? Amelia? Susan? I want an answer." She thought she was seeing horror, dismay, fear, when actually all the faces held something she couldn't see—pride.

"Good girl," Cary said loudly. "I'm with you and so is Amelia."

"Me, too. And include Jessie in my vote," Susan said happily.

"I agree and so does Thad," Billie said, rushing up to Sawyer. "I'm so glad."

It was Maggie's turn. She looked around wildly, tears sliding down her cheeks. Rand reached out to her. Riley handed her his handkerchief. "So, you do know how to fight. You have my vote."

"One more thing," Sawyer told them. "If I don't make it, I want you all to know that . . . I . . ." She swayed dizzily, then her knees crumpled as she started to slip to the floor. Rand was there first, his arms outstretched. Adam came around the side of the table a second too late. He bent down, his eyes locking with Rand's. What he saw there made him nod and stand up. It was Rand who carried Sawyer to the waiting ambulance.

Cole stood next to Riley in the driveway. "This is big shit, you know," he said. "They're putting everything on the line for us." He sat down on the garage steps where Luana always sat. "I think we just grew up."

"My grandfather will assist in whatever way he can. I wish he hadn't come here though. I see the way he looks at me. I've caused him trouble."

"I saw him look at you, too. He doesn't believe you did it, and no one else thinks so, either. He's . . ." Cole groped for the right word. "Sad."

"Do you think Sawyer'll make it?"

"Hell, I don't know. She did real good in there, didn't she?"

"She sure did. Maybe we can still go to Hawaii when she's better."

"Yeah, maybe," Cole said glumly.

"I was thinking about something," Riley said uneasily. "If I ask your opinion, will you give me a truthful answer?"

"Sure."

"I was thinking about getting my eyes fixed, Westernized. What do you think?" He held his breath, waiting for Cole to answer.

Cole turned to stare at his cousin, looking at him closely from different angles. Finally he said, "Why the hell would you want to do a dumb thing like that?"

Riley laughed. "You mean it?"

"Hell, yes. You can't do that to the old man in there. He'd lay down and die. You're who you are and I'm who I am."

"I'd look more like a Coleman," Riley said defensively.

"Man, being a Coleman is being one. It doesn't matter how you look. I'm only half, too. When push comes to shove, that's when you know who you are. I hated your guts in the beginning. Guess you know that."

"Yeah. Well, I wasn't too fond of you, either. I thought you were a real jerk."

"I thought you were a real fag myself. You had it all. At least I thought you did. You didn't have it so easy, either, did you?"

"No," Riley replied. He wasn't about to tell his cousin he'd had a wonderful life till he came here. They were even now, starting from square one.

"We're it, you know. The last of the Colemans. Little Jessie doesn't count, because she's ... she's different. I don't think Susan will have any more children. She might adopt. And we don't know about Sawyer. So, cousin, we're it."

"Yeah, look where we are."

"I have a gut feeling we're gonna make it," Cole said with more confidence than he felt. "With a family like this, how can we lose? Your grandfather is okay, too," Cole added generously. "Maybe that's what set me off about you. He bailed out the Colemans when the going got tough."

"Don't you think your family would have done the same thing?" Riley asked curiously.

"Back then, when you first got here, I probably would have said no. Now I know differently." He leaned back, resting on his elbows.

"How do you think you're going to like Yale?"

"Probably the same as you're going to like Notre Dame. I'll think of you doing all that praying."

"Ah, shit." Cole grinned.

"How fast does that Cougar go?"

"Just as fast as that Berlinetta. Do you drink and drive?" Cole asked curiously.

"No way, man, do you?"

"Nope. You ever score with a chick?" Cole asked slyly.

"Nope. Did you?"

"No. Guess we do have a lot in common."

"You wanna keep in touch when we go off to college?" Riley asked.

"Sure. Maybe we can even visit each other. I think it's time we started spending some of this Coleman money. Did anyone say anything to you about allowances?"

"Don't worry. What's mine is yours," Riley said generously.

Cole stuck out his hand. Riley gripped it. Both boys grinned.

While the boys were coming to terms with each other, the remaining Colemans sat around the dining room table, waiting as Valentine Mitchell opened her briefcase and took out a legal pad, then fished for a pen. "Okay, let's hear it."

Two minutes later she got up, looked around, and said, "You want to do *what*?"

"You heard right," Maggie said firmly. "We're all in agreement. And we're prepared for anything. You do your job, and we'll handle the rest."

Valentine sat down heavily. "I guess I don't have to tell you—"

"No, you don't. We know. Now, who's going to the newspapers, you or us?" Valentine read the determination in Maggie's expression.

"I'll do it." The leaf-green eyes looked around the table. "You have guts; I'll say that for you. Procedure is that I go to Simms's attorney."

"We aren't interested in procedure. You go for the jugular," Maggie said coldly.

"What if they want to make a deal; what if—"

"No deals. Not a penny. We want the press. We want our lives back."

The Gucci briefcase snapped shut. Maggie thought it looked a little more worn since she'd seen it last.

The following morning every newspaper in the state of Texas carried the banner headline: COLEMAN FAMILY FIGHTS BACK. Maggie winced several times when she read the printed words to the family over breakfast.

The phone had to be taken off the hook shortly after the story broke. Three ranch hands, armed with rifles, stood guard at the entrance to Sunbridge. The Colemans were prisoners in their own home.

Maggie packed her bag carefully, putting in enough clothes for at least a week. If she needed more, she could buy them. She was New York bound. There was nothing more she could do here, and she needed to go to Sawyer.

"You understand," she said to Shadaharu Hasegawa, "why I have to go to New York."

The old Japanese bowed and nodded. "But of course, Mrs. Tanner. We will handle everything in your absence."

"I know that. If you need them, there are two other phones in the study. Both private lines." She embraced the old man and looked deeply into his dark eyes. "Riley will come out of this just fine. Trust us. My daughter wouldn't have asked us to do what we did otherwise."

"You will please give her my best wishes for a speedy recovery."

"I'll do that, Mr. Hasegawa," Maggie said in a choked voice.

Martin, the chauffeur, blew the horn in front of the house. "Mam, you should be the one going, not me," Maggie said.

"No. It's you Sawyer needs."

Maggie kissed them all and hugged Jessie. "I'm not deserting you, boys. It's just that Sawyer needs me more. Or I need her. Rand, take care of my boys," she said, kissing him lightly on the cheek.

"My best to Sawyer."

"Our love," everyone chorused.

A few minutes later the Mercedes 300 SD roared down the road to the arched gate. The guards moved back, and the car shot through as though jet-propelled. The reporters standing guard hopped in their cars and followed. Forty-five minutes later, Maggie climbed aboard a Coleman Lear jet and was airborne in less than ten minutes.

When she landed at Kennedy Airport, she went straight to Adam's apartment. He answered the door. "I wasn't sure you'd be here," she said nervously. "How is she?"

"Holding her own. They're running tests. I'm going to the hospital later. They want her a little stronger before they operate, my guess would be at least five days. What are we standing here for? Come on up."

"I can stay someplace else if—"

"No way. You're staying here. I even think we have clean towels."

"The price sounds right," Maggie said quietly.

"I heard the news. How's it going?"

Maggie shrugged. "It's only been a day and a half. I wanted to be here; they can all ... The boys ... There's Mr. ..."

"I understand. Coffee?"

"Yes, I could use a cup. How are you?" Maggie asked, noticing the dark circles under his eyes.

"Hey, I'm t-u-f-f! I'm from Texas."

"Sometimes I wish I'd never heard of the state," Maggie said wearily, then grimaced. "This coffee is terrible! How old is it?"

Adam shrugged. "Yesterday, I guess. Let me make some fresh. It'll give me something to do."

"Have you spoken to the doctors?"

"No. I thought maybe this evening I'd get a chance. Sawyer is comfortable. They're medicating her and she isn't in too much pain. She's drowsy most of the time."

"I want to go with you this evening."

"Good," Adam said as he measured coffee into the wire basket. "I think you should talk to the doctor, too."

"How upset do you think Sawyer is going to be when she sees that I'm here?"

"I don't know. She isn't exactly with it, if you know what I mean."

While the situation in Texas brewed and simmered, Maggie made daily treks to the hospital. Most of the time Sawyer was sleeping, but she'd stay and try to read. Once Sawyer woke and stared across at Maggie. "You remind me of a vulture, just waiting to descend," Sawyer said through clenched teeth. "If I had any strength, I'd tell them to throw you out."

"Not a vulture, Sawyer. How about a mother hen? I wouldn't let them throw me out."

"Vulture."

"Mother hen."

"Damn you."

"Why are you damning me?"

"For never being there when I needed you," Sawyer said, tears slipping through her lashes.

"I can't change that time in our lives. I'm here now."

"It's too late."

"Do you want me to grovel? I will. Do you want me to kiss your feet? I will. If you want me to leave, I won't."

"You left the boys, knowing what was going on," Sawyer said, mustering all the anger she could.

"It was a question of priorities. The boys will be fine. I believe that, and I know you do, too. If you hadn't had the guts to do this, we'd all still be sucking our thumbs. You're my daughter and I'm proud of you."

"Is this where we kiss and make up, and I say I'm proud to have you for my mother?"

"Only if you want to. I don't expect anything from you, Sawyer. I just want you to understand. If only you'd try, we might be able to go on from there."

"Just me and you. And Rand."

"Don't bring Rand into this. It's just you and me, kid."

"Go home, Maggie. I can't give you what you want."

"What is it you think I want?"

"You know what you want," Sawyer said uncertainly.

"No, you tell me. Tell me what it is you think I want. I want to hear it from you."

"Go away. Nurse," she called weakly.

"What is it I want, Sawyer?"

"To pretend you're my mother. To pretend you are. You want me to believe that. Well, I don't. You never cared. You never even tried."

"That was then and this is now. Give me a chance. Please, Sawyer."

When Sawyer didn't respond, Maggie panicked and called the nurse. "What happened? Is anything wrong?" She asked anxiously.

"No, Mrs. Tanner. She does that. Just slips into a deep sleep for a while. Why don't you go home and get some rest."

"I guess I will. You'll call if..."

"Of course we will," the nurse said compassionately.

"How do you do it?" Maggie whispered. "How can you take care of dying patients day after day?"

"I like to think I make their days a little better. I do my best; we all do here. There are some days when I say I'm not coming back tomorrow, and then someone like your daughter comes in who has a fighting chance, and I want to be sure she gets it. I guess that's it."

"Bless you," Maggie said hoarsely. "Take care of her."

"We will."

Adam looked up from his worktable as Maggie let herself into the loft. "Not a good evening, huh?" he said sympathetically.

"I might have been too hard on her. She fought me. Then she slipped off to sleep. The nurse told me to come home."

"At least you're obedient. Want a sandwich?"

"I suppose so. How old is the coffee?"

"Fresh."

"Adam, where are my diaries?"

"In the hall closet in the bag you brought them in. I wouldn't let her burn them."

"Thank you for that. I think maybe I'm spinning my

wheels trying to talk to her. I can never convince her that
I . . . Oh, what's the use?"

Adam nodded to show he understood as he slapped
mustard on some tired-looking bologna. Maggie ate her
sandwich mechanically, not tasting anything. She drank
cup after cup of coffee. "How's your work going?"

"Okay, I guess. Actually, my editor told me it's some
of my best yet. I can't figure that out. The stuff I turned
out in Texas really had grit in it."

"You're telling me. I think it helped, though. You really
love her, don't you?"

"Body and soul. I think she cares for me, too. Not a
dependent kind of caring, either. Hell, I know the difference. If she'd just let go, we might have a shot at something really good. If only we had more time."

Maggie snorted. "Time. It's everyone's enemy." She
stood up wearily. "I guess I should call home."

"Oh, hell, I almost forgot. Billie called while you were
at the hospital. You made the headlines. The newspapers
said you cut and ran. Deserted the kiddies and are seeking sanctuary here, in the city where millions can get lost.
A whole bunch of bullshit, if you'll excuse the expression."

"What's going on?" she asked sourly.

"Just what you'd expect. Ben Simms was interviewed
on the morning news, the noon news, the six-o'clock news,
and the evening news. The Colemans are standing fast
and speaking only through their attorneys. By tomorrow
everyone'll know why you're here. There are some decent
reporters out there. If and when you want to make a
statement, I'd appreciate it if you'd do it through a buddy
of mine. It'll be printed just the way you give it to him.
He's an ace."

"When it's time. I'm tired now. I think I'll turn in if
you don't mind."

At five-thirty the following morning, the phone rang.
Adam got it on the first ring and craned his neck. Good,
it hadn't wakened Maggie.

It was Sloan-Kettering. Sawyer wanted to see him. He

dressed hurriedly, fishing his running clothes from the
closet. His eyes fell upon the bag with Maggie's diaries
and he grabbed it on impulse.

Sawyer was wide awake when he arrived, more coher-
ent than she'd been in days. "They want to operate this
afternoon. One o'clock, they said." Adam nodded. He
felt a lump in his throat. "I said okay." Adam nodded.
The lump was getting bigger. "Maybe I do love you. You're
so goofy, who could help but love you? That cat has to
go, though." He couldn't swallow past the lump, nodded,
and wondered if he was drooling. "What's in the bag? The
diaries?" Another nod. "Okay, read them to me."

"You want me to read them?" Adam asked, startled
into speech.

"I can barely see, so who else is there?"

Adam opened the first little journal and began to read.
He felt terrible, as if he were prying into Maggie Coleman's life. He knew she hadn't intended the diaries for
anyone's eyes but her daughter's. Somehow, though, he
didn't think she would mind. He read on, finishing one
and picking up another. Sawyer lay still, her eyes closed.
One time he looked up, thinking she was asleep. "Keep
going. Don't stop," she said weakly.

He read on, from time to time noticing a tear roll down
her cheeks. When he'd finished the last page and closed
the journal, Sawyer opened her eyes. "What time is it?"
she asked.

"Eleven o'clock. Why? Are you going somewhere?"

"They'll be coming in to give me a shot soon. And they
have to shave my hair. Will you do something for me?"

"Name it."

"Call my mother. Tell her I want to see her."

"Okay, sure." God, there was so little time left. He
might never see her again. They might never be able to
banter back and forth. He might not be able to yell at her
to wash the towels. They now had eighty-four of them.

"Adam, what are you thinking?"

Adam told her.

"I'm glad you didn't lie to me. We have eighty-four

towels, though." They both laughed. "Will you hold my hand a minute? You know, I can hardly see you."

"Why would you want to look at me?" he asked huskily as he squeezed her hand.

Sawyer didn't answer. "Will you wait? It's going to be a long operation."

"I'll read a book, maybe one of those trashy romances you read."

"Okay. Are you going to call Ma—my mother?"

"As soon as you let go of my hand. You know I love you, right?"

"Yeah, I know. Tell the boys . . . You know what to tell them. You know, in case . . . And Adam . . ."

"Yes?"

"Sometimes first loves aren't what they're cracked up to be. Sometimes it's the last love that counts."

Shit, he was crying. It was a good thing she couldn't see him. He bent down to kiss her cheek and was surprised when she turned so his lips would find hers. It was a long kiss, and by the time it was over, the blood was roaring through his veins.

Sawyer heard the door close behind him. "Good-bye, Adam," she said softly.

The nurse came in, her starched uniform crackling busily. She readied a hypodermic. Another nurse came in with a covered tray to shave her head. She prayed silently.

Maggie picked up the phone and listened to Adam. "She said *what*?"

"She said, call my mother. In fact, she said it twice. Not Maggie, 'my mother.' Hurry up. I don't know what the shot will do to her."

Maggie was out of the apartment and down the stairs within minutes. She ran up the street and across and out onto the road. She flagged a cab and told him where she wanted to go. The driver took one look at her face and sped away. When he pulled to the curb minutes later, Maggie handed him some crumpled bills. She had no idea if it was too much or too little—she couldn't even read the meter.

"Good luck, ma'am."

"Thank you," Maggie whispered. "Thank you very much." She was breathless when she got out of the elevator. The first person she saw was Adam. Part of her registered that he was carrying the flight bag that contained her diaries. Quickly he told her what he'd done.

Outside Sawyer's room, she stopped long enough to take several deep breaths, then went inside.

She thought she could feel death in the room. So close. She wanted to shout, to scream, "Not yet!" She walked over to the bed where Sawyer lay so still. There was a puckered cap on her head. She'd never really noticed before how long and thick Sawyer's lashes were. It was hard to tell now where they started, with the sooty smudges under her eyes. "Sawyer, are you awake?" she whispered.

Sawyer heard the words and tried to make her tongue work. She felt as if there were cotton balls in her mouth. She tried again. Her arms flailed at the air around her.

Maggie, sensing what was wrong, reached for her hand and clasped it tightly in both of hers. "I'm here." Sawyer squeezed slightly. Maggie tried to find her own voice and had to clear her throat twice. "Adam told me he read you the diaries. All I want, Sawyer, is for you to tell me you understand. Later, we'll work on the rest. Blink, baby, if you understand." Sawyer's eyelashes fluttered faintly.

Maggie's head bowed. All the years slipped behind her, the weight suddenly lifted from her shoulders. Almost home free. Almost.

"You'll have to leave now, Mrs. Tanner," said the nurse. "Mr. Jarvis is waiting for you at the end of the hall. Dr. Marlow will be out shortly to speak with you."

Sawyer summoned every ounce of strength left in her. She was so groggy, she just wanted to sleep, but she had to do something, say something. No one else would have understood the mangled word that came out through her dry mouth.

"M-mam."

Maggie heard. She thought she could hear a choir of angels singing when she walked down the hall to join Adam. Taking him by the arm, she asked, "Do you hear them, the angels singing?"

Adam stared at her, bewildered. He realized she was deadly serious. "No, I don't," he said slowly, "but if you do, that's okay with me. That's a plus for our side."

Maggie walked around the waiting room, her gaze sweeping the ceiling. Adam shivered when she said, "It could mean they're getting ready to take her."

"Don't talk like that," he said sharply.

When the surgeon arrived Maggie and Adam listened to him. When he left, they looked at each other. "Do you know what he said?" Maggie asked crazily. Adam shook his head.

"Seven hours. Then, if she comes through it, it'll take another seventy-two till they know if it was a success."

They waited. The minutes ticked by; the hours crawled. Twice Maggie called Sunbridge just to hear her mother's voice. "I really do have two children, Mam," she cried before she hung up.

"Be strong, Maggie."

"I am."

"Call me later."

"Mam ... I heard angels sing. I really heard them. I know Adam thinks I'm crazy, but I did hear them; I know I did. Say you believe me," Maggie pleaded.

"Darling, if you say you heard them, then I believe you. I, for one, still believe in miracles."

"What if ... what if it means they're getting ready to take her?" Maggie cried.

"Then, baby, you have to let them take her."

Maggie cried, great huge sobs that ripped at her insides. Adam found her in the phone booth and led her back to the waiting room.

More minutes and hours crawled by. They smoked and drank coffee. Adam scrounged in his pockets for some stale M&M's, which he offered to share with Maggie. She refused. "How long has it been?" she asked hoarsely.

"Six hours."

"One more to go. It must be going all right, or we would have heard by now. Don't you think so?" Maggie asked, looking at him imploringly.

"I think so." Jesus, one more hour. Sixty minutes. Three thousand six hundred seconds. A lifetime.

Forty-five minutes later the surgeon entered the waiting room, a cup of coffee in his hands. He ripped off his green skullcap, his mask dangling around his neck. He looked tired, Maggie thought. She waited for him to speak.

He took a long swallow of the horrible coffee. "She came through it, and she's in recovery now. We'll know in seventy-two hours. I'd say her chances are better than I first thought. I've seen people that should be dead still living because they will it. When she first came to me, Sawyer had given up. I was dumbfounded when you called and said she wanted the operation," he said to Adam. "Something happened to that girl along the way. I'm confident she'll fight now. I would have liked her to be a little stronger, but we simply couldn't wait to build her up. She's got round-the-clock nurses. I can be back here within fifteen minutes at any time. One of my associates is staying the night. Is there anything you want to ask me?"

Maggie's mind was full of questions, but she couldn't voice them. She looked at Adam, who was just as mute. Both of them shook their heads. Then, when he saw Maggie glance up, Adam closed his eyes.

"Do you hear them?" she asked, smiling at the doctor.

"Who?" he asked tiredly.

"The choir of angels. This is the second time I've heard them today."

The doctor smiled, his eyes warm and gentle. "I hear them every day. I'd say they're a little louder than usual, though. A good sign." He held out his hand, first to Adam and then to Maggie. "Go home now and get some rest. You both look like I feel."

Adam and Maggie linked arms and walked to the elevator. In the main lobby they stopped to call Sunbridge.

Maggie reported happily that Sawyer had come through the operation. She could hear Billie repeat the news to the others. "The next seventy-two hours are crucial. Pray, Mam. I heard the angels again. Even Dr. Marlow says he hears them. The surgeon—he said they were louder than usual. A good sign. Mam, I'm not crazy."

"I know you aren't. Take care, Maggie. Go home and get some rest."

"Anything new?"

"Not a thing. When Sawyer comes to, give her our love."

"I will. Good night."

In the taxi Adam stewed and fretted. "Why didn't I hear them? What does it mean?"

"I wish I could explain it to you, but I can't. Perhaps it has something to do with life and death. I gave Sawyer life. The doctor deals in life and death all the time. It's the best I can do."

"Damn, I wish I'd heard them. I'd feel so much better."

"Maybe you don't need an angel to sing for you. Maybe you're supposed to do your own singing. I don't know. . . . I'm so tired, I can't think. Can we discuss this tomorrow?" Adam nodded.

Billie called a family meeting. "Things are on hold here. How would all of you like to go to New York and be there when they pronounce Sawyer's operation a success? I'll call Valentine and see if she can get permission for Cole and Riley to go. Amelia, you know Judge Bellows, don't you?" At her nod, Billie said, "See what you can do. Make it easy for Valentine. Tell him we'll be back in forty-eight hours."

Twenty-four hours after Sawyer's operation, the Coleman jet took off with all the Colemans aboard. They camped out in the hospital waiting room, returning to Adam's to freshen up, then going immediately back to the hospital to watch the sleeping girl through the glass in the intensive care unit.

It was Maggie who kept vigil across from the clock.

In just four hours the time limit would be up. How still Sawyer looked, how pale and wan. She wished she could hear the angels again. She was so tired, she could barely keep her eyes open.

Suddenly she caught a movement out of the corner of her eye and looked through the glass. Sawyer's hand fluttered, but the thumbs-up salute was unmistakable. Maggie's own thumb went up in response.

Sobbing, Maggie ran back to the others and fell into Rand's arms. "She's okay! She just did this." She demonstrated the cocky salute that had been a favorite of her father's. Adam collapsed on the sofa. Cole and Riley took off and pressed their faces up against the glass. Both boys shot their fists into the air. Sawyer again stuck her thumb up.

"You hear something?" Cole asked.

"Yeah, a radio. I didn't think you could play radios in this unit."

"That's no radio. It sounds like the choir at school."

"Yeah, it does," Riley agreed. He shrugged it off as they made their way back to the others.

"She's got a long road ahead of her, but I'm confident she'll make it," Dr. Finley said heartily. "Now, I think all of you should go home and let our patient begin her recovery. She knows you've all been here; I told her. I also told her I was sending you home. She understands. I want all of you to get at least eight hours of sleep, and that's an order. . . . Damn, they're at it again," he muttered as he left the room. Maggie smiled happily.

Kisses and hugs were the order of the day in the lobby. "Tell Sawyer I'll be back, Adam," Maggie said. "I have business at home. And take good care of her."

"I still didn't hear them," he whispered.

"Don't worry. Sawyer will sing a song for you. Just for you. Call us."

"Will do."

{{{{{{{{{{ CHAPTER THIRTY }}}}}}}}}}

It was almost midnight when the Coleman jet touched ground. The tired but happy clan climbed into the waiting cars that would take them back to Sunbridge. Amelia immediately placed a call to Judge Bellows, informing him the boys were back in Texas and would soon be asleep in their own beds. She also reported on Sawyer's progress and hung up feeling better than she had in days. Maybe that little talk she'd had with Sawyer had helped.

That night they slept, all of them. If their sleep was invaded by demons in the shape of Ben and Luana Simms, no one ever knew.

It was two-thirty the following afternoon when Maggie sent Rand out to invite the reporters and news media to the house. Valentine Mitchell was in attendance. Maggie read a statement and then waited for questions.

"Are you serious, Mrs. Tanner? You really want a face-to-face confrontation with Luana Simms? What if her lawyers won't go for it?"

"We have nothing to hide. If they have nothing to hide and the girl is telling the truth, why wouldn't they? Unless, of course, this is all for money."

"You said you'd offer ten thousand dollars to anyone who would come forward and tell what they know about that night. You mean only if it clears Cole and Riley. Is that right?"

"Absolutely right," Maggie said tightly.

"Does that include Luana herself?"

"It includes anyone who can clear Riley and Cole," Valentine said clearly.

"How's your daughter, Mrs. Tanner?" asked a young woman.

"On this side of the angels. Thank you for asking."

"Then that's it, ladies and gentlemen," Valentine said, dismissing the reporters. "We'll be here at the same time tomorrow. Hopefully, the Simmses will be here, too."

When the door closed behind them, Valentine put her hands on her hips, glowering. "That's probably the dumbest, the stupidest, thing I've ever done in my life. That goes for you, too. If you think for one minute that the Simmses' attorneys are going to let them come out here, you're all out of your minds."

"You're probably right," Maggie said ruefully. "What I'm hoping for is that Luana will come forward. Ten thousand dollars will get her away from here. If she tells the truth, Social Services will take her from Simms, where she'll be safe. When she's of age, she'll have ten thousand dollars plus the interest it gathers." She shrugged. "It was worth a shot. I saw that child after one of her father's beatings, and it's something I'll never forget. We have absolutely nothing to lose." The others nodded.

Valentine left the ranch shaking her head. It was so damn dumb, it just might work. She couldn't allow herself to think beyond this time tomorrow.

"Cole, take the pickup, and you and Riley go to the line shack and bring that old couch back here. Put it in the garage and cover it up."

Ben Simms watched the six-o'clock news with his daughter, his face dark and full of rage. Luana cowered in her chair. "Don't you go gettin' no funny ideas, you hear, girl?" he snapped. "I'm going out to call our lawyer. You stay right here with Louise."

Sullenly, Luana looked at the woman sitting across from her. They'd been staying with Louise since they'd moved from the dirty apartment they were in. This place was clean and Louise was a good cook. But she was mean, just like Pa—watching her every move as though she were some kind of thief.

Luana stared moodily at the TV. Nothing was working right. The lady she was supposed to work for had canceled her, summer school had never materialized, and she'd been cooped up here like a prisoner. All because of her pa and what he'd done to her. If there was only some way she could get out of here, she'd go to the police and tell the truth. She often thought of Cole and Riley and wondered if they hated her. They sure had a right to.

Ben Simms came back in, a look of joviality on his face. "Our lawyers said them Colemans are just grabbin' at straws because they know we got 'em cornered. He said we could expect more tricks like this one." Luana didn't say anything. She hadn't been able to look her father in the eye since that night. She didn't even want to be in the same room with him. "He said we ain't goin' out there tomorrow, so don't go thinkin' we are, girl."

"Yes, Pa," she said obediently, keeping her eyes on the TV. If she could just get to the Coleman ranch . . .

That night, Luana lay awake in her bed for a long time, listening to the sounds coming from the room next to hers. When the bedsprings finally stopped groaning, she waited another fifteen minutes, then stole out of bed and threw on a pair of jeans, a T-shirt, and sneakers. Then she crept into the other bedroom, pocketed two quarters from Louise's purse, and quietly let herself out the front door.

Once outside, she ran, tears flowing down her cheeks. She ran till she came to Bill's Sunoco Station, which was brightly lit but closed. She went right to the phone booth and called information to get the number for Maggie Coleman Tanner of Sunbridge. She repeated it aloud five or six times, then dropped the returned quarter back into the slot. Her hands were shaking so badly, she could barely punch out the numbers.

The phone was picked up on the tenth ring. "Miz Tanner? This is Luana," she said, her voice trembling. "Can you come get me? I'm at Bill's Sunoco Station on the highway. Please, Miz Tanner."

"I'll be right there. Are you all right?"

"I will be soon as I tell the truth. I can't stay out here in the light. I'll be across the road in the dark. You stop, and if I see it's you, I'll come out. My pa might find me gone, and he knows the first place I'd go is to you."

"It'll take us about twenty minutes. Just stay there."

"Was that who I think it was?" Rand demanded when she'd hung up.

"It certainly was. We have to get dressed. Do you think we should call a doctor or a nurse or somebody?"

"Or somebody. I think you should call Valentine and let her pick Luana up. Simms might accuse you of kidnapping her. Christ only knows what that bastard will do."

Maggie shook her head. "Luana will think it's some kind of trick. I promised her I'd be there. I think she trusts me; otherwise she wouldn't have called."

"Maybe it was the ten thousand dollars," Rand said sourly.

"That was bait. It made her move, didn't it? It must have taken some of the fear out of her. I don't care about the money. I can't imagine what it must be like to be raped by your own father."

"Are we going by car or horseback?"

"Horseback. Luana can ride with me. I don't dare drive through the gate. Let them figure it out in the morning. Be quiet, though. Voices carry when it's quiet like this."

They saddled their horses silently and led them on foot for a good quarter of a mile. Then they mounted and raced off. Lotus whickered softly as her mistress urged her on.

Five minutes later, Maggie reined in her horse. "We have to cross the highway. Bill's station is about a quarter of a mile down the road," Maggie whispered softly. "Wait until there's no sign of a car and then go for it."

Luana gasped when Maggie called out to her from behind. "Over here, Luana. We're on horseback. Hurry. There're cars coming and we have to get on the other side of the highway."

They'd no sooner crossed the road and were in the

shadows than they saw two police cars race by, sirens blaring.

"I knew it. I knew it. Pa heard me sneak out. Don't send me back. God, Mrs. Tanner, don't send me back."

"No one is sending you anywhere. Hang on. You're going to find out what it's like to ride with the wind. I think we can make it back to the ranch before they get there." Maggie gave Lotus her head and the horse galloped off.

Soon they were walking back from the barn, keeping well in the shadows. The flashing lights could be seen from the driveway. "Shhh," said Maggie, laying a finger against her lips. "I told you voices carry."

Rand grimaced. Luana shivered against Maggie. They all listened.

"Any cars come or go out of here in the past two hours?"

There was a chorus of nos. "What's up?" a brash reporter shouted.

"The Simms girl split. Her father thinks the Colemans snatched her. You sure no one came or left here?"

"Would we be standing here if there was any action going on?" the same voice demanded.

"Back to the barn," Maggie ordered quietly. "We're going to have to sleep out here. The others will think we went out for a while and just aren't back yet. It's better if we don't have to lie to the police."

Rand unsaddled the horses while Maggie and Luana watched from one of the barn windows. The flashing red and blue lights lit up the entire driveway. A few minutes later, lights came on in Sunbridge. Then someone was at the back door; the porch light went on. Mam.

Fifteen minutes later the porch light went out. The police cars backed up, their blue and red lights twirling like batons.

"What we've just done is probably illegal," Maggie whispered to Rand. Luana was asleep in the straw, her cheek resting on her hands. Rand stared at her for a long time before answering.

"I suppose it is. As soon as the Social Service Office—
or whoever is in charge of things like this—opens, get on
the phone. I don't think it would hurt to . . . what is it you
Texans say?—call in a few favors. That judge Amelia was
talking to: call him again, too. And for God's sake, make
sure Valentine is here. The police will be back as soon as
it gets light." He cradled Maggie's head against his chest.
"Sleep, Maggie. I'll keep watch." He·stroked her hair
gently and thought he could hear her purr. For one crazy
second he felt as though he were back in the RAF.

Rand shook Maggie gently. "It's going to be light in a
few minutes. Go back to the house. I'll stay here with
Luana. Send somebody out with some food when you
can."

Maggie dusted off the straw. "You're being a real brick.
Are you sorry you got tangled up with this crew and all
our problems?"

"No way. We're seeing daylight now. By this time
tomorrow things should be settled with the boys. Sawyer
is on the mend. This isn't exactly the time to say this,
but how would you like to honeymoon back in Hawaii?"

"I'd love it!" She kissed Rand soundly. "Now, keep
your eye on that little girl in case her feet turn cold." With
that, Maggie raced back to the house. She let herself in
quietly and watched as Martha eyed her up and down.

"I think I'll have breakfast now. Everything. Flapjacks,
eggs, ham, toast, and coffee. Make enough for three."

"Three?"

"Three," Maggie repeated.

Maggie ate and waited while Martha carried a steaming
tray to the barn. Shortly after seven the police arrived.
Maggie listened to Deputy Pierson's explanations. "You're
welcome to search the house, Deputy," she said cour-
teously, "but I must ask you to be quiet. Martha and I
are the only ones awake."

"Where were you last night, Mrs. Tanner?"

"At what time?"

"All evening. My men were here after midnight, and

your mother said you must have gone out. Your room was empty."

"Well, I was here till around eleven or so. Then I went riding. I do that when I can't sleep."

"Did you ride alone?"

"No, as a matter of fact, Rand Nelson was with me."

"Would you get him for me, or is he asleep, too?"

Maggie could feel her neck start to prickle. "As a matter of fact, he's in the barn rubbing down the horses. I'll call him for you."

Her heart fluttering, Maggie walked out to the back porch, onto the driveway, and cupped her hands to her mouth. "Rand . . . will you come here, please?" She almost fainted with relief when Rand walked out of the barn with a curry brush in his hand.

He sauntered over to Maggie as though he had all the time in the world. "What's wrong?"

Maggie motioned to the kitchen and said, "The police want to talk to you." They walked inside.

"Where were you last night, Mr. Nelson?" asked Deputy Pierson.

"With the others right here in the house till after eleven. Mrs. Tanner wanted to go riding, and I didn't think she should go alone, so I joined her. I was rubbing down the horses."

"Is Luana Simms here?"

"Look," Maggie interrupted, "I told you you could search the house if you wanted."

"No," Rand said coldly. "He only searches if he has a warrant."

"I can get one in an hour."

"Then get one. Maggie, I'd like some breakfast."

Martha was already whipping eggs in a bowl. She saw Deputy Pierson glance at the open dishwasher and the frying pans on the stove. "I always eat before the family," she said, eyeing him coldly.

Pierson knew he was being conned, but there wasn't anything he could do. "Enjoy your breakfast," he said coolly, and left.

"I thought he was going to click his heels there for a minute," Rand muttered.

"He's only doing his job," Maggie said. "I almost feel sorry for him." She looked out the window at the departing police car. "Where's Luana?"

"Don't worry about her. She's so petrified, she isn't moving a muscle. We had a long talk after you went into the house. She'll come through for you and the boys. She wanted to know what was going to happen to her. I told her you'd make sure she was well taken care of. So, as far as she's concerned, you're the white knight now, or is that knightess?"

"She's a minor. We snatched her," Maggie said fretfully.

"We didn't snatch her—we picked her up. She called us. There will be a record of that from the phone booth. Under the circumstances, her being a minor will work in your favor if she tells the truth. She shouldn't be allowed to stay with a father who abused her sexually."

"I'm frightened, Rand."

"So am I," Rand said, laying his cheek on Maggie's dark hair. "I have to get back to the barn before Luana gets itchy. Don't forget to make those calls."

Maggie looked at the clock: 7:50 A.M. She climbed the stairs and walked into Susan's room, shaking her awake gently. "Shhh, it isn't Jessie. I need your help." She explained what had happened. "Call Ferris. He must know someone in Social Services we can trust. Do it now, okay?"

Susan was already dialing when Maggie closed the door behind her. She walked on down the hall into the nursery, smiling as she bent over the crib. Jessie was sucking her thumb, her blanket clutched in her hand. "Nothing is ever going to hurt you, little one. Not while I'm around, anyway. Sleep," she crooned.

Next she stopped at Amelia's door and knocked softly. Cary opened it and stood aside. Amelia was slipping into a robe. Again Maggie explained the situation.

"Grandpap would say it's time to palaver a little. This family is owed a lot of favors, and it's time to call them in. Seth kept a book on who owed who; it's still in his desk. Will you do the honors?"

Amelia grinned. "Could you fortify me with some coffee while I'm doing it?"

"I'll get it for you, honey," Cary said. "You go down to the study and do what you do best. I love that word 'palaver'." He laughed. "What can I do?"

Maggie opened the door. "After you get her the coffee, stand around and listen to how the Colemans have survived all these years. You're going to need the experience if you plan to stay in Texas. Your wife is a pro."

Maggie tripped down the steps, her mind clicking. Maybe she was playing by different rules, Coleman rules, but two boys' futures were at stake. Fair was fair. Sometimes you had to pull out all the stops. Money couldn't buy happiness, but maybe it could buy truth. And that was all she wanted—the truth. They would all be seven-day wonders for a while, but they'd all survive.

"I think we're going to have guests for lunch, Martha. A buffet. I can help you or we can have it sent it. What do you think?"

"I think I can handle it. I have a lot in the freezer. About a ton of fried chicken." She laughed. "Those boys of yours can eat two at a time. I'll just pop it all in the oven, make a mess o' salads, and order some fresh cold cuts from Ferdie's. You do whatever you have to do, ma'am; I'll take care of this. And ma'am, I'm real happy about Miss Sawyer. I like her young man."

"Thank you, Martha. Yes, Adam is a fine young man. We all like him."

"This is all going to be all right, isn't it, ma'am?"

"I hope so, Martha. We've had our little family problems with the boys, but they don't deserve this; none of us do. The Simmses just marched into our lives and are trying to ruin us. Making a very good job of it, too."

Martha snorted. "And him pretending to be so virtuous, reading the Bible and all. Always preaching to the girl. She's not what we're used to around here. I knew

they were trouble the minute I saw them. You can preach—
if you practice what you preach."

Maggie backed out of the kitchen, hoping Martha had
finished her monologue. She was right, though. Loyal
Martha. If anyone knew the Colemans, she did.

At one o'clock Valentine Mitchell arrived, Dudley
Abramson shuffling alongside her. Maggie noticed with
amusement that he carried not only his own briefcase but
hers as well. Later that afternoon, Amelia personally welcomed the lieutenant governor and poured him a drink.
They chatted like old friends. The police chief shook Billie's hand and kissed her lightly on the cheek. Maggie
could hear them discuss Thad's indecision about running
for Congress. Susan introduced everyone to Rita Introne,
the head of Social Services, Juvenile Division. Maggie
watched out of the corner of her eye. As soon as Rita's
introductions were over and the small talk had trailed off,
Rita followed Susan to the kitchen. From there, Maggie
knew, they would go to the barn. Luana would be in good
hands.

Maggie remembered her promise to Adam and greeted
Steve Axelrod at the kitchen door. She showed him into
the study and offered to keep one of the private lines open
for his newspaper. Then she talked. Steve made squiggles
on his notepad. He listened. He wrote. He showed neither
approval nor disapproval. .

"May I talk to the boys?" he asked. "I'd like to get
their views."

Maggie hesitated. "I'll ask them. It's their decision."
She summoned the boys and explained the situation.

"Okay," Cole said.

"Why not. Maybe it's time we got to say something,"
Riley said agreeably.

Steve leaned back in Seth's chair. He was so skinny,
he looked almost lost in it. Riley grinned. Cole smirked.
It would take one hell of a man to fill that chair, and he
said so to Steve.

"Hell, I'm just resting my butt. I've heard tales of Seth

Coleman all my life. You're right; there's no one around
here who could fit that chair. Give me a break, huh, and
let me sit here. You guys into baseball?"

"I am," Riley said shyly. "Cole here is an expert archer.
He's also an expert marksman," he added generously.

"You trying to warm us up or something?" Cole asked
suspiciously.

"Yeah, as a matter of fact, I am. I'm a good friend—
and by good I mean grade school, high school, and college—of Adam Jarvis. Does that help?"

Cole grinned. "Shit, why didn't you say so?" He pulled
up two chairs and both boys sat, each rotating his chair
to straddle the seat.

"So talk. Tell me what it's like to see your life shot to
hell. Tell me what you thought, what you felt. Tell me
what it's like to be a Coleman with all this money. There's
all kinds of people out there on your terrace that I only
read about in the paper. Powerful people. They're here
for you. Tell me about Luana Simms. Tell me what you
know about Ben Simms. Tell me about your dreams, your
ambitions. I want it all."

They gave it to him.

Steve hooked a gadget to the phone and played the
tape to an associate on the other end of the line. He shook
their hands. They weren't kids; they were young men.
Colemans, true; but they were something else. The future.
From the Texas panhandle to Yale and Notre Dame. East
and West.

The Colemans gathered together at exactly two-thirty.
Sid Jackson, the anchorman for the six-o'clock news, held
out a microphone. Maggie stepped forward. She spoke
haltingly at first, and then the words flowed. Out of the
corner of her eye she could see both boys, Shadaharu
Hasegawa behind them.

"Luana Simms called me last night and asked for my
help. I brought her here. Rita Introne from Social Services
is with her. They're coming now."

They were like a gaggle of geese, firing questions like
machine-gun bullets. Cameras clicked and the news sta-

tions fought for clear shots. Luana licked her dry lips. She searched the crowd for Riley and Cole, then broke free from Rita's grasp and walked over to them.

Her conversation, because it was brief and no one expected it, was not overheard. "I couldn't spoil your chances to go to Yale and Notre Dame. I bet you thought I was so dumb, I didn't know they were the best Ivy League schools going. I'm sorry. Real sorry."

"Just tell the truth, Luana," Cole said softly. "Don't worry about us."

"You'll be okay. That lady with you, she'll make sure nothing happens to you," Riley whispered.

Cole thought the girl's back was a little straighter as she returned to Rita Introne. They listened as she told her story, trying to keep the horror from their faces. When it was all over and Luana was taken to the children's shelter, Riley bowed low to his grandfather. "I have regained our honor, have I not, Grandfather?" he asked anxiously.

"There is no one who walks this earth who could ever convince me otherwise. Come. I think we must eat some ...fried chicken." He made a slight grimace. "I wonder if it is as bad as Yankee bean soup."

Cole smiled. "Sir, my mother made something special for you. You won't have to eat fried chicken."

"My boy, you have just saved my life," the Japanese said heartily.

"Will you stay on, Grandfather, just for a little while? I must remember to return the money to you for the trip."

"I will go to New York and see Sawyer. I want to see with my own eyes this miracle that was performed. I have seen that you are fine. I came only to show support." Both boys beamed when he kissed them. "Come. I can't wait to see what Mrs. Tanner has prepared for me."

When the last car left the driveway, Cole and Riley stood alone, one dark, one fair. Neither could see the family watching them from the terrace. "We almost lost all of this," Cole said softly as he waved his arm about.

Riley reached into his back pocket and pulled out his baseball cap. He settled it carefully on his head. "Now it feels right." He bent down and reached inside the Berlinetta and pulled out a cap. He shoved it at Cole.

Cole looked at the yellow letters. Notre Dame. Son of a gun. He clapped it on his head. "It's not so bad being a Coleman."

"Not bad at all." Riley grinned.